D0759453

THE YEAR'S BEST

SCIENCE FICTION

ALSO BY GARDNER DOZOIS

ANTHOLOGIES

A DAY IN THE LIFE

ANOTHER WORLD

BEST SCIENCE FICTION STORIES OF THE
  YEAR Vols. 6–10

THE BEST OF ISAAC ASIMOV'S SCIENCE
  FICTION MAGAZINE

TIME-TRAVELERS FROM ISAAC ASIMOV'S
  SCIENCE FICTION MAGAZINE

TRANSCENDENTAL TALES FROM ISAAC
  ASIMOV'S SCIENCE FICTION MAGAZINE

ISAAC ASIMOV'S ALIENS

ISAAC ASIMOV'S MARS

ISAAC ASIMOV'S SF LITE

ISAAC ASIMOV'S WAR

ROADS NOT TAKEN (with Stanley Schmidt)

THE YEAR'S BEST SCIENCE FICTION, Vols. 1–30

FUTURE EARTHS: UNDER AFRICAN SKIES (with
  Mike Resnick)

FUTURE EARTHS: UNDER SOUTH AMERICAN
  SKIES (with Mike Resnick)

RIPPER! (with Susan Casper)

MODERN CLASSIC SHORT NOVELS OF
  SCIENCE FICTION

MODERN CLASSICS OF FANTASY

KILLING ME SOFTLY

DYING FOR IT

THE GOOD OLD STUFF

THE GOOD NEW STUFF

EXPLORERS

THE FURTHEST HORIZON

WORLDMAKERS

SUPERMEN

COEDITED WITH SHEILA WILLIAMS

ISAAC ASIMOV'S PLANET EARTH

ISAAC ASIMOV'S ROBOTS

ISAAC ASIMOV'S VALENTINES

ISAAC ASIMOV'S SKIN DEEP

ISAAC ASIMOV'S GHOSTS

ISAAC ASIMOV'S VAMPIRES

ISAAC ASIMOV'S MOONS

ISAAC ASIMOV'S CHRISTMAS

ISAAC ASIMOV'S CAMELOT

ISAAC ASIMOV'S WEREWOLVES

ISAAC ASIMOV'S SOLAR SYSTEM

ISAAC ASIMOV'S DETECTIVES

ISAAC ASIMOV'S CYBERDREAMS

COEDITED WITH JACK DANN

ALIENS!	SORCERERS!	DRAGONS!	HACKERS
UNICORNS!	DEMONS!	HORSES!	TIMEGATES
MAGICATS!	DOGTALES!	UNICORNS 2!	CLONES
MAGICATS 2!	SEASERPENTS!	INVADERS!	NANOTECH
BESTIARY!	DINOSAURS!	ANGELS!	IMMORTALS
MERMAIDS!	LITTLE PEOPLE!	DINOSAURS II	

FICTION

STRANGERS

THE VISIBLE MAN (COLLECTION)

NIGHTMARE BLUE
  (with George Alec Effinger)

SLOW DANCING THROUGH TIME
  (with Jack Dann, Michael Swanwick,
  Susan Casper and Jack C. Haldeman II)

THE PEACEMAKER

GEODESIC DREAMS (collection)

NONFICTION

THE FICTION OF JAMES TIPTREE, JR.

THE YEAR'S BEST

SCIENCE FICTION

thirty-first annual collection

edited by Gardner Dozois

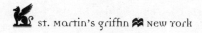 st. martin's griffin ✖ new york

These short stories are works of fiction. All of the characters,
organizations, and events portrayed in these stories are either
productions of the authors' imaginations or are used fictitiously.

THE YEAR'S BEST SCIENCE FICTION: THIRTY-FIRST ANNUAL COLLECTION.
Copyright © 2014 by Gardner Dozois. All rights reserved.
Printed in the United States of America.
For information, address St. Martin's Press, 175 Fifth Avenue,
New York, N.Y. 10010.

www.stmartins.com

Library of Congress Cataloging-in-Publication Data

 Year's Best Science Fiction : Thirty-First Annual Collection / edited by
Gardner Dozois.
        pages   cm
    ISBN 978-1-250-04620-8 (hardcover)
    ISBN 978-1-250-04621-5 (trade paperback)
    ISBN 978-1-4668-6529-7 (e-book)
 1. Science fiction.   I. Dozois, Gardner R., editor of compilation.
    PN6071.S33Y43 2014
    808.83'8762—dc23

                                                    2014008569

St. Martin's Griffin books may be purchased for educational, business,
or promotional use. For information on bulk purchases, please contact
Macmillan Corporate and Premium Sales Department at 1-800-221-7945,
extension 5442, or write specialmarkets@macmillan.com.

First Edition: July 2014

10   9   8   7   6   5   4   3   2   1

contents

permissions

acknowledgments

The editor would like to thank the following people for their help and support: Susan Casper, Jonathan Strahan, Sean Wallace, Gordon Van Gelder, Andy Cox, John Joseph Adams, Ellen Datlow, Kathleen Ann Goonan, Jay Lake, Sheila Williams, Trevor Quachri, John Klima, Peter Crowther, Nick Gevers, William Shaffer, Ian Whates, Paula Guran, Tony Daniel, Liza Trombi, Mike Resnick, Niall Harrison, Pat Cadigan, Peter Coleborn, Brian White, Shahid Mahud, Mecurio R. Rivera, Jerimy Colbert, Kristine Kathryn Rusch, Allyson Longeuira, David Moore, Michael Smith, C. Joshua Villines, A. C. Wise, David Sweeney, Charlene Brusso, Fran Wilde, Bryan Thomas Schmidt, Carl Engle-Laird, Steve Cameron, Stephen Cass, Robert Wexler, Patrick Nielsen Hayden, Tom Bouman, Amanda Brown, Mary Anne Mohanraj, Vandana Singh, Susan Palwick, Matthew Kressel, Paul Cornell, Mathew Bennado, Alec Nevala-Lee, Russell B. Farr, Brian White, Eric Reynolds, Ivor W. Hartman, Correio do Fantastico, Steve Dameron, Robert Mendes, Athena Andreadis, Carl Rafala, Christopher Barzak, Edwina Harvey, Roger Gray, Erin Underwood, Gabrielle Harbowy, Torie Atkinson, George Mann, Jennifer Brehl, Peter Tennant, Susan Marie Groppi, Karen Meisner, Wendy S. Delmater, Jed Hartman, Rich Horton, Mark R. Kelly, Tehani Wessely, Michael Smith, Tod McCoy, Brian White, Andrew Wilson, Robert T. Wexler, Ian R. MacLeod, Aliette de Bodard, Lavie Tidhar, Nancy Kress, Sunny Moraine, Geoff Ryman, Paul McAuley, Robert Reed, Sean McMullen, Carrie Vaughn, Alastair Reynolds, Ken Liu, James Patrick Kelly, Allen M. Steele, Greg Egan, Martin L. Shoemaker, Jake Kerr, Sandra McDonald, Michael Swanwick, Alexander Jablokov, Val Nolan, Neal Asher, Stephen Baxter, Melissa Scott, Ian McDonald, Brendan DuBois, Damien Broderick, Liz Gorinsky, Jeff VanderMeer, David Hartwell, Kelly Link, Gavin Grant, John O'Neill, Charles Tan, Rodger Turner, Tyree Campbell, Stuart Mayne, John Kenny, Edmund Schubert, Tehani Croft, Karl Johanson, Ian Randall Strock, Nick Wood, Sally Beasley, Tony Lee, Joe Vas, John Pickrell, Ian Redman, Anne Zanoni, Kaolin Fire,

Ralph Benko, Paul Graham Raven, Nick Wood, Mike Allen, Jason Sizemore, Karl Johanson, Sue Miller, David Lee Summers, Christopher M. Cevasco, Vaughne Lee Hansen, Mark Watson, Katherine Canfield, and special thanks to my own editor, Marc Resnick.

Thanks are also due to the late, lamented Charles N. Brown and to all his staff, whose magazine *Locus* (Locus Publications, P.O. Box 13305, Oakland, CA 94661; $60 in the United States for a one-year subscription, twelve issues, via second class; credit card orders: [510] 339-9198) was used as an invaluable reference source throughout the summation. *Locus Online* (www.locusmag.com), edited by Mark R. Kelly, has also become a key reference source.

Some commentators have been predicting for several years now that digital books, e-books, are going to drive physical print books into extinction, and although e-books continue to gain an increasing share of the market, the driving-print-books-into-extinction thing didn't happen in 2013—and I don't think it is going to happen. What seems to be happening instead is that we're reaching some kind of equilibrium, where people who buy e-books continue to buy print books as well.

A study by PEW Research Center, released at the beginning of 2014, noted that half of American adults now own either a tablet or an e-reader, and even those who don't own either a tablet or an e-reader sometimes read e-books on their cell phones or smartphones. The percentage of adults who have read an e-book in the past year has risen to 28 percent, up from 23 percent at the end of 2012, and 14 percent of adults have listened to an audiobook.

However, the study also says: "Though e-books are rising in popularity, print remains the foundation of Americans' reading habits. Most people who read e-books also read print books, and just 4 percent of readers are 'e-book only.' Among adults who read at least one book in the past year, just 5 percent said they read an e-book in the last year without also reading a print book."

The PEW Research study goes on to elaborate that "87 percent of e-book readers also read a print book in the past twelve months, and 29 percent listened to an audiobook. "Eighty-four percent of audiobook listeners also read a print book in the past year, and 56 percent also read an e-book.

"A majority of print readers read only in that format, although 35 percent of print book readers also read an e-book and 17 percent listened to an audiobook.

"Overall, about half (52 percent) of readers only read a print book, 4 percent only read an e-book, and just 2 percent only listened to an audiobook. Nine percent of readers said they read books in all three formats."

So it seems fairly obvious to me that none of these formats is going to drive the others into extinction anytime soon. For the foreseeable future, most readers will buy books both in electronic and print forms during the year, choosing one format or the other depending on the circumstances, convenience, their needs of the moment, even their whim. There are strong indications that in some cases people will buy both e-book *and* print versions *of the same book*.

Far from killing literacy, as prophets back in the 'eighties and nineties were confidently assuring us that it was going to, the Internet and e-books may actually be enhancing it.

Brick-and-mortar bookstores are not going to disappear either (although online bookselling is certainly not "a passing fad," as some people were claiming only a decade or so back). An odd but interesting fact is that although big chain stores like

Barnes & Noble have closed some of their stores, independent bookstores are springing up again in many places. Bookstore sales held moderately stable in 2013. U.S. Census Bureau figures for September show bookstore sales of $1.298 billion, up 6.3 percent from September 2012. For the year-to-date, bookstore sales were down slightly, but only by 1.6 percent, to $13.19 billion. Pretty good for an industry that was supposed to be extinct by now, according to some cyberprophets.

The biggest story in the publishing world in 2013 was certainly the merger of publishing giants Random House and Penguin to form Penguin Random House, something that was announced in 2012 but only finalized this year, at a stroke reducing the so-called "Big Six" publishing houses to the "Big Five." Rumors of further possible mergers to come constantly swirl, so it's entirely possible that we could end up with the "Big Four" or even the "Big Three" eventually. What effect all of this will have on the genre, and on publishing as a whole, remains to be seen. In the year's other big news, Simon & Schuster has announced a new imprint, not yet named, that will focus on science fiction, fantasy, and horror for "YA and above"; Justin Chanda is publisher, Joe Monti is executive editor, and Navah Wolfe of Simon & Schuster Books for Young Readers has been promoted to full-time editor for the new line. Springer has also announced a new science fiction book line. On the downhill side, the busy genre publisher Night Shade Books went bankrupt and was purchased by Skyhorse Publishing and Start Publishing, who will split print publishing and digital publishing of future Night Shade Books between them; Night Shade founders Jason Williams and Jeremy Lassen will work for Skyhorse and Start as consultants, under an editor to be named later. Start also purchased Salvo Press. Underland Press was purchased by Resurrection House. Hachette Book Group purchased most of the Hyperion adult backlist from Disney. David Fickling left Random House Children's UK to found his own imprint, David Fickling Books. Longtime editor James Frenkel left Tor.

Otherwise, it was a fairly quiet year, with the other prominent news being the scramble of print publishing houses to establish digital imprints to publish e-books. Prime Books is launching a digital imprint called Masque Books. Bloomsbury Children's launched a new digital imprint, Bloomsbury Spark. Harlequin UK announced a new digital imprint, Carina UK. Telos Publishing launched a new digital imprint, Telos Moonrise. Audiobook publisher Brilliance is branching out into print and e-books with their new Grand Harbor Press imprint.

It was another fairly stable year in the professional print magazine market, after years of sometimes precipitous decline. Sales of electronic subscriptions to the magazines are continuing to creep up, as well as sales of individual electronic copies of each issue, and this is making a big difference to profitability. It may be that the Internet will ultimately save the genre print magazine market, as I predicted it might years ago when I first agitated for the *Asimov's* Web site and Forum to be created.

Asimov's Science Fiction had another strong year, probably the strongest of the genre print magazines, publishing excellent fiction by Ian R. MacLeod, Robert Reed, Neal Asher, Kristine Kathyrn Rusch, Karl Bunker, Lavie Tidhar, Alexander Jablokov, M. Bennardo, Carrie Vaughn, Tom Purdom, and others. As usual, their SF was considerably stronger than their fantasy, the reverse of *The Magazine of Fantasy & Science Fiction*. *Asimov's Science Fiction* registered a 7.3 percent loss in overall circulation, down to 23,192 from 2012's 25,025. Subscriptions were 20,327, down from 21,380. Newsstand sales were down to 2,385 copies from 2012's 3,207, plus 480 digital copies sold on average each month in 2013, up from 438 in 2012. Sell-through fell from 42 percent to 39 percent. Sheila Williams completed her ninth year as *Asimov's* editor.

Analog Science Fiction and Fact published good work by Lavie Tidhar, Martin L. Shoemaker, Alec Nevala-Lee, Joe Pitkin, Sean McMullen, Linda Nagata, Stephen Baxter, Paul Di Filippo, and others. *Analog* registered a 2.0 percent loss in overall circulation, down to 27,248 from 2012's 27,803. There were 23,630 subscriptions, down slightly from 2012's 24,503 subscriptions; newsstand sales were up to 3,235 from 2012's 2,854; digital sales were down from 446 digital copies sold on average each month in 2013 to 383 copies. Sell-through rose from 31 percent to 41 percent. Stanley Schmidt, who had been editor there for thirty-three years, retired in 2012, winning his first Hugo Award at the 2013 Worldcon. He has been replaced by Trevor Quachri. The magazine's eighty-third anniversary was in 2013.

The Magazine of Fantasy & Science Fiction was almost exactly the reverse of *Asimov's*—lots of good fantasy work appeared there in 2013, but relatively little strong SF. *F&SF* had first-class work by Geoff Ryman, Eleanor Arnason, Rachel Pollack, Brendan DuBois, Robert Reed, Susan Palwick, Alex Irvine, Andy Stewart, and others. *F&SF* registered a 7.2 percent drop in overall circulation from 11,510 to 10,678, slowing the previous year's precipitous drop of 20.4 percent. Subscriptions dropped from 8,300 to 7,762. Newsstand sales dropped from 3,210 to 2,916. Sell-through fell from 39 percent to 23 percent. Figures are not available for digital subscriptions and digital copies sold, but editor and publisher Gordon Van Gelder said that they were "healthy." Gordon Van Gelder is in his seventeenth year as editor, and thirteenth year as owner and publisher.

Interzone is technically not a "professional magazine," by the definition of the Science Fiction Writers of America (SFWA), because of its low rates and circulation, but the literary quality of the work published there is so high that it would be ludicrous to omit it. *Interzone* had good work by Lavie Tidhar, Sean McMullen, Aliette de Bodard, Jim Hawkins, John Shirley, Jason Sanford, Tim Lees, Sarah Dodd, and others this year. Exact circulation figures are not available, but it is guessed to be in the 2,000 copy range. TTA Press, *Interzone's* publisher, also publishes straight horror or dark suspense magazine *Black Static*, which is beyond our purview here, but has a similar level of professional quality. *Interzone* and *Black Static* changed to a smaller trim size in 2011, but maintained their slick look, switching from the old 7¾"-by-10¾" saddle-stitched semigloss color cover sixty-four-page format to a 6½"-by-9¼" perfect-bound glossy color cover ninety-six-page format. The editors include publisher Andy Cox and Andy Hedgecock.

If you'd like to see lots of good SF and fantasy published every year, the survival of these magazines is essential, and one important way that you can help them survive is by subscribing to them. It's never been easier to do so, something that these days can be done with just the click of a few buttons, nor has it ever before been possible to subscribe to the magazines in as many different formats, from the traditional print copy arriving by mail to downloads for your desktop or laptop available from places like Amazon (www.amazon.com), to versions you can read on your Kindle, Nook, or iPad. You can also now subscribe from overseas just as easily as you can from the United States, something formerly difficult to impossible.

So in hopes of making it easier for you to subscribe, I'm going to list both the Internet sites where you can subscribe online and the street addresses where you can subscribe by mail for each magazine: *Asimov's* site is at www.asimovs.com, and subscribing online might be the easiest thing to do, and there's also a discounted rate for online subscriptions; its subscription address is **Asimov's Science Fiction**, Dell Magazines, 267 Broadway, Fourth Floor, New York, N.Y., 10007–2352—$34.97 for annual subscription in the U.S., $44.97 overseas. *Analog's* site is at www.analogsf .com; its subscription address is **Analog Science Fiction and Fact**, Dell Magazines, 267 Broadway, Fourth Floor, New York, N.Y. 10007–2352—$34.97 for annual subscription in the U.S., $44.97 overseas. **The Magazine of Fantasy & Science Fiction's** site is at www.sfsite.com/fsf; its subscription address is **The Magazine of Fantasy & Science Fiction**, P.O. Box 3447, Hoboken, N.J., 07030, annual subscription—$36.97 in the U.S., $48.97 overseas. **Interzone** and **Black Static** can be subscribed to online at www.ttapress.com/onlinestore1.html; the subscription address for both is TTA Press, 5 Martins Lane, Witcham, Ely, Cambs CB6 2LB, England, UK, 45.00 Pounds Sterling each for a twelve-issue subscription, or there is a reduced rate dual subscription offer of 80.00 Pounds Sterling for both magazines for twelve issues; make checks payable to "TTA Press."

Most of these magazines are also available in various electronic formats through the Kindle, Nook, and other handheld readers.

The print semiprozine market continues to shrink. Many have transitioned to online all-electronic formats, although that's not a guarantee of success either—in 2011, *Zahir, Electric Velocipede,* and *Black Gate* made the switch to only-online format; *Zahir* and *Electric Velocipede* have subsequently died, and *Black Gate* has stopped posting fiction on a regular basis, although it continues to refresh its nonfiction content. Australian semiprozine *Aurealis* has transitioned to a downloadable format. *Bull Spec* has announced that 2014 will be their last year of publication.

Many of the semiprozines that remain in print format struggle to bring out their scheduled issues. The Canadian *On Spec*, the longest-running and most reliably published of all the print fiction semiprozines, which is edited by a collective under general editor, Diane L. Walton, met their production schedule as usual, bringing out four issues in 2013. Another collective-run SF magazine with a rotating editorial staff, Australia's *Andromeda Spaceways Inflight Magazine* managed only two issues this year. *Lady Churchill's Rosebud Wristlet*, the long-running slipstream magazine edited by Kelly Link and Gavin Grant, managed two issues in 2013, as did *Shimmer*, Ireland's long-running *Albedo One, Space and Time Magazine,* and the small British SF magazine *Jupiter. Weird Tales*, under new editor Marvin Kaye, managed one issue, as did *Neo-opsis. Tales of the Talisman*, edited by David Lee Summers, produced three issues this year.

Little really memorable fiction appeared in any of the surviving print semiprozines this year, which were far outstripped by the online magazines (see below).

The venerable newszine *Locus: The Magazine of the Science Fiction and Fantasy Field*, now in its forty-seventh year of publication, is about all that's left of the popular print critical magazine market, following the departure of *The New York Review of Science Fiction* to the electronic world in mid-2012. It has long been your best bet for value in this category anyway, a multiple Hugo winner, for decades an indispensible source of news, information, and reviews. The magazine has survived the death of founder, publisher, and longtime editor Charles N. Brown and has continued strongly and successfully under the guidance of a staff of editors headed by Liza Groen Trombi, and including Kirsten Gong-Wong, Carolyn Cushman, Tim Pratt, Jonathan Strahan, Francesca Myman, Heather Shaw, and many others.

I saw two issues this year (although there may have been more that I missed) of an interesting new feminist print magazine of reviews and critical essays, *The Cascadia Subduction Zone: A Literary Quarterly*, edited by L. Timmel Duchamp and Nisi Shawl.

Most of the other surviving print critical magazines are professional journals more aimed at academics than at the average reader. The most accessible of these is probably the long-running British critical zine *Foundation*.

Subscription addresses are: **Locus, The Magazine of the Science Fiction & Fantasy Field**, Locus Publications, Inc., P.O. Box 13305, Oakland, CA 94661, $76.00 for a one-year first-class subscription, twelve issues; **Foundation**, Science Fiction Foundation, Roger Robinson (SFF), 75 Rosslyn Avenue, Harold Wood, Essex RM3 ORG, UK, $37.00 for a three-issue subscription in the U.S.A; **On Spec, The Canadian Magazine of the Fantastic**, P.O. Box 4727, Edmonton, AB, Canada T6E 5G6, for subscription information, go to Web site www.onspec.ca; **Neo-opsis Science Fiction Magazine**, 4129 Carey Rd., Victoria, BC, V8Z 4G5, $25.00 for a three-issue subscription; **Albedo One**, Albedo One Productions, 2, Post Road, Lusk, Co. Dublin, Ireland; $32.00 for a four-issue airmail subscription, make checks payable to "Albedo One" or pay by PayPal at www.albedo1.com; **Lady Churchill's Rosebud Wristlet**, Small Beer Press, 150 Pleasant St., #306, Easthampton, MA 01027, $20.00 for four issues; **Andromeda Spaceways Inflight Magazine**, see Web site www .andromedaspaceways.com for subscription information; **Tales of the Talisman**, Hadrosaur Productions, P.O. Box 2194, Mesilla Park, NM 88047–2194, $24.00 for a four-issue subscription; **Jupiter**, 19 Bedford Road, Yeovil, Somerset, BA21 5UG, UK, 10 Pounds Sterling for four issues; **Shimmer**, P.O. Box 58591, Salt Lake City, UT 84158–0591, $22.00 for a four-issue subscription; *Weird Tales*, see Web site www .weirdtalesmagazine.com for subscription and ordering information; **The Cascadia Subduction Zone: A Literary Quarterly**, subscription and single issues online at www.thecsz.com, $16 annually for a print subscription, print single issues $5, Electronic Subscription—PDF format—$10 per year, electronic single issue, $3, to order by check, make them payable to Aqueduct Press, P.O. Box 95787, Seattle, WA 98145–2787.

In the last few years, the world of online-only electronic magazines has become at least as important as a place to find good new fiction as the traditional print market.

One of the most promising of the electronic magazines was *Eclipse Online*, edited by Jonathan Strahan late in 2012 as an online continuation of Strahan's critically acclaimed anthology series *Eclipse*. *Eclipse Online* published several of 2012's best stories, and then unfortunately died early in 2013, killed by the economic upheaval at parent publishing company Night Shade Books, a heavy loss to the genre.

Lightspeed (www.lightspeedmagazine.com), edited by John Joseph Adams, had a good year, featuring strong work by Jake Kerr, Matthew Kressel, Carrie Vaughn, M. Bennardo, Matthew Hughes, and others. Late in the year, a new electronic companion horror magazine, *Nightmare* (www.nightmare-magazine.com), also edited by John Joseph Adams, was added to the Lightspeed stable.

Clarkesworld (www.clarkesworldmagazine.com), edited by Sean Wallace and Neil Clarke, featured good stuff by James Patrick Kelly, Aliette de Bodard, Vandana Singh, Ian McDonald, Robert Reed, Benjanun Sriduangkaew, and others. They also host monthly podcasts of stories drawn from each issue. Clarkesworld won its third Hugo Award as Best Semiprozine this year, and also issued three volumes of stories from the magazine, *Clarkesworld: Year Three*, *Clarkesworld: Year Four*, and *Clarkesworld: Year Five*. *Clarkesworld* co-editor Sean Wallace, along with Jack Fisher, launched another new online horror magazine, *The Dark Magazine* (http://thedark magazine.com).

Subterranean (http://subterraneanpress.com), edited by William K. Schafer, had first-class work by K. J. Parker, Ted Chiang, Jay Lake, Lewis Shiner, Ian Tregillis, and others. Schafer has recently announced that he will be shutting down *Subterranean* the online magazine after 2014 to concentrate on running the Subterranean book line, which I think is a real loss to the field. Some fine material has appeared on *Subterranean* over the years, and they've been one of the few online markets receptive to running novellas, which (for some reason I don't entirely understand) are rarely found on the Internet.

Tor.com (www.tor.com), edited by Patrick Neilsen Hayden and Liz Gorinsky, with additional material purchased by Ellen Datlow, Ann VanderMeer, and others, published some outstanding work by Nancy Kress, Carrie Vaughn, Ken Liu, Andy Duncan and Ellen Klages, Michael Swanwick, Garth Nix, Karin Tidbeck, Charles Stross, and others. There was a collection of stories from the site, *Some of the Best from Tor.com, 2013 Edition*, issued as a free e-book anthology this year.

Strange Horizons (www.strangehorizons.com), the oldest continually running electronic genre magazine on the Internet, started in 2000, had a change of editorial staff this year. Longtime editors Jed Hartman and Susan Marie Groppi stepped down; the new editor-in-chief there is Niall Harrison, with Brit Mandelo, Julia Rios, and An Owomoyela as fiction editors. This year, they had strong work by Kate MacLeod, Anaea Lay, Lavie Tidhar, Sunny Moraine, Lara Elena Donnelly, and others.

Longtime print semiprozine *Electric Velocipede*, edited by John Klima, transitioned to being an electronic magazine (www.electricvelocipede.com), but then died after publishing two final issues that featured excellent work by Val Nolan, Sam Miller, and others.

Apex Magazine (www.apexbookcompany.com/apex-online) had good work by Indrapramit Das, Lavie Tidhar, Patricia C. Wrede, Michael Griffin, Emily Jang, and others. Lynne M. Thomas stepped down as editor-in-chief, and was replaced by Sigrid Ellis.

Abyss & Apex (www.abyssapexzine.com) ran interesting work by Ruth Nestvold, Damien Broderick and Paul Di Filippo, E. Lily Yu, Cat Rambo, Ken Altabef, Jay Castleberg, and others. New editor Carmelo Rafala stepped down to be replaced by the former longtime editor, Wendy S. Delmater, who returned to the helm.

An e-zine devoted to "literary adventure fantasy," *Beneath Ceaseless Skies* (http://beneath-ceaseless-skies), edited by Scott H. Andrews, ran nice stuff by Richard Parks, M. Bennardo, Gemma Files, Naim Kabir, Marissa Lingen, and others. They published their fourth *Best of BCS* reprint e-book anthology this year.

Long-running Sword & Sorcery print magazine *Black Gate*, edited by John O'Neill, transitioned into an electronic magazine in September of 2012 and can be found at www.blackgate.com. This year they put up stories by Michael Shea, Vera Nazarian, Mary Catelli, Nina Kiriki Hoffman, Dave Gross, and others, but they have recently announced that they will no longer be regularly running new fiction, although they will be regularly refreshing their nonfiction content, essays, and reviews; the occasional story will continue to appear.

A new online SF magazine was launched, *Galaxy's Edge* (www.galaxysedge.com), edited by Mike Resnick, featuring work by Stephen Leigh, Jack McDevitt, Martin L. Shoemaker, as well as lots of reprints by Jack Dann, Larry Niven, Maureen McHugh, Nancy Kress, C. L. Moore, Robert Silverberg, and others. A print edition is available from BN.com and Amazon.com for $5.99 per issue.

The Australian popular science magazine *Cosmos* (www.cosmosmagazine.com) is not an SF magazine per se, but for the last few years it has been running a story per issue (and also putting new fiction not published in the print magazine up on its Web site), and interesting stuff by Damien Broderick, Terry Dowling, Nick Mamatas, Thoralya Dyer, and others appeared there this year. The new fiction editor is SF writer Cat Sparks.

Ideomancer Speculative Fiction (www.ideomancer.com), edited by Leah Bobet, published interesting work, usually more slipstream than SF, by Sunny Moraine, Leah Thomas, Bonnie Jo Stufflebaum, and others.

Orson Scott Card's Intergalactic Medicine Show (www.intergalacticmedicine show.com), edited by Edmund R. Schubert under the direction of Card himself, ran interesting stuff from Ian Creasey, Matthew S. Rolundo, Robert J. Howe, and others.

SF/fantasy e-zine *Daily Science Fiction* (http://dailysciencefiction.com) publishes one new SF or fantasy story *every single day* for the entire year. Unsurprisingly, many of these were not really up to professional standards, but there were some good stories here and there by Robert Reed, M. Bennardo, Ken Liu, Colin P. Davies, Cat Rambo, and others. Editors there are Michele-Lee Barasse and Jonathan Laden.

Redstone Science Fiction (http://redstonesciencefiction.com) has gone "on hiatus," which usually means that a magazine isn't coming back.

GigaNotoSaurus (http://giganotosaurus.org), now edited by Rashida J. Smith, taking over from Ann Leckie, published one story a month by writers such as C.S.E. Cooney, Caroline M. Yoachim, Ken Liu, Cat Rambo and Ben Bergis, and others.

The World SF Blog (http://worldsf.wordpress.com), edited by Lavie Tidhar, was a good place to find science fiction by international authors, and also published news, links, round table discussions, essays, and interviews related to "science fiction, fantasy, horror, and comics from around the world." The site is no longer being updated, but an extensive archive is still accessible there.

A similar site is *International Speculative Fiction* (http://internationalSF.wordpress .com), edited by Roberto Mendes.

Weird Fiction Review (http://weirdfictionreview.com), edited by Ann VanderMeer and Jeff VanderMeer, which occasionally publishes fiction, bills itself as "an ongoing exploration into all facets of the weird," including reviews, interviews, short essays, and comics.

There's been a relaunch of *Amazing Stories* (amazingsoriesmag.com), edited by Steve Davidson, but to date it doesn't seem to have actually published much fiction.

Below this point, most of the stories are slipstream or surrealism, and it becomes harder to find center-core SF, or even genre fantasy/horror. Such sites include Rudy Rucker's *Flurb* (www.flurb.net) which hasn't been refreshed since the spring of 2012, and may well be dead, *Revolution SF* (www.revolutionsf.com), *Heliotrope* (www.he liotropemag.com), *Fireside Magazine* (www.firesidemag.com), edited by Brian White, *Interfictions Online* (http://interfictions.com), edited by Christopher Barzak and Meghan McCarron, *Michael Moorcock's New Worlds* (www.newworlds.co.uk), edited by Roger Gray, and the somewhat less slipstreamish *Bewildering Stories* (www .bewilderingstories.com)

But there's also a lot of good *reprint* SF and fantasy stories out there on the Internet, in addition to original work. *Fictionwise* and *Electric Story* have died, but there are sites where you can access formerly published stories for free, including *Strange Horizons, Tor.com, Lightspeed, Subterranean, Abyss & Apex, Apex*, and most of the sites that are associated with existent print magazines, such as *Asimov's, Analog*, and *The Magazine of Fantasy & Science Fiction*, make previously published fiction and nonfiction available for access on their sites as well, and also regularly run teaser excerpts from stories coming up in forthcoming issues. Hundreds of out-of-print titles, both genre and mainstream, are also available for free download from *Project Gutenberg* (http://promo.net/pc), and a large selection of novels and a few collections can also be accessed for free, to be either downloaded or read on-screen, at the *Baen Free Library* (www.baen.com/library). Sites such as *Infinity Plus* (www.infinity plus.co.uk) and *The Infinite Matrix* (www.infinitematrix.net) may have died as active sites, but their extensive archives of previously published material are still accessible (an extensive line of new Infinity Plus Books can also be ordered from the Infinity Plus site).

Even if you're not looking for fiction to read, though, there are still plenty of other reasons for SF fans to go on the Internet. There are many general genre-related sites of interest to be found, most of which publish reviews of books as well as of movies and TV shows, sometimes comics or computer games or anime, many of which also feature interviews, critical articles, and genre-oriented news of various kinds. The best such site is *Locus Online* (www.locusmag.com), the online version of the newsmagazine *Locus*, where you can access an incredible amount of information—including book reviews, critical lists, obituary lists, links to reviews and essays appearing outside the genre, and links to extensive database archives such as the Locus Index to Science Fiction and the Locus Index to Science Fiction Awards. The previously mentioned *Tor.com* is also one of the most eclectic genre-oriented sites on the Internet, a Web site that, in addition to its fiction, regularly publishes articles, comics, graphics, blog entries, print and media reviews, book "rereads" and episode-by-episode "rewatches" of television shows, as well as commentary on all the above. The long-running and eclectic *The New York Review of Science Fiction* has ceased print publication, but can be purchased in PDF, epub, mobi formats, and POD editions through Weightless Press (http://weightlessbooks.com; see also www.nyrsf.com for information). Other major general-interest sites include Io9 (www.io9.com), *SF Site* (www.sfsite.com), although it's no longer being regularly updated, *SFRevu* (www.sfsite.com/sfrevu), *SFCrowsnest* (www.sfcrowsnest.com), *SFScope* (www.sfscope.com), *Green Man Review* (http://greenmanreview.com), *The Agony Column* (http://trashotron.com/agony), *SFFWorld* (www.sffworld.com), *SFReader* (forums.sfreader.com), and *Pat's Fantasy Hotlist* (www.fantasyhotlist .blogspot.com). A great research site, invaluable if you want bibliographic informa- tion about SF and fantasy writers, is *Fantastic Fiction* (www.fantasticfiction.co.uk). Another fantastic research site is the searchable online update of the Hugo-winning *The Encyclopedia of Science Fiction* (www.sf-encyclopedia.com), where you can ac- cess almost four million words of information about SF writers, books, magazines, and genre themes. Reviews of short fiction as opposed to novels are very hard to find anywhere, with the exception of *Locus* and *Locus Online*, but you can find reviews of both current and past short fiction at *Best SF* (www.bestsf.net), as well as at pio- neering short-fiction review site *Tangent Online* (www.tangentonline.com). Other sites of interest include: SFF NET (www.sff.net) which features dozens of home pages and "newsgroups" for SF writers; the Science Fiction Writers of America page (www.sfwa.org); where genre news, obituaries, award information, and recommended reading lists can be accessed; *Ansible* (http://news.ansible.co.uk/Ansible), the online version of multiple Hugo winner David Langford's long-running fanzine *Ansible*; *Book View Café* (www.bookviewcafe.com) is a "consortium of over twenty professional authors," including Vonda N. McIntyre, Laura Ann Gilman, Sarah Zittel, Brenda Clough, and others, who have created a Web site where work by them—mostly reprints, and some novel excerpts—is made available for free.

There are also a number of sites where podcasts and SF-oriented radio plays, an area which has been growing in popularity in recent years, can be accessed: at *Au- dible* (www.audible.com), *Escape Pod* (http://escapepod.org, podcasting mostly SF), *SF Squeecast* (http://sfsqueecast.com), *The Coode Street Podcast* (http://jonathan strahan.podbean.com), *The Drabblecast* (www.drabblecast.org), *StarShipSofa* (www .starshipsofa.com), *SF Signal Podcast* (www.sfsignal.com), *Pseudopod* (http: //pseudo pod.org), podcasting mostly fantasy, and *Podcastle* (http://podcastle.org), podcasting mostly fantasy). *The Agony Column* (http://agonycolumn.com) also hosts a weekly podcast. There's also a site that podcasts nonfiction interviews and reviews, *Dragon Page Cover to Cover* (www.dragonpage.com).

The year 2013 was not an exceptionally strong one for short fiction overall, although so much of it is now published in so many different mediums—print, electronic, audiobooks, print-on-demand, downloadable files, chapbook novellas—that it still wasn't difficult to find a lot of good stories to read.

There weren't many strong trade original SF anthologies this year; rather than coming from trade publishers, the best SF anthologies of the year were issued by ultrasmall presses, or in nontraditional formats.

One of the best of these was *Twelve Tomorrows* (Technology Review), edited by Stephen Cass, the second in a series of special all-fiction issues produced by the magazine *MIT Technology Review*. Like the first volume, the twelve stories in *Twelve Tomorrows* are all solid core SF, most of them near-future stories that deal with the possibilities (and threats) of emerging technologies, most set within the next twenty or thirty years. You won't find any far future or flamboyant space opera stories here, which does give the volume a certain similarity if read all at once, but the literary quality of the individual stories is quite high, featuring excellent work by Nancy Kress, Paul McAuley, Greg Egan, Kathleen Ann Goonan, Peer Watts, and others, and, considered as an anthology, *Twelve Tomorrows* would certainly have to qualify as one of the year's best SF anthologies, certainly the most consistent in overall quality. Also good was *The Other Half of the Sky* (Candlemark & Gleam), edited by Athena Andreadis, coedited by Kay Holt, featuring stories about "heroes who happen to be women, doing whatever they would do in universes where they're fully human," which had first-rate work by Melissa Scott, Alexander Jablokov, Aliette de Bodard, Vandana Singh, Ken Liu, Joan Slonczewski, C. W. Johnson, Cat Rambo, and others. (Another all-women anthology, mostly fantasy rather than SF, was *One Small Step: An Anthology of Discoveries* [FableCroft], edited by Tehani Wessely.)

Another good small-press anthology was *We See a Different Frontier: A Postcolonial Speculative Fiction Anthology*, edited by Fabio Fernandes and Djibril al-Ayad. The emphasis here was more political than feminist, insomuch as the two can be separated, the idea being to give a voice to the native races who are usually conquered and subjugated by earthmen in much science fiction, especially golden age SF and the SF of the fifties and sixties. Not all the stories here are science fiction; there are a few alternate histories and fantasy stories as well (in both of which, imperialistic Western nations, often Britain, stand in for the "earthmen" of the SF stories), and the book is a bit more uneven overall in literary quality than *The Other Half of the Sky*, but there's still some excellent stuff here by Sunny Moraine, Sandra McDonald, Lavie Tidhar, J. V. Yang, Rahul Kanakia, Dinesh Rao, and others. Another eccentric small press anthology is *Pandemonium: The Lowest Heaven*, edited by Anne C. Perry and Jared Shurin, an original SF anthology produced to coincide with the exhibition *Visions of the Universe* at Royal Museums Greenwich; each story is illustrated with a picture from the exhibition, which used more than a hundred astronomical photographs and drawings to show "how advances in imaging technology have repeatedly transformed our understanding of the Universe and our own place within it." The idea behind *The Lowest Heaven* was to demonstrate "what happens when a group of today's most imaginative writers are let loose in the gigantic playground of the Solar System," which sounds great—the result, however, is not as impressive as it might have been, as the anthology produced is extremely uneven in literary quality, with some excellent material by writers such as Alastair Reynolds, Lavie Tidhar, Adam Roberts, and others nestled in among a number of noticeably weaker stories. For an anthology with close ties to astronomy and technological progress, it's somewhat disappointing that the science in some of the stories is as nonrigorous as it is; I would also have liked to have seen more core science fiction used, since many of the stories here are fantasy, some are slipstream, and some are straight mainstream, with only the faint traces of a connection to the anthology's supposed theme.

Not available in print form at all was the audiobook anthology *METAropolis: Green Space* (Audible), edited by Jay Lake and Ken Scholes. This is the third of three volumes in the *METAtropolis* series of audiobook anthologies, dealing with intrigue and conspiracies in a twenty-second century world that has suffered a disastrous ecological crash and been rebuilt to adhere to strict Green principles, producing a relatively stable worldwide society—but one threatened by radical ecoterrorists who will not be satisfied until the earth is rid of its human population altogether. You may lose a little nuance if you start with this volume rather than listening to the other two audiobook anthologies first, but most of the backstory you can pick up interstitially, on the fly, without having it diminish your enjoyment of the seven novellas here. All of the stories—by Jay Lake, Elizabeth Bear, Karl Schroeder, Seanan McGuire, Tobias S. Buckell, Mary Robinette Kowal, and Ken Scholes—are entertaining and well worth listening to. I'm not sure that *Extreme Planets* (Chaosium), edited by David Conyers, David Kerndt, and Jeff Harris, is available in print form either; I only saw it in e-book form, and although a print edition was announced, a quick search of Amazon didn't turn it up. At any rate, *Extreme Planets* features stories set on "alien worlds that push the limits of what we once believed possible in a planetary environment." There's nothing really exceptional here, although the anthology does contain a lot of solid, entertaining core SF by Peter Watts, Brian Stableford, Meryl Ferguson, and others.

Much the same could be said of *Beyond the Sun* (Fairwood Press), edited by Bryan Thomas Schmidt, that featured interesting work by Nancy Kress, Brad R. Torgeson, Jaleta Clegg, Nancy Fulda, and others, and of *Rayguns Over Texas* (FACT, Inc.) edited by Rick Klaw, that has solid work by Mark Finn, Lawrence Person, Aaron Allison, Chris N. Brown, and others. *Starship Century* (Microwave Sciences), edited by Gregory Benford and James Benford, was a mixed fiction-nonfiction anthology where the nonfiction was generally stronger than the fiction, although there were interesting stories by Neal Stephenson, Allen M. Steele, Gregory Benford, and others. Publisher WGM Publishing debuted Fiction River, an "original Anthology Magazine," with a series of volumes, some SF, some fantasy; the SF volumes included *Fiction River: Unnatural Worlds*, edited by Kristine Kathryn Rusch and Dean Wesley Smith, *Fiction River: How to Save the World*, edited by John Helfers, and *Fiction River: Time Streams*, edited by Dean Wesley Smith.

One of the few general, nonspecifically themed SF anthologies from a trade publisher was the long-awaited *Solaris Rising 2: The New Solaris Book of Science Fiction* (Solaris), edited by Ian Whates. Somewhat disappointingly after all the anticipation, there's little here that is really exceptional, but it's still a good solid SF anthology, with solid work by Paul Cornell, Liz Williams, Adrian Tchaikovsky, Mecurio D. Rivera, Vandana Singh, and others.

Most of the other original anthologies from trade publishers this year that had SF stories in them also contained fantasy and other types of fiction, and were somewhat specialized in theme: *Shadows of the New Sun: Stories in Honor of Gene Wolfe* (Tor), a tribute anthology to Gene Wolfe, edited by. J.E. Mooney and Bill Fawcett, *Oz Reimagined: New Tales from the Emerald City and Beyond* (47 North), edited by John Joseph Adams and Douglas Cohen, *The Mad Scientist's Guide to World Domination* (Tor), edited by John Joseph Adams, *The Worlds of Edgar Rice Burroughs* (Baen), edited by Mike Resnick and Robert T. Garcia, *Lonely Souls* (Spilogate), edited by Gordon Van Gelder; *Clockwork Phoenix 4* (funded by Kickstarter), edited by Mike Allen, and *Postscripts 30/31: Memoryville Blues* (PS Publishing), edited by Nick Givers and Peter Crowther. All of these anthologies featured a few good stories apiece, but were uneven in overall quality, and most mixed SF with fantasy, soft horror, and slipstream.

A YA SF anthology was *Futuredaze* (Underwood Press) edited by Hannah Strom-Martin and Erin Underwood.

Noted without comment are retro-SF anthology *Red Mars* (Random House) and cross-genre anthology *Dangerous Women* (Tor), both edited by George R. R. Martin and Gardner Dozois.

The best original fantasy anthology of the year was probably *Fearsome Journeys* (Solaris), edited by Johnathan Strahan, which featured excellent stories by Elizabeth Bear, K. J. Parker, Daniel Abraham, Scott Lynch, Ellen Kushner and Ysabeau Wilce, Kate Eliot, and others. Also first-rate was the somewhat steampunk-flavored *Queen Victoria's Book of Spells* (Tor), edited by Ellen Datlow and Terri Windling, which featured strong stories by Delia Sherman, Maureen McHugh, Jeffrey Ford, Elizabeth Bear, Jane Yolen, Theodora Goss, and others.

Eclectic anthologies that existed on the borderland between SF, fantasy, and slipstream included *Glitter & Mayhew* (Apex), edited by John Klima, Lynne M. Thomas, and Michael Damian Thomas, and *Unfettered* (Grim Oak Press), edited by Shawn Speakman. A book of Canadian superhero stories was *Masked Mosaic: Canadian Super Stories* (Tyche Books), edited by Claude Lalumiere and Camille Alexa.

There were several books that retold classic fairy tales in updated modern versions, including *Rags & Bones* (Little, Brown), edited by Melissa Marr and Tim Pratt; *Shards and Ashes* (HarperCollins), edited by Melissa Marr and Kelley Armstrong; *Impossible Monsters* (Subterranean Press), edited by Kasey Lansdale; *Clockwork Fairy Tales* (Roc), edited by Stephen L. Antczak and James C. Basset; *Once Upon a Time: New Fairy Tales* (Prime Books), edited by Paula Guran; and *Fearie Tales* (Jo Fletcher), edited by Stephen Jones. Other pleasant original fantasy anthologies included *Halloween: Magic, Mystery, and the Macabre* (Prime Books), edited by Paula Guran; *Fiction River: Christmas Ghosts* (WMG Publishing), by Kristine Grayson; and *Hex in the City* (WMG Publishing), edited by Kristine Kathryn Rusch and Dean Wesley Smith.

I don't keep a close eye on the horror genre, but original horror anthologies included *The End of the Road* (Solaris), edited by Jonathan Oliver; *Mister October, Volume I: An Anthology in Memory of Rich Hautala* (JournalStone), edited by Christopher Golden; *Mister October, Volume II: An Anthology in Memory of Rich Hautala* (JournalStone), edited by Christopher Golden; *Into the Darkness: An Anthology*

Vol. 1 (Necro Publications), edited by Dennis C. Moore and David G. Barnett; and *After Death* (Dark Moon), edited by Eric J. Guignard.

Anthologies that provided an overview of what's happening in fantastic literature in other countries, outside the usual genre boundaries (in addition to *We See a Different Frontier*) included *Mothership: Tales from Afrofuturism and Beyond*, edited by Bill Campbell and Edward Austin Hall, *Pathlight: New Chinese Writings*, edited by Li Jingze, and *International Speculative 2013 Annual Anthology of Fiction*, edited by Roberto Correio do Fantastico.

Shared-world anthologies included *Wild Cards II: Aces High* (Tor), edited by George R. R. Martin; *Man-Kzin Wars XIV* (Baen), edited by Larry Niven; *Beginnings* (Baen) edited by David Weber; *Elementary: All-New Tales of the Elemental Masters* (DAW), edited by Mercedes Lackey; and *1636: The Devil's Opera* (Baen), edited by Eric Flint and David Carrico.

L. Ron Hubbard Presents Writers of the Future Volume XXIX (Galaxy), edited by Dave Wolverton, taking over from the late K. D. Wentworth, is the most recent in a long-running series featuring novice work by beginning writers, some of whom may later turn out to be important talents.

Lavie Tidhar and Ken Liu were the most prolific authors at short-fiction lengths again this year, followed by Robert Reed, Nancy Kress, Kristine Kathryn Rusch, Albert E. Cowdrey (who I believe placed a story in every single issue of *F&SF* in 2013) and new writer M. Bennardo; all published good stories all over the place, in many different markets.

SF· continued to appear in places well outside accepted genre boundaries, from the science magazines *Cosmos* and *Nature* to *The New Yorker*.

(Finding individual pricings for all of the items from small presses mentioned in the Summation has become too time-intensive, and since several of the same small presses publish anthologies, novels, *and* short-story collections, it seems silly to repeat addresses for them in section after section. Therefore, I'm going to attempt to list here, in one place, all the addresses for small presses that have books mentioned here or there in the Summation, whether from the anthologies section, the novel section, or the short-story collection section, and, where known, their Web site addresses. That should make it easy enough for the reader to look up the individual price of any book mentioned that isn't from a regular trade publisher; such books are less likely to be found in your average bookstore, or even in a chain superstore, and so will probably have to be mail-ordered. Many publishers seem to sell only online, through their Web sites, and some will only accept payment through PayPal. Many books, even from some of the smaller presses, are also available through Amazon.com. If you can't find an address for a publisher, and it's quite likely that I've missed some here, or failed to update them successfully, Google it. It shouldn't be that difficult these days to find up-to-date contact information for almost any publisher, however small.)

Addresses: **PS Publishing**, Grosvener House, 1 New Road, Hornsea, West Yorkshire, HU18 1PG, England, U.K, www.pspublishing.co.uk; **Golden Gryphon Press**, 3002 Perkins Road, Urbana, IL 61802, www.goldengryphon.com; **NESFA Press**, P.O. Box 809, Framingham, MA 01701–0809, www.nesfa.org; **Subterranean Press**, P.O. Box 190106, Burton, MI 48519, www.subterraneanpress.com; **Old Earth**

Books, P.O. Box 19951, Baltimore, MD 21211–0951, www.oldearthbooks.com; Tachyon Press, 1459 18th St. #139, San Francisco, CA 94107, www.tachyonpublications .com; Night Shade Books, 1470 NW Saltzman Road, Portland, OR 97229, www .nightshadebooks.com; Five Star Books, 295 Kennedy Memorial Drive, Waterville, ME 04901, www.galegroup.com/fivestar; NewCon Press, via www.newconpress .com; Small Beer Press, 176 Prospect Ave., Northampton, MA 01060, www.small beerpress.com; Locus Press, P.O. Box 13305, Oakland, CA 94661; Crescent Books, Mercat Press Ltd., 10 Coates Crescent, Edinburgh, Scotland EH3 7AL, UK, www .crescentfiction.com; Wildside Press/Borgo Press, P.O. Box 301, Holicong, PA 18928–0301, or go to www.wildsidepress.com for pricing and ordering; Edge Science Fiction and Fantasy Publishing, Inc. and Tesseract Books, Ltd., P.O. Box 1714, Calgary, Alberta, T2P 2L7, Canada, www.edgewebsite.com; Aqueduct Press, P.O. Box 95787, Seattle, WA 98145–2787, www.aqueductpress.com; Phobos Books, 200 Park Avenue South, New York, NY 10003, www.phobosweb.com; Fairwood Press, 5203 Quincy Ave. SE, Auburn, WA 98092, www.fairwoodpress.com; BenBella Books, 6440 N. Central Expressway, Suite 508, Dallas, TX 75206, www.benbella books.com; Darkside Press, 13320 27th Ave. NE, Seattle, WA 98125, www.darkside press.com; Haffner Press, 5005 Crooks Rd., Suite 35, Royal Oak, MI 48073–1239, www.haffnerpress.com; North Atlantic Press, P.O. Box 12327, Berkeley, CA, 94701; Prime Books, P.O. Box 36503, Canton, OH, 44735, www.primebooks.net; Monkey Brain Books, 11204 Crossland Drive, Austin, TX 78726, www.monkeybrainbooks .com; Wesleyan University Press, University Press of New England, Order Dept., 37 Lafayette St., Lebanon, NH 03766–1405, www.wesleyan.edu/wespress; Agog! Press, P.O. Box U302, University of Wollongong, NSW 2522, Austrailia, www.uow.ed.au /~rhood/agogpress; Wheatland Press, via www.wheatlandpress.com; MirrorDanse Books, P.O. Box 3542, Parramatta NSW 2124, www.tabula-rasa.info/MirrorDanse; Arsenal Pulp Press, 103–1014 Homer Street, Vancouver, BC, Canada V6B 2W9, www.arsenalpress.com; DreamHaven Books, 912 W. Lake Street, Minneapolis, MN 55408; Elder Signs Press/Dimensions Books, order through www.dimensions books.com; Chaosium, via www.chaosium.com; Spyre Books, P.O. Box 3005, Radford, VA 24143; SCIFI, Inc., P.O. Box 8442, Van Nuys, CA 91409–8442; Omnidawn Publishing, order through www.omnidawn.com; CSFG, Canberra Speculative Fiction Guild, www.csfg.org.au/publishing/anthologies/the_outcast; Hadley Rille Books, via www.hadleyrillebooks.com; Suddenly Press, via suddenlypress@yahoo. com; Sandstone Press, P.O. Box 5725, One High St., Dingwall, Ross-shire, IV15 9WJ; Tropism Press, via www.tropismpress.com; SF Poetry Association/Dark Regions Press, www.sfpoetry.com, send checks to Helena Bell, SFPA Treasurer, 1225 West Freeman St., Apt. 12, Carbondale, IL 62401; DH Press, via diamondbookdistributors .com; Kurodahan Press, via Web site www.kurodahan.com; Ramble House, 443 Gladstone Blvd., Shreveport LA 71104; Interstitial Arts Foundation, via www.inter stitialarts.org; Raw Dog Screaming, via www.rawdogscreaming.com; Three Legged Fox Books, 98 Hythe Road, Brighton, BN1 6JS, UK; Norilana Books, via www .norilana.com; coeur de lion, via coeurdelion.com.au; PARSECink, via www.parsec ink.org; Robert J. Sawyer Books, via www.sfwriter.com/rjsbooks.htm; Rackstraw Press, via http://rackstrawpress.nfshost.com; Candlewick, via www.candlewick.com; Zubaan, via www.zubaanbooks.com; Utter Tower, via www.threeleggedfox.co.uk;

Spilt Milk Press, via www.electricvelocipede.com; **Paper Golem**, via www.paper golem.com; **Galaxy Press**, via www.galaxypress.com; **Twelfth Planet Press**, via www.twelfhplanetpress.com; **Five Senses Press**, via www.sensefive.com; **Elastic Press**, via www.elasticpress.com; **Lethe Press**, via www.lethepressbooks.com; **Two Cranes Press**, via www.twocranespress.com; **Wordcraft of Oregon**, via www.word craftoforegon.com; **ISFiC Press**, 456 Douglas Ave., Elgin, IL 60120 or www.isfic press.com.

According to the newsmagazine *Locus*, there were 2,643 books "of interest to the SF field" published in 2013, down 10 percent from 2,951 titles in 2012. Overall new titles were down 9 percent to 1,850 from 2012's 2,030, while reprints dropped 14 percent to 793 from 2012's 921. Hardcover sales fell by 6 percent to 819 from 2012's 875, while the number of trade paperbacks declined by 5 percent to 1,280 to 2012's 1,343; as has been true for the last couple of years, the big drop was in mass-market paper-backs, which dipped a whopping 26 percent to 544 from 2012's 733, probably because of competition with e-books, which seem to be cutting into mass-market sales more than they are in any other category. The number of new SF novels was up to 339 titles from 2012's 318. The number of new fantasy novels fell slightly, to 620 from 2012's 670. Horror novels were down to 181 from 2012's 207 titles. Paranormal ro-mances were down to 237 titles from 2012's 314—although it should be noted that sometimes it's a subjective call whether a particular novel should be pigeonholed as paranormal romance, fantasy, or horror.

Young Adult SF novels continued to boom, especially dystopian and postapoca-lyptic SF, perhaps at least in part because of the popularity of *The Hunger Games* novels and films. The 339 original SF novels include 122 YA novels, 36 percent of the new SF total, up from 28 percent in 2012; this also includes 38 SF first novels, 11 percent of the new SF total, down from 13 percent last year. Fantasy's 620 origi-nal novels include 233 YA novels, 36 percent of the new fantasy total, up from 2012's 33 percent; this includes 57 fantasy first novels, 9 percent of the fantasy total, down from 2012's 10 percent.

It's worth noting that in spite of slight declines, this is still an enormous number of books—far more than the entire combined total of genre titles only a few decades back. And these totals don't count e-books, media tie-in novels, gaming novels, nov-elizations of genre movies, print-on-demand books, or self-published novels—all of which would swell the overall total by hundreds if counted.

As usual, busy with all the short-story reading I have to do, I didn't have time to read many novels myself this year, so I'll limit myself to mentioning novels that re-ceived a lot of attention and acclaim in 2013 including, *On the Steel Breeze* (Gollancz), by Alastair Reynolds; *Shaman* (Orbit), by Kim Stanley Robinson; *Protector* (DAW), by C. J. Cherryh; *Evening's Empires* (Gollancz), by Paul McAuley; *Abaddon's Gate* (Orbit), by James S. A. Corey; *The Human Division* (Tor), by John Scalzi; *Burning Paradise* (Tor), by Robert Charles Wilson; *The Last President* (Ace), by John Barnes; *Zero Point* (Tor), by Neal Asher; *The Ocean at the End of the Lane* (Morrow), by Neil Gaiman; *Blood of Dragons* (Harper Voyager), by Robin Hobb; *Proxima* (Gollancz), by Stephen Baxter; *River of Stars* (Roc), by Guy Gavriel Kay; *Without a*

Summer (Tor), by Mary Robinette Kowal; *Life on the Preservation* (Solaris), by Jack Skillingstead; *Neptune's Blood* (Ace), by Charles Stross; *The Long War* (Harper-Collins), by Terry Pratchett and Stephen Baxter; *Fiddlehead* (Tor), by Cherie Priest; *Kalimpura* (Tor), by Jay Lake; *The Republic of Thieves* (Del Rey), by Scott Lynch; *Blood of Tyrants* (Del Rey), by Naomi Novik; *The Best of All Possible Worlds* (Del Rey), by Karen Lord; *Cold Steel* (Orbit), by Kate Elliott; *The Shambling Guide to New York City* (Orbit), by Mur Lafferty; *Transcendental* (Tor), by James Gunn; *Allegencies* (Tor), by Beth Bernobich; *Zombie Baseball Beatdown* (Little, Brown), by Paolo Bacigalupi; *Starhawk* (Ace), by Jack McDevit; *Prophet of Bones* (Henry Holt), by Ted Kosmatka; *The Land Across* (Tor), by Gene Wolfe; *Homeland* (Tor Teen), by Cory Doctorow; *The Girl Who Soared Over Fairyland and Cut the Moon in Two* (Macmillan), by Catherynne M. Valente; *The Serene Invasion* (Solaris), by Eric Brown; *On the Razor's Edge* (Tor), by Michael Flynn; *Impulse* (Tor), by Steven Gould; *London Falling* (Tor), by Paul Cornell; *The Tyrant's Law* (Orbit), by Daniel Abraham; *The Emperor of All Things* (Bantam Press), by Paul Witcover; *Mending the Moon* (Tor), by Susan Palwick; *Necessary Evil* (Tor), by Ian Tregillis; *Kill City Blues* (Harper Voyager), by Richard Kadrey; *NOS4A2* (Morrow), by Joe Hill; and *Doctor Sleep* (Scribner), by Stephen King.

As usual, this list contains fantasy novels and some hard to classify items, but there is also plenty of core SF, and even hard science fiction, including the Reynolds, the McAuley, the Scalzi, the Kim Stanley Robinson, the Skillingstead, the C. J. Cherryh, the Corey, the Robert Charles Wilson, the Pratchett and Baxter, and many others, and many more could be cited from the lists of small-press novels and first novels. Science fiction has not vanished from the bookshelves yet, no matter what you hear—there's still more good core SF out there than any one person could possibly have time to read in the course of a year.

Small presses are active in the novel market these days, where once they published mostly collections and anthologies. Novels issued by small presses this year included: *Martian Sands* (PS Publishing), by Lavie Tidhar; *Finches of Mars* (The Friday Project), by Brian W. Aldiss; *The Red: First Light* (Mythic Delirium Books), by Linda Nagata; *Snipers* (WMG Publishing), by Kristine Kathryn Rusch; *Leave Your Sleep* (PS Publishing), by R. B. Russell; *The Aylesford Skull* (Titan Books), by James Blaylock; *Growing Pains* (PS Publishing), by Ian Whates; *Sister Mine* (Grand Central), by Nalo Hopkinson; *The Village Sang to the Sea: A Memoir of Magic* (Aeon Press Books), by Bruce McAllister; and *Joyland* (Hard Case Crime), by Stephen King.

The year's first novels included *The Scroll of Their Years* (Pyr), by Chris Willrich; *Ancillary Justice* (Orbit) by Ann Leckie; *Sulway* (Tartarus), by Naomi Rupetta; *A Stranger in Olondria* (Small Beer Press), by Sofia Samatar; *The Bone Season* (Bloomsbury), by Samantha Shannon; *Sea Change* (Tor), by S. M. Wheeler; *Billy Moon* (Tor), by Douglas Lain; *Delia's Shadow* (Tor), by Jamie Lee Moyer; *The Age of Ice* (Scribner), by J. M. Sidorova; *The Golem and the Jinni* (HarperCollins), by Helene Wecker; *The Six-Gun Tarot* (Tor), by R. S. Belcher; *The Darwin Elevator* (Del Rey), by Jason M. Hough; *Terra* (Gollancz), by Mitch Benn; *Taken* (HarperTeen), by Eric Bowman; *Shadows Cast by Stars* (Atheneum Books), by Catherine Knutsson; *No Return* (Night Shade Books), by Zachary Jernigan; *Wolfhound Century* (Gollancz), by Peter

Higgins; *Seoul Survivors* (Jo Fletcher Books), by Naomi Foyle; *All Our Yesterdays* (Hyperion), by Cristin Terrill; *The Genesis Code* (DarkFuse), by Lisa von Biela; *Dreams and Shadows* (Gollancz), by Robert C. Cargill; and *The Thinking Woman's Guide to Real Magic* (Viking), by Emily Crow Barker. None of these novels seemed to draw an unusual amount of attention.

Good novella chapbooks in 2013 included *The Reparateur of Strasbourg* (PS Publishing), by Ian R. MacLeod, *Love in the Time of Metal and Flesh* (Prime Books), by Jay Lake, *Spin* (Spin), by Nina Allen, *Balfour and Meriwether in the Incident of the Harrowmoor Dogs* (Subterranean Press), by Daniel Abraham, *Strangers at the Room of Lost Souls* (WMG Publishing), by Kristine Kathryn Rusch, *Six-Gun Snow White* (Subterranean Press), by Catherynne M. Valente, *Free Fall* (Immersion Press), by Mecurio D. Rivera, *Cry Murder! In a Small Voice* (Small Beer Press), by Gilman Greer, *Land of Dreams* (Prime/Masque), by Yellowboy Erzebet, *Summer's End*, by Lisa Morton (JournalStone), *Forbidden* (Subterranean Press), by Kelly Armstrong, and *The Last Full Measure* (Subterranean Press), by Jack Campbell.

Novel omnibuses this year included the following: *SF Gateway Omnibuses: Nightwings, A Time of Changes, Lord Valentine's Castle*, by Robert Silverberg; *Tactics of Mistake, Time Storm, The Dragon and the George*, by Gordon R. Dickson; *The Pellucidar Omnibus*, by Edgar Rice Burroughs; *The Last Coin, The Paper Grail, All the Bells on Earth*, by James Blaylock; *Black Easter, The Day After Judgement, The Seedling Stars*, by James Blish; *Orbitville, The Ragged Astronauts, A Wreath of Stars*, by Bob Shaw; *After Long Silence, Shadow's End, Six Moon Dance*, by Sheri S. Tepper; *The Skylark of Space, Skylark Three, Skylark of Valeron, Skylark DuQuesne*, by E. E. "Doc" Smith.

Novel omnibuses are also frequently made available through the Science Fiction Book Club.

Not even counting print-on-demand books and the availability of out-of-print books as e-books or as electronic downloads from Internet sources, a lot of long out-of-print stuff has come back into print in the last couple of years in commercial trade editions. Here's some out-of-print titles that came back into print this year, although producing a definitive list of reissued novels is probably impossible.

In addition to the novel omnibuses already mentioned, Gollancz reissued *Transformations*, by Michael Bishop, *No Enemy But Time*, by Michael Bishop, *The Falling Woman*, by Pat Murphy, *AEgypt*, by John Crowley, *The Deep*, by John Crowley, *Deus Irae*, by Philip K. Dick and Roger Zelazny, *Last Call*, by Tim Powers, *Von Beck*, by Michael Moorcock, *The Gods Themselves*, by Isaac Asimov, and *This Is the Way the World Ends*, by James Morrow; Tor reissued *Ha'penny, Farthing* and *Half a Crown*, by Jo Walton, *The Path of Daggers*, by Robert Jordan, and *The River Awakens*, by Steven Erikson; Tor Teen reissued *Farseed*, by Pamela Sargent; Subterranean Press reissued *The Deadly Streets*, by Harlan Ellison, *Gentleman Junkie and Other Stories of the Hung-Up Generation*, by Harlan Ellison; Baen reissued *Transgalactic*, by A. E. Van Vogt, and *The Man Who Sold the Moon/Orphans of the Sky*, by Robert A. Heinlein; Bantam reissued *Tuf Voyaging*, by George R. R. Martin; Ace reissued *Daughter of Regals and Other Tales*, by Stephen R. Donaldson; Titan reissued *Flesh*, by Philip Jose Farmer, and *The Steel Czar*, by Michael Moorcock; Lethe Press reissued *Minions of the Moon*, by Richard Bowes, *Point of Dreams*, by Melissa

Scott and Lisa A. Barnett, and *Fatal Women*, by Tanith Lee; NonStop Press reissued *Lord of Darkness*, by Robert Silverberg; Knopf reissued *Eragon*, by Christopher Paolini; Muchelland Books reissued *Darwin's Blade*, by Dan Simmons; PM Press reissued *Jerusalem Commands*, by Michael Moorcock; CreateSpace reissued *The Iron Dream*, by Norman Spinrad; EReads reissued *Ribofunk*, by Paul Di Filippo; Chizine Press reissued *The Warrior Who Carried Life*, by Geoff Ryman; Roc reissued *Valentine Pontifex*, by Robert Silverberg; Morrow reissued *Declare*, by Tim Powers; Small Beer Press reissued *Death of a Unicorn*, by Peter Dickinson; Fairwood Press reissued *Ancient of Days*, by Michael Bishop, and *The Terrorists of Irustan*, by Louise Marley; Tartarus Press reissued *Sub Rosa*, by Robert Aickman; Bison Books reissued *The End of the Dream*, by Philip Wylie.

Many authors are now reissuing their old back titles as ebooks, either through a publisher or all by themselves, so many that it's impossible to keep track of them all here. Before you conclude that something from an author's backlist is unavailable, though, check with the Kindle and Nook stores, and with other online vendors.

2013 was another moderately strong year for short-story collections, although perhaps not as strong overall as the last few years have been.

The year's best collections included *A Very British History: The Best of Paul McAuley* (PS Publishing), by Paul McAuley; *The Best of Joe Haldeman* (Subterranean Press), by Joe Haldeman, edited by Jonathan Strahan and Gary K. Wolfe; *Horse of a Different Color* (Small Beer Press), by Howard Waldrop; *The Best of Connie Willis* (Ballantine Del Rey), by Connie Willis; *Good-bye Robinson Crusoe and Other Stories* (Subterranean Press), by John Varley; *Beyond the Rift* (Tachyon), by Peter Watts; *Universes* (PS Publishing), by Stephen Baxter; *Big Mama Stories* (Aqueduct), by Eleanor Arnason; *In the Company of Thieves* (Aqueduct), by Kage Baker; *Bleeding Shadows* (Subterranean Press), by Joe R. Lansdale; *Sir Hereward and Mister Fitz: Three Adventures* (Subterranean Press), by Garth Nix; Tales of Majipoor (Roc), by Robert Silverberg; *Conservation of Shadows* (Prime Books), by Yoon Ha Lee; *Adam Roberts* (Orion/Gollancz), by Adam Roberts; and *Five Autobiographies and a Fiction* (Subterranean Press), by Lucius Shepard. Two of the year's best collections were available only as ebooks: *Snodgrass and Other Illusions: The Best Short Fiction of Ian R. MacLeod* (Open Road Media), by Ian R. MacLeod, and *Life After Wartime* (Amazon Digital Services), by Paul McAuley.

Also good were *Yamada Monogatari: Demon Hunter* (Prime Books), by Richard Parks; *North American Lake Monsters* (Small Beer Press), by Nathan Ballingrud; *The Bread We Eat in Dreams* (Subterranean Press), by Catherynne M. Valente; *The Beautiful Thing That Awaits Us All and Other Stories* (Night Shade Books), by Laird Barron; *The Ape's Wife and Other Stories* (Subterranean Press), by Caitlin R. Kiernan; *Before and Afterlives* (Lethe Press), by Christopher Barzak; *What the Doctor Ordered* (Centipede Press), by Michael Blumlein; *The Queen, the Cambion, and Seven Others* (Aqueduct), by Richard Bowes; *Her Husband's Hands* (Prime Books), by Adam-Troy Castro; *WikiWorld* (ChiZine), by Paul Di Filippo; *Jewels in the Dust* (Subterranean Press), by Peter Crowther; *Space Is Just a Starry Night* (Aqueduct Press), by Tanith Lee; *The Hunter from the Woods* (Subterranean Press), by Robert

McCammon; *The Human Front* (PM Press), by Ken MacLeod; *Kabu Kabu* (Prime Books), by Nnedi Okorafor; *Antiquities and Tangibles and Other Stories* (Merry Blacksmith), by Tim Pratt; *New Taboos* (PM Press), by John Shirley; and *How the World Became Quiet: Myths of the Past, Present, and Future* (Subterranean Press), by Rachel Swirsky.

Career-spanning retrospective collections this year included *The Complete Short Stories: Volume One—The 1950s* (HarperCollins), by Brian W. Aldiss; *The Collected Short Works of Poul Anderson, Volume 5: The Door to Anywhere* (NESFA Press), by Poul Anderson; *Magic Highways: The Early Jack Vance, Volume Three* (Subterranean Press), by Jack Vance, edited by Terry Dowling and Jonathan Strahan; *The Collected Stories of Philip K. Dick Volume Four: The Minority Report (1954–1963)* (Subterranean Press), by Philip K. Dick; *The Story Until Now* (Wesleyan University Press), by Kit Reed; *The Collected Stories of Carol Emshwiller, Volume 2* (Nonstop Press), by Carol Emshwiller; *The Classic Horror Stories* (Oxford University Press), by H. P. Lovecraft, edited by Roger Luckhurst; *The Very Best of Barry N. Malzberg* (Nonstop Press), by Barry N. Malzberg; *The Collected Stories of Robert Silverberg, Volume Eight: Hot Times in Magma City* (Subterranean Press), by Robert Silverberg; *The Best of Robert Silverberg: Stories of Six Decades* (Subterranean Press), by Robert Silverberg; and *The Complete John Thunstone* (Haffner Press), by Manly Wade Wellman.

As usual, small presses again dominated the list of short-story collections, with trade collections having become almost as rare as the proverbial hen's teeth.

A wide variety of "electronic collections," often called "fiction bundles," too many to individually list here, are also available for downloading online at many sites. The Science Fiction Book Club continues to issue new collections as well.

The most reliable buys in the reprint anthology market, as usual, are the various Best of the Year anthologies. At the moment, science fiction is being covered by three anthologies (actually, technically, by two anthologies and by two separate half anthologies): the one you are reading at the moment, *The Year's Best Science Fiction* series from St. Martin's, edited by Gardner Dozois, now up to its thirty-first annual collection; the *Year's Best SF* series (Tor), edited by David G. Hartwell, now up to its eighteenth annual volume; by the science fiction half of *The Best Science Fiction and Fantasy of the Year: Volume Seven* (Night Shade Books), edited by Jonathan Strahan; and by the science fiction half of *The Year's Best Science Fiction and Fantasy: 2013 Edition* (Prime Books), edited by Rich Horton (in practice, of course, Strahan's and Horton's books probably won't divide neatly in half with their coverage, and there's likely to be more of one thing than another). The annual Nebula Awards anthology, which covers science fiction as well as fantasy of various sorts, functions as a de facto Best of the Year anthology, although it's not usually counted among them; this year's edition was *Nebula Awards Showcase 2013* (Pyr), edited by Catherine Asaro. There were three Best of the Year anthologies covering horror: *The Best Horror of the Year: Volume Five* (Night Shade), edited by Ellen Datlow; *The Mammoth Book of Best New Horror 24* (Robinson), edited by Stephen Jones; and *The Year's Best Dark Fantasy and Horror: 2013 Edition* (Prime Books), edited by Paula

Guran. Fantasy, which used to have several series devoted to it, is now only covered by the fantasy halves of the Stranhan and Horton anthologies, plus whatever stories fall under the "Dark Fantasy" part of Guran's anthology; as commercially successful at novel lengths as fantasy is, it seems odd that it doesn't have a Best of the Year of its own devoted to it. Also functioning as a somewhat specialized Best of the Year was *Imaginarium 2013: The Best Canadian Speculative Writing* (ChiZine Publications), edited by Sandra Kasturi and Samantha Beiko. There was also *The 2013 Rhysling Anthology* (Hadrosaur Productions), edited by John Mannone, which compiles the Rhysling Award–winning SF poetry of the year.

The best stand-alone reprint anthology of the year was undoubtedly *Twenty-First Century Science Fiction* (Tor), edited by David G. Hartwell and Patrick Nielsen Hayden, a book that clearly gives the lie to the idea that there are no good new science fiction writers coming along anymore. This huge anthology contains stories by Elizabeth Bear, Charles Stross, Cory Doctorow, Paolo Bacigalupi, Catherynne M. Valente, Hannu Rajaniemi, John Scalzi, Ken Liu, Yoon Ha Lee, Tobias S. Buckell, Vandana Singh, Peter Watts, Paul Cornell, Liz Williams, Ian Creasey, Karl Schroeder, David Moles, Jo Walton, Neal Asher, Rachel Swirsky, and many others, and belongs in the library of everyone who is interested in the evolution of the genre. Another good overview of young talent is provided by *Telling Tales: The Clarion West 30th Anniversary Anthology* (Hydra House), edited by Ellen Datlow, a compendium of tales written during the Clarion West Writers Program, where they've been grooming new writers with an intensive six-week training seminar in Seattle, Washinton, for more than thirty years; the book contains strong stories by Andy Duncan, Benjamin Rosenbaum, David Marusek, Mary Rosenblum, Kij Johnson, Ysabeau S. Wilce, Kathleen Ann Goonan, Louise Marley, Margo Lanagan, Susan Palwick, Ian McHugh, Daniel Abraham, David D. Levine, Christopher Rowe, Rachel Swirsky, and Nisi Shawl, plus essays here about the authors and the workshop process itself by Vonda N. McIntyre, Greg Bear, Pat Murphy, Howard Waldrop, Samuel R. Delany, Maureen F. McHugh, Lucy Sussex, Connie Willis, Geoff Ryman, Elizabeth Hand, Terry Bisson, Andy Duncan, Pat Cadigan, Nancy Kress, Ursula K. LeGuin, Paul Park, and editor Ellen Datlow herself, all of whom have either been instructors at Clarion West, or, in some cases, students there themselves, once upon a time.

There were also two big reprint anthologies for fans of the time-travel story, *The Time Traveller's Almanac* (Head of Zeus), edited by Jeff VanderMeer and Ann VanderMeer and *The Mammoth Book of Time Travel SF* (Running Press), edited by Mike Ashley; two books of superhero stories, *Superheroes* (Prime Books), edited by Richard Horton and *Super Stories of Heroes and Villains* (Tachyon), edited by Claude Lalumiere; a book of ape stories, *The Apes of Wrath* (Tachyon), edited by Richard Klaw; a book of cyberpunk stories, *Cyberpunk: Stories of Hardware, Software, Wetware, Evolution and Revolution* (Underland Press), edited by Victoria Blake; a book of stories about aliens, *Aliens: Recent Encounters* (Prime Books), edited by Alex Daily MacFarlane; a book of end of the world stories, *After the End: Recent Apocalypses* (Prime Books) edited by Paula Guran; and a book about future games, *Future Games* (Prime Books), edited by Paula Guran.

Reprint fantasy anthologies were a bit scant on the ground this year, but they did include a mixed reprint (mostly) and original anthology, *Unnatural Creatures* (Harper-Collins), edited by Neil Gaiman and Maria Dahvana Headley; *The Mammoth Book of Angels and Demons* (Running Press), edited by Paula Guran; *Weird Detectives: Recent Investigations* (Prime Books), edited by Paula Guran; and a mixed reprint (mostly) and original anthology of Christmas stories, *A Cosmic Christmas 2 You* (Baen), edited by Hank Davis. A big book of stories by older writers, most from the nineteenth and twentieth centuries, is found in *The Treasury of the Fantastic* (Tachyon), edited by David Sander and Jacob Weisman.

Reprint horror anthologies included *Hauntings* (Tachyon), edited by Ellen Datlow; a mixed reprint and original anthology of Lovecraft pastiches, *Weirder Shadows Over Insmouth* (Fedogan & Bremer), edited by Stephen Jones; *Shades of Blue and Gray: Ghosts of the Civil War* (Prime Books), edited by Steve Berman; *Zombies: Shambling through the Ages* (Prime Books), edited by Steve Berman; *Bad Seeds: Evil Progeny* (Prime Books), edited by Steve Berman; a mixed reprint and original anthology of Jack the Ripper stories, *Tales of Jack the Ripper* (Word Horde), edited by Ross E. Lockhart; and a mixed reprint (mostly) and original anthology of outer space horror stories, *In Space No One Can Hear You Scream* (Baen), edited by Hank Davis.

Anthologies of gay SF and fantasy and/or erotica included: *Heiresses of Russ 2013: The Year's Best Lesbian Speculative Fiction* (Lethe Press), edited by Tenea D. Johnson and Steve Berman; *Fantastic Erotica: The Best of Circlet Press 2008–2012* (Circlet), edited by Cecilia Tan and Bethay Zalatz; *Where Thy Dark Eye Glances: Queering Edgar Allen Poe* (Lethe Press), edited by Steve Berman; *Suffered from the Night: Queering Stoker's Dracula* (Lethe Press), edited by Steve Berman; and *Wilde Stories 2013* (Lethe Press), edited by Steve Berman.

It was another somewhat weak year in the genre-oriented non-fiction category, with the two most interesting books being studies of the early roots of the genre and one of its strangest prominent figures, controversial SF magazine editor Ray Palmer, *The Man from Mars* (Penguin/Tarcher), by Fred Nadis and *War Over Lemuria: Richard Shaver, Ray Palmer and the Strangest Chapter of 1940s Science Fiction* (McFarland), by Richard Toronto.

Other books about genre authors included *William Gibson* (University of Illinois Press), by Gary Westfahl, *John Brunner* (University of Illinois Press), by Jad Smith, *Dragonwriter: A Tribute to Anne McCaffrey and Pern* (BenBella/Smart Pop), by Todd McCaffery, *The Lady and Her Monsters: A Tale of Dissections, Real-Life Dr. Frankensteins, and the Creation of Mary Shelley's Masterpiece* (Morrow), by Rosanne Montillo, *H. P. Lovecraft's Dark Arcadia: The Satire, Symbology and Contradiction* (McFarland), by Gavin Callaghan, and *As I Knew Him: My Dad, Rod Serling* (Kensington/Citadel), by Anne Serling. An autobiography was *Miracles of Life: Shanghai to Shepperton, An Autobiography* (Norton/Liveright), by J. G. Ballard. Books of essays *by* writers, sometimes examining their own work or providing errata about it, included *The Wit and Wisdom of Tyrion Lannister* (Bantam), by George R. R. Martin, *Dodger's Guide to London* (Doubleday UK), by Terry Pratchett, *Ender's World: Fresh Perspectives on the SF Classic Ender's Game* (BenBella/Smart Pop), edited by

Orson Scott Card, *House of Steel: The Honorverse Companion* (Baen), by David Weber, *Benchmarks Continued: 1975–1982* (Ansible), by Algis Budrys, *Doctor Who: Who-ology* (BBC) by Cavan Scott and Mark Wright, *The Mallet of Loving Correction: Selected Writings from Whatever, 2008–2012* (Subterranean Press), by John Scalzi, and *Make Good Art* (Morrow), by Neil Gaiman.

Critical studies about the genre included *Parabolas of Science Fiction* (Wesleyan University Press), by Brian Attebery and Veronica Hollinger, *Strange Matings: Science Fiction, Feminism, African American Voices, and Octavia E. Butler* (Aqueduct), by Rebecca J. Holden and Nisi Shawl, *Afrofuturism: The World of Black Sci-Fi and Fantasy Culture* (Lawrence Hill Books), by Ytasha Womack, *We Modern People: Science Fiction and the Making of Modern Russia* (Wesleyan University Press), by Anindita Banerjee, *Los Angeles Review of Books—Digital Editions #12: Science Fiction* (Los Angeles Review of Books), edited by Jerome Winter, *Here Be Dragons: Exploring Fantasy Maps and Settings* (Wesleyan University Press), by Stefan Ekman, and *Out in the Dark: Interviews with Gay Horror Filmmakers, Actors and Authors* (Lethe Press), edited by Sean Abley. *Past Masters, and Other Bookish Natterings* (The Merry Blacksmith Press), is a collection of columns about yesterday's SF and author profiles by Bud Webster.

Wonderbook: The Illustrated Guide to Creating Imaginative Fiction (Abrams Image), by Jeff VanderMeer may be the most eccentric and entertaining book of writing advice ever produced, profusely and imaginatively illustrated by Jeremy Zerfoss, with additional advice from Ursula K. Le Guin, Neil Gaiman, Kim Stanley Robinson, Peter Straub, Lev Grossman, and others.

The World Until Yesterday: What We Can Learn from Traditional Societies (Viking Press), by Jared Diamond, will be of interest to anyone who likes anthropological SF. Fans of the ever-increasing volume of apocalyptic and postapocalyptic SF will probably find a lot of food for thought in *Scatter, Adapt, and Remember: How Humans Will Survive a Mass Extinction* (Doubleday), by Annalee Newitz.

My two favorite nonfiction books of the year have no direct connection to the genre, but I think will be of interest anyway to most genre readers, *One Summer: America, 1927* (Doubleday) by Bill Bryson, is a fascinating look at the hidden interconnections between the major players in world and local history during one American summer, and has perhaps a minor genre connection by containing a great deal of information about the early pioneering days of powered flight, and showing the impact that technological innovation rapidly had on the world. One of the funniest books of the year is *Hyperbole and a Half: Unfortunate Situations, Flawed Coping Mechanisms, Mayhem, and Other Things That Happened* (Touchstone), by Allie Brosh, a collection of her Web comics and blog entries from her popular site, which do—as weak justification for inclusion here—contain a lot of fantasy elements in their depiction of the world of childhood. The section entitled "The God of Cake" is one of the funniest things I ever read on the Internet, and most of the other entries are comic gems as well.

The year 2013 was a weak one in the art book market. As usual, your best bet was probably the latest in a long-running "best of the year" series for fantastic art, *Spec-*

trum 20: The Best in Contemporary Fantastic Art (Underwood Books), edited by Cathy Fenner and Arnie Fenner. Also good were *Expose 11: The Finest Digital Art in the Universe* (Ballistic Publishing) edited by Paul Hellard and Mark Thomas; *The Art of Brom* (Flesk Publications), by Brom; *Frazetta Sketchbook* (Vanguard Productions), by Frank Frazetta and J. David Spurlock; and, a bit out on the edge, *The Eye of the World: The Graphic Novel, Volume Three* (Tor), by Robert Jordan, Chuck Dixon, Marcio Fiorito, and Francis Nuguit.

According to the Box Office Mojo site (www.boxoffice.com), as was also true of last year, nine out of ten of the year's top-earning movies were genre films of one sort or another (if you're willing to count animated films, fantasy films, and superhero movies as being "genre films"), as were fourteen out of the top twenty, and fifty (more or less, I might have missed something here and there) out of the top one hundred.

The year's six top box-office champs were all genre movies, seven if you're willing to accept *Gravity* as a genre movie (most would, as it takes place in space; some sticklers say it's not SF because everything that happens in it could happen today in the real world, and it has no speculative element). Only one nongenre movie, *Fast and Furious 6*, appears on the top ten list, in eighth place. The ninth and tenth places are also taken by genre films, as are, if we were to extend the list beyond the Top Ten, the eleventh, twelfth, thirteenth, and fourteenth places.

This has been true for several years now—genre films of one sort or another have dominated the box-office top ten for more than a decade. You have to go all the way back to 1998 to find a year when the year's top-earner was a nongenre film, *Saving Private Ryan*.

This year's number one box-office champ was a superhero movie, a sequel at that, *Iron Man 3*, which so far has raked in $1,215,439,994 worldwide (it was a good year for Marvel, their *Thor: The Dark World*, another superhero sequel, just missed the top ten, coming in at twelfth place and earning another $638,542,579). In second place was an SF movie—also a sequel—drawn from a dystopian YA book series, *The Hunger Games: Catching Fire*. Third and fourth places were taken by animated fantasy movies, *Frozen* and *Despicable Me 2*. Fifth place was taken by a superhero "reboot," *Man of Steel*, which sharply divided Superman fans everywhere and started them squabbling about whether it departed too far from canon or not, outraging many. Sixth place was another animated fantasy film, *Monsters University*, seventh place the aforementioned space thriller (maybe SF, maybe not, depending on who you ask) *Gravity*, which was almost certainly the best-reviewed movie on this list, and the one taken the most seriously as a "serious film" by critics. Ninth place goes to Oz "reimagining" *Oz: The Great and Powerful*, and tenth place to another sequel, *The Hobbit: The Desolation of Smaug*, which divided Tolkien fans even more sharply than *Man of Steel* divided Superman fans, as had the first movie, *The Hobbit: An Unexpected Journey* (*The Hobbit: The Desolation of Smaug* was only released just before Christmas, and will almost certainly make a lot more money as 2014 rolls on).

The top twenty list included several more genre films, including *Star Trek: Into Darkness* (a sequel to a reboot which didn't do as well as the first one and didn't seem to be received with as much enthusiasm by *Star Trek* fans), in eleventh place, *Thor: The Dark World* in twelfth place, big-budget zombie movie *World War Z* in thirteenth place, animated caveman comedy *The Croods* in fourteenth place, and supernatural horror movie *The Conjuring* in eighteenth place. Rounding out the top twenty are the nongenre movies, mostly caper/con man/slob road movies (with one "literary" movie), *The Heat* in fifteenth place, *We're the Millers* in sixteenth place, *The Great Gatsby* in seventeenth place, *Identity Thief* in nineteenth place, and *Grown Ups 2* in twentieth place.

It's worth noting that the only movies on the whole top ten list that weren't a sequel, a reboot, or a "reimagining" (including the nongenre *Fast & Furious 6*) were *Frozen* and *Gravity*. Looking over the whole top twenty list, only *Frozen*, *Gravity*, *World War Z*, *The Heat*, *We're the Millers*, *The Conjuring*, and *Identity Thief* weren't sequels, reboots, or reimaginings—a lesson that certainly won't be lost on Hollywood.

It's quite possible that genre movies earned more money this year than they ever have before. But they weren't all successful; several A-list big budget genre movies that cost multiple millions to make "performed under expectations," as the polite phrase has it, and some outright failed at the box office. The giant robots versus Godzilla-like monsters movie, *Pacific Rim*, which I had tagged last year as a sure box-office champ, came in somewhat disappointingly in thirty-fourth place in the list of the year's hundred top earners, although I enjoyed it myself. *Elysium*, the less critically acclaimed follow-up movie by the director of the critically acclaimed movie *District 9*, made it only to thirty-eighth place, futuristic after-the-apocalypse movies *Oblivion* and *After Earth* to forty-first and fifty-ninth place respectively, the big-screen version of Orson Scott Card's famous novel *Ender's Game* (one of the year's most severe box-office disappointments, since it cost a *lot* of money to make) only to fifty-seventh place, *Jack the Giant Slayer*, a splashy fairy-tale "reimagining," to fifty-fourth place, horror reboot *Carrie* to seventy-eighth place, space thriller *Riddick* to seventy-sixth place, special effects–heavy fantasy/kung fu movie *47 Ronin* to seventy-eighth place, and *Kick-Ass 2*, the sequel to cult favorite *Kick-Ass*, to ninety-third place. If you want to consider reboot *The Lone Ranger* a genre film, a somewhat dubious proposition, it made it to fortieth place, but had the distinction of being perhaps the most critically savaged and poorly reviewed movie of the year.

As usual, there were few movies this year that could be considered *science fiction* movies, as opposed to fantasy movies, animated films, and superhero movies. If you consider *Gravity* to be a science fiction movie (see earlier), then it was by far the best reviewed and most commercially successful SF movie of 2013. *The Hunger Games: Catching Fire* wasn't taken quite as seriously by the critics, perhaps because it's drawn from a Young Adult novel, but it raked in the bucks, and, although not a space movie, is certainly legitimate dystopian SF. Unfortunately, most of the year's other movies that could come closest to claiming to be core science fiction were among the year's most costly failures or "underperforming" films: *Pacific Rim*, *Elysium*, *Oblivion*, *After Earth*, *Ender's Game*, *Riddick*, even to some extent *Star Trek: Into Darkness*, which did pretty well but perhaps not quite as well as it had been hoped it would do. Hollywood will no doubt take note of this as well.

A little-seen core SF film that got reviews almost as good as those garnered by

Gravity was *Europa Report*—but it was a small-budget independent film that flew so far under the commercial radar that it made it only to 314th place on the list of the year's 400 top-earning movies.

There were at least thirty other genre movies of various sorts out in 2013, far too many to individually list here, including two end-of-the-world slob comedies/road pictures, *The World's End* and *This Is the End*.

Dozens of genre movies are in the pipeline for release in 2014. At this point in time, as I write these words in January, the most buzz seems to be generated by *Captain America: The Winter Soldier*, *The Hobbit: There and Back Again* sequel, *The Hunger Games: Mockingjay—Part I* sequel, *The Amazing Spider-Man 2*, the *Godzilla* reboot, the *RoboCop* reboot, the new *Avatar* movie, and the upcoming Disney *Star Wars* sequel (although that may be longer than a year away).

As many genre movies as there were out in 2013, there were even more genre TV shows that debuted in 2013, joining the large number of them already on the air, with yet another big wave of genre shows coming along for 2014. Genre shows of various sorts—fantasy, SF, superhero, supernatural horror—are now as common as cop/forensic shows were in the nineties and the Oughts, or as cowboy shows were in the fifties. There's so many of them now that it's become hard to keep track of them all, but we'll do the best that we can.

A lot of new genre shows hit the airwaves in 2013. They included *Dracula*, *Sleepy Hollow*, *Believe*, *Agents of S.H.I.E.L.D*, *Almost Human*, *Once Upon a Time in Wonderland* (a spin-off from *Once Upon a Time*), *The Witches of East End*, *The Originals* (a spin-off from *The Vampire Diaries*), and *Ravenswood* (a spin-off from *Pretty Little Liars*), *Believe*, *Resurrection*, *The Originals*, *The Tomorrow People*, *The 100*, and *Star-Crossed*. Of these, the surprise hit seems to be *Sleepy Hollow*, a show about an inadvertent time traveler from Colonial days hunting a supernatural menace, a rather silly concept that I don't think anybody really expected to be as popular as it is; it's already been renewed for a second season. *Almost Human*, a show about a human cop with a robot partner, seems to also have pretty solidly established itself, although I don't know whether it's been renewed. The most hopes for the season going in were probably pinned on *Agents of S.H.I.E.L.D.*, the Joss Whedon–produced spin-off from *The Avengers* movie that brings the long-running Marvel comic to the screen; certainly this was the new show with the biggest buzz about it, and expectations for it were high—perhaps too high. *Agents of S.H.I.E.L.D.* has certainly not been a failure, and has received an order for a complete season, but it doesn't seem to have been the blockbuster, runaway hit that the producers were hoping for either, and Joss Whedon fans, Marvel fans, and *S.H.I.E.L.D.* fans (who don't seem to be all the same audience, which may be part of the problem) are fiercely divided (with each camp very vocal) about whether the show is any good or not. Oddly, almost everyone loves Agent Coulson, the lead character—but not everybody loves the *show* he's embedded in. As I type these words, the first season is half over, and they have another half-season left to turn things around and get more of the audience on their side; if they can't, being renewed for a second season may be problematical, although I wouldn't be entirely surprised to see the network give them another shot even if the ratings are shaky. Myself, I love the character of Agent Coulson and the actor who plays him, but am lukewarm about everything else about the show—but considering that it often takes shows a couple of seasons to really hit their stride, I'm willing to give them the benefit of the doubt and time to develop. Whether or not the network will be, is the question.

The new shows join the continuing genre shows, of which there were already quite a few. Of course, one of the big hits of 2013, as it had been for the previous two years, was HBO's *A Game of Thrones*, based on the best-selling *A Song of Ice and Fire* series of fantasy novels by George R.R. Martin and now a full-fledged cultural phenomenon, with references to it, jokes about it, and even cartoons featuring it permeating the culture; needless to say, it's coming back in 2014. That other perennial cultural phenomenon, *Dr. Who*, had a big year in 2013, and will be returning in 2014, with yet another new actor in the title role. HBO's other genre show, the campy vampire show *True Blood*, is coming back for a final season in 2014, and then will be canceled, much to the dismay of those viewers who enjoyed seeing hunky Viking vampire Eric with his shirt off. (Charlaine Harris also ended her long-running series of Sookie Stackhouse novels, which leaves Bon Temps fans totally destitute.)

Among the other newish shows, the superhero show *Arrow*, about the adventures of Green Arrow, seems to be the strongest, and will be back in 2014. *Person of Interest, Orphan Black, Falling Skies, Grimm,* and *Once Upon a Time* all seem to be doing well (although the future of spin-off *Once Upon a Time in Wonderland* may be in doubt), and will continue, as will *Teen Wolf, The Vampire Diaries, The Walking Dead, Being Human, Defiance, American Horror Story,* and the perennial *Supernatural,* which is now entering its eighth season. *Warehouse 13* is having a final partial season, then dying, and *Star Wars: The Clone Wars* has already died. *Beauty and the Beast, Dracula, Continuum, The Neighbors, Revolution, Zero Hour,* and others are said to be "on the bubble," which means they may or may not be continuing in 2014.

Returning for 2014 is *Under the Dome,* a miniseries, taken from a Stephen King novel, which follows people imprisoned under a dome by mysterious forces.

Other coming new shows are *Intelligence, The Leftovers, Resurrection, Salem, Star-Crossed, Sense8, The Lost Girl, Bitten, Helix, Outlander, Penny Dreadful, Legends, Helix,* two pirate shows with supernatural elements, *Black Sails* and *Crossbones,* and a spin-off from *Arrow* called *The Flash* and starring a superhero you can probably guess. Some of these will thrive, many will die, and it's impossible at this point to tell which will be which. If forced to bet, I'd put my money of *The Flash,* and maybe *Intelligence.*

There's also a science-oriented nonfiction show coming up, *Cosmos: A Space-Time Odyssey,* starring Neil deGrasse Tyson.

The 71st World Science Fiction Convention, LoneStarCon 3, was held in San Antonio, Texas, USA, from August 29 to September 2, 2013. The 2013 Hugo Awards, presented at LoneStarCon 3, were: Best Novel, *Redshirts: A Novel with Three Codas,* by John Scalzi; Best Novella, "The Emperor's Soul," by Brandon Sanderson; Best

Novelette, "The Girl-Thing Who Went Out for Sushi," by Pat Cadigan; Best Short Story, "Mono no aware," by Ken Liu; Best Graphic Story, *Saga, Volume 1*, by Brian K. Vaughn, illustrated by Fiona Staples; Best Related Work, *Writing Excuses, Season 7*, by Brandon Sanderson, Dan Wells, Mary Robinette Kowal, Howard Tayler, and Jordan Sanderson; Best Professional Editor, Long Form, Patrick Nielsen Hayden; Best Professional Editor, Short Form, Stanley Schmidt; Best Professional Artist, John Picacio; Best Dramatic Presentation (short form), *Game of Thrones*, "Blackwater"; Best Dramatic Presentation (long form), *The Avengers*; Best Semiprozine, *Clarkesworld*; Best Fanzine, *SF Signal*; Best Fancast: SF Squeecast; Best Fan Writer, Tansy Rayner Roberts; Best Fan Artist, Galen Dara; plus the John W. Campbell Award for Best New Writer to Mur Lafferty.

The 2012 Nebula Awards, presented at a banquet at the San Jose Hilton in San Jose, California, on May 18, 2013, were: Best Novel, *2312*, by Kim Stanley Robinson; Best Novella, "After the Fall, Before the Fall, During the Fall," by Nancy Kress; Best Novelette, "Close Encounters," by Andy Duncan; Best Short Story, "Immersion," by Aliete de Bodard; Ray Bradbury Award, *Beasts of the Southern Wild*; the Andre Norton Award to *Fair Coin*, by E. C. Myers; Solstice Awards to Ginjer Buchanan and Carl Sagan; the Service to SFWA Award to Michael Payne; and the Damon Knight Memorial Grand Master Award to Gene Wolfe.

The 2013 World Fantasy Awards, presented at a banquet on November 4, 2013, in Brighton, England, United Kingdom, during the Thirty-Ninth Annual World Fantasy Convention, were: Best Novel, *Alif the Unseen*, by G. Willow Wilson; Best Novella, "Let Maps to Others," by K. J. Parker; Best Short Fiction, "The Telling," by Gregory Norman Bossert; Best Collection, *Where Furnaces Burn*, by Joel Lane; Best Anthology, *Postscripts #28/#29: Exotic Gothic 4*, edited by Danel Olson; Best Artist, Vincent Chong; Special Award (Professional), to Lucia Graves; Special Award (Non-Professional), to S. T. Joshi; plus the Life Achievement Award to Susan Cooper and Tanith Lee, and Special Awards to Brian W. Aldiss and William F. Nolan.

The 2013 Bram Stoker Awards, presented by the Horror Writers of America on June 15, 2013, in New Orleans, Louisiana, were: Best Novel, *The Drowning Girl*, by Caitlin R. Kiernan; Best First Novel, *Life Rage*, by L. L. Soares; Best Young Adult Novel, *Flesh and Bone*, by Jonathan Maberry; Best Long Fiction, *The Blue Heron*, by Gene O' Neill; Best Short Fiction, "Magdala Amygdala?" by Lucy Snyder; Best Collection, *New Moon on the Water*, by Mort Castle and *Black Dahlia and White Rose: Stories*, by Joyce Carol Oates (tie); Best Anthology, *Shadow Show*, edited by Mort Castle and Sam Weller; Best Nonfiction, *Trick or Treat: A History of Halloween*, by Lisa Morton; Best Poetry Collection, *Vampires, Zombies and Wanton Souls*, by Marge Simon and Sandy DeLuca; Graphic Novel, *Witch Hunts: A Graphic History of the Burning Times*, by Rocky Wood and Lisa Morton; Best Screenplay, *The Cabin in the Woods*, by Joss Whedon and Drew Goddard; plus Lifetime Achievement Awards to Clive Barker and Robert R. McCammon.

The 2013 John W. Campbell Memorial Award was won by *Jack Glass: The Story of a Murderer*, by Adam Roberts.

The 2013 Theodore Sturgeon Memorial Award for Best Short Story was won by "The Grinnell Method," by Molly Gloss.

The 2013 Philip K. Dick Memorial Award went to *Lost Everything*, by Brian Francis Slattery.

The 2013 Arthur C. Clarke award was won by *Dark Eden*, by Chris Beckett.

The 2012 James Tiptree, Jr. Memorial Award was won by *The Drowning Girl*, by Caitlin R. Kiernan and *Ancient, Ancient*, by Kiini Ibura Salaam (tie).

The 2012 Sidewise Award for Alternate History went to *Dominion*, by C. J. Sansom (Long Form) and "Something Real," by Rick Wilber (Short Form).

The Cordwainer Smith Rediscovery Award went to Wyman Guin.

Dead in 2013 or early 2014 were:

JACK VANCE, 96, one of the true giants of the field, seminal to the development of the science fiction and fantasy genres as we know them (he also wrote mysteries, winning an Edgar Award for *The Man in the Cage*), multiple Hugo and Nebula Award–winner, recipient of the World Fantasy Award for Lifetime Achievement and the SFWA Grand Master Award, inducted into the Science Fiction Hall of Fame, author of novels such as *The Dying Earth, Big Planet, Emphyrio, The Star Kings, The Dragon Masters, Night Lamp*, and many others; **FREDERIK POHL**, 93, another of the seminal giants of the field as both writer and editor, winner of multiple Hugo and Nebula Awards, as well as the SFWA Grand Master Award and an inductee into the Science Fiction Hall of Fame, onetime editor of *Galaxy* and *Worlds of If* magazine as well as the *Star* original anthology series, the author of sixty-five novels and thirty short-story collections, including the landmark *The Space Merchants* (with C. M. Kornbluth), *Gateway, Man Plus*, and many others, a friend; **RICHARD MATHESON**, 87, author and screenwriter, winner of the World Fantasy Award, the Bram Stoker Life Achievment Award, an inductee into the Science Fiction Hall of Fame, author of *I Am Legend* and *The Shrinking Man*, as well as many screenplays for *Twilight Zone* episodes; British writer **IAIN M. BANKS**, 59, author of the influential SF novel series about the far-future society known as the Culture, such as *Consider Phlebas, The Player of Games*, and *Use of Weapons*, as well as stand-alone SF novels such as *Feersum Endjin* and *The Algebraist*, and, writing as **IAIN BANKS**, best-selling mainstream novels such as *The Wasp Factory, The Bridge*, and *The Crow Road*; brilliant and eclectic writer **NEAL BARRETT JR.**, 84, whose best known among his many novels was probably *The Hereafter Gang* (which critic John Clute called "The great American novel"), but who was even better known for his quirky short fiction, recently collected in *Other Seasons: The Best of Neal Barrett, Jr.*, a friend; **PARKE GODWIN**, 84, World Fantasy Award–winner, author of the Arthurian *Firelord* trilogy, among others; **DORIS LESSING**, 94, Noble Prize–winner, famous for her mainstream fiction, but who also produced many science fiction novels and books with fantastic elements, including the books in the *Canopus in Argos* sequence such as *The Marriages Between Zones Three, Four and Five* and *The Making of the Representative for Planet 8*, as well as *Briefing for a Descent into Hell, The Summer Before the Dark*, and many others; **BASIL COPPER**, 89, prolific British author of horror and mystery fiction; **JAMES HERBERT**, 69, British author, author of twenty-three novels, most horror, including international bestsellers *The Rats* and *The Fog*; **MICK FARREN**, 69, author and musician, author of the cult favorite *The DNA Cowboys* trilogy, as well as *The Long Orbit, Their Master's War,* and *The Renquist Quartet*; **BOYD BRADFIELD UPCHURCH**, 93, who wrote as **JOHN BOYD**, author of *The Last Starship from Earth* and a dozen other SF novels; **DOUGLAS R. MASON**, 94, British SF author who wrote as **JOHN RANKINE**; **ANN CRISPIN**, 63, SF writer, author of the *Starbridge* series as well as many *Star Trek* and *Star Wars* novels and other media tie-in novels, cofounder of the watchdog group Writer Beware, a friend; **PATRICIA ANTHONY**, 66, SF writer, author of novels such as *Brother Termite, Happy Policeman, God's Fires,* and *Conscience of the Beagle,* as well as much short fiction; **DOUGLAS R. MASON**, 94, who also wrote as **JOHN RANKINE**, prolific SF novelist; **ANDREW J. OFFUTT**, 78, author of more than seventy-five books of fantasy, SF, and erotica; **RICK HAUTALA**, 64, horror writer, author of thirty books including *Night Stone* and *Mockingbird Bay*; **NICK POLLOTTA**, 58, prolific author of many SF and action adventure novels, including *Damned Nation* and *Belle, Book and Candle*; **ANGEL ARANGO**, 86, Cuban SF writer, considered to be one of the founders of Cuban SF; **DAVID B. SILVA**, 62, horror writer and editor, editor of the influential magazine *The Horror Show*; **JAN HOWARD FINDER**, aka "**THE WOMBAT,**" 73, writer, anthologist, and longtime fan; **DANIEL PEARLMAN**, 77, SF writer, prolific short-story writer and author of fantasy novel *Memini*; **WILLIAM HARRISON**, 79, author of the story "Roller Ball Murder," which was made into the movie *Rollerball*; **ANDREW GREELEY**, 85, best-selling Chicago author, columnist, and priest; British author **DEBORAH J. MILLER**, 50, who also wrote as **MILLER LAU**; **ELMORE LEONARD**, 87, a writer whose genre credentials were limited to the novel *Touch* and the YA animal fantasy *A Coyote's in the House,* but a towering figure in the mystery field, where he was a best-selling author and a grandmaster, author of dozens of famous mystery novels such as *Get Shorty, Stick, Out of Sight,* and *Rum Punch*; **TOM CLANCY**, 66, best-selling author of technothrillers such as *The Hunt for Red October, Red Storm Rising,* and *Clear and Present Danger*; **BARBARA MERTZ**, 85, well-known mystery novelist who wrote as **ELIZABETH PETERS**, as well as under other pseudonyms; **GARY BRANDNER**, 80, horror writer, best known for *The Howling*; **JON MANCHIP WHITE**, 89, Welsh horror writer; **PHILIP NUTMAN**, 50, writer, journalist, and critic; **T. R. FEHRENBACH**, 88, Texas historian and occasional SF writer; **COLIN WILSON**, 82, English philosopher and novelist, author of the well-known nonfiction book *The Outsider,* as well as novels such as *The Mind Parasites* and *The Space Vampires*; **JOEL LANE**, 50, British author, poet, critic, and anthology editor; **HUGH NISSENSON**, 80, mainstream author who occasionally wrote SF; **GOKULANANDA MAHAPATRA**, 91, Indian SF author and science writer; **JOSEPH J. LAZZARO**, 56, SF writer and science essayist, mostly for *Analog*; **MARY-LYNN REED**, 64, author; **PAUL WILLIAMS**, 64, editor, author, and fan, founder of the groundbreaking music magazine *Crawdaddy!* as well as of the Philip K. Dick Society, editor of the thirteen-volume series of *The Complete Stories of Theodore Sturgeon* as well as one of the first critical studies of the work of Philip K. Dick; **ANNE JORDAN**, 69, author and anthologist, former managing editor of *The Magazine of Fantasy & Science Fiction*; **JACQUES SADOUL**, 78, prominent French editor; **ANNE C. PETTY**, 68, novelist and Tolkien scholar; **RICHARD E. GEIS**, 85, author, editor, longtime fan, multiple Hugo

Award–winner, editor of the influential fanzines *Science Fiction Review* and *The Alien Critic*; **LELAND SAPIRO**, 89, editor, SF scholar, fanzine fan, teacher; **NICK ROBINSON**, 58, chairman of publishing house Constable & Robinson; **RICHARD GALLEN**, 80, publishing financier who backed the start-ups of Tor, Baen, and Bluejay; **ANTONIO CARONIA**, 69, Italian SF translator and critic; **ROGER EBERT**, 70, film critic, author, and fan, whose film criticism for *The Chicago Sun-Times* and on television programs such as *Siskel and Ebert at the Movies* and *Roger Ebert and the Movies* made him the most famous film critic in America; **ROBERT MORALES**, 55, writer, editor, and journalist, author of the miniseries *Truth: Red, White and Black Marvel Comics*; **DOROTHY "DOT" LUMLEY**, 64, British literary agent, and former wife of writer Brian Lumley; **SCOTT CARPENTER**, 88, astronaut, one of the original *Mercury 7* crew; **RAY HARRYHAUSEN**, 92, pioneering stop-motion animator and world-famous special effects artist who created the special effects for such classic genre movies as *Jason and the Argonauts* and *The Seventh Voyage of Sinbad*; **MITCHELL HOOKS**, 89, SF cover artist; **DAVID FAIRBOTHER-ROE**, SF cover artist; **CARMINE INFANTINO**, 87, renowned comic book artist, best known for his work on *The Flash* and *Adam Strange*; **JOHN DAVID WILSON**, 93, Disney animator who worked on *Lady and the Tramp* and others; **EDWARD LEVITT**, 97, animator; **JOAN HANKE-WOODS**, 67, cover artist, winner of the Best Fan Artist Hugo; **JEAN-CLAUDE SUARES**, 71, graphic designer and illustrator; **DAN ADKINS**, 76, illustrator and comic book artist; **AL PLASTINO**, 91, longtime comic book artist; **JANICE VALLEAU WINKLEMAN**, 90, longtime comic book artist; **STUART FREEBORN**, 98, makeup artist on *Dr. Strangelove*, *2001: A Space Odyssey*, and *Star Wars*; **JANE HENSON**, 79, one of the cocreators of the Muppets, former wife of the late Jim Henson; **RAY MANZAREK**, 74, keyboardist for The Doors, perhaps the best keyboardist in rock music; **PETER O' TOOLE**, 81, famous stage and screen actor whose genre connections are slight, but whom everyone knows from films such as *The Lion in Winter*, *Lawrence of Arabia*, *The Stunt Man*, and *The Ruling Class*; **MICHAEL ANSARA**, 91, TV actor, best known for playing Kang in *Star Trek*, who also had roles in many other genre shows such as *Babylon 5*, *The Outer Limits*, and *Lost in Space*; **ANNETTE FUNICELLO**, 70, actress with roles in genre movies such as *The Shaggy Dog*, best known for her participation in the original *The Mickey Mouse Club* in the fifties; **ROBIN SACHS**, 61, stage, film, and television actor, best known to genre audiences for his roles as evil sorcerer Ethan in TV's *Buffy the Vampire Slayer* and as Sarris in *Galaxy Quest*; **JONATHAN WINTERS**, 87, improvisational comedian and actor, best known to genre audiences for his role as Mearth in *Mork and Mindy*; **JAMES GANDOLFINI**, 51, TV actor with no real genre connection, but known to everyone for his role in *The Sopranos*; **EILEEN BRENNAN**, 80, film actor, best known for roles in *The Sting* and *Murder by Death*; **DENNIS FARINA**, 69, best known for roles in *Get Shorty* and *Law & Order*; **ALLAN ARBUS**, 95, best known for his role in TV's *M*A*S*H*, who also appeared in genre productions such as *Wonder Woman* and *Damien: Omen II*; **JEAN STAPLETON**, 90, stage and film actor, best known as Edith from TV's *All in the Family*, who also appeared in genre film *Damn Yankees!*; **KAREN BLACK**, 74, film actress, known for her role in *Five Easy Pieces* and in many horror movies; **MEL SMITH**, 60, actor, best known to genre audiences for his role as the Albino in *The Princess Bride*; **RICHARD GRIFFITHS**, 65, actor, best known to genre audiences as Uncle Vernon from the *Harry Potter* movies; **MILO O'SHEA**, 87, actor, best known for playing Durand-Durand in *Barbarella*; **LEE THOMPSON YOUNG**, 29, television actor on *Smallville* and *Rizzoli & Isles*; **MICHAEL BURGESS**, 65, better known as **ROBERT REGINALD**, author, editor, and publisher, founder of Borgo Press; **GRAHAM STONE**, 87, Australian scholar, librarian, bibliographer, longtime fan, founder of the Australian Science Fiction Society; **MARTY GEAR**, 74, longtime fan and costumer; **KEITH ARMSTRONG-BRIDGES**, longtime British fan, cofounder of the Tolkien Society, a friend; **DAN MCARTHY**, 78, New Zealand fan, writer, artist, and con-runner; **ELLIOT K. SHORTER**, 74, fan, bookseller, former Locus editor; **FRANK DIETZ**, longtime fan, fanzine editor, convention organizer, cofounder of the Lunarians; **JERRY WRIGHT**, 67, founding editor of Web zine *Bewildering Stories*; **JIM GOLDFRANK**, 80, longtime fanzine fan; **BOBBIE DUFAULT**, 55, convention organizer and fan; **ANDREA M. DUBNICK**, 63, editor and fan; **BOB BOOTH**, 66, writer, editor, and convention organizer; **ROBERT BRIDGES**, 83, longtime fan, one of the founding members of the Washington Science Fiction Society; **PAMELA BOAL**, 78, writer and longtime British convention fan; **ALICE S. CLARESON**, 83, editor and teacher, widow of SF critic Thomas D. Clareson; **RUTH NIMERSHEIM BAMBACH**, 96, mother of SF writer Jack Nimersheim; **RICHARD BALLANTINE**, 72, son of publishers Ian and Betty Ballantine, an editor and author in his own right; **MARY ANN PORTER** , 103, mother of small-press publisher Marianne Porter; **BETTY DeHARDIT**, 88, daughter of the late Will Jenkins, who wrote SF as Murray Leinster; **ALAN BRUCE SAWYER**, 51, producer, brother of SF writer Robert Sawyer; **ROSEMARY WOLFE**, 82, wife of SF writer Gene Wolfe; **MARION STURGEON**, 83, third wife of late SF writer Theodore Sturgeon; **RUTH SPEER**, 90, wife of longtime fan Jack Speer; **NANCY KEMP**, 90, former wife of longtime fan Earl Kemp.

the piscovered country

IAN R. MACLEOD

*British writer Ian R. MacLeod was one of the hottest new writers of the nine-
ties, publishing a slew of strong stories in* Interzone, Asimov's Science Fiction, Weird Tales, Amazing, The Magazine of Fantasy and Science Fiction,
*and elsewhere, and his work continues to grow in power and deepen in matu-
rity as we move through the first decades of the new century. Much of his work
has been gathered in four collections:* Voyages By Starlight, Breathmoss and
Other Exhalations, Past Magic, *and* Journeys. *His first novel,* The Great
Wheel, *was published in 1997. In 1999, he won the World Fantasy Award
with his novella "The Summer Isles," and followed it up in 2000 by winning
another World Fantasy Award for his novelette "The Chop Girl." In 2003, he
published his first fantasy novel and his most critically acclaimed book,* The
Light Ages, *followed by a sequel,* The House of Storms, *in 2005, and then by*
Song of Time, *which won both the Arthur C. Clarke Award and the John W.
Campbell Award in 2008. A novel version of* The Summer Isles *also appeared in 2005. His most recent books are a new novel,* Wake Up and Dream,
and a big retrospective collection, Snodgrass and Other Illusions: The Best
Short Stories of Ian R. MacLeod. *MacLeod lives with his family in the West
Midlands of England.*

*Here he tells an evocative and emotionally powerful story of someone sent
on a mission to a virtual utopia reserved only for the superrich who have died
on our mundane Earth, a sort of literal afterlife. It's a smart, tense, and tricky
story in which the stakes are high and nothing is what it seems.*

T he trees of Farside are incredible. Fireash and oak. Greenbloom and maple. Shot
through with every colour of autumn as late afternoon sunlight blazes over the
Seven Mountains' white peaks. He'd never seen such beauty as this when he was
alive.

The virtual Bentley takes the bridge over the next gorge at a tyrescream, then
speeds on through crimson and gold. Another few miles, and he's following the
coastal road beside the Westering Ocean. The sands are burnished, the rocks silver-
threaded. Every new vista a fabulous creation. Then ahead, just as purple glower sweeps

in from his rear-view over those dragon-haunted mountains, come the silhouette lights of a vast castle, high up on a ridge. It's the only habitation he's seen in hours.

This has to be it.

Northover lets the rise of the hill pull at the Bentley's impetus as its headlights sweep the driveway trees. Another turn, another glimpse of a headland, and there's Elsinore again, rising dark and sheer.

He tries to refuse the offer to carry his luggage made by the neat little creature that emerges into the lamplit courtyard to greet him with clipboard, sharp shoes and lemony smile. He's encountered many chimeras by now. The shop assistants, the street cleaners, the crew on the steamer ferry that brought him here. All substantially humanoid, and invariably polite, although amended as necessary to perform their tasks, and far stranger to his mind than the truly dead.

He follows a stairway up through rough-hewn stone. The thing's name is Kasaya. Ah, now. The east wing. I think you'll find what we have here more than adequate. If not . . . Well, you *must* promise to let me know. And this is called the Willow Room. And *do* enjoy your stay . . .

Northover wanders. Northover touches. Northover breathes. The interior of this large high-ceilinged suite with its crackling applewood fire and narrow, deep-set windows is done out in an elegantly understated arts-and-craftsy style. Amongst her many attributes, Thea Lorentz always did have excellent taste.

What's struck him most about Farside since he jerked into new existence on the bed in the cabin of that ship bound for New Erin is how unremittingly *real* everything seems. But the slick feel of this patterned silk bedthrow . . . The spiky roughness of the teasels in the flower display . . . He's given up telling himself that everything he's experiencing is just some clever construct. The thing about it, the thing that makes it all so impossibly overwhelming, is that *he's* here as well. Dead, but alive. The evidence of his corpse doubtless already incinerated, but his consciousness— the singularity of his existence, what philosophers once called "the conscious I," and theologians the soul, along with his memories and personality, the whole sense of self which had once inhabited pale jelly in his skull—transferred.

The bathroom is no surprise to him now. The dead do so many things the living do, so why not piss and shit as well? He strips and stands in the shower's warm blaze. He soaps, rinses. Reminds himself of what he must do, and say. He'd been warned that he'd soon become attracted to the blatant glories of this world, along with the new, young man's body he now inhabits. Better just to accept it that rather than fight. All that matters is that he holds to the core of his resolve.

He towels himself dry. He pulls back on his watch—seemingly a Rolex, but a steel model, neatly unostentatious—and winds it carefully. He dresses. Hangs up his clothes in a walnut panelled wardrobe that smells faintly of mothballs, and hears a knock at the doors just as he slides his case beneath the bed.

"Yes? Come in . . ."

When he turns, he's expecting another chimera servant. But it's Thea Lorentz.

This, too, is something they'd tried to prepare him for. But encountering her after so long is much less of a shock than he's been expecting. Thea's image is as ubiquitous as that of Marilyn Monroe or the Virgin Mary back on Lifeside, and she really hasn't changed. She's dressed in a loose-fitting shirt. Loafers and slacks. Hair tied back. No obvious evidence of any make-up. But the crisp white shirt with its rolled up cuffs shows her dark brown skin to perfection, and one lose strand of her tied back hair plays teasingly at her sculpted neck. A tangle of silver bracelets slide on her wrist as she steps forward to embrace him. Her breasts are unbound and she still smells warmly of the patchouli she always used to favour. Everything about her feels exactly the same. But why not? After all, she was already perfect when she was alive.

"Well . . . !" That warm blaze is still in her eyes, as well. "It really *is* you."

"I know I'm springing a huge surprise. Just turning up from out of nowhere like this."

"I can take these kind of surprises any day! And I hear it's only been—what?—less than a week since you transferred. Everything must feel so very strange to you still."

It went without saying that his and Thea's existences had headed off in different directions back on Lifeside. She, of course, had already been well on her way toward some or other kind of immortality when they'd lost touch. And he . . . Well, it was just one of those stupid lucky breaks. A short, ironic keyboard riff he'd written to help promote some old online performance thing—no, no, it was nothing she'd been involved in—had ended up being picked up many years later as the standard message-send fail signal on the global net. Yeah, that was the one. Of course, Thea knew it. Everyone, once they thought about it for a moment, did.

"You know, Jon," she says, her voice more measured now, "you're the one person I thought would never choose to make this decision. None of us can pretend that being Farside isn't a position of immense privilege, when most of the living can't afford food, shelter, good health. You always were a man of principle, and I sometimes thought you'd just fallen to . . . Well, the same place that most performers fall to, I suppose, which is no particular place at all. I even considered trying to find you and get in touch, offer . . ." She gestures around her. "Well, this. But you wouldn't have taken it, would you? Not on those terms."

He shakes his head. In so many ways she still has him right. He detested—no, he quietly reminds himself—*detests* everything about this vast vampiric sham of a world that sucks life, hope and power from the living. But she hadn't come to him, either, had she? Hadn't offered what she now so casually calls *this*. For all her fame, for all her good works, for all the aid funds she sponsors and the good causes she promotes, Thea Lorentz and the rest of the dead have made no effort to extend their constituency beyond the very rich, and almost certainly never will. After all, why should they? Would the gods invite the merely mortal to join them on Mount Olympus?

She smiles and steps close to him again. Weights both his hands in her own. "Most people I know, Jon—most of those I have to meet and talk to and deal with, and even those I have to call friends—they all think that I'm Thea Lorentz. Both Farside and Lifeside, it's long been the same. But only you and a very few others really know who I am. You can't imagine how precious and important it is to have you here . . ."

He stands gazing at the door after she's left. Willing everything to dissolve, fade, crash, melt. But nothing changes. He's still dead. He's still standing here in this Farside room. Can still even breathe the faint patchouli of Thea's scent. He finishes dressing—a tie, a jacket, the same supple leather shoes he arrived in—and heads out into the corridor.

Elsinore really is *big*—and resolutely, heavily, emphatically, the ancient building it wishes to be. Cold gusts pass along its corridors. Heavy doors groan and creak. Of course, the delights of Farside are near-infinite. He's passed through forests of mist and silver. Seen the vast, miles-wide back of some great island of a seabeast drift past when he was still out at sea. The dead can grow wings, sprout gills, spread roots into the soil and raise their arms and become trees. All these things are not only possible, but visibly, virtually, achievably real. But he thinks they still hanker after life, and all the things of life the living, for all their disadvantages, possess.

He passes many fine-looking paintings as he descends the stairs. They have a Pre-Raphaelite feel, and from the little he knows of art, seem finely executed, but he doesn't recognise any of them. Have these been created by virtual hands, in some virtual workshop, or have they simply sprung into existence? And what would happen if he took that sword which also hangs on display, and slashed it through a canvas? Would it be gone for ever? Almost certainly not. One thing he knows for sure about the Farside's vast database is that it's endlessly backed up, scattered, diffused and re-collated across many secure and heavily armed vaults back in what's left of the world of the living. There are very few guaranteed ways of destroying any of it, least of all the dead.

Further down, there are holo-images, all done in stylish black and white. Somehow, even in a castle, they don't even look out of place. Thea, as always, looks like she's stepped out of a fashion-shoot. The dying jungle suits her. As does this war-zone, and this flooded hospital, and this burnt-out shanty town. The kids, and it is mostly kids, who surround her with their pot bellies and missing limbs, somehow manage to absorb a little of her glamour. On these famous trips of hers back to view the suffering living, she makes an incredibly beautiful ghost.

Two big fires burn in Elsinore's great hall, and there's a long table for dinner, and the heads of many real and mythic creatures loom upon the walls. Basilisk, boar, unicorn . . . Hardly noticing the chimera servant who rakes his chair out for him, Northover sits down. Thea's space at the top of the table is still empty.

In this Valhalla where the lucky, eternal dead feast forever, what strikes Northover most strongly is the sight of Sam Bartleby sitting beside Thea's vacant chair. Not that he doesn't know that the man has been part of what's termed *Thea Lorentz's inner circle* for more than a decade. But, even when they were all still alive and working together on *Bard On Wheels*, he'd never been able to understand why she put up with him. Of course, Bartleby made his fortune with those ridiculous action virtuals, but the producers deepened his voice so much, and enhanced his body so ridiculously, that it was a wonder to Northover they bothered to use him at all. Now, though, he's chosen to bulk himself out and cut his hair in a Roman fringe. He senses Northover's gaze, and raises his glass, and gives an ironic nod. He still has the self-regarding manner of someone who thinks themselves far more better looking, not to mention cleverer, than they actually are.

Few of the dead, though, choose to be beautiful. Most elect for the look that ex-presses themselves at what they thought of as the most fruitful and self-expressive period of their lives. Amongst people this wealthy, this often equates to late middle age. The fat, the bald, the matronly and the downright ugly rub shoulders, secure in the knowledge that they can become young and beautiful again whenever they wish.

"So? What are you here for?"

The woman beside him already seems flushed from the wine, and has a homely face and a dimpled smile, although she sports pointed teeth, elfin ears and her eyes are cattish slots.

"For?"

"Name's Wilhelmina Howard. People just call me Will . . ." She offers him a claw-nailed hand to shake. "Made my money doing windfarm recycling in the non-federal states. All that lovely superconductor and copper we need right here to keep our power supplies as they should be. Not that we ever had much of a presence in England, which I'm guessing is where you were from . . . ?"

He gives a guarded nod.

"But isn't it just so *great* to be here at Elsinore? *Such* a privilege. Thea's every-thing people say she is, isn't she, and then a whole lot more as well? *Such* compassion, and all the marvellous things she's done! Still, I know she's invited me here because she wants to get hold of some of my money. Give back a little of what we've taken an' all. Not that I won't give. That's for sure. Those poor souls back on Lifeside. We really have to do something, don't we, all of us . . . ?"

"To be honest, I'm here because I used to work with Thea. Back when we were both alive."

"So, does that make you an *actor*?" Wilhelmina's looking at him more closely now. Her slot pupils have widened. "Should I *recognise* you? Were you in any of the famous—"

"No, no." As if in defeat, he holds up a hand. Another chance to roll out his story. More a musician, a keyboard player, although there wasn't much he hadn't turned his hand to over the years. Master of many trades, and what have you—at least, until that message fail signal came along.

"So, pretty much a lucky break," murmurs this ex take-no-shit businesswoman who died and became a fat elf, "rather than a any kind of lifetime endeavour . . . ?"

Then Thea enters the hall, and she's changed into something more purposefully elegant—a light grey dress that shows her fine breasts and shoulders without seem-ing immodest—and her hair is differently done, and Northover understands all the more why most of the dead make no attempt to be beautiful. After all, how could they, when Thea Lorentz does it so unassailably well? She stands waiting for a mo-ment as if expectant silence hasn't already fallen, then says a few phrases about how pleased she is to have so many charming and interesting guests. Applause follows. Just as she used to do for many an encore, Thea nods and smiles and looks genuinely touched.

The rest of the evening at Elsinore passes in a blur of amazing food and superb wine, all served with the kind of discreet inevitability which Northover has decided only chimeras are capable of. Just like Wilhelmina, everyone wants to know who he's with, or for, or from. The story about that jingle works perfectly; many even claim to have heard of him and his success. Their curiosity only increases when he explains his and Thea's friendship. After all, he could be the route of special access to her famously compassionate ear.

There's about twenty guests here at Elsinore tonight, all told, if you don't count the several hundred chimeras, which of course no one does. Most of the dead, if you look at them closely enough, have adorned themselves with small eccentricities; a forked tongue here, an extra finger there, a crimson badger-stripe of hair. Some are new to each other, but the interactions flow on easy rails. Genuine fame itself is rare here—after all, entertainment has long been a cheapened currency—but there's a relaxed feeling-out between strangers in the knowledge that some shared acquaintance or interest will soon be reached. Wealth always was an exclusive club, and it's even more exclusive here.

Much of the talk is of new Lifeside investment. Viral re-programming of food crops, all kinds of nano-engineering, weather, flood and even birth control—although the last strikes Northover as odd considering how rapidly the human population is decreasing—and every other kind of plan imaginable to make the earth a place worth living in again is discussed. Many of these schemes, he soon realises, would be mutually incompatible, and potentially incredibly destructive, and all are about making money.

Cigars are lit after the cheeses and sorbets. Rare, exquisite whiskeys are poured. Just like everyone else, he can't help but keep glancing at Thea. She still has that way of seeming part of the crowd yet somehow apart—or above—it. She always had been a master of managing social occasions, even those rowdy parties they'd hosted back in the day. A few words, a calming hand and smile, and even the most annoying drunk would agree that it was time they took a taxi. For all her gifts as a performer, her true moments of transcendent success were at the lunches, the less-than-chance-encounters, the launch parties. Even her put-downs or betrayals left you feeling grateful.

Everything Farside is so spectacularly different, yet so little about her has changed. The one thing he does notice, though, is her habit of toying with those silver bangles she's still wearing on her left wrist. Then, at what feels like precisely the right moment, and thus fractionally before anyone expects, she stands up and taps her wineglass to say a few more words. From anyone else's lips, they would sound like vague expressions of pointless hope. But, coming from her, it's hard not to be stirred.

Then, with a bow, a nod, and what Northover was almost sure is a small conspiratorial blink in his direction—which somehow seems to acknowledge the inherent falsity of what she has just done, but also the absolute need for it—she's gone from the hall, and the air suddenly seems stale. He stands up and grabs at the tilt of his chair before a chimera servant can get to it. He feels extraordinarily tired, and more than a little drunk.

In search of some air, he follows a stairway that winds up and up. He steps out high on the battlements. He hears feminine chuckles. Around a corner, shadows tussle. He catches the starlit glimpse of a bared breast, and turns the other way. It's near-freezing up out on these battlements. Clouds cut ragged by a blazing sickle moon. Northover leans over and touches the winding crown of his Rolex watch and studies the distant lace of waves. Then, glancing back, he thinks he sees another figure behind him. Not the lovers, certainly. This shape bulks far larger, and is alone. Yet the dim outlines of the battlement gleam though it. A malfunction? A premonition? A genuine ghost? But then, as Northover moves, the figure moves with him, and he realises that he's seeing nothing but his own shadow thrown by the moon.

He dreams that night that he's alive again, but no longer the young and hopeful man he once was. He's mad old Northy. Living, if you call it living, so high up in the commune tower that no one else bothers him much, and with nothing but an old piano he's somehow managed to restore for company. Back in his old body, as well, with is old aches, fatigues and irritations. But for once, it isn't raining, and frail sparks of sunlight cling to shattered glass in the ruined rooms, and the whole flooded, once-great city of London is almost beautiful, far below.

Then, looking back, he sees a figure standing at the far end of the corridor that leads through rubble to the core stairs. They come up sometimes, do the kids. They taunt him and try to steal his last few precious things. Northy swears and lumbers forward, grabbing an old broom. But the kid doesn't curse or throw things. Neither does he turn and run, although it looks as if he's come up here alone.

"You're Northy, aren't you?" the boy called Haru says, his voice an adolescent squawk.

He awakes with a start to new light, good health, comforting warmth. A sense, just as he opens his eyes and knowledge and who and what he is returns, that the door to his room has just clicked shut. He'd closed the curtains here in the Willow Room in Elsinore, as well, and now they open. And the fire grate has been cleared, the apple-wood logs restocked. He reaches quickly for his Rolex, and begins to relax as he slips it on. The servants, the chimeras, will have been trained, programmed, to perform their work near-invisibly, and silently.

He showers again. He meets the gaze of his own eyes in the mirror as he shaves. Whatever view there might be from his windows is hidden in a mist so thick that the world beyond could be the blank screen of some old computer from his youth. The route to breakfast is signalled by conversation and a stream of guests. The hall is smaller than the one they were in last night, but still large enough. A big fire crackles in a soot-stained hearth, but stream rises from the food as cold air wafts in through the open doors.

Dogs are barking in the main courtyard. Horses are being led out. Elsinore's battlements and towers hover like ghosts in the blanketing fog. People are milling, many wearing thick gauntlets, leather helmets and what look like padded vests and kilts. The horses are big, beautifully groomed but convincingly skittish in the way that Northover surmises expensively pedigreed beasts are. Or were. Curious, he goes over to one as a chimera stable boy fusses with its saddle and reins.

The very essence of equine haughtiness, the creature tosses its head and does that lip-blubber thing horses do. Everything about this creature is impressive. The flare of its nostrils. The deep, clean, horsy smell. Even, when he looks down and under, the impressive, seemingly part-swollen heft of its horsey cock.

"Pretty spectacular, isn't he?"

Northover finds that Sam Bartleby is standing beside him. Dressed as if for battle, and holding a silver goblet of something steaming and red. Even his voice is bigger and deeper than it was. The weird thing is, he seems more like Sam Bartleby than the living Sam Bartleby ever did. Even in those stupid action virtuals.

"His name's Aleph—means alpha, of course, or the first. You may have heard of him. He won, yes didn't you . . . ?" By now, Bartleby's murmuring into the beast's neck. "The last ever Grand Steeple de Paris."

Slowly, Northover nods. The process of transfer is incredibly expensive, but there's no reason in principle why creatures other than humans can't join Farside's exclusive club. The dead are bound to want the most prestigious and expensive toys. So, why not the trapped, transferred consciousness of a multi-million dollar racehorse?

"You don't ride, do you?" Bartleby, still fondling Aleph—who, Northover notices, is now displaying an even more impressive erection—asks.

"It wasn't something I ever got around to."

"But you've got plenty of time now, and there are few things better than a day out hunting in the forest. Suggest you start with one of the lesser, easier, mounts over there, and work your way up to a real beast like this. Perhaps that pretty roan? Even then, though, you'll have to put up with a fair few falls. Although, if you really want to cheat and bend the rules, and know the right people, there are shortcuts . . ."

"As you say, there's plenty of time."

"So," Bartleby slides up into the saddle with what even Northover has to admit is impressive grace. "Why are you here? Oh, I don't mean getting *here* with that stupid jingle. You always were a lucky sod. I mean, at Elsinore. I suppose you want something from Thea. That's why most people come. Whether or not they've got some kind of past with her."

"Isn't friendship enough?"

Bartleby is now looking down at Northover in a manner even more condescending than the horse. "You should know better than most, Jon, that friendship's just another currency." He pauses as he's handed a long spear, its tip a clear, icy substance that could be a diamond. "I should warn you that whatever it is you want, you're unlikely to get it. At least, not in the way you expect. A favour for some cherished project, maybe?" His lips curl. "But that's not *it* with you, is it? We know each other too well, Jon, and you really haven't changed. Not one jot. What you really want is Thea, isn't it? Want her wrapped up and whole, even though we both know that's impossible. Thea being Thea just as she always was. And, believe me, I'd do anything to defend her. Anything to stop her being hurt . . ."

With a final derisory snort and a spark of cobbles, Bartley and Aleph clatter off.

The rooms, halls and corridors of Elsinore are filled with chatter and bustle. Impromptu meetings. Accidental collisions and confusions that have surely been long planned. Kisses and business cards are exchanged. Deals are brokered. Promises offered. The spread of the desert which has now consumed most of north Africa could be turned around by new cloud-seeding technologies, yet still, there's coffee, or varieties of herb tea if preferred.

No sign of Thea, though. In a way she's more obvious Lifeside, where you can buy as much Thea Lorentz tat as even the most fervent fanatic could possibly want. Figurines. Candles. Wallscreens. Tee shirts. Some of it, apparently, she even endorses. Although always, of course, in a good cause. Apart from those bothersome kids, it was the main reason Northover spent so much of his last years high up and out of reach of the rest of the commune. He hated being reminded of the way people wasted what little hope and money they had on stupid illusions. Her presence here at Elsinore is palpable, though. Her name is the ghost at the edge of every conversation. Yes, but Thea . . . Thea . . . And Thea . . . Thea . . . Always, always, everything is about Thea Lorentz.

He realises this place she's elected to call Elsinore isn't any kind of home at all—but he supposes castles have always fulfilled a political function, at least when they weren't under siege. People came from near-impossible distances to plead their cause, and, just as here, probably ended up being fobbed off. Of course, Thea's chimera servants mingle amid the many guests. Northover notices Kasaya many times. A smile here. A mincing gesture there.

He calls after him the next time he sees him bustling down a corridor.

"Yes, Mister Northover . . . ?" Clipboard at the ready, Kasaya spins round on his toes.

"I was just wondering, seeing as you seem to be about so much, if there happen to be more than one of you here at Elsinore?"

"That isn't necessary. It's really just about good organisation and hard work."

"So . . ." Was that *really* slight irritation he detected, followed by a small flash of pride? ". . . you can't be in several places at once?"

"That's simply isn't required. Although Elsinore does have many short cuts."

"You mean, hidden passageways? Like a real castle?"

Kasaya, who clearly has more important things than this to see to, manages a smile. "I think that that would be a good analogy."

"But you just said think. You *do* think?"

"Yes." He's raised his clipboard almost like a shield now. "I believe I do."

"How long have you been here?"

"Oh . . ." He blinks in seeming recollection. "Many years."

"And before that?"

"Before that, I wasn't here." Hugging his clipboard more tightly than ever, Kasaya glances longingly down the corridor. "Perhaps there's something you need? I could summon someone . . ."

"No, I'm fine. I was just curious about what it must be like to be you, Kasaya. I mean, are you always on duty? Do your kind *sleep*? Do you change out of those clothes and wash your hair and—"

"I'm sorry sir," the chimera intervenes, now distantly firm. "I really can't discuss these matters when I'm on duty. If I may . . . ?"

Then, he's off without a backward glance. Deserts may fail to bloom if the correct kind of finger food isn't served at precisely the right moment. Children blinded by onchocerciasis might not get the implants that will allow them to see grainy shapes for lack of a decent meeting room. And, after all, Kasaya is responding in the way that any servant would—at least, if a guest accosted them and started asking inappropriately personal questions when they were at work. Northover can't help but feel sorry for these creatures, who clearly seem to have at least the illusion of consciousness. To be trapped forever in crowd scenes at the edges of the lives of the truly dead . . .

Northover comes to another door set in a kind of side-turn that he almost walks past. Is this where the chimera servants go? Down this way, Elsinore certainly seems less grand. Bright sea air rattles the arrowslit glass. The walls are raw stone, and stained with white tidemarks of damp. This, he imagines some virtual guide pronouncing, is by far the oldest part of the castle. It certainly feels that way.

He lifts a hessian curtain and steps into a dark, cool space. A single barred, high skylight fans down on what could almost have been a dungeon. Or a monastic cell. Some warped old bookcases and other odd bits of furniture, all cheaply practical, populate a roughly paved floor. In one corner, some kind of divan or bed. In another, a wicker chair. The change of light is so pronounced that it's a moment before he sees that someone is sitting there. A further beat before he realises it's Thea Lorentz, and that she's seated before a mirror, and her fingers are turning those bangles on her left wrist. Frail as frost, the silver circles tink and click. Otherwise, she's motionless. She barely seems to breathe.

Not a mirror at all, Northover realises as he shifts quietly around her, but some kind of tunnel or gateway. Through it, he sees a street. It's raining, the sky is reddish with windblown earth, and the puddles seem bright as blood. Lean-to shacks, their gutters sluicing, line something too irregular to be called a street. A dead power pylon leans in the mid-distance. A woman stumbles into view, drenched and wading up to the knee. She's holding something wrapped in rags with a wary possessiveness that suggests it's either a baby or food. This could be the suburbs of London, New York or Sydney. That doesn't matter. What does matter is how she falls to her knees at what she sees floating before her in the rain. Thea . . . ! She almost drops whatever she's carrying as her fingers claw upward and her ruined mouth shapes the name. She's weeping, and Thea's weeping as well—two silver trails that follow the perfect contours of her face. Then, the scene fades in another shudder of rain, and Thea Lorentz is looking out at him from the reformed surface of a mirror with the same soft sorrow that poor, ruined woman must have seen in her gaze.

"Jon."

"This, er . . ." he gestures.

She stands up. She's wearing a long tweed skirt, rumpled boots, a loose turtle-neck woollen top. "Oh, it's probably everything people say it is. The truth is that, once you're Farside, it's too easy to forget what Lifeside is really like. People make all the right noises—I'm sure you've heard them already. But that isn't the same thing."

"Going there—being seen as some virtual projection in random places like that—aren't you just perpetuating the myth?"

She nods slowly. "But is that really such a terrible thing? And that cat-eyed woman you sat next to yesterday at dinner. What's her name, Wilhelmina? Kasaya's already committed her to invest in new sewerage processing works and food aid, all of which will be targeted on that particular area of Barcelona. I know she's a tedious creature—you only have to look at her to see that—but what's the choice? You can stand back, and do nothing, or step in, and use whatever you have to try to make things slightly better."

"Is that what you really think?"

"Yes. I believe I do. But how about *you*, Jon? What do you think?"

"You know me," he says. "More than capable of thinking several things at once. And believing, or not believing, all of them."

"Doubting Thomas," she says, taking another step forward so he can smell patchouli.

"Or Hamlet."

"Here of all places, why not?"

For a while, they stand there in silence.

"This whole castle is designed to be incredibly protective of me," she says eventually. "It admits very few people this far. Only the best and oldest of friends. And Bartleby insists I wear these as an extra precaution, even though they can sometimes be distracting . . ." She raises her braceletted wrist. "As you've probably already gathered, he's pretty protective of me, too."

"We've spoken. It wasn't exactly the happiest reunion."

She smiles. "The way you both are, it would have been strange if it was. But look, you've come all this incredible way. Why don't we go out somewhere?"

"You must have work to do. Projects—I don't know—that you need to approve. People to meet."

"The thing about being in Elsinore is that things generally go more smoothly when Thea Lorentz isn't in the way. You saw what it was like last night at dinner. Every time I open my mouth people expect to hear some new universal truth. I ask them practical questions and their mouths drop. Important deals fall apart when people get distracted because Thea's in the room. That's why Kasaya's so useful. He does all that's necessary—joins up the dots and bangs the odd head. And people scarcely even notice him."

"I didn't think he likes it much when they do."

"*More* questions, Jon?" She raises an eyebrow. "But everything here on Farside must still seem so strange to you, when there's so much to explore . . ."

Down stairways. Along corridors. Through storerooms. Perhaps these are the secret routes Kasaya hinted at, winding through the castle like Escher tunnels in whispers of sea-wet stone. Then, they are down in a great, electric-lit cavern of a garage. His Bentley is here, along with lines of other fine and vintage machines long crumbled to rust back on Lifeside. Maseratis. Morgans. Lamborghinis. Other things that look like Dan Dare spaceships of Faberge submarines. The cold air reeks of new petrol, clean oil, polished metal. In a far corner and wildly out of place, squatting above a small black pool, is an old VW Beetle.

"Well," she says. "What do you think?"

He smiles as he walks around it. The dents and scratches are old friends. "It's perfect."

"Well, it was never *that*. But we had some fun with it, didn't we?"

"How does this work? I mean, creating it? Did you have some old pictures of it? Did you manage to access—"

"Jon." She dangles a key from her hand. "Do you want to go out for a drive, or what?"

"The steering even *pulls* the same way. It's amazing . . ."

Out on roads that climb and camber, giving glimpses through the slowly thinning mist of flanks of forest, deep drops. Headlights on, although it makes little difference and there doesn't seem to be any other traffic. She twiddles the radio. Finds a station that must have stopped transmitting more than fifty years ago. Van Morrison, Springsteen and Dylan. So very, very out of date—but still good—even back then. And even now, with his brown-eyed girl beside him again. It's the same useless deejay, the same pointless adverts. As the road climbs higher, the signal fades to bubbling hiss.

"Take that turn up there. You see, the track right there in the trees . . . ?"

The road now scarcely a road. The Beetle a jumble of metallic jolts and yelps. He has to laugh, and Thea laughs as well, the way they're being bounced around. A tunnel through the trees, and then some kind of clearing, where he stops the engine and squawks the handbrake, and everything falls still.

"Do you remember?"

He climbs out slowly, as if fearing a sudden movement might cause it all to dissolve. "Of course I do . . ."

Thea, though, strides ahead. Climbs the sagging cabin steps.

"This is . . ."

"I know," she agrees, testing the door. Which—just as it had always been—is unlocked.

This, he thinks as he stumbles forward, is what it really means to be dead. Forget the gills and wings and the fine wines and the spectacular food and the incredible scenery. What this is, what it means . . .

Is *this*.

The same cabin. It could be the same day. Thea, she'd called after him as he walked down the street away from an old actors' pub off what was still called Covent Garden after celebrating—although that wasn't the word—the end of *Bard on Wheels* with a farewell pint and spliff. Farewell and fuck off as far as Northover was concerned, Sam Bartleby and his stupid sword fights especially. Shakespeare and most other kinds of real performance being well and truly dead, and everyone heading for well-deserved obscurity. The sole exception being Thea Lorentz, who could sing and act and do most things better than all the rest of them combined, and had an air of being destined for higher things that didn't seem like arrogant bullshit even if it probably was. Out of his class, really, both professionally and personally. But she'd called to him, and he'd wandered back, for where else was he heading? She'd said she had a kind of proposal, and why didn't they go out for a while out in her old VW? All the bridges over the Thames hadn't yet been down then, and they'd driven past the burnt-out cars and abandoned shops until they came to this stretch of woodland where the trees were still alive, and they'd ended up exactly here. In this clearing, inside this cabin.

There's an old woodburner stove that Northover sets about lighting, and a few tins along the cobweb shelves, which he inspects and settles on a tin of soup, which he nearly cuts his thumb struggling to open, and sets to warm on the top of the fire as it begins to send out amber shadows. He goes to the window, clears a space in the dust, pretending to check if he turned the VW's lights off, but in reality trying to grab a little thinking time. He didn't, doesn't, know Thea Lorentz that well at this or any point. But he knows her well enough to understand that her spontaneous suggestions are nothing if not measured.

"Is this how it was, do you think?" she asks, shrugging off her coat and coming to stand behind him. Again, that smell of patchouli. She slides her arms around his waist. Nestles her chin against his shoulder. "I wanted you to be what I called producer and musical director for my Emily Dickinson thing. And you agreed."

"Not before I'd asked if you meant roadie and general dogsbody."

He feels her chuckle. "That as well . . ."

"What else was I going to do, anyway?" Dimly, in the gaining glow of the fire, he can see her and his face in reflection.

"And how about now?"

"I suppose it's much the same."

He turns. It's he who clasps her face, draws her mouth to his. Another thing about Thea is that, even when you know it's always really her, it somehow seems to be you.

Their teeth clash. It's been a long time. This is the first time ever. She draws back, breathless, pulls off that loose-fitting jumper she's wearing. He helps her with the shift beneath, traces, remembers, discovers or rediscovers, the shape and weight of her breasts. Thumbs her hardening nipples. Then, she pulls away his shirt, undoes his belt buckle. Difficult here to be graceful, even if you're Thea Lorentz, struggle-hopping with zips, shoes and panties. Even harder for Northover with one sock off and the other caught on something or other, not to mention his young man's erection, as he throws a dusty blanket over the creaky divan. But laughter helps. Laughter always did. That, and Thea's knowing smile as she takes hold of him for a moment in her cool fingers. Then, Christ, she lets go of him again. A final pause, and he almost thinks this isn't going to work, but all she's doing is pulling off those silver bracelets, and then, before he can realise what else it is she wants, she's snapping off the bangle of his Rolex as well and pulling him down, and now there's nothing else to be done, for they really are naked.

Northover, he's drowning in memory. Greedy at first, hard to hold back, especially with the things she does, but then trying to be slow, trying to be gentle. Or, at least, a gentleman. He remembers, anyway—or is it now happening?—that time she took his head between her hands and raised it to her gaze. *You don't have to be so careful,* she murmurs. Or murmured. *I'm flesh and blood, Jon. Just like you . . .*

He lies back. Collapsed. Drenched. Exhausted. Sated. He turns from the cobweb ceiling and sees the Rolex lies cast on the gritty floor. Softly ticking. Just within reach. But already, Thea is stirring. She scratches, stretches. Bracelet hoops glitter as they slip back over her knuckles. He stands up. Pads over to a stained sink. There's a trickle of water. What might pass for a towel. Dead or living, it seems, the lineaments of love remain the same.

"You never were much of a one for falling asleep after," Thea comments, straightening her sleeves as she dresses.

"Not much a man, then."

"Some might say that . . ." She laughs as she fluffs her hair. "But we had something, didn't we, Jon? We really did. So why not again?"

There it is. Just when he thinks the past's finally over and done with. Not Emily Dickinson this time, or not only that project, but a kind of greatest hits. Stuff they did together with *Bard on Wheels*, although this time it'll be just them, a two-hander, a proper double act, and, yes Jon, absolutely guaranteed no Sam fucking Bartleby. Other things as well. A few songs, sketches. Bits and bobs. Fun, of course. But wasn't the best kind of fun always the stuff you took seriously? And why not start here and see how it goes? Why not tonight, back at Elsinore?

As ever, what can he say but yes?

Thea drives. He supposes she did before, although he can't really remember how they got back to London. The mist has cleared. She, the sea, the mountains, all look magnificent. That Emily Dickinson thing, the one they did before, was a huge commercial and critical success. Even if people did call it a one-woman show, when he'd written half the script and all of the music. To have those looks, and yet to be able to hold the stage and sing and act so expressively! Not to mention, although the critics generally did, that starlike ability to assume a role, yet still be Thea Lorentz. Audrey Hepburn got a mention. So did Grace Kelly. A fashion icon, too, then. But Thea could carry a tune better than either. Even for the brief time they were actually living together in that flat in Pimlico, Northover sometimes found himself simply looking—staring, really—at Thea. Especially when she was sleeping. She just seemed so angelic. Who are you really? he'd wondered. Where are you from? Why are you here, and with me of all people?

He never did work out the full chain of events that brought her to join *Bard on Wheels*. Of course, she'd popped up in other troupes and performances—the evidence was still to be found on blocky online postings and all those commemorative hagiographies, but remembrances were shaky and it was hard to work on the exact chain of where and when. A free spirit, certainly. A natural talent. Not the sort who'd ever needed instructing. She claimed that she'd lost both her parents to the Hn3i epidemic, and had grown up in one of those giant orphanages they set up at Heathrow. As to where she got that poise, or the studied assurance she always displayed, all the many claims, speculations, myths and stories that eventually emerged—and which she never made any real attempt to quash—drowned out whatever had been the truth.

They didn't finish the full tour. Already, the offers were pouring in. He followed her once to pre-earthquake, pre-nuke Los Angeles, but by then people weren't sure what his role exactly was in the growing snowball of Thea Lorentz's fame. Flunky, and neither was he. Not that she was unfaithful. At least, not to his knowledge. She probably never had the time. Pretty clear to everyone, though, that Thea Lorentz was moving on and up. And that he wasn't. Without her, although he tried getting other people involved, the Emily Dickinson poem arrangements sounded like the journeymen pieces they probably were. Without her, he even began to wonder about the current whereabouts of his other old sparring partners in *Bard on Wheels*.

It was out in old LA, at a meal at the Four Seasons, that he'd met, encountered, experienced—whatever the word for it was—his first dead person. They were still pretty rare back then, and this one had made its arrival on the roof of the hotel by veetol just to show that it could, when it really should have just popped into existence in the newly-installed reality fields at their table like Aladdin's genie. The thing had jittered and buzzed, and its voice seemed over-amplified. Of course, it couldn't eat, but it pretended to consume a virtual plate of quail in puff pastry with foie gras in a truffle sauce, which it pretended to enjoy with virtual relish. You couldn't fault the thing's business sense, but Northover took the whole experience as another expression of the world's growing sickness.

Soon, it was the Barbican and the Sydney Opera House for Thea (and how sad it was that so many of these great venues were situated next to the rising shorelines) and odd jobs or no jobs at all for him. The flat in Pimlico went, and so, somewhere, did hope. The world of entertainment was careering, lemming-like, toward the cliffs of pure virtuality, with just a few bright stars such as Thea to give it the illusion of humanity. Crappy fantasy-dramas or rubbish docu-musicals that she could sail through and do her Thea Lorentz thing, giving them an undeserved illusion of class. At least, and unlike that idiot buffoon Bartleby, Northover could see why she was in such demand. When he thought of what Thea Lorentz had become, with her fame and her wealth and her well-publicised visits to disaster areas and her audiences with the Pope and the Dalai Lama, he didn't exactly feel surprised or bitter. After all, she was only doing whatever it was that she'd always done.

Like all truly beautiful women, at least those who take care of themselves, she didn't age in the way that the rest of the world did. If anything, the slight sharpening of those famous cheekbones and the small care lines that drew around her eyes and mouth made her seem even more breath-takingly elegant. Everyone knew that she would mature slowly and gracefully and that she would make—just like the saints with whom she was now most often compared—a beautiful, and probably incorruptible, corpse. So, when news broke that she'd contracted a strain of new-variant septicemic plague when she was on a fact-finding trip in Manhattan, the world fell into mourning as it hadn't done since . . . Well, there was no comparison, although

JFK and Martin Luther King got a mention, along with Gandhi and Jesus Christ and Joan of Arc and Marilyn Monroe and that lost Mars mission and Kate and Diana.

Transfer—a process of assisted death and personality uploading—was becoming a popular option. At least, amongst the few who could afford it. The idea that the blessed Thea might refuse to do this thing, and deprive a grieving world of the chance to know that somehow, somewhere, she was still there, and on their side, and sorrowing as they sorrowed, was unthinkable. By now well ensconced high up in his commune with his broom and his reputation as an angry hermit, left with nothing but his memories of that wrecked piano he was trying to get into tune, even Northover couldn't help but follow this ongoing spectacle. Still, he felt strangely detached. He'd long fallen out of love with Thea, and now fell out of admiring her as well. All that will-she won't-she crap that she was doubtless engineering even as she lay there on her deathbed! All she was doing was just exactly what she'd always done and twisting the whole fucking world around her fucking little finger. But then maybe, just possibly, he was getting the tiniest little bit bitter . . .

Back at Elsinore, Kasaya has already been at work. Lights, a low stage, decent mikes and pa system, along with a spectacular grand piano, have all been installed at the far end of the great hall were they sat for yesterday's dinner. The long tables have been removed, the chairs re-arranged. Or replaced. It really does look like a bijou theatre. The piano's a Steinway. If asked, Northover might have gone for a Bechstein. The action, to his mind, and with the little chance he's even had to ever play such machines, being a tad more responsive. But you can't have everything, he supposes. Not even here.

The space is cool, half-dark. The light from the windows is settling. Bartleby and his troupe of merry men have just returned from their day of tally-ho slaughter with a giant boar hung on ropes. Tonight, by sizzling flamelight out in the yard, the dining will be alfresco. And after that . . . Well, word has already got out that Thea and this newly arrived guy at Elsinore are planning some kind of reunion performance. No wonder the air in this empty hall feels expectant.

He sits down. Wondrous and mysterious as Thea Lorentz's smile, the keys—which are surely real ivory—gleam back at him. He plays a soft e-minor chord. The sound shivers out. Beautiful. Although that's mostly the piano. Never a real musician, Northy. Nor much of a real actor, either. Never a real anything. Not that much of a stagehand, even. Just got lucky for a while with a troupe of travelling players. Then, as luck tends to do, it ran out on you. But still. He hasn't sat at one of these things since he died, yet it couldn't feel more natural. As the sound fades, and the gathering night washes in, he can hear the hastening tick of his Rolex.

The door at the far end bangs. He thinks it's most likely Kasaya. But it's Thea. Barefoot now. Her feet sip the polished floor. Dark slacks, an old, knotted shirt. Hair tied back. She looks the business. She's carrying loose sheaves of stuff—notes, bits of script and sheet music—almost all of which he recognises as she slings them down across the gleaming lid of the piano.

"Well," she says, "shall we do this thing?"

Back in his room, he stands for a long time in the steam heat of the shower. Finds he's soaping and scrubbing himself until his skin feels raw and his head is dizzy. He'd always wondered about those guys from al-Qaeda and Hezbollah and the Taliban and New Orthodoxy. Why they felt such a need to shave and cleanse the bodies they would soon be destroying. Now, though, he understands perfectly. The world is ruined and time is out of joint, but this isn't just a thing you do out of conviction. The moment has to be right, as well.

Killing the dead isn't easy. In fact, it's near impossible. But not quite. The deads' great strength is the sheer overpowering sense of reality they bring to the sick fantasy they call Farside. Everything must work. Everything has to be what it is, right down to the minutest detail. Everything must be what it seems to be. But this is also their greatest weakness. Of course, they told Northy when they took off his blindfold as he sat chained to a chair which was bolted to the concrete floor in that deserted shopping mall, we can try to destroy them by trying to tear everything in Farside apart. We can fly planes into their reactors, introduce viruses into their processing suites, flood their precious data vaults with seawater. But there's always a backup. There's always another power source. We can never wreck enough of Farside to have even a marginal effect upon the whole. But the dead themselves are different. Break down the singularity of their existence for even an instant, and you destroy it forever. The dead become truly dead.

Seeing as it didn't exist as a real object, they had to show him the Rolex he'd be wearing through a set of VR gloves and goggles. Heavy-seeming of course, and ridiculously over-engineered, but then designer watches had been that way for decades. This is what you must put on along with your newly assumed identity when you return to consciousness in a cabin on board a steamer ferry bound for New Erin. It many ways, the watch is what it appears to be. It ticks. It tells the time. You'll even need to remember to wind it up. But carefully. Pull the crown out and turn it backwards—no, no, not now, not even here, you mustn't—and it will initiate a massive databurst. The Farside equivalent of an explosion of about half a pound of semtex, atomising anything within a three metre radius—yourself, of course, included, which is something we've already discussed—and causing damage, depending on conditions, in a much wider sphere. Basically, though, you need to be within touching distance of Thea Lorentz to be sure, to be certain. But that alone isn't enough. She'll be wearing some kind of protection which will download her to a safe backup even in the instant of time it takes the blast to expand. We don't know what that protection will be, although we believe she changes it regularly. But, whatever it is, it must be removed.

A blare of lights. A quietening of the murmurous audience as Northover steps out. Stands centre stage. Reaches in his pocket. Starts tossing a coin. Which, when Thea emerges, he drops. The slight sound, along with her presence, rings out. One thing to rehearse, but this is something else. He'd forgotten, he really had, how Thea raises her game when you're out here with her, and it's up to you to try to keep up.

A clever idea that went back to *Bard on Wheels*, to re-reflect *Hamlet* through some of the scenes of Stoppard's *Rozencrantz and Guildenstern Are Dead*, where two minor characters bicker and debate as the whole famous tragedy grinds on in the background. Northover doubts if this dumb, rich, dead audience get many of the references, but that really doesn't matter when the thing flows as well as it does. Along with the jokes and witty wordplay, all the stuff about death, and life in a box being better than no life at all, gains a new resonance when it's performed here on Farside. The audience are laughing fit to bust by the end of the sequence, but you can tell in the falls of silence that come between that they know something deeper and darker is really going on.

It's the same when he turns to the piano, and Thea sings a few of Shakespeare's jollier songs. For, as she says as she stands there alone in the spotlight and her face glows and those bangles slide upon her arms, The man that hath no music in himself, the motions of his spirit are dull as night. She even endows his arrangement of Under the Greenwood Tree, which he always thought too saccharine, with a bittersweet air.

This, Northover thinks, as they move on to the Emily Dickinson section—which, of course, is mostly about death—is why I have to do this thing. Not because Thea's fake or because she doesn't believe in what she's doing. Not because she isn't Thea Lorentz any longer and has been turned inside out by the dead apologists into some parasitic ghost. Not because what she does here at Elsinore is a sham. I must do this because she is, and always was, the treacherous dream of some higher vision of humanity, and people will only ever wake up and begin to shake off their shackles when they realise that living is really about forgetting such illusions, and looking around them, and picking up a fucking broom and clearing up the mess of the world themselves. The dead take our power, certainly—both physically and figuratively. The reactors that drive the Farside engines use resources and technologies the living can barely afford. Their clever systems subvert and subsume our own. They take our money, too. Masses and masses of it. Who'd have thought that an entirely virtual economy could do so much better than one that's supposedly real? But what they really take from us, and the illusion that Thea Lorentz will continue to foster as long as she continues to exist, is hope.

Because I did not stop for death . . . Not knowing when the dawn will come, I open every door . . . It all rings so true. You could cut the air with a knife. You could pull down the walls of the world. Poor Emily Dickinson, stuck in that homestead with her dying mother and that sparse yet volcanic talent that no one even knew about. Then, and just when the audience are probably expecting something lighter to finish off, it's back to Hamlet, and sad, mad Ophelia's songs—which are scattered about the play just as she is; a wandering, hopeless, hopeful ghost—although Northover has gathered them together as a poignant posy in what he reckons is some of his best work. Thea knows it as well. Her instincts for these things are more honed than his ever were. After all, she's a trouper. A legend. She's Thea Lorentz. She holds and holds the audience as new silence falls. Then, just as she did in rehearsal, she slides the bangles off her arm, and places them atop the piano, where they lie bright as rain circles in a puddle.

"Keep this low and slow and quiet," she murmurs, just loud enough for everyone in the hall to hear as she steps back to the main mike. He lays his hands on the keys. Waits, just as they always did, for the absolute stilling of the last cough, mutter and shuffle. Plays the chords that rise and mingle with her perfect, perfect voice. The lights shine down on them from out of sheer blackness, and it's goodnight, sweet ladies, and rosemary for remembrance, which bewept along the primrose path to the grave where I did go . . .

As the last chord dies, the audience erupts. Thea Lorentz nods, bows, smiles as the applause washes over her in great, sonorous, adoring waves. It's just the way it always was. The spotlight loves her, and Northover sits at the piano for what feels like a very long time. Forgotten. Ignored. It would seem churlish for him not to clap as well. So he does. But Thea knows the timing of these things better than anyone, and the crowd loves it all the more when, the bangles looped where she left them on the piano, she beckons him over. He stands up. Crosses the little stage to join her in the spotlight. Her bare left arm slips easy around his waist as he bows. This could be Carnegie Hall. This could be the Bolshoi. The manacling weight of the Rolex drags at his wrist. Thea smells of patchouli and of Thea, and the play's the thing, and there could not, never could be, a better moment. There's even Sam Bartleby, who sat grinning but pissed-off right there on the front row and well within range of the blast.

They bow again, *thankyouthankyouthankyou*, and by now Thea's holding him surprisingly tightly, and it's difficult for him to reach casually around to the Rolex, even though he knows it must be done. Conscience doth make cowards of us all, but the time for doubt is gone, and he's just about to pull and turn the crown of his watch when Thea murmurs something toward his ear which, in all this continuing racket, is surely intended only for him.

"What?" he shouts back.

Her hand cups his ear more closely. Her breath, her entire seemingly living body, leans into him. Surely one of those bon mots that performers share with each other in times of triumph such as this. Just something else that the crowds love to see.

"Why don't you do it now?" Thea Lorentz says to Jon Northover. "What's stopping you . . . ?"

He's standing out on the moonlit battlements. He doesn't know how much time has passed, but his body is coated in sweat and his hands are trembling and his ears still seem to be ringing and his head hurts. Performance come-down to end all performance come-downs, and surely it's only a matter of minutes before Sam Bartleby, or perhaps Kasaya, or whatever kind of amazing Farside device it is that really works the security here at Elsinore, comes to get him. Perhaps not even that. Maybe he'll just vanish. Would that be so terrible? But then, they have cellars here at Elsinore. Dungeons, even. Put to the question. Matters of concern and interest. Things they need to know. He wonders how much full-on pain a young, fit body such as the one he now inhabits is capable of bearing . . . He fingers the Rolex, and studies the drop, but somehow he can't bring himself to do it.

When someone does come, it's Thea Lorentz. Stepping out from the shadows into the spotlight glare of the moon. He sees that she's still not wearing those bangles, but she keeps further back from him now, and he knows it's already too late.

"What made you realise?"

She shrugs. Shivers. Pulls down her sleeves. "Wasn't it one of the first things I said to you? That you were too principled to ever come here?"

"That was what I used to think as well."

"Then what made you change your mind?"

Her eyes look sadder than ever. More compassionate. He wants to bury his face in her hair. After all, Thea could always get more out of him than anyone. So he tells her about mad old Northy, with that wrecked piano he'd found in what had once been a rooftop bar up in his eyrie above the commune, which he'd spent his time restoring because what else was there to do? Last working piano in London, or England, most likely. Or the whole fucking world come to that. Not that it was ever that much of a great shakes. Nothing like here. Cheaply built in Mexico of all places. But then this kid called Haru comes up, and he says he's curious about music, and he asks Northy to show him his machine for playing it, and Northy trusts the kid, which feels like a huge risk. Even that first time he sits Haru down at it, though, he knows he's something special. He just has that air.

"And you know, Thea . . ." Northover finds he's actually laughing. "You know what the biggest joke is? Haru didn't even *realise*. He could read music quicker than I can read words, and play like Chopin and Chick Corea, and to him it was all just this lark of a thing he sometimes did with this mad old git up on the fortieth floor . . .

"But he was growing older. Kids still do, you know, back on Lifeside. And one day he's not there, and when he does next turn up, there's this girl downstairs who's apparently the most amazing thing in the history of everything, and I shout at him and tell him just how fucking brilliant he really is. I probably even used the phrase *God-given talent*, whatever the hell that's supposed to mean. But anyway . . ."

"Yes?"

Northover sighs. This is the hard bit, even though he's played it over a million times in his head. "They become a couple, and she soon gets pregnant, and she has a healthy baby, even though they seem ridiculously young. A kind of miracle. They're so proud they even take the kid up to show me, and he plongs his little hands on my piano, and I wonder if he'll come up one day to see old Northy, too. Given a few years, and assuming old Northy still alive, that is, which is less than likely. But that isn't how it happens. The baby gets sick. It's winter and there's an epidemic of some new variant of the nano flu. Not to say there isn't a cure. But the cure needs money—I mean, you know what these retrovirals cost better than anyone, Thea—which they simply don't have. And this is why I should have kept my big old mouth shut, because Haru must have remembered what I yelled at him about his rare, exceptional musical ability. And he decides his baby's only just starting on his life, and he's had a good innings of eighteen or so years. And if there's something he can do, some sacrifice he can make for his kid . . . So that's what he does . . ."

"You're saying?"

"Oh, come on, Thea! I know it's not legal, either Lifeside or here. But we both know it goes on. Everything has its price, especially talent. And the dead have more than enough vanity and time, if not the application, to fancy themselves as brilliant musicians, just the same way they might want to ride an expensive thoroughbred, or fuck like Casanova, or paint like Picasso. So Haru sold himself, or the little bit that someone here wanted, and the baby survived and he didn't. It's not that unusual a story, Thea, in the great scheme of things. But it's different, when it happens to someone you know, and you feel you're to blame."

"I'm sorry," she says.

"Do you think that's enough?"

"Nothing's ever enough. But do you really believe that whatever arm of the resistance you made contact with actually wanted me, Thea Lorentz, fully dead? What about the reprisals? What about the global outpouring of grief? What about all the inevitable, endless let's-do-this-for-Thea bullshit? Don't you think it would suit the interests of Farside itself far better to remove this awkward woman who makes unfashionable causes fashionable and brings attention to unwanted truths? Wouldn't *they* prefer to extinguish Thea Lorentz and turn her into a pure symbol they can manipulate and market however they wish? Wouldn't that make far better sense than whatever it was you thought you were doing?"

The sea heaves. The whole night heaves with it.

"If you want to kill me, Jon, you can do so now. But I don't think you will. You can't, can you? That's where the true weakness of whoever conceived you and this plan lies. You *had* to be what you are, or were, to get this close to me. You had to have free will, or at least the illusion of it . . ."

"What the hell are you saying?"

"I'm sorry. You might think you're Jon Northover—in fact, I'm sure you do—but you're not. You're not him really."

"That's—"

"No. Hear me out. You and I both know in our hearts that the real Jon Northover wouldn't be here on Farside. He'd have seen through the things I've just explained to you, even if he had ever contemplated actively joining the resistance. But that isn't it, either. Not really. I loved you, Jon Northover. Loved *him*. It's gone, of course, but I've treasured the memories. Turned them and polished them, I suppose. Made them into something realer and clearer than ever existed. This afternoon, for instance. It was all too perfect. You haven't changed, Jon. You haven't changed at all. People, real people, either dead or living, they shift and they alter like ghosts in reflection, but you haven't. You stepped out of my past, and there you were, and I'm so, so, sorry to have to tell you these things, for I fully believe that you're a conscious entity that feels pain and doubt just like all the rest of us. But the real Jon Northover is most likely long dead. He's probably lying in some mass grave. He's just another lost statistic. He's gone beyond all recovery, Jon, and I mourn for him deeply. All you are is something that's been put together from my stolen memories. You're too, too perfect."

"You're just saying that. You don't know."

"But I do. That's the difference between us. One day, perhaps, chimeras such as you will share the same rights as the dead, not to mention the living. But that's one campaign too far even for Thea Lorentz—at least, while she still has some control over her own consciousness. But I think you know, or at least you *think* you do, how to tune a piano. Do you know what inharmonicity is?"

"Of course I do, Thea. It was me who told you about it. If the tone of a piano's going to sound right, you can't tune all the individual strings to exactly the correct pitch. You have to balance them out slightly to the sharp or the flat. Essentially, you tune a piano ever so marginally out of tune, because of the way the strings vibrate and react. Which is imperfectly . . . Which is . . . I mean . . . Which is . . ."

He trails off. A flag flaps. The clouds hang ragged. Cold moonlight pours down like silver sleet. Thea's face, when he brings himself to look at it, seems more beautiful than ever.

The trees of Farside are magnificent. Fireash and oak. Greenbloom and maple. Shot through with every colour of autumn as dawn blazes toward the white peaks of the Seven Mountains. He's never seen such beauty as this. The tide's further in today. Its salt smell, as he winds down the window and breathes it in, is somehow incredibly poignant. Then the road sweeps up from the coast. Away from the Westering Ocean. As the virtual Bentley takes a bridge over a gorge at a tyrescream, it dissolves in a roaring pulse of flame.

A few machine parts twist jaggedly upward, but they settle as the wind bears away the sound and the smoke. Soon, there's only sigh of the trees, and the hiss of a nearby waterfall. Then, there's nothing at all.

the book seller

Lavie Tidhar

Lavie Tidhar grew up on a kibbutz in Israel, has traveled widely in Africa and Asia, and has lived in London, the South Pacific island of Vanuatu, and Laos. He is the winner of the 2003 Clarke-Bradbury Prize (awarded by the European Space Agency), was the editor of Michael Marshall Smith: The Annotated Bibliography, *and the anthologies* A Dick & Jane Primer for Adults, The Apex Book of World SF, *and* The Apex Book of World SF 2. *He is the author of the linked story collection* HebrewPunk, *the novella chapbooks* An Occupation of Angels, Gorel and the Pot-Bellied God, Cloud Permutations, Jesus and the Eighfold Path, *and, with Nir Yaniv, the novel* The Tel Aviv Dossier. *He is a prolific short story writer; his stories have appeared in* Interzone, Clarkesworld, Apex, Asimov's Science Fiction, Sci Fiction, Strange Horizons, Chizine, Postscripts, Fantasy, Nemonymous, Infinity Plus, Aeon, The Book of Dark Wisdom, Fortean Bureau, *and elsewhere, and have been translated into seven languages. His latest novels include* The Bookman *and its sequels,* Camera Obscura *and* The Great Game, Osama: A Novel, *which won the World Fantasy Award as the year's best novel in 2012,* Martian Sands, *and* The Violent Century. *After a spell in Tel Aviv, he's currently living back in England.*

"The Book Seller" is another of his interconnected Central Station stories, set in a complex, evocative, multicultural future during a time when humanity—including part-human robots, AIs, cyborgs, and genetically engineered beings of all sorts—is spreading through the solar system. This one deals with a humble, introspective book dealer in Old Tel Aviv, whose shop is in the shadow of the immense Central Station, where spaceships come and go, and who gives shelter to a strigoi against the advice of everyone he knows, and the odd, ever-deepening relationship that develops between them.

Achimwene loved Central Station. He loved the adaptoplant neighbourhoods sprouting over the old stone and concrete buildings, the budding of new apartments and the gradual fading and shearing of old ones, dried windows and walls flaking and falling down in the wind.

Achimwene loved the calls of the alte-zachen, the rag-and-bone men, in their traditional passage across the narrow streets, collecting junk to carry to their immense junkyard-cum-temple on the hill in Jaffa to the south. He loved the smell of sheesha-pipes on the morning wind, and the smell of bitter coffee, loved the smell of fresh horse manure left behind by the alte-zachen's patient, plodding horses.

Nothing pleased Achimwene Haile Selassi Jones as much as the sight of the sun rising behind Central Station, the light slowly diffusing beyond and over the immense, hour-glass shape of the space port. Or almost nothing. For he had one overriding passion, at the time that we pick this thread, a passion which to him was both a job and a mission.

Early morning light suffused Central Station and the old cobbled streets. It highlighted exhausted prostitutes and street-sweeping machines, the bobbing floating lanterns that, with dawn coming, were slowly drifting away, to be stored until nightfall. On the rooftops solar panels unfurled themselves, welcoming the sun. The air was still cool at this time. Soon it will be hot, the sun beating down, the aircon units turning on with a roar of cold air in shops and restaurants and crowded apartments all over the old neighbourhood.

"Ibrahim," Achimwene said, acknowledging the alte-zachen man as he approached. Ibrahim was perched on top of his cart, the boy Ismail by his side. The cart was pushed by a solitary horse, an old grey being who blinked at Achimwene patiently. The cart was already filled, with adaptoplant furniture, scrap plastic and metal, boxes of discarded house wares and, lying carelessly on its side, a discarded stone bust of Albert Einstein.

"Achimwene," Ibrahim said, smiling. "How is the weather?"

"Fair to middling," Achimwene said, and they both laughed, comfortable in the near-daily ritual.

This is Achimwene: he was not the most imposing of people, did not draw the eye in a crowd. He was slight of frame, and somewhat stooped, and wore old-fashioned glasses to correct a minor fault of vision. His hair was once thickly curled but not much of it was left now, and he was mostly, sad to say, bald. He had a soft mouth and patient, trusting eyes, with fine lines of disappointment at their corners. His name meant "brother" in Chichewa, a language dominant in Malawi, though he was of the Joneses of Central Station, and the brother of Miriam Jones, of Mama Jones' Shebeen on Neve Sha'anan Street. Every morning he rose early, bathed hurriedly, and went out into the streets in time to catch the rising sun and the alte-zachen man. Now he rubbed his hands together, as if cold, and said, in his soft, quiet voice, "Do you have anything for me today, Ibrahim?"

Ibrahim ran his hand over his own bald pate and smiled. Sometimes the answer was a simple, "No." Sometimes it came with a hesitant, "Perhaps . . ."

Today it was a "Yes," Ibrahim said, and Achimwene raised his eyes, to him or to the heavens, and said, "Show me?"

"Ismail," Ibrahim said, and the boy, who sat beside him wordless until then, climbed down from the cart with a quick, confident grin and went to the back of the cart. "It's heavy!" he complained. Achimwene hurried to his side and helped him bring down a heavy box.

He looked at it.

"Open it," Ibrahim said. "Are these any good to you?"

Achimwene knelt by the side of the box. His fingers reached for it, traced an opening. Slowly, he pulled the flaps of the box apart. Savouring the moment that light would fall down on the box's contents, and the smell of those precious, fragile things inside would rise, released, into the air, and tickle his nose. There was no other smell like it in the world, the smell of old and weathered paper.

The box opened. He looked inside.

Books. Not the endless scrolls of text and images, moving and static, nor full-immersion narratives he understood other people to experience, in what he called, in his obsolete tongue, the networks, and others called, simply, the Conversation. Not those, to which he, anyway, had no access. Nor were they books as decorations, physical objects hand-crafted by artisans, vellum-bound, gold-tooled, typeset by hand and sold at a premium.

No.

He looked at the things in the box, these fragile, worn, faded, thin, cheap paper-bound books. They smelled of dust, and mould, and age. They smelled, faintly, of pee, and tobacco, and spilled coffee. They smelled like things which had *lived*.

They smelled like history.

With careful fingers he took a book out and held it, gently turning the pages. It was all but priceless. His breath, as they often said in those very same books, caught in his throat.

It was a *Ringo*.

A genuine Ringo.

The cover of this fragile paperback showed a leather-faced gunman against a desert-red background. RINGO, it said, it giant letters, and below, the fictitious author's name, Jeff McNamara. Finally, the individual title of the book, one of many in that long running Western series. This one was *On The Road To Kansas City*.

Were they all like this?

Of course, there had never been a 'Jeff McNamara.' Ringo was a series of Hebrew-language Westerns, all written pseudonymously by starving young writers in a bygone Tel Aviv, who contributed besides it similar tales of space adventures, sexual titillation or soppy romance, as the occasion (and the publisher's cheque book) had called for. Achimwene rifled carefully through the rest of the books. All paperbacks, printed on cheap, thin pulp paper centuries before. How had they been preserved? Some of these he had only ever seen mentioned in auction catalogues, their existence, here, now, was nothing short of a miracle. There was a nurse romance; a murder mystery; a World War Two adventure; an erotic tale whose lurid cover made Achimwene blush. They were impossible, they could not possibly exist. "Where did you *find* them?" he said.

Ibrahim shrugged. "An opened Century Vault," he said.

Achimwene exhaled a sigh. He had heard of such things—subterranean safe-rooms, built in some long-ago war of the Jews, pockets of reinforced concrete shelters caught like bubbles all under the city surface. But he had never expected . . .

"Are there . . . many of them?" he said.

Ibrahim smiled. "Many," he said. Then, taking pity on Achimwene, said, "Many vaults, but most are inaccessible. Every now and then, construction work uncovers one . . . the owners called me, for they viewed much of it as rubbish. What, after all, would a modern person want with one of these?" and he gestured at the box, saying, "I saved them for you. The rest of the stuff is back in the Junkyard, but this was the only box of books."

"I can pay," Achimwene said. "I mean, I will work something out, I will borrow—" the thought stuck like a bone in his throat (as they said in those books)—"I will borrow from my sister."

But Ibrahim, to Achimwene's delight and incomprehension, waved him aside with a laugh. "Pay me the usual," he said. "After all, it is only a box, and this is mere paper. It cost me nothing, and I have made my profit already. What extra value you place on it surely is a value of your own."

"But they are precious!" Achimwene said, shocked. "Collectors would pay—" imagination failed him. Ibrahim smiled, and his smile was gentle. "You are the only collector I know," he said. "Can you afford what you think they're worth?"

"No," Achimwene said—whispered.

"Then pay only what I ask," Ibrahim said and, with a shake of his head, as at the folly of his fellow man, steered the horse into action. The patient beast beat its flank with its tail, shoeing away flies, and ambled onwards. The boy, Ismail, remained there a moment longer, staring at the books. "Lots of old junk in the Vaults!" he said. He spread his arms wide to describe them. "I was there, I saw it! These . . . books?" he shot an uncertain look at Achimwene, then ploughed on—"and big flat square things called televisions, that we took for plastic scrap, and old guns, lots of old guns! But the Jews took those—why do you think they buried those things?" the boy said. His eyes, vat-grown haunting greens, stared at Achimwene. "So much *junk*," the boy said, at last, with a note of finality, and then, laughing, ran after the cart, jumping up on it with youthful ease.

Achimwene stared at the cart until it disappeared around the bend. Then, with the tenderness of a father picking up a new-born infant, he picked up the box of books and carried them the short way to his alcove.

Achimwene's life was about to change, but he did not yet know it. He spent the rest of the morning happily cataloguing, preserving and shelving the ancient books. Each lurid cover delighted him. He handled the books with only the tips of his fingers, turning the pages carefully, reverently. There were many faiths in Central Station, from Elronism to St. Cohen to followers of Ogko, mixed amidst the larger populations—Jews to the north, Muslims to the south, a hundred offshoots of Christianity dotted all about like potted plants—but only Achimwene's faith called for this. The worship of old, obsolete books. The worship, he liked to think, of history itself.

He spent the morning quite happily, therefore, with only one customer. For Achimwene was not alone in his—obsession? Fervour?

Others were like him. Mostly men, and mostly, like himself, broken in some fundamental fashion. They came from all over, pilgrims taking hesitant steps through the unfamiliar streets of the old neighbourhood, reaching at last Achimwene's alcove, a shop which had no name. They needed no sign. They simply knew.

There was an Armenian priest from Jerusalem who came once a month, a devotee of Hebrew pulps so obscure even Achimwene struggled with the conversation—romance chapbooks printed in twenty or thirty stapled pages at a time, filled with Zionist fervour and lovers' longings, so rare and fragile few remained in the world. There was a rare woman, whose name was Nur, who came from Damascus once a year, and whose speciality was the works of obscure poet and science fiction writer Lior Tirosh. There was a man from Haifa who collected erotica, and a man from the Galilee collecting mysteries.

"Achimwene? Shalom!"

Achimwene straightened in his chair. He had sat at his desk for some half an hour, typing, on what was his pride and joy, a rare collectors' item: a genuine, Hebrew typewriter. It was his peace and his escape, in the quiet times, to sit at his desk and pen, in the words of those old, vanished pulp writers, similarly exciting narratives of daring-do, rescues, and escapes.

"Shalom, Gideon," he said, sighing a little. The man, who hovered at the door, now came fully inside. He was a stooped figure, with long white hair, twinkling eyes, and a bottle of cheap arak held, like an offering, in one hand.

"Got glasses?"

"Sure . . ."

Achimwene brought out two glasses, neither too clean, and put them on the desk. The man, Gideon, motioned with his head at the typewriter. "Writing again?" he said.

"You know," Achimwene said.

Hebrew was the language of his birth. The Joneses were once Nigerian immigrants. Some said they had come over on work visas, and stayed. Others that they had escaped some long-forgotten civil war, had crossed the border illegally from Egypt, and stayed. One way or the other, the Joneses, like the Chongs, had lived in Central Station for generations.

Gideon opened the bottle, poured them both a drink. "Water?" Achimwene said.

Gideon shook his head. Achimwene sighed again and Gideon raised the glass, the liquid clear. "L'chaim," he said.

They clinked glasses. Achimwene drank, the arak burning his throat, the anis flavour tickling his nose. Made him think of his sister's shebeen. Said, "So, nu? What's new with you, Gideon?"

He'd decided, suddenly and with aching clarity, that he won't share the new haul with Gideon. Will keep them to himself, a private secret, for just a little while longer. Later, perhaps, he'd sell one or two. But not yet. For the moment, they were his, and his alone.

They chatted, whiling away an hour or two. Two men old before their time, in a dark alcove, sipping arak, reminiscing of books found and lost, of bargains struck and the ones that got away. At last Gideon left, having purchased a minor Western, in what is termed, in those circles, Good condition—that is, it was falling apart. Achimwene breathed out a sigh of relief, his head swimming from the arak, and returned to his typewriter. He punched an experimental heh, then a nun. He began to type.

The g.

The girl.

The girl was in trouble.

A crowd surrounded her. Excitable, their faces twisted in the light of their torches. They held stones, blades. They shouted a word, a name, like a curse. The girl looked at them, her delicate face frightened.

"Won't someone save me?" she cried. "A hero, a—"

Achimwene frowned in irritation for, from the outside, a commotion was rising, the noise disturbing his concentration. He listened, but the noise only grew louder and, with a sigh of irritation, he pulled himself upwards and went to the door.

Perhaps this is how lives change. A momentary decision, the toss of a coin. He could have returned to his desk, completed his sentence, or chosen to tidy up the shelves, or make a cup of coffee. He chose to open the door instead.

They are dangerous things, doors, Ogko had once said. You never knew what you'd find on the other side of one.

Achimwene opened the door and stepped outside.

The g.

The girl.

The girl was in trouble.

This much Achimwene saw, though for the moment, the *why* of it escaped him. This is what he saw:

The crowd was composed of people Achimwene knew. Neighbours, cousins, acquaintances. He thought he saw young Yan there, and his fiancé, Youssou (who was Achimwene's second cousin); the greengrocer from around the corner; some adaptoplant dwellers he knew by sight if not name; and others. They were just people. They were of Central Station.

The girl wasn't.

Achimwene had never seen her before. She was slight of frame. She walked with a strange gait, as though unaccustomed to the gravity. Her face was narrow, indeed delicate. Her head had been done in some other-worldly fashion, it was woven into dreadlocks that moved slowly, even sluggishly, above her head, and an ancient name rose in Achimwene's mind.

Medusa.

The girl's panicked eyes turned, looking. For just a moment, they found his. But her look did not (as Medusa's was said to) turn him to stone.

She turned away.

The crowd surrounded her in a semi-circle. Her back was to Achimwene. The crowd—the word *mob* flashed through Achimwene's mind uneasily—was excited, restless. Some held stones in their hands, but uncertainly, as though they were not sure why, or what they were meant to do with them. A mood of ugly energy animated them. And now Achimwene could hear a shouted word, a name, rising and falling in different intonations as the girl turned, and turned, helplessly seeking escape.

"Shambleau!"

The word sent a shiver down Achimwene's back (a sensation he had often read about in the pulps, yet seldom if ever experienced in real life). It arose in him vague, menacing images, desolate Martian landscapes, isolated kibbutzim on the Martian tundra, red sunsets, the colour of blood.

"Strigoi!"

And there it was, that other word, a word conjuring, as though from thin air, images of brooding mountains, dark castles, bat-shaped shadows fleeting on the winds against a blood-red, setting sun . . . images of an ageless Count, of teeth elongating in a hungry skull, sinking to touch skin, to drain blood . . .

"Shambleau!"

"Get back! Get back to where you came from!"

"Leave her alone!"

The cry pierced the night. The mob milled, confused. The voice like a blade had cut through the day and the girl, startled and surprised, turned this way and that, searching for the source of that voice.

Who said it?

Who dared the wrath of the mob?

With a sense of reality cleaving in half, Achimwene, almost with a slight *frisson*, a delicious shiver of recognition, realised that it was he, himself, who had spoken.

Had, indeed, stepped forward from his door, a little hunched figure facing this mob of relatives and acquaintances and, even, perhaps, a few friends. "Leave her alone," he said again, savouring the words, and for once, perhaps for the first time in his life, people listened to him. A silence had descended. The girl, caught between her tormentors and this mysterious new figure, seemed uncertain.

"Oh, it's Achimwene," someone said, and somebody else suddenly, crudely laughed, breaking the silence.

"She's Shambleau," someone else said, and the first speaker (he couldn't quite see who it was) said, "Well, she'd be no harm to *him*."

That crude laughter again and then, as if by some unspoken agreement, or command, the crowd began, slowly, to disperse.

Achimwene found that his heart was beating fast; that his palms sweated; that his eyes developed a sudden itch. He felt like sneezing. The girl, slowly, floated over to him. They were of the same height. She looked into his eyes. Her eyes were a deep clear blue, vat-grown. They regarded each other as the rest of the mob dispersed. Soon they were left alone, in that quiet street, with Achimwene's back to the door of his shop.

She regarded him quizzically; her lips moved without sound, her eyes flicked up and down, scanning him. She looked confused, then shocked. She took a step back.

"No, wait!" he said.

"You are . . . you are not . . ."

He realised she had been trying to communicate with him. His silence had baffled her. Repelled her, most likely. He was a cripple. He said, "I have no node."

"How is that . . . possible?"

He laughed, though there was no humour in it. "It is not that unusual, here, on Earth," he said.

"You know I am not—" she said, and hesitated, and he said, "From here? I guessed. You are from Mars?"

A smile twisted her lips, for just a moment. "The asteroids," she admitted.

"What is it like, in space?" Excitement animated him. She shrugged. "Olsem difren," she said, in the pidgin of the asteroids.

The same, but different.

They stared at each other, two strangers, her vat-grown eyes against his natural-birth ones. "My name is Achimwene," he said.

"Oh."

"And you are?"

That same half-smile twisting her lips. He could tell she was bewildered by him. Repelled. Something inside him fluttered, like a caged bird dying of lack of oxygen.

"Carmel," she said, softly. "My name is Carmel."

He nodded. The bird was free, it was beating its wings inside him. "Would you like to come in?" he said. He gestured at his shop. The door, still standing half open.

Decisions splitting quantum universes . . . she bit her lip. There was no blood. He noticed her canines, then. Long and sharp. Unease took him again. Truth in the old stories? A Shambleau? Here?

"A cup of tea?" he said, desperately.

She nodded, distractedly. She was still trying to speak to him, he realised. She could not understand why he wasn't replying.

"I am un-noded," he said again. Shrugged. "It is—"

"Yes," she said.

"Yes?"

"Yes, I would like to come in. For . . . tea." She stepped closer to him. He could not read the look in her eyes. "Thank you," she said, in her soft voice, that strange accent. "For . . . you know."

"Yes." He grinned, suddenly, feeling bold, almost invincible. "It's nothing."

"Not . . . nothing." Her hand touched his shoulder, briefly, a light touch. Then she had gone past him and disappeared through the half-open door.

The shelves inside were arranged by genre.

> Romance.
> Mystery.
> Detection.
> Adventure.
> And so on.

Life wasn't like that neat classification system, Achimwene had come to realise. Life was half-completed plots abandoned, heroes dying half-way along their quests, loves requited and un-, some fading inexplicably, some burning short and bright. There was a story of a man who fell in love with a vampire . . .

Carmel was fascinated by him, but increasingly distant. She did not understand him. He had no taste to him, nothing she could sink her teeth into. Her fangs. She was a predator, she needed *feed*, and Achimwene could not provide it to her.

That first time, when she had come into his shop, had run her fingers along the spines of ancient books, fascinated, shy: "We had books, on the asteroid," she admitted, embarrassed, it seemed, by the confession of a shared history. "On Nungai Merurun, we had a library of physical books, they had come in one of the ships, once, a great-uncle traded something for them—" leaving Achimwene with dreams of going into space, of visiting this Ng. Merurun, discovering a priceless treasure hidden away.

Lamely, he had offered her tea. He brewed it on the small primus stove, in a dented saucepan, with fresh mint leaves in the water. Stirred sugar into the glasses. She had looked at the tea in incomprehension, concentrating. It was only later he realised she was trying to communicate with him again.

She frowned, shook her head. She was shaking a little, he realised. "Please," he said. "Drink."

"I don't," she said. "You're not." She gave up.

Achimwene often wondered what the Conversation was like. He knew that, wherever he passed, nearly anything he saw or touched was noded. Humans, yes, but also plants, robots, appliances, walls, solar panels—nearly everything was connected, in an ever-expanding, organically growing Aristocratic Small World network, that spread out, across Central Station, across Tel Aviv and Jaffa, across the interwoven entity that was Palestine/Israel, across that region called the Middle East, across Earth, across trans-solar space and beyond, where the lone Spiders sang to each other as they built more nodes and hubs, expanded farther and farther their intricate web. He knew a human was surrounded, every living moment, by the constant hum of other humans, other minds, an endless conversation going on in ways Achimwene could not conceive of. His own life was silent. He was a node of one. He moved his lips. Voice came. That was all. He said, "You are strigoi."

"Yes." Her lips twisted in that half-smile. "I am a monster."

"Don't say that." His heart beat fast. He said, "You're beautiful."

Her smile disappeared. She came closer to him, the tea forgotten. She leaned into him. Put her lips against his skin, against his neck, he felt her breath, the lightness of her lips on his hot skin. Sudden pain bit into him. She had fastened her lips over the wound, her teeth piercing his skin. He sighed. "Nothing!" she said. She pulled away from him abruptly. "It is like . . . I don't know!" She shook. He realised she was frightened. He touched the wound on his neck. He had felt nothing. "Always, to buy love, to buy obedience, to buy worship, I must feed," she said, matter-of-factly. "I drain them of their precious data, bleed them for it, and pay them in dopamine, in ecstasy. But you have no storage, no broadcast, no firewall . . . *there is nothing there.* You are like a simulacra," she said. The word pleased her. "A *simulacra*," she repeated, softly. "You have the appearance of a man but there is nothing behind your eyes. You do not broadcast."

"That's ridiculous," Achimwene said, anger flaring, suddenly. "I speak. You can hear me. I have a mind. I can express my—"

But she was only shaking her head, and shivering. "I'm hungry," she said. "I need to feed."

There were willing victims in Central Station. The bite of a strigoi gave pleasure. More—it conferred status on the victim, bragging rights. There had never been strigoi on Earth. It made Achimwene nervous.

He found himself living in one of his old books. He was the one to arrange Carmel's feeding, select her victims, who paid for the privilege. Achimwene, to his horror, discovered he had become a middleman. The bag man.

There was something repulsive about it all, as well as a strange, shameful excitement. There was no sex: sex was not a part of it, although it could be. Carmel leeched knowledge—memories—stored sensations—anything—pure uncut data from her victims, her fangs fastening on their neck, injecting dopamine into their blood as her node broke their inadequate protections, smashed their firewalls and their security, and bled them dry.

"Where do you come from?" he once asked her, as they lay on his narrow bed, the window open and the heat making them sweat, and she told him of Ng. Merurun, the tiny asteroid where she grew up, and how she ran away, on board the Emaciated Messiah, where a Shambleau attacked her, and passed on the virus, or the sickness, whatever it was.

"And how did you come to be here?" he said, and sensed, almost before he spoke, her unease, her reluctance to answer. Jealousy flared in him then, and he could not say why.

His sister came to visit him. She walked into the bookshop as he sat behind the desk, typing. He was writing less and less, now; his new life seemed to him a kind of novel.

"Achimwene," she said.

He raised his head. "Miriam," he said, heavily.

They did not get along.

"The girl, Carmel. She is with you?"

"I let her stay," he said, carefully.

"Oh, Achimwene, you are a fool!" she said.

Her boy—their sister's boy—Kranki—was with her. Achimwene regarded him uneasily. The boy was vat-grown—had come from the birthing clinics—his eyes were Armani-trademark blue. "Hey, Kranki," Achimwene said.

"Anggkel," the boy said—*uncle*, in the pidgin of the asteroids. "Yu olsem wanem?"

"I gud," Achimwene said.

How are you? I am well.

"Fren blong mi Ismail I stap aotside," Kranki said. "I stret hemi kam insaed?"

My friend Ismail is outside. Is it ok if he comes in?

"I stret," Achimwene said.

Miriam blinked. "Ismail," she said. "Where did you come from?"

Kranki had turned, appeared, to all intents and purposes, to play with an invisible playmate. Achimwene said, carefully, "There is no one there."

"Of course there is," his sister snapped. "It's Ismail, the Jaffa boy."

Achimwene shook his head.

"Listen, Achimwene. The girl. Do you know why she came here?"

"No."

"She followed Boris."

"Boris," Achimwene said. "Your Boris?"

"My Boris," she said.

"She knew him before?"

"She knew him on Mars. In Tong Yun City."

"I . . . see."

"You see nothing, Achi. You are blind like a worm." Old words, still with the power to hurt him. They had never been close, somehow. He said, "What do you want, Miriam?"

Her face softened. "I do not want . . . I do not want her to hurt you."

"I am a grown-up," he said. "I can take care of myself."

"Achi, like you ever could!"

Could that be affection, in her voice? It sounded like frustration. Miriam said, "Is she here?"

"Kranki," Achimwene said, "Who are you playing with?"

"Ismail," Kranki said, pausing in the middle of telling a story to someone only he could see.

"He's not here," Achimwene said.

"Sure he is. He's right here."

Achimwene formed his lips into an O of understanding. "Is he virtual?" he said.

Kranki shrugged. "I guess," he said. He clearly felt uncomfortable with—or didn't understand—the question. Achimwene let it go.

His sister said, "I like the girl, Achi."

It took him by surprise. "You've met her?"

"She has a sickness. She needs help."

"I *am* helping her!"

But his sister only shook her head.

"Go away, Miriam," he said, feeling suddenly tired, depressed. His sister said, "Is she here?"

"She is resting."

Above his shop there was a tiny flat, accessible by narrow, twisting stairs. It wasn't much but it was home. "Carmel?" his sister called. "Carmel!"

There was a sound above, as of someone moving. Then a lack of sound. Achimwene watched his sister standing impassively. Realised she was talking, in the way of other people, with Carmel. Communicating in a way that was barred to him. Then normal sound again, feet on the stairs, and Carmel came into the room.

"Hi," she said, awkwardly. She came and stood closer to Achimwene, then took his hand in hers. The feel of her small, cold fingers in between his hands startled him and made a feeling of pleasure spread throughout his body, like warmth in the blood. Nothing more was said. The physical action itself was an act of speaking.

Miriam nodded.

Then Kranki startled them all.

Carmel had spent the previous night in the company of a woman. Achimwene had known there was sex involved, not just feeding. He had told himself he didn't mind. When Carmel came back she had smelled of sweat and sex and blood. She moved lethargically, and he knew she was drunk on data. She had tried to describe it to him once, but he didn't really understand it, what it was like.

He had lain there on the narrow bed with her and watched the moon outside, and the floating lanterns with their rudimentary intelligence. He had his arm around the sleeping Carmel, and he had never felt happier.

Kranki turned and regarded Carmel. He whispered something to the air—to the place Ismail was standing, Achimwene guessed. He giggled at the reply and turned to Carmel.

"Are you a *vampire?*" he said.

"Kranki!"

At the horrified look on Miriam's face, Achimwene wanted to laugh. Carmel said, "No, it's all right—" in asteroid pidgin. *I stret nomo.*

But she was watching the boy intently. "Who is your friend?" she said, softly.

"It's Ismail. He lives in Jaffa on the hill."

"And what is he?" Carmel said. "What are you?"

The boy didn't seem to understand the question. "He is him. I am me. We are . . ." he hesitated.

"Nakaimas . . ." Carmel whispered. The sound of her voice made Achimwene shiver. That same cold run of ice down his spine, like in the old books, like when Ringo the Gunslinger met a horror from beyond the grave on the lonesome prairies.

He knew the word, though never understood the way people used it. It meant black magic, but also, he knew, it meant to somehow, impossibly, transcend the networks, that thing they called the Conversation.

"Kranki . . ." the warning tone in Miriam's voice was unmistakable. But neither Kranki nor Carmel paid her any heed. "I could show you," the boy said. His clear, blue eyes seemed curious, guileless. He stepped forward and stood directly in front of Carmel and reached out his hand, pointing finger extended. Carmel, momentarily, hesitated. Then she, too, reached forward and, finger extended, touched its tip to the boy's own.

It is, perhaps, the prerogative of every man or woman to imagine, and thus force a *shape,* a *meaning,* onto that wild and meandering narrative of their lives, by choosing genre. A princess is rescued by a prince; a vampire stalks a victim in the dark; a student becomes the master. A circle is completed. And so on.

It was the next morning that Achimwene's story changed, for him. It had been a Romance, perhaps, of sorts. But now it became a Mystery.

Perhaps they chose it, by tacit agreement, as a way to bind them, to make this curious relationship, this joining of two ill-fitted individuals somehow work. Or perhaps it was curiosity that motivated them after all, that earliest of motives, the most human and the most suspect, the one that had led Adam to the Tree, in the dawn of story.

The next morning Carmel came down the stairs. Achimwene had slept in the bookshop that night, curled up in a thin blanket on top of a mattress he had kept by the wall and which was normally laden with books. The books, pushed aside, formed an untidy wall around him as he slept, an alcove within an alcove.

Carmel came down. Her hair moved sluggishly around her skull. She wore a thin cotton shift; he could see how thin she was.

Achimwene said, "Tell me what happened yesterday."

Carmel shrugged. "Is there any coffee?"

"You know where it is."

He sat up, feeling self-conscious and angry. Pulling the blanket over his legs. Carmel went to the primus stove, filled the pot with water from the tap, added spoons of black coffee carelessly. Set it to cook.

"The boy is . . . a sort of *strigoi*," she said. "Maybe. Yes. No. I don't know."

"What did he do?"

"He gave me something. He took something away. A memory. Mine or someone else's. It's no longer there."

"What did he give you?"

"Knowledge. That he exists."

"Nakaimas."

"Yes." She laughed, a sound as bitter as the coffee. "Black magic. Like me. Not like me."

"You were a weapon," he said. She turned, sharply. There were two coffee cups on the table. Glass on varnished wood. "What?"

"I read about it."

"Always your *books*."

He couldn't tell by her tone how she meant it. He said, "There are silences in your Conversation. Holes." Could not quite picture it, to him there was only a silence. Said, "The books have answers."

She poured coffee, stirred sugar into the glasses. Came over and sat beside him, her side pressing into his. Passed him a cup. "Tell me," she said.

He took a sip. The coffee burned his tongue. Sweet. He began to talk quickly. "I read up on the condition. Strigoi. Shambleau. There are references from the era of the Shangri-La Virus, contemporary accounts. The Kunming Labs were working on genetic weapons, but the war ended before the strain could be deployed—they sold it off-world, it went loose, it spread. It never worked right. There are hints—I need access to a bigger library. Rumours. Cryptic footnotes."

"Saying what?"

"Suggesting a deeper purpose. Or that Strigoi was but a side-effect of something else. A secret purpose . . ."

Perhaps they wanted to believe. Everyone needs a mystery.

She stirred beside him. Turned to face him. Smiled. It was perhaps the first time she ever truly smiled at him. Her teeth were long, and sharp.

"We could find out," she said.

"Together," he said. He drank his coffee, to hide his excitement. But he knew she could tell.

"We could be detectives."

"Like Judge Dee," he said.

"Who?"

"Some detective."

"Book detective," she said, dismissively.

"Like Bill Glimmung, then," he said. Her face lit up. For a moment she looked very young. "I love those stories," she said.

Even Achimwene had seen Glimmung features. They had been made in 2D, 3D, full-immersion, as scent narratives, as touch-tapestry—Martian Hardboiled, they called the genre, the Phobos Studios cranked out hundreds of them over decades if not centuries, Elvis Mandela had made the character his own.

"Like Bill Glimmung, then," she said solemnly, and he laughed.

"Like Glimmung," he said.

And so the lovers, by complicit agreement, became detectives.

MARTIAN HARDBOILED, genre of. Flourished in the CENTURY OF DRAGON. Most prominent character: Bill GLIMMUNG, played most memorably by Elvis MANDELA (for which see separate entry). The genre is well-known, indeed notorious, for the liberal use of sex and violence, transplanted from old EARTH (also see MANHOME; HUMANITY PRIME) hardboiled into a Martian setting, sometimes realistically-portrayed, often with implicit or explicit elements of FANTASY.

While early stories stuck faithfully to the mean streets of TONG YUN CITY, with its triads, hafmek pushers and Israeli, Red Chinese and Red Soviet agents, later narratives took in off-world adventures, including in the BELT, the VENUSIAN NO-GO ZONE and the OUTER PLANETS. Elements of SOAP OPERA intruded as the narratives became ever more complex and on-going (see entry for long-running Martian soap CHAINS OF ASSEMBLY for separate discussion).

"There was something else," Carmel said.

Achimwene said, "What?"

They were walking the streets of old Central Station. The space port rose above them, immense and inscrutable. Carmel said, "When I came in. Came down." She shook her head in frustration and a solitary dreadlock snaked around her mouth, making her blow on it to move it away. "When I came to Earth."

Those few words evoked in Achimwene a nameless longing. So much to infer, so much suggested, to a man who had never left his home town. Carmel said, "I bought a new identity in Tong Yun, before I came. The best you could. From a Conch—"

Looking at him to see if he understood. Achimwene did. A Conch was a human who had been ensconced, welded into a permanent pod-cum-exoskeleton. He was only part human, had become part digital by extension. It was not unsimilar, in some ways, to the eunuchs of old Earth. Achimwene said, "I see?" Carmel said, "It worked. When I passed through Central Station security I was allowed through, with no problems. The . . . the digitals did not pick up on my . . . nature. The fake ident was accepted."

"So?"

Carmel sighed, and a loose dreadlock tickled Achimwene's neck, sending a warmth rushing through him. "So is that likely?" she said. She stopped walking, then, when Achimwene stopped also, she started pacing. A floating lantern bobbed beside them for a few moments then, as though sensing their intensity, drifted away, leaving them in shadow. "There are no strigoi on Earth," Carmel said.

"How do we know for sure?" Achimwene said.

"It's one of those things. Everyone knows it."

Achimwene shrugged. "But *you're* here," he pointed out.

Carmel waved her finger; stuck it in his face. "And how likely is that?" she yelled, startling him. "I believed it worked, because I *wanted* to believe it. But surely they know! I am not human, Achi! My body is riddled with nodal filaments, exabytes of data, hostile protocols! You want to tell me they *didn't know*?"

Achimwene shook his head. Reached for her, but she pulled away from him. "What are you saying?" he said.

"They let me through." Her voice was matter of fact.

"Why?" Achimwene said. "Why would they do that?"

"I don't know."

Achimwene chewed his lip. Intuition made a leap in his mind, neurons singing to neurons. "You think it is because of those children," he said.

Carmel stopped pacing. He saw how pale her face was, how delicate. "Yes," she said.

"Why?"

"I don't know."

"Then you must ask a digital," he said. "You must ask an Other."

She glared at him. "Why would they talk to me?" she said.

Achimwene didn't have an answer. "We can proceed the way we agreed," he said, a little lamely. "We'll get the answers. Sooner or later, we'll figure it out, Carmel."

"How?" she said.

He pulled her to him. She did not resist. The words from an old book rose into Achimwene's mind, and with them the entire scene. "We'll get to the bottom of this," he said.

And so on a sweltering hot day Achimwene and the strigoi left Central Station, on foot, and shortly thereafter crossed the invisible barrier that separated the old neighbourhood from the city of Tel Aviv proper. Achimwene walked slowly; an electronic cigarette dangled from his lips, another vintage affectation, and the fedora hat he wore shaded him from the sun even as his sweat drenched into the brim of the hat. Beside him Carmel was cool in a light blue dress. They came to Allenby Street and followed it towards the Carmel Market—"It's like my name," Carmel said, wonderingly.

"It is an old name," Achimwene said. But his attention was elsewhere.

"Where are we going?" Carmel said. Achimwene smiled, white teeth around the metal cigarette. "Every detective," he said, "needs an informant."

Picture, then, Allenby. Not the way it was, but the way it is. Surprisingly little has changed. It was a long, dirty street, with dark shops selling knock-off products with the air of disuse upon them. Carmel dawdled outside a magic shop. Achimwene bargained with a fruit juice seller and returned with two cups of fresh orange juice, handing one to Carmel. They passed a bakery where cream-filled pastries vied for their attention. They passed a Church of Robot node where a rusting preacher tried to get their attention with a sad distracted air. They passed shawarma stalls thick with the smell of cumin and lamb fat. They passed a road-sweeping machine that warbled at them pleasantly, and a recruitment centre for the Martian Kibbutz Movement. They passed a gaggle of black-clad Orthodox Jews; like Achimwene, they were unnoded.

Carmel looked this way and that, smelling, looking, *feeding*, Achimwene knew, on pure unadulterated *feed*. Something he could not experience, could not know, but knew, nevertheless, that it was there, invisible yet ever present. Like God. The lines from a poem by Mahmoud Darwish floated in his head. Something about the invisibles. "Look," Carmel said, smiling. "A bookshop."

Indeed it was. They were coming closer to the market now and the throng of people intensified, and solar buses crawled like insects, with their wings spread high, along the Allenby road, carrying passengers, and the smell of fresh vegetables, of peppers and tomatoes, and the sweet strong smell of oranges, too, filled the air. The bookshop was, in fact, a yard, open to the skies, the books under awnings, and piled up, here and there, in untidy mountains—it was the sort of shop that would have no prices, and where you'd always have to ask for the price, which depended on the owner, and his mood, and on the weather and the alignment of the stars.

The owner in question was indeed standing in the shade of the long, metal bookcases lining up one wall. He was smoking a cigar and its overpowering aroma filled the air and made Carmel sneeze. The man looked up and saw them. "Achimwene," he said, without surprise. Then he squinted and said, in a lower voice, "I heard you got a nice batch recently."

"Word travels," Achimwene said, complacently. Carmel, meanwhile, was browsing aimlessly, picking up fragile-looking paper books and magazines, replacing them, picking up others. Achimwene saw, at a glance, early editions of Yehuda Amichai, a first edition Yoav Avni, several worn *Ringo* paperbacks he already had, and a Lior Tirosh semizdat collection. He said, "Shimshon, what do you know about vampires?"

"Vampires?" Shimshon said. He took a thoughtful pull on his cigar. "In the literary tradition? There is *Neshikat Ha'mavet Shel Dracula*, by Dan Shocker, in the Horror series from nineteen seventy two—" *Dracula's Death Kiss*—"or Gal Amir's *Laila Adom*—" *Red Night*—"possibly the first Hebrew vampire novel, or Vered Tochterman's *Dam Kachol*—" *Blue Blood*—"from around the same period. Didn't think it was particularly your area, Achimwene." Shimshon grinned. "But I'd be happy to sell you a copy. I think I have a signed Tochterman somewhere. Expensive, though. Unless you want to trade . . ."

"No," Achimwene said, although regretfully. "I'm not looking for a pulp, right now. I'm looking for non-fiction."

Shimshon's eyebrows rose and he regarded Achimwene without the grin. "Mil. Hist?" he said, uneasily. "Robotniks? The Nosferatu Code?"

Achimwene regarded him, uncertain. "The what?" he said.

But Shimshon was shaking his head. "I don't deal in that sort of thing," he said. "*Verboten.* Hagiratech. Go away, Achimwene. Go back to Central Station. Shop's closed." He turned and dropped the cigar and stepped on it with his foot. "You, love!" he said. "Shop's closing. Are you going to buy that book? No? Then put it down."

Carmel turned, wounded dignity flashing in her green eyes. "Then take it!" she said, shoving a (priceless, Achimwene thought) copy of Lior Tirosh's first—and only—poetry collection, *Remnants of God*, into Shimshon's hands. She hissed, a sound Achimwene suspected was not only in the audible range but went deeper, in the non-sound of digital communication, for Shimshon's face went pale and he said, "Get . . . out!" in a strangled whisper as Carmel smiled at him, flashing her small, sharp teeth.

They left. They crossed the street and stood outside a cheap cosmetics surgery booth, offering wrinkles erased or tentacles grafted, next to a handwritten sign that said, *Gone for Lunch.* "Verboten?" Achimwene said. "Hagiratech?"

"Forbidden," Carmel said. "The sort of wildtech that ends up on Jettisoned, from the exodus ships."

"What you are," he said.

"Yes. I looked, myself, you know. But it is like you said. Holes in the Conversation. Did we learn nothing useful?"

"No," he said. Then, "Yes."

She smiled. "Which is it?"

Military history, Shimshon had said. And no one knew better than him how to classify a thing into its genre. And—*robotniks.*

"We need to find us," Achimwene said, "an ex-soldier." He smiled without humour. "Better brush up on your Battle Yiddish," he said.

"Ezekiel."

"Achimwene."

"I brought . . . vodka. And spare parts." He had bought them in Tel Aviv, on Allenby, at great expense. Robotnik parts were not easy to come by.

Ezekiel looked at him without expression. His face was metal smooth. It never smiled. His body was mostly metal. It was rusted. It creaked when he walked. He ignored the proffered offerings. Turned his head. "You brought *her*?" he said. "*Here*?"

Carmel stared at the robotnik in curiosity. They were at the heart of the old station, a burned down ancient bus platform open to the sky. Achimwene knew platforms continued down below, that the robotniks—ex-soldiers, cyborged humans, preset day beggars and dealers in Crucifixation and stolen goods—made their base down there. But there he could not go. Ezekiel met him above-ground. A drum with fire burning, the flames reflected in the dull metal of the robotnik's face. "I saw your kind," Carmel said. "On Mars. In Tong Yun City. Begging."

"And I saw *your* kind," the robotnik said. "In the sands of the Sinai, in the war. Begging. Begging for their lives, as we decapitated them and stuck a stake through their hearts and watched them die."

"Jesus Elron, Ezekiel!"

The robotnik ignored his exclamation. "I had heard," he said. "That one came. Here. *Strigoi*. But I did not believe! The defence systems would have picked her up. Should have eliminated her."

"They didn't," Achimwene said.

"Yes . . ."

"Do you know why?"

The robotnik stared at him. Then he gave a short laugh and accepted the bottle of vodka. "You guess *they* let her through? The Others?"

Achimwene shrugged. "It's the only answer that makes sense."

"And you want to know why."

"Call me curious."

"I call you a fool," the robotnik said, without malice. "And you not even noded. She still has an effect on you?"

"*She* has a name," Carmel said, acidly. Ezekiel ignored her. "You're a collector of old stories, aren't you, Achimwene," he said. "Now you came to collect mine?"

Achimwene just shrugged. The robotnik took a deep slug of vodka and said, "So, nu? What do you want to know?"

"Tell me about Nosferatu," Achimwene said.

SHANGRI-LA VIRUS, the. Bio-weapon developed in the GOLDEN TRIANGLE and used during the UNOFFICIAL WAR. Transmission mechanisms included sexual intercourse (99%-100%), by air (50%-60%), by water (30%-35%), through saliva (15%-20%) and by touch (5%-6%). Used most memorably during the LONG CHENG ATTACK (for which also see LAOS; RAVENZ; THE KLAN KLANDESTINE). The weapon curtailed aggression in humans, making them peaceable and docile. All known samples destroyed in the Unofficial War, along with the city of Long Cheng.

"We never found out for sure where Nosferatu came from," Ezekiel said. It was quiet in the abandoned shell of the old station. Overhead a sub-orbital came in to land, and from the adaptoplant neighbourhoods ringing the old stone buildings the sound of laughter could be heard, and someone playing the guitar. "It had been introduced into the battlefield during the Third Sinai Campaign, by one side, or the other, or both." He fell quiet. "I am not even sure who we were fighting for," he said. He took another drink of vodka. The almost pure alcohol served as fuel for the robotniks. Ezekiel said, "At first we paid it little enough attention. We'd find victims on dawn patrols. Men, women, robotniks. Wandering the dunes or the Red Sea shore, dazed, their minds leeched clean. The small wounds on their necks. Still. They were alive. Not ripped to shreds by Jub Jubs. But the data. We began to notice the enemy knew where to find us. Knew where we went. We began to be afraid of the dark. To never go out alone. Patrol in teams. But worse. For the ones who were bitten, and carried back by us, had turned, became the enemy's own weapon. Nosferatu."

Achimwene felt sweat on his forehead, took a step away from the fire. Away from them, the floating lanterns bobbed in the air. Someone cried in the distance and the cry was suddenly and inexplicably cut off, and Achimwene wondered if the street sweeping machines would find another corpse the next morning, lying in the gutter outside a shebeen or No. 1 Pin Street, the most notorious of the drug dens-cum-brothels of Central Station.

"They rose within our ranks. They fed in secret. Robotniks don't sleep, Achimwene. Not the way the humans we used to be did. But we do turn off. Shut-eye. And they preyed on us, bleeding out minds, feeding on our feed. Do you know what it is like?" The robotnik's voice didn't grow louder, but it carried. "We were human, once. The army took us off the battlefield, broken, dying. It grafted us into new bodies, made us into shiny, near-invulnerable killing machines. We had no legal rights, not any more. We were technically, and clinically, dead. We had few memories, if any, of what we once were. But those we had, we kept hold of, jealously. Hints to our old identity. The memory of feet in the rain. The smell of pine resin. A hug from a new-born baby whose name we no longer knew.

"And the *strigoi* were taking even those away from us."

Achimwene looked at Carmel, but she was looking nowhere, her eyes were closed, her lips pressed together. "We finally grew wise to it," Ezekiel said. "We began to hunt them down. If we found a victim we did not take them back. Not alive. We staked them, we cut off their heads, we burned the bodies. Have you ever opened a strigoi's belly, Achimwene?" he motioned at Carmel. "Want to know what her insides look like?"

"No," Achimwene said, but Ezekiel the robotnik ignored him. "Like cancer," he said. "Strigoi is like robotnik, it is a human body subverted, cyborged. She isn't human, Achimwene, however much you'd like to believe it. I remember the first one we cut open. The filaments inside. Moving. Still trying to spread. Nosferatu Protocol, we called it. What we had to do. Following the Nosferatu Protocol. Who created the virus? I don't know. Us. Them. The Kunming Labs. Someone. St. Cohen only knows. All I know is how to kill them."

Achimwene looked at Carmel. Her eyes were open now. She was staring at the robotnik. "I didn't ask for this," she said. "I am not a *weapon*. There is no fucking *war*!"

"There was—"

"There were a lot of things!"

A silence. At last, Ezekiel stirred. "So what do you want?" he said. He sounded tired. The bottle of vodka was nearly finished. Achimwene said, "What more can you tell us?"

"Nothing, Achi. I can tell you nothing. Only to be careful." The robotnik laughed. "But it's too late for that, isn't it," he said.

Achimwene was arranging his books when Boris came to see him. He heard the soft footsteps and the hesitant cough and straightened up, dusting his hands from the fragile books and looked at the man Carmel had come to Earth for.

"Achi."

"Boris."

He remembered him as a loose-limbed, gangly teenager. Seeing him like this was a shock. There was a thing growing on Boris' neck. It was flesh-coloured, but the colour was slightly off to the rest of Boris's skin. It seemed to breathe gently. Boris's face was lined, he was still thin but there was an unhealthy nature to his thinness. "I heard you were back," Achimwene said.

"My father," Boris said, as though that explained everything.

"And we always thought you were the one who got away," Achimwene said. Genuine curiosity made him add, "What was it like? In the Up and Out?"

"Strange," Boris said. "The same." He shrugged. "I don't know."

"So you are seeing my sister again."

"Yes."

"You've hurt her once before, Boris. Are you going to do it again?"

Boris opened his mouth, closed it again. He stood there, taking Achimwene back years. "I heard Carmel is staying with you," Boris said at last.

"Yes."

Again, an uncomfortable silence. Boris scanned the bookshelves, picked a book at random. "What's this?" he said.

"Be careful with that!"

Boris looked startled. He stared at the small hardcover in his hands. "That's a Captain Yuno," Achimwene said, proudly. "*Captain Yuno on a Dangerous Mission*, the second of the three Sagi novels. The least rare of the three, admittedly, but still . . . priceless."

Boris looked momentarily amused. "He was a kid taikonaut?" he said.

"Sagi envisioned a solar system teeming with intelligent alien life," Achimwene said, primly. "He imagined a world government, and the people of Earth working together in peace."

"No kidding. He must have been disappointed when—"

"This book is *pre-spaceflight*," Achimwene said. Boris whistled. "So it's old?"

"Yes."

"And valuable?"

"Very."

"How do you know all this stuff?"

"I read."

Boris put the book back on the shelf, carefully. "Listen, Achi—" he said.

"No," Achimwene said. "You listen. Whatever happened between you and Carmel is between you two. I won't say I don't care, because I'd be lying, but it is not my business. Do you have a claim on her?"

"What?" Boris said. "No. Achi, I'm just trying to—"

"To what?"

"To warn you. I know you're not used to—" again he hesitated. Achimwene remembered Boris as someone of few words, even as a boy. Words did not come easy to him. "Not used to women?" Achimwene said, his anger tightly coiled.

Boris had to smile. "You have to admit—"

"I am not some, some—"

"She is not a woman, Achi. She's a strigoi."

Achimwene closed his eyes. Expelled breath. Opened his eyes again and regarded Boris levelly. "Is that all?" he said.

Boris held his eyes. After a moment, he seemed to deflate. "Very well," he said. "Yes."

"I guess I'll see you."

"I guess."

"Please pass my regards to Carmel."

Achimwene nodded. Boris, at last, shrugged. Then he turned and left the store.

There comes a time in a man's life when he realises stories are lies. Things do not end neatly. The enforced narratives a human impinges on the chaotic mess that is life become empty labels, like the dried husks of corn such as are thrown down, in the summer months, from the adaptoplant neighbourhoods high above Central Station, to litter the streets below.

He woke up in the night and the air was humid, and there was no wind. The window was open. Carmel was lying on her side, asleep, her small, naked body tangled up in the sheets. He watched her chest rise and fall, her breath even. A smear of what might have been blood on her lips. "Carmel?" he said, but quietly, and she didn't hear. He rubbed her back. Her skin was smooth and warm. She moved sleepily under his hand, murmured something he didn't catch, and settled down again.

Achimwene stared out of the window, at the moon rising high above Central Station. A mystery was no longer a mystery once it was solved. What difference did it make how Carmel had come to be there, with him, at that moment? It was not facts that mattered, but feelings. He stared at the moon, thinking of that first human to land there, all those years before, that first human footprint in that alien dust.

Inside Carmel was asleep and he was awake, outside dogs howled up at the moon and, from somewhere, the image came to Achimwene of a man in a spacesuit turning at the sound, a man who does a little tap dance on the moon, on the dusty moon.

He lay back down and held on to Carmel and she turned, trustingly, and settled into his arms.

pathways

NANCY KRESS

Here's a suspenseful story about a smart but uneducated woman taking part in an experimental program that's attempting to find a cure for the degenerative inherited disease that will inevitably kill her—with the clock rapidly running out.

Nancy Kress began selling her elegant and incisive stories in the mid-seventies. Her books include the novel version of her Hugo– and Nebula–winning story, Beggars in Spain, *and a sequel,* Beggars and Choosers, *as well as* The Prince of Morning Bells, The Golden Grove, The White Pipes, An Alien Light, Brain Rose, Oaths & Miracles, Stinger, Maximum Light, Crossfire, Nothing Human, The Flowers of Aulit Prison, Crucible, Dogs, Steal across the Sky, *and the space opera trilogy* Probability Moon, Probability Sun, *and* Probability Space. *Her short work has been collected in* Trinity and Other Stories, The Aliens of Earth, Beaker's Dozen, Nano Comes to Clifford Falls and Other Stories, The Fountain of Age, Future Perfect, AI Unbound, *and* The Body Human. *Her most recent books are the novels* Flash Point, *and, with Therese Pieczynski,* New Under the Sun. *In addition to the awards for "Beggars in Spain," she has also won Nebula awards for her stories "Out of All Them Bright Stars" and "The Flowers of Aulit Prison," the John W. Campbell Memorial Award in 2003 for her novel* Probability Space, *and another Hugo in 2009 for "The Erdmann Nexus." Most recently, she just won another Nebula Award in 2013 for her novella* After the Fall, Before the Fall, During the Fall. *She lives in Seattle, Washington, with her husband, writer Jack Skillingstead.*

The Chinese clinic warn't like I expected. It warn't even Chinese.

I got there afore it opened. I was hoping to get inside afore anybody else came, any neighbors who knew us or busybodies from Blaine. But Carrie Campbell was already parked in her truck, the baby on her lap. We nodded to each other but didn't speak. The Campbells are better off than us—Dave works in the mine up to Allington—but old Gacy Campbell been feuding with Dr. Harman for decades and

Carrie was probably glad to have someplace else to take the baby. He didn't look good, snuffling and whimpering.

When the doors opened, I went in first, afore Carrie was even out of the truck. It was going to take her a while. She was pregnant again.

"Yes?" said the woman behind the desk. Just a cheap metal desk, which steadied me some. The room was nothing special, just a few chairs, some pictures on the wall, a clothes basket of toys in the corner. What really surprised me was that the woman warn't Chinese. Blue eyes, brown hair, middle-aged. She looked a bit like Granmama, but she had all her teeth. "Can I help you?"

"I want to see a doctor."

"Certainly." She smiled. Yeah, all her teeth. "What seems to be the problem, miss?"

"No problem." From someplace in the back another woman came out, this one dressed like a nurse. She warn't Chinese either.

"I don't understand," the woman behind the desk said. From her accent she warn't from around here—like I didn't already know that. "Are you sick?"

"No, ma'am."

"Then how can I—"

Carrie waddled into the door, the baby balanced on her belly. Now my visit would be table-talk everywhere. All at once I just wanted to get it over with.

"I'm not sick," I said, too loud. "I just want to see a doctor." I took a deep breath. "My name is Ludmilla Connors."

The nurse stopped walking toward Carrie. The woman behind the counter half stood up, then sat down again. She tried to pretend like she hadn't done it, like she warn't pleased. If Bobby were that bad a liar, he'd a been in jail even more than he was.

"Certainly," the woman said. I didn't see her do nothing, but a man came out from the back, and he *was* Chinese. So was the woman who followed him.

"I'm Ludmilla Connors," I told him, and I clenched my ass together real hard to keep my legs steady. "And I want to volunteer for the experiment. But only if it pays what I heard. Only if."

The woman behind the desk took me back to a room with a table and some chairs and a whole lot of filing cabinets, and she left me there with the Chinese people. I looked at their smooth faces with those slanted, mostly closed eyes, and I wished I hadn't come. I guess these two were the reason everybody here-abouts called it the "Chinese clinic," even if everybody else there looked like regular Americans.

"Hello, Ms. Connors," the man said and he spoke English real good, even if it was hard to understand some words. "We are glad you are here. I am Dr. Dan Chung and this is my chief technician Jenny."

"Uh huh." He didn't look like no "Dan," and if she was "Jenny," I was a fish.

"Your mother is Courtney Connors and your father was Robert Connors?"

"How'd you know that?"

"We have family trees for everyone on the mountain. It's part of our work, you know. You said you want to aid us in this research?"

"I said I want to get paid."

"Of course. You will be. You are nineteen."

"Yeah." It warn't a question, and I didn't like that they knew so much about me. "How much money?"

He told me. It warn't as much as the rumors said, but it was enough. Unless they actually killed me, it was enough. And I didn't think they'd do that. The government wouldn't let them do that—not even this stinking government.

"Okay," I said. "Start the experiment."

Jenny smiled. I knew that kind of smile, like she was so much better than me. My fists clenched. Dr. Chung said, "Jenny, you may leave. Send in Mrs. Cully, please."

I liked the surprised look on Jenny's face, and then the angry look she tried to hide. Bitch.

Mrs. Cully didn't act like Jenny. She brought in a tray with coffee and cookies: just regular store-bought Pepperidge Farm, not Chinese. Under the tray was a bunch of papers. Mrs. Cully sat down at the table with us.

"These are legal papers, Ms. Connors," Dr. Chung said. "Before we begin, you must sign them. If you wish, you can take them home to read, or to a lawyer. Or you can sign them here, now. They give us permission to conduct the research, including the surgery. They say that you understand this procedure is experimental. They give the university, myself, and Dr. Liu all rights to information gained from your participation. They say that we do not guarantee any cure, or even any alleviation, of any medical disorder you may have. Do you want to ask questions?"

I did, but not just yet. Half of me was grateful that he didn't ask if I can read, the way tourists and social workers sometimes do. I can, but I didn't understand all the words on this page: *indemnify, liability, patent rights.* The other half of me resented that he was rushing me so.

I said something I warn't intending: "If Ratface Rollins warn't president, this clinic wouldn't be here at all!"

"I agree," Dr. Chung said. "But you Americans elected a Libertarian."

"Us Americans? Aren't you one?"

"No. I am a Chinese national, working in the United States on a visa arranged by my university."

I didn't know what to say to that, so I grabbed the pen and signed everything. "Let's get it over with, then."

Both Dr. Chung and Mrs. Cully looked startled. She said, "But . . . Ludmilla, didn't you understand that this will take several visits, spread out over months?"

"Yeah, I know. And that you're going to pay me over several months, too, but the first bit today."

"Yes. After your interview."

She had one of those little recording cubes that I only seen on TV. They can play back an interview like a movie, or they can send the words to a computer to get put on screen. Maybe today would be just talking. That would be fine with me. I took a cookie.

"Initial interview with experimental subject Ludmilla Connors," Dr. Chung said, and gave the date and time. "Ms. Connors, you are here of your own free will?"

"Yeah."

"And you are a member of the Connors family, daughter of Courtney Ames Connors and the late Robert Connors?"

"Did you know my dad at the hospital? Were you one of his doctors?"

"No. But I am familiar with his symptoms and his early death. I am sorry."

I warn't sorry. Dad was a son-of-a-bitch even afore he got sick. Maybe knowing it was coming, that it was in his genes, made him that way, but a little girl don't care about that. I only cared that he hit me and screamed at me—hit and screamed at everybody until the night he took after Dinah so bad that Bobby shot him. Now Bobby, just four months from finishing doing his time at Luther Luckett, was getting sick, too. I knew I had to tell this foreigner all that, but it was hard. My family don't ask for help. "We don't got much," Granmama always said, "but we got our pride."

That, and the Connors curse. Fatal Familial Insomnia.

It turned out that Dr. Chung already knew a lot of my story. He knew about Dad, and Bobby, and Mama, and Aunt Carol Ames. He even knew which of the kids got the gene—it's a 50-50 chance—and which didn't. The safe ones: Cody, Patty, Arianna, Timothy. The losers: Shawn, Bonnie Jean, and Lewis. And me.

So I talked and talked, and the little light on the recording cube glowed green to show it was on, and Mrs. Cully nodded and looked sympathetic so damn much that I started wishing for Jenny back. Dr. Chung at least sat quiet, with no expression on that strange ugly face.

"Are you showing any symptoms at all, Ms. Connors?"

"I have some trouble sleeping at night."

"Describe it for me, in as much detail as you can."

I did. I knew I was young to start the troubles; Mama was forty-six and Bobby twenty-nine.

"And the others with the FFI gene? Your mother and Robert, Jr. and"—he looked at a paper—"Shawn Edmond and—"

"Look," I said, and it came out harsher than I meant, "I know I got to tell you everything. But I'm not going to talk none about any of my kin, not what they are or aren't doing. Especially not to a Chinaman."

Silence.

Then Dr. Chung said quietly, "I think, Ms. Connors, that you must not know how offensive that term is. Like 'spic' or 'nigger.'"

I didn't know. I felt my face grow warm.

He said, "I think it's like 'hillbilly' is to mountain people."

My face got even warmer. "I . . . I'm sorry."

"It's okay."

But it warn't. I'm not the kind to insult people, even Chinese people. I covered my embarrassment with bluster. "Can *I* ask some questions for a change?"

"Of course."

"Is this Chi—did this clinic come to Blaine and start treating people for what ails them, just to get my family's trust so you all can do these experiments on our brains?"

That was the scuttlebutt in town and I expected him to deny it, but instead he said, "Yes."

Mrs. Cully frowned.

I said, "Why? Because there are only forty-one families in the whole world with our sickness? Then why build a whole clinic just to get at us? We're just a handful of folk."

He said gently, "You know a lot about fatal familial insomnia."

"I'm not stupid!"

"I would never think that for even a moment." He shifted in his chair and turned off the recorder. "Listen, Ms. Connors. It's true that sufferers from FFI are a very small group. But the condition causes changes in the brain that involve neural pathways which everybody has. Memory is involved, and sleep regulation, and a portion of the brain called the thalamus that processes incoming sensory signals. Our research here is the best single chance to gain information beyond price about those pathways. And since we also hope to arrest FFI, we were able to get funding as a medical clinical trial. Your contribution to this science will be invaluable."

"That's not why I'm doing it."

"Whatever your reasons, the data will be just as valuable."

"And you know you got to do it to me fast. Afore the Libertarians lose power."

Mrs. Cully looked surprised. Why was she still sitting with us? Then I realized: Dr. Chung warn't supposed to be alone with a young woman. Well, fine by me. But at least *he* didn't seem surprised that I sometimes watch the news.

"That's true," he said. "If Rafe Bannerman wins this presidential election, and it certainly looks as if he will, then all the deregulations of the present administration may be reversed."

"So you got to cut into my skull afore then. And afore I get too sick." I said it nasty, goading him. I don't know why.

But he didn't push back. "Yes, we must install the optogenetic cable as soon as possible. You are a very bright young woman, Ms. Connors."

"Don't try to butter me up none," I said.

But after he took blood samples and all the rest of it, after we set up a whole series of appointments, after I answered ten million more questions, the Chinaman's—no, *Chinese man's*—words stayed in my head all the long trudge back up the mountain. Not as bright, those words, as the autumn leaves turning the woods to glory, but it was more praise than I'd gotten since I left school. That was something, anyway.

When I got back to the trailer, about noon, nobody wouldn't speak to me. Carrie must of dropped by. Bobby's wife, Dinah, sewed on her quilt for the women's co-op: the Rail Fence pattern in blue and yellow, real pretty. Mama sat smoking and drinking Mountain Dew. Granmama was asleep in her chair by the stove, which barely heated the trailer. It was cold for October and Bobby didn't dig no highway coal again. The kids were outside playing, Shawn warn't around, and inside it was silent as the grave.

I hung my coat on a door hook. "That quilt's coming nice, Dinah."

Nothing.

"You need some help, Mama?"

Nothing.

"The hell with you all!" I said.

Mama finally spoke. At least today she was making sense. "You better not let Bobby hear where you been."

"I'm doing it for you all!" I said, but they all went back to pretending I didn't exist. I grabbed my coat, and stomped back outside.

Not that I had anyplace to go. And it didn't matter if I was inside or out; Mama's words were the last ones anyone spoke to me for two mortal days. They hardly even looked at me, except for scared peeps from the littlest kids and a glare from Bonnie Jean, like nobody except a ten-year-old can glare. It was like I was dead.

But half the reason I was doing this was the hope—not strong, but there—that maybe I wouldn't end up dead, after first raving and thrashing and trying to hurt people and seeing things that warn't there. Like Dad, like Aunt Carol Ames, like Cousin Jess. And the other half of the reason was to put some decent food on the table for the kids that wouldn't look at me or speak to me from fear that Bobby would switch them hard. I had hopes of Shawn, who hadn't been home in a couple of days, out deer hunting with his buddies. Shawn and I always been close, and he was sweeter than Bobby even afore Bobby started showing our sickness. I hoped Shawn would be on my side. I needed somebody.

But that night in bed, with Patty on my other side as far away as she could get without actually becoming part of the wall, Bonnie Jean spooned into me. She smelled of apples and little kid. I hugged onto her like I warn't never going to let go, and I stayed that way all through the long cold night.

"We have good news," Dr. Chung said. "Your optogenetic vectors came out beautifully."

"Yeah? What does that mean?" I didn't really care, but my nerves were all standing on end and if I kept him talking, maybe it would distract me some. Or not.

We sat in his lab at the Chinese clinic, a squinchy little room all cluttered with computers and papers. No smoking bottles or bubbling tubes like in the movies, though. Maybe those were in another room. There was another Chinese doctor, too, Dr. Liu. Also Jenny, worse luck, but if she was the "chief technician" I guess she had to be around. I kept my back to her. She wore a pretty red shirt that I couldn't never afford to buy for Patty or Bonnie Jean.

"What does that mean?" I said, realized I'd said it afore, and twisted my hands together.

"It means we have constructed the bio-organism to go into your brain, from a light-sensitive opsin, a promoter, and a harmless virus. The opsin will be expressed in only those cells that activate the promoter. When light of a specific wavelength hits those cells, they will activate or silence, and we can control that by—Ms. Connors, you can still change your mind."

"What?" Jenny said, and Dr. Chung shot her a look that could wither skunkweed. I wouldn't of thought he could look like that.

"My mind is changed," I said. His talking warn't distracting me, it was just making it all worse. "I don't want to do it."

"All right."

"She signed the contracts!" Jenny said.

I whirled around on my chair to face her. "You shut up! Nobody warn't talking to you!"

Jenny got up and stalked out. Dr. Liu made like he would say something, then didn't. Over her shoulder Jenny said, "I'll call Dr. Morton. Although too bad she didn't decide that before the operating room was reserved at Johnson Memorial."

"I'm sorry," I said, and fled.

I got home, bone-weary from the walk plus my worst night yet, just as Jimmy Barton's truck pulled up at the trailer. Jimmy got out, looking grim, then two more boys, carrying Shawn.

I rushed up. "What happened? Did you shoot him?" Everybody knew that Jimmy was the most reckless hunter on the mountain.

"Naw. We never even got no hunting. He went crazy, is what. So we brought him back."

"Crazy how?"

"You know how, Ludie," Jimmy said, looking at me steady. "Like your family does."

"But he's only seventeen!"

Jimmy didn't say nothing to that, and the other two started for the trailer with Shawn. He had a purpled jaw where somebody slugged him, and he was out cold on whatever downers they made him take. My gut twisted so hard I almost bent over. *Shawn*. Seventeen.

Dinah and Patty came rushing out, streaming kids behind them. Dinah was shrieking enough to wake the dead. I looked at Shawn and thought about how it must of been in the hunting camp, him going off the rails and "expressing" that gene all over the place: shouting from the panic, grabbing his rifle and waving it around, heart pounding like mad, hitting out at anyone who talked sense. Like Bobby had been a few months ago, afore he got even worse. Nobody in my family ever lasted more than seven months after the first panic attack.

Shawn.

I didn't even wait to see if Mama was coming out of the trailer, if this was one of the days she could. I went back down the mountain, running as much as I could, gasping and panting, until I got to the Chinese clinic and the only hope I had for Shawn, for me, for all of us.

Dr. Morton turned out to be a woman. While they got the operating room ready at Johnson Memorial in Jackson, I sat with Dr. Chung in a room that was supposed to look cheerful and didn't. Yellow walls, a view of the parking lot. A nurse had shaved off a square patch on my hair. I stared out at a red Chevy, trying not to think. Dr. Chung said gently, "It isn't a complicated procedure, Ms. Connors. Really."

"Drilling a hole into my skull isn't complicated?"

"No. Humans have known how to do that part for thousands of years."

News to me. I said, "I forgot a hat."

"A hat?"

"To cover this bare spot in my hair."

"The first person from your family to visit, I will tell them."

"Nobody's going to visit."

"I see. Then I will get you a hat."

"Thanks." And then, surprising myself, "They don't want me to do none of this."

"No," he said quietly, and without asking what I meant, "I imagine they do not."

"They think you conduct experiments on us like we're lab animals. Like with the Nazis. Or Frankenstein."

"And what do you think?"

"I think they are . . . unknowing." It felt like a huge betrayal. Still, I kept on. "Especially my Granmama."

"Grandmothers are often fierce. Mine is." He made some notes on a tablet, typing and swiping without looking at it.

I hadn't thought of him—of any of them—as having a grandmother. I demanded, like that would make this grandmother more solid, "What's her name?"

"Chunhua. What is the name of your grandmother?"

"Ludmilla. Like me." I thought a minute. "'Fierce' is the right word."

"Then we have this in common, yes?"

But I warn't yet ready to give him that much. "I bet my granmama is more fierce than any of your kin."

He smiled, a crinkling of his strange bald face, eyes almost disappearing in folds of smooth skin. "I would—what is it you say, in poker?—'see that bet' if I could."

"Why can't you?"

He didn't answer, and his smile disappeared. I said, "What did your granmama do that was so fierce?"

"She made me study. Hours every day, hours every night. All spring, all summer, all winter. When I refused, she beat me. What does yours do?"

All at once I didn't want to answer. Was beating better or worse? Granmama never touched me, nor any of us. Dr. Chung waited. Finally I said, "She freezes me. Looks at me like . . . like she wants to make a icy wind in my mind. And then that wind blows, and I can't get away from it nohow, and then she turns her back on me."

"That is worse."

"Really? You think so?"

"I think so."

A long breath went out of me, clearing out my chest. I said, "Bobby warn't always like he is now. He taught me to fish."

"Do you like fishing?"

"No." But I liked Bobby teaching me, just the two of us laughing down by the creek, eating the picnic lunch Mama put up for us.

A nurse, masked and gowned like on TV, came in and said, "We're ready."

The last thing I remember was lying on the table, breathing in the knock-out gas, and thinking, *Now at least I'm going to get a long deep sleep.* Only at the very last minute I panicked some and my hand, strapped to the table, flapped around a bit. Another hand held it, strong and steady. Dr. Chung. I went under.

When I woke, it was in a different hospital room but Dr. Chung was still there, sitting in a chair and working a tablet. He put it down.

"Welcome back, Ms. Connors. How do you feel?"

I put my hand to my head. A thick bandage covered part of it. Nothing hurt, but my mouth was dry, my throat was scratchy, and I had a floaty feeling. "What do you got me on? Oxycontin?"

"No. Steroids to control swelling and a mild pain med. There are only a few nerve receptors in the skull. Tomorrow we will take you back to Blaine. Here."

He handed me a red knit hat.

All at once I started to cry. I never cry, but this was so weird—waking up with something foreign in my skull, and feeling rested instead of skitterish and tired, and then this *hat* from this strange-looking man. . . . I sobbed like I was Cody, three years old with a skinned knee. I couldn't stop sobbing. It was awful.

Dr. Chung didn't high-tail it out of there. He didn't try to there-there me, or take my hand, or even look embarrassed and angry mixed together, like every other man I ever knowed when women cry. He just sat and waited, and when I finally got myself to stop, he said, "I wish you would call me 'Dan.'"

"No." Crying had left *me* embarrassed, if not him. "It isn't your name. Is it?"

"No. It just seems more comfortable for Westerners."

"What is your damned name?"

"It is Hai. It means 'the ocean.'"

"You're nothing like any ocean."

"I know." He grinned.

"Do all Chinese names mean something?"

"Yes. I was astonished when I found out American names do not."

"When was that?"

"When I came here for graduate school."

I was talking too much. I never rattled on like this, especially not to Chinese men who had me cut open. It was the damn drugs they gave me, that thing for swelling or the "mild pain med." I'd always stayed strictly away from even aspirin, 'cause of watching Mama and Bobby. Afore I could say anything, Dr. Chung said, "Your meds might induce a little 'high,' Ludmilla. It will pass soon. Meanwhile, you are safe here."

"Like hell I am!"

"You are. And I apologize for calling you 'Ludmilla.' I have not received permission."

"Oh, go the fuck ahead. Only it's 'Ludie.'" I felt my skull again. I wanted to rip off the bandage. I wanted to run out of the hospital. I wanted to stay in this bed forever, talking, not having to deal with my family. I didn't know what I wanted.

Maybe Dr. Chung did, because he went on talking, a steadying stream of nothing: graduate school in California and riding busses in China and his wife's and daughters' names. They were named after flowers, at least in English: Lotus and

Jasmine and Plum Blossom. I liked that. I listened, and grew sleepy, and drifted into dreams of girls with faces like flowers.

I was two days in Johnson Memorial and two more in a bed at the clinic, and every single one of them I worried about Shawn. Nobody came to see me. I thought Patty might, or maybe even Dinah if Bobby'd a let her, but they didn't. Well, Patty was only twelve, still pretty young to come alone. So I watched TV and I talked with Dr. Chung, who didn't seem to have a whole lot to do.

"Don't you got to see patients?"

"I'm not an M.D., Ludie. Dr. Liu mostly sees the patients."

"How come Blaine got so many Chinese doctors? Aren't Americans working on optogenetics?"

"Of course they are. Liu Bo and I became friends at the university and so applied for this grant together."

"And you brought Jenny."

"She is Bo's fiancé."

"Oh. She warn't—there he is, the bastard!"

President Rollins was on TV, giving a campaign speech. Red and blue balloons sailed up behind him. My hands curled into fists. Dr. Chung watched me, and I realized—stupid me!—that of course he *was* working. He was observing me, the lab rat.

He said, "Why do you hate the president so?"

"He stopped the government checks and the food stamps. It's 'cause of him and his Libbies that most of Blaine is back to eating squirrels."

Dr. Chung looked at the TV like it was the most fascinating thing in the world, but I knew his attention was really on me. "But under the Libertarians, aren't your taxes lower?"

I snorted. "Five percent of nothing isn't less to pay than fifteen percent of nothing."

"I thought the number of jobs in the coal mines had increased."

"If you can get one. My kin can't."

"Why not?"

I didn't tell him why not. Bobby and Uncle Ted and maybe even now Shawn—they can't none of them pass a drug screen. So I snapped, "You defending Ratface Rollins?"

"Certainly not. He has drastically and tragically cut funding for basic research."

"But here you all are." I waved my arm to take in the room and the machines hooked up to me and the desk in the lobby where Mrs. Cully was doing something on a computer. I was still floating.

"Barely," Dr. Chung said. "This study is funded as part of a grant now four years old and up for renewal. If—" He stopped and looked—for just a minute, and the first time ever—a little confused. He didn't know why he was telling me so much. I didn't know, either. *My* excuse was the pain drugs.

I said, "If Ratface wins, you lose the money for this clinic?"

"Yes."

"Why? I mean, why this one specially?"

He chewed on his bottom lip, something else I didn't see him do afore. I thought he warn't going to say any more, but then he did. "The study so far has produced no publishable results. The population affected is small. We obtained the current grant just before President Rollins came into office and all but abolished both the FDA and research money. If the Libertarians are re-elected, it's unlikely our grant will be renewed."

"Isn't there someplace else to get the money?"

"Not that we have found so far."

Mrs. Cully called to him then and he left. I sat thinking about what he said. It was like a curtain lifted on one corner, and behind that curtain was a place just as dog-eat-dog as Blaine. Bobby scrambled to dig coal from the side of the highway, and these doctors scrambled to dig money out of the government. Dinah worked hard to make it okay that Bobby hit her ("It ain't him, it's the fucking sickness!"), and Dr. Chung worked hard to convince the government it was a good idea to put a bunch of algae and a light switch in my skull. Then I thought about how much I liked him telling me all that, and about the bandages coming off and the real experiment starting tomorrow, and about lunch coming soon. And then I didn't think about nothing because Bobby burst into the clinic with his .22.

"Where is she? Where's my fucking sister?"

"Bobby!"

He didn't hear me, or he couldn't. I scrambled out of bed but I was still hooked up to a bunch of machines. I yanked the wires. Soothing voices in the lobby but I couldn't make out no words.

The .22 fired, sounding like a mine explosion.

"Bobby!"

Oh sweet Jesus, no—

But he hadn't hit nobody. Mrs. Cully crouched on the floor behind her counter. The bullet hole in the wall warn't anywhere near her or Dr. Chung, who stood facing Bobby and talking some soothers that there was no way Bobby was going to hear. He was wild-eyed like Dad had been near the end, and I knew he hadn't slept in days and he was seeing things that warn't there. "Bobby—"

"You whore!" He fired again and this time the bullet whizzed past Dr. Chung's ear and hit the backside of Mrs. Cully's computer. Bobby swung the rifle toward me. I stood stock still, but Dr. Chung started forward to grab the barrel. That would get Bobby's attention and he would—God no *no* . . .

But afore I could yell again, the clinic door burst open and Shawn grabbed Bobby from behind. Bobby shouted something, I couldn't tell what, and they fought. Shawn didn't have his whole manhood growth yet, but he didn't have Bobby's waygone sickness yet, neither. Shawn got the rifle away from Bobby and Bobby on the ground. Shawn kicked him in the head and Bobby started to sob.

I picked up the rifle and held it behind me. Dr. Chung bent over Bobby. By this time the lobby was jammed with people, two nurses and Dr. Liu and Jenny and Pete Lawler, who must a been in a examining room. All this happened so fast that Shawn was just preparing to kick Bobby again when I grabbed his arm. "Don't!"

Shawn scowled at the bandage on my head. "He's going to get us all put behind bars. Just the same, he ain't wrong. You're coming home with me."

The breath went out of me. I warn't ready for this. "No, Shawn. I'm not."

"You come home with me or you don't never come home again. Granmama says."

"I'm not going. They're going to help me here, and they can help you, too! You don't need to get like Bobby, like Dad was—"

He shook off my arm. And just like that, I lost him. The Connors men don't hardly never change their minds once they make them up. And soon Shawn wouldn't even have a mind. Seven months from the first sleeplessness to death.

Shawn yanked Bobby to his feet. Bobby was quiet now, bleeding from his head where Shawn kicked him. Dr. Liu started to say, "We must—" but Dr. Chung put a hand on his arm and he shut up. Shawn held out his other hand to me, his face like stone, and I handed him Bobby's gun. Then they were gone, the truck Shawn borrowed or stole roaring away up the mountain.

Dr. Chung knew better than to say anything to me. I looked at the busted computer and wondered how much it cost, and if they would take it out of my pay. Then I went back into my room, closed the door, and got into bed. I would a given anything, right up to my own life, if I could a slept then. But I knew I wouldn't. Not now, not tonight, not—it felt like at that minute—ever again. And by spring, Shawn would be like Bobby. And so would I.

"You need a pass-out," I said to Dr. Chung.

He paused in his poking at my head. "A what?"

"When Bonnie Jean got a fish at a pet store once, they gave her a pass-out paper, TAKING CARE OF YOUR GOLDFISH. To tell her how to do for the fish— not that she done it. You need a pass-out, TAKING CARE OF YOUR BRAIN ALGAE."

Dr. Chung laughed. When he did that, his eyes almost disappeared, but by now I liked that. Nobody else never thought I was funny, even if my funning now was just a cover for nerves. Dr. Liu, at the computer, didn't laugh, and neither did Jenny. I still didn't like *her* eyes.

I sat on a chair, just a regular chair, with my head bandage off and the shaved patch on my head feeling too bare. All my fingers could feel with a tiny bit of something hard poking above my skull: the end of the fiber-optic implant. Truth was, I didn't need a pass-out paper. I knew what was going to happen because Dr. Chung explained it, as many times as I wanted, till I really understood. The punchpad in his hand controlled what my "optrode" did. He could send blue or yellow laser light down it, which would make my new algae release tiny particles that turned on and off some cells in my brain. I'd seen the videos of mice, with long cables coming from their skulls, made to run in circles, or stop staggering around drunk-like, or even remember mazes quicker.

Last night I asked Dr. Chung, "You can control me now, can't you?"

"I have no wish to control you."

"But you *could.*"

"No one will control you."

I'd laughed then, too, but it tasted like lemons in my mouth.

"Ready?" Dr. Liu said.

"Ready." I braced myself, but nothing happened. I didn't feel nothing at all. But at the screen Jenny went, "Aaaaaaaahhh."

"What?" I said.

"It works," Dr. Chung said quietly. "We are getting a good picture of optrode response."

On the screen was a bunch of wavy lines, with a lot of clicking noises.

That went on for a long bit: me sitting in the chair feeling nothing, Dr. Chung turning lights on and off in my head that I didn't see, lines and numbers on the computer, and lots of long discussions with words I didn't understand. Maybe some of them were Chinese. And then, just when I was getting antsy and bored both at the same time, something happened. Another press of the punchpad and all at once I saw the room. Not like I saw it afore—I mean I really *saw* it. Every little thing was clear and bright and separate and itself: the hard edge of the computer screen, the way the overhead light made a shadow in the corner, a tiny brown stain on the hem of Jenny's white coat—*everything*. The room was like Reverend Baxter said the world looked right when God created it: fresh and new and shining. I could feel my mouth drop open and my eyes get wide.

"What?" Dr. Chung said. "What is it, Ludie?"

I told him. He did something with the switch in his hand and all the fresh clearness went away. "Oh! Bring it back!"

"Hyperawareness," Dr. Liu said. "The opsins could be over-expressing?"

"Not that quickly," Dr. Chung said. "But—"

"Bring it back!" I almost shouted it.

He did. But after a minute it was almost too much. Too bright, too clear, too strange. And then it got clearer and brighter, so that it almost blinded me and I couldn't see and everything was wrong and—

It all stopped. Dr. Chung had pressed some switch. And then I wanted it back.

"Not yet, Ludie," he said. He sounded worried. "You were injected with multiple opsins, you know, each responding to a different wavelength of light. We're going to try a different one. Would you stand up, please? Good . . . now walk toward me."

I did, and he did something with his switch, and all at once I couldn't move. I was frozen. The computer started clicking loud as a plague of locusts.

Jenny said, "Pronounced inhibitory motor response."

I said, "Stop!"

Then I could move again and I was pounding on Dr. Chung with my fists. "You said you warn't going to control me! You said!"

He grabbed my wrists and held them; he was stronger than he looked. "I didn't know that would happen, Ludie. This is all new, you know. Nobody wants to control you."

"You just did, you bastard!"

"I did not know the inhibitory neurons would fire that strongly. Truly, I did not."

Jenny said something in Chinese.

"No," Dr. Chung said sharply to her.

"I'm done here," I said.

"Yes, that's enough for a first session," Dr. Liu said. Which warn't what I meant. I meant I was going home.

But I didn't. Instead I went to my room in the clinic, got into bed, and slept a little. Not long, not real hard, but enough to calm me down. Then I got up and found Dr. Chung in his office.

If he was glad to see me, he didn't let on. Instead he handed me an envelope. "This came for you in the mail."

Inside was a single page torn from the Sears catalogue, a page with kids' coats on the top and enough white space at the bottom for Dinah to print THANK U. So she got the money I been sending her from my pay. Where did she tell Bobby the warm clothes come from, the coats and stuff for Lewis, Arianna, Timmy, Cody, Bonnie Jean? No, that was stupid—Bobby was too far gone to notice even if the kids ran around buck naked.

I turned on Dr. Chung. "Did you give me this right now so's I'd stay?"

"Ludie, how could I know what was in your envelope? I still don't know."

"You know sure enough what's in my head!"

"I know there are abnormal FFI prions, which we hope to arrest. I know, too, that there is valuable information about how the brain works."

"You told me afore that you can't get them prions out of my head!"

"We cannot, no. What we hope is to disrupt the formation of any more. For your sake, as much as ours."

"I don't believe that crap!"

Only I wanted to believe it.

"Okay," I said, "here's the deal. I stay and you do your experiments, but the minute I tell you to stop something, you do it." It was lame bluster, and he knew it.

"Yes. I already did so, you know. You told me to stop the inhibition of motor activity, and I did."

"And another thing. I want a pass-out, after all."

He blinked. "You want—"

"I want you to write out in words I can understand just what you're doing to me. So's I can study on it afore we do it again."

Dr. Chung smiled. "I will be glad to do that, Ludie."

I flounced out of there, knowing I hadn't told him the whole truth. I wanted to keep sending money to Dinah, yes. I wanted him to not freeze me no more, yes. I wanted a pass-out paper, yes. But I also wanted that shining clearness back, that thing Jenny had called hyper-awareness. I wanted it enough to go on risking my brain.

If that's really what I was doing.

> Ludie—you have Fatal Familial Insomnia. Inside a part of your brain called the thalamus, some proteins called prions are folding up wrong. The wrongly folded proteins are making other proteins also fold wrong. These

are sticking together in clumps and interfering with what cells are supposed to do. The main thing thalamus cells are supposed to do is process communications among different parts of the brain. The thalamus is like a switchboard, except that it also changes the communications in ways we are trying to learn about. Things which the thalamus communicates with the rest of the brain about include: moving the body, thinking, seeing, making decisions, memory formation and retrieval, and sleeping. When you get a lot of sticky, misfolded proteins in the thalamus, you can't go into deep sleep, or move properly, or think clearly. You get hallucinations and insomnia and sometimes seizures.

We are trying to do three things: (1) Stop your brain making more misfolded prions, even if we can't get rid of the ones that are already there. We are trying to do this by interfering with the making of a protein that the prions use to fold wrong. Unhappily, the only way we will know if this happens is if your symptoms do not get worse. (2) Your brain works partly by sending electrical signals between cells. We are trying to map how these go, called "neural pathways." (3) We want to find out more about what the special algae (opsins) we put in your brain can do. They release different chemicals when we put different laser lights down the cable. We want to know the results of each different thing we do, to aid science.

Well, Dr. Chung wrote good, even though I didn't know what a "switchboard" might be.

I thought of Mama, her brain full of these misfolded proteins, gummed up like a drain full of grease and hair. And Bobby's brain, even worse. Mine, too, soon?

It was dark outside by the time I finished reading that damn paper over and over and over. Everybody'd gone home from the clinic except the night nurse, a skinny rabbitty-looking girl named Susannah. I knowed that she was mountain-born the minute I laid eyes on her, and that somehow she'd got out, and I'd tried not to have nothing to do with her. But now I marched out to where she was reading a magazine in the lobby and said, "Call Dr. Chung. Now."

"What's wrong?"

"Never you mind. Just call him."

"It's ten o'clock at—"

"I know what time it is. Call him."

She did, and he came. I said, "We're going to work now. Now, not in the morning. Them proteins are folding in me right this second, aren't they? You call Jenny and Dr. Liu if you really need them. We're going to work all night. Afore I change my mind."

He looked at me hard. Funny how when you know a person long enough, even a strange and ugly person, they don't look so bad no more.

"Okay," he said. "Let's work."

We worked all night. We worked all week. We worked another week, then another. And I didn't get no worse. No better, but no worse. What I got was scared.

Nobody ought to be able to do those things to somebody else's brain, using nothing except little bits of light.

Dr. Chung froze me again while I was walking around.

Dr. Liu said, "Filtering signals is an important thalamic function, and any change in filtering may give rise to physiological effects."

Dr. Chung made the "hyperawareness" come back, even stronger.

Jenny said, "Interfering with action potentials on cell membranes changes the way cells process information."

Dr. Chung made me remember things from when I was really little—Mama singing to me. Shawn and me wrestling. Granmama telling me troll stories while I sat on her knee. Bobby teaching me to fish. The memories were so sharp, they felt like they was slicing into my brain. Good memories but too razored, making my mind bleed.

Dr. Liu said, "Are the opsins in the anterior nuclei over-expressing? That could cause problems."

Dr. Chung did something that made me stutter so's I couldn't get a word out whole no matter how much I tried.

Jenny said, "Neural timing—even the shift of a few milliseconds can reverse the effect of the signal on the rest of the nervous system. Not good."

I didn't think any of it was good. But I warn't going to say anything in front of that Jenny; I waited until I got Dr. Chung alone.

"I got to ask you something."

"Of course, Ludie." He had just finished checking on my heart and blood pressure and all that. "Are you pleased by the way the study is going? You say your FFI symptoms aren't any worse, and with the usual rapid progression of the disease in your family, that may mean genuine progress."

"I'm happy about that, yeah, if it goes on like now. But I got a different question. I been reading in that book you gave me, how the brain is and isn't like a computer." The book was hard going, but interesting.

"Yes?" He looked really caught on what I was saying. For the first time, I wondered what his wife was like. Was she pretty?

"A computer works on teeny switches that have two settings, on and off, and that's how it knows things."

"A binary code, yes."

"Well, those laser switches on the bundle of optic cables you put in my head—they're off and on, too. Could you make my head into a computer? And put information into it, like into a computer—information that warn't there afore?"

Dr. Chung stood. He breathed deep. I saw the second he decided not to lie to me. "Not now, not with what we know at present, which isn't nearly enough. But potentially, far down the road and with the right connections to the cortex, it's not inconceivable."

Which was a fancy way of saying yes.

"Good night," I said abruptly and went into my room.

"Ludie—"

But I didn't have nothing more to say to him. In bed, though, I used the tablet he loaned me—that's what I been reading the book on—to get the Internet and find

Dr. Chung. I got a lot of hits. One place I found a picture of him with his wife. She was pretty, all right, and refined-looking. Smart. He had his arm around her.

Sleep was even harder that night than usual. Then, the next day, it all happened.

We were in the testing room, and my hyperawareness was back. Everything was clear as mountain spring water, as sharp as a skinning knife. I kept rising up on my tip-toes, just from sheer energy. It didn't feel bad. Dr. Chung watched me real hard, with a little frown.

"Do you want a break, Ludie?"

"No. Bring it on."

"Hippocampal connection test 48," Jenny said, and Dr. Chung's hand moved on his punchpad. The computer started clicking louder and louder. The door burst open and Bobby charged in, waving a knife and screaming.

"Whore! Whore!" He plunged the knife into Jenny and blood spurted out of her in huge, foaming gushes. I shouted and tried to throw myself in front of Dr. Chung, but Bobby got him next. Dr. Liu had vanished. Bobby turned on me and he warn't Bobby no more but a troll from Granmama's stories, a troll with Bobby's face, and Bonnie Jean hung mangled and bloody from his teeth. I hit out at the troll and his red eyes bored into me and his knife raised and—

I lay on the floor, Dr. Chung holding me down, Jenny doubled over in pain, and the computer screen laying beside me.

"Ludie—"

"What did you do?" I screamed. "What did you do to me? What did I do?" I broke free of him, or he let me up. "*What?*"

"You had a delusional episode," Dr. Chung said, steady but pale, watching me like I was the Bobby-troll. And I was. I had hit Jenny and knocked over the computer, only it was—

"Don't you touch me!"

"All right," Dr. Chung said quietly, "I won't." Dr. Liu was picking up the computer, which was still clicking like a crazy thing. Mrs. Cully and a nurse stood in the doorway. Jenny gasped and wheezed. "You had a delusional episode, Ludie. Perhaps because of the FFI, perhaps—"

"It was you, and you know it was you! You done it to me! You said you wouldn't control my brain and now you—" I pulled at the optrode sticking up from my skull, but of course it didn't budge. "You can't do that to me! You can't!"

"We don't know what the—"

"You don't know nothing! And I'm done with the lot of you!" It all came together in me then, all the strangeness of what they was doing and the fear for my family and them throwing me out and the lovely hyperawareness gone when the switch went off and Dr. Chung's pretty wife—*all of it.*

I didn't listen to nothing else they said. I walked straight out of that clinic, my legs shaking, without even grabbing my coat. And there was Shawn pulling up in Jimmy Barton's truck, getting out and looking at me with winter in his face. "Bobby's dead," he said. "He killed himself."

I said, "I know."

The funeral was a week later—it took that long for the coroner to get done fussing with Bobby's body. It was election day, and Ratface Rollins lost, along with the whole Libertarian party.

The November wind blew cold and raw. Mama was too bad off to go to the grave-yard. But Shawn brought her at the service where she sat muttering, even through the church choir singing her favorite, "In the Sweet Bye and Bye." I don't know if she even knew what was going on; for sure she didn't recognize me. It warn't be long afore she'd be as bad as Bobby, or in a coma like Aunt Carol Ames. Granmama recognized me, of course, but she didn't say nothing when I came into the trailer, or when I stayed there, sleeping in my old bed with Patty and Bonnie Jean, or when I cleaned up the place a bit and cooked a stew with groceries from my clinic money. Granmama didn't thank me, but I didn't expect that. She was grieving Bobby. And she was Granmama.

Dinah kept to her room, her kids pretty much in there with her day and night.

I kept a hat on, over my part-shaved head. Not the red knit hat Dr. Chung gave me, which I wadded up and threw in the creek. In the trailer I wore Bobby's old baseball cap, and at the funeral I wore a black straw hat that Mama had when I was little.

"'The Lord is my Shepherd; I shall not want. He maketh me to lie down in green pastures . . .'" Reverend Baxter did funerals old-fashioned. Bobby's casket was low-ered into the hole in the churchyard. The last of the maple leaves blew down and skittered across the grass.

Dinah came forward, hanging onto Shawn, and tossed her flower into the grave. Then Granmama, then me, then Patty. The littlest kids, Lewis and Arianna and Timothy and Cody, were in relatives' arms. The last to throw her flower was Bonnie Jean, and that's when I saw it.

Bonnie Jean wore an old coat of Patty's, too big for her, so's the hem brushed the ground. When she stood by the grave that hem was shaking like aspen leaves. Her face had froze, and the pupils of her eyes were so wide it looked like she was on something. She warn't. And it warn't just the fear and grief of a ten-year-old at a fu-neral, neither.

"Ashes to ashes, dust to dust. . . ."

Neighbors brought cakes and covered dishes to the trailer. Nobody didn't stay long 'cause they knew we didn't want them to. Dinah went back into her room with her two kids, Mama was muttering beside the stove, Shawn sat smoking and drink-ing Bud. I told Patty to watch Timmy and Cody and I took Bonnie Jean into our bedroom.

"How long since you slept through the whole night?"

She was scared enough to give me lip. "I sleep. You been right there next to me!"

"How long, Bonnie Jean?"

"I don't got to tell you nothing! You're a whore, sleeping with them Chinese and letting them do bad things to you—Bobby said!"

"How long?"

She looked like she was going to cry, but instead she snatched Bobby's baseball hat off my head. It seemed to me that my optrode burned like a forest fire, though of course it didn't. Bonnie Jean stared at it and spat, "Chink Frankenstein!"

Probably she didn't even know what the words meant, just heard them at school. Or at home.

Then she started to cry, and I picked her up in my arms and sat with her on the edge of the bed, and she let me. All at once I saw that the bed was covered with the Fence Rail quilt Dinah had been making for the women's co-op. She'd put it on my bed instead.

I held Bonnie Jean while she cried. She told me it had been two weeks since she couldn't sleep right and at the graveyard was her second panic attack—what she called "the scared shakes." She was ten years old, and she carried the gene Granmama and God-knows-who-else had passed on without being affected themselves. Insomnia and panic attacks and phobias. Then hallucinations and more panic attacks and shrinking away to hardly no weight at all. Then dementia or coma or Bobby's way out. Ten years old. While I was nineteen and I hadn't even felt her restless beside me in the long cold night.

I knowed, then, what I had to do.

The Chinese clinic was almost empty.

A sign outside said CLOSED. Through the window I could see the lobby stripped of its chairs and pictures and clothesbasket of toys. But a light shone in a back room, bright in the drizzly gray rain. I rattled the lock on the door and shouted "Hey!" and pretty soon Mrs. Cully opened it.

She wore jeans and a sweatshirt instead of her usual dress, and her hair was wrapped in a big scarf. In one hand was a roll of packing tape. She didn't look surprised to see me. She looked something, but I couldn't read it.

"Ludie. Come in."

"You all leaving Blaine?"

"Our grant won't be renewed. Dr. Chung found out the day after the election from a man he knows in Washington."

"But Rollins lost!"

"Yes, but the new president made campaign promises to reinstate the FDA with tight regulations on studies with human subjects. Under Rollins there was too much abuse. So Doctors Chung and Liu are using their remaining money for data analysis, back at the university—*especially* since we have no research subjects here. I'm packing files and equipment."

The rooms behind her, all their doors open, were full of boxes, some sealed, some still open. A feeling washed over me that matched the weather outside. The clinic never had no chance no matter who won the election.

Mrs. Cully said, "But Dr. Chung left something for you, in case you came back." She plucked a brown envelope off the counter, and then she went back to her packing while I opened it. Tact—Mrs. Cully always had tact.

Inside the envelope was a cell phone, a pack of money with a rubber band around it, and a letter.

Ludie—

This is the rest of what the clinic owes you. Along with it, accept my deepest
gratitude for your help with this study. Even though not finished, it—and
you—have made a genuine contribution to science. You are an exceptional young woman, with exceptional intelligence and courage.

This cell phone holds the phone number for Dr. Morton, who implanted
your optrode, and who will remove it. Call her to schedule the operation.
There will of course be no charge. The phone also holds my number.
Please call me. If you don't, I will call this number every day at 11:00 a.m.
until I reach you. I want only to know that you are all right.

Your friend,
Hai Chung

The phone said it was 9:30 a.m. Mrs. Cully said, "Is that your suitcase?"

"Yeah. It is. I need Dr. Chung's address, ma'am."

She looked at me hard. "Call him first."

"Okay." But I wouldn't. By the time the phone rang, I would be on the 10:17
Greyhound to Lexington.

She gave me his university address but wouldn't give out his home. It didn't really matter. I knew he would give it to me, plus whatever else I needed. And not just
for the study, neither.

Dr. Chung told me, one time, about a scientist called Daniel Zagury. He was
studying on AIDS, and he shot himself up with a vaccine he was trying to make, to
test it. Dr. Chung didn't do no experiments on himself; he used me instead, just like
I was using him for the money. Only that warn't the whole story, no more than
Bobby's terrible behavior when he got really sick was the whole story of Bobby. The
Chinese clinic warn't Chinese, and I'm not no Frankenstein. I'm not all that "courageous," neither, though I sure liked Dr. Chung saying it. What I *am* is connected to
my kin, no matter how much I used to wish I warn't. Right now, connected don't
mean staying in Blaine to help Dinah with her grief and Shawn with his sickness
and the kids with their schooling. It don't mean waiting for Mama's funeral, or living
with Granmama's sour anger at what her genes did to her family. Right now, being
connected means getting on a Greyhound to Lexington.

It means going on with Dr. Chung's study.

It means convincing him, and everybody else, to put a optrode in Bonnie Jean's
head, and Shawn's, and maybe even Lewis's, so laser light can "disrupt their neural
pathways" and they don't get no more misfolded prions than they already got.

It means paying for this with whatever work I get.

And maybe it even means going to Washington D.C. and talking to my
congressman—whoever he is—about why this study is a good thing. I read on
Dr. Chung's tablet that other scientists sometimes do that. Maybe I could take Bonnie
Jean with me. She's real pretty, and I can teach her to look pathetic. Maybe.

I never had no thoughts like this afore, and maybe that's the opsins, too. But maybe
not. I don't know. I only know that this is my path and I'm going to walk it.

I hike to the highway, suitcase in one hand and cell phone in the other, and I flag
down the bus.

A Heap of Broken Images

SUNNY MORAINE

Here's a moving, disquieting, unsettling look at the psychological effects of attempted genocide on those fortunate enough—or perhaps unfortunate enough—to survive.

Sunny Moraine is an occasional author of various flavors of speculative fiction; the flavor in question depends upon a complex conjunction of different variables, the exact nature of which they have yet to specify or untangle. Sunny's short fiction has appeared or is forthcoming in Clarkesworld, Strange Horizons, Shimmer, Apex, Lightspeed, Daily Science Fiction, Ideomancer, *and the anthologies* Long Hidden: Speculative Fiction from the Margins of History *and* We See a Different Frontier: A Postcolonial Speculative Fiction Anthology, *among other places. They are also responsible for the novels* Line and Orbit *(cowritten with Lisa Soem) and* Crowflight, *the sequel to which,* Ravenfall, *will be released in 2014. They live just outside Washington, DC, in a reasonably creepy house with two cats and a husband. They are on Twitter as @dynamicsymmetry and can be found making words at sunnymoraine.com.*

> Odette nodded at my notebook, where I was writing as she spoke. 'Do the people in America really want to read this? People tell me to write these things down, but it's written inside of me. I almost hope for the day when I can forget.
> —*Philip Gourevitch*, We Wish to Inform You That Tomorrow We Will Be Killed with Our Families

Are you going to take a picture?"

I ask it because it seems like a sensible question. The shorter of the two humans has brought his camera with him and since we entered the houses of the dead he has held it in his hands and a little close to his chest, as though he's afraid that someone might snatch it away from him, or that he might drop it and it might shatter.

I ask it because I am their guide and it is my task to show them what they ask to see, and I am wondering, now, if they really wish to see this.

The shorter man—I have been told that his name is *Jacob* but the syllables feel strange in my mouth and I have to struggle with them a little—looks at me as though he is only just now seeing me. He nods once. He lifts the camera to his face and I hear the soft *whir* of its processor. And then, as though he performed the act entirely for my benefit, he shows me the image he has captured.

Here: It's not well framed. He clearly gave little thought for the arrangement of it. Half a skull takes up the lower left-hand corner, pushed most of the way under a desk. The fractured curve of a broken spine extends into the middle-foreground, disappearing into a fold of old blue cloth from which ribs protrude. On the right, a severed arm stretches into the frame as if reaching for the skull and the spine. It clearly isn't from the same corpse. It's much too small. Draped and tangled over everything, heavy flowers in brilliant red and pink, green vines, and dried skin of no color whatsoever.

There are other bodies. Look closer and you will see that the floor is nothing but bodies. That you can't see the floor at all. That you cannot, in fact, be absolutely sure that the floor is even there. If you walk into this room, you'll walk on the dead. So we don't invite them to walk inside, and without invitation they never do. We all stand in the doorway and I deliver the information I have to share about this place, and then there is silence.

I feel their discomfort. I was raised in the *jodenja klimenji*—the Way of Welcoming. It is our highest calling to give comfort to a guest, to put them at ease. But it is also our highest calling to give them whatever they ask for, within reason. And if they ask to come here, I cannot do anything for what I know they must feel. I cannot unmurder the murdered. I cannot change who did the murdering. And I cannot tell them how they should feel, a generation after the fact. There are things I wish I could say, things I *would* say if everything were different, but I also cannot change who I am. So we stand in silence, and the dead are also silent, and I wait for one of the living to speak.

The first sun is low and tosses our shadows out in a long diagonal across the room. The second sun is rising behind us. The light is shifting and strange, and it makes it difficult to be sure just how big the room is. How much death it can hold.

The taller one—I think his name is *Aaron*—points to a stack of crates in one corner next to a row of bookshelves. Another corpse is slumped against it, scraps of dried paper skin, the head gone. "Shairoven, what are those?"

"Goods," I say. "Clothes, probably. Foodstuffs. They thought that they could buy their lives from their attackers. You must understand that such things are not strange to us; in our culture there is an idea of a blood price. Life has monetary value."

"Why didn't the colonists take them?"

I shrug—it is a very human gesture but I can't help it. Five full cycles as a *klimenjiani*—what I have heard them call a *tour guide*—and I have adopted many human habits. "There are many things about what was done in those months that we do not understand."

What I do not say is that I suspect that the killing distracted them. It must have been very distracting. It must have been very tiring, also. It's said that all throughout the time of killing, the rank and file were urged on by overseers of death with bull-horns and amplifiers. They were given rhythms by which to work, to make it easier for their bodies to move without the burden of thought.

I have tried to understand this. When I run I think of the beating of my own heart. But then I think of blood and falling bodies and my imagination fails me. How can they be the same?

How could they have done it? Were they blind?

The flowers nod in the breeze that comes in through the open windows. It should not be as lovely as it is—all those long bones. The large, elongated skulls. The vines and the blossoms. Graceful and clean. Even the faded blood on the walls looks like an abstract mural in dark swoops and swirls. I have heard the humans say that our people are beautiful. I wonder if that is a truth that is not always true.

"We should go," I say gently. At my sides, my hands are clenched into fists. I hope they will not see. It would shame me. "You will be late for supper at the hotel."

Much like the killing itself, it remains a puzzle to us, that the humans come to Lejshethra for this. Why they come. Why they want to look. These are not their dead. They pay no respects, they make no offerings. They just stare with their tiny eyes, and I can never say for sure what they're thinking.

They have told us that there are entire pathways of schooling back on Earth that deal with nothing but the killing, that try to pull it apart like a corpse and understand how it happened, why so much murderous hate could arise so suddenly in the human colonists. I have heard that they believe that it was not sudden. That it built over years, that there was tension where my people could perceive none. Two cycles ago when I first heard of this I took it to my body-sire and told her of it, and I think I was lucky to escape the back of her hand.

"Ignore such things, Shairoven," she said to me. She turned back to the *tijath* she was cutting for the meal of second sun. "The humans fixate on what's past, even after blood-price is paid. Mind your manners and ignore their habits. They can't help what they are."

My body-sire's right arm is missing. Her back is a mass of crisscrossing scars. We were told—not by her, for she never speaks of those months—that she survived the massacre of her district by hiding herself under the corpses of her neighbors. There were many who survived that way, but we don't speak much of the ones with visible scars. The blatantly accusing nature of the evidence they carry with them is a form of rudeness that can't be erased or undone.

My body-sire makes her place secure through her denial.

I have never discovered how to tell her that this makes me so *sad-angry-trapped* all at once, that it makes me feel as though I am buried under a pile of corpses and I am being cut with long knives and I do not understand why. We have no word in our language for such an impolite emotion.

I arrive at the hotel after the meal of first sun to collect the humans. They have told me that today they wish to travel to the city center to see the memorial that the human government erected to the dead of the killings—or to the killings themselves, but the difference has never been adequately explained to me, and I am afraid to ask. I am afraid that my people would see it as overtly accusatory, and I am afraid of what the humans might say.

In the groundcar on the way from my home to the hotel, I think about all the questions I would like to ask and never will. *Why do you remember? What do you think? Do you feel guilty? Do you think that you should? Do you hate us now? Will you hurt us again?*

Their leaders said, of course, that they did not hate us and that the killings will never be repeated. But I am not sure I find this convincing. I am full of doubt both impolite and inconvenient and it pulls at me like a hungry child. Many hungry children. There were camps full of them after the killings, orphans all with no mate-sire or body-sire and often missing siblings. I have seen images, and in those images what stands out most are their enormous eyes. All the confusion of an entire people could be held inside such eyes. *Why?* This is what they would ask the humans I am going to see. In this we are alike.

I would also like to ask whether the humans live with ghosts as we do. I wonder whether it is forbidden for them to acknowledge or speak to the ghosts. I wonder whether they can put the ghosts here aside and leave them behind. In the end most of them return home to Earth; very few humans live here now. They thinned our numbers, but in the end they were the ones who ran.

In the groundcar, the humans and I ride in silence. My head is still buzzing with questions. My mouth is sealed by my raising.

Every time, this is a little more difficult.

"How long have you been a guide?" Jacob asks me eventually, and I am relieved because this is a question that I can answer without offense. I tell him five cycles, and he smiles and pats the knee of his companion.

"We're lucky to get someone so experienced."

I incline my head at the compliment.

"Aaron and I have been studying the massacre since college," Jacob says after another few moments of silence. "We're both writers—did we tell you that? We're doing a series on what it's like for the children of the colonists now, so this is excellent material."

I nod again. "I am glad to be able to help," I say, and inside the eyes of the hungry children are growing and growing and for an instant I am afraid they will swallow me. I am glad that the groundcar is on automatic because I could not see to direct it now. Everything is questions, beating against the inside of me, smothering me like a mound of corpses, and really all the questions are a single question: *Why?*

Why did you kill us? Why do you come here now? Why did you build the monument, why are you writing about it, why are you sitting here and smiling at me like that when my body-sire has lost her arm and my life is all of the ghosts I will never welcome, and instead I welcome you?

We keep the houses of the dead but we would never go there if it weren't for you and every time I am there I feel that I might fall apart into hacked-up pieces and lie there among the dead because I cannot make any of these other pieces fit.

I smile at them, at these writer humans who walk oblivious among the ghosts. It is said among my people that the *jodenja klimenji* is the most demanding of all the disciplines, and the most pure, because it means the utter denial of self. And every moment of it I wonder if I am really strong enough.

And every moment of it I wonder if it is right for me to be so.

The memorial itself is a single black spike one hundred feet high. It impales the sky. Every time I come here, I think, *It looks so angry*. And I am never sure where the anger comes from or where it is going. Perhaps it is my anger that I am feeling. Inside the spike, it is apart from me and safe to face. It stabs and stabs blindly, forever.

The spike is bounded by a circular plaza dotted with stone benches. There are no trees. We three are the only ones there. We stay for a few minutes, and then we return to the hotel in silence.

There is a river that alternately circles around and cuts through our city. Its banks are part of what make this region so excellent for farming, and I understand why this was the initial locus for the human colonization. The river is the center of many things. After second sun, after I have returned to my home and bathed and oiled my skin, I dress in the lighter clothing of repose and walk down the broad path that leads from my street to the river where it touches the edge of my home district. The bank is paved here, lined with flowerbeds and hanging colored lanterns.

It is lovely. It is all that I remember seeing here, but I have been told by humans and by human texts that the paving and the flowerbeds and the lanterns are all recent additions. Before, this was all rich red soil and black rocks, like other points along the river's bank, and then at the time of the killings it was paved with bodies as people tried to flee across it and were cut down or trampled or carried away and drowned.

There was a major sanitation problem in the weeks after the greatest bloom of killing, which added to the already rising tide of human refugees flooding back to Earth ahead of their fear and their shame. The water was choked with bloated corpses and undrinkable. This is what I have been told, by humans and by those of my own people to whom I know I should not listen. But though they tell the same story, the humans and a few of my people, the telling is so different that I cannot think of it as the same.

It is the river Laijan, which means purveyor of life. I stand at the edge of the paved bank and I look into its depths. In the twilight the water looks like black blood, calm and placid and flowing without a heart to pump it.

Tomorrow is the last day that the humans will be here, and before I said goodbye to them today they asked me for a favor. It is not the first time I have been asked for what they want. But I have always said no, *impossible, it cannot be done, no one will agree to it*.

And I have been lying.

And today I said that I would try.

I do not know if this is dishonor or a fulfilling of my raising. I am pulled between what I have been taught and what I have been taught; again I think I could fall to pieces, and then I think that maybe I have always been in pieces, broken apart from myself, and so there is no more damage to be done.

I look into the flowing black water and I think of empty eyes and outstretched hands reaching up from those depths and beckoning me. There were many bodies that were swept away by the river in the growing-season flood that year and many were never found. They are all still there in the life of the river. There are other people strolling, idling along the bank in the cool of the evening; I could call, *Don't you see them? Don't you hear? How can we deny our own spilled blood, whatever price has been paid?*

My mouth is full of ghosts. I place my hand against it and hold them in until they are silent again, and the ones in the water fall silent as well.

I am in pieces but I am alive. Tell me how this is a reasonable thing.

Before first sun I am awake and back in the streets, leaving my body-sire and my two siblings sleeping at home. They do not know what I intend; if they did they would try to stop me, for this is not shame of any accidental kind but shame that is sought for, and that is the most profound shame of all.

The streets are still mostly deserted but I keep to the shadows, moving as quietly as I can. I live in one of the more affluent districts and I am passing into places that are clearly less so, with waste uncollected by the entranceways and roofs in need of repair. And on, further, into a place of real destitution, where the cracked and dirty street is dotted here and there with people who have no roof at all but sleep surrounded by whatever they can carry with their mangled limbs—in whatever sleep their rage allows them.

This is the district of the self-exiled. They Who Will Not Release Their Grasp. I was taught to pity them and fear them, for they carry the specter of what was done to us in their minds and bodies like a plague and they will not give themselves over to denial as my body-sire has done. They stand and they insist that we look on them, and the pain is too great, and we fear what the humans would do or say, despite the fact that the humans themselves seem to want to see such things.

Sometimes I think our ways have become confused, like tangled limbs that no longer fit the body to which they were attached.

Three cycles ago I came here for the first time because of a request like the one that sends me here now. I turned away then, at the cusp of fulfilling what was asked of me. I could not bear it. I am not sure what has made me decide to try again, but I know that all night I tried to resist it and it would not be held back.

Down a narrow, stinking alley I find the door I am looking for. I lift my head at the same moment that I raise my hand to press the call-bell and I see the sky lightening for first sun, pale pink. I think of blood just under thin skin, warm and alive.

The door opens and the sky seems to fall away again.

She is missing an arm like my body-sire is, but there the resemblance of their scars ends: her face is practically half gone, twisted with scar tissue, hairless and purple and swollen. One of her eyes is not there at all. The scars wind down her long neck and vanish under her worn tunic but I know they continue. She is stooped with pain that never goes away. Her ghosts are vengeful and they tear at everything that comes near, including her.

"Shairoven," she says. She sounds unsurprised to see me. I incline my head; I am not sure how much respect is due to her, and again my heart says one thing while my raising says another. She is lower than a beggar, lower than a criminal, because she has committed the unforgivable sin of inhospitality to those who have, in the end, observed the proper rites and dues, and paid the owed blood price.

And what I cannot tell anyone, not even her, is that my heart tells me that she is braver than anyone I have ever met.

"Jaishevkin," I say. With clear effort, she stands aside from the door and invites me in.

Inside is dim and cramped and smelling strongly of old rotting grass. I can barely see the chair she motions me into. Thin light seeps in through the threadbare curtains that cover her single window. She sinks down onto the cot that serves as her bed and leans over her knees. Whenever she moves I am freshly reminded of how thin she is, as though she is already one of the dried corpses in the houses of the dead, animated by the sheer magnitude of her indignation. Whereas they remain quietly and unobtrusively dead, as is right.

"You have come to ask me to meet them," she says. I am not astonished that she should guess this; there is really no other reason for me to be here. So I nod.

"Before, you ran away." She has only one remaining eye but it is like a knife, cutting away pieces of me and letting them fall to the floor. I cannot move under its edge. "Every time you run away. Will you run now?"

I am not sure how to answer that. The directness, the bluntness—close to brutality. No delicacy in her approach. It has been cut and burned out of her.

"I don't wish to run," I say finally. My hands are turning over and over each other in my lap, as though I am washing them.

"You all run," she says. At last she looks away from me, turning her horribly scarred face to that thin light. "They run too, even if they think they do not. They study and they write and they talk, and they congratulate themselves on their bravery, but they are still running. And they are putting it all into little boxes with clear tops, so they can look at it without feeling any pain or dirtying their hands. They don't *feel*."

She turns back to me and her single eye is blazing. "None of you feel. You have forgotten how. We remember. And we frighten you."

I did not come here for this. I came here to ask her to accompany me back to the hotel, and to offer her payment for her time and her effort. Now I am not sure why I am here at all. I am sitting under a knife; I am drowning in a river of old blood; I am buried under the pieces of myself and I cannot breathe, and I was never even part of this, does she understand that? I bear no scars. *When it happened I was not even born.*

I open my mouth to say *I am sorry that I disturbed you. If you will not come with me I will go now.* And then I think *I am running again*, and *I don't wish to*, and what comes out of my mouth instead is, "Why?"

Jaishevkin looks at me for a long time. I cannot read her face under the scars and this is only part of why I have never felt easy around her. But her eye is still a heated knife and I am still trapped under its edge.

And, strangely, part of me is content to be so.

"They have very many reasons, don't they?" she says at last. The words are accusing but all the bile has gone out of her voice and now she sounds only sad and very, very tired. I think that I have never been as tired as that. But I am beginning to feel how one becomes so. "They say that it was land restrictions. They say that talks broke down. They say that it was many accumulated *cultural misunderstandings*." And there again is the bile, the bite, just for a moment and gone again, like something emerging briefly from black water before sinking back out of sight. "I have heard them say that it was the delayed mental strain of encountering a new sentient species. I have heard them say that it was simple fear, that they thought that we would attack them and so they struck at us first. I have heard every reason, Shai-roven. I have heard them all."

"And which do you believe?" My voice is very soft. Suddenly I feel breathless. I am afraid. I am on the edge of a great unknown expanse. I am spreading my arms because I am just mad enough to think that I might fly.

"I believe all of them," she says. "Or I believe that *they* believe them. And now I think you will ask me what I really believe."

Jaishevkin gets slowly to her feet and makes her way over to the little window, pushing aside the ragged curtains with her remaining hand. In the brightening light of first sun the scars on her face are sharper, darker, but their jagged lines are also smoothed out into something almost beautiful.

I wait. I don't ask.

"I don't know why," she says softly. "I have thought and read and argued and I do not know. There are all the reasons. And then there is what happened. And in between . . ." She falls silent.

And I am silent. I am trying to understand this. I have taken this—the Not Knowing—for granted, because while I have asked the question I have never seriously pursued an answer. It has never until now occurred to me that perhaps there is no answer, no one answer, that any one person can find.

And now I am wondering about the questions. About the right ones.

"Will it happen again?"

Again, she does not answer at once. Her fingers move across the curtains, dancing in a vague kind of pattern—it seems strangely appropriate that the hand they left her would be entirely unmarked, graceful, lovely.

"That all depends," she says at last, "on how we remember."

I want to ask more, because now I am full of new questions. How we remember? How should we remember? In the human way? In our way? In the houses of the dead or in their studies and writing? In the ghosts that float in the river Laijan and dance on their banks? In the flesh of my body-sire? In that black spike stabbing always up into the sky? In the way we make it so heavy and so big with our careful silence and our smiles and bows? In the way that I fear it might crush us one day, once it is too big and too angry with being ignored?

How do we remember?

But Jaishevkin is already shaking her head. "No more questions." She turns away from the window and she is blanketed in shadows. "I will not meet with your humans."

Everything in me sinks in disappointment. I am confused, I am breathless with fear, and I feel as though everything is slipping away from me and whirling into a mess of color and time, but I had hoped to at least be able to fulfill the *jodenja kli-menji* and bring my guests what they want. I was holding to the idea of it like the one solid thing I can see. "I understand, Jaishevkin," I say. "I will—"

"You should meet them instead."

I stare at her. I do not understand this at all. Have I not already met with them? Have I not been meeting with them every day for over a week? Have we not spoken, do they not know my name and the pertinent details of my personal history, have I not given them all the information they require?

"You should meet with them," Jaishevkin says again. "You should meet them as you are. You should let yourself *feel*."

Our farewell is mostly silent. I am so confused as I make my way back through the dirty streets that I barely see them at all and more than once I nearly make a wrong turning. That I should meet with the humans? That I should *meet* them? I think about everything that Jaishevkin said, about what she might have said if she had agreed to meet them after all. About their writing. About how they smile at me.

About how they remember.

And I think, *My body-sire will never be whole again.*

I listen to the soft padding sound of my feet against the pavement and I think about that sound multiplied a hundred-fold, a thousand-fold, as we all ran for the river. For Laijan, for life, with death following behind.

When it happened, I was not yet born. From what I know of human lifespans, neither were Aaron and Jacob. We are looking back behind us at the death that follows us wherever we go, and we have all three been told *here is how you are to look at so much death so that it never catches you and here is what you are never to do. And here is how you should look at the ghosts.*

And here is how you should look at each other.

They smile at me that way because they are trying very hard to not see me at all.

When I am home I am still the only one awake. I bathe myself and dress in my formal *klimenjiani* clothing, light and softly hued. I do not know exactly what I will say or how I will find the words to tell what I feel. I do not know what my body-sire will say when she hears of it, and I do not know if I will be allowed to remain a *kli-menjiani*. I do not know what will happen after today. I do not know if my body-sire will ever be whole, or if I will ever be whole, or if any of us will. I do not know what Aaron and Jacob will say to me. I do not know if the death that follows us will catch us someday, or if Laijan will carry life, or if the ghosts that surround us will ever truly be seen.

But I am going to meet the humans.

rock of ages

jay lake

Highly prolific writer Jay Lake seems to have appeared nearly everywhere with short work in the past few years, including Asimov's, Interzone, Jim Baen's Universe, Tor.com, Clarkesworld, Strange Horizons, Aeon, Post-scripts, Electric Velocipede, *and many other markets, producing enough short fiction that he already has released four collections even though his career is only a few years old:* Greetings from Lake Wu, Green Grow the Rushes-Oh, American Sorrows, Dogs in the Moonlight, *and* The Sky That Wraps. *His novels include* Rocket Science, Trial of Flowers, Mainspring, Escapement, Green, The Madness of Flowers, *and* Pinon, *as well as three chapbook novellas,* Death of a Starship, The Baby Killers, *and* The Specific Gravity of Grief. *He's the coeditor, with Deborah Layne, of the prestigious* Polyphony *anthology series, now in six volumes, and has also edited the anthologies* All-Star Zeppelin Adventure Stories, *with David Moles,* Other Earths, *with Nick Gevers, and* Spicy Slipstream Stories, *with Nick Mamatas. His most recent books include* Endurance, *a sequel to* Green, *and a chapbook novella* Love in the Time of Metal and Flesh. *Coming up are new novels* Kalimpura *and* Sunspin. *He won the John W. Campbell Award for Best New Writer in 2004. Lake lives in Portland, Oregon.*

Here he give us a thriller about an embattled Green future that is besieged by sinister enemy conspiracies and in which a deep-cover agent must surface to try to prevent an asteroid strike on Seattle.

I: YEARS OF LIFE BEARING DOWN ON HIM LIKE A SLOW RAIN OF ANVILS

Reports of Bashar's death were greatly exaggerated. Reports of his death had *always* been greatly exaggerated. Even here in the oh-so-elegant precincts of the J. Appleseed Foundation, his bastard corporate stepchild that had broken free decades ago to make its own way in the world.

Daddy was coming home one more time after decades of absence. And he had hard questions. It took a special kind of hate to think up something like the island plagues. That his own creation might be behind the greatest incipient atrocity in human history was too much to bear. He wanted answers.

This outer office was a first stop. Surrounded by antique paintings and an ancient carpet, it signaled wealth in the symbolic language of a bygone age.

"I've been working with J. Appleseed since before you were born," Bashar said to the pert young man who stared at him in thin-lipped exasperation. Pale skinned, smelling of cologne and laundry detergent, the little bastard had damned near had himself starched, he was so white.

Bashar hadn't set foot in these offices in over a decade, but he wasn't going to let himself be stopped now. Just *being* here was risky as hell. Not being here was worse, given what he'd learned. "I've been working with you people since before Administrator Lang was born, for that matter. If I want to see the administrator, I'll see the damned administrator."

He leaned forward, knuckles planted on the milled Douglas fir on the assistant's desk. Some artisan had collaged the slab with shredded bits of classic currency, so that Ben Franklin and Queen Elizabeth II stared owlishly out of ripped interruptions in the wood grain from beneath a thick layer of hand-applied lacquer. It smelled of age and wood and musty paper, those olfactory cues doubtless as carefully designed as the visual.

Bashar's hands were as old as the rest of him, pushing toward his thirteenth decade of life. And if that wasn't a miracle in and of itself, almost enough to make a theist out of him, he didn't know what was. But at close to one hundred and twenty years of age, he simply wasn't as *scary* as he used to be.

This young twit didn't have the sense to be frightened anyway.

"You're not on the cleared list, sir," the assistant said, the first edge of nerves creeping into his voice. He glanced at a projected virteo datacloud which was nothing more than a faint shimmer from Bashar's perspective.

"Little boy, I *wrote* the damned cleared list. Back in the day. If I'm not on it now, someone will be breathing through their asshole by nightfall."

By the sound of it, several burly men and women were clattering through the door of Administrator Lang's outer office. Bashar turned, the twit's very old fashioned and deliberately archaic papermail letter opener now in his hand. It didn't even rise to the cutting standards of a dull-edged prison shiv, but would do for his current purposes.

He seized the initiative. "May I help you?"

"Ah, sir . . ." The head of the security detail obviously knew perfectly well who Bashar was. And how dangerous he could be. She and her three goons stood on the worn Persian rug over the antique warehouse flooring, shifting their weight as uneasily as elementary school pranksters caught with a databomb and a can of smartpaint. "Um. Is there a problem?"

"You're flubbing your lines, sister." He smiled, over a century's hard practice at looking and being sinister in the lines of his face. "Reddy Kilowatt here at the desk is having trouble telling friend from foe. I suggest you take him downstairs for some re-education." Tapping the lettermail opener against the palm of his left hand, Bashar added, "He'll like your beatdown a hell of a lot better than he'll like my beatdown."

He trusted this security squad to know the difference between promises and threats.

"Um, sir . . ." The woman glanced around before she realized that her three subordinates were all trying to hide behind her. "That's not what my orders say."

Bashar stopped tapping the world's dullest knife. "What orders?"

"The ones we have *now*, sir." A message strained urgently in the detail leader's eyes.

He knew that message. And there was no point in shooting the messenger. Besides which, at his age, he was out of practice taking on armed and armored squaddies at four to one odds.

Never one to fight beyond his point of no return, Bashar knew it was time to give up on his questions. For now at least, J. Appleseed's connection to some of the worst epidemiological die-offs of the past few decades would have to remain a bitter mystery.

He fucking hated mysteries, at least ones he wasn't behind himself.

Turning around, Bashar carefully set the lettermail opener back down on the assistant's desk. He smiled again, ignoring the reek of sweat. Exasperation had fled the twit's face to be replaced by the healthy panic of self-preservation. "My apologies, son. I didn't get the memo about which way the wind was blowing." He gave the assistant a sharp nod. "Let me know if you need the name of a good dry cleaner."

The security squad escorted him out of the office, keeping a polite distance every step of the way. Bashar was certain this was against their shiny new orders, which almost certainly included words such as "detention" and "with prejudice." Years of respect and a fearsome reputation as a stone killer had its advantages. He'd take his courtesies where he found them. Thanks to the squaddies, he passed through two human-staffed checkpoints and three automated ones without further challenge.

Bashar didn't start breathing easily again until he was outside under an overcast Seattle sky all by himself. As easily as he ever breathed these days. His skin warmed quickly even with the cloud cover—the UV filter tattoos that covered most of his body were doing their work, converting waste energy to radiant heat, much of which was trapped by the thermal battery fibers in his clothing. Who needed an ozone layer when you had tattoo guns and micron-scale engineering embedded in your transparent ink?

Sometimes the future still boggled him.

Headed down the Fourth Avenue waterfront promenade accompanied by the usual reek of low tide and—even now in this oil-starved age—marine bunker fuel, Bashar entered walking meditation. He needed to dial down the adrenaline the confrontation had dumped into his bloodstream. *Lose the shakes*, he told himself. *Otherwise you'll stand out to the cameras and the profilers.* Though one advantage to being old was a lot less attention paid to him by the more casual idiots who populated the world's security apparatus.

After all these years, Bashar didn't look a day over seventy-five. William Silas Crown, dead longer ago than he liked to think about, had had a lot to do with *that*. In a day and age when average life expectancy struggled to top five decades, he knew he was unusually blessed with some experimental and now long lost medical nanotech tending to his telomeres and stem cells and whatnot. Unusually blessed all the more so given his lifelong choice of occupations and obsessions.

Interest in the island plagues wasn't likely good for his health, either.

The New Seawall groaned to his left, holding back tides several meters above Bashar's head. A few ships loomed there, mostly gyre-runners towed in from the California Current to offload and onload along their endless, circling journeys. Powered on the open ocean by kite sails and current-generated electricity, *they* certainly weren't the source of the ubiquitous hydrocarbon reek.

He slipped a throwaway earbud from his sleeve stash. Single-use frequency hoppers, they were helpful for calls Bashar didn't want traced back to his personal *sensorium electronica*. What the kids today called iSys. If no one was looking for him, they were rated for ten minutes of secured talktime. At this point, so close to the now-presumed unfriendlies at J. Appleseed's Madison Street headquarters, he figured on two minutes of secured talk.

Bashar turked into the earbud's nanopower network—range, about three hundred centimeters, if you didn't stand near anything that shed EM trash. He tapped up Charity's comms address.

"Hey there," she said warmly. One of the few women Bashar had ever met who was as tough as he was. Few people of any flavor, in truth; not just cisgendered women. It wasn't a male-female issue, either. She'd been less than half his age when they had first encountered one another. Now, well . . . time was the great leveler.

And despite his best efforts, he'd never been able to hook his wife up with any of Crown's diamond-grade medtech. The sole-source supply and supplier were both gone in a hard Green bombing decades ago. It wasn't as simple as transfusing from him to her. Or he would have done that in years past. Pushing seventy, Charity Oxham looked and felt a hell of a lot older than Bashar did at well past a century.

"Babe." He smiled despite himself. "I'm on a code McQueen here." She'd know that meant his clock was short. "Just got frozen out by the pips." The data was explosive—his darwin file, the island plagues, a hint of any of it could have set J. Appleseed off. "They nearly went hard on me." That they hadn't gone all the way hard still amazed him. "Light up your perimeter and firm your assets."

After a moment, she said, "One and done."

"And, ah . . . check up on Sooboo, too?" It wasn't like J. Appleseed didn't know whose daughter worked in their analysis section. He just hoped whatever security stain he'd spilled on himself wasn't going to follow family lines. After all, she and the rest of the foundation thought him ten years dead.

"Samira's fine." Reproof now, old family arguments that transcended security and politics and a century of being one of the hardest of hard men. "You'll need to talk to her again some day, Bashar."

"Safer this way. Don't tell her . . ." He wasted precious seconds searching for words he didn't have. "Never mind. Here's what's going down: check out your data mirror, my file code 'darwin.'"

"You coming in from the cold?" she asked, almost matter of factly.

"Why start now?" After a moment, he added, "Love you."

"Love you, too."

Missing Charity a lot, Bashar dropped the earbud and smashed it with his heel without a break in his stride. The pressure stimulated the thermal fibers embedded in the bud's soft electronic matrices. A smoking dot of ash in the gravel of the sidewalk was all that remained a moment later.

He began to walk uphill, away from the ocean, his back to the J. Appleseed Foundation and much of his life's work.

From greenwiki:

Island Plague. Refers to the population-specific epidemics and pandemics which began emerging in the 2070s. The first documented instances were in Tonga, the Grand Caymans and Iceland, hence the name. Outbreaks of island plague targeted specific genetic groups, typically the demographically dominant one in each locus. Some researchers consider the St. Louis Flu which ravaged the North American Midwest and prairie polities in 2092 to be an example of island plague, given that it targeted persons of eastern European ancestry almost exclusively.

The major open question about island plague is whether the disease is artificially engineered or not. Detailed microbiological research has been spotty at best, with suppression of such results as may exist for both political and competitive reasons. The involved virii are certainly of a single, common class, but are also quite fragile outside their hosts. This of course begs the question of what the viral reservoir within the ecosystem might be, and how the virus continues to be reintroduced to geographically and genetically diverse human populations after extended gaps of time. That issue alone has persuaded many commentators as to the artificial origins of the island plague.

The primary countervailing argument has been that the island plague appears to serve no coherent political, economic or ideological agenda, and is therefore more likely to be a natural event.

Bashar had never been much for biological warfare. He preferred to ladle out his violence the old fashioned way, making his points one wound at a time. Focused application of force could, like Archimedes' lever, move the world.

Population kill was *inefficient*. If he'd spent his life doing anything, it was promoting efficiency. Looked at from the perspective of physics, that's what the Green movement was all about. Hard Greens and soft Greens alike could agree on that, whatever their other schisms. The late, lamented Cascadiopolis and her daughter cities ran on energy budgets that wouldn't have powered a Sunday morning church service in the days of Bashar's youth.

Tygre Tygre had been something . . . else. An experiment on the part of someone, never proven who. Tygre Tygre could have changed Cascadiopolis and everyone in it if Lightbull hadn't bombed them with a kinetic strike from orbit.

And what had those secret bastards ever wanted? Destructive change? Creative preservation?

The late twen-cen model of infrastructure preservation during wholesale warfare as exemplified in the neutron bomb was even sillier, to his perspective. Rewilding through macroscale infrastructure destruction wasn't particularly elegant, but it *was* effective. That had certainly been proven in the Middle East and South Asia over the course of the last century. Low-yield nuclear exchanges took on the climate modifying role of megavolcanoes.

There had been some cold years after that, and the climate models were borked beyond all recognition, but planetary stasis had managed to reassert itself.

Now, the darwin file bothered him. In its way, that was as destructive as Tygre Tygre, Lightbull, or the tactical ambitions of 1980s American generals.

It was time to put some physical distance between himself and J. Appleseed. Someone, somewhere had been stirred up against Bashar. Despite his best efforts, he'd left footprints in the plundered data from which the darwin file had been built. Sometimes the best security lay in simply not being where they were looking for you, after all. And Seattle was J. Appleseed's home turf. Their ground zero.

So he walked away. Hard to track a man who didn't take the train, or hop an airship, or even ride a bicycle with registry transponders that left breadcrumbs in the iSys of every passing tourist. Walking took time, time that let the hunt find its own way elsewhere, and perhaps best of all, carried Bashar toward an old friend who could be a lot of quiet help.

So he'd strolled out of Seattle, spent a couple of days walking down the I-5 corridor and out past Seatacalong the rewilded right of way. Not much there but fresh air and the sharp scent of evergreens. Bashar was just another old man sharing the trails and the winding little road that was the last concession to vehicular traffic other than the buried rail line. Bikers, walkers, seggers—his fellow travelers were a busy cross-section of Pacific Northwest types. Even a band of solar stilters, who didn't normally approach the urban cores much at all.

But even his own countermeasures left traces. A man who wasn't present could sometimes be as visible as a fire on a nighttime cliff. Rolling surveillance blackouts drew attention and inferences as surely as a fart in a staff meeting.

So mostly he was just an old man who ambled along with the simplest of security blockers to defeat the widespread surveillance present even out here in the wilderness. Smart dust was everywhere, after all.

Gait recognition could be countered with training and a walking stick. The right hat broke up his profile. A slump changed his height. The ultimate in high tech surveillance was vulnerable to security spoofing so old that Niccolò Machiavelli would have recognized the techniques. He couldn't do much about DNA sniffers, but those didn't work too well away from climate-controlled interiors.

As he walked, he considered the truism that everything evolves. In a sense, this was the first law of Green. Yet the island plagues had not evolved. He was increasingly certain of that.

At his age, meatspace memory wasn't what it once had been, but Bashar still didn't have a problem keeping in his head the salient summaries of all his work creating the darwin file. The viral reservoir problem was the central issue with the island plagues. It didn't make evolutionary *sense*.

Where did they come from, and where did they go?

His wife had dealt with that problem once before, back around the time they'd first met. Some whackjob Christian terrorists had targeted the United States government with a high-kill virus, using a politician's son as the vector.

In the end, thanks to some extremely quick thinking on the part of Charity, patient zero had also been the last patient. Edgewater had caught up to Ibrahim bin Yosef, the Yemeni virologist behind the microbiological engineering of the virus. He'd disappeared down a security hole so deep even the shadows around it were classified "kill before reading."

Was there a connection between bin Yosef's virus and the island plagues?

Bashar was finally ready talk to someone. Charity again, or any of a handful of AIs he knew. He needed data and he needed headroom to think. And his destination was close.

A grove loomed ahead. Shadows-In-Line-With-the-Moon was the human name for the trees' natural entity—their collective corporate and legal identity anthropomorphized. Warm weather opportunists like so many species, the torrey pines had been creeping northward since the early twenty-first century, following the shifting climate and the changes in growth bands. He knew this grove, had slept under its protection a few times. There was trust between himself and these trees, insofar as that concept could apply in this situation.

He could find secure bandwidth there, and take the temperature of events back in Seattle.

Bashar slipped off the trail and moved deeper among the pines along a narrow cobblestone path. The trees were straighter here than in their native California, protected from the winds by Seatac's Valley Ridge just to their west. Their needles carpeted the ground, interspersed with an engineered hardy, low-moisture moss that a lot of the trees in this region contracted to have laid down. It reduced the feral competition for sunlight and soil resources by keeping the ground cover tight and hampering seedlings of whatever species. Including their own, but plants in general seemed to take a different view of their progeny than animals did.

The result was a forest far cleaner than the wild ever produced, one that smelled of pinesap and old needles. Data ghosts flickered as well from a handful of virteo projectors, and at least one text stream so old school it would have been archaic in the days of Bashar's youth.

He sat down on an artfully careless piece of basalt. Many of the groves and forests had adapted to a philosophy that translated to humans as resembling Zen Buddhism. For all he knew, the rock symbolized universal transubstantiation.

Right now, it symbolized a place to put his tired butt.

"Hello," he said calmly. "Thank you for the grant of shelter to me."

They didn't talk much, the trees, but it almost always paid to be polite.

Bashar flexed the muscles of his face in a specific order. An embedded ultra low power data transceiver powered by a combination of his body heat and piezoelectric charging as his muscles moved began to hunt for friendly turked signals within the same three hundred-centimeter radius as his implanted microearbuds. All his gear was battery-free, so as not to show up on most sensors. This was the electronic equivalent of know-your-neighbor security, without the disposable convenience of his single-use phones.

Shadows-In-Line-With-the-Moon accepted the connection. His optics flared briefly, then cycled through a disorienting sequence of images of daylight, darkness and fuzzy logic models of organic molecules. *Esters*, he thought, but chemistry wasn't exactly Bashar's long suit. At least, not chemistry that didn't involve explosives, propellants or fuels.

That was a tree's way of saying hello. Or more to the point, several hundred trees' way of saying hello.

His communication wizard requested a cloaked ping out to a persistent data pipe. The rewilded I-5 corridor had a strong quantum fiber backbone running underneath the one-lane walkway, with shunts and repeaters every few hundred meters or so. That was how both the tourists and the permanent residents talked to the wider world around them. Infrastructure was pervasive, even deep in the wilderness.

Price. There would always be a price.

An electric green text stream floated into his sensorium via his optic nerves, complete with a blinking block cursor. The trees were being very retro. A packagewalkssouth, their message read.

Now? But the natural entities were known to be indirect in many of their dealings. He'd wanted to talk, this was a conversation. They had something to tell him.

So Bashar went along with it. "Fair enough." He could carry it himself or turk it, depending on how far south the package needed to walk. Turking was effective but slow, sort of the land-based equivalent of the gyre-runners that cruised the oceanic currents. Hand to hand, person to person, the package might move a few hundred meters one day and dozens of kilometers the next. Or it might sit by the side of the trail in a cache for weeks. It would get there, through the peer-to-peer osmosis that was turking.

Furthermore, today, in this place, there was probably a good reason for him to take this assignment. "Destination?"

California Suisun Bay.

Whoops. That was over seven hundred miles as the feet wandered. Not at all what he had in mind.

It was a weird destination in any case. Bashar was pretty sure Suisun Bay was long gone. Just a shallow water feature of Greater San Pablo Bay in these degenerate days, but he wasn't going to argue with Shadows-In-Line-With-the-Moon. Besides, the package would presumably be tagged with an address that would make sense to the locals once it got there.

"You want me to see something south of here?" Bashar asked.

See what is before you. The grove flashed images of a forest fire, of people fleeing a city.

It was worried about something. Very worried.

"I don't expect to go to California personally, but I'll get it there."

Nobody turked in a hurry. But people usually turked for a reason. And Shadows-In-Line-With-the-Moon wanted him headed south.

Your proposal is acceptable.

With those words, he found his own data tendrils insinuating into the I-5 corridor carrier signal. In accepting the package, he'd paid the grove's price for anonymous access into the datastream. Insofar as Bashar could tell from the inside, he was embedded in a feed of archive weather-and-climate data. That was good enough for him.

He pinged his wife. Voice wouldn't cut it here, too much traceable bandwidth required, but he needed to talk to her again about darwin and what was happening to him now. That Shadows-In-Line-With-the-Moon would hear everything seemed a fairly low-risk trade, given the degree of anonymity the grove was granting him.

Trees were good secret keepers. For the most part, they simply didn't care at all.

Charity's ack came back as scrolling text wrapped in Shadows-In-Line-With-the-Moon's crazy retro interface.

cox:: ¿¿¿bashar???

The world's oldest security operative smiled.

From greenwiki:

Lightbull. Alleged cover identity of a long-term conspiracy to achieve world domination, much in the tradition of the Illuminati or the Bilderberg Group. This strain of theorizing is notable mostly for its intermingling with soft and hard Green history, including a putative role in the unsolved bombing of Cascadiopolis.

Even the best evidence for Lightbull is indirect, having been described as "a string of words." Tauroctony. Mexico City. Tygre Tygre. A dead satellite and a pair of orbital kinetic bombings. Devotees of the theory have drawn a crooked line back through Enlightenment conspiracies and the Eastern Roman Empire and Mithraic mysteries back to Minoan Crete. For those who believe, much of history comes down to who was on the wrong side of the Battle of Salamis, and who survived the eruption of Thera. The underlying questions of what any secret society of such age would want to accomplish in the modern world is not usually answered. Like almost all conspiracy theories, Lightbull is a heady compound of wishful thinking, paranoia and outright fantasy.

II: SOME PEOPLE WOULD RATHER THAT YOU DIE FOR THEIR BELIEFS THAN THAT THEY RE-EXAMINE THOSE BELIEFS

Charity Oxham hated her nasal oxygen concentrator. Her every breath reeked of a curious combination of slightly musty plastic and that strange, fresh smell of O_2.

Bashar had commented once—just once—that she lived now the way William Silas Crown had died. "In a small room wallpapered by medicine," were his exact words. Colorful as her partner of almost four decades always was. She smiled in fond memory of the old bastard.

And *old* didn't even begin to cut it, when talking about Bashar.

She'd long ago passed through jealousy at his extended good health and lack of senescence. Even now, barely seventy herself, Charity had seen most of her friends and family long dead. Except for Samira and Bashar, she had almost no one left. And Bashar had been legally dead for the third time this past decade. That he called her up periodically, and interfaced data with her quite regularly, was no substitute for his warm-bodied company.

At least someone was still out doing good in the world.

Her current project, likely her last, was to make additional effort to run down the old Lightbull leads. That was a set of threads Bashar had picked up back around the time the two of them had first met. He'd been following them ever since, as time and new evidence permitted.

Charity finally realized the increased medical bleating was a reminder to breathe. She sucked down another noseful of oxygen and its olfactory discontents. The stuff very nearly made her high. Which was either a blessing or a sin, she couldn't be sure which.

Malik, the human nurse on this shift, cracked open the sealed door to her room and stuck his head in. "You can't be doing that, lady." His teeth shoaled within his quick, mobile smile, bright in the dark skin of his face. His accent was warm and liquid and curious, some mysterious regionalism that had arisen since she was young. "Woman needs air to live."

"Woman needs peace and quiet to live, too," Charity grumped, but she didn't mean it. And she knew that Malik knew that as well. "Any papermail?"

"Nothing hard copy since those chocolates turked in last week from your daughter."

Samira barely talked to Charity any more. A grown woman, that was her own business, but it saddened her mother's heart. The girl had been born angry and she'd probably die angry. Admittedly, the relationship between herself and Bashar hadn't exactly been a comfort to their daughter in her youth. Still, Samira had only been scrambled on one black ops raid that Charity could remember now.

Arranging for baby sitters *had* been a stone bitch.

"You enjoy 'em, Malik?" Charity had been strictly off sweets for years thanks to her long-surrendered pancreas, something Samira knew perfectly well.

He mocked a pout. "Niranjana ate half the box, then left the rest in the staff room."

Charity snickered. She'd known some first sergeants like that, back in the day. *Way* back in the day. "She's the charge nurse, I guess she can do what she wants."

"Some secrets tell themselves." Malik winked. "Some never get told at all. Don't forget to breathe."

"Breath is life." Charity wondered who she was quoting.

Bashar's darwin file made a nice contrast to tweaking the long-dead threads of Lightbull. Why her husband concerned himself with viral reservoirs of fatal plagues was the kind of question Charity had given up asking decades ago. Bashar was interested in *everything*, and had never been much for offering any of his own secrets in return. Not even to her. She was convinced that he'd lived so long as much out of sheer bloody-mindedness and preternaturally good security as out of whatever medtech Crown's legacy had left him with.

Despite Malik's parting words, that meant more secrets kept. A lot of them. And a lot of those for reasons even Bashar might not be certain of anymore.

Her right hand shook, tremula again, so that the microthin data tablet wavered in her grip like waves on the ocean. Being old was *frustrating*. Most of what she wanted to do she couldn't, and the rest took three or four times longer than it had any right to. Charity gulped down another noseful of oxygen before the monitors went off once more. Malik was a good kid, but he had an entire ward to watch, not just her.

Everything hurt, not much worked right, and the smell . . . Gah. She was living in the future. Surely they could get better disinfectants.

Her husband's notes within the darwin file were as cryptic as ever. The attachments and outside references were more verbose in painting a picture of the island plagues. The phenomenon itself wasn't hard to understand. The mystery was all, and always, in the causation.

Bashar was clearly convinced of human agency. Just as clearly, he was angrily baffled as to motive.

She had to laugh out loud at that. Sometimes Bashar was so simple. "A century and a half since the Trinity atomic bomb test, and you have to wonder why someone would come up with a new way to kill?" she asked the empty room.

The machines around her bore Charity no answer. Silent witnesses to her decline, they offered scarce comforts at the best of times.

The genomic targeting was admittedly an angle a little more troublesome than the usual run of biowar horrors. Planetary population was down to a bit over a third of the early twenty-first century peak of almost eight billion. That had been accomplished wholesale, though, through the time honored means of famine and economic collapse. Not ethnic extermination.

No one could have a political or religious grudge that extended to both Tongans and Icelanders at the same time. Those had been testbed populations. Bashar didn't think otherwise, to judge from his notes. And the vectoring made no sense. *How* would a virus naturally migrate from the south Pacific to the north Atlantic, years apart, leaving no intermediate traces along the way? What was the vector? Epidemiology just didn't work like that.

This was rather like pulling the strings on Lightbull. Thinly scattered evidence displayed just enough pattern to invite the paranoid pareidolia to which the human mind was so readily suspect.

The outbreaks must have been test efforts, with increasingly large and uncontrolled populations as the project went on. That culminated in the misnamed St. Louis flu that could have wiped out half of two continents if it hadn't been contained.

What if that had been the goal?

Some secrets keep themselves, after all.

She had to ask herself: who stood to benefit from that sort of death toll?

Hard Greens, of course. The edge of the Green movement, on the far side of J. Appleseed and its ideological kin. Zero-population rewilding of the terrestrial biosphere wasn't exactly a new concept. But up to now, they hadn't run so close to the edge as to engage in genocide.

Or had they?

The darwin file was frustratingly similar to the Lightbull problem. There was far more physical evidence for the island plagues than there ever had or would be for Lightbull, but that didn't lead her any closer to the truth. Just more threads that broke off and unraveled as soon as you got near them.

It wasn't just the sheer secrecy involved. The world was made of secrets. She and

Bashar still kept more than a few of them. The problem here was the lack of agency. Causation. Motivation.

Who benefited?

The hard Greens hadn't bombed Cascadiopolis all those years ago. Tygre Tygre had died, Bashar had nearly been killed. The green city movement had been shattered, only to be reborn in a hundred other places as Cascadiopolis' shards had spread across western North America.

Or had the hard Greens meant that all along?

Charity felt a cold sinking in her chest. These days, the Cascadian daughter-cities ran from the Brooks Range in Alaska to Mexico's Sierra Madre Occidental. They were the ultimate in soft Green power. Low-impact living in close integration with the hyperlocal climate, ecosystem and resource base. In a sense, the opposite of zero-population rewilding.

Close cousins to the hard Greens in some ways. In others, when looked at from the hard Green perspective, the daughter-cities were traitors of the sort only someone so close could be.

And now Shadows-In-Line-With-the-Moon was pushing Bashar south, farther away from the J. Appleseed manhunt and towards something. Another piece of the puzzle, and if the natural entities were getting involved, a whole different player. What did Lightbull and the hard Green movement look like to them, she wondered?

The answer came as if from an outside voice: "one and the same." People plotting for power over one another, but also over the biosphere. Which affected the natural entities profoundly. On a life-and-death basis.

What if the forests and their kin were right? What if Lightbull and the hard Green movement were one and the same, or at least overlapping . . .

Horror dawned on her like nuclear fire in the night.

"How many years have we been played?" Charity asked her machines. She already knew part of the answer to her own question: All her life at the very least. Lightbull almost certainly stretched back before she was born. Years before. Decades. If only some of what Bashar believed was true, centuries, or perhaps millennia.

Even the trees understood this.

Her mind raced. The problem was figuring out what the hard Greens behind the island plagues meant to accomplish. Charity just couldn't credit them with being literally suicidal. Not in their own lifetimes. And even the most radical of activists often as not had children, and thus slowly acquired a different view of the future through the lens of their genetic propagation.

Bashar, for example.

She dropped him a "call me" ping, then spent some time correlation mapping different configurations of the available evidence and her speculations.

"Hello."

It was Bashar. His voice was deep and mellow with age, and still made her shiver all the way down into her loins. Besides which, Charity had never in her life heard the man say "hi."

"You've got bandwidth this time," she observed. "You don't sound like Elmer Fudd piped through a noise filter."

"Hah. Let's just say I've been tree hugging, and leave it at that."

"Hippie."

"Pig."

"Love you, too," she said. "Besides, I was a soldier, not a cop."

"Fascist pig, then." The fondness in his voice nearly brought her to tears.

"Okay, I'll own that." She wondered if he would ever come in from the cold and see her again. It wasn't like she could get out much stuck here in Chelan Heights, a Federal retirement home and high security medical facility tucked in the Cascades more or less due east of Seattle.

"Miss you."

He laughed. "Get a scope. It'll improve your aim."

"Chauvinist." She stopped, reined herself in. They didn't have time. Ten minutes, tops, for a secured line, and she'd burned the better part of the first minute on their version of 'I love you.' "I've been sailing your *Beagle*."

He caught the toss. Obvious enough as a reference to darwin. "Find any interesting finches?"

"Oh, yes." Charity checked her security filters, dialed up the encoding. The line squealed a moment before the audible tone that indicated deeper encryption. Both their voices would flatten now, picking up latency ghosts and losing the nuance of emotion. "I've been thinking. Are we pulling on opposite ends of the same thread? I think maybe your tree friends believe that the people behind the island plagues and the people behind Lightbull are one and the same."

"Lots of things are possible," he replied.

She couldn't hear his inflection, not over the quantum-encrypted line that currently burned up bandwidth like a kilometers-long, electrons-wide bonfire, but Charity knew Bashar well enough to fill in what was missing from their connection.

"Yes," Charity said. "But there's a common m.o. of deep secrecy here, with dead end threading. And there's maybe a common set of goals. If you're a zero-pop hard Green with a reductionist agenda, the island plagues make sense as test runs for a bid to take the biosphere back to pre-human in a fairly constrained amount of time. Cascadiopolis was a demonstration project of the compromise version of that hard Green agenda. Radicals hate their squishy allies a lot more than they hate their implacable enemies."

"What about Tygre Tygre," her husband asked, skipping ahead half a dozen steps down the logic trail.

"I haven't the least idea. You knew him. I didn't. But if you're right about the deep origins of Lightbull, isn't it possible they have their own dissenters?"

"Everybody has dissenters. Says so right here in the big handbook of movement security."

Even through the flattened line, she could catch the humor in his voice.

"There's more," Charity said, suddenly reluctant to push her intuition forward.

"More what?"

Always a practical man, her husband.

Charity continued: "I think maybe we've all been played. Played hard, from the beginning. If Lightbull has a planning baseline that runs beyond decades, to centuries or more, that's not inconceivable."

"Paranoid, are we?"

"*You* lived through the last century. Tell me another series of worldwide economic and technical collapses isn't something to be paranoid about."

"Our hard Green friends would say that just proves their point. Human culture is unsustainable beyond a certain threshold."

"Do you believe that?"

"No," Bashar said. Then, slowly: "When is zero-population not suicide?"

"Never?" she hazarded.

"Not after a certain point, no. Not never. Think, Charity. Green Space. The habitats they've been building up there in high orbit."

"They?" Charity snorted. "*We*, Bashar. J. Appleseed funded a lot of that directly, and funneled much of the rest. And if we've all been played since before day one, maybe that was part of the plan."

"They've got two great, big rocks up there," he said, "and how much headcount?"

"Bashar, there are people working in orbit who were *born* in space. Young people, admittedly."

"What, ten thousand at least?"

Charity pulled some data threads. "Current estimate of human presence in space is approximately seventeen thousand, four hundred permanent residents in orbit, another eleven hundred on the Moon. Plus as many as five thousand transients at any given time."

She could practically hear Bashar thinking before he spoke again: "We've brought back plant and animal species here on Earth from a few cloned cells harvested out of museums. A genetic reservoir of over twenty thousand people is enough to preserve our species in good health. It's not like *Homo sapiens* has all that much genetic variation to start with."

The species was weirdly single-threaded, from a genomic perspective.

"So this is all directed from space?" Charity wondered how that worked.

"Or at least reliant on orbital resources, yes." Bashar sounded impatient. As usual, he was out ahead of her. "I'm more curious about how all this was directed from deep in the past. Zero-population rewilding isn't exactly a staple of classical thought."

"Agendas change," she reminded her husband. "Ours certainly has over the years."

"Yes, but *this* agenda . . . It's world-spanning, with a very long time base. You don't shift that easily." He fell silent a moment. Then: "How soon?"

"How soon what?"

"How soon until Lightbull releases the final plague? Assuming Lightbull and darwin are one and the same, like you seem to believe."

You believe it, too, she thought, before replying, "If we stipulate that the prerequisite is a self-sustaining population in space, their state of readiness been achieved."

"How many of the folks in orbit know about this?"

Charity could practically hear Bashar point at the sky. "I haven't a clue."

"I'm going to find out. Thank you, dear."

"I love you," she told her husband.

"I love you, too." Uncharacteristically, Bashar added, "Remember that."

She watched her own monitors a while after the connection dropped, fading into stochastic bursts of electrical energy. Everything descended into clouds of unknowing eventually.

Sometimes she was glad she was old and sick and almost dying. The idea of trying to stop the island plagues from going global sounded absolutely overwhelming. Charity considered drawing on some of her own resources, whether to call in favors decades old.

Not yet. Not until she knew precisely what it was that Bashar intended to do.

From Green Space and Your World, Pyloric Publishing, 2081:

If you watch the skies at the right time of night, you may see the glimmer of Orbital Zero being constructed. That is your future, right there, in the sky high above you. Paid for by concerned citizens the world over, Green Space Operations is building that future one launch at a time, one pair of hands at a time.

Soon you'll be able to visit. Gardens in the sky. Microgravity swimming pools. Asteroids brought to Earth for their wealth, so that we can mine cold rocks from the beginning of creation instead of continuing to disturb our planet's natural environment. It will all come together by the time you're old enough to work your passage into orbit and take up a gainful trade with the rest of us building the future.

Are you ready to learn more? Good. In the first chapter, we'll talk about the GSO launches, how our heavy lift vehicles work, and the environmental remediation that Green Space puts into effect every time we push a launch into the sky.

III: SOMETIMES THE DEAD WERE EASIER TO DEAL WITH THAN THE LIVING

What went on in orbit had never interested Bashar too much. When he was a kid, NASA had been dying on the vine, victim of the American conservative anti-science fixation. The Russians and the Chinese had done their thing, of course, until they'd run out of money and motivation. Eventually, space had gone strictly commercial and military. Both of which Bashar had always considered to be cultural perversions.

But now . . .

Maybe he'd been wrong all along.

He walked further south along the I-5 corridor, turking the package for Shadows-In-Line-With-the-Moon. It was small, about twice the size of a deck of cards, sealed in resin which probably carried the grove's DNA as a signature. Thankfully, stabilizer had been oversprayed so the thing didn't stick to his fingers.

Walking, Bashar kept his eyes open for whatever the grove might have been directing him toward. *All* his eyes, not just the meatware in his face.

Occasional undirected movement made for good security, and exercise always helped his thinking. The weather was a bit brisk for late spring, and something was in bloom that scented the wind with unsubtle perfume. Bashar was pretty sure given his conversation with Charity that he'd wind up back in Seattle soon. That was all the more reason to be out of town right now. Let J. Appleseed's squads hunt him where he wasn't, if their orders had gone beyond the foundation's own premises. By the time he got back, they'd be looking somewhere else.

The foundation's play against him was a problem, too. Something had already been in the wind at J. Appleseed from the darwin file. The same accrual of evidence that had brought Bashar in from the street must be pushing them toward their trigger point. Certainly the orbital allies were ready.

His enemies list was much, much longer than his friends list. For the most part, Bashar preferred things that way. He could ration his trust accordingly, and make reasonable assumptions about where everyone else stood. But it rendered the old motivation/method/opportunity triad a tad less useful when most everyone had motivation to spare.

There were still people on the inside he could talk to. Starting and ending with his daughter. But to reach out to J. Appleseed right now . . . Not without a strike force at his back, and some notion of how to stop their plague release. If that was what was really going on.

He shouldn't have let himself fade out like he had this past decade and more. It was just that being dead was so convenient. Not that Bashar had ever paid taxes in his life, but death cut down on the mail, too. He got a lot more done when people weren't looking for him, asking him to do things.

"Orbit," he told the stand of Japanese maples he was currently passing through. Feral ornamentals, it looked like, almost certainly without any corporate structure to their natural entity yet, so no answer would be forthcoming. "Why take it to orbit?"

Charity had the right of things. Orbit was all about a genetic reservoir. The ultimate island, in a sense. If their speculation had any basis, Lightbull had built a virtual ark high overhead, and was now in the process of permanently exporting the problem of human existence from the terrestrial biosphere.

The *why* mattered, but not so much as the how, let alone the *when*.

The *when* gnawed at him.

As he walked, Bashar began to methodically retune his data traps, changing the keywords to include some new concepts. There were security trapdoors out there almost as old as he was. And he had friends in the virtual world.

He wondered what the hard Greens intended for the infrastructure after the zero-population level had been achieved. A lot of the biosphere was online now in the form of natural entities, instantiated as legal and economic actors in their own right. Was the plan for a post-human infosphere, automated systems and species agents interacting over time? Somebody still had to site the repeaters and repair storm damage, after all. Even if the storms themselves paid their own bills, they didn't have opposable thumbs.

There were some powerful, genuinely green entities who might not be so pleased at all with this plan. Even sleepy bystanders such as Shadows-In-Line-With-the-Moon would probably have a thing or two to say about subtracting humans from the world completely.

Hence him turking this package.
Could trees get bored, he wondered.

The trees had sent him south for a reason. Bashar found someone who might be his contact amid the ruins of an overpass down around what used to be the town of Federal Way. An androgynous teen sunbathed nude, no visible genitalia to speak of, their groin sort of like that of an old fashioned toy doll. He was both old enough and old-fashioned enough to be uncomfortable with androgynes.

They stirred from their rest as soon as he ambled into sight. The kid's tall bike was parked casually enough, lying on one side amid some black-eyed Susans, but the artfully distressed frame members had the sheen of nanotech over their rust-and-mud patina.

No modern primitive this one, he thought.

"Yo." The kid shrugged into their t-shirt. Oversized and threadbare to the point of being more mesh than cloth, it was screenprinted with a pixelated image of the twen-cen actor Peter Lorre in a jacket and bow tie.

"You looking for me?" Bashar asked. Sometimes it paid to be blunt. And to be honest, he was tired of messing around in the woods.

The kid tugged on a pair of biking shorts and some toe shoes, picked up a hardbook—actual paper—then skittered down the rotten concrete to meet him. "Might be." They flashed the book like a gang sign.

Bashar controlled his reaction. It was *A Symmetry Reframed.* Written by him, decades ago. The soft Green bible, some people had called it. That book had been the J. Appleseed foundation's calling card much longer than this . . . child . . . had been alive.

Symmetry was either his greatest work or his greatest mistake, depending on how he thought about things.

"I got a package needs turking south." He hefted the evidence in his left hand. "Sent by a friend."

The kid shrugged. "Who's got friends? Turkin's easy. Life is hard."

"Truth," Bashar acknowledged. "You got anything for me? I'm headed north."

"You just came from north, moonshadow," the kid pointed out.

That was probably as much explicit recognition as he would get. "And now I'm headed back north."

Standing up their bike, they extended a hand. That close, the teen smelled of marijuana and machine oil. "No. West."

Bashar paused as he handed over the grove's package. "What?"

"Go west, young man."

Close to a century of security work, he knew a touch when he heard one. This was what Shadows-In-Line-With-the-Moon had sent him south for. "What's west?"

The teen shrugged. "People you ought to meet. Friends of Mr. Cairo."

Who? Bashar tugged his chin, thinking. "Friends. Does anyone have friends these days?"

"Nobody. Give you this for free, though: Saw someone take a dirt nap today. Went down the hard way. Shooter was a cyranoid, working for someone else. Heavy stuff, not a local spat." They flipped *Symmetry* into a messenger bag with a grin, tucking the package after it. "Man like you, would know what it all meant."

So much for his cover.

Who knew what the grove had told this kid, or who this kid really worked for? For a moment, Bashar wondered if he was seeing a cyranoid right now—had the kid done the killing themself, on behalf of some distant puppetmaster? But that much bandwidth would have stood out like a flare this far into the sticks. And the kid had none of the peripheral oddities of a human-hosted avatar. "Mind the road," Bashar finally said.

"And watch your wheels." With that, the kid kicked up on top of a shattered concrete pillar to mount their tall bike, then headed south, whistling tunelessly. Bashar watched a while but received no backward glances.

Killings in the woods. And a cyranoid wouldn't be operating out here without consent and assistance from the natural entities. It was hard to imagine Shadows-In-Line-With-the-Moon hiring contract killers, but depending on how badly the grove and its peers wanted to protect the infrastructure that gave them civil rights and economic power, one human life was just a small step.

What did he know, at least at the moment?

Bashar knew he had to head west. The trees had all but told him that. He supposed he was working for them now. But the only thing around here besides dope growers and survivalists who liked to go shopping less than once a year was Schaadt's Shack, a roadhouse that had a good reputation as neutral territory. For the most part, you didn't get far off the I-5 corridor without specific business in hand and someone's permission to do that business. Schaadt's Shack was an exception. People who would shoot each other on sight out in the hills would sit down to drink together in a place like that. Peer pressure, a weapons check, and a small stable of fearsome bouncers kept the bar in business on those terms.

He walked. The trees were worried. Bashar was worried. Friends of Mr. Cairo? What did that mean?

It was less than thirty minutes on foot from the corridor trail to his destination. People liked their drinking convenient.

So far as Bashar could tell, the place had been originally built as a tiltwall shopping mall. How it survived the comprehensive rewilding movement of the middle of the last century was anybody's guess. The outer walls were covered with layers of granite stacked like a riprap breakwater. The roof was a Medieval classic, hand-logged Douglas fir beams supporting honest-to-god slate tiles. Bashar wouldn't have hesitated to airdrop a cargo load onto it.

The tamped clay apron in front even held a few vehicles. Unusual in these parts. He slacked his pace and scanned. A couple of small, battered hovercraft that would run slow and fat on dense, long range fuel cells. The usual assortment of bikes and seggers. An honest-to-God Hummer body, though this one was crowded with an alcohol-fueled boiler and wouldn't drive much faster than he could run. Not that *he* could run with a couple of metric tons of cargo on his back.

And strangely enough, a rather peculiar helicopter. Something *very* new. Insectile airframe, rotors folded politely, bristling with enough stingers of one kind or another to melt everything else in the yard and punch more than a few holes in Schaadt's Jack-the-giant-killer slate roof in the process.

Finding such a machine out here was like finding a silenced carbon fiber pistol in a child's toy box.

Somebody took their drinking seriously.

Precisely who had taken a dirt nap and how they had been killed became much more interesting questions to Bashar.

He paged his own alerts. Nothing with any meaningful priority sought his attention. Whatever this was, it likely wasn't here for him.

Right. Cairo's ride, he'd bet, whoever Mr. Cairo was. "You're not the only bad ass in the world," Bashar reminded himself out loud.

He was here for this killer chopper and whoever had flown in on it. Still, he made a wide circle around the helo as he approached the front door.

From greenwiki:

Mining Packages. While many people are familiar with Orbital Zero as an effort to ensure long-term human space habitation, the real economic driver was always the Luna-Lagrange Consortium's Project Precious. Two separate efforts, both successful, were made to capture and tow two asteroids known to contain significant quantities of high value and precious metals into high Earth orbit for intensive mining and mineral recovery.

Project Precious was an unusual effort as it had a significant positive return when expressed within the budgetary frameworks of the old state-capital system by which many polities still manage their fiscal processes, while also having a significant positive return within the Green accounting frameworks as codified in the Catalina Accords of 2051. This combination of monetary value and abstracted resource extraction returns was rarely seen in the twenty-first century, and never on a project of this scale, with trillions of Euros at stake.

The problems with Project Precious emerged when attempting to transfer the extracted minerals back down the gravity well for surface-based industrial and economic use. Simply put, while heavy lift has been a challenge since the first days of the rocket age, ultraheavy return was never seriously contemplated prior to Project Precious. Especially not in kiloton quantities.

After much debate, the delivery of resources to the Earth's surface was finally accomplished via guided airfoil-shaped "mining packages" covered with sufficient waste material cast as tiles to provide an ablative heat shield. These are sent to the surface on a shallow angle of re-entry to minimize loss due to re-entry stress, as well as minimize surface impact effect. The mining packages are guided to land in fairly shallow water splash zones offering substantial west-to-east clearance (Gulf of Mexico, the Great Lakes, the Baltic Sea, the Black Sea, various littorals, and so forth). Materials thus delivered are then retrieved through various conventional means as appropriate to the local tech base and Green priorities.

Early in the project's history, one re-entry in Lake Superior experienced an unplanned "skip" which resulted in the mining package coming to rest outside the planned impact zone, and causing the near-complete destruction to the city of Sault Sainte Marie, Michigan. This is considered the costliest peacetime human-caused destruction of property in history. As a result of this disaster, landing protocols for the mining packages were altered, and onboard control systems with a variety of override capabilities were added.

IV: TYGRE TOLD ME ONCE IN PASSING THAT HE CAME FROM A SECRET SCHOOL

Bashar let the bouncer pat him down. A woman he vaguely recognized, Blue Alice. "I got to ask," he said conversationally, "who's the fly-in customer?"

She shrugged, an activity which bordered on the tectonic. "Seattle money, maybe. Walked in clean. All I care about."

Walked in clean with hot, flaming death on wings parked outside. Anybody with the *cojones* to fly low over this airspace was heavy stuff indeed, or awfully well defended.

"Not Cairo money, huh?"

That sally produced no visible reaction at all. He pushed on inside.

Schaadt's Shack boasted a lot of square footage, rough-hewn Douglas fir pillars interspersed with separate tables and booth clusters. That much wood had to cost a pretty penny from the forest collectives. The layout made space for privacy and room to have fist fights. Not to mention break them up. A big kitchen loomed at the back, running off a combination of wood-fired and solar. Somebody had been baking just recently, though yeasty-beastie beer reek underlay the rest of the interior fug.

They were known for their food here. People even came down from Seattle just to eat.

Like the flyboys who'd parked outside.

Huge bars lined each side of the cavernous hall. The brewery bulked behind the bar to his right. Everything was underlit, so the individual clusters of tables and booths resembled candelaria scattered through a musty dusk.

Bashar found a stretch of stools at the bar by the east wall, the one without the brewery. It was a slow day, which was fine with him. Better chance to find this Mr. Cairo. A menu of beer and food was scrawled across a wide chalkboard. Where the hell did anyone get colored chalk these days, he wondered. Maybe they fabbed it from feedstock.

A barback finally drifted over. "Yeah?"

Customer service at its finest. Bashar didn't bother to not smile. "Pint of Burn Scar Bitter, and the Brie tempura with wild game charcuterie, please."

"On the way."

He turned to watch the room. Mostly Bashar was curious to spot the flyboys.

There wasn't much to see. Drinkers and diners kept to themselves. There'd be a band tonight, and the usual local sports of poker, dancing and brawling. Right now it was the casual lunch trade—basically himself—and a few locals doing whatever locals did around here. Plus some tables deep in the shadowed corners and bays of the vast room.

No one he could see looked like they'd dropped in riding twenty million Euros worth of combat hardware. If Bashar had been security for Schaadt's Shack, that would make him awfully twitchy.

His food turned up warm and smelling like protein heaven. Food had gotten a lot better after the early twenty-first century distribution networks had collapsed. Farm-to-table was how most of the human race existed these days.

Bashar raised his Burn Scar Bitter and offered an old toast to no one in particular. "Consumers of the world unite, you have nothing to lose but your supply chains."

"You some kind of capitalist?" asked the barback suspiciously.

The question—close to a killing insult in many circumstances—amused Bashar. "I'm older than your grandma's bunions, and ain't never yet had a bank account. What do you think?"

"Original Green, huh?" She leaned against her side of the bar and gave him a long look.

Bashar returned the favor, with his security eyes this time. Female, mixed race but probably Pacific Islander and East African, pretty-but-hard in the way of most young women these days. Hair buzzed short with something sparkly rubbed in for looks. Or more. He could think of half a dozen offensive and defensive applications for reflective shavings, depending on the materials involved. Wore no scent at all but her sweat and a trace of bar rag from being on shift at least a few hours. Modest facial tattoos, faux-Celtic abstracts around her orbital ridges and down her nose. Three tiny studs in the left nostril, each winking with a single dull green pixel—*there* was cultural code he couldn't read without a data dip. Her shirt was a torn collared tee in a style so old it had been out of fashion when he was her age, black bamboo cloth with smart fiber image of the late American President Chamnansatol.

Presumably before her assassination by hemorrhagic fever, though with the noisily pixelated art it was hard to tell.

"You're young," Bashar said pleasantly, indulging his not-so-cold read, "radical but not extreme, no hard Green or you wouldn't be working in here." They tended to be puritanical, among their other faults and virtues. "Tired of both the new world order and the old one, and probably the one before that. You're part of something that meets evenings or weekends that gives you purpose. Out here it's likely not all that political, but I could be wrong. Infrastructure pirates, maybe?"

She growled, but there was a twinkle in her eye. "Smart old man, huh? Older than you look. Extreme and radical. O.G., like I said, but no hard Green or you wouldn't be drinking in here. You've seen the last two or three world orders, and you got that patina of well-worn power. You were part of something big once, but you aren't any more. Working one last scam, maybe?"

He had to laugh. Would that she knew. "Every scam is my last one. If I didn't think that way, I'd have been dead a long time ago."

"And if you were less than three times my age, I'd give you something else to work." She winked and walked away, calling over her shoulder, "Tab's on the house this time, old man."

"Huh," Bashar observed to no one in particular. "A free lunch. How about that?" He wondered which one of them had played the other.

"Nothing's free," said a waiter, approaching from among the pillars at the center of the room.

No, not a waiter. A man with a tray and a gun underneath that tray. In here. Middle-aged, fit, frowning face under a head so bald it might have been waxed. And white as any Georgia cracker.

"Security?" Bashar asked mildly. *Or Mr. Cairo.*

"No thanks, I already got some." He stopped next to Bashar.

The gun was between them, not pointed anywhere in particular. Threat by implication.

Several responses passed through Bashar's thoughts, but he left them there. He was too damned old to go starting fights. And if the waiter seriously meant to kill him, the trigger would have already been pulled.

Instead he applied the universal conversational solvent: silence.

The bald man obliged. "You're Credence." It wasn't a question.

Credence was one of his aliases, though he usually employed that name a lot further south in the Cascades. Someone had been buying data. "Possible," Bashar allowed in a drawl that his mother wouldn't have recognized.

Another non-question. "You're wired high up with a lot of security."

Another non-answer. "Possible."

"We got a problem here. Thousand loonies on top of that free lunch for a little consulting on your part."

Here comes that helicopter, he thought. Was Baldie here Mr. Cairo, or had the handsome stranger flown in on that well-armed broom stick? *Interesting.* And the barback had played him. Of course she was part of local security. Anybody behind one of these bars had to be. "Don't take jobs blind," Bashar said.

"Just some talk-and-think. No black bag, no wet work."

This was what he was here for. The next step in the chain back to Lightbull and darwin. Plus money was money, and Canadian dollars spent a hell of a lot better than American dollars. It never hurt to get paid for what you were going to do anyway. "All right."

The bald man collected Bashar's pint glass and plate before leading him off into the deeper shadows.

"Table C-13."

The low-lux video sensors actually did a good job. It meant Schaadt's Shack security could see more than their patrons. He had to wonder about the surveillance booth. Cramped and loaded with gear, featuring that special scorched air scent of electronics hard at work. This seemed like a lot more tech than restaurant cash flow should be able to afford. Not to mention a lot more trouble than even a hard knocks bar ought to go to. Even more so not to mention a thousand loonies dropped as a consulting fee on a passing stranger.

In the view, Baldie-with-no-name was pointing to with a light pen, Bashar saw four young men he hadn't been able to spot from his perch at the bar. Well, probably men. Brushy mohawks, abstractly tattooed scalps, pierced foreheads. They wore a uniform, or at least identical razzle dazzle cammies. "That an urban color scheme?" he asked—everything was shades of gray on the low-lux virteo.

"No. Blue and silver. Whoever they are, these aren't city boys. That cloth won't hide you in Seattle."

Not in these woods, either, Bashar thought. "And they flew in on the rig outside."

Baldie snorted. "No one from around here is dumb enough to loiter in a clear fire zone like the sky."

"I didn't recognize the make on the helo," he admitted.

"You're not alone. We can't even get a match on Jane's."

Bashar looked over at Baldie-with-no-name and thought for a moment. Then: "I can't decide whether to be more impressed that a hick bar in the country bothers with Jane's, or that there's no match for that hardware out there."

"Don't worry about our business model. Definitely not your problem."

"No. You got that right. So why are *these* guys a problem?"

Baldie shrugged. "Been here five hours drinking."

Which could have meant they'd dirt napped someone this morning, per the bike punk.

"You worried they're likely to walk their check?"

"Laid down a card."

That would cover charges, presumably. Not much of an answer, though. It was twenty questions time, obviously. Bashar assumed this was something in the nature of a test of whether *he* was worth a thousand loonies. "Care to tell me what bothers you about the card?"

"Face of the card says Cascadia Credit Interchange." Like most commercial and consumer finance cards in this area, Bashar knew. Baldie-with-no-name went on. "Down in the encryption, it says Federated Luna Credit."

"You decrypt all your customers' cards?" Bashar asked mildly.

"Just the ones that scare the piss out of us."

"Space-based money, drinking in this joint. With a flying bomb of no known origin parked outside." He stared at the display. "What the hell are they doing *here*? More to the point, who or what are they waiting for?" *Whoever had been killed earlier that day out in the woods, almost certainly.* They hadn't done the dirt-napping, then. He'd found the other end of the string.

And this string stank. It wasn't his kind of stench. Not with darwin and Lightbull loose out there. And Cairo somewhere in the middle.

Baldie-with-no-name answered him. "You tell me, Mr. Thousand-Loonie Credence the security consultant."

"Well, in the old days I would have just capped them, then sifted their pocket lint for evidence. If I had any need for evidence."

Baldie snorted. "Not precisely an option for those of us in the restaurant business."

"You could always try talking to them," Bashar offered.

"Been there. Done that. Got nowhere."

"That barback was on top of it with me."

"Godiva?" Baldie almost smiled this time. "She's good for her age and experience, but these guys weren't buying anything she had to sell."

Bashar was briefly distracted by the idea that the barback's name had been Godiva. He couldn't even imagine who would do that to their kid.

This wasn't his deal, not no how, not no wise. But that biker had known *something*. Had known who he was, for one thing. Which even Baldie didn't seem to. Whoever the hell *this* guy was. Running a scam? Or the victim of it? Bashar had to follow the string a little further. "Want me to rumble them up? Politely."

"How are your interview skills?"

Now it was his turn to smile. "Let's find out."

"Hey, boys." Bashar approached the table with the four mohawks.

They all looked up at him with a shared, dead-eyed hostility. Troops, not officers, given that response to a perimeter intrusion. Anyone with real authority who was camped to wait for a contact would be a bit more open about it.

He tugged over an empty chair, ignoring the silent anger and the odor of spilled liquor. Bashar let his voice slip into Southern white mud mouth. Even now, in the twenty-second century, that was homeboy jive to a lot of North America's more violent weirdoes. "How about I buy the next round and y'all tell me what brings y'all to town?"

"Fuck off," one began, before another interrupted him with an outstretched hand. The corporal of this little half-squad, maybe. At least, the thinker. Genius gave Bashar a long, hard look. "Who's asking?"

"A friendly stranger." He wasn't ready to drop the Cairo name yet.

Baldie-with-no-name swept in, gun out of sight, tray stacked with five shot glasses. Bashar's would-be apple juice, by arrangement. The new booze hit the table with a series of faint plinks, bearing the paint thinner odor of what passed for Scotch whisky in these benighted days. Bashar could remember twenty-five year old Laphroaig. One of globalism's few benefits had been the widespread availability of high quality booze.

"Ain't no friendly strangers here," said the corporal, but he picked up his shot glass anyway.

"All them friendlies stranger, dear," Bashar replied. It was an old jody, a marching chant.

"Drink to that," said one of the others. They slammed their glasses. Bashar's apple juice went down warm and sweet. Something was odd about the way these guys held their liquor. Literally, as in the way they handled their glasses.

"Waitin' for someone who like to never gonna drop by," the corporal added, almost meditative. He gave Bashar a long, slow stare.

He thinks it might be me, Bashar thought. *Run with it.* "Anyone I might know? Could help you spot them."

"'S a pick up," confided the corporal's now-chatty friend. "Got to see a dog about a man."

"Four hard boys in an assault chopper? Must be a big dog. Odd sort of pick up for out here in the woods."

"Odd sort of world, downside."

These guys were fresh from high orbit, Bashar realized. *That* was an interesting thought. Cairo or no Cairo, he was suddenly a lot more interested in this string than he had been. He would owe Shadows-In-Line-With-the-Moon big when this was all over with. "You didn't fly in here, did you? You *dropped* in from on high."

"Like mother fucking angels dangling from God's dick," the corporal declared proudly.

"Long way to come to see that dog about a man," said Bashar.

"Shit don't target itself," observed their fourth with a belch.

The corporal slapped him on the shorn temple. "Shut up."

This conversation had drifted into dangerous territory. "You vacuum breathers don't need a terrain survey to target orbital kinetics," Bashar observed. He hoped like hell Baldie-with-no-name was close by. And who in their right mind would send this little crew of moron muscle in to do a pick up? "Earth's been fully satellite mapped for fifteen decades. Plus you've got the God's eye view from upstairs."

"You our man?" asked the corporal.

"Sure." Bashar had no idea what their countersigns and recognition codes were, but he knew how to run a bluff. He went on sarcastically, "That's me, wandering around loose in the Washington woods looking for a skyhook." Now was the time to try. "I'm a friend of Mr. Cairo's."

"Ah." With a knowing look, the corporal cleared his throat, and recited in the manner of one who'd been cudgeled to rote memorization. "Of man's first dis-disobedience, and the fruits of the forbidden tree, who, uh, whose . . . immortal, I mean, immoral taste brought death into the world. Um, and all our woe."

John Milton. *Paradise Lost.* Sort of, at least. Was some high school student upstairs running these fools?

Never one to let his own eccentric education go to waste, Bashar answered with the rest of the passage. "With loss of Eden, till one greater Man restore us, and regain the blissful seat, sing heavenly muse." His delivery was way better. *And* he knew all the words right.

"You got the maps?" the corporal asked.

Maps, thought Bashar. *What maps? What the hell was he talking about?* Time to bluff some more, on an empty hand. "In my head." Bashar tapped his temple and grinned. "And none of this iSys or cloud server crap. Good old fashioned meat memory." In other words, they needed him. Assuming they believed him in the first place.

"You want to ride the ride with your meatware data?" asked the corporal mildly. A sharp focus burned in his eyes. This one might be playing a part, but he wasn't as stupid as he looked. Or as his squadmates were.

This was where the string led, but Bashar was getting an awfully long way from Seattle if he went with them.

The corporal spoke again: "Drop's in about thirty hours. A lift with us is your fastest way out of the kill zone."

A cold fear passed hard down Bashar's spine, shivering from neck to hips. *Seattle.* "Lot of geography around here," he said.

The corporal answered with a shrug. "You're the man with the maps. I don't know from Elliott Bay. We've got the big rocks. You've got the big maps. That's why we're here."

"Your operational security sucks, son," Bashar told him. Cairo must have been the dead man the androgynous kid on the bike had talked about. And this was a set-up that stunk higher than last week's fish and chips.

But . . . Seattle. This was about J. Appleseed and the darwin file. It *had* to be. He had no choice but to follow the string through.

"Let's go for a ride," the corporal said.

Lightbull had killed Cascadiopolis from orbit. He was heading for orbit. There were no coincidences in this life.

From greenwiki:

Orbital Evolution, or OrbEv. The name given to forward planning for genetic drift and founder effect shifts to be expected in a permanent non-terrestrial human population.

By the eighth decade of the twenty-first century, most observers were agreed that there was a sufficiently large human population in space to be self-perpetuating in the event of a collapse of surface-to-orbit travel. Even though at that time approximately eighty percent of permanent space residents were male, this was considered valid. Consensus has firmed in the intervening decades, especially given the growth rate in space-based births at the usual roughly even gender ratios prevailing in human populations.

Even with this widening genetic base, there is still a pronounced island ecology aspect to human expansion off Earth. Crewed surface-to-orbit capabilities have dwindled, and are almost non-existent among surface-based populations, nation-states and non-state actors. Virtually all upward lift traffic is now a return trip, managed and sponsored by any of over a dozen orbital agencies and polities, Green Space Mining being the largest of those. This means Earth-to-space migration has slowed to almost a standstill, which in turns means the current non-terrestrial genetic reservoir is close to fixed.

Geneticists and anthropologists both on Earth and in orbit (GSM Institute, University of Lagrange and Luna University) have seized on this natural experiment, with its attendant extensive medical records and close monitoring of the vast majority of subjects, to both study human microevolution in realtime and to develop increasingly higher degrees-of-confidence in longer scale projections. This study with its presumed eventual real world outcomes is known as orbital evolution.

V: THE USUAL MISDIRECTIONS AND INNUENDOES AND PLAUSIBLE DENIABILITY

Bashar had not packed for a trip to orbit. Wouldn't be his first time to go commando. "Let's hit it," he told the corporal. "Time to fly."

They all stood up. Two chairs fell backward to slam loudly into the sawdust-strewn floor. Baldie-with-no-name finally caught Bashar's eye from a distance in the shadows. Bashar nodded and began herding his newfound friends toward the front door. Baldie approached with his tray.

"Your change, sir." A thousand loonies, in the waiter's hand.

Bashar slacked his pace to exchange a quick word as he slipped the cash into his own pocket. "I'm taking the problem off your hands. Anyone else comes looking for Mr. Cairo's friends, I'd appreciate it if they waited as long as possible for directions where to look next."

That earned him a surprised look from Baldie. "Better you than me."

"So it goes."

He caught up with the orbital troopies at the exit. All Bashar had time for now was a quick, coded message to Charity to let her know he would be even *more* off the grid than usual, and that he didn't expect to be safe or check in for a while.

People who went up to orbit didn't tend to come back down.

"What's it like out there?" Bashar asked the corporal.

"No dirt." The young man scuffed his boot in the gravel of the parking apron. "Not much to hide behind. You see everyone coming, good and bad, from thousands of klicks away."

"Makes securing your perimeter a whole different proposition, I guess," Bashar replied.

"You people have *plants*." The corporal sounded disgusted.

In front of them, the helicopter unfolded with a faint whine. It swelled, left and right, puffing out like one of those Japanese fish, while the rotors extended and stiffened.

"I'd been wondering," Bashar said. "It looked a little small for five."

"Rated to six butts and seven hundred kilos of passenger," said one of the other troopies.

"Which one of you is an atmosphere-rated rotary wing pilot?"

All four orbital troops laughed as they climbed in through a strangely soft and rounded access hatch. Oddly tiny for such an aircraft. Bashar wondered exactly who they worked for, whose hands he was putting himself in.

This had to be one of the stupidest stunts he'd ever pulled.

No one flew.

It couldn't be remotely operated, not with the transmission lag from orbit. No, the helicopter had an onboard AI smart enough to cope with a combat-grade take off that scrambled Bashar's internal organs, but was also probably pretty good at outrunning anything shoulder-launched.

Not that anybody was shooting at them just now. *Mirable dictu.*

The blades whirred in a buzzsaw whine like Bashar had never heard from a helicopter. Not stealthed. Something else. Hypersonic, maybe? Schaadt's Shack dropped away fast below them, tilted hard as they banked through their steep, juking climb.

He was stuck in the back between the belching drunk and the silent one. Booze and boys, a familiar set of smells. The corporal sat right seat, up front, but didn't touch anything. His other troopie stared out the windscreen as they hit turbulence.

"Atmosphere sucks," shouted the corporal over the racket of their rough ascent. "How do you people live down here?"

"At least I can step outside for a walk," Bashar shouted back. Half-wit banter with morons wasn't his thing, but he was trying to work at their level.

A *drop on Elliott Bay*. Seattle. Somebody was going to make a big, hard splash, and kill about a million people doing it.

The orbital troops laughed. "Who'd want to?" asked the drunk to his left, before, improbably, he fell asleep.

To Bashar's surprise, they were still climbing hard. The little helicopter clawed for altitude. No one but him seemed worried—the interior smelled of plastic and that strange, musty scent of nanotech, but not the reek of fear. No flop sweat here.

"Where's our pick up?" he asked. Truth be told, he wasn't sure how people in orbit got down to the surface any more. Well, fall bags. Everybody knew about those low-tech nightmares. But how they got down when they also planned to climb back out of the gravity well again.

Not in helicopters, he was fairly certain of that at least.

"High dive," said the corporal, as if that actually explained anything.

Bashar decided that ignorance was the better part of valor. He didn't think he'd like the answer anyway.

They still climbed. Time passed with a frantic unspooling only he could hear. The drunk snored. The silent one stared out the window. Up front, the corporal hummed. Mount Rainier loomed below them off to the starboard. To the north he could see Glacier Peak and Mount Baker. How *high* were they?

The buzz saw whine trailed off, to be followed by a whipping noise as the helicopter tossed once, twice, then settled into a silent, slinging arc.

"Blades folding," shouted the corporal helpfully.

So far as Bashar could tell, they were in ballistic flight now. An aerodynamic rock, fifteen or twenty thousand meters up.

Something aft kicked in, and they weren't ballistic any more. The horizon swiftly acquired a distinctly multitoned look, not to mention a pronounced curvature. He was seeing the top of the sky. For the first time in his life, Bashar found himself at the edge of motion sickness.

Higher still they went. He thought he could spot the Great Plains.

Another bulletin from the front seat: "Hang on, it's gonna get weird."

The drunk stirred, the silent troopie turned to Bashar with a sickly, tense grin.

"Have you ever done this before?" Bashar asked him.

"Hell no," whispered the troopie. Kid, in fact. Bashar had whipped hundreds like him into line over the decades.

The kid went on: "We train, a lot. High gravity gym, drop-and-lift simulations. Got to build up bone density and muscle tone for one-gee operations. But even high rez VR ain't the same." He sounded ready to panic.

"Just nerves," Bashar said with the tough unsympathy of a drill sergeant. "Keep your mission in mind and close your eyes if you think you need to. Too late to walk home now."

That cracked the kid up with the edged laughter of hysteria. It also kept him focused on Bashar instead of the increasingly curved horizon outside.

No wonder the drunk was sleeping. And now he understood the tiny hatch. Air pressure differential was a real issue for this craft.

Then the boost cut out, and they were ballistic once more. High up. Very high up. Bashar felt lightweight and ill in his seat. He strained against the straps and wondered quite seriously if this were a rather baroque assassination plot.

Something big and dark moved above them, barely visible at first from his seat. He saw a pointed nose ahead of theirs.

"Mommy's come to gather us up, boys," said the corporal with a tone of relieved and nervous satisfaction.

They slammed upward, hard. Everything went dark outside and in except the control panel lights, which painted the corporal's face with a sickly orange underglow just shy of demonic.

About ninety uncomfortable minutes later the lights came back on outside. Two figures in pressure suits crowded into a tiny bay that was barely larger than the helicopter itself. Or whatever this machine was—"helicopter" was a grossly insufficient description. One pointed an instrument at them while the other rather incongruously waved, as if saying hello to friends in a boat.

Bashar had no particular urge to wave back, but the corporal was apparently happy to do so.

After a minute or two of whatever sweep was being performed, their little round hatch opened. Unstrapping, Bashar found himself on the loose in microgravity for the first time in his life. His gut flopped twice, then settled. That was a small mercy, as he didn't want to barf cheese tempura and elk salami all over the interior. He was third through, after the corporal and his front seat passenger, being boosted from the back by the scared kid. Bashar tried to avoid windmilling his arms or otherwise making a touristic hazard of himself.

One of the pressure suited types propelled him out of the tiny bay and through another hatch. That opened onto a corridor with all four surfaces padded and grab rails running along them. The air here smelled weirdly clean, like glass would if it had an odor.

"No gravity ever?" Bashar asked.

"Not here." The woman in front of him was dark-skinned, grey-eyed, shaven-headed and deeply suspicious. "Who the hell are you?"

"The map man," he said pointedly.

"Ah, Mr. Biòu. The other one, whom we were not expecting."

Biòu? Who the hell was Biòu? "I, well, took over the franchise. Decided it was better to come in person."

"Mr. Franchise, I hope you like it here in orbit. You're going to be a permanent resident. However long it is you wind up staying."

A woman after his own heart. Time to act like he belonged in this place. "I need a briefing."

"Everybody needs something," she said unsympathetically. "A lucky few even get it."

She turned and swarmed along the corridor, which curved upward. Bashar started after the woman, trying to mimic her hand-over-hand grip on the rails. He got himself moving in the right direction but slipped loose to bounce twice off the padding before he could get a firm grasp. Someone behind him laughed.

We're all new once, son, he thought. *You try this for the first time at my age.*

At least he was inside the perimeter. Bashar followed the woman, attempting to figure out why anyone had thought those four clowns were good security at the entry point. Life in orbit had to be the ultimate in know-your-neighbor security. Maybe these people just didn't have procedures for infiltrators.

Was that degree of laxness even possible?

He wound up seated—with a strap to keep him there against microgravity—on one of a semicircle of chairs facing a large virteo monitor in a small and otherwise featureless room. The woman who'd met him was present, along with a hard-bitten, whipcord thin Asian man who could almost have been Bashar's age, and a much younger and doughier man—another kid, in truth—with pink eyes and brittle hair who seemed to be suffering from a metabolic disorder. He smelled like it, too.

"I'm Moselle," said his host. "That's Lu," she pointed at the Asian man. Then a negligent wave toward the albino. "Bibendum."

"I'm Credence," Bashar said. It was the name he'd wound up using at Schaadt's Shack, and thus, at least in a sense, a verifiable identity. These people might be strangely naïve about physical security, but he'd bet every Euro he'd ever possessed that they were at the razor's edge on data security.

"Credence today, Mr. Biòu. Where's Feeney?"

That was the recently deceased, presumably. "Dead." Killed by trees, he had become fairly certain. The other possibility was the mysterious and possibly nonexistent Mr. Cairo. His voice freighted with the conviction of a truly bald-faced lie, Bashar went on. "Caught in a dope grower's cross-fire two days ago. I knew he had the meet up at Schaadt's Shack. So I went to keep it. Sorry, I'm a little short on countersigns and secret plans."

"Hmm." She glanced at Lu and Bibendum, then back at Bashar. "I trust you have the maps?"

"Depends," said Bashar. "Which maps do you need?"

"We can handle the blast distribution and hydrological calculations from geophysical survey data. We need the *locations.* Those AIs are not to be trusted with telling us everything."

J. Appleseed's AIs, he thought, *she had to mean them.* What he said was: "Maps of how far Elliott Bay will splash? I'm not playing stupid, Ms. Moselle. Remember, I'm filling in here for Feeney, who never told me your objectives. Just that you needed confidential Seattle location data that wasn't available in the cloud."

That was his best approximation of what they were seeking. Based on the slight relaxation from both Moselle and Lu, he figured he'd guessed close enough to right. Bibendum kept staring not quite at him with unblinking pale-pink eyes. Bashar wondered if the kid was blind.

"Our friends at Appleseed want to appear to have been wiped out," Lu said. Bashar could have shouted for the confirmation of the connection. Lu went on:

"We need to ensure that enough force gets applied to crack the foundation's deep vaults, down in the bedrock. That's in our contract with them. But we strongly suspect them of hiding additional resources, with the intention of surviving the blast and emerging to shift blame to us."

Bashar's mind raced ahead. Blame? For the island plagues? Making the orbital Greens into history's greatest villains instead of J. Appleseed. When you were bent on wiping out the human race anyway, who cared about getting the credit? "Not that this is any of my business," he said, "but aren't there better ways to take out a small cluster of known sites than nuking an entire metropolitan area?"

"You're right," said Moselle. "It's not any of your business, Mr. Biòu. But as it happens, we aren't nuking anybody."

"Just a rock," said Bibendum in an unexpectedly gravelly voice. Somehow, Bashar had figured on a piping squeak.

Then he put it all together. "You're about to drop a mining package on them. It's the biggest orbital kinetic strike in history." This would be the destruction of Cascadiopolis all over again, but writ oh so very large.

"Biggest *human-targeted* orbital kinetic strike in history," Moselle corrected. "Now, let us speak of the offices of J. Appleseed."

From greenwiki:

Green Space. Refers to the privately funded Earth-to-orbit heavy lift initiative that placed almost two hundred launches into orbit over a four-decade period between 2077 and 2115. Each launch series is referred to by the code GSO, for Green Space Operations, followed by a number signifying the program year. Individual missions are numbered within their launch year, so the very first launch was GSO-01-01, while the final launch was GSO-28-09.

The entire project was defined as a closed-ended solution dedicated to placing sufficient heavy manufacturing capacity into orbit to allow boot strapping of long term, self-sustaining, space-based industrialization with minimal further launch requirements from the Earth's surface. All spacecraft were controlled by a combination of onboard automation and remote command, and the vast majority of the launches were uncrewed. However, a limited number of crew capsules were boosted to orbit as part of the cargo payload. Green Space never experienced a catastrophic failure during any operational launches.

The Green Space project has been considered a success by outside observers. Highly visible program outcomes include the Curiosity asteroid tug program, as well as the Lagrange-G refineries, both dedicated to mining of asteroidal resources placed in high Earth orbit. The stated purpose of this effort was to provide for minerals and resource extraction which inflicted minimal waste processes on the terrestrial biosphere. The less widely acknowledged longer-term goal appears to be development of a permanent human space presence with a sufficiently deep population base to serve as a long term reservoir for species preservation and genetic diversity.

The primary funders of Green Space have never stepped forward for formal comment, and thus all discussion of these goals is inherently speculative. From a technical perspective, Green Space for the most part leveraged the abandoned United States Air

Force infrastructure at the site of the former Vandenberg Air Force Base in California. Launch and orbit control was managed from remote facilities spread throughout Cascadia. A limited number of launches, in the GSO-19 through GSO-24 series, were conducted under contract with the Reformed China National Space Administration through their Xichang launch complex.

VI: EIGHTY WAS NOT SO OLD, IF ONE'S BODY WAS NOT CONSPIRING AGAINST ONE'S SELF

Charity contemplated Bashar's most recent message. He'd *been* downstate, she knew that much. Talking to trees and what not. She'd even received a polite note from Shadows-In-Line-With-the-Moon, along with a gift certificate to Harry and David that the grove had thoughtfully sent along for vegetable reasons of its own.

Trees were weird but considerate. You got that way if it took dozens of you thinking together to finish a sentence.

But now . . . ? Where in the hell was he? How could a man who'd lived off the grid for almost a century go even *more* off the grid?

Following either darwin or Lightbull, of course. Bashar hadn't needed to say that. But where was he?

So far as Charity knew, her husband had never left North America in his life. Intercontinental travel was either too regulated and monitored, or simply too slow. The gyre-runners were about as anonymous as one got, but a whole year to get from San Diego to Osaka just wasn't the speed at which Bashar moved.

Mexico City, maybe, chasing a new thread on the long-stale Lightbull satellite lead. That was far enough outside his usual Cascadian haunts to be considered more off the grid. Except these days Mexico City was just as wired as Seattle, maybe even more so. The old economic divides between north and south had melted with the climate shifts and the slow collapse of the industrialized West. The Green movement knew no bounds.

It wasn't as if the *Distrito Federal* wasn't just as gridded as the rest of the world. And the Cascadiopolis daughter-cities extended down into the Sierra Madre Occidental. He'd have friends that far south.

So, not Mexico.

North? Bashar didn't like being cold. Charity just couldn't see her husband headed for Alaska or the Yukon, even if the Greens were so thick on the ground there that the old-school statists had long since decamped for the Great Plains and other areas more supportive of recidivism. Besides which, what was up there anyway?

Maybe he had hopped an airship bound for somewhere more distant.

Tired of chasing darwin and Lightbull in circles, Charity put some more of her resources into chasing her husband instead. She had the advantage of knowing he was still out there with his head down, and roughly where he was last to be found.

And if this *didn't* have something to do with the problem of stopping the island plagues, she would skin him alive. Or at least have Malik do it.

Shavonne, one of the relief nurses, woke her much later. Charity never could keep track of time in her head anymore—another of those subtle penalties of aging which drove her half-crazy.

She managed to form a coherent question. "What?"

"You have a visitor, ma'am." Shavonne was a quiet Afro-Irish immigrant whose parents had fled some round of European purges or another. The girl wasn't ever able to be as comfortable with Charity as Malik managed. Charity's personal theory was that something about herself signaled "authority" and short-circuited any sociable tendencies that might otherwise be lurking in the nurse's subconscious.

"I don't get visitors," Charity said, bleary-eyed and bleary-brained. Her location wasn't precisely a secret, but neither was it something she cared to have known. Being effectively immobilized by medical science was a hell of a security problem, and one of the reasons she and Bashar had agreed to part ways these past years, regardless of their feelings for one another. "Who is it?"

"Can't rightly say, ma'am." Shavonne sometimes let herself be a bit overly rulebound, Charity knew from experience.

"Are they cleared?"

"Site security passed him up to the ward."

After a quiet, exasperated moment, Charity asked, "Him *who*?"

"Says his name is Joel Cairo."

"Right, and I'm Ruth Wonderly."

Shavonne's bushy ginger eyebrows drew up. "Who?"

Charity sighed. "Never mind, just send him in." If this was a hit, simply declining to see the man wasn't going to change much. Anyone who could get through site security could get through Shavonne, not to mention Charity's door. On the other hand, if this was a legitimate visit, at . . . she checked the virteo display by her bed—four in the morning? . . . well, she was beyond curious at this point.

Joel Cairo proved to be a compact, fit man so bald he might be suffering from alopecia. And possibly the whitest man she'd seen in a long time. Aryan Bund recruiting poster white.

"You're a hard woman to find, Ms. Oxham," he said.

"And you've been dead a century and a half, Mr. Lorre."

Cairo chuckled. "No one ever gets it."

"A bit flashy, for an alias?"

His chuckle broadened to a smile. "Do you know how many James Bonds I've met over the years?"

She had to ask. "Were they any *good*?"

"You have a point. Some of them did become grave men on the morrow."

"Spare me the horrors of a classical education," Charity said tartly. "If you're here for a hit, get it over with. Otherwise, speak your piece. I'm old and sick and want to go back to sleep."

"You're connected to Bashar." Cairo's voice was flat, all business now.

A flutter of fear stirred within her. "You wouldn't ask me that if you didn't already know."

"I wasn't asking."

"So?"

He continued: "I saw your husband yesterday."

Interesting, thought Charity. "Not many people ever realize they've seen Bashar. At least not the ones who live to talk about it later."

"He was using the name Credence."

"My husband always was the man of a thousand faces." Or a thousand names, more to the point.

"Bashar ever use the alias Lon Chaney?"

"Some people aren't so in love with their cleverness as you are, Mr. Cairo. *Why are you telling me this?*"

"Because you've been pulling searches and asking questions that point to something I care about deeply." Cairo frowned. "I shot a messenger yesterday so Mr. Credence could get a ride in her place. The messenger will be missed, but she'll never be found."

"We've all killed people." Memories of Charity's time in Tehran drifted through her head. A lot of blood and screaming back in her army days. "That doesn't impress me."

"This will impress you: the late messenger was from Lightbull."

Charity's heart fluttered all over again, to the point where the medical alarms began complaining. She closed her eyes and controlled her breathing. *Center, center, center.*

The door cracked open. "You all right in there, Ms. Oxham?" Shavonne asked nervously.

"Yes, thanks. We're just talking."

After long moment, the door clicked shut again. Malik would have been more . . . demonstrative . . . in his attentions. But she didn't need rescuing. Nor medical intervention. Not here and now.

Charity took a long look at the man who called himself Joel Cairo. "Perhaps you and I do have much to discuss, sir."

"Yes. For one thing, Samira Bashar Oxham is going to die in . . ." His stare unfocused briefly as Mr. Cairo checked some internal data feed. "Twenty-three hours, forty-two minutes and eleven seconds. Plus or minus ten minutes." His stare focused on her. "She and about a million other people. Unless your husband can do something to stop it."

"Even Bashar can't turn back a nuke," Charity said sadly.

"Not that. Bigger. Much bigger." Cairo leaned closer, investing his personal energy into her social space. "The zero-pop kill is coming."

"City killers? Not the island plagues?" She bit back her next words, knowing she'd already given away too much.

"Yes and yes." His hand raised as if to touch her, then paused. "I had to work with Bashar because there was no time for anything but improvisation. Your husband happens to be a world-class expert at improvisational problem solving."

"Does he know why you're working with him?" Charity asked.

"No." Cairo's smile was bleak. "A mutual friend helped Bashar find his way. Is there anyone else you'd rather have trying to stop this?"

Her answering smile was as wintry as his, Charity knew. "No, not really." *Me in the old days,* she thought but did not say. "What will you do if he can't stop it?"

"We—I—have someone on the inside of this. Work with them, you can do more than lie here and trip data alarms. So much more, Charity Oxham."

VII: WE'RE DEFINITELY IN MEATSPACE

Bashar thought very, very fast. Around eleven thousand tons of rock was going to make a damned big splash wherever it landed. They didn't drop mining packages anywhere in Cascadia—wrong hydrography for it. Except the eastern end of the Gulf of Alaska, but no one would ever get the environmental clearances needed to make that big a mess in the vicinity of Glacier Bay. Not to mention affording the fines and fees from the oceanic wildlife and coastal forest natural entities.

Seattle.

His daughter Samira.

Hell.

He knew where and what and now even why. J. Appleseed wanted a rock dropped on their hide, to hide their tracks with darwin. These guys wanted the rock to be more accurate than J. Appleseed's data, in case of a double-cross. Lightbull probably won either way. That would be how a conspiracy of that nature thought.

No matter how it came out, the losers were Seattle first, the human race second.

Bashar would have to find some way to stop this. His mouth moved distinctly from his thoughts. Even at his current age, he could still multitask well enough to spin convincing bullshit. "J. Appleseed's distributed. It's not like they have an office building downtown."

"Well of course they're distributed," wheezed Bibendum.

There was something damned unnerving about that boy. If this was what very many of the orbit-born looked like, then the hard Greens would have to rethink their whole genetic reservoir concept.

The strange, pale kid continued, "None of this would work if they weren't. But we need to eliminate the computing cores and all the pre-virtualization infrastructure. Now. Get them out of there. If anything survives, even if the AIs don't double cross us, somebody might find enough evidence to stop the plans."

Which would be too damned bad if the island plagues didn't happen world wide, Bashar told himself. He held his tongue this time.

Lu called up a street-and-infrastructure map of the Seattle metro area on the virteo projection. With a few flicks of his fingers, a series of red spots and dots overlaid the intertwined grids of roads and pathways and core data pipes.

J. Appleseed. All of it. The 4th Avenue offices he'd so recently been ejected from. The computing cores he'd helped secrete within the city's telecommunications infrastructure some decades back. As well as various warehouses, training facilities and satellite offices. The dots, Bashar realized, were the home locations of remote workers.

Darwin and Appleseed came together here. No wonder they'd bounced him hard from the offices. Somebody high up must have believed he'd twigged to what was coming. Which, in a sense, he had, but not to this degree of detail.

Moselle spoke up as she traced the red overlays with a light pen. "That's our intel from about two weeks ago, per the Appleseed AIs. Obviously we have the inside material, but we also know that J. Appleseed has a lot of right and left hands that don't communicate very well. Our sources are the highest, but given that parts of the organization run on the classic cell system, even the top doesn't know everything about what its various tentacles are doing." Her grin owed much to sharks and hyenas. "We're told you people do."

"Nobody knows everything," Bashar temporized. He took a shot, adding, "Not even *us*."

"Organizational modesty is a new vector for you," Moselle observed with some obvious surprise.

Who precisely did these people think he worked for? Or with? He tried another shot. "The appearance of infallibility has its uses, but we're down to targeting time here. Clarity trumps propaganda."

Bibendum laughed. His mirth was as grating as his speech. "You're a contractor. Or maybe a convert. None of the birthright Bull Dancers would ever say anything like that."

The world cracked open inside Bashar's head. He felt like a man who'd stopped to pick up a twig on the beach and discovered it was the least extension of a huge log buried in the sand.

The Bull Dancers.

Lightbull.

And it all came together for him in an implosion of insight. J. Appleseed and Lightbull cooperating to spread the island plague. A hidden hard Green agenda behind his life's work with the foundation, not to mention everyone else's. They planned to crack Seattle like an egg to cover their tracks. Not just J. Appleseed's tracks. Lightbull's tracks using the foundation as a front. Which meant the zero-pop rewilding plan hadn't passed the tipping point yet.

The world could still be saved.

The whole business made a horrific sense. These people had been hired to fake the destruction of J. Appleseed by creating a disaster on an epic scale, that would bury the evidence forever beneath a mountain of hot rock, steam and ash, with a million bodies to keep the alleged corpse of the foundation company. A million bodies who'd done nothing to deserve a stone dropped on them from heaven.

Except they wanted to destroy the infrastructure for real. Leave no pockets undisturbed. Which would free Lightbull to go into a radical metastasis and begin the process of launching the island plagues and pursuing zero population. With Seattle a cauldron of hot ash, no one in a position to stop the plan would be able to uncover any evidence in time to be useful.

That was *never* what they were about. Lightbull had to have suborned the foundation and its AIs decades ago. Perhaps even back when William Silas Crown was alive, Bashar realized, recollecting some of the irregular behavior of the triplet AIs near the end of Crown's life, when the two of them had briefly been in contact one last time.

He swept the room with his best staff meeting stare, what a colleague used to call his "speaker-to-morons" look. These people thought he was one of *them*. One of the Bull Dancers who had destroyed his beloved Cascadiopolis all those years ago. That gang of idiots with the helicopter-rocket down at Schaadt's Shack had been waiting for a contact from Lightbull. Instead, they'd got him.

Everybody eventually made a terminal error. Bashar would do his level best to make sure that taking him into orbit had been theirs.

"*You* don't know what kinds of things I'd say, Mr. Bibendum." He used his coldest voice. A century of being a hard man gave Bashar a tone of authority few could match.

The pink-eyed kid shrank back for the first time. Perhaps no one ever pushed him hard.

Live and learn, Bashar thought with a vicious glee. "Light pen?" he snapped at Moselle.

She tossed him hers. In the microgravity of the conference room, it flew oddly. "Where are we headed right now, by the way?" he asked, with a nod toward the bulkhead.

The look she gave him told Bashar he'd almost blown his newfound cover with that question. "Orbital Zero. Where else?"

The larger of the two asteroids was being gutted by Green Space Mining for minerals while simultaneously being hollowed out for long-term habitats. Where the mining packages came from. "Not GSO Prime?"

Moselle grunted and exchanged an unreadable-to-Bashar glance with Lu. Bibendum just glowered.

Bashar turned his attention to the map, still thinking furiously. As a site consultant, he had no power here. He was just a data source and a form of verification. But playing the role of a representative of Lightbull, he could wield their power. Perhaps even authority, depending on who'd precisely contracted this job.

"You've got most of the coverage correct here." He traced the same series of hotspots Moselle had minutes earlier.

She glared at him. "All major infrastructure, distributed as it is, has been accounted for."

The AIs were the core of J. Appleseed. Crown's old triumvirate of Heinlein, Hubbard, and Kornbluth, supplemented by the rest of the board of directors. There hadn't been a human seated on that board in forty years or more. And AIs could live, well, anywhere their code was compiled and running and properly hardened.

Like cores embedded in Seattle's subterranean infrastructure.

Or anywhere with enough processing power. In a grove of trees. Inside someone's head.

Anywhere at all.

"You're missing some physical plant." He picked a random location in Bellevue, across Lake Washington from Seattle proper. They wouldn't have time to do spot checks on the ground. Bashar hoped. "Even J. Appleseed has motor pools, maintenance shops, that kind of thing." Another random location in the Queen Anne district. He stared at the map a long moment as his thoughts continued to race ahead.

"Mr. Bìòu?" prompted Moselle.

"Apologies." Bashar pulled himself abruptly back to the discussion. He could die here, at any time, for a moment's inattention, or just the wrong word. He wondered what the first name of his cover alias was supposed to be. Damn it, he hadn't been in this deep with this little preparation since, well, ever. "I was just thinking about the blast shadow of Capitol Hill. You drop your rock in Elliott Bay, you won't hit Bellevue with enough force to wipe it. You've only got eleven thousand tons, and you're coming in shallow. That's admittedly a damned big kinetic payload, but we're not talking the Chicxulub dinosaur killer here. I can't think your crater will be more than a few hundred yards wide."

"About a kilometer, actually." Lu said, "We're not trying to nail the whole West Coast with this one. We did consider a strike on Capitol Hill, but that doesn't bring enough impact into downtown Seattle where our critical targets are concentrated."

The AIs would be getting out, Bashar thought. There must be physical evidence they're concerned about, one-and-done stuff stored as single-copy security in the buried server rooms of J. Appleseed.

"The seawall," muttered Bibendum.

"What he means," Moselle added, "is that we want to strike Elliott Bay immediately west of the seawall. The resultant flooding will significantly confuse the issue."

"What if you come in shallow and skip?" asked Bashar. "Like what happened to Sault Sainte Marie. Nail the bay, then drop the payload on top of or behind Capitol Hill?"

Bibendum fluttered his eyes. "Math on the skip isn't reliable."

Moselle nodded. "The degree of confidence on a direct strike is high. Anything else is too complex."

"And," Bibendum added, "we won't be putting enough kinetic energy into the bay with a skip. It'll make an unholy mess, but not big enough."

Bashar could appreciate the problem, even from the other side of it. "Then you'll need to content yourself with obliterating the downtown targets and hope no one cares too much about the outlying locations." He glanced at the map again. "All the old computing cores are downtown."

The conversation devolved into an hour's discussion of precise locations of particular facilities, and their known purposes as well as likely occupants. *Such as his daughter.* At least Charity was tucked away far enough from Seattle to avoid the direct consequences of such a strike.

Most of what he said was even true, within the context of a certain desperation.

Could he somehow make a secure, anonymous data connection out of this spaceship that his hosts wouldn't know about? He knew how to tap comsats from the surface, but the channels he relied on weren't listening for orbit-to-orbit signals.

Bashar realized desperately that he didn't understand nearly enough about the orbital infrastructure to make a sensible move. He *had* to be away from these people.

"When we arrive at Orbital Zero, I will inspect the mining package," he finally announced.

"Why?" Moselle's voice was flat and hostile.

Bashar stared her down. "So my report will be as complete as possible."

Bibendum stirred again. "Let him. You know how the damned Bull Dancers are. And we'll be living with *them* for a long, long time."

Which confirmed what he'd already suspected—*these* people weren't Lightbull.

How many of the hard Greens were? Bashar let his grin grow feral once more. All three of his putative colleagues shrank back.

"I'll . . . I'll need clearance," Moselle said weakly.

"Lady," Bashar told her, "we're the people who *issue* clearances."

From greenwiki:

Earth-to-orbit and orbit-to-Earth transport. Since the end of the sponsored heavy lift era at the conclusion of the GSO project, the vast majority of Earth-to-orbit launches are via lighter-than-air vehicles carrying booster sleds to 30,000 meters or higher, then dropping them for independent burn-to-orbit. A few very large corporations and still functional governments have preserved limited classic heavy lift functionality for essentially strategic purposes, but as most non-crewed space assets are now in the form of cube sats or pebble swarms, demand for such heavy lift is infrequent. Space-based industrial capacity has expanded to the point that with the available resources from the Project Precious asteroids, it is generally cheaper to manufacture or construct additional required infrastructure in situ. This is increasingly true at higher mass tiers. The exception to this trend is the limited number of orbital weapons platforms still maintained by the remnants of the 20th and 21st century great powers.

Re-entry is of course another proposition entirely. With the notable exception of the mining packages themselves, there tends to be very little justification for dropping mass back down Earth's gravity well. The orbital population practices an intense re-use/recycle ethic that meets or exceeds even that of the most dedicated terrestrial Green communities. Human beings are the primary orbit-to-Earth payload, and most of them are returned either via glider or fall bag. Fall bags are a far more expeditious re-entry path than orbital gliders, but plummeting a hundred kilometers to the ground in a sealed environment the size of a small camping tent is a psychological challenge for a surprisingly large percentage of travelers.

VIII: MINOAN WOMEN AND ROMAN MYSTERY CULTS AND THE CORRIDA AND THE AMERICAN STOCK MARKET

A number of questions cascaded through Charity's head. She cursed her perpetual mild fuddlement—a gift of aging, and the medications that helped keep her alive now.

She picked one that seemed safer than pursuing Cairo's request for her assistance. "How would you know that the messenger you killed was from Lightbull? Bashar's been looking for Lightbull for decades and has never yet found a lead that solid."

"Your husband should have listened more closely to William Silas Crown when he was alive." Cairo tugged the rollaway stool the nurses used close to her bed and sat down. "Crown nearly had it right."

"Lightbull doesn't get found unless it wants to be found." She paused, her thoughts drifting in a dangerous direction. "Or are you one of the Bull Dancers?" Everything seemed ready to collapse in on itself, all the old paranoias and conspiracy theories.

Cairo laughed, his amusement seeming genuine. "I am with Lightbull, yes. But never a Bull Dancer. I have neither the right genetics nor the right sponsors to become one of them, Mrs. Charity Oxham. You have to be born and raised into *that* lineage. The rest of us are just . . . agents of destiny."

Charity set that thought aside for very careful review at some future point.

He continued: "Consider this—every organization has many hands. They do not all communicate. Or agree. The Greens come in hard and soft varieties, yes?"

"Of course." She and Bashar had been aligned with the soft Greens all along. That agenda had worked through J. Appleseed since Crown's death had swollen the foundation's funding with the bequest of his rather considerable fortune. Not to mention his trio of emancipated AIs.

"You might imagine that while all the Bull Dancers leap the horns of fate, if not of an actual bull, they do not all follow the same beat."

"Bashar always thought Tygre Tygre had come from you," Charity told him.

"Which 'you' do you mean?" asked Cairo. "Our name is legion, for we are many."

"Many but few. Conspiracies don't last when they're run by committee."

Cairo's voice dropped. "Minoan Crete was a very, very long time ago."

"And why are you telling me all of this?" Charity demanded. "Or any of it, for that matter?"

"So you will believe me when I say that thirty-eight centuries of effort comes to a head tomorrow. Not everyone who dances believes this is how the measure should be brought to a close." He leaned toward her again. "And you can help those of us who oppose this effort."

It was her turn to laugh. "You expect me to believe that some Bronze Age cult planned to nuke Seattle four thousand years in their future?"

"No." Patience loomed in Cairo's voice."That would be stupid. I hope you will believe that a Bronze Age cult survived, pursuing one end then another, to evolve into something that has an effect on the modern world. The Catholic Church has been around for over two thousand years. How much more improbable is this?"

Charity stared at him. "And after almost four thousand years of secrecy, you decide to come out to me now?"

Cairo shrugged. "How secret is secret? Ever seen the statue of the Bowling Green Bull on Wall Street? We've always been here. Always been visible for those with the right eyes. But now . . . Let me get to the point. Your darwin file is correct but incomplete. Lightbull is behind that effort, working through J. Appleseed."

"You've done something to make Bashar disappear," Charity said. "He's gone to ground somewhere."

"Oh, quite the opposite of going to ground, I assure you. He's in orbit right now. Trying to keep thousands of tons of rock from dropping on Seattle."

She was rarely at a loss for words, but that news was just bizarre. ". . . Bashar? In orbit?"

"If you'd like, I can probably open a low bandwidth channel to him."

"Yes," Charity said unthinking. Then: "No. I don't want to compromise him. And I have to understand. How will him stopping that rock from hitting Seattle keep the island plague from being released worldwide?"

"It won't," said Cairo simply. "It will just keep the people behind the island plague from effecting an undetectable disappearance. Then, maybe, they can be dealt with before it's too late. Cures may be possible, but only with all the relevant records and research in hand as swiftly as possible. Like I said, we have . . . someone . . . inside. But they cannot work alone."

"You couldn't have done this sooner?" Charity asked.

"These were contingency plans until quite recently. Subject to much disputation. I wasn't willing to betray my trust for possibilities. Now, well, it is all becoming real. And so treason is born."

She thought about that for a little while. "Do you have a ride into orbit yourself, Mr. Cairo? Or are you in the hard Green death camp with the rest of us?"

His smile was thin that time. "Well, and that would be another problem with zero population rewilding, wouldn't it? And so we come to here and now. Where I need your help."

"What's in it for me?" Charity asked.

He shrugged. "Saving the world? Some justice for Cascadiopolis." Cairo pulled a small vial from his pocket, the frosted silver sheen of a nanomed carrier catching her eye. "And perhaps the fountain of youth." That was accompanied by a wink bordering on the lascivious. "William Silas Crown was not the only one with good medical tech."

She cleared her throat, feeling her pulse pound to a heady mix of panic, hope and dread. "I think I would like to speak to my husband after all, if I can do so without compromising him."

IX: THEY BOMBED YOU FROM ORBIT JUST TO MAKE THEIR POINT?

Bashar was discovering the hard way that it was impossible to fake expertise in handling himself in microgravity. Neither Lu nor Bibendum seemed to expect anything better from him, so presumably his cover identity didn't include any history of orbital operations.

They were hand-over-handing down a series of corridors aboard Orbital Zero itself. He'd assumed rock tunnels, but what he saw didn't look much different from the corridors on the carrier ship that had snagged the Earth-to-orbit rocket copter he'd ridden up on. It even smelled the same. Bashar was desperate to ask questions, but didn't dare.

"Mining control is already in late countdown," Lu said over his shoulder. "You won't be able to make a long inspection."

Long inspection, short inspection, it didn't matter. Bashar wanted to *see* the damned thing, figure out if there was anything he could do to stop or even redirect it. Not that a rock drop inland would be much of an improvement, but he could at least reduce the body count. As well as keeping these clowns from covering whatever tracks they planned to cover with the strike.

And Samira. His Sooboo.

He didn't figure on being able to influence the rock drop directly, but maybe he could talk his way into mining control afterward, and . . . what? Take on an entire habitat's worth of experienced microgravity dwellers in hand-to-hand combat?

If he ever saw Baldie-with-no-name again, Bashar promised himself he'd beat the man blue, then extract a forced if retroactive briefing from that smiling little bastard.

"Suits," Lu announced, as they fetched up against a heavy metal door. "Bibendum will take you through the safety drill."

"You're not coming?" Bashar was in fact relieved, as the pudgy and indifferent Bibendum was someone he could probably handle even in microgravity. Not Lu, whose physique and style of movement showed all the signs of being an extremely old school ass kicker. With the emphasis on *old*, but Bashar was perfectly well aware of what an old guy could do. It took one to know one.

"I don't go Outside much," Lu admitted.

"Kenophobe," Bibendum put in. He couldn't keep the sneer out of his voice. "Fear of the void. A lot of people get seriously jittered Outside."

Lu said nothing, but Bashar wouldn't have cared to be on the receiving end of the look he gave Bibendum. Should the kid meet with an accident Outside, here was one man who wouldn't mourn long.

Belatedly, it occurred to Bashar to wonder if he himself was kenophobic.

Suit drill took about fifteen minutes. It covered everything from breathing patterns to the external emergency purge-and-pop switch meant to be used for rapid extraction in dire situations. Bashar was acutely aware of time crawling, of knowing the launch was in final countdown, of being as badly out of place as he'd ever been in his adult life. Every word, every movement up here in orbit, was him faking it.

Undercover wasn't a problem. He'd spent literally decades undercover. Being under a cover he didn't understand in a location he had no information about made him crazy.

At least it was that idiot Bibendum who was droning through the safety precautions and handling instructions. Not Moselle or Lu, who were far more dangerous to him personally. Bashar paid attention—he wasn't suicidally stupid—but still his mind raced.

The next unstupid thing he needed to do was stop thinking of Bibendum as an idiot. The kid wouldn't have been tasked to his reception team if he was. Slow and doughy didn't mean foolish. Or even not dangerous. If nothing else, it was Bibendum who knew all those little things like the airlock passcodes and the pressure suit safety margins. This kid could kill Bashar simply by not speaking up.

"I gave you an all-purpose suit," Bibendum told him near the end of the safety lecture.

"Why?" asked Bashar.

"Cheaper than the mission-specific equipment. If you find some new way to hurt it or yourself, less of a problem for the rest of us."

Bashar was momentarily diverted by sheer intellectual curiosity. "What's the difference between the suit types?"

"There's engineering suits, and mining suits, and long-duration suits. Those last ones are basically tiny little shuttles in their own right. Each type carries tools and equipment appropriate to the job. What you've got? Rated to seventy-two hours for use in re-entry applications." Bibendum giggled. "Takes a long time to get down by glider. And they have basic atmospheric capabilities, for escape if a re-entry goes wrong. But minimally powered here in orbit. Don't go jetting around. You'll run out of juice and have three days to be real sorry about it before you die of asphyxiation."

"Surely you have search-and-rescue capabilities."

"All depends on the priority. You've already validated the target maps, after all."

That was an unambiguous statement of his current importance in the local scheme of things. Not to mention a nicely veiled threat. Well, in truth, not even all that veiled.

Then they went Outside.

After about two minutes of being towed by the little booster sled Bibendum was piloting, Bashar recovered his wits. The Earth was . . . huge. And blue. None of the photography and virteography he'd seen over the years did this view even the remotest justice. The Moon was somewhere else, not in his line of sight, but Orbital Zero stood close and big.

And the stars. The cold, unblinking stars. It wasn't hard to see where Lu got his terror from. This was like looking down a well the size of the Universe and wondering why you weren't falling in. Still, Bashar didn't think he shared Lu's kenophobia.

Just a respect for the depth of the tumble he'd take if he missed his step up here.

"Nice view, huh?" Bibendum's voice crackled over a dedicated suit-to-suit channel as he towed both of them through empty space with a little powered sled to which the suits were closely tethered.

"You're orbit-born, aren't you?" Bashar asked, confirming an earlier thought. *How had he gone all his life without ever seeing this view in person?*

The kid's reply was disgusted. "You think they'd bother to lift someone like *me* out of the gravity well?"

"Is everyone born up here like you?"

"No." Then, reluctantly: "I have Yonami syndrome. It's a genetic disorder unrelated to conception or gestation in orbit. One or more of my grandparents got into some pretty toxic stuff. I also have friable bones, from growing up here without being healthy enough to use the high-gee workout rooms. That can be an orbit-born problem. I'll never go down the gravity well. Not if I want to keep on living." It sounded like a rehearsed speech.

Bashar could almost feel sorry for the kid. At least, he would have if Bibendum weren't neck deep in an effort to murder a million people on Bashar's home turf.

"So what's in it for you?" he asked softly. "The rock drop on Seattle. Everything that will come after. Are you actually dedicated to zero population rewilding? Or is this all in a day's work for Bibendum?"

The response was a while in coming. "It's just math," the kid finally said. "That's what I do. Calculate deorbits and payload trajectories. I'm something of a savant. One of Yonami's few benefits." Pride crept into his voice as he spoke. "The computers are smarter and faster than all of us put together, but I'm better at framing the problems and interpreting the results than anyone."

"You know your math is going to kill a million people not too long from now?" Then three billion more in the next year or two, given the evidence in the darwin file.

"So what? I'll still be here. Besides, what do you care?" His head twisted to look at Bashar directly, though glare made Bibendum's visor brilliantly opaque. "It's *your* plan, Bull Dancer."

"Just curious about all our places in history," Bashar said slowly. He'd often had that same *so what, I'll still be here* thought.

The carrier on his subcutaneous relays began to blink in Bashar's visual field, tweaking his optic nerve. *What the hell? Up here?*

He twitched the appropriate muscle sequence to accept the transmission. Words began to scroll across his visual field.

cox:: ¿¿¿bashar???
bas:: charity . . . busy here
cox:: lightbull in my room now
bas:: you going to live?
cox:: not a hit . . . you know about seattle?
bas:: rock is in front of me

Which was true. They approached something that looked like a tiled-covered sculpture of a big, stubby glider.

cox:: you in orbit?
bas:: yes . . . trying to stop this
cox:: lightbull says tied to darwin
bas:: short bald man?
cox:: yes

Bashar had a lot he could say to that, but any threats would be empty, any warnings redundant.

bas:: check on schaadts shack . . . dont know if ill make it home
cox:: save seattle . . . then come home
bas:: to darwin
cox:: one crisis at a time

That was also certainly true. He realized Bibendum was speaking.

". . . not a hell of a lot to see. It's a rock, covered with heat-resistant tiles, with some attitude jets and control surfaces stuck on. World's heaviest glider, basically."

bas:: must go
cox:: love you

"Fly by wire from orbit?" Bashar asked.

"Not if I've done my job right," Bibendum responded with some irritation. "Can't get a signal through during re-entry burn off, so fly by wire wouldn't work in any case. That's where I come in. My job is to plot orbital insertions. Plus this thing has onboard manual control for minor course corrections or relocations before we drop it."

Onboard manual control? Ah-ha. "Show me the jets and controls. We may need targeting flexibility if there's another drop like this."

"You people are idiots," hissed Bibendum. But he steered the two of them around the blunt end of the mining package and began to point out strapped-on pieces of hardware. Bashar wondered why they bothered, as surely it all burned off during re-entry, but maybe not. He didn't know anything about this kind of engineering. He wasn't in a position to learn it now.

Besides, what he really wanted to see was the manual control. Could this hunk of rock possibly have a cockpit? Bashar studied the exterior of Bibendum's suit, thinking over the safety drill. How quickly could he disable the kid and take control of the situation?

A laconic voice with a thick Australian accent crackled over Bashar's suit comms. "You blokes got another ten minutes before we nudge her out of here and on her way."

"Roger that," Bibendum said. "Tourists," he added after a moment.

I'll show you some tourism, Bashar thought. Maybe he'd make the kid ride the rock down.

Then they came upon the little teardrop metal cabin on the dorsal surface of the mining package, tucked far back from the leading edge.

"See?" said Bibendum. "Now let's get out of here."

"Hold on a moment," Bashar replied. He laid one hand on the arm of Bibendum's pressure suit as if to steady himself. The kid didn't react, so Bashar's other hand reached for the emergency purge-and-pop switch.

He hadn't been sure what to expect. The actual result wasn't much of anything at all. Just a rush of air that fogged, crystallized and vanished. Bibendum didn't even make a sound over the suit comms.

"Next time, kid, don't mess with my people," Bashar said. It would do, for an elegy.

He unhooked himself from the tow sled, wishing like crazy he had a spare suit to latch on. Before he wrestled with the sled any further, Bashar made sure to hook his safety line to the mining package's control cockpit. He didn't think the traffic controller had any telemetry on their suits—Bibendum certainly hadn't hooked *him* up to anything that would have done that job.

Bashar got the sled pointed back in the general direction of Orbital Zero. He then discovered the go-button was a dead man rig. Well, that made sense. You wouldn't want uncontrolled acceleration up here. He made a slipknot out of the slack in Bibendum's safety line, which was beastly slow work in his own suit gloves, especially given that the line had obviously been engineered to be kink resistant, and therefore was largely knot resistant as well. With any luck, it would spring free fairly quickly and cut the acceleration so as to leave the tow sled moving on its own without further power. That ought to look like a normal flight pattern.

The Australian's voice eventually crackled over the comms once more. "You two moving out, or headed home the hard way?"

Bashar hazarded a response. "Bibendum's getting us headed home right now."

"Roger that. Initial burn in one minute, forty-two seconds."

These people relied on instrumentation far more than visual contact, he realized. If someone were eyeballing him, they'd already be on to what he was up to.

Bashar re-aimed the sled, which had been drifting, and tugged his slip knot tight. The sled's compressed gas motors puffed and it slid away, dragging Bibendum's corpse along.

The absolute *silence* would eventually drive him mad, he realized. All he could hear was his own breathing, and the occasional whir of some relay or motor in the structure of his suit. Bibendum's death should have made a noise. The sled ought to whoosh.

He'd seen too many movies and virteos. And they never got the smell right either. His suit stank like an old fashioned gym locker room. Did all space suits reek like this?

Pushing the thought aside, he contemplated the control cockpit's tiny hatch. *That* they surely would have wired into telemetry. He didn't dare open it until the mining package was far enough into its de-orbit process to be past the point of no return.

Instead he huddled as low as he could so as not to profile himself to any casual visual observation, and studied the hatch mechanism. At home, back on Earth, with just a few not-so-simple mechanical and electronic tools, he could bypass most entry sensors. Here, in space, with nothing but blunt-fingered suit gloves, he didn't dare risk it.

Bashar wedged himself in tightly and watched the planet loom above him. It was the world, the whole damned world, glowing blue and brown and white and green as night swept in from the curve of the east and clouds danced across the central Pacific.

He wondered how many wars would have been stopped if everyone had been shipped upstairs once in their life for *this* view.

Finally he just waited for the rock's initial de-orbiting burn, his breath echoing in his ears as the sweat sock stench of the suit crowded his nose, watching the world drift and reflecting on what a terrible, terminal idea this was.

Moselle's voice crackled over the suit comms. She sounded worried. "Biòu. Where the hell are you!?"

It took Bashar a moment to recall that Biòu was him. The cover identity to which Baldie-with-no-name hadn't tipped him. He didn't see much point in answering her, as that would constitute passing intelligence to the enemy. It seemed unlikely that they didn't know where he was by now.

"Biòu." She sounded calmer. "Don't be an idiot. You will die out there. We can still pick you up."

She was right about one thing. Bashar knew he would die out here. He had no idea if that business about being able to pick him up was true, but he wasn't going to encourage a test from this end. Besides which, she sounded like she was fishing. Bashar left the control cockpit's hatch alone a little longer, just in case they thought he was floating around outside Orbital Zero somewhere with the late, unlamented Bibendum.

Her voice crackled a third time. "Damn it, answer me."

If I could drop a rock on you, lady, I would, he thought, then returned to his contemplation of the eye-boggling majesty of Earth.

The pleas ran on for a while, every minute or two.

When after about fifteen minutes, they shifted to a roaring spate of enraged profanity, Bashar figured his latest cover was well and truly blown, and so he let himself in to the cockpit.

If they could still catch him, well, he'd done everything he could.

Piloting an artificial asteroid in a decaying orbit wasn't very much like flying a microlight at treetop level over the Cascade forests. But that was all the aviation experience he had.

"Not a hell of a lot to work with here," Bashar told himself. Then he realized if he could open a comms link to the surface, he might be able to get some advice.

Unfortunately, being tucked into thousands of tons of rock meant his line-of-sight options were severely reduced.

Did the mining package even have a comms capability? *That* was a technology he did understand fairly well.

The cabin wasn't pressurized, so all the equipment must be hardened against vacuum and radiation. Which in turn meant nothing looked quite like he expected it to. Still, the rock had to have communications capability—how else would the traffic controllers at Orbital Zero be able to signal for burns and course corrections prior to atmospheric insertion? Bashar suddenly became very interested in cutting off that access.

He finally settled for depowering and unracking the comms rig completely. Then he jacked his suit comms into the antenna line that connected to something somewhere out on the surface of the mining package. Bashar couldn't imagine using a directional dish on a high velocity throwaway deployment like this—it had to be meters of omnidirectional antenna, hopefully on multiple faces of the rock.

Unsurprisingly, the orbital tech was fundamentally the same as the downside tech. That meant he could use his implanted ultra low power gear to interface to the suit comms, then boost with the suit comms to the mining package's antenna.

Bashar told his communication wizard to find a terrestrial connection, and left it to hop bands and ping for handshakes. He then turned his attention to the flight controls.

"The Wright brothers would recognize this." The rock was flown, if that was indeed the word, by a pair of joysticks and a small rank of thruster controls. They were labeled, but the labels didn't mean much to him. "Ventral Boost 2" didn't exactly tell him what it *did*.

And what was *he* going to do? Assuming he could alter course, was it better to undershoot or overshoot? If he couldn't undershoot far enough to put the mining package down in deep Pacific waters, he was probably better off overshooting as far as possible. They wouldn't be too happy about it in Wenatchee or wherever it was this thing hit in central Washington, but the major damage would be at the impact site and eastward, clear of Seattle and behind some nice, sheltering mountains. With a *hell* of a lot fewer people involved as either corpses or disaster refugees.

Bashar tried very hard not to think about who else was out there as well.

The problem was knowing what to do. He wasn't even sure if the right move was to speed the rock up or slow it down.

Then he had a connection. Bashar squirted out Charity's comms address.

She answered quickly enough. But then, his wife knew where he was and what he was doing. "You still alive?"

Her voice was like a balm to him. The comm lag from surface to orbit and through several satellite bounces was a lot less calming. "A little while longer," Bashar said.

The response to that was annoying seconds later. "You must still be in orbit." Charity couldn't keep the fright from her voice.

"Yes. Coming home the hard way. I'm riding the rock right now." One last plunge, like Milton's Satan without a lake of ice to land in.

Nine times the space that measures day and night
To mortal men, he with his horrid crew
Lay vanquished, rolling in the fiery gulf,
Confounded though immortal.

Another lag, some of it emotional, some of it imposed by the relentless laws of physics. "They after you up there?" Charity asked.

"Oh, surely. No idea if they can catch me. I have to assume not." There hadn't been any more cursing from Moselle for a while, at least. "I want your help."

That answer came as fast as the electrons permitted. "What do you need?"

"Someone who knows a lot about orbital mechanics." He'd killed his last expert an hour or so ago, Bashar realized. But he still didn't see any way he could have either suborned Bibendum or forced the boy to help him. "I have to find a way to drive this thing not to hit Seattle. All it's got are attitude jets, and airfoils for the upper atmosphere. So I can't repoint it at, say, Wake Island."

Lag. "Where are you going to put it?"

"Pacific, by preference. Otherwise as far east of Seattle as I can make the rock fly."

She took a long time replying to those words. "That's, um . . ."

"Where you are. Yes." Charity's med facility, Chelan Heights, was on that vector. "A lot fewer people there," he said ruthlessly, his heart breaking slowly.

More lag. "I'll find you a pilot. Can I call you back?"

"Operational security is well and truly buggered on this one," Bashar said. "Doesn't matter who's listening in now. Just use the usual address. It'll find me."

More lag, emotional again, he thought. "All right," she added after a moment. "It will be okay."

"I love you, too. It's been a good life."

He set about calling his daughter at work in Seattle. Bashar knew he needed to warn Sooboo to get out of whatever J. Appleseed subbasement she worked in these days. Just in case none of this made a damned bit of difference and the rock came down hard there after all.

X: OBSERVING HER FATHER'S MINDLESS DECAY FOR SOME YEARS NOW

Samira Bashar Oxham felt her earbud buzz again. She ignored it again. Whoever it was had to be an insistent bastard. Not to mention in possession of some righteous comms code overrides. J. Appleseed wasn't the easiest organization in the world to just call up.

She was tracking a bug in the mass accounting somewhere within the final three years of heavy lift launch budgets under the now-defunct Green Space project. It was quite unclear if the bug was a numbers problem on the data analysis side, or someone had been filching ground-to-orbit throw weight by the tens of kilograms per flight. The GSO-26 through GSO-28 mission series were all suspect.

Even though the last launch, GSO-28-09, was six years in the past, this continued to be an issue. The possibilities for espionage from black cargo were immense, for one thing.

Dataflow ghosts spun around Sabo, weighted by relevance and degree-of-confidence, interconnected with thin webs of color- and intensity-coded audit trails. At the moment, she was most interested in the physical audits, actual weights-and-measures checks on launch payloads. Translucent virteo images of men and women in bunnysuits stuttered in the background, synthesized from the GSO launch facility's ubiquitous surveillance. Much as would be found in virtually any industrial premises. She could almost smell the ozone-and-cleanser scent of a highly secured facility.

Her own workspace wasn't nearly that secure. Just a base model productivity pit with drink dispensers and a cocoon bag, like any wage slave anywhere. Even if she slaved for something different from most office drones.

Sabo's earbud buzzed again. Same haptic encoding as the last two attempts. The damned thing was stupidly retro, but it had its uses.

"Sweet Jesus and the twelve," she muttered, finally tapping in the call. "What!?" The sharp bark disturbed the data that swirled translucent around her.

"My dear Sooboo." An eerily familiar voice crackled on the other end of a low bandwidth circuit afflicted by lightspeed lag. Or at least, filtered to sound like it.

"You . . ." That voice was the touch of a warm autumn wind, the scent of samosas crackling in oil over a wood fire—a key to memory. Her father's face. His dense, old arms around her as a little girl. Her parents laughing over some joke too ancient even for the expert systems in the datacloud to explain. "I thought you were dead," she snapped. *Hoped*, more like it, but even now, Sabo could not say that to her father.

No one else had ever called her "Sooboo." Even some black hat messaging her with a voice simulator wouldn't have known to do so. It was better than any password. The ultimate in know-your-neighbor security.

Her father was a man whose first posthumous biography had been written a decade before she was born. Sabo should have known better than to believe he was gone from the Earth. Bashar was fucking immortal, insofar as she could tell.

"Life is more convenient that way," he admitted.

That was her dad, all right. Classic Bashar. Funny as a thrown knife, serious as a heart attack. "What in the name of Wall Street do you want?"

More line crackle, more lightspeed lag. "I've only got a little time. Listen . . ." he drew a long breath. "Get out of Seattle. Now. This minute. Get the hell away from Elliott Bay. At least thirty miles north or south if possible. Behind the highest elevation you can find. Do *not* head east."

Miles? Miles? Who the fuck talked about miles anymore? Except century-old men with bad attitudes.

Her own anger, never far from view, bobbed to the surface. "*Now?* I'm busy, God damn it. What are you on? I don't hear from you for over ten years, Mom won't talk about whatever happened between you two, and you call me up and tell me to leave town *now*!?"

Something blipped hard on the line, interference or monitoring, Sabo couldn't tell. Again that lag. Was he bouncing off a daisy chain of comsats? With her father, anything was possible.

"I'm coming home the hard way, Sooboo. Nobody's going to like this splash."

She groaned. "Oh, god, Dad. Are you nuking Seattle?"

"Just about. Get out." Another deep breath. "Please." That was followed by a burst of static.

Sabo hadn't heard her father say "please" since she was four years old. "Bugger off, Dad. Call someone who gives a shit."

He had no answer, just more static and the kind of voice ghosts that turned up when the latency went off the map and the circuit wasn't sufficiently filtered to compensate.

She cut the line and went back to the mass accounting data. After a couple of minutes chasing phantoms in the visualization, she gave up and instantiated a window into the current open source low earth orbit tracking.

If something was moving out of place up there, maybe, just maybe, she'd take her father seriously.

He'd said "please," after all.

And Elliott Bay.

Really?

Many hours later, the mining package skipped roughly across the upper atmosphere. Behind him, and immediately above him, Bashar could see a blaze of heat and light. "It's shallow angle entry with a semicontrolled glide," he told himself out loud. Small reassurance.

At least Moselle and Lu couldn't get at him here. Slightly more reassurance.

The noise was ungodly. To think he'd complained that space was silent. Even inside the cockpit, enclosed in the pressure suit, the howling and buffeting threatened to stun him. Bashar repeatedly shut his eyes and tried to meditate. This was about as effective as doing so in the middle of a firefight, but it was still more constructive than screaming his head off in pain and terror.

He was out of comms, as well, for the duration. Too much interference from the raw chaos of the burn, as well the mining package's ablative coating ablating, or whatever it was doing. Not to mention the racket onboard would have kept him from hearing anything anyway.

Did people ride this down at other times? That would explain the cockpit. A potentially less traceable surface insertion than a fall bag or a glider either one, especially when the lucky pilot bailed out at a fairly low altitude and deployed a wingsuit or microlight glider.

Bashar refused to wonder if he would survive the ride. That hadn't been much of an option from the beginning of this misbegotten affair. What information Charity had come up with before he'd lost comms hadn't been helpful. Using the boosters in a decaying orbit wouldn't do much, she'd told him. Minor course adjustments intended to ensure the attitude of the mining package was correct when it encountered the thicker layers of the atmosphere. Even Bashar knew how critical that was. And the rock had no capacity for large-scale course redirects—that was done with the initial positioning, which had been completed long before he'd even gotten into orbit. Otherwise he could have just flown it into the Canadian Rockies or something.

Any control he achieved would be with the airfoils in atmosphere.

So Bashar divided his time between not-panicking about the rough ride and a hunt for the autopilot, or whatever autonomous system managed the lower stages of descent. The late, unlamented Bibendum had made it clear they weren't controlling *that* from orbit.

He wound up unhooking every component that was obviously not a flight control. Five pieces of rack-mounted equipment in all. Loose they were a terrible hazard, so he slotted them back into their racks reversed. The empty circuit connections stared at him like baleful silver eyes.

When the mining package stopped jouncing and howling so much, and the fire above his head guttered to mixed streaks of brightness and ash, Bashar figured they had gone from a ballistic mode to at least semi-controlled atmospheric flight. He took over the joysticks to see if there was anything like wing bite.

The problem now was an almost complete lack of navigational instruments. This wasn't intended to be flown from the cockpit. There was no forward view. All he had was an altimeter, a compass, an airspeed indicator and a GPS readout.

Which at the moment told him he was at 81,400 meters, headed almost due east, making Mach ten somewhere over the Pacific Ocean.

No one bailed out at this altitude and airspeed. Not anyone who wanted to survive the first step.

Bashar fought the controls in an effort to keep the nose up as high as possible. He wanted to make the glide path shallower, so as to overshoot the landing zone. Surely he'd already messed up their careful calculations to drop this into Elliott Bay just west of the New Seawall, but he needed to miss by miles. Kilometers. A lot of them, whichever they were.

His sensorium flickered as text came into being, superimposed on his visual field.

cox:: ¿¿¿bashar???
cox:: they bombed Schaadts shack

Schaadt's? Had Baldie-with-no-name been a victim or the perp? He'd bet vinos-to-dollars he knew the answer to that, given what a slick bastard Baldie had turned out to be. Trail of bodies in his wake kind of guy. Everything at Schaadt's had been a set up. Lightbull, the hard Greens, did it even matter who?

No.

More to the point, Charity'd found some bandwidth that could reach him. Well, he had lost a lot of his burn. But this just wasn't the time.

bas:: not now . . . im saving the world
cox:: one more thing . . . samira is getting out of seattle

His relief at that news was bone deep. His daughter had listened to him. Something had been salvaged. *I have won*, Bashar thought. At least the smallest and most important of victories. But time was slipping, fast.

bas:: thank god and all the little fishes
cox:: love you
bas:: this isnt goodbye

God, he wished that was true.

He kept pulling the nose up. *Was he going to make it?*

No matter what happened, someone would have to deal with Lightbull, with the hard Greens in orbit, with the darwin file and the island plagues, with J. Appleseed's rogue AIs.

A few governments still had surface-to-orbit missiles. Could he convince the United States Air Force to nuke Orbital Zero? As for the rest of it . . .

bas:: dump everything to sooboo . . . all data . . . all of it
bas:: someone has to take on lightbull and finish this
bas:: ¿¿¿charity???
bas:: ¿¿¿charity???
bas:: ¿¿¿charity???

Had she received that?

At 4,000 meters, the mining package's airspeed dropped below Mach one. Bashar figured he was close to the Olympic peninsula. Even a hard stop in the mountains there would be better than nailing Seattle. But he was pretty sure he'd clear the peaks, and if he cleared the peaks, he'd clear Seattle.

Mt. Howard east of Seattle was a little over 2,000 meters. Bashar figured it was even money on striking the Cascades there or just clearing them as well to nail some poor bastard farmer in the Palouse.

Or his own wife.

It was nut-cutting time. Ride the rock down, keeping the nose up as hard as he could, or step outside and check the weather? Bashar had no way to know for sure. All he could do was guess. Bibendum had said the suit had basic atmospheric capabilities. He'd have ten or fifteen seconds to figure it out. Must be a wingsuit, since there wasn't enough mass on the back to hold a pop-up microlight.

Unfortunately, he knew how to fly a microlight. Wingsuits were a mystery to him.

Bashar hoped like hell Samira would take the larger problem and run with it as she escaped the drop zone. He wasn't sure he would ever hit the ground alive. And Charity . . .

"I'm sorry," he said to no one in particular as he popped the cockpit's hatch, and stepped out into the screaming wind that snatched him away from the rock like the hand of God.

His suit was smoldering, Bashar realized as he spun high in the air over the rugged terrain of the Olympic Peninsula, buffeted by the searing trail of his erstwhile craft.

The suit stiffened and puffed to slam him hard where he'd expected to fall. Now he was spinning, not plunging.

Bashar spread his arms wide like a starfish. Did this damned rig have jets?

Well, of course it did, for maneuvering in microgravity, but they wouldn't likely be affecting him here.

His spin turned into a swooping curve. Ahead of him, the mining package left a contrail of smoke and debris as it crossed Puget Sound. Behind him was . . . he bent his head . . . smoke.

No wonder his legs were getting hot. His suit was on fire.

Damn it.

Stop, drop and roll wouldn't cut it. Not here two miles up in the air.

If he'd simply fallen, he'd have hit the ground by now. Instead, Bashar was in a kind of spiral glide over what looked like the eastern end of the Olympic National Forest. Not a good landing zone for a man coming in hot, hard and aflame. He tried to steer toward Puget Sound, or at least the Hood Canal.

Looking up again, he watched the mining package drop toward Seattle as the eastern sky faded to dusk.

"Oh shit oh shit oh shit oh shit," Bashar said.

It cleared the downtown skyscrapers like the fist of God, then, also like the fist of God, barely cleared Capitol Hill.

A cloud of steam and ash shot up when the rock hit Lake Washington. Even as he watched, the blast tore the top off Capitol Hill. Most of Bellevue was toasted, too, surely. But Seattle . . .

Seattle hadn't died. Knocked hard, yes. Fucked, yes. But not dead. And people would come looking *now* to figure out what happened. Hard people, like the man he had been.

He had won. His daughter was still alive, and so was Seattle.

His suit aflame, his eyes full of tears, Bashar turned his face toward the sparkling waters and let himself plunge. Milton's words came into his mind as he fell.

I toiled out my uncouth passage, forced to ride the untractable abyss, plunged in the womb of unoriginal night and chaos wild.

"Good-bye, Samira," he told the world.

cox:: ¿¿¿bashar???
cox:: ¿¿¿bashar???
cox:: ¿¿¿bashar???

GEOFF RYMAN

Here's an eccentric and lyrical alternate history concerning a life path for William Shakespeare different than the one he followed—one that takes him to some very strange destinations indeed.

Although born in Canada, Geoff Ryman now lives in England. He made his first sale in 1976, to New Worlds, *but it was not until 1984, when he made his first appearance in* Interzone *with his brilliant novella* The Unconquered Country *that he first attracted any serious attention.* The Unconquered Country, *one of the best novellas of the decade, had a stunning impact on the science-fiction scene of the day and almost overnight established Ryman as one of the most accomplished writers of his generation, winning him both the British Science Fiction Award and the World Fantasy Award; it was later published in a book version:* The Unconquered Country: A Life History. *His novel* The Child Garden: A Low Comedy *won both the prestigious Arthur C. Clarke Award and the John W. Campbell Memorial Award, and his later novel* Air *also won the Arthur C. Clarke Award. His other novels include:* The Warrior Who Carried Life; *the critically acclaimed mainstream novel* Was; Coming of Enkidu; The King's Last Song; Lust; *and the underground cult classic* 253, *the "print remix" of an "interactive hypertext novel" that in its original form ran online on Ryman's home page, www.ryman.com, and which in its print form won the Philip K. Dick Award. Four of his novellas have been collected in* Unconquered Countries. *Most recently, he edited the anthology* When It Changed; *his latest books are the novel* The Film-Makers of Mars *and the collection* Paradise Tales: and Other Stories.

T HE ROOM WAS WOOD—floor, walls, ceiling.

The doorbell clanged a second time. The servant girl Bessie finally answered it; she had been lost in the kitchen amid all the pans. She slid across the floor on slippers, not lifting her feet; she had a notion that she polished as she walked. The front door opened directly onto the night: snow. The only light was from the embers in the fireplace.

Three huge men jammed her doorway. "This be the house of Squire Digges?"

the smallest of them asked; and Bessie, melting in shyness, said something like, "Cmn gud zurs."

They crowded in, stomping snow off their boots, and Bessie knelt immediately to try to mop it up with her apron. "Shoo! Shoo!" said the smaller guest, waving her away.

The Master roared; the other door creaked like boots and in streamed Squire Digges, both arms held high. "Welcome! Good Count Vesuvius! Guests! Hah hah!" Unintroduced, he began to pump their hands.

Vesuvius, the smaller man, announced in Danish that this was Squire Digges, son of Leonard and author of the lenses, then turned back and said in English that these two fine fellows were Frederik Rosenkrantz and Knud Gyldenstierne.

"We have corresponded!" said Squire Digges, still smiling and pumping. To him, the two Danes looked huge and golden-red with bronze beards and bobbed noses, and he'd already lost control of who was who. He looked sideways in pain at the Count. "You must pardon me, sirs?"

"For what?"

The Squire looked harassed and turned on the servant. "Bessie! Bessie, their coats! The door. Leave off the floor, girl!"

Vesuvius said in Danish, *"The gentleman has asked you to remove your coats at long last. For this he is sorry."*

One of the Danes smiled, his face crinkling up like a piecrust, and he unburdened himself of what must have been a whole seal hide. He dumped it on Bessie, who could not have been more than sixteen and was small for her years. Shaking his head, Digges slammed shut the front door. Bessie, buried under furs, began to slip across the gleaming floor as if on ice.

"Bessie," said Digges in despair then looked over his shoulder. "Be careful of the floors, Messires, she polishes them so. Good girl, not very bright." He touched Bessie's elbow and guided her toward the right door.

"He warns us that floors are dangerous."

Rosenkrantz and Gyldenstierne eyed each other. *"Perhaps we fall through?"* They began to tiptoe.

Digges guided Bessie through the door, and closed it behind her. He smiled and then unsmiled when there was a loud whoop and a falling crash within.

"All's well, Bessie?"

"Aye, zur."

"We'll wait here for a moment. Uh, before we go in. The gentlemen will excuse me but I did not hear your names."

"He's forgotten your names. These English cannot speak." Vesuvius smiled. "Is so easy to remember in English. This be noble Rosary and Goldenstar."

"Sirs, we are honored. Honored beyond measure!"

Mr. Goldenstar sniffed. *"The whole place sags and creaks. Haven't the English heard of bricks?"*

Mr. Rosary beamed and gestured at the panelling and the turd-brown floor. "House. Beautiful. Beautiful!"

Squire Digges began to talk to them as if they were children. "In. Warm!" He beat his own arms. "Warrrrrrrrrrm."

Goldenstar was a military man, and when he saw the room beyond, he gave a cry and leapt back in alarm.

It was not a dining hall but a dungeon. It had rough blocks, chains, and ankle irons that hung from the wall. *"It's a trap!"* he yelped, and clasped young Rosary to pull him back.

From behind the table a tall, lean man rose up, all in black with a skull cap and lace around his neck. *Inquisitor.*

"Oh!" laughed the Squire and touched his forehead. "No, no, no, no alarms, I beg. Hah hah! The house once belonged to Philip Henslowe; he owns the theater out back; this is like a set from a play."

Vesuvius blinked in fury. *"This is his idea of a joke."*

"You should see the upstairs; it is full of naked Venuses!"

"I think he just said upstairs is a brothel."

Goldenstar ran his fingers over the walls. The rough stones, the iron rings and the chains had all been frescoed onto plaster. He blurted out a laugh. *"They're all mad."*

"They are all strolling players. They do nothing but go to the theater. They pose and declaim and roar."

Digges flung out a hand toward the man in black. "Now to the business at hand. Sirs! May . . . I . . . introduce . . . Doctor John DEE!"

For the Doctor, Vesuvius had a glittery smile; but he said through his teeth, *"They mime everything."*

"Ah!" Mr. Rosary sprang forward to shake the old man's hand. He was in love, eyes alight. "Queen Elisabetta. Magus!"

Dr. John Dee rumbled, "I am called Mage, yes, but I am in fact the Advisor Philosophical to her Majesty."

Digges beamed. "His *Parallaticae commentationis* and my own *Alae seu scalae mathematicae* were printed as a pair."

Someone else attended, pale skinned, pink cheeked, and glossy from nose to balding scalp, with black eyes like currants in a bun and an expression like a barber welcoming you to his shop.

"And this example," growled Digges, putting his hand on the young man's shoulder, "will not be known to you, but we hold him in high esteem, a family friend. This is Guillermus Shakespere."

The young man presented himself. "A Rosary and a Goldenstar. These are names for poetry. Especially should one wish to contrast Religion and Philosophy."

Vesuvius's lip curled. "You mock names?"

"No no, of course not. I beg! Not that construction. It is but poetic . . . convenience. My own poor name summons up dragooned peasants shaking weapons. Or, or, an actor whose only roles are those of soldiers." The young man looked back and forth between the men, expecting laughter. They blinked and stood with their hands folded not quite into fists.

"My young friend is a reformed Papist and so thinks much on issues of religion and philosophy. As do we." Digges paused, also waiting. "Please sit, gentlemen."

Cushions, food, and wine all beckoned. Digges busied himself pouring far too much wine into tankards. Mr. Rosary hunkered down with pleasure next to Dr. Dee, and even took his hand. He then began to speak, sometimes closing his eyes. "My dear Squire Digges and honorabled Doctor Dee. My relative Tycho Brahe sends his greatest respects and has entrusted us to give you this, his latest work."

He sighed and chuckled, relieved to be rid of both a small gray printed pamphlet, and his speech. Digges howled his gratitude, and read a passage aloud from the pamphlet and passed it to Dr. Dee, and pressed Rosary to pass on his thanks.

Rosary began to recite again. "I am asked by Tycho Brahe to say how impress-ed with your work. Sir. To describe the universe as infinite with mathematical argument!" His English sputtered and died. "Is a big thing. We are all so amuzed."

"Forgive me," said the young man. "Is it the universe or the argument that is infinite?"

"Guy," warned Digges in a sing-song voice. He pronounced it with a hard "G" and a long eeee.

"And is it the universe or the numbers that are amusing?"

Mr. Rosary paused, understood, and grinned. "The two. Both."

"We disagree on matters of orbitals," said Squire Digges.

Vesuvius leaned back, steepling his fingers; his nails were clean and filed. "A sun that is the circumference of Terra." He sketched with his finger a huge circle and shook his head.

Almost under his breath the young man said, "A sonne can be larger than his father."

Digges explained. "My young friend is a poet."

Vesuvius smiled. "I look forward to him entertaining us later." Then he ventriloquized in Danish, *"And until then, he might eat with the servants."*

Mr. Rosary looked too pleased to care and beamed at Digges. "You . . . have . . . lens."

Digges boomed. "Yes! Yes! On roof." He pointed. *"Stierne. Stierne."*

Rosary laughed and nodded. "Yes! *Stierne!* Star."

"Roof. We go to roof." Squire Digges mimed walking with his two fingers. Blank looks, so he wiped out his gesture with a wave.

Vesuvius translated with confidence. *"No stars tonight, too cloudy."*

"No stars," said Mr. Rosary, as if someone's cat had died.

"Yes." Digges looked confused. *"Stierne.* On roof."

Everything stalled: words, hands, mouths and feet. Nobody understood.

Young Guy made a sound like bells, many of them, as if bluebells rang. His fingers tinkled across an arch that was meant to be the Firmament. Then his two flat hands became lenses and his arms mechanical supports that squeedled as they lined up his palms.

Goldenstar gave his head an almost imperceptible shake. *"What the hell is he doing?"*

Vesuvius: *"I told you they have to mime everything."*

"No wonder that they are good with numbers. They can't use words!"

"It's why there will never be a great poet in English."

Rosary suddenly rocked in recognition. He too mimed the mechanical device with its lenses. He twinkled at young Guy. Young Guy twinkled back.

"Act-or," explained Digges. "Tra-la! Stage. But poet. Oh! Such good poet. New poem. *Venus and Adonis!*" He kissed the tips of his fingers. Vesuvius's eyes, heavy and unmoved, rested on his host.

"Poet. Awww," Rosary said in sympathy. "No numbers."

John Dee, back erect, sipped his wine.

Bessie entered, rattling plates and knives in terror. Goldenstar growled, and his hands rounded in the air the curvature of her buttocks. She noticed and fled, soles flapping, polishing no more.

The Squire poured more wine. "Now. I want to hear more of your great relation, Lord Tycho. I yearn to visit him. He lives on an island? Devoted to philosophy!" He pronounced the name as "Tie-koh."

Vesuvius corrected him. "Teej-hhho."

"Yes yes yes, Tycho."

"The island is called *Hven*. You should be able to remember it as it is the same word as 'haven.' It is called in Greek Uraniborg. Urania means study of stars. Perhaps you know that?"

Digges's face stiffened. "I do read Greek."

Rosary beamed at Guy. "Your name Gee. In Greek is Earth."

Guy laughed. "Is it? Heaven and Earth. And I was born Taurus." He waited for a response. "Earth sign?" He looked at them all in turn. "You are all astrologers?"

Dr. Dee said, "No."

"And your name," said Guy, turning suddenly on the translator as if pulling a blade. "You are called Vesuvius?"

"A pseudonym, Guy," said Digges. "Something to hide. A *nom de plume.*"

"What's that?"

"French," growled Vesuvius. "A language."

Rosary thought that was a signal to change languages, and certainly the subject. "*Mon cousin a un nez d'or.*"

Squire Digges jumped in to translate ahead of Vesuvius. "Your cousin has a . . ." He faltered. "A golden nose."

Rosary pointed to his own nose. "*Oui. Il l'a perdu ça par se battre en duel.*"

"In . . . a . . . duel."

Goldenstar thumped the table. "Over *matematica!*"

Squire Digges leaned back. "Now that is a good reason to lose your nose."

"*Ja! Ja!*" Goldenstar laughed. "*Principiis mathematicis.*"

"I trust we will not come to swords," said Digges, half-laughing.

Rosary continued. "*De temps en temp il port un nez de cuivre.*"

Vesuvius translated. "Sometimes the nose is made of copper."

Guy's mouth crept sideways. "He changes noses for special occasions?"

Vesuvius glared; Goldenstar prickled. "Tycho Brahe great man!"

"Evidently. To be able to afford such a handsome array of noses."

Squire Digges hummed "no" twice.

Rosary pressed on. "*Mon cousin maintain comme un animal de familier un élan.*"

Vesuvius snapped back, "He also has a pet moose."

Digges coughed. "I think you'll find he means elk."

"*L'élan peut danser!*" Rosary looked so pleased.

Digges rattled off a translation. "The elk can dance." He paused. "I might have that wrong."

Goldenstar thought German might work better. *"Der elch ist tot."*

Digges. "The elk is dead."

"Did it die in the duel as well?" Guy's face was bland. "To lose at a stroke both your nose and your moose."

Rosary rocked with laughter. *"Ja-ha-ha. Ja! Der elch gesoffenwar von die treppen gefallen hat."*

Sweat tricked down Digges's forehead. "The elk drank too much and fell down stairs."

Guy nodded slightly to himself. "And you good men believe that the Earth goes around the sun." His smile was a grimace of incredulity and embarrassment.

Dr. Dee tapped the table. "No. Your friend Squire Digges believes the Earth goes around the sun. Our guests believe that the sun goes around the Earth, but that all the other planets revolve around those two central objects. They believe this on the evidence of measurements and numbers. This evening is a conference on numbers and their application to the ancient study of stars. Astronomy. But the term is muddled."

Guy's face folded in on itself.

"Language fails you. Thomas Digges is described as a designer of arms and an almanacker. Our Danish friends are called astrologers, I am called a mage. I call us philosophers, but our language is numbers. Numbers describe, sirrah, with more precision than all your poetry."

Shakespere bowed.

"The Queen herself believes this and thus so should you." Dee turned away from him.

"But the numbers disagree," said Shakespere.

BESSIE LABORED into the room backwards, bearing on a trencher a whole roast lamb. It was burnt black and smelled of soot. The company applauded nonetheless. The parsnips and turnips about it were cinders shining with fat.

Digges continued explaining. "Now, this great Tycho saw suddenly appear in the heavens. . . ."

Goldenstar punched the air and shouted over the last few words, "By eye! By eye!"

"Yes, by eye. He saw a new light in the heavens, a comet he thought, only it could not be one."

"Numbers by eye!"

"Yes, he calculated the parallax and proved it was not a comet. It was beyond the moon. A new star, he thought."

"Nova!" exclaimed Goldenstar.

"More likely to be a dying one, actually. But it was a change to the immutable sphere of the stars!"

"Oh. Interesting," said Shakespere. "Should . . . someone carve?"

"You're as slow as gravy! Guy! The sphere of the stars is supposed to be unchanging and perfect."

"Spheres, you mean the music of the spheres?"

Goldenstar bellowed. *"Ja.* It move!"

"I rather like the idea of the stars singing."

Digges's hand moved as if to music. "It means Ptolemy is wrong. It means the Church is wrong, though why Ptolemy matters to the Church I don't know. But there it was. A new light in the heavens!"

Guy's voice rose in panic. "When did this happen?"

John Dee answered him. "1572."

Shakespere began to count the years on his fingers.

John Dee's mouth twitched and he squeezed shut Shakespere's hand. "Twenty. Years. And evidently the world did not end, so it was not a portent." As he spoke, Vesuvius translated in an undertone.

Squire Digges grinned like a wolf. "There are no spheres. The planets revolve around the sun, and we are just another planet."

"Nooooooooooo ho-ho!" wailed Rosary and Goldenstar.

Digges bounced up and down in his chair, still smiling. "The stars are so far away we cannot conceive the distance. All of them are bigger than the sun. The universe is infinitely large. It never ends."

The Danes laughed and waved him away. Goldenstar said, "Terra heavy. Sit in center. Fire light. Sun go around Terra!"

"Could we begin eating?" suggested Guy.

"Terra like table. Table fly like bird? No!" One of Goldenstar's fists was matter, the other fire and spirit.

"I'll carve. Shall I carve?" No one noticed Shakespere. He stood up and sharpened the knife while the philosophers teased and bellowed. He sawed the blackened hide. "I like a nice bit of crackling." He leaned down hard on the knife and pushed; the scab broke open and a gout of blood spun out of it like a tennis ball and down Guy's doublet. The meat was raw. He regained his poise. "Shall we fall upon it with lupine grace?"

Vesuvius interpreted. *"He says you have the manners of wolves."*

Rosary said, "Hungry like wolves."

The knife wouldn't cut. Guy began to wrestle the knuckle out of its socket. Like a thing alive, the lamb leapt free onto the floor.

"Dear, dear boy." Digges rose to his feet and scooped up the meat, and put it back on the board. "Give me the knife." He took it and began with some grace to carve. "He really is a very good poet."

"Let us hope he is that at least," said Vesuvius.

Digges paused, about to serve. "He's interested in everything. History. Ovid. Sex. And then spins it into gold."

He put a tranche onto Goldenstar's plate. Knud did not wait for the others and began to press down with his knife. The meat didn't cut. He speared it up whole and began to chaw one end of it. The fat was uncooked and tasted of human genitals; the flesh had the strength of good hemp rope. He turned the turnip over in his fingers. It looked like a lump of coal and he let it fall onto his plate. *"I suggest we sail past this food and go and see the lenses."*

Rosary tried to take a bite of the meat. "Yes. Lenses."

Thomas Digges's house stood three stories high, dead on Bankside opposite the spires of All Hallows the Great and All Hallows the Lesser. Just behind his house, beyond a commons, stood Henslowe's theater, The Rose, which was why Guy was such a frequent houseguest. Digges got free tickets in the stalls as a way of apologizing for the groundlings' noise and litter and the inconvenience of Guy sleeping on his floor. Guy didn't snore but he did make noises all night as if he were caressing a woman or jumping down from trees.

No noise in February at night. The wind had dropped, and a few boats still plied across the river, lanterns glowing like planets. The low-tide mud was luminous with snow. The sky looked as if it had been scoured free of cloud.

Over his slated roof, Digges had built a platform. Its scaffolding supports had splintered; it groaned underfoot, shifting like a boat. The moon was full-faced and the stars seemed to have been flung up into the heavens, held by nets.

The cold had loosened Guy's tongue. "S-s-s-size of lenses, you look with both eyes. No squinting. C-c-can you imagine f-f-f-folk wearing them as a collar, they lift up the arms and have another set of eyes to see distant things. W-w-w-would that make them philosophers?"

"The gentlemen are acquainted with the principle, Guy." Digges was ratcheting a series of mechanical arms that supported facemask-sized rounds of glass.

"But not the wonder of it. D-do you sense wonder, Mr. Rosary?"

Rosary's red cheeks swelled. "I do not know."

"Many things I'm sure, Rosie, are comprehended by you. Are you married, perchance?"

"Geee-eee—heee," warned Digges. He bent his knees to look through the corridor of lenses and made an old-man noise.

Goldenstar answered. "Married."

"As am I. That signifies, b-b—but not much." Guy arched back around to Rosary. "Come by day the morrow and walk alongside the river with me. The churches and the boats, moorhens, the yards of stone and timber."

Vesuvius shook his head. "We have heard about you actors."

Goldenstar said, "We leave tomorrow." Rosary shrugged.

Digges stood up and presented his lenses to them. "Sirs." Vesuvius and Rosary did a little dance, holding out hands for each other, until the Count put a collegial hand on Rosary's back and pushed. Rosary crouched and stared, blinking.

Squire Digges sounded almost sad. "You see. The moon is solid too. Massy with heft."

Rosary was still. Finally he stood up, shaking his head. "That is . . ." He tried to speak with his hands, but that also failed. "Like being a sea." He looked sombre. "The stars are made of stone."

Goldenstar adopted a lunging posture as if grounding a spear against an advancing horde. *"This could get us all burnt at the stake."*

John Dee answered in Danish. Vesuvius looked up in alarm. *"Yes, but not here, not while my Queen lives."*

Shakespere understood the tone. "Everything is exploding, exploding all at once. When I was in Rome—it's so important to g-g-get things right, don't you think? Research is the best part of the j-job. Rome. Verona. Carthage. I was in a room with a man who was born the same year I was and his first name was the same as his last, G-G-Galileo Galilei. I told him about Thomas and he told me that he too has lenses. He told me that Jupiter has four moons and Saturn wears a rainbow hat. He is my pen pal, Galileo, I send him little things of my own, small pieces you understand—"

Vesuvius exploded. "Please you will stop prattle!" He ran a hand across his forehead. "We are meeting of great astrological minds in Europe, not prattle Italian!"

Digges placed an arm around Guy as if to warm him. Rosary phalanxed next to them as though shielding him from the wind. "Please," Rosary said to Vesuvius.

John Dee thought: People protect this man.

Guillermus Shakespere thought:

I can be in silence. My source is in silence. Words come from silence.

How different they be, these Danes, one all stern and leaden, forceful with facts, the other leavening dough. Their great cousin. All by eye? Compromise by eye, just keep the sun going around the Earth, to pacify the Pope and save your necks. Respect him more if he declared for the Pope forthrightly and kept to the heavens and Earth as we knew them. Digges digs holes in heaven, excavating stars as if they were bones. Building boats of bone. He could build boxes, boxes with mirrors to look down into the heart of the sea, show us a world of narwhales, sharks, and selkies.

All chastened by Mr. Volcano. All silent now. Stare now—by eye—you who think you see through numbers, stare at what his lenses show. New eyes to see new things.

How do rocks hang in the sky?

How will I tell my groundlings: the moon is a mountain that doesn't fall? The man with gap in his teeth; the maid with bruised cheek, the oarsman with rounded back? What can I say to them? These wonders are too high for speaking, for scrofulous London, its muddy river. Here the moon has suddenly descended onto our little eye-land. Here where the future is hidden in lenses and astrolabes. The numbers and Thomas's clanking armatures.

"Guy," says old Thomas, full of kindness. "Your turn."

I bow before the future, into the face of a new monarch of glass who overturns. I look through his eyes; see as he sees, wide and long. I blink as when I opened my eyes in a basin of milk. Dust and shadow, light and mist cross and swim and I look onto another world.

I can see so clearly that it's a ball, a globe. Its belly swells out toward me, a hint of shadow on its crescent edge.

It is as stone as any granite tor. Beige and hot in sunlight. The moon must see us laced in cloud but no clouds there, no rain, no green expanse. Nothing to shield from the shriveling sun. No angels, nymphs, orisons, bowers, streams, butterflies, lutes. Desiccated corpses. No dogs to devour. A circle of stone. Avesbury. A graveyard. Breadcrumbs and mold.

Not man in the moon, but a skull.

Nothing for my groundlings. Or poetry.

I look on Digges's face. He stares as wide as I do; no comfort there. He touches my sleeve. "Dear Guy. Look at the stars."

He hoists the thing on some hidden bearing, and then takes each arm and gears into a new niche. The lenses rise and intersect at some new angle, and I look again, and see the stars.

Rosie was right, it is an ocean. What ship could sail there? Bejeweled fish. That swallow Earth. Carry it to God. I can see. I can see they are suns, not tiny torches, and if suns then about those too other Earths could hang. Infinite suns, infinite worlds, deeper and deeper into bosom of God, distances vast, they make us more precious because so rare and small, defenseless before all that fire.

Here is proof of church's teaching. God must love us to make any note of us when the very Earth is a mote of soot borne high on smoky gas.

My poor groundlings.

John Dee watched.

The boy pulled back from the glass, this actor-poet-playwright. Someone else for whom there is no word. In the still and icy air, tears had frozen to his cheeks. Digges gathered him in; Rosary stepped forward; Goldenstar stared astounded. Only the spy stood apart, scorn on his face.

"You are right, Squire Digges," said the boy. "It is without end. Only that would be big enough for God." He looked fallen, pale and distracted. "The cold bests me. I must away, gentlemen."

"The morrow?" Rosary asked. "We meet before we go?"

The wordsmith nodded, clasped Rosary's hand briefly and then turned and trundled down the steps. The platform shook and shuddered. Dee stood still and dark for a moment, decided, and then with a swirl, followed.

Winding down the stairwell past people-smelling bedrooms, through the dungeon of a dining room. The future that awaited them? Out into the paneled room, flickering orange.

"Young Sir! Stay!"

The boy looked embarrassed. "Nowhere else to go."

Such a poor, thin cloak. Was that the dust of Rome on it? Or only Rome wished for so hard that mind-dust fell upon it? But his eyes: full of hope, when I thought to see despair. "Young master. Have you heard of the Brotherhood of Night?"

Hope suspended like dust, only dust that could see.

"I see you have not, for which I am thankful. We are a brotherhood devoted to these new studies late from Germany and Denmark, now Austria and Italia. None of us can move, let alone publish, without suspicion. That man Vesuvius is as much spy as guide, the Pope's factotum. How, young Guillermus, would you like to see Brahe's island of philosophy, in sight of great Elsinore? Uraniborg, city of the heavens, though in fact given over to the muse of a study that has late been revived. And all this by a man with a golden nose. Would you like to see again your starry twin Galileo? See Rome, Verona, Athens? Not Carthage, not possible, don't say that in good company again. But Spain, possible now. The courtship of Great Elizabeth by Philip makes travel even there approved and safe."

"My . . . I'm an actor. I used to play women."

"You still do." Dee's grim smile lengthened. "Men like Vesuvius dismiss you. Bah! Religion is destroying itself. The Protestants prevent the old Passion Plays, and in their stead grow you and Marlowe. You write the history of tragic kings. That has not happened since the Greeks."

Guy shook his head. "Ask Kit to do this."

He is, thought Dee, a good, faithful, fragile boy. And something in his thin shoulders tells me that he's contemplating going into Orders. That must be stopped.

Dee said aloud, "Kit draws enemies." The boy's eyes stared into his. "Men who want to kill him. They love you."

Out of cold policy, Dee took the boy into his arms and kissed him full on the lips, held him, and then pushed him back, to survey the results in the creature's eyes: yes: something soft, something steel.

Guy said, "You taste of gunpowder."

"You would still be able to write your poetry. Send it to Kit in packets to furnish out the plays. In any case he will be undone, caught up in these Watchmen unless we hide him. As you might well be undone if you stay here and miss your chance to see the world blossom. Move for us and write it down. And learn, boy, learn! See where Caesar walked; breathe the scents of Athens's forest. Go to high Elsinore."

Shakespere stood with his eyes closed. The old house crackled and turned about them. The world was breaking. "Are there tales in Denmark of tragic kings?"

Dr. Dee nodded. "And things as yet undreamt of." He took up his long staff and the black cloak that was taller than himself. He put his arm around the slender shoulders and said, "Riverwalk with me."

The door shut tight behind them, and only then did Bessie come to open it.

Outside, white carpeted everything, and Bessie stepped into the hush. Somehow it was snowing again, though the sky overhead was clear. She kicked snow off the stone step and sat down, safe and invisible. It looked as if the stars themselves were falling in flakes. The idea made her giggle. She saw thistledown: stars were made of dandelion stuff.

As so often once it starts to snow, the air felt warmer. The blanket of white would be melted by morning; if she were abed now she'd have missed it. So she warmed the stone step by sitting on it, and let the snow tingle her fingertips. She scooped up a ridge of it and tasted: cold and fresh, sweeter than well water.

She looked up, and snow streaked past her face like stars. Her stomach turned over and it felt as if she were falling upward, flying into heaven where there would be angels. She could see the angels clearly; they'd be tall and thin with white hair because they were so old, but no wrinkles, with the bodies of men and the faces of women. The thought made her giggle, for it was a bit naughty trying to picture angels. She lifted up her feet, which made her feel even more like she was flying.

An hour later and Guy came back to find her still seated on the step.

"Hello, Bessie." He dropped down next to her and held up his own pink-fingered ridge of snow. "It's like eating starlight."

She gurgled with the fun of it and grabbed her knees and grinned at him. She was missing a tooth. "Did you see the old gent'man home?"

"Aye. He wants me to go to Denmark. He'll pay."

"Oooh! You'll be off then!"

He hugged his knees too and rested his head on them, saying nothing.

She nudged him. "Oh. You should go. Chance won't come again."

"I said I would think on it. He wants me to spy. Like Kit. I'd have to carry a knife."

"You should and all. Round here." She nudged him again. "Wouldn't want you hurt."

"You're a good lass, Bessie."

"Aye," wistfully, as if being good had done her no good in return. He followed her eyeline up into the heavens, that had been so dreary and cold. The light of stars sparkled in her eyes and she had a sweet face: long nosed, with a tiny mouth like a little girl, stray hair escaping her kerchief, a smudge of ash on her face. He leaned forward and kissed her.

"Hmm," she said happily and snuggled in. These were the people he wanted to make happy; give them songs, dances, young blades, fine ladies in all their brocade, and kings halfway up the stairs to God.

"What do you see when you look at stars, Bessie?"

She made a gurgling laugh from deep within. "You know when the sun shines on snow and there's bits on it? Other times it's like I've got something in my eye, like I'm crying. But right now, I'm flying through 'em. Shooting past!"

"Are you on a ship?" He glimpsed it, like the royal barge all red and gold, bearing Queen Elizabeth through the Milky Way, which wound with a silver current. Bessie sat on the figurehead, kicking her heels.

"Oh, I don't know!"

"Like Sir Walter Raleigh with a great wind filling the sails."

"That'll be it," she said and kicked her heels. She leaned forward for another kiss, and he gave it to her, and the rising of her breath felt like sails.

"Wind so strong we're lifted up from the seas, and we hang like the moon in the air." He could see the sails fill, and a storm wave that tossed them free of the sea, up into the sky, away from whatever it was held them to the Earth. "We'll land on the moon first, beaching in sand. It's always sunny there, no clouds. We'll have taken salt pork and hardtack."

"Oh no, we'll take lovely food with us. We'll have beer and cold roast beef."

"And we'll make colonies like in the Caribbean now, on Mars, and then Jupiter. They'll make rum there out of a new kind of metal. We'll go beyond to the stars."

Bessie said, "There'll be Moors on Mars."

Shakespeare blinked. She was a marvel. They all were, that's why he wrote for them. He loved them.

That old man: *like the Greeks had done,* he said. Their great new thing that he and Kit were doing. And the others, even miserable old Greene; their *Edwards* and their *Henrys.* Mad old John Dee had made them sound old-fashioned, moldy from the grave. Bessie didn't care about the past. She was traveling to Araby on Mars.

So why write those old things from the grammar school? Write something that was part of the explosion in the world.

I need to bestir myself. I need to learn; I can turn their numbers into worlds, such as Bessie sees, where stars are not crystals, where the moon is a beach of gravel and ice.

Dee would be gone by dawn. He and the Danes were sailing. Were the Danes still in the house? If they were he could leave with them.

As if jabbed, Guy sat up. "Bessie, I'm going to go."

"I knew you would," she said, her face dim with pleasure for him.

Go to that island of philosophy, be there with Rosary; he liked Rosie, wanted to kiss him too—and Rosie could explain the numbers. Guy jittered up to his feet, slipping on the slush. He saw Fortune: a salmon shooting away under the water. He nipped forward, gave Bessie a kiss on the cheek, and ran into the house, shouting, "Squire. My good sirs!"

From inside the house came thumps and racketing and shouts, the Squire bellowing "Take this coat!" and the Danes howling with laughter. Outside, it started to snow again, drifting past Bessie's face.

Well, thought Bessie, *I never had him really.*

She was falling between stars again on a silver ship shaped like a swan with wings that whistled. They docked on a comet that was made not of fire, but ice; and they danced a jig on it and set it spinning with the lightness of their feet; and they went on until clouds of angels flew about them with voices like starlings and the voyagers wouldn't have to die because they already were in Heaven, and on the prow stood Good Queen Bess in silver armor and long red hair, but Good Queen Bess was her.

Shakespere's next play was called *A Midwinter's Nonesuch on Mars.*

gray wings

KARL BUNKER

New writer Karl Bunker is currently a software engineer and has been a jew-
eler, a musical instrument maker, a sculptor, and a mechanical technician.
His writing has appeared in Asimov's, Cosmos, Abyss & Apex, Electric
Velocipede, Writers of the Future, Neo-Opsis, *and elsewhere. His story*
"Under the Shouting Sky" won him the first Robert A. Heinlein Centennial
Short Story Contest. Bunker lives with his dog in Boston, Massachusetts.

Here he gives us a quiet but poignant demonstration that we are likely to
be divided into the haves and have-nots even in an opulent high-tech future.

It was just carelessness. I'd gotten into the wake turbulence of an old jetliner that was still low after taking off from Lagos. The wingtip vortices off of those old buckets can trail behind them for fifty or a hundred kilometers, and . . . well, I was careless.

So I tumbled and spun and twisted and generally had a bad time of it, and then I fell. By the time I was wings-up and face-down again, I didn't have much altitude left and the ground was rushing up to greet me. My wings had folded in tight during my tumble, and at the speed I was falling I'd rip my sternum open if I tried to unfurl them too quickly. So I went easy, feathering open slowly. I turned into the wind, trying to translate my downward momentum into forward. I furled out more and more, listening to the fibers that held my chest together go snap, snap, snap.

But it was working; I was falling slower. There was a treeless valley to my right, so I teased out a banking turn in that direction. I skimmed over the crest of a low hill, glancing down to watch the ground blur past me with two meters to spare. Then I looked up again—too late.

There was a building straight ahead of me, and all I had time to do was close my eyes. I hit the thatched roof and ripped through it with a whooshing, crunching sound. Then there was another fraction of a second of blind freefall, and then my hands and chest and stomach hit a hard-packed dirt floor and I skidded to a stop.

I was lying inside a low building. There were broken lengths of wood and piles of straw scattered around me, underneath me, on top of me. I took a slow breath, then started looking at my body, moving as little as possible. There was a long ragged

gash across my shoulder and partway down my right breast, but it was already closing. My left leg was worse, with both bones below the knee broken, the tibia piercing the skin and the fabric of my unitard. That seemed to be it for body damage. I
turned my head carefully and looked back at my wings. "Shit!" I yelled. The main
spar of both wings was snapped just before the elbow joint, the bloody carbon fibers
extending like brush bristles from the broken ends.

I lay still for a while, just breathing. Then I sat up and grabbed my left shin above
and below the break. I shut off all pain and deadened the muscles, and then started
pulling and twisting. After a few attempts I got the broken ends of the bones lined
up. I clamped both hands over the break and held, counting out 120 elephants.
Somewhere around ninety my nerve-shutoff timed out and pain came roaring back,
and I groaned and whimpered and sniffled.

When I was done counting, and a while after that, I opened my eyes again. I was
lying on my side and there was an old woman looming over me. Black-skinned and
deeply wrinkled, her mouth was open in what might have been a smile, showing
several missing teeth. She said something in a language I didn't understand, then in
thickly accented English: "An anchel, yes? We have a little girl-child anchel fallen
from heaven, eh?" She laughed, then straightened up and walked away, kicking
aside a pile of straw as she went to a door and left.

I looked around at the building I was in. It seemed to be a small barn, with a
hayloft and unglazed windows on all four walls. Beyond those walls, I was in the
dead center of nowhere. I didn't know where I was to within two hundred kilometers, and wouldn't until I hit the Niger River sometime in the next day or so, where
the beacon buoys would tell me whether to head upstream or down.

The door swung open again and two people came through it: The old woman
and a young man. The woman spoke in her unknown language to the man, pointed
at me, then at the hole in the roof. She laughed her thin, dry laugh. The man
walked up to me and bent over at the waist, examining me. Belatedly, I thought to
check the front of my unitard to see if my breasts were showing. Not that there's
much to look at there, but some cultures are touchy about that sort of thing. He
systematically looked me over: legs, torso, arms, face, and finally the broken wings
that sprouted from my back. Then he spoke, his accent not as thick as the old woman's. "How bad you are hurt?" he said.

"I—I'm all right. My leg was . . . But it will heal." I realized that he was in fact
almost a boy, possibly still in his teens. He was tall and very thin and dressed in blue
jean shorts and a T-shirt. "My name is Amy," I said. "I'm flying in the Kitaroharo
Race—do you know it?"

The young man looked up, through the hole in the roof to the sky beyond. "Yes,"
he said slowly. "The flyer races. They give you wings and you fly; sometimes you
race. I have heard of this—seen videos." Suddenly he dropped to his knees. He bent
his head, looking closely at my leg in the dim light. "Are you sure is okay? There is
much blood."

"Yes, it will be fine." I peeled up the soggy leg of my unitard to reassure him. The
pain had subsided to a dull throb by now.

With one finger he traced a path in the air, close to my skin but not touching it,
following the line of the scar that showed where the bone had come through. It was

a swollen, light-colored streak against the darker ash-gray of my skin. He withdrew his hand, closing his fingers. "You fix yourself? Of course—you have healing nanos, yes? Good. Very good." He stood up again. "Dabir is me—is my name," he said, touching his chest. He smiled, his teeth bright in the gloom. His face was beautiful, with wide, innocent eyes, high cheekbones, and a long nose that flared at the nostrils. "I am please to meet you, Amy." The smile flashed again and he waved vaguely in the direction of the door he had come through. "Our connection is dead right now, but I can go to the village, to the computers there. Shall I call to Lagos maybe? Or you have family I should call? People who come get you?"

"No!" I blurted. "If you do that they'll take me out of the race, and I won't qualify for the Asiatics this season. I can't win this race now, probably can't even place in the top ten, but the time limit for finishing is still six days away. I can make it to Casablanca by then—" I twisted around to look at where my wings were broken, the upper parts of the spars dangling limply, "if I can repair my wings fast enough."

"You can fix your wings yourself?" Dabir asked. "Like your leg?"

"Not quite. They need to be splinted until they self-repair, and I can't reach them to do that. I'll need help."

Dabir went around behind me and crouched down again. A moment later he made a soft grunting sound. "You are bleeding," he said. "The broken part of the wings—it bleeds."

"Yes. They're a part of me, connected to my blood supply. But it's okay; they'll only bleed a little, and it doesn't hurt." This wasn't entirely true; I could feel the two breaks in the main spars, especially when the broken ends flexed, and while it wasn't anything like the pain in my leg had been, it was damned unpleasant.

He came around in front of me again and squatted. He looked at me, meeting my eyes for a moment and then shyly looking away. He was sitting with his knees up and his forearms resting on them. His hands were long and delicate-looking, with tapering fingers. "Okay," he said. "If you can explain to me how to make this splint, I will try to do it."

Over the next hour or so, Dabir found four suitable pieces of wood and some heavy string. He got squeamish when I told him he'd have to punch a row of holes through the wing membrane so he could wrap the string around the spar and the two pieces of splint, but after some hesitation he did it. By the time he was finished my neck was stiff from craning to look around behind me to watch what he was doing. "Thank you," I said when he was finally done. "That's great. By tomorrow this time they should be strong enough to fly."

"That soon?" Dabir shook his head, smiling. "Is amazing."

As I rubbed the ache out of my neck I realized I was thirsty, hungry, and exhausted. The day had taken a lot out of me. "Could I have some water?" I said.

"Oh!" Dabir practically leapt to his feet, and then flinched, something in his leg or hip hurting him. His hands were covered with my blood, some of it dried and some still wet. "I am sorry," he said. "I should have brought you water sooner. And food." He left, walking quickly and with a limp. Crouching down to work on my wings must have aggravated something in his leg. A few moments later he was back with a big mug full of water, which he handed to me before hurrying away again.

This time he was gone for several minutes, and when he came back he had a plate of food. There were boiled greens and some kind of meat with a thick sauce. He held the plate out to me with one hand and a fork with the other.

"Oh, you didn't have to do that, Dabir. There's no need, really. I can eat anything. My nanos can digest cellulose—grass, raw leaves, anything. You don't have to give me your . . ." I stopped, feeling stupid. As I'd been speaking, Dabir's hand and the plate it was holding drifted down and toward his side, until it looked like all the plate's contents were about to spill onto the ground.

"You do not want?" he said.

I held my hands out for the plate and the silverware. "Yes, I do," I said. "Thank you. It's very kind of you."

Once I started eating, I could barely shovel the food into my mouth fast enough. Dabir sat cross-legged—as I was sitting—on the dirt floor a few feet away from me. He wasn't watching me eat, but wasn't not watching either.

"What is this building?" I asked, partly to force myself to slow down my gobbling and partly just for something to say.

"A barn for goats we used to have," he said. He made a loose-jointed wave of his arm that seemed to indicate more than just the building. "We had many goats. Then they all get a disease, last year. They all die."

"Ah, that's too bad," I mumbled, staring down at my plate. I was trying to decide if the meat underneath the tamarind sauce was real or a synthetic, maybe from a UN-Aid rations pack. I went on eating.

A minute later the old woman came in, carrying another plate of food like mine, but with less meat. She handed it to Dabir, grinning her gap-toothed smile at some secret joke. She glanced at me, croaked a few dry, laughing words at Dabir in their language, grinned some more, and then went away. Dabir avoided my eyes after she was gone, and began to eat, deftly plucking food from his plate with his long, thin fingers.

I looked down at my own hands, at my charcoal-gray skin. I wondered if he thought I was born with skin this color, thought it had anything to do with race.

"My grandmother likes you," Dabir said after a little while. "She calls you our little wounded angel."

"That's what she called me when she found me," I said. "'A little girl-child angel, fallen from heaven' she said." I paused. "Does she really think . . . ?"

He looked at me with a smile that made me feel like the idiot I was. "No, is only a joke," he said. "Most strangers she doesn't like very much." His smile grew into a soft chuckle. "But you know, most strangers don't fall out of the sky and land in our barn."

I looked up at the roof of the barn. I'd broken through some of the timbers that supported the thatching, and about a third of the roof was slumping inward precariously. "I'm sorry about the damage," I said. "Before I leave, give me your information and I'll send money to you for repairs."

He made a dismissive motion with his head. "Damage doesn't matter. There are no goats now."

"But you'll be getting more, won't you?"

"Tell me about flying," he said. "What is it like?"

"It's . . . pretty much what you would expect." I got to my feet as I spoke, stretching myself out straight, testing my weight on the newly-repaired bones of my left leg. I took a few tentative steps, looking behind me at my wings to make sure Dabir's splints were holding. Luckily the peaked roof of the barn was tall enough that I didn't have to worry about the elbows of my wings hitting anything. "You're up high, you look down, it's quiet, it's cold and windy, it's wet when you fly into a cloud . . ." I glanced at Dabir, feeling awkward. I didn't talk about the feeling of the wings pulling at the air, catching it, clutching at it like it was some huge living thing carrying me on its back, the feeling of inhuman strength in my wings, the roaring, screaming, blazing intoxication of it all, burning through me with every flight, every liftoff, like a drug.

I stared down hard at the ground. When I looked at Dabir a moment ago I'd noticed for the first time that he had a long, ragged scar along the outside of his right leg, starting at the knee and stretching down halfway to his ankle. The skin was rough and puckered, the two sides of the gash misaligned; the wound must not have even been sutured, much less nano-healed.

"I'd like to walk around outside, if I may," I said.

"Of course!" He bounced to his feet and walked with me to the door. With both of us standing, I barely came up to his shoulder. "You are small—tiny!" he laughed down at me. "But you are not so young as you look, yes? I mean, not a girl, like my grandmother thought at first."

"No, Dabir, not so young as I look." Moving carefully, I bent low to angle my folded wings through the doorway ahead of me. I thought of my friend Nila, and the party she'd thrown for me to celebrate my new wings. She'd had every door and doorway in her home modified into a gothic arch with a peak three meters high, so I could walk from room to room without bending over. And the next day, the party over, she'd had them all changed back.

Outside, the sun was getting low. Ahead of us was a sprawling field of some kind of crop; meter-high stalks of something dry and yellowing, with lots of bare dirt between each plant. To the right, not far away, was a tiny, unpainted wooden house with a flat roof of corrugated metal. It was crudely built, like the barn, but beyond that there was something about it that screamed of poverty and misery and ugliness. Looking at it made me feel hollowed out inside, and when I suddenly realized that Dabir might invite me in there, the thought terrified me.

"Not a good year for the millet," Dabir said, as if apologizing, looking out over the field. "Good rain at first, but then not enough. Next year be better, we think."

I walked in a mock-aimless direction, away from the house, taking deep breaths, waving my arms and flexing my wings slowly. I could feel energy from the sun soaking into my skin, coursing into the storage cells distributed through my body. But more than that I could feel that terrible little house, crouching behind me like a gargoyle. I was wishing desperately, frantically, that I could lift into the air and fly away now. That I could be back up in the cold sky where I belonged, where all of this would be far, far down, invisible below me.

Of course I'd known what I was flying over. I'd known people lived like this. Like this, and a hundred times worse than this in some places. There was famine in Sudan, the epidemic in New Guinea, collapsing economies here and there around the world. I knew all that, had known it since I was a child. But . . . But . . . But something.

Dabir was still at my side. "Are the splints holding okay?" I asked, half turning my back to him.

"Yes, they seem good," he said after looking.

"This race I'm in, the Kitaroharo, is a solo race," I said. "That means the racers have no support crew, no electronics, and we aren't allowed to make contact with the local people. At least not on purpose. It's okay if it happens by accident, if a racer makes a forced landing like I did. But normally we only land in remote areas, and we spend nights in the open, usually sleeping in trees. That's why the race is only over sparsely populated areas." I was saying all this with the plan of mumbling something about it being against the rules for me to spend the night in Dabir's house, should he invite me.

"I am glad you crashed here," he said, and then dipped his head in a gesture of embarrassment and apology. "I mean, I'm sorry you were hurt, but if you were going to crash somewhere . . ." He grinned, waving his long, graceful hand as a way of finishing the sentence. "I am . . . happy to be able to help you."

"You've been very generous, and I'm grateful," I said. "With any luck I'll be out of your hair tomorrow. Please let me know how I can send you some money, to pay for the barn, and to thank you for all your help."

Dabir was looking at an angle into the sky, where there was nothing to look at. "And tomorrow . . . tomorrow I see you fly, yes?"

"Yes, tomorrow I fly."

We walked around for a while in silence, ending up back at the barn as it was getting dark. Dabir went into his little house and came back out a few minutes later carrying a small, thin mattress and a blanket. "The roof in the house is low," he said, holding his free hand palm-down a few inches over his head. "You would hit your wings. So you okay to sleep in here?" He nodded at the barn.

"Yes, that's fine."

Dabir went into the barn and laid the little mattress out on the floor. It was really just a blanket that had been folded in half and stitched up with something stuffed inside, probably dried millet leaves. "I'm sorry we have no better bed for you," Dabir said, flipping out the blanket over the mattress.

"Dabir . . . Is this your bed?"

He tugged at the corners of the blanket, pretending not to hear me.

"I don't need this, Dabir, really. I'm used to sleeping on the ground, and my body doesn't get cold." That last bit was pretty stupid of me, since the nighttime temperatures in this region are warm by anyone's standards. Still feigning deafness, Dabir was backing away from the bed and from me, moving toward the door. "Damnit, Dabir . . ." I said. I thought about picking the bed up and forcing it back into his arms, but I didn't.

"Good night," he said, smiling shyly and backing out the door.

As I lowered my face to his mattress there was the sweet smell of hay, and faintly beneath that, his sweat; a warm, living, human smell. I slept, jolting awake once through the night with my heart pounding from a dream I couldn't remember.

The next morning I was up early, pacing around outside and slowly flexing my wings while keeping them mostly furled. There was barely a hint of dew on the ground, and it was evaporating away with the smell of wet dust. I heard someone coughing in the house. It was wet, hacking, feeble, coming from old lungs. It seemed it was never going to stop, and finally I went back into the barn and sat on the dirt floor and put my hands over my ears.

Some time later, Dabir came in with a bowl of porridge for my breakfast. While I ate, sitting cross-legged on the ground, I asked him to unlace the splints on my wings. When he was done with that I felt him running his hand over the wing membrane, feeling the texture of it. And then his hand was on my shoulder, near my neck, grazing over a part of me that wasn't covered by my unitard.

"The wings, they look good," he said. "The places where they were broken, there is only a small bump now."

I went outside and made some experimental flaps with the wings half-unfurled, feeling for any twinges at the break sites. Nothing, or nothing too bad anyway. I flapped harder and harder, until Dabir was flinching and blinking his eyes at the rush of air and dust I was blowing up. The weight on my feet was becoming less and less, became nothing for a moment, and then another moment. I held my arms to the sides, tipped my body forward . . . And stopped, furling my wings in so quickly that I lost my balance, dropping to my knees and pitching forward to catch myself on my hands.

Dabir was at my side instantly, one hand on my arm and the other on my back. "Are you okay? Did you hurt something?" he asked.

"I'm all right." I stayed on my hands and knees for a few moments. The left break site had flexed dangerously, and now it was throbbing with an ache that kept time with my heartbeat. "I just overdid it a little. I need a few more hours to heal." I let Dabir help me to my feet, feeling his dry, callused hands holding me with gentleness and strength.

"Such power in your wings!" he said. "And they are huge when they open all the way! Amazing!" He was still holding me with one arm across my back, and with the word "huge" he swung his free arm over his head, sweeping it across the sky. "And your eyes!" he said.

"Eyes?"

"Your eyes, when you started to fly . . ." He didn't finish.

I went and sat on a bare patch of ground, spreading my wings out to the sun to gather energy and let the breaks finish healing. I fell asleep again.

When I woke I could see it was past noon already. I looked around for Dabir and found him in the millet field, deepening a dry irrigation ditch. "I'm ready to leave, Dabir," I said.

"Ah." He looked at me for a long time, and then smiled. "I get to see you fly. You finish this race and you qualify for the Asiatics, yes?"

"Yes," I said, wishing I had his certainty about what I was going to do. We walked up to a small hillside where the high ground would help with my takeoff. Dabir's grandmother was standing outside the doorway of the house, and when she saw me looking she lifted a hand and made one of her open-mouthed grins. "Dabir," I said. "If you just tell me your last name, and the name of the nearest village, then I'll be able to send you some money. It will pay for repairs to the barn, and enough so you could get some more goats, get medical care for your grandmother . . ." My voice trailed away. He was just looking at me with that blank, boyish smile. Or maybe it was an old man's smile. Maybe it was a smile of pity for the stupid, silly child who'd landed in his goat barn and who knew nothing, nothing, nothing about the world.

And then suddenly my arms are around him, my face pressed to his bony chest, my eyes wet. His hands touch my shoulders, my back, the side of my face, and then I turn away from him and I run down the hill, flapping frantically, tearing at the air, clawing my way up, and up, and up, then circling around to look down at him, both of his hands pressed to his mouth as he looks back up at me, his arm suddenly flailing out in a wave, piercingly childlike in the wild joy of it, and I climb up, straight up, pulling myself higher and higher to make him smaller, to make him smaller, to make him disappear.

THE BEST WE CAN

CARRIE VAUGHN

New York Times *bestseller Carrie Vaughn is the author of a wildly popular series of novels detailing the adventures of Kitty Narville, a radio personality who also happens to be a werewolf, and who runs a late-night call-in radio advice show for supernatural creatures. The Kitty books include* Kitty and the Midnight Hour, Kitty Goes to Washington, Kitty Takes a Holiday, Kitty and the Silver Bullet, Kitty and the Dead Man's Hand, Kitty Raises Hell, Kitty's House of Horrors, Kitty Goes to War, Kitty's Big Trouble, Kitty Steals the Show, Kitty Rocks the House, *and a collection of her Kitty stories,* Kitty's Greatest Hits. *Her other novels include:* Voices of Dragons, *her first venture into young adult territory; a fantasy,* Discord's Apple; Steel; *and* After the Golden Age. *Vaughn's short work has appeared in* Lightspeed, Asimov's Science Fiction, Subterranean, Wild Cards: Inside Straight, Realms of Fantasy, Jim Baen's Universe, Paradox, Strange Horizons, Weird Tales, All-Star Zeppelin Adventure Stories, *and elsewhere; her non-Kitty stories have been collected in* Straying from the Path. *Her most recent books include a new Kitty novel,* Kitty in the Underworld, *and* Dreams of the Golden Age, *a sequel to* After the Golden Age. *She lives in Colorado.*

Here she gives us a quiet but moving story about an all-too-plausible reaction to the age-old dream of first contact.

In the end, the discovery of evidence of extraterrestrial life, and not just life, but intelligence, got hopelessly mucked up because no one wanted to take responsibility for confirming the findings, and no one could decide who ultimately had the authority—the obligation—to do so. We submitted the paper, but peer review held it up for a year. News leaked—NASA announced one of their press conferences, but the press conference ended up being an announcement about a future announcement, which never actually happened and the reporters made a joke of it. Another case of Antarctic meteorites or cold fusion. We went around with our mouths shut waiting for an official announcement while ulcers devoured our guts.

So I wrote a press release. I had Marsh at JPL's comet group and Salvayan at Columbia vet it for me and released it under the auspices of the JPL Near Earth

Objects Program. We could at least start talking about it instead of arguing about whether we were ready to start talking about it. I didn't know what would happen next. I did it in the spirit of scientific outreach, naturally. The release included that now-famous blurry photo that started the whole thing.

I had an original print of that photo, of UO-1—Unidentified Object One, be-cause it technically wasn't flying and I was being optimistic that this would be the first of more than one—framed and hanging on the wall over my desk, a stark focal point in my chronically cluttered office. Out of the thousands of asteroids we tracked and photographed, this one caught my eye, because it was symmetrical and had a higher than normal albedo. It flashed, even, like a mirror. Asteroids aren't symmet-rical and aren't very reflective. But if it wasn't an asteroid . . .

We turned as many telescopes on it as we could. Tried to get time on Hubble and failed, because it sounded ridiculous—why waste time looking at something inside the orbit of Jupiter? We *did* get Arecibo on it. We got pictures from multiple sources, studied them for weeks until we couldn't argue with them any longer. No one wanted to say it because it was crazy, just thinking it would get you sacked, and I got so frustrated with the whole group sitting there in the conference room after hours on a Friday afternoon, staring at each other with wide eyes and dropped jaws and no one saying anything, that I said it: It's not natural, and it's not ours.

UO-1 was approximately 250 meters long, with a fan shape at one end, blurred at the other, as if covered with projections too fine to show up at that resolution. The rest was perfectly straight, a thin stalk holding together blossom and roots, the lines rigid and artificial. The fan shape might be a ram scoop—Angie came up with that idea, and the conjecture stuck, no matter how much I reminded people that we couldn't decide anything about what it was or what it meant. Not until we knew more.

We—the scientific community, astronomers, philosophers, writers, all of humanity—had spent a lot of time thinking about what would happen if we found definitive proof that intelligent life existed elsewhere in the universe. All the sce-narios involved these other intelligences talking to us. Reaching out to us. Sending a message we would have to decipher—would be eager to decipher. Hell, we sure wouldn't be able to talk to them, not stuck on our own collection of rocks like we were. Whether people thought we'd be overrun with sadistic tripods or be invited to join a greater benevolent galactic society, that was always the assumption—we'd know they were there because they'd talk to us.

When that didn't happen, it was like no one knew what to do next. No one had thought about what would happen if we just found a . . . a *thing* . . . that happened to be drifting a few million miles out from the moon. It didn't talk. Not so much as a blinking light. The radiation we detected from it was reflected—whatever propul-sion had driven it through space had long since stopped, and inertia carried it now. No one knew how to respond to it. The news that was supposed to change the course of human history . . . didn't.

We wouldn't know any more about it until we looked at it up close, until we brought it here, brought it home. And that was where it all fell apart.

I presented the initial findings at the International Astronomical Union annual meeting. My department gathered the data, but we couldn't do anything about implementation—no one group could implement *anything*. But of course, the first argument was about whom the thing belonged to. I nearly resigned.

Everyone wanted a piece of it, including various governments and the United Nations, and we had to humor that debate because nothing could get done without funding. The greatest discovery in all of human history and funding held it hostage. Several corporations, including the producers of a popular energy drink, threatened to mount their own expeditions in order to establish naming and publicity rights, until the U.S. Departments of Energy, Transportation, and Defense issued joint restrictions on privately-funded extra-orbital spaceflight, which caused its own massive furor.

Meanwhile, we and the various other groups working on the project tracked UO-1 as it appeared to establish an elliptical solar orbit that would take it out to the orbit of Saturn and back on a twenty-year cycle. We waited. We developed plans, which were presented and rejected. We took better and better pictures, which revealed enough detail to see struts holding up what did indeed appear to be the surface of a ram scoop. It did not, everyone slowly began to agree, appear to be inhabited. The data on it never fluctuated. No signals emanated from it. It was metal, it was solid, it was inert. We published papers and appeared on cable documentaries. We gritted our teeth while websites went up claiming that the thing was a weapon, and a survivalist movement developed in response. Since it was indistinguishable from all the existing survivalist movements, no one really noticed.

And we waited.

The thing is, you discover the existence of extraterrestrial intelligence, and you still have to go home, wash up, get a good night's sleep, and come up with something to eat for breakfast in the morning. Life goes on, life keeps going on, and it's not that people forget or stop being interested. It's that they realize they still have to change the oil in the car and take the dog for a walk. You feel like the whole world ought to be different, but it only shifts. Your worldview expands to take in this new information.

I go to work every day and look at that picture, *my* picture, this satellite or spacecraft, this message in a bottle. Some days I'm furious that I can't get my hands on it. Some days I weep at the wonder of it. Most days I look at it, sigh, and write another round of emails and make phone calls to find out what's going to happen to it. To *make* something happen.

"How goes the war?" Marsh leans into my office like he does every afternoon, mostly to try to cheer me up. He's been here as long as I have; our work overlaps, and we've become friends. I go to his kids' birthday parties. The brown skin around his eyes crinkles with his smile. I'm not able to work up a smile to match.

"The Chinese say they're sending a probe with a robotic arm and a booster to grab it and pull it back to Earth. They say whoever gets there first has right of salvage. It's a terrible idea. Even if they did manage to get it back without breaking it, they'd never let anyone else look at it."

"Oh, I think they would—under their terms." He doesn't get too worked up about it because nobody's managed to do anything yet, why would they now? He would say I take all of this too personally, and he'd be right.

"The IAU is sending a delegation to try to talk the Chinese government into joining the coalition. They might have a chance of it if they actually had a plan of their own. Look, if you want me to talk your ear off, come in and sit, have some coffee. Otherwise, leave now. That's your warning."

"I'll take the coffee," he says, claiming the chair I pulled away from the wall for him before turning to my little desktop coffee maker. His expression softens, his sympathy becoming genuine rather than habitual. "You backing any particular plan yet?"

I sigh. "Gravity tractor looks like our best option. Change the object's trajectory, steer it into a more convenient orbit without actually touching it. Too bad the technology is almost completely untested. We can test it first, of course. Which will take years. And there's an argument against it. Emissions from a gravity tractor's propulsion may damage the object. It's the root of the whole problem: we don't know enough about the thing to know how much stress it can take. The cowboys want to send a crewed mission—they say the only way to be sure is to get eyeballs on the thing. But that triples the cost of any mission. Anything we do will take years of planning and implementation anyway, so no one can be bothered to get off their asses. Same old, same old."

Two and half years. It's been two and a half years since we took that picture. My life has swung into a very tight orbit around this one thing.

"Patience, Jane," Marsh says in a tone that almost sets me off. He's only trying to help.

Truth is, I've been waiting for his visit. I pull out a sheet of handwritten calculations from under a manila folder. "I do have another idea, but I wanted to talk to you about it before I propose anything." His brow goes up, he leans in with interest.

He'll see it faster than I can explain it, so I speak carefully. "We can use Angelus." When he doesn't answer, yes or no, I start to worry and talk to cover it up. "It launches in six months, plenty of time to reprogram the trajectory, send it on a flyby past UO-1, get more data on it than we'll ever get sitting here on Earth—"

His smile has vanished. "Jane. I've been waiting for Angelus for five years. The timing is critical. My comet won't be this close for another two hundred years."

"But Angelus is the only mission launching in the next year with the right kind of optics and maneuverability to get a good look at UO-1, and yes, I know the timing on the comet is once-in-a-lifetime and I know it's important. But this—this is once in a *civilization*. The sooner we can look at it, answer some of our questions . . . well. The sooner the better."

"The better *you'll* be. I'm supposed to wait, but you can't?"

"Please, Marsh. I'll feel a lot better about it if you'll agree with me."

"Thank you for the coffee, Jane," he says, setting aside the mug as he stands.

I close my eyes and beseech the ceiling. This isn't how I want this to go. "Marsh, I'm not trying to sabotage your work, I'm just looking at available resources—"

"And I'm not ultimately the one who makes decisions about what happens to

Angelus. I'm just the one depending on all the data. You can make your proposal, but don't ask me to sign off on it."

He starts to leave and I say, "Marsh. I can't take it anymore. I spend every day holding my breath, waiting for someone to do something truly stupid. Some days I can't stand it that I can't get my hands on it."

He sits back down, like a good friend should. A good friend would not, however, steal a colleague's exploratory probe away from him. But this is *important*.

"You know what I think? The best bet is to let one of these corporate foundations mount an expedition. They won't want to screw up because of the bad publicity, and they'll bring you on board for credibility so you'll have some say in how they proceed. You'll be their modern-day Howard Carter."

I can see it now: I'd be the face of the expedition, all I'd have to do is stand there and look pretty. Or at least studious. Explain gravity and trajectories for the popular audience. Speculate on the composition of alien alloys. Watch whatever we find out there get paraded around the globe to shill corn chips. Wouldn't even feel like I was selling my soul, would it?

I must look green, or ill, or murderous, because Marsh goes soothing. "Just think about it, before you go and do something crazy."

I've kept a dedicated SETI@home computer running since I was sixteen. Marsh doesn't know that about me. I don't believe in extraterrestrial UFO's because I know in great, intimate detail the difficulties of sending objects across the vast distances of space. Hell, just a few hundred miles into orbit isn't a picnic. We've managed it, of course—we are officially extra-solar system beings, now, with our little probes and plaques pushing ever outward. Will they find anything? Will anything find *them*?

Essentially, there are two positions on the existence of extraterrestrial intelligence and whether we might ever make contact, and they both come down to the odds. The first says that *we're* here, humanity is intelligent, flinging out broadcasts and training dozens of telescopes outward hoping for the least little sign, and the universe is so immeasurably vast that given the odds, the billions of stars and galaxies and planets out there, we can't possibly be the only intelligent species doing these things. The second position says that the odds of life coming into being on any given planet, of that life persisting long enough to evolve, then to evolve intelligence, and then being interested in the same things we are—the odds of all those things falling into place are so immeasurably slim, we may very well be the only ones here.

Is the universe half full or half empty? All we could ever do to solve the riddle was wait. So I waited and was rewarded for my optimism.

In unguarded moments I'm certain this was meant to happen, I was meant to discover UO-1. Me and no one else. Because I understand how important it is. Because I'm the one sitting here every day sending emails and making phone calls. I ID'd the image, I made the call, I had the guts to go public, I deserve a say in what happens next.

I submit the paperwork proposing that the Angelus probe be repurposed to perform a flyby and survey of UO-1. Marsh will forgive me. I wait. Again.

I've kept track, and I've done a hundred fifty TV interviews in the last two years. Most of them are snippets for pop-documentaries, little chunks of information delivered to the lowest common denominator audience. I explain over and over again, in different settings, sometimes in my office, sometimes in a vague but picturesque location, sometimes at Griffith Observatory, because for some reason nothing says "space" like Griffith Observatory. I hold up a little plastic model of UO-1 (they're selling the kits at hobby stores—we don't see any of the money from that) to demonstrate the way it's traveling through space, how orbital mechanics work, and how we might use a gravity tractor to bring it home. Sometimes, the segments are specifically for schools, and I like those best because I can give free rein to my enthusiasm. I tell the kids, "This is going to take more than one lifetime to figure out. If we find a way to go to Alpha Centauri, it's going to take lifetimes. You'll have to finish the work I've started. Please grow up and finish it."

I call everyone I can think of who might have some kind of influence over Angelus. I explain that a picture of a metal object taken from a few million miles away doesn't tell us anything about the people who made it. Not even if they have thumbs or tentacles. Most of them tell me that the best plan they can think of is to build bigger telescopes.

"It's not the size," I mutter. "It's how you use it."

NASA thinks they will be making the decision because they've got the resources, the scientists, the experience, the hardware. Congress says this is too important to let NASA make decisions unilaterally. A half dozen private U.S. firms would try something if the various cabinet departments weren't busy making anything they could try illegal by fiat. There are already three court cases. At least one of them is arguing that a rocket launch is protected as freedom of speech. The IAU brought a complaint to the United Nations that the U.S. government shouldn't be allowed to dictate a course of action. The General Assembly nominated a "representative in absentia" for the species that launched UO-1—some Finnish philosopher I'd never heard of. It should have been me.

After a decade of international conferences I have colleagues all over the world. I call them all. Most are sympathetic. A South African cosmologist I know tells me I'm grandstanding, then laughs like it's a joke, but not really. They all tell me to be patient. Just wait.

Life goes on. My other research, the asteroid research I was doing, has piled up, and I get polite but firm hints that I really ought to work on that if I want to keep my job. I go to conferences, I publish, I do another dozen interviews, holding up the plastic model of the object that I'll likely never get close to. The ache in my heart feels just like it did when Peter left me. That was three years ago, and I can still feel it. The ache that says: I can't possibly start over, can I?

The ache faded when I found UO-1.

"JPL rejected your proposal to repurpose Angelus. Thank God." Marsh leans on my doorway like usual. He's grinning like he won a prize.

I got the news via email. The bastards can't even be bothered to call. I'd called them back, thinking there must have been a mistake. The pitying tone in their voices didn't sound like kindness anymore. It was definitely condescension. I cried. I've been crying all afternoon, as the pile of wadded-up tissues on my desk attests. My eyes are still puffy. Marsh can see I've been crying; he knows what it looks like when I cry. He was there three years ago. I take a breath to keep from starting up again and stare at him like he's punched me.

"How can you say that? Do you know what they're talking about now? They're talking about just leaving it! They're saying the orbit is stable, we'll always know where it is and we can go after it when we have a better handle on the technology. But what if something happens to it? What if an asteroid hits it, or it crashes into Jupiter, or—"

"Jane, it's been traveling for how many hundreds of billions of miles—why would something happen to it now?"

"I don't know! It shouldn't even be there at all! And they won't even *listen* to me!"

He sounds tired. "Why should they?"

"Because it's *mine*!"

His normally comforting smile is sad, pitying, smug, and amused, all at once. "It's not yours, not any more than gravity belonged to Newton."

I want to scream. Because maybe this isn't the most important thing to happen to humanity. That's probably, oh, the invention of the wheel, or language. Maybe this is just the most important thing to happen to me.

I grab another tissue. Look at the picture of UO-1. It's beautiful. It tells me that the universe, as vast as we already know it is, is bigger than we think.

Marsh sits in the second chair without waiting for an invitation. "What do you think it is, Jane? Be honest. No job, no credibility, no speaking gig for Discovery on the line. What do you think when you look at it?" He nods at the picture.

There are some cable shows that will win you credibility for appearing on them. There are some that will destroy any credibility you ever had. I have been standing right on that line, answering the question of "What is it?" as vaguely as possible. We need to know more, no way to speculate, et cetera. But I know. I *know* what it is.

"I think it's Voyager. Not *the* Voyager. *Their* Voyager. The probe they sent out to explore, and it just kept going."

He doesn't laugh. "You think we'll find a plaque on it? A message? A recording?"

"It's what I want to find." I smile wistfully. "But what are the odds?"

"Gershwin," he says. I blink, but he doesn't seem offended by my confusion. He leans back in the chair, comfortable in his thick middle-aged body, genial, someone who clearly believes all is well with the world, at least at the moment. "We've had fourteen billion years of particles colliding, stars exploding, nebulae compressing, planets forming, all of it cycling over and over again, and then just the right amino acids converged, life forms, and a couple of billion years of evolution later—we get Gene Kelly and Leslie Caron dancing by a fountain to Gershwin and it's beautiful. For no particular evolution-driven reason, it's beautiful. I think: what are the odds? That they're dancing, that it's on film, and that I'm here watching and thinking it's gorgeous. If the whole universe exists just to make this one moment happen, I wouldn't be at all surprised."

"So if I think sometimes that maybe I was meant to find UO-1, because maybe there's a message there and that I'm the only one who can read it—then maybe that's not crazy?" Like thinking that the universe sent me UO-1 at a time in my life when I desperately needed something to focus on, to be meaningful . . .

"Oh no, it's definitely crazy. But it's understandable." This time his smile is kind.

"Marsh—this really is the most important thing to happen to humanity ever, isn't it?"

"Yes. But we still need to study and map near-Earth asteroids, right?"

I don't tell Marsh that I've never seen *An American in Paris*. I've never watched Gene Kelly in anything. But Marsh obviously thinks it's important, so I watch the movie. I decide he's right. That dance at the fountain, it's a moment suspended in time. Like an alien spacecraft that shouldn't be there but is.

Two things happen next.

At the next IAU meeting an archaeologist presents a lecture on UO-1, which I think is very presumptuous, but I go, because I go to everything having to do with UO-1. She talks about preservation and uses terms like "in situ," and how modern archaeological practice often involves excavating artifacts, examining them—and then putting them back in the ground. She argues that we don't know what years of space travel have done to the metal and structures of UO-1. We don't know how our methods of studying it will impact it. She showed pictures of Mayan friezes that were excavated and left exposed to the elements versus ones that remained buried for their own protection, so that later scientists with better equipment and techniques will be able to return to them someday. The exposed ones have dissolved, decayed past recognition. She gives me an image: I reach out and finally put my hand on UO-1, and its metallic skin, weakened by a billion micrometeoroid impacts gathered over millennia, disintegrates under my touch.

I think of that and start to sweat. So yes, caution. I know this.

The second thing that happens: I turn my back on UO-1.

Not really, but it's a striking image. I write another proposal, a different proposal, and submit it to one of the corporate foundations because Marsh may be right. If nothing else, it'll get attention. I don't mind a little grandstanding.

We already have teams tracking a best-guess trajectory to determine where UO-1 came from. It might have been cruising through space at nonrelativistic speed for dozens of years, or centuries, or millions of centuries, but based on the orbit it established here, we can estimate how it entered the solar system and the trajectory it traveled before then. We can trace backward.

My plan: to send a craft in that direction. It will do a minimal amount of science along the way, sending back radiation readings, but most of the energy and hardware is going into propulsion. It will be fast and it will have purpose, carrying an updated variation of Sagan's Voyager plaques and recordings, digital and analog.

It's a very simple message, in the end: Hey, we found your device. Want one of ours?

In all likelihood, the civilization that built UO-1 is extinct. The odds simply aren't good for a species surviving—and caring—for long enough to send a message and receive a reply. But our sample size for drawing that conclusion about the average lifespan of an entire species on a particular world is exactly one, which isn't a sample size at all. We weren't supposed to ever find an alien ship in our backyard, either.

I tear up when the rocket launches, and that makes for good TV. As Marsh predicted, the documentary producers decide to make me the human face of the project, and I figure I'll do what I have to, as best as I can. I develop a collection of quotes for the dozens of interviews that follow—I'm up to two-hundred thirty-five. I talk about taking the long view and transcending the everyday concerns that bog us down. About how we are children reaching across the sandbox with whatever we have to offer, to whoever shows up. About teaching our children to think as big as they possibly can, and that miracles sometimes really do happen. They happen often, because all of this, Gershwin's music, the great curry I had for dinner last night, the way we hang pictures on our walls of things we love, are miracles that never should have happened.

It's a hope, a need, a shout, a shot in the dark. It's the best we can do. For now.

transitional forms

PAUL J. McAULEY

Paul J. McAuley was born in Oxford, England, in 1955, and now makes his home in London. He has been a professional biologist for many years, sold his first story in 1984, and went on to be a frequent contributor to Interzone, *as well as to markets such as* Asimov's Science Fiction, SCI FICTION, Amazing, The Magazine of Fantasy and Science Fiction, Skylife, The Third Alternative, When the Music's Over, *and elsewhere.*

His first novel, Four Hundred Billion Stars, *won the Philip K. Dick Award, and his novel* Fairyland *won both the Arthur C. Clarke Award and the John W. Campbell Award in 1996. His other books include the novels* Of the Fall, Eternal Light, *and a major trilogy of ambitious scope and scale set ten million years in the future,* Pasquale's Angel, Confluence; *it comprises the novels* Child of the River, Ancient of Days, *and* Shrine of Stars. *Others include* Life on Mars, The Secret of Life, Whole Wide World, White Devils, Mind's Eye, Players, Cowboy Angels, The Quiet War, Gardens of the Sun, *and* In the Mouth of the Whale. *His short fiction has been collected in* The King of the Hill and Other Stories, The Invisible Country, Little Machines, *and* Stories From the Quiet War, *and he is the coeditor, with Kim Newman, of an original anthology,* In Dreams. *His most recent books are a new novel,* Evening's Empire, *and two collections,* Life After Wartime *and* A Very British History: The Best of Paul McAuley, *a big retrospective collection.*

In the tense story that follows he takes us along with a ranger patrolling the borders of a Hot Zone, in which bizarre forms of artificial life have mutated and run riot—but in which, as always, the most dangerous forms of life prove to be other human beings.

At night, the hot zone was patched with drifts of soft pastel light. Violets and indigos; dark reds, translucent greens. Jellyfish genes for luminescence had been used as markers for tweaks in the first genetically modified organisms, and that tradition had been adopted by alife hackers. The colours were tags, territorial claims that pulsed and twinkled like spring blossom in an alien and verdant land.

Ray Roberts had been patrolling the hot zone and the desert around its perimeter for two years now, and he still thought it beautiful, at night. During the day, the trees and other alife organisms baked under the sunbleached sky. Black twisted lattices like the charred skeletons of cacti; carbonised spikes and spurs like the armatures of nuclear-blasted buildings. Tangles of burnt wire. Fields of grim sculpture. But at night, shrouded in soft clouds of colour, it was a fairyland.

That particular night, about a week after a salvage gang had infiltrated the zone and stripped copper and molybdenum beads from about twenty hectares of metal-concentrating trees, Ray was riding his bay gelding, Winston, along the dirt roads that switchbacked over the dump rock hills. He was plugged into the surveillance grid of cameras and drones. GPS tracked him to within a metre. He reported to dispatch every thirty minutes, and the reports of the other patrols crackled in his earpiece. The zone was on amber alert because the salvage gang would almost certainly be back for more, but that night everyone was reporting they'd nothing to report.

Around midnight, he met up with two colleagues at one of the monitoring stations near the pit of the exhausted copper mine at the core of the zone. They watered their horses from the standpipe, exchanged gossip, moved on. At sunup, Ray and Winston were heading home along the old boundary road when he spotted something up on a ridge. A glint, a speck in the eye, a dead pixel in a heads-up display. He glassed it in UV and infra-red, called up dispatch and sent a good shot from the camera built into his glasses, got permission to check it out.

He kept a wary eye on the spot, let Winston pick his way between rocks and mini-cathedrals of black spikes and clumps of prickly pear. At the top of the ridge, he reined in his horse and sat and waited, one hand close to the taser holstered at his hip. He'd never yet used it in anger, but you never could tell.

To the naked eye, the tent's canvas perfectly matched the ground's dry pebbly texture. Pretty soon a woman emerged, as if climbing out of a rent in the air. T-shirt and jeans, dirty blond hair in a ponytail, sunglasses heliographing early morning sun as she looked up at him.

Ray asked her if she was alone. "Neither of us need any surprises."

"There's no one here but me and the ants."

"They do thrive out here."

"I saw an owl, too."

"This area's been cleaned up by the alife, pretty much. The desert's coming back in."

Ray's glasses had grabbed the woman's face by now, checked it against the government databases. Janine Childs. B.Sc, Ph.D, both degrees from UCLA. A spell of employment in the California Department of Fish and Game, then some startup funded by South Korea, working in Kazakhstan. Currently freelance. The usual traffic citations, a divorce, no criminal record. Thirty-one, five eleven, blond hair, blue eyes.

She didn't flinch when Ray swung down from his saddle. She was exactly his height.

He said, "You know why I came up here?"

"I guess I picked the wrong place to camp."

"I guess you did. You're about ten kilometres inside a state-designated exclusion zone."

"I'll pack up and move on right away. Unless you're going to arrest me," Janine Childs said, with a nice smile. "Are you going to arrest me?"

"That depends on what you have cached up yonder."

"Oh. I was hoping you hadn't spotted that."

"Your camo is good, but it's military surplus. And it's surplus because someone figured out how to detect it. Let's go see what you've got."

After Janine Childs had pulled back the camo tarp, Ray studied the fans and the tubing and the rolling strips of sticky paper, then said, "You're collecting spores."

"Suppose I said I was doing pollen counts?"

"In September? I'd say you're either six months late or six months early. I'd also say you should have picked a spot a couple of kilometres further in, if you were expecting to pick up anything from the core. The spores don't travel far, even on a good wind."

"Then I guess I've only broken the law a little bit. Will I get to keep my equipment?"

"That's not for me to say, ma'am."

"Janine."

"Yes ma'am."

She was one of those who liked to play the good sport when busted, asking Ray if he got a bonus for bringing in bandits, asking him how long he'd been riding the range, asking him where he'd bought his cowboy hat.

"It's a Stetson. Western Straw. There's a place in Yuma sells them."

"It suits you better than the yellow safety jacket and black coveralls combo. Do they sell cowboy boots, in that place in Yuma?"

"They sell just about everything in that line."

Ray couldn't tell if she was serious or was ragging on him, discovered he didn't mind.

She said, "I was thinking of buying a pair. I bet you wear them, off-duty."

Eventually the backup arrived, two troopers in a Blazer. Janine Childs handed over the keys to the rented 4x4 she'd hidden under a camo tarp on the back slope, submitted to being cuffed, and allowed Ray to help her into the rear seat of the Blazer.

"Maybe I'll see you again," she said.

Ray filed papers back at the station, heard a couple of days later that Janine Childs' equipment had been confiscated and she'd been freed with a caution.

"Think she has a taste for it?" the section supervisor said.

"She seemed to be having fun," Ray said.

"Then she'll be back," the supervisor said. "You ask me, people like her are being given too much slack, these days. We catch them and hand them over the troopers, and instead of prosecuting them the state throws them right back into the mix."

"I guess it keeps everyone in business," Ray said.

Everyone knew that most of the hackers and ware pirates were funded by the skunk works of biotech companies. The state confiscated the data and samples and equipment of everyone caught infiltrating the zone, sold it back to the companies. It was the only way anyone could make any money until ownership of the zone was resolved.

The supervisor was an old-time guy who'd been laid off the Phoenix police force when it had been privatised. He said, "It's policy, and we get paid to enforce it, but I don't have to like it."

Two months passed. Ray helped round up the salvage gang when they came back for more, and caught a pair of ware pirates with rucksacks packed with samples sawn from alife trees and shrubs, but saw no sign or trace of Janine Childs. Then, early in November, a new tweak caused a serious stepwise change in the dense ecology of alife organisms growing in the core of the hot zone.

The original alife organisms had been designed to extract low levels of copper, gold, silver and molybdenum from the bench terraces of the old copper mine and the dump rock hills around it. Powered by various forms of artificial photosynthesis, they put down long roots that ramified through bedrock like the threads of fungus through rotten wood, and selectively grabbed heavy metals and concentrated them in "berries" strung along their branches.

The process had worked pretty well until the third major recession since the turn of the century had bankrupted both the company that had planted the alife organisms and Arizona's state government. The alife organisms had spread unchecked into the desert around the mine, and the biotech company that had purchased a license to use the site as an experimental facility was discovered to have been performing all kinds of clandestine work. Some of the original alife trees were still down in the mine's pit, grown in tall tottering lattices like mediaeval siege towers, but most had been swamped by vigorous new forms of alife. The rogue company had set loose an uncatalogued variety of organisms, many infected with so-called cut-up and misprint hacks that not only allowed the organisms to swap and recombine loops of their artificial DNA, but also created random transcription errors: mutations. Introducing a kind of sex into the mix; turning the core of the hot zone into an uncontrolled evolutionary experiment. While ownership of the area and responsibility for cleaning it up was disputed in the courts, new varieties of alife organism spread through the zone like bacterial colonies growing across an agar plate, and hackers and hackers and ware pirates tried to infiltrate the zone and quarry its biodiversity, or use it as a testbed for new tweaks.

Most organisms in the zone had already acquired the capability of shedding spores or live fragments. Now, this was a new twist, instead of becoming copies of their parents, airborne fragments of at least eight varieties were generating intermediate motile forms that ran off in every direction before settling down and developing into the adult form. The change had been quick and systemic, spreading like an old-fashioned computer virus, threatening to disperse rogue alife far beyond the quarantine strip bulldozed around the perimeter of the hot zone. No one knew if it had been caused by a hacker who'd managed to infiltrate the core, or by previously unexpressed code made active by some new, random recombination event. While government scientists scrambled to isolate and understand it; every security officer was seconded to firefighting, one shift on, one shift off.

Ray spent two weeks working in the area around the core, helping to locate and dig up and burn alife organisms that were spreading the new spores, then spent two weeks more riding through the zone, hunting down the so-called rollers. Things like pygmy tumbleweeds spun from wire; little latticed spheres like pillbugs. Ray captured some for analysis, sizzled the rest with a lance equipped with an arc-weld tip.

There were hard winds blowing from the north, driving the rollers fast and far, and whipping up dust and sand. Ray and the others wore masks and goggles; at the end of every shift Ray knocked about a pound of desert out of his Stetson. The fun of the chase quickly wore off. It became work. Hard, repetitive, frustrating work.

There was a place where guards and hackers and ware pirates drank, at a crossroads where an enterprising family had set up a charge station, a motel, and a bar, the Rattler's Nest. It was an old-fashioned roadhouse, with a pine board floor and a long counter and a couple of pool tables. A pickup band played Friday nights; it was playing the night Ray came in, two days before Christmas, just off a shift chasing down rollers, and saw her. Janine Childs.

She was sitting by herself in the corner by the unplugged jukebox, blond hair loose around the shoulders of a black riding jacket slashed with zipper pockets. Long legs in blue jeans and brown leather boots. Ray leaned against the bar, watched her watching the band. She seemed to be alone. After a while, one of the hackers drifted up to her, said something. She shook her head and after a brief exchange the hacker shrugged and drifted back to the knot of his buddies, bumping fists, and Ray bought a couple of bottles of Dos Equis from a barkeep wearing a Santa hat and walked over and stood there until she looked up.

"Hey, cowboy."

"Ma'am."

"If that beer's for me, you can call me Janine."

Her eyes were bright blue, with flecks of grey around the edges of the irises.

They sat and talked, awkwardly at first, finding it hard to fit into each other's rhythms.

Janine said, "I see you favour the full-on cowboy look when you're off duty. The boots and jeans, the sheepskin-collar jacket, that hat . . . In California they take off hats, in restaurants. In Arizona, I notice that they generally don't. Can I try it?"

He gave her his hat, showed her how to handle it by the brim front and back, how to pinch the brim to pull it down over her eyes.

She looked good in it. Ray told her so. He said, "I notice you bought some good boots."

"I can picture myself living out here. You on one side of the law and me on the other. Like one of the old songs."

"Is that what this is about?" Ray said.

"It's whatever we want it to be," Janine said.

There was a silence they covered by drinking beer. The band was some kind of mutant Western swing deal. It wasn't bad: two guitars and a stand-up bass, an accordion, a fiddle, a guy whaling a minimal drum kit. A few couples were dancing, shuffling and turning in a two-step.

Janine asked Ray how he'd come to work for the state; he told her how he'd joined the army and got into private security after he'd served his four years active duty, but hadn't much liked it.

"The people I worked with were okay, mostly, but some of the clients weren't. The second time one of them put me in a bad situation, I walked. After that, I did all kinds of jobs. Construction. Painting houses. I've always worked. One time I stood on a street corner with one of those big signs, pointing people to a sale of golfing equipment. And then someone told me about the company that provides security for the zone, and here I am. I thought I'd stick it out for six months," Ray said. "But it stretched to two years, somehow. And since it doesn't look like the lawyers are about to come to any kind of agreement about who owns the zone, I guess I'll be here a while. Maybe I found my level. How about you?"

"I think that you don't get on in life by sticking around in the same place," Janine said.

"So this is just temporary," Ray said.

"You're wondering how I got into it."

"I'm wondering why someone so smart isn't working for one of the biotech companies."

"When I was much younger and the ink was still wet on my Ph.D., I thought I could make a difference. I worked for a government project at the Salton Sea, using alife organisms to remove arsenic from the lake bed of the part that was allowed to evaporate. After that, I was recruited by a Korean biotech company. Have you ever been to Kazakhstan?"

"Not yet."

"There's a genuine space port, at Baikonor. And I'm sure some parts of the country are lovely. But the place where I was working was anything but. It was out on the steppe, nothing but grass and dust for hundreds of miles in any direction. It wouldn't have been so bad if the research had been interesting, but it was production line stuff, testing varieties of alife organism for their ability to extract residual metals from the tailings of a uranium mine. And not as well paid as you might think. But I managed to save enough to try my luck here. And you know how that went."

There was another space of silence while Ray wondered what to say to that. Janine asked him how the roller hunt was going; he said, "You heard about that, uh?"

He was relieved, in a way, that she'd finally gotten around to the point.

She said, "The same way everyone else did."

"You know, only government scientists are allowed in the core. And grunts like me are watched all the time. The little cameras in our glasses, drones . . . There are pat-downs at the end of every shift, dogs trained to sniff out alife stuff. And if anyone approaches us, on the outside, chances are it's a company agent."

"I'm not an agent, Ray. And I'm not asking you to do anything illegal. Really. I'm just expressing an interest in your work."

"As far as that goes, I guess you know we have it under control."

"I know that's what the spokesman for the Department of Agriculture has been saying for the past two weeks."

"Well, it's true," Ray said. "We'll soon have things back to normal."

"But it isn't over yet, and when it's over, it won't be over. It'll be the new normal."

Ray thought about that, said, "One of the scientists told me everything out there is a transitional form. On its way to becoming something else."

"We haven't started to find out what we can do with alife organisms. Or what they can do, given the chance. 'From so simple a beginning endless forms most beautiful and wonderful have been, and are being, evolved.'"

"Nice."

"Charles Darwin."

They clinked bottles, drank to good old Charlie Darwin.

"Do you dance?" Janine Childs said.

They danced. He discovered all over again that she was exactly his height. They drank a couple more beers, danced again. Around midnight the band segued into "Rudolph the Red-nosed Reindeer" and every drunk in the place whooped onto the little dance floor.

Janine leaned against Ray and said into his ear, "I have a room, in the motel."

He made the mistake of accepting her offer of a drink, in the motel. A generous shot of tequila in a glass she fetched from the bathroom. He remembered her watching him knock it back, and then he woke with a foul headache, alone on the untouched bed. Her stuff was gone. So was his Stetson.

He didn't tell anyone about it. He wasn't even sure exactly what had happened, but he had the feeling that he'd been fooled, somehow.

The roller hunt in the core of the hot zone continued over Christmas and into the New Year. Every shift, Ray found and dispatched fewer rollers than the last. There came a time when he spent three shifts in succession without spotting a single one. Soon afterwards, the Governor declared that the emergency was over.

The next day, Ray handed in his resignation. He told himself he'd put in enough time chasing down hackers and salvage gangs. He told himself that Janine Childs was right: it doesn't pay to stick around in the same place for too long.

He tried to trace her, but had no luck. She was in the wind, as they said.

He drifted from job to job, ended up working security for the Salton Sea plantations where she had once worked. It was a monoculture of pretty basic alife organisms, but even so, hackers were slipping under the wire, inserting rogue traits. At night, patches of red or green bioluminescence showed where they'd been at work.

Ray had been there about a year when he saw a brief item in the news. The State of Arizona was suing an experimental alife facility that had recently started up in South Korea, on the grounds that the organisms it was using were based on code stolen from the hot zone. The head of the place was Dr. Janine Childs. Ray emailed her, expecting to hear nothing. A reply hit his inbox the next day.

It wasn't an apology or an explanation, but a tall story about this old scientist in Denmark who was into yeast and wanted to do research on the strains lager makers used, each one slightly different, each one producing a different brew. He wrote to the breweries, asking for samples, and without exception every one declined, citing commercial reasons. But the old scientist had what he wanted anyway: he took swabs from the rejection letters, swiped the swabs on agar plates, and cultured the yeasts that grew up. The air of each brewery was full of floating yeast cells, which had contaminated the paper of the letters.

Ray thought about this, and realised that he had an answer to his little mystery. And the next day went back out on the line. Only a few forms are ready to make the transition into something new. Most have to make do with what they already are.

precious mental

ROBERT REED

Robert Reed sold his first story in 1986 and quickly established himself as one of the most prolific of today's writers, particularly at short lengths, and he has managed to keep up a very high standard of quality while being pro-lific, something that is not at all easy to do. Reed's stories count as among some of the best short work produced by anyone in the last few decades; many of his best have been assembled in the collections The Dragons of Springplace *and* The Cuckoo's Boys. *He won the Hugo Award in 2007 for his novella* A Billion Eves. *Nor is he nonprolific as a novelist, having turned out eleven since the end of the eighties, including* The Lee Shore, The Hormone Jungle, Black Milk, The Remarkables, Down the Bright Way, Beyond the Veil of Stars, An Exaltation of Larks, Beneath the Gated Sky, Marrow, Sister Alice, *and* The Well of Stars, *as well as two chapbook novellas,* Mere *and* Flavors of My Genius. *His most recent books are a chapbook novella,* Eater-of-Bone, *a novel,* The Memory of Sky, *and a collection,* The Greatship. *Reed lives with his family in Lincoln, Nebraska.*

The novella that follows is part of Reed's long-running series of stories about the Great Ship, a Jupiter-sized spaceship created eons ago by enig-matic aliens that travels the galaxy endlessly with its freight of millions of passengers from dozens of races, including humans. This one takes us far from the Great Ship when an immortal captain, who has lived under an as-sumed identity for centuries, is shanghaied onto a desperate mission to find and salvage a derelict ship that's been lost for millions of years, and where a secret of immense importance is hidden.

1

The man came to Port Beta carrying an interesting life.

Or perhaps that life was carrying him.

Either way, he was a strong plain-faced human, exceptionally young yet already dragging heavy debt. Wanting honest, reliable employment, he wrestled with a series of aptitude tests, and while scoring poorly in most categories, the newcomer showed promise when it came to rigor and precision and the kinds of courage required by the mechanical arts. Port Beta seemed like a worthy home for him. That was where new passengers arrived at the Great Ship, cocooned inside streakships and star taxis, bomb-tugs and one-of-a-kind vehicles. Long journeys left most of those starships in poor condition. Many were torn apart as salvage, but the valuable and the healthiest were refurbished and then sent out again, chasing wealthy travelers of every species.

A local academy accepted the newcomer, and he soon rose to the most elite trade among technicians. Bottling up suns and antimatter was considered the highest art. Drive-mechanics worked on starship engines and dreamed about starship engines, and they were famous for jokes and foul curses understandable only to their own kind. Their work could be routine for years, even decades, but then inside the monotony something unexpected would happen. Miss one ghost of a detail and a lasting mistake would take hold, and then centuries later, far from Port Beta, a magnificent streakship would explode, and the onboard lives, ancient and important, were transformed into hard radiation and a breakneck rain of hot, anonymous dust.

That was why drive-mechanics commanded the highest wages.

And that was why new slots were constantly opening up in their ranks.

According to official records, the academy's new student was born on the Great Ship, inside a dead-end cavern called Where-Peace-Rains. Peculiar humans lived in that isolated realm, and they usually died there, and to the soul, they clung to preposterous beliefs, their society and entire existence woven around one linchpin idea:

The multiverse was infinite.

There was no denying that basic principle. Quantum endlessness was proven science, relentless and boundless and beautiful. Yet where most minds saw abstractions and eccentric mathematics, those living inside Where-Peace-Rains considered infinity to be a grand and demanding gift. Infinity meant that nothing could exist just once. Whatever was real, no matter how complicated or unlikely, had no choice but to persist forever.

In that way, souls were the same as snowflakes.

A person's circumstances could seem utterly, yet he was always surviving in limitless places and dying in limitless places, and he couldn't stop being born again in every suitable portion of the All.

Life had its perfect length. Most humans and almost every sentient creature believed in living happily for as long as possible. But the archaic souls inside that cave considered too much life to be a trap. One or two centuries of breathing and sleeping were plenty. Extend existence past its natural end, and the immortal soul was debased, impoverished, and eventually stripped of its grandeur. Only by knowing that you were temporary could life be stripped of illusion and the cloaks of falsegodhood, and then the blessed man could touch the All, and he could love the All, and if his brief existence proved special, a tiny piece of his endless soul might earn one moment of serene clarity.

Where-Peace-Rains constantly needed babies. Like primitive humans, its citizens were built from water and frail bone and DNA full of primate instincts. The outside world called them Luddites—an inadequate word, part insult and part synonym for madness. But the young drive-mechanic was remarkable because he grew up among those people, becoming an important citizen before relinquishing their foolish ways.

Stepping alone into the universe, the man was made immortal.

But immortality was an expensive magic.

It had to be.

Archaic muscles and organs needed to be retrofitted. The body had to be indifferent to every disease, ready to heal any wound. Then the soggy soft and very fragile human brain was transformed into a tough bioceramic wonder, complex enough to guarantee enough memory and quick intelligence to thrive for eons.

But transformation wasn't the only expense. The boundless life never quit needing space and food and energy. Eternal, highly gifted minds relished exotic wonders, yet they also demanded safety and comfort—two qualities that were never cheap. That's why the Great Ship's captains demanded huge payments from immortals. Passengers who never died would never stop needing. And that was why the one-time Luddite was impressive: Fresh inside his new body, consumed by his many debts, he was using a new brain to learn how to repair and rebuild the most spectacular machines built by any hands.

Every student was soon hired as a low-wage trainee. The newcomer did small jobs well, but more importantly, he got out of the way when he wasn't needed. People noticed his plain, unimpressive face. It was a reasonable face; fanatics didn't need beauty. The man could be brusque when displeased, and maybe that quality didn't endear him with his superiors. But he proved to have an instinct for stardrives, and he knew when to buy drinks for his colleagues, and he was expert in telling dry old jokes, and sometimes, in a rare mood, he offered stories about Where-Peace-Rains. Audiences were curious about the cavern and its odd folk, the left-behind family and their ludicrous faith. Years later, co-workers thought enough of their colleague to attend his graduation, and if the man didn't show enough pride with the new plasma-blue uniform, at least he seemed comfortable with the steady work that always finds those who know what they are doing.

Decades passed, and the reformed Luddite acquired responsibilities and then rank, becoming a dependable cog in the Tan-tan-5 crew.

Then the decades were centuries.

One millennium and forty-two years had steadily trickled past. Port Beta remained a vast and hectic facility, and the Great Ship pushed a little farther along its quarter-million year voyage around the galaxy, and this man that everybody knew seemed to have always been at his station. His abandoned family had died long ago. If he felt any interest in the generations still living inside Where-Peace-Rains, he kept it secret. Skill lifted him to the middle ranks, and he was respected by those that knew him, and the people who knew him best never bothered to imagine that this burly, plain-faced fellow might actually be someone of consequence.

2

His name used to be Pamir.

Wearing his own face and biography, Pamir had served as one of the Great Ship's captains. Nothing about that lost man was cog-like. In a vocation that rewarded charm and politics, he was an excellent captain who succeeded using nothing but stubborn competence. No matter how difficult the assignment, it was finished early and without fuss. Creativity was in his toolbox, but unlike too many high-gloss captains, Pamir used rough elegance before genius. Five projects wearing his name were still taught to novice captains. Yet the once-great officer had also lost his command, and that was another lesson shared with the arrogant shits who thought they deserved to wear the captains' mirrored uniform: For thousands of years, Pamir was a rising force in the ranks, and then he stupidly fell in love with an alien. That led to catastrophes and fat financial losses for the Ship, and although the situation ended favorably enough, passengers could have been endangered, and worse than that, secrets had been kept from his vengeful superiors.

Sitting out the voyage inside the brig was a likely consequence, but dissolving into the Ship's multitudes was Pamir's solution. The official story was that the runaway captain had slipped overboard thirty thousand years ago, joining colonists bound for a new world. As a matter of policy, nobody cared about one invisible felon. But captains forgot little, and that's why several AIs were still dedicated to Pamir's case—relentless superconductive minds endlessly sifting through census records and secret records, images dredged up from everywhere, and overheard conversations in ten thousand languages.

Every morning began with the question, "Is this the day they find me?"

And between every breath, some piece of that immortal mind was being relentlessly suspicious of everyone.

"Jon?"

Tools froze in mid-task, and the mechanic turned. "Over here."

"Do you have a moment?"

"Three moments," he said. "What do you want, G'lene?"

G'lene was human, short and rounded with fat—a cold-world adaptation worn for no reason but tradition. One of the newest trainees, she was barely six hundred years old, still hunting for her life's calling.

"I need advice," she said. "I asked around, and several people suggested that I come to you first."

The man said nothing, waiting.

"We haven't talked much before," she allowed.

"You work for a different crew," he said.

"And I don't think you like me."

The girl often acted flip and even spoiled, but those traits didn't matter. What mattered was that she was a careless technician. It was a common flaw worn by young immortals. Carelessness meant that the other mechanics had to keep watch over her work, and the only question seemed when she would be thrown out of the program.

"I don't know you much at all," said Pamir. "What I don't like is your work."

She heard him, took a quick breath, and then she pushed any embarrassment aside. "You're the Luddite, aren't you?"

There were various ways to react. Pamir told the nearest tool to pivot and aim, punching a narrow hole through the center of his palm.

Blood sprayed, and the hole began to heal instantly.

"Apparently not," he said.

G'lene laughed like a little girl, without seriousness, without pretense.

Pamir didn't fancy that kind of laugh.

"Jon is a popular name with Luddites," she said.

Pamir sucked at the torn flesh. He had worn "Jon" nearly as long as he had worn this face. Only in dreams was he anybody else.

"What kind of advice are you chasing?" he asked.

"I need a topic for my practicum."

"Ugly-eights," he said.

"That's what you're working on here, isn't it?"

He was rehabilitating the main drive of an old star-taxi. Ugly-eights were a standard, proven fusion engine. They had been pushing ships across the galaxy longer than most species were alive. This particular job was relentlessly routine and cheap, and while someone would eventually find some need for this old ship, it would likely sit inside a back berth for another few centuries.

"Ugly-eights are the heart of commerce in the galaxy," said Pamir.

"And they're ugly," she said.

"Build a new kind of ugly," he said. "Tweak a little function or prove that some bit or component can be yanked. Make this machine better, simpler or sexier, and a thousand mechanics will worship you as a goddess."

"Being worshipped," she said. "That would be fun."

She seemed to believe it was possible.

The two of them were standing in the middle of an expansive machine shop. Ships and parts of ships towered about them in close ranks. Port Beta was just ten kilometers past the main doors, and the rest of Pamir's crew and his boss were scattered, no other face in sight.

"I know what you did for your practicum," said G'lene. "You built a working Kajjas pulse engine."

"Nobody builds a working Kajjas pulse," he said. "Not even the Kajjas."

"You built it and then went up on the hull and fired the engine for ninety days."

"And then my luck felt spent, so I turned it off."

"I want to do something like that," she said. "I want something unusual."

"No," he said. "You do not, no."

She didn't seem to notice his words. "It's too bad that we don't have any Kajjas ships onboard. Wouldn't it be fun to refab one of those marvels?"

Kajjas space had been left behind long ago. Not one of their eccentric vessels was presently berthed inside Beta. But the Great Ship had five other ports, reserved for the captains and security forces. Did G'lene know facts that weren't public knowledge? Was the girl trying to coax him into some kind of borderline adventure?

"So you want to play with a real Kajjas ship," Pamir said.

"But only with your help. I'm not a fool."

Pamir had never given much thought to G'lene's mind. What he realized then, staring at that pretty ageless and almost perfectly spherical face, was that she didn't seem to be one thing or another. He couldn't pin any quality to his companion.

"The Kajjas are famous explorers," she said.

"They used to be, but the wandering urge left them long ago."

"What if I knew where to find an old Kajjas starship?"

"I'd have to ask where it's hiding."

"Not here," she said.

The way she spoke said a lot. "Not here." The "here" was drawn out, and the implications were suddenly obvious.

"Shit," said Pamir.

"Exactly," she said.

"It's not on the Great Ship, is it?"

The smile brightened, smug and ready for the next question.

"Who are you?" he asked.

"Exactly who I seem to be," she said.

"A lipid-rich girl who is going to fail at the academy," he said.

To her credit, she didn't bristle. Poise held her steady, and she let him stare at her face a little longer before saying, "Maybe I was lying."

"You aren't talking about your practicum, are you?"

"Not really," she said. "No, I have friends who need to hire a drive-mechanic."

"Friends," he said.

"Best friends," she said. "And like all best friends, they have quite a lot of money."

Pamir said, "No."

"Take a leave of absence," she said. "The bosses like your work. They'll let you go. Then in a little while . . . well, a long while . . . you can come back again with enough money to wipe away all of your debts."

"What do you know about my debts?"

The smile sharpened. "Everything," she said.

"No, I don't want this," he said.

Then a little meanness crept into her laugh. "Is it true what they say?"

"It often is."

"Luddite minds are better than others," she said. "They work harder because they have to start out soft and simple."

"We all start simple," he said.

"You need to go with me," she insisted.

There was a threat woven into the words, the tone. Pamir started to gauge his surroundings as well as this peculiar creature, but he never heard the killer's approach. One moment, the drive-mechanic was marshaling his tools for some ad hoc battle, but before he was ready, two impossibly strong hands were clasped around his neck, reaching from behind, calmly choking the life out of a thousand year-old body.

3

The Kajjas home sun was a brilliant F-class star circled by living worlds, iron-fattened asteroids, and billions of lush comets. Like humans, the Kajjas evolved as bipeds hungry for oxygen and water, and like most citizens of the galaxy, biology gave them brief lifespans and problematic biochemistries. Independent of other species, they invented the usual sciences, and after learning the principles of the Creation, they looked at everything with new eyes. But their solar system happened to be far removed from the galactic plane. The nearest star was fifty light-years away. Isolated but deeply clever, the Kajjas devised their famous pulse engines—scorching, borderline-stable rockets built around collars of degenerate matter. Kajjas pulses were as good as the best drives once they reached full throttle, but stubborn physics still kept them from beating the relativistic walls. Every voyage took time, and worse still, those pulse engines had the irksome habit of bleeding radiation. Even the youngest crew would die of cancers and old age before the voyage was even half-finished.

Faced the problem of spaceflight, every species realized that there were no perfect answers, at least so long as minds were mortal and the attached bodies were weak.

A consensus was built among the Kajjas. Alone, they began reengineering their basic nature. With time they might have invented solutions as radical as their relentless star-drives, but not long after the project began, a river of laser light swept out at them from the galaxy's core—a dazzling beacon carrying old knowledge, including the tools and high tricks necessary to build the bioceramic mind.

A similar beacon would eventually find the Earth, unleashing the potentials of one wild monkey.

But that event was a hundred million years in the future.

Human history was brief and complicated—a few hundred thousand years of competing, combustible civilizations. By comparison, the Kajjas built exactly one technological society. War and strife were unimaginable. Unity rode in their blue blood. Once armed with immortal minds and the infamous engines, their starships rained down across a wide portion of the galaxy, setting up colonies and trade routes while poking into ill-explored corners. The Kajjas were curious and adaptable explorers, and it was easy to believe that they would eventually rule some fat portion of local space. But the species reached its zenith while the dinosaurs still ran over one tiny world, and then their slow decline began. Colonies withered. Their starships began keeping to the easy, well-mapped routes. Some of the Kajjas never even went into space. And what always bothered Pamir, and what always intrigued him, was that these ancient creatures had no clear idea what had gone wrong.

A few Kajjas rode onboard the Great Ship. They were poorer than the typical passenger, but each had a love for brightly lit taverns, and in moderation, drinks made from hot spring waters and propanol salted liberally with cyanide.

Philosophers by nature and cranky philosophers at that, the Kajjas made interesting company. Pamir approved of their irritable moods. He liked cryptic voices and far-sighting reflections. This was a social species with clear senses of hierarchies. If you wanted respect, it was important to sit near your Kajjas friend, near enough to taste the poison on his breath, and to wring the best out of the experience, you had to act as if he was the master of the table and everyone sitting around it.

Pamir's favorite refugee was ageless to the eye, but eyes were easily fooled.

"We were courageous voyagers," said the raspy voice.

"You were," Pamir agreed.

His companion had various names, but in human company, he preferred to be called "Tailor."

"Do you realize how many worlds we visited?"

"No, Tailor, I don't."

"You do not know, and we can only guess numbers." The words were tumbling out of an elderly, often repaired translator. "Ten million planets? Twenty billion? I can't even count the places that I have walked with these good feet."

The Kajjas suddenly propped his legs on the tabletop.

Knowing what was proper, Pamir leaned between the toe-rich, faintly kangaroo-style feet. "I would tolerate your stories, if you could tolerate my boundless interest."

The alien's head was narrow and extremely deep, like the blade of a hatchet. Three eyes surrounded a mouth that chewed at the air, betraying suspicion. "Do I know you, young human?"

"No," Pamir lied. "We have never met."

He was wearing that new face and the name Jon, and he was cloaked in a fresh life story too.

"You seem familiar to me," said the Kajjas.

"Because you're ancient and full of faces, remembered and imagined too."

"That feels true."

"I beg to know your age," Pamir said.

The question had been asked before, and Tailor's answer was always enormous and never repeated. If the alien felt joyous, he claimed to be youthful forty million years old. But if angry or despairing, he painted himself as being much, much older.

"I could have walked along your Cretaceous shoreline," said Tailor that evening, hinting at a very dark disposition.

"I wish you had," said Pamir.

"Yet I can do that just the same," the Kajjas said, two eyes turning to mist as the mind wove some private image.

Pamir knew to wait, sipping his rum.

The daydream ended, and the elderly creature leaked a high trilling sound that the translator turned into a despairing groan.

"My mind is full," Tailor declared.

"Should I envy you?"

Iron blades rubbed hard against one another—the Kajjas laugh. "Fill your mind with whatever you wish. Envy has its uses."

"Should my species envy yours?"

Every eye cleared. "Are you certain we haven't met?"

"Nothing is certain," said Pamir.

"Indeed. Indeed."

"Perhaps you know other humans," Pamir said.

"I have sipped drinks with a few," Tailor said. "Usually male humans, as it happens. One or two of them had your bearing exactly."

The focus needed to be shifted. "You haven't answered me, my master. Should humans envy your species' triumphs?"

A long sip of poison turned into a human-style nod. "You should envy every creature's success. And if you wish my opinion—"

"Yes."

"In my view, our greatest success is the quiet grace we have shown while making our plunge back to obscurity. Not every species vanishes so well as the Kajjas."

"Humans won't," said Pamir.

"On that, we agree."

"And why did your plunge begin?" the human asked. "What went wrong for you, or did something go right?"

Pamir had drunk with this entity many times over the millennia. Tailor gave various answers to this question, each delivered without much faith in the voice. Usually he claimed that living too long made an immortal cowardly and dull. Too many of his species were ancient, and that antediluvian nature brought on lethargy, and of course lethargy led to a multifaceted decline.

Wearing the Jon face, Pamir waited for that reliable excuse again.

But the alien said nothing, wiggling those finger-like toes. Then with an iron laugh, fresh words climbed free of his mouth.

"I think the secret is our minds," he began.

"Too old, are they?" asked Pamir.

"I am not talking about age. And while too many memories are jammed inside us, they are not critical either."

"What is wrong with your mind?"

"And yours too." Tailor leaned forward. A hand older than any ape touched Pamir's face, tracing the outlines of his forehead. "Your brain and mine are so similar. In its materials and the nanoscopic design, and in every critical detail that doesn't define our natures."

"True, true," said the worshipful Pamir.

"Does that bother you?"

"Not at all."

"Of course not, no," said the alien. "But have you ever asked yourself . . . has that smart young mind of yours ever wondered . . . why doesn't this sameness leave you just a little sick in your favorite stomach?"

4

Choke an immortal man, pulverize the trachea and neck bones and leave the body starved of oxygen, and he dives into a temporary coma. But the modern body is more sophisticated than machines, including star-drives, and within their realm, humans can be far more durable, more self-reliant. Choke the man and a nanoscopic army rises from the mayhem, knitting and soothing, patching and building. Excess calories are warehoused everywhere, including inside the bioceramic mind, and despite the coma and the limp frame, nothing about the victim is dead. Pamir wasn't simply conscious. He was lucid, thoughts roaring, outrage in full stride as he guessed about enemies and their motives and what he would do first when he could move again, and what he would do next, and depending on the enemies, what color his revenge would take.

But there were many states between full life and true death.

He was sprawled out on the shop floor, and standing over him, somebody said, "Done."

Then he felt himself being lifted.

A woman said, "Hurry."

G'lene?

His body was carried, but not far. There was a maze of storage hangers beneath the shop. Pamir assumed that he was taken into one of those rooms, and once set down again he found the strength to strike a careless face, once and then twice again before someone shoved a fat tube down his ruined throat.

Fiery chemicals cooked his flesh.

Too late, he tried to engage his nexuses. But their voices had been jammed, and all that came back to him was white noise and white deathly light.

In worse ways than strangling, his body was methodically killed.

Deafness took him, and his sense of smell was stripped away, and every bit of skin went numb. In the end, the only vision remaining was imagination. A body couldn't be left inside a storage hanger. Someone would notice. That's why he imagined himself being carried, probably bound head to toe to keep him from fighting again. But he didn't feel any motion, and nothing changed. Nothing happened. Lying inside blackness, his thoughts ran on warehoused power, and when no food was offered those same thoughts began to slow, softening the intensities of each idea, ensuring a working consciousness that could collapse quite a bit farther without running dry.

The streakship's launch was never noticed, and the long, fierce acceleration made no impression.

But Pamir reasoned something like that would happen. Clues and a captain's experience let him piece together a sobering, practical story. If any Kajjas ship was wandering near the Great Ship, it would have been noticed. That news would have found him. And since it wasn't close, and since the universe was built mostly from inconvenient trajectories, the streakship would probably have to burn massive amounts of fuel just to reach the very distant target—assuming it didn't smash into a comet while plunging through interstellar space.

This kind of mission demanded small crews and fat risks, and Pamir was going to remain lost for a very long time.

"Unless," he thought. "Unless I'm not lost at all."

Paranoia loves darkness. Perhaps this ugly situation was a ruse. Maybe the relentless AI hunters had finally found him, but nobody was quite sure if he was the runaway captain. So instead of having him arrested, the captains decided to throw the suspect inside a black box, trying to squeeze the secrets out of him.

Bioceramic minds were tiny and dense and utterly unreadable.

But a mind could be worn down. A guilty man or even an innocent man would confess to a thousand amazing crimes. Wondering if prison was better than dying on some bizarre deep-space quest, Pamir found the temptation to say his old name once, just to see if somebody had patched into his speech center. But as time stretched and the thoughts slowed even more, he kept his mind fixed on places and days that meant something to a man named Jon. He pictured Port Beta and the familiar machinery. He spoke to colleagues and drank with them, the routine, untroubled life of the mechanic lingering long past his death. Then when he was miserably bored, he imagined Where-Peace-Rains, spending the next years with a life and beliefs that before this were worn only as camouflage.

For the first time, he missed that life that he had never lived.

Decades passed.

Oxygen returned without warning, and flesh warmed, and new eyes opened as a first breath passed down his new throat.

A face was watching him.

"Hello, Jon," said the face, the hint of a smile showing.

Pamir said, "Hello," and breathed again, with relish.

G'lene appeared to be in fine health, drifting above the narrow packing crate where his mostly dead body had been stowed.

Pamir sat up slowly.

A thoroughly, wondrously alien ship surrounded them. Its interior was a cylinder two hundred meters in diameter and possibly ten kilometers long. Pamir couldn't see either end of this odd space. The walls were covered with soft glass threads, ruddy like the native Kajjas grass, intended to give the Kajjas good purchase for kicking when they were in zero gravity, like now. But when the ship's engines kicked on, the same threads would come alive, lacing themselves into platforms where the crew could work and rest, the weaves tightening as the gees increased. That was standard Kajjas technology. Kajjas machines were scattered about the curved, highly mobile landscape, each as broken as it was old. There were control panels and what looked like immersion chambers, none of them working, and various hyperfiber boxes were sealed against the universe. Every surface wore a vigorous coat of dust. Breathing brought scents only found in places that had been empty forever. Rooms onboard the Great Ship smelled this way. But the air and the bright lights felt human, implying that his abductors had been onboard long enough to reconfigure the environment.

G'lene kept her distance. "How do you feel, Jon?"

"Can you guess?" he asked.

She laughed quietly, apparently embarrassed.

In the distance, three entities were moving in their direction. Two of them were human.

"Our autodoc just spliced a fast-breaker pipe into your femoral," she said. "You'll be strong and ready in no time."

Pamir studied legs that didn't look like his legs, and he looked at a rib-rich chest and a stranger's spidery hands. Starvation and nothingness had left him eroded, brittle and remarkable.

"Our captain wants you to start repairing the pulse drive," G'lene said.

"And I imagine that our captain wants enthusiasm on my part."

She blinked. She said, "Hopefully."

"You know a little something about machines," he said. "How does the old engine look?"

"I'm no expert, as you like to tell me. But it looks like the last crew put everything to sleep in the best ways. Unfortunately there's no fuel onboard, and none of the maintenance equipment is functioning."

"I hope our captain considered these possibilities."

"We brought extra fuel and tools, yes."

"Enough?"

She stared at his skinny legs.

Pulse engines, like flesh, were adaptable when it came to nutrition. Any mass could be fed through the collars, transformed into plasma and light.

Pamir wiggled his bare toes.

The other crewmembers were kicking closer.

"I'm guessing that the Kajjas crew is also missing," he said.

"Oh, yes," she said.

"How long missing?"

The question made her uneasy.

"How long have we been here?" he asked.

That was another difficult topic, but she nodded when she said, "Nineteen days."

The autodoc beneath him was a small field model, serviceable but limited. Pamir studied it and then the girl, and then he flexed one leg while leaving the other perfectly still. Asked to work, the atrophied muscles took the largest share of the new food, and the leg grew warmer, sugars burning and lipids burning until the slippery blood began to glow.

"How about the sovereigns?" he asked.

"Sovereigns?"

"The ship's AIs." Most species patterned their automated systems after their social systems, and the Kajjas preferred noble-minded machines in charge of the automated functions.

"We've tried talking to the AIs," said G'lene. "They don't answer."

Tossing both legs out from the tiny growth chamber, Pamir dragged the fast-break pipe with them. "And what are we? A salvage operation?"

She said, "Yes."

"And at the end of the fun, am I paid? Or am I murdered for good?"

"Paid," she blurted. "The offer from me was genuine, Jon. There's a lot of money to be made here."

"For a badly depleted Kajjas ship," he said, sighing. "It's more than hopeful, believing this derelict can earn much on the open market."

She said nothing.

"But it is exceptionally old, isn't it?"

"That's what our captain says."

"Sure, the Kajjas sent missions everywhere," he said. "They were even happy to poke far outside the Milky Way."

"Which makes this a marvelous relic," she said.

"To a species inflicted with hard times. Nobody with a genuine purse would give a little shit about this lost wreck."

The two other humans were arriving—a woman and a man. They were closely related, or they loved to wear faces that implied some deep family bond.

"This is Maxx," G'lene said, referring to the man.

"And I'm Rondie," the woman offered.

Powerful people, each as muscular as G'lene was round, their every motion and the flash of their eyes proved they were youngsters.

Pamir wondered whose hands had strangled him.

"It's great to finally meet you," Maxx said, nothing but pure, undiluted happiness in his voice. "We keep hearing that you can make this ship healthy again."

"Who says that?" Pamir asked.

"The only one who matters," the fellow said, laughing amiably.

What was more disturbing: Being kidnapped for a mission that he didn't want to join, or being trapped in the company of three earnest, inexperienced near-children?

Next to the humans, the drive-mechanic was utterly ancient.

But compared to their captain, Pamir was a newborn.

"Hello to you, Jon," said the Kajjas.

"Why me?" Pamir asked. "You should know how to fix your own beast."

One last kick made the glass crinkle and flow, bringing the captain into the group. The sound of grinding iron preceded the words, "I have never mastered the peculiar genius to be a worthy engineer."

"Too bad," said Pamir.

Then Tailor touched his own head above the eyes. "And to learn the necessary talents now would require empty spaces inside my head, which means discarding some treasured memories. And how could I do such to pieces of my own self?"

5

Pamir knew that nobody was clever enough or worthy enough, much less lucky enough to truly disappear.

The tiniest body still possessed mass and volume, shadow and energy.

And a brilliant mind was never as clever as three average minds sniffing after something of interest.

The wise fugitive always kept several new lives at the ready.

But every ready-made existence carried risks of its own, including the chance that someone would notice the locker jammed with money and clothes, the spare face and a respectable name never used.

Like real lives, each false life had its perfect length, and there was no way to be sure how long that was.

No matter how compromised the current face, transitions always brought the most perilous days.

Paranoia was a fugitive's first tool.

But panic could make the man break from cover at the worst possible moment.

Love meant trust, which meant that no face should be loved.

Most of all, the wanted man should be acutely suspicious of the face in the mirror.

Patterns defined each life, and old patterns were trouble.

Except acquiring the new walk and voice, pleasures and hates was the most cumbersome work possible. And even worse, fine old strategies could be left behind, and the best instincts were corroded by the blur of everything new.

In a crowd of ten million strangers, nobody cared about the human who used to be many things, including a captain. And among the millions were four exceptions, or perhaps one hundred and four, or just that one inquisitive soul standing very close.

Now look into that sea of faces, stare at humans and aliens, machines and the hybrids between. Look hard at everything while pointing one finger—a finger that has been worn for some little while—and now against some very long odds, pick out which of those souls should be feared.

Humans found the derelict machine drifting outside the Milky Way, and after claiming the Great Ship as their own, loyal robots proceeded to map the interior. Each cavern was named using elaborate codes. Even excluding small caves and holes, there were billions of caverns on the captains' maps. Positions and volumes were included each name, but there was also quite a lot of AI free verse poetry. Then as the Great Ship entered the galaxy, one paronomasia-inspired AI savant was ordered to give a million caverns better designations—words that any human mouth could manage—and one unremarkable hole was named:

Where-Peace-Rains.

Peace ruled inside the dark emptiness, but there was no rain. Remote and unspectacular, the cavern remained silent for long millennia. Communities of archaic humans were established in other locations. Some failed, others found ways to prosper. Mortal passengers had one clear advantage; being sure to die, they paid relatively small sums to ride the Great Ship. And unlike their eternal neighbors, they could pay a minimal fee to have one child. Three trifling payments meant growth, and the captains soon had to control populations through laws and taxes as well as limiting the places where those very odd people could live.

Forty-five thousand years ago, human squatters claimed Where-Peace-Rains, setting up the first lights and a hundred rough little homes in the middle of the bare granite floor. They told themselves they were clever. They assured each other that they were invisible, stealing just a trickle of power from the Ship. But an AI watchdog noticed the theft, and once alerted to the crime, the Master Captain sent one of her more obstinate officers to deal with the ongoing mess.

Pamir was still a captain—an entity full of authority and the ready willingness to deploy his enormous powers.

Wearing a mirrored uniform, he walked every street inside the village, telling the strangers that they were criminals and he wasn't happy. He warned that he could order any punishment that could be imagined, short of genocide. Then he demanded that the Luddites meet him in the round at the village's heart, bags packed, and ready for the worst.

Three hundred people, grown and young, assembled on the polished red granite.

"Explain your selves," the captain demanded.

A leader stepped forward. "We require almost nothing," the old/young man began, his voice breaking at the margins. "We are simple and small, and we ask nothing from the captains or the sacred Ship."

"Shut up," said Pamir.

Those words came out hard, but what scared everyone was the captain's expression. Executions weren't possible, but a lot of grim misery lay between slaughter and salvation, and while these people believed in mortality, they weren't fanatics chasing martyrdom or some ill-drawn afterlife.

Nobody spoke.

Then once again, the captain's voice boomed.

"Before anything else, I want you to explain your minds to me. Do it now, in this place, before your arbitrary day comes to an end."

Nobody was allowed to leave and reset the sun. With little time left, a pretty young woman was pressed into service. Perhaps the other squatters thought she would look appealing to the glowering male officer. Or maybe she was the best, bravest voice available. Either way, she spoke about the limits of life and the magic of physics and the blessings of the eternal, boundless multiverse. Pamir appeared to pay attention, which heartened some. When she paused, he nodded. Could they have found an unlikely ally? But then with a low snort, he said, "I like numbers. Give me mathematics."

The woman responded with intricate, massive numbers wrapped around quantum wonders, invoking the many worlds as well as the ease with which fresh new universes sprang out of the old.

But the longer she spoke, the less impressed he seemed to be. Acting disgusted, then enraged, Pamir told the frightened community, "I know these theories. I can even believe the crazy-shit science. But if you want this to go anywhere good, you have to make me believe what you believe. You have to make me trust the madness that we aren't just here. There are an infinite number of caves exactly like this stone rectum, and infinite examples of you, and there is no measurable end of me. And all of us have assembled in these endless places, and this meeting is happening everywhere exactly as it is here.

"Convince me of that bullshit," he shouted.

The woman's infinite future depended on this single performance. Tears seemed like a worthy strategy. She wept and begged, dropping to her knees. Her skin split and the mortal blood flowed against the smooth stony ground, and every time she looked up she saw an ugly immortal dressed in that shiny garb, and every time she looked down again, the world seemed lost. No words could make this blunt, brute of a man accept her mind. No action or inaction would accomplish any good. Suddenly she was trying only to make herself worthy in the eyes of the other doomed souls, and that was the only reason she stood again, filling her body with pride, actively considering the merits of rushing the captain to see if she could bruise that awful face, if only for a moment or two.

Yet all that while, Pamir had a secret:

He had no intention of hurting anyone.

This was a tiny group. A captain of his rank had the clout to give each of them whatever he wished to give them. And later, if pressed by his superiors, Pamir could blame one or two colleagues for not adequately defending this useless wilderness. Really, the scope of this crime was laughably, pathetically tiny—a mild burden more than an epic mess, regardless what these bright terrified eyes believed.

Out of fear or born from wisdom, the woman didn't assault him.

Then the captain reached into a pocket on his uniform.

The object hadn't been brought by chance. Pamir came with a plan and options, and eons later, novice captains would stand in their classroom, examining all the aspects of the captain's scheme.

Out from the pocket came his big hand, holding what resembled a sphere.

He explained, "This is a one hundred-and-forty-four faced die, diamond construction, tear-shaped weights for a rapid settling, each number carrying its own unique odds."

Luddite faces stared at the object.

Nobody spoke.

"I'm going to toss it high," said Pamir. "And then you, baby lady . . . you call out any number. And no, I won't let you look at the die first. You'll make your guess, and you will almost certainly lose. But then again, as you understand full well, any fraction of the endless is endless. And regardless of my toss, an infinite number of you are going to win this game."

Swallowing, the woman discovered a thin smile.

"And if I am right?" she asked.

"You stay here. And your people stay here. The entire cavern is granted to you, under my authority. But you aren't allowed to steal power from our reactors, and your water has to be bought on the common markets, and you will be responsible for your food and your mouths, and if you overpopulate this space, the famines and plagues will rest on your little shoulders.

"Is that understood?" he asked.

Everybody nodded, and everybody had hope.

But when Pamir threw the die, the girl offered the most unlikely number.

"One," she shouted.

One was riding on the equator, opposite 144—the smallest facets on the diamond face.

Up went the die.

And then was down, rattling softly as it struck, bouncing and rolling, slowing as sandals and boots and urgent voices pulled out of the way.

Looking at the number was a formality.

The cave would soon be empty and dark.

Yet odd as it seemed, Pamir wasn't particularly surprised to find the simplest number on top, in plain view: As inevitable as every result must be.

6

Reaching with a nexus, Pamir discovered an elaborate star chart waiting for him. The galaxy was stuffed inside a digital bottle, the nearest million suns translated into human terms and human clocks. At the center was the Kajjas ship—a long dumbbell-shaped body with a severely battered shield at one end, the pulse engine and drained fuel tanks behind. Its hull was slathered with black veneers and stealth poxes and what looked like the remnants of scaffolding. The captains never spotted this relic; too many light-years lay between their telescopes and this cold wisp of nothing. Even the Great Ship was too distant to deserve any size—the core of a jovian world rendered as a simple golden vector. Sixty years had been invested reaching the Kajjas vessel, and home was receding every moment. Hypothetical courses waited to be studied. Pamir gave them enough of a look to understand the timetables, and then he seasoned the quiet with a few rich curses.

A second nexus linked him to this ship's real-time schematics. Blue highlights showed areas of concern. An ocean's worth of blue was spread across the armored, badly splintered prow. High-velocity impacts had done their worst. Judging by ancient patches, smart hands had once competently fixed the troubles. But then those hands stopped working—a million years ago, or twenty million years ago. Since then the machine had faithfully chased a line that began in the deepest, emptiest space, only recently slicing its way across the Milky Way.

Pamir referred back at the star chart, discovering that it was far larger than he assumed. The blackness and the stars encompassed the Local Group of galaxies, and some patches were thoroughly charted.

A quiet, respectful curse seemed in order.

A small streakship was tethered to the dumbbell's middle. Pamir knew the vessel. It arrived at Port Beta in lousy shape, where it was rehabbed but never rechristened. Someone higher ranking than the mechanics decided that nothing would make the vessel safe, which was when the high-end wreck was dragged inside a back berth, waiting for an appropriately desperate buyer.

Tailor.

Pamir warmed the air with blasphemies and moved on to the manifests.

And all along, the Kajjas had been watching him.

"I remember a different boy," the alien said. "You aren't the polite, good-natured infant with whom I drank."

"That boy got strangled and packed up like cargo."

"Each of us flew in hibernation," said Tailor. "There was no extra space, no room for indulgences. I was very much like you."

Pamir cursed a fourth time, invoking Kajjas anatomy.

The alien reacted with silence, every eye fixed on the angry mechanic.

"Your streakship is tiny and spent," Pamir said. "Something half again better than this, and we could have strapped this artifact on its back and used those young engines to carry us home quickly."

"Except our financing was poor," said Tailor.

"No shit."

"We have rich options," said Tailor. "We will use our remaining fuel and then carve up the streakship like a sweet meat, dropping its pieces through the pulse engine."

"With a troop of robots, that's easy work," Pamir said.

Tailor remained silent.

"Only you neglected to bring any robots, didn't you?"

"Worthy reasons are in play."

"I doubt that."

The other humans were watching the conversation from a safe distance.

"So why?" asked Pamir. "Why is this fossil so important?"

Two eyes went pale.

"You're going to tell me," the human said.

"Unless I already have, Jon. I explained, but you chose not to hear me."

Scornful laughter chased away the quiet, and then Pamir turned his attentions elsewhere. The manifest was full of news, good and otherwise. "At least you spent big for tools and fuel."

"They were important," the alien said.

Pamir chewed his tongue, tasting blood.

"I am asking for your expert opinion," said Tailor. "Can we meet our goals and return to the Ship?"

"There is an answer, but I damn well don't know it."

"You aren't the boy with whom I drank."

Pamir said nothing.

"Perhaps I should have cultivated that boy's help at the outset," said Tailor. "He could have plotted my course and devised my methods too."

"That would have been smart."

Tailor showed his plate-like teeth, implying concern. "I cannot help but notice, sir. You have been studying our ships and vectors, but you have barely paid attention to either engine."

"Engines aren't the worst problem."

"But your specialty is the drive machinery," said Tailor. "That should be your first concern. Instinct alone should put your eyes and mind on those elements, not the state of a hull that has survived quite well on its own."

Pamir looked away. The other humans looked confident, relaxed, flashing little smiles when they whispered to one another. Maxx and Rondie did most of the whispering. G'lene floated apart from the others, and she smiled the most.

"Are they supposed to help me?" Pamir asked.

"Each will be useful, yes," said Taylor. "The twins are general starship mechanics, and they have other training too."

"I don't recognize them. They haven't worked near Beta."

Silence.

"So they must be from a different port, different background. Probably military. Soldiers love to be strong, even if their bulk gets in the way."

Tailor started to reply.

"Also, I see six thousand kilos that's blue-black on the manifest," Pamir continued. "You're not letting me see this. But since indulgences were left behind, the mass is important. So I'll guess that we're talking about weapons."

"I will admit one truth to you, Jon. About you, sir, I have a feeling."

"Is that feeling cold blue dread?"

Iron clawed against iron. "There never was a boy, it occurs to me. I think that you are somewhat older than your name claims, and maybe, just perhaps, we have met each other in the past."

"Who's the enemy?" Pamir asked.

"If only I knew that answer," the alien began.

Then Tailor said nothing more, turning and leaping far away.

7

Forty-four thousand years was a sliver of time. The galaxy had moved only in little ways since people dared slip inside Where-Peace-Rains, and nothing inside but the least stubborn, most trivial details had changed within the cave. The same genetics and honored language were in play. Stock beliefs continued to prosper. And there was still a round expanse of cool red granite where the captain had once played one round of chance, the stone dished in at the middle by generations of worshippers and their mortal feet.

Of course there were many more faces, and there was far less peace. Following the terms of the ancient agreement, archaics produced their own power and clean water and rough, edible foodstuffs. Carefully invested funds had allowed them to purchase a scrap star-drive—an ugly-eight reconfigured to generate electricity, not thrust. The drive was set on the cavern floor, not a thousand meters from the holy place where a chunk of diamond determined the world. The machinery was designed to run forever without interruption, provided that it was maintained regularly. And the ugly-eight had run for thousands of years without trouble. But it was being used in an unusual capacity, and not all of its wastes were bottled up. Lead plates and hyperfiber offered shielding, but the occasional neutron and gamma blast found ways to escape, and the childless men working nearby were prone to murderous cancers.

One engineer had worked fifty years in the most critical job in the world. A bachelor named Jon, he was still holding out hope that the tumor in his liver could be cut out of him, and then smarter, friendlier radiations would have a fighting chance to kill the cancers that had broken loose.

Jon lived inside a small apartment within walking distance of the reactor.

Everyone in Where-Peace-Rains lived in a small apartment, and everyone lived close to their important places.

Jon arrived home early. The foreman told him that he looked especially tired and needed to sleep, and Jon had agreed with the prognosis. Nothing felt unusual when he arrived. A key worn smooth by his fingers went into the lock, and the lock gave way with a solid click. But as the door swung inwards, he smelled a stranger, and a strange voice spoke out of the darkness.

"Just be aware," it said. "You're not alone."

Robberies weren't uncommon in the world, and sometimes thieves turned violent. But this was no robbery. The intruder was sitting in Jon's best chair, the seat reserved for guests. The human was relaxed enough to appear lazy. That was the first quality Jon noticed as the room's single light came on. The second detail was the man's appearance, which was substantial, and the beautiful face, even and clean-shaven. His clothes looked like the garb worn by fancy hikers and novice explorers who occasionally passed through the local caverns. Some of those people asked to come inside the archaic community. A few of the immortal passengers were intrigued by archaics, and the best of the interlopers left behind money and little favors.

But there were bad immortals too. They came for one reason, to coax people out of their home, out into the true world—as if one place was truer than another, and as if a person could simply choose his life.

"I let myself in," the stranger said.

Jon took off the daily dosage badge. "You want something," he guessed.

"Yes, I do."

"From me."

"Absolutely, yes."

Nuclear engineers earned respectable salaries, but nobody in this world was wealthy. Jon's fanciest possession was an old ceramic teapot, precious to him because it had been in his family for three thousand years.

The stranger was surely older than the pot.

Stories came back to Jon, unlikely and probably crazy stories. He had never believed such things could involve him, but when he met the man's blue eyes, something passed between them. Suddenly they had an understanding, the beginnings of a relationship. Jon found himself nodding. He knew what this was. "You think that I am dying," he said.

"You are dying."

"But how could you know?"

The immortal shifted his weight, perhaps a little uncomfortable with the subject. Or maybe quite a lot was balanced on the next moments, and he was making his rump ready for whatever Fate saw fit to throw at them.

"I've seen your doctor's files," the man said. "She tells you that you might survive to the end of the year, but I know she's being generous."

Jon had sensed as much. Yet it hurt to hear the news. A new burden, massive and acidic, was burning through his frail, middle-aged body.

He dropped into his own chair.

"I'm sorry," said the man.

Maybe he was sorry, because he sounded earnest.

"You want my life," Jon said.

The pretty face watched him, and after a moment he said, "Maybe."

"Why maybe?"

"Or if you'd rather, I'll pay for your treatments elsewhere."

"I can't abandon Peace," said Jon. "And even if I did, your doctors and your autodocs can't legally cure me."

"Cancer is not the problem," the man said. "I am talking about full treatments. I'm ready to give you that gift, if you want it. Leave your realm and live forever anywhere you want inside the Great Ship, inside the endless universe . . . except for here . . ."

"No."

Did Jon think before answering? He wasn't sure.

But giving the offer serious consideration, he said, "Never, no."

"Good," the stranger said.

Jon leaned forward. The room was small and the chairs were close together, and now they were close enough to kiss. "Are you wearing a mask?"

"Not much of one, if you can see it," said the man, laughing.

"You want my life," Jon repeated.

"Apparently you don't want to hold onto it. Why shouldn't I ask the question?"

They sat and stared at one another. Next door, a newborn was starting to feel her empty stomach, and her cry quickly built until there was no other sound in the world.

Suddenly she fell silent, her mouth full of nipple.

Jon thought about that mother's fine brown nipple. Then he wasn't thinking about anything, waiting for whatever happened next.

Out from a hiker's pocket came a weapon—a sleek gun designed by alien hands. "Except it's not a gun," the man explained. "In my realm, this is a camper's torch and portable grill. For me, the worst burns would heal inside an hour. But the torch can transform ninety kilos of your flesh and bone into a fine white ash, and I can place your remains in whatever garden or sewage plant you want on my way out of town."

Jon stared at the alien machine.

The man dropped it into Jon's lap, and then he sat back.

Its weight was a surprise. The machine was more like a sketch of a weapon, lightweight to the brink of unreal.

"I won't use the tool on you," the stranger promised. "You'll have to use it on yourself."

"No."

Did he think that time?

Jon hadn't, and after hard deliberation, he said, "Maybe."

"And for your trouble," the man began.

He stopped talking.

"I would want something," Jon said.

Not only did his companion have an offer waiting, he knew everything about Jon's living family. Nuclear technicians didn't dare make babies, what with mutations and cancers and the genuine fear that their sons and sons-in-law would follow them into this grim business. But he had siblings and cousins and a dozen nephews, plus even more nieces. Accepting this illegal arrangement meant that each limb of his family would receive enough extra money, dressed up in various excuses, and their lives would noticeably improve.

Jon passed the fierce machine from one hand to the other.

What looked like a trigger was begging to be tugged.

"No, not like that," the man said, patiently but not patiently. Something in this business was bothering him. "And when you do it, if you do it," he said, "stand in the middle of the room. We don't want to set a wall on fire."

Jon considered standing and then didn't.

The man watched him, weighing him, probably using an outsider's magic as well as his eyes.

"It's not enough," Jon said at last.

"It probably isn't," the man agreed.

"If I do this, you walk out of here with my life. Is that what happens?"

"Yes."

"So this isn't nearly enough. Everybody that I will think . . . they'll have no choice but believe . . . that I abandoned them and our cause . . ."

"That can't be helped," the man said. "It sucks, but what other way is there?"

Jon studied the machine once more.

"I picked you and just you," said the man. "Nobody else fits my needs. And sure, yes, the others will be free to tell themselves that you got weak and gave up. But you know that won't be true, and I'll live forever knowing that it wasn't true. And besides, when I give up this life of yours, I can send a confession back here. I'll tell them that you died in your home. Hell, if you want, I can tell the world that I murdered you, which will sure make everybody smile."

Jon started to hand back the alien hardware.

He paused.

The stranger reached up, and in one sloppy motion he tore off the mask, revealing a new face, a genuine face. It was Jon's face, rendered completely—the washed-out, hollow-eyed face already halfway to ash.

"Now I have one more gift, if you want it," said the man.

"What is that?"

"I'll tell you who I am."

Jon shrugged. "What do I care? Your real name doesn't matter."

Reaching into a pocket, his tormentor and salvation brought out a diamond with one hundred and forty-four faces.

Jon jumped up, and then he nearly keeled over, fainting. The alien machine hit the dirty carpet, humming for a moment, leaving an arc of charred fiber.

"Careful," said the one-time captain.

"Let me hold it," Jon said.

The man placed the diamond into his palm and closed the hand around it. The immortal's flesh was exactly as cool and sick as Jon's flesh, which was another wonderful detail.

"Is this the same die?" Jon asked.

"No, that trinket got left behind long ago," Pamir said.

Inspiration came to the dying man. Forcing the diamond into the fugitive's hand, he said, "Throw it. Or roll it. Pick your number either way, and if she stands on top, I will do whatever you want."

Pamir closed his hand.

He breathed once, deeply.

"No, I played that game once," the lost captain said, and with that he dropped the diamond back into his pocket. "I'm done letting chance run free."

8

Three hours of sleep and the humans were sharing the day's first meal. Tailor wasn't with them. Since boarding on the fossil ship, the alien had spent most of his time cuddling with a distant control panel, trying to coax the sovereigns into saying one coherent word. But despite ample power and reassuring noise, the AIs remained lost, crazy or rotted and probably gone forever.

G'lene felt sorry for the old beast, chasing what wasn't there.

And that was where her empathy ended. Like most aliens, the Kajjas man was a mystery and always would be. She accepted that fact. Dwelling on what refused to make sense was senseless. What G'lene cared about, deeply and forever, were human beings. That was true onboard the Great Ship, and her desires were even more urgent here in the wilderness.

But her three human companions were burdens, odd and vexing, usually worse than useless. The twins never stopped whispering in each other's ears. They went so far as creating their own language, and deciphering their private words was a grave insult. Yet despite their vaunted closeness, they did nothing sexual. With a defiant tone, Rondie claimed that sex was an instinct best thrown aside. "That's what my brother did, and I did, and you should too." Preaching to a woman who couldn't imagine any day without some lustful fun, the muscle-bound creature said, "Each of us would be stronger and five times happier if we gave up every useless habit."

G'lene was entitled to feel sorry about her loneliness. That's why she kept smiling at Jon, the Luddite. She smiled at him one hundred times every day. Not that it helped, no. But he was the only possibility in a miserably poor field, and she reasoned that eventually, after another year or maybe a decade, she would wear some kind of hole in his cold resolve.

This was Jon's third breakfast as a living crewmember.

G'lene smiled as always, no hope in her heart. Yet this morning proved to be different. The odd homely conundrum of a man suddenly noticed her expression. At least he met her eyes, answering with what might have been the slyest grin that had ever been tossed her way.

She laughed, daring to ask, "Are you in a good mood, Jon?"

"I am," he said. "I'm in a lovely, spectacular mood."

"Why's that?"

"Last night, I realized something very important."

"Something good, I hope."

"It is. And do you want to you know what my epiphany was?"

"Tell it," she said, one hand scratching between her breasts.

But then Jon said, "No," and his eyes wandered. "I don't think that you really do want to know."

G'lene knew thousands of people, but this Luddite was the most bizarre creature, human or otherwise.

The twins were sharing their breakfast from the same squeeze-bowl. They stopped eating to laugh with the same voice, and then Rondie said, "Give up the game, dear. That boy doesn't want you."

What a wicked chain of words to throw at anyone.

"But you can tell us your epiphany," Maxx said.

Jon glanced at the twins.

G'lene felt uneasy in so many ways, and she had no hope guessing why.

Tipping her head, Rondie said, "Whisper your insight inside my ear. I promise I won't share it with anyone."

Her brother gave a hard snort, underscoring her lie.

"No, I think I should tell everyone," said Jon. "But first, I want to hear a confession from you two. Which one of you strangled me?"

Maxx laughed, lifting a big hand.

But his sister grabbed his arm, bracing her feet inside the glass strands before flinging him aside. "No, I'm quieter, and I have the better grip. So I did it. I broke your little neck."

Jon nodded, and then he glanced at G'lene.

"All right, that's done," G'lene said. "What's the revelation?"

"Starting now," said Jon, "we are changing priorities."

"Priorities," Maxx repeated, as if his tongue wanted to play with the word.

"You've been spending your last few days assembling weapons," Jon said to the twins. "That crap has to stop."

Similar faces wore identical expressions, puzzled and amused but not yet angry.

"Our enemies won't arrive inside a starship," said Jon. "Unless I'm wrong, and then I doubt that we could offer much of a fight."

"Our enemies," Maxx repeated.

"Do you know who they are?" G'lene asked.

Jon shook his head. "I don't. Do any of you?"

Nobody spoke.

Jon teased a glob of meal-and-milk from his breakfast orb, spinning the treat before flicking it straight into his mouth.

The ordinary gesture was odd, though G'lene couldn't quite see why.

"Tailor claims that we have to be ready for an attack," said Jon. "Except our sovereign isn't particularly forthcoming about when and where that might happen. His orders tell us nothing specific, and that's why they tell us plenty. For instance, this crazy old wreck is worth nothing, which means that it's carrying something worth huge risks and lousy odds."

The twins didn't look at each other. Thinking the same thoughts, they glanced at G'lene, and she tried to offer a good worried smile. And because it sounded a little bit reasonable, she said, "That Kajjas is so old and so strange. I just assumed that he's just a little paranoid. Isn't that what happens after millions of years?"

"My experience," said Jon. "It doesn't take nearly that long."

"You want to change priorities," Rondie said, steering the subject.

"Change them how?" Maxx asked.

"Forget munitions and normal warfare," said the Luddite. "We have one clear job, and that's to finish loading the fuel and dismantling the streakship. Its entire mass has to be ready to burn, when the time comes."

"That would be crazy," said Maxx. "If you can't get the pulse engine firing, then the other ship becomes our lifeboat."

"Except we aren't going to fly any streakship," said Jon. "Streakships are brilliant and very steady and we love them because of it. But if we have enemies, then they'll spot us at a distance, and believe me, streakships are easy targets. On the other hand, the Kajjas pulse engine is a miserable mess full of surges and little failures. Teaching us will be a very difficult proposition. And that's why today, in another ten minutes, I want the two of you to start mapping the minimum cuts to make that other ship into a useable corpse."

"But you promised," said Maxx. "Our enemies aren't coming inside a warship."

"What I promised is that we can't beat them if they do come. We don't have the munitions or armor to offer any kind of fight. My little epiphany, for what it's worth, is that our foes, if they are real, will have one of two strategies: They don't want anybody to have this ship or its cargo, which means they destroy us out here, in deep space. In which case, boarding parties are a waste. Or they want to have whatever we have here, and that's why we have to make ourselves a lousy target."

Rondie scoffed. "Again, we know nothing."

"Or there's nothing worth knowing," G'lene added.

"Physics and tactics," Jon said. "I see our advantages as well as our weaknesses, which is why my plan is best."

"Impressive," said Maxx with a mocking tone, one leg kicking him a little closer to Jon.

G'lene didn't like anybody's face. Where was Tailor? In the distance, hands and long feet working at a bank of controls—controls that hadn't been used since she was a broth of scattered DNA running in the trees, waiting for mutations and the feeble tiny chance to become human.

Jon's gaze was fixed in the middle of the threesome.

"You know quite a lot for a simple drive-mechanic," Maxx said.

"Simple can be good." Jon winked at that empty spot of air. "Now ask yourselves this: Why did our captain hire children?"

"We're not children," Rondie said.

Maxx said.

But G'lene sighed, admitting, "I wondered that too."

"Real or imagined, Tailor's enemy is treacherous," said Jon. "Our Kajjas wants youth. He brought only humans, which is a very young species. And he wants humans that aren't more than a thousand years old, give or take. That way he could study our entire lives, proving to his satisfaction that we aren't more than we seem to be."

"I'm not a little girl," said Rondie.

"You're not," Maxx said.

But Jon was a thousand and the siblings weren't even five centuries old, making them the babies in this odd group.

G'lene watched the angry faces and Jon's face, alert but weirdly calm. Then she noticed the twins' sticky breakfast floating free of its orb. G'lene was born on the Great Ship. Everybody had been. This was their first genuine experience with zero-gee, and she hated it. Without weight, everything small got lost inside the same careless moment, and she didn't know how to move without thinking, and she wasn't moving now, remembering how the Luddite so easily, so deftly, made that bite of his breakfast spin and drift into his waiting mouth.

Jon had been in zero gravity before this.

When?

She nearly asked. But then Maxx said, "I'm going back to work. Plasma guns need to be secured and powered up."

"No, you're not," said Jon.

Rondie kicked closer to the Luddite, hands flexing. "Who put you in charge?" she asked.

"Life," Jon said.

Everybody laughed at him.

But then he asked, "Do you know what I did last night? While you slept, I changed the pass-codes on every gun. Nothing warms an egg without my blessing."

The twins cursed.

Jon shrugged and said, "By the way, I've convinced our human-built AIs that the only voice of reason here is me. Me."

The twins wrapped some brutal words around, "Luddite," and "mutiny."

The mysterious human showed them nothing. He didn't brace for war or smile at his victory. The milky water from a glacier was warmer and far more impatient. Then the twins' anger finally ebbed, and Jon looked at G'lene. Again, from somewhere, he found the sly grin that unsettled her once more. But it also had a way of making her confident, which she liked.

"You never were a Luddite," she blurted.

Jon didn't seem to notice. "Sleep is an indulgence," he told everyone. "We're working hard and smart from this instant, and we'll launch eighteen days earlier than you originally planned. Everybody can sleep, but only when we're roaring back to the Great Ship."

"You're somebody else entirely," she said. "Who are you?"

"I'm Jon, the drive-mechanic," he told them. "And I'm Jon, the temporary captain of this fossil ship.

"Everything else is electrons bouncing inside a box."

9

The field kitchen had no trouble generating propanol and cyanide, and for that matter, spitting out passable rum—an archaic drink that Pamir had grown fond of. What was difficult was finding the moment when the ship's new captain and the Kajjas could drink without interruption. The streakship was being gutted and sliced up, each piece secured against the scaffolding on the old ship's hull. Pamir's three-body crew was working with an absence of passion, but they were working. When everything was going well enough, he offered some calibrated excuse about his lifesuit malfunctioning. Then alone, he slipped back inside the long interior room, grabbing the refreshments and joining Tailor, drifting before that bank of murmuring and glowing, deeply uncooperative machines.

"For you, my sovereign," said the human, handing over a bulb of poison.

The Kajjas was fondling the interfaces, using hands and bare toes, using touch and ears. But his eyes were mist and dream, and the long neck held the head back in a careless fashion that hinted at deep anguish.

The bulb drifted beside him, unnoticed.

Pamir cracked his bulb, sipping the liquor as he waited.

Then the eyes cleared, but Tailor continued to stare into the machinery.

"I have two questions," said the human.

"And I have many," the Kajjas said. "Too many."

"'The army is one body masquerading as many,'" Pamir quoted. "'You are at war with one puzzle, and it just seems like a multitude.'"

"Whose expression is that?"

"Harum-scarums use it," Pamir said.

"I know a few harum-scarums," said Tailor. "They are a spectacularly successful species."

"You should have hired them, not us."

"Perhaps I should have."

Pamir sipped the rum again.

"I'm not oblivious, blind or stupid," the alien said. "I understand that you have taken control of my ship and its future."

"Your plans were weak, and I did what was necessary. Do you approve?"

"Have I contested this change?"

"Here is your chance," said Pamir.

Tailor steered the conversation back where it began. "You wish to ask two questions."

"Yes."

Tailor claimed the other bulb, sipping deeply. "You wish to know if I am making progress."

"I don't care," Pamir said.

"You are lying."

"I have a talent in that realm."

Iron crashed against iron, leaving the air ringing. "Well, I am enjoying some small successes. According to the rough evidence, this is a cargo vessel transporting something precious. But the various boxes and likely cavities are empty, and the sovereigns' language began ancient and then changed over time, and meanwhile these machines have descended into codes or madness, or both."

"How old are you?" Pamir asked.

The Kajjas' three eyes were clear as gin, and each one reached deep inside the head, allowing light to pour into a shared cavity where images danced within a tangle of lenses and mirrors, modern neurons and tissues older than either species.

"You have posed that question before," Tailor said. "You've asked more than once, if my instincts are true."

Pamir confessed how many times they had met over drinks.

"Goodness." Laughter followed, and a sip. "I have noticed. You are suddenly acting and sounding like a captain. Maybe that was one of your disguises, long ago."

"There was no disguise," he said. "I was a fine captain."

"Or there was, and you were fooled as well."

Pamir liked the idea. He didn't believe it, but the meme found life inside him, cloying and frightening and sure to linger.

"I'm a few centuries older than ninety-three million years," Tailor said. "And while I can't claim to have walked your earth, I have known souls—Kajjas and other species—who saw your dinosaurs stomping about on your sandy beaches."

"Lucky souls."

The Kajjas preferred to say nothing.

"I'm waking our engine tomorrow," Pamir said.

"According to your own schedule, that's far too soon."

"It is. But I've decided that we can fly and cut apart the streakship at the same time. We'll use our hydrogen stocks until they're nine-tenths gone, and then we'll throw machine parts down the engine's mouth."

"Butchering the other ship will be hard work, under acceleration."

"Which brings me to my second question: Will you help my crew do the essential labor?"

"And give my important work its sleep," Tailor said.

"Unless you can do both at once."

The mouth opened to speak, but then it closed again, saying nothing as two eyes clouded over.

Pamir finished his drink, the bulb flattened in his hand.

Tailor spoke. Or rather, his translator absorbed the soft musical utterances, creating human words and human emotions that struggled to match what could never be duplicated. Honest translations were mythical beasts. On its best day, communication was a sloppy game, and Pamir was lucky to know what anyone meant, including himself.

"This starship," said the alien. "It is older than me."

"How do you know?"

"There are no markings, no designations. I have looked, but there is no trace of any name. Yet the ship is identical to vessels built while my sun was far outside the galaxy. Those ships were designed for the longest voyages that we could envision, and then they were improved beyond what was imaginable. They had one mission. They were to carry brave and very patient crews into the void, out beyond where anyone goes, in an effort to discover our galaxy's sovereigns."

"Our galaxy's sovereigns," Pamir repeated. "I don't understand."

"But the concept is obvious."

"Someone rules the galaxy?"

"Of course someone does."

"And how does leaving the galaxy prove anything?"

"That's a third question," Tailor pointed out.

"It's your query, not mine. Not once in my life have I ever thought that way."

"And which life is that?"

"Talk," said Pamir.

"Onboard your Great Ship, I once met a Vozzen historian of considerable age and endless learning. The two of us spent months discussing the oldest species of intelligent life, those bold first examples of technological civilizations, and what caused each to lose its grip on Forever and die away. The historian's mind was larger and far wiser than mine. I admit as much. But you can appreciate how the same principles are at work inside both of us, and inside you. The bioceramic mind is the standard for civilized worlds. It was devised early, and several founding worlds have been given credit, although none of them exist anymore. And since the mind's introduction into the galaxy, no one has managed more than incremental improvements on its near-perfection."

"The brain works," said Pamir.

"One basic design is shared by twenty million species. Of course intellect and souls and the colors of our emotions vary widely, even inside the human animal. At first look and after long thought, one might come to the conclusion that it is as you say: We have what's best, and there isn't any reason to look farther."

"We don't look farther," Pamir agreed.

"Humans don't. But the Kajjas once did. That is the point: Our nameless fleet was buried inside a great frozen dwarf world, every pulse engine blazing, driving that shrinking world toward our Second Eye, your Andromeda. The survivors of that epic were under orders to investigate what kind of minds those natives employed, and if another, perhaps worthier mind was found, the fleet would return home immediately.

"At the very most," said Tailor, "that mission would have demanded eight million years. I was born near the end of that period, and I spent my youth foolishly watched for those heroes to return and enlighten us. But they did not appear, even as an EM whisper. Ten and twenty and then fifty million passed, yet just by their absence, much was learned. We assumed that they were dead and the ships were lost, or the explorers had pushed farther into the void, seeking more difficult answers.

"Few civilizations ever attempt such wonders. I have always believed that, and the Vozzen happily agreed with my assessment.

"Don't you find that puzzling? Intriguing? Wrong? The resources of a galaxy in hand, and few of us ever attempt such a voyage.

"But my brethren did. And afterward, living inside my galaxy, I have tried my best to answer the same questions. It is the burden and blessing of being Kajjas: Each of us knows that he rules only so much, and every ruler has worthy masters of his own, wherever they might hide."

"Sovereigns to the galaxy," said Pamir, his voice sharpening.

"You don't believe in them," Tailor said.

"Have you found them?"

"Everywhere, and nowhere. Yes." The laugh was brief, accompanied by a sad murmuring from the translator. "Everywhere that I travel, there are rumors of deeds that claim no father, legends of creatures that wear any face and any voice. There is even talk about invisible worlds and hidden realms, conspiracies and favored species and species that diminish and succumb to no good opponent.

"About our masters, I have little to say. Except that they terrify me, and because I am Kajjas, I wish that I could lie between their mighty feet and beg for some little place at their table."

Pamir had too many questions to ask or even care about. His crew was noticing his absence. One nexus rewarded him with a string of obscenities from the twins, and with those words, promises to turn him over to the Great Ship's captains as soon as they arrived home.

It was no secret that Pamir could hear them, and Rondie and Maxx didn't care.

And all that while, G'lene said nothing.

"Suddenly," said Tailor, almost shouting the word.

"What?"

"Just two million years ago, suddenly and with the barest of warnings, our old fleet began to return home."

Pamir nodded, and waited.

"The ships appeared as individuals. I won't explain how a person might know in advance where such a derelict will show itself, but there is a pattern and we have insights, and there have been some little successes in finding them before anyone else. The crews are always missing. Dead, we presume. But 'missing' is a larger, finer word. Empty ships return like raindrops, scattered and almost unnoticed, and their AIs are near death, and nothing is learned, and sometimes tragic events find the salvage teams that come out to meet these relics."

"Your enemies strike," Pamir said.

"Yet disaster isn't certain," the alien said. "That might imply that there are no masters of the galaxy. Or it means that they are the ultimate masters, and better than us, they know what is and is not a threat to their powers."

Pamir drifted closer, placing his body in a submissive pose.

Long feet pulled away from the display panel, surrounding the human head. "The old fleet had one additional command," Tailor said. "If no equal or at least different mind could be found in the wilderness, then the Kajjas had to assemble at some sunless world, preferably a large moon stirred by a brown dwarf sun, and there, free of interference and ordinary thoughts, our finest minds would build a colony. Then in that nameless place, they and their offspring would kill preconceptions and create something else.

"They were to build a different way of thinking, yes."

"And that is what they were to send home, however they could and in the safest way possible."

Approximating the Kajjas language, the human said, "Shit."

Tailor stroked the panel with one hand, watching a thousand shades of blue swirl into fancy shapes that collapsed as soon as the fingers lifted. "I don't know this language," he said. "It is older than me and full of odd terms, and maybe it has been corrupted. There are fine reasons to believe that there is no meaning inside these machines. But it is possible, weak as the chance seems, that the truth stands before me, and my ordinary mind, and yours, are simply unable to see what is."

The alien was insane, Pamir hoped.

The hand released the display, and Tailor said, "Yes."

"Yes what?"

"I will help make the ship ready for flight. Obviously, nothing I do here can be confused for good."

10

A brick of metallic hydrogen plunged into the first collar, the widest collar, missing the perfect center by the width of a small cold atom. Compression accompanied the hard kick of acceleration, and then a second collar grabbed hold, flinging it through ten of its brothers. Neutronium wire wrapped inside high-grade hyperfiber made the choke points, each smaller and more massive than the ones before, and the cycle continued down to where the brick was burning like a sun—a searing finger of dense plasma that still needed one last inspiration to become useful, reliable fuel.

Pulse engines relied on that final collar of degenerate matter. From outside, the structure looked like a ceramic bottle shaped by artisan hands—a broad-mouthed bottle where it began and then tapering to a point that magically dispensed the ultimate wine. Plasma flowed into the bottle's interior, clinging to every surface while being squeezed. But what was smooth to the eye was vast and intricately shaped at the picometer scale—valleys and whorls, high peaks and sudden holes. Turbulence yielded eddies. The birth of the universe was replicated in tiny realms, and quantum madness took hold. Casimir fields and antiproton production triggered a lovely apocalypse that ended with the obliteration of mass and a majestic blast of light and focused neutrinos.

Then the next moment arrived, bringing another brick of hydrogen.

Twelve thousand and five bricks arrived in order. There were no disasters, but the yields proved fickle. Then the ship's captain killed the engine, invoking several wise reasons for recertifying a control system that was, despite millions of years of sleep, running astonishingly well.

But who knew what a healthy pulse engine could accomplish?

The human captain wasn't sure, and he confessed that loudly, often and without any fear of looking stupid.

Pamir had settled into a pattern. His nameless ship would accelerate hard, pushing at four gees for ten minutes or three days. Bodies ached. Muscles grew in response to the false weight. Then they would coast for a few minutes or for an hour, except the time they drifted for a week, every easy trajectory slipping out of reach.

The ship's sovereigns must have done this good work once, but they remained uncooperative. The streakship's AIs had been salvaged to serve as autopilots, but they weren't confident of their abilities. Pamir gave his crew reasons that wanted to be believed. He offered technical terms and faked various solutions that were intended to leave the children scared of this ancient, miserably unhappy contraption. Tailor required a bit more honesty, and that was why the captain invoked the Kajjas' faceless enemies. Pamir explained that he didn't want other eyes knowing where they would be tomorrow and thirty years from now. "The wounded bandelmoth is hunted by a flock of ravenous tangles," Pamir explained. "The moth flies a quick but utterly random course, letting chance help fend off the inevitable."

"Why not tell the others what you tell me?" the Kajjas asked. "Why invent noise about 'damned stuck valves' and 'damned chaotic flows'?"

"I don't trust my crew," he said flatly.

The Kajjas tapped one foot, agreeing with the sentiment.

"If our children thought they could fly home, they might try it."

"But what I wish to know: Do you have faith in our new captain?"

"More than I have in the rest of you," Pamir said. "I don't believe what you believe, old friend. Not about the galaxy's mysterious rulers. Not about the peculiar sameness of our brains. Not about mysterious foes diving out of the darkness to kill us."

"I believe quite a lot more than that," Tailor said.

"Of course our enemy could be more treacherous than you can imagine. For example, maybe toxic memes have taken control over me, and that's why I took charge of this primordial ship."

"I hope that isn't the case," said the Kajjas.

"And I'll share that wish, or I'll pretend to."

"And what's your impression of Tailor?"

Pamir shrugged. "The ancient boy dances with some bold thoughts. He sounds brave and a little wise, and on his best days profound. But really, I consider him to be the dodgiest suspect of all."

"Then we do agree," said Tailor. "I trust none of us."

They laughed for a moment, quietly, without pleasure.

"But again," Pamir concluded. "I don't accept your galactic sovereigns. Except when I make myself believe in them, and even then, I always fall back on the lesson that every drive-mechanic understands."

"Which lesson?"

"A reliable star-drive doesn't count every hydrogen atom. The machinery doesn't need to know the locations of every proton and electron. No engineer, sane or pretending to be, would design any engine that attempts to control every element inside its fire. And for all of their chaos and all of their precision, star-drives are far simpler than any corner of the galaxy.

"Maybe I'm wrong. You're right, and some grand game is being played with the Milky Way and all of us. But you and I, my friend: We are two atoms of hydrogen, if that. And no engine worth building cares about our tiny, tiny fates."

Robots could have been trusted with this work, if someone brought them and trained them and then insulated each of them from clever enemies. No, maybe it was better that the crew did everything. They worked through the boost phases, and they picked up their pace during the intervals of free fall. G'lene was the weakest: Clad in an armored lifesuit, suffering from the gees, she could do little more than secure herself to the hull's scaffolding, slicing away at the scrap parts set directly in front of her. Complaining was a crucial part of her days, and she spent a lot of air and imagination sharing her epic miseries. By comparison, the twins were stoic soldiers who reveled in their strength, finding excuses to race one another between workstations and back to the airlock at the end of the day. But Tailor proved to be the marvel, the prize. The Kajjas world was more massive than the earth, but his innate physical power didn't explain his dependability or the polish of his efforts. Pamir told him what needed to be cut and into what shapes and where the shards needed to be stored, and looking at the captain as his sovereign, he never grumbled, and every mistake was his own.

One day, Tailors' shop torch burped and burnt away his leg. He reacted with silence, sealing the wound with the same flame before dragging himself inside, stripping out of the lifesuit and eating one of the bottled feasts kept beside the airlock, waiting to supercharge any healings.

"Captains have a solemn duty," the twins joked afterwards. "They should sacrifice the same as their crew."

"Yeah, well, my leg stays on," said Pamir.

The laughter was nearly convincing.

Two years were spent slowly dismantling the streakship. Every shard of baryonic matter had been shaped and put away, waiting to be shoved down the engine's throat after the hydrogen was spent. The only task left was to carve up the streakship's armored prow. Better than hydrogen, better than any flavor of baryonic matter, a slender smooth blade of hyperfiber would ignore compression and heat, fighting death until its instantaneous collapse and a jolt of irresistible power. But hyperfiber was a better fuel in mathematics than it was in reality, subject to wildness and catastrophic failure—a measure waiting for desperate times.

Shop torches were too weak. Sculpting hyperfiber meant deploying one of their plasma guns. Pamir ordered his crew to remaining indoors, the humans maintaining the lights and atmosphere while Tailor was free to return to his obsessions. For five months, Pamir began every day by passing through the airlock to wake a single gun. A block of armor was fixed into a vice, waiting to be carved into as many slips of fuel as possible. The work lasted until his nerves were shot. Then the gun had to be secured, and he crawled back inside the ship. G'lene always threw a smile at him. The twins pretended to ignore him, their curses still echoing in the bright air. Tailor was muttering to the sovereigns or searching for cargoes that didn't exist, or he did nothing but sit and think. Pamir needed to sit and think. But first he had to kick his way to the engine, attacking its inevitable troubles.

When the sixth month began, the twins stopped cursing him.

Even worse, they started to smile. They called him, "Sir," and without prompting, they did their duties. One evening Rondie was pleasant, almost charming, grinning when she said that she knew that his jobs were difficult and she was thankful, like everyone, for his help and good sense.

Pamir wasn't sure what to believe, and so he believed everything.

Tailor continued fighting with the sovereigns.

"I have a verdict," he said one day.

"And that is?" asked Pamir.

"These machines are not insane. They pretend madness to protect something from someone. And the problem is that they won't tell me what either might be."

"Can you break through?"

"If I was as wise as my ancestors, I would, yes." The Kajjas laughed. "So I am convinced and a little thankful that I never will be."

Three years and a month had passed since their launch, the voyage barely begun. Pamir shook himself out of a forty minute nap, ate a quick breakfast and then donned a lifesuit that needed repairs. But the hyperfiber harvest would end in another nine days, and the suit was still serviceable. So alone, he trudged through the airlock and onto a gangway. The plasma gun was locked where he had left it six hours ago. The gun welcomed him with a diagnostic feed, and while it was charging, Pamir used three nexuses to watch the interior. The twins were sleeping. G'lene was studying a mechanic's text, boredom driving her toward competency. And Tailor was staring into a display panel, trying to guess the minds of his ancestors.

Sensors were scattered around the huge cabin. Some were hidden, others obvious. And a few were self-guided, wandering in random pathways that would surprise everyone, including the captain who let them roam.

The peace had held for months.

But Pamir had been strangled and packed away with the luggage, and every day, without fail, he considered the smart clean solution to his worries. Three minutes, and the problem would be finished, with minimal fuss.

Kill the crew before they killed him.

Temporarily murder them, of course.

But those cold solutions had to be avoided. Despite temptations, he clung to the idea that kindness and compassion were the paths to prove your sanity.

Everybody seemed to hold that opinion. G'lene still flirted with the only available man. Maxx offered to drink heavily with his friend Jon, once his hard work was done. And just last week, his sister tried defining herself to this tyrannical captain: Rondie and her brother shared very weak but wealthy parents. They had wanted strong children. Genes were tweaked, giving both of them muscles and strong attitudes. Rondie said that she was beautiful even if nobody else thought so. She said that her parents had wisely kept their wealth away from their children, which was why they joined the military. And then in the next breath, the girl confessed to hating those two ageless shits for being so wise and looking out for their souls.

At that point she laughed. Pamir couldn't tell at whom.

He said, "In parts of the multiverse, both of you are weak and happy."

"A Luddite perspective," she said.

"It is," he agreed.

"Who are you really?" she asked.

"I'm you in some other realm."

"What does that mean?"

"Think," he said, liking the notion then and liking it more as he let it percolate inside his old mind.

That was a good day, and so far this day had proved ordinary.

The twins slept but that didn't keep them from conversing—secret words bouncing between each other's dreams. Tailor was on a high platform, muttering old words that his translator didn't understand. G'lene was the quiet one. She studied. She fell asleep. Then she was awake and reading again, and that was when the pulse engine fell silent.

Pamir lifted from the gangway. Then he caught himself and strapped his body down, focusing on the white-hot shard of hyperfiber before him.

The airlock opened.

He didn't notice.

Three average people, working in concert, could easily outthink the weary fugitive. Pamir saw nothing except what his eyes saw and what the compromised sensors fed to him. The twins slept, and while studying, G'lene played with herself. Pamir looked away, but not because of politeness. At this point, those other bodies were as familiar and forgettable as his. No, his eyes and focus returned to the brilliant slip of hyperfiber that had almost, almost achieved perfection.

From a distant part of the cabin, Tailor called out.

The shout was a warning, or he was giving orders. Or maybe this was just another old word trying to subvert the security system, and it didn't matter in the end.

The ex-soldiers had cobbled together several shop torches, creating two weak plasma guns. The first blast struck Pamir in his left arm, and then he had no arm. But Maxx had responsibility for the captain's right arm, and the boy tried too hard to save the plasma gun. Wounded, Pamir spun as the second blue-white blast peeled back the lifesuit's skin, scorching his shoulder but leaving his right hand and elbow alive.

Quietly and deliberately, Pamir aimed with care and then fired.

Charged and capable, his weapon could have melted the ship's flank. But it was set for small jobs, and killing two muscular humans was a very small thing.

The first blast hit Rondie in her middle, legs separating from her arms and chest. Cooked blood exploded into the frigid vacuum while the big pieces scattered. Maxx dove into the blood cloud to hide, and he fired his gun before it could charge again, accomplishing nothing but showing the universe where he was hiding.

Pamir turned two arms into ash and a gold-white light.

But where was G'lene?

Pamir spun and called out, and then he foolishly tried to kick free of the gangway. But he forgot the tie-downs. Clumsier than any bouncing ball, he lurched in one direction and dropped again, and G'lene shot him with a series of kinetic charges. Lifesuits were built to withstand high-velocity impacts, but the homemade bullets had hyperfiber jackets tapering to needles that pierced the suit's skin, bits of tungsten and iron diving inside the man's flailing sorry body.

The plasma gun left Pamir's grip, spinning as it fled the gangway.

A woman emerged from shadow, first leaping for the gun and securing it. She was crying, and she was laughing. The worst possibilities had been avoided, but she still had the grim duty of retrieving body parts. The plasmas hadn't touched the twins' heads, and they remained conscious, flinging out insults in their private language, even as their severed pieces turned calm, legs and organs and one lost hand saving their energies for an assortment of futures.

G'lene grabbed Maxx first, sobbing as she tied the severed legs to his chest.

Rondie said, "Leave," and then, "Him."

"You're next," G'lene promised.

"No no look," Rondie muttered.

Too late, the crying woman turned.

Every lifesuit glove was covered with high-grade hyperfiber. Pamir was holding his own dead limb with living fingers, using those dead fingers like a hot pad. That was how he could control the slip of hyperfiber that he had been carving on. A kiss from the radiant hyperfiber was enough to cut the tie-downs that secured him, and then he leaped at G'lene. The crude blade was hotter than any sun. He jabbed it at her belly, aiming for the biggest seam, missing once and then planting his boots while shoving harder, searing heat and his fine wild panic helping to punch the beginnings of a hole into the paper-thin armor.

G'lene begged for understanding, not mercy, and she let go of body parts, trying to recover her own weapon.

Pamir shoved again, and he screamed, and the blade vanished inside the woman.

Flesh cooked, and G'lene wailed.

He let her suffer. With his flesh roaring in misery, Pamir set to work tying down body parts and weapons. All the while the girl's round body was swelling, the fire inside turning flesh into gas, and then empathy stopped him. He finally removed her helmet, the last scream emerging as ice, the round face freezing just before a geyser of superheated vapor erupted out of her belly.

"You had some role," Pamir said.

They were sharing a small platform tucked just beneath the ship's prow. The alien had been crawling through an access portal where nothing had ever been stowed. The glass threads had pulled together, building the platform that looked like happy red grass. Pamir hated that color just now. The alien's eyes were clear, and he didn't pretend to look anywhere but at the battered, mostly-killed human.

"Each of us has a role," Tailor said.

"You helped them," said the captain.

"Never," he said.

"Or you carefully avoided helping, but you neglected to warn me."

"I could have done more," the creature admitted. "But why are you distressed? They intended a short death for you, just long enough for you to reconsider."

Every situation had options. The captain's first job was to sweep away the weakest options.

What remained was grim.

"I should kill you too," he said.

"Can you fly this ship alone?"

"It's an experiment that I am willing to run."

Tailor had fewer options, and only one was reasonable. "Secure me," he said. "Each day, please, you can tie me to one place. I'll work where you trap me. If I can go nowhere, what harm do I pose?"

"What if you talk to the sovereigns? You could turn them against me."

"Or you can separate their influences with the ship," the Kajjas said. "Feed them power, of course. But please, let this conundrum have its way with me."

"No."

The three eyes went opaque, blind.

"No," Pamir repeated.

"You once said something important," Tailor said.

"Once?"

"I overheard you. When you came back to life the last time, you were talking to the children. You claimed that there was a reason why youthful souls interested me."

"Young minds can't hide secrets," Pamir said.

"But that isn't their major benefit." Iron knives struck one another inside that long throat. "Just finding the treasure may not be enough. A young mind, unburnished and willing, often proves more receptive to mystery."

"And to madness," Pamir said.

Tailor let one eye clear. "Whoever you are, you hold a strong mind."

"Thank you," Pamir said.

"On the whole," said the Kajjas, "I believe that strength is our universe's most overprized trait."

11

Of course there were sovereigns. Pamir always knew that. The sovereigns were vast and relentless, and they were immortal, and he knew their faces: The kings of vacuum and energy, and their invincible children, time and distance. Those were the masters of everything. Their stubborn uncharitable sense of the possible and the never-can-be was what ruled the Creation. All the rest of the players were little souls and grand thoughts, and that was the way it would always be.

The Great Ship was obeying the kings. It remained no better than a point, a conjecture, crossing one hundred thousand kilometers every second. Reaching the Ship was life's only purpose. Pamir thought of little else. The human-made AIs thought of nothing else. The hydrogen had been consumed until only a thin reserve remained, and then the streakship's corpse was thrown to oblivion, each bit unique in shape and composition. Calculations demanded to be made. Adjustments never ended. Slivers of a cabin wall exploded differently than the plumbing ripped out of fuel pump, and while the Kajjas engine ate each gladly, there was sloppiness, and sometimes the magic would fail, leading to silence as the nameless ship once again began to drift.

Every day had its sick machines.

No week was finished without the engine dying unexpectedly, ruining the latest trajectory.

Anyone less competent than Pamir would have been defeated. Anyone more talented would have known better and given up in this idiot venture on the first day. A soul less proud or more clear-headed would have happily aimed for one of the solar systems on the Kajjas' charts—a living place that would accept the relic starship and two alien species of peculiar backgrounds. But Pamir clung to his stations, and the AIs found new solutions after every hiccup, while Tailor filled his lucid moments moving from platform to cubbyhole, talking to the madness.

Several decades of furious work brought them halfway home.

And then the engine was silenced on purpose, and their ship was given half a roll, preparing to slow its momentum before intercepting the Great Ship.

"You have to pay attention to me," said Tailor.

Pamir was in earshot, barely. But his companion was talking to himself, or nobody.

"I see your stares," the Kajjas said.

Pamir ignored him. From this point on, they had even less play in their trajectories and the remaining time. The Great Ship was swift, but the Kajjas ship had acquired nearly twice its velocity. Very few equations would gently drop them into the berth at Port Beta, while trillions of others shot them ahead of the Great Ship, or behind.

"Do you hear me?" Tailor asked.

Yes, but Pamir pressed on. His companion was another one of the thousand tasks that he could avoid for the time being, and maybe always. What the captain needed to do next was prepare a test-firing of the hyperfiber fuel, and the fuel feeds begged to be recalibrated, and one of his AIs had developed an aversion to an essential algorithm, and he hadn't eaten his fill in three days, and meanwhile the small, inadequate telescopes riding the prow had to be physically carried to the stern and fixed to new positions so that they could look ahead, eating the photons and neutrinos that never stopped raining and never told him enough.

Eating was the first priority.

Pamir was finishing a huge meal when the first note of a warning bell arrived, followed immediately by two others.

Those bells were announcing intruders.

Pamir made himself enjoy his dessert, a slab of buttery janusian baklava, and then, keeping his paranoia in check, he examined the data and first interpretations. The half-roll had revealed a different sky. The telescopes had spotted three distinct objects traversing local space. None were going to collide with Pamir, yet each could well have been aimed at this ship while it moved on an earlier tangent. Each was plainly artificial. The smaller two were the most distant, plunging from different directions, visible only because they were using their star-drives. Measuring masses and those fires, Pamir guessed about likely owners. An enormous coincidence was at hand, three strangers appearing at the perfect place for an attack. The roll-over left him predictable, exposed. It would be smart to conjure up a useful dose of fear. But the fear didn't come. Pamir wasn't calm, and he couldn't recall the last time when he was happy. But he wasn't properly worried either. A thousand ships could be lurking nearby, each with their engines off—invisible midges following his every possible course. But that possibility didn't scare him. His heartbeat refused to spike, right up until the nearest vessel suddenly unleashed a long burn.

Their neighbor was a huge, top-of-the-line streakship, and if Pamir followed the best available trajectory, that luxury ship and his own thumping heart would soon pass within twenty million kilometers of one another.

But the heart was quiet, and Pamir knew why: The universe did not care about him, or this relic, or even crazy old Tailor.

A loud transmission arrived thirteen hours later, straight from the streakship. In various languages and in data, its owners were named as well as the noble species onboard, both by number and their accumulated wealth. Then a synthetic voice asked for Pamir's identity, and with words designed to sound friendly to as many species as possible, it asked if the two of them were perhaps heading toward the same destination? "Are we joining on the Great Ship together, my lovely friend?"

Pamir invented new lies, but he didn't use them. Instead, he identified himself as Human Jon. With his own weary voice, he explained that this was a salvage operation and he was alone, and his ship was little better than a bomb. That's why he kept trying to maneuver out from the path of others. Invoking decency, he decided to delay his test firings, watching the interloper, wondering what it would do in response.

Devoted to its own course, the other voice wished him nothing but the best and soon blasted into the lead.

And three weeks later, the streakship's central engine went wrong. Containment failed or some piece of interstellar trash pierced the various armors. Either way, the universe was suddenly filled with one spectacular light, piercing and relentless, along with the wistful glow from a million distant suns.

Pamir knew a thousand sentient species well enough to gather with them, drinking and eating with them, absorbing natures and histories and the good jokes while sharing just enough of his blood and carefully crafted past. Bioceramic minds didn't merely absorb memories. They organized the past well enough that sixty thousand years later, a bored man doing routine work could hear the song from a right-talisman harp and the clink of heavy glasses kissing each other, and with the mind's eye he saw the face of the most peculiar creature sitting across from him: A withered face defined by crooked teeth and scars, fissures where the skin sagged and sharp bones where muscle had once lived.

That Pamir was younger than many captains, while his companion was a fraction of his age and probably no more than ten years from death. She was as human as Pamir, though he had trouble seeing her that way. Archaics living on the stormy shore of the Holiday Seas had sent delegates to meet with this captain. These citizens were to come to terms on tiny matters of babies and fees paid for those babies, and where their people could travel, and where the other passengers could not.

Pamir already possessed the famous snarl.

"You're stranger to me than most aliens," said the novice captain, finishing his first Mist-of-Tears. "If I try, I understand an extraterrestrial's thought process. But if I look at you and try to figure you out, I get tangled. I end up wanting to scream."

The archaic was drinking rum. Maybe it was the taste in the old woman's mouth, or maybe it was his words. Or perhaps she enjoyed the music coming from an exotic instrument. Whatever the reason, she offered a smile, and then looking down at the swirling dark liquor, she told the glass, "Scream. You won't hurt my feelings."

"You're dying. Right in front of me, you are dying."

The grin lifted. "And you feel for me, how dear."

"A hundred years isn't enough time." Pamir wouldn't scream, but he couldn't sit comfortably either. "I know what you people believe, and it's crazy. Religious scared mad foolish shit-for-brains crazy."

"I'm one hundred and forty years-old," she said with her slow, careful voice. Then after a weirdly flirtatious wink, she added, "I personally believe in modest genetic engineering, ensuring good health and a swift decline at the end."

"Good for you," he said.

She sipped and said nothing.

The young captain ordered another round. Their bartender was a harum-scarum,

gigantic, covered with scales and spines and a sour-temper, ready to battle any pa-
tron who gave her any excuse. Pamir felt closer and much warmer toward that creature than he did to the frail beast beside him.

"There is another way for you," he told her.

A little curious, the old woman looked at him.

"Employ limited bioceramic hardware. A single thread is all that you'd need.
Thinner than a hair, planted deep inside that fatty organ of yours, and you could
spend one hundred and forty years learning everything quickly and remembering
all of it. Then you'd die, just like you want, and your family could have their funeral.
A ceremony, an ornate spectacle, and your grandchildren could chop the implant
out of your skull. Maybe they could pretend it was a treasure. Wouldn't that be nice?
They can drop your intellect into a special bottle and set it on some noble high
shelf, and if they ever needed your opinion, about anything, they could bring you
down for a chat. That's the better way to live like a primitive."

Cheerfully, almost giggling, the old woman said, "I am not a Luddite."

Pamir hadn't used the word, and he didn't intend to use it now.

"'Archaic' isn't an adequate word either," she said.

"What's the best word?" he asked.

"Human," she said instantly, without hesitation or doubt.

Pamir snorted and leaned forward, wondering if this unfriendly back-and-forth
was going to help their negotiations. Probably not, he decided. Oh well, he decided.
"If that's what you are, what am I?" he asked.

"A machine," she said.

He leaned back, hard. "Bullshit."

The old woman shrugged and smiled wistfully.

"Is that the word you use? When we're not present, do you call us cyborgs?"

With a constant, unnerving cheeriness, she said, "Cyborgs are partly human,
and you are not. Your minds, and your flesh, and the basic nature of your bones and
brains: Everything about you is an elaborate manifestation of gears and electrical
currents with just enough masquerading in place to keep you ignorant of your own
nature."

"I don't like you," said the young captain.

"Try the rum," she said.

He played with the mirrored hat on his head.

Then she said, "But as you helpfully pointed out, I shouldn't be around much
longer. So really, what can my opinion weigh?"

Theory claimed that hyperfiber would make a potent fuel. But every theory involved modeling and various flavors of mathematics and usually a fair share of hope.
Truth demanded tests, which was why Pamir dropped a single blade of fuel into the
ship's mouth. And when the engine survived that experiment, he sent in three others,
followed by a hundred more closely-packed slivers.

The old model proved wildly pessimistic.

Yields were at the high end of predictions, and more importantly, each explosion
was set inside a tiny piece of time. Brutal kicks passed through the Kajjas ship. Plas-

mas were spewed ahead, velocities pushing against light-speed, and Pamir let himself breathe while the AIs celebrated with party paradoxes and new models of annihilation, plus fresh crops of trajectories that took into account this unexpected power.

Pamir began slowing the ship with high-gee burns, randomly spaced, and despite premonitions for the worst, the old engine never complained.

Was this how the vanished Kajjas explored the far galaxies? Building hyperfiber only to burn it again?

Three months into the deceleration, the ship was in a coasting phase. Glass strands were pulled to the round cabin walls while Pamir worked on another recalibration. Space appeared normal, benign and cold and vast, and then suddenly an adjacent portion of space became hot. Distant lasers were firing on wandering comets and dust, and the nameless grit responded by boiling, turning to gas and wild ions. Within minutes, a billion cubic kilometers had been engulfed by a bright cobalt glow that looked lovely to the scared human eye.

The Kajjas was wearing smart-manacles and three watchdog sensors. The nearest display panel was busy, gold and mauve wrapped around symbols that looked like a genuine language. But Tailor was standing apart from every machine, closely watching something in one hand, something quite small. Pamir had to call his name several times to be noticed.

The clear eyes rose, and the alien called out, "This is a wondrous day."

"But not especially pleasant," said Pamir. "Somebody is shooting at us, and now I'm starting to believe you."

"Then this day is even better," the creature proclaimed.

A single strand of red glass was dangling from his hand. At a distance and even up close, it looked like every other stalk of fake grass.

Pamir didn't ask about glass or symbols.

"I'm here to warn you," was all that he had time to say. "We're still aiming for the Great Ship. I'm not giving that up. But no sane predictable brain would ever try it this way."

12

Modern bodies didn't easily rot.

Trillions of bacteria lived inside the guts and pores, but they weren't simple beasts waiting for easy meals. Every microbe was a sophisticated warrior tailored to serve its host. Service meant protecting the flesh in life, and if that life was cut to pieces by a plasma blast, then the surviving trillions worked as one, fending off wild bacteria while pulling out the excess moisture, rendering the temporarily dead man as a collection of perfectly mummified pieces.

Even broken, Maxx was a tough looking fellow. Pamir gave the autodoc every chunk, every burnt shred, and he kept close tabs on the progress. Dried tissues were rehydrated and then fed. Stem cells cultured themselves, and they built what was missing, and two days later the growth chamber was filled to overflowing with a naked man, hairless and massive. An earthly gorilla would be proud of that body.

Leaving Maxx trapped inside the chamber seemed wise, but there was little choice. Pamir opened the lid before the boy was ready to move, and he stood over him, starting to explain what he wanted.

Maxx interrupted. "Where's my sister?"

"She'll be next," the captain promised. "But only after you make a promise, or you lie well enough to fool me."

Too soon, Maxx tried to sit up.

Two fingers and a quiet, "Stay," were enough to coax him back down again.

"I was awake," the boy said. "When I was dead, I was thinking."

"Thinking about Rondie," Pamir guessed.

"Not always, no."

The words carried implications.

Pamir quickly explained what had happened since their fight and what might happen if they held the same conventional course. He said that he had considered using Tailor, but the alien was useless. An insight had infected him, and he was even crazier than usual. As a precaution, Pamir had limited his tools and chained him nearby.

Maxx glanced at the Kajjas.

Then with a slower voice, the captain laid out the basics of his mad plan.

Some part of Maxx listening. Yet more compelling matters had to be considered. The boy's voice was uneasy, shrill at the edges when he asked, "When will my sister be back?"

Rondie's remains were more numerous and in worse condition, and the autodoc was limited. "Six days, or with luck, five," he said.

"Take your time," Maxx advised.

Pamir said, "I don't do sloppy work."

"That isn't what I mean." Then with a shy smile, Maxx said, "I rather liked it, being alone."

"Solitude has its pleasures," Pamir said.

"Yeah, I promise, I'll do whatever you want me to do," said the resurrected man. "Just please, don't tell my sister what I just confessed to you."

The ship had rolled again, and denying every commonsense vector, it was once more accelerating, hard.

Pamir and Maxx were out of sight, out of reach. Tailor wore manacles and tethers, and an ordinary tool kit was in easy reach. Standing took too much work. Against the thundering engine, it was better to sit deep in the grassy glass. The drill lay between his feet, recharging itself. Five times, the Kajjas had ordered the drill to cut a single precise hole, and then with his own trembling hands, he fed one of the treasures into the breach.

Momentous times, that's what these were. His species had labored for one hundred million years, searching for enlightenment. Tailor couldn't remember when he wasn't preparing for this day. And at long last, he broke every code and deciphered old, vanished technologies. No barriers remained. The magic had no choice but to work, and that's what he was doing.

Five times he overrode the drill's safeties, coaxing a slender beam of high-UV light to evaporate his flesh and then his bone before eating slowly, carefully into the living template of his mind.

Each hole was perfect.

Into each hole went one of the rare treasures.

During the first four attempts, he emptied his mind of thought, making ready for lightning and epiphanies. Tailor was relaxed and rested, fortunate beyond all measure, thinking about nothing, ready to be seized by truth in whatever serene form it came. And something did happen. Four times, there were sensations, the painful roiling of electrons that became familiar and intense to a point where much more was promised . . . and then the intensity slackened and slipped, nothing remaining but the residues one endures when rising from a deep, perishable dream.

On the fifth attempt, Tailor changed tactics.

He purposefully thought about quite a lot. Perhaps engaging old memories would open the necessary gateway. Who knew? That's why he built lost rooms in his head, and why he spoke to family members who were dead or so distant that they might as well be. He recalled his first journey in space and his first new sun, and buried inside that flood of old, rarely-touched remembrance he discovered a nameless world, watery and deliciously warm but not available to colonize. Why was that? Because there were rules, yes. Supposedly the galaxy had no sovereigns, but the rising civilizations, young and otherwise, had carved laws and punishments out of the potential. This wet world was too promising to be claimed. The furry souls hiding inside their burrows and up on the high tree branches held promise—just enough of this and not too much of that—and their world was stable enough to survive comet blasts and the next half billion years. That was why the Kajjas scout team was just visiting. It had already been decided to move to another nearby solar system, harsher and far more promising.

Tailor couldn't remember when he last thought about that world.

It might have been the human homeland. Who would know? The galaxy never stopped moving, suns marching in every direction. Certainty it would take work and patience, and he didn't have either to spare.

He considered calling to Jon. This memory would be a gift.

But the scorching laser had burrowed deep into his mind, much deeper than the others, and the fifth thread had to be eased into position and then sealed in place. Tailor accomplished both tasks with fingers and a torch. The thread only looked like the red glass. Years had been spent walking on the cargo, sleeping with it and ignoring it, and he never suspected: One strand in eight million was glass on the outside, mimicking their mates, but it was bioceramic at the core. Each core employed an architecture that was nothing like the standard mind. How it worked was just another mystery. Tailor had found six odd threads already, there were probably several hundred more, and this thread was inside him and talking to his soul, bringing nothing but pain, pure simple dumb pain, as the brain felt the grievous injury, more and more of his ancient memories thrown to oblivion.

Tailor dipped his head, and the translator transformed his noble sobs into sick human sobs.

All the while, the nameless ship was filled with motion, with purpose. The invincible engine was eating hyperfiber and shitting out the remnants. And Jon and Maxx were far away, making ready for the last portion of this desperate scheme.

Despair was a shroud, and through the shroud came a human voice.

"What are you doing?" she asked.

"Healing," the Kajjas said.

The new patient was lying inside the growth chamber. The autodoc had lifted its lid, allowing her flesh to grow while she breathed freely.

Rondie turned onto her side.

With a paternal voice, the autodoc told its patient to do nothing but rest.

"Shut up," she said.

Tailor laughed, but not because of her.

"Where's my brother?" she asked.

"Helping our insane captain," he said. "Jon has decided to harvest our own ship's armor and employ it as fuel."

"No," she said.

"It is a strange tactic, yes," he said.

"I mean, why isn't Maxx with me?"

Looking at any human, looking at the beast deeply and with all of his experience, it often occurred to Tailor that each of these creatures was a species onto herself. "Human" was just a convenience applied to a pack of disagreeable, dissimilar fur-bearers.

"You look strong," he said.

She said, "I'm feeling better."

"Wonderful," he said. "Can you climb out of that device now?"

Rondie was exceptionally powerful. Even unfinished, she sat up easily and the naked legs came out without much trouble. But death had made her cautious, and she moved slowly until an alarm sounded, the autodoc trying to coax her to behave with nothing but loud, brash sounds.

She jumped free and slapped the controls, earning silence.

"Come here," Tailor said.

Five slivers were inside him, and he had no idea what enlightenments they were carrying.

"When will my Maxx come back?" she asked.

Tailor said, "Come here and I will call your brother."

She took slow steps against the thundering of the engine. "So our bastard captain tied you down," she said, looking at the manacles and tethers.

"This is a verdict which I deserved and embraced." Then he reached with one hand and a foot, which was a blunder.

Rondie stopped, keeping out of his reach.

"You look as if you're hurting," she said.

"A few wounds, yes. But the mind is durable and profound, and I will heal soon enough."

"I'm going to get dressed," she said. "I want to find Maxx."

"But first," said Tailor.

She stared at him, waiting.

"G'lene is waiting inside the box, that packing crate lying just past the autodoc."

The sixth thread felt light and cool in his palm and between his long fingers. "Would you unpack G'lene for me, please?"

"Let the bastard cure her."

"But I don't want you to feed her to the autodoc," he said. "No, I very much want the girl for myself. And I have a good reason, if that matters."

She shrugged, absolutely unmotivated.

"If you did this," he said, "the Luddite will be exceptionally angry with you. I promise."

"Okay," she allowed.

And as she walked toward the boxes, Tailor called out, "If it is easier, you may cut off the head. I desire nothing else."

13

The mad plan was to burn up their original fuel stocks in order to bring them home on a short vector. All that while, they would carve away a portion of the ship's prow, holding back those shards for later. If they survived the boost phase, the ship would be rolled again at the last possible moment, and then the engine's muscle and endurance would be severely tested. Hyperfiber would be shoved into oblivion and expelled before them—a long spike of plasma and radiations slicing through the blackness. Every local eye would see their arrival, and that was part of Pamir's scheme: If someone tried to kill this ship, it would be a loud public act, a revealing act. If some secret power was at large, it would surely prefer to settle this matter in more private ways.

Pamir had explained his plan, and to one degree or another, the others accepted his rule if not his logic. Besides, everyone knew that they were far off course, and at this velocity and in this place, there was simply no other route home.

Every hand was needed. The original crew was at work, infuriating yet predictable. But now a second crew shared the ship with them. The twins could follow their usual script, sometimes for a full day or two. But then the boy suddenly begged to be left alone, please. Except his sister came out of death lonely, famished for more touches than ever and private words known only to her and maybe even the first stirrings of lust for the only object of value in her brief life.

The Kajjas remained the ancient puzzle. Freed of manacles and his studies, Tailor helped slice apart the least critical portions of the ship's armor. But without warning, he would suddenly turn fearless, risking millions of years of existence by stepping onto the open prow. Grains of dust would explode on all sides while he did nothing but sing, throwing old songs into the vacuum, eyes gazing up at the blue-shifted starlight that fell inside his joyous soul.

Even Pamir was two people. Long habit and the ingrained personality usually held him where he belonged—a blunt strong-willed soul that could sleep minutes every day and push three days' work into two. He ruled a minor realm inside the boundless universe governed by faceless, amoral laws. Those laws were too powerful and too perfect to give a shit about little him, and wasn't that the least awful existence imaginable?

But the other Pamir, the new man, was much less certain about everything.

Invisible, potent sovereigns held sway over the galaxy. Except in Pamir's mind, they weren't Kajjas sovereigns. They wore the faces and attitudes of captains. They were bold opinionated creatures looking splendid in their bright uniforms, each one ambitious, each a rival to all of the others, and somewhere there sat a world-sized Master Captain holding a godly feast every million years, just to prove to her nervous self that she was genuinely in charge.

The imagery had its charms, its humor.

Laughing, he could deny everything. One senile alien from a vanquished race was not much of an authority, and there were explanations waiting to be invoked. Their ship was nothing but a derelict, and its sovereigns were crazy, and nothing here was worth two drops of blood or any reputation. Those bits of glass that Tailor found were just that. They were glass. The alien had installed them, and what changed about him? The new boldness was nothing but Tailor's anguish for a thoroughly wasted life. The streakship following them was one mild coincidence, and its detonation was another. And that final attack—the wild flash of laser light—was just some local species running experiments in deep space, or a factory ionizing the dust to harvest it, or maybe someone was trying to kill them. But what did that mean? There were endless reasons to destroy another ship, and saving the universe for the sovereigns was far down on the list.

Wild thoughts kept running where they wanted inside the captain's exhausted mind. But he suppressed the worst of them, and he learned to ring the humor out of the paranoia and push on.

But whatever his burdens, G'lene's were immeasurably worse.

Through his nexuses, Pamir had watched Rondie cut the woman's head off of her boiled corpse. Then she handed the head to Tailor, and he watched what Tailor did with that gift. But the prow was far away and the high-gee acceleration had to be maintained. It took only minutes to carve a fresh hole into G'lene's mind, and then the final thread—one last piece of glass—was implanted.

Change the time or change the circumstances, and Pamir would not have brought her back to life. Better autodocs onboard the Great Ship would repair the damaged intellect first. But he needed G'lene's hands, her back. He fit the surviving pieces inside the growth chamber, and they remembered their original self, knitting together and building connections, swelling with water and fat until the girl emerged on schedule, seemingly unharmed.

Pamir didn't tell her about the rough surgery. As far as he could see, nobody else mentioned it either. The inserted glass had done nothing to change the girl's complaining attitude, and she still had bouts of laziness. But there was a quiet that had gotten inside her and wouldn't let her free. She stopped flirting, and more alarming, she stopped masturbating too.

Dreaming, she wept.

Awake, the girl used her nexuses for most peculiar functions. Everybody was near the prow, everybody carving hyperfiber, but her attentions were focused on textbooks and general how-to files. She used to fitfully study. Now she acted focused if not happy. She said that she was the same, by feeling and by thought, except she had a sudden passion for stardrives and the ships that surrounded those engines. Pamir asked why. Everyone asked. Explaining herself, G'lene claimed that she had to think about something while she was dead. Contemplating her life seemed reasonable. And in the darkness, she told herself: "Quit making a mess of your existence and do your damned work."

It was easy to accept the girl's reasoning. Pamir took the role of tutor, if only to keep close tabs on her progress. Each month, G'lene researched a different drive, exhausting its basics before trying to master some subsystem that other drive-mechanics found cumbersome or boring. She wasn't notably smarter than before, and her memory was no sharper. She would still be one of the weakest students in any class. But G'lene was focusing her skills on rockets and power sources, and the months became several years, and then suddenly, without comment, she quit accessing the texts and manuals.

Pamir mentioned the change.

The girl shrugged and finished polishing the latest slip of hyperfiber. Then she stepped away, saying, "I realized. I'll never be good doing your job."

"No?"

With a slow, untroubled voice, she said, "If we survive this, I will quit the program."

Her captain had never seen her make any smart choice, until now.

During those intense years, their ship ate the last of its hydrogen stocks and the final bits of the streakship guts, and then most of the streakship's hyperfiber was tossed into oblivion. No invisible hand tried to murder them. No truly vital system failed. The ship's huge prow was degraded, pierced with tunnels and little caverns, and several lumps of comet ice managed to punch deep. But the frame remained sound, and the engine was in fair shape when they gave it one fast rest, and as the slow final roll-over began, the captain decided that this was the moment when their ship deserved to finally wear some kind of name.

He let Tailor master the honor.

A moment of consideration led to a Kajjas phrase—an honored term meaning wisdom and deep, profound sanity. Then with a most respectful voice, the translator said, "Precious Mental."

They wrote that name on various bare surfaces, in a thousand distinct languages.

"I don't know this tongue," G'lene said.

She was reading over Pamir's shoulder. "The language is mine," he said. "It's the dialect we use inside Where-Peace-Rains."

She touched the lettering, and a painful murmur came out of her.

"I've been watching you," he said.

"All of you keep staring at me."

"Do you know why?"

"Because you're worried."

"There's a lot to worry about," he said.

She tried to leave.

"Stay here," he said.

"Is that an order?"

"If it keeps you here, it is." Pamir didn't want to touch her, but a hand to the shoulder seemed important. Then he forgot that he was holding her, saying, "I know what you're studying now."

"You know everything," she said, bristling slightly.

"Mathematics," he said.

"Yes."

"But not just any numbers," Pamir said. "You're dabbling with the big, scary co-nundrums, the old problems about existence and the shape of the universe."

"Yes," she said.

He kept quiet, waiting.

"What's wrong with that?" she asked.

"Why are you?" he asked.

She shrugged. "I've also developed a taste for poetry."

"Bleak poems about death," he said. "Yeah, I'm eavesdropping. Each of us is wor-ried about you, G'lene."

"Including me."

He waited for a long moment. Then he quietly asked, "What happened? When you were dead in the box, what happened?"

"I thought about you," she said calmly. "I could have killed you on the gangway, and you could have killed me. Again and again, I relived all of that. And then at the end, just before you put me inside the autodoc—just before the darkness broke—this idea came to me. From the middle of my regrets and stupidity, it came."

"What idea?"

She shook her head.

"Tell me," Pamir insisted.

She looked at her captain and then at the archaic words—white lines smoothly drawn across a coal-black housing. "Have you ever noticed, sir? There are so many ways to push a ship across space. Dozens of engines are popular, and thousands have been tried at least once. But most of us wear the same basic brain. And shouldn't thought be more important than action?"

"Is that your epiphany?" he asked.

"No," she said. "That's me wishing that my brain was smarter."

He nodded, weighing his next words.

But then she pushed aside her doubts. "I was alive but only barely, trapped inside a room without light or ends," she said. "I was thinking about you, Jon. You're not the person that you pretend to be. You're no Luddite or drive-mechanic, but you're doing a very fine job of pretending.

"And then all of the sudden, out of nowhere, I thought: 'What if everyone is the same as Jon?

"'What if everything is that way?

"'Not just people, but the universe?' I thought. 'What if everything we see and everything we know is one grand lie, an extraordinary mask, and waiting behind the mask is something else entirely?'"

14

The Great Ship was close enough to see and close enough to fear.

Approaching from behind, the Kajjas ship was tracing a rigorous line, a very pe-culiar line, and if nothing changed their tiny vessel would miss every Port and the emergency landing sites on the hull. If the pulse engine never fired, the five of them would pass in front of their home and continue onwards, eventually leaving the galaxy for places that not even Tailor's charts would show.

But if their engine ignited, a collision was possible. That's why they were studied, and that's why various voices called out to them. Captains demanded to know the ship's history and intentions. The Great Ship's best weapons were directed forwards, fending off lost moons and the like. But there was ample firepower on the backside, ready to eviscerate their little craft. Pamir assured his crew that crosshairs were locked on them, probably for some time. He also confessed that ignoring the first pleas was his strategy. Those captains needed to feel ignored, which made them worry. There was a tradition to command and rank and the corrosive strategies of those who wore the mirrored uniforms. Worry was what helped the five of them. A captain's responsibilities grew heavier when nobody was listening. And then at the ripe moment, Pamir told their audience a story—a sweet balance of truth and lie, pieces of it practiced for a thousand years.

Early on, Pamir had considered making a full confession.

But what would that help? A nervous captain might believe him too well, and smelling commendations, sprinkle the space between them with arrest warrants and nuclear mines.

No, he was still Jon. He was the drive-mechanic hired to bring home one lost ship. Playing to every bias held by those mirrored uniforms, he admitted that he was an idiot far from his native habitat. Taking no credit for himself, he thanked his AIs for finding this odd route home. Captains would always accept genius in machines before genius in a tool-bearing grunt. Then as the pivotal moment approached, Pamir added a long, faintly sentimental message aimed at his descendants wearing his blood and his name. And for no reason but that it felt true, he told Where-Peace-Rains that he was miserably sorry for his crime of living far too long.

The rest of Pamir's crew was in place, waiting. Each wore the best available life-suit, and each suit was set on a tall bed of shock absorbers. Those beds would do almost nothing, and the glassy grass heaped around them was mostly for show. Gee-forces of this magnitude would kill most machines. Hyperfiber and bioceramics would survive, if barely. There was only the slenderest of room for error, but then again, as experience showed, some guesses were pessimistic, and if you took a risk, sometimes the results were golden.

Pamir was inside his suit, securing himself to his bed.

Nearby, Rondie said private words to Maxx.

Her brother responded with silence.

Injured, she said his name twice, and then Maxx spoke out, but not to her. "So Jon," he said with a loud, clear voice. "For the record, what's your real name?"

He said it. For the first time in decades, he said, "Pamir," aloud, and then added, "If you survive and I survive, turn me in. There's going to be an ample reward."

The man laughed. "If I survive, that's the reward."

Mournfully, Rondie said, "Maxx."

"If we live, I mean," he said.

Then the twins were talking again, dancing with words devised in just the last few hours.

Tailor was closer to him, and G'lene was the closest.

"Thank you," said the Kajjas. "Without you, nothing ends properly."

Pamir made a polite noise about helping hands and interesting conversations.

G'lene said nothing.

Pamir said her name.

Nothing.

He repeated the word, but with a captain's tone behind it.

She sniffed once, and then very quietly, almost sweetly, she admitted, "I can't get comfortable yet. How much longer will this be?"

Quite a lot occurred, most of it happening slowly.

And seven months later, a famous man returned to his childhood home.

Every citizen wanted to see him, but of course that was impossible. A lottery identified the luckiest few, and certain people of power bought slots or invented places for themselves, and of course there were cameras in position, feeding views to every apartment and tavern and even the hospital beds. The energy demands were enormous. The old stardrive was laboring at ninety percent capacity. But if anything should go wrong, some joked, at least they had an expert on hand who could fix the machine, probably with his eyes closed.

Yet despite fame and warm feelings, Jon sensed the doubts that came with the crowd. They were staring at a creature that had left their ranks long ago. Every face resembled his face, except he was something else. He was a machine. He was a monster and a traitor to the most suspicious ones, and Pamir was ready to admit as much to anyone who wanted to start a brawl.

"I'm not like you," he began. "And anymore, after everything, I don't know who I resemble."

The story they wanted was spectacular, and like most good stories, it was already known to everyone, here and throughout the Great Ship. So that's where Pamir began: He was a lump of tissue and fear inside a lifesuit, and following preprogrammed instructions, the Kajjas ship let loose with its one old engine. But unlike every other firing, there were no millisecond breaks between each sliver of fuel. Tons and tons of hyperfiber passed through the collars and out the magic wine bottle, and a blaze that rivaled the Great Ship's engines slowed their descent, twisting their motion into a course that could be adjusted only in the tiniest, most fractional ways.

The storyteller remembered nothing after the first damning jerk of the engine.

Encased inside hyperfiber, his body turned to mush and then split apart, dividing according to density. Teeth settled at the bottom of the suit, pulverized bits of bone laid over them. And floating on top was the water that began inside his body, inside his cells—a dirty brew distinctly unlike the stuff that ran out of pipes and that fell as rain, denser and stranger in a realm where gravity was thousands of times stronger than was right.

In the end, good wise captains were debating what to do about this unwelcomed piece of museum trash. Do they shoot it apart to be careful, or shoot it apart as a warning to whoever tried to repeat this maneuver? But Pamir had been very careful about his aim, and once his destination was assured, the argument ended. A few moments later, Precious Mental rode down on the last gasps of its engine, entering the centermost nozzle of the Ship's own rockets.

Each nozzle was impervious to these whiffs of heat and raw light.

Three kilometers off target, the old ship touched down and split wide, the debris field larger than the floor of this old cavern.

Jon was pulled from the rubble, his lifesuit cracked but intact.

Four more suits were found, but only two other survivors.

"My friend Tailor died," he told his audience. "And my very good friend G'lene was killed too. Their minds had recently undergone surgery. The nanofractures spread and grew, and everything shattered. Bioceramic is a wonderful substance, right up until it breaks. And nothing brings anyone back from that kind of damage."

His sadness was theirs. His grief and anguish made every face hurt. At that point, Pamir could have ended this chore. His plan was to walk out of this place and invent his death, using a stand-in body and fake damage from the crash landing. But the earnest smart watchful faces didn't want him to leave, and he didn't want solitude just now.

He was standing in the middle of the red granite round.

At the edge of the crowd was one young woman. She was Jon's relative. This many generations after his leaving, everybody was part of his family. And in her hand was a teapot that someone had remembered. Careful hands had taken it off its shelf and cleaned it up, and there was even cold tea inside, ready to be given in some little ceremony devised for this very peculiar occasion.

Pamir smelled the tea, and at that moment, for endless good reasons, he confessed.

No, he didn't name himself. Nor did he mention that his namesake died more than ten centuries ago. What he told them was the story that he had revealed only in pieces to the investigators and the overseeing captains. He told about Tailor's quest for enlightenment, and he described a fleet of exploratory ships racing out to neighboring galaxies. With minimal detail and words, he explained how the Kajjas was afraid of invisible sovereigns, and Jon admitted that he was temporarily sick with that fear, but then at the end, waiting for the engine to fire once more, he decided that there was no ground or heart to any of these wild speculations.

It took weeks for his pulverized body to be made into something living, and then into a man's shape, and finally into his old body.

After months of care, he was finally awake again. He was eating again. His attendant was a harum-scarum. The alien told him that two of his companions were sharing a room nearby, each a little farther in the healing than he was, and when the human asked about the other two, a grave sound emerged from the attendant's eating mouth. Then she explained that both had died instantly, and they had felt nothing, which was a sorry way to die, oblivious to the moment.

But his two wonderful friends had not died, of course.

In that bed, restrained by lousy health and the watchful eyes of doctors, Jon could suddenly see everything clearly. G'lene's own words came back to him. Why would the galaxy have a thousand stardrives but only one basic mind? And how can the thousand or ten thousand original civilizations all vanish together in the remote past? Why can't there be forces at work and different minds at work, hidden in myriad ways?

Jon paused.

Where-Peace-Rains listened to his silence.

He coughed weakly into a shaking fist, and the girl, urged by others, started forward with her offering of cold water infused with ordinary tea.

He stopped her.

"It's like this," he said. "If there are hidden captains, and in one measure or another they are steering our galaxy, then how can I deny the possibility—the distinct probability—that they would be naturally curious about some one hundred million year-old vessel that was getting washed up on our shore? Tailor believed that this mission was his, but that doesn't make it so. Maybe it never was. And in the end, our masters got exactly what they wanted, which was a viable sample of novel technologies, and with G'lene, a creature with whom they could talk to and perhaps learn from."

When did the man begin to cry?

Jon wasn't certain, but he was definitely crying now.

Encouragement was offered, and once again, the girl and the tea came forward. She had a nice smile. He had seen that same smile before, more than forty millennia ago. He was crying and then he had stopped crying, wiping his face dry with a sleeve, and he said to the girl, "Give me the pot. I want to hold, like old times."

She was happy to relinquish the chore.

But as she pulled back, she saw what was in her hands now. She felt the glass threads squirming of their own volition. Laughing nervously, she said, "What are these things?"

He offered his best guess.

Everybody wanted to see, including the cameras.

But he waved the others off, and then just to her, he muttered, "They could be a danger. G'lene had one inside her, and it made her halfway crazy. Tailor found several hundred more before we crashed, but on my own, on the sly, I found a few. I never told anybody, and that's five of them. You keep them. Put them somewhere safe, and give them to your next thousand generations. Please."

The girl nodded solemnly, putting the threads into her best pocket.

"What if?" he said.

"What if what, Jon?" she asked.

He sighed and nodded.

"What if this brain of mine is designed to be stupid?" he asked. "What if the obvious and important can't be seen by me, or by anyone else?"

A sorrowful face made her prettier. She wasn't yet twenty, which was nothing. It was barely even born by the man's count. But after struggling for something to say—something kind or at least comforting—she touched the man with her cool little hand. "Maybe you're right," she said. "But when you talk about that poor friend of yours, the girl and her suffering . . . I wonder if perhaps there is no treachery, no conspiracy. Maybe it is a kindness, making all of you a little foolish.

"Letting you forget the awful truth about the universe.

"Isn't that what you do with children, lending them the peace that lets them sleep through their nights . . . ?"

Martian Blood

ALLEN M. STEELE

Allen Steele made his first sale to Asimov's Science Fiction *magazine in 1988, soon following it up with a long string of others not only to* Asimov's *but to markets such as* Analog, The Magazine of Fantasy and Science Fiction, *and* Science Fiction Age. *In 1990, he published his critically acclaimed first novel,* Orbital Decay, *which subsequently won the Locus Poll as best first novel of the year, and soon Steele was being compared to Golden Age Heinlein by no less an authority than Gregory Benford. His other books include the novels* Clarke County Space, Lunar Descent, Labyrinth of Night, The Weight, The Tranquility Alternative, A King of Infinite Space, Oceanspace, Chronospace, Coyote, Coyote Rising, Spindrift, Galaxy Blues, Coyote Horizon, Coyote Destiny, Hex, *and a YA novel,* Apollo's Outcast. *His short work has been gathered in three collections,* Rude Astronauts, Sex and Violence in Zero G, *and* The Last Science Fiction Writer. *His most recent book is a new novel,* V-S Day. *He has won three Hugo Awards, in 1996 for his novella* The Death of Captain Future, *in 1998 for his novella* Where Angels Fear to Tread, *and most recently in 2011 for his novelette* The Emperor of Mars. *He was born in Nashville, Tennessee, and has worked for a variety of newspapers and magazines covering science and business; he is now a full-time writer and lives in Whately, Massachusetts with his wife, Linda.*

Here he takes us to a Mars very different from the Mars of his Hugo-winning novelette, the Old Mars of ancient dreams, and deep into the Martian Badlands on a mission that could plunge two races, and two worlds, into all-out war.

The most dangerous man on Mars was Omar al-Baz, and the first time I saw him, he was throwing up at the Rio Zephyria spaceport.

This happens more frequently than you might think. People coming here for the first time often don't realize just how thin the air really is. The cold surprises them, too, but I'm told the atmospheric pressure is about the same as you'd find in the Himalayas. So they come trooping down the ramp of the shuttle that transported them from Deimos Station, and if the ride down didn't make them puke, then the shortness of breath, headaches, and nausea that comes with altitude sickness will.

I didn't know for sure that the middle-aged gent who'd doubled over and vomited was Dr. al-Baz, but I suspected that he was; I hadn't seen any other Middle Eastern men on his flight. There was nothing I could do for him, though, so I waited patiently on the other side of the chain-link security fence while one of the flight attendants came down the ramp to help him. Dr. al-Baz waved her away; he didn't need any assistance, thank you. He straightened up, pulled a handkerchief from his overcoat pocket, and wiped his mouth, then picked up the handle of the rolling bag he'd dropped when his stomach revolted. Nice to know that he wasn't entirely helpless.

He was one of the last passengers to step through the gate. He paused on the other side of the fence, looked around, and spotted the cardboard sign I was holding. A brief smile of relief, then he walked over to me.

"I'm Omar al-Baz," he said, holding out his hand. "You must be Mr. Ramsey."

"Yes, I'm your guide. Call me Jim." Not wanting to shake a hand that just wiped a mouth which had just spilled yuck all over nice clean concrete, I reached forward to relieve him of his bag.

"I can carry this myself, thank you," he said, not letting me take his bag from him. "But if you could help me with the rest of my luggage, I'd appreciate it."

"Sure. No problem." He hadn't hired me to be his porter, and if he'd been the jerk variety of tourist some of my former clients had been, I would've made him carry his own stuff. But I was already beginning to like the guy: early 50's, skinny but with the beginnings of a pot belly, coarse black hair going grey at the temples. He wore round spectacles and had a bushy mustache beneath a hooked aquiline nose, and looked a little like an Arab Groucho Marx. Omar al-Baz couldn't have been anything but what he was, an Egyptian-American professor from the University of Arizona.

I led him toward the terminal, stepping around the tourists and business travelers who had also disembarked from the 3 p.m. shuttle. "Are you by yourself, or did someone come with you?"

"Unfortunately, I come alone. The university provided grant money sufficient for only one fare, even though I requested that I bring a grad student as an assistant." He frowned. "This may hinder my work, but I hope that what I intend to do will be simple enough that I may accomplish it on my own."

I had only the vaguest idea of why he'd hired me to be his guide, but the noise and bustle of the terminal was too much for a conversation. Passenger bags were beginning to come down the conveyer belt, but Dr. al-Baz didn't join the crowd waiting to pick up suitcases and duffel bags. Instead, he went straight to the PanMars cargo window, where he presented a handful of receipts to the clerk. I began to regret my offer to help carry his bags when a cart was pushed through a side door. Stacked upon it were a half-dozen aluminum cases; even in Martian gravity, none small enough to be carried two at a time.

"You gotta be kidding," I murmured.

"My apologies, but for the work I need to do, I had to bring specialized equipment."

He signed a form, then turned to me again. "Now . . . do you have a means of taking all this to my hotel, or will I have to get a cab?"

I looked over the stack of cases and decided that there weren't so many that I couldn't fit them all in the back of my jeep. So we pushed the cart out to where I'd parked beside the front entrance, and managed to get everything tied down with elastic cords I carried with me. Dr. al-Baz climbed into the passenger seat and put his suitcase on the floor between his feet.

"Hotel first?" I asked as I took my place behind the wheel.

"Yes, please . . . and then I wouldn't mind getting a drink." He caught the questioning look in my eye and gave me a knowing smile. "No, I am not a devout follower of the Prophet."

"Glad to hear it." I was liking him better all the time; I don't trust people who won't have a beer with me. I started up the jeep and pulled away from the curb. "So . . . you said in your email you'd like to visit an aboriginal settlement. Is that still what you want to do?"

"Yes, I do." He hesitated. "But now that we've met, I think it's only fair to tell you that this is not all that I mean to do. The trip here involves more than just meeting the natives."

"How so? What else do you want?"

He peered at me over the top of his glasses. "The blood of a Martian."

When I was a kid, one of my favorite movies was *The War of the Worlds*—the 1953 version, made about twelve years before the first probes went to Mars. Even back then, people knew that Mars had an Earthlike environment; spectroscopes had revealed the presence of an oxygen-nitrogen atmosphere, and strong telescopes made visible the seas and canals. But no one knew for sure whether the planet was inhabited until Ares I landed there in 1977, so George Pal had a lot of latitude when he and his film crew tried to imagine what a Martian would look like.

Anyway, there's a scene in the movie where Gene Barry and Ann Robinson have made their way to L.A. after escaping the collapsed farmhouse where they'd been pinned down by the alien invaders. Barry meets with his fellow scientists at the Pacific Tech and presents them with a ruined camera-eye he managed to grab while fighting off the attackers. The camera-eye is wrapped in Ann Robinson's scarf, which was splattered with gore when Gene clobbered a little green monster with a broken pipe.

"And this—" he says melodramatically, showing the scarf to the other scientists "—blood of a Martian!"

I've always loved that part. So when Dr. al-Baz said much the same thing, I wondered if he was being clever, copping a line from a classic movie that he figured most colonists might have seen. But there was no wink, no ironic smile. So far as I could tell, he was as serious as he could be.

I decided to let it wait until we had that drink together, so I held my tongue as I drove him into Rio Zephyria. The professor's reservation was at the John Carter Casino Resort, located on the strip near the Mare Cimmerium beach. No surprise there: it's the most famous hotel in Rio, so most tourists try to book rooms there.

Edgar Rice Burroughs was having a literary renaissance around the time it was built, so someone decided that A *Princess of Mars* and its sequels would be a great theme for a casino. Since then it's become the place most people think of when they daydream about taking a vacation trip to Mars.

Good for them, but I want to throw a rock through its gold-tinted windows every time I drive by. It's a 10-story monument to every stupid thing humans have done since coming here. And if I feel that way, as someone who was born and raised on Mars, then you can well imagine what the *shatan* think of it . . . when they come close enough to see it, that is.

It was hard to gauge Dr. al-Baz's reaction when we pulled up in front of the hotel lobby. I was beginning to learn that his normal expression was stoical. But as a bellhop was unloading his stuff and putting it on a cart, the professor spotted the casino entrance. The doorman was dark-skinned and a little more than two meters in height; he wore the burnoose robes of an aborigine, with a saber in the scabbard on his belt.

Dr. al-Baz stared at him. "That's not a Martian, is he?"

"Not unless he used to play center for the Blue Devils." Dr. al-Baz raised an eyebrow and I smiled. "That's Tito Jones, star of the Duke basketball team . . . or at least until he came here." I shook my head. "Poor guy. He didn't know why the casino hired him to be their celebrity greeter until they put him in that outfit."

Dr. al-Baz had already lost interest. "I was hoping he might be a Martian," he said softly. "It would have made things easier."

"They wouldn't be caught dead here . . . or anywhere near the colonies, for that matter." I turned to follow the bellhop through the revolving door. "And by the way . . . we don't call them 'Martians.' 'Aborigines' is the preferred term."

"I'll keep that in mind. And what do the Mar . . . the aborigines call themselves?"

"They call themselves *shatan* . . . which means 'people' in their language." Before he could ask the obvious next question, I added, "Their word for us is *nashatan*, or 'not-people,' but that's only when they're being polite. They call us a lot of things, most of them pretty nasty."

The professor nodded and was quiet for a little while.

The University of Arizona might not have sprung for a grad student's marsliner ticket, but they made up for it by reserving a two-room suite. After the bellhop unloaded his cart and left, Dr. al-Baz explained that he'd need the main room, a large parlor complete with a bar, for the temporary lab he intended to set up. He didn't unpack right away, though; he was ready for that drink I'd promised him. So we left everything in the room and caught the elevator back downstairs.

The hotel bar is located in the casino, but I didn't want to drink in a place where the bartender is decked out like a Barsoomian warlord and the waitresses are dolled up as princesses of Helium. The John Carter is the only place on Mars where anyone looks like that; no one in their right mind would wear so few clothes outside, not even in the middle of summer. So we returned to the jeep and I got away from the strip, heading into the old part of town that the tourists seldom visit.

There's a good watering hole about three blocks from my apartment. It was still late afternoon, so the place wasn't crowded yet. The bar was quiet and dark, perfect for conversation. The owner knew me; he brought over a pitcher of ale as soon as the professor and I sat down at a table in the back.

"Take it easy with this," I told Dr. al-Baz as I poured beer into a tallneck and pushed it across the table to him. "Until you get acclimated, it might hit you pretty hard."

"I'll take your advice." The professor took a tentative sip and smiled. "Good. Better than I was expecting, in fact. Local?"

"Hellas City Amber. You think we'd have beer shipped all the way from Earth?" There were more important things we needed to discuss, so I changed the subject. "What's this about wanting blood? When you got in touch with me, all you said was that you wanted me to take you to an aboriginal settlement."

Dr. al-Baz didn't say anything for a moment or so. He toyed with the stem of his glass, rolling it back and forth between his fingers. "If I'd told you the entire truth," he finally admitted, "I was afraid you might not agree to take me. And you come very highly recommended. As I understand, you're not only native-born, but your parents were among the first settlers."

"I'm surprised you know that. You must have talked to a former client."

"Do you remember Ian Horner? Anthropologist from Cambridge University?" I did indeed, although not kindly; Dr. Horner had hired me to be his guide, but if you'd believed everything he said, he knew more about Mars than I did. I nodded, keeping my opinion to myself. "He's a friend of mine," Dr. al-Baz continued, "or at least someone with whom I've been in contact on a professional basis."

"So you're another anthropologist."

"No." He sipped his beer. "Research biologist . . . astrobiology, to be exact. The study of extraterrestrial forms of life. Until now, most of my work has involved studying Venus, so this is the first time I've been to Mars. Of course, Venus is different. Its global ocean is quite interesting, but . . ."

"Professor, I don't want to be rude, but do you want to get down to it and tell me why you want the blood of a—" damn, he almost got me to say it! "—an aborigine?"

Sitting back in his chair, Dr. al-Baz folded his hands together on the tabletop. "Mr. Ramsey . . ."

"Jim."

"Jim, are you familiar with the panspermia hypothesis? The idea that life on Earth may have extraterrestrial origins, that it may have come from somewhere in outer space?"

"No, I've never heard that . . . but I guess that when you say 'somewhere,' you mean here."

"That is correct. I mean Mars." He tapped a finger firmly against the table. "Have you ever wondered why there's such a close resemblance between humans and Martian aborigines? Why the two races look so much alike, even though they're from worlds over 70 million kilometers apart?"

"Parallel evolution."

"Yes, I expect that's what you've learned in school. The conventional explanation is that, because both planets have similar environments, evolution took approximately the same course on both worlds, the differences being that Martians . . . aborigines, sorry . . . are taller because of lower surface gravity, have higher metabolisms because of colder temperature, have significantly darker skin because of the thinner ozone layer, so forth and so on. This has been the prevalent theory because it's the only one that seems to fit the facts."

"That's what I've heard, yeah."

"Well, my friend, everything you've know is wrong." He immediately shook his head, as if embarrassed by his momentary burst of arrogance. "I'm sorry. I don't mean to sound overbearing. However, several of my colleagues and I believe that the similarities between *homo sapiens* and *homo aresian* cannot be attributed to evolution alone. We think there may be a genetic link between the two races, that life on Earth . . . human life in particular . . . may have originated on Mars."

Dr. al-Baz paused, allowing a moment to let his words sink in. They did, all right; I was beginning to wonder if he was a kook. "Okay," I said, trying not to smile, "I'll bite. What leads you to think that?"

The professor raised a finger. "First, the geological composition of quite a few meteorites found on Earth is identical to those of rock samples brought from Mars. So there's a theory that, sometime in the distant past, there was a cataclysmic explosion on the Martian surface . . . possibly the eruption of Mt. Daedalia or one of the other volcanoes in the Albus range . . . which ejected debris into space. This debris travelled as meteors to Earth, which was also in its infancy. Those meteors may have contained organic molecules which seeded Earth with life where it hadn't previously existed."

He held up another finger. "Second . . . when the human genome was sequenced, one of the most surprising finds was the existence of DNA strands which have no apparent purpose. They're like parts of a machine that don't have any function. There's no reason for them to be there, yet nonetheless they are. Therefore, is it possible that these phantom strands may be genetic biomarkers left behind by organic material brought to Earth from Mars?"

"So that's why you want a blood sample? To see if there's a link?"

He nodded. "I have brought equipment that will enable me to sequence, at least partially, the genetic code of an aborigine blood sample and compare it to that of a human. If the native genome has non-functional archaic strands that match the ones found in the human genome, then we'll have evidence that the hypothesis is correct . . . life on Earth originated on Mars, and the two races are genetically linked."

I didn't say anything for a few seconds. Dr. al-Baz didn't sound quite as crazy as he had a couple of minutes earlier. As far-fetched as it may seem, what he said made sense. And if the hypothesis were true, then the implications were staggering: the *shatan* were close cousins to the inhabitants of Earth, not simply a primitive race that we'd happened to find when we came to Mars.

Not that I was ready to believe it. I'd met too many *shatan* to ever be willing to accept the idea that they had anything in common with my people. Or at least so I thought . . .

"Okay, I get what you're doing." I picked up my glass and took a long drink. "But let me tell you, getting that blood sample won't be easy."

"I know. I understand the aborigines are rather reclusive . . ."

"Now *that's* an understatement." I put down my glass again. "They've never wanted much to do with us. The Ares 1 expedition had been here for almost three weeks before anyone caught sight of them, and another month before there was any significant contact. It took years for us to even learn their language, and things only got worse when we started establishing colonies. Wherever we've gone, the *shatan* have moved out, packing up everything they owned, even burning their villages so that we couldn't explore their dwellings. They've become nomads since then. No trade, and not much in the way of cultural exchange . . ."

"So no one has ever managed to get anything from them on which they may have left organic material? No hair samples, no saliva, no skin?"

"No. They've never allowed us to collect any artifacts from them, and they're reluctant to even let us touch them. That outfit you saw Tito Jones wearing? It's not the real thing . . . just a costume based on some pictures someone took of them."

"But we've learned their language."

"Just a little of one of their dialects . . . pidgin *shatan*, you might call it." I absently ran a finger around the rim of my glass. "If you're counting on me to be your native interpreter . . . well, don't expect much. I know enough to get by and that's about it. I may be able to keep them from chucking a spear at us, but that's all."

He raised an eyebrow. "Are they dangerous?"

"Not so long as you mind your manners. They can be . . . well, kinda aggressive . . . if you cross the line with them." I didn't want to tell him some of the worst stories—I'd scared off other clients that way—so I tried to reassure him. "I've met some of the local tribesmen, so they know me well enough to let me visit their lands. But I'm not sure how much they trust me." I hesitated. "Dr. Horner didn't get very far with them. I'm sure he's told you that they wouldn't let him into their village."

"Yes, he has. To tell the truth, though, Ian has always been something of an ass—" I laughed out loud when he said this, and he gave me a quick smile in return "—so I imagine that, so long as I approach them with a measure of humility, I may have more success than he did."

"You might." Ian Horner had come to Mars with the attitude of a British army officer visiting colonial India, a condescending air of superiority that the *shatan* picked up almost immediately. He learned little as a result, and had come away referring to the "abos" as "cheeky bahstahds." No doubt the aborigines felt much the same way about him . . . but at least they'd let him live.

"So you'll take me out there? To one of their villages, I mean?"

"That's why you hired me, so . . . yeah, sure." I picked up my beer again. "The nearest village is about a hundred and fifty kilometers southeast of here, in a desert oasis near the Laestrygon canal. It'll take a couple of days to get there. I hope you brought warm clothes and hiking boots."

"I brought a parka and boots, yes. But you have your jeep, don't you? Then why are we going to need to walk?"

"We'll drive only until we get near the village. Then we'll have to get out and walk the rest of the way. The *shatan* don't like motorized vehicles. The equatorial desert is pretty rough, so you better prepare for it."

He smiled. "I ask you . . . do I look like someone who's never been in a desert?"

"No . . . but Mars isn't Earth."

I spent the next day preparing for the trip: collecting camping equipment from my rented storage shed, buying food and filling water bottles, putting fresh fuel cells in the jeep and making sure the tires had enough pressure. I made sure that Dr. al-Baz had the right clothing for several days in the outback and gave him the address of a local outfitter if he didn't, but I need not have worried; he clearly wasn't one of those tourists foolish enough to go out into the desert wearing Bermuda shorts and sandals.

When I came to pick him up at the hotel, I was amazed to find that the professor had turned his suite into a laboratory. Two flatscreen computers were set up on the bar, a microscope and a test-tube rack stood on the coffee table, and the TV had been pushed aside to make room for a small centrifuge. More equipment rested on bureaus and side tables; I didn't know what any of it was, but I spotted a radiation symbol on one and a WARNING - LASER sticker on another. He'd covered the carpet with plastic sheets, and there was even a lab coat hanging in the closest. Dr. al-Baz made no mention of any of this; he simply picked up his backpack and camera, put on a slouch cap, and followed me out the door, pausing to slip the DO NOT DISTURB sign over the knob.

Tourists stared at us as he flung his pack into the back of my jeep; it always seemed to surprise some people that anyone would come to Mars to do something besides drink and lose money at the gaming tables. I started up the jeep and we roared away from the John Carter, and in fifteen minutes we were on the outskirts of town, driving through the irrigated farmlands surrounding Rio Zephyria. The scarlet pines that line the shores of Mare Cimmerium gradually thinned out as we followed dirt roads usually travelled by farm vehicles and logging trucks, and even those disappeared as we left the colony behind and headed into the trackless desert.

I've been told that the Martian drylands look a lot like the American southwest, except that everything is red. I've never been to Earth, so I wouldn't know, but if anyone in New Mexico happens to spot a six-legged creature that looks sort of like a shaggy cow or a raptor that resembles a pterodactyl and sounds like a hyena, please drop me a line. And stay away from those pits that look a little like golf course sand-traps; there's something lurking within them that would eat you alive, one limb at a time.

As the jeep weaved its way through the desert, dodging boulders and bouncing over small rocks, Dr. al-Baz clung to the roll bars, fascinated by the wilderness opening before us. This was one of the things that made my job worthwhile, seeing familiar places through the eyes of someone who'd never been there before. I pointed out a Martian hare as it loped away from us, and stopped for a second to let him take pictures of a flock of *stakhas* as they wheeled high above us, shrieking their dismay at our intrusion.

About seventy kilometers southeast of Rio, we came upon the Laestryum canal, running almost due south from the sea. When Percival Lowell first spotted the Martian canals through his observatory telescope, he thought they were excavated waterways. He was half-right; the *shatan* had rerouted existing rivers, diverting them so that they'd go where the aborigines wanted. The fact that they'd done this with the simple, muscle-driven machines never failed to amaze anyone who saw them, but Earth people tend to underestimate the *shatan*. They're primitive, but not stupid.

We followed the canal, keeping far away from it so that we couldn't be easily spotted from the decks of any *shatan* boats that might be this far north. I didn't want any aborigines to see us before we reached the village; they might pass the word that humans were coming, and give their chieftain a chance to order his people to pack up and move out. We saw no one, though; the only sign of habitation was a skinny wooden suspension bridge than spanned the channel like an enormous bow, and even that didn't appear to be frequently used.

By late afternoon, we'd entered hill country. Flat-topped mesas rose around us, with massive stone pinnacles jutting upward between them; the jagged peaks of distant mountains lay just beyond the horizon. I drove until it was nearly dusk, then pulled up behind a hoodoo and stopped for the night.

Dr. al-Baz pitched a tent while I collected dead scrub brush. Once I had a fire going, I suspended a cookpot above the embers, then emptied a can of stew into it. The professor had thought to buy a couple of bottles of red wine before we left town; we opened one for dinner and worked our way through it after we ate.

"So tell me something," Dr. al-Baz said once we'd scrubbed down the pot, plates, and spoons. "Why did you become a guide?"

"You mean, other than getting a job as a blackjack dealer?" I propped the cook-ware up against a boulder. A stiff breeze was coming out of the west; the sand it carried would scour away the remaining grub. "Never really thought about it, to be honest. My folks are first-generation settlers, so I was born and raised here. I started prowling the desert as soon as I was old enough to go out alone, so . . ."

"That's just it." The professor moved a little closer to the fire, holding out his hands to warm them. Now that the sun was down, a cold night was ahead; we could already see our breath by the firelight. "Most of the colonists I've met seem content to stay in the city. When I told them that I was planning a trip into the desert, they all looked at me like I was mad. Someone even suggested that I buy a gun and take out extra life insurance."

"Whoever told you to buy a gun doesn't know a thing about the *shatan*. They never attack unless provoked, and the surest way to upset them is to approach one of their villages with a gun." I patted the utility knife on my belt. "This is the closest I come to carrying a weapon when there's even a possibility that I might run into aborigines. One reason why I'm on good terms with them . . . I mind my manners."

"Most people here haven't even seen an aborigine, I think."

"You're right, they haven't. Rio Zephyria is the biggest colony because of tourism, but most permanent residents prefer to live where there's flush toilets and cable TV." I sat down on the other side of the fire. "They can have it. The only reason I live there is because that's where the tourists are. If it wasn't for that, I'd have a place out in the boonies and hit town only when I need to stock up on supplies."

"I see." Dr. al-Baz picked up his tin cup and mine and poured some wine into each. "Forgive me if I'm wrong," he said as he handed my cup to me, "but it doesn't sound as if you very much approve of your fellow colonists."

"I don't." I took a sip and put the cup down beside me; I didn't want to get a headful of wine the night before I was going to have to deal with *shatan* tribesmen. "My folks came out here to explore a new world, but everyone who's come *after* those original settlers . . . well, you saw Rio. You know what it's like. We're building hotels and casinos and shopping centers, and introducing invasive species into our farms and dumping our sewage into the channels, and every few weeks during conjunction another ship brings in more people who think Mars is like Las Vegas only without as many hookers . . . not that we don't have plenty of those, too."

As I spoke, I craned my neck to look up the night sky. The major constellations gleamed brightly: Ursa Major, Draco, Cygnus, with Denes as the north star. You can't see the Milky Way very well in the city; you have to go out into the desert to get a decent view of the Martian night sky. "So who can blame the *shatan* for not wanting to have anything to do with us? They knew the score as soon as we showed up." Recalling a thought I'd had the day before, I chuckled to myself. "The old movies got it wrong. Mars didn't invade Earth . . . Earth invaded Mars."

"I didn't realize there was so much resentment on your part."

He sounded like his feelings were wounded. That was no way to treat a paying customer.

"No, no . . . it's not you," I quickly added. "I don't think you'd be caught dead at a poker table."

He laughed out loud. "No, I don't think the university would look very kindly upon me if my expense report included poker chips."

"Glad to hear it." I hesitated, then went on. "Just do me a favor, will you? If you find something here that might . . . I dunno . . . make things worse, would you consider keeping it to yourself? Humans have done enough stupid things here already. We don't need to do anything more."

"I'll try to remember that," Dr. al-Baz said.

The next day, we found the *shatan*. Or rather, they found us.

We broke camp and continued following the Laestrygon as it flowed south through the desert hills. I'd been watching the jeep's odometer the entire trip, and when we were about fifty kilometers from where I remembered the aborigine settlement being, I began driving along the canal banks. I told Dr. al-Baz to keep a sharp eye out for any signs of habitation—trails, or perhaps abandoned camps left behind by hunting parties—but what we found was a lot more obvious: another suspension bridge, and passing beneath it, a *shatan* boat.

The canal boat was a slender catamaran about ten meters long, with broad white sails catching the desert wind and a small cabin at its stern. The figures moving along its decks didn't notice us until one of them spotted the jeep. He let out a warbling cry—"*wallawallawalla!*"—and the others stopped what they were doing to gaze in the direction he was pointing. Then another *shatan* standing atop the cabin yelled something and everyone turned to dash into the cabin, with their captain disappearing through a hatch in its ceiling. Within seconds, the catamaran became a ghost ship.

"Wow." Dr. al-Baz was both astounded and disappointed. "They really don't want to see us, do they?"

"Actually, they don't want us to see *them*." He looked at me askance, not understanding the difference. "They believe that, if they can't be seen, then they've disappeared from the world. This way, they're hoping that, so far as we're concerned, they've ceased to exist." I shrugged. "Kind of logical, if you think about it."

There was no point in trying to persuade the crew to emerge from hiding, so we left the boat behind and continued our drive down the canal bank. But the catamaran had barely disappeared from sight when we heard a hollow roar from behind us, like a bullhorn being blown. The sound echoed off the nearby mesas; two more prolonged blasts, then the horn went silent.

"If there are any more *shatan* around, they'll hear that and know we're coming," I said. "They'll repeat the same signal with their own horns, and so on, until the signal reaches the village."

"So they know we're here," Dr. al-Baz said. "Will they hide like the others?"

"Maybe. Maybe not." I shrugged. "It's up to them."

For a long time, we didn't spot anyone or anything. We were about eight kilometers from the village when we came upon another bridge. This time, we saw two figures standing near the foot of the bridge. They appeared unusually tall even for an aborigine, but it wasn't until we got closer that we saw why: each of them rode a *hattas*, enormous buffalo-like creatures with six legs and elongated necks that the natives tamed as pack animals. It wasn't what they were riding that caught my attention, though, so much as the long spears they carried, or the heavy animal-hide outfits they wore.

"Uh-oh," I said quietly. "That's not good."

"What's not good?"

"I was hoping we'd run into hunters . . . but these guys are warriors. They can be a little . . . um, intense. Keep your hands in sight and never look away from them."

I halted the jeep about twenty feet from them. We climbed out and slowly walked toward them, hands at our sides. As we got closer, the warriors dismounted from their animals; they didn't approach us, though, but instead waited in silence.

When the owners of the John Carter hired a basketball star to masquerade as a *shatan*, they were trying to find someone who might pass as a Martian aborigine. Tito Jones was the best they could get, but he wasn't quite right. The *shatan* standing before us were taller; their skin was as dark as the sky at midnight, their long, silky hair the color of rust, yet their faces had fine-boned features reminiscent of someone of northern European descent. They were swathed in dusty, off-white robes that made them look vaguely Bedouin, and the hands that gripped their spears were larger than a human's, with long-nailed fingers and tendons which stood out from wrists.

Unblinking golden eyes studied us as we approached. When we'd come close enough, both warriors firmly planted their spears on the ground before us. I told Dr. al-Baz to stop, but I didn't have to remind him not to look away from them. He stared at the *shatan* with awestruck curiosity, a scientist observing his subject up close for the first time.

I raised both hands, palm out, and said, "*Issah tas sobbata shatan* (Greetings, honored *shatan* warriors). "*Seyta nasahtan habbalah sa shatan heysa*" (Please allow us human travelers to enter your land).

The warrior on the left replied, *"Katas nashtan Hamsey. Sakey shatan habbalah fah?"* (We know you, human Ramsey. Why have you returned to our land?)

I wasn't surprised to have been recognized. Only a handful of humans spoke their language—albeit not very well; I probably sounded like a child to them—or knew the way to their village. I may not have met these particular warriors before, but they'd doubtless heard of me. And I tried not to smile at the mispronunciation of my name; the *shatan* have trouble rolling the "r" sound off their tongues.

"(I've brought a guest who wishes to learn more about your people)," I replied, still speaking the local dialect. I extended a hand toward the professor. "(Allow me to introduce you to Omar al-Baz. He is a wise man in search of knowledge.)" I avoided calling him "doctor"; that word has a specific meaning in their language, as someone who practices medicine.

"(Humans don't want to know anything about us. All they want to do is take what doesn't belong to them and ruin it.)"

I shook my head; oddly, that particular gesture means the same thing for both *shatan* and *nashatan*. "(This is not true. Many of my people do, yes, but not all. On his own world, al-Baz is a teacher. Whatever he learns from you, he will tell his students, and therefore increase their knowledge of your people.)"

"What are you saying?" Dr. al-Baz whispered. "I recognize my name, but . . ."

"Hush. Let me finish." I continued speaking the native tongue. "(Will you please escort us to your village? My companion wishes to beg a favor of your chieftain.)"

The other warrior stepped forward, walking toward the professor until he stood directly before him. The *shatan* towered above Dr. al-Baz; everything about him was menacing, yet the professor held his ground, saying nothing but continuing to look straight in the eye. The warrior silently regarded him for several long moments, then looked at me.

"(What does he want from our chieftain? Tell us, and we will decide whether we will allow you to enter our village.)"

I hesitated, then shook my head again. "(No. His question is for the chieftain alone.)"

I was taking a gamble. Refusing a demand from a *shatan* warrior guarding his homeland was not a great way to make friends. But it was entirely possible that the warriors would misunderstand me if I told them that Dr. al-Baz wanted to take some of their blood; they might think his intent was hostile. The best thing to do was have the professor ask the chieftain directly for permission to take a blood sample from one of his people.

The *shatans* stared at us for a moment without saying anything, then turned away and walked off a few feet to quietly confer with each other. "What's going on?" the professor asked, keeping his voice low. "What did you tell them?"

I gave him the gist of the conversation, including the risky thing I'd just said. "I figure it can go one of three ways. One, they kick the matter upstairs to the chieftain, which means that you get your wish if you play your cards right. Two, they tell us to get lost. If that happens, we turn around and go home, and that's that."

"Unacceptable. I've come too far to go away empty-handed. What's the third option."

"They impale with their spears, wait for us to die, then chop up our bodies and scatter our remains for the animals to find." I let that sink in. "Except our heads," I added. "Someone will carry those back to the city in the middle of the night, where they'll dump them on the doorstep of the nearest available house."

"Please tell me you're joking."

I didn't. The professor was scared enough already, and he didn't need any stories about what had happened to explorers who'd crossed the line with the *shatan*, or the occasional fool stupid enough to venture onto aboriginal territory without someone like me escorting them. I hadn't exaggerated anything, though, and he seemed to realize that, for he simply nodded and looked away.

The *shatan* finished their discussion. Not looking at us, they walked back to their *hattases* and climbed atop them again. For a moment, I thought that they were taking the second option, but then they guided their mounts toward Dr. al-Baz and me.

"*Hessah*," one of them said (Come with us).

I let out my breath. We were going to meet the village chieftain.

The village was different from the last time I'd seen it. Since the *shatan* became nomads, their settlements are usually tent cities which can be taken down, packed up, and relocated when necessary. This one had been there for quite a while, though; apparently the inhabitants had decided that they'd stay at the oasis for some time to come. Low, flat-roofed adobe buildings had taken the place of many of the tents, and scaffolds surrounded a stone wall being built to enclose them. But if the place had a name, I wasn't aware of it.

Dr. al-Baz and I were footsore and tired by the time we reached the village. As expected, the warriors had insisted that we leave the jeep behind, although they allowed us to retrieve our packs. They'd slowly ridden abreast of us all the way, only reluctantly letting us stop now and then to rest. Neither of them had spoken a word since we'd left the bridge, but when we were within sight of the settlement, one of them raised a whorled shell that looked like a giant ammonite. A long, loud blast from his horn was answered a few seconds later by a similar call from the village. The professor and I exchanged a wary glance. Too late to turn around now; the inhabitants knew we were coming.

The village seemed empty as we entered through a half-built gate and walked down packed-dirt streets. No one to be seen, and the only thing that moved were *hattases* tied up to hitching posts. The tent flaps were closed, though, and the narrow windows of the adobe houses were shuttered. No, the place wasn't deserted; it was just that the people who lived there had gone into hiding. The silence was eerie, and even more unsettling than the spears our escorts pointed at our backs.

The village center was a courtyard surrounding an aresian well, with a large adobe building dominating one side of the square. The only *shatan* we'd seen since our arrival peered down at us from a wooden tower atop the building. He waited until we'd reached the building, then raised an ammonite horn of his own and blew a short blast. The warriors halted their *hattases*, dismounted, and silently beckoned for us to follow them. One of them pushed aside the woven blanket which served as the building's only door, and the other warrior led us inside.

The room was dim, its sole illumination a shaft of sunlight slanting down through a hole in the ceiling. The air was thick with musky incense that drifted in hazy layers through the light and made my eyes water. Robed *shatan* stood around the room, their faces hidden by hoods they'd pulled up around their heads; I knew none of them were female, because their women were always kept out of sight when visitors arrived. The only sound was the slow, constant drip of a waterclock, with each drop announcing the passage of two more seconds.

The chieftain sat in the middle of the room. Long-fingered hands rested upon the armrests of his sandstone throne; golden eyes regarded us between strands of hair turned white with age. He wore nothing to indicate his position as the tribal leader save an implacable air of authority, and he let us know that he was the boss by silently raising both hands, then slowly lowering them once we'd halted and saying nothing for a full minute.

At last he spoke. "*Essha shakay Hamsey?*" (Why are you here, Ramsey?)

I didn't think I'd ever met him before, but obviously he recognized me. Good. That would make things a little easier. I responded in his own language. "(I bring someone who wants to learn more about your people. He is a wise man from Earth, a teacher of others who wish to become wise themselves. He desires to ask a favor from you.)"

The chieftain turned his gaze from me to Dr. al-Baz. "(What do you want?)"

I looked at the professor. "Okay, you're on. He wants to know what you want. I'll translate for you. Just be careful . . . they're easily offended."

"So it seems." Dr. al-Baz was nervous, but he was hiding it well. He licked his lips and thought about it a moment, then went on. "Tell him . . . tell him that I would like to collect a small sample of blood from one of his people. A few drops will do. I wish to have this because I want to know . . . I mean, because I'd like to find out . . . whether his people and mine have common ancestors."

That seemed to be a respectful a way of stating what he wanted, so I turned to the chief and reiterated what he'd said. The only problem was that I didn't know the aboriginal word for "blood." It had simply never come up in any previous conversations I'd had with the *shatan*. So I had to generalize a bit, calling it "the liquid that runs within our bodies" while pantomiming a vein running down the inside of my right arm, and hoped that he'd understand what I meant.

He did, all right. He regarded me with cold disbelief, golden eyes flashing, thin lips writhing upon an otherwise stoical face. Around us, I heard the other *shatan* murmuring to one another. I couldn't tell what they were saying, but it didn't sound like they were very happy either.

We were in trouble.

"(Who dares say that shatan and nashtan have the same ancestors?)" he snapped, hands curling into fists as he leaned forward from his throne. "(Who dares believe that your people and mine are alike in any way?)"

I repeated what he'd said to Dr. al-Baz. The professor hesitated, then looked straight at the chieftain. "Tell him that no one believes these things," he said, his tone calm and deliberate. "It is only an hypothesis . . . an educated guess . . . that I want to either prove or disprove. That's why I need a blood sample, to discover the truth."

I took a deep breath, hoped that I was going to get out of there alive, then translated the professor's explanation. The chieftain continued to glare at us as I spoke, but he seemed to calm down a little. For several long seconds, he said nothing. And then he reached a decision.

Reaching into his robes, he withdrew a bone dagger from a sheath on his belt. My heart skipped a beat as the light fell upon its sharp white blade, and when he stood up and walked toward us, I thought my life had come to an end. But then he stopped in front of Dr. al-Baz and, still staring straight at him, raised his left hand, placed the knife against his palm, and ran its blade down his skin.

"(Take my blood)," he said, holding out his hand.

I didn't need to translate what he'd said. Dr. al-Baz quickly dropped his backpack from his shoulders and opened it. He withdrew a syringe, thought better of it, and pulled out a plastic test tube instead. The chieftain clenched his fist and let the blood trickle between his fingers, and the professor caught it in his test tube. Once he'd collected the specimen, he pulled out a tiny vial and added a couple of drops of anticoagulant. Then he capped the tube and nodded to the chieftain.

"Tell him that I greatly appreciate his kindness," he said, "and that I will return to tell him what I have found."

"Like hell we will!"

"Tell him." His eyes never left the chieftain's. "One way or another, he deserves to know the truth."

Promising the chieftain that we intended to return was the last thing I wanted to do, but I did it anyway. He didn't respond for a moment, but simply dropped his hand, allowing his blood to trickle to the floor.

"(Yes)," he said at last. "(Come back and tell me what you've learned. I wish to know as well.)" And then he turned his back to us and walked back to his chair. "(Now leave.)"

"Okay," I whispered, feeling my heart hammering against my chest. "You got what you came for. Now let's get out of here while we still have our heads."

Two days later, I was sitting in the casino bar at the John Carter, putting away tequila sunrises and occasionally dropping a coin into the video poker machine in front of me. I'd discovered that I didn't mind the place so long as I kept my back turned to everything going on around me, and I could drink for free if I slipped a quarter into the slots every now and then. At least that's what I told myself. The fact of the matter was that there was a certain sense of security in the casino's tawdry surroundings. This Mars was a fantasy, to be sure, but just then it was preferable to the unsettling reality I'd visited a couple of days earlier.

Omar al-Baz was upstairs, using the equipment he'd brought with him to analyze the chieftain's blood. We'd gone straight to the hotel upon returning to the city, but when it became obvious that it would take awhile for the professor to work his particular kind of magic, I decided to go downstairs and get a drink. Perhaps I should have gone home, but I was still keyed up from the long ride back, so I gave Dr. al-Baz my cell number and asked him to call me if and when he learned anything.

I was surprised that I stuck around. Usually when I return from a trip into the outback, all I really want to do is get out of the clothes I'd been wearing for days on end, open a beer, and take a nice, long soak in the bathtub. Instead, there I was, putting away one cocktail after another while demonstrating that I knew absolutely nothing about poker. The bartender was studying me and the waitresses were doing their best to stay upwind, but I could have cared less about what they thought. They were make-believe Martians, utterly harmless. The ones I'd met a little while ago would have killed me just for looking at them cross-eyed.

In all the years that I'd been going out in the wilderness, this was the first time I'd ever been really and truly scared. Not by the desert, but by those who lived there. No *shatan* had ever threatened me, not even in an implicit way, until the moment the chieftain pulled out a knife and creased the palm of his hand with its blade. Sure, he'd done so to give Dr. al-Baz a little of his blood, but there was another meaning to his actions.

It was a warning . . . and the *shatan* don't give warnings lightly.

That was why I was doing my best to get drunk. The professor was too excited to think of anything except the specimen he'd just collected—all the way home, he'd babbled about nothing else—but I knew that we'd come with an inch of dying, and that ours would have been a really nasty death.

Yet the chieftain had given his blood of his own free will, and even asked that we return once the professor learned the truth. That puzzled me. Why would he be interested in the results, if the thought of being related to a human was so appalling?

I threw away another quarter, pushed the buttons and watched the machine tell me that I'd lost again, then looked around to see if I could flag down a princess and get her to fetch another sunrise. Dejah or Thuvia or Xaxa or whoever she was had apparently gone on break, though, because she was nowhere to be seen; I was about to try my luck again when something caught my eye. The TV above the bar was showing the evening news, and the weatherman was standing in front of his map. I couldn't hear what he was saying, but he was pointing at an animated cloud system west of Rio Zephyria that was moving across the desert toward the Laestrygon canal.

It appeared that a sandstorm was brewing in Mesogaea, the drylands adjacent to the Zephyria region. This sort of weather isn't uncommon in the summer; we call them haboobs, the Arabic name for sandstorms on Earth that somehow found its way to Mars. From the looks of things, it would reach the Zephyria outback sometime tomorrow afternoon. Good thing I'd come home; the last thing anyone would want is to be caught out in the desert during a bad storm.

A waitress strolled by, adjusting a strap of her costume bikini top. I raised my glass and silently jiggled it back and forth, and she feigned a smile as she nodded and headed for the bar. I was searching my pockets for another quarter so that she'd see that I was still pretending to be a gambler when my cell buzzed.

"Jim? Are you still here?"

"In the bar, professor. Come down and have a drink with me."

"No! No time for that! Come upstairs right away! I need to see you!"

"What's going on?"

"*Just come up here! It's better if I show you!*"

Dr. al-Baz opened the door at the first knock. Spotting the cocktail glass in my hand, he snatched it from me and drained it in one gulp. "Good heavens," he gasped, "I needed that!"

"Want me to get you another one?"

"No . . . but you can buy me a drink when I get to Stockholm." I didn't understand what he meant, but before I could ask he pulled me into the room. "Look!" he said, pointing to one of the computers set up on the bar. "This is incredible!"

I walked over to the bar, peered at the screen. Displayed upon it were rows of A's, C's, G's, and T's, arranged in a seemingly endless series of combinations, with smears that looked a little like dashes running in a vertical bar down the right side of the screen. A five-line cluster of combinations and smears was highlighted in yellow.

"Yeah, okay," I said. "Professor, I'm sorry, but you're going to have to . . ."

"You have no idea what you're looking at, do you?" he asked, and I shook my head. "This is the human genome . . . the genetic code present in every human being. And these—" his hand trembled as he pointed to the highlighted cluster "—are strands that are identical to the partially-sequenced genome from the aborigine specimen."

"They're the same?"

"Exactly. There is no error . . . or at least none that the computers can detect." Dr. al-Baz took a deep breath. "Do you see what I'm getting at? The hypothesis is correct! Human life may have originated on Mars!"

I stared at the screen. Until then, I hadn't really believed anything that Dr. al-Baz had told me; it seemed too unlikely to be true. But now that the evidence was in front of me, I realized that I was looking at something that would shake the foundations of science. No, not just science . . . it would rattle history itself, forcing humankind to reconsider its origins.

"My god," I whispered. 'Have you told anyone yet? On Earth, I mean."

"No. I'm tempted to send a message, but . . . no, I need to confirm this." The professor walked over to the window. "We have to go back," he said, his voice quiet but firm as he gazed out at the city lights and, beyond them, the dark expanse of the desert. "I need to get another blood sample, this time from a different *shatan*. If the same sequence appears in the second sample, then we'll know for sure."

Something cold slithered down my spine. "I'm not sure that's a good idea. The chieftain . . ."

"The chieftain told us that he wanted to know what we discovered. So we'll tell him, and explain that we need more blood . . . just a little . . . from one of his tribesmen to make sure that it's the truth." Dr. al-Baz glanced over his shoulder at me. "Not an unreasonable request, no?"

"I don't think he's going to be very happy about this, if that's what you're asking."

He was quiet for a few moments, contemplating what I'd just said. "Well . . . that's a risk we'll just have to take," he said at last. "I'll pay you again for another trip, if that's your concern . . . double your original fee, in fact. But I must go back as soon as possible." He continued to gaze out the window. "Tomorrow morning. I want to leave tomorrow morning."

My head was beginning to ache, dull blades pressing upon my temples. I shouldn't have had so much to drink. What I should have done was turn him down right then and there. But his offer to double my fee for a return trip was too good to pass up; I needed the money, and that would pay my rent for a couple of months. Besides, I was too drunk to argue.

"Okay," I said. "We'll head out first thing."

I went back to my place, took some aspirin, stripped off my filthy clothes, and took a shower, then flopped into bed. But I didn't fall asleep for quite a while. Instead, I stared at the ceiling as unwelcome thoughts ran an endless loop through my mind.

What would the chieftain do when Omar al-Baz informed him that *shatan* blood and *nashtan* blood were very much alike and that our two races might be related? He wouldn't be pleased, that much was certain. The aborigines never wanted to have anything to do with the invaders from Earth; as soon as our ships had arrived, they had retreated into the wilderness. This was the reason why they'd become nomads . . .

But they weren't any more, were they? The significance of what I'd seen at the village suddenly became clear to me. Not only had this particular tribe built permanent houses, but they were also erecting a wall around them. That meant they were planning to remain where they were for some time to come, and were taking measures to defend themselves. They were tiring of running from us; now they were digging in.

Until now, the human colonists had been content to ignore the *shatan*, thinking of them as reclusive savages best left alone. This would change, though, if humans came to believe that *homo sapiens* and *homo aresians* were cousins. Suddenly, we'd want to know all about them. First would come more biologists like Dr. al-Baz, more anthropologists like Dr. Horner. Maybe that wouldn't be so bad . . . but right behind them would be everyone *else*. Historians and journalists, tour buses and camera safaris, entrepreneurs looking to make a buck, missionaries determined to convert godless souls, real estate tycoons seeking prime land on which to build condos with a nice view of those quaint aborigine villages . . .

The *shatan* wouldn't tolerate this. And the chieftain would know that it was inevitable the moment Dr. al-Baz told him what he'd learned. First, he'd order his warriors to kill both him and me. And then . . .

In my mind's eye, I saw the horrors to come. Wave upon wave of *shatan* warriors descending upon Rio Zephyria and the other colonies, hell-bent on driving the invaders from their world once and for all. Oh, we had superior weapons, this was true . . . but they had superior numbers, and it would only be a matter of time before they captured a few of our guns and learned how to use them. Ships from Earth would bring soldiers to defend the colonies, but history is unkind to would-be conquerors. Either we would be driven back, step by inexorable step, or we would commit genocide, exterminating entire tribes and driving the few survivors further into the wilderness.

Either way, the outcome was inevitable. War would come to a world named for a god of war. Red blood would fell upon red sand, human and Martian alike.

A storm was coming. Then I thought of a different storm, and knew what I had to do.

Two days later, I was found staggering out of the desert, caked with red sand from my hair to my boots save for raccoon-like patches around my eyes where my goggles had protected them. I was dehydrated and exhausted to the point of delirium.

I was also alone.

Ironically, the people who rescued me were another guide and the family from Minneapolis whom he'd escorted into the desert just outside Rio Zephyria. I remember little of what happened after I collapsed at their feet and had to be carried to the guide's land rover. The only things I clearly recall were the sweet taste of water within my parched mouth, a teenage girl gazing down at me with angelic blue eyes as she cradled my head in her lap, the long, bouncing ride back into the city.

I was still in my hospital bed when the police came to see me. By then, I'd recovered enough to give them a clear and reasonably plausible account of what had happened. Like any successful lie, this one was firmly grounded in truth. The violent haboob that suddenly came upon us in the desert hills. The crash that happened when, blinded by wind-driven sand, I'd collided with a boulder, causing my jeep to topple over. How Dr. al-Baz and I had escaped from the wreckage, only to lose track of each other. How only I had managed to find shelter in the leeside of a pinnacle. The professor becoming lost in the storm, never to be seen again.

All true, every word of it. All I had to do was leave out a few facts, such as how I'd deliberately driven into the desert even though I knew that a haboob was on its way, or that even after we saw the scarlet haze rising above the western horizon, I'd insisted upon continuing to drive south, telling Dr. al-Baz that we'd be able to outrun the storm. The cops never learned that I'd been careful to carry with me a pair of sand goggles and a scarf, but refrained from making sure that the professor took the same precautions. Nor did they need to know that I'd deliberately aimed for that boulder, even though I could have easily avoided it.

I broke down when I spoke about how I'd heard Omar al-Baz calling my name, desperately trying to find me even as the air was filled with stinging red sand and visibility was reduced to only arm's length. That much, too, was true. What I didn't say was that Dr. al-Baz had come within three meters of where I was huddled, my eyes covered by goggles and a scarf wrapped around the lower part of my face. And yet I remained silent as I watched his indistinct form lurch past me, arms blindly thrust out before him, slowly suffocating as sand filled his nose and throat.

My tears were honest. I liked the professor. But his knowledge made him too dangerous to live.

As an alibi, my story worked. When a search party went out into the desert, they located my overturned jeep. Omar al-Baz's body was found about fifteen meters away, face-down and covered by several centimeters of sand. Our footprints had been erased by the wind, of course, so there was no way of telling how close the professor had been to me.

That settled any doubts the cops may have had. Dr. al-Baz's death was an accident. I had no motive for killing him, nor was there any evidence of foul play. If I was guilty of anything, it was only reckless and foolish behavior. My professional reputation was tarnished, but that was about it. The investigation was officially concluded the day I was released from the hospital. By then, I'd realized two things. The first was that I would get away with murder. The second was that my crime was far from perfect.

Dr. al-Baz hadn't taken the chieftain's blood specimen with him when he'd left the hotel. It was still in his room, along with all his equipment. This included the computers he'd used to analyze the sample; the results were saved in their memories, along with any notes he might have written. In fact, the only thing the professor had brought with him was his room key . . . which I'd neglected to retrieve from his body.

I couldn't return to his hotel room; any effort to get in would have aroused suspicion. All I could do was watch from the hotel lobby as, a couple of days later, the bellhops wheeled out a cart carrying the repacked equipment cases, bound for the spaceport and the shuttle which would ferry them to a marsliner docked at Deimos Station. In a few months, the professor's stuff would be back in the hands of his fellow faculty members. They would open the digital files and inspect what their late colleague had learned, and examine the blood specimen he'd collected. And then . . .

Well. We'll just have to see, won't we?

So now I sit alone in my neighborhood bar, where I drink and wait for the storm to come. And I never go into the desert any more.

zero for conduct

GREG EGAN

Looking back at the century that's just ended, it's obvious that Australian writer Greg Egan was one of the big new names to emerge in SF in the nineties, and he is probably one of the most significant talents to enter the field in the last several decades. Already one of the most widely known of all Australian genre writers, Egan may well be the best new "hard-science" writer to enter the field since Greg Bear, and he is still growing in range, power, and sophistication. In the past few years he has become a frequent contributor to Interzone *and* Asimov's Science Fiction *and has made sales as well as to* Pulphouse, Analog, Aurealis, Eidolon, *and elsewhere; many of his stories have also appeared in various "best of the year" series, and he was on the Hugo final ballot in 1995 for his story "Cocoon," which won the Ditmar Award and the* Asimov's Readers' Award. *He won the Hugo Award in 1999 for his novella* Oceanic. *His first novel,* Quarantine, *appeared in 1992; his second novel,* Permutation City, *won the John W. Campbell Memorial Award in 1994. His other books include the novels* Distress, Diaspora, Teranesia, Zendegi, *and* Schild's Ladder, *and four collections of his short fiction,* Axiomatic, Luminous, Our Lady of Chernobyl, *and* Crystal Nights and Other Stories. *His most recent books are part of the Orthogonal trilogy, consisting of* The Clockwork Rocket, The Eternal Flame, *and* The Arrows of Time. *He has a Web site at http://www.netspace.netau/^gregegan/.*

In the story that follows he takes us to a repressive near-future Iran where a young girl makes a fundamental scientific discovery that could change the world. Which is when her troubles start.

1

Latifa started the web page loading, then went to make tea. The proxy she used convinced her internet provider that every page she accessed belonged to a compendium of pious aphorisms from uncontroversial octogenarians in Qom, while to the sites themselves she appeared to be a peripatetic American, logging on from Pittsburgh one day and Kansas City the next. Between the sanctions against her true host country and that host's paranoia over the most innocent interactions with the West, these precautions were essential. But they slowed down her already sluggish connection so effectively that she might as well have been rehearsing for a flight to Mars.

The sound of boiling water offered a brief respite from the televised football match blaring down from the apartment above. "Two nil in favor of the Black Pearls, with fifteen minutes left to play! It's looking like victory for the home team here in Samen Stadium!" When the tea had brewed, she served it in a small glass for her grandfather to sip through a piece of hard sugar clenched between his teeth. Latifa sat with him for a while, but he was listening to the shortwave radio, straining to hear Kabul through the hum of interference and the breathless commentary coming through the ceiling, and he barely noticed when she left.

Back in her room after fifteen minutes, she found the scratched screen of the laptop glistening with a dozen shiny ball-and-stick models of organic molecules. Reading the color coding of the atoms was second nature to her by now: white for hydrogen, black for carbon, cherry red for oxygen, azure for nitrogen. Here and there a yellow sulfur atom or a green chlorine stood out, like a chickpea in a barrel of candy.

All the molecules that the ChemFactor page had assigned to her were nameless—unless you counted the formal structural descriptions full of cis-1,3-dimethyl-this and 2,5-di-tert-butyl-that—and Latifa had no idea which, if any of them, had actually been synthesized in a lab somewhere. Perhaps a few of them were impossible beasts, chimeras cranked out by the software's mindless permutations, destined to be completely unstable in reality. If she made an effort, she could probably weed some of them out. But that could wait until she'd narrowed down the list of candidates, eliminating the molecules with no real chance of binding strongly to the target.

The target this time was an oligosaccharide, a carbohydrate with nine rings arranged in pleasingly asymmetric tiers, like a small child's attempt to build a shoe rack. Helpfully, the ChemFactor page kept it fixed on the screen as Latifa scrolled up and down through the long catalog of its potential suitors.

She trusted the software to have made some sensible choices already, on geometric grounds: all of these molecules ought to be able to nestle reasonably snugly against the target. In principle she could rotate the ball-and-stick models any way she liked, and slide the target into the same view to assess the prospective fit, but in practice that made the laptop's graphics card choke. So she'd learned to manipulate the structures in her head, to picture the encounter without fretting too much about precise angles and distances. Molecules weren't rigid, and if the interaction with the target liberated enough energy the participants could stretch or flex a little to accommodate each other. There were rigorous calculations that could predict the upshot of all that give and take, but the equations could not be solved quickly or easily. So ChemFactor invited people to offer their hunches. Newcomers guessed no better than random, and many players' hit rates failed to rise above statistical noise. But some people acquired a feel for the task, learning from their victories and mistakes—even if they couldn't put their private algorithms into words.

Latifa didn't over-think the puzzle, and in twenty minutes she'd made her choice. She clicked the button beside her selection and confirmed it, satisfied that she'd done her best. After three years in the game she'd proved to be a born chemical match-maker, but she didn't want it going to her head. Whatever lay behind her well-judged guesses, it could only be a matter of time before the software itself learned to codify all the same rules. The truth was, the more successful she became, the faster she'd be heading for obsolescence. She needed to make the most of her talent while it still counted.

Latifa spent two hours on her homework, then a call came from her cousin Fashard in Kandahar. She went out onto the balcony where the phone could get a better signal.

"How is your grandfather?" he asked.

"He's fine. I'll ask him to call you back tomorrow." Her grandfather had given up on the shortwave and gone to bed. "How are things there?"

"The kids have all come down with something," Fashard reported. "And the power's been off for the last two days."

"*Two days?*" Latifa felt for her young cousins, sweltering and feverish without even a fan. "You should get a generator."

"Ha! I could get ten; people are practically giving them away."

"Why?"

"The price of diesel's gone through the roof," Fashard explained. "Blackouts or not, no one can afford to run them."

Latifa looked out at the lights of Mashhad. There was nothing glamorous about the concrete tower blocks around her, but the one thing Iran didn't lack was electricity. Kandahar should have been well-supplied by the Kajaki Dam, but two of the three turbines in the hydroelectric plant had been out of service for more than a year, and the drought had made it even harder for the remaining turbine to meet demand.

"What about the shop?" she asked.

"Pedaling the sewing machine keeps me fit," Fashard joked.

"I wish I could do something."

"Things are hard for everyone," Fashard said stoically. "But we'll be all right; people always need clothes. You just concentrate on your studies."

Latifa tried to think of some news to cheer him up. "Amir said he's planning to come home this Eid." Her brother had made no firm promises, but she couldn't believe he'd spend the holidays away from his family for a second year in a row.

"Inshallah," Fashard replied. "He should book the ticket early though, or he'll never get a seat."

"I'll remind him."

There was no response; the connection had cut out. Latifa tried calling back but all she got was a sequence of strange beeps, as if the phone tower was too flustered to offer up its usual recorded apologies.

She tidied the kitchen then lay in bed. It was hard to fall asleep when her thoughts cycled endlessly through the same inventory of troubles, but sometime after midnight she managed to break the loop and tumble into blackness.

"Afghani slut," Ghamzeh whispered, leaning against Latifa and pinching her arm through the fabric of her manteau.

"Let go of me," Latifa pleaded. She was pressed against her locker, she couldn't pull away. Ghamzeh turned her face toward her, smiling, as if they were friends exchanging gossip. Other students walked past, averting their eyes.

"I'm getting tired of the smell of you," Ghamzeh complained. "You're stinking up the whole city. You should go back home to your little mud hut."

Latifa's skin tingled between the girl's blunt talons, warmed by broken blood vessels, numbed by clamped nerves. It would be satisfying to lash out with her fists and free herself, but she knew that could only end badly.

"Did they have soap in your village?" Ghamzeh wondered. "Did they have underwear? All these things must have been so strange to you, when you arrived in civilization."

Latifa waited in silence. Arguing only prolonged the torment.

"Too stuck up to have a conversation?" Ghamzeh released her arm and began to move away, but then she stopped to give Latifa a parting smile. "You think you're impressing the teachers when you give them all the answers they want? Don't fool yourself, slut. They know you're just an animal doing circus tricks."

When Latifa had cleared away the dinner plates, her grandfather asked her about school.

"You're working hard?" he pressed her, cross-legged on the floor with a cushion at his back. "Earning their respect?"

"Yes."

"And your heart is still set on engineering?" He sounded doubtful, as if for him the word could only conjure up images of rough men covered in machine oil.

"Chemical engineering," she corrected him gently. "I'm getting good grades in chemistry, and there'd be plenty of jobs in it."

"After five more years. After university."

"Yes." Latifa looked away. Half the money Amir sent back from Dubai was already going on her school fees. Her brother was twenty-two; no one could expect him to spend another five years without marrying.

"You should get on with your studies then." Her grandfather waved her away amiably, then reached over for the radio.

In her room, Latifa switched on the laptop before opening her history book, but she kept her eyes off the screen until she'd read half the chapter on the Sassanid kings. When she finally gave herself a break the ChemFactor site had loaded, and she'd been logged in automatically, by cookie.

A yellow icon of a stylized envelope was flashing at the top of the page. A fellow player she'd never heard of called "jesse409" had left her a message, congratulating "PhaseChangeGirl" on a cumulative score that had just crossed twenty thousand. Latifa's true score was far higher than that, but she'd changed her identity and rejoined the game from scratch five times so far, lest she come to the notice of someone with the means to find out who she really was.

The guess she'd made the previous night had paid off: a rigorous model of the two molecules showed that the binding between them was stable. She had saved one of ChemFactor's clients the time and expense of doing the same calculations for dozens of alternatives, and her reward was a modest fraction of the resources she'd effectively freed. ChemFactor would model any collection of atoms and molecules she liked, free of charge—up to a preset quota in computing time.

Latifa closed her history book and moved the laptop to the center of her desk. If the binding problems were easy for her now, when it came to the much larger challenge she'd set herself the instincts she'd honed on the site could only take her so far. The raw computing power that she acquired from these sporadic prizes let her test her hunches and see where they fell short.

She dug out the notebook from her backpack and reviewed her sketches and calculations. She understood the symmetries of crystals, the shifts and rotations that brought any regular array of atoms back into perfect agreement with itself. She understood the thrillingly strange origins of the different varieties of magnetism, where electrons' spins became aligned or opposed—sometimes through their response to each other's magnetic fields, but more often through the Exclusion Principle, which linked the alignment of spin to the average distance between the particles, and hence the energy they needed in order to overcome electrostatic repulsion. And after studying hundreds of examples, she believed she had a sense for the kind of crystal that lay in a transition zone where one type of magnetism was on the verge of shifting to another.

She'd sketched her ideal crystal in the notebook more than a year before, but she had no proof yet that it was anything more than a fantasy. Her last modeling run had predicted something achingly close, but it had still not produced what she needed. She had to go back one step and try something different.

Latifa retrieved the saved data from that last attempt and set the parameters for the new simulation. She resisted the urge to stab the CONFIRM button twice; the response was just taking its time weaving its way back to her through the maze of obfuscation.

Estimated time for run: approximately seven hours.

She sat gazing at the screen for a while, though she knew that if she waited for the prediction to be updated she'd probably find that the new estimate was even longer.

Reluctantly, she moved the laptop to the floor and returned to the faded glory of the Sassanids. She had to be patient; she'd have her answer by morning.

"Whore," Ghamzeh muttered as Latifa hurried past her to her desk.

"You're ten minutes late, Latifa," Ms Keshavarz declared irritably.

"I'm very sorry." Latifa stood in place, her eyes cast down.

"So what's your excuse?"

Latifa remained silent.

"If you overslept," Ms Keshavarz suggested, "you should at least have the honesty to say so."

Latifa had woken at five, but she managed a flush of humiliation that she hoped would pass for a kind of tacit admission.

"Two hours of detention, then," Ms Keshavarz ruled. "It might have been half that if you'd been more forthcoming. Take you seat, please."

The day passed at a glacial speed. Latifa did her best to distract herself with the lessons, but it was like trying to chew water. The subject made no difference: history, literature, mathematics, physics—as soon as one sentence was written on the blackboard she knew exactly what would follow.

In detention with four other girls, she sat copying pages of long-winded homilies. From her seat she could see a driveway that led out from the staff car park, and one by one the vehicles she most needed to depart passed before her eyes. The waiting grew harder than ever, but she knew it would be foolish to act too soon.

Eighty minutes into her punishment, she started holding her breath for ever longer intervals. By the time she raised her hand there was nothing feigned in her tone of discomfort. The supervising teacher, Ms Shirazi, raised no objections and played no sadistic games with her. Latifa fled the room with plausible haste.

The rest of the school appeared deserted; the extra time had been worth it. Latifa opened the door to the toilets and let it swing shut, leaving the sound echoing back down the corridor, then hurried toward the chemistry lab.

The students' entrance was locked, but Latifa steeled herself and turned into the warren of store rooms and cubicles that filled the north side of the science wing. Her chemistry teacher, Ms Daneshvar, had taken her to her desk once to consult an old university textbook, to settle a point on which they'd both been unsure.

Latifa found her way back to that desk. The keys were hanging exactly where she remembered them, on labeled pegs. She took the one for the chemistry lab and headed for the teachers' entrance.

As she turned the key in the lock her stomach convulsed. To be expelled would be disastrous enough, but if the school pressed criminal charges she could be imprisoned and deported. She closed her eyes for a moment, summoning up an image of the beautiful lattice that the ChemFactor simulation had shown her. For a week she'd thought of nothing else. The software had reached its conclusion, but in the end the only test that mattered was whether the substance could be made in real life.

Late afternoon sunlight slanted across the room, glinting off the tubular legs of the stools standing upside-down on the black-painted benches. All the ingredients Latifa needed—salts of copper, barium and calcium—sat on the alphabetized shelves that ran along the eastern wall; none were of sufficient value or toxicity to be kept locked away, and she wouldn't need much of any of them for a proof of principle.

She took down the jars and weighed out a few grams of each, quantities too small to be missed. She'd written down the masses that would yield the right stoichiometry, the right proportions of atoms in the final product, but having spent the whole day repeating the calculations in her head she didn't waste time now consulting the slip of paper.

Latifa mixed the brightly colored granules in a ceramic crucible and crushed them with a pestle. Then she placed the crucible in the electric furnace. The heating profile she'd need was complicated, but though she'd only ever seen the furnace operated manually in class, she'd looked up the model number on the net and found the precise requirements for scripting it. When she pushed the memory stick into the USB port, the green light above flickered for a moment, then the first temperature of the sequence appeared on the display.

The whole thing would take nine hours. Latifa quickly re-shelved the jars, binned the filter paper she'd used on the scales, then retreated, locking the door behind her.

On her way past the toilets she remembered to stage a creaking exit. She slowed her pace as she approached the detention room, and felt cold beads of sweat on her face. Ms Shirazi offered her a sympathetic frown before turning back to the magazine she'd been reading.

Latifa dreamed that the school was on fire. The blaze was visible from the balcony of her apartment, and her grandfather stood and watched, wheezing alarmingly from the toxic fumes that were billowing out across Mashhad. When he switched on the radio, a newsreader reported that the police had found a memory stick beside the point of ignition and were checking all the students for a fingerprint match.

Latifa woke before dawn and ate breakfast, then prepared lunch for the two of them. She'd thought she'd been moving silently, but her grandfather surprised her as she was opening the front door.

"Why are you leaving so early?" he demanded.

"There's a study group."

"What do you mean?"

"A few of us get together before classes start and go over the lessons from the day before," she said.

"So you're running your own classes now? Do the teachers know about this?"

"The teachers approve," Latifa assured him. "It's their lessons that we're revising; we're not just making things up."

"You're not talking politics?" he asked sternly.

Latifa understood: he was thinking of the discussion group her mother had joined at Kabul University, its agenda excitedly recounted in one of the letters she'd sent him. He'd allowed Latifa to read the whole trove of letters when she'd turned fourteen—the age her mother had been when he'd gone into exile.

"You know me," Latifa said. "Politics is over my head."

"All right." He was mollified now. "Enjoy your study." He kissed her goodbye.

As Latifa dismounted from her bicycle she could see that the staff car park was empty except for the cleaners' van. If she could bluff her way through this final stage she might be out of danger in a matter of minutes.

The cleaners had unlocked the science wing, and a woman was mopping the floor by the main entrance. Latifa nodded to her, then walked in as if she owned the place.

"Hey! You shouldn't be here!" The woman straightened up and glared at her, worried for her job should anything be stolen.

"Ms Daneshvar asked me to prepare something for the class. She gave me the key yesterday." Latifa held it up for inspection.

The woman squinted at the key then waved her on, muttering unhappily.

In the chemistry lab everything was as Latifa had left it. She plucked the memory stick from the port on the furnace, then switched off the power. She touched the door, and felt no residual heat.

When she opened the furnace the air that escaped smelled like sulfur and bleach. Gingerly, she lifted out the crucible and peered inside. A solid gray mass covered the bottom, its surface as smooth as porcelain.

The instruments she needed to gauge success or failure were all in the physics lab, and trying to talk her way into another room right now would attract too much suspicion. She could wait for her next physics class and see what opportunities arose. Students messed around with the digital multimeters all the time, and if she was caught sticking the probes into her pocket her teacher would see nothing but a silly girl trying to measure the electrical resistance of a small paving stone she'd picked up off the street. Ms Hashemi wouldn't be curious enough to check the properties of the stone for herself.

Latifa fetched a piece of filter paper and tried to empty the crucible onto it, but the gray material clung stubbornly to the bottom where it had formed. She tapped it gently, then more forcefully, to no avail.

She was going to have to steal the crucible. It was not an expensive piece of equipment, but there were only four, neatly lined up in a row in the cupboard below the furnace, and its absence would eventually be missed. Ms Daneshvar might—just might—ask the cleaners if they'd seen it. There was a chance that all her trespasses would be discovered.

But what choice did she have?

She could leave the crucible behind and hunt for a replacement in the city. At the risk that, in the meantime, someone would take the vessel out to use it, find it soiled, and discard it. At the risk that she'd be caught trying to make the swap. And all of this for a gray lump that might easily be as worthless as it looked.

Latifa had bought a simple instrument of her own in the bazaar six months before, and she'd brought it with her almost as a joke—something she could try once she was out of danger, with no expectations at all. If the result it gave her was negative that wouldn't really prove anything. But she didn't know what else she could use to guide her.

She fished the magnet out of the pocket of her manteau. It was a slender disk the size of her thumbnail, probably weighing a gram or so. She held it in the mouth of the crucible and lowered it toward the bottom.

If there was any force coming into play as the magnet approached the gray material, it was too weak for her to sense. With a couple of millimeters still separating the two, Latifa spread her fingers and let the magnet drop. She didn't hear it strike the bottom—but from such a height how loud would it have been? She took her fingers out of the crucible and looked down.

It was impossible to tell if it was touching or not; the view was too narrow, the angle too high.

Latifa could hear the woman with the mop approaching, getting ready to clean the chemistry lab. Within a minute or less, everything she did here would take place in front of a witness.

A patch of morning sunlight from the eastern window fell upon the blackboard behind her. Latifa grabbed an empty Erlenmeyer flask and held it in the beam, tilting it until she managed to refract some light down into the crucible.

As she turned the flask back and forth, shifting the angle of the light, she could see a dark circle moving behind the magnet. Lit from above, an object barely a millimeter high couldn't cast a shadow like that.

The magnet was floating on air.

The door began to open. Latifa pocketed the crucible. She put the Erlenmeyer flask back on its shelf, then turned to see the cleaner eyeing her suspiciously.

"I'm all done now, thanks," Latifa announced cheerfully. She motioned toward the staff entrance. "I'll put the key back on my way out."

Minutes later, Latifa strode out of the science wing. She reached into her pocket and wrapped her hand around the crucible. She still had some money Amir had given her last Eid; she could buy a replacement that afternoon. For now, all she had to do was get through the day's lessons with a straight face, while walking around carrying the world's first room-temperature superconductor.

2

Ezatullah was said to be the richest Afghani in Mashhad, and from the look of his three-story marble-clad house he had no wish to live down that reputation. Latifa had heard that he'd made his money in Saudi Arabia, where he'd represented the mujahedin at the time of the Soviet occupation. Wealthy Saudi women with guilty consciences had filed through his office day after day, handing him bags full of gold bullion to help fund the jihad—buying, they believed, the same promise of paradise that went to the martyrs themselves. Ezatullah, being less concerned with the afterlife, had passed on their donations to the war chest but retained a sizable commission.

At the mansion's gate, Latifa's grandfather paused. "I promised your mother I'd keep you out of trouble."

Latifa didn't know how to answer that; his caution came from love and grief, but this was a risk they needed to take. "Fashard's already started things rolling on his side," she reminded him. "It will be hard on him if we pull out now."

"That's true."

In the sitting room Ezatullah's youngest daughter, Yasmin, served tea, then stayed with Latifa while the two men withdrew to talk business. Latifa passed the time thinking up compliments for each rug and item of furniture in sight, and Yasmin replied in such a soft, shy voice that Latifa had no trouble eavesdropping on the conversation from the adjoining room.

"My nephew owns a clothing business in Kandahar," her grandfather began. "Some tailoring, some imports and exports. But recently he came across a new opportunity: a chance to buy electrical cable at a very fair price."

"A prudent man will have diverse interests," Ezatullah declared approvingly.

"We're hoping to on-sell the wire in Mashhad," her grandfather explained. "We could avoid a lot of paperwork at the border if we packed the trucks with cartons labeled as clothing—with some at the rear bearing out that claim. My granddaughter could run a small shop to receive these shipments."

"And you're seeking a partner, to help fund this venture?"

Latifa heard the rustle of paper, the figures she'd prepared changing hands.

"What's driven you to this, haji?" Ezatullah asked pointedly. "You don't have a reputation as a businessman."

"I'm seventy years old," her grandfather replied. "I need to see my daughter's children looked after before I die."

Ezatullah thought for a while. "Let me talk to my associates in Kandahar."

"Of course."

On the bus back to the apartment, Latifa imagined the phone calls that would already be bouncing back and forth across the border. Ezatullah would soon know all about the new electrification project in Kandahar, which aimed to wire up a dozen more neighborhoods to the already-struggling grid—apparently in the hope that even a meager ration of cheap power would turn more people against the insurgents who bombed every convoy that tried to carry replacement parts to the hydroelectric plant.

International donors had agreed to fund the project, and with overhead cables strung from pole to pole along winding roads, some discrepancy between the surveyed length and the cable used was only to be expected. But while Fashard really had come to an agreement with the contractor to take the excess wire off his hands, with no family ties or prior connection to the man he had only managed to secure the deal by offering a price well above the going rate.

Latifa didn't expect any of these details to elude their partner, but the hope was that his advisers in Kandahar would conclude that Fashard, lacking experience as a smuggler, had simply underestimated his own costs. That alone wouldn't make the collaboration a bad investment: she'd structured the proposal in such a way that Ezatullah would still make a tidy return even if the rest of them barely broke even.

They left the bus and made their way home. "If we told him the truth—" her grandfather began as they started up the stairs.

"If we told him the truth, he'd snatch it from our hands!" Latifa retorted. Her words echoed in the concrete stairwell; she lowered her voice. "One way or another he'd get hold of the recipe, then sell it to some company with a thousand lawyers who could claim they'd invented it themselves. We need to be in a stronger position before we take this to anyone, or they'll eat us alive." A patent attorney could do a lot to protect them before they approached a commercial backer, but that protection would cost several thousand euros. Raising that much themselves—without trading away any share in the invention—wasn't going to be easy, but it would make all the difference to how much power they retained.

Her grandfather stopped on a landing to catch his breath. "And if Ezatullah finds out that we've lied to him—"

His phone buzzed once, with a text message.

"You need to go to the house again," he said. "Tomorrow, after school."

Latifa's skin prickled with fear. "*Me?* What for?" Did Ezatullah want to quiz her about her knowledge of retail fashion for the modern Iranian woman—or had his digging already exposed her other interests?

"Most of the money's going straight to Fashard, but we'll need some cash at our end too," her grandfather explained. "He doesn't want me coming and going from the house, but no one will be suspicious if you've struck up a friendship with his daughter."

Latifa had asked the electricians to come at seven to switch on the power to the kilns, but when they hadn't shown up by eight she gave up any hope of making it to her history class.

For the first hour she'd killed time by sweeping; now she paced the bare wooden floor, optimistically surveying her new fiefdom. Finding the factory had been a huge stroke of luck; it had originally produced ceramic tableware, and when the tenants went out of business the owner of the premises had taken possession of the kilns. He'd been on the verge of selling them for scrap, and had parted with them for a ridiculously low price just to get her grandfather to sign the lease. The location wasn't perfect, but perhaps it was for the best that it wasn't too close to the shop. The separation would make it less likely that anyone would see her in both places.

When the electricians finally arrived they ignored Latifa completely, and she resisted the urge to pester them with odd questions. *What would you do if you cut into an overhead power line and found that its appearance, in cross-section, wasn't quite what you were used to?*

"Delivery for Bose Ceramics?" a man called from the entrance.

Latifa went to see what it was. The courier was already loading one box, as tall as she was, onto his trolley. She guided him across the factory floor. "Can you put it here? Thank you."

"There are another two in the truck."

She waited until the electricians had left before finding a knife and slicing away the cardboard and styrofoam—afraid that they might recognize the equipment and start asking questions of their own. She plugged in one of the cable winders and put it through a test sequence, watching the nimble motorized arms blur as they rehearsed on thin air.

One machine would unpick, while the other two wove—and for every kilometer of cable that came into the factory, two kilometers would emerge. With half as many strands as the original, the new version would need to be bulked out from within to retain the same diameter. The pellets of ceramic wound in among the steel and aluminum wouldn't form a contiguous electrical path, but these superconducting inclusions would still lower the overall resistance of the cable, sharing the current for a large enough portion of its length to compensate for the missing metal.

So long as the cable was fit for use, the Iranian contractors who bought it would have no reason to complain. They'd pocket the difference in price, and the power grid would be none the worse for it. Everyone would get paid, everyone would be happy.

Latifa checked her watch; she'd missed another two classes. All she could do now was write the whole day off and claim to have been sick. She needed to chase down the heat-resistant molds that would give the ceramic pellets their shape, and try again to get a promise from the chemical suppliers that they could deliver the quantities she was going to need to keep the kilns going day after day, week after week.

"Do you have this in size sixteen?" the woman asked, emerging from the changing room. Latifa looked up from her homework. The woman was still wearing the over-sized sunglasses that she hadn't deigned to remove as she entered the shop, as if she were a famous singer afraid of being mobbed by fans.

"I'm sorry, we don't."

"Can you check your storeroom? I love the colors, but this one is a bit too tight."

Latifa hesitated; she was certain that they didn't stock the blouse in that size, but it would be impolite to refuse. "Of course. One moment."

She spent half a minute rummaging through the shelves, to ensure that her search didn't seem too perfunctory. It was almost six o'clock; she should close the shop and relieve her grandfather at the factory.

When she returned to the counter, the customer had left. The woman had taken the blouse, along with two pairs of trousers from the rack near the door. Latifa felt a curious warmth rising in her face; most of all she was annoyed that she'd been so gullible, but the resentment she felt at the brazen theft collided unpleasantly with other thoughts.

There was nothing to be done but to put the incident out of her mind. She looked over her unfinished essay on the Iran-Iraq war; it was due in the morning, but she'd have to complete it in the factory.

"Are these goods from your shop?"

A policeman was standing in the doorway. The thief was beside him, and he was holding up the stolen clothes.

Latifa could hardly deny it; the trousers were identical to the others hanging right beside him.

"They are, sir," she replied. He must have seen the woman emerging, hastily stuffing everything into her bag. Why couldn't she have done that out of sight?

"This lady says she must have dropped the receipt. Should I look for it, or will I be wasting my time?"

Latifa struggled to choose the right answer. "It's my fault, sir. She must have thought I'd given her the receipt along with the change—but she was in a hurry, she didn't even want one of our bags . . ."

"So you still have the receipt?"

Latifa pointed helplessly at the waste-paper basket beside the counter, full to the brim with discarded drafts of her essay. "I couldn't leave the shop and chase after her, so I threw it in there. Please forgive me, sir, I'm just starting out in this job. If the boss learns what I've done, he'll fire me straight away." It was lucky that the thief was still wearing her ridiculous glasses; Latifa wasn't sure how she would have coped if they'd had to make eye contact.

The policeman appeared skeptical: he knew what he'd seen. Latifa put the back of her hand to her eyes and sniffed.

"All right," he said. "Everyone makes mistakes." He turned to the woman. "I'm sorry for the misunderstanding."

"It's nothing." She nodded to Latifa. "Good evening."

The policeman lingered in the doorway, thinking things over. Then he approached the counter.

"Let me see your storeroom."

Latifa gestured to the entrance, but stayed beside the cash register. She listened to the man moving about, rustling through discarded packaging, tapping the walls. What did he imagine he'd find—a secret compartment?

He emerged from the room, stony faced, as if the lack of anything incriminating only compounded his resentment.

"ID card."

Latifa produced it. She'd rid herself of her accent long ago, and she had just enough of her father's Tajik features that she could often pass as an Iranian to the eye, but here it was: the proof of her real status.

"Ha," he grunted. "All right." He handed back the ID. "Just behave yourself, and we'll get along fine."

As he walked out of the shop, Latifa began shaking with relief. He'd found an innocent explanation for her reticence to press charges: the card entitled her to remain in the country at the pleasure of the government, but she wasn't a citizen, and she would have been crazy to risk the consequences if the woman had called her a liar.

Latifa wheeled her bicycle out of the storeroom and closed the shop. The factory was six kilometers away, and the traffic tonight looked merciless.

"I had a call from Ezatullah," Latifa's grandfather said. "He wants to take over the transport."

Latifa continued brushing down the slides from the superconductor hopper. "What does that mean?"

"He has another partner who's been bringing goods across the border. This man has a warehouse in Herat."

Herat was just a hundred kilometers from the border, on the route from Kandahar to Mashhad. "So he wants us to make room for this other man's merchandise in our trucks?" Latifa put the brush down. It was an unsettling prospect, but it didn't have to be a disaster.

"No," her grandfather replied. "He wants us to bring the wire across in this other man's trucks."

"Why?"

"The customs inspectors have people coming from Tehran to look over their shoulders," her grandfather explained. "There's no fixing that with bribes, and the clothes make too flimsy a cover for the real cargo. This other man's bringing over a couple of loads of scrap metal every week; hiding the wire won't be a problem for him."

Latifa sat down on the bench beside the winders. "But we can't risk that! We can't let him know how many spools we're bringing in!" Ezatullah had kept his distance from their day-to-day operations, but the black market contacts to whom they passed the altered wire had long-standing connections to him, and Latifa had no doubt that he was being kept apprised of every transaction. *Under-reporting their sales* to hide the fact that they were selling twice as much wire as they imported would be suicidal.

"Can we shift this work to Kandahar?" her grandfather asked.

"Maybe the last part, the winding," Latifa replied. So long as they could double the wire before it reached Herat, there'd be no discrepancies in the numbers Ezatullah received from his informants.

"What about the kilns?"

"No, the power's too erratic. If there's a blackout halfway through a batch that would ruin it—and we need at least two batches a day to keep up."

"Couldn't we use a generator?"

Latifa didn't have the numbers she needed to answer that, but she knew Fashard had looked into the economics of using one himself. She texted him some questions, and he replied a few minutes later.

"It's hopeless," she concluded. "Each kiln runs at about twenty kilowatts. Getting that from diesel, we'd be lucky to break even."

Her grandfather managed a curt laugh. "Maybe we'd be better off selling the rest of the wire as it is?"

Latifa did a few more calculations. "That won't work either. Fashard is paying too much for it; we'd be making a loss on every spool." After sinking money into the factory's lease and other inputs to the doubling process, any attempt to get by without the benefits of that doubling would leave them owing Ezatullah more cash than the remaining sales would bring in.

"Then what choice is left to us?"

"We could keep making the superconductor here," Latifa suggested.

"And get it to Kandahar how?" her grandfather protested. "Do you think we can do business with anyone working that route and expect Ezatullah not to hear about it? Once or twice, maybe, but not if we set up a regular shipment."

Latifa had no answer to that. "We should talk about this in the morning," she said. "You've been working all day; you should get some sleep now."

At her insistence he retired to the factory's office, where they'd put in a mattress and blankets. Latifa stood by the hopper; the last batch of superconductor should have cooled by now, but she was too dejected to attend to it. If they moved the whole operation to Kandahar, the best they could hope for was scraping through without ending up in debt. She didn't doubt that Fashard and her other cousins would do whatever needed to be done—working unpaid, purely for the sake of keeping her grandfather out of trouble—but the prospect of forcing that burden onto them filled her with shame.

Her own dawdling wasn't helping anyone. She put on the heat-proof gloves, took the molds from the kiln and began filling the hopper. She'd once calculated that if Iran's entire grid were to be replaced with a superconducting version, the power no longer being lost in transmission would be enough to light up all of Afghanistan. But if that was just a fantasy, all her other plans were heading for the same fate.

Latifa switched on the winders and watched the strands of wire shuttling from spool to spool, wrapping the stream of pellets from the hopper. Of all the wondrous things the superconductor made possible, this had seemed the simplest—and the safest way to exploit it without attracting too much attention.

But these dull gray beads were all she had. If she wanted to rescue the whole misbegotten venture, she needed to find another way to turn them to her advantage.

Latifa's grandfather ran from the office, barefoot, eyes wide with fear. "What happened? Are you hurt?"

Latifa could see dents in the ceiling where the pellets had struck. "I'm all right," she assured him. "I'm sorry, I didn't mean to wake you." She looked around; the kilns and the winders were untouched, and there was no damage to the building that a plasterer couldn't fix.

"*What did you do?* I thought something exploded—or those machines went crazy." He glared at the winders, as if they might have rebelled and started pelting their owners with shrapnel.

Latifa switched off the power from the outlet and approached what remained of her test rig. She'd surrounded it with workbenches turned on their sides, as safety shields. "I'm going to need better reinforcement," she said. "I didn't realize the field would get so strong, so quickly."

Her grandfather stared at the shattered assembly that she'd improvised from a helix of copper pipe. The previous tenants had left all kinds of junk behind, and Latifa had been loathe to discard anything that might have turned out to be useful.

"It's a storage device," she explained. "For electricity. The current just sits there going round and round; when you want some of it back you can draw it out. It's not all that different from a battery."

"I'd say it's not all that different from a bomb."

Latifa was chastened. "I was careless; I'm sorry. I was impatient to see if I could make it work at all. The current generates a strong magnetic field, and that puts the whole thing under pressure—but when it's built properly, it will be a solid coil of superconductor, not a lot of pellets stuffed inside a pipe. And we can bury it in the ground, so if it does shatter no one will get hurt."

"How is this meant to help us?" her grandfather asked irritably. He lifted his right foot to examine the sole; a splinter of superconductor was poking through the skin.

Latifa said, "The mains power in Kandahar is unreliable, but it's still far cheaper than using a generator. A few of these storage coils should be enough to guarantee that we can run the kilns through a blackout."

"You're serious?"

Latifa hesitated. "Give me a few days to do some more experiments, then we'll know for sure."

"How many days of school have you missed already?"

"That's not important."

Her grandfather sat on the ground and covered his eyes with one hand. "School is not important now? They *murdered your mother* because she was teaching girls, and your father because he'd defended her. When she grew so afraid that she sent you to me, I promised her you'd get an education. This country is no paradise, but at least you were safe in that school, you were doing well. Now we're juggling money we don't have, living in fear of Ezatullah, blowing things up, planning some new madness every day."

Latifa approached him and put a hand on his shoulder. "After this, there'll be nothing to distract me. We'll close the factory, we'll close the shop. My whole life will be school and homework, school and homework all the way to Eid."

Her grandfather looked up at her. "How long will it take?"

"Maybe a couple of weeks." The coils themselves didn't have to be complicated, but it would take some research and trial and error to get the charging and discharging circuitry right.

"And then what?" he asked. "If we send these things to Kandahar—with the kilns and everything else—do you think Fashard can put it all together and just take over where we left off?"

"Maybe not," Latifa conceded. Fashard had wired his own house, and he could repair a sewing machine blindfold. But this would be tricky, and she couldn't talk him through the whole setup on the phone.

She said, "It looks like Eid's coming early for me this year."

In Herat, in the bus station's restroom, Latifa went through the ritual of replacing her headscarf and manteau with the burqa and niqab that she'd need to be wearing when she arrived in Kandahar.

She stared through the blue gauze at the anonymous figure reflected in the restroom's stained mirror. When she'd lived in Kabul with her parents, she'd still been young enough to visit Kandahar without covering her hair, let alone her face. But if anything, she felt insufficiently disguised now. On top of her anxiety over all her new secrets, this would be her first trip home without Amir traveling beside her—or at least, ten meters ahead of her, in the men's section of the bus. Fashard had offered to come and meet her in Herat, but she'd persuaded him to stay in Kandahar. She couldn't help being nervous, but that didn't mean she had to be cowed.

It was still early as the bus set out. Latifa chatted with the woman beside her, who was returning to Kandahar after visiting Herat for medical treatment. "I used to go to Quetta," the woman explained, "but it's too dangerous there now."

"What about Kabul?" Latifa asked.

"Kabul? These days you'll wait six months for an appointment."

The specialists in Herat were mostly Iranian; in Kabul, mostly European. In Kandahar, you'd be lucky to find anyone at all with a genuine medical degree, though there was a wide choice of charlatans who'd take your money in exchange for pharmaceuticals with expiry dates forged in ballpoint.

"Someone should build a medical school in Kandahar," Latifa suggested. "With ninety percent of the intake women, until things are evened out."

Her companion laughed nervously.

"I'm serious!" Latifa protested. "Aren't you sick of traveling to every point of the compass just to get what other people have at home?"

"Sister," the woman said quietly, "it's time to shut your mouth."

Latifa took her advice, and peered past her out the scratched window. They were crossing a barren, rock-strewn desert now, a region infamous for bandits. The bus had an armed guard, for what that was worth, but the first time Latifa had made the journey Amir had told her stories of travelers ambushed on this road at night. One man on a motorbike, carrying no cash, had been tortured until he phoned his family to deposit money into his assailant's account.

"Wouldn't that help the police catch the bandits?" Latifa had asked him, logical as ever but still naive.

Amir had laughed his head off.

"When it comes to the police," he'd finally explained, *"money in the bank* tends to have the opposite effect."

Fashard was waiting for Latifa in the bus station. He spotted her before she saw him—or rather, he spotted the bright scarf, chosen from the range she sold in the shop, that she'd told him she'd be tying to the handle of her suitcase.

He called out, then approached her, beaming. "Welcome, cousin! How was your trip?" He grabbed the suitcase and hefted it onto his shoulders; it did have wheels, but in the crowded station any baggage at foot level would just be an impediment.

"It was fine," she said. "You're looking well." Actually, Fashard looked exhausted, but he'd put so much enthusiasm into his greeting that it would have been rude to mention anything of the kind.

Latifa followed him to the car, bumping into people along the way; she still hadn't adjusted to having her peripheral vision excised.

The sun was setting as they drove through the city; Latifa fought to keep her eyes open, but she took in an impression of peeling advertising posters, shabby white-washed buildings, crowds of men in all manner of clothing and a smattering of women in near-identical garb. Traffic police stood at the busiest intersections, blowing their whistles. Nothing had changed.

Inside the house, she gratefully shed her burqa as Fashard's five youngest children swarmed toward her. She dropped to her knees to exchange kisses and dispense sweets. Fashard's wife, Soraya, his mother, Zohra, eldest daughter, sister, brother-in-law and two nephews were next to greet her. Latifa's weariness lifted; used as she was to comparative solitude, the sense of belonging was overpowering.

"How is my brother?" Zohra pressed her.

"He's fine. He sends his love to you especially."

Zohra started weeping; Fashard put an arm around her. Latifa looked away. Her grandfather still had too many enemies here to be able to return.

When Latifa had washed and changed her clothes, she rejoined the family just as the first dizzying aromas began escaping from the kitchen. She had fasted all day and the night before, knowing that on her arrival she was going to be fed until she burst. Soraya shooed her away from the kitchen, but Latifa was pleasantly surprised: Fashard had finally improved the chimney to the point where the wood-fired stove no longer filled the room with blinding smoke.

As they ate by the light of kerosene lamps, everyone had questions for her about life in Mashhad. What did things cost now, with the new sanctions in place? What were her neighbors like? How were the Iranians treating Afghanis these days? Latifa was happy to answer them, but as she looked around at the curious faces she kept thinking of eight-year-old Fatema tugging on her sleeve, accepting a sweet but demanding something more: *What was school like? What did you learn?*

In the morning, Fashard showed Latifa the room he'd set aside for their work. She'd sent the kilns, the winders, and the current buckets to him by three different carriers. Fashard had found a source for the superconductor precursors himself: a company that brought a variety of common industrial chemicals in through Pakistan. It was possible that news of some of these shipments had reached Ezatullah, but Latifa was hoping that it wouldn't be enough to attract suspicion. If Fashard had decided to diversify into pottery, that hardly constituted a form of betrayal.

The room opened onto the courtyard, and Fashard had already taken up the paving stones to expose a patch of bare ground. "This is perfect," Latifa said. "We can run some cable out along the wall and bury the current buckets right here."

Fashard examined one of the halved diving cylinders she'd adapted to the purpose. "This really might burst?" he asked, more bemused than alarmed.

"I hope not," Latifa replied. "There's a cut-off switch that should stop the charger if the magnetic field grows too strong. I can't imagine that switch getting jammed—a bit of grit or friction isn't going to hold the contacts together against a force that's threatening to tear the whole thing apart. But so long as you keep track of the charging time there shouldn't be a problem anyway."

It took a couple of hours to dig the holes and wire up the storage system. Late in the morning the power came on, giving them a chance to test everything before they covered the buckets with half a meter of soil.

Latifa switched on the charger and waited ten minutes, then she plugged a lamp into the new supply. The light it produced was steadier and brighter than that it had emitted when connected to the mains: the voltage from the buckets was better regulated than the incoming supply.

Fashard smiled, not quite believing it. The largest of the components inside the cylinders looked like nothing so much as the element of an electric water heater; that was how Latifa had described the ceramic helices in the customs documents.

"If everyone had these . . ." he began enthusiastically, but then he stopped and thought it through. "If everyone had them, every household would be drawing more power, charging up their buckets to use through the blackouts. The power company would only be able to meet the demand from an even smaller portion of its customers, so they'd have to make the rationing periods even shorter."

"That's true," Latifa agreed. "Which is why it will be better if the buckets are sold with solar panels."

"What about in winter?" Fashard protested.

Latifa snorted. "What do you want from me? Magic? The government needs to fix the hydro plant."

Fashard shook his head sadly. "The people who keep bombing it aren't going to stop. Not unless they're given everything they want."

Latifa felt tired, but she had to finish what she'd started. She said, "I should show you how to work the kilns and the winders."

———

It took three days for Latifa and Fashard to settle on a procedure for the new factory. If they waited for the current buckets to be fully charged before starting the kilns, that guaranteed they could finish the batch without spoiling it—but they could make better use of the time if they took a risk and started earlier, given that the power, erratic though it was, usually did stay on for a few hours every day.

Fashard brought in his oldest nephew, Naqib, who'd be working half the shifts. Latifa stayed out of these training sessions; Naqib was always perfectly polite to her, but she knew he wasn't prepared to be shown anything by a woman three years younger than himself.

Sidelined, Latifa passed the time with Fatema. Though it was too dangerous for Fatema to go to school, Fashard had taught her to read and write and he was trying to find someone to come and tutor her. Latifa sat beside her as she proudly sounded out the words in a compendium of Pashtun folk tales, and practiced her script in the back of Latifa's notebook.

"What are these?" Fatema asked, flicking through the pages of calculations.

"Al-jabr," Latifa replied. "You'll understand when you're older."

One day they were in the courtyard, racing the remote-control cars that Latifa had brought from Mashhad for all the kids to share. The power went off, and as the television the other cousins had been watching fell silent, Fatema turned toward the factory, surprised. She could hear the winders still spinning.

"How is that working?" she asked Latifa.

"Our cars are still working, aren't they?" Latifa revved her engine.

Fatema refused to be distracted. "They use batteries. You can't run anything big with batteries."

"Maybe I brought some bigger batteries from Iran."

"Show me," Fatema pleaded.

Latifa opened her mouth to start explaining, her mind already groping for some simple metaphors she could use to convey how the current buckets worked. But . . . *our cousin came from Iran and buried giant batteries in the ground?* Did she really want that story spreading out across the neighborhood?

"I was joking," Latifa said.

Fatema frowned. "But then *how* . . . ?"

Latifa shrugged. Fatema's brothers, robbed of their cartoons, were heading toward them, demanding to join in the game.

The bus station was stifling. Latifa would have been happy to dispense a few parting hugs and then take her seat, but her cousins didn't do quiet farewells.

"I'll be back at Eid," she promised. "With Amir."

"That's months away!" Soraya sobbed.

"I'll phone every week."

"You say that now," Zohra replied, more resigned than accusing.

"I'm not leaving forever! I'll see you all again!" Latifa was growing tearful herself. She squatted down and tried to kiss Fatema, but the girl turned her face away.

"What should I bring you from Mashhad next time?" Latifa asked her.

Fatema considered this. "The truth."

Latifa said, "I'll try."

3

"I did my best to argue your case," Ms Daneshvar told Latifa. "I told the principal you had too much promise to waste. But your attendance records, your missed assignments . . ." She spread her hands unhappily. "I couldn't sway them."

"I'll be all right," Latifa assured her. She glanced up at the peg that held the key to the chemistry lab. "And I appreciate everything you did for me."

"But what will you do now?"

Latifa reached into her backpack and took out one of the small ceramic pots Fashard had sent her. Not long after the last spools of wire had left Kandahar, two men had come snooping on Ezatullah's behalf—perhaps a little puzzled that Fashard didn't seem quite as crushed as the terms of the deal should have left him. He had managed to hide the winders from them, but he'd had to think up an alibi for the kilns at short notice.

"I'm going to sell a few knickknacks in the bazaar," Latifa said. "Like this." She placed the pot on the desk and made as if to open it. When she'd twisted the lid through a quarter-turn it sprung into the air—only kept from escaping by three cotton threads that remained comically taut, restraining it against the push of some mysterious repulsive force.

Ms Daneshvar gazed in horror at this piece of useless kitsch.

"Just for a while!" Latifa added. "Until my other plans come to fruition."

"Oh, Latifa."

"You should take a closer look at it when you have the time," Latifa urged her. "There's a puzzle to it that I think you might enjoy."

"There are a couple of magnets," Ms Daneshvar replied. "Like pole aimed at like. You were my brightest student . . . and now you're impressed by *this*?" She turned the pot over. "Made in Afghanistan. Patent pending." She gave a curt laugh, but then thought better of mocking the idea.

Latifa said, "You helped me a lot. It wasn't wasted." She stood and shook her former teacher's hand. "I hope things go well for you."

Ms Daneshvar rose and kissed Latifa's cheek. "I know you're resourceful; I know you'll find something. It just should have been so much more."

Latifa started to leave, but then she stopped and turned back. The claims had all been lodged, the details disclosed. She didn't have to keep the secret any more.

"Cut one thread, so you can turn the lid upside-down," she suggested.

Ms Daneshvar was perplexed. "Why?"

Latifa smiled. "It's a very quick experiment, but I promise you it will be worth it."

The waiting stars

ALIETTE DE BODARD

Aliette de Bodard is a software engineer who lives and works in Paris, where she shares a flat with two Lovecraftian plants and more computers than warm bodies. Only a few years into her career, her short fiction has appeared in Interzone, Asimov's, Clarkesworld, Realms of Fantasy, Orson Scott Card's Intergalactic Medicine Show, Writers of the Future, Coyote Wild, Electric Velocipede, The Immersion Book of SF, Fictitious Force, Shimmer, *and elsewhere, and she has won the British SF Association Award for her story* "The Shipmaker," *the Locus Award, and the Nebula Award for her story* "Immersion." *Her novels include* Servant of the Underworld, Harbinger of the Storm, *and* Master of the House of Darts, *all recently reissued in a novel omnibus,* Obsidian and Blood. *Her most recent book,* On a Red Station, Drifting, *is a chapbook novella set in the same universe as the following story. Her Web site, www.aliettedebodard.com, features free fiction, thoughts on the writing process, and entirely too many recipes for Vietnamese dishes.*

The engrossing story that follows takes us to the far future of an alternate world, where a high-tech conflict is going on between spacefaring Mayan and Chinese empires and women give birth to children who are prenatally altered in the womb to become the control systems of living spaceships—and it takes us along on an unusual kind of rescue mission to a graveyard of dead spaceships, where one turns out to be not quite as dead as it seems.

The derelict ship ward was in an isolated section of Outsider space, one of the numerous spots left blank on interstellar maps, no more or no less tantalising than its neighbouring quadrants. To most people, it would be just that: a boring part of a long journey to be avoided—skipped over by Mind-ships as they cut through deep space, passed around at low speeds by Outsider ships while their passengers slept in their hibernation cradles.

Only if anyone got closer would they see the hulking masses of ships: the glint of starlight on metal, the sharp, pristine beauty of their hulls, even though they all lay quiescent and crippled, forever unable to move—living corpses kept as a reminder of how far they had fallen; the Outsiders' brash statement of their military might, a reminder that their weapons held the means to fell any Mind-ships they chose to hound.

On the sensors of *The Cinnabar Mansions*, the ships all appeared small and diminished, like toy models or avatars—things Lan Nhen could have held in the palm of her hand and just as easily crushed. As the sensors' line of sight moved—catching ship after ship in their field of view, wreck after wreck, indistinct masses of burnt and twisted metal, of ripped-out engines, of shattered life pods and crushed shuttles—Lan Nhen felt as if an icy fist were squeezing her heart into shards. To think of the Minds within—dead or crippled, forever unable to move . . .

"She's not there," she said, as more and more ships appeared on the screen in front of her, a mass of corpses that all threatened to overwhelm her with sorrow and grief and anger.

"Be patient, child," *The Cinnabar Mansions* said. The Mind's voice was amused, as it always was—after all, she'd lived for five centuries, and would outlive Lan Nhen and Lan Nhen's own children by so many years that the pronoun "child" seemed small and inappropriate to express the vast gulf of generations between them. "We already knew it was going to take time."

"She was supposed to be on the outskirts of the wards," Lan Nhen said, biting her lip. She had to be, or the rescue mission was going to be infinitely more complicated. "According to Cuc . . ."

"Your cousin knows what she's talking about," *The Cinnabar Mansions* said.

"I guess." Lan Nhen wished Cuc was there with them, and not sleeping in her cabin as peacefully as a baby—but *The Cinnabar Mansions* had pointed out Cuc needed to be rested for what lay ahead; and Lan Nhen had given in, vastly outranked. Still, Cuc was reliable, for narrow definitions of the term—as long as anything didn't involve social skills, or deft negotiation. For technical information, though, she didn't have an equal within the family; and her network of contacts extended deep within Outsider space. That was how they'd found out about the ward in the first place . . .

"There." The sensors beeped, and the view on the screen pulled into enhanced mode on a ship on the edge of the yard, which seemed even smaller than the hulking masses of her companions. *The Turtle's Citadel* had been from the newer generation of ships, its body more compact and more agile than its predecessors: designed for flight and manoeuvres rather than for transport, more elegant and refined than anything to come out of the Imperial Workshops—unlike the other ships, its prow and hull were decorated, painted with numerous designs from old legends and myths, all the way to the Dai Viet of Old Earth. A single gunshot marred the outside of its hull—a burn mark that had transfixed the painted citadel through one of its towers, going all the way into the heartroom and crippling the Mind that animated the ship.

"That's her," Lan Nhen said. "I would know her anywhere."

The Cinnabar Mansions had the grace not to say anything, though of course she could have matched the design to her vast databases in an eyeblink. "It's time, then. Shall I extrude a pod?"

Lan Nhen found that her hands had gone slippery with sweat, all of a sudden; and her heart was beating a frantic rhythm within her chest, like temple gongs gone mad. "I guess it's time, yes." By any standards, what they were planning was madness. To infiltrate Outsider space, no matter how isolated—to repair a ship, no matter how lightly damaged . . .

Lan Nhen watched *The Turtle's Citadel* for a while—watched the curve of the hull, the graceful tilt of the engines, away from the living quarters; the burn mark through the hull like a gunshot through a human chest. On the prow was a smaller painting, all but invisible unless one had good eyes: a single sprig of apricot flowers, signifying the New Year's good luck—calligraphied on the ship more than thirty years ago by Lan Nhen's own mother, a parting gift to her great-aunt before the ship left for her last, doomed mission.

Of course, Lan Nhen already knew every detail of that shape by heart, every single bend of the corridors within, every little nook and cranny available outside— from the blueprints, and even before that, before the rescue plan had even been the seed of a thought in her mind—when she'd stood before her ancestral altar, watching the rotating holo of a ship who was also her great-aunt, and wondering how a Mind could ever be brought down, or given up for lost.

Now she was older; old enough to have seen enough things to freeze her blood; old enough to plot her own foolishness, and drag her cousin and her great-great- aunt into it.

Older, certainly. Wiser, perhaps; if they were blessed enough to survive.

There were tales, at the Institution, of what they were—and, in any case, one only had to look at them, at their squatter, darker shapes, at the way their eyes crinkled when they laughed. There were other clues, too: the memories that made Catherine wake up breathless and disoriented, staring at the white walls of the dormitory until the pulsing, writhing images of something she couldn't quite identify had gone, and the breath of dozens of her dorm-mates had lulled her back to sleep. The craving for odd food like fish sauce and fermented meat. The dim, distant feeling of not fitting in, of being compressed on all sides by a society that made little sense to her.

It should have, though. She'd been taken as a child, like all her schoolmates— saved from the squalor and danger among the savages and brought forward into the light of civilisation—of white sterile rooms and bland food, of awkward embraces that always felt too informal. Rescued, Matron always said, her entire face transfigured, the bones of her cheeks made sharply visible through the pallor of her skin. Made safe.

Catherine had asked what she was safe from. They all did, in the beginning—all the girls in the Institution, Johanna and Catherine being the most vehement amongst them.

That was until Matron showed them the vid.

They all sat at their tables, watching the screen in the centre of the amphitheatre— silent, for once, not jostling or joking among themselves. Even Johanna, who was always first with a biting remark, had said nothing—had sat, transfixed, watching it.

The first picture was a woman who looked like them—smaller and darker- skinned than the Galactics—except that her belly protruded in front of her, huge and swollen like a tumour from some disaster movie. There was a man next to her, his unfocused eyes suggesting that he was checking something on the network through his implants—until the woman grimaced, putting a hand to her belly and calling out to him. His eyes focused in a heartbeat, and fear replaced the blank expression on his face.

There was a split second before the language overlays kicked in—a moment, frozen in time, when the words, the sounds of the syllables put together, sounded achingly familiar to Catherine, like a memory of the childhood she never could quite manage to piece together—there was a brief flash, of New Year's Eve firecrackers going off in a confined space, of her fear that they would burn her, damage her body's ability to heal . . . And then the moment was gone like a popped bubble, because the vid changed in the most horrific manner.

The camera was wobbling, rushing along a pulsing corridor—they could all hear the heavy breath of the woman, the whimpering sounds she made like an animal in pain; the soft, encouraging patter of the physician's words to her.

"She's coming," the woman whispered, over and over, and the physician nodded—keeping one hand on her shoulder, squeezing it so hard his own knuckles had turned the colour of a muddy moon.

"You have to be strong," he said. "Hanh, please. Be strong for me. It's all for the good of the Empire, may it live ten thousand years. Be strong."

The vid cut away, then—and it was wobbling more and more crazily, its field of view showing erratic bits of a cramped room with scrolling letters on the wall, the host of other attendants with similar expressions of fear on their faces; the woman, lying on a flat surface, crying out in pain—blood splattering out of her with every thrust of her hips—the camera moving, shifting between her legs, the physician's hands reaching into the darker opening—easing out a sleek, glinting shape, even as the woman screamed again—and blood, more blood running out, rivers of blood she couldn't possibly have in her body, even as the *thing* within her pulled free, and it became all too clear that, though it had the bare shape of a baby with an oversized head, it had too many cables and sharp angles to be human . . .

Then a quiet fade-to-black, and the same woman being cleaned up by the physician—the thing—the baby being nowhere to be seen. She stared up at the camera; but her gaze was unfocused, and drool was pearling at the corner of her lips, even as her hands spasmed uncontrollably.

Fade to black again; and the lights came up again, on a room that seemed to have grown infinitely colder.

"This," Matron said in the growing silence, "is how the Dai Viet birth Minds for their spaceships: by incubating them within the wombs of their women. This is the fate that would have been reserved for all of you. For each of you within this room." Her gaze raked them all; stopping longer than usual on Catherine and Johanna, the known troublemakers in the class. "This is why we had to take you away, so that you wouldn't become brood mares for abominations."

"We," of course, meant the Board—the religious nuts, as Johanna liked to call them, a redemptionist church with a fortune to throw around, financing the children's rescues and their education—and who thought every life from humans to insects was sacred (they'd all wondered, of course, where they fitted into the scheme).

After the class had dispersed like a flock of sparrows, Johanna held court in the yard, her eyes bright and feverish. "They faked it. They had to. They came up with some stupid explanation on how to keep us cooped here. I mean, why would anyone still use natural births and not artificial wombs?"

Catherine, still seeing the splatters of blood on the floor, shivered. "Matron said that they wouldn't. That they thought the birth created a special bond between the Mind and its mother—but that they had to be there, to be awake during the birth."

"Rubbish." Johanna shook her head. "As if that's even remotely plausible. I'm telling you, it has to be fake."

"It looked real." Catherine remembered the woman's screams; the wet sound as the Mind wriggled free from her womb; the fear in the face of all the physicians. "Artificial vids aren't this . . . messy." They'd seen the artificial vids; slick, smooth things where the actors were tall and muscular, the actresses pretty and graceful, with only a thin veneer of artificially generated defects to make the entire thing believable. They'd learnt to tell them apart from the rest; because it was a survival skill in the Institution, to sort out the lies from the truth.

"I bet they can fake that, too," Johanna said. "They can fake everything if they feel like it." But her face belied her words; even she had been shocked. Even she didn't believe they would have gone that far.

"I don't think it's a lie," Catherine said, finally. "Not this time."

And she didn't need to look at the other girls' faces to know that they believed the same thing as her—even Johanna, for all her belligerence—and to feel in her gut that this changed everything.

Cuc came online when the shuttle pod launched from *The Cinnabar Mansions*—in the heart-wrenching moment when the gravity of the ship fell away from Lan Nhen, and the cozy darkness of the pod's cradle was replaced with the distant forms of the derelict ships. "Hey, cousin. Missed me?" Cuc asked.

"As much as I missed a raging fire." Lan Nhen checked her equipment a last time—the pod was basic and functional, with barely enough space for her to squeeze into the cockpit, and she'd had to stash her various cables and terminals into the nooks and crannies of a structure that hadn't been meant for more than emergency evacuation. She could have asked *The Cinnabar Mansions* for a regular transport shuttle, but the pod was smaller and more controllable; and it stood more chances of evading the derelict ward's defences.

"Hahaha," Cuc said, though she didn't sound amused. "The family found out what we were doing, by the way."

"And?" It would have devastated Lan Nhen, a few years ago; now she didn't much care. She *knew* she was doing the right thing. No filial daughter would let a member of the family rust away in a foreign cemetery—if she couldn't rescue her great-aunt, she'd at least bring the body back, for a proper funeral.

"They think we're following one of Great-great-aunt's crazy plans."

"Ha," Lan Nhen snorted. Her hands were dancing on the controls, plotting a trajectory that would get her to *The Turtle's Citadel* while leaving her the maximum thrust reserve in case of unexpected manoeuvres.

"I'm not the one coming up with crazy plans," *The Cinnabar Mansions* pointed out on the comms channel, distractedly. "I leave that to the young. Hang on—" she dropped out of sight. "I have incoming drones, child."

Of course. It was unlikely the Outsiders would leave their precious war trophies unprotected. "Where?"

A translucent overlay gradually fell over her field of vision through the pod's windshield; and points lit up all over its surface—a host of fast-moving, small crafts with contextual arrows showing basic kinematics information as well as projected trajectory cones. Lan Nhen repressed a curse. "That many? They really like their wrecked spaceships, don't they."

It wasn't a question, and neither Cuc nor *The Cinnabar Mansions* bothered to answer. "They're defence drones patrolling the perimeter. We'll walk you through," Cuc said. "Give me just a few moments to link up with Great-great-aunt's systems . . ."

Lan Nhen could imagine her cousin, lying half-prone on her bed in the lower decks of *The Cinnabar Mansions*, her face furrowed in that half-puzzled, half-focused expression that was typical of her thought processes—she'd remain that way for entire minutes, or as long as it took to find a solution. On her windshield, the squad of drones was spreading—coming straight at her from all directions, a dazzling ballet of movement meant to overwhelm her. And they would, if she didn't move fast enough.

Her fingers hovered over the pod's controls, before she made her decision and launched into a barrel manoeuvre away from the nearest incoming cluster. "Cousin, how about hurrying up?"

There was no answer from Cuc. Demons take her, this wasn't the moment to overthink the problem! Lan Nhen banked, sharply, narrowly avoiding a squad of drones, who bypassed her—and then turned around, much quicker than she'd anticipated. Ancestors, they moved fast, much too fast for ion-thrust motors. Cuc was going to have to rethink her trajectory. "Cousin, did you see this?"

"I saw." Cuc's voice was distant. "Already taken into account. Given the size of the craft, it was likely they were going to use helicoidal thrusters on those."

"This is all fascinating—" Lan Nhen wove her way through two more waves of drones, cursing wildly as shots made the pod rock around her—as long as her speed held, she'd be fine . . . She'd be fine. . . . "—but you'll have noticed I don't really much care about technology, especially not now!"

A thin thread of red appeared on her screen—a trajectory that wove and banked like a frightened fish's trail—all the way to *The Turtle's Citadel* and its clusters of pod-cradles. It looked as though it was headed straight into the heart of the cloud of drones, though that wasn't the most worrying aspect of it. "Cousin," Lan Nhen said. "I can't possibly do this—" The margin of error was null—if she slipped in one of the curves, she'd never regain the kinematics necessary to take the next.

"Only way." Cuc's voice was emotionless. "I'll update as we go, if Great-great-aunt sees an opening. But for the moment . . ."

Lan Nhen closed her eyes, for a brief moment—turned them towards Heaven, though Heaven was all around her—and whispered a prayer to her ancestors, begging them to watch over her. Then she turned her gaze to the screen, and launched into flight—her hands flying and shifting over the controls, automatically adjusting the pod's path—dancing into the heart of the drones' swarm—into them, away from them, weaving an erratic path across the section of space that separated her from *The Turtle's Citadel*. Her eyes, all the while, remained on the overlay—her fingers speeding across the controls, matching the slightest deviation of her course to the set trajectory—inflecting curves a fraction of a second before the error on her course became perceptible.

"Almost there," Cuc said—with a hint of encouragement in her voice. "Come on, cousin, you can do it—"

Ahead of her, a few measures away, was *The Turtle's Citadel*: its pod cradles had shrivelled from long atrophy, but the hangar for docking the external shuttles and pods remained, its entrance a thin line of grey across the metallic surface of the ship's lower half.

"It's closed," Lan Nhen said, breathing hard—she was coming fast, much too fast, scattering drones out of her way like scared mice, and if the hangar wasn't opened . . . "Cousin!"

Cuc's voice seemed to come from very far away; distant and muted somehow on the comms system. "We've discussed this. Normally, the ship went into emergency standby when it was hit, and it should open—"

"But what if it doesn't?" Lan Nhen asked—the ship was looming over her, spreading to cover her entire windshield, close enough so she could count the pod cradles, could see their pockmarked surfaces—could imagine how much of a messy impact she'd make, if her own pod crashed on an unyielding surface.

Cuc didn't answer. She didn't need to; they both knew what would happen if that turned out to be true. Ancestors, watch over me, Lan Nhen thought, over and over, as the hangar doors rushed towards her, still closed—ancestors watch over me . . .

She was close enough to see the fine layers of engravings on the doors when they opened—the expanse of metal flowing away from the centre, to reveal a gaping hole just large enough to let a small craft through. Her own pod squeezed into the available space: darkness fell over her cockpit as the doors flowed shut, and the pod skidded to a halt, jerking her body like a disarticulated doll.

It was a while before she could stop shaking for long enough to unstrap herself from the pod; and to take her first, tentative steps on the ship.

The small lamp in her suit lit nothing but a vast, roiling mass of shadows: the hangar was huge enough to hold much larger ships. Thirty years ago, it had no doubt been full, but the Outsiders must have removed them all as they dragged the wreck out there.

"I'm in," she whispered; and set out through the darkness, to find the heartroom and the Mind that was her great-aunt.

"I'm sorry," Jason said to Catherine. "Your first choice of posting was declined by the Board."

Catherine sat very straight in her chair, trying to ignore how uncomfortable she felt in her suit—it gaped too large over her chest, flared too much at her hips, and she'd had to hastily readjust the trouser-legs after she and Johanna discovered the seamstress had got the length wrong. "I see," she said, because there was nothing else she could say, really.

Jason looked at his desk, his gaze boring into the metal as if he could summon an assignment out of nothing—she knew he meant well, that he had probably volunteered to tell her this himself, instead of leaving it for some stranger who wouldn't care a jot for her—but in that moment, she didn't want to be reminded that he worked for the Board for the Protection of Dai Viet Refugees; that he'd had a hand, no matter how small, in denying her wishes for the future.

At length Jason said, slowly, carefully—reciting a speech he'd no doubt given a dozen times that day, "The government puts the greatest care into choosing postings for the refugees. It was felt that putting you onboard a space station would be—unproductive."

Unproductive. Catherine kept smiling; kept her mask plastered on, even though it hurt to turn the corners of her mouth upwards, to crinkle her eyes as if she were pleased. "I see," she said, again, knowing anything else was useless. "Thanks, Jason."

Jason coloured. "I tried arguing your case, but . . ."

"I know," Catherine said. He was a clerk; that was all; a young civil servant at the bottom of the Board's hierarchy, and he couldn't possibly get her what she wanted, even if he'd been willing to favour her. And it hadn't been such a surprise, anyway. After Mary and Olivia and Johanna . . .

"Look," Jason said. "Let's see each other tonight, right? I'll take you someplace you can forget all about this."

"You know it's not that simple," Catherine said. As if a restaurant, or a wild waterfall ride, or whatever delight Jason had in mind could make her forget this.

"No, but I can't do anything about the Board." Jason's voice was firm. "I can, however, make sure that you have a good time tonight."

Catherine forced a smile she didn't feel. "I'll keep it in mind. Thanks."

As she exited the building, passing under the wide arches, the sun sparkled on the glass windows—and for a brief moment she wasn't herself—she was staring at starlight reflected in a glass panel, watching an older woman running hands on a wall and smiling at her with gut-wrenching sadness . . . She blinked, and the moment was gone; though the sense of sadness, of unease remained, as if she were missing something essential.

Johanna was waiting for her on the steps, her arms crossed in front of her, and a gaze that looked as though it would bore holes into the lawn.

"What did they tell you?"

Catherine shrugged, wondering how a simple gesture could cost so much. "The same they told you, I'd imagine. Unproductive."

They'd all applied to the same postings—all asked for something related to space, whether it was one of the observatories, a space station; or, in Johanna's case, outright asking to board a slow-ship as crew. They'd all been denied, for variations of the same reason.

"What did you get?" Johanna asked. Her own rumpled slip of paper had already been recycled at the nearest terminal; she was heading north, to Steele, where she'd join an archaeological dig.

Catherine shrugged, with a casualness she didn't feel. They'd always felt at ease under the stars—had always yearned to take to space, felt the same craving to be closer to their home planets—to hang, weightless and without ties, in a place where they wouldn't be weighed, wouldn't be judged for falling short of values that ultimately didn't belong to them. "I got newswriter."

"At least you're not moving very far," Johanna said, a tad resentfully.

"No." The offices of the network company were a mere two streets away from the Institution.

"I bet Jason had a hand in your posting," Johanna said.

"He didn't say anything about that—"

"Of course he wouldn't." Johanna snorted, gently. She didn't much care for Jason; but she knew how much his company meant to Catherine—how much more it would come to mean, if the weight of an entire continent separated Catherine and her. "Jason broadcasts his failures because they bother him; you'll hardly ever hear him talk of his successes. He'd feel too much like boasting." Her face changed, softened. "He cares for you, you know—truly. You have the best luck in the world."

"I know," Catherine said—thinking of the touch of his lips on hers; of his arms, holding her close until she felt whole, fulfilled. "I know."

The best luck in the world—she and Jason and her new flat, and her old haunts, not far away from the Institution—though she wasn't sure, really, if that last was a blessing—if she wanted to remember the years Matron had spent hammering proper behaviour into them: the deprivations whenever they spoke anything less than perfect Galactic, the hours spent cleaning the dormitory's toilets for expressing mild revulsion at the food; or the night they'd spent shut outside, naked, in the growing cold, because they couldn't remember which Galactic president had colonised Longevity Station—how Matron had found them all huddled against each other, in an effort to keep warm and awake, and had sent them to Discipline for a further five hours, scolding them for behaving like wild animals.

Catherine dug her nails into the palms of her hands—letting the pain anchor her back to the present; to where she sat on the steps of the Board's central offices, away from the Institution and all it meant to them.

"We're free," she said, at last. "That's all that matters."

"We'll never be free." Johanna's tone was dark, intense. "Your records have a mark that says 'Institution.' And even if it didn't—do you honestly believe we would blend right in?"

There was no one quite like them on Prime, where Dai Viet were unwelcome; not with those eyes, not with that skin colour—not with that demeanour, which even years of Institution hadn't been enough to erase.

"Do you ever wonder . . ." Johanna's voice trailed off into silence, as if she were contemplating something too large to put into words.

"Wonder what?" Catherine asked.

Johanna bit her lip. "Do you ever wonder what it would have been like, with our parents? Our real parents."

The parents they couldn't remember. They'd done the maths, too—no children at the Institution could remember anything before coming there. Matron had said it was because they were really young when they were taken away—that it had been for the best. Johanna, of course, had blamed something more sinister, some fix-up done by the Institution to its wards to keep them docile.

Catherine thought, for a moment, of a life among the Dai Viet—an idyllic image of a harmonious family like in the holo-movies—a mirage that dashed itself to pieces against the inescapable reality of the birth vid. "They'd have used us like brood mares," Catherine said. "You saw—"

"I know what I saw," Johanna snapped. "But maybe . . ." Her face was pale. "Maybe it wouldn't have been so bad, in return for the rest."

For being loved; for being made worthy; for fitting in, being able to stare at the stars without wondering which was their home—without dreaming of when they might go back to their families.

Catherine rubbed her belly, thinking of the vid—and the *thing* crawling out of the woman's belly, all metal edges and shining crystal, coated in the blood of its mother—and, for a moment she felt as though she were the woman—floating above her body, detached from her cloak of flesh, watching herself give birth in pain. And then the sensation ended, but she was still feeling spread out, larger than she ought to have been—looking at herself from a distance and watching her own life pass her by, petty and meaningless, and utterly bounded from end to end.

Maybe Johanna was right. Maybe it wouldn't have been so bad, after all.

The ship was smaller than Lan Nhen had expected—she'd been going by her experience with *The Cinnabar Mansions*, which was an older generation, but *The Turtle's Citadel* was much smaller for the same functionalities.

Lan Nhen went up from the hangar to the living quarters, her equipment slung over her shoulders. She'd expected a sophisticated defence system like the drones, but there was nothing. Just the familiar slimy feeling of a quickened ship on the walls, a sign that the Mind that it hosted was still alive—albeit barely. The walls were bare, instead of the elaborate decoration Lan Nhen was used to from *The Cinnabar Mansions*—no scrolling calligraphy, no flowing paintings of starscapes or flowers; no ambient sound of zither or anything to enliven the silence.

She didn't have much time to waste—Cuc had said they had two hours between the moment the perimeter defences kicked in, and the moment more hefty safeguards were manually activated—but she couldn't help herself: she looked into one of the living quarters. It was empty as well, its walls scored with gunfire. The only colour in the room was a few splatters of dried blood on a chair, a reminder of the tragedy of the ship's fall—the execution of its occupants, the dragging of its wreck to the derelict ward—dried blood, and a single holo of a woman on a table, a beloved mother or grandmother: a bare, abandoned picture with no offerings or incense, all that remained from a wrecked ancestral altar. Lan Nhen spat on the ground, to ward off evil ghosts, and went back to the corridors.

She truly felt as though she were within a mausoleum—like that one time her elder sister had dared her and Cuc to spend the night within the family's ancestral shrine, and they'd barely slept—not because of monsters or anything, but because of the vast silence that permeated the whole place amidst the smell of incense and funeral offerings, reminding them that they, too, were mortal.

That Minds, too, could die—that rescues were useless—no, she couldn't afford to think like that. She had Cuc with her, and together they would . . .

She hadn't heard Cuc for a while.

She stopped, when she realised—that it wasn't only the silence on the ship, but also the deathly quiet of her own comms system. Since—since she'd entered *The Turtle's Citadel*—that was the last time she'd heard her cousin, calmly pointing out about emergency standby and hangar doors and how everything was going to work out, in the end . . .

She checked her comms. There appeared to be nothing wrong; but whichever frequency she selected, she could hear nothing but static. At last, she managed to find one slot that seemed less crowded than others. "Cousin? Can you hear me?"

Noise on the line. "Very—badly." Cuc's voice was barely recognisable. "There—is—something—interference—"

"I know," Lan Nhen said. "Every channel is filled with noise."

Cuc didn't answer for a while; and when she did, her voice seemed to have become more distant—a problem had her interest again. "Not—noise. They're broadcasting—data. Need—to . . ." And then the comms cut. Lan Nhen tried all frequencies, trying to find one that would be less noisy; but there was nothing. She bit down a curse—she had no doubt Cuc would find a way around whatever blockage the Outsiders had put on the ship, but this was downright bizarre. Why broadcast data? Cutting down the comms of prospective attackers somehow didn't seem significant enough—at least not compared to defence drones or similar mechanisms.

She walked through the corridors, following the spiral path to the heartroom—nothing but the static in her ears, a throbbing song that erased every coherent thought from her mind—at least it was better than the silence, than that feeling of moving underwater in an abandoned city—that feeling that she was too late, that her great-aunt was already dead and past recovery, that all she could do here was kill her once and for all, end her misery . . .

She thought, incongruously, of a vid she'd seen, which showed her great-grandmother ensconced in the heartroom—in the first few years of *The Turtle's Citadel*'s life, those crucial moments of childhood when the ship's mother remained onboard to guide the Mind to adulthood. Great-grandmother was telling stories to the ship—and *The Turtle's Citadel* was struggling to mimic the spoken words in scrolling texts on her walls, laughing delightedly whenever she succeeded—all sweet and young, unaware of what her existence would come to, in the end.

Unlike the rest of the ship, the heartroom was crowded—packed with Outsider equipment that crawled over the Mind's resting place in the centre, covering her from end to end until Lan Nhen could barely see the glint of metal underneath. She gave the entire contraption a wide berth—the spikes and protrusions from the original ship poked at odd angles, glistening with a dark liquid she couldn't quite identify—and the Outsider equipment piled atop the Mind, a mass of cables and unfamiliar machines, looked as though it was going to take a while to sort out.

There were screens all around, showing dozens of graphs and diagrams, shifting as they tracked variables that Lan Nhen couldn't guess at—vital signs, it looked like, though she wouldn't have been able to tell what.

Lan Nhen bowed in the direction of the Mind, from younger to elder—perfunctorily, since she was unsure whether the Mind could see her at all. There was no acknowledgement, either verbal or otherwise.

Her great-aunt was in there. She had to be.

"Cousin." Cuc's voice was back in her ears—crisp and clear and uncommonly worried.

"How come I can hear you?" Lan Nhen asked. "Because I'm in the heartroom?"

Cuc snorted. "Hardly. The heartroom is where all the data is streaming from. I've merely found a way to filter the transmissions on both ends. Fascinating problem . . ."

"Is this really the moment?" Lan Nhen asked. "I need you to walk me through the reanimation—"

"No you don't," Cuc said. "First you need to hear what I have to say."

The call came during the night: a man in the uniform of the Board asked for Catherine George—as if he couldn't tell that it was her, that she was standing dishevelled and pale in front of her screen at three in the morning. "Yes, it's me," Catherine said. She fought off the weight of nightmares—more and more, she was waking in the night with memories of blood splattered across her entire body; of stars collapsing while she watched, powerless—of a crunch, and a moment where she hung alone in darkness, knowing that she had been struck a death blow—

The man's voice was quiet, emotionless. There had been an accident in Steele; a regrettable occurrence that hadn't been meant to happen, and the Board would have liked to extend its condolences to her—they apologised for calling so late, but they thought she should know . . .

"I see," Catherine said. She kept herself uncomfortably straight—aware of the last time she'd faced the board—when Jason had told her her desire for space would have been unproductive. When they'd told Johanna . . .

Johanna.

After a while, the man's words slid past her like water on glass—hollow reassurances, empty condolences, whereas she stood as if her heart had been torn away from her, fighting a desire to weep, to retch—she wanted to turn back time, to go back to the previous week and the sprigs of apricot flowers Jason had given her with a shy smile—to breathe in the sharp, tangy flavour of the lemon cake he'd baked for her, see again the carefully blank expression on his face as he waited to see if she'd like it—she wanted to be held tight in his arms and told that it was fine, that everything was going to be fine, that Johanna was going to be fine.

"We're calling her other friends," the man was saying, "but since you were close to each other . . ."

"I see," Catherine said—of course he didn't understand the irony, that it was the answer she'd given the Board—Jason—the last time.

The man cut off the communication; and she was left alone, standing in her living room and fighting back the feeling that threatened to overwhelm her—a not-entirely unfamiliar sensation of dislocation in her belly, the awareness that she didn't belong here among the Galactics; that she wasn't there by choice, and couldn't leave; that her own life should have been larger, more fulfilling than this slow death by inches, writing copy for feeds without any acknowledgement of her contributions—that Johanna's life should have been larger . . .

Her screen was still blinking—an earlier message from the Board that she hadn't seen? But why—

Her hands, fumbling away in the darkness, made the command to retrieve the message—the screen faded briefly to black while the message was decompressed, and then she was staring at Johanna's face.

For a moment—a timeless, painful moment—Catherine thought with relief that it had been a mistake, that Johanna was alive after all; and then she realised how foolish she'd been—that it wasn't a call, but merely a message from beyond the grave.

Johanna's face was pale, so pale Catherine wanted to hug her, to tell her the old lie that things were going to be fine—but she'd never get to say those words now, not ever.

"I'm sorry, Catherine," she said. Her voice was shaking; and the circles under her eyes took up half of her face, turning her into some pale nightmare from horror movies—a ghost, a restless soul, a ghoul hungry for human flesh. "I can't do this, not anymore. The Institution was fine; but it's got worse. I wake up at night, and feel sick—as if everything good has been leeched from the world—as if the food had no taste, as if I drifted like a ghost through my days, as if my entire life held no meaning or truth. Whatever they did to our memories in the Institution—it's breaking down now. It's tearing me apart. I'm sorry, but I can't take any more of this. I—" she looked away from the camera for a brief moment, and then back at Catherine. "I have to go."

"No," Catherine whispered, but she couldn't change it. She couldn't do anything.

"You were always the strongest of us," Johanna said. "Please remember this. Please. Catherine." And then the camera cut, and silence spread through the room, heavy and unbearable, and Catherine felt like weeping, though she had no tears left.

"Catherine?" Jason called in a sleepy voice from the bedroom. "It's too early to check your work inbox . . ."

Work. Love. Meaningless, Johanna had said. Catherine walked to the huge window pane, and stared at the city spread out below her—the mighty Prime, centre of the Galactic Federation, its buildings shrouded in light, its streets crisscrossed by floaters; with the bulky shape of the Parliament at the centre, a proud statement that the Galactic Federation still controlled most of their home galaxy.

Too many lights to see the stars; but she could still guess; could still feel their pull—could still remember that one of them was her home.

A lie, Johanna had said. A construction to keep us here.

"Catherine?" Jason stood behind her, one hand wrapped around her shoulder—awkwardly tender as always, like that day when he'd offered to share a flat, standing balanced on one foot and not looking at her.

"Johanna is dead. She killed herself."

She felt rather than saw him freeze—and, after a while, he said in a changed voice, "I'm so sorry. I know how much she meant . . ." His voice trailed off, and he too, fell silent, watching the city underneath.

There was a feeling—the same feeling she'd had when waking up as a child, a diffuse sense that something was not quite right with the world; that the shadows held men watching, waiting for the best time to snatch her; that she was not wholly back in her body—that Jason's hand on her shoulder was just the touch of a ghost, that even his love wasn't enough to keep her safe. That the world was fracturing around her, time and time again—she breathed in, hoping to dispel the sensation. Surely it was nothing more than grief, than fatigue—but the sensation wouldn't go away, leaving her on the verge of nausea.

"You should have killed us," Catherine said. "It would have been kinder."

"Killed you?" Jason sounded genuinely shocked.

"When you took us from our parents."

Jason was silent for a while. Then: "We don't kill. What do you think we are, monsters from the fairytales, killing and burning everyone who looks different? Of course we're not like that." Jason no longer sounded uncertain or awkward; it was as if she'd touched some wellspring, scratched some skin to find only primal reflexes underneath.

"You erased our memories." She didn't make any effort to keep the bitterness from her voice.

"We had to." Jason shook his head. "They'd have killed you, otherwise. You know this."

"How can I trust you?" Look at Johanna, she wanted to say. Look at me. How can you say it was all worth it?

"Catherine . . ." Jason's voice was weary. "We've been over this before. You've seen the vids from the early days. We didn't set out to steal your childhood, or anyone's childhood. But when you were left—intact . . . accidents happened. Carelessness. Like Johanna."

"Like Johanna." Her voice was shaking now; but he didn't move, didn't do anything to comfort her or hold her close. She turned at last, to stare into his face; and saw him transfixed by light, by faith, his gaze turned away from her and every pore of his being permeated by the utter conviction that he was right, that they were all right and that a stolen childhood was a small price to pay to be a Galactic.

"Anything would do." Jason's voice was slow, quiet—explaining life to a child, a script they'd gone over and over in their years together, always coming back to the same enormous, inexcusable choice that had been made for them. "Scissors, knives, broken bottles. You sliced your veins, hanged yourselves, pumped yourselves full of drugs . . . We had to . . . we had to block your memories, to make you blank slates."

"Had to." She was shaking now; and still he didn't see. Still she couldn't make him see.

"I swear to you, Catherine. It was the only way."

And she knew, she'd always known he was telling the truth—not because he was right, but because he genuinely could not envision any other future for them.

"I see," she said. The nausea, the sense of dislocation, wouldn't leave her—disgust for him, for this life that trapped her, for everything she'd turned into or been turned into. "I see."

"Do you think I like it?" His voice was bitter. "Do you think it makes me sleep better at night? Every day I hate that choice, even though I wasn't the one who made it. Every day I wonder if there was something else the Board could have done, some other solution that wouldn't have robbed you of everything you were."

"Not everything," Catherine said—slowly, carefully. "We still look Dai Viet."

Jason grimaced, looking ill at ease. "That's your *body*, Catherine. Of course they weren't going to steal that."

Of course; and suddenly, seeing how uneasy he was, it occurred to Catherine that they could have changed that, too, just as easily as they'd tampered with her memories; made her skin clearer, her eyes less distinctive; could have helped her fit into Galactic society. But they hadn't. Holding the strings to the last, Johanna would have said. "You draw the line at my body, but stealing my memories is fine?"

Jason sighed; he turned towards the window, looking at the streets. "No, it's not, and I'm sorry. But how else were we supposed to keep you alive?"

"Perhaps we didn't want to be alive."

"Don't say that, please." His voice had changed, had become fearful, protective. "Catherine. Everyone deserves to live. You especially."

Perhaps I don't, she thought, but he was holding her close to him, not letting her go—her anchor to the flat—to the living room, to life. "You're not Johanna," he said. "You know that."

The strongest of us, Johanna had said. She didn't feel strong; just frail and adrift. "No," she said, at last. "Of course I'm not."

"Come on," Jason said. "Let me make you a tisane. We'll talk in the kitchen—you look as though you need it."

"No." And she looked up—sought out his lips in the darkness, drinking in his breath and his warmth to fill the emptiness within her. "That's not what I need."

"Are you sure?" Jason looked uncertain—sweet and innocent and naïve, everything that had drawn her to him. "You're not in a state to—"

"Ssh," she said, and laid a hand on his lips, where she'd kissed him. "Ssh."

Later, after they'd made love, she lay her head in the hollow of his arm, listening to the slow beat of his heart like a lifeline; and wondered how long she'd be able to keep the emptiness at bay.

"It goes to Prime," Cuc said. "All the data is beamed to Prime, and it's coming from almost every ship in the ward."

"I don't understand," Lan Nhen said. She'd plugged her own equipment into the ship, carefully shifting the terminals she couldn't make sense of—hadn't dared to go closer to the centre, where Outsider technology had crawled all over her great-aunt's resting place, obscuring the Mind and the mass of connectors that linked her to the ship.

On one of the screens, a screensaver had launched: night on a planet Lan Nhen couldn't recognise—an Outsider one, with their sleek floaters and their swarms of helper bots, their wide, impersonal streets planted with trees that were too tall and too perfect to be anything but the product of years of breeding.

"She's not here," Cuc said.

"I—" Lan Nhen was about to say she didn't understand, and then the true import of Cuc's words hit her. "Not here? She's alive, Cuc. I can see the ship; I can hear her all around me . . ."

"Yes, yes," Cuc said, a tad impatiently. "But that's . . . the equivalent of unconscious processes, like breathing in your sleep."

"She's dreaming?"

"No," Cuc said. A pause, then, very carefully: "I think she's on Prime, Cousin. The data that's being broadcast—it looks like Mind thought-processes, compressed with a high rate and all mixed together. There's probably something on the other end that decompresses the data and sends it to . . . Arg, I don't know! Wherever they think is appropriate."

Lan Nhen bit back another admission of ignorance, and fell back on the commonplace. "On Prime." The enormity of the thing; that you could take a Mind—a beloved ship with a family of her own—that you could put her to sleep and cause her to wake up somewhere else, on an unfamiliar planet and an alien culture—that you could just transplant her like a flower or a tree . . . "She's on Prime."

"In a terminal or as the power source for something," Cuc said, darkly.

"Why would they bother?" Lan Nhen asked. "It's a lot of power expenditure just to get an extra computer."

"Do I look as though I have insight into Outsiders?" Lan Nhen could imagine Cuc throwing her hands up in the air, in that oft-practised gesture. "I'm just telling you what I have, Cousin."

Outsiders—the Galactic Federation of United Planets—were barely comprehensible in any case. They were the descendants of an Exodus fleet that had hit an isolated galaxy: left to themselves and isolated for decades, they had turned on each other in huge ethnic cleansings before emerging from their home planets as relentless competitors for resources and inhabitable planets.

"Fine. Fine." Lan Nhen breathed in, slowly; tried to focus at the problem at hand. "Can you walk me through cutting the radio broadcast?"

Cuc snorted. "I'd fix the ship, first, if I were you."

Lan Nhen knelt by the equipment, and stared at a cable that had curled around one of the ship's spines. "Fine, let's start with what we came for. Can you see?"

Silence; and then a life-sized holo of Cuc hovered in front of her—even though the avatar was little more than broad strokes, great-great-aunt had still managed to render it in enough details to make it unmistakably Cuc. "Cute," Lan Nhen said.

"Hahaha," Cuc said. "No bandwidth for trivialities—gotta save for detail on your end." She raised a hand, pointed to one of the outermost screens on the edge of the room. "Disconnect this one first."

It was slow, and painful. Cuc pointed; and Lan Nhen checked before disconnecting and moving. Twice, she jammed her fingers very close to a cable, and felt electricity crackle near her—entirely too close for comfort.

They moved from the outskirts of the room to the centre—tackling the huge mount of equipment last. Cuc's first attempts resulted in a cable coming loose with an ominous sound; they waited, but nothing happened. "We might have fried something," Lan Nhen said.

"Too bad. There's no time for being cautious, as you well know. There's . . . maybe half an hour left before the other defences go live." Cuc moved again, pointed to another squat terminal. "This goes off."

When they were finished, Lan Nhen stepped back, to look at their handiwork.

The heartroom was back to its former glory: instead of Outsider equipment, the familiar protrusions and sharp organic needles of the Mind's resting place; and they could see the Mind herself—resting snug in her cradle, wrapped around the controls of the ship—her myriad arms each seizing one rack of connectors; her huge head glinting in the light—a vague globe shape covered with glistening cables and veins. The burn mark from the Outsider attack was clearly visible, a dark, elongated shape on the edge of her head that had bruised a couple of veins—it had hit one of the connectors as well, burnt it right down to the colour of ink.

Lan Nhen let out a breath she hadn't been aware of holding. "It scrambled the connector."

"And scarred her, but didn't kill her," Cuc said. "Just like you said."

"Yes, but—" But it was one thing to run simulations of the attack over and over, always getting the same prognosis; and quite another to see that the simulations held true, and that the damage was repairable.

"There should be another connector rack in your bag," Cuc said. "I'll walk you through slotting it in."

After she was done, Lan Nhen took a step back; and stared at her great-aunt—feeling, in some odd way, as though she were violating the Mind's privacy. A Mind's heartroom was their stronghold, a place where they could twist reality as they wished, and appear as they wished to. To see her great-aunt like this, without any kind of appearance change or pretence, was . . . more disturbing than she'd thought.

"And now?" she asked Cuc.

Even without details, Lan Nhen knew her cousin was smiling. "Now we pray to our ancestors that cutting the broadcast is going to be enough to get her back."

Another night on Prime, and Catherine wakes up breathless, in the grip of another nightmare—images of red lights, and scrolling texts, and a feeling of growing cold in her bones, a cold so deep she cannot believe she will ever feel warm no matter how many layers she's put on.

Johanna is not there; beside her, Jason sleeps, snoring softly; and she's suddenly seized by nausea, remembering what he said to her—how casually he spoke of blocking her memories, of giving a home to her after stealing her original one from her. She waits for it to pass; waits to settle into her old life as usual. But it doesn't.

Instead, she rises, walks towards the window, and stands watching Prime—the clean wide streets, the perfect trees, the ballet of floaters at night—the myriad dances that make up the society that constrains her from dawn to dusk and beyond—she wonders what Johanna would say, but of course Johanna won't ever say anything anymore. Johanna has gone ahead, into the dark.

The feeling of nausea in her belly will not go away: instead it spreads, until her body feels like a cage—at first, she thinks the sensation is in her belly, but it moves upwards, until her limbs, too, feel too heavy and too small—until it's an effort to move any part of her. She raises her hands, struggling against a feeling of moving appendages that don't belong to her—and traces the contours of her face, looking for familiar shapes, for anything that will anchor her to reality. The heaviness spreads, compresses her chest until she can hardly breathe—cracks her ribs and pins her legs to the ground. Her head spins, as if she were about to faint; but the mercy of blackness does not come to her.

"Catherine," she whispers. "My name is Catherine."

Another name, unbidden, rises to her lips. *Mi Chau*. A name she gave to herself in the Viet language—in the split instant before the lasers took her apart, before she sank into darkness: Mi Chau, the princess who unwittingly betrayed her father and her people, and whose blood became the pearls at the bottom of the sea. She tastes it on her tongue, and it's the only thing that seems to belong to her anymore.

She remembers that first time—waking up on Prime in a strange body, struggling to breathe, struggling to make sense of being so small, so far away from the stars that had guided her through space—remembers walking like a ghost through the corridors of the Institution, until the knowledge of what the Galactics had done broke her, and she cut her veins in a bathroom, watching blood lazily pool at her feet and thinking only of escape. She remembers the second time she woke up; the second, oblivious life as Catherine.

Johanna. Johanna didn't survive her second life; and even now is starting her third, somewhere in the bowels of the Institution—a dark-skinned child indistinguishable from other dark-skinned children, with no memories of anything beyond a confused jumble . . .

Outside, the lights haven't dimmed, but there are stars—brash and alien, hovering above Prime, in configurations that look *wrong*; and she remembers, suddenly, how they lay around her, how they showed her the way from planet to planet—how the cold of the deep spaces seized her just as she entered them to travel faster, just like it's holding her now, seizing her bones—remembers how much larger, how much wider she ought to be . . .

There are stars everywhere; and superimposed on them, the faces of two Dai Viet women, calling her over and over. Calling her back, into the body that belonged to her all along; into the arms of her family.

"Come on, come on," the women whisper, and their voices are stronger than any other noise; than Jason's breath in the bedroom; than the motors of the floaters or the vague smell of garlic from the kitchen. "Come on, great-aunt!"

She is more than this body; more than this constrained life—her thoughts spread out, encompassing hangars and living quarters; and the liquid weight of pods held in their cradles—she remembers family reunions, entire generations of children putting their hands on her corridors, remembers the touch of their skin on her metal walls; the sound of their laughter as they raced each other; the quiet chatter of their mothers in the heartroom, keeping her company as the New Year began; and the touch of a brush on her outer hull, drawing the shape of an apricot flower, for good luck . . .

"Catherine?" Jason calls behind her.

She turns, through sheer effort of will; finding, somehow, the strength to maintain her consciousness in a small and crammed body alongside her other, vaster one. He's standing with one hand on the doorjamb, staring at her—his face pale, leeched of colours in the starlight.

"I remember," she whispers.

His hands stretch, beseeching. "Catherine, please. Don't leave."

He means well, she knows. All the things that he hid from her, he hid out of love; to keep her alive and happy, to hold her close in spite of all that should have separated them; and even now, the thought of his love is a barb in her heart, a last lingering regret, slight and pitiful against the flood of her memories—but not wholly insignificant.

Where she goes, she'll never be alone—not in the way she was with Jason, feeling that nothing else but her mattered in the entire world. She'll have a family; a gaggle of children and aunts and uncles waiting on her, but nothing like the sweet, unspoiled privacy where Jason and she could share anything and everything. She won't have another lover like him—naïve and frank and so terribly sure of what he wants and what he's ready to do to get it. Dai Viet society has no place for people like Jason—who do not know their place, who do not know how to be humble, how to accept failure or how to bow down to expediency.

Where she goes, she'll never be alone; and yet she'll be so terribly lonely.

"Please," Jason says.

"I'm sorry," she says. "I'll come back—" a promise made to him; to Johanna, who cannot hear or recognise her anymore. Her entire being spreads out, thins like water thrown on the fire—and, in that last moment, she finds herself reaching out for him, trying to touch him one last time, to catch one last glimpse of his face, even as a heart she didn't know she had breaks.

"Catherine."

He whispers her name, weeping, over and over; and it's that name, that lie that still clings to her with its bittersweet memories, that she takes with her as her entire being unfolds—as she flies away, towards the waiting stars.

A MAP OF MERCURY

ALASTAIR REYNOLDS

Alastair Reynolds is a frequent contributor to Interzone, Asimov's Science Fiction, Spectrum SF, Arc, *and elsewhere. His first novel,* Revelation Space, *was widely hailed as one of the major SF books of the year; it was quickly followed by* Chasm City, Redemption Ark, Absolution Gap, Century Rain, *and* Pushing Ice, *all big sprawling space operas that were big sellers as well, establishing Reynolds as one of the best and most popular new SF writers to enter the field in many years. His other books include a novella collection,* Diamond Dogs, Turquoise Days *and a chapbook novella,* The Six Directions of Space, *as well as three collections of short stories,* Galactic North, Zima Blue and Other Stories, *and* Deep Navigation. *His other novels include* The Prefect, House of Suns, Terminal World, Blue Remembered Earth, *and a Doctor Who novel,* Harvest of Time. *His most recent book is a new novel,* On the Steel Breeze. *As a professional scientist with a Ph.D. in astronomy, he worked for the European Space Agency in the Netherlands for a number of years, but has recently moved back to his native Wales to become a full-time writer.*

Here he takes us to the broiling, inhospitable planet Mercury, in the company of an emissary who must find a way to negotiate with groups of artists who are in the process of renouncing and abandoning their organic human existence altogether.

When at last his ship had escaped Mercury's gravitational pull and aligned itself for the long cruise back to Jupiter space, Oleg unstrapped from his launch couch and floated through the cabin until he reached the aft stowage rack where he had slotted the artwork. It had been a fight against temptation, not opening the box until now, but he had promised himself that he would not do so until he had reached space. Perhaps it was unwise to open it at all, and certainly before he surrendered it to his Jovian masters. But he had been given no special instructions in the matter.

The box was light, almost too light, as if it contained no more than air or packing. Was it a last trick on the world, he wondered? An empty container? A box full of high-grade vacuum?

He would have to open it to know.

The container was an unprepossessing object. It was a plain white in colour. Its upper third was hinged and secured by a simple metal clasp. It was the kind of thing, he reflected, in which one might receive a hat or perhaps a new space helmet.

The clasp released easily under his fingers. He hinged open the top of the box. Immediately beneath the lid lay, as anticipated, a wadding of packaging. He plucked the cottony material away, until a harder form began to reveal itself. It was the upper part of a rough-textured sphere. It was beautifully shaded and coloured—a warm grey, relieved by blue and gold mottling and the circles and sprays of fine white cratering. The polar region glittered with tiny embedded diamonds, signifying motherlodes of frozen water, locked in shadowed craters for mindless aeons.

Well, of course. It was a globe. The clue had been there in the title all along.

A Map of Mercury.

He had come in with high expectations—unrealistically high, perhaps.

The artists kept the place clean. Being cyborgs they could tolerate both the lit and unlit faces of the slow-turning world, but they moved anyway—camping and then travelling on, endlessly. Except for their artforms, littering the crust like Ozymandis heads, they left no trace of themselves. On airless Mercury the shadows of these things clawed out to the limit of the world's curvature.

From orbit he had locked onto their moving caravan. It had only been a little distance ahead of the terminator, the dividing margin between day and night.

"Hello," he declared cheerfully. "I have come from Jupiter. I would like permission to land and speak with Rhawn."

"This is the Cyborg Artistic Collective," came back the reply. "Thank you for your interest, but your request to speak with Rhawn is declined."

Oleg smiled, for this was nothing more or less than he had anticipated. "I'd still like to land. Is that possible?"

"Do you have tradeable goods?"

"Yes, and I'd also like to barter for fuel. I can set my ship down a little ahead of your caravan and cross the remaining ground on foot."

"That is acceptable," the voice said eventually. "One of us will meet you. Bring your tradeables."

He lowered on thrust until his little ship pinned itself to the face of Mercury like a brooch. Once down, it flicked a parasol across itself and began to cool down.

Oleg emerged from an airlock in a bulky spacesuit patterned with active mirror facets and fanlike cooling vanes. He went around to the back of the ship and unpacked two scuttling chrome spiders. The robots helped him unload the tradeable goods from the ship's belly hatch. Then he orientated himself and set off for the caravan, with the spiders following.

Here the Mercurean terrain was as flat as a salt lake. The caravan was a huge, raggedy thing composed of many travelling elements. Some as small as a person— some, indeed, were cyborgs jogging next to the procession—while others were as big as mansions or beached spacecraft. The larger structures were made up of a bits of scavenged vehicle, fuel tank and pressure module, cut-and-shut into rococo dwellings. Sails, banners and penants whipped high into the airless black. On one platform travelled the huge, lacy outline of a two hundred metre high stallion. Inside the horse's geodesic chest cavity, tiny figures worked with nova-bright welding torches. Another form, equally tall, was a naked human woman balancing on one leg. She had her arms cantilevered out for balance, one ahead and one behind. Jammed into her torso at odd, disruptive angles were repurposed cargo modules.

One of the cyborgs broke from the pack and jogged out to meet him. Beneath its knees, the cyborg's legs were springy prosthetics that sent it metres into the sky with each stride.

"Welcome, Oleg," said a synthetic voice. "We spoke earlier. I am Gris. Have you been to Mercury before?"

"No, this is my first time. Thank you for allowing me to land."

"That is a very impressive suit," Gris said. "I imagine it could keep you alive for quite a while?"

"Not as long as yours, I'd wager," Oleg said.

"Ah, but we don't think of our suits as *suits*." Gris touched a fist to its chest, in a kind of salute. "This is my skin, now and forever. I'm wired into it on a profound sensory level—full haptic and proprioceptive integration. I don't just *live* in it—it's part of me. I trust that doesn't unsettle you?"

"If it did, I'd be the wrong person to come to Mercury. And definitely the wrong person to speak to the Cyborg Artistic Collective."

Gris's suit—or skin, if that was the proper way to think of it—was a mechanical integument giving little hint of the organic contents within. The armour was multicoloured and baroquely patterned. Gris's helmet had become a beak-faced gargoyle, with multiple cameras wedged into its eye-sockets. There was no glass or visor.

"I know you've come a long away," Gris said. "But you mustn't take Rhawn's disinterest personally."

They walked under the Sun. In Oleg's view it had no business being *that big* or *that bright*. The intensity of its illumination, averaged over an orbit, was a hundred times stronger than he was normally used to. That bloated inflamed Sun was an affront to his sensibilities. It would be very good to be on his way from Mercury, back to the civilised polities of Jovian Space.

But not without the thing he had come for.

"Rhawn's star has risen," he observed.

"It makes no difference to her. Mercury is her home now. The sooner people accept that, the happier everyone will be. Are those your tradeables?"

"It's not much, I know. But there are some rare alloys and composites in there, which you may find of value."

When they were at the caravan cyborgs were waiting to pick through his offerings. A value would be placed on the items, which Oleg was free to accept or decline.

"You can come aboard," Gris said casually. "We have provision for guests, if you wish to get out of the suit. It will take a little while to give you a value for your goods, so you may as well."

"Thank you," Oleg agreed.

Gris brought him to one of the sliding, sledge-like platforms. They vaulted up onto a catwalk, then found an airlock leading into the side of a chequered structure made from an old fuel tank. Oleg satisfied himself by just removing the helmet and gloves, placing them next to him on a kind of combination sofa and padded mattress. Gris, squatting on the other side of a table, had removed no part of its suit except the spring extensions of its legs, presently racked by the door. Now it busied itself pouring herbal infusions into little alloy cups.

"Were you an artist before you came here?" Oleg asked, to be making conversation.

"Not at all. In fact I came to trade, just like you. My spaceship needed some repairs, so my stay turned from days into weeks. I had no intention of becoming part of the Collective."

"Were you . . . like this?"

"Cyborgized, you mean? No, not at all. A few simple implants, but they don't really count." The goggled face was inscrutable, even as it decanted tea into a little receptacle on the end of its beaklike mandible. "It was a difficult decision to stay, but one that in hindsight was almost inevitable. There's nowhere like this anywhere else in the system, Oleg—nowhere as simultaneously lawless and civilised. Around Jupiter, you're bound up in rigid hierarchies of wealth and power. Here we have no money, no legal apparatus, no government."

"But to become what you are now . . . that can't have been something you took lightly."

"There's no going back," Gris admitted. "The crossing—that's what we call it—is far too thorough for that. I sold my skin to the flesh banks around Venus! But the benefits are incalculable. On Mars, they're remaking the world to fit people. Here, we're doing something much nobler: remaking ourselves to fit Mercury."

"And was Rhawn already here, when you were transformed?"

"Ah," Gris said, with a miff of disappointment. "Back to that now, are we?"

"I've been sent to make contact. My masters will be very disappointed in me if I fail."

"Masters," Gris dismissed. "Why would you ever work for someone, if you had a choice?"

"I had no choice."

"Then I am afraid you had best prepare to disappoint your masters."

Oleg smiled and sipped at his tea. It was quite sweet, although not as warm as he would have liked. He presumed that Gris still had enough of a digestive tract to process fluids. "Rhawn's early work, what she did before she came here, was just too original and unsettling to fit into anyone's existing critical framework. They wanted her to be something she was not—more like the artists they already valued. In time, of course, they began to realise her worth. Her stock began to rise. But by then Rhawn had joined your Collective."

"None of this is disputed, Oleg. But Rhawn has had her crossing—become one of us. She has no interest in your world of investors and speculators, of critics and reputations."

"Nonetheless, my masters have a final offer. I would be remiss if I did not try everything in my power to bring it to Rhawn's attention."

"Forget dangling money before her."

"It isn't money." Oleg, knowing he had the momentary advantage, continued to sip his tea. "They know that wouldn't work. What they are offering, what they have secured, is something money almost couldn't buy—not without all the right con-nections, anyway. A private moon, a place of her own—the space to work unob-structed, with limitless resources. More than that, she'll have the attentions of the system's best surgeons. Their retro-transformative capabilities are easily sufficient to undo her crossing, if that's what she desires."

"I assure you it would not be."

"When she completed the crossing," Oleg said patiently, "she would have sur-rendered to the total impossibility of ever undoing that work. But the landscape has changed! The economics of her reputation now allow what was forbidden. She must be informed of this."

"She'll say no."

"Then let her! All I request—all my masters ask of me—is that Rhawn gives me her answer in person. Will you allow me that, Gris? Will you let me meet with Rhawn, just the once?"

Gris took its time answering. Oleg speculated that some dialogue might be tak-ing place beyond his immediate ken, Gris communing with its fellow artists, per-haps even Rhawn herself. Perhaps they were working out the best way to give him a brush-off. The Collective needed to trade with outsiders, so they would not want to be too brusque. Equally, they were obviously very protective of their most feted member.

But at length Gris said: "There is a difficulty."

Oleg stirred on his mattress. The suit was starting to chafe—it was not built for lounging around in. "What sort? I'm here, aren't I? Why can't I have a moment with Rhawn? Is she unwell?"

"No," Gris answered carefully. "Rhawn is perfectly well. But she is not here."

"I don't understand. She can't have left Mercury—no one would have missed that. And the Collective is all there is. Has she gone off on her own?"

"Not exactly. But you are wrong in one matter. The Collective is not all that there is. Or at least, it isn't any more. There has been . . ." And now Oleg had the sense that Gris was choosing its words with particular care, and not a small measure of distaste, as if it found the whole business painful. "A division within our ranks. The formation of a second caravan. A breakaway movement, springing from within the Collective."

Oleg listened intently. His masters either knew nothing of this, or they had failed to brief him adequately. "When, what, how?"

"It would probably be easier if I showed you," Gris said.

Soon the caravan had fallen behind them, receding over the horizon until even the stallion and the balancing woman were lost. Their shadows, Oleg noticed, were slowly lengthening, stretching ahead of the fast little surface vehicle Gris had com-mandeered. Mercury was a small world and they were covering ground very rapidly, pushing the Sun toward the horizon. Beyond, but closer by the moment, was the transition zone of the terminator and the extreme cold of the unlit face. He thought of his delicate little ship, how far he was from it now, how totally at the mercy of his cyborg host.

"Tell me about Rhawn."

"There's not much to say. She was always restless—in her art and her soul. It's what brought her to Mercury. She found contentment with us, for a while. But always there was that need to push against her own limits, to break out of existing formalisms. It was only a matter of time before she attached herself to the Totalists."

"The breakaway movement?"

"Of course."

"You said they'd formed a second caravan. Do they move around Mercury, the same way you do?"

"Most of the time. They're camped now."

"What's so special about them, that Rhawn had to leave the rest of you? Aren't you radical enough?"

"They are purists. Extremists, if you will. We have accepted extensive physiological alteration to adapt to life on the Playa. It enables us to work almost without restriction, to submit ourselves to the act of artistic creation. But even we have limits."

"Really?"

"Our bodies and minds are still hampered by the design compromises of biology. In the Totalists' view, that makes us inefficient and in need of radical improvement."

"What could be more efficient than you?" Oleg asked.

"Robots," Gris said.

At length they traversed the terminator and entered the starlit nightside of Mercury. In his suit Oleg felt nothing of the precipitous temperature drop, seven hundred awesome kelvins of it, but the faceplate markers recorded the transition from appalling heat to appalling cold clearly enough, and now the suit was having to work just as competently to keep him from freezing to death. He supposed that Gris's life-support mechanisms were coping with a similar shift in demands.

"They keep away from us, mostly," Gris said. "We aren't enemies, as such. We are obliged to conduct a certain amount of business, and of course the Totalists have no contact with the outside world at all. On the rare occasions when they need something, they have to rely on our cooperation. But I would not say our relationship is an easy one. There have been . . . acts of artistic sabotage. Denied, of course. But it's no secret that the Totalists view our work as decadent, corrupted, mired in a state of creative exhaustion."

"I suppose it was inevitable," Oleg said. "There can't have been an artistic movement in history that hasn't eventually fractured into two or more creative poles. If it's any consolation, they'll have their own splitters sooner or later!"

"No," Gris said. "It's no consolation at all. We made something beautiful here, Oleg. There's no reason in the world it had to break up like this."

As they approached the Totalists' encampment Oleg was struck by how profoundly the scene resembled an exact negative image of the dayside caravan. The sky was a nearly faultless black, its perfection only marred (or improved upon, perhaps) by a sprinkling of stars and planets, the great glittery arch of the Milky Way and the faint dust haze of the solar system's zodiacal light.

Whereas the caravan had moved under the full blaze of day, here the only lights were those provided by the Totalists themselves. The encampment was smaller than the caravan, but the essentials were similar: it was a cluster of things which could be dragged or self-propelled across Mercury, when the time came to move. They also had sails and pennants, except that these were picked out in edges of colourful neon: reds and yellows, blues and greens, purples and oranges. The figures moving around the camp's periphery were also outlined in bright hues. Oleg had been expecting something austere, but the proliferation of colours and shapes elevated his spirits.

"It's marvellous!" he said.

Rising from the illuminated camp was what Oleg took to be a piece of large-scale art in the same spirit as the stallion and the balancing woman. It was a cluster of spires, or perhaps a single main spire attended by a large number of smaller ones, linked by a connecting tissue of arches and flying buttresses. The pale structure had a knobby, rough-cast haphazardness about it. It might almost have been glued together from millions of sea-shells, or fossils.

"The Bone Cathedral," Gris said, with a hint of dismissiveness.

"Do they move that around with them? It looks much too fragile."

"No, it stays fixed to this spot. They've been building it for several years now. The day and night cycles don't seem to do it any harm. When it is time for a new Totalist to complete their crossing, the caravan circles the Bone Cathedral." Gris applied the brakes and brought the vehicle to a halt. They were still a decent kilometre from the Totalist encampment. "You'd best go the rest of the way yourself."

"What do I do?"

"You need do nothing. They will either talk to you or ignore you. They already know that you are here."

He disembarked from the vehicle. He looked up at the goggle-faced creature that had become his companion, fully aware that if Gris abandoned him here—and the Totalists disdained to help—he would be in a great deal of trouble. They had come much too far for the range of his suit.

"I would not be too long about it," Gris warned.

So Oleg wandered across the black Playa. His suit projected a terrain overlay. It was still functioning properly. He kept looking back, making sure the vehicle and the cyborg still waited. But Gris remained. And as the Totalist camp loomed larger, so one of the neon forms broke away from the blaze of colour and came loping over to meet him.

The thing had arms and legs, a body and a head in roughly the right proportions, but there was no possibility that it was anything but a robot. There was no room in it for anything human. The thing's chassis was an open exoskeleton, offering an easy view of its internal mechanisms. Oleg saw lots of machinery in there, much of it lit up and flashing in pretty colours, but there was nothing that looked biological. Its head was a cage that he could see all the way through, only loosely stuffed with instruments and modules.

"I'd like to speak to Rhawn," Oleg said confidently.

"Who are you, and why have you come?" The robot's voice, picked up by his helmet, was lighter in tone than that of Gris.

"I am Oleg. I've come from Jupiter to offer Rhawn a moon of her own and the chance at reverse cyborgisation—to become fully human again."

The robot emitted a noise like fading static. It took Oleg a moment to realise he was being laughed at.

"Go home, meat boy. Be on your merry way."

"I realise that my offer's likely to be rejected. But my masters won't be satisfied until I have the answer from Rhawn herself. She's here, isn't she? I won't take more than a few minutes of her time."

"Your timing," the robot said, "is either very fortuitious or very poor."

"My timing is sheer luck," Oleg said. "Until just now I didn't even know that Rhawn had joined the Totalists."

"She hasn't."

"I was told . . ."

"Rhawn has *commenced* her second crossing. But until it is complete, she will not be one of us. It will happen soon, though. We are confident in the force of her conviction. It is certainly much too late for reversal."

"Can I at least talk to her?"

Again Oleg had the sense that matters were being discussed. Lights flickered and strobed in the cagelike enclosure of the robot's head. Oleg risked a glance back, satisfying himself that the vehicle and its driver were still there.

"Rhawn is . . . receptive," the robot said. "You will have your audience. But it will be brief. Rhawn has readied herself for the final phase of the crossing. She will not be detained."

"I only need an answer."

The robot brought him into the encampment. Up close, he saw that it was not as similar to the caravan as he had first assumed. There were hardly any enclosed spaces—just a few sealed modules which may or may not have been airtight. The remainder of the structures—most of them wheeled or skid-mounted, even as they were now parked around the Bone Cathedral—were for the most part skeletal frames. Their roofs were parasols and solar-collectors, their walls either absent or no more than concertina-hinged magnetic screens which could be drawn across when required. Gathered around and inside these treehouse-like forms were many similar-looking robots, lounging or reclining like overfed monkeys. They were plugged into bits of architecture via their abdomens—recharging from stored power, Oleg supposed, or perhaps pushing energy back into the community. There seemed little in the way of artistic creation going on. But perhaps the robots had been furiously preoccupied before his arrival.

"Is Rhawn one of these?"

"They are what Rhawn will become. It will not be long now."

"You all look the same."

"You all look like tinned meat."

Through the thicket of skeletal structures Oleg was at last brought to an upright green block the size of a small house. It was a round-ended cylinder that might once have been a fuel tank or reactor chamber, before being anchored to a moving platform and gristled over with access ladders, catwalks and power conduits. In contrast to its surroundings this dumpy, windowless flask seemed entirely enclosed. Oleg's robot host spidered up a ladder and looked down as Oleg completed his clumsy ascent. The robot opened a door in the side of the chamber, then stood aside to allow Oleg to pass through first.

It was not an airlock, for the interior of the green flask was still depressurised. Oleg had emerged onto a platform running around the circumference of the interior, with a circular gap in the middle. Supported in the chamber's middle, with a large part of it beneath the level of the platform, was a hefty piece of biomedical machinery. Many cables and pipes ran into the upright, wasp-shaped assemblage. Three robots, much like his host, were stationed around the machinery at what Oleg took to be control pedestals. They were not moving, but the robots had plugged in to the pedestals via their abdomens. Oleg presumed that they were directing whatever complicated procedure was going on inside the machine.

The wasp-shaped machine culminated in a glass dome. Inside the glass was a beaked and goggled head much like that of Gris, except that it was encased within a bulky surgical clamp. Beneath the head, enclosing the neck, was a tight metal collar separating it from the rest of the machine.

Oleg surveyed the beaked and goggled face with deep dread and apprehension.

"Rhawn will speak to you now," the robot said.

"Thank you, Rhawn, for agreeing to listen to me," Oleg said hastily. "I have come from Jupiter, with . . ."

"I know where you came from, you spineless little shit."

Oleg bristled. He had listened to enough recordings to recognise the voice as belonging to Rhawn, despite a deliberate machinelike filtering.

"I . . ." he began.

"Stop cowering. What are you, a piece of bacteria? A vegetable? The Totalists horrify you, but you are the puppet, the thing with no free will."

"I only need an answer."

"I studied your background, when I knew you were approaching. Oleg the failed artist. Oleg the supine instrument of market forces. Oleg the pliable little turd, shat out by Jupiter. Why do you imagine your insolent little piss streak of an offer would be of the remotest interest to me? Why should I not have your suit drilled through now?"

"My masters thought . . ." His throat was as parched as the sunlit Playa itself. "They didn't know that you'd left the Collective. They thought there might still be a possibility to . . ."

"To do what? To make me normal again? To bring me back to the condition of meat?"

"To undo what has been done."

"As if it were a mistake, that I now regretted?"

"I didn't mean it like that."

"But your masters did. Did it never occur to question this mission? To doubt its idiotic purpose? To show the slightest sign of independent thought?"

One of the robots at the control plinths turned its head slowly in his direction.

"Things have changed since you came to Mercury," Oleg persisted, refusing to waver under the robot's eyeless regard. "No one knew what to make of your art, when you joined the Collective. It was too different, too hard to assess."

"If they were idiots then, they are idiots now."

"But idiots with money and influence. Do you understand the terms of the offer, Rhawn?"

"My understanding is irrelevant. I can no more be 'undone' than an egg can be unsmashed, or meat uncooked. Let me demonstrate. Have you a strong stomach?"

"I . . ."

But Oleg had barely begun to give his answer. The surgical clamp around Rhawn's cyborg head was reconfiguring itself, pulling away to separate the tight-fitting segments of her armour. Oleg thought back to what he had learned from Gris, of how the cyborg exoskeleton had become its living skin. This was how it must have been for Rhawn, before she exiled herself to the Totalists. There was a human head under the metal plates, but it was a head already skinned back to an anatomical core of muscle and sinew and nervous system. She had been blind, without the cameras. She had no nose or mouth or ears, for she did not need to breathe or speak or hear. Her cyborg senses were wired directly into deep brain structure, bypassing the crude telemetry of ancient nerve channels. Machinery was plumbed directly into her heart and lungs.

"Are you horrified? You should not be. This is the state of being that Mercury demands of us. There is no pain, no discomfort, in being what we are. Far from it. We revel in our new strength, our bold new senses—our resilience. To each other, we have become beautiful. We drink in the sustenance of the dayside Sun and glory in the stellar cold of the Mercurean night. But why come this far, and not go all the way?"

"They tell me that your crossing is nearly done."

"It's true." And for the moment her spite seemed to move off him. "There is almost nothing left of my old self now—the old vehicle in which I moved. What use are lungs and a heart, on Mercury? What use is a digestive system? What use is meat? These things are simply waiting to go wrong, waiting for their moment to fail us. To undermine us in our absolute, unblinking dedication to art. So we gladly discard that which the Collective fears to surrender. The flesh. Every organic part of ourselves. We donate our bones to the Bone Cathedral! The Playa was made for robots, Oleg—not 'mere mortals,' or their half-way cousins. We are the true heirs of Mercury—we the Totalists!"

Something in him snapped in that moment. "You're committing suicide, in other words. Being taken apart, until there's nothing left of you. You can't *become* a robot, any more than you can become air, or sunlight!"

"What is this—a glimmer of contradiction? The faintest signs of a spine? Keep at it—there may be hope for you yet."

"This isn't about me. This is about you, throwing yourself away—wasting what you are."

"How little you understand of us. What would be the *last* thing I clung to, do you think? The last, most sacrosanct piece of myself?"

"Your mind," he stated firmly. "You do not reside in your heart and lungs, but without your brain, there is no Rhawn."

"What you mean is, without the encoding of my personality implied by my detailed idiosyncratic brain structure, there is no Rhawn. How could there be? But that encoding doesn't care about the terms of its own embodiment."

"I would," Oleg said, with fierce certainty.

"Weeks ago, at the commencement of my second crossing, small volumes of my brain structure were duplicated by artifical connective structures located outside my body. Machine circuits, in other words. When neural signals passed through the interfaces of these brain volumes, my Totalist peers had the freedom to choose whether those signals continued to pass through my existing anatomy, or were instead shunted through the exosomatic structures. The change was made, and then switched back—and made again, over and over! The key thing is that I felt no change in my perception of self, regardless of whether my thoughts were running inside my head, or in the exterior circuitry! Electricity doesn't mind which route it takes, as long as it gets to the same destination! And so, step by step, volumes of my own brain were switched out—supplanted and discarded! This continued. Over the weeks, fifty, sixty, seventy percent of my old architecture was supplanted by exosomatic machinery. And now you arrive. I stand now on the cusp of absolute machinehood— ready to make the final transition to Totality. Only the last ten percent of my mind is still inside my head. You see now why it is far, far too late to reverse what I have become?"

"There's still active brain tissue inside you?" he asked. "Still some meat, inside the head I'm looking at?"

"What is left of me, you could squeeze between your fingers, like a handful of wet grey sand."

"Then where is the rest of you? Executing inside one of these machines? Already in a robot, waiting for you to take control?"

"You misunderstand. Ninety percent of me has already completed the transition. And one hundred percent of me is already in control. My robot body is not 'waiting' for me. I am already mostly in it. And we have already met."

He turned from the globed head, conscious that the robot that had brought him in from outside was still there. He looked with renewed fascination at the symphony of flickering coloured lights.

"I should have guessed. You never did give me your name."

"And you never asked," the robot said, nodding. "But here I am. This is me. I am Rhawn. That *thing* that you have been talking to, that is just the place where I used to live."

"You could have given me your answer outside."

"I thought it would help if you understood. I am ready now, you see. But that last ten percent of me—I won't pretend that there has not been hesitation. I could have completed the transition days ago. On the brink, I quailed! Foolishly, I could not quite bring myself to submit to Totality. The meat's pathetic last twitch! But you have been the spur I needed. For that alone, Oleg, you have my undying gratitude."

"I've done nothing!"

"You have come, and now you may observe. Suffer one useful moment in your miserable existence. Are you prepared?"

"For what?"

"To bear witness. To document my becoming. In a moment, the last traces of my living neural tissue will cease to serve any useful function. And I will have transcended myself." But when he thought she might be done, Rhawn added: "You may thank your masters, Oleg, for their kind offer. I spit it back at them, all the same. They were much too late, of course, but it would have made no difference if they had sent you years ago. I have been on this path for much too long for that. I have always felt the pull of Totality, even before I knew it in my self. The more I move from the meat, the more the meat repulses me."

"And one day," Oleg said, "you'll feel the need to go beyond this as well. It's in your nature."

"What could possibly lie beyond the perfection of robotic embodiment?"

"The greater perfection of non-embodiment. The flawless condition of non-existence."

"You mean that I would kill myself."

"I'm sure you will. You can't ever accept what you are, Rhawn. It's just not in your nature."

A new light came on in the robot's head. It was a pale green, rising and falling in brightness without ever quite dimming completely. Oleg was quite sure it had not been activated earlier on.

"Even now?" she asked.

"Even now."

"Well, you're mistaken. But then, you are only human. And now that I have completed my second crossing, I feel my conviction more forcefully than ever before. We shall have to see who is wrong, won't we? I hope you have a great deal of patience, not to mention a solid medical plan. You are a bag of cells with an expiration date. Parts of you are already starting to rot. It will take me centuries to begin to exhaust the possibilities of Totality."

"You'll burn through them quickly enough. And then what?"

"Something beyond this. But not death. There is no art in death, Oleg. Only art's supreme negation."

He smiled thinly. "The world will await your next masterpiece with interest, Rhawn. Even if it never leaves Mercury."

"Well, something shall. Does this surprise you? And you shall be its custodian."

"I don't understand."

"It is . . . traditional . . . among the Totalists. At the time of our second crossing, we concieve of a new piece. A celebration of transition, if you will. The work is initiated before the crossing's start, and not fully completed until the crossing is done. I have . . . planned such a work. I call it A Map of Mercury. It is a minor piece, in the scheme of things. Almost beneath me. But since you have gone to such pains to find me, I should consider it fitting if it should fall upon you, the great and glorious Oleg, to bring the work to public attention."

"A new piece by Rhawn?"

"Exactly that," she said proudly. "A new piece by Rhawn. And, as far as the outside world is concerned, the last. No, I shan't be abandoning art. But the realms into which I expect to push . . . these will shortly lie beyond your conceptual horizon. You would not only fail to recognise my art as art, you would fail to recognise that it was anything at all. But this last piece will be my gift to you—and your meat cousins. You will find it comprehensible. Take it to your masters. Fight over it like dogs. I will enjoy watching the overheated spasms of your Jovian economy."

"It's not what they asked for," Oleg said.

"But they won't be displeased with you?"

"No," he supposed. "I came for you, but never with much expectation that you'd agree to the offer. They'll hand that moon over to someone else, I suppose. But to return with a new piece by Rhawn . . . that was never in my plans. They'll be pleased, I think."

"And will their pleasure be of benefit to you? Will you also profit from this?"

"I should imagine."

"Then we are all satisfied. You will return to the Collective? Delay your departure by a couple of days, and the work will be packaged and delivered to you. It really is a trifling little thing."

She had not been exaggerating, Oleg reflected.

He tugged more of the packaging away. The upper quarter of A Map of Mercury was now visible. But everything below that was concealed by a thin layer of protective material with a circular hole cut into it. He dug his fingers around the layer until it began to come free. He grew incautious. If he damaged the material, he could always say it had been that way when he found it.

Besides, he was starting to suspect that his masters would think very little of this offering no matter the condition in which it had arrived. It wasn't the sort of thing they had been hoping for at all. Yes, it was a late Rhawn. But a globe? A Map of Mercury?

Something that literal?

The layer came free. He could see more of the globe now. There was in fact something a bit odd about it. Instead of continuing with the shape of the sphere he had been expecting, the object began to bulge in some directions and turn inwards in others. There was more packaging material to be discarded. He tugged it away with increasing urgency. There were two cavities opening up in one side of the no longer very spherical thing. Above the cavities was the fine swell of a brow ridge. Beneath the cavities—the eye-sockets—was the slitted absence where her nose would have been, and beneath that the toothy crescent of the upper jaw. There was no lower part.

He pulled the whole thing from its box. The colours of the top part, the emulation of the planet's surface features and texturing, continued across every part of it. There were ochres and tangerines and hues of jade and turquoise. It had a fine metallic lustre, sprinkled with a billion glints of stardust. It was simultaneously lovely and horrible.

A Map of Mercury.

That was exactly what it was. She had not lied. Nor would this piece—this piece of her—dent Rhawn's reputation in the slightest. No wonder she had needed a couple of days to make it ready. At the start of their conversation, ten percent of her had still been inside this skull.

Oleg had to smile. It was not exactly what he had come for, and not exactly what his masters had been after either. But what was art without an audience? She had made him her witness, and she had made art of herself, and she was still there, down on Mercury, having crossed twice.

Clever, clever Rhawn.

But then a peculiar and impish impulse overcame Oleg. He thought back to their conversation again. It was true, much of what she had said about him. He had been supine. He had tried and failed at art, and allowed himself to become the servant of powers to whom he was no more than an instrument. He had become spineless. He did what they told him—just as he was now executing Rhawn's wishes.

A tool. An instrument.

A machine made of meat.

A little while later a little door opened in the side of Oleg's spacecraft. It was a disposal hatch, the kind he used for waste dumps. A small grey nebula coughed out into vacuum. The nebula, for an instant, glittered with hints of reflectivity and colours that were not entirely grey.

Then it dispersed, and the ship continued on its merry way.

one

NANCY KRESS

Here's another novella by Nancy Kress, whose "Pathways" appears elsewhere in this anthology. This one is about a battered and embittered professional boxer who finds, initially to his chagrin, that he's developing what amounts to a superpower—and that's only the beginning of his journey, for both better and worse.

> I doubt if anyone ever touches the limits at either end of his personality. We are not our own light.
> —*Flannery O'Connor, private letter, 1962*

I.

"It's a long way to fall, Zack."

Zack scowled up at her, wishing Anne would go away. Bad enough to be lying on this damn hospital bed in a thin cotton dress that left his ass bare. Bad enough to be going into surgery for something wrong in his brain. Bad enough to not understand what that something was, not even after one of all those doctors had explained it, just the same way he'd never understood that kind of intellectual crap his whole stupid life. But having his sister loom over him, upright when he was down—well, wasn't that just the icing on this particular shit cake?

"I'm fine," he said shortly.

"Of course you'll be fine," Anne said.

"So go back to work. I don't need you here."

"I'm on break anyway," Anne said. She wore her nurse's scrubs, her brown curls tied back. She, or the curtained cubicle, smelled of disinfectant trying to smell like pine trees. "I just wanted to remind you that when they put you under the anesthetic, it can feel like a long way to—"

"I got it, I got it already! Now go away!"

Behind her Gail—and who invited *her* to be here anyway?—said, "Knock it off, Murphy. She's just trying to be nice to you."

"Nobody asked you!"

"If anything happens to you in there, do you really want your last words to Anne to be 'go away'?"

Gail was right, the bitch. Gail was right, Anne was right, the doctors were right, only Zack was wrong. Just like he'd been wrong his whole life. But if they'd just leave him alone for five fucking minutes to think, he couldn't *think* with both of them jabbering at him . . . And it wasn't like Gail cared what happened to him in surgery. She might love Anne, she might have married Anne in a state where they could do that, but Zack was just so much spoiled meat to Gail. Always had been, ever since she and Anne got together. Gail, lean and muscled and as welcome here as a bad uppercut to the chin.

A second later, the other too-familiar feeling swamped him: regret that he hadn't been nicer to Anne. Why was that always so hard to do?

"Please," Anne said in her soft, pleading voice. "Please don't fight again, you two."

"I'm sorry, Anne," Gail said.

"Sorry," Zack muttered. Sorry, sorry, sorry, he was always apologizing to Anne.

"I know you didn't mean it," Anne said.

Another, older nurse came into the curtained cubicle and glanced quizzically at Anne, who began explaining that she was a relative, Zack's next of kin, not a member of the surgical team. The other nurse nodded, not interested. "Ready, Mr. Murphy?"

"Yeah."

"Wait—what's that black eye? Does Dr. Singh know about this?"

How should Zack know what Dr. Singh did or didn't know? Zack wasn't a damn mind reader. He said, "I box. We get hit. We get black eyes." It came out nastier than he intended. So, all right, maybe he was nervous about this operation. It was on his *brain*, after all. Maybe his brain wasn't much, but it was the only one he had.

His sister, the brainy one, launched into a history of all the doctors Zack had seen in the last week, what they'd said about the tumor in Zack's head, the concussion he'd gotten in the fight against DeShawn Jeffers, a bunch of other medical bullshit. Finally—finally!—the women finished talking and an orderly wheeled him into the operating room. Almost a relief. Anne, Gail—it was too much sometimes. And Jazzy not there only because he'd forbidden her to come. She hadn't liked that, but he'd been firm. Three months of seeing each other, even with great sex, didn't mean she could invade every corner of his life.

The last thing he saw before the OR doors closed was Gail, her arm around Anne, staring fixedly at Zack like she could erase him from the Earth. He wanted to give her the finger, but he didn't get his arms free of the blanket in time.

He transferred himself from the gurney to a table, someone holding his IV tubes out of the way. The room was full of masked people, only their eyes visible. A bright light overhead like a mirrored UFO with a handle sticking out of it. Humming machinery. One nurse lifted Zack's wrist to read his name band; another assisted a doctor with gloves.

Another doctor sat on a stool beside Zack's head while something was injected into his IV. "Relax, Mr. Murphy," she said. "You're just going to take a little nap. Now, count backwards from a hundred."

Don't tell me what to do. He counted forward instead, picturing Jeffers lying there in the ring, that was it, Zack should have won that fight, *one two three four* . . .

A weird drifting took him. What the . . . he wasn't . . . this . . .

It's a long way to fall, Zack.

He woke in a cubicle with a curtain around it and a bedside table holding a barf bowl shaped like a fancy swimming pool. Plastic tubing ran all over him. From somewhere came the smell of coffee. Everything seemed fuzzy. Someone— not Anne, not Jazzy—fussed with machines. Zack tried to say something, and couldn't.

"Rest," the someone said. He slept.

But the next time he woke, he was in a different room, and it was full of people. Scrubs, white coats, two men in suits. None of them were looking at him. They clustered around a screen, looking at something Zack couldn't see.

"Not possible," someone said.

"It has to be possible because there it is," someone else said, irritated and impressed and scared.

How do I know all that from looking at his back? Zack thought drowsily, and slept again.

The third time, he came fully awake. The plastic tubing was all gone. The room had pale blue curtains and a view of the parking lot. Only Anne, wearing an off-duty skirt and top, sat beside his bed, her head bent over a magazine. Unexpectedly, gladness at seeing her flooded him. "Hey," Zack said. It came out a croak.

Anne looked up. Instantly Zack thought: *She's scared. Really scared.*

"You're awake!"

"Yeah. What's wrong?"

"What do you mean?"

"Don't lie to me, Anne! Something's wrong and it's, like, major. Am I . . . am I dying?"

Her hand shot out to rest on his. "Oh, no, Zack, nothing like that! You came through the surgery just fine. Nothing's wrong."

"I said don't lie to me!" He could feel her fear—no, wait, what did that mean? But it was true.

He knew she was afraid, and wary of him, and at the same time—oh, curious, her mind open and searching for answers . . . How could Zack know all that? He was no mind reader. No, he knew it from the way Anne held her head, the way her eyebrows shifted, the set of her mouth. . . . He simply *knew.* Just like he knew a second before she stood up that was what she'd do next.

"I have to get Dr. Jakowski," she said. "I told him I'd send for him as soon as you woke up."

"Who's Dr. Jakowski?" Hadn't his surgeon had some Indian name, not a Polack one?

Anne didn't answer. She left, and Zack lay in the bed testing his hands and arms and legs. Everything seemed to work all right. He made a fist, two fists, sat up. Still in that damn bare-ass cotton dress. A man in white coat strode into the room ahead of Anne.

Eager as a rookie before his first fight. Thinks he's way better than anybody else. Looks at me like a lab rat. He's going to ask me a lot of questions but tell me nothing.

"You're quite an interesting phenomenon, Mr. Murphy. I'm going to ask you some questions now."

"No, you're not," Zack snapped. *The man was going to hold up his left hand.* Cold slid down Zack's spine, icing his bones. *How do I know what he's going to do before he does it?*

Jakowski held up his left hand. "Purely routine, Mr. Murphy. Now, when you—"

"It's not routine and you know it, you bastard."

"Zack!" Anne said. She turned to the doctor. "I apologize on behalf of my brother, doctor. He—"

"Don't apologize for me, Anne. You've done it my whole fucking life. I'll talk to somebody, but somebody who isn't a high-and-mighty prick."

The doctor mottled maroon. Another man in a white coat entered the room. "Mr. Murphy is awake?"

As eager as the other one, but this guy's human. Hasn't got a stick up his ass. Quiet but not timid, he'd go the distance in a fight, featherweight maybe, good shoulders. . . . He's going to reach out his right hand, ask me how I'm doing. . . .

"How are you feeling? I'm Dr. John Norwood, a neurologist." He held out his right hand to shake hands with Zack.

Zack shook and nodded, all at once too confused to speak.

Anne said, "Zack, does your head hurt?"

"No." Something easy, something he could answer. Zack clung to it like a life raft in a choppy sea.

"Good," Norwood said. "I'd like to ask you some questions, if that's all right with you. May I sit down?"

"Sure. But Dr. King-of-the-World there, he goes."

Anne looked startled. Jakowski stalked out. Norwood sat and smiled, so slightly that no one could have seen the tiny movement of his lips, too brief for interpretation.

He thinks Jakowski's a prick, too.

He's going to lean forward, shift his weight to the left . . .

Norwood leaned forward and shifted his weight to the left. "All your vital signs look excellent. Mr. Murphy. But I'd like to hear from you how you're feeling. Does anything ache, even a little?"

"No."

"Does your vision seem altered in any way?"

"No."

"Hearing?"

"No."

"The feel of that blanket?"

"No."

"We're going to do formal tests, now that you're awake, but I wanted to get your initial impressions before we tell you that there is something *to* explain. Does anything about you seem different from before the operation?"

"Well, my ass wasn't hanging out before."

Anne laughed, a high startled sound that held relief and fascination and fear all at once. Norwood smiled. Zack didn't look at his sister. He said, "Doc, you tell me right now what all this is about, or nothing else gets talked about at all. You hear me?"

"Certainly. Mr. Murphy, the meningioma was successfully removed. As you were told before, it wasn't malignant and there's no reason to think it will return. Everything connected to the surgery was routine. But something connected to the anesthetic was not. Is not. You had some kind of allergic reaction, your pressure dropped, and we couldn't ventilate you. We thought we were going to lose you. But you responded to a steroid bolus, fortunately."

"Yeah?" His last, confused memory was of counting down DeShawn Jeffers, a memory somehow connected to Anne. . . . *It's a long way to fall, Zack.*

"During surgery we use a machine called a CRI—for 'consciousness registration index"—to measure how far you've gone under the anesthetic. What the machine does, basically, is bombard your brain with electromagnetic waves, then record how your brain reacts. Through something called—"

"Wait, wait," Zack said. "You shoot electricity at my brain?"

"Not electricity, no." Norwood paused, and Zack saw him—felt him, *knew* him—thinking how to explain clearly and simply, just like people had been trying to explain things clearly and simply to him all Zack's stupid life. This time, though, Zack didn't resent it. He was too confused.

Norwood said, "A human brain operates in electrochemical waves. You know those measurements they take when you get a concussion, using an EEG? It shows your brain waves in patterns. Have you seen that?"

"Yeah. On a computer screen."

"Precisely. Well, a measure of how conscious you are uses those patterns. Specifically, it shows two things: how complex the patterns are, and how much the different parts of the brain are communicating with each other. 'Integration,' we call it. The less integration—the less that different parts of the brain are sending information to each other—the more unconscious you are. The entire underlying concept is called 'integrated information theory' and it's only a few decades old. Am I being clear, Mr. Murphy?"

"Yeah," Zack said, although he was struggling to keep up. Too much like school. *Dummy, dummy . . . Why don't you work harder . . . Your sister had no trouble with history or math . . .*

"The reason we measure consciousness during an operation is to make sure patients are out deeply enough so that they won't wake up while the operation is in progress."

"That can happen?" Christ, it would be worse than a kick in the nuts. Knives tearing at your flesh while you're strapped down and helpless. . . . *He's going to lean forward and say something important now . . .*

Norwood leaned forward. "It can happen, but it almost never does since CRI came into wide use. Your post-operative CRI shows patterns we've never seen before. Not so much in wave complexity as in integration. Various parts of your brain are sending information to each other at an unprecedented rate."

"What parts?" *He's going to raise his right hand to his head . . . He's excited and confused. . . .*

Norwood raised his hand and ran it through his thinning hair. "Many different structures are involved, Mr. Murphy, because the brain is, after all, an integrated whole. But mainly, your sensory input areas are working overtime—sight and sound and touch and smell—sending the signals they receive to places where those signals are processed and interpreted. Do you understand?"

"No." Zack hesitated. "But I kind of know what you're going to do before you do it. And I know what . . . what you think. No, I don't mean any mind-reading bullshit. I mean . . . fuck, I don't know. What you feel. Like, right now you're surprised and not surprised at the same time. You believe me, but you wish I was smarter so I could tell you more. And you don't want to embarrass me by saying that."

It had all just blurted out of him, and immediately Zack wished it hadn't. You didn't give away your guts like that, he'd known that since he was ten, so what the hell had all that been . . . Well, it wouldn't happen again. Give away your guts and you were a sitting target for people to use.

"Mr. Murphy—"

"When do I get out of here?"

Anne said, "Zack, you can't—"

"Don't tell me what I can or can't do!" Anger was the familiar armor, welcome as an unprotected opening on your opponent in the ring. Immediately the regret followed. Anne was not the opponent here. He scowled at Norwood. "When do I go home?"

Norwood said, "You can leave at the end of the week if there are no complications and if you so choose, but we're hoping you'll stay to let us—"

"Let you study me? I'm no lab rat, doc. No way. Now, you should leave and let me rest. I'm supposed to rest, right?"

He doesn't want to go . . . Looking for something to say to convince me . . . Coming up empty. Resolve to try again later. Bye, bye, doc.

Norwood stood. "Perhaps you should rest. I'll stop by later, if I may."

"Don't bother," Zack said.

But when Norwood had gone, Zack turned to Anne for one more question. "What do they say caused all this?"

She was staring at him, biting her lip. *Scared, interested . . .* He was a lab rat to her, too. But also her brother, and she came closer to Zack's bed and took his hand. His fingers tightened on hers.

Anne said, "They don't know. Some weird combination of the CRI action, your recent concussion, and the way the tumor pressed on tissue and maybe altered it before they removed the mass, or maybe released some unknown enzymes. Or maybe your age—at twenty the brain isn't even done growing. But you're integrating sensory input more fully than most people. Maybe reading body language and minute facial expressions and tones of voice and processing them into . . . I don't know, Zack. Everybody does that, but you're doing it to an unprecedented degree. Maybe."

Okay, one *more* question. "Is it going to last or go away?"

She spread her hands wide, palms up, and any idiot could have read her. "How should I know? Your consciousness has reached an unknown level of integration. Nobody knows anything about it! Which is why you should let Dr. Norwood and the neurological team—"

"Thanks," Zack said, and turned his face to the wall, away from all the sensory-whatever she was putting out.

The voices started the day he left the hospital.

They weren't really voices, just faint, whispery swishings in his head, no louder than a breeze in trees or the hum of hospital machinery, although not as monotonous. Zack found them easy to ignore. He had too much else on his mind.

For four days, he had resisted being interviewed or tested or anything else by any doctors. Suspicious even of the nurses, he'd objected when they changed his IV, gave him pills to swallow, or even brought him meals. How could he tell what was in the food? He'd seen movies and TV shows with truth drugs and shit like that, and what if the doctors were ordering him stuff the nurses didn't even understand? He ate as little as he could. The nurses' exasperation came through in every movement they made. The only one he liked was a dumpy middle-aged woman from whom he picked up complete indifference to him and everyone else. She was just doing her job, and she didn't need anybody to say *Atta girl* to her. Zack approved.

Anne said, "At least let a nurse wash you, Zack."

"Yeah, you stink to high hell," Gail said, because of course she was with Anne, horning in. Gail carried her yellow hard hat from whatever construction site she was engineer on this month. Flaunting her job. *She's going to turn her back on me, look out the window, pat Anne's back, give me the finger behind it.* . . . Whatever Anne had told her about his "condition," Gail wasn't impressed. It didn't make Zack like her any better.

"I'll shower when I get home this afternoon."

Anne frowned. "You can't, not without—"

"I checked myself out."

"Against medical advice?" On the last word her voice scaled upward like she'd been goosed. Zack held his temper. She meant good, and even bossy and a pain in the ass, she was his sister. Christ, she'd practically raised him after their parents bought it. He had a sudden memory, sharp and sweet as a lemon drop on the tongue, of walking with Anne to some candy store, his small hand in hers, her head bent protectively toward him. *"The only person you've ever loved, and only on your terms,"* Gail had once said to him. Screw that. Gail should keep her nose out of Zack's business.

"They're doing the paperwork now. Annie, I'm fine. Really. That shit they gave me made all the brain swelling go down. I'm fine and I'm going home."

But not before he had two more visitors, neither of which he wanted to see.

Jerry, at least, had no idea of Zack's "condition of integrated consciousness" and wouldn't have cared if he did. Huge, shambling, a former heavyweight gone to fat, Jerry's tattoos had expanded with his fat until the naked girl on his forearm looked as bloated as he did. Nothing in Jerry's life had quite worked: not the brief boxing career, not the even briefer mob involvement that earned him five-to-ten in federal prison, not the seedy gym, always on the verge of going under, where Jerry trained and matched boxers who were never going anywhere bigger. For the past six months, ever since Zack had started fighting for Jerry on Saturday nights, he had thought: *I'm not going to end up like you.* He just hadn't known how to avoid it.

Until now.

"So, champ, how you doing?" Jerry called all his fighters "champ." None of them ever were. Jerry stared at the side of Zack's head, shaved around the bandages.

"Going home."

"Yeah? When you coming back to the gym?"

"Real soon," Zack said, glad that Anne wasn't there. Jerry said nothing. *He's got more to say, something he needs to ask but don't want to, he's going to scratch his head first . . .*

Jerry scratched his head, his flabby arm coming up like a hydraulic lift. "Champ, I hate to ask this, but I got a problem. Week from Saturday, Bobby Marks was on the slate to fight Tom Cawkins. Not at the gym—at a real venue. Magnolia Gardens. But Bobby, stupid kid, got himself nabbed for possession, won't be out in time. Cawkins's manager's trying to pull him out of the fight cause ever since Cawkins beat C.P. James, manager thinks he's bigger shit than he'll ever really be. I don't have a fighter to put against him week from Saturday, contract's void and I gotta C&R."

Cancel and Refund—the boogie man that chased Jerry every struggling accounting period. Zack knew that Jerry needed every scheduled fight to make expenses, even though the fights were mostly lame and the customers, neighborhood punks and old guys who remembered better, only filled half the seats. Jerry especially needed this fight; he'd hoped it might move his gym up a notch. Personally, Zack doubted it.

Jerry went on, looking everywhere but at Zack's bandages. "So—you think you'll be well enough to be slotted in? Bandages off and all?"

Zack said, "Sure. Why not?"

Jerry blinked. *He's really afraid I'll get hurt . . . why, the sentimental fat old bastard! He's going to go all sappy. . . .*

"Look, champ, I don't want you to do nothing that'll interfere with getting better. You're a good kid even if you are so mouthy. You want to wait to fight, we'll wait. I can get DeShawn, maybe, though he—"

"I'll do it," Zack said, and watched Jerry go through a complicated series of emotions during which Jerry kept a poker face.

"Well, if you're sure, then good. Prize money ain't great, but—"

"I said I'll do it."

Jerry knew when a deal was closed. A rare smile quirked his lips, drowned in his usual anticipation of the worst, and propelled him shambling out the door.

Zack poked gently at the bandages on his head and stared at the ceiling.

His last, most unwelcome visitor was Jasmine.

He was out of bed, dressed in his own clothes again, a little headachy but upright. Five more minutes and he could have escaped. He should have known better—you couldn't outrun women. Anne, Jazzy, even fucking Gail. And a part of him was glad to see Jazzy, or at least might have been glad if she hadn't looked mad enough to chew his head off.

"Why did you tell the nurses to not let me in? Huh, Zack? *Why?*"

"Didn't want to upset you."

"Like I'm not upset now?"

Damn, she looked good. She had on the tight jeans he liked and a low-cut top with some sort of creamy ruffles that shimmered against her chocolate breasts. Body like a porn star, big dark eyes, seventeen years old and no slut. She kept her nights for Zack, her days for finishing high school (more than he had done), and next year's eye on a training school in medical technology. Jazzy had plans. She didn't want a baby daddy and a welfare check, she wanted a job and an apartment she could pay for herself. Zack had been afraid since they started hanging out together that she also wanted him in that future apartment, tethered and leashed. So he'd tried a few other hook-ups, but nobody else had Jazzy's pull on him.

Also—and this was the surprising thing—they had fun together even out of bed. They went to movies, laughed, took walks together just to walk, not to get someplace. She was funny and she got him, got who he was. He *liked* her. But even so—

"Look, Jazzy, I didn't want you here because I didn't want any big scene. Bad enough I got Anne wringing her hands over me. She works here, so I was stuck. But I just wanted to rest and get better and go home. Is that so hard to understand, huh? Is it?"

"Don't get all huffy with me, Zack Murphy. Don't you dare. I know you needed rest. I wouldn't have made a scene."

She was telling the truth. Zack felt it from her. But, given the scene she'd made when they were last together ("Who was that slutty girl? When are you going to give up fighting and get your shit together? You need a real job and a real future!"), he'd been sure that she would keep it up in the hospital. But—clearly he'd been wrong. Concern for him poured off her—Zack could see it, feel it, almost taste it.

He hated it. It was a rope, tying him down.

"I gotta go, Jazzy. Anthony's picking me up."

"I can drive you home."

"I already called Anthony."

Anger, held in check. Concern that he was all right. The gentleness he'd glimpsed once or twice underneath her fierceness; each time he'd hated that gentleness. Another rope. She was going to cross the floor, hug him gently. . . .

He brushed past her. "Call you later, baby, okay?" In the hallway, he regretted his rudeness—how many people did he actually like? Fewer than corners in a boxing ring. Nonetheless, he strode as quickly as his aching head would allow to get to the elevator, to the outside, to the welcome indifference of Anthony, one of his two roommates in the apartment filled with beer and sagging couches and pizza boxes and freedom from women.

"*Zack*," the voices said. "*Zack. . . .*"

No, they didn't. Lying awake three days before his fight with Cawkins, Zack knew perfectly well that the voices were the thrumming of the music coming through the thin walls of the apartment. Was the breeze from the open window, wafting the faint scent of garbage cans in the alley. Was that ringing in your ears that everybody got sometimes. It wasn't even voices, it was his imagination, and he damn well better stifle it and get some sleep. But it was only midnight, and he wasn't anywhere near sleepy.

"You leaving the party so early?" Anthony had said. But the truth was, Zack had been leaving early all the time. Leaving parties at night, leaving Pizza Hut at dinner, even leaving the goddamn 7-11 before he found the Cheerios on the shelves. Too many people, all flinging emotions at him in the way their bodies moved, the way their mouths worked, the tones of their voices. *I'm scared, I'm so happy, I'm disgusted, I'm starting something that might not work, I'm going to talk to that guy over there or boost that nail polish or give that bum a dollar or find somebody to fight with or brush against that babe's tits or buy these roses even though I can't afford it . . .* Stop!

But they never did. All the information about everybody just kept coming, and Zack didn't even know how he knew any of it.

He had to get it under control. Now.

Heaving himself up from his mattress on the floor, Zack put his clothes back on. Outside, the non-voices seemed even more persistent, like the sweet spring night gave them more to work with. Well, screw that. Zack was having enough trouble with live people without dealing with imaginary ones.

People spilled out from the bars and clubs on Belmont Street. Zack leaned against a lamp post, lit one of the twenty or so cigarettes he allowed himself every month, and pretended to be absorbed in it while a couple walked past, holding hands and talking softly.

He loves her, she doesn't love him, she wants out and he doesn't know it yet. . . . How do I know?

Forget that. It didn't matter how. Concentrate on not seeing them, not noticing all the "sensory information" that Anne said he was getting and "integrating." Concentrate . . .

It didn't work. Zack was aware of everything the couple didn't know they were telling him, until they turned the corner and disappeared.

He tried next with three high school kids who got off a bus and peered into a bar where, of course, they knew they wouldn't be allowed in. *Anger, envy, thinking that if only they could get in they'd show up everybody there but not even believing it themselves, horny as hell . . .* The redhead is going to say something full of bullshit . . .

The redhead said, "Couldn't I just give that babe there a thick foot of happiness!" His buddies jeered.

Zack tried to both see and not see them. He didn't turn his back, but he concentrated on his cigarette: how it felt, smelled, looked as the ash lengthened and fell to the sidewalk. The boys walked past him, arguing. Concentrate on the cigarette. . . .

The information about the boys was still there, but now it felt more like rap playing in the house next door. You could hear it, but you could also sort of block it out. The cigarette mattered, the information from the boys didn't.

He practiced for a few more hours, sitting in the corner of a bar. He didn't always succeed; sometimes the only way he could break the overwhelming flow of information was to close his eyes. Even then, it seemed like he could *smell* attitudes around him. But as the night wore on, he got better at it.

The next day, better still.

He could control it.

The day before the fight, Friday, Jazzy showed up in his bedroom before Zack was even out of bed.

"How'd you get in?" Zack said, sitting up woozily on his mattress and glancing at the glowing red numbers on the clock sitting on the floor. 12:00. Midnight? No, noon.

"Anthony or Lou didn't lock the door," Jazzy said. Zack had nailed a blanket over the window and light from the living room silhouetted her. He couldn't see her face. He didn't need to.

"Why . . . why aren't you in school?"

"Because this is more important."

Alarm bells sounded in Zack's head. When Jasmine thought something was more important than school, it meant trouble.

She put her hands on her hips. "I'm only going to ask you once, Zack, and I want an honest answer. Are you done with me? Are we over?"

Were they? Peering at her, Zack didn't want them to be over. On the other hand, he'd been avoiding her for days. Quick phone calls full of bogus excuses: doctor's appointment for my head, Anne's got a situation I got to see to, Jerry's got a situation, Anthony's got a situation, I need to rest baby I'm just so tired since the operation—

She was serious. He got that from every line in her back-lit body: a whole lot of inner conflict, but she was dead serious. If he said it was over, this time it would be. He could be free.

She looked so damn good. And when they had good times, they were really good times. The sweet way she'd looked at him that time he'd bought her those earrings for no holiday or birthday, just because the earrings reminded him of her . . .

But he could be free.

"We're not over," he said slowly, wondering if he meant it, "but I need some time. Some space."

"Some space I'm not in." Now her arms were crossed across her chest, which he knew she was going to do before she did it.

"Jazzy . . ." All at once he felt tears prickle his eyes. What the fuck! He hadn't cried since the last time his father beat him, when Zack was nine, just before the bastard died. Zack blinked hard to dash away the tears. He didn't want Jazzy to see.

Maybe she did, maybe she didn't. But all at once she was kneeling beside him on the mattress, and then he was kissing her, and then clothes were coming off and she was the one with tears on her face and . . .

He *felt* her. Not just near him, taking him in, like normally in sex. No, he knew what she was going to move before she moved it, knew what she wanted without her whispering anything, knew when his touch wasn't getting it done and when he was exactly in the right place, doing the right thing, for how long she wanted it done. It was like he was her as well as himself, and when he exploded, right after she did, he cried out, something he never did.

He hated every second of it.

Jazzy lay face down, jeans still circling one ankle, tee shirt up over her ears. She gasped, "That was . . . incredible."

When he had control of his voice, he said, "No."

She twisted to look at him. "What?"

"You kayoed me. I don't like that."

"What are you talking about?"

"You . . . *erased* me."

"I—"

"It's over, Jazzy. Go away." He snatched up his clothes and stalked into the bathroom, locking the door before she could say anything more, before he could take in any "sensory input" and know what she was going to do next, what she was feeling, where he ended and she began.

He spent the afternoon in the public library, a place he hadn't been since the third grade, trying to find things on the Internet that would explain what was happening to him. He Googled the words he remembered Dr. Norwood or Anne using: "sensory input," "consciousness," "brain patterns," "CRI." CRI got him "Carpet and Rug Institute," "color rendering index," and "Community Rowing, Inc." Googling "consciousness" resulted in 88,000,000 hits, "brain patterns" almost as many. He tried to read some of them but the terminology was too hard and anyway none of it seemed to apply to his problem. Which was what? Norwood said that Zack had some sort of new level of consciousness. If so, why was he still too stupid to find out what was happening to him?

He wasn't going to call Norwood or Anne. His cell had two calls from the doctor, six from his sister. He wasn't going to go crawling to either one of them for information he'd rejected when they offered it before. He texted Anne *I'm fine stop worrying* and left the library to go get drunk instead.

Dusk bathed downtown in a pink glow, neon through light fog. The air smelled sweet. Zack picked a bar he never went to, where nobody would find him. He sat at the bar and practiced shutting out everybody except the bartender, a handsome young guy who might have made a welterweight: long legs and arms, heavy sloping shoulders, thick neck. Zack knew when the bartender was going to sweep his eyes around everyone's drinks to offer refills, when he was irked by the almost-but-not-quite-falling-down drunk on the end stool, when he was going to flirt with the middle-aged brunette sitting alone. Zack knew it all before the bartender did it, maybe even before the guy himself knew he was going to do anything. Just as important, Zack was able to not let the other people in the bar distract him from this one guy, at each one moment.

And after three drinks, the non-voices in his head went away.

When the bartender shot him a glance that said *You're looking at me too much, wrong team, no luck here buddy,* Zack paid his tab and left. He wasn't as drunk as he wanted to be, but drunk enough. On to the next test.

The hooker wasn't all that young, and she wasn't all that pretty, which meant she was cheap. Zack followed her to her room and undressed. She did the same, not bothering to look at him. Zack pulled her down onto the bed.

And the thing happened again. Even through the alcohol, Zack knew what would make her happy. Not at first, because she was so sullen that nothing would make her happy. But when he picked up on faint movements and expressions she probably didn't even know she was making, and then he followed through, the thing happened again. He could anticipate every one of her secret needs, hidden desires. Another minute and he would be her.

"Hey," she said softly, the word carrying a world of surprise and shock.

He got up, threw her money on the bed, and left, more furious than he'd ever been in his life. To ruin sex! If Norwood had been in that room, on that steep flight of stairs, beside that sidewalk stained with somebody's vomit, Zack would have torn the doc's balls off and stuffed them down his throat. And enjoyed it.

The fight against Cawkins was at Magnolia Gardens, a small and dingy arena on the edge of the industrial district. Despite what Jerry had said, Zack knew it wasn't an important fight and Cawkins wasn't an important fighter. Nothing Jerry arranged was important in the world of boxing that started with clubs like Jerry's and rose upward to dizzying heights: Madison Square Garden and title fights and TV movies about Ali or Tyson. Those were places Zack had never even thought about. Until now.

He got to the Gardens an hour ahead of fight time, only slightly hung over. There, sitting on the pavement by the alley door as if they'd been there for hours, were Anne and Gail. *Shit.* Anne jumped up when she saw Zack. Gail got to her feet more slowly, her eyes on Zack's face. He didn't need any new level of consciousness to know what his sister would say.

"You can't fight today! The doctor said—"

"Let me go by, Anne. How did you even know about the fight?"

"It was in the paper. *Zack*—"

Of course it was, but who knew Anne would look at the sports section? No, she hadn't—Gail had, the interfering bitch. Gently Zack took hold of Anne's hands. Fear poured off her like tarry oil. "Don't worry, Annie. Really. I got it covered."

She's going to make that sister-mouth and hug me.

Anne did. "You can't get this 'covered' by wish-fulfillment, Zack! Your head isn't healed yet, you can't risk getting hit, you—"

Gail said, "Give it up, Anne. I told you. Anyway, he won't get hit, will you, Zack? Nobody'll even lay a glove on him."

Zack shot her a glance, trying to remember how much he'd said to Anne, to anybody, when Gail was around. Whatever it was, Gail understood. She knew. Her contempt for him was still there, in spades, but now it was mixed with an uneasy wariness. Behind Anne's back, Zack shot her the finger.

He peeled Anne off him, went inside, and shut the door firmly behind him. Jerry waited in a tiny dressing room with fist-sized holes in its peeling walls. One look and Zack knew that Jerry not only expected Zack to lose this fight, but also that Jerry had bet against him.

Think again, old man.

The rest of the hour before the fight, as he got dressed and warmed up and heard the crowd fill the Garden, Zack focused on not focusing on anyone. He kept his head down—although even the stance and shifts of people's *feet* told him more than he wanted to know about them. Then he was walking, head down, along the aisle to climb into the ring. The corner man, who was also the cut man because Jerry was too cheap to pay for both, spread a thin layer of petroleum jelly over Zack's face to help control cuts that Zack wasn't planning on getting.

"In this corner, weight one-seventy-one, Zack Murphy!"

Zack raised his glove.

"In this corner, weight one-seventy-three, Thomas Cawkins!"

Cawkins was taller than Zack, with a longer reach. A dancer, moving in and out, jabbing at the air for effect even before he left his corner. A shit-eating grin.

He's going to move in suddenly and fast.

Cawkins did, counting on his longer reach to punch at Zack's head. But Zack was already inside, under the jab. Surprise jerked on Cawkins's face.

He's going to step back and bring up his right in an uppercut.

Zack circled away.

He's going to bring up his right—no, it's a feint, he's going for a left hook—

It grazed Zack but only a graze, and now Zack was sure he would know Cawkins's every move a fraction of a second before he made it. Zack began to attack.

The crowd was screaming but Zack barely heard it. Rather, he did hear it, but only distantly, like waves crashing on rocks. The ref was there, circling and hovering, but he barely registered on Zack. Only Cawkins filled his senses. Cawkins couldn't get near Zack, but his defenses were still good, and it took a while for Zack to land a punch. The crowd noise died down: nobody was pounding anybody. A few boos arose.

Then Zack saw it: the opening he needed. He went in low, looping a left to Cawkins's side, following it with a right to the head. The fighters closed and Zack held Cawkins tight and began to batter. This had always been Zack's ace: he was incredibly strong. Cawkins had reach and speed instead of strength, and now both were neutralized. Zack hit him again and again. The watchers screamed.

When the ref made them separate, Cawkins fell to his knees. He got up, and

Zack felt elation lift him onto the balls of his feet. He had the son of a bitch. The bell rang.

In the next round he played with Cawkins, anticipating his every move, putting on a show for the crowd, enjoying himself immensely. When Zack finally went in for the big hit, Cawkins was bloody and exhausted. Zack didn't have a mark on him. The medic rushed over to Cawkins. The announcer was screaming what any idiot could see, that Zack had won.

He walked back down the aisle, savoring the shouts of *Mur-phy! Mur-phy!* In his dressing room, Jerry looked dazed.

Zack said, "Don't let my sister in here. And don't you ever bet against me again."

To Zack's surprise, Anne didn't try to see him again. But she sent him texts every day. He read them, because she was his sister, because she had practically raised him after Mom took a powder and the old man bought it, because he owed her. But he only read each of them once.

I want to explain this to you, Zack, at least as much as I understand it. Think of a brain like a city. Part of it has houses, part has shops, part of it factories, part of it is a newspaper printing office. Now think of your consciousness like police. The part of the city that has houses doesn't know every minute what's going on in the part that has the factories, but the cops can go to any part of the city. Even if they can't get into the factories or the houses.

Not without a warrant, Zack thought.

Somehow, your brain is different. The police do *know what's going on in the news office. News comes in all the time, huge amounts of it, and you know consciously what it is. The news comes through your senses: sight, hearing, touch, taste. The news is about other people, their body language and facial expressions and so on. Everybody reads other people's sensory signals, but you do it in a more integrated way than other people do: the input sensory signals and your conscious ability to use them to predict. Does this sound to you like what's happening to you?*

Zack didn't reply.

You never answer my texts. I just want to know you're reading them!

Zack had another beer in a bar on Third Avenue, with older fighters who'd never given him the time of day before now.

I talked again to Dr. Norwood and there is such a thing as "acquired savantism," where some kinds of brain damage actually bring out talents in patients that they didn't have before. It's even been demonstrated in controlled experiments. Dr. Norwood wants to see you again. Please answer me!

Zack was surprised by how much he missed Jazzy. One night, he picked up a girl who had seen him fight the night before. He didn't even have to pay for it. If he was drunk enough, he found, he didn't get her "sensory signals" and didn't have to become her. Sex was just sex again.

Zack, do you understand what I'm telling you? Please answer!

Zack understood, all right. He understood that Anne was dumbing down everything she told him, trying to make it fit to his slow, stupid, little-brother brain.

Zack, here's my last text on this subject. Just think about it, please. Integrated consciousness—a part of the city knowing what other places are doing—might involve other sections of the brain, too. Are you experiencing that? Is anything else happening in your brain besides your being able to predict how people are going to move and feel?

The non-voices.

Most of the time Zack had learned to ignore them, just as he'd learned to ignore "sensory input" from people he didn't want to focus on. Once he'd seen a horse with blinders on so it wouldn't be spooked by traffic on either side of it. This was like that. He didn't even like to think about the non-voices, until Anne's texts made him. Were they another part of his brain trying to get in touch with his police?

Christ, if he kept on thinking like this, he'd end up as loopy as his sister. No, that wasn't fair—Anne wasn't the one going loopy. Frustrated, guilty, overwhelmed—he *should* answer her texts!—Zack ordered another drink.

He won more fights, all spring and all summer, each time against fighters rated a lot higher than he was. Going up the ladder. The last one was even picked up for reshowing by ESPN. For the first time in his life, he had a bank account rather than using the blood-sucking check-cashing joints. There was even money in the account. Jerry was exultant, talking about title fights. In one fight, Zack got hit in the head, which made him afraid that he might lose his "integrated consciousness," but nothing happened except a blinding headache. Well, it hadn't been that hard of a hit. The path upward looked dazzling, and Zack was loving every minute of it: the attention, the parties, the girls (after enough booze). He stayed away from the offers of drugs, though. That shit was always the beginning of the end. Zack wasn't going to have an end.

Then he saw the dog.

There weren't many dogs in this part of the city, just dirty feral cats that lived on rats and garbage and hissed at any human fool enough to approach them. This dog looked out of place. Big, the color of dead leaves, short hair—Zack didn't know anything about breeds of dogs. It wore a leather collar with tags and looked well cared for, its fur glossy as it sat in the middle of the sidewalk in front of Jerry's office building. The animal blocked the crumbling cement steps up to the front door.

"Move," Zack said. He didn't like dogs, especially large dogs. One had bitten him badly when he was four, a monster belonging to a neighbor when he and Anne still lived on Tremaine Street with drunken old dad, who had only taken Zack to the ER when Anne, eleven, got hysterical.

The dog stood up and growled at Zack. It didn't like him, either.

Zack froze. Was it going to attack? No. How did he know that? He just did. This dog was scared, not mad. Despite himself, Zack took a step forward. It felt like his body moved itself. Weight shifted, spine straight, shoulders squared, breathing even and steady, eyes on the mutt.

The dog lay down on its belly and put its head on his paws.

What the fuck? How did he know how to make the dog do that? The mutt was acting like Zack was God, or at least leader of the pack. What pack? What part of Zack's brain city was integrating with his cruising head cops to produce this behavior?

Unnerved, Zack stepped over the prostrate dog and went into the building. "Jerry, there's a damn dog outside and—"

Jerry wasn't alone. Two men sat in the soiled arm chairs of Jerry's tiny office; both rose when Zack entered. They wore expensive suits. Jerry wore a dazed look.

"Zack, this is Mr. Donovan and, um—"

"Jim Solkonov, Mr. Murphy. May I call you Zack?"

He's going to hold out his hand and smile. He's intensely interested in me. He has something he wants to offer.

Jerry blurted, "They're from TV!"

"USNAF," Solkonov said. "United Sports Network for America's Fans. We're fairly new, committed to bringing America more, and more interesting, choices in sports. Maybe you already watch us. Zack—" he paused, brought up his hand, smiled widely "—have you ever watched any bouts of ultimate fighting?"

"Yeah, sure."

"Then you know how the sport has been watered down. Twenty-five years ago they started with 'No rules!' Then they added in more and more rules until now a fighter can hardly do anything: no head butting, no elbow strikes, only approved kinds of kicks. Foot stomping out, foot stomping in, gotta wear gloves—it might as well be a dance recital! We want to start something new, a genuinely exciting sport."

"Yeah? Like what?" Zack wasn't sure he liked Solkonov, but the guy was going to offer him something big. It showed in every line of him.

"We're calling it Level Fighting. Matches will take place on a stage, not a ring or Octagon, with four different levels at varying heights, and no rules at all. I saw you fight, Zack, and you're uncanny—it's almost like you can read your opponent's mind and know what he's going to do. In that last fight, Saladino never touched you, not even once. You'd be a natural for level fighting."

Jerry blurted, "No rules at all? You'll never get it through. Authorities will shut you down."

"Not if the matches take place in another country. We already have an island country that wants us."

If that was true, it meant big money was involved. Well, duh—these guys had a *TV network.* But Zack kept his face neutral. "I'm not a martial arts fighter. Those ultimate-fighting guys all have years of training in that stuff."

"Yes, we know. But we're not looking for fancy moves. We want this to feel primitive, like guys in a jungle. The basic aggressive primate."

Donavan said, "We're thinking of animal-skin costumes."

"No," Solkonov said irritably, "we're not. Nothing gimmicky. This is going to be raw and basic. We think they'll be a huge world-wide audience."

"No rules?" Jerry said. *He was going to scratch his head the way he did when he was worried, he was going to lean forward, he was going to lift his chin . . .*

"Well, two," Solkonov said. "No drugs of any kind, and we're serious about that. Major, state-of-the-art testing. And no killing. But that's it."

Zack said, "What if someone dies by mistake?"

Donavan said, "Like that never happens in boxing?"

Zack said nothing, knowing as well as anybody the list of men who had died shortly after matches, from head trauma or internal bleeding. Sisnorio, Alcázar,

Flores, Johnson, Sanchez. More. Jerry shifted his hams on his chair; he was going to ask about money.

"What kind of cash are we talking about here, gentlemen? And prize money with or without signing sweeteners and bonuses?"

"All the good things, Jerry," Solkonov said, pulling a paper from his pocket. "Here's our offer."

Jerry took the paper, which had printing large enough for Zack to read it over Jerry's shoulder. Zack felt his mouth fall open.

"Listen," Solkonov said earnestly, "we know that our potential fighters are taking enormous risks. We're looking for risk takers, because those are the guys that don't surrender, not even when the situation is dangerous. Those are the guys with courage and balls, am I right? Those are the guys we want, and our backer knows that to get them, he's got to pay well."

Jerry managed to get out, "Who is the backer?"

"I'm not at liberty to tell you that. All·I can say is that he's not American, he's a fan of true courage, and he thinks it should be adequately rewarded."

Bullshit. But the money wasn't. Zack tried to stop his mind from racing ahead to the life he could have with that kind of money. My God, the life he could have. . . .

Jerry said, "We need to talk it over, of course. Where can we reach you?"

"The Plantagenet Hotel. Our number's on the bottom of the offer, which of course is not a contract—that comes from our lawyer. But we need to know by tonight, gentlemen. We're talking to other fighters who are close to signing."

He wasn't lying, Zack knew. There were other candidates. Zack was not at the top of their list.

Jerry said, "We'll call by tonight."

"Great."

When they'd left, Jerry turned to Zack. Jerry said nothing; he didn't have to. His old, paunchy body had become a young kid's yearning toward a pony.

Zack said, "I don't know yet. Don't crowd me. I need to think."

"About what?"

Zack didn't answer. He went out, tossing back over his shoulder, "Back by six o'clock. Plenty of time."

"Zack—"

"Six o'clock."

On the sidewalk, the dog was gone.

The non-voices were stronger now. His own mind, warning him about self-preservation? His ancestors, doing the same damn thing? That explanation was one of the crackpot hits he'd gotten when he Googled "voices in the head." Another was "schizophrenia." Zack stopped Googling.

He headed into the nearest bar, an Irish pub blessedly dim. Three men sat at the bar, spaced well away from each other, drinking away their troubles at two in the afternoon. Zack downed three double Scotches in quick succession, which shut up the non-voices. Then he took out his phone and played with it while he tried to think.

Good money—really good—just for signing. And if he won fights, more money than he'd ever dreamed of.

No rules, with all the viciousness that implied.

His Gift—that was how he thought of it now—which would always tell him what his opponents were about to do.

Going against fighters who were trained in mixed martial arts, because Solkonov had been lying when he'd said the owners "weren't looking for fancy moves."

More money than he'd ever dreamed of.

No rules.

All at once he wanted to talk this over with somebody. Not Jerry, who always followed the money. Not Anne, who would be horrified and would lecture. Not Anthony or Lou, who both had started acting so jealous and huffy that Zack had moved into his own place. His fingers moved almost by themselves to call Jazzy.

The call went straight to voice mail. He left a message: "Hi, it's Zack. Will you call me?" And then the thing that, he'd learned as young as fifteen, always worked with women: "I really need you."

"You can't," Jazzy said. "It's way too dangerous."

They sat on either side of a campfire somewhere way the hell up in the mountains. Jazzy was at an off-season ski lodge with, of all things, a bunch of middle-school kids, some sort of volunteer work in a community center. Jazzy did that kind of do-good shit. When Zack had been in middle school, nobody had ever organized a weekend field trip to any damn ski lodge.

But he'd been able to persuade Jazzy to leave her charges with the other counselors for a few hours. He'd called Jerry and said he'd give him an answer by 8:00 p.m. He'd borrowed Anthony's wheezy old Chevy and followed Jazzy's directions up winding roads, through dark woods that crowded each side of the road, to the ass end of the world, and then he'd let her lead him away from the lighted lodge to this clearing where they'd have some privacy. He had muck on his shoes and damp on his ass from sitting on the ground, and his side closest to Jazzy's fire was too hot while his other side was too cold, and after all that, Jazzy said the same thing Anne would have. Although without Anne's nurse-list of injuries he could get plus all the reasons he didn't want them.

But damn, she looked good, hugging her knees in tight jeans, the firelight playing on her warm brown skin. He'd been startled by the intensity of his pleasure at seeing her again.

He said, "It's a lot of money, Jazzy."

"You only got one body. Which already gets pounded enough as it is."

He stayed quiet. Right now, he didn't have to do anything. Every line of her, every movement, said she wanted him, no matter how grim she tried to keep her face. His erection was so strong it hurt. And he'd been practicing on controlling the Gift, so if he shut out everything but the sex the way he did with hookers, the way he shut out the non-voices . . . If only he'd had a few drinks! But he hadn't brought anything, and anyway, only a moron would drive down those dark mountain roads half-sloshed. So if he just focused on the sex . . .

She was going to move toward him.

She moved toward him, and her lips were as soft and sweet as he remembered. His arms went around her and then he'd eased her onto the ground and it didn't matter which side of him was by the hot fire because he was hot all over, they both were, and—

It happened again. He anticipated what she wanted and he gave it to her, and then he *was* her but he couldn't stop, his own need was too great, and when it was over she lay purring in his arms and he lay wanting to be somewhere else, anywhere else, away from her and the fucking perversion that turned fucking into something that fucked him over by robbing him of himself.

"I love you," Jazzy murmured, and there it was, the golden rope. Just like always. Women!

This time she was the one who sensed what he was feeling. She sat up. "Zack?"

"This was a mistake."

"Why?"

"I don't want this!" It came out harsher than he intended, out of his own anger and bewilderment and fear. She was going to jump up and leave—

"Fuck you," Jazzy said, and stalked off. Zack didn't try to stop her, didn't even watch her as she disappeared into the trees. But there was a big black hole when she'd gone.

He kicked dirt onto the fire and started back toward the lodge, where he'd left Anthony's car. Five minutes into the woods and he was lost.

"Jazzy!" he called. "Jazzy! Hey, anybody? I'm lost!"

An owl hooted someplace.

There was a moon but under the trees it was still dim. His cell phone flashed NO SERVICE—he was too far from a tower, or blocked by the hills, or something. Zack stumbled on. Nothing looked familiar—all the damn trees looked like trees!

Eventually he came to a place he knew he hadn't been before, a sort of mini-meadow, thick with weeds and brush but at least moonlight could shine down. The air was growing colder, and he shivered. Where the hell was he? And what if he couldn't find his way back? People died lost in the mountains, didn't they? But maybe not in September. He hoped not in September.

A shape stepped out of the woods into the moonlight.

A city boy, Zack could nonetheless recognize a wolf. Dimly he remembered Anne saying something about a pack having come down from Canada and killing chickens or sheep or something. Did wolves attack people? Zack had no idea, but his hands curled into fists. Which probably wouldn't be of any use anyway—

He and the wolf stared at each other.

All at once an idea came into Zack's head, from wherever ideas started. A wolf was just a kind of dog, right? Zack took a step toward the wolf and moved his body, without thinking about it, the way he had with the dog on the sidewalk. Commanding. In charge.

The wolf snarled softly.

Zack kept staring, in challenge.

The wolf hesitated, then lay down on the brush and lowered its head.

My God, he could dominate a wolf.

Not that he really wanted to. After a long, wholly satisfying moment, Zack turned and walked away. Twenty minutes later he glimpsed light through the woods and came to the lodge. His cell phone worked again. He got into the car and started the engine and the heater. It was two minutes to nine.

"Jerry? Call Solkonov. I'm in."

II.

Zack stepped out onto the fourth, highest level of the huge stage. Immediately the crowd shouted and stamped. Zack couldn't see them; everything beyond the stage was in darkness. But the stage itself was bright, and he easily spotted the other three fighters, one on each level where they couldn't get at each other until the bell rang. Zack looked past the edge of the rough wooden board at the three men arrayed near the front edges of the levels below.

It's a long way to fall, Zack.

He pushed Anne's voice out of his head and concentrated. The stage, covered in canvas printed with a pattern of rocks, was supposed to look like some sort of cliff with four staggered ledges that overlapped in the center:

_____

_____

_____

_____

At the overlap, the ledges were only three and a half feet above each other, which meant not only that you had to crouch if you were idiot enough to move up or down that way, but also that you could jump, or throw a man, from levels four to two or three to one. Each ledge was set back a few feet from the one above. At each of the ends were fake palm trees of concrete with green plastic fronds; in the middle of each ledge was a man-sized hole. Zack wore shorts printed in leopard (Donavan had won on that), with a jock strap but no cup. Ramon Romero had zebra, Julian Browne tiger, Serge Luchenko, who spoke almost no English, snakeskin. Nobody wore shoes or gloves. Everybody had shaved their heads.

The announcer introduced the fighters and spent a few minutes excitedly explaining what everyone there already knew: No rules! Raw and primitive! A brand new sport! The first match ever! Zack took deep breaths and looked down at Romero, on the broad and deep level one. All four fighters were welterweights, but Romero had the long, muscled legs of a jumper. Zack had checked them all out on the Internet, and he hadn't liked what he'd read. Romero had almost qualified for gymnastics in the Olympics. Browne was a black belt in Tae Kwan Do. Luchenko, who Solkonov had dug up somewhere in Russia, was a mystery, with almost no web presence. But he had more muscles than Zack had known it was possible to pack onto a human body. If the blond Russian caught you in any kind of grip, you wouldn't leave conscious, or possibly alive. Zack was insane to be here.

The bell rang.

The men on the lower three levels faded back under the ledges above, to avoid being jumped on. Zack moved back, too, and waited. At the highest level, drawn by lottery, he had the advantage. Seconds passed, which seemed like hours. Then shouts erupted from the audience and grunts from below Zack, on the left edge of the stage.

He ran to the center and leapt onto the third level, far enough out that if anyone were crouching there to grab his feet, they wouldn't get him. No one crouched. The third level was empty, and Zack peered through its hole to the first. Luchenko advanced on Romero while Browne rushed toward them from the other side. Zack caught the quick glance between Romero and Browne.

They had formed an alliance. *No rules.* Together take down Luchenko, then Zack, and only then fight each other.

Luchenko is going to feint left and trip Romero, but Romero's already seen it . . .

Browne is going to come at Luchenko with some fancy martial-arts move that throws him . . .

Another second and the Russian was on the ground. Romero and Browne began kicking him and then dancing away. Luchenko wasn't as fast as they were. He put up his arms to protect his head, but not soon enough. Still, he got one good grab, which Zack anticipated, and caught Romero's ankle. Browne bent and elbow-jabbed Luchenko in his now vulnerable face. The Russian couldn't handle them both at once and he was too vulnerable on the ground. A few more vicious kicks and murderous jabs, and he went still.

Half the crowd shouted, the other half booed at how quickly one fighter was out.

Browne had a clear shot at Romero while Romero was freeing his ankle, *but he's not going to take it.* They were still in alliance, and Zack knew, the moment before that they were going to turn toward him.

He shimmied up the palm tree to level three. Romero, the jumper, leapt easily onto recessed level two and then three, but by that time Zack had dropped back through the level-three hole to level one, jumping down the seven feet to face Browne, whom Zack had known was going to move back under the overhang of level two.

This was risky. Browne was the one trained in martial arts, and Zack had only seconds before Romero leapt back down to join his ally. But if Zack let them corner him on a higher level, Browne could fancy-move throw him off a ledge, which might break his back. Zack had to face him here, and fast.

He rushed Browne, who side-stepped easily . . . but Zack had known he was going to. He counter-feinted, grabbed Browne in a choke hold, and began to batter him in the head. Browne shifted his weight to try for advantage, but Zack sensed every move he would make and counter-shifted—clumsily, maybe, but Browne didn't get out of the hold. He was trained in graceful kicks and chops, not brutal battering. In a few moments he screamed and stopped trying to fight. Zack didn't know if the scream was a feint, too, so he kept punching at the face, head, chin. It felt terrible, but Zack was afraid for his life, and that made him afraid to stop. Fear fueled rage—he hated feeling afraid!—and he kept on punching as his knuckles bled and throbbed. Browne went slack in his arms.

Romero rushed up. Zack threw Browne's body on him and climbed to the third level.

For three minutes, they chased each other up and down and around. Romero was more agile but Zack more tireless; he'd spent months training to build up his stamina. In a proper boxing match, the bout would have ended at five minutes, with a one-minute rest between bouts. Not here. Zack caught Romero's puzzlement; he couldn't understand how Zack kept escaping him. Zack knew every move Romero would make.

The crowd loved it. They roared wordlessly, a beast without language *my non-voices have no words either and they're not beasts*—

The thought distracted him for a fraction of a second, and Romero caught him.

But the jumper was tired. Zack broke away with less trouble than he'd expected and climbed a palm tree. It had real coconuts wired to its plastic fronds. Zack tore one free; it was surprisingly heavy. He hurled it at Romero. *Put on a show.* The coconut missed, but now the crowd screamed a real word: Murphy! Murphy! Murphy! Zack threw more coconuts.

It took him another two minutes to confuse Romero enough for Romero to lose track of Zack. Zack dropped through the fourth-level hole, on top of Romero, and started punching. The man's training in boxing was minimal. He fell to his knees. Zack let him get up and then crashed a left hook to his head. Romero went down and stayed down.

Zack stepped to the edge of the second level and held up his arms. All at once they felt too light without gloves. Blood streamed into one eye; he'd been hit in the head. His left knee, which he hadn't even noticed before, was ready to buckle. His knuckles were scraped raw.

"Murphy! Murphy! Murphy!"

"And the winner is . . . Zack Murphy!"

His cornerman—or at least that's what he would have been if this stage had corners—brought Zack a robe and led him away. Pretty girls wearing almost nothing lined up across the front of level one to dance to raucous music. Men with mops appeared behind them to clean the stage of blood and pick up the shattered coconuts. A doctor bent over Romero, said, "OK," then moved swiftly to Browne. As Zack and the cornerman passed by them, Zack just caught the doctor's words over the music and the crowd:

"This one's dead."

Julian Browne had been beaten so badly around the head and neck that he had choked on blood and broken teeth and other assorted body bits. That had taken five or six minutes. If the doctor had gotten to him—had been permitted to interrupt the drama on stage—while Zack was throwing coconuts at Romero, Browne might have lived.

The prize money, a percentage of the gate plus the broadcast pay-per-view plus a variable bonus, was supposed to be substantial. Zack didn't ask if it was. He walked past Jerry, past the back-stage reporters, past the doctor and his dressing room. No fans stood by the back entrance, not yet: There were two more fights to go tonight.

"Zack! Zack! Where are you going? You can't just leave, kid!" Jerry, sputtering and worried. Zack didn't answer.

"You feeling dizzy? Wait, I'll get the doc!"

Zack didn't wait. In his leopard-printed shorts and bare chest he raised his hand, bloody still, and a cab stopped. It never would have stopped in the States. He was not in the States. He was on a tropical island someplace—he didn't even know which island—and he had just killed a man.

"Yeah, mon?" the cabbie said.

Zack mumbled the name of the hotel and the cabbie drove through the warm, flower-scented tropical night. Zack had no money with him. The cabbie went with him through the lobby, where guests turned and stared, up to Zack's room. Zack paid him. Then he stood under a shower as hot as he could get it, which wasn't very hot, for as long as the water held out, which wasn't very long. His phone buzzed insistently. As soon as it stopped, pounding started on his door.

"Go away, Jerry," Zack said. "That's it. I'm not fighting any more. Break the contract."

"*Zack—*"

"Go away."

Jerry didn't. He began his spiel about all the fighters—boxers, ultimate fighters, anybody he could think of—who'd happened to die in the ring or shortly after a bout. It was the risk you took, the risk Browne had known he was taking, it was nobody's fault, it wasn't such a—

Zack called hotel security and had the old man removed. When he accessed his bank account on his phone, the prize money from the first fight—the only fight!—was already there. Zack bought a ticket on a 6:00 a.m. flight home, bandaged his fists as well as he could with washcloths from the hotel, and packed. The airport bar stayed open all night. Zack had two double Scotches, and then he couldn't hear the voices anymore. By 5:30 a.m. he was on a plane headed Stateside.

Fighters take risks in the ring. Browne knew the risks. Not anybody's fault.

He couldn't make himself believe it.

And it easily could have been him. A fraction of a second slower in reading the other fighters' signals, in "integrating sensory data" with his "acquired savantism" and it would have been him.

He slept until 4:00 p.m. in his one-bedroom apartment. It had an actual bed, but nearly nothing else. Somehow Zack had never gotten around to shopping for furniture. The walls were the pristine white of snow before stumbling drunks, urinating kids, or car exhaust got at it. Zack's cheap Wal-Mart clock sat on the floor. He peered at it, sat up, and gazed at the blood from his cuts, which had stained his new sheets before he'd properly, if awkwardly, bandaged his hands. On each, fingers stuck out of a thick wad of padding.

He had killed Julian Browne.

He punched at his phone, grimacing at the screen as if it were toxic. "Gail? It's Zack."

"Well, well. A call from On High."

Zack gritted his teeth. But what else did he expect? "I need to ask a favor."

Surprise colored Gail's voice, even as she pressed her attack. "Yes, I'm fine, thank you for asking, and so is Anne. Who has been out of her mind with worry about you."

"I'm going to call her."

"Really? Then why call me at work, where you knew she wouldn't be able to wrench the phone from me so she could talk to her worthless brother?"

"Never mind. Forget the whole thing!"

"No, wait, don't hang up—Anne really is worried about you. Let me at least tell her you're all right. Are you all right?"

Yes. No. I don't know any more what "all right" even means. "I'm fine."

"Where are you? Still on St. Aimo?"

A horrible idea took Zack. "You mean Anne watched the fight?"

"Of course Anne watched the fight! Did you think it escaped Google? She cried all night afterward."

Zack closed his eyes. "I'm sorry."

"Wow, there's something I never thought I'd hear from you."

"I'm not going to fight again. Ever."

Gail's silence was more shocked than words would have been. Zack took his temporary advantage. "I need to borrow your camping stuff."

"My what?"

"Your tent and shit. Maybe a little stove thing. Whatever I need for a week in the mountains."

"Why?"

"I want to spend a week in the mountains."

Silence. Then, "Is this really Zack I'm talking to?"

"Stuff it, Gail. Can I borrow the things or not? I'm asking because if I went to a store and bought all that stuff, I still wouldn't know what the fuck to do with it. I need you to show me."

"So you can spend a week in the mountains."

"Yes."

"Alone."

"Yes."

"In late October."

"Yes!"

"Too risky, Zack. They already have snow in the passes. A neophyte could easily get himself killed."

"Forget it. I'll buy the stuff and figure it out."

"As if. Anne would never forgive me if you froze to death or got attacked by a bear or fell off a cliff. You'll never last a week, but you could maybe do a few days. I'll bring the stuff tonight. Give me an address. When are you leaving?"

"Tomorrow."

"You're bat-shit crazy, Zack."

Like I didn't already know that.

He had the rest of the afternoon to kill. His apartment was above a sports bar—very convenient. But all at once Zack didn't want to go there. It was the kind of place where men and a few women watched extreme sports; he might be recognized, especially with his bandaged hands. He pulled his cap low over his face, stuck his hands in his pockets, and found a bar so dark that entire stables of fighters could have gone unnoticed. He gulped two Scotches and then nursed a third, trying to not see Julian Browne choking on his own blood on level one of the First Ever Level Fighting Match.

At six o'clock he started home on dark streets that had half their street lamps broken.It was cold; he turned up the collar of his jacket. Occasionally he passed little "sidewalk altars," pictures painted or glued onto building walls of people who had been killed in gang-war violence, with clumps of dead flowers on the cracked cement beneath them.

In an alley, three punks about eleven or twelve were throwing stones at a little dog.

They had it backed up, cowering and whimpering, between two overflowing garbage cans. The stones were heavy; the bastards meant business. A gash had opened in the dog's side.

"Hey! Knock it off!"

Their heads snapped around, peering through the darkness. When they saw it was only one man, their postures eased a little. When they saw his bandaged hands, Zack knew they were going to start something.

"Yeah? Who says so? You, old man?"

The leader. That he called Zack the same name that Zack called Jerry—that didn't help. The boy's lieutenant half-turned, making sure Zack was watching, and hurled another stone at the dog. It hit and the animal yelped.

Zack rushed them. It was no contest, of course, not even when the head punk drew a knife. Zack knew what clumsy move each untrained kid was going to make, and he was fueled by a rage he didn't even try to understand. At the same time, he didn't want to really hurt them. So he pulled his punches, tripped but didn't kick, only waved the knife when he'd captured it, which took about ten seconds. Another ten and they were all running away, one limping but nothing serious. Not crippling them had taken every inch of self-control Zack hadn't even known he possessed.

"Okay, mutt, scram. Go home."

The dog didn't move. Maybe it was hurt too bad?

But when Zack approached warily—he didn't want to get bit, not even by a mutt this small—the dog got to its feet all right.

"I said go home!"

The dog lay down again, this time on its belly, and looked up at Zack.

What the—he hadn't been trying to dominate the animal. Actually, it didn't look dominated. It looked adoring. The dog crept forward and licked his shoe.

"Stop that, you know what shit can be on shoes?"

The dog went on licking.

Gingerly, Zack squatted beside the dog. It didn't bite. How did you tell how bad a dog was hurt? He had no idea. Maybe he could take it to a shelter. Were there shelters for dogs? Would the shelter people think he had hurt it?

"I gotta go," he told the dog, and did. When he looked over his shoulder, it was following him. Under a street lamp that actually worked, he saw how thin and scruffy it looked, its fur coming out in patches. This wasn't a dog with a home to go to.

"Damn it to fucking hell," Zack said to the dog. It wagged its tail.

In his apartment, he washed the little dog's wound and tied a thick bandage around its middle. The dog, a neutered male, let him. It seemed to be of no breed—not that Zack would know otherwise—and a middling sort of animal: middle-long fur, middle brownish color, middle-thick tail. Zack gave it half a pizza and a some water in the plastic tray from a frozen TV dinner. By the time he finished, Gail was at the door. She wasn't carrying anything. She looked around the apartment and snorted.

Zack said, "Where's the camping stuff?"

"You'll get it in the morning. We're not driving up until it's light in the morning."

"'We'? No way."

"Oh, yeah, and believe me, I don't like it any better than you do. But you're ignorant about camping and you're not the deepest carrot in the garden anyway. I took tomorrow off. I'll drive up with you, set up the tent, show you how to keep your food in a hang-bag, basic survival stuff, and leave. Wear warm clothing and bring a parka, hat, gloves, changes of wool socks, and boots, no matter how warm it seems in the city. We'll need two cars."

"I don't want you there."

"That makes two of us. But I'm doing it. Not for you—for Anne."

"Does she know about this?"

"No. She'd have a cow. Hey, I didn't know you have a dog!" Before Zack could say *I don't*, Gail added, "What's wrong with his side?"

"He got into a fight."

"Males," Gail said. "Is he going with us?"

Zack looked at the dog. It gazed back at him with an adoration he never got, not from boxing fans, not from Anne or Jazzy, and certainly not from Gail. "Yeah. I guess he is."

"What's his name?"

From a deep place inside that Zack instantly hated but could not control, he said, "Browne. His name is Browne."

They took both cars, the second-hand Ford Focus Zack had just bought and Gail's four-wheel-drive jeep. Their only conversation occurred in the street before they left the city. Gail said, "You're really not going to do that maximum fighting crap anymore?"

"Yeah. I'm done."

"Why?"

"I just am."

She didn't answer. Zack felt her curiosity: about his decision, about this trip, even about the dog, who had jumped happily onto the passenger seat of Zack's Ford. Zack disliked Gail as much as ever, but he'd give her this: unlike Anne or Jazzy, she didn't crowd him.

Jazzy. The last time he'd gone up to the mountains, they'd done it. Her luscious body warm in the firelight . . . but it hadn't been any good, not for him. He'd had to get way too far inside her skin. The price was too high. Still . . .

He was astonished to realize that right now he didn't want to fuck Jazzy as much as he wanted to talk to her. Well, that wasn't happening. Another price too high.

He followed Gail. After a few hours of ascent, they reached a small parking lot. Below them spread hills of red and gold trees dotted with dark-green firs. Beyond that, the city lay hazy and unreal. A sign with an arrow said AMBER NATURE TRAIL, followed by a lot of small print that Zack didn't read. Browne leapt happily from the car.

Gail said, "This is as far as we can drive. Now we pack it in. Do you know where you want to camp?"

Zack shook his head and Gail rolled her eyes, an action repeated when she saw the Safeway brown bag of groceries on the passenger seat."You really thought you could just carry that stuff in?"

"It's food," he said, lamely. He filled his pockets with two bananas and handfuls of dog kibble before she handed him things from the trunk to carry, including a big jug of water with straps that slung over his back. She put on a backpack that rose far above her head, and they set off along the trail.

In half an hour he felt as if he'd just gone three bouts in the ring. Gail strode on, tireless. Zack said, "This spot looks good."

Gail snorted, led him off the trail, and kept hiking. It was even harder here, rougher ground and branches all over the place. Eventually she stopped in a clearing. "Okay, this has good drainage, a place for the hang-bag, wood for the fire. Now pay attention. There are bears around here, and you need to do this right."

Bears? That wasn't the animal Zack was hoping for.

She put up the tent. She showed him how to keep his food in a hang-bag when he wasn't eating it and how to reconstitute and cook the dried stuff when he was. The hang-bag was suspended high above ground from a line stretching between two trees. She built him a fire and showed him how to start another one with the Nanostriker, a device he hadn't even known existed. She found wood and told him to keep the woodpile replenished during daylight. She gave him a GPS, a powerful flashlight, a hunting knife, a miniature first-aid kit, and a sleeping bag "good to ten below zero, and it won't get anywhere near that. I always bring a handgun up here but I can't loan it to you, you're not licensed to carry."

"I can take care of myself without a gun."

She snorted. "Does your phone work up here?"

It didn't. Gail looked around the camp she'd made, shrugged, and disappeared into the trees. "Thank you, Gail," he called after her retreating form, but she didn't look back.

He couldn't sleep. He sat very late by the fire, feeding it from Gail's woodpile. Browne lay beside him, and Julian Browne filled Zack's thoughts. The non-voices whispered in his head. The forest made strange sounds. By firelight he read the only book he'd brought, a second-hand paperback titled *Wolves and Their Ways*.

"*Within the genus Canis, the gray wolf (Canis lupus) represents a more specialized* *and progressive form than either Canis latrans or Canis aureus, as can be seen from its morphological adaptations to hunting larger prey—"*Christ! Why couldn't they write in English?

He did learn that wolves traveled in packs, were constantly in search of prey, were smart, and covered nine percent of their territory daily, about fifteen miles. So what were the odds of a pack, or even a single wolf, strolling into Zack's camp? Also, wouldn't they avoid the fire or maybe even a flashlight? But if he doused the fire and turned off the flashlight, he couldn't see any wolves if they did come. And he'd be sitting alone in the dark, which was deeper here than he could have imagined. Bottom-of-a-cave dark, devil's soul dark. There wasn't even a moon.

It did rise, eventually, a little after midnight, an almost-full globe that flooded the clearing with silver. But no wolves. The non-voices swirled and hummed in his head. Zack gave up and went to bed.

The next day he was profoundly bored. What the hell was a person supposed to do up here? He emptied his pocket flask of Scotch, cooked his mushy meals and rehung the food bag. He read as much of *Wolves and Their Ways* as he could stand. He threw a stick for Browne. The dog brought it back. Zack experimented, teaching the mutt to shake paws, to "stay" on command. It was easy; Zack knew everything Browne would do before he did it, just by watching the animal's movements, and somehow Zack also knew what movements he himself should make to control the dog. When Zack said "No," Browne obeyed instantly.

Zack was still bored. This had been a stupid idea, in a life of stupid ideas. Give it one more night, then pack up Gail's stuff and go home. The drinking water was almost gone, anyway.

No wolf pack that night, either.

Sometime after midnight, Browne barked sharply and Zack awoke. There was someone outside the tent.

He picked up the hunting knife and turned on the flashlight, briefly regretting the lack of Gail's gun. Fully dressed except for boots, he unzipped the tent and jumped out, to take the intruder by surprise. It was a bear, up one of the trees that anchored the line holding his hang-bag of food.

"Holy shit," Zack said. Browne, zipped inside the tent, barked hysterically.

The bear was going to climb down the tree.

It did, faster than Zack thought anything could move. At the bottom it stared at him. *It's uncertain. . . . It's going to take a step toward me . . .*

It did, and through his panic and fear, Gail's advice rushed into his head: *If you encounter a bear, make all the noise you can and wave your arms. It will probably go away, unless you're between a she-bear and her cubs or you have the supreme bad luck to encounter a grizzly in a bad mood. Then you're dead.*

Was this a grizzly? Zack didn't know one bear from another. He shouted and waved his arms, and his shouts came out high-pitched and shrill. "Go away, leave me alone, I didn't ask for this, *shut the hell up!*"

Dimly, he wondered who he was screaming at.

But the bear didn't respond to him as Browne had, or the wolf last summer. It tried again to grab the hang-bag, failed, and eventually ambled off into the woods. Zack went back into his tent, knife still clutched so tight in his damaged fist that the blood had left his knuckles. Browne was still barking. Zack picked up the dog and held him tight. The bear didn't return. Zack knew this because he stayed awake the rest of the night. In the morning he took down the tent, carrying it in his arms when he couldn't figure how to fold it enough to fit into the backpack along with the sleeping bag and everything else. He left the hang-bag with its remaining food and the water jug with straps. He'd pay Gail for them.

On the drive back to the city, Zack realized that he'd gotten what he'd come for, after all. Just not in the way he'd expected. But he had it. The information had been not in the woods, not in the bear, but in a stray, almost irrelevant sentence in the book about wolves.

For the first time since he'd killed Julian Browne, Zack smiled.

III.

The MGM Grand Arena in Las Vegas was filled to capacity. From his dressing room Zack could hear the noise of sixteen thousand people. All waiting for him.

"Ready?" Jerry said.

"Ready." For the hundredth time, Zack wondered why he kept Jerry on as his manager. The old man had managed fighters all his life; there were better people to manage the new career Zack had pursued for over two years now. Much better people, more knowledgeable about the field and more used to the big time. But Zack owed Jerry, from back in the day. And he trusted Jerry, which was more than you could say for the usual eye-gouging Vegas promoter.

Just as Zack was making sure his headdress didn't wobble, Marissa pushed her way into the dressing room. Zack shot Jerry a glance that said *You're supposed to keep her out before a fight*. Zack didn't need the Gift to read Jerry's shrug: *Didn't want another scene*. Browne, who loved everybody, barked happily and licked the silver-painted toes showcased by Marissa's four-inch high heels.

"I just thought I'd give you a big ol' sloppy kiss for luck," Marissa said. "Ugh, your breath reeks of liquor."

Marissa, unusual for a showgirl, didn't drink. She ate only organic, carefully nourishing that spectacular body. She wasn't that great of a dancer, but for her erotic act at After Hours Vegas, she didn't have to be. Not with the way she looked.

Jerry, radiating fearful worry, made a face at Zack. But if Zack didn't drink, the non-voices got distracting. It was a fine line: enough Scotch to tamp them down but not so much he got muddled. The hell with Jerry.

"Gotta go, honey."

"Break a leg!"

He could never get her to stop the stupid show-business clichés.

When Zack walked onto the runway, the crowd noise rose to a crescendo. *Focus, focus.* There was no room for distraction, or error. Not here.

He focused. There was nothing but the cage door, not even Karoly as he unlocked it. Karoly and his brothers resented Zack tremendously. All three of them had spent their lives at this, raising and training and working with the animals, and then Zack waltzed in and did what none of them could do, for bigger audiences and a lot more money.

Not exactly. Not Karoly, Anton, or Henryk Bajek—not even Jerry—knew anything of the year in Florida, before Zack had returned to Jerry's stable. Zack had started with the rinky-dink, semi-illegal carnivals that spring up in the South like mushrooms after rain. Those were the only places that had what he looked for, and were willing to let him be killed facing it. The Bajek brothers knew nothing of Zack's struggles to banish the fear that ruined his phrasing, to learn what phrasing even was, to achieve the right state of mind from which his Gift could do this. The first time Henryk had seen the scar down Zack's left arm, without a thick covering of make-up, Henryk's eyes had widened.

"From an alligator," Zack lied. He had never tried alligators, not since reading that one sentence in the wolf book.

He stepped into the cage and faced the big cats.

"Of the Felidae, only lions exhibit, and to an astonishing degree considering the morphological and evolutionary differences, many of the same social needs and pack behaviors as Canis lupus."

Four lions, three females and a young male. They were a pack, the females all related to each other. Thin bars of unbreakable steel separated the audience from the cats, the lingering legacy of an on-stage tiger mauling twenty years ago. Entirely different, as far as Zack was concerned. Roy Horn had not had Zack's Gift. But the crowd remembered, and at least half of them hoped Zack wouldn't emerge alive. Cell phones stood ready to record the gore. A robo-cam, somehow smuggled through Security, hovered overhead. The Arena's drone captured it silently and flew off with it.

Goldie, the young male lion, got to his feet. For a few weeks now, he'd been getting ready to challenge Zack. Probably the announcer was putting that into his excited spiel, along with the facts that the lions had been given no tranquilizers, Zack was unarmed, some ancient pharaoh had taken a lion into battle with him as a mascot. This last was the reason Zack was wearing an elaborately wrapped white loincloth, gladiator sandals, and a towering fake-gold headdress.

He didn't listen to the announcer's garbage. He took a step toward Goldie.

Goldie, Fluffy, Fuzzball, Lulu. The Bajek brothers hated the cutesy names Zack had given the lions and called them by more "dignified" names. But Zack had chosen these to minimize the beasts' power in his own mind. It wasn't like the lions responded to their names. They weren't dogs.

Fluffy, who'd given birth a few months ago and didn't like having her cub left behind backstage, opened her cavernous mouth and roared.

Zack held no chair, no clicking spoons, none of the other gizmos that lion tamers used to distract the animals and break up their concentration. Except that the MGM Grand insisted, Zack wouldn't even have allowed Anton or Henryk to stand behind the barred shield, a cage within a cage, with canisters of CO_2 to blast any lion that attacked. No lion was going to attack. Nor did Zack carry a whip. He carried himself.

His legs were straight under his torso, shoulders squared, gait leisurely, facial muscles relaxed and breathing calm and regular. Everything about his phrasing, the critical combination of posture and gesture, said *I am powerful and in charge. You cannot hurt me.* The lions must believe this. Even a quarter of an inch off in the angle of Zack's head, the set of his body, the position of his fingers, would have sent a different message, but Zack didn't have to think about any of that; the sensory signals that Zack sent were fully integrated with those he received. Had lions' intense social needs resembled those of tigers or cheetahs or house cats, instead of wolves, what Zack did would have been impossible. Lions were the only big cats with dog-like pack behavior.

But they were still lions. Goldie had just turned two years old. The pride, run by the females, was getting ready to drive Goldie out, since he was no longer a cub and the pride now had Zack as leader. The females might still mate with Goldie, but soon they wouldn't share food with him or let him into their "territory." From deep instinct, Goldie knew this. He didn't want it. The only way to stay in the pack was to kill Zack and take over.

Goldie, well fed, was big for his age, with a black mane designed to intimidate other males from a distance. He snarled and flashed his claws at Zack. Goldie had omitted the stilted walk that would signal to another cub that this was a mock fight. Goldie was serious.

Zack took another step forward.

Fluffy got to her feet. Her tail lashed back and forth.

Goldie took a step forward.

Zack stopped, but without altering his posture or expression. He had reached what the Bajeks called "the office," that invisible line the animal must not be allowed to cross or it would believe it held the power. But Zack could cross it, and did.

Goldie roared a challenge.

Every atom of Zack's being concentrated on the lions. There was no crowd, no Arena, no steel bars. Only the lions, and they were faster, stronger, bloodier than he would ever be. But his integrated consciousness, receiving and processing and sending out sensory information as no human ever had before, knew what each of them would do, would feel. Almost he *was* the lions, controlling them from inside. Almost, but not quite. Goldie responded to his own inner signal to challenge or be ousted from the pack that was his life.

Zack moved to Fluffy, the new mother, and laid a hand on her head.

Fuzzball and Lulu got to their feet.

Zack knew the second before Goldie would attack. He dodged behind Fluffy, moving fluidly, with no jerks or other indications of stress. Female lions ordinarily didn't interfere with challenge fights between males, but Fluffy's cub was not Goldie's and changes in pack males were traumatic for any pride because the new male typically killed all cubs to make way for his own. Also, the cage, although not cramped, was a far more restricted environment than the savannah, or even the habitat, and Fluffy felt the tension of limited space for two leaders. She launched herself at Goldie.

Zack walked calmly to Lulu, the most placid of the lionesses, and put his hand on her head. Henryk and Karoly rushed forward with blasts of CO_2 to break up Goldie and Fluffy, a fight that didn't need breaking up because Fluffy had backed off, gashed, and Goldie had again turned his attention to Zack. Zack put his other hand on Fuzzball, the aging but far-from-toothless matriarch, who snarled at Goldie.

The young lion was only two. With Zack gazing at him from between two lionesses, a hand on either one's head, Goldie backed away.

Zack stared at him steadily, a clear challenge: Fight or submit.

Goldie roared, feebly. Then he lay on his belly and put his head on the ground.

And Zack played with Lulu and Fuzzball while Fluffy, not badly hurt, licked her bloody side. He played ball with them. He had Lulu jump through the traditional hoop. He played peek-a-boo with Fuzzball and a chain-mail blanket. Finally he walked to the cage door with the two lionesses, patting them both on their heads as if they'd been kittens. Leisurely he unlocked the cage door, stepped outside, and smiled at Anton, who did not smile back. Only then did Zack look at the 16,000 people on their feet, screaming themselves hoarse. Only then did he become aware again of the non-voices, stronger than ever, tugging at the inside of his head.

In the newly refurbished Skyline Terrace Suite of the MGM Grand, Anne, Gail, and Marissa sat on the veranda, twenty-six stories in the air and almost as big as the suite itself. The terrace was furnished with sofa, dining table, and huge TV. The TV played the Torres-Lucito boxing match at The Wynn, on mute. Below and around the terrace, the Strip glittered and twinkled and shone. From the roller coaster on top of New York–New York came screams of delight.

"It's something, isn't it?" Marissa said, stirring her club soda with a celery stick.

"Something," Anne said. Zack knew that his sister hated Vegas. She'd come to see him, and he'd tried to show her a good time. They'd taken a plane tour to the Grand Canyon, gone to see Cirque de Soleil, eaten lunch at places where the slot machines stayed in discreet alcoves. Gail, meanwhile, had spent all her time in the casinos. She radiated the quiet, non-dazed satisfaction of someone who'd won but not really big.

Anne was going to say something Zack didn't want to hear.

"I went to your show tonight."

He drained his drink. "I asked you not to."

"Why ever not!" Marissa cried. "It was wonderful! He's so brave, the way he just goes in there with all those big ol' cats!"

Gail's lean, quick body said, *So your girlfriend doesn't know about you. Still the same old Zack.*

"I know you asked me not to go," Anne said, "but I needed to see it. It was. . . . impressive."

"Thanks." She disapproved, and there was no way she could hide it, even though she was trying. As if she knew what he was thinking, she said, "I'm sorry."

Marissa said, puzzled, "What for?"

No one answered her. Instead Anne finished her drink, some awful vodka thing loaded with fruit, and blurted, "There's so much else you could have put your . . . talent to. Aiding law enforcement. Some kind of business office, interpreting people. Even playing poker!"

Marissa looked at Zack. "I didn't know you like poker, honey."

"I don't," Zack said. "Anne, I have a suspended-sentence conviction, remember? No law enforcement. And I'd hate any office job. I'd hate any *office*. I need to move, get physical."

Gail said dryly, "Well, lions are certainly physical. Zack, you've got something on your mind. Why don't you just spit it out?"

Zack looked at her in surprise. It always startled him when someone else, someone normal, knew what he intended. He said, "Marissa, will you leave us alone for a few minutes? Family stuff."

Marissa stuck out her bottom lip. Before she could protest, Gail stood. "Show me the rest of this place, Marissa, will you? It's so big I think I'd get lost by myself."

Marissa looked mutinous, but eagerness to play hostess won out. "Well, the master suite is this way. . . ."

On the TV screen, Jose Torres hit Wayne Luciter a wicked uppercut to the chin.

Zack said, "You remember that doctor who wanted to give me an MRI way back when I was in your hospital, three and a half years ago? NorSomething? Well, I want it now."

Anne said quietly, "What's happening?"

"I don't know. Nothing. Something. It's like I . . . I'm not sure. But I think there's more of that integration stuff going on."

"Why do you think that? Because you can control those lions so well?"

"I'm not controlling them. They're . . . well, okay, maybe I am. Indirectly. But it's not that."

"What then?"

Zack grimaced. Anne was prepared to wait all night for a good answer, but Zack didn't have all night. Marissa and Gail passed by the open doorway to the terrace, Marissa saying condescendingly, "And of course we have a whirlpool and—"

All at once Zack was sick of Marissa. She had a nasty temper, she was interested mainly in his money, and he could only fuck her if he was drunk. Before he knew he was going to, he blurted out, "How is Jazzy?"

Anne looked startled. Even before she spoke, he knew what, and how, she was going to say. "She's married, Zack. A year after you . . . nearly two years ago. Last I heard, she was expecting a child."

And then, in response to what must have been on his face, "I'm sorry."

"Don't be, it's fine," he rasped. "I don't care, I was just curious, is all."

"She—"

"It doesn't matter!" He didn't need Jazzy, he didn't need anybody. There was a little silence.

Anne said gently, "You wanted to tell me about the 'more integration stuff' going on."

All at once, he didn't want to. And yet this was why he'd paid to bring Anne and Gail out here, wasn't it? "Nah. Changed my mind."

"I don't think so," Anne said, but Marissa and Gail had finished their tour and sat back down. Anne—submissive Anne!—said firmly, "Marissa, it was lovely meeting you, but Zack and I need to talk some more. Gail will get you a cab."

"Hey!" Marissa said. "Who the hell do you think you are to—"

"Go, Marissa," Zack said.

"Listen, *sweetheart*, don't think you can order me around like some—"

Gail took her elbow, lifted her from her chair, and dragged her off the terrace. Marissa began to shout protests and then obscenities. Gail paid no attention whatsoever, tossing over her shoulder, "'Night, Annie. See you much later."

"Wow," Zack said, caught somewhere between admiration and resentment. But if *he'd* tried to manhandle Marissa, it would have had an entirely different meaning. All of a sudden you would have had domestic abuse.

Anne said, "Talk to me, Zack."

Even in the sudden calm, it was harder than he'd anticipated. His throat seemed to close up, and for a second he was afraid of strangling.

Anne's body and face said: *Trust me.*

When was the last time Zack had trusted someone to hear his fears? He'd never trusted anyone like that, not even Anne. Not even Jazzy. But Anne was the only person who'd been there for him his whole life. She'd been the big sister set above him, the brainy bar he could never reach, the sparring partner he could never touch—but she'd been there.

"I hear voices," he said, and after that, it was easier. Anne shifted suddenly and Zack added, "No, not like that, not crazy stuff. I mean, it *is* crazy, but they aren't voices telling me to kill myself or anything. Actually, they aren't voices at all. They're a sort of . . . Christ, this is going to sound so stupid . . . they're like something big. Inside my mind."

The alarm rising off her like an odor didn't let up. "What kind of something big?"

"How the fuck should I know? I just know it's there, and it's getting stronger, and I don't like it! Maybe an MRI can tell what it is and the doctors can get rid of the damn thing."

"Is it . . . does it feel like a religious presence?"

"Religious? You mean, like God or spirits or demons? No."

"What does it feel like?"

"I told you. Something really big. Oh, Christ, Anne, forget it. I don't need an MRI. I'm doing fine. I mean, look at all this!" He waved his hand vaguely at the terrace, the vaulted ceilings of the suite beyond, Las Vegas. "I'm making more money than you would believe!"

But she wasn't impressed, he could tell. Damn it, he'd wanted her to be impressed! That was, he realized, the true reason why he'd brought her out here. To finally impress Anne.

"I can arrange for an MRI, Zack, and I will. For as soon as possible." She smiled painfully and put her hand over his. She really cared. So why was what he heard in his brain Anne's voice from over two years ago, saying, "*It's a long way to fall, Zack.*" Why?

He looked over the terrace railing at the Strip, twenty-six stories below. Down there on a huge marquee his name flashed in gaudy lights. On the TV, Luciter had Torres on the mat, and Torres didn't get up.

———

For the MRI, he had to fly home. Norwood had arranged for time on some sort of super-scanner that, Zack figured, was probably like arranging sparring time at an elite gym. This super scanner, some under-doctor-type told him, "paired functional MRI with connectome imaging, through high-angular diffusion and diffusion spectrum imaging combined with neurocognitive tests." Show-off prick. Norwood just said they were going to take pictures of how and when different parts of his brain worked, including how it was wired to other parts.

Zack couldn't be drunk, he couldn't be on any junk, he couldn't be anything but himself and whatever else was inhabiting his head. Zack clenched his fists as the exam table slid into the machine like slab into a drawer in the morgue.

"Try to relax," a tech said from somewhere outside. Yeah, right. Stupid bastard.

His head was held immobile by a brace. The brace wasn't painful but he hated it anyway, just for the way it cut his freedom. He wore goggles that could project images in front of his eyes.

"Ready, Zack?" the tech said. "Please tap your right thumb against each of the fingers on your right hand."

Zack did, followed by a lot of other dumb little tasks. Each time, the coils in the machine thumped softly. His head felt slightly warm. Eventually an image flashed on the screen.

"What do you see, Zack?"

"A kid's ball. Red."

"Fine. Now what?"

A house, a campfire, an ice-cream cone, a dog, a car. Zack felt back in kindergarten: C is for car, D is for dog. Zack had brought Browne with him to Anne's place. A computer, a church, a tree, a table, the seashore. When he'd been eleven, Zack, who couldn't swim, had nearly drowned in rough surf. A rocket ship, a rose, a book, a refrigerator.

A boxing ring.

Now they're getting to it.

A cloud, a rosary, a star of David, a pencil.

A lion.

Two lions.

A statue of Jesus, a sailboat, a pyramid, a starry sky.

The images started to include videos of people doing things: eating, dancing, singing, praying, walking along the beach, kissing, driving a car, boxing. Animals ran and hunted and slept. Zack waited to see them either humping or tearing apart prey, but there were no images like that. He smiled.

"What's funny, Zack?" the tech said, and Zack told him. The tech didn't reply.

A building blew up. A speeder was arrested. Two children pushed at each other, their faces angry. Something else blew up, Zack wasn't exactly sure what. A fire raged in a building. A firefighter carried out a little girl, unhurt. A minister led a congregation in prayer.

"Hey," Zack said, "are we almost done?"

"Just a little longer."

It was a lot longer. Anne had told him the typical imaging lasted about 45 minutes, but this took hours. By the end, Zack was thoroughly bored. What did describing yet another tree ("Do you know what kind of tree it is, Zack?") have to do with his non-voices? This was stupid.

When they finally let him out, he went straight to the nearest bar and got drunk. He thought of looking up Jazzy's address on his phone and taking a cab to her house, just to see where she lived now, but even drunk, he realized how dumb that was. Instead he took a cab to Anne's. She'd been waiting up and looked worried, but all she said was, "I walked Browne just fifteen minutes ago, so you don't have to do that before you go to bed."

He thanked her, torn between gratitude and the wish that she didn't always do everything so fucking *right*. In bed, with the dog curled against his back, he dreamed that he held Jazzy again, before she pulled away and went into the arms of a dead, bleeding Julian Browne.

Dr. Norwood's office held Zack, Anne, Norwood, and a Dr. Keller, who looked too young, pretty, and blonde to be what she was. Zack couldn't remember the term, but it meant a doctor who analyzed and interpreted the scanner results. She looked a little dazed. The room was small, chaotic with computers, piles of print-outs, and a lot of equipment Zack couldn't identify, all interspersed with used coffee cups. One of these was growing greenish mold, which couldn't be good. Weren't doctors supposed to be super clean?

Norwood was going to lean forward, going to clasp his hands on his lap, going to speak—

"Mr. Murphy, the results of your scan are very interesting. Let me start by telling you what we thought we might see but didn't, and then what we didn't expect to see but did."

"Okay," said Zack, unable to think of any other response. The non-voices had been pummeled into silence by two double Scotches.

"Often when people report sensing a 'presence' in their mind, we see increased activity in the temporal lobe, and more than usual wiring to that area of the brain. That correlates with certain kinds of religious experience, including mysticism and meditation and out-of-body sensations. Neither your responses to religious imagery nor your scan show that."

"You mean it isn't God in my voices. Well, I told you *that*."

Norwood smiled. "So you did. The other usual source of hearing voices is schizophrenia, which doesn't feature brain-structure abnormalities but does include certain patterns of neural wiring. Your scans don't show those, either."

"So I'm not nuts."

"You are not schizophrenic."

"They aren't really voices anyway," Zack said. "I told you that. They don't have words. I just call them that . . . because." Because there wasn't anything else to call them. He really wanted this conference over, even though he was the one who'd asked for it.

Dr. Keller spoke for the first time. "What do they seem like, Zack, if not voices?"

He shrugged. "I don't know. Presences, like Anne said. Or maybe one really big presence. Only not really. It's like . . . it's like *everything* is there. In my head."

Anne said, "Everything? What do you mean?"

"I don't know what I mean! That's what you're supposed to tell me! Christ!"

Norwood said soothingly, "Let's go on to what your scan *does* show. We expected to see greater integration among the sensory input areas, the motor areas, and a section of the brain associated with interpreting and responding to people and animals, including the fear centers. We saw that integration, which is what lets you so effectively work with the lions."

And with you, Zack didn't say aloud. The signals coming from everyone practically shouted at him: Norwood's excited interest, that he was trying and failing to mask; the blonde's dazed fearfulness; Anne's concern so strong it was almost despair. Christ, she should lighten up. But none of them were all that different from the big cats. Which was depressing to think about, so he didn't.

"Some of your neural profile matches that of highly creative people who—"

"Creative? You mean like painters and writers and all them? I don't create anything."

Norwood went on, "Stronger, and more surprising, are other results of the scan. Mr. Murphy, you present a neural profile remarkably like a person who is asleep and dreaming, with—"

"What the hell! I wasn't asleep inside that machine!"

"I know you weren't. But your connectome and functional data show the pattern of dreams: heightened activity in the oldest parts of the brain, in memory, and in emotion, along with decreased activity in areas governing reason and decision-making. The biggest surprise was how much the scan reflects a dream-like state usually associated with dealing with internal situations, not external ones. In other words, whatever is going on, and it includes some very unusual neural pathways, you are connecting with something that is inside your mind, like dreams are. But not anything we can name."

Anne said, "The unconscious?"

"In part. But much more than the usual patterns that tap subconscious responses. Somehow the parts of the brain that respond to other people is heavily involved, even when Mr. Murphy is reacting to imagery like trees or rocks or stars."

Anne said, "A . . . I almost can't say this . . . a collective unconscious?"

The blonde said primly, "That lies outside our purview, Ms. Murphy."

Zack demanded, "What is collective unconscious?"

Norwood smiled. "That's a good question, Mr. Murphy. But we don't know the answer, any more than we know what consciousness is. We're all conscious, we experience the world as 'I, me,' but nobody knows how the brain gives rise to that consciousness. It's the great mystery of neuroscience: What are we experiencing when we think, 'Cogito, ergo sum'?"

Think what? All at once Zack had enough of this. Talk, talk, talk, that's all they could offer him. He glared at them, even Anne. "So what does it mean? Can you cure me?"

Norwood said, "You're not ill, Mr. Murphy."

Dr. Keller said, "The brain's incredible plasticity—"

Anne said, "Maybe meds to completely disrupt everything the—"

"No drugs to completely disrupt everything!" Zack shouted. He didn't even know why he was so furious. "I only wanted the voices to stop! You want to take away what I can do? How I make my living? What's wrong with you people? We're done here!"

Anne grabbed his arm. Zack shook her off and stalked out of the room.

On the plane back to Vegas, he paid for in-flight wi-fi. The flight attendant had already brought him two Scotches. He Googled "collective unconscious" and got "Psychology: in Jungian psychological theory, a part of the unconscious mind incorporating patterns of memories, instincts, and experiences common to all mankind. These patterns are inherited, may be arranged into archetypes, and are observable through their effects on dreams, behavior, etc."

Bullshit. If there was one thing his non-voices were not, it was "common to all mankind." He was the only sap blessed, or cursed, with the Gift. Which even after two drinks and at 30,000 feet, was growing stronger and stronger. It was like it was trying to take him over, like he could take over the lions. And the doctors had been no help at all.

He ordered a double.

All the next day, the thing in his head grew. He had a show that night and couldn't drink. He refused to see Jerry, ignored messages from Marissa and Anne, spent the day sitting on the huge terrace of his Las Vegas suite, holding Browne on his lap. The dog was the only thing that made sense to him. Browne didn't even squirm, only giving one polite bark when he needed to use the doggie poo-pad in the corner. Zack ate nothing all day. His head felt as if it could explode.

No, not explode. Expand, to take in whatever else was in there. Expand as big as the universe. Almost it seemed to Zack that he could feel—what had Norwood called them?—"neural pathways" multiplying like rabbits in his brain. Ridiculous, but . . . Christ, his head *hurt*.

It still ached when he went on stage at 8:00, but he gave the best show ever, effortlessly controlling even Goldie. He had Fuzzball and Lulu jump over each other, Fluffy fetch a spangled baton and drop it at his feet as if she were Browne. And all the while Zack felt that he was only partly there, or only partly himself. Power flowed through him—but from where? Whose?

The consciousness of the universe itself.

The words formed in his mind, scaring him so badly that he ended the show ten minutes early and walked out of the cage. The audience, on its feet and roaring his name, didn't mind. Even Henryk, the least resentful of the Bajek brothers, glanced at Zack with something like awe. Zack didn't answer whatever Henryk said to him. He had to get out of there, or his head would explode.

He took a car right to the MGM Grand and bolted to his suite, locking the door behind him. He hardly knew what he was doing, or why. He put his hands to his head and groaned.

Everything *was* there, in his head—everything that had ever existed, or would exist, and he was both its observer and a part of it: the entire universe laid bare in a second. He felt possessed, taken over, even though he knew he wasn't. But it was too much, the pressure—the pressure!—of *everything*! It was going to crush him, to burst him apart like a balloon filled with too much air, a wine bottle left too long in the freezer until the wine expanded and shattered. . . .

Browne, bounding forward to greet him, stopped so short that his feet slid on the marble floor. The dog whimpered.

"Hey, Brownie, good dog . . ."

Browne backed away from Zack, tail between his legs.

It was the last insult to his autonomy, to him, to Zack Murphy, his own person. He didn't want to be everything, he didn't want the consciousness of the universe woven through and into his mind. Norwood had said that Zack's brain had the same cells in it as anybody else's, just arranged differently and doing different things—did that mean that anybody could be what he was becoming? Well, let them have it! He didn't want to be everything, he didn't want to be anything but himself, alone and independent the way he'd always been . . . Zack screamed in rage, in frustration, in fear. His eye fell on the foyer table, marble and wrought iron.

And he *saw* it. Saw the table so vividly it almost burned his eyeballs, every curve and line of it. He saw the pattern in the marble as if etched into his brain. He felt the flow of the arched iron legs. He saw the table as it was now, and as it had been when new, and as it would be in a few years' time when someone had scratched it and someone else had stained the top and one leg was bent. He knew what the table would become, just as he knew when Goldie would raise a paw and bat at him. The table was part of him because the same force inhabited it as inhabited him, and in that force, time was an illusion. The past and present and future of the table were simultaneous and they were now in Zack's head.

With the past and present and future of the floor.

And the vase.

And the stars in the sky above the terrace.

And Browne, who cowered before Zack and who was a mewling puppy, a full-grown mutt, an old dog barely able to move his paralyzed hind legs, a small inert corpse, a fresh bit of soil in a grave, even as he continued to romp and play in puppyhood. Time itself possessed Zack, and everything in his head, which was everything that existed, was one thing.

Just One.

He screamed and rushed onto the terrace. Above him the stars glittered and below the lights of Vegas glittered, and there was no difference, nor any difference between all that and himself. It was too much, it was intolerable, he would not have it . . . He threw one leg over the railing.

It's a long way to fall, Zack.

"No! No! No! Not me! You got the wrong guy! Go away!"

Everything, with its past and present and future, filled his head. Zack clung to the railing. Behind him, on the wall of the terrace, a mirror exploded, sending shards of glass flying twenty feet. In that instance, Zack knew he could explode the terrace, explode the MGM Grand, explode Las Vegas. And what else? *What else?*

"Mr. Murphy? Mr. Murphy!" Pounding on the locked door.

"No," Zack whispered. "Please, no. *I don't want it.*"

He never remembered what happened next. Everything went black. When he came to, the hotel manager and Security were prying his fingers off the railing. Mirror glass had cut his chest, his arms. "A . . . accident," he gasped. "Go . . . away."

They did, or maybe they didn't. But when Zack woke again, in his bed, it wasn't the hotel manager with him. It was Jerry, shaking his shoulder and saying, "Hey, champ. Wake up. That must have been some bender last night. You got any idea what time it is?"

Zack looked at the clock beside the bed: 7:00 p.m. He had been asleep, or passed out, or dead, for twenty hours.

"You got a show in an hour, kid."

"I—"

"Come on, get dressed!"

He wore clean pajamas. There were bandages over the cuts on his chest. He remembered almost nothing of the night before. There had been a mirror . . . hadn't there? Moving heavily, feeling as if the air were damp cotton wool, Zack let Jerry get him dressed, get him downstairs, get him into the waiting car. In his dressing room at The Wynn, Jerry got him into costume, the Egyptian pharaoh headdress and the gladiator sandals and ridiculous white loincloth. Zack walked out during the announcer's spiel, crossing the catwalk to the cage. Goldie roared.

Anton, on duty, sullenly unlocked the cage door.

Karoly stood inside, behind the barred shield, holding the CO_2 canister.

The crowd stopped screaming Zack's name and quieted, waiting.

Zack looked at the lions, Goldie and Lulu and Fluffy and Fuzzball. No: at Rex, Majesty, Artemis, Lilith. He looked at Anton, holding open the cage door. Zack had no idea what gesture or expression Anton would make next. Zack looked at Karoly, who stared back at him.

Karoly is going to. . . .

Is going to . . .

He didn't know what Karoly was going to do.

There were no non-voices, no presences in his head.

Zack looked again at the big cats, at their huge teeth and sleek long muscles and claw tips like ice picks. He looked at Rex's intent eyes and dark mane, at Artemis's lashing tail, at Majesty's poised stillness. He turned and walked back down the catwalk away from the cage, head tipped so far down that his headdress, sloppily fastened, fell off and lay in a heap of shining imitation gold.

IV.

Winter came swiftly in the mountains. At first snowfall, Zack looked for a shovel to dig out the car. Not that he was going anywhere; he hadn't gone anywhere in the nearly two months he'd been here. But there ought to be a shovel. It irritated him, and he phoned Loffman.

"Where's the snow shovel kept?"

"It should be in the laundry room, in the cupboard with the other maintenance stuff," Loffman said.

"It's not."

"Well, maybe—"

"Loffman, when I rent an entire mountain lodge, ten rooms, for three months right in the ski season, I expect there to be a goddamn snow shovel!"

"I know, but—"

"No buts, get one up here!"

Loffman sighed. Zack could picture his whole, tall, stooping, incredibly thin figure shaking with the sigh. Loffman always looked insubstantial as fog.

"Yes, Mr. Murphy. Oh, and somebody called looking for you. A woman."

"What did you say to her? Part of our agreement was that you tell nobody I'm here, that's what I'm paying your blood-sucking rent for—"

"I said nothing, I swear. I said I never even heard of you. And someone will bring a shovel today."

"They better."

The minute he broke the connection with Loffman, the stupidity of the entire exchange hit Zack. He didn't want a snow shovel. He didn't want anyone bringing him one. He didn't want to see anybody, talk to anyone.

Or had he called Loffman just to hear a human voice?

That was stupid, too. He'd come up to not hear any voices, not on the TV or the radio or even his cell phone. The third-rate lodge, the same one where Jazzy had once taken her middle-school charges, had no cable, no direct TV, no Internet, and cell coverage only in the immediate vicinity of the lodge. Zack was alone, free of anything but himself and Browne, just as he wanted.

Except for in his head.

There was no presence, no non-voices. But every time he got out of bed, made a cup of coffee, put on his parka and went out into the woods, Jazzy's image was there. Was this, the biggest apartment in the lodge, the same one that the adults had used on that field trip three years ago? Had Jazzy slept in this bed? Opened this refrigerator door? Sat on this chair, staring at this gas fireplace?

He hated it. He didn't want to think about her. Certainly not think about her more than when they'd actually been sleeping together. Jazzy's naked body, creamy chocolate and dark whorly hair. . . .

He was horny, was all! But he wasn't going down the mountain to find a hooker. No place he might be recognized, no act that required anyone else. Fuck that. Besides, he didn't have a snow shovel.

"Come on, Browne!"

The dog leapt off the rug by the fireplace and trotted after Zack. Every morning they went for a walk in the woods together. Every afternoon Zack went again, alone. That's all it was, a walk. Nothing else. No matter what he saw.

That afternoon, it was a deer. Zack had sat very still for a long time beside a deadfall at the edge of a clearing, cold eventually seeping through even his parka, waiting for whatever came along. The deer stepped hesitantly into the far edge of the clearing, downwind.

It's going to move left. . . .

The deer moved right, stepping daintily on delicate hooves.

It's going to push aside some snow and look for grass the way they do . . .
The deer lifted its head and sniffed the air.
It's going to run away, I know it, it's getting ready to run . . .
The deer stayed in the clearing another three minutes, until Zack jumped up and cursed the stupid thing and it fled, silent and swift as thought.
Zack stomped home, slammed the door, and got drunk.

He was acting crazy, and when he was sober he knew it, and when he was sober he got drunk so that he didn't care that he was acting crazy.

He built a wall of snow, using the shovel delivered by a sullen teenage boy driving an SUV, and lay down on top of the wall until he passed from shivering to drowsing. His lips were blue, he could barely walk on his frozen feet, and he understood that if he'd stayed there five more minutes, he might have died.

He lured a chipmunk to the porch with stale Sara Lee and failed to predict when it would scamper away.

He drew pictures of Jazzy, despite the fact that he couldn't draw, and burned each one in the gas fireplace, first prying off its glass cover. That created acrid odors that made Browne move indignantly away.

He boxed with a tree, an oak at least fifty years old, whose dry, sere leaves rattled with his blows while Zack's knuckles ended up bloody and his left thumb got broken.

In the woods he came across an animal he couldn't identify, something brown and furry the size of a large wastebasket. It rose on its hind legs and snarled at him. Zack took one step closer, knowing that it would attack. It didn't, dropping to all fours and lumbering off over the snow.

He buried his cell phone under a pile of snow-damp leaves, as deeply and carefully as if conducting a funeral for a beloved child.

He woke at night from dreams he couldn't remember, with tears that shamed him so much he raged at himself and rammed his broken fist into the unforgiving wall.

Then he found the wolves.

It was morning, which meant Browne was with him, which meant there should have been no animals around because Browne's joyous barking usually scared them all away. Snow had just started to fall in cold, gray flakes. Zack, with a long thick oak branch as a walking stick, trudged behind the lodge. He turned the corner and there, just before the tree line and the bottom of the idle ski lift, a pack of wolves dotted bloody snow. They had brought down a fawn and were tearing it apart.

One looked up and saw Zack and Browne.

They stared at each other—was this the same wolf he'd seen years before? How long did wolves live? Zack began to back away. The fawn's empty black eyes gazed at him. Its exposed entrails twisted like greasy ropes.

Then a small wolf—young?—jumped forward and raced at Browne.

The dog yelped and ran in circles, terrified. The rest of the wolf pack stayed motionless, watching its murderous whelp, watching Zack. The young wolf's jaws closed on Browne's tail.

Browne's cry of surprised pain galvanized Zack. He leapt at Browne, hitting out at the wolf with his oak branch. The branch connected, hard, and the wolf gave a single sharp yelp and fell on its side.

The pack left the fawn and moved forward, snarling.

Zack tried to grab Browne, and failed. The little dog was too terrified. Two wolves slipped between Zack and the lodge.

Wolves don't attack people, Loffman had told Zack. *They're scareder of you, boy, than you are of them.* But that wasn't the way it looked now.

He concentrated, his heart gonging faster than it ever had in the ring, trying to anticipate what the pack would do. They weren't attacking—score one for Loffman— but they were watching him intently, and he was surrounded. So was Browne, who chose that moment to streak toward Zack.

Instantly the young wolf was in pursuit. He caught Browne in his jaws. Browne shrieked, a sound Zack had not known a dog could make, and Zack threw himself on both of them, trying to tear Browne free.

"Let go, you fucker, let go—"

A claw raked his cheek, and the pack moved forward.

He was going to be torn apart by wolves, he and Browne both, "wolves don't attack people, boy," *but I faced lions. . . .* He was Browne, the fighter not the dog, and he was being murdered by himself in the ring.

The smell of wolf filled his nostrils, gamey and primitive. Jaws snapped close to Zack's flailing hands. A shot pierced the cold winter air.

The wolves scattered, the whelp dropping Browne. Zack picked him up. The dog still shrieked like something human. Gail ran from the lodge, her nine millimeter in her hand.

"What the fuck!" she shouted, and to Zack it sounded like a prayer.

In the animal-hospital waiting room, after Gail had driven her jeep down the mountain like she or it was possessed, they finally spoke. The vet had rushed Browne into surgery. Gail looked at Zack and said, "What did you do to your hand?"

"Broke the thumb." After a silence he added, "Boxing with a tree."

"Huh," Gail said.

"Why were you there at the lodge?"

"The same reason I always come—to check on you for Anne. I didn't tell her I'd located you, because she would have wanted to come and I thought you might refuse to talk to her, or be even crazier than you are, or be dead."

"How did you find me?"

"It wasn't that hard. I know people, still." And after another long silence she said, "Did Anne ever tell you how we met?"

What? Zack didn't care how Gail and Anne had met. He cared about Browne, and about nothing else except being so tired. Why was he so tired? It was only morning.

Gail said, "I had a shitty life. I know you think you did, too, with your parents and all, but you aren't nearly the bad-ass you think you are. Weird, yes, but not a genuine bad-ass. I was on crack, and in jail, and turning tricks to survive. Then I O.D.ed. Anne was my nurse in the hospital and all I wanted was for her to leave me alone so I could get back out on the street and do more crack. But then I assaulted a cop, never a good idea, and so I was back in the can. And Anne came to see me. Once, twice, a lot. It didn't happen all at once. Or maybe it did, but I didn't want to see it. Committing to Anne, to a drug-free life, to normalcy—it was a long way for me to fall. Into trust. I had to fall into trust, and into needing somebody, and it felt like such a long way to fall."

"I'm not interested in your lame story," Zack said coldly.

"Sure you are. You just don't know it yet."

Zack said nothing, staring at his boots. They had on them snow, dead leaves, muck, blood.

Gail said, "I'm going home now. I'm not telling Anne about this, although I will tell her you're all right even if you're cruel enough to not return her calls. You got your credit card? Good. You can get a cab back up the mountain, if you want to spend more of your undeserved fortune, or to someplace down here, I don't care which. Where's your phone?"

"Six feet underground."

Gail didn't even blink. She stood and stretched leisurely, and Zack saw the bulge of the nine millimeter at her waist. She walked away. Over her shoulder she said, "Jazzy's husband left her. He was no good in the first place. She and the baby are at her mother's."

Zack sat there another hour. He didn't touch the cell phone that Gail had left on her plastic seat. Eventually the vet emerged, dressed in scrubs and a paper hat, just like a doctor for people.

"Your dog will be fine, Mr. Murphy. He needs to stay here a few days. The receptionist will tell you when you can take him home, and she'll give you discharge instructions when you do. What happened to your hand?"

"Nothing."

"That's not nothing. You should go to an ER and have that looked at."

"Okay," Zack lied.

His hand hurt, but not much. The vet had not recognized him. Neither had the receptionist, nor the old lady holding a cat, nor the child and its mother with a rabbit restless in a red carrier. There was a whole world of people who didn't know what Zack had been able to do—any of the things he'd been able to do—and didn't care. Normal people, in a normal world.

Trust, Gail had said.

Zack picked up her phone and took it out to the parking lot. It was winter here, too, but not the snowy freezing winter of the mountains. Rain spat at him from an overcast sky. He stood between the animal hospital and a Dodge Caravan, and keyed in a number. With his left thumb broken and his right hand bloody, it was awkward. It should have been Anne first, Zack knew that; Anne had earned the right to be first. But that wasn't the way it worked, because about one thing at least, Gail had been wrong.

You didn't fall a long way. Falling wasn't enough. You had to *leap*.

He waited through the ringing, the answer, the normal voice saying "Hello?"

"Jazzy," he said. "Please don't hang up. It's me, just me. It's Zack."

murder on the *aldrin* express

MARTIN L. SHOEMAKER

In the clever story that follows we're treated to a murder mystery set on a spaceship, one which focuses strongly on believable future technology and which gives us an ingenious and classically satisfying mystery to unravel, one peopled with vivid characters who are convincing as real people, with all their varying strengths, weaknesses, and foibles.

 Martin L. Shoemaker is a writer with a lucrative programming habit. He always expected to be a writer, right up to the day when his algebra teacher said, "This is a computer. This is a program. Why don't you write one?" He has programmed computers professionally for thirty years and has also written articles and two books on software design. He has recently returned to his fiction-writing roots. His works have appeared in Analog Science Fiction and Fact, Galaxy's Edge, *the Digital Science Fiction Anthology series,* The Glass Parachute *anthology, and* The Gruff Variations: Writing for Charity Anthology, Volume 1.

Are you sure about this, Riggs?"

Midshipman Riggs nodded. "The micrographs don't lie, Chief Carver. There are nanos all over that cable."

I scratched my neck under my stiff white uniform collar. It was hard to keep my uniform clean within the water rations on the ship. Besides an inescapable slight stink—inescapable because the whole ship had the same stink of bodies confined for months—I was developing a bit of a rash. "But are you *sure*? We're going to have to take this to Captain Aames."

I saw the young British astronaut turn pale, almost as pale as his close-cropped blonde hair, and I managed to conceal my amusement. Riggs was new to the *Aldrin*, but already he lived in fear of Nick. Half the crew did the same, while the other half would never dare go to space without Nick in command. Some days I wasn't sure which half I was in.

Riggs was understandably nervous: being challenged by the Chief Officer was bad enough, and bringing bad news to Nick would be even worse. But the midshipman hesitated only briefly before he swallowed and answered. "Yes, sir. Take a look. The micrographs don't lie."

I did take a look, pulling Riggs's report onto my comp. I wasn't an expert in nano-machines any more than Riggs was, but I could read the computer analysis easily enough. The frayed S3 cables were infested with dormant nanobots.

Well, I had been hoping for a distraction so I could stop thinking about Tracy. I had managed to avoid her even in the close confines of the Mars cycler, but I couldn't avoid the memory of her without some distraction. This would certainly fit the bill. "All right, then. No sense in delay. Let's go see the Captain." I stood from my desk chair, automatically correcting to avoid rising too fast in the ship's quarter gravity. As we headed out of my office, I noticed that Riggs still moved with exaggerated care. Eventually he would adjust—if Nick didn't break him first.

Nick had broken more men than any three other commanders in the Corps. He loves to push a crew in drill: "Again. Again. Do it again, and get it right this time." Sometimes that seems like the only word he knows: "Again". Again and again until you break; but those he doesn't break, we *know* our stuff. We have to. Being the best is the only way to get Nick to shut the hell up.

Probably Riggs would break, but I hoped not. He was a good kid, endearingly eager to be in space even if only as crew of a Mars cycler. We would never make planetfall, just follow a complex pseudo-cometary Solar orbit that took us back and forth between Earth and Mars every eleven months. We orbited the Sun; but as we got close to Earth, she grabbed us, swung as around a couple of times, and then tossed us back toward Mars; and then Mars grabbed us and tossed us back in a complicated dance that took only trivial amounts of fuel for occasional course corrections. It was a mathematically elegant and efficient way to travel; but it was about as exciting and eventful as driving a subway train. Most in the Corps saw cycler service as pretty low duty for an astronaut, tantamount to punishment. And working under Nick didn't make that duty any more popular, which added to our attrition rate. I couldn't guess whether Riggs would last or not. Nick couldn't, either, which was why he insisted on testing people until he found out. Nick hated not knowing.

We walked through the ship as I ruminated, passing through one brownish-gray corridor after another. I had seen pictures of the ship when she was new, all orange-yellow ("ochre" the designers called it) and with the Holmes Interplanetary logo prominently displayed in most rooms. It had been a bit ostentatious, but it had looked polished. Then Holmes had gone out of business and Mission Control had scooped up their assets and repurposed them for government missions. One of the first things they had done was to paint over the ochre with government-issue gray; but because they had skimped on the gray, the result had a brownish tinge that looked grimy even when we cleaned it as best we could. We got used to the grimy look eventually, but we prized any little bit of color that broke up the dullness.

Eventually we arrived at Nick's outer office—empty, since I was the one who usually manned the desk there—and passed through to the command office. The door opened as I approached. I ushered Riggs in and we stood before the display desk. Where most of the ship was brownish-gray, Nick had had his office painted in darker tones, mostly black. He also kept the lights low, except for the glow from his computer desk. He liked the room dark, with one giant window behind the desk showing the star field outside.

A chair was behind the desk, its high back facing us, and it didn't budge as we entered and the door closed behind us. Nick was staring at the stars and probably ignoring us, but it was possible he hadn't heard us. As usual, the office was filled with mellow Brazilian music. Many of us in the Corps have trained in Brazil and picked up a little Portuguese; but Nick had thoroughly adopted the country and its culture. I recognized "Brigas Nunca Mais," one of Nick's favorites. I always found some irony in that: the title translated roughly as "Never Fight Again," and Nick was a tenacious fighter.

The chair back swayed slightly. Despite the music, I was sure Nick knew we were there. He was just ignoring us. Fine. I would wait him out.

Finally the song ended, and Nick's voice came from behind the chair. "Are you going to stand there all day, Chief Carver? I know you didn't leave."

"How did you know it was me?" Did he analyze the sound of my walk? I couldn't see how over the music.

"Elementary, my dear Carver. After Margo Azevedo's breakdown at last month's maudlin dinner, I would rather avoid any unnecessary contact with our passengers. That door is currently programmed to open for only one other person on this ship besides myself; and that one other person is you, Chief."

"Someone could have broken your lock program and entered that way."

"True. But there's only one person on this ship whose programming skills are up to that task. And that person is also you. Ergo, if someone intrudes on my solitude, it could only be you. Oh, and Mr. Riggs, of course." I saw Riggs flinch when Nick said his name. He looked at me and mouthed the word "how," but I didn't respond. I didn't want to give Nick the satisfaction. Besides, he likely had a camera hidden in his office, so it wasn't any big mystery.

Over the years I had learned the value of having more patience than Nick. It's not easy, but I've done it. He has nearly zero patience when he wants something from you, but nearly infinite when he's avoiding someone. So I just stood silently and waited him out. At last he spoke again. "So what is it, Chief Carver? More of the incessant mourning? Have our passengers decided they want to regale us with yet more stories of the late, great Professor and his botched expedition?"

"No, sir, but it does involve the expedition. Riggs has found evidence that Professor Azevedo's S3 cable was sabotaged."

It's rare that I get to surprise Nick, even with bad news; so I took a secret, perverse delight in the way he spun the chair around. Instead of his usual casual slouch, he leaned intently forward: a medium-short man, fit and wiry with bushy red-gray hair and short beard. When he got like this, his energy seemed likely to burst out in a random direction on the smallest provocation. Again Riggs flinched as if Nick might leap at him or throw something at him; and I had to admit, it had happened to others in the crew.

Nick fixed Riggs with his best contemptuous stare. "Mr. Riggs, Synthetic Spider Silk breaks. It is incredibly strong, but it also breaks when not properly maintained over time. And Paolo Azevedo was notoriously sloppy—exactly as I warned his backers before the expedition, not that anyone listened to me. Half of his maintenance reports never got filed. So I have no doubt he fell behind on S3 inspections, and the cable broke as a result. Why would you suggest otherwise?"

Riggs straightened to attention under Nick's stare, and he stood his ground. I could really get to like the kid. He had spunk. "Captain, I was performing the quarantine inventory, as per Chief Officer Carver's orders." We were less than two days away from Earth orbit, so it was standard practice to scan all transported gear for contaminants—including nanos, since many Earth jurisdictions have pretty strict laws about unlicensed nanomachines. "I inspected Professor Azevedo's S3 cable, and I found a small colony of scavenger nanos. If I may, sir?"

Nick nodded, and Riggs swiped his finger across the comp in his sleeve, pushing his report to Nick's display desk. Nick gestured us closer as he leaned over the electron micrograph, an image of several parallel gray tubules dotted with miniscule magenta specks. Riggs tapped his comp, and several circles zoomed out of the image for more detail. The tubules began to show as a fine matrix; and the specks became a number of small structures, false colored in shades of magenta to stand out against the gray background. "There they are, sir. Scanner says they conform 99.993% to the structure of standard scavenger nanos, one of the same lines that the expedition took along for scavenging raw materials. This particular line scavenges salt ions and fixes them to a substrate, manufacturing salts and salt-based compounds. And these—" Riggs tapped the comp again, and small flecks were highlighted in yellow. "—are salt ions trapped in the glycine matrix."

Nick sneered at Riggs. "And why are you wasting my time over a bunch of salt ions?" But I knew that sneer from long experience: it meant that Nick was testing Riggs. Nick already knew the answer, and he suspected that just *maybe* Riggs wasn't a complete incompetent. If Riggs could just keep his cool and make a thorough, professional report, he might actually impress Nick. And I knew as well as anyone how difficult it is to impress Nick.

Riggs held up under the sneer and continued his report. "Captain, the salt ions depolymerize the glycine, reverting it from a fibrous state to more of a gel. The silk becomes liquid again, Captain, and it stretches like taffy. It pulls thinner and thinner until it just wisps away. If the Captain is done with this micrograph?" Nick waved his hand dismissively, and Riggs brought up the next image. "This is the same zone, zoomed out by a factor of ten." There were a number of gray strands, too small now to see the magenta specks; but the strands became progressively more yellow as they approached the upper right corner. They also narrowed dramatically. When the strands had diminished to roughly half their width, they started to bend and warp. And suddenly, almost in the corner of the image, they became a knotted yellow tangle, and they reached no further.

Nick turned one wide eye up at Riggs. "So, Mr. Riggs, you're telling me that although Azevedo *was* an utter fool who had no business leading that expedition, he wasn't at fault in his own death? You're telling me that I was wrong?"

Riggs swallowed before he spoke. "Yes, Captain."

"Good!" Nick looked back down at the desk. You would have to know him as well as I did to see the slight edge of a smile at the corner of his mouth. Riggs had impressed him. "Riggs, it is my job to be right. This ship and all aboard depend on that. It is *your* job to tell me when I'm not doing *my* job. I *will* tear you into small bloody bits when you do, because I'm *never* wrong; and I expect you to do so anyways, because sometimes I *am* wrong, and I will *not* tolerate that. If you can accept that, you might have a future on this ship. Can you?"

Riggs didn't hesitate again. "I don't know, Captain. We'll find out."

This time Nick even let his smile show. "Honesty. Another mark in your favor. Don't ever lie to me, Riggs, and we'll get along fine. So I trust you did research on these nanos. You know how they're activated."

"Concentrated UV light, Captain, of specific frequencies. The light excites certain outer electrons in the structure, ionizing the nanos and initiating a chain reaction that starts them in motion. I'm afraid chemistry isn't my best subject, Captain, so I can explain how to activate them but not the details. The frequency and intensity required are such that they don't occur naturally in the solar spectrum."

"So they can't activate by accident. Someone has to use an emitter." Riggs nodded. "And that's why you believe the break must have been sabotage."

I decided Riggs had had enough of Nick's attention, and it was time to draw some fire of my own. "Yes, Captain, and that's why we had to bring this straight to you. Until we reach Earth's gravipause, you are the highest legal authority aboard this ship."

"Much as it chaps Lee Klein's ass." Nick had negotiated that clause in his contract with Holmes Interplanetary before he had accepted command of the *Aldrin*: while the ship was in free fall around Sol, Nick had nearly the sovereign power of an old British sea captain. Oh, he couldn't have you flogged, but he had pretty broad authority to run his ship as he saw fit. When Mission Control bought out Holmes, Director Klein discovered that Nick had fashioned the contract with all of his trademark attention to detail. Nick's autonomy survived the end of Holmes unless the new owner wanted to dismiss Nick and pay him his full wage for five years plus bonuses while Nick sat on a beach in Brazil and drank caipirinhas. Klein was not about to do that, and so Nick's authority was pretty much total until Earth's gravitational force acting on us exceeded Sol's.

Nick didn't continue, so I did. "And so it is your responsibility to investigate, Captain. Secure the evidence, prepare a report for the authorities on Earth, and make sure whoever is behind this isn't a danger to our passengers and crew."

"My responsibility?" Nick turned one glaring eye upon me.

"Yes, sir. And I guess this changes at least one thing."

"Oh?"

"You were wrong about the expedition. The failure wasn't their fault."

"Oh, really?"

"Well, clearly, it was deliberate. It wasn't an accident."

"Oh, really? And what does that change?"

"Well . . . everything!" Nick exasperated me. As usual. I think exasperating was one of his primary joys in life. Defying expectations and challenging beliefs was one of his many ways of testing people.

"Does it change the fact that they didn't plan for adequate backup water? Does it change the fact that they didn't plan for the possible temperature extremes? Does it change the fact that they were completely unprepared for a Category V dust storm? Does it change the fact that they had no plan for what would happen if they lost their orbital platform *like we lost ours?*"

"Nnnnno." I had intended to needle Nick, but I hadn't expected him to react so strongly. Riggs was squirming. The crew didn't usually see Nick and I duel like this.

"Then I wasn't wrong! They had a poorly planned mission from start to finish. Though I grant you there's one failure even I overlooked: they didn't plan for a criminal on board."

I saw my opening. "And that's *another* reason why only you can investigate this murder. You understand their expedition and you know what to look for."

Nick sighed, and I knew I had him. "Very well, then, Chief Carver. I guess I must end my exile here and deal with the members of the expedition. Interview them and find out who might have a motive for this crime."

"So should I bring them in, sir?"

"Oh not all at once, one at a time. That's all I want to deal with. Let us start with . . . I think we'll start with Ms. Wells."

Tracy! I tried to stall. "Nick, surely you don't think she had anything to do with this."

"What I think is none of your concern. Has she already messed up your head so much that you've forgotten how to follow orders?"

Damn it, Nick, get out of my head! "No, Captain, if that's your order, I shall carry it out, *sir.*"

"That's good, man, because I need to know if you're going to have a problem with this. I need to know if you're thinking with your brain, or somewhere lower."

I had manipulated Nick into taking charge of the investigation, and he was going to make me suffer for that; but I wasn't going to let that impair my performance of my duties. "Sir, I shall carry out my responsibilities exactly as expected."

I left, Riggs in tow, and the door closed behind us. Facing off to Nick must have emboldened Riggs. Normally I wouldn't expect personal questions from such a junior crewman, so his next question hit me by surprise. "Is there a problem with Ms. Wells, sir?"

"No, we just have a . . . history. I've been avoiding her. Too many uncomfortable memories."

"He knows this? And he's putting you in this bind deliberately? He's a right bastard, isn't he?"

"That he is, Mr. Riggs. That he is." We reached the tube to the berthing ring, and I turned off while Riggs continued back to his post. Under my breath, I echoed Riggs. "A right bastard he is."

I had dreaded that encounter, but I couldn't put it off. Three months ago I had looked up the cabin number where Tracy bunked with Arla Simms, another member of the Azevedo expedition. I had managed to stop myself from going there, but the number was lodged firmly in my brain.

And now I stood before 32-A and held my finger on the door buzzer. *Nearly four years . . .* Too soon, and far too long. I pressed the buzzer.

Arla opened the door: a trim young woman in a simple blue jumpsuit from the expedition, her blonde curls cut functionally short. We had met several times during the voyage, but never for very long. I had avoided prolonged contact with the passengers almost as thoroughly as Nick had. Arla seemed surprised to have a visitor. "Yes, Chief Carver?"

I straightened to attention, hiding behind formality as best I could. "Begging your pardon, ma'am, but the Captain has sent me. He has asked me to fetch Ms. Wells—" I managed not to stammer at her name "—so that he may ask some questions about the expedition."

"The expedition? Is there something wrong?"

"Nothing I can speak of, ma'am. The Captain is just thorough." It wasn't precisely a lie. Not that I would hesitate to lie to keep the investigation under control, but I would stick as close to the truth as I could.

"Well, come in, Chief. Tracy's in here." *Damn.* I had been afraid she would invite me in, and I hadn't figured out a polite excuse to refuse. Arla stepped aside, and I entered the cabin.

Instantly my eyes were pulled to Tracy where she sat on her bunk, a desk folded out from the cabin wall. She was editing expedition videos, and she paused them as I came in. Tracy wore a blue jumpsuit like Arla's, but she had altered the legs to thigh-length shorts. She had always liked her legs free, and I had never minded the chance to see them. She looked just as I had glimpsed her in random moments since the expedition came aboard: a little older than when we had parted, and a little thinner from the tight rations on Mars, and somehow that made her even more beautiful than the day we had met. Her face was the same cocoa shade that I remembered. Her hair was the same black that I knew so well, but pulled back in a bun to keep it out of ship's air systems. The auburn highlights that fascinated me so were only visible when she let her hair flow free, so I was safe from them for the moment. Her eyes . . . Her deep brown eyes looked up at mine, and I looked just a bit away.

And her scent . . . It wasn't possible, but the cabin smelled of lilacs. After months on Mars and more months on the trip there and back, she couldn't possibly still have any of the lilac water she liked so much. I concentrated, and the odor faded away. It had been only a memory.

Tracy still knew all of my tricks, too. She shifted her head to meet my eye line. "What is it, Anson?" My pulse leapt. Practically no one called me by my first name, and no one at all since we had broken up.

I couldn't look away. I didn't want to. I had to—but I couldn't. "The Captain is conducting an investigation of the accident, and he has asked me to escort you to his office so that he may ask some questions." There. I had gotten out a whole sentence.

"Certainly, Anson. Anything I can do to help." Tracy folded up the desk and stood from her bunk. I managed not to analyze how her body moved in the low gravity. "If you'll lead the way. I have no idea how to find the Captain's office."

Glad of the excuse, I turned on my heel and faced the door. I touched my cap. "My apologies for the intrusion, Ms. Simms."

I left the cabin. I heard Tracy's soft tread behind me, and then the door closed. I waited until she was almost beside me, and then I set off through the passageway.

I knew the silence wouldn't last forever, but I still felt a stab when Tracy broke it. "You said there's nothing you can speak of; so I assume there's something you *can't* speak of?"

I never could fool Tracy. "I'm sorry you heard that."

"'I'm sorry you heard that, *Tracy.*' It's okay to say my name, you know."

I missed my stride, but only by a fraction of a second. I tried for casual: "Why waste words? We both know who I'm talking to."

Tracy sped up, edged around me in the narrow passageway, and stopped in front of me, forcing me to stop as well. "You're *not* talking, not really. You're *avoiding* talking."

Before I knew what was happening, I answered: "We talked four years ago. That didn't turn out so well." I should've let it rest, I knew I should've. This could only get worse.

And it did. "And you're still angry? After four years?"

"Still angry that you left me? Absolutely!"

"I left you for Mars! My chance to film the documentary of my dreams! I couldn't pass up that opportunity! You should know, you did the same to me when you left on the *Bradbury.*"

"That was different!" I tried to control my emotions, but they were building higher.

"Different? Different how?"

"We barely knew each other then. We had only been together for a couple months. We hardly meant anything to each other then. Not like . . . Not like breaking our engagement."

"I had to break it! It wasn't fair. I was going to Mars for nearly four years, with training and travel. I couldn't ask you to wait that long!"

"You couldn't . . . ?" And suddenly my restraints broke. "You couldn't ask me? Why not? *That* made me angry, the way you just decided without asking me. But oh, I got past angry." That took nearly a year. Then I tried hurt for a while. Hurt and drunk. Then just drunk, and then drunk and bitter. Eventually Nick dried me out and kicked my tail and got me to focus on work again. That's what I have now: my work, and I'm damned good at it. "I ferry passengers to and from Mars now, and that's all that's going on here."

Tracy was silent for almost a minute; and when she did speak, I could barely hear her. "I thought maybe . . . maybe you joined this crew so you could . . . see me . . ."

I looked away. I didn't want to give her the satisfaction of seeing how much that had touched me. She wasn't my reason, though part of me wished she had been.

Trying to keep a steady tone, I answered, "No, I joined this crew to serve under Captain Aames."

"Nick? He's a bastard!"

"That 'bastard' is the only reason I'm alive today. Me and the twelve other survivors from the second *Bradbury* expedition."

"Yes, but . . . The way he treats you! How can you put up with that abuse?"

How could I explain it to her when sometimes I couldn't even explain it to myself? But I had to try. "The safest place to be in this Solar System is under the command of Nick Aames—but just outside of shouting distance."

"And inside shouting distance?"

"Third safest. Second safest if you can get him shouting at somebody else."

Tracy smiled. Despite myself, I did, too. *Damn it!* I couldn't do this. I had to keep my distance. If I relaxed, if I let myself loose, it would happen all over again. I couldn't take another round of losing her.

I squeezed past her. "Come on. The bastard is waiting."

Nick's door opened, and the liquid notes of a trumpet emerged, accompanied by a soft drum beat and guitar. It was a sad, sweet tune, "Mue Esquema." Now *there* was a title that suited Nick: "My Scheme." We entered. Nick looked up and silenced the music.

I stood by the door. "As you requested, Captain, Ms. Wells is here to speak with you. I'll be in my office."

"No, Chief Carver, stay. I need your perspective on these interviews."

Nick had me right where he wanted me, but I wasn't going to acknowledge it. "As the Captain wishes."

"Ms. Wells, have a seat."

"Thank you, Nick." Tracy had never been big on formality, and it looked like she wasn't going to play by Nick's rules. No surprise there. She casually dropped into the guest chair, settling easily in the low gravity.

Nick stared directly at Tracy, his hands clasped on the desk. "So . . . You've had quite an expedition. It's been a long time. How long?"

"Almost four years, as you know. You *always* know details like that."

"Certainly! Attention to detail *is* my specialty. And yours, apparently, is distract- ing and ruining my best officer."

Tracy held her casual pose, but I could see the rising ire in her eyes. "*I* ruined him?"

"Look at him standing there, all tense, ready to flinch at any moment."

"*I* wasn't the one who talked him out of his opportunity to go back to Mars! And . . ."

"I did no such thing."

"You know full well you did!" Tracy leaned forward. Despite her resolve, Nick was getting to her. He always did. "When you turned down the Liaison post on the Azevedo expedition, you knew there was no way Anson would go with us if you didn't! Of course he wanted to go back to Mars! What member of the Corps didn't? Three-quarters of your crew were on our applicant list. I've seen it! But not Anson, nooooo! He wouldn't go on any expedition where you didn't approve. He wouldn't leave you."

"Not even to be with you."

"Not even to be with me."

"And that bothers you."

"No, not any more. It stopped bothering me a long time ago. But it bothered me then."

"And that's why you broke up with him."

"Captain!" I had had enough of the two of them arguing over me as if I weren't there. "You're supposed to be investigating—"

"Chief Carver, I *am* investigating, and I'll do it my way. I expect you to respect my line of questioning and trust that I have my reasons."

I sighed, but not loudly. "Aye, Captain."

Tracy glared at me. "'Aye, Captain.' It's still like that? All right, if you want to pretend this is germane, I won't give you the satisfaction of fighting with you. I broke up with Anson because it would've been unfair to ask him to wait for me for nearly four years through the training and the expedition. It would've been different if we were together, but you made sure that wouldn't happen. He had to get on with his life, even if his 'life' was following you and taking your orders."

"Taking orders. Discipline. Concepts you never really understood, aren't they? That's why you fit in so perfectly in the Azevedo expedition." Tracy didn't respond, but I could see she wanted to. "Carver tried to warn you about their poor planning, I know he did; but you were Mars struck. Or should I say star struck, perhaps? The great Professor Azevedo was going to Mars, the first mission of the Civilian Exploration Program, and he was taking the best of the best with him! Or at least that's what his press releases said. And he chose you, a practically unknown film student, to record his journey! You weren't about to let anything stop you from going. The dazzle of the spotlight blinded you to the actual state of the mission."

"It didn't blind me."

"No?"

"All right, it sounded glamorous and exciting at the start. All my life, I had dreamed of shooting documentaries on other planets and between planets. I wanted to capture life in space and on ships and space stations. That's how I met Anson, when I was filming at Mission Control one time."

Nick didn't interrupt, but I knew what he was thinking. He had told me often that he thought Tracy had used me as a stepping stone for her video ambitions. Tracy's admissions came uncomfortably close to proving his point.

"But I took my training *seriously*. Azevedo didn't train us, you know, we had training from the Corps. From *your* protocols! And oh, I took notes, and I *learned*. I wanted to understand what Anson thought was so important, so vital that he would turn down a promotion if he thought the mission was poorly planned. I wanted to learn what made *your way* so important to him."

"And did you learn?"

Tracy paused. I knew her face too well, I could read the reluctance there; but then she nodded. "I did. I learned the value of precision and protocol and observation. And . . . your way *is* right. So I learned."

"Uh-huh. And your proof is . . . ?"

Tracy pushed a file from her comp to Nick's desk. "Here's a list of my reports. And notice in particular the variances: every time I observed a deviation from protocols, I filed a variance. Every variance includes a risk assessment as well, and also my contingency recommendations. Every one filed with Professor Azevedo and also with Gale as the Corps Liaison. It got so they both stopped reviewing my reports. I was never wrong, but still they just kept doing what they wanted. Despite them, I did *everything* by the book. By *your* book, Nick."

"Hmmm . . . We'll see, won't we? These records *do* look impressive. I've had Bosun Smith running an inventory of the expedition gear. It's sloppy, poorly maintained, articles are missing or misplaced . . . . As I expected, most of your team weren't as meticulous as you've been here."

Tracy stared blankly. She was used to abuse and criticism from Nick; but something close to a compliment seemed to baffle her.

When Tracy didn't respond, Nick prompted her to continue. "All right . . . Tell me about the Chronius Mons trip, and the accident." I relaxed a bit. *Finally* we were moving on from personal matters—*my* personal matters—to the actual subject of the investigation.

Tracy, on the other hand, became less relaxed. As she started into her report, she sat up and looked alert and . . . *serious*, in a way I wasn't accustomed to from her. "As you know, Professor Azevedo selected Terra Cimmeria for the first CEP expedition due to two unusual phenomenon observed there, one measured and one inferred. The Mars Global Surveyor measured large magnetic stripes in Cimmeria and Terra Sirenum, which are hypothesized to be evidence of ancient tectonic activity; and albedo spectroscopy had indicated possible carbonate deposits that could be evidence of ancient life. The Professor hoped that by choosing that locale, he would double the chances of a momentous discovery that would bring in new investors for future expeditions.

"But by our hundredth day on Mars, Terra Cimmeria had proven frustrating and disappointing. It wasn't even that we had negative data to report, just no statistically valid conclusions either way. The magnetic stripes didn't conform exactly to any of the three standard tectonic models; but they didn't vary far enough to disprove any of the models, either, nor enough to choose between them. All our data really told us was we would need a lot more data. In the same way, the carbonate deposits were largely albedo spectres; and what deposits we *did* find were too small, too dispersed for us to make much sense of. They could've been remnants of ancient biotics, but they could just be natural mineral phenomena."

I managed not to stare, but I was surprised. Tracy had never shown much science knowledge before. Oh, she had always been smart, but she had concentrated on filmmaking and project management. She was an artist, not a researcher, and Azevedo had hired her for her video skills. Somehow in the past four years she had developed a whole new side to her.

Tracy continued, "So the Professor decided to make the trek to Chronius Mons. He . . . Well, it might be easier if I just played back my journal."

Tracy tapped her sleeve comp, and a strange voice emerged. It was *almost* recognizable, but pitched to a high octave like a cartoon character. "*Azevedo Expedition Journal, Day 106. Videographer Wells reporting. After considering my advice—refer variance report 104-27w—Professor Azevedo has filed a revised exploration plan for a two-day hike to Chronius Mons. He believes we may find—*"

"Stop!" Nick shouted, and Tracy paused the log. "Enough with the chipmunk log!"

"I'm sorry," Tracy said, "I don't even notice it any more. After five months of breathing heliox, I speak 'chipmunk' fluently." To reduce payload mass, Azevedo's team had brought a helium-oxygen breathing gas mix rather than standard air. It massed only one-third as much, but it had the unfortunate side effect of raising human voices by an octave or more due to the thinner gas. We didn't bother with it on the *Aldrin*, since our orbit required almost zero fuel to maintain; but the choice had made a huge impact on Azevedo's mass budget.

"Well, I hate heliox," Nick said. "For the sake of my ears, I'd like you to summarize. We can skip the journals."

"If I have to do a lot of talking, can I get some water? I got spoiled by the heliox, it's easier to breathe. I'm still readjusting to normal air. My throat *always* seems dry."

Nick looked at me. "Carver, fetch the lady some water." I went to the sink in the corner, poured a glass, and brought it to Tracy. Our fingers touched briefly as she took the glass. I managed to keep my hand from trembling.

Tracy took a drink, and then she resumed. "With the carbonates disappointing and the plate tectonics inconclusive, Professor Azevedo didn't have much to show for the expedition. So he announced a *new* mission objective. I told him that was clearly outside of *all* protocols; but he overruled my objections, as usual, and said we had plenty of safety margin for a trek to Chronius Mons. He said we had spectroscopic evidence of significant and unusual phosphorus outcroppings on the upper slopes. We had no particular theory to test, no reason for scouting for phosphorus. It was data gathering and grandstanding, nothing more. And the spectroscopic assay was *far* from conclusive, as I told him."

"Oh? And when did you get a degree in chemistry?"

Nick's question had been mocking, so Tracy's answer surprised him as well as me. "I started the program during mission training, and then I got my degree on the trip out on the *Collins*. I had to do something to fill my spare time." She glanced in my direction, then looked back to Nick. "Anson always told me how important it is for expedition members to cross train so that critical skills have backups. 'Videographer' isn't a critical mission skill, even if the Professor saw it as such; but a grounding in chemistry made me a backup for a number of personnel."

I actually saw Nick nod at Tracy's answer. That was as close to praise as she was likely to get.

When Tracy realized Nick had nothing to say, she continued. "So Professor Azevedo insisted on Chronius Mons. In truth, I think he was looking for challenge and adventure. He kept talking about scaling the highest point on the Terra and the great panoramas I could film from up there. He wanted something that would make great publicity. This wasn't really for the scientists, it was all for the money folks and the media back home.

"He also insisted that we could hike the distance in two days and make the climb in two more, rather than risk a lander flight in the questionable winds. We had no ground vehicles, so it was hike or fly or stay at the camp; and he wouldn't consider the last two choices.

"Professor Azevedo selected Lieutenant Gale and Dr. Ivanovitch for the hike, and also myself to record it. Gale selected himself, really: as Astronaut Corps Liaison, he had supervisory authority over any trip outside the bounds of the camp. He didn't always exercise that authority, but he insisted for that trip. Margo also insisted on coming, and the Professor wasn't inclined to say no to his wife—especially since she financed much of the expedition.

"We loaded up sledges with supplies. I personally prepared the equipment plan, but then was overruled time and again by the Professor and Gale. Still, I think we were adequately prepared when we left. We had three Mars tents—"

Nick's eyebrow raised. "Three tents? For five people?"

"I know, protocols call for two: a primary for all of us, and a backup. But again, I was overruled. We also had food, water, tanks of heliox, spare clothes, comm gear, spare clothes, the doctor's med kit, a telescope, a microscope, shovels, sample bags, pitons, hammers, plenty of S3 cable, computers, a satellite locator, flare guns, an emergency beacon, a chemical mini lab, a mineralogical kit, videography gear, suit repair kits.

"Despite the frequent stops for photo ops, the hike to the mountain went quickly, and it was pretty uneventful. Even pulling the loaded sledges, it was light work in the Martian gravity. We walked all day and set up camp, two nights in a row as scheduled. Inevitably Dr. Ivanovitch broke out his vodka. I had long since given up fighting that, and he was too professional to drink to excess when he was the sole medic on that trip. But I had to nag him and Gale to see to equipment maintenance before they started drinking each night."

"And did they?"

"See the reports, here. I didn't have the opportunity to inspect the gear stored in the other two tents. I encouraged the others to do standard inspections. As you can see, the inspections were spotty; but in aggregate, most of the gear was covered. Except . . ." She paused and pointed.

"Except the Professor's climbing gear, including the S3 cables."

"Mmmhmmm. It hadn't been unpacked since we left Earth, so he saw no need to inspect that.

"And then we reached the mountain. Chronius Mons, the highest peak in that quadrant. We had done mountaineering training in Peru, all in full Mars suits. The mountain was tall, but it looked like only an average difficulty climb, and even less thanks to the gravity. And I'll give the team credit: while they were lax on most mission protocols, they took the climb seriously. They tested every handhold, double checked every piton. And so . . . it came as a complete shock to me . . . when . . ." Tracy stopped, her face anguished. Old instincts kicked in, and I wanted to comfort her; but before I had to decide whether to follow those instincts, she gathered her strength and continued. "Professor Azevedo's cable snapped. Any one of us could've been on that cable at that time, but it happened to be him. He . . . fell. He fell so slowly in the Martian gravity. He had plenty of time to cry out for help. But even on Mars, three-hundred feet is . . . too far. His cries ended in a sickening crunch before his suit comm cut out.

"Margo wanted to rush down to him, and it was all we could do to restrain her so we didn't end up with another casualty. Carefully we rappelled and climbed down to him, taking nearly five minutes. Thanks to his suit's automatic seals and med systems, he was still alive; but the doctor shook his head. He said the Professor needed emergency surgery immediately.

"And that just wasn't possible. We had to descend another hundred feet to a ledge large enough to set up a Mars tent. Despite our best efforts, the climb inflicted further injuries. Then we had to set up the tent, pressurize it, and get the Professor out of his suit. Dr. Ivanovitch set up for emergency surgery, and Gale and I assisted. The doctor gave his best effort, but it was far too late." Tracy swallowed drily. "The Professor died twenty minutes after the start of surgery. He had never really stood a chance."

I was . . . puzzled. Puzzled but impressed. The old Tracy would often be overwhelmed by her empathy. Sometimes I thought she used the camera to put up a layer between her and the suffering she observed. But now . . . Now she was distraught, but she reported the incident in full, maintaining her composure for the most part. She had grown stronger—but not, I hoped, less empathetic.

As I thought on this, Tracy continued. "With the Professor dead, Gale assumed command. Oh, Margo might have contested that if she had tried, but she was in no shape to make any decisions. We bundled the Professor back into his suit for transport, and Gale led us back down the slope. There we had to rest for another night. We were physically and emotionally spent. The next day we double-timed it back to the camp.

"The rest is in my reports over the remaining month and a half until your pickup. We did our best to continue exploration and sampling, trying to salvage what we could for our objectives. Margo slowly regained enough energy to argue about who was in charge of the expedition. Legally she had the stronger case, but Gale kept arguing that we needed a professional in charge."

Nick nodded. "You did. Too bad all you had was Gale."

Tracy almost smiled at that. "The camp was pretty small, so their arguments made the place very unpleasant, with different members of the expedition lining up with her or with him. Dr. Ivanovitch and I eventually managed to calm things down by appealing to Azevedo's memory. His personality had united the expedition in the first place, and it was enough in the end to keep us alive until you arrived. The rest is in my reports."

Tracy took one last drink of water and then set her glass down on Nick's desk. "So that's my summary. Is that what you need?"

"Yes, if you've told me the whole story, then we're done here."

"I wouldn't keep anything secret. That's against mission protocols."

"Ms. Wells, I have learned in my command career that people keep all sorts of things secret when they're trying to protect their own careers and their own reputations. If they have a guilty conscience or they think perhaps they contributed to some mistake, they keep secrets, and they lie. I've learned to ferret out details that people would rather hide. I won't be lied to on my ship."

"You will find that my reports are complete in every detail, and as factual as I could make them. I did everything I could, but I lacked the authority to override Professor Azevedo's decisions."

Nick looked over his comp. "I wouldn't have expected it, but it does seem that way. So considering everything, I have to say that perhaps your training wasn't wasted. You mastered the protocols, which is more than I can say for your leadership."

Tracy stared blankly at Nick. I did as well. He had just come very close to complimenting her, at least by Nick's standards.

But she quickly recovered. "Then if you don't mind, I still have videos to edit before we get to Earth." Tracy stood to leave, but she stopped and turned at the door. "Goodbye, Anson." And then she left.

After Tracy was gone, I turned on Nick. "You never once asked her about the cable and the nanos! The . . . the murder!"

"I didn't need to."

"What?"

"I heard what I needed to hear. Now I know the basic outline of the trip and Azevedo's death: who was present, what their roles were, and so on. I'll talk to her again later if I need more details."

I knew better than to push Nick. He would keep his secrets until he saw a need to reveal them. Besides, I had something else on my mind. I didn't like it, but I couldn't stop myself from asking: "Did you have to be so hard on her?"

"Yes, Mr. Carver, I did. I have my reasons."

"And you had to drag *me* into it? What was the point of that?"

"Carver, I am conducting a criminal investigation. Didn't you ever read mysteries? Means, motive, opportunity: those are the classic requirements for solving a crime, and a key part of that is motives. I have to understand the people involved and what drives them. So I had to know where she stood in regards to you and in regards to that expedition. I had to know everything about her."

I was in no mood to be mollified. "You just can't resist picking at old wounds, can you?"

"Your wounds or hers? I'm not convinced she has any."

"What did she do to deserve that?"

"What did she do? You ought to remember! Are you going to let her do this to you again?"

"What are you talking about?"

"You are! You're going to let her just use you for whatever it is she's up to: chew you up, spit you out, and leave you crying in your beer. Again!"

"It's not like that!"

"It's *always* like that!"

"Look, just because *your* wife and *your* kids aren't talking to you any more doesn't mean it's like that for everyone!"

"It was last time!"

"It wasn't like that last time, either. Relationships just sometimes . . . They just sometimes end!"

"Yep, it ended when she got what she wanted."

"That's not fair! She had the chance to go to Mars, and she took it! I did the same thing when I had the chance. I can't blame her for that."

"Uh-huh. You went with *me*. She went with Azevedo, and now he's dead. That was mighty poor judgment on her part. She's lucky she's still alive."

"That's not fair! You heard her. She studied! She learned *your* mission protocols. She did everything possible to ensure the success of that expedition."

"Hmmm . . . Yes, she did, didn't she? I have to admit, that surprised me. A chemistry degree? Surprising, yes."

Nick sat in silence, clasping his hands and staring at his fingers. I realized he had gotten to me again. He always probed for weakness, always had to know where someone might fail him. I stood, fuming but patient, determined not to give in to his testing.

At last Nick looked up. "All right, Ms. Wells has given her report, and that's a start. But I need another perspective. Carver, express my condolences, but bring me Margo Azevedo."

I found Mrs. Azevedo alone in her cabin. She had it to herself, a luxury we normally couldn't spare even for important passengers such as her. But on this trip, I had triple-berthed some junior crew to open up a private cabin for her. I figured she deserved some solitude if she needed it. The ship might be too damned crowded for her otherwise.

When I signaled the door, it took Mrs. Azevedo almost a minute to open it. She was a tall, dark-toned woman with dark hair that showed some gray. In her pre-mission photos there had been no gray, but hair dye was just another luxury not to be found on Mars. Despite the gray, she still looked much like the fashion model she had been in her youth, back before she turned her earnings into shrewd business investments and a major fortune.

Her once elegant face was lined with grief. She wasn't red-eyed from crying like she had been earlier in the voyage. Five months of travel from Mars had gotten her past the deepest grief. But she still looked very weary, and I felt guilty for having to disturb her. But guilty feeling or no, Nick had his reasons and I had my orders.

Mrs. Azevedo summoned the energy to speak. "Yes, Chief Carver, can I help you?"

"Begging your pardon, ma'am. I hate to disturb you, but I have orders from the Captain. He has sent me to request that you come to his office. He has some matters to discuss."

"What . . . What's it about?"

"I'm sorry, ma'am, I'm not at liberty to comment on the Captain's business." That was a lie, of course, but I didn't want to explain to her that someone had killed her husband. And I didn't want to even consider that she might be a suspect. But as we walked through the ship, I realized I had an obligation to prepare her for Nick's investigation. "Ma'am, you know that Captain Aames can be a bit . . . brusque."

"'Brusque' hardly goes far enough."

"Ma'am, I don't think you understand."

"Please, Chief, don't treat me like a china doll. This is a rough time for me, but believe me, I'll get by. I've been making my fortune the hard way since before you were born: first on the fashion runways, and then on the spaceplane runways. And I saw plenty of ugly corporate battles in between, I survived all of them, and I triumphed. I've faced opponents far ruder than Captain Aames."

Despite myself, I grinned. "There's no one ruder than Captain Aames."

She laughed; and for a moment I saw the charm she had used to win backing for this expedition. "Nick Aames can be a smug, self-righteous asshole, no doubt. I appreciate your concern. But don't worry. I've handled Nick before, and I can handle him today."

"Of course." I knew the basics, so she didn't have to explain; but she seemed to need to talk, like the silence was too much for her.

"Nick was . . . Paolo's first choice for the Astronaut Corps Liaison for our expedition. I thought it was a done deal, but Nick and Paolo couldn't agree on terms. Nick insisted on rewriting the entire mission plan to his exacting standards."

I nodded. "The Captain would do that."

"But his standards . . . were *too* exacting. Too much redundancy, too much expense. Paolo wanted a streamlined mission—still a *safe* mission!—so that we could keep to an affordable budget. He said a mission to Nick's standards would never get launched; and Nick said that was fine with him, and he hoped Paolo's mission would never launch, either. He said the Civilian Exploration Program couldn't afford to have its first expedition go wrong, and that that would undermine support for the program. And now . . . I fear he'll be proven correct." Her face darkened, and I looked discreetly away. "Nick stormed out that day, and we had to hire Lieutenant Gale instead. Gale is a fine officer, and he gave us none of Nick's troubles. But rest assured, I know Nick's moods, and I'm ready for him."

"I hope so, ma'am."

We arrived at Nick's outer office. We entered the command office in the middle of a samba tune. Nick stood to the side of the desk, absently bouncing to the beat. If we had been alone, I would've told him what a lousy dancer he is, even in one-quarter G. That's a common jibe in our ongoing duels. But I would never disrespect an officer in his official capacity.

The song soon ended, and Nick sat down. I pulled out the visitor chair for Mrs. Azevedo.

Nick leaned on his desk. "Ah, Mrs. Azevedo. Much as I wish otherwise, I'm afraid I've opened an investigation into the tragic incident on your expedition. Some information has come to me about your equipment, and it's very troubling."

Mrs. Azevedo started to speak, looking agitated; then she paused and regained her control. "Captain Aames, are we going to discuss this again?"

"I have some concerns."

"Yes, Nick, I'm well aware of your concerns from before."

"And now you can see that I was right, and Paolo's carelessness has gotten someone killed. At least it was him, not someone who trusted him."

"Nick!" I couldn't help myself. That was over the line, even for Nick.

But Mrs. Azevedo wasn't disturbed. "No, Chief, he's just trying to provoke me. I won't let him do that. Yes, Captain, you predicted a disaster, and it happened. But *none* of your dire predictions came to pass. What happened was something you never foresaw, a freak cable accident and nothing more. I stand by my original decision that your fears were groundless, and you were afflicted with your usual excess of caution and your pathological need for control."

"And I stand by my original decision. I wanted nothing to do with your poorly planned vanity expedition. Only a fool would take your offer, and I'm no fool. But you found your fool in Gale, didn't you?"

"All right, Nick, if it makes you happy: I wish you *had* taken my offer. Maybe if you had been our Liaison . . ." She trailed off, but we all knew what went unspoken: maybe Nick could've gotten Azevedo safely back to shelter in time to save his life. Or maybe Nick would've prevented the accident in the first place.

Nick's face turned more serious. Perhaps his conscience was tweaking him just a bit. "I'm sorry, Margo, that would never happen. I can't take a mission I don't believe in."

"And so you took this instead?" Mrs. Azevedo leaned forward. "I know there are some in the Corps and in Mission Control who will *never* forgive you for the second

Bradbury incident, even though the review board ratified your every decision. There were many who told me I was a fool for wanting you for Liaison for this expedition. I wanted you anyway. Okay, you turned me down, you explained your reasons. But then, to take *this* job . . . Nick, you're throwing away your talents here. You're better than this! You're more than . . . more than a glorified subway conductor! If you didn't want to be on my mission, you would've been invaluable in program management."

"And work with fools like Lee Klein? Not a chance."

"Judgmental as always, aren't you? Everyone in your eyes is a loser or a fool."

"No, not everyone. There are fifteen billion people back there on those two worlds. They're not *all* losers. Ninety percent of them are ordinary folks, minding their own business, going about their day, not causing me any trouble. And there's maybe half a dozen people worth actually spending time with. But that leaves that 10 percent—one and a half *billion*—idiots, jerks, losers, and *psychopaths*."

"And so you'll lock yourself up here with only a couple of dozen."

"Yep. A couple of dozen, and I'm smarter than all of 'em. And I'm in charge."

"All right. You're the Captain, you're in charge here. Are you happy now?"

Nick paused. When he started again, his tone was lower and more reserved. Nick can be respectful when he chooses. "Margo, I know we clash. And I clashed with Paolo, too. It's my nature, not anything to do with you. I call them like I see them, and sometimes I neglect how people might feel. So please accept my condolences. I didn't agree with Paolo's plans, but it wasn't personal. He was a good man. I'm very sorry."

Mrs. Azevedo stared down at the floor, but she nodded. "Thank you, Nick. That means . . . a lot. Chief Carver says you have questions for me?"

Nick hesitated again. "This will be . . . difficult, I'm afraid. But I need to hear about the trip to Chronius Mons."

Mrs. Azevedo's tone was flat. "It's in our reports."

"I know. It's . . . important that I hear it in your own words."

She nodded; and then she started slowly retelling the story. She echoed Tracy's version, but without Tracy's critical judgments about mission protocols. In fact she made every effort to portray her husband in a positive light. On the subject of Terra Cimmeria, she saw the site selection as a great success: "Oh, we didn't find evidence to decide among the competing theories, but we have radically improved on the precision of the orbital data. Now we know exactly where we should plan new expeditions to definitively rewrite the geological history of Mars. Paolo already submitted a paper on that before . . . the accident." She similarly saw the carbonate data as eliminating a lot of possibilities, pointing the way to new research.

And then she got to a crucial point: the reasons for the Chronius Mons trip. She saw it very differently than Tracy had. "That was in the back of Paolo's mind all along. That was why he insisted on bringing Wells on the expedition in the first place: he wanted to show humanity the grandeur of Mars, the grand vistas and the sweep of the unknown. He wanted . . . He wanted to excite people, ignite their sense of adventure."

"Yes," Nick agreed, "he was a visionary. Or that's how he saw himself, which is visionary enough. That was what worried me about him: that vision blinded him to flaws in his plans. He had this sense that 'destiny' would see him past any prob-lems." Mrs. Azevedo didn't answer, but her face turned down. "And he would tackle any obstacle, follow any path for that destiny. How fortunate for him that he mar-ried into enough money to fund his visions."

"Nick!" Again I was stunned that even Nick could be so callous; but before I could say more, Mrs. Azevedo held up a hand to stop me. She glared at Nick.

"So that comes up again." Her tone was bitter. "You said as much during expedi-tion planning. You think he married me for money?"

"Well, there are always many motivations that lead into a decision like that. You were young and attractive, and you bought into his vision. The money was just an added benefit; but as it happened, it was a crucial benefit in order for him to succeed."

She paused; and when she answered, she spoke slowly, restraining her emotions. "I know you're a cynic, Nick. I know you would never understand what Paolo and I had. But to question it . . . now . . . I didn't think even you could be that cruel."

Nick leaned back in his chair and shrugged. "You call it cruel, I call it diligent. I have to get some answers."

"Fine, here are your answers. I love Paolo. He . . . loved me. We had problems, everyone does, but we shared so much more than just Mars plans."

Nick looked down at his desk. "So noted. My apologies, but I have to be thor-ough. Please, continue."

Mrs. Azevedo looked at Nick, considered, and then went on. Soon she got to the subject of supplying the expedition, and Nick again asked about the three tents. She seemed surprised by the question. "Why is that important?"

"I can't tell what's important," Nick explained. "Details matter. That's what I tried to tell your husband: details matter, and you can't guess which ones. So why three tents?"

"Well, we had them to spare, so why not? Paolo and I had a tent for ourselves. The command tent, as it were. Besides, we were entitled to our privacy. Ivan and Gale shared another tent, and Wells slept in the third. We divided supplies among the three tents so that an accident with one wouldn't affect other supplies. You should approve of precautions like that."

"Hmmm. Yes, I approve of precautions; but protocol here is entirely different. For a mission that size, two tents would have been proper: one for all of you to share, and one as a backup for that. It might be less comfortable to squeeze five into a tent, but it would've given adequate safety margins and less mass to transport."

"Yes, yes, I've read your recommendation. We decided we could handle the mass, and we wanted the comfort. And ultimately it had nothing to do with Paolo's accident, so can we just *drop it?*"

Nick didn't answer. He had made his point, so he let her continue. He also didn't comment when Mrs. Azevedo discussed their stops for the night; but even I could see that Tracy had been correct: the team had performed only perfunctory equip-ment inspections. Their uneventful time on Mars to that point had made them sloppy—or sloppier, as Nick would say.

And there was something else: something about the expedition had distressed her, and she had difficulty discussing it. She drew out the discussion with a lot of trivialities, stopping and repeating points. It took her twice as long to describe the trip as it had Tracy, and yet she revealed less. Was she just postponing the discussion yet to come? Maybe; but I saw Nick eyeing her carefully as if he suspected something more.

And then finally she discussed the climb; and then the fall and the attempted rescue. She started to choke up when she got to the surgery, tears flowing; and Nick showed unexpected kindness by stopping her there. "That's enough, Margo. I only need to know what led to the incident. I have a clear picture of what came after. Carver, give her your handkerchief." I did, and she dabbed her eyes.

Nick was being uncharacteristically kind, but I knew it couldn't last. Sooner or later, he would point out again how this was all Professor Azevedo's fault. Before he could get the chance, I spoke up. "Captain, if we're done, Mrs. Azevedo has had a long day. Can I escort her back to her cabin?"

Nick seemed a little distant. "What?" Then he recovered. "Oh, yes, we're done here. But I've summoned Bosun Smith. She can see to Margo. I have more duties for you."

Just then the office door opened, and Smith came in: a large, competent woman who I knew to also have a compassionate side when she needed it. Nick was right: Mrs. Azevedo might appreciate having a woman's support after putting up with him. But he would never admit that was his motive.

Bosun Smith stood at attention. Nick looked at her, a questioning look on his face. "Well?"

Smith lifted her sleeve comp and pushed a file to Nick's desk. "There's my full report, Captain. A number of items are missing, as indicated, and the necessary maintenance reports haven't been filed for much of the rest."

Nick nodded at Smith, and then rose. "Margo, again, I'm sorry. If I could've prevented this pain for you, I would've. We'll talk again. Ms. Smith, please see Mrs. Azevedo to her cabin." Smith saluted and then offered an arm. Mrs. Azevedo took it and leaned on Smith's shoulder as they left the office.

When the door closed, I turned back to Nick. My questions were the same as before. "I hate to repeat myself—"

"Then don't," Nick interrupted. "Everything is going as I planned."

"This is a plan?" I couldn't see how Nick could learn anything about the murder this way.

"Yes. I'm learning what I need to know. Besides, didn't you hear that undertone? There's something she's not saying, something she feels guilty about."

I hadn't heard it. I mean, I'd heard something wrong, and noted it; but I hadn't picked up on guilt. She was a grieving widow! I expected some distress. But Nick had always been better at reading people than I was. He himself might come across as a one-note scold and a control junkie, but he was excellent at ferreting out hidden motivations and secrets.

"What would she have to feel guilty about?" I asked.

"I don't know. I've no idea. For that I need the help of an incurable gossip. And so I guess it's time to speak with Horace Gale."

I tracked down Lieutenant Gale in the Rec Lounge. As had been the norm on this trip, knots of expedition crew occupied the tables, and our off-duty crew hung near, each imagining what it must have been like to be down on Mars. But strangely, when I found Gale in the corner with Riggs they were discussing football, not Mars.

"Yes sir, Lieutenant." Riggs's enthusiasm was all over his face. He was eager to talk about football leagues with a fellow Brit. "Absolutely it's Manchester's year. They've been rebuilding for five now. It's their time!"

"Well, Karl, I'm not so sure. Liverpool is looking pretty strong."

"Liverpool?" Riggs nearly exploded with laughter. "They'll barely finish the season. They're old and tired."

"You're right, you're right. Still, they have experience."

Riggs raised an eyebrow. "In football, sir, isn't that just another word for 'old'?"

"All right, they're old, I'll admit it." Gale laughed. "But just remember: in the Astronaut Corps, it's not age, it's seniority." Riggs joined the laughter on that line, though I thought his sounded a bit forced.

I cleared my throat, and Gale looked up. "Yes, Chief Carver?"

"Lieutenant Gale, the Captain would like to see you, sir."

"Oh, Nick causing trouble again, eh?"

"It's not my place to comment on what trouble the Captain might cause, sir. If you'll come with me, please."

"I suppose. I knew this was coming eventually. Well, Mr. Riggs, it has been a pleasure. See you at SP?"

Riggs raised a glass to Gale. "Indeed, sir. Thank you!"

We set off to the Captain's cabin. As soon as we were alone, Gale turned to the subject I knew was coming. "So, Carver, have you had enough of Aames and this tin can yet?"

I deflected. "The *Aldrin* is no 'tin can', sir. It's a masterwork of engineering, and it gets better every cycle as we add rings and capacity."

But Gale wasn't about to let up so easily. "Yes, yes, but it's still a glorified transport ship. You're a fine officer, Carver, you deserve better. If you had the Space Professionals behind you, you might get a better posting."

The SPs were something of an "astronauts' guild", though they never used that term. They advocated for more influence over mission planning. Ideally that would be something Nick would support. His feuds with Mission Control were legendary in the Corps. But Nick had laughingly rebuffed their efforts to recruit him, saying that they were more Politicals than Professionals. And that included Gale, who had a lot of influence in the movement. As Nick explained it to me: "It's the only way a bumbler like Gale can hope to get work. Before long they'll have work rules that say I can't dismiss any crew member any damned time I please; and next thing you know someone'll get killed because of those rules. Why would I be part of that?"

Since they had failed to recruit Nick, the SPs had worked on me, hoping I might influence him; but I found Nick's arguments to be irrefutable as usual. There were some good people in the SPs, but a lot of them were just looking for more money for less work. I was tempted to answer as bluntly as Nick would; but instead I simply said, "I'm sorry, Lieutenant, but I can't imagine a better posting than this, or a better commander than Captain Aames."

And with that, I opened the door to Nick's office. We entered to the sounds of bossa nova, but this time Nick didn't make us wait, turning off the music immediately. "Ah, Horace . . ." Nick exaggerated the name: "*Horace.*"

"Hello, Nick. So this is where you say 'I told you so'?"

Nick waved his hand dismissively. "Waste of my time. We both know it."

"Yes, but I'm sure you've just been waiting for the chance."

"No, I've been avoiding the lot of you as best I can. I may have to transport you, but that doesn't mean I have to sit here and listen to the mistakes I *knew* would happen."

Gale sat in the visitor chair while I remained standing. "So, Nick, what's this about?"

"Well, *Horace*, we do need some discussion regarding the fate of your ill-planned mission."

"Yes." Gale sighed. "Get on with it."

"That final trip across the desert . . . It was just the five of you?"

"Yes: me, Paolo, Margo, Ivan, and Tracy."

"So you had five people, and yet you had three Mars tents. Wasn't that a little bit of excess weight to carry? You could've carried more consumables?"

I was confused. *Again* with the tents? What did that have to do with the sabotage of Azevedo's cable? But Gale didn't seem to find the question unusual. "The Mars protocols—*which you wrote*—say we should have a backup for every piece of essential equipment. Mars isn't Earth, where we might survive without a tent."

"Yes, so two tents would give you a backup. But three? Those tents will hold six."

"Yes . . ."

"So why did you have three? You didn't need them for storage."

"Well, we did store supplies separately in each tent. 'No single point of failure,' that's in the protocols, too. If something happened to one supply cache, we would still have the others."

"Oh, so you didn't even reserve them as backups? You deployed all three tents?" Nick already knew that from Tracy and Mrs. Azevedo. I could only assume he was feigning ignorance to keep Gale talking.

"Yes. Paolo and Margo wanted their privacy, you know." Nick looked up, but Gale shook his head. "No, not for sex, for fighting. They did an awful lot of arguing on the expedition . . . I'm sure Margo regrets it now."

I nodded. That might explain the guilt that Nick had detected. But Nick showed no reaction and continued his questioning. "So the lovebirds insisted on their own tent. And the three of you remaining needed two tents because . . . ?"

"Well, Tracy insisted we should share a tent. 'That's the protocol,' she said, 'and I don't want to write up another variance.' The girl is almost as mad as you, Nick, always writing up variances and insisting on following protocols to the letter. She acted like *she* was in charge, not just a videographer. But Ivan said he wanted more space."

"I see. And you bunked with Ivan because . . ."

"Well, because Tracy was making such a row about protocols, I finally got fed up with her."

"But why, Horace? You knew she was right."

"Of course she was 'right'."

"Then why—"

"Because I didn't want to keep fighting about it!" Gale was red-faced. I could tell that Nick knew his buttons; and Nick can never resist pushing buttons, testing to see where your breaking point is. It looked like he had found Gale's. "Why make such a big deal about it?"

Nick steepled his fingers and looked up at the ceiling. "I'm finding I have a new respect for Ms. Wells. If she annoyed you this much, she must've been doing something right." Gale scowled, and Nick smiled. "Same old Horace . . . You're smart enough to know what the right thing is, but you're too weak to fight for it."

"I heard enough of this from you before the expedition, and I am tired of it now!"

"Good! If I provoke you enough, you *can* show a little backbone. But you never seem to when it matters. That's why Paolo chose you as Corps Liaison, you know."

"What?"

"You won't argue with the wrong decision, even if you know it might get somebody killed. You're too eager to get along. You're too nice. Space doesn't give a damn about nice."

"If you're going to bring that up again, then I think this conversation is over."

"No. I'm still Captain on this ship, and we're still outside the gravipause. This conversation is over when I say it's over. Chief Carver?"

I straightened. "Yes, Captain."

"If he tries to leave, sit on him."

"Yes, Captain."

"Horace, you are a weak man. I wouldn't send my worst enemy on an expedition where you made the decisions. You won't stand up for what's right, and that may have gotten Paolo killed." Gale's face showed dismay, but not shock. Suddenly I was sure he had already reached the same conclusion, and guilt was tearing at him. And then I was also sure: if he felt his mistakes might be responsible for Paolo's death, and he felt remorse at the possibility, then he couldn't be the murderer.

Gale seemed to rally, mounting a weak counter offense. "I needn't worry about sending men on an expedition with you, since no one in the Corps will have you."

"Nope, they won't. Klein and the rest of Mission Control want a bunch of yes men and toadies."

Gale sat in silence, looking at the floor in sullen silence. Nick let the silence hang for several seconds before continuing. "One more thing . . . What did Paolo and Margo argue about?"

It took Gale a few moments to answer. Finally he looked up at Nick. "I shouldn't . . . shouldn't say. It's a personal matter, and it's in bad form to mention it now. But I know you, Nick. You're going to gnaw on this until you get an answer, aren't you?" Nick just stared at Gale. Gale looked away. "All right . . . Margo was jealous of Tracy. She said several times that she was sure Paolo and Tracy were sleeping together." I winced, but I managed to control my reaction beyond that. "I'm not sure when they would've had the opportunity. It's very close quarters on Mars, and very tight schedules, as you know. But she was sure they were grabbing spare moments here and there. Certainly Paolo showed an excessive interest in Tracy."

"Ah, there we go! A classic motivation for mischief, eh?"

"Mischief? Who said anything about mischief?"

"Oh, I'm looking for motivations. That was one of Azevedo's biggest mistakes, you know, he didn't consider the range of interpersonal problems that might arise. And you didn't help him any." Gale glared again, and Nick returned to his previous tack. "So you have no reason to suspect foul play?"

"Oh, no! And especially not Margo! She couldn't have. Oh, they fought, but . . ."

"So she couldn't have. And you, no doubt, will proclaim your innocence. You're narrowing down the list of suspects."

"What's all this about suspects, Nick? What, you think some sort of crime was committed?"

"Oh, I am *certain* that a crime has been committed. Now I'm just trying to determine by whom. All right, Mr. Carver, I'm through with him. You can let him leave."

Gale stood stiffly and headed for the door. He glanced at me, but he turned away at my impassive response; and then he left.

I looked at Nick. "So I suppose you want me to summon Dr. Ivanovitch next?"

"Oh? No, I have no need to talk with the good doctor."

"You don't think he could've killed Azevedo? Maybe he sabotaged the cable; and then after Azevedo survived, he did a poor job of treating him?"

"No, I am quite certain that Dr. Ivanovitch is much too smart for this crime."

I didn't understand what intelligence had to do with it; but I knew Nick would explain when he was ready, and not until. So I tried another line of questioning. "At last you've gotten around to the subject of the crime; but why didn't you ask Gale about the cable?"

"Oh, trust me, I'm very curious about the cable. But I was waiting to see if he would bring it up."

"What? Why would he do that?"

"Why, indeed? That's what I've been waiting for: one of them to bring up the cable."

"Nick, that makes no sense. The *last* thing the murderer would want to do is draw attention to the cable. That's evidence!"

"Ummhmmm." But Nick said no more. He just stared at me as if waiting for me to reach some obvious conclusion. But whatever that conclusion was, it eluded me.

Besides, I had another concern tugging at my mind. "What's with your obsession with their sleeping arrangements? You don't seriously believe that . . . that Tracy was . . ."

"Whether *I* believe it or not is inconsequential. And I'm not sure why it matters to you, either, if you're over her like you say you are. But if it soothes your worries any: no, I don't believe it. Unless she's fooling me—and she's not—she has changed. She's too professional to risk the expedition over an affair.

"But what matters is: does Margo believe it? If so, that might have motivated her anger during the expedition, as Gale said; and perhaps it motivates her guilt now. This is a complex case, and it's all about motivations at this point. I understand the crime, so now I just need to understand who had a motive."

"So what now? More interviews? Whom do I fetch next?"

Nick shook his head. "No more interviews quite yet. I need to think. Tell Bosun Smith I have some errands for her, and then you can go about your duties."

Nick didn't bother dismissing me. I knew him well enough to know I was dismissed when he turned on the music. It was another classic, "Parece Mentira," from an old Brazilian saying: "It seems like a lie."

But instead of going about my duties, my watch was over. Not that that really mattered: on Nick's ship, you were off duty when Nick said you were off duty, and not until. And that was doubly true for me as his second in command. Still, I had nothing on my schedule; and I had had a long, emotionally draining day already. I needed to unwind like I hadn't needed in nearly . . . four years. So I headed back to the Rec Lounge.

But when I got there, I knew I wouldn't be able to escape my troubles after all. Tracy was there, and she had a large audience gathered for a preview of the final cut of her big documentary. There was a large mix of expedition members and *Aldrin* crew. Tracy opened with some production notes and then started the show; but she stopped occasionally for more notes or to invite comments from expedition members. Riggs sat in the front, right next to Gale, and he asked lots of questions and took notes on Gale's answers.

But my attention was reserved for Tracy. She had cleaned up for this presentation, switching to a freshly pressed jumpsuit. She had let her hair down so it hung around her shoulders the way I always liked it. Again I smelled lilac water, and I tried to shake it out of my memory; but it wouldn't go away. Her eyes lit up as she explained details of the expedition and her filming; and she was an engaging speaker, as always. I knew that wasn't just my heart speaking, as the crowd hung on her every word. But the documentary stood on its own just fine even without her production notes and her enthusiasm.

It was *really* good. She covered the highlights of planning and training. She showed just enough of the flight out on the *Collins* to give the flavor without losing the viewer in the tedium of five months in orbit. She vividly captured the blend of exhilaration and terror of landing in the Ishiro-class shuttles. She showed the camp setup and the scientific experiments, including both the disappointments and the tantalizing hints for the future.

And she covered Professor Azevedo's death. Oh, she had no film of the incident itself. The rescue had taken all their efforts, so there was no film. But she had a computer animation of the scene, with stick figures tastefully substituted for the real participants. She showed exactly what went wrong—except, of course, that she didn't mention the salt contamination. Nick hadn't revealed that yet; and if Tracy knew . . . No, I didn't want to contemplate how she might know.

I was still wrapped up in these thoughts, not even noticing that the film had ended, when I felt a tap on my shoulder. Before I turned, the scent of lilacs swept over me. It was Tracy. Old habits took over before I could even think, and I smiled at her. When she smiled back at me, I almost reached out for her; but at least I held that reaction in check.

"So what did you think?" she asked as she sat across from me.

"I . . ." I searched for the words. Then I decided to just be upfront. "It's brilliant. Your best work ever."

"Thank you, Anson. That means a lot."

"Except . . . In your report to Nick, you were so harsh on Azevedo and his team for their poor planning. You didn't miss a note, and you didn't pull a punch. And yet none of that came through here."

Tracy hesitated. I could see that I had caught her in a conflict. "Anson, there are two stories of the expedition: the story of what went wrong, and the story of what went right. A lot went wrong, and that's all in my reports; but even with all the inconclusive experiments, even with the Professor's death, he accomplished his primary goals. He showed that Mars is a place where *people* will go, not just an elite group of professional astronauts. And where people go, people will die. People make mistakes. We're not all perfect robots. We're . . . We're not all Nick Aames. If we let imperfection stop us, we'll never go anywhere."

"Imperfection gets people killed."

"Yes, and perfection can't always save them, either. Have you forgotten the *Bradbury*?"

I would never forget the *Bradbury*, and she knew that. We had lost a lot of good crew in that incident. "But don't you feel like this is a lie?"

"No, it's the other side of the story. When we get to Earth, I know the media will be full of reports of the accident again—my *own* reports. They're going to give Gale and that bunch another weapon to use in their argument: 'Space isn't safe for ordinary people. Leave it to us professionals.' They will find reasons to be safe, to avoid risks. We can't afford that. We need people to take chances. That was the Professor's goal and Margo's goal, and it's still my goal. I thought . . . it was a goal you understood."

I understood; but I understood Nick's point of view as well. I felt like they were doing it to me again, forcing me to choose all over again between his caution and her dreams.

I couldn't choose, so I said nothing; and I saw disappointment in her face. Once more, I hadn't chosen her. I hadn't chosen Nick, either, but I hadn't chosen her.

But it seemed she wasn't ready to give up, not again. She pulled her chair around beside mine, uncomfortably close. The lilac water couldn't be imaginary, as clear as the scent was. She must've preserved a vial. I remembered other nights when I smelled it so close, and I squirmed; but Tracy didn't seem to notice. "We were there for seven months. I've got months of footage to work with. This won't be my only documentary coming out of the expedition. There will be one that tells the mistakes quite thoroughly. But this is the one that I need to tell now. The one that shows: *We can do this!*" She opened her comp so I could see it. "Here. This is my *real* last scene. I haven't included it yet because I want to get Margo's approval first. But it's important that you see this, that you understand."

She tapped her comp, and a new scene appeared. It was Mrs. Azevedo in a shelter in the camp. Her eyes were red from recent tears, but she had a defiant look on her face. The shelter was darkened with a hint of red, probably from natural Martian daylight outside; but a mild light shone down on her from above, accentuating the shadows in her face. She leaned forward, directly into the camera. "Am I going to give up? No. Never! If I give up, *then* Paolo is dead. When his dream dies, then I bury him in my heart. Until then . . . No, there is no then. I won't give up, not ever.

But maybe others will. Maybe I'll have no choice. But my words, my money, my time, my power . . . I'll use them all for Paolo's dream. People *will* come here, they'll keep coming here. And they'll remember . . . They'll remember Paolo, and how his spirit calls them to come here and live here and work here. And some of them . . . Well, they'll be brave like Paolo. They'll know the risks."

And then the scene rolled back in time and space, all the way back to Earth, back to the earliest days of training. Professor Azevedo sat in a tent that bore a superficial resemblance to the Mars shelter; but the light was bright and blue-white, and Azevedo sat back in his chair. He wore a stubbly beard of gray with flecks of white, much like the hair that stuck out from his knit cap. I suspected they were on a mountain trip. He looked into the camera, and he smiled that smile that had won over so many skeptics. "Will people die in this program? Of course they'll die, what kind of question is that? It's the old Pioneers' Creed: 'The cowards never started, and the weak died along the way.' People die on the frontier, and that's no reason not to go. The ones who survive will be the strong and the smart and the lucky and the just-too-tough-to-kill."

From off screen, Tracy asked, "And which are you?"

His grin broadened. "There's only one way to find out. And no matter what, I *will* find out. Gladly. How about you?" And he laughed. And the screen faded to black, and white letters appeared: *Paolo Azevedo, Ph.D., Founder of the Civilian Expedition Program. 1994–2037.*

I stared at the simple words, dumbstruck. Tracy's video made her argument far more eloquently than her words had. In that moment, I wanted to take her in my arms and tell her I was wrong. I wanted to take her to Mars.

And so, with his usual uncanny timing, that was the moment Nick's voice came from my comm. "Chief Carver, we're almost to the gravipause, and I'm ready to conclude our business. Please bring Mrs. Azevedo, Lieutenant Gale, and Ms. Wells to my office immediately."

I ushered the expedition members into Nick's office. By unspoken understanding, the others left the sole guest chair to Mrs. Azevedo. She sat and looked at Nick.

Nick stood behind his desk. In his hand he held a coil of S3 cable. He looked across the faces and then began to speak. "Well, here we are. One last time together. We're entering Earth's orbit, we've passed the gravipause, so this ship is now back under the authority of Mission Control. So I guess that wraps up my investigation."

"Investigation?" They were all thinking it, but Mrs. Azevedo was the one who asked. "What investigation?"

"Oh, the investigation into this S3 cable. It has been an internal matter to this point, but now it's time to present my findings to you all before I report to Mission Control. Midshipman Riggs has found conclusive evidence that this cable has been contaminated with salt ions, destroying its integrity; and then it stretched until it broke." Mrs. Azevedo turned pale, but Nick gave her no time to interrupt. "Furthermore, there's no doubt that this contamination was *deliberate.*"

This time Mrs. Azevedo did break in. "Deliberate? Paolo . . . ?"

But she got no further, and Nick continued. "Someone wanted it to break. It's also clear that the cable is from your trip to Chronius Mons. Ms. Wells's inventory reports are quite thorough, and they document precisely which gear you took with you."

Tracy said, "But Mrs. Azevedo couldn't—"

Nick interrupted her, nodding. "You're right, she couldn't. Oh, people do surprising things, angry spouses especially. Gale told me how Margo was jealous of you, Tracy, jealous that Paolo had his eye on you."

Mrs. Azevedo stood, too fast for the low gravity. "That's a lie!" In her anger, she ignored her unexpected bounce, but Nick seemed amused. "We were past all of that months ago! Paolo convinced me he had no interest in this . . . this little *girl*. We made up, and we were . . . We were closer than . . ." She glared at Nick. "But how could I convince a cynic like you? You always believe the worst of people. What would you know about two people in love?"

That stopped Nick cold; and his face showed something close to sympathy. Then he shook his head. "No, I believe you. A gossip like Horace always exaggerates what he knows. But just because Paolo had no interest doesn't mean *Tracy* had no interest."

This time it was Tracy who was angry. "That's ridiculous! I . . . I would *never* let personal feelings endanger the team. I admired the Professor, and I was grateful to be on this expedition; but that's *all* there was between us!"

"Is it? Did you know, Ms. Wells, that when you broke up with Carver he wondered if perhaps you had your sights set on Professor Azevedo?"

"What?" Tracy practically shouted; and at the same time I said, "Nick, that's out of line!"

"Oh, he was quite sure of that for a while. He said a lot of bitter things when he was drunk."

"Anson! You didn't believe that?"

"Tracy, I was hurt. I . . . No, I didn't believe it, I just didn't know what to believe. I wanted some explanation."

"And maybe . . ." Nick broke back in. "Maybe he was correct. Motivations, that's what we're after here. Was it perhaps the woman scorned? And that brings us back to this cable." Nick held up the cable for us all to see. "I had Bosun Smith bring me this cable from the lab because there was one piece of information missing from our earlier report: the RFID tag woven into the cable end. And guess what? It's *not* one that Professor Azevedo packed in his gear."

"What do you mean?"

"Ms. Wells, the RFID tag is clear, and your meticulous inventory is equally clear: this cable came from your personal supplies. You had it stowed in your tent each night before the climb. Oh, and Bosun Smith also searched the rest of the expedition's supplies very carefully; and the Professor's cable is nowhere to be found. She checked the tag on every cable. Someone swapped this sabotaged cable for his."

Someone swapped . . . And Tracy had packed this cable . . . And . . .

No. I couldn't believe that. Tracy had surprised me before. She had disappointed me. She had broken my heart. But this? No. I knew that was impossible. I loved her, it couldn't be possible.

But Nick was drawing the conclusions I refused to draw. "So the cable Paolo packed, the cable that would've been in his tent every night where Margo had access to it: that cable's missing. And the cable you packed, Ms. Wells: that cable's sabotaged."

Tracy grew livid. "What are you implying?"

"I'm presenting facts, not implications. Now that we're in Earth orbit, it's up to Mission Control to make decisions from these facts. My duty is to report what I know, not to speculate."

"So what will you report?"

"The facts exactly as I know them. I will report that this cable is not Professor Azevedo's, it is yours. I will report that it was under your control the entire time it was on Mars. Professor Azevedo's cable is missing, and no one in the expedition crew admits to knowing where it's at. I will report that this cable has been contaminated with salt-affixing nanomachines. And I'll report all the rest of our findings, and they can draw whatever conclusions they may."

"And I will get a good lawyer to ensure that your accusations never make it into my record."

"I'm not making accusations. The conclusions should be obvious to anyone with half a brain, so I expect the review board to miss them entirely."

"And what are *you* going to do, Captain?" Tracy asked.

"Nothing, and you know it. Now that we've passed the gravipause, my powers are strictly curtailed. I can't hold you. I have no authority here over anyone but my crew."

"Well, that's good news, because I'm innocent. As soon as the funeral's done, I'll clear my name."

I knew that determined look on Tracy's face. Every bit of self-control was at work, holding back her anger, and maybe her tears. I wanted to comfort her, but I had to stand my post. She looked at me, and I almost broke; but then she left for the docking bay.

No one else spoke. Mrs. Azevedo stood. She stared at Nick, her expression unreadable. Then Gale offered her an arm, and they left.

I stood where I was. I hadn't been dismissed, and I had no orders, so I had nothing to do but stand there and stew over all that I had just heard. Stand and stew and stare at Nick.

Nick ignored me for almost a minute and a half; but finally he spoke. "Don't stand there glowering at me. Can't you make yourself useful?"

"'Glowering'? Really?"

"It's the perfect word to describe your expression, and I get to use it so seldom. But get over it already. Ms. Wells will be fine. In fact, I've entered a commendation into her record." I must have looked puzzled, so Nick explained. "The silly little girl who broke your heart is gone. That woman who just left here is the only one on that whole team who understands how to properly plan a mission. I can't guess what changed her, but I can't deny the change. Azevedo was an ass. He chose his expedition members for their willingness to fawn over him and for how popular they would be in the press. Plus a bunch of other *entirely* personal reasons: camaraderie, influence, favors . . . You name it, anything but competence. But with her, despite himself he got lucky. The only one whom he chose who was worth a damn was Ms. Wells, and even I wouldn't've guessed that. She surprised me."

"What?"

"Look at her reports, Carver. Look at what she's done. Look at everything. Despite my doubts, that woman has shown that the discipline that we need in space can be found far outside the Corps. The people who want to go to space, the ones who really *should* be there, are going to do it right. I couldn't have predicted it four years ago; but if I had to staff a mission and my choices were 'professionals' like Gale or an amateur like Ms. Wells, I would choose her without hesitation."

"But I thought—I thought you blamed Tracy! You practically accused her of murder!"

Nick sighed, his "you are beyond an idiot" sigh. "There was no murder here, Carver."

"No murder?"

Nick tapped his desk and the comm chime sounded. "Mr. Riggs, you can come in now." The door to the outer office opened, and Riggs entered, looking nervous as usual when crewmen are summoned before Nick. I ushered him in, and he stood at attention before Nick's desk.

Nick wasted no time on pleasantries. He sat and looked up at Riggs, who stood neatly at attention. "Midshipman Karl Riggs . . . What do you know about salts in chemistry?"

"Not much, Captain, I'll admit. I know I like salt on my chips!" It was a weak joke, and weaker in Riggs's delivery. Nick had the man nervous, which wasn't unusual.

"Ah, that's right, you said you're weak in chemistry. Unlike Ms. Wells, say. Quite a surprise, that chemistry degree of hers, it gave me a whole new perspective on that discovery of yours.

"Mr. Riggs, a salt is a compound wherein a positive and a negative ion exactly counter each other, yielding a neutral end product. They can be quite useful both biologically and in other reactions, and it's very hard for us to get by without them. That's why we've manufactured nano lines that can scavenge or even assemble the necessary ions from available stock."

"I . . . see, sir."

"But nano machines don't have *brains*, Riggs. They only have simple chemical sensors, valence detectors particularly. They look for the proper valences, grab the ions, and affix them to other ions or to a substrate. They're really just glorified enzymes in a sense. If they can't find the precise valence signature and yet they're still active, some of them will grab the nearest equivalent they can find: something close enough to the right ionic properties.

"Ah, but something close electrically can still be chemically a very different salt. For instance . . ." Nick pulled up Riggs's report on his desk comp. "These nanos in these micrographs you took, they were designed to scavenge carbonate items out of Mars's atmosphere, with its high concentration of carbon dioxide. It's almost 95% CO_2, did you know that?"

"Well, I . . . I knew something like that, sir."

"Yes. And in fact, Azevedo chose his site because of the high presence of carbonates, perfect for these nanos. But if they can't find the carbon ions they're designed for, many of them will find the next closest valence. For example, a nitrite ion would be electrically identical to a carbonate ion, and a nitrate might be close enough for a nano's detectors.

"Now there's something interesting about these micrographs you took. If you look at the chemical analysis attached—as I did when you brought them to me—you will find that the S3 cables have been contaminated with *nitrite* salts, and also a smaller proportion of nitrate salts, *not* carbonate salts. That means that when those nanos were active, they found predominantly nitrogen stock, not carbon dioxide. Nitrogen, you know, the stuff that makes up 79% of standard air mix."

Riggs was silent. His normally fair complexion had turned even more pale.

"In fact, since they get much of their stock from the surrounding air, that implies that this contamination happened in a nitrogen atmosphere. Now you won't find that on Mars, as I said. It's nearly all CO_2. And you wouldn't even find it in the expedition's shelters. They used heliox as their breathing gas to lower their payload mass. That, by the way, is why I was so insistent on confirming the details of which Mars tents were used and where and how the gear was stowed. I needed to be *certain* that I knew where these cables had been and what they might've been exposed to; and all three expedition members confirmed for me that the gear was safely stored in the Mars tents every night, in the heliox conditions. There would be trace amounts of nitrogen, surely, but it should be completely dominated by carbon dioxide. There was no chance for contamination there, so there's only one place this contamination could have happened."

I couldn't keep quiet. "On the ship!"

"Yes, on the ship, Chief Carver. And since these cables were very thoroughly inspected and recorded by Ms. Wells—I'm quite astonished at her meticulous records, Carver, you could learn something from her—we can be certain that the cables were not contaminated when they left the *Collins*. And so the contamination could only have happened aboard the *Aldrin*—*after* Professor Azevedo's all-too-avoidable death."

Riggs found his voice. "I . . . see, sir."

"Oh, I'm quite sure you do. And Mr. Carver is starting to see as well, though I think you had a head start on him. I knew right away: I wasn't investigating a murder, I was investigating a frame-up. Someone is trying to frame someone for Azevedo's death, and I needed to know who the someones were.

"So I had to ask myself the traditional questions: who had means, who had motive, and who had opportunity? At first I thought Ms. Wells had opportunity. She could've gotten to the cable at any time; and once we learned it was *her* cable, the opportunities expanded. But no, even before that, I learned of her chemistry degree. No chemist would make that mistake with the atmospheric ions. They would know it was a waste of time.

"As for Margo . . . What would she gain by making Azevedo's death look like murder? Not much. For one thing, the spouse is *always* the first, most likely suspect in a homicide, especially given their well-known fights. Oh, in theory she might have tried to frame Ms. Wells by swapping the cables; but Margo had too much to lose either way. Her whole media campaign is about Azevedo's great judgment, his people instincts that helped him to select an elite team of scientist explorers, the best of the best. If people think he let a murderer onto his crew, his entire myth falls apart. Not that I put any stock in that myth, mind you, but her investors do. She wouldn't do anything to endanger that myth. It would ruin her.

"And Horace?" Nick chuckled. "What would he gain out of it? Cast suspicion on Margo, maybe? Hardly. He needs her. He's a joke in the Corps. Yes, I know he's a bigwig to you SPs, but no one in Mission Control trusts his decisions. He needs this Civilian Exploration Program to succeed if he wants to stay employed. Oh, I considered briefly that Horace might have a motive: if Azevedo's death was murder, then it couldn't be blamed on Horace's poor planning. He could've been trying to duck responsibility. But Horace just isn't that clever. Besides, he may be a damned fool, but he's well versed in the atmospheric chemistry of Mars. He couldn't make that mistake any more than Ms. Wells could."

I broke in. "And that's why you didn't question Dr. Ivanovitch, either. You knew his chemistry knowledge ruled him out as a suspect."

"Yes."

"Then why'd you interview Gale at all?"

Nick grinned. "Because it amuses me to rub his nose in his mistakes. *And* I wanted his perspective on the personalities of the expedition. Horace Gale may be a pompous ass, but he's also a political climber. He always knows the gossip.

"But that was before I realized I was looking in *entirely* the wrong direction, because I was only looking at the expedition personnel. If the sabotage happened here, that added dozens of potential suspects from our own crew. Mr. Riggs?"

Riggs was slow to respond. "Captain?"

"Reports are that you seem to be very friendly with Gale."

"Yes, sir. We . . . worked together in the past. I trained under him on my first post. And besides, he's the only other Brit on board. It's nice to talk football with someone."

"Indeed. My reports are that you've spent pretty much all of your free time with him."

"Can you blame me, sir? It's a chance to talk to a real explorer. Someone different on this ship, you know."

"Um-hmmm. Perhaps you forget: both I and Chief Carver have already been to Mars on the second *Bradbury* expedition. I do hope we're 'real' enough for you." Riggs took the rebuke without blinking, and Nick continued. "And you—and you're not alone in this, so don't take offense—you've voiced concern in the past that the CEP is a mistake, and missions like this should be Corps missions. 'Leave space to the professionals,' I believe that's what the SP activists say."

"I'm entitled to my opinion, Captain. As you say, I'm not alone. We Space Professionals have a lot of influence in the Corps command."

"Yes, yes, just what we need: more politics in the space program. Be that as it may . . . It looks like, despite poor planning and one unfortunate death, *this* expedition met most of their mission objectives. I would hazard a guess that Ms. Azevedo's investors will be pleased over all, and will invest in further CEP expeditions. Once she buries her husband, Margo still has the clout and the drive and the financing to mount another expedition, and another."

"I wouldn't know, sir."

"Oh, trust me, she does. These decisions are being made politically these days, not sensibly. And I'm sure you believe it as well."

"Y-yes, sir."

"But now *if* Margo were to be implicated in a murder—or for that matter, if any of the senior staff were, it hardly matters who—it would throw everything into disarray. Suddenly there would be investigations, there would be questions, there would be doubts . . . Investors would get nervous and pull financing. The Corps would feel pressure from the Space Professional contingent, and would likely push to cancel the CEP. The next mission would likely be under Corps command, probably under Horace Gale himself; and he would pick his loyal crew."

Nick still held the coil of S3 cable in his hand, looking down at it, not at Riggs. "I have a report from your supervisor that you may be leaving us."

"Sir?"

"He says you've applied for a transfer."

"Well . . . Yes, sir, just . . . considering it."

"Yes, and a chance to ingratiate yourself with them as well, especially with Horace Gale. Looking at the letters of recommendation you've requested—"

"Sir!"

"Pshht. You think any communication goes out from this ship without me knowing about it? Please. What kind of a Captain would I be if I didn't keep up with details on my vessel? So it looks like in fact you're hoping for reassignment to the Mars expedition on their next trip."

"Well . . ."

"And lo and behold, with the news from this expedition, there are sure to be some vacancies on that crew. Azevedo dead, and now Miss Wells tied up in legal battles, the whole CEP in jeopardy . . . There should be a complete shakeup. It's likely the Space Professionals will get their way. Gale will end up in charge, and there could be an opening for the right man."

"Well, I . . . guess . . ."

"Oh, most certainly. Horace would want to take his chosen crew with him, men he knew and trusted. And you hope to be one of them."

"Captain . . ."

"Oh, don't deny it. As I was told, three-quarters of my crew applied for that last expedition, you included. But there will be some difficulty with your transfer, I'm afraid." Nick touched the comm control on his desk. "Bosun, come in, please."

The office door opened, and Bosun Smith came in. She carried another coil of S3 cable.

"Well?" Nick looked from Smith to the cable.

Smith nodded. "It was in his cabin, sir, just like you said it would be. I found it coiled up in his pillowcase, crammed in between the bunk and the wall. You'd never notice it without a search. Well, *you* might, Captain, but not the average person." She handed the cable to Nick. "The RFID tag confirms: that's Professor Azevedo's cable."

Nick stood slowly, came around his desk, and stood nose to nose with Riggs. He didn't yell. That's when I know Nick is *really* angry, not just domineering: he gets very calm. He looked at Riggs and said, "Get off my ship."

Riggs swallowed. "Sir?"

"You lied to me, Mr. Riggs."

"Captain, I—"

"Don't bother denying or explaining. We may be inside the gravipause; but when it comes to my crew, I am still judge, jury, and lord high executioner. And I do *not* want to hear more lies. I'm a realist, I know people lie for all sorts of stupid reasons. It's part of their nature. But *not* to me, and *not* on my ship. That gets people dead, and I won't tolerate that. Bosun, escort Mr. Riggs to his cabin. Watch him pack his kit. If he tries to go anywhere else or talk to anyone else, slam him into the nearest bulkhead. Twice. Once he's packed, escort him to the docking bay and confine him there until the ferry arrives."

"Yes, Captain." Smith didn't grin, but her eyes did. She was half again as large as Riggs, and she knew how to fight dirty. I think she wanted Riggs to make trouble. But he didn't: he just left, and Smith followed.

My head spun. It was like my head was tossed into microgravity and all the facts I thought I had learned that day had been tumbled into space and rearranged themselves. I had been wrong. About all of it. And about Tracy. But Nick—I looked at him. "But if you knew this already, why didn't you say so? Why did you let Tracy twist in the wind? Why did you let her suffer? She left here practically in tears!"

Nick sat in his chair, leaned back, knotted his fingers before him, and looked at me for several seconds. "Carver, you may have gotten over what she put you through, but I still had a bit of a grudge to work out. She almost cost me the best junior officer I've ever had. She appears to have grown up since then, but she still had earned a little suffering for that. And I knew *you* would never give her what she deserved, so I had to do it."

"You . . . You planned that?"

"It was a simple calculation. I had nothing to gain. It's not like exonerating her is going to endear me to her. It's far too late for that. But I had nothing to lose as well. It's not like she could hate me any more than she already did. So I might as well play the villain."

"So you were cruel to her just because you had nothing to lose?"

"You missed the final line in my calculation: *I* would gain nothing by exonerating her; but if *you* get on that shuttle and present the evidence that clears her name, you're her hero. You'll come in and save her from my vile accusation."

I blinked. Nick playing matchmaker? But . . . "No. I can't play games like that with her. I won't lie to her."

"Oh, don't be a complete ass, Carver. Tell her a lie, tell her the truth for all I care, but don't you *dare* let her leave you behind the way she did last time. That woman is going to space, with or without you. So get going before you miss that shuttle. I don't need you moping around for another six months. Go work out whatever it is you two have to work out."

"Thank you, sir." I leapt for the door.

"Oh, one last thing . . ." Nick halted me on the threshold. "The *Aldrin* leaves Earth for Mars in three months, with or without you. If I'm wrong, and she's not going back to space . . . If I'm going to need a new Chief Officer, please try to give me enough time to find a replacement who can measure up to your standards."

"Yes, Nick. Permission to go ashore, Captain?" But Nick ignored me, turning his music on instead. Once again I heard "Brigas Nunca Mais." Without waiting for an answer, I was already in the outer office and heading for the corridor.

I *would* be back on the *Aldrin*, I was certain of that. And I was just as sure that next time I wouldn't be alone. That would give Nick something to complain about, so everyone would be happy.

Biographical Fragments of the Life of Julian Prince

JAKE KERR

After a long career as a journalist, Jake Kerr turned to fiction in 2011. That year his first published story, "The Old Equations," was nominated for a Nebula Award for Best Novelette, the storySouth Million Writers Award, *and the Theodore Sturgeon Memorial Award. His stories have been published by* Lightspeed, Fireside, *and other magazines and anthologies.*

Here he delivers a story that's just what it says it is: a collection of Wikipedia articles and other essays and news pieces about a famous author, along with book reviews and critical analysis of his work. But he's also a writer who becomes famous some years after an asteroid crashes into the Earth and obliterates most of North America.

JULIAN PRINCE

From Wikipedia, the free encyclopedia

Julian Samuel Prince (March 18, 1989–August 20, 2057) was an American novelist, essayist, journalist, and political activist. His best works are widely considered to be the post-Impact novels *The Grey Sunset* (2027) and *Rhythms of Decline* (2029), both of which won the Pulitzer Prize. He was awarded the Nobel Prize for Literature in 2031.

Prince was a pioneer of Impact Nihilism, a genre that embraced themes of helplessness and inevitable death in the aftermath of the Meyer Impact. His travelogue, *Journey Into Hopelessness* (2026), outlined Prince's return to North America, ostensibly to survey the damage to his home state of Texas. The book's bleak and powerful language of loss and devastation influenced musicians, artists, and writers worldwide, giving voice to the genre as a counter to the rising wave of New Optimism, which sprang out of the European Union as a response to the Meyer Impact and the enormous loss of life.[1] [2]

Early Life

Not much is known of Prince's early life. He spoke rarely of his childhood, and with the loss of life and destruction of records during the Meyer Impact, little source material remains. What is known is that Prince was an only child, the son of Margaret Prince (maiden name unknown) and Samuel Prince. He was born in Lawton, Oklahoma, but moved to Dallas, Texas, when he was eight years old.[3] In an interview before his death, Prince noted:

I was a good kid, a boring kid. I didn't cause trouble, and trouble didn't find me. I studied hard and planned on being a journalist, figuring that I was better at observing the world than shaping it. I graduated high school, and continued with my journalism classes via the net. Up until the Impact, I was thoroughly and utterly average.[4]

Upon earning a bachelor's degree from Khan University in journalism, Prince embarked on a career as a web reporter.[5]

EXCERPT FROM JULIAN PRINCE'S NOBEL PRIZE ACCEPTANCE SPEECH, 2031

So it is that life, to which we all cling with desperation and joy, prevails. Yet I cannot let go of the memories, the experiences, and the physical reality of those that have passed away. The ghosts are all around us, even as we squint to see through them. It has been said that I deny optimism and ignore our future, but that is not true. It is just that I refuse to let the difficult questions remain unasked. I refuse to conveniently ignore the graveyard that is now half our planet. And I refuse to feel joy that so many have lived when so many—so many—have died.

It is with humility that I accept this award, not for myself, but for the hundreds of millions who are not here with us today. I did my best to tell their story, but they deserve so much more than I can possibly give. If I achieved even a small part in doing so, I am glad.

Pre-Impact Career

Prince spent the decade before the Meyer Impact crossing the globe courtesy of a series of freelance journalism jobs. His first writing job was with AOL Local/Patch in 2010, where he aggregated citizen journalism stories from North Texas and rewrote them for syndicated release to the net. He continued to work for AOL Local for seven years, until he quit in 2017.[6] He wrote about this transition in an essay on the carefree lives of the pre-Impact world in 2031:

I quit because I wasn't excited. Can you imagine such a thing today? To leave security and stability because your life just isn't dangerous or crazy or exciting enough? Such was the innocence before the Impact. So I left the boring to move to Africa, where the excitement was, and where I could write about things that shed light on life and death, not ennui or entertainment.[7]

Prince took a job with European news agency Star News in 2017. His writing up until the Impact in 2023 was spare and fact-driven, although flashes of Prince's eye for emotion could occasionally be seen. Prince would say of those years, "Everything I wrote back then was worthless, but it was also worth everything—because it was the mind-numbing limitation of facts and cold description that allowed me to view the Impact in its true light." [8] [9]

EXCERPT FROM "MALDIVES' LAST GRAIN OF SAND," REPORTED BY JULIAN PRINCE (STAR NEWS, 2018)

Ahmed Manik sits in a rickety wooden boat, watching as a wave crests over a strip of sand. Manik is the grandson of Maldives' last President, Mohammed Manik, and the strip of sand is all that's left of the island country of Maldives, a country wiped away by global warming, rising water levels, and decades of mismanagement. Scientists don't even bother estimating how long this last remnant of the former island nation will remain before it is washed away. It may be weeks, perhaps even days.

Manik shrugs when asked about the lost legacy of his family and former country. "We are all grains of sand, just waiting to be washed away," he says and smiles, which accentuates the heavy creases around his eyes and mouth. He may have accepted the inevitable force of the rising waters, but it has taken a toll.

Impact Year

Prince was already in Africa during the six-month preparation for the Impact and thus didn't have to take part in the Expatriation Lottery. He wrote many news articles during this time, but no fiction or essays. There is no record of Prince's life for the 18 months following the Impact and the immediate global environmental catastrophe it caused. Prince would write about this time often, but never about his own life—only what he had seen.[citation needed]

EXCERPT FROM "IMMIGRATION CONCERNS DOMINATE SOUTH AFRICAN PRESIDENTIAL DEBATE," REPORTED BY JULIAN PRINCE (STAR NEWS, 2023)

Cheers followed South African presidential candidate Maxwell Mahlangu on each stop of his tour of the country, despite deep concerns that his endorsement of the United Nations Emergency Emigration Plan for North America would upset the entire framework of the country. "Our country's motto is 'Unity in Diversity,'" Mahlangu said at a rally in Port Elizabeth. "How can we let these people die simply because we refuse to accept more diversity?"

Later in his speech, Mahlangu touched upon a common theme expressed by leaders across the globe as countries prepared to take in refugees from

North America—no one really knows what the Meyer Asteroid will do to the world. With a massive death toll a certainty, the real economic unit of the future may be people, so taking in immigrants is a good idea: "No one knows what God has in store for us and what life will be like. In the future, with more people, South Africa will be stronger!"

Sitting president Jacob Sisulu rejected Mahlangu's moral and economic argument. He continued to object to the UN's current plan for South Africa to accept up to a million expatriates from the United States. "Such a wave of people would severely stress every part of our country," Sisulu explained during a press conference in Pretoria. "They will starve! China or Russia or Europe should take them!"

"Coming Home"

In 2025, Prince's essay "Coming Home" was published in *Der Spiegel*.[10] It became a worldwide sensation and ironically helped create the New Optimism movement that Prince's later work would reject. In the essay, Prince described the unloading of thousands of North American refugees in various cities along the African Coast, using the metaphor of humanity leaving its doomed colonial past to come home to Africa.

Literary critic Gerald King described the essay as the perfect origin point for both Impact Nihilism and New Optimism, and its publication immediately marked Prince as the leading light of post-Impact literature:

The central concept of "Coming Home" is warm and welcoming. Africa, the cradle of civilization, is welcoming home its wayward sons and daughters, even after their many sins. The deep themes of forgiveness and generosity fed directly into the New Optimism being loudly voiced in Europe. But many overlook that Prince did not flinch in describing the gaunt, guilty looks of those that exited the boats—a few million survivors while hundreds of millions of their friends and family members were doomed to die back home. The language that Prince uses in describing those left behind is very stark and makes it clear to the close reader that one should mourn, as well as celebrate.[11]

The reception of "Coming Home" led directly to Prince tackling the difficult subjects of the Impact and "the Lost," a term for those who died in the Impact that Prince coined himself in *Journey Into Hopelessness*.[citation needed]

EXCERPT FROM "COMING HOME" BY JULIAN PRINCE
(*DER SPIEGEL*, 2025)

Not one person who landed in Africa looked over his or her shoulder. It was as if the direction labeled "West" no longer existed. Sunsets were no longer a thing of beauty but a painful reminder of those doomed across the ocean, a literal dying light. Thoughts stopped at the ocean. It was overwhelming to consider friends and family alive yet suffering with the knowledge of their impending deaths.

Denial was the coping mechanism of choice. No one that landed in Africa could remember having any family or friends remaining in North America.

I asked dozens of refugees, and none would admit to having left anyone behind. Friends, neighbors, colleagues, family—they all somehow made it into the expatriation program.

In Mogadishu I met a man I used to work with. I asked him about several of our former colleagues and whether he knew if they had been chosen to expatriate. He denied ever having known them. I was shocked for a moment, but recovered and asked about his family. He smiled and said that they all made it and were settling across various cities in Europe. He didn't know anyone that had been left behind.

No one knew of anyone left behind.

To know was to be a participant in their death sentence, and that was too painful, too sad, too horrific. But the guilt existed, nonetheless. So they did what they could to avoid it. They didn't look West. They didn't watch sunsets. They never called or messaged North America, even as it still lived. They cut off their former lives and looked ahead to their new ones.

And thankfully, mercifully, Africa was there with open arms. A return to home and hearth, as it had for time immemorial, made everything better.

"THE CONSCIENCE OF A GENERATION"

Prince traveled back to North America to survey the damage from the impact in early 2026. He spent six months traveling across the continent with a United Nations Blue Team, observing and sometimes helping as they assessed the damage. This experience was the basis for his worldwide best-selling travelogue, *Journey Into Hopelessness*. His stark and often graphic descriptions of a barren landscape, littered with dead flora and fauna, were described by critics as "poetic," "beautiful," "poignant," and "chilling." Prince himself described the trip as the "hardest six months of my life. It was like performing an autopsy on your own parent."[12][13][14]

After returning from North America, Prince spent the next six months working on his first piece of fiction, the novel *The Grey Sunset*. The novel follows the life of Phil Gumm, who is a working class truck driver from Kansas and a winner of the Expatriation Lottery. The novel is highly introspective, and the narrative follows Gumm's descent from exhilaration at being one of the lucky few to the depths of guilt over those he left behind. The bulk of the novel takes place on the journey from Galveston, Texas, to Capetown, South Africa, and the physical journey is an extended metaphor for the emotional and spiritual journey that Gumm also takes. As Gumm physically gets closer to safety and a new life in Africa, he emotionally and spiritually gets closer to guilt, despair, and, eventually, suicide.[15]

The book was released at the height of the New Optimism movement and was immediately heralded as a compelling counter. The phrase Impact Nihilism had already been in use since the publication of *Journey Into Hopelessness* and similar works, but it was *The Grey Sunset* that defined the genre and helped propel its popularity.[citation needed] *The Grey Sunset* won the Pulitzer Prize in 2027, which had been re-established by the Expatriation Heritage Foundation the year before.[16]

Prince shied from publicity, and spent the bulk of the next two years working on what many consider his masterpiece, *Rhythms of Decline*. The novel is a complicated narrative of five families, each of whom lives on a different continent. The centerpiece is the impending impact of the Meyer Asteroid, and how each family deals with an uncertain future. Only one family survives the Impact, although their future is full of doubt as the novel ends.

Literary critic Malcolm Spencer described the book as "the work of unparalleled genius." He described the American Smith family, as "the definitive representation of our times. They face impending death with a kind of sad and yet warm acceptance. They live one day at a time, knowing that days are all they have left." Spencer described Prince as "the conscience of a generation" for his unflinching look at the tragedy of the Impact and the guilt and pain it left behind.[17]

Some critics saw the book as a complete repudiation of New Optimism, and this led to significant criticism of Prince. London web daily *The Beacon* called Prince "The Prince of Doom and Gloom."[18] *The Paris Review* printed a scathing review of *Rhythms of Decline*, describing it as "one man's self-absorbed journal of guilt over surviving the Impact."[19]

Prince did a series of interviews in the wake of the criticism. His most famous appearance was on the popular holo *The New Day*, broadcast out of Berlin. When asked about his critics, his reply became one of the most quoted lines of the post-Impact era: "I'll listen to them when they've walked among the three hundred million ghosts that I have."[20]

Despite the controversy, *Rhythms of Decline* won the Pulitzer Prize and led directly to Prince being awarded the Nobel Prize for Literature two years later.[21]

EXCERPT FROM *JOURNEY INTO HOPELESSNESS*
BY JULIAN PRINCE (VINTAGE/ANCHOR, 2026)

Finally we landed in Texas.

When I was young my parents took me to Palo Duro Canyon in northwest Texas. It was a massive rift in the Earth that my mother told me God himself had carved out of the Texas plains. I didn't see it that way. I saw it as a broken land born of violence, something left behind when the plains and hills had collided. But broken as it was, I saw it as natural and beautiful. The sharp angles and the bare rock acted as a balance to the plains that spread into the distance. And despite the wound in the land, life continued to thrive around it.

There is nothing natural or beautiful in the tortured land that now covers North Texas. The force of the impact stripped away everything. There are no trees, no plants, no grass. There is nothing but scarred land, windburned ridges, and fetid water. Everywhere there is decay, death, and the certainty that this is a barren land with no future.

EXCERPT FROM AN INTERVIEW ON
THE NEW TONIGHT SHOW (CANAL+, JANUARY 18, 2030)

Phil Preston: Speaking of your trip, there are rumors that you didn't get along with the UN team during your visit to North America.

Julian Prince: Well, we spent six months together, so there were the normal conflicts, but I wouldn't say that I didn't get along with the team. I actually have a funny story about it.

Preston: *You* have a funny story? This I've got to hear.

Prince: Since this was officially a military mission for some idiotic reason, the scientists and I—all the civilians—had to take part in an orientation. The orientation was basically our team leader, Colonel Cooper, telling us over and over again that he was in charge and we had to listen to him. He was this husky bald guy with a kind of soft voice, but he had an intensity that made it clear he was used to people doing what he told them to do. His look and demeanor reminded me of Marlon Brando's character of Kurtz from the movie *Apocalypse Now*, so when he finished I said something like, "Sure thing, Kurtz."

[Audience laughter]

Prince: I thought it was funny, too, but he didn't seem to get it, and he marched over to me, put his nose right up to mine, and said, "The name is Cooper, and you can call me Colonel or Colonel Cooper." Of course I called him Kurtz for the entire six months.

[Audience cheers and laughter]

Preston: I'm surprised he didn't do anything.

Prince: I just assumed that he had no idea who Kurtz was, but during the last few days of the mission I said to him "I'm going to miss you, Kurtz." No one else was around, so I hoped he realized that I meant it. He then shook his head and said—and I remember every word to this day—"You have been calling me Kurtz this entire trip, and I had hoped by now that you would have realized how foolish that has been." He then leaned in and whispered in my ear, "You can't go native when there *are* no natives."

Preston: Wow. That's intense.

Prince: I know. And people call *me* the Prince of Doom and Gloom!

[Scattered audience laughter]

Preston: Actually, do you mind that—when people call you the Prince of Doom and Gloom?

Prince: [Pause] Yes.

Preston: Well, you've dated Janet Skillings, so I'm guessing that being the Prince of Doom and Gloom hasn't interfered much with your love life.

[Audience laughter]

Prince: Well, being rich and famous helps.

[Audience laughter]

Preston: So is there anyone in your life right now?

Prince: I'm afraid not. I live life one day at a time.

Preston: So what you're saying is you're only up for one-night stands.

[Audience laughter]

Prince: Life is a one-night stand.

[Uncomfortable silence]

Political Activism

The next ten years of Prince's life were marked by political activism. Violence in Africa and Asia led to the rise of the Repatriation Movement, which fought for the return of former North Americans to their home continent. While most countered the movement on practical grounds—North America simply wasn't habitable yet—Prince saw the movement as something deeper and darker. He felt the movement was about rejecting Africa and Asia and the expatriates' hosts more than a desire to return to their devastated homeland.[21][22]

In a widely quoted speech in 2034, Prince said:

> This is not a movement about returning home. This is a movement about rejecting friends. This is not a movement about finding comfort in familiar lands. This is a movement about fearing those who wish to help. This is not about repatriation. This is about rejection.[23]

Prince was a prolific essay writer during this period, but nothing ever approached the popularity and power of his earlier work. His essay "Rejecting Home" (*Der Spiegel*, 2035) an acerbic and politically pointed update of his essay "Coming Home," was described by critic Gerald King as "a sad attempt by Prince to leverage his earlier brilliance to make a point about what many are starting to see in him as a naïve perception of unity in people who want no such thing."[24]

Prince ceased his anti-repatriation activism when parts of North America were re-opened for settlements in 2038.[*citation needed*]

EXCERPT FROM *RHYTHMS OF DECLINE* BY JULIAN PRINCE (KNOPF, 2029)

Simon had hoped that all would be normal in the end. He would tuck Annie into bed, pat Arthur on the head, and then kiss them both goodnight. Jason would wander off, falling asleep to the dull glow of some video game or another. Later, Simon would poke his head in, mutter a goodnight, and then turn the electronics off. Finally, he and Annie would hold each other and let the night take them. That was his dream—that they would fall asleep as a family and never wake up.

Yet, somehow, this seemed better. Their tears, their grief, and their fear tapped into a well deeper than family ritual. They were together in a moment when being alone seemed profane and wrong.

Jason joined Simon and began to cry as they all held each other. No one said anything. They breathed the air that gave them life. They shared the love that made them family. They cried the tears that made them human.

And then they died.

Later Life and Novels

Prince lived the rest of his life in Capetown, South Africa. He only published three more novels; all were well-received but garnered far less praise than *The Grey Sunset* and *Rhythms of Decline*.[*citation needed*]

Countdown (Knopf, 2040) told the story of a young man named Franklin Proudman who had decided to repatriate to North America. Proudman lands and finds life a lot different than he expected. Much of the book is a rambling series of anecdotes around the hopeless efforts of Proudman to build a life. He eventually dies from starvation, the ground still too damaged to produce crops.

Lost in North America (Knopf, 2045) is Prince's only foray into the science fiction genre.[25] The novel tells the story of the Winkler family, who hide in a fallout shelter in Rapid City, South Dakota. Despite Rapid City being ground zero for the Meyer Impact, the family survives and exit the shelter a year later to rebuild their lives. When it becomes clear that there is no food or wildlife, the family begins a journey, foraging for food across North America. The book has clear allusions to Cormac McCarthy's *The Road*, but the emptiness of the landscape provides for a uniquely Princean view. The book generated significant positive critical press. [26][27]

Prince's final novel, *Crater* (Knopf, 2056), was released the year before his death. The book continued his exploration of the dark aspects of repatriation.[28] The novel follows a scientist, William Ho, and his assistant Wendy Singh, as they attempt to descend to the bottom of the Meyer Crater. Like Prince's other novels, *Crater* is rife with introspection. As Ho and his assistant get closer to the bottom, they realize they are in love. It is when they have reached ground zero of the Meyer Impact when the two realize they have found their future together. The novel's ending is ambiguous, as the two are attempting to climb out of the crater but are uncertain if they will ever escape. While thematically similar to his earlier novels, *Crater* employs a denser prose style, with long paragraphs that often include a stream-of-consciousness technique. Despite its ambiguity and often dark scenes, the novel was marked by some as a return to the optimism of "Coming Home." *Crater* was a bestseller and re-established Prince as a popular figure in post-Impact literature. [29][30]

Personal Life

Prince was romantically connected to several celebrities during his life, including actresses Renee Diaz[*citation needed*] and Janet Skillings.[31] None of these relationships lasted more than a few weeks, however. In 2050, unofficial Prince biographer Susan Nillson announced that she had uncovered proof that Prince had left a girlfriend and child behind in North America. The document, a digitized copy of a Texas State birth certificate backed up on a European server, showed that Prince fathered a child named Samuel to a mother named Wendy Reynolds. Prince never acknowledged Nillson's allegations, although most contemporary historians consider the claim accurate.[32]

EXCERPT FROM JULIAN PRINCE'S
FINAL INTERVIEW (*PARIS LIVE!*, 2056)

Aliette Rameau: You've achieved so much, Monsieur Prince. Do you have any regrets?

[Pause]

Rameau: Monsieur Prince?

Julian Prince: I'm sorry. Your question is a bit overwhelming. My life is full of regrets.

Rameau: Is there anything specific you could share with us?

Prince: No. [Takes drink of water] I'm sorry. Could we change the subject, please?

Death and Legacy

Prince died on August 20, 2057 in Capetown, South Africa, from a self-inflicted gunshot wound. He left no suicide note. Having died without any heirs, Prince bequeathed his literary estate and assets to The 300 Million Ghosts Foundation, which was founded to record, research, and archive the stories of those who died during the Meyer Impact.[33][34]

Prince's legacy continues to define and influence artists to this day. While Impact Nihilism has fallen out of fashion, Prince's stark images and deep themes can be seen in everything from the paintings of Ellen Winslow to the music of the Bluefins. His use of introspection and stream-of-consciousness has influenced writers as diverse as Joe Lguyen and Isabel Shoeford.[citation needed]

The play "Coming Home" debuted on the anniversary of Prince's death in 2058 at the Globe Theater in London. Adapted by Nobel-winning playwright Andrew Hillsborough, the play was an unabashedly optimistic look at a world that survived an extinction event and came away smiling. Hillsborough noted on BBC, "Oh, I'm sure old Prince would have hated it. But the words are all his. Somewhere along the way he changed. Just because he decided that facing the abyss meant that we were all doomed to fall in, doesn't mean we have to agree with him."[35]

EPITAPH ON JULIAN PRINCE'S GRAVESTONE
Finally home.

the plague

KEN LIU

Ken Liu is an author and translator of speculative fiction, as well as a lawyer and programmer. His fiction has appeared in The Magazine of Fantasy & Science Fiction, Asimov's Science Fiction, Analog Science Fiction and Fact, Clarkesworld, Lightspeed, *and* Strange Horizons, *among many other places. He has won a Nebula, two Hugos, a World Fantasy Award, and a Science Fiction & Fantasy Translation Award and been nominated for the Sturgeon and the Locus awards. He lives with his family near Boston, Massachusetts.*

In the short, sharp shocker that follows he demonstrates how people are kept apart as much by their preconceptions as by the mutual incompatibilities of their environments.

I'm in the river fishing with Mother. The sun is about to set, and the fish are groggy. Easy pickings. The sky is bright crimson and so is Mother, the light shimmering on her shkin like someone smeared blood all over her.

That's when a big man tumbles into the water from a clump of reeds, dropping a long tube with glass on the end. Then I see he's not fat, like I thought at first, but wearing a thick suit with a glass bowl over his head.

Mother watches the man flop in the river like a fish. "Let's go, Marne."

But I don't. After another minute, he's not moving as much. He struggles to reach the tubes on his back.

"He can't breathe," I say.

"You can't help him," Mother says. "The air, the water, everything out here is poisonous to his kind."

I go over, crouch down, and look through the glass covering his face, which is naked. No shkin at all. He's from the Dome.

His hideous features are twisted with fright.

I reach over and untangle the tubes on his back.

I wish I hadn't lost my camera. The way the light from the bonfire dances against their shiny bodies cannot be captured with words. Their deformed limbs, their malnourished frames, their terrible disfigurement—all seem to disappear in a kind of nobility in the flickering shadows that makes my heart ache.

The girl who saved me offers me a bowl of food—fish, I think. Grateful, I accept.

I take out the field purification kit and sprinkle the nanobots over the food. These are designed to break down after they've outlived their purpose, nothing like the horrors that went out of control and made the world unlivable . . .

Fearing to give offense, I explain, "Spices."

Looking at her is like looking into a humanoid mirror. Instead of her face I see a distorted reflection of my own. It's hard to read an expression from the vague indentations and ridges in that smooth surface, but I think she's puzzled.

"*Modjasaf-fuotapoiss-you,*" she says, hissing and grunting. I don't hold the devolved phonemes and degenerate grammar against her—a diseased people scrabbling out an existence in the wilderness isn't exactly going to be composing poetry or thinking philosophy. She's saying "Mother says the food here is poisonous to you."

"Spices make safe," I say.

As I squeeze the purified food into the feeding tube on the side of the helmet, her face ripples like a pond, and my reflection breaks into colorful patches.

She's grinning.

The others do not trust the man from the Dome as he skulks around the village enclosed in his suit.

"He says that the Dome dwellers are scared of us because they don't understand us. He wants to change that."

Mother laughs, sounding like water bubbling over rocks. Her shkin changes texture, breaking the reflected light into brittle, jagged rays.

The man is fascinated by the games I play: drawing lines over my belly, my thigh, my breasts with a stick as the shkin ripples and rises to follow. He writes down everything any one of us says.

He asks me if I know who my father is.

I think what a strange place the Dome must be.

"No," I tell him. "At the Quarter Festivals the men and women writhe together and the shkins direct the seed where they will."

He tells me he's sorry.

"What for?"

It's hard for me to really know what he's thinking because his naked face does not talk like shkin would.

"All this." He sweeps his arm around.

When the plague hit fifty years ago, the berserk nanobots and biohancers ate away people's skins, the soft surface of their gullets, the warm, moist membranes lining every orifice of their bodies.

Then the plague took the place of the lost flesh and covered people, inside and outside, like a lichen made of tiny robots and colonies of bacteria.

Those with money—my ancestors—holed up with weapons and built domes and watched the rest of the refugees die outside.

But some survived. The living parasite changed and even made it possible for its hosts to eat the mutated fruits and drink the poisonous water and breathe the toxic air.

In the Dome, jokes are told about the plagued, and a few of the daring trade with them from time to time. But everyone seems content to see them as no longer human.

Some have claimed that the plagued are happy as they are. That is nothing but bigotry and an attempt to evade responsibility. An accident of birth put me inside the Dome and her outside. It isn't her fault that she picks at her deformed skin instead of pondering philosophy; that she speaks with grunts and hisses instead of rhetoric and enunciation; that she does not understand family love but only an instinctual, animalistic yearning for affection.

We in the Dome must save her.

"You want to take away my shkin?" I ask.

"Yes, to find a cure, for you, your mother, all the plagued."

I know him well enough now to understand that he is sincere. It doesn't matter that the shkin is as much a part of me as my ears. He believes that flaying me, mutilating me, stripping me naked would be an improvement.

"We have a duty to help you."

He sees my happiness as misery, my thoughtfulness as depression, my wishes as delusion. It is funny how a man can see only what he wants to see. He wants to make me the same as him, because he thinks he's better.

Quicker than he can react, I pick up a rock and smash the glass bowl around his head. As he screams, I touch his face and watch the shkin writhe over my hands to cover him.

Mother is right. He has not come to learn, but I must teach him anyway.

fleet

SANDRA McDONALD

Sandra McDonald's first collection of fiction, Diana Comet and Other Improbable Stories, was a Booklist Editor's Choice, an American Library Association Over the Rainbow Book, and winner of a Lambda Literary Award. Her story "Sexy Robot Mom" recently won the Asimov's Readers' Poll award. Four of her stories have been noted on the James A. Tiptree Award Honor List that acknowledges writing that explores gender stereotypes. She is the published author of several novels and more than sixty short stories for adults and teens, including the award-winning Fisher Key Adventures and the gay asexual thriller City of Soldiers. She graduated from Ithaca College in New York and the University of Southern Maine and lived on the island of Guam as an ensign in the United States Navy. She holds an MFA in creative writing from the University of Southern Maine and teaches college in Florida.

Here she takes us to a postapocalyptic Guam, which has been abandoned by the Western powers, for a sly lesson in what it takes to survive when those powers become interested in colonizing again.

W hen I officially became a girl, I took the new name of Isa. At the time I was nine years old. In the Umatac village records I'm still a male named Magahet Joseph Howard USN. It's good luck to be given the name of an ancestor from Before Silence. My brother calls me Shithead, because he's my brother. But most people call me Bridge, because the governors gave me that. Someone in every village is appointed to stand with one dusty foot in the past and the other planted in the Great Future, ready to take action when ships appear on the blue horizon.

Sounds important. Don't be fooled. We're not some backwards cargo cult, building mock radio towers in the magical hope of luring back civilization. Civilization will come again regardless. We're sure of it.

It's hot today, late afternoon. I'm sitting on the beach and thinking hard about taking a nap. A dozen yards offshore, blue waves roll around Fouha Rock, where the gods created mankind. No kidding: it's a giant limestone phallus jutting out of the sea.

"What are you staring at, Shithead?" my brother Rai shouts when the canoes return.

"Your tiny shriveled-up balls," I yell back.

The men laugh. Among them is my husband Pulan Robert, who comes to me at night with reverence and good humor. He has a second wife, Kami Brittany, who bears him our children and hopes that one day I'll be gored to death by a boonie pig. She can't say that too loudly, though, for fear I'll call down upon her a vengeful taotaomo'na. Those are the spirits that slink through the nunu trees under moonlight, and moan during storms as if in great pain, and brush their invisible cold hands over your nape when you least expect it.

She's right to worry. I know the names of seven thousand taotaomo'na. Seven thousand ancestors who perished here in the After Silence. There's a man in Yigo who knows twelve thousand. The oldest woman on the island lives in Dededo, and she knows fifteen thousand. The governors gave them to her, just like they gave them to me, through white caps clamped to our skulls.

I try not to think about the white caps too much.

The men beach the canoes and haul out their catches. Pulan Robert smiles at me and waves over to where Kami waits with our youngest daughter bouncing on her hip. A moment later his smile dims. Our visitors have arrived. Four men, tall and lean, with walking sticks wrapped in copper wire and the green ribbons of Agat village.

Rai stops beside me and frowns. "They're late."

"They're on time."

"Late," he insists. "They'll slow us down tomorrow."

"Two days to get there," I tell him. "Then you'll see Angelina again."

At sunset our entire village dines on roasted fruit bats, fresh rabbit fish, breadfruit, cakes, and tuba. The musicians play nose flutes and drums for the children dancing around the bonfire. Three of the men from Agat know of me, but the fourth keeps sliding glances my way. Beneath my blouse, my bra is stuffed with soft grass. I wear a wig of long hair, dark and straight.

"Babae?" he asks his companions in Tagalog. Many Filipinos clustered in Agat in the After Silence.

"Oo," his friends say.

He wants to know if I'm a girl. Yes, they say. But he looks at me doubtfully. Wondering what's under my skirt, maybe wondering if he can put his hands under there to squeeze and rub.

Pulan Robert puts his arm around my shoulder. He smells like salt and fish and Kami.

"You should stay here," he says that night, in our bed, as we stare up at the tin and thatch ceiling. Kami's hut is bigger, but mine is closer to the cooling ocean breeze. Mosquitoes nibble on our arms.

"I have to go. Someone has to remember the dead," I remind him.

"I'll come along and keep you company."

"Rai is coming."

"Rai is too impatient. He won't pay attention."

I kiss his nose. "Rai will always pay attention to me."

Rai's impatient because it's been six months since he's held his wife in his arms. In the morning, he's awake before anyone else. At breakfast, somber Irao speaks quietly to his crying children. The fourth from our village is Husto, who has spent the last week pleading to our little governor that he should be excused from this duty. She stands firm. The lottery is fair and the gods have picked him to take his turn digging. I wonder if we're going to have to physically lift Husto in the air and carry him away, but finally he pries himself away from his weeping mother.

"Travel safely," Pulan Robert says, with a final warm kiss.

"I will," I promise.

The men from Agat lead the way down the road. We follow, and only Husto looks back.

Despite the solemn occasion, I like these trips. Before Silence, you could drive all over Guahan on asphalt roads, from the turquoise waters of Cocos Lagoon all the way north to the limestone cliffs at Ritidian Point. The shrine for the Japanese soldiers who killed themselves, the international airport for big jets, the army tanks abandoned after the war—you could visit them all in just one day. Now the roads are all rubble, and bandits control the bridges, and some of the white villages up north won't let you pass over their lands without payment. Rai and I tried rowing around the island once when we were young. We nearly shredded ourselves on the reefs. Ours is the age of footpaths and walking sticks, and many people die without ever having stepped outside the villages they were born in.

The coastal route to Layon is pretty enough, but I'd like to see more of the old military bases. My namesake Joseph Howard USN worked on one of those. The concrete shells of the buildings are all gutted and stripped out, the roofs blown away by typhoons or leveled by earthquakes. Those ruins are less sad, somehow, than the iron skeletons of hotel high-rises in Hagatna, the resorts where the tourists honeymooned and gambled away their fortunes until the Night of Fire.

Imagine it: two hundred thousand people drinking or dreaming or fucking or hunched over military equipment in the middle of the night, in the middle of the endless ocean, and in the gap from one minute to the next, all the technology died. No telephones, radios, satellites, computers. All the power stations erupted into fire. All the transformers and electrical wires sizzled and fried themselves into charred metal. In the skies above, enormous waves of green light shimmered against the moon and stars. The governors gave me just enough science to know what the Northern Lights are, and why they should never be seen this close to the equator.

I rub my head, remember the tight white caps, and keep walking.

Our first step is Fort Nuestra, high on the bluff, to make our offers to the Lady. She's not the oldest of our gods, but she's the one Magellan and the Spanish gave to us while they burned our huts and killed our chiefs. When I was very small, I would pray to the Lady to take away my cock. She never did. I don't hold it against her, though, not much anyways, because Pulan Robert likes it well enough in the dark.

After praying and leaving gifts we continue on to Merizo. Only a few families are left to great us. Merizo went to war with Inarajan last year and came out on the poorer end. The fight was supposedly over the ownership of a prized carabao, but was probably about skin color or religion. For now Merizo only has one worker to send to the landfill, a teenage boy with a topknot dangling from his otherwise bare skull.

"I'm going to dig up a radio and battery," he tells me as we drink tuba by the ruins of a church. "I'm going to call Jesus Christ."

Merizo's always been known for this kind of talk. I don't mind it. Husto, though, announces that Jesus Christ died on the Night of Fire, and this makes the boy's parents angry. While they argue, I walk away to piss. A woman with limestone white hair follows me. Her left leg drags in the dirt.

"You're the 'idge," she says, the words slurred.

Her name is Nena and she should be dead now, or so the story goes. While working at the landfill she was accidentally buried by the shifting, stinking debris. By the time they pulled her out, she'd been breathing bad air for too long. A quick death might have been more merciful, but Nena's father carried his only child back to Merizo and cared for her until he died in the war.

"I'm Isa," I tell her, pulling down my skirt.

"I 'ound the 'eet," she says.

I shake my head, not understanding.

She waves her good hand toward the ocean. "The 'eet."

Fleet. She found the Fleet. She wouldn't be the first. Usually, though, there's a lot of tuba involved, or smoked weeds, or the fanciful imagination of children.

"I don't see any ships, Nena."

"'ailor," she says, and gestures toward the jungle.

"Show me."

Chickens scatter before our feet on a narrow path. From the vines and bushes peek out old cement houses on cracked foundations. One hut without doors or a roof is so overgrown you'd miss it if you weren't looking closely. Inside sits a white man, his face ghastly with pain and his eyes half-lidded. He smells like shit and urine. In his right hand is a sharp curved knife.

"The 'eet," Nena repeats.

The rips in his clothing and long scrapes on his arms say he washed in over the reef, but any fool fisherman from the north can fall over the side of a boat. I kneel in the doorway.

"Good day, sir," I say. "Can you tell me your name? Your village?"

He struggles to focus. Twitches the knife, as if trying to raise his arm. He starts to ramble—short, disconnected words, none of them in English or Chamorro or Tagalog.

But I know these words. The governors gave me nations and languages before they gave me names to carry. This man is speaking Russian.

My throat goes tight.

To Nena, I say, "He comes from Yona. They speak strange up there. Nothing more than that."

Her expression falls. "Not 'eet?"

"Not Fleet, no," I say confidently. "When the Fleet returns, an armada of ships will sail into the bay bearing food and wine. They'll set off fireworks and play the United States anthem. This is just a lost fisherman who needs our help. Return to the beach and find my brother Rai. He's the tallest, the most handsome. Bring him here. But don't let anyone else see you. They'll claim the reward his village has for him."

A new light gleams in her eyes at the mention of reward, and she hurries off.

If Nena had bothered to examine the Russian's clothes, she would have seen that even stiff with sea salt, the fabric is newer and finer than anything we can weave or dig up here. He's wearing lightweight boots with fresh rubber soles. For a white man he's pale—a sailor who doesn't see much sun. Maybe he came from a submarine. The governors showed us pictures of those.

"Who are you?" I ask in Russian.

His rambling stops. A hairy brown spider crawls down his leg. He doesn't brush it off.

"Did you come alone? Can I call someone for help?"

"Sergei," he murmurs.

Maybe that's his name, maybe someone else's. Before I can ask his head slumps over and the knife tumbles from his lax fingers. I see dark blood on the back of his skull. There's a swelling there, a stone-like bump. No other major injuries on him, no jewelry or electronics, only the knife and its leather sheath strapped under his left trouser leg.

He may not have much time left, or he could recover enough to cause serious damage.

As always, I am sworn to uphold Rule Number One.

I squeeze his nose shut and clap my hand over his mouth.

Life is a stubborn habit to break. It's a sacred thing, to watch the spirit struggle to take flight. You can see it in the flopping fish pulled from the sea, or in the panicking pig as the knife pierces its throat. The Russian makes muffled sounds and jerks his head, but has no strength to fight me off. I pray to the gods and governors for him. No one here will mourn his death with a nine day feast. But most living things deserve kindness in their last moments, to hear words ushering them to arms of their ancestors.

When she returns with Rai, Nena's eyes turn accusatory.

"He passed quietly, without pain," I say. "His people from Yona will want to come and retrieve his bones. Rai, bury him in a shallow grave. But don't tell anyone, or let them help, or they'll want the reward, too."

Rai balks. "What reward?"

I squeeze his arm. "The people of Yona will be grateful to know what happened to him."

He opens his mouth, maybe to say the people of Yona are nothing but swindlers and drunkards. My fingers dig deeper into his skin. He's not an idiot, my brother, so he goes silent. Nena, bent over the naked corpse, sniffs in grief.

"'is clothes," she says.

"I took them for his people," I tell her. "His last words were to thank you, Nena. His spirit rests in peace because of your kindness. He asked that you seclude yourself and say rosaries for him. If you don't, his taotaomo'na will be very angry. Will you do it?"

She nods emphatically. "Yes."

Back at the church, the others want to know where Rai is. "Too much feasting last night," I lie, and they sympathize. Everyone here has suffered from the squats before.

Husto gestures to the folded fern leaves in my arms. "What's that?"

"A gift for the taotaomo'na," I warn him. "Don't touch."

We bid farewell to Merizo and detour into the valley to visit both Tinta and Faha Caves. I worry that Nena won't do as told. Or that Rai will discover something incriminating that I left behind. But the caves require my full concentration. Back in World War II, the Japanese soldiers spent years raping the women, killing old and young alike, forcing people from their homes to concentration camps. Here, as the end of the war drew near, they herded villagers into caves and tossed grenades in after them. Other victims were tied up and beheaded and left in the dirt.

I don't have their names—no Bridge does—but we know that the Japanese brutality made the people of Merizo rise up in rebellion. We honor them, too, in this sacred place heavy with memory.

"You tell the story well," Irao comments, afterward.

"I wish I didn't have to tell it at all," I reply.

After the ceremonies we trek back to the coast, where dark gray clouds are rolling in from the south. We make it to Achang Bay before the rain starts. The only shelter is an old fueling station with two walls and a sand floor. Irao and Husto sit to one side of me, and on the other sits the man from Agat who doesn't believe I'm a woman.

"The gods don't want us to go to Layon," Husto says as water pelts down.

"You whine like a child," Irao tells him.

The man from Agat looks like he's thinking of putting his hand on my thigh. I slide my fingers along the sheath of my knife, and he decides to stare at the rain instead.

By dusk the weather is clear but it's too late to continue on. The men look for wood dry enough to burn while I worry about Rai. It doesn't take that long to dig a shallow grave, and the detour to Tinta and Faha cost us time.

Irao knows me well. "He'll be along soon."

"Hmm," I say.

Eventually the men build a fire, and we eat supper quietly, and afterward they smoke and drink more tuba. Rai does not come. We all stretch out under the dark, starry sky and rising full moon. I'm halfway through the first thousand names in my head when from the jungle arises a long, low, awful moan of pain. Someone—or something—in agony, in torment.

We all sit up in fear.

"It's a pig," says one of the men from Amat.

"It's Anufat," says Husto, naming the ugliest and meanest of the taotaomo'na. Anufat has fangs and claws, and sometimes not even a head.

Irao tosses sand at Husto. "Stop telling stories."

"He wants his gift," Husto insists, pointing to the fern leaves I'd forbidden anyone to touch. "You said it was for him."

"It's for another," I protest.

The moan again: drawn out agony that makes my stomach flutter. Not Rai, I tell myself. But that fear grabs me and doesn't let go, and after the third terrible time, I stand up.

"I'll come with you," Irao offers.

"No. I'll go alone." I pick up the folded leaves. "Stoke the fire and stay here."

By the time I reach the edge of the jungle the fire is bright again, the men nothing but silhouettes. A narrow path, mostly overgrown, curves from behind the fueling station into the nunu trees. Brown snakes curl away from my bare feet. The knife in my hand won't do anything against a spirit, but I have salt, too, and words, and if I have to run I can run, too, faster than anyone can imagine.

The steady sea breeze shifts the trees and leaves, makes shadows flicker, tricks my eyes with movement—and then a hand clamps down over my mouth, yanks me backward. The dead man's clothes and knife spill from their leafy envelope and scatter on the ground. My knife gets lost in the bushes. Someone speaks low against my ear, a command of some kind. I stop struggling.

"Who are you?" I ask in Russian, muffled, garbled.

He repeats his command. Be quiet, he's saying. He pulls me backward through brush into a small clearing where Rai is curled up on the ground, his hands and ankles bound, his mouth gagged.

"I'm a friend," I insist, the words mostly unintelligble. "Friend."

His free hand gropes my hips and ass. Looking for a weapon. He finds my cock instead and makes a startled noise. A moment later he yanks me down to the ground against Rai and lays a sharp blade against my exposed throat. My skin stings. Rai grunts. The moonlight illuminates the stranger's pale face but I can't see his eyes, or what emotion might be in them.

"Who are you?" he demands in Russian.

"Isa."

He yanks at my wig, rips at my skirt. My cock hangs out, long and soft. He slaps at it and says, "Not a woman."

If I had my knife, I'd cut his hand off. Instead I keep my chin up and stare straight at him. "Sergei?"

He hesitates. The slightest flick of his wrist and he can end my life. I'm breathing fast and my insides are watery. Some things you can't control.

"That's the last thing he said," I tell him. "Sergei."

Another long moment. Then, "How did he die?"

"From his head injury. He said you might come, that you'd tell us everything. Not that you'd attack and try to kill us."

The Russian sits back on his haunches. Rai grunts against his gag. Carefully I put my hand on his leg. He can't understand what we're saying. He thinks that we're only a few moments from death, and I wouldn't call him wrong.

"You're Sergei?" I repeat.

"Yes. He was Vasilly."

"You're from Russia?"

"There's no Russia." His voice is flat.

"You're the first visitors from the outside world in a hundred years," I say, and the thrill of it runs through me. No other Bridge has ever found a man from away. The governors will be happy with me. Maybe I can finagle a reward; fewer workers to the dump each season, perhaps, or some other special favor.

Sergei points his finger and says, "Don't move."

He retreats to search through Vasilly's scattered clothing and boots. In the darkness I tug on Rai's knots, but my fingers are trembling and the cords are wound too well.

Sergei returns with Vasilly's knife. He unscrews the base of the hollow grip. Inside are blue fireflies. Electric lights. I haven't seen those in a long time. The weapon is some kind of tracking or communication device, designed for stealth. He slides out a narrow part and wedges free a luminescent strip. Quick, efficient moves.

"We've hoped for your return," I say, trying to sound awed. "Prayed for it."

Sergei pockets the strip. "Forget prayers. We're only here for information."

"Honored visitor, our governors would be happy to share anything we know."

He snorts, though I'm the one who should laugh. Information. Fishing reports, maybe? Average daily rainfall? No man treks across the Pacific, dares to swim between the reefs, and subsequently avoids the local population without good reason.

"How is it that you speak Russian?" he asks.

I duck my head. "There was a man, many years ago. He washed ashore the way your friend did. He recovered and lived in the jungle by himself. I would visit him, bring him companionship, and he taught me to speak it."

He looks at my cock and shakes his head. Imaging perversion, maybe. Defending his imaginary countryman from the likes of me. The truth is much worse, of course. Those white caps, burning hot. My hair never grew back.

"Our governors would greet you with open arms," I insist. "They've kept all the records from the Before time. They know everything about the island and what was here when the world went silent."

Behind me, Rai struggles quietly against his bonds.

"What governors?" Sergei asks. "Where?"

"I'll take you," I tell him.

Sergei wants to leave Rai behind. I can't risk it. Despite Rai's many fine qualities, he's terrible at keeping secrets. Sooner or later he'll tell Irao and Husto what he's seen. They'll tell people at the landfill. Those people will go back to their villages and spread word. And the governors will most definitely not be pleased.

So instead I convince Sergei that the governors despise me and consider me crazy, an insult to their masculinity. They'll only allow us near their village if a local man guides us. Sergei looks doubtful, but it's not hard for him to believe that here I'm an abomination. Eventually he unties Rai and lets him stand. I try to soothe over their unfortunate introduction to one another.

"He's Fleet," Rai says, both angry and amazed.

"No, not Fleet," I tell him. "Just a fisherman lost in a storm. He come from Hawaii."

Of course, we haven't had contact with Hawaii since Before Silence. Any stray fisherman would have to survive four thousand miles of open sea to reach our shore. But no one ever taught Rai geography.

Still, he's skeptical. "If he's a fisherman, why did he want to kill us?"

"He thought we killed his brother. He was afraid."

Sergei watches us. He can't understand a word of Chamorro, or maybe he's just pretending not to. Perhaps they don't have white caps where he comes from.

"Hawaii," Rai muses. "We could go there. We could trade, maybe, and no one would have to dig at the landfill anymore. My children, your children—Isa, this could change everything for them."

"The governors will decide," I say. "I have to take him there."

Rai hesitates. He's my big brother. He used to fight bullies for me when we were dusty children. He cried the day our uncles took me away to Talofofo. He came to walk me home when they were finished burning knowledge into my head. But the mother of his children is waiting for him at Layon.

"I'll take him by myself," I tell him. "Go get Angelina."

He frowns. "No. I'll come."

"You don't have to—"

"I'll come," he says curtly.

We circle through the jungle to avoid Irao, Husto and the men from Agat. For hours we walk along the old highway. No sentries or dog raise an alarm as we ghost through Inarajan. I wish we had water. Sergei's careful to walk behind us, never letting Rai or me out of his sight.

"Is there an army?" Sergei asks.

"Not anymore," I tell him. "Most of the military evacuated or died off After Silence."

"What about an army of your own people?"

I don't think that he wants an entire history of the militia here, how the local men trained under the Spanish and fought the Japanese and eventually became the Guam National Guard.

"There's no need. We only fight each other once in awhile. Do they have armies where you come from?"

"No," he says, but I think he's lying.

We trudge on. Boonie pigs trample away in the bushes when our feet come too close. To stay awake, I recite the second thousand of the names in my head. In my fatigue, some syllables slip out.

"What are you saying?" Sergei asks tightly.

"I'm praying," I tell him. "For your friend. You were very close?"

He grunts.

"He said your name before he died. He sounded . . . fond."

"He was only a man from my—" Sergei says, and stops. From his ship? From his base? Maybe from his bed.

Carefully I say, "If there are others of your people nearby, they are welcome as well."

Nothing. I glance back. Sergei has stopped to stare at a faint orange glow in the hills. Rai glances, too, but only for a moment. Those are the lights of Layon. The last gift of the old world. There aren't many options for garbage on an island like this. You have to pile it somewhere, otherwise you dump it into the ocean—all those car batteries and paint cans, light bulbs and lead pipes, the plastic wrap from food, the dirty diapers and soiled cat litter, generations of toxic messes.

"What's up there?" Sergei asks.

"An old landfill. They burn off the gasses so they can dig."

He swats at a bug on his neck. "What are they digging for?"

I shrug. "Anything useful."

The sky is pink-gold by the time we reach the old satellite tracking station above Inarajan. It's just a bunch of concrete buildings now, long abandoned, but Sergei pokes around in interest.

"What was this place?" he asks.

"Something called NASA," I tell him. "People used to visit the moon and this place helped them not get lost."

"A tracking station."

"Do people still live up there? On the moon?"

He kicks at an old fencepost. "If there are, they don't answer when we call them."

For the first time I really think about the world Sergei comes from. Out there they've had the raw materials, factory resources, and technical know-how to manufacture new transformers and power stations. By now they've rebuilt the radio stations, the telephone systems, and maybe even the Internet. They probably have medicines like aspirin and insulin, and no one dies of illnesses like appendicitis or childbirth.

All of these things would make life on Guahan easier.

But at a cost. Magellan taught us that.

"Do you trust me?" I ask Rai once we're walking again.

"What's kind of stupid question is that?" he asks, brushing thick green leaves from the path.

Sergei says, "Stop talking."

"You must be completely honest with anything the governors ask you," I tell him. And then, to Sergei, in Russian, "I'm sorry. I asked my brother not to let them beat me when we reach our leaders. I shame them, the men."

Sergei says, "If they beat you, why do you dress that way?"

He reminds me of the villagers when I was still Magahet Joseph Howard USN. Dress like a boy. Act like a boy. Can you teach a stone to act like a tree, or a bird to act like a dolphin? The governors said many long-ago ancestors were proud to be Fa'afafine, in the manner of male and female alike. Their approval made the criticism go silent, or at least less vocal.

"I follow my heart," I tell Sergei. "As all men and women should. Don't your people do that?"

Sergei coughs. "Perhaps."

"Vasilly was more than your friend, wasn't he?" And some of this is just guessing, but a name murmured in longing is hard to forget.

His face turns hard. "It doesn't matter. He's gone now."

Several minutes later we reach the outskirts of Talofofo Park. The parking lot has long returned to vegetation, and the gondalas disassembled or left to rust. Here the governors live in the old history museum, flanked by ramshackle huts and old latte stones and the fresh waters of the Ugum River. It's all small, unimpressive, nothing to look at twice. A sentry yawns when he sees us.

"Who comes?" he asks.

"Rai of Umatuc," Rai says. "And my sister the Bridge."

The sentry yawns again and scratches his ass. "What business?"

"This man comes from away," I say.

Sergei nudges me nervously. "Tell your governors to come out here."

"The governors are old men who believe in tradition," I reply. "They'll give you all the old records here, but we have to do things their way."

He continues to look skittish. But the sentry shrugs as if unimpressed with our visitor and pushes open the museum door. Inside all is dim and empty. I remember being nine years old and standing here with the children of other villages, waiting for our education from the wise governors. We all thought we'd been picked for a special destiny.

There's no such thing as destiny. Only inevitability.

The sentry takes us into a courtyard with woven mats circled around a cooking fire. "Wait here."

Sergei shuffles his feet, undecided, but I plop down and Rai follows.

An old man in a threadbare shirt shuffles from the house a few minutes later. "Isa," he says, a toothless smile on his face. He shakes Rai's hand, nods respectfully at Sergei. Behind him, a hunched servant brings out tea. The old man, Kepuha, sits with a creaking of his knees.

I introduce Sergei in Russian and explain that Kepuha, too, knew the mythical old stowaway, learned this strange foreign language.

"We must celebrate your arrival," Kepuha says, all kindness. "Such a momentous day."

"They say you can help me with information, sir," Sergei says.

Kepuha nods. "Yes, much information. All the old missiles. All those other terrible weapons. It'll be a relief to be rid of them."

Sergei relaxes. He's close, now, to what he came for.

Rai can't follow their words, but he knows some kind of agreement is being discussed. "Honored uncle, will they trade with us?"

"A good question to ask," Kepuha says.

We all drink our cool, sweetened tea. More servants bring toasted bread, boiled eggs, and strips of bacon. Kepuha turns to Sergei and talks more about weapons. On the roof of the museum, another sentry appears. Some young men carry large baskets through the far end of the courtyard. The skin on my neck prickles.

"Honored Kepuha, my brother and I have family business in Layon," I say in Chamorro. "We should depart."

Kepuha waves his gnarled hand. "There's time to rest. You must be exhausted."

Even as I watch, Rai's eyes slide shut. He leans sideways and sprawls into the dust. Sergei realizes at the same time I do that our food is drugged. He leaps up, tries to dart away, but gets no farther than a few feet before a guard knocks him down and kicks him in the ribs.

"My brother—" I say, slurred. "He didn't—"

"Sleep," Kepuha says. "You did well, Bridge."

My ears fill with a rushing noise and the sluggish crawl of my own heart. A sweet cool river, just like the river Ugum, carries me away to darkness.

The next time I see Sergei, he's screaming. The soldiers have him naked and strapped to a table, a white cap affixed to his head. I know what it's like to writhe as knowledge is forced into neural connections. Like lightning striking the brain, over and over. But Sergei's pain is worse because they're not putting data into his brain. They're yanking it out.

The back of my throat burns with bile.

Colonel Kepuha of the Guahan Militia stands beside me, watching through the mirrored window. Electric lights illuminate the rooms down here under the museum. Fresh, cool air circulates from pumps. The entire base runs off the power from recycled material dug out of the Layon landfill. Trash converted to fuel. One of the last great technological achievements of the old world. After Silence, our ancestors couldn't fix the whole island. But they could fix this place.

Sergei screams again.

"Is this . . . necessary?" I ask.

"He wouldn't answer questions about his homeland," Kepuha says. "But we'll find out."

Take a hump of land in the middle of the Pacific Ocean. Build a fort on it. Build another. Keep building, decade after decade, ports and airfields and depots of concrete and steel. Swap ownership during wartime. Swap it back. Add secret research labs dedicated to memory research. The future looks unlimited. But then civilization collapses, all of it, swallowed up by solar megaflares, and that hump of land has to fend for itself.

"You did well, bringing him here," Kepuha says. "We'll dig up the body of the one you killed and find out what we can from it."

With effort, I keep my voice steady. "Who says I killed him?"

He turns to me. "Of course you did. You learned your lessons well."

One foot rooted in the past. One planted in the future. The job of a Bridge isn't to greet the Fleet, but to stop it.

"What of my brother, sir?" I ask. "He thinks the strangers were fisherman from Hawaii. I'll make him swear not to tell, and if he does, no one will believe him anyway."

Kepuha smiles indulgently and starts walking down the hall. "Your brother is a good man?"

I follow. "Yes. Very good and honorable."

"Even honorable men can have loose tongues."

"You can trust him as much as you trust me," I promise.

We've reached another window and another memory room. The table inside is empty.

"When you finished your training as a child, how many names did you leave with?" Kepuha asks casually.

I rub the goose bumps on my arms. "Seven thousand."

"You left with one thousand," he says. "We give you another thousand more every time you bring us someone from Fleet. A reward for good service. A way to fill the gaps."

"But that's not—" I gulp against a new surge of bile. "That's not possible. I'd remember."

The doors in the room open and two guards drag Rai inside. He fights them, my brother does, but they're much stronger. They strap him down and reach for a cap.

Colonel Kepuha says, "No, you won't remember. You never do."

the she-wolf's hidden grin

michael swanwick

Michael Swanwick made his debut in 1980, and in the years that have followed he has established himself as one of SF's most prolific and consistently excellent writers at short lengths, as well as as one of the premier novelists of his generation. He has won the Theodore Sturgeon Memorial Award and the Asimov's Readers' Award poll. In 1991, his novel Stations of the Tide *won him a Nebula Award as well, and in 1995 he won the World Fantasy Award for his story "Radio Waves." He won the Hugo Award five times between 1999 and 2006, for his stories "The Very Pulse of the Machine," "Scherzo with Tyrannosaur," "The Dog Said Bow-Wow," "Slow Life," and "Legions in Time." His other books include the novels* In the Drift, Vacuum Flowers, The Iron Dragon's Daughter, Jack Faust, Bones of the Earth, *and* The Dragons of Babel. *His short fiction has been assembled in* Gravity's Angels, A Geography of Unknown Lands, Slow Dancing Through Time, Moon Dogs, Puck Aleshire's Abecedary, Tales of Old Earth, Cigar-Box Faust and Other Miniatures, Michael Swanwick's Field Guide to the Mesozoic Megafauna, *and* The Periodic Table of Science Fiction. *His most recent books are a massive retrospective collection,* The Best of Michael Swanwick, *and a new novel,* Dancing with Bears. *Swanwick lives in Philadelphia with his wife, Marianne Porter. His Web site is www.michaelswanwick.com and he maintains a blog at www.floggingbabel.com.*

In the sly and cruelly elegant story that follows, Swanwick spins off of my favorite Gene Wolfe story, "The Fifth Head of Cerberus," to produce a story that feels like it actually might have been written by Wolfe himself—high praise in my book.

When I was a girl my sister Susanna and I had to get up early whether we were rested or not. In winter particularly, our day often began before sunrise; and because our dormitory was in the south wing of the house, with narrow windows facing the central courtyard and thus facing north, the lurid, pinkish light sometimes was hours late in arriving and we would wash and dress while we were still uncertain whether we were awake or not. Groggy and only half coherent, we would tell each other our dreams.

One particular dream I narrated to Susanna several times before she demanded I stop. In it, I stood before the main doorway to our house staring up at the marble bas-relief of a she-wolf suckling two infant girls (though in waking life the babies similarly feeding had wee chubby penises my sister and I had often joked about), with a puzzled sense that something was fundamentally wrong. "You are anxious for me to come out of hiding," a rasping whispery voice said in my ear. "Aren't you, daughter?"

I turned and was not surprised to find the she-wolf standing behind me, her tremendous head on the same level as my own. She was far larger than any wolf from ancestral Earth. Her fur was greasy and reeked of sweat. Her breath stank of carrion. Her eyes said that she was perfectly capable of ripping open my chest and eating my heart without the slightest remorse. Yet, in the way of dreams, I was not afraid of her. She seemed to be as familiar as my own self.

"Is it time?" I said, hardly knowing what I was asking.

"No," the mother-wolf said, fading.

And I awoke.

Last night I returned to my old dormitory room and was astonished how small it was, how cramped and airless; it could never had held something so unruly and commodious as my childhood. Yet legions of memories rose up from its dust to batter against me like moths, so thickly that I was afraid to breathe lest they should fly into my throat and lungs to choke me. Foremost among them being the memory of when I first met the woman from Sainte Anne who was the last in a long line of tutors bought to educate my sister and me.

Something we had seen along the way had excited the two of us, so that we entered the lesson room in a rush, accompanied by shrieks of laughter; only to be brought up short by a stranger waiting there. She was long-legged, rangy, lean of face, dressed in the dowdy attire of a woman who had somehow managed to acquire a university education, and she carried a teacher's baton. As we sat down at our desks, she studied us as a heron might some dubious species of bait fish, trying to decide if it were edible or not. Susanna recovered first. "What has happened to Miss Claire?" she asked.

In a voice dry and cool and unsympathetic, the stranger said, "She has been taken away by the secret police. For what offenses, I cannot say. I am her replacement. You will call me Tante Amélie."

"'Tante' is a term of endearment," I said impudently, "which you have done nothing to earn."

"It is not yours to decide where your affection is to be directed. That is your father's prerogative and in this instance the decision has already been made. What are your favorite subjects?"

"Molecular and genetic biology," Susanna said promptly.

"Classical biology." I did not admit that chiefly I enjoyed the wet lab, and that only because I enjoyed cutting things open, for I had learned at an early age to hold my cards close to my chest.

"Hmmph. We'll begin with history. Where were you with your last instructor?"

"We were just about to cover the Uprising of Sainte Anne," Susanna said daringly.

Again that look. "It is too soon to know what the truth of that was. When the government issues an official history, I'll let you know. In the meantime we might as well start over from the beginning. You." She pointed at Susanna. "What is Veil's Hypothesis?"

"Dr. Aubrey Veil posited that the abos—"

"Aborigines."

Susanna stared in astonishment, then continued, "It is the idea that when the ships from Earth arrived on Sainte Anne, the aborigines killed everyone and assumed their appearance."

"Do you think this happened? Say no."

"No."

"Why not?"

"If it had, that would mean that we—everyone on Sainte Anne and Sainte Croix both—were abos. Aborigines, I mean. Yet we think as humans, act as humans, live as humans. What would be the point of so elaborate a masquerade if its perpetrators could never enjoy the fruits of their deceit? Particularly when the humans had proved to be inferior by allowing themselves to be exterminated. Anyway, mimicry in nature is all about external appearance. The first time an aborigine's corpse was cut open in a morgue, the game would be over."

Turning to me, Tante Amélie said, "Your turn. Defend the hypothesis."

"The aborigines were not native to Sainte Anne. They came from the stars," I began.

Susanna made a rude noise. Our new tutor raised her baton and she lowered her eyes in submission. "Defend your premise," Tante Amélie said.

"They are completely absent from the fossil record."

"Go on."

"When they arrived in this star system, they had technology equal to or superior to our own which, due to some unrecorded disaster, they lost almost immediately. Otherwise they would have also been found here on Sainte Croix." I was thinking furiously, making it all up as I went along. "They rapidly descended to a stone age level of existence. As intelligent beings, they would have seen what was going on and tried to save some aspect of their sciences. Electronics, metallurgy, chemistry— all disappeared. All they could save was their superior knowledge of genetics. When humans came along, they could not resist us physically. So they interbred with us, producing human offspring with latent aboriginal genes. They would have started with pioneers and outliers and then moved steadily inward into human society, spreading first through the lower classes and saving the rich and best-defended for last. Once begun the process would proceed without conscious mediation. The aborigines would not awaken until their work was done."

"Supporting evidence?"

"The policies of the government toward the poor suggest an awareness of this threat on their part."

"I see that I have fallen into a den of subversives. No wonder your last tutor is no more. Well, what's past is over now. Place your hands flat on your desks, palms down." We obeyed and Tante Amélie rapped our knuckles with her baton, as all our tutors had done at the beginning of their reigns. "We will now consider the early forms of colonial government."

Tante Amélie was the daughter of a regional administrator in a rural district called Île d'Orléans. As a girl, she had climbed trees to plunder eggs from birds' nests and trapped beetles within castles of mud. She also gigged frogs, fished from a rowboat, caught crabs with a scrap of meat and a length of string, plucked chickens, owned a shotgun, hunted waterfowl, ground her own telescope lenses, and swam naked in the backwater of a river so turbulent it claimed at least one life every year. This was as alien and enchanting as a fairy tale to my sister and me and of an evening we could sometimes coax her into reminiscing. Even now I can see her rocking steadily in the orange glow of an oil lamp, pausing every now and again to raise a sachet of dried herbs from her lap so the scents of lemon, vanilla, and tea leaves would help her memory. She had made it to adulthood and almost to safety before her father "inhaled his fortune," as the saying went on our sister planet. But of the years between then and her fetching up with us, she would say nothing.

It may seem odd that my sister and I came to feel something very close to love for Tante Amélie. But what alternative did we have? We only rarely saw our father. Our mother had produced two girls and multiple stillbirths before being sent away and replaced with the woman we addressed only as Maitresse. None of the other tutors, even those who resisted the temptation to sample father's wares, lasted very long. Nor were we allowed outside unaccompanied by an adult, for fear of being kidnapped. There were not many objects for our young hearts to fasten upon, and Tante Amélie had the potent advantage of controlling our access to the outside world.

Our house at 999 Rue d'Astarte doubled as my father's business, and so was redolent of esters, pheromones, and chemical fractions, most particularly that of bitter truffle for he held a monopoly over its import and used it in all his perfumes as a kind of signature. There were always people coming and going: farmers bringing wagons piled high with bales of flowers, traders from the Southern Sea bearing ambergris, slave artisans lugging in parts for the stills, neurochemists summoned to fine-tune some new process, courtesans in search of aphrodisiacs and abortifacients, overfed buyers almost inevitably accompanied by children with painted faces and lace-trimmed outfits. Yet Susanna and I were only rarely allowed beyond the run of the dormitory, classroom, and laboratory. Freedom for us began at the city library, the park, the slave market, and the like. Tante Amélie was a vigorous woman with many outside interests, so our fortunes took an immediate uptick at her arrival. Then we discovered quite by accident that she had opened a bank account (legal but interest-free) in hope of one day buying her freedom. This meant that she was amenable to bribery, and suddenly our horizons were limited only by our imaginations. The years that Tante Amélie spent with us were the happiest of my life.

For my sister too, I believe, though it was hard to tell with her. That was the period in which her passion for genetics peaked. She was always taking swabs of cell samples and patiently teasing out gene sequences from stolen strands of hair or nail clippings. Many an afternoon I trailed after her, in Tante Amélie's bought company, as she scoured the flesh market for some variant of Sainte-Anne's ape or rummaged in disreputable antique shops for hand-carved implements that might be made from—but never were—genuine abo bone. "You think I don't know what you're doing," I told her once.

"Shut up, useless."

"You're trying to prove Veil's Hypothesis. Well, what if you did? Do you think anyone would listen to you? You're just a child."

"Look who's talking."

"Even if they took you seriously, so what? What difference would it make?"

Susanna stared nobly into a future only she could see. "Madame Curie said, 'We must believe that we are gifted for something and that this thing, at whatever cost, must be attained.' If I could make just one single discovery of worth, that would atone for a great deal." Then she lowered her gaze to look directly at me, silently daring me to admit I didn't understand.

Baffled and resentful, I lapsed into silence.

I did not notice the change in my sister at first. By slow degrees she became sullen and moody and lost interest in her studies. This, for an irony, happened just as I was growing serious about my own and would have welcomed her mentorship. It was not to be. A shadow had fallen between us. She no longer confided in me as she once had; nor did we share our dreams.

Rummaging in her desk for a retractor one day, I discovered the notebook, which previously she had kept locked away, recording her great study. I had never been allowed to look at it and so I studied it intensely. Parts of it I can still recite from memory:

> This implies a congeries of recessive sex-linked genes; they, being dependent on the x-chromosome, will necessarily appear only in women.

and

> Under the right conditions, activating the operon genes in the proper sequence, the transformation would occur very rapidly, even in adults.

and

> Colonization of the twin planets entailed an extreme constriction of genetic plasticity which renders heritability of these recessives at close to one hundred percent.

and most provocative of all

> All this presupposes that abos and humans can interbreed & thus that they spring from a common star-faring (most likely extinct) race. H. sapiens and H. aboriginalis are then not two separate species but specializations of the inferred species H. sidereus.

The bulk of the notebook was filled with gene sequences which despite Susanna's tidy schoolgirl script I could barely make sense of. But I journeyed through to the end of the notes and it was only when I fetched up against blank pages that I realized that she hadn't added to them in weeks.

That was the summer when Susanna conceived a passion for theater. She went to see *Riders to the Sea* and *Madame Butterfly* and *Anthony and Cleopatra* and *The Women* and *Mrs. Warren's Profession* and *Lysistrata* and *Hedda Gabler* and *The Rover* and I forget what else. She even got a small part in *The Children's Hour*. I attended one rehearsal, was not made to feel welcome, and never showed up again.

Thus it was that when I had my first period (I had been well prepared so I recognized the symptoms and knew what to do), I did not tell her. This was on a Sunday morning in early spring. Feeling distant and unhappy, I dressed for church without saying a word to my sister. She didn't notice that I was withholding something from her, though in retrospect it seems that I could hardly have been more obvious.

We went to Ste. Dymphna's, sitting as usual in a pew halfway to the altar. Tante Amélie, of course, sat in the back of the church with the other slaves. Shortly after the Mass began a latecomer, a young woman whom I felt certain I had seen before, slipped into our pew. She was dressed in black, with fingerless lace gloves and had a round, moon-white face dominated by two black smudges of eyes and a pair of carmine lips. I saw her catch my sister's eye and smile.

I endured the service as best I could. Since the rebellion, the Québécois liturgy had been banned and though I understood the reasons for it the vernacular sounded alien to my ear. Midway through the monsignor's interminable sermon something—a chance shift of light through the stained glass windows, perhaps, or the unexpected flight of a demoiselle fly past my head—drew my attention away from his impassioned drone, and I saw the stranger stifle a yawn with the back of her hand, then casually place that hand, knuckles down on the pew between her and my sister. A moment later, Susanna looked away and placed her own hand atop it. Their fingers intertwined and then clenched.

And I knew.

The components for a disaster had been assembled. All that was needed was a spark.

That spark occurred when Susanna returned from cotillion in tears. I trailed along in the shadow of her disgrace, feeling a humiliation that was the twin of hers though I had done nothing to earn it. Nevertheless, as always happened in such cases, as soon as our escort had returned us to our father's house and made his report, we were summoned as a pair before Tante Amélie. She sat on a plain wooden chair, her hands overlapping on the knob of a cane she had recently taken to using, looking stern as a judge.

"You spat in the boy's face," she said without preamble. "There was no excuse for that."

"He put his hand—"

"Boys do those things all the time. It was your responsibility to anticipate his action and forestall it without giving him offense. What else do you think you go to cotillion to learn?"

"Don't bother sending me back there, then. I'm not going to become that kind of person."

"Oh? And just what kind of person do you imagine you can be?"

"Myself!" Susanna said.

The two women (it was in that moment that I realized my sister had stolen yet another march on me and left her childhood behind) locked glares. I, meanwhile, was ignored, miserable, and unable to leave. I clasped my hands behind my back and let my fingers fight with one another. The injustice of my being there at all gnawed at me, growing more and more acute.

Angrily, Tante Amélie said, "I despair for you. Why are you behaving like this? Why can't I get a straight answer out of you? Why—"

"Why don't you ask her girlfriend?" I blurted out.

Tante Amélie's lips narrowed and her face turned white. She lifted up her cane and slammed it down on the floor with a *thump*. Then she was on her feet and with a swirl of skirts was gone from the room, leaving Susanna shivering with fear.

But when I tried to comfort my sister, she pushed me away.

The summons came later than I expected, almost a week after Tante Amélie's abrupt cane-thump and departure. Tante Amélie escorted us to Maitresse's austere and unfeminine office—she had been the company doctor, according to gossip, before catching father's eye—and with a curtsey abandoned us there. Maitresse was a pretty woman currently making the transition to "handsome," very tall and slender, and that evening she wore a pink dress. When she spoke, her tone was not angry but sorrowful. "You both know that your place in life is to marry well and increase the prestige of our house. A great deal of money has been invested in you." Susanna opened her mouth to speak, but she held up a hand to forestall her. "We are not here to argue; the time for that is long past. No one is angry at you for what you have done with that young lady. I have performed for your father with other women many times. But you must both learn to look to your futures without sentiment or emotion.

"We are going out. There is something you must see."

Into the lantern-lit night streets of Port-Mimizon we sallied. This was a pleasure I had almost never experienced before, so that my apprehension was mingled with a kind of elation. A light breeze carried occasional snatches of music and gusts of laughter from unseen revelries. Maitresse had dressed us in long cloaks and Venetian carnival masks—undecorated *voltos* for us girls and for her a *medico della peste* with a beak as long as Pinocchio's—as was the custom for unescorted females.

The slave market at night was dark and silent. No lanterns were lit along its length, making the windowless compound seem a malevolent beast, crouching in wait for unwary prey to chance by. But Maitresse did not hurry her step. We turned a corner and at the end of an alley dark as a tunnel, saw a bright blaze of light and well-dressed men and women hurrying up the steps of a fighting club.

Maitresse led us around to the side, where we were let in at her knock. A dwarfish man obsequiously led the way to a small private waiting room with leather armchairs and flickering lights in mother-of-pearl sconces. "We'll have tea," she told the little man and he left. While we waited, for what I could not imagine, Maitresse addressed us once again.

"I spoke of the trouble and expense that went into your educations. You probably think that if you don't make good marriages, you will simply be sold for courtesans. That was a reasonable expectation a generation ago. But times have changed. Male infants have become rarer and even the best-brought-up girls are a glut on the market. Increasingly more men have taken to pederasty. The reasons are not well understood. Social? Cumulative poisoning from subtle alien compounds in the environment over the course of generations? No one knows."

"I will not give up Giselle," Susanna said almost calmly. "There is nothing you can do or threaten that will change my mind. She and I . . . but I imagine you know nothing about such passion as ours."

"Not know passion?" Maitresse laughed lightly, a delicate trill of silver bells. "My dear, how do you think I got involved in this mess in the first place?"

Our tea came and we drank, a quiet parody of domesticity.

What felt like hours dragged by. Finally, there came a roar of many voices through the wall and the dwarf deferentially reappeared at the door. "Ah." Maitresse put down her teacup. "It is time."

We entered our theater box between bouts, as the winner was being wrestled to the ground and sedated and his opponent carried away. Susanna sat stiffly in her seat, but I could not resist leaning over the rails to gawk at the audience. The theater smelled of cigar smoke and human sweat, with an under-scent of truffle so familiar that at first I thought nothing of it. As I watched, people wandered away from their seats, some to buy drinks, others retiring by pairs into private booths, while yet others . . . My sight fixed on a large man as he snapped a small glass vial beneath his nose. His head lolled back and a big loutish grin blossomed on his heavy face. I had never witnessed anyone sampling perfume in public before but having seen it once I immediately recognized its gestures being repeated again and again throughout the room. "Your father's wares," Maitresse observed, "are extremely popular." I was not sure if she wanted me to feel proud or ashamed; but I felt neither, only fearful and confused.

After a time the audience, alerted by cues undetectable to me, reassembled itself in the tiered rows of chairs wrapped around a central pit with canvas-lined walls. The loud chatter turned to a dwindling murmur and then swelled up again in a roar of unclean approval as two girls, naked, were led stumbling down opposing aisles. Their heads were shaved (so they could not be seized by the hair, I later learned) and one had her face painted red and the other blue. Because they were both of slender build and similar height, this was needed to tell them apart.

Several slaves, nimble as apes, lowered the girls into the pit, then jumped down to rub their shoulders, chafe their hands, speak into their ears, and break vial after vial of perfume under their noses. By degrees the fighters came fully awake and then filled with such rage that they had to be held back by four men apiece to keep them from prematurely attacking each other. Then a bell rang and, releasing their charges, the slaves scrambled up the canvas walls and out of the pit.

The audience below came to their feet.

"Do not look away," Maitresse said. "If you have any questions, I will answer them."

The two girls ran together.

"How do they get them to fight?" I asked even though I was certain I would be told simply that they had no choice. Because were I in their place, knowing that the best I could hope for was to survive in order to undergo the same ordeal again in a week, I would not fight someone of my trainers' choosing. I would leap up into the audience and kill as many of them as I could before I was brought down. It was the only reasonable thing to do.

"Your father creates perfumes for myriad purposes. Some cure schizophrenia. Some make it possible to work a forty-hour shift. Some are simple fantasies. Others are more elaborately crafted. Those below might think they are dire-wolves fighting spear-carrying primitives, or perhaps abos defending their families from human ravagers. Their actions seem perfectly rational to them, and they will generate memories to justify them." As commanded, I did not look away but I could feel her gaze on the side of my face nonetheless. "I could arrange for you to sample some of your father's perfumes, if you're curious. You would not like them. But if you persisted, after a time you would find yourself liking them very much indeed. My best advice to you is not to start. But once would not hurt."

I shook my head to blink away my tears. Misinterpreting the gesture, Maitresse said, "That is wise."

We watched the rest of the fight without further comment. When it ended, the survivor threw back her head and howled. Even when burly slaves immobilized and then tranquilized her, her mad grin burned triumphantly.

"May I stop watching now?" Susanna asked. I could tell she meant it to be defiant. But her voice came out small and plaintive.

"Soon." Maitresse leaned over the rail and called down to the pit-slaves, "Show us the body."

The pit workers started to hoist up the naked corpse for her examination.

"Clean her up first."

They produced a dirty cloth and rubbed at the girl's face, wiping away most of the red paint. Then they lifted her up again. In death, she seemed particularly childlike: Slender, small-breasted and long-legged. The hair on her pubic mound was a golden mist. I could not help wondering if she had experienced sex before her premature death and, if so, what it had been like.

"Study her features," Maitresse said dryly.

I did so, without results. Turning to my sister with a petulant shrug, I saw in the mirror of her horrified expression the truth. There came then a shifting within me like all the planets in the universe coming into alignment at once. When I looked back at the dead fighter I saw her face afresh. It could have been a younger version of my sister's face. But it was not.

It was my own.

Susanna said nothing during the long walk home, nor did I.

Maitresse, however, spoke at length and without emotion. "Your mother made many children. You—" (she meant Susanna) "—were natural. You—" (me) "were the first of many clones commissioned in an attempt to create a male heir, all failures.

When your mother was sent away, your father resolved to get rid of everything that reminded him of her. I argued against it and in the end we compromised and kept the two of you while selling off the others. I have no idea how many survive. However, the economic realities of the day are such that, were either of you to be sold, you would fetch the highest price here." She said a great deal more as well but it was unnecessary; we already well understood everything that she had to tell us.

When we arrived home, Maitresse took our masks from us and bid us both a pleasant good-night.

We went to sleep, my sister and I, cradled in each other's arms, the first time we had done so in over a year. In the morning, Tante Amélie was gone and our formal educations were done forever.

Last night, as I said, I returned to my old dormitory room. It took me a while to realize that I was dreaming. It was only when I looked for Susanna and found nothing but dust and memories that I recollected how many years had gone by since my childhood. Still, in the way of dreams, there was a pervasive sense that the entire world was about to change. "You know what to do now," a rasping whispery voice said. "Don't you, daughter?"

I turned and the she-wolf was not there. But I felt sure of her presence anyway. "Is it time?" I asked.

She did not reply. Her silence was answer enough.

I *grinned* for I now understood where the she-wolf had been hiding all this time.

Not so much awakening as taking my dream-state with me into the waking world, I got up out of bed and walked down the hall to my husband's room. Then I paid a visit to the nursery, where my twin sons were sleeping. Finally, I went out into the night-dark streets to look for my sister.

The night is almost over now, and we must hurry to finish what we have begun. At dawn we will leave the cities behind and return to the swamps and forests, the caverns and hills from which the humans had driven us, and resume our long-interrupted lives. I have taken off my skin and now prowl naked through the streets of Port-Mimizon. In the shadows about me I sense many others who were once human and I devoutly pray that there are enough of us for our purpose. In the back of my mind, I wonder whether all this is real or if I have descended into the pit of madness. But that is a minor concern. I have work to do.

I have freed the she-wolf from within her hiding place and there is blood on her muzzle.

Only . . . why does the world smell as it does? Of canvas and bitter truffle.

Bad Day on Boscobel

ALEXANDER JABLOKOV

With only a handful of stories, mostly for Asimov's Science Fiction *and a few well-received novels, Alexander Jablokov established himself as one of the most highly regarded new writers of the nineties. His first novel,* Carve the Sky, *was released in 1991, and was followed by other successful ones, such as* A Deeper Sea, Nimbus, River of Dust, *and* Deepdrive, *and a collection of short fiction,* The Breath of Suspension. *Jablokov fell silent through the decade of the oughts, but in the past couple of years has been returning to print, in 2010 publishing his first novel in over ten years,* Brain Thief, *and popping up in the magazines again with elegant, coolly pyrotechnic stories such as the one that follows, which spins a suspenseful tale of espionage and intrigue in a world whose inhabitants live in giant trees.*

Dunya stopped just outside Phineus's unit to calm herself down. Otherwise she would burst in and start screaming at him. That was no way to start a check-in meeting with one of her refugees.

That gave her a chance to realize that she looked like hell. She'd already had one fight that morning, with her daughter, Bodil, and afterwards she had rushed out, unsnapped and unbrushed. It was hard enough to manage someone like Phineus, all Martian and precise, without giving him more ammunition about how lax things were here, among the asteroids.

She stepped out of the foot traffic, pulled out her kit, sharpened her eyebrows, got her pale hair in some semblance of order, and cleaned sleep and tears out of the corners of her eyes.

They'd put Phineus low-down, not far above actual rock, in a line of wooden cubicles along a root. Leaves rustled overhead. But there was no dramatic view up past the trunks to the spreading branches of the famed Boscobel axis, just some fibrous safety panels and a moving ladderway. Phineus sometimes grouched about what it said about his status.

There. Bodil had gone straight to bed after their fight. Dunya had a full day ahead of her. Looking good might be poor revenge on an ungrateful child, but that was what she had. And it had relaxed her enough. Now she was ready for that idiot.

When she got into his narrow space, her most difficult refugee sat on his bed, bony knees against his chest. Phineus's cliff of a face swept up into an impressive brow and forehead. It was almost too big for the room.

"I didn't expect you for a couple more days," he said.

So she'd been getting predictable. And he wanted her to know it, which was interesting. "I have something to talk to you about."

"Am I in trouble?" He smiled.

She didn't answer.

"Look," he said. "I'm happy to see you. It's kind of a treat. Not a lot happens down here."

"I was just over in Lower Cort. In the Wendell Beech, about a third of the way up."

"Nice spot," he said. "If you're the sort who likes nice spots, that is. I never pegged you for the type."

"The branches sag down there," she said. "Thick growth. If you climb up bough 73, then slide a bit down the branches there, you'll find a bunch of these." She flipped something across to him. He caught it. "All hanging from strings, blowing in the breeze. They're getting tangled up in the twigs. Someone should have given them a bit more weight in the lower parts."

Phineus looked expressionlessly at the doll in his hand. It was made from human hair, looped and woven together, with the loose ends bursting from the top of its head in a huge fall. Its face was miserable, with downturned mouth and squinted eyes, like a child with a stomach ache. It might have been almost cute, but it was all held together by something thick and sticky.

"You know that's blood, right?" she asked.

"Look, I don't—"

"It's gang sign, Phineus. Green Burnings. They jump the boughs around here. Sometimes keeping order, sometimes tearing it up. They're Root & Branch party supporters, field workers, and enforcers. Things have been fairly balanced lately. But if the Green Burnings push up into Five Boughs, there's going to be trouble with the Trunk. I don't know how things are on Mars, but it's not just about gang territory here on Boscobel. It's always got another dimension. The Trunkers are losing support from small businesses who think the party's not protecting their interests. Burnings jumping through Five Boughs will only make that more obvious. Things might get rough."

"I still don't understand local politics," he said.

"That's exactly why you shouldn't be messing around with it."

"Me? What do I have to do with it?"

That expression of outraged innocence was the last straw. Dunya snatched the doll from his hand, startling the old Martian corridor fighter with her speed, and stuck it back in her pocket. "You know them. Hang out with them. Give them a bit of training. Just keeping your Martian hand in? Or something more? In any case, you're going to get into trouble. Not just with some rival group. With me."

"How did—"

"My sources are none of your business." She wasn't going to reveal that she had learned it entirely by chance, by fighting with her daughter just that morning, not because she had previously had any interest in what he was doing.

"You've got the wrong guy. I see that detritus, sure. Green Burnings, whatever. They flip off branches above me while I'm catching some breakfast out at Kumar's. We got to talking. So maybe I gave them some tactical tips, just to keep my hand in. But I don't drill them or anything like that. Maybe they hired from outside. I mean, there are Martians hanging around Preem Bough. Maybe they've set up a school or something."

This was unexpected. "You're the only Martian in Boscobel."

"Piece of information, Dunya: there is always another Martian. We're tricky that way."

"So you've seen other Martians out there?" she said.

"Oh, you know, rumors. Someone uncomfortable with all the plant life is up there, looking for trouble. It would be nice to see someone from the old dustball." He looked bleak. "But it's probably false. I'm the only Martian here. Stuck down in the roots, going nowhere."

Once Phineus started feeling sorry for himself, he usually went all the way and ended up lying face down on the floor, refusing to respond. It could last for days.

She didn't have time for that. "Phineus. Let me be clear. No more combat training. From now on. And no contact with anyone who jumps with Green Burnings. It will endanger your status if you do. Do you understand?"

"What does that mean? Say I want to go up to Kumar's. If a Burning comes in and gets coffee while I'm there, do I have to pack it up and leave?"

"If you're going to ask, I'm going to tell you. Yes. Don't even share a common space with them until I say otherwise." Phineus kept himself clean, but his room was a mess, with clothes shoved places that must have taken more work than just putting them away properly. He even had a couple of noodle-parlor containers under a cushion. She resisted the urge to lecture him about it. "You like to bring your food home. If you see a gang member, just do that. Any more questions?"

"If I ask, I'll find out I have to stay in my room. So, no."

"Smart man. Just find yourself a better hobby."

He didn't raise his head as she left.

Bodil had sauntered in that morning just as Dunya was getting ready to leave for work. She smelled of trees far from where she was supposed to be, with a couple of girlfriends: every spot in Boscobel had its own combination of gums, saps, pollens, nectars, and oils. Bodil relied too much on the fact that her mother wasn't a native, and sometimes had trouble with the more subtle signals.

When Bodil tried to just brush past her mother on her way to her room, Dunya had blocked her path with an outstretched leg. First Bodil had denied she had been anywhere. Then she said she'd told her mother about it, but she, distracted and too busy, had forgotten. Then she denied that her mother had any authority that meant anything.

"And where is Dad?" Bodil had said, through too-ready tears. "Why isn't he ever here? What's he trying to get away from?"

Bryn *was* away a lot. Dunya didn't like it either.

But the fight had come with one unexpected benefit. After Dunya had started in about Bodil's on-again, off-again boyfriend Unray, who jumped with the Green Burnings, Bodil had burst out with a defense of his capabilities. "He's the one who figures out their tactics. He's learned a lot, don't think he hasn't. Martian stuff, not like the other gangs. It's a whole other level of activity. You should see how he's marked their territory over at Wendell Beech . . ."

Her mother's sudden interest told Bodil she'd made a mistake boasting about that. But it was too late. Dunya connected that information with other things she'd learned, and understood something of what Phineus was up to. She let her daughter go, already planning a detour to Lower Cort on her way to Phineus.

Bodil could try to use Bryn as a weapon, she thought now, as she climbed to her next appointment. It would still be just the two of them for quite some time. They'd have to fight it out on their own.

She rose through several layers of the great branches that made up the dwelling levels of Boscobel. Sometimes the view went out a great distance, revealing a group of people at a table, a prowling cat, a vortex of rain renewing pockets of water in the great branches. Usually it was compacted, held in by leaves and lattice. She finally stepped off onto a busy pathway and made her way between shops and the small personal gardens people here kept in front of their units.

No matter where you were, most of Boscobel was invisible, but from this level, about a third of the way up, you got the best feel for what this world was. Boscobel was trees, the biggest trees in the solar system. They stuck their roots deep into the crust, flung themselves across the axis of the spinning cylinder of the asteroid, and then plunged into the opposite side, where their upper branches became roots. In between, vast boughs spread, providing living and production areas. Some had developed leaves meters across or complex meshes of interlaced branches. Though they still bore names like sycamore and juniper, they bore only slight resemblances to their earth-rooted ancestors.

"I started out late," she said, as she came up to Fama's dining area. "I'm not catching up."

"That's okay, you can help me get things ready. Let's roll this out."

Dunya pushed hot tables loaded with steaming pots out onto the balcony that looked out over a wide opening among the trees. Nothing dramatic, but a nice spot. It was shaded by a couple of gigantic leaves, each of which had bugs scurrying in its furry underside. To any asteroid-dweller eye, Boscobeli or not, that was comforting. It meant that, no matter what else happened, you wouldn't starve.

Fama was a big woman who seemed to wear all of her clothes at the same time. The outer garment was always different, but Dunya thought she recognized a couple of the layers underneath. It was cooler than average here, where a breeze came down from the distant North Pole. But she didn't think that was the explanation. Fama was still ready to flee, and wanted to make sure she had everything she needed with her when the time came.

"Any shakedowns recently?" Dunya asked.

"None, thanks to your suggestion."

Dunya tried to remember what she had come up with.

"Ah, Strop."

Fama shrugged. "He knows his food, I'll give him that."

Merv Strop was an agent of the Office of Adversary Knowledge, Boscobel's internal security force. Fama had been getting harassed by some low-level thugs from the Dead Roots, competitors to those Green Burnings Phineus gave tactics classes to. Dunya had suggested that she invite agent Strop to dine, in a visible way. The Dead Roots had moved off to find an easier target, while Strop had stayed.

"He's actually got a real crime to solve, I hear," Fama said. "Someone took off with an ancient emergency kit from some secure area. It's sweating his skull, making him ornery."

Dunya had to get to business. "I'm curious about someone. In the area. A Martian, I've heard."

"Anything else? Martians don't got red dots on their foreheads to make them easy to spot."

Dunya had found a few minutes to check up on available tourist entries. She had access because tourists were sometimes refugees in disguise—or ended up as refugees when a political shift back home left them unable to return after their relaxing vacation lounging in a tree branch. No Martians had turned up, but there was one good possibility, from the innerbelt asteroid Fortuna. Fortuna had close relations with Mars, and might have been willing to cooperate in screening someone's identity. If so, this person had some connections to the Martian government, but was probably operating unofficially.

"It's someone a fairly tough guy would still be nervous about. One possibility is a woman, supposedly from Fortuna." And Phineus had been nervous. Who knew what enemies Phineus might have made back on Mars?

"I need some critters," Fama said. "Soup's kind of bland."

Dunya helped pluck bugs from the underside of the leaf. Most of them escaped her fingers. Fama grabbed writhing handfuls and dumped them into the steaming pot. Their shells puffed, and their dissolving legs gave the stock the saffron color that marked its quality. A restaurant depended on the diet of its feedbugs as much as it did on the skill of its chef.

"That might actually explain a few things, though." Fama tasted, and nodded in satisfaction. "That's enough now. Let the rest go."

The bugs scurried into the fibers. "You've seen someone?" Dunya said.

"Didn't think 'Martian' 'til you said. A woman. Tall. Does claim to be from Fortuna but moves like she grew up in gravity. No obvious business. Has a drink here, chats with someone there. But she's working hard the whole time. No relaxation in her." Fama was desperate to expand her business, kept her eye on competitors and potential customers.

"Any idea where I can find her?"

"She sleeps at the Moss, I think."

Fama was looking over Dunya's shoulder to see who might have come in. She should let the woman get to her business.

"Anything else you need to talk about?" Dunya said.

"Well . . ." Fama was suddenly reluctant. "Tell me. How long did it take you to feel that you fit in?"

"Here in Boscobel?" Dunya made it a principle to be honest with her clients. Sometimes that was difficult. "Most days I don't feel I fit in at all. But sometimes, when I stand under a dripping leaf and watch the white gibbons jump the gap at Gantan, I think I should never have been anywhere else."

Fama scooped a bug out of the soup and sucked thoughtfully on its head. "Hope for me yet, then."

"Hope for us all."

A couple of clients later, Dunya was at the Moss, a set of rental rooms on stilts above the mosses that gave the name. This woman was after Phineus for something, and Phineus was nervous about it. His casualness had been unconvincing. If she was keeping Phineus under observation, Dunya had a chance to maybe spot her.

Phineus wouldn't listen to a thing Dunya had told him. He'd go to breakfast, meeting with a Green Burning or two, maybe in a corner, so as not to be obvious. If this woman, whoever she was, meant to keep him under observation, that would be an easy spot. If Phineus then went back to sulk in his unit, the woman might take the opportunity to come back to the Moss to take care of other business. If she did, she would most likely skirt the roots of the big ash tree.

That was a lot of assumptions. But Boscobel was incredibly resistant to travel if you didn't know it well. Once visitors learned a useful route, they tended to stick to it. Dunya found a spot by a mossy root where she could watch, get work done, and have someone bring her a coffee every now and then.

After an hour or so, she had updated everyone's files. Just as she was considering giving it up, she saw an odd bit of movement. Someone had started down the stairs from the direction of Phineus, glanced across the open area below, then stepped back. Somehow, Dunya had been spotted.

Now Dunya was even more interested. Who was this woman? And why was she so anxious to avoid an interview?

She'd been successful in predicting the Martian's route home, at least. Where would the woman go now? She'd probably planned out some escape route and bolt-hole, for contingencies. Dunya was used to people trying to avoid her.

What choices would have seemed smart to a Martian corridor dweller who hadn't had the time to work out the intricacies of Boscobel? The main question was: up or down? Right here was a mazelike sprawl of roots. Concealment would seem easier, and it was just the kind of place that would give comfort to a Martian.

But she would have thought past that. She'd try to be unpredictable, at least to herself. And she'd want to use the ways in which Boscobel differed from her home. She'd want things to be interesting. She'd climb.

There were three good routes up from here. The closest one was exposed in most directions, easily seen. One of the other two, then.

As it happened, both those routes hit a bottleneck in the understory, in a volume that had suffered a fire a couple of decades before. Several branches had not re-grown to useful size, so both those routes would kink back to near the ash trunk.

Dunya knew another way up. It was longer and involved climbing higher, into the crown. There was no on-bough route there, where a high wind swept the branches. To the inexperienced eye, it looked impassable. But Dunya knew a tunnel *inside* a bough, the result of a cleared-out fungal infection, that sometimes served as swing housing for low-status new dwellers. She'd have to step over people's shitpots, but they knew her there. After that a drop-down would put her across where the Martian would have to go. That should persuade her that Dunya was someone she had to pay attention to.

No matter what, after that she had to get home, find her daughter, and try to keep the rest of her life under repair. She grabbed a ladderway and rose up.

The sunglobe had moved past its brightest point and lunchtime had gone past when Dunya found herself in a wet space under massive leaves. Water burped up onto the ridged surfaces, and cascaded down to the hanging gardens below. Only a few misguided frogs clinging to strands of pale fungus gave hints of life elsewhere.

This was part of Boscobel's secret support equipment. Fluid-filled tubes along the walls carried nourishment to the higher reaches of the impossible trees. Light fibers pumped photons into photosynthetic centers to support metabolisms that couldn't possibly get all their energy from the mostly decorative sunglobe.

The woman now dodged through a small café that hung from the rough bark of the oak bough just below here. It was a good spot to check for pursuit.

Too bad for her that Dunya was ahead of her, not behind.

She was a long-limbed woman with big hands and feet. With the strength in her shoulders she looked like she could have picked up the entire café and shaken everything out of it. But instead of revealing any force, she moved smoothly, sliding past people before they even knew she was there. She wore her dark brown hair loose, a style more suitable to a Martian corridor than leafy Boscobel. She'd clearly bought that treesilk jacket here, though, and it suited the length of her torso. Dunya pulled herself back into concealment.

The chase had taken her out of herself. Now all the worries of the day came back to her. As cold water dripped on the back of her neck, she worried about her afternoon schedule, about her next encounter with Bodil, about whether Bryn would send her a message today. The longer he was away, the more entertaining his messages got, a bad sign. A poorly healed pipe with a lumpy joint vibrated under her boot, and she saw that it had shaken a couple of the big leaves loose from their adhesive connections with each other. Pushing back with her elbow and feeling the leaves peel away from each other was like childishly poking at a loose tooth with your tongue, pleasant and disturbing at once. Looked at too closely, much of Boscobel was falling apart.

She slid out of concealment. Where was the woman? Had Dunya miscalculated?

She felt the breath behind her. There was no time to respond. Something hit the back of her head and knocked her forward. She rolled, and found herself looking up at a long boot that pushed on her throat, and beyond it, slowly coming into focus, the Martian.

The woman wasn't beautiful, but she was certainly striking, with dark skin, high cheekbones, and big eyes the color of moss agate.

"Who the hell are you?" Dunya said.

"I could ask you the same thing," the Martian said.

"You could, but you have no right to. I'm a citizen of Boscobel trying to get through my day. You're the one who snuck in here in pursuit of Phineus Gora."

"And who is Phineus Gora to you?"

"My client. He's a refugee. I'm responsible for grafting him onto Boscobel."

"Good luck with that." The woman was amused. "So you look out for him."

"I look out for all my refugees. It's my job. He's worried about why you're here."

"But he didn't give you any details, hoping your sense of responsibility would put you in my way." The amused look disappeared. "He had no right to risk you that way. His problems should stay his own." She pulled her boot off Dunya's throat.

For a second, Dunya didn't know what to do.

"Get up, get up." The woman was impatient. "You've tempted me into . . . actually, I think you've tempted me into exactly what Phineus hoped. Exposing myself. Giving the OAKs a reason to throw me out of Boscobel. Maybe he's smarter than he seems."

Dunya sat up. What *had* Phineus gotten her to do?

"He knows who you are," Dunya said.

The woman laughed. "He thinks he does."

"But I still have no idea."

"It may not matter. But . . . my name is Miriam Kostal. I'm from Mars."

"Dunya Hautala."

"Let me be short. Phineus is the inside man for a filibustering expedition that left Mars orbit two months ago and will be here within a day. Does that mean anything to you?"

Anarchic Mars had turned into a menace to everyone between the orbits of Jupiter and Earth. A weak central government, recovering from assassination and attempted revolution, was unable to stop ambitious groups from putting together military expeditions to seize individual asteroids and set themselves up as ruling juntas. As a girl, Dunya had fled just such a takeover, finally fetching up on Boscobel.

"And so you take a room at the Moss and follow Phineus around?" Dunya said. "How much sense does that make? Do the OAKs know? Anyone else?"

"No one knows. Even on Mars. Filibustering expeditions rarely succeed without cooperation from their targets, either tacit or explicit. On Mars, the expedition has some official support. Here . . . I have no idea who might be involved. Anyone could have an interest in rearranging things to end up closer to the top. Phineus is a technician, not anyone involved in political discussions. He's got a specific mission, assisting the initial penetration by the attacking force. I can't trust anyone here. But I don't need to. All I need to do is figure out what he's doing, and stop it. Then I can be on my way."

Miriam was almost persuasive. It was always tempting to skip the mess of political compromise and get straight to the decisive action. And Boscobel sure was a mess. Dunya didn't even try to deny it. But decisive action always left its own mess, to be cleaned up by people like her, while people like Miriam strode off in search of some other dramatic problem to fix.

Dunya slid herself to sit with her back against the loose leaves.

"The complexities of corruption are all we've got," Dunya said. "I'm sure not everyone's looking forward to being ruled by someone else. If you have information that will help our government fend off an attack, you should share it."

"No. I'll be arrested. And now you. Any investigation will be ended by the new regime. End of story. End of us."

That was plausible enough. But Miriam hadn't even tried getting cooperation. Dunya found herself irritated at the woman, impressive though she was. Boscobel was her home. She didn't like thinking of it as a clump of trees run by people instantly eager to betray it for a better deal.

The bottom of the leaves was loose. The top still stuck. She didn't have time to work on it more. She had no real reason to trust Miriam. She had to make contact with someone. She leaned her head back, as if thinking it over, and pushed harder. She knew there was a branch about ten feet below, where she could find a quick route down. The leaves parted behind her and she fell through.

From the last glimpse of her face, Miriam was taken completely by surprise. But she recovered almost instantly. She dove forward, whipped out a long arm, and just managed to snag Dunya's ankle as she fell. Stopping Dunya's fall almost jerked her out of the gap. She braced one foot against the ripping leaf and swung Dunya to the side, until she dangled over a much longer drop. The endless network of tree boughs circled around her.

She could tell Miriam was considering it. People would pretty much assume that Dunya had tried something too difficult for a non-native to do properly. "Poor Dunya never quite got the hang of it . . ."

With a sudden effort, Miriam hauled her in. Dunya curled up and grabbed the edge of the leaf. Finally, she lay on the floor next to Miriam, sucking in air.

"Nice move," Miriam said. "You practice that?"

"A sudden inspiration."

"Look," Miriam said. "You want to go to the OAKs for help? I can't stop you. It won't help, and it might put this whole world at hazard. But it's up to you."

"Would you really have killed me?" Dunya said.

"An impolite question. We've been slashing each other's faces on Mars for a decade or more now, trying to solve problems by eliminating the people we think are causing them. Hasn't worked for us, but it's habit now."

"Not for you, though."

"I wouldn't rely on the quality of my habits, if I were you. Go. Go now. Before I get sensible."

Dunya could feel the stare of those agate eyes like something physical. She thought about saying something else, but nothing, not even "good luck," made sense. Without another word, she turned and went.

"Eh?" Strop looked up from his soup. "Dunya. What are you doing here?"

"I want to ask you some questions."

"Well, I . . ." Strop grunted in annoyance as Dunya pulled a chair up and joined him at his table. "Suit yourself, then."

Strop's pale hair lay plastered to a soft-looking skull. He was the local OAK agent, and as OAKs went, he was a decent sort. OAKs didn't go very far, Dunya reminded herself.

"What do you know about Phineus?" she said. "I mean, what drove him from Mars, why he's here. Who he's in contact with."

Strop swallowed a spoonful of the soup and closed his eyes. He was known for his devotion to food, and his presence at a restaurant actually served as a sign of approval. So maybe Fama wasn't quite the victim she made herself sound.

"Phineus is your client, isn't he?"

"Of course," Dunya said.

"So it's your job to make sure he stays out of trouble. What we pay you for. Didn't you do some kind of intake when you got him? Then you know he's a protected exile. Unable to return to Mars, but protected by Martian law. A Martian trying to kill him would be in serious trouble on return home. Anyone after him would have an unusual devotion to justice. Please be more vigilant about your intakes. They give you at least little preliminary information. Too bad we don't get to do one when we have a child. That's why children can surprise you. They never fill out the proper forms."

Strop had two well-liked and successful children, both older than Bodil. It was just exasperating.

She thought about giving him Miriam Kostal. *That* he'd have to pay attention to. But Miriam had gauged her right. She couldn't do it.

And she was reflecting that there were probably good reasons why Phineus had been dumped on her without much background information. Did Strop know those reasons? In any event, bringing that up would either sound like whining or be actively dangerous.

"Look, Dunya." Fama had whisked away the soup, careful to show no sign she'd seen Dunya earlier, and the sculpted pyramid that steamed in front of him smelled delicious. "I appreciate that you've gotten a yen to get better at your job. These impulses never last. If you don't mind a bit of friendly advice, I'd say that you should look after your own family situation instead."

"My family situation?" Dunya said. "What the hell is that supposed to mean?"

He pursed his disconcertingly full lips, pleased that he'd pissed her off. "Children can be a handful. Sometimes they can even do things that pass beyond the childish, and get in real trouble. Are you heading home soon?"

"I don't think that's your business."

"If you're hoping to find your daughter there, give up on that notion. She's found herself a hidey hole. She seems to think it's secret. Secrets can lead to trouble."

This was too much. Not only was she not going to get any action out of Strop, he was going to punish her for trying by implying that she was a bad mother.

And what was even more irritating was how right Miriam Kostal had been. There would be no help in the OAKs. Whether or not there was some high-level interest in a change of regime, field agents like Strop knew better than to wander into delicate political situations. It might interfere with their digestion. So Strop would fight as hard as he could to hear nothing about Phineus.

She pushed her chair back, ready to stand. But she couldn't just leave. He had her, just as he intended.

"Do you know where she is?" Dunya said.

"In the crust. Near the Xanthus airball. Her boyfriend has run into trouble from his Green Burnings buddies, big surprise. Bodil might easily end up in the same trouble. If those kids broke into where I think they did, they're all in serious trouble. Stop worrying about what plausible Martians might be up to and give your daughter some thought. This isn't official advice, by the way. One parent to another."

"Thanks, Strop." Dunya had to consciously loosen her jaw to speak. "I hope I can return the favor someday."

"Not likely, Dunya. Not likely."

Her daughter was definitely a Boscobel native, Dunya thought. An immigrant like her would have tried to hide in the trees. Bodil knew the many ways of getting found there, and had instead burrowed into Boscobel's neglected shell, which she thought of as invisible.

Dunya looked up into the shaft above. Boscobel had a huge volume in its shell, but only the poorest lived in it. The air rumbled. Just beyond was the vast space of Xanthus, one of the pressure equalization spaces excavated after the newly expanded shell of Boscobel had cooled.

The only illumination came from infrequent light bumps. There was no way she was going to stumble around this ridiculous space searching for her daughter. She stood in the center of the shaft and said, "Come down, Bodil. Now."

Before a minute was out, she wanted to say something more. She stopped herself. The silence grew as hollow as the space around her. The best way to get a client to say something was to say nothing. That conversational vacuum could suck out the most amazing things.

There was a rustle. A pair of shoes appeared in a hole about ten meters up. Bodil slid into view and then slowly climbed down to the level where her mother stood.

Bodil favored her father, Bryn. She was taller than Dunya, but with softer features, big eyes, and downturned mouth. She looked gentle. Maybe someday she would be.

"It's your fault." Bodil spoke quietly, the way she showed she was really angry.

"What? What's my fault?"

"Don't pretend you don't know!" The other way she showed she was really angry was by yelling. "You got that information about that Martian out of me, and now Unray's been beaten. They knew it had to come from him. They hit him, momma. A lot. I never trusted them. I want to hurt them."

"You think that's bad?" Dunya said. "Things are way worse than you think. Every one of us is in trouble. I don't have time for this. You don't have time for it. If we're not careful, we might all end up as slaves, or refugees, or something worse."

"What are you talking about?"

"I need your help, Bodil. I'm sorry about what happened to Unray. Probably not as sorry as you'd like me to be. But we've got Martians crawling around our home that might rip the whole thing apart and I don't have time to worry about your stupid boyfriend and his lame-ass buddies."

For the first time in a long time, Bodil clearly didn't know what to say. She'd hoped her mother would feel guilty and help her. Instead, her mother was asking for help herself. That hadn't happened in an equally long time.

Dunya realized she'd gotten up against her daughter, looking up at her, feeling like a knife pointed at her belly. She stepped back, looked around. "Isn't this their territory? You shouldn't be here."

"I don't care what they call their territory. They don't deserve anything. I thought . . . I can do something to them, make them feel it, the way they made me feel it."

"Well, Bodie," a voice said from the gloom. "Good luck for you 'cause here's your chance."

Phineus had trained the Green Burnings well. They appeared all around, blocking every route of escape, while moving as casually as if just out for a stroll.

"Eger," Bodil said. "Eger!"

"Yeah?" A young man slouched from the shadows. He wore a long jacket decorated with silver loops and pins. Pieces of the stolen emergency kit, Dunya thought, the parts they thought weren't good for anything.

"My mother doesn't have anything to do with any of this," Bodil said.

Eger looked Dunya up and down, raised his eyebrows. "Doesn't look that way to me. Like she said, this is Burnings' territory. Doesn't matter who's messing with it. Or why."

"Why you—"

Eger blocked Bodil's blow with a forearm and threw her back. Dunya took a step forward, and found herself looking at a blade that seemed to reflect more light than there was in that dark place.

Eger shook his head. "Nah, Mom. Not a good idea."

Bodil was puffing next to her. Dunya thought she was crying, but when she glanced at her daughter, she realized that it was the breath of rage. Knife or not, greater fighting skill or not, she looked like she was going to throw herself at Eger.

Did she know this girl?

"You can define your territory with respect to some other gang," Dunya said. "Not for ordinary citizens."

"Ordinary citizens?" Eger was in her face. "You telling me you don't know what's what? You come here, know all our business, what we do." He looked even younger close up, with smooth skin and curly reddish hair.

"We'll get out," Dunya said.

"'We' won't do anything. Bodil and us got to talk."

"No."

"No?"

"Stop it, Eger," Bodil said. "Don't be an idiot. My mom doesn't have anything to do with this. You're the one who beat Unray. Right?"

Eger grinned. "I got some licks in, sure. But we had to share. Everyone wanted a piece. You know what it's like when everyone wants a piece. We share, in the Burnings."

Even though he was genuinely dangerous, Dunya found his leer too deliberate, like he practiced it in front of the mirror.

"Because Unray could have taken you alone," Bodil said. "That's why?"

Dunya knew that tone of lazy insolence well. It made her want to hit her daughter. She never had.

Eger had less restraint. Bodil dodged his first, overhand blow, but he moved fast and punched her in the side. She *oof*ed and bent over and Dunya slid away from her position, looking for an opening, even as she knew they weren't going to get out of this—

There was a wail from somewhere overhead, and a body came hurtling down out of the dangling roots. It hit so hard it bounced.

Dunya moved as if she had expected exactly that to happen. She hit Eger with her shoulder and, off balance, he fell.

She turned to tell Bodil to run. Bodil was gone, already moving at full tilt, slashing at the face of the young Green Burning who tried to stop her. The boy dodged back, automatically covering his face. By the time he realized he still had his looks, it was too late, and she was past.

Behind, another crash, as another scout fell from above, followed by shouts.

Her daughter ran beautifully, also like her father. Dunya's own legs were shorter, and she had to pump them hard to keep up. She kept expecting resistance, but the Burnings had been confident enough not to set pickets out this far.

And if it hadn't been for that sudden intervention, they wouldn't have needed them. Who had flung that scout down? He seemed to have been flung with some force, by someone with muscles. Martian muscles.

She just managed to keep Bodil in view as she dodged, first into this corridor, then that, then up a ramp, first shallow, then steep, then stairs. Stairs covered with moss and ferns. They were out, in the shadows amid the roots. Around was the rustle of leaves, the green glow, air thick with pollen. Bees flickered in the light that made it through from high overhead.

Bodil turned and fell against her mother, almost knocking her over. She was laughing. Unbelievably, she was laughing, almost helpless.

"Ah!" Bodil said. "Did you see the look on his face?"

"I was too busy panicking."

"He always thinks he's got it all under control. Jerk." The savage look Bodil threw back down the black hole of the stairs was beautiful and terrifying. "I visited stupid Unray in the hospital. He talked all tough too, and blamed it all on me."

"Okay, it was my fault. Right now I need your mind working. Someone was above us in that shaft. She's just a visitor, doesn't know Boscobel. She's going to be moving out of that area, fast. Where would she go, and can we intercept her?"

"There's really only one way. Come on."

The route turned out to be fairly simple, involving just a climb up to a living bridge between a twisted olive tree and a baobab whose hollow interior held a playground filled with shrieking children.

Dunya grabbed her daughter's shoulder and pointed. Below them, tall above the crowd, Miriam Kostal strolled. Dunya could sense that Bodil instantly picked her out.

Without hesitation, Bodil jumped off the stubby branch of a baobab. Dunya followed, hitting a mossy spot that would have been softer if it hadn't been so worn. The gravity was highest here, near the roots, and Dunya really felt the impact as she landed.

Bodil slid ahead, and up again, on the aerial root of a mangrove. They were now ahead of Miriam, though Dunya had been in that position before, and it hadn't helped her. Just below them was a noodle shop, Cairngorm's, sending up puffs of aromatic steam and making her hungry. She looked down at the bubbling pots, the patrons with their heads bent over bowls. She'd never been there, but it seemed familiar to her—

"Mind telling me why we're after her?" Bodil plopped down in a tangled mass of vines and looked up at the hummingbirds that investigated a flower just above her.

"Your buddies the Green Burnings are being used by someone else," Dunya said. "A Martian. Phineus. Who happens to be one of my clients."

"You never talk about your clients."

"They appreciate my silence. You should too. But he's kind of moved himself out of the confidential category by trying to get me killed. And you, now."

"Nah. I don't know about this Phineus. Eger was on his own, just being his usual jerk of a self. Defending Burning territory. I was just hiding out there. Hoping no one would ever find me. But you did."

Dunya had already resolved never to tell her daughter how she had found out. It was too humiliating.

Fortunately, Miriam rescued her again.

"You think that was smart?" Miriam Kostal stood over them, casting more shadow than it seemed reasonable for her lean form. "Putting yourself at risk was bad enough. Putting my mission at risk might be fatal."

Instead of being intimidated by the other woman's anger, Dunya found herself just as mad. "I don't need to justify myself to you."

"Protecting your offspring." Miriam eyed Bodil. "How do you feel about being defended, little girl?"

"Don't try to set us against each other." Bodil's insolence was more pleasant when applied to someone else. "That's our own, on our own time. Nothing for you. And my name's Bodil."

Miriam looked the girl over, then smiled, an expression as tight as a wrestler's grip. "Pleased to meet you, Bodil. Have you had a chance to figure out what it is you are now involved in?"

"No. Not that much."

"If I knew what your mother was up to, I might be able to fill in some of the gaps for you."

Bodil and Miriam turned to look at her, and Dunya found herself nettled. That had been a nice bit of solidarity with her daughter, but it was over. Now that they were standing side by side, she fancied she saw similarities between her daughter and the rangy Martian. They both had sharp jaws, and an easy stance. Assuming that Dunya was perversely withholding information seemed to be another thing they had in common.

"Bodil. That trim Eger was wearing, some of the others. What was it? Where did they get it?"

"Those loops? They grabbed some kind of gear from some old locker."

"Emergency gear?"

"I . . . I don't know. They were all excited about it, though. First real operation. Tactics, penetration of secure areas. Martian training, they said."

"You have information about it?" Miriam said in Dunya's ear.

"A friend who runs a restaurant heard about it. Someone took off with a complete emergency kit. An old one, probably ignored and forgotten."

"Where did they run their operation?" Miriam asked Bodil.

"Imperial Valley. There's an access lock there, not used much now. This was in the storage area nearby. Secure, I guess. Not as secure as the OAKs thought, though." She couldn't suppress a hint of pride in what her boyfriend and his unpleasant friends had accomplished. "But . . . what's going on?"

Dunya could feel Miriam waiting. This was up to her, how much to tell. "Phineus, the guy they've been getting their lessons from. He's the inside man in a Martian filibustering expedition that means to take over Boscobel. He's using them as some kind of screen."

"He's using them to gain access to an airlock," Miriam said. "A place they can make entry. And their vessel will be here soon."

Bodil looked at Dunya. "Momma. What do we do?"

"There's really no need for you two to do anything," Miriam said.

"Really?" Dunya had thought about how to argue this. Practicality was the best way. "Does that give you the best chance of success?"

"Are you going to help me by going back to the OAKs again?" Sarcasm didn't suit Miriam.

"The theft of safety equipment is a real crime, one the OAKs can enforce without any concern about who is hoping the Martians will give him a better office. If they hold Phineus for that, it will give you some breathing space. And Bodil . . . do you think you could face Unray again?"

"Sure. I have to go there and tell him we're through. I was too mad the last time."

"Well, that will give you a good reason to pump him on what the Green Burnings are up to. I'll bet it isn't at all what Phineus thinks they're doing."

"I have the perfect outfit," Bodil said. "I've been waiting for the opportunity to wear it. I'll break his heart."

"That's my girl."

"Do I get to say anything about the help I need?" Miriam was surprisingly patient.

"I waited for that," Dunya said. "I finally went without it."

"We're making a lot of assumptions. Some are bound to be wrong. Be ready to switch direction as necessary. Keep your OAKs on the emergency kit, and leave any mention of Martians to me."

"You got it."

"I have to handle Phineus carefully," Miriam said. "He's got support back home, and harming him would have bad consequences. But preventing him from acting will achieve what I need. Then, maybe, Martians can start hashing out their problems with each other, rather than exporting them. It's a dream, of course. But it's one I share with my husband."

"You're married?"

"Don't sound so shocked. Hektor doesn't get to see much of me, unfortunately. While he's trying to build a stable coalition at home, I'm usually out trying to keep each leak from turning into a blowout."

"I'm sure he misses you."

"I wish he was out here with me. He'd be better at working with people than I am."

"Oh, I don't know," Dunya said. "You seem to be doing fine."

Dunya could see that, despite herself, the fierce Martian was pleased. Dunya wanted to meet the man who could keep someone like that in his bed.

"The sooner we take care of Phineus and his ridiculous ambitions, the sooner I can get home," Miriam said.

Dunya would have loved to order Bodil home, to prepare dinner and perhaps ready for a siege. That would just result in Bodil's running off to do something on her own. She hoped she would not regret the choice that she had made.

"See you, momma." Bodil gave her a kiss, and was gone.

By this time, with the sunglobe getting red, Strop would have moved up and over and been holding court at a restaurant high up in an aromatic cedar. She'd have to find a way to get him on that missing emergency kit without getting herself arrested—

"Twice in one day." Phineus blocked the twisting ladder ahead of her. "How about that?"

He was the last person Dunya wanted to see. "I'm in kind of a hurry right now."

"Sure, sure." He moved as if to go around her, then leaned in, his big forehead looming. "Did you get a chance to check out my fellow Martian?"

"It's on my list, Phineus."

"I'm in danger! It's not at all like you not to take the concerns of your clients seriously."

Unfortunately, that was true. He knew her too well. "I think you just made her up."

"Maybe I did. But was my imagination good enough for you to notice if the Martian pursuing me was a man or a woman?"

No way she could remember how precisely he'd described who was after him. It didn't matter. He knew that she would have checked his story out by now, and that Miriam would have done something about it. As far as he was concerned, no explanation for why Dunya was walking around healthy and alive was a good one.

"I might have a chance to get out there before I go to bed." If he wasn't going to move, she would swing around him. She glanced up at a convenient branch, to find two long-jacketed kids hanging over her, one girl, one boy. How long had they been there?

Phineus shook his head. "She doesn't miss, Dunya. That's why I'm afraid of her. I was hoping she'd make a mistake and get herself in trouble. Instead of killing you, she recruited you. And here I thought you were on my side."

Before Dunya could move, the two kids grabbed her and swung her into the leaves.

To her surprise, there were fish here. A carp bumped its snout into her mask.

Within five minutes of grabbing her they had bound her, put her into a mask and air supply, tied her legs to an elastic band, and sucked her down under a water drop. It was half local water supply, half wildlife reserve—and now her prison. Phineus had not looked her in the eye as the Green Burnings had done their work, but just before the water had closed over her head, he had muttered, "The new administration will free you."

He had made her complicit with his plot. Only his success would bring someone here to keep her from suffocating. If he failed she would be left here to become food for these fish.

Dunya breathed slowly and carefully. She had no idea how much air she had, and struggle would just shorten the time she had left. She'd curled herself down a couple of times. She could find no way to influence her bonds. She could only plan for what she would do if someone rescued her, or compose her soul for death.

The facemask, with its blinking indicators, smelled old. It had to be from the stolen emergency kit. So it was designed for vacuum, not underwater use, yet another thing to worry about. It did have an eyeball-controlled display that she ran through. No comm, and no "cut my bonds" command. It did have an inventory list of the kit of which it was a part, some things marked as "exhausted" or "damaged-unrepairable." It included two spacesuits, of which this was presumably one, an exoshelter, fuel cells, enough procal bars to live on for a few months while awaiting rescue . . . and a full emergency airlock. Without her consciously willing it, the faceplate showed her an exploded view of the airlock and listed all of its many components. Good to go, it told her with satisfaction.

Phineus had gotten the Green Burnings to steal the old emergency kit because he wanted the airlock. Dunya was sure of it. That the kit had been stored near the Imperial Valley airlock was just a distraction. Miriam was wasting her time there.

But he needed a place to link inside and outside. Asteroid environments didn't survive by being easy to punch through. Dammit. It was one thing to resolve to be calm and meditative and accepting. It was another to keep on doing it. Where was Bryn? Why wasn't he around, at least to comment mordantly on affairs? Her husband had been increasingly given to mordant commenting. Doing something about things was less his line.

But she was being unfair. He worked with cultural development in various asteroids, as far sunward as Phobos. He was respected, and busy. When he came home he was loving, attentive, and everything he needed to be.

And then he was gone again. And she found herself just as happy. Could she imagine some other man who she would want around more? Sometimes she thought she could. But she, too, was too busy to spend too much time on that.

Bryn's absence was equally hard on Bodil, of course. So she ran with losers like Unray, getting rudimentary political education with the Green Burnings. That seemed a reasonable explanation. Nothing to do with anything Dunya herself had done.

Did this facemask have a setting that sucked away all illusions? Clever, some of

these old gadgets. A rough way to die, though, facing the absolute truth about everything you'd been so careful to keep under control.

She thought about Bryn's own dusty and peppery scent, which had eventually
faded from his side of the bed, careful though she'd been not to move anything, and
only breathe it when she absolutely had to. She'd smelled something else recently,
associated with quite a different man. Peppery as well, but damper, and tanged
with . . . cilantro. She remembered the noodle shop she'd parked herself above to
get a drop on Miriam.

Phineus had shoved leftover containers under his cushions. From that same
place, Cairngorm's.

He was working with his airlock somewhere down in Xanthus. The crust was
thinner down there, sure, but it was still nothing you could just hack through.

Something splashed above her. A larger fish? Since the carp, she hadn't seen
much more than larvae. But now it was dark, and she couldn't see anything. Someone yanked on her. She stretched up, then was pulled back by the cable holding her
bound feet. She sensed swearing, hearing nothing. Arms reached far in, grabbed
her, and pulled hard. She rose and rose . . . and finally pulled free. Then she was
lying on a seeping bank of wildflowers. Her facemask was pulled off.

"Momma!" Bodil said. "Are you still breathing?"

Unray had given Bodil her mother's location. He was out of the loop as far as Green
Burning tactical operations were concerned. But someone had felt it right to tell
him that his soon-to-be-ex-girlfriend's mother had been captured and imprisoned in
a water tank in the cedars.

You found virtue in the oddest places.

"I guess they sometimes hide stuff in here," Bodil said. "Contraband. Not usually
people, though."

"What's that?" Dunya looked at a bundle of steaming leaves that lay amid dew-
covered yellow flowers.

"Mom! You have no idea how hard it was for me growing up, to have a mom that
didn't know anything."

"God, of course I know what it is. Should I eat it, or nap on it?"

It was the wrong tone to take, even if she was newly resurrected and should be
cut some slack. Bodil pushed her lower lip out and looked about to cry.

Dunya hugged her daughter. "We're on a mission," she whispered. "And we have
a lot to do. Unwrap it."

"You're cold." Bodil pulled off her jacket and put it around her soaked, shivering
mother. Then she dropped to her knees and unwrapped the leaves, letting steam
rise into the dark air.

This lozenge cake was traditional Boscobeli food for a journey. The leaves were
from a modified fig and added a spice to the outer layers of the dough, which cooked
enzymatically when tugged in just the right way. Dunya had never cared for it, finding it too sour for a decent dessert, and, uncooked, too hard as a pillow, the use the
ancient and fictional tradition had for it.

Of course, a people defined itself by those things no sensible individuals would pick on their own. And Bodil was Boscobel born and bred. So Dunya sat on a branch in a world she had not chosen, happy to be alive, and shared the almost inedible cake with her daughter.

Bodil had figured it out instantly. Any airball had an expulsion pore, through which the waste rock had been expelled. And above that, a series of baffles. All safe, no danger from the ancient weakness.

Except that, at the base of Xanthus, the baffles had collapsed into useless piles of cracked rock, another sign of the deferred maintenance that put the entire world at risk.

Dunya climbed down the tumbled slabs alone. Bodil had gone to find Miriam. She wouldn't succeed, of course. But Miriam would find her. Dunya only hoped that would happen before she got herself into serious trouble down here.

One other thing Bodil had learned from Unray: there was no one from the Green Burnings down here. They'd gotten irritated with their mysterious guru, and had dumped Phineus in preference to mixing it up with their competitors over in Five Boughs. After that, a party. Phineus was on his own down here.

It didn't really matter. He could take her easily. She had to wait for Miriam, who knew what to do. Miriam would have told her that herself.

She couldn't listen to Miriam, even though what Miriam had not actually said made perfect sense. Phineus was still her client, making bad choices. Even as she knew she had to stop him, she recognized him as her responsibility.

There he was, working with a small light. The airlock was in. She could see the rubble from the sealed pore all around it. Being so small, it had to be secret. It could fit, at most, two people at a time. It was next to impossible to get an army in position and deployed using that. But, as she had learned from both Phineus and Miriam, next to impossible was a Martian's favorite spot to get a seat.

She thought she was moving quietly. Phineus heard her, and jerked around. The light caught her.

"Aren't you cold?" he said. "You're all wet."

"Oh, how thoughtful, Phineus," she said.

He muttered something.

"What?" she said.

"I said I'm sorry. It had to be done."

"Please stop, Phineus. Just stop. Do you really think you're still going to get a force of Martians in here?"

He shook his head. "You think what you see is what there is. I have support, here in Boscobel. It's really my place, not yours."

She tried not to think about how much he was right. "Contingent support. If-you-win support. If there's any problem, it will vanish. I walked right in here. The gang you trained up is gone, you're here alone. That should tell you something."

He'd never done his own dirty work. First he'd sent Dunya into Miriam's path in the hopes that Miriam would take her out, then he'd used his gang. Now he was pretending to be too busy to bother with her. No wonder he'd left Mars. He just wasn't up to it.

"There's no way to advance on Mars," he said. "Everything's owned or closed off. The only way to get somewhere is to come out here. There's a lot of unrealized value in the asteroids."

If he was arguing, there was a chance. But it was too late for him. At the last instant it seemed he knew that, because he stopped and stared at her. Before he could say anything else, Miriam dropped from somewhere overhead and kicked him in the head.

Not straight on, though. Phineus reacted fast. He tilted his head so that the force of her kick grazed past, then tried to help her on her way with a slap at her heel.

Miriam was fast too. She spun and landed in a crouch.

Dunya wished she could help. But she knew all she could do was get in the way or become a hostage.

The struggle was brief and vicious. Then Phineus whipped a rock at Miriam, and when she dodged he rolled and launched himself into a black gap among the dry roots.

Without hesitating, Miriam went after him. Both vanished among the rocks.

Dunya stepped down to the airlock. The least she could do was deactivate it while Miriam did her work.

"I need to return that in good working order," Strop said. He stood among the rocks, looking miserable and sweaty. Stumbling around in the high-gravity area in the dark wasn't usually his way of getting things done.

"Did it get too public?" Dunya said. "Too hard to deny?"

She hadn't expected him to answer, and he didn't. He lumbered forward and slapped a Maintenance Required sticker across the airlock.

"What's going to happen?" Dunya said.

"I can at least tell you something that *won't* happen. No Martian vessel will approach Boscobel. If one does, it will get a warning shot, and know to go elsewhere."

"Thus ensuring no one ever has to testify to who knew what."

He shrugged. "A lot of people would prefer that. You might even be one of them. If Phineus is still alive, he won't get a trial either. He'll be expelled. He can go to Mars, where they'll kill him. Or he can go somewhere else. Not our problem. I do need to say that your inability to control him will be a black mark on your record. Not a lot I can do, but I'll put in a good word for you." He smiled at her.

She'd take a shower when she got home. That might do something about the greasy film he left on her, even as he was helping her out.

"As staff is rotated off the entry and departure airlocks to be re-vetted and cleared, coverage will be affected. Pretty much anyone who wants to get out of Boscobel without interference will be able to do so."

She glanced up. Bodil stood on a rock high above. She smiled and gave her mother the thumbs-up.

"Go ahead," Strop said. "Get your girl home. I'll pick up our unfortunate Martian invader."

She'd have to use Bodil to communicate with Miriam and get her off Boscobel. Too dangerous for Dunya to do it directly. That was too bad. That woman was someone to know.

Someday, she guessed, Bodil would want an off-Boscobel school. Deliberately exposing her daughter to Miriam's influence would be dangerous, of course. But she had heard that there really was nothing like a Martian education.

She climbed up the shattered slabs of rock, back toward the trees she had come to rely on.

тhe ιrιsh asτronαuτ

VAL NOLAN

*The lyrical and compassionate story that follows takes a man to Ireland to
perform a last sad duty for a fallen comrade—one that may ultimately prove
as important to the living as to the dead.*

*Val Nolan lectures at the National University of Ireland, Galway. His fic-
tion has previously appeared on the Futures page of* Nature *and in magazines
and newspapers such as* Cosmos, The Irish Times, *and* The Daily Telegraph.
His academic publications include "Flann, Fantasy, and Science Fiction:
O'Brien's Surprising Synthesis" *(The Review of Contemporary Fiction,* Flann
O'Brien *special edition, 2011) and* "If it was Just Th' ol Book . . . : A History of
the John McGahern Banning Controversy" *(Irish Studies Review, 2011).
Forthcoming work includes* "Break Free: Understanding, Reimagining, and
Reclaiming Stories in Grant Morrison's* Seven Soldiers of Victory" *(Journal of
Graphic Novels and Comic Books, 2014) and a chapter on* Lost *and* Battle-
star Galactica *in* Godly Heretics: Essays on Alternative Christianity in Literature and Popular Culture *(McFarland, 2013). He is a regular literary critic
for the* Irish Examiner.

By his second week in the village with the unpronounceable name, Dale had
taken up with the old men fishing out beyond the rocks. The place was called the
Blue Pool and people died there, he was told, freak waves being known to carry
them away. Fierce tragic, as his new friends had it.

"Saw a man plucked from the earth here once," Gerry McGovern said. "Looked
off at a girl in a summer dress and then, well—"

"Gone?" asked Dale.

"Gone."

"Christ."

McGovern blessed himself.

Beside him, Bartley tapped his pipe upside-down against his hand. "Every one of
your stories starts like that, Gerry. Every one."

McGovern sneered. "Won't be long now," he said to the American.

"Hopefully," said Dale, who had been waiting ten days for the parish priest. "I should have called ahead, but . . . I wasn't sure."

"Bad luck, surely," Bartley said. He cut thin strips of tobacco from a block with his penknife and rolled the tar curls between filthy palms until the nest was finely shredded. "Though you could hardly blame the Father," he said. "'Tis the first holiday that man has taken since God-knows-when."

"Well his timing's incredible," Dale said, "just incredible." He followed the thread of his borrowed line down into the water and watched a tiny ripple stir around it. It was a fine morning on the coast of Ireland, cool beneath a naked sun. Dale felt like he'd been sitting there since he first trundled through the airport, catching nothing and talking about airplanes or weather. Every day he ate his breakfast in the B&B and every night he drank at a small bar in the centre of the village. He had yet to go into the grey stone hills which loomed above the crooked, multicoloured houses. There was just something about them, something he couldn't quite put his finger on.

"I wonder," Bartley said, "D'you think they'd ever have one of our lads up there?" He plucked a pebble from the ground and placed it in the bowl of his pipe. "They're fierce small, you know, because of our planes. They'd fit them tin cans of yours awful easy."

Dale laughed. "Height really isn't . . . " He looked around. "It doesn't matter. The program's shut down."

"Aye," Bartley said, serious all of a sudden. "Because of the crash?"

"It wasn't a crash."

"The accident then?" He held a match towards his face and cupped both hands above the pipe.

"Yeah," Dale said. "Because of the accident." He drank from the plastic bottle beside him and stared out across the water. As we set sail on this new ocean, he thought . . .

"Terrible thing," Bartley was saying. "Terrible altogether. Did you know any of them boys, you did?"

"I knew them all," Dale said. "Davis, O'Neil, Rodriguez . . . " He took a deep breath and looked up at the sky. It was two years later and the president's speech still rang in his ears: "Aquarius is lost. There are no survivors."

Ireland. The slide-rule rigidity of Houston had not prepared him for it. Dale was used to clean lines and order, but this little village was a bow tie of crooked streets knotted where their paths crisscrossed with those of history and want. The first time Dale saw it he had thought it was a theme park. Even after fourteen days on the ground, its true arrangement continued to elude him. One wrong turn, what he thought might make a sensible shortcut, and Dale would find himself on the shoulder of the potted two-lane to another parish, would suddenly be in the company of dirty hens by a half-finished house on the edge of the arid countryside.

He had taken a room in the centre of the village, on what passed for the main drag. It was a rambling nook-and-cranny job, an anarchic spiderweb of low doors and high ceilings rebuilt and renovated many times. Thomas and Catherine, the elderly couple who owned it, had gleefully explained the building's history to him; how it had consumed outhouse after outhouse, how it had gone from farmhouse to townhouse, from boarding house to B&B, and Dale was sure his room had once been among the rafters of a forge or stable. Standing in the guesthouse doorway, one could go only left or right—to the pub or the sea—and still Dale always managed to get lost.

"The streets all move around at night," Catherine told him one morning.

"Nice try," Dale said.

"It's true," Thomas added, cocking his head towards the window. "The village used to be up there, in the hills."

Dale looked over his shoulder. It was as much limestone as he had ever seen. "I don't think so," he said at last.

"Oh yeah." Thomas winked at his wife. "'Twas a deal made with the devil, you know? Sealed with a hoof. And pretty soon the whole lot of us are to be sucked right down the Blue Pool, like one of them black spots of yers."

Dale thought for a moment. "A black hole?"

"Aye, a black hole."

The American laughed. At least the food was always good. "I appreciate the effort," he said, "but I'm not buying it."

"Then tell me this so." Thomas hunched over his plate. "Did ye really go up there? To the Moon, like?"

"Thomas," Dale said, "I'll let you know." He excused himself as he always did, climbing the bare staircase back to his room where a copy of the county paper lay yellowing in the sun. "Spaceman Dale" had made page five, and he had cringed when he saw it, his life unspooled as lies and inexplicable exaggeration, the gross embellishment of an undistinguished record. To read it one would think him a Borman or a Conrad, if not the equal of Armstrong himself. Dale had not looked at it since Thomas first produced it one morning over breakfast.

"I didn't know you gave an interview," the old man had teased at the time.

"I didn't," Dale had said, staring at the picture they had printed alongside the article, a publicity snap of him at the initial rollout of Aquarius, his arm around Rodriguez's shoulder and both men grinning. He supposed it was easily sourced.

"'Twas a slow week," Thomas said.

"Excuse me?"

"Slow enough now," the old man went on. "Though Maggie Kelleher's ewe drowned down by the shore last evening. That's two now."

"I'm sorry, what?"

"Two," he said. "Careless, that woman. Not like her husband, God bless him."

"God bless him," repeated Catherine, drifting through the room with a plate piled high with toasty strips of bacon.

Dale had watched this all with amusement. After breakfast he had asked Thomas for the paper though he didn't know why. Vanity, probably, though when he went back to his room he refused to open it again, merely threw it on the dresser beside the tin flask he had brought across the ocean. It irked him, the usurpation of his life. He had never even met this reporter and yet her fanciful invention now defined him to everyone he met.

Catherine told him not to worry. Every morning after breakfast she would meet him at the bottom of the stairs, he with a satchel to see him through his fishing; she with a little foil package of sandwiches, moist, crustless feasts of dark bread and thick-cut meats painted heavily in relish. It was a peculiar, motherly gesture with which she earned Dale's gratitude forever.

"Sure, we have to keep you fed," she said.

Somewhere Thomas coughed violently. Dale smiled, and let himself out.

Down by the Blue Pool, the American explained his theory about his room having once been a forge, but McGovern only smirked.

"What?"

"Ah now," McGovern said, turning to Bartley.

Puffing his pipe, his cheeks an artful bellows, Bartley shook his head. "Didn't they tell you, Dale?" he asked. "Sure everybody knows, that part of Tom's used be the undertakers."

For years he had heard Rodriguez talk of coming here, of green hills and red-headed girls. It was a fantasy, colourful and wild, and by definition it bore scant resemblance to what met Dale as he rolled his battered hardside off the plane. Not a fertile field or a dancing lass in sight, instead a murky tonnage of dull cloud which weighted on the whole country like a fat palm pressed upon a chest. At customs, a sneering, grey-haired policeman stamped his passport without a word. At the car hire desk, a woman with food stains on her blouse went on and on about the foulness of the weather, about the worst summer in a generation and how the crops were rotting in the ground.

"Twas far from the ground the likes of her were raised," Bartley said when Dale recounted him the story. Hell of an introduction, the American thought later. It was the first time they had met, the old man seemingly oblivious to the fact that it had indeed been raining steadily since Dale's arrival, weather which had confined them all inside the gloomy local.

"It was late," Dale said. "I'm sure she was just tired."

"No excuse for that kind of behaviour, and you a guest of this great little nation." Bartley daubed at the beige moustache left by his pint and leaned into his new acquaintance. "What was it you said you did again?"

Dale cleared his throat. "Aeronautics," he said warily.

"No," Bartley said, squinting. "No, that's not it . . . Too much bearing, too . . . clean cut." A ripple of laughter passed through the bar.

"I'm sorry?" Dale said. He hadn't realised anyone was listening.

"Not that you should have to be," the old man said, "but I appreciate it."

Dale looked around, though no one met his eyes. He turned back to Bartley. "And what's your line?"

"When you're ready, Pat," Bartley said, grinning at the barman and sinking a bony finger deep into his empty glass.

"You'll not get an answer out of him," the barman told Dale.

"Yeah, I'm starting to see that."

Beside him, Bartley cleared his throat. "So," he said, "is it a pilot or an engineer you are?" he asked.

"First one," Dale said, "and then the other." He was getting the hang of Bartley.

"Test pilot?" the old man said, narrowing his eyes. He was sharp.

Dale shook his head, sipped his drink and allowed himself a tiny smile.

"He's toying with me," Bartley announced.

The barman said nothing.

"You really want to know?" Dale asked at last.

"I do," Bartley said.

"He does," the barman echoed, elbows on the counter.

Dale sighed. "Alright." He tapped the little silver pin on his lapel. "Astronaut Corps.," he said.

"Well now," Bartley said.

The barman whistled quietly.

Dale sipped his drink. "It's a job like any other."

"A job like any other, he says." Bartley cocked his thumb in Dale's direction. "Bring him another whiskey, will you, Pat?"

The American shifted his weight on the barstool. "Hospitality?"

"Generosity of spirit," Bartley said, a gleam in his eye. He began on the fresh pint before him with a kind of practiced reverence.

"Well then," Dale said, raising his own glass, "I believe I'm supposed to say sláinte."

"Aye," said Bartley, "you've got it, sláinte indeed." And so their conversation drifted into trivialities, the price of stout and the state of county games, things which were the heartbeat of the local. Dale left when the bar was almost empty and the barman started to look restless. He had no better grasp on who Bartley was, the old man foxing him at every turn. He walked back to the B&B beneath a loaned umbrella, shaking the rain off out on the step.

"Gallivanting, was it?" Thomas asked, stirring from the shadows in the hallway.

"Only as far as the bar."

"How'd you find it?"

"Your directions were perfect."

The old man smiled patiently. His teeth were crooked and yellow. "I mean," he said softly, "how was it?"

"Ah . . . It was good. I enjoyed it. Met a man named Bartley, I'm sure you know him."

"Oh, Bartley's a cute one alright. Wiley, like."

Dale rubbed the side of his head. "I gathered that."

"Fierce interested in you now, I'd say."

"He was. Though less forthcoming about himself. I wonder, what is it he does exactly?"

"His brother killed three Tans in that business with the British."

"Right. But Bartley?"

Thomas laughed as he began up the stairs, slapping Dale on the back. "Sure, isn't he his brother's keeper, Dale? His brother's keeper."

When the downpours finally ended the little village came into its own. Stone walls caught the new light and turned it back upon the darkest corners of the place. The streets began to glow, and, on their outskirts, brave flowers sprung from a frugal soil. Everywhere became warm and the sky assumed a welcome, almost Texan hue.

"This is our summer now," Bartley announced in the bar that afternoon, wiping his hands on his thighs and standing up. His crooked frame drew nods of approval from the other patrons. It seemed an event of some importance.

"You going somewhere?" Dale asked. The half-full glass in front of Bartley was conspicuous.

"The Blue Pool," the old man said. "Come on, if you like and we'll stand you the line."

That was how it started.

"You seem awful content," Bartley said at the end of that first week's fishing.

"Must be the company."

"All the same," McGovern said, cocking his head towards the grey hills, "would you not see The Burren?"

"I've no interest."

"'Tis a place of beauty."

"So I've heard."

"You're a strange man, Dale."

"I've been called worse."

Their lines hung heavy in the water. Nothing was biting.

"I heard once," Bartley said, "that spaceships were tiled, and that 'twas Irish students working over there that glued them on."

Dale smiled. "Sure, on the outside. Ceramics to survive re-entry, but I don't know who glued them on."

"Pity," Bartley said. "Pity now."

Beside him, McGovern shrugged.

"Twould be nice," Bartley went on, "to think of the contribution, like."

"Twould a'course," said McGovern.

Dale looked at the two of them, this grizzled pair, then shook his head and smiled. He closed his eyes and raised his head towards the sun. So unremarkable, he thought, and still so great. Turning away, he opened his eyes and caught the ghost face of the Moon in daylight peeking through the afternoon. He allowed himself a look of happiness.

"What's that now?" Bartley asked. He never took his eyes off his line.

"I remember he was on the radio," Dale said. "Loud and clear. His first words out of the lander were Man, that's beautiful."

"Who was that, then?"

"A friend of mine," Dale said. "Rodriguez. One of the men who died."

Bartley nodded.

Beside him, McGovern asked what it was like. He too was looking at the Moon now, the withered veins on his unshaven neck coaxed back to elasticity by the tilt of his blunt chin.

"Rock," said Dale. "He went on and on about the rock, the mountains and the boulders and the dust."

"Rock?" McGovern said. "Mountains and dust?"

"Sure you could see that here," said Bartley.

Dale grinned. "Could you see the colours in the grey? The red and orange and the yellow tints from the sun?" He laughed. "God, he wouldn't shut up about that. We could hardly get him to carry out his orders."

The two old Irishmen exchanged a look. Dale couldn't read it.

"You'd get the most of it here anyway," Bartley said. "The sun on the stone and all that. No knowing what you'd see."

"Sure isn't it all they go on about above in them hills?" McGovern added. "And they don't need any of them helmets or big white suits to see it in."

"They're lucky," Dale said.

"Terrible lucky," Bartley nodded.

Dale smiled. "But can they see the Earth rising over the horizon the way the moon does here? That's what Rodriguez saw. He said he was standing there, looking up at planet Earth, this great, blue oasis in the black velvet sky, and he said it was just too beautiful to have happened by accident . . ."

They were listening to him now, he saw, Bartley and McGovern with their grey heads cocked, though Dale didn't know what else to tell them. Technical particulars and numbers and dry facts would only spoil it, and Rodriguez only shared so much that anyone would call poetic.

Instead, Dale reeled in his line and watched ripples echo all across the surface as his bait broke through from underneath. Earth, he mused, was covered mostly of water. A blue pool in the night of space. Its name was suddenly inadequate, powerless to convey its sheer, inexplicable abundance. Staring into the water, he found himself speaking without realizing.

"Rodriguez was talking to us afterwards," he said, "when he was back aboard Aquarius, and he told me he'd seen the whole world, all of it, all at once. Imagine that, every human being in existence, everything we are, all of it a size that if he reached out he could have plucked it from the sky. I'll never forget that," he said. "It was almost as good as being there."

"Almost?"

"Almost." Dale laughed again. He wasn't sure which one of them had said it, but it didn't matter. "We're explorers," he said. "Or at least we were; we should be. And no explorer ever knows exactly what he's going to find when he gets to where he's going, but every time we fly we add to what's known. Rodriguez, he helped me to learn something, you understand? About the grand scheme of things. Perspective, that's what I learned from him."

"Aye," McGovern said, licking his lips, "but what have you learned from us, I wonder?"

"I've learned," Dale said slowly, "that there aren't any fish in this pond, are there?" He looked from McGovern to Bartley and back again, but the two old men had already started laughing.

Blue skies and bright light. It was outdoors that Dale felt most at home in. All Irish people seemed to regard the world through doors and windows, he had noticed. Their view was blinkered, like the draw-horses in the etchings which hung on the walls of Catherine's dining room. When people here spoke of the land they did not mean the country or the state, they meant the field, some small enclosure within which they were snared by circumstance or greed. Whole lives here were bounded by the whitewashed sovereignties of dated bungalows or played out in discontent behind the cobweb-covered lens of guilty window panes.

And yet Dale surprised himself with what he loved about them, their history, their rancour hardening around them into flakes or scales, of all things their certainty in what cannot be seen. For everyone he had met here, a palm's rough lines were no less truthful than the dotted contours of a map. Myth and fact were interchangeable, reality a personal affliction.

"What was it like," he asked McGovern, "growing up around here?"

They sat with Bartley by the Blue Pool, the sun baking all of them.

"I suppose it was the same as anywhere," the old man said. "We chased girls and went to matches and swam in the sea."

"Aye," said Bartley, "going round with your tongue hanging out."

"We played hurling," McGovern added. "Fastest field game in the world."

Dale squinted at him. "Is that a fact?"

"Oh yeah. But don't think we didn't know what it was ye were up to."

"Ye . . . ?"

"Oh, he's been workin' on this one," Bartley said.

"'Twas before my sister was married," McGovern began. "And she was still living with us, which is a long time ago now. I'd just started inside at Callaghan's and I was driving in and out of the city every day."

Dale turned to Bartley. "What's he talking about?"

"Your friends," the old man said, raising his eyebrows. "The men above."

"We'd to go to the neighbours," McGovern went on. "We'd still no TV ourselves."

Dale smiled. "The Moon landings," he said, getting it.

"Momentous!" McGovern was in full flight now. "No thought of course to the risks involved. Just those two lads bouncing 'round the place, like kangaroos the pair of them. The boys were all trying it at work the next day. I swear, old Roddy Callaghan himself, leppin' around the yard . . ." He looked at Dale.

"I'm sorry," the American said. "I don't know who that is."

"Ah," McGovern said sadly, "sure it doesn't . . . Never mind."

Between them, Bartley was shaking his head. "There was no television where I was. Had to see it in the papers next day. Yer lad Aldrin like the Michelin Man, setting up the flag as if he owned the damn place." He laughed. "I have to hand it to ye, that was a good one." He laid a hand on Dale's arm and nodded. A livery of age adorned his skin. McGovern's too, and Dale suddenly felt out of place.

"Why is it," the American asked, "that everyone's so old here?"

"Say what?"

"I mean," Dale said, "where are all the young people?"

"Sure here's one now," McGovern said, elbowing Dale gently in the ribs and indicating the path from the road where a meek spectre with a Methuselan gait tottered in their direction. It was Regan, a venal leprechaun of a man whom Dale had seen around the village.

"Is it yourself?" Bartley asked without looking away from the water.

"It is," Regan said, standing above them as if in judgment. "And tell me, gentlemen, how's the fishing?"

"Could be worse," McGovern said beneath his breath. "Could be better too."

Regan glowered at him. He stood crooked, with his weight resting on a walking stick. One eye, Dale saw, was perpetually narrower than the other. "We've never really had the chance to talk," he said to the American, "and I've been meaning to ask you, what was it like up there?"

Dale clinched his jaw. Someone must have told him. "I don't know," he said at last.

Regan leaned closer. "Sure, how could you forget a thing like that?"

"I was an alternate," he said. "A backup. I've never been up there."

"Some other lad went?"

"Yeah, some other lad."

Regan licked his lips. "So you never flew?"

"I flew combat over Iraq. I flew experimental planes to the edge of space. I earned my wings."

"But not . . . up there?"

"No."

"They told me," Regan said slowly, "you were an astronaut."

"That's right."

"But then—"

"The criteria," Dale said, "is altitude." He held Regan's stare.

"Ah now," McGovern said, "would you ever leave the man alone."

"I'll not be told what to do," the interloper snapped back.

"The fish," Bartley said quietly, "are finally biting."

Dale ignored him and turned to the newcomer. "And you are?"

"He's a Peace Commissioner," McGovern said, spitting the words. "It's nothing what you think."

"The criteria," Regan said, "is good character."

"The criteria is arse-licking," McGovern said. "And no better man for it."

"I take offence to that."

"'Tis a pity you won't take it somewhere else."

Twisted over his line, Bartley cackled quietly and Dale turned his gaze back out to sea. Regan drew himself away from three fishermen, as if to say well then, so be it.

"I might see you later," he declared to no one in particular, and gradually he shuffled off until he disappeared into the middle distance.

McGovern shook his head. "Thinks he's lord and master, that man does." He leaned in close to the American, "You should fight him."

"Fight him?" It was Bartley, cackling so loud that the pipe nearly left his lips. "'Tis not a movie, Gerry."

McGovern folded his arms. "'Twould still be right."

"I'm not here to start fights," Dale said.

"Sure twas that begrudger started it." He raised an arm and pointed after Regan.

"There's guys like that all over," Dale said.

"The Man on the Moon," Bartley said, rocking back and forth, and laughing to himself. He stabbed at the sky with his pipe.

"Would you ever put that thing away?" McGovern said.

The old man grinned at him through yellow teeth. "Sure, why would I?" he asked. "Don't I like my poison neat?"

Regan was a troublemaker, but there was no denying he was good at it. What he said had stuck in the American's craw and the rest of the day hadn't shaken it. To most of these people, Dale realised, he was just the astronaut—the astronaut—and he had gotten used to that even though it wasn't true. To have had it called out unsettled him because Rodriguez had been the astronaut, a number one aviator with nothing ruffled but his hair. Beside him Dale was only competent, next on the rotation for sure, but not flying at anything like that altitude. Regan had shown him up, and Dale felt sick that it had taken someone like that to bring him back to Earth. He shook his head. Ego was a part of his job, but he had let it run amuck here. Where was his control, the better part of being a pilot?

When he walked back into the village he was angry, angry about Regan, angry about the priest's continued absence; he was angry at himself by how quickly he had succumbed to his own tacit celebrity. He sat in the bar until it was dark outside and thought of that damn newspaper lying in his room. He resolved to burn it and called for another whiskey.

Regan, when he arrived hours later, quickly smelt his opportunity on the American's breath. "Well now," he said, "we can finally have that chat."

"I'm not really in the mood."

"Ah, we'll have none of that," Regan motioned to the bartender for a pint.

Dale sighed deeply. He hunkered over his drink and resigned himself to Regan's company. Sometimes in flight you go into a spin; nothing to do but throttle down, flatten out your surfaces, turn your rudder the opposite way and hold. He readjusted himself to face the old man.

"What do you want to know?" he said.

"Would you have gone?"

"Yes sir, I would."

"If the other lad hadn't flown, like?"

Dale drained his glass. "If Rodriguez had been pulled, I'd have taken his seat. If the programme had continued, I'd have had a flight of my own."

"And you'd have gone—"

"Wham, bam, straight to the Moon. That's where I was going. That's where Rodriguez went."

"Jasus," Regan said. "Tis a quare thing." He returned his attention to the pint in front of him. "You tell it well though, you tell it well."

Dale couldn't figure out if he was being serious or not. He stared at the empty glass in his hand, how it caught the light. "Rodriguez," he said at last.

Regan looked at him. "What's that now?"

"Rodriguez was a better pilot than I was. Christ, he flew that bird the whole way down without a pair of wings to carry him."

"This was the crash, it was?"

"Disintegration," Dale said. "Aquarius didn't crash, it disintegrated mid-flight." Around him, the regulars had grown quiet. No one had gotten this much out of Dale before.

"I thought they all died when it came apart," Regan said gently. "'Tis what the papers said."

"They didn't die until they hit the water," Dale said. "Everything else came apart, but the crew module retained integrity until it hit the ocean. Which is more than I can say for those penny-pinchers in Congress, those smooth-talking Washington slicks scurrying to avoid the blame. 'Organisational causes,' they called it, 'poor technical decision-making,' and after all the times we tried to warn them. Ah," he said, "I don't know." He slid his glass back to the bartender who looked quickly at Regan before refilling it.

"I was the CAPCOM," Dale said. "You know, in the movies, when they say, Houston, we have a problem? Well I was the guy they're talking to, I was Houston. They like to have the alternates wear that headset. The thinking is that we're best trained to understand what's going on up there."

"And what was?" Regan whispered. "Going on up there, I mean?"

"Rodriguez and the others were alive for two minutes, thirteen seconds," Dale said. "Thermal protection failure. Loss of RCS. He couldn't alter his approach, couldn't tip the capsule those vital few degrees. And all the while they knew exactly what was happening."

"What did they say?"

"All Rodriguez said was uh-oh." Dale emptied his glass again. "The downlink went dead then and that was it," he said.

"And?"

Dale looked Regan in his hooded eyes. "And that was it," he said again. "Aquarius suffered what they call 'failure of vehicle with loss of human life.' I saw it myself, dozens of sources blossoming on the radar. I saw it again later on, laid out on the floor of a hanger at the Cape. Everything reduced to slag. We all understood the risks, but—"

"But you thought it'd never happen to someone that you knew?"

Dale shook his head. "I never knew how I was going to feel when it happened. God," he said, "when I could think about it clearly, when I could process it, you know, I was relieved."

". . ."

"I thought to myself, that could have been me up there." His head sunk deep between his shoulders.

"Ole human beings are strange," Regan said.

Down the bar, a heavy, bovine man was listening intently. He nodded.

"You can't be expected to be rational," Regan went on. "Not with the likes of that going on around you."

But Dale wasn't paying any attention. "Rodriguez walked on the Moon," he said.

"And he was alive the whole way down, I know it." He held up his glass to the bartender.

"Go home," was the reply.

"He's right," Regan said. "You'll pay no respects like this."

"Ah," said Dale, standing up. He missed Bartley and McGovern, and couldn't imagine where they might have got to. He thought of them as crewmates, strapped in beside him in the nose of some heavy-lifting firecracker and bickering about the running of the parish or talking about the weather like it was a new event. He laughed at that to himself all the way to the B&B, his mood darkening then in the vagueness of the empty room.

Sitting on the edge of the bed, he stared at the small black canister which stood upright on the dresser. "I bet you've got something smart to say," he muttered before he fell asleep.

Morning. Scraping birdsong and the hot, fierce lantern of a disappointed sun. A dull halo of the night before hung crooked on Dale's skull when he woke, a liquor-dog, as Rodriguez would have said. It was not without cause that Dale seldom touched the hard stuff.

With great, unshaven indignity he presented himself for breakfast but by some small mercy it was quiet, his hosts tuned obsessively to the conditions of their guests. They had seen it all before, of course.

"Fr. O'Grady's back," Thomas said, nose deep in his newspaper.

"Saw him last evening," Catherine said. "He's looking forward to meeting you." There were no sandwiches from her this morning. It was as though she knew his days of fishing were at an end. "He should be out of mass within the hour," she added.

"Thanks."

Outside a soft breeze rolled in from the Atlantic. Dale took his time walking through the village, stopping along the way to buy a bottle of water. When he reached the church he stood outside for almost twenty minutes. Clouds limped slowly through the sky and it felt wrong to go in so he walked on, circling around for many hours. Bartley and McGovern were nowhere to be found, not even by the shore.

At dusk, with a gold Moon shining overhead, he returned to the limestone church and stood in the doorway as a young man in black fussed around the altar.

"Evening, Padre," Dale said.

O'Grady started at him as if trying to place the countenance. "Yes," he said at last. "You must be the spaceman." His eyes had the smallest pupils Dale had ever seen, mere pinpricks, though with a curious, inviting depth. "Strange visitor from another planet, eh?" He waved the American inside. "Dale, isn't it?" He did not pause for a reply. "What can I do for you, Dale?"

"It's about Rodriguez," Dale said. "A friend of mine. He died in an accident."

"The, ah, the Aquarius pilot, yes?"

Dale nodded. He put his hands in his pockets. The air felt heavier in here. "This . . . " he said. "Well . . . This is where his people were from, I guess you'd say."

O'Grady moved down among the pews. He smelt faintly of the sacristy. "Rodriguez," he said carefully. "Not really many of them this side of the Shannon."

"Fitzpatricks," said Dale, "on his mother's side. Grandparents came out a long time ago. I don't know when."

"Well, how about that," O'Grady said. "An Irish astronaut. Now isn't that something?"

"He was hardly Irish," said Dale.

"If he could play for the soccer team he was Irish," the priest said firmly.

Dale couldn't help but smile at the man's excitement. "That's not really the point."

"That's always the point." He was back on the altar now, pottering around, adjusting the position of plates and candles and embroidery to suit his own baffling idiosyncrasies.

"No," said Dale, following to the edge of the marble steps. "The point is . . . I brought him home. It's what he wanted."

The priest's frantic motions ceased. His eyes drifted across the empty chapel and then back to Dale. "I didn't know there was a body," he said.

"There wasn't."

"Then—"

Dale allowed himself sit down in the front pew. "Most of what was recovered was unidentifiable," he said. "The temperatures, the impact. The undifferentiated remains were interned in Arlington."

"And those that were . . . differentiated?"

Dale removed the small black canister from his jacket and stood it on the seat beside him. "Identified remains were returned to family," he said. "But Rodriguez didn't have family."

O'Grady looked at the small metal can. He very gently picked it up, surprised at its weight. "And this—"

"The surviving remains of Commander Mike Rodriguez, USN. NASA Astronaut Group 19."

The priest blessed himself.

"We flew off the Truman together in the war," Dale said.

O'Grady frowned.

"That's what you do in a war, Padre. But wanting to go into space, that was different. We go in peace and all that?"

O'Grady was quiet for a long moment. "It occurs to me," he said at last, "that there's something I should show you." Still holding the canister, he led Dale back into a dark corner of the church, through an old low door with a gothic arch.

"Where are we going?"

"You'll see." The priest started on the tight spiral of the bell tower stairs and Dale trailed after him, his hand feeling the way along the undressed stone. It was dark and cold, the walls showing evidence of damp, and at the top was a cramped, shuttered room, the floor of which had been boarded out. There was no bell.

"We replaced it," O'Grady said, as if reading Dale's mind. He patted a fat loudspeaker affixed with brackets to the wall. "Bullhorn," he said, delighted with himself. "You'd never know the difference."

"Then what do you use this place for?"

"Ah . . ." O'Grady knelt by the far wall, beside a long bundle Dale had failed to notice. "I use it for this," the priest said, unwrapping the canvass and displaying its contents to the American.

"A telescope?"

O'Grady grinned.

"You have a telescope?"

"Help me set it up." He passed Dale the tripod and then the mount as he went about inspecting the reflector.

Dale stood the tripod in the centre of the floor and began locking it into place.

"A little higher," the priest said. "Yes, there. Perfect." He handed Dale the telescope itself. "Here," he said. "You know how to do this?"

"Uh-hu."

"Great." He stood back and began to open up the wooden shutters.

The bright night streamed in, and beneath the colour of the Moon Dale could see the grey hills rolling off above the village. O'Grady caught him staring and took over assembly of the telescope.

"The Burren," the priest said. "Bare stone for as far as you can see. No soil only in the cracks between the rocks, no rivers or lakes. Not enough water to drown a man, not enough wood to hang him—"

"And not enough flat ground for him to land his aircraft." Dale shook his head and smiled. "Rock and mountains and boulders and dust."

"Sorry?"

"Something Rodriguez told me once."

"You know," O'Grady said quietly, "you can't wear the armband forever."

"Copy that." Dale thought about the hearings, the investigation, the names cut into the granite wall at Kennedy. He thought about those pieces of Aquarius laid out across the hanger floor, little more than scrap and garbage. Rodriguez, the tone of his voice; no worry or no anger, just surprise. Uh-oh.

There was nothing anybody could have done.

"Here," O'Grady said, stepping back from the telescope. The American took his place above the instrument, turned the focus slightly and watched another world jump sharply into view. The Moon, itself a great mirror bathing in the sun; its soft mountains rising off romantic maria, the Ocean of Storms, the Sea of Rains, the Lakes of Excellence and Perseverance . . .

"Man," Dale said, "that's beautiful."

O'Grady took a turn and murmured his agreement while Dale stood back and looked up at the sky. Mark-one eyeball, they called it in flight school. Sometimes there's just no substitute.

"There," he said suddenly, raising his arm to the southern sky where a new star bloomed and flew in a short arc before fading back again into the darkness. "The Space Station," Dale said. "Will you look at that."

The priest peered up just in time. "Impressive," he said.

Dale laughed. "I could have gone there once, you know."

"You can't still go?"

"I suppose. Take a ride with the Russians. Ah, but it wouldn't be the same. I'm a pilot, an explorer. I'm not a hitchhiker."

O'Grady nodded.

"You know," Dale said, "I can still remember going to the Space Centre as a kid and asking my mom if I could stay up all night when they landed the first man on Mars." He laughed. "I really thought they'd do it too. Hell, I thought I'd get to do it once I joined the programme."

"Could happen yet."

"Maybe," said Dale, "but then again maybe it's as well I'm out. Space is hungry, Padre. This business, it devours people. I've been devoured by it. It mightn't hurt to take the time to . . ." He trailed off. "I don't know."

"Yes you do."

The astronaut smiled. "To consider it, I suppose. To get my head around it."

O'Grady leaned back against the wall. "You know," he said, "I'll bury your friend here if you like. But are you sure that's what he wanted?"

Dale stared at the canister where the priest had placed it on the floor and considered the sad strange journey which had brought it here, all the questions which surrounded it. He looked out through the open shutters, across the otherworldly hills. Nothing was certain anymore, nothing at all.

Rodriguez, if he could have seen him, would have laughed his ass off.

Soon after that he left O'Grady in the tower. There'd been a chaplain of the same mold aboard the Truman, he recalled; could get inside your head like nobody's business. It was not a shock to find another here; priests were all of a kind, Dale thought, though even so there was something very likeable about O'Grady. Not the astronomy or even the rudimentary philosophy. No, it was completely separate. He dared to call it enthusiasm and immediately felt bad.

Making his way down the narrow stairs and out through the church, Dale found Bartley and McGovern waiting outside for him, the latter with the palm of his hand pressed firm against the wall.

"Heard you'd finally gone to see the priest," McGovern said.

"This one was worried for ya," Bartley added, shaking his head.

McGovern shrugged. "Civility never broke a man's jaw."

"Clearly you've never been in a pilots' ready room," Dale said. "But thank you, Gerry. I appreciate it."

"Come on now," said Bartley. "Tell us, is your business done?"

"My business is done here," he said. "But I've got one more thing to do, if you want to join me . . ."

"You'll stand us the line?" the old man asked with a wink.

Dale grinned, the keys to his rental car already in his hand. "Sure."

Ten minutes later they were out of the village, crystal moonlight making everything unreal as they drove into The Burren. The pale-faced sky-child of earlier was gone, as was the golden hue of dusk, the Moon's disc having slipped to a colder, sterner blue which cast long, chaotic shadows all round them. Hills squeezed the twisting road and each shape was another sculpture in a garden of demented stone where everything became reverent and cruel. In a field by the road with the light streaming through it, the silhouette of a horse stood proud on the hilltop. Dale thought he glimpsed an empty saddle on its back but couldn't know for sure. They drove on.

He remembered, back in training, Rodriguez and himself; still young men, men who had fought together, who had chosen a most dangerous profession.

"You'll take me back to Houston?" Dale had said.

"If you take me back to County Clare."

Beer-bottle necks had clinked at the arrangement, but Dale never thought he'd have to see it through, never once reckoned that he'd end up here with his friend in a metal can.

"What'd'ya think," McGovern said. "Does this look good?"

Dale nodded, "Yeah." He pulled in from the road and stopped the engine. Everything was silent. Leaning over the steering wheel, he stared into the sky where the spirit of his friend flew free. The image of disintegration was burned into his mind. The whirling debris, the cloud of vapour when the remaining hydrogen and oxygen collapsed against each other. Aquarius, he thought; the water carrier.

The president had made a speech which came back to him from time to time. "The cause for which they died will go on," he'd said. "Our journey into space will continue." He quoted it to Bartley and McGovern.

"Always liked him," Bartley said. "A good lad, now. A good lad."

"Yes," said Dale, who had met him once, a tall, sad man whose ambition had surpassed his reach. "I guess he always seemed to be." He picked up the canister and opened the door of the car. "Let's go." He led them out onto the bare shoulder, through the stile and up into a steep, rocky field. There was no soil, or very little anyway, and it was odd, he thought, to recognise the kind of features he had been trained to see on lunar missions, erratics and stratigraphic markers. He picked up a stone from the rough surface and turned it over in his hand.

"What's that?" McGovern asked.

"The technical term is FLR. At least according to Rodriguez."

"FLR?"

"Funny Looking Rock." He smiled as he dropped it to the ground. Rodriguez always said that levity was appropriate in a dangerous trade and he was right, Dale realized, as he picked his way through loose stones, careful not to lose his footing on the crumpled ground. One had to be able to laugh at one's self, at the job, at the danger.

"Woah," he said, catching his toe in one of the great, deep cracks which slithered everywhere.

Bartley sniggered. "You alright there, Dale?"

"Yeah," the American said. "Thanks."

They were on the true Burren now, a vast, wrinkled plain of undulating stone weathered into near oblivion. A kaleidoscope of grey, it spread on and on, beyond history, beyond the night, out of sight beyond Dale's unrelenting dreams. Behind them, the few stray streetlights of the village sparkled in the distance, and, above, the wash of moonlight made it seem another world entirely.

It was, Dale decided, as good a place as any. "Here," he said.

Beside him Bartley nodded. "When they buried my brother it wasn't like this," he said, "it was a fine spring day."

Dale and McGovern both turned to look at him, startled by his openness.

"He was a hero," Bartley went on. "Of the kind they name streets after, you know? Brought down a lot of them lot here at the time."

"The Tans," McGovern said. "The British."

"Aye," said Bartley. "And they'd men from his column there to see him away, draping the tricolour across his box, a few of them with rifles that they let off. The noise of it all," he said. "'Twas a fierce honour."

Dale cast him an unsure look. "You're not . . . armed now, are you Bartley?"

The old man laughed, a booming ho-ho as loud as any shot. "Not at all. Not at all, a'course. I'm just saying, you know, the moment should be marked."

"And what had you in mind?" McGovern asked.

Bartley grinned, and with great effort brought himself to his full height. He raised his right arm and bent his elbow, bringing his hand to his head in a salute. McGovern quickly did the same.

Dale nodded, and carefully he opened up the flask, tipping its cremated contents out onto the breeze. The cloud flattened out at once, dove towards the rocky pavement, and then took flight, specks of ash like busy stars exploding all around him while the world turned overhead. Dale straightened up and saluted too, the remains of Rodriguez taking wing into the night.

When it was over he brought his hand down and, behind him, his two friends mumbled something as they let their own arms fall, Bartley rubbing at his shoulder.

"We should take a stroll now," McGovern said quietly.

"What?" Bartley said.

"You know, as we're here, we should give Dale the air of the place."

"Ah, will you not be—"

"No," Dale said. He laid his hand on Bartley's shoulder, "I'd like that." He was tired, that was true, it was late, and yet some new energy was coming to him. It compelled him to move, to walk, to see what he could find.

"Well then," McGovern said, "come on so," and he led them out across the hillside.

They were at last, Dale thought, the crew he had imagined, ambling across this odd terrain with the strange, loping gait required to leap from one great limestone block to another. Step-by-step the three of them picked their way across the broken surface, away from the road, away from the lights of the village and everything that Dale had come to know. This was a separate place, severe and beautiful and altogether alien. There, in the stone, were red and orange tints which he could not explain. In the sky, the universe's mechanism whirled while the three men drifted on, and, as the grey rock fell off toward the close horizon, they could have been walking on the moon.

the other gun

NEAL ASHER

Neal Asher was born in Essex, England, but now lives in Crete. He started writing at the age of sixteen but didn't explode into public print until a few years ago; a quite prolific author, he now seems to be everywhere at once. His stories have appeared in Asimov's Science Fiction, Interzone, The Agony Column, Hadrosaur Tales, *and elsewhere, and have been collected in* Runcible Tales, The Engineer, *and* Mason's Rats. *His extremely popular novels include* Gridlinked, Cowl, The Skinner, The Line of Polity, Brass Man, Voyage of the Sable Keech, The Engineer Reconditioned, Prador Moon: A Novel of the Polity, *and* Hilldiggers. *His most recent books are a novel,* The Line War, *and a collection,* The Gabble and Other Stories.

Here he gives us a typical Asher story: fast-paced, ultraviolent, grim, highly inventive, sometimes gruesome, and thoroughly entertaining.

As the bathysphere landed I fought to regain my humanity, even though my latest communication with the Client had been some hours ago. Talking to that entity was always a bizarre and confusing experience, and one I would never get used to, didn't want to. Every time afterwards it felt to me like I was a new occupant of my old and battered body. I blinked, remembering the lack of eyelids, held up my hand to clench and unclench it and remembered a lack of fingers, or at least fingers like these, then, with the bathysphere settling, reached out and pressed a thumb against the door control.

The twenty-foot-wide circular door thumped away from me, releasing from its seals to allow in a waft of vapour and smell like rotting vegetables, turned its inner locking ring to unlock then slowly hinged down, first exposing a yellow sky bruised with brown clouds.

"Don't take anything for granted," I said to my companion.

"I never do," sighed Harriet, her voice as always surprisingly gentle from such a large mouth full of so many teeth.

I glanced at her and wondered how the people of this colony would react to her. Harriet was a Mesozoic era dinosaur, a troodon in the style of those dinosaurs from one of the paleo-history fashions when feathers were out and colourful skin was back in. She was jade on her upper surfaces and mustard yellow below and her back mackerel patterned with hints of navy blue. To add to her gaudy appearance she had painted her claws gold, and wore a variety of silver and gold bangles and neck rings. I was glad that in recent years she'd lost interest in applying eye-shadow. She now stood up on her toes and extended her long neck to raise her sharp reptilian head, which was first at a level with mine, to peer over the door at the landscape lying beyond, and blinked bright slot-pupil eyes.

"Tasty," she said, which was often her response to overly muscled humans. She then clicked her fore-claws in frustration and ducked back down. This probably meant the humans concerned were armed.

The door finally came down to rest on boggy ground mounded with heather-like plants and nodular mosses, stabbed through here and there with black reeds. The colony raft sat about a mile beyond, a structure a mile wide and bearing some resemblance to an ancient aircraft carrier. Members of the Frobishers, who were the family I had come to trade with, stood between the bathysphere door and the vehicle they'd come over in—a swamp car with cage wheels. Four heavies clad in quilted body suits and rain capes stood out there, three of them carrying light laser carbines and a fourth holding something that looked suspiciously like a proton weapon. Before these stood a woman, clad much the same as them but studying an ancient computer tablet. This must be the woman I had come to see, scourge of the Cleaver family and a character with growing off-world interests. I moved forwards, raindrops spattering against my crocodile-skin jacket and thick canvas trousers, my heavy boots sinking into the boggy ground as I stepped off the door.

"Madeleine Frobisher?" I enquired.

She was already looking up, studying both me and my companion warily. I advanced towards her and held out my hand, trying to ignore the laser carbines tracking my progress. "I'm Tuppence."

She didn't offer her hand in return, instead nodding towards the bathysphere behind.

"Novel form of transport," she opined.

I lowered my hand and turned to look back. The spherical craft was shifting—adjusting its gravmotors to pull itself back up out of the soft ground. Those motors were far too inefficient to support the entire weight of the craft and send it airborne, not because of their decrepitude, for even though they were centuries old they still functioned as they always had, but because when they were made the prador had only just begun inventing the technology. This was why the craft's main method of ascent and descent was attached to its crown: a wrist-thick stent-weave diamond-filament cable that speared upwards to disappear into the bruised sky. Hundreds of miles of it attached at its further end to a giant reel in the underbelly of the *Coin Collector*—an ancient prador tug that had once born a very different name under previous ownership.

"It is," I replied, "but it serves."

"And what is this?" Madeleine gestured to Harriet.

Pointing to my troodon companion, I replied, "Let me introduce Harriet, who by her appearance you would not realize was once an exotic dancer on Cheyne III."

Harriet dipped her head in acknowledgement. "Pleased to eat you."

"She of course means 'pleased to meet you' since her artificial vocal chords sometimes struggle with the shape of her mouth." I eyed Harriet. The changes her brain had undergone, having been compressed in that reptilian skull, were a worry. Though, at that point, I couldn't figure out whether that "pleased to eat you" was a Freudian slip due to her lost intelligence or just a little joke at my expense.

"Is she . . . alien?"

I turned back to Madeleine. "Harriet is just the result of an extreme desire for change using adaptogenic drugs, zooetics and nanodaption, and is, if you were to stretch the term almost to breaking point, a human being."

"She will remain here," said Madeleine.

I shook my head. "She comes with me—that's not negotiable."

"Then our negotiations are over before they have truly started."

"Very well," I smiled at her congenially. "I have to admit to being disappointed, but if you're going to grandstand by setting pointless conditions . . ." I shrugged and began to turn back to my bathysphere. I was halfway back up the ramp door before she relented.

"Oh, if she must," she finally said.

I turned back to see her waving a dismissive hand, this all obviously being a matter of no consequence.

"It's just that there's little room in the ATV," she added.

"That's not a problem. Harriet is more than capable of keeping up on foot." I gestured to her vehicle as I returned to her. "Shall we?"

She held up one hand. "I do hope you've brought payment and are not wasting my time."

"Of course," I replied. "Twenty pounds of prador diamond-slate, etched sapphires to the value of one million New Carth Shillings and the fusion reactor parts you detailed."

"Good." She nodded.

Catching her speculative glance towards the bathysphere I remembered to send the signal to close the door, and heard it groaning shut as I followed two of the heavies up the steps leading inside the swamp car. Within, seats lined the two sides with plenty of room for Harriet to squat between, but I didn't point this out. The heavies sat down, silent and watchful, while Madeleine sat beside the driver who was obviously another of the Frobisher line. This weedy looking individual bore similar facial features as the rest in here but also had a wart growing in precisely the same position on each of his eyelids—a sure sign of interbreeding. He started up the car—a hydrogen turbine engine by the sound of it—and set it into motion. I stretched up to look out of the narrow heavily scratched plastic windows to see Harriet bounding along beside the vehicle, then settled down patiently. Within five minutes we were in the shadow of the family raft then driving up a ramp and parking, the engine winding down to silence.

"So where did you find the artefact?" I asked as I followed Madeleine out into a crammed tube of a swamp-car park.

"It's been here in our raft for as long as I can remember," she replied, "but it was only when one of my people studied your broadcast was it identified . . . that was about ten years ago."

"Solstan?"

Madeleine paused, glanced round at me. "I haven't heard that expression in a while . . . no, it's maybe seventeen solstan years ago."

I grimaced. I'd been chasing rumours about the elements of the farcaster in the Wasteland for twenty years now and found nothing. I often wondered if they truly existed because why, as the Client claimed, would the Polity AIs have ordered it broken up and scattered? If they had truly considered it such a danger why hadn't they just destroyed it completely? I also often considered the unlikelihood of Polity AIs ridding themselves of such a potentially potent weapon, because that seemed very unlike them. But I could only obey and keep on searching, meanwhile slowly plotting my route to freedom.

Harriet had now re-joined us, panting but probably invigorated by the run. The armed escort closed in all around, seemingly a lot more confident now. I wondered if this indicated that they were thinking of doing something stupid. Past experience of trades like this told me they probably were, and knowing the Frobisher's history did not make me optimistic.

Confirmation came just a minute later as Madeleine led the way up steps so worn the plating was gone to expose closed-cell bubble-metal. Concentrating on my footing with my body's eyes I also looked through other eyes at the two swamp cars that had just pulled up by my bathysphere. I then watched some Frobishers unloading a heavy atomic shear from one of them, and wondered if this family had become so interbred there had been a loss of intelligence. It would be interesting to see what would happen when the atomic shear hit the prador alloy of the vehicle. The metal might not be the kind that armoured their war ships, but it was very tough, and the defence system might be old, but had proven effective on many occasions.

"So what's its condition?" I asked, so as to keep up the pretence. Of course, by the data package Madeleine had sent there had been a good chance that this could have been the real deal, but not now.

"I can't really say. It produces the power signatures you detailed and it's of the shape you described." Madeleine shrugged. "Hopefully you know your stuff and will be able to tell me." She then added, "But we still get the agreed first payment."

"Of course," I said.

I did know my stuff, perhaps more so than she would want. A century of research and experimentation and of perpetual mental updates of the latest research in the Polity since the war had made me an expert in many fields. I would also recognize a fake which, as I had been at pains to stress during my broadcast across the Wasteland, would result in no payment at all and quite likely some extreme response.

The stairs terminated in a long hall lined with heavy doors, each with a barred window. No doubt at all that this was a prison. Madeleine led the way across to one of them, punched a code into a panel beside it and the door popped open.

"We keep it here for the security." She gestured me inside.

Without hesitating, I stepped through, Harriet coming in behind me. It was fairly obvious what would happen next, and I was glad that they had not yet tried violence. I walked up to plinth at the centre of the cell and gazed at the object resting under a dome of chainglass. A curved chunk of white crystal lay there, rather like the sepal of some huge flower, but with a disc-shaped plug at its base from which protruded hundreds of micro-bayonets for data and power. I pinged it and received a facsimile of the supposed power signature of a farcaster element, but straight away I could see the joins. I peered at it closer, ramping up the magnification of my eyes and probing with a spectroscopic laser. The crystal was plain white quartz cut and polished to the required shape, while the base plug was just a not very good mock-up made of bonded resin. I turned as if to address my host, but just then the door slammed shut.

"Disappointing," I said.

Harriet was also peering at the object. She gave it a dismissive sniff then turned to face me.

"No good?" she enquired eagerly.

"Another fake," I said. "The Client will not be pleased at all."

Harriet, opened her mouth and licked her long red tongue over her white teeth. Evidently *she* wasn't displeased.

Through my other eyes—the cams on the bathysphere I'd linked to via my internal transceiver—I watched the Frobishers apply their atomic shear to the door. The door reacted by lifting off its seal then slamming down, smashing the shear and its two operators into the ground, then lifting and dropping slowly above the mess as if like a beckoning hand it was inviting the rest to try again. One of them decided to fire some kind of explosive inside, but the door whipped up to send it bouncing back and it detonated by one swamp car, blowing off one cage wheel. The bathysphere defence system then decided to stop playing. Two hatches opened in the ring girdling the vehicle above the door, extruded two Gatling cannons and began firing. The two cars, their liquid hydrogen tanks soon peppered with holes, exploded, but by then all the humans had become bloody smears across the boggy ground.

"Stupid," I said, then landed a heavy boot squarely in the centre of the cell door. The force of my kick buckled the floor underneath my other boot and the door tumbled clanging into the space beyond.

"Can I?" asked Harriet, stepping from one clawed foot to the other. "Can I now?"

She had slipped into childlike eager pet mode again. Was that what she was destined to be or was it just a deliberate pose?

"Off you go," I conceded, and she shot through the opening, her claws leaving scratches in the metal floor.

She'll get herself killed one day, I thought, *but not today.*

All the Frobishers had seen was a big and slightly ridiculous lizard, easy to kill with their weapons and only capable of using the natural weapons with which she had been endowed. I agreed, for I knew that with her long claws she wasn't even capable of picking up a gun let alone firing one. However, Harriet had survived and prevailed during many encounters like this one. I put this down to the fact that she had been a canny and experienced bounty hunter in her time and that though her intelligence had, apparently, dropped a few tens of IQ points, she hadn't lost that edge.

I stepped back from the door and pulled open the studs in my canvas trousers, peeled back a patch over my right thigh, and watched the skin there etch out a frame and pop open. Next I reached inside my leg and took out a heavily redesigned QC laser, held it in my right hand and plugged its superconducting power cable into the socket in my right wrist. After a pause I then looked down to a similar patch over my left thigh. I hesitated, then decided otherwise.

No, not today; not the *other* gun.

I stepped up to the plinth, straight-armed the chainglass dome and sent it clanging like a bell across the cell floor. I then extended my other arm and fired the laser, the beam invisible until vapour from the burning artefact etched it out of the air. Playing the high-energy-density beam over the thing, I watched the quartz shatter into hot fragments and the supposed base plug slump into molten ruin, then took my finger off the trigger. The momentary fit of pique had cost me time and I'd wasted more than enough of it on this world and in the Wasteland entire.

I grimaced, then stepped out of the door to the sounds of distant screams and the cracking and sawing of laser carbines.

The *Coin Collector* was a pyramid of brassy metal, its edges rounded and measuring a mile long, the throats of its fusion engines nearly covering one face and possessing enough drive power to fry a small moon. As the giant reel inside its EVA bay, which lay a quarter of a mile up from the fusion engines, wound in the bathysphere, I turned to watch Harriet clumsily using a suction sanitizer on her body to clean off all the blood now she'd licked off everything she could reach with her tongue.

As the bathysphere drew closer to the ancient prador tug, I considered the debacle below. The Frobishers had been utterly unprepared for Harriet and utterly unprepared for me. Harriet had torn into them quickly, leaving the route to the car park scattered with body parts, and had been munching on the same when I had arrived there. More Frobishers had turned up while I was stealing a swamp car and they had managed to get off a few shots before my QC laser fire drove them back and before Harriet finished off the stragglers. I had then taken one of the cars out and set it on automatic before abandoning it. A proton blast had turned it to wreckage about half a mile out, but by then we were well beyond it and soon safe inside the bathysphere. Still, the Client would not be pleased and I did not look forward to that.

I peered down at the holes burned through my jacket and into the artificial parts of my body, which was most of its parts. My sight was slightly blurred, my other senses dull and my right arm wasn't working properly. It seemed likely that as well as structural damage there might be some problem with my smart plasm component. This meant I would have to go into a mould and level two consciousness for nerve reintegration, which also increased the likelihood of the Client communicating with me. This annoyed me intensely, as did the Frobisher's ludicrous attempt to rip me off.

Had Madeleine Frobisher really thought she could just lure me down, capture me, break into my bathysphere and steal the payment I had brought? Had she completely neglected to factor this ship up here into her plans? Then again perhaps she *had* factored it in. Perhaps her aim had been not only theft of the payment I had brought but seizure of my ship as well. How naïve. I stood, walked over to one of the array of hexagonal screens and human consoles plugged into prador pit-controls and made a call.

"Madeleine," I said, the moment her face appeared in one of the screens. "That was really a rather silly thing to do."

"You destroyed the artefact," she replied. "Why did you do that? It's something you've been hunting down for ages."

Odd, I thought, she seemed genuinely puzzled. Working the controls I called up a view of the Frobisher colony raft from a remote I'd dropped on the surface before descent.

"As you should be well aware, the item you showed me wasn't genuine," I replied. "It has not been sitting in your raft over the ages, but was recently made there."

"It was not!"

"Whatever. Your subsequent attempt to imprison me and break into my craft demonstrated your intent."

"My intent was to ensure you had brought payment. It was you who started killing my brothers!"

"Weak Madeleine, very weak." I paused, a suspicion nagging at me. I relayed an instruction to the *Coin Collector* for a search of the area surrounding the colony raft. "So, if you didn't make the thing, where did you really get it from?"

She gazed at me for a long moment, perhaps realizing her predicament and understanding that lies would not help now. Meanwhile the search produced results: a group of Cleavers watching from around an ancient tripod-mounted holocorder mounted on a platform that was itself fixed to a swamp car. This could not be a regular activity of the Cleavers for surely they would have automatic systems in place to keep watch on their enemies.

I further worked some controls to bring up an image, from orbit, of the Cleaver colony raft as Madeleine replied, "We stole it from the Cleavers. We found out they were bringing in something valuable from the North and ambushed them."

I glanced round at Harriet, who had moved with eerie silence to stand at my shoulder.

"Squabbling children," she said, in one of her moments of clarity.

So it seemed, and a plot by the Cleavers to put the Frobishers in my bad books, nicely exacerbated by Madeleine Frobisher's greed and intent to extend her off-world interests. I'd been dragged into a silly feud, my time had been wasted, my body had been damaged and the Client would be pissed off. However, before I could further consider what the Client's reaction would be, the bathysphere arrived with a shuddering crash in its docking cage. I would find out soon enough, I decided.

"Goodbye, Madeleine," I said, and cut the connection.

The bathysphere door opened into an oval tube twenty feet across and ten high. Everything aboard the *Coin Collector* was of a similar scale—this tube apparently matching the size of burrows made by prador yet to grow into huge father-captains and lose their legs in that process. The interior was plain metal, the lower half roughened with fingertip size pyramidal spikes for grip, tubes of varying sizes branching off for the different iterations of prador children. Its design was obviously an old one made long before the prador started designing the décor of their ships to match their home environment and long before the father-captains dared to come out of their lairs. As I strode into it, the human lighting from induction blisters grew brighter, revealing a group of about twenty thetics marching in perfect synchronization across a junction. I headed over to a parking platform for various designs of scooter, Harriet pacing at my side like some faithful hound.

I mounted a gyroscope-balanced mono-scooter, engaged its drive, and using the detached throttle and steering baton guided it from the platform and up along the tunnel to the end where a steep switchback took me up another level. Harriet followed me all the way, still hound-faithful for, except on the odd occasions when I allowed her to let her instincts reign, she never left my side. Five levels later I arrived at a massive oval door, dismounted and walked towards it. With a loud crump it separated diagonally and the two halves revolved up into the walls, whereupon I entered a small captain's sanctum packed with human equipment plugged into the ancient prador controls. As I approached the consoles, with their hexagonal screens above, they abruptly came on to show me the views I had been seeing in the bathysphere. I stared at them for a long time, utterly certain now of what was to come, then I turned away.

Now it was time for me to deal with my injuries and the inevitable upbraiding from the Client—a prospect I did not relish at all. I walked over to a case against one wall, a thing that looked very much like an iron maiden, woodenly stripping off my jacket as I went. I tossed the jacket into a bin beside it, then struggled with my boots, trousers, shirt and undergarments—a thetic would collect them later and clean and repair them. Naked, I opened the front door of the case to reveal a human-shaped indentation inside, turned round and backed into it, Harriet watching me like a curious puppy. I closed up the lid and immediately I felt the bayonet connections sliding into my body, then everything began to shut down.

Next I gazed from old dying eyes, reality broken into thousands of facets easily interpretable to a distributed mind, even though the dimensions it could perceive were beyond reason to a human one. However, the facets were going out. Pheromone receptors were stuttering too, and synaesthetic interpreters churning nonsense. Meanwhile, down below, the hot tightness came in peristaltic waves and something was snapping open. In hot orange vastness I screamed chemical terror and shed. Nerve plugs and sockets parted and a mass of dry chitin fell, a hollow waspish thing bouncing amidst many of the same, doubled iridescent wings shattering like safety glass.

And next all was clear again with new eyes to see. Thirty-two wings beat and pheromone receptors began receiving again, while the synaesthetic interpreters turned the language and code of the Client into something I could understand. The creature rose up, a hundred feet tall, opened its beak and with its new black tongue tasted the air of its furnace.

"You have failed again," it said.

As the Polity knew to its cost, the prador were vicious predators not prepared to countenance other intelligent entities in their universe. What had not been known, until a year in to the start of the war when it seemed that humanity, the Polity and its AIs faced extinction, was that the prador were already practiced in the art of extermination.

I was working in bioweapons—the natural place in the war for a parasitologist and bio-synthesist—trying to resurrect a parasite of those giant crablike homicidal maniacs, when I was abruptly reassigned. I later learnt that the parasite was resurrected and delivered as a terror weapon by assassin drones made in its shape. They sneaked aboard prador ships or into their bases, and injected parasite eggs—prador Father-Captains extinguished by the worms chewing out their insides.

Only once I was aboard the destroyer ferrying me to my destination, along with a large and varied collection of other experts, did I get the story. Before the prador encountered the Polity they had encountered another alien species whose realm encompassed just three or four star systems. Being the prador they had attacked at once, but then found themselves in a long drawn-out war against a hive species who even in organic form approached AI levels of intelligence, and who quickly developed some seriously nasty weaponry in response to the attack. The war had dragged on for decades but, in the end, the massive resources of the prador Kingdom told against the hive creatures. It was during this conflict that the prador developed their kamikazes, and not during the prador-human war, and it was with kamikazes that the prador steadily annihilated the hive creatures' worlds. However, one of these multifaceted beings, a weapons developer no less, managed to steal a prador cargo ship and get out through the prador blockade of the systems of its kind. And now, this creature, which the AI's referred to as the Client, wanted to ally itself with the Polity for some payback.

My memories of my time with the Client are vague. I'm sure we worked together on bioweapons while other experts there worked on the more knotty problem of delivery systems, and other weapons arising from the Client's science. A bioweapon capable of annihilating every prador it came into contact with was perfectly feasible, but getting it into contact with enough of them wasn't so easy. Though the prador fought under one king to destroy the Polity, they were often physically isolated. The father-captains remained aboard their ships only coming into physical contact with their own kin, many prador wore atmosphere sealed armour perpetually, while others had been surgically transplanted into the aseptic interiors of their war machines. A plague would not spread and, to be effective, would have to be delivered across millions of targets. This seemed impossible, until the farcaster . . .

U-space tech has always been difficult. A runcible gate will only open into another runcible gate and a U-space drive for a ship is effectively its own gate. Open ended runcibles had been proposed, developed, and had failed. Without the catcher's mitt there at the other end nothing without its own integral U-space drive could surface from underspace. It couldn't work. It wasn't possible. *Except it was.*

Because of the vagueness of my memories of the time I am assuming that the AIs developed the farcaster. The device could, using appalling amounts of energy, generate an open-ended gate. It was possible to point this thing anywhere in the prador Kingdom, inside their seemingly invulnerable ships, even inside the armour of individuals, and send something. But there was a problem: the energy requirement ramped exponentially with the size of the portal. To send something the size of a megaton contra terrene device, would require the full energy output of a G-type sun for a day, even if the iteration of the farcaster we had was capable of using that amount of energy, which it wasn't. This was completely unfeasible and, if we could have utilized such massive amounts of power it could have been directed in a much more effective way. However, there were other possibilities. The output of a stacked array of fifty fusion reactors could deploy the device as it stood, and it was possible to open microscopic portals—ones that though small were large enough to send through something like a virus, a spore or a bacterium.

Working together the Client and I made something that could kill the prador. I don't know precisely what it was—the vagueness of my memories was due to the accident that destroyed most of my body, for it had also destroyed part of my mind. We were ready. We had our weapon and we had our delivery system. But things had changed in the intervening years. The prador had begun to lose and even as we lined up the farcaster for its first tests, the old prador king was displaced and they began to retreat, and to negotiate. The AIs put a hold on our project, then they cancelled it, seizing the farcaster and breaking it into separate elements, which were cast away all across known space.

What happened then? The war ended, apparently. I never knew because my remains were clinging to life in one of the Client's growth tanks as it fled into hiding aboard the *Coin Collector*. Apparently there had been some contention about the breaking up of the farcaster during which some unstable weapons activated. I don't know. I just don't know.

Consciousness returned to me while I was alone aboard the *Coin Collector*, my mind somehow enslaved, my task to search out and recover the elements of the farcaster, and to one day take them to the Client, when it allowed me to know its location, so it could at last have its revenge against the prador. I waited patiently for that day, for I wanted revenge too and I wanted freedom, and I knew that the only way I could have them would be to finish the job the prador started so long ago.

The Client had spoken and now, with my connection to it renewed and affirmed, or maybe some parts of my mind reprogrammed and updated, I had no choice but to obey. As I stepped out of the repair cabinet and donned newly cleaned and repaired clothing, I felt sick, bewildered by my human form, and still wishing I could change the past.

"Time to finish this now," I said.

"Finish it?" Harriet perked up.

I did worry about her love of mayhem for it seemed her main interest now. Once she had been an "exotic dancer" who used various reptiles in her act and then, like many such people for whom appearance is all, she acquired an accelerating addiction to change. First had been changes of skin colour and the addition of snake eyes, then scales, claws and numerous internal changes, adaptogenic drugs and enhancements, and change thereafter for its own sake. At some point the jobs she had taken to supplement her wealth had displaced the dancing, and she became a full-time bounty hunter, and she further adapted herself to that work. I had employed her to hunt down a rogue war drone said to possess some strange piece of U-space tech which just might have been part of the farcaster, but as it turned out wasn't. The drone fried her, leaving not much more than her brain and a bit of nerve tissue. I managed to get her out, in an ab-zero stasis bottle, and thence to a hospital in the Graveyard. I didn't hold out much hope for her. Had we access to a Polity hospital her chances would have been better but, since quite a few of her bounties were paid upon delivery of a corpse, or parts thereof, she couldn't return to the Polity. But the next time I saw I got a bit of a shock.

Her change into a troodon dinosaur had been out of a catalogue that explored the "limits of the feasible" apparently, and she was idiotically delighted with it. They'd shoe-horned her brain into this reptile body, where it didn't seem to fit right. They'd turned her into something like an upgraded pet that could speak, but didn't possess the hands to do anything more complicated than tear at meat. I felt responsible, and so allowed her to stay at my side.

"Yes, finish it," I said, the feeling that I occupied some nightmare form slowly receding as I worked the controls, targeting both colony rafts and the Cleaver watch post, then pausing to study the only weapons option.

The Frobishers and Cleavers were nasty and certainly deserved some sort of response, but there had to be innocents amidst them. What I was about to do sickened me, but I simply had no choice . . . or did I? I now struggled against my own mind, because my instructions did offer me some leeway, and I opened com channels covering all the radio and microwave frequencies the two families used, and set the equipment for record and repeat.

"This is a message from Tuppence aboard the *Coin Collector* for all Frobishers and Cleavers," I said. "You have both wasted my time and threatened my life." And now the unscripted bit, "You therefore have one hour to abandon your colony rafts and watch stations. At the end of that hour I will destroy them all." I paused while a knife of pain lanced through my skull, then faded as I selected the single particle cannon for the chore. The pain returned as I set a timer for firing, then continued with, "Perhaps, after this, those of you who might be innocent in this matter will carefully consider your choice of leadership. That is all."

"You are being merciful?" Harriet enquired.

I stepped back from the controls, the pain redoubling in my skull, and slumped into an acceleration chair. I was aware that I had gone, if only a little, contrary to my orders, and now, somehow, I was punishing myself. Paralysed, I watched lights flashing and icons appearing on the screen indicating increasingly desperate attempts from both families to get in contact with me. Ever so slowly the pain faded—just a small punishment for a minor infringement, and not the agony that could leave me crippled in hell for days on end. The leeway around my orders enabled me to do such things, enabled me to do many things. I rested a hand on my thigh—the one containing the *other* gun.

"Yes, maybe I'm getting old," I finally managed to rasp in reply to Harriet.

Realizing there would be no immediate action, Harriet paced around the room for a while, before coming back to stand beside my chair, her head dipping as she nodded off into one of her standing dozes.

A quarter of an hour later I observed swamp cars, ATVs, heavy crawlers and people on foot, loaded down with belongings, abandoning both rafts. A further half hour passed, and as the end of the hour approached I heaved myself out of the chair, my head still throbbing with post punishment pain, and approached the controls. The last minutes counted down, the last seconds, and then the particle cannon fired—any effects here on the ship unfelt.

The side view of the Frobisher's raft showed a beam as wide as a tree trunk stabbing down, its inner core bright blue but shrouded in misty green. Molten metal and debris exploded out from the impact point then, when the beam cut right through the raft to the boggy ground below, the whole thing lifted on an explosion, its back breaking and the two halves heaving upwards on a cloud of fire and superheated steam, before collapsing down as the beam cut out. Another screen showed those on the watching swamp car just gone—a smoking hollow where they had been, while the Cleaver's raft was now just as much a mess as the Frobisher's, though viewed from a different perspective. Harriet was at my side of course, watching with fascination, before turning away in disappointment.

"Tank." I turned now to face precisely such an object over the far side of the sanctum: a cylindrical tank much like one used for fuel oil or gas, but covered with an intricate maze of pipes and conduits. "Take us out of orbit and put us on course for the Graveyard."

"As you instruct," replied a frigid voice.

I immediately felt the vibration through my feet as the fusion engines fired up. The thing inside that tank, which might or might not have been the usual ganglion of a press-ganged prador first- or second-child, could take over.

Everything fell into stillness aboard the *Coin Collector* during U-space jumps. Without orders the thetics just became somnolent, without action and prey to hunt Harriet spent her time dozing or following me about like a lost puppy. On this occasion she was in lost puppy mode, easily keeping pace with my scooter as I drove through the ship, finally pulling up beside yet another massive diagonally slashed elliptical door that opened ponderously as I dismounted. Just outside this door I surveyed twenty thetics standing ready clad in impact armour with pulse-rifles shouldered. They were somnolent but at a word from me would wake and be ready. In two more U-jumps I would give that word as we tracked down yet another possible element of the farcaster. I bit down on my frustration. When would the Client finally give up and summon me back? When could I finally end this? I walked through the door.

The cauldron was a pale pink glass sphere twenty feet across supported in a scaffold of gold metal extending from the floor to the ceiling fifty feet above. Across the back wall of the chamber were the doors to rows of chemical reactors. Catalytic cracking columns stood guard to one side while on the other squatted an object like a mass of stacked aluminium luggage woven together with tubes. Each case was a nano-factory in itself and the whole generated the smart-plasm being fed into the cauldron—the distillation of a billion processes. Gazing upon this set-up I felt it just did not seem sufficiently high-tech, but looked like something Jules Verne might have dreamed up in a moment of insanity.

Next I lowered my gaze to the rows of moulds bracketing the catwalk leading to the cauldron itself. The ones to my right were closed, like sarcophagi, their contents incubating. To the left half of them were closed, a robot arm running on rails to inject plasm into each. The others were open to reveal polished interiors in the shape of humans, a thetic peeling itself up out of one of them assisted by two more of its kind, while thetics from the other open moulds stood in a group behind observing the whole procedure with blue eyes set in milk-white faces, mouths opening and closing as if miming the speech they were incapable of producing.

"I wish we could extend their lives," I said.

"Why?" asked Harriet, completely baffled.

"Four years and two days seems to be the point beyond which returns diminish," I replied. "I wonder if that limitation is why the Polity scrapped the idea?"

"The Polity?" wondered Harriet, her thinking even slower in these periods of inaction.

The thetics had been an attempt by the Polity to produce large quantities of disposable soldiers—a project with which I felt sure the Client and I had been involved during the war. Or perhaps we weren't? There had been other researchers, scientists and experts of every kind on that ship sent to that first meeting with the Client, so perhaps the thetics were the result of some research by one of them? Perhaps when the Client had run, just after the farcaster had been broken up, it had stolen data and equipment too? How else had it obtained the samples with which to rebuild all this here? I shook my head, frustrated by the confusion. Where the thetic technology had come from and what my involvement had been were questions that would probably remain unanswered—they probably lay in that portion of my mind taken away by the accident.

Unfortunately, as well as the thetics' life-span being limited, both the amount of programming they could take and the damage they could withstand was limited too. Smart-plasm was all very well for quick production of disposable hominids, but on receiving damage under fire such constructs tended to quickly revert to their original form, and crawl out of their uniforms like particularly nervous slime moulds.

"Golem chasses," I said as I walked on through the cauldron room towards the back corner.

My own body was an amalgam of a Golem base frame, smart-plasm and an early form of syntheskin outer covering—as a whole a more rugged combination. I wasn't entirely sure what human parts I had retained: perhaps my brain, perhaps only part of my brain, maybe just some crystal recording from that original flesh. I wondered if it had been a bioweapon that had taken away the rest of me, and wondered if it had been one I had designed.

"Golem chasses," Harriet repeated, with less intelligence than a parrot.

I decided not to bother making a suggestion I had made before, of giving her prosthetic Golem hands to replace her unwieldy claws. She wasn't interested when her mind was at a high point, and would be less interested now.

A smaller door at one rear corner of this chamber took me into my private laboratory. Here I felt the tension begin to ebb. It wasn't as if I could somehow be disobedient here, ignore the Client's orders or cease my endless search for farcaster elements, but somehow its grip on my existence seemed less rigid in this place. Perhaps it was because here I occupied those parts of my mind not concerned with that search—those being the parts wholly focused on my original interests so long ago.

Oddly, the effect here seemed the same for Harriet, though she had no alien entity controlling her mind. Her interest perked up as she surveyed all the complicated equipment, peered at nanoscope screens and clumsily tried to pick up objects made for human hands and not claws pained with shocking pink polish. I say oddly because elsewhere her interests didn't often stray into the scientific.

I checked on a brain worm first; version 1056 and now a long way away from the parasite that forced ants to climb to the top of stalks of grass when a sheep might be strolling by and thus pass itself on to said sheep. This particular beauty would make a prador, if it was aboard a space ship, suffer terminal claustrophobia. Not only would it want to get out of the ship, it would be completely unable to wear any kind of protective suit. Of course, prador could survive in vacuum for an appreciable time, but still the victim of this parasite would eventually die. I'd yet to test it out, and didn't think I ever would.

The next bug was one that caused a prador's carapace to grow as soft as sponge, and the next was a fungus that dined on their nerve tissue. I only checked on them briefly before moving on to the latest version of my favourite fungus—perfect now in every detail and perhaps a precise copy of a fungus that the Client possessed. Thus I occupied my spare time pursuing my interests in parasites and biological weapons. Thus, by pursuing the lines of research I had followed with the Client I tried to restore some lost memory. Staring at the latest nanoscope images and latest computer models of the function of this last fungus, in all its different genetic settings, I tried to remember seeing them before, but there was nothing.

"The gun?" queried Harriet.

"One day," I said.

Really, it should be tested, but I needed some victim deserving of such an end. Perhaps, during this latest search, if all the data was correct, I would find such.

The Graveyard lay in the intersection point of two spheres of interstellar occupation, everything beyond its edge being called the Wasteland or the Reaches, or having no name at all. As the *Coin Collector* heaved out of U-space I knew we had arrived upon sensors picking up high amounts of space debris across many light years and upon gazing at a screen image of the devastated world called Molonor. This world possessed its own orbital ring of debris that had once been space stations and, also orbiting it, its small moon was half subsumed by a base that seemed a conglomerate mass of those same debris. I eyed the ships orbiting that moon, along with the various ground-based coil-gun emplacements then, after a short contemplation, focused in on one of those ships. Here was an in-system cargo hauler the shape of an ancient shouldered rifle bullet sitting in a U-space carrier shell like a hexagonal threaded nut. I pinged it and got a confirmation of identity: the *Layden*— one of Gad Straben's haulers. Straben was my target now—the Client had made that abundantly clear during one of our frequent drops out of U-space to let the *Coin Collector*'s engines cool and realign.

"Harriet," I said, opening com. "Where are you?"

"The Cauldron," she replied.

"I'll be with you shortly." I considered how like a dog being taken on a familiar walk she had rushed ahead, then I experienced a moment of puzzlement. Harriet didn't often get this far ahead of me, usually stayed by my side, so she had to be *very* eager. I shook my head, dismissing the thought before inputting a course to take the

Coin Collector down into close orbit, conveniently close to the *Layden*. With that done, I stood up and headed out of the captain's sanctum, finally arriving at the door outside the Cauldron.

"Gad Straben," said Harriet, dancing from clawed foot to foot. "The gun!"

I nodded solemnly, perhaps so. Gad Straben was evil enough.

Through its various other contacts about the Graveyard the Client had learned that, after the disappearance of a black AI called Penny Royal, salvagers had finally plucked up the courage to venture to the AI's original home base. This was a wanderer planetoid wormed through with numerous tunnels. As always they had gone there for technology and, before some event burned up everything inside that small world, it was rumoured that Gad Straben had managed to obtain some objects of value, things that might be an elements of some war time weapon, and he had begun to put out feelers, make enquiries . . . The Client wanted them. The Client hoped pieces of the farcaster could at last be obtained.

"But scraping the barrel," Harriet opined.

I studied her carefully. It must be one of her good days because she was showing a lot more intelligence than usual.

I nodded. After searching for so long it seemed increasingly unlikely we would ever find any part of the farcaster, or that it even existed at all. This item supposedly obtained by Gad Straben might even be our last shot and I might be recalled at last. My hand strayed down to my hip, fingers tapping there for a moment. I noted Harriet watching closely and quickly withdrew it.

"Yes, we are," I agreed. "The Client has less chance of finding what it wants now than before." I paused for a second, then shuddered, feeling a little stab of the Client's influence over my mind. It was time to start acting.

Straben's organisation was a criminal one, salvage being a mere sideline, and he was as paranoid as all who ran such concerns in the Graveyard had to be if they were to survive, so I had to both act fast, but take care. There were risks associated with getting too drastic in the Graveyard. It might be styled as a kind of anything-goes no-man's-land but that wasn't true. It was a volume of space in critical balance; a buffer zone between the Polity and the prador and both sides watched it intently.

"Do we have enough for Hobbs' Street?" Harriet asked.

I nodded. "One hundred ready to go," I surveyed the twenty thetics in the corridor, now no longer somnolent but not really showing any inadvertent movements associated with real life.

"Have you spoken to John Hobbs yet?" she asked.

I looked at her again. She had suddenly become a lot more coherent, a lot more intelligent, just like the Harriet I had used to know. She was asking the right questions now when all I had come to expect of her was child-like demands for her version of fun.

The Molonor moon base, until thirty years ago, had been essentially lawless, but then one salvage hunter became much annoyed with protection costs and damage to his operation by the constant squabbles between the criminal elements there. After a particularly rich find he used his newly acquired wealth to hire in some hoopers to make the place more amenable to his operation. After a brief year of chaotic readjustment which resulted in many crime lords ending up being processed into fertilizer, John Hobbs became the ruler there. He allowed criminals to come and do business, spend their wealth there, establish their bases, but did not allow them to bring their fights with them.

"He was surprisingly helpful."

She tilted her head slightly to one side, waiting for an explanation.

"He could have been a problem, but for his hoopers and our old association," I explained. "Hobbs tolerates a lot, but some of the criminals down there he doesn't like at all. He's only too willing to turn a blind eye to anything that might happen in Straben's headquarters."

Still that tilted head.

"Coring," I finished.

Harriet straightened up. "I see."

"Meanwhile," I continued, "we might not have to go to Hobb's Street at all, since a less risky opportunity has presented itself. I'm taking us into orbit close to one of Straben's ships, the *Layden*, which is here."

"Sphere Two?" Harriet suggested.

"Certainly," I nodded, then stabbing a thumb towards the twenty thetics. "These are programmed for basic obedience and combat—nothing fancy. They'll do." I now turned to face the thetics. "Automatics should have the rest ready for Hobbs Street should we need them."

The thetics hadn't been humanized, but that was not necessary for what I intended. I checked the coloured bar codes on their combat armour then selected the commander of this unit.

"Bring your men with me," I instructed.

The commander, unable to speak, dipped its head in acquiescence. When I mounted my scooter and set off the whole unit turned neatly as one and broke into a jog to keep up. By the time I reached an access tube to Sphere Two they were panting and their white skins were sheened with sweat. Harriet wasn't out of breath at all. I dismounted and walked over to palm the control to the tunnel door. As it slid open I stepped to one side and again addressed the thetic commander. "Enter and secure yourselves in the acceleration chairs."

The thetics trooped inside.

"Are they necessary?" Harriet asked.

"Straben's carriers usually have a crew of between five and ten." I glanced at Harriet. "I know that's not too many for you and I but I want to be sure. Also, if we don't find what we're after here this can act as a test of this new batch so we can be sure of them before we hit Hobbs' Street. You remember the last time?"

Harriet dipped her reptilian head in acknowledgement. I'd sent a group of armed thetics against a single prador first-child—one of the many renegade prador in the Graveyard—guarding a store said to contain a Polity weapon, from the war, as usual. The moment the first-child fired on the thetics they had collapsed into a bubbling mass. Unstable plasm, and a perfect demonstration of why the Polity might have dumped this technology. I took out the prador with a particle cannon blast from the *Coin Collector*, but it had all been yet another waste of time. The Polity weapon had been the carcase of some insectile war drone—its mind burnt out long ago.

I turned away from Harriet, glad she had bought the lie I had just told her. The reality was that I didn't want her going first into that ship. She might be fast and deadly but armed only with claws and teeth she might well end up on the bad end of a pulse-rifle in such an enclosed environment. It hadn't happened before, but the feeling I had that things were somehow coming to an end was making me more protective of her.

Moving aside I now gazed through the slanting windows overlooking the bathysphere bay. Bathysphere Two—the *Coin Collector* had only two of these vehicles— had first been adapted for inter-ship travel, its line detached and chemical boosters affixed all around its rim. Its second adaptation had been mine: a big metal mouth extending around its main door, a leech-lock. This could attach to the hull of any ship, its rim digging in with microscopic diamond hooks and making a seal. It had come in very handy over the years.

Harriet followed the thetics in and, after a pause, I followed too. Inside, the thetics were, as instructed, sitting down in the concentric rings of seats and strapping down tightly, their rifles slotted into containers beside them. I headed over to the single seat before the adapted prador controls, sat down and hit the release button. Even as I secured my own straps the bathysphere jerked and set into motion. I turned on the screens and observed the space doors opening, then laid in the correct course. Harriet, meanwhile, squatted down beside me, her claws clenched around the floor grid.

"Shouldn't be too bumpy," I said.

"One I've heard before," Harriet replied.

In a moment we were out in vacuum, the chemical rockets firing to put us on the pre-programmed course. I glanced over to the door leading into the leech lock, hit a control and the door irised open. Within this, running on rails around the inner face of the lock, was a robot cutter that wielded a carbon-titanium thermic lance, tubed for feed-through of laser heating, oxygen, peroxide and catalytic nanospheres. It was the fastest way to cut through just about anything. I closed the iris door again. It was also messy, producing thick searing smoke and poisonous gases.

"Approaching vessel, what is your purpose!" a voice demanded from my console.

"I've got something for Gad Straben," I replied, now calling up an image of Straben's hauler on my array of hexagonal screens.

"Identify yourself!"

I turned on the visual feed and gazed at an unshaven face displayed in just one of the hexagons. The man's head was partially submerged in a half-helmet augmentation, and the one eye I could see widened in shocked recognition.

"I'm Tuppence," I said, just to be sure.

"Gad Straben is not here," said the man.

"Not a problem—I'll leave his gift with you."

"You are not to approach this ship. I will not allow docking!"

I lined up the boost and paused with my finger over the control to operate it. "Don't be so hostile. I'm sure Mr. Straben will be very interested in what I am bringing him."

"I know exactly who you are, Tuppence," replied the man. "If you approach any closer you will be fired upon."

Of course, many in the Graveyard knew of me, even though I'd been away for a couple of decades. Many had dealings with me, some coming off worse and some better. The likes of Straben had generally been the former kind.

"Oh well," I said, and hit boost.

The sudden acceleration tried to lever me sideways out of my chair, but I locked my body in place. Behind me a couple of the thetics made an odd warbling sound. At the same time I saw the *Layden* fire up its own engines to move away and two flashes on its hull marking the departure of two missiles. I watched them curve round and head towards Bathysphere Two, their drive flames growing in intensity like angry eyes.

"Incoming," I stated.

"No shit," said Harriet.

Gee forces now tried to throw me into the screens as the bathysphere turned to present its thickest armour to the missiles. They hit one after the other with shuddering crashes. The screens whited out for a second, then gradually came back on with sparkles of burning metal shooting past. It would take a lot more than what the hauler had available to penetrate even ancient prador armour. The *Layden* was now up very close, still trying to accelerate away but just having too much mass to shift quickly. I pointed at the screens with one finger and drew a target frame over part of its hull just behind the carrier shell.

"Impact in three, two, one . . ."

The force of the crash bent the supports of my chair so it hung sideways. A thetic, emitting a short squeal, slammed against the curved wall opposite the leech lock then, as the bathysphere rocked into stillness, dropped to the floor with a soggy thud. I checked on Harriet and saw that she'd torn up some of the floor grid, but had still managed to hang on. I unstrapped myself just as the thermic lance kicked off behind the iris door, roaring and hissing like some trapped demon. Standing, I checked on the rest of the thetics. One of them was reverting, its face now a shapeless mass, one of its gauntlets on the floor below and a white worm oozing from the sleeve of its combat armour. Another of them had completely deliquesced. Its suit was empty, a milky pool scattered with pink offal around its boots.

"Unstrap and prepare your weapons," I instructed the remainder.

As they obeyed, the thermic lance finished its work and a loud crash ensued. That was the hydraulic hammer smashing a disk of hull into the ship beyond. I reached down and hit the control for the iris door and it slid open to release a cloud of stinking smoke, slowly clearing as air filtration ramped up to a scream. The interior of the other ship was devastated: a burned and melted mess of interior walls, crash foam and fire retardants snowing, some fires still burning.

"Thetics," I called, while pointing into the other ship. "Go in there and secure the ship, try not to kill the one you saw me speaking to." They had just about enough intelligence to follow such an instruction. If there weren't any survivors it wouldn't matter too much—would just mean a bit more work inspecting the cargo, and checking the ship's log and other data stores.

In good order they moved into the other ship, silently passing instructions between themselves and splitting into two parties, one heading forwards and one to the stern. Just a minute later I heard a laser carbine firing, then pulse-rifle fire in return.

"Not too bad," said Harriet, now standing at my side and eyeing the two thetics that had failed, then the one that had smashed into the wall and was now slowly oozing from its suit.

"Standard ten per cent," I agreed, moving towards the iris door. I meant the two failures—the one that smashed into the wall could be counted as a casualty.

"What are you going to use?" Harriet asked. "Demolition charges?"

"In good time, Harriet," I replied. "We're here after information and, if we're lucky, maybe even the item salvaged from Penny Royal's planetoid—I want to check up on the cargo first."

Grav was out inside the *Layden*, so from the leech lock I propelled myself inwards to find my way to a central drop-shaft. The cargo area on ships like this was usually positioned ahead of the engines, so I turned right, soon having to push aside a floating corpse that could have served as a sieve. Shortly after that I observed a group of four thetics heading back towards me, and pulled myself to one side to allow them past. Further on I found two of their number leaking out of their suits, then another member of the crew—most of his head missing.

"In there," said Harriet, pausing at a side tube and sniffing.

I entered the tube and eyed the palm-locked doors, then drove my fist through one of them and tore it out of its frame and tossed it aside. The room within was racked out, the plastic frameworks filled with simple aluminium boxes the size of coffins. On seeing these I first felt disappointment, then a growing anger. There would be no salvage aboard this ship for its cargo was of a very different kind. I dragged one of the coffins out, pushed it down against the floor and tore off its lid.

Inside lay a naked woman, her body marked with circular blue scars and her head bald. Her eyes were open and she was breathing gently, but she showed utterly zero response to me. I slapped her face, hard, but all she did was slowly return her head to its original position. I reached in, cupped the back of her neck in one hand and hauled her up into a sitting position and studied the scars on her head.

"Fully cored and thralled, I reckon," said Harriet.

"So it would seem," I replied, releasing the woman and watching her slowly lie back like a damped box lid closing.

I pulled out another box and checked the contents of that, shoved it back in the rack and moved on to a square box at the end, pulled that out and opened it. This contained hexagonal objects each the size of a soup bowl, prador glyphs inscribed in their upper surfaces.

"Thrall control units," I said tightly, pausing to look at the number of those other coffin-sized boxes around me and wondering if the same number lay behind each door. "Let's see if our thetics managed to get us a captive."

Making my way up to the bridge of the hauler I noted another two thetics down and returning to their original form, but there were also two more crewmen riddled with pulse-rifle fire. Finally, entering the bridge I found four thetics pinning their captive to the floor, the rest milling about aimlessly, and another three of their kind floating through the air, partially dismembered and reverting—obviously having run afoul of their captive's laser carbine before they could bring him down.

"I want two of you to remain here to restrain the captive," I instructed. "The rest of you go back to the bathysphere, now."

The milling immediately ceased and the most of the thetics departed.

"Get him up off the floor," I instructed to the two remaining. The fight seemed to have gone out of him now, probably because of the shots to each of his legs and his right biceps. He was obviously in a great deal of pain.

"I have some questions," I said.

"Fuck . . . you," the man managed.

"My first question is: does your cargo consist of fully cored humans only? That is, are there any included who have been spider thralled."

"Why the hell . . . should I answer you?"

"Curious question to which I'm sure the answer must be obvious," I said. "If you don't answer me I will torture you until you either do answer me or you die. Harriet." I beckoned with one finger and Harriet turned away from a deliquescing thetic she had been sniffing. "His right hand do you think?"

Harriet walked right up to the man, nose to nose, then sniffed down his right arm, pausing for a while at the wound in his biceps them moving on down to his hand. She licked his hand, then lifted her head back up to gaze into his eyes.

"Crunchy," she said, exposing her teeth.

"Why do you want to know?" the man asked, trying to focus his gaze on me.

"Why do you want to know why I want to know?"

"I don't want to die."

I smiled tiredly turning away and heading over to the ship's controls. As I began to search for the ship's log and other data storage, I said, "All you need to know right now is that if you do not answer my question Harriet here will bite off and eat your right hand."

I glanced round in time to see the man seeming to brace himself, pull himself more upright. Returning to the controls I found myself puzzled by the lack of security, quickly locating the ship's log and transmitting it to the *Coin Collector* and receiving confirmation a moment later.

"The customer for this shipment . . . did not want spider thralls used because after a period of time they can be rejected by the body." The man paused, then continued in a rush, "I'm just the pilot—I'm not involved in the rest of it."

Ah, here's something, I thought to myself as I uncovered a number of encrypted files, then feeling slightly impatient, turned back to our prisoner.

"The customer presumably being a prador . . . So let me clarify," I said. "Each and every human being in your cargo has suffered the removal of both the brain and a portion of the spinal cord so is essentially just technologically animated meat. They're all dead."

"Yes . . . it's best . . . they don't suffer."

"I see." No one here to rescue then. I had done some questionable things in my time but what was being done here was utterly beyond the pale. I'd known that Straben's organisation was involved in the coring trade which was why I'd had no reservations about sending the thetics in like I had, and now I had complete confirmation.

"Next question." I held up a finger, then brought it down on the touch controls. The encrypted files refused to transmit. I stared at them for a moment, then banished them from the screen and called up a ship's schematic. "What did the salvagers find in Penny Royal's planetoid and where will that find be located now?"

"I don't know . . . I don't know what you're . . . talking about."

The schematic showed the location of this ship's mind—a second-child ganglion that was barely sentient. It merely acted as a data processor and stored none at all in itself. However, it had to store it somewhere. After a moment I had it. Smiling, I reached down and tore off the panel in front of my seat. In there I located a series of crystals plugged in like test-tubes in a rack. I detached optics, switched the rack over to its own power supply before detaching the external power feed and pulling the whole thing out. I now had the ship's collimated diamond data store. I could try to break into the files it contained and sort through the data myself, but there were terabytes of it here. Best to hand it over to Tank.

"You don't know about some item or items obtained from Penny Royal's planetoid?"

"No . . . I don't."

The man seemed to be telling the truth and really I didn't feel I had the time to check. Hobbs' Street had to be our next target and we needed to move swiftly.

"Thank you." I dipped my head in acknowledgement, then patted a hand against my left thigh. I could try out the *other* gun now, but that seemed mean, since Harriet hadn't seen much action here. I relented. "Harriet, you may kill him now."

The man shrieked as I stood up with the ship's data store and headed for the door glimpsing, as I went, Harriet pulling on something like a dog worrying a length of bloody rope. As I headed back towards the bathysphere I decided that first I would have the prador mind removed from this ship and transferred over to my own—a useful replacement should that thing in the tank finally expire, or should I, for whatever reason, want a ship mind that did not owe its loyalty to the Client. The best option then would be a kiloton thermite scatter bomb on a timer set to go off sometime after our visit to Hobbs Street. It would completely gut this ship, burn up its cargo and destroy its workings, including its U-drive and fusion reactor. The ship would then only have any value as scrap and one portion of Straben's organization would be defunct—and during this mission I would have cleaned up at least a small portion of the crap scattered about the Graveyard.

Hobbs' Street smelled odd, damp and sweet, but that wasn't due to the residents here but to an odd mutation of a terran honey fungus that had spread throughout the moon colony, running its mycelia through air vents, electrical ducting or any other opening available, sucking nutrients from spillages on the floors of hydroponics units or out of the soil of private gardens. I paused in my study of a clump of honey mushrooms sprouting from a crack in the foamstone pavement and considered the workings of coincidence. I had decided that here I would use the *other* gun, and there was a connection . . .

As I looked up an ancient hydrocar motored past. It was the cops, and I was surprised to see them. The car, a by-blow of flying saucer and Mercedes, had an assault drone like a huge grey copepod squatting on its roof. The vehicle was painted white with fluorescent blue circles decorating it—a colour scheme that had come to mean much the same as the black and white stripes of a wasp: danger. The driver and his mate, respectively a hulking man and an equally lethal looking woman, eyed me as they passed, the blue ring-shaped scars on their faces visible in the street lights.

"Probably here in the hope of picking up any strays," I said.

"There won't be any," said Harriet.

"They would probably like to join in," I continued. "John told me that he had some trouble dissuading his hoopers from contacting me and offering assistance."

Harriet dipped her head in acknowledgement. "Understandable, considering the history. Jay Hoop, his pirates and their coring operation weren't very popular on Spatterjay."

Weapons grade understatement, I thought. It surprised me that Straben had managed to keep his headquarters here at all.

"Here they come," said Harriet.

Hobbs' Street was crowded, it being one of the most popular thoroughfares here, and now it was becoming even more crowded. The thetics in the street where clad in a wide variety of clothing and their faces were concealed by syntheskin, but they hadn't managed to suppress their inclination to march along in neat squads like the soldiers they were meant to be. There were five street doors to Straben's conjoined buildings, which extended five floors up with the chainglass street roof attached across on top of the fifth. Fifty thetics were in the street, ten to each door, while a further seventy thetics clad in light space suits were, even now, moving into position up on the building's roofs, which were exposed to vacuum.

I watched, through the eyes of my artificial body and through pin-cams the thetics all wore in their clothing. I saw those up on the roof avoiding the heavily secured airlocks, consulting building blueprints and selecting areas over which they glued down atmosphere shelters, before beginning to cut through below, thus making their own airlocks. They would be inside within five minutes. Meanwhile, those down on the street were moving in on the doors with sticky bombs or sausages of thermite, depending on the design of door concerned. I began walking.

"So, Harriet," I said. "You seem a lot more coherent lately."

She glanced at me, her reptilian face unreadable. "Do I?"

"Undoubtedly," I said, watching her.

"I've never been incoherent," she argued.

"Not as such but—."

I couldn't take that further because a loud bang ensued, the explosion as bright as a welding arc and a gust of smoke blowing out into the street and then rising up towards the glass roof. People started yelling and running. It might have been thirty years since John Hobbs took control but there had still been incidents, and the people here still knew when it was best just to run. I noted that one of the doors had disappeared just as thermite flared further down the street and two more explosions ensued. I watched thetics pouring into three of the buildings, pulling short wide-blast sawn-off pulse rifles from under their coats. I saw thermite burn in a fast ring around an armoured door then a central charge blow it inwards. Just one more . . .

I glanced over towards the door concerned as a machine gun began firing in short bursts. An explosion took out the door, but from a stone-effect arch above it a lumpish ugly security drone had dropped on a pole and begun firing a miniature version of the Gatling cannons prador favoured. In annoyance I saw thetics being torn apart, even one civilian who had been a bit tardy going down. I reached down and flipped open the patches on my trousers, drew my QC laser and plugged in its power lead, then I drew the *other* gun, noting Harriet now watching me intently. Meanwhile a thetic opened out a telescopic launcher, shouldered it and put a missile into the door arch. The drone arced smoking and bouncing out into the street.

"Harriet—" I began, but didn't get to finish as she shot off and went through the door concerned. Obviously the most secure doorway was the one into the building I most wanted to enter because, if my data was correct, Gad Straben himself had entered here just a few hours ago. I now entered to be greeted by the sound of gunfire and the commingled screams of pain and terror which were the usual result of Harriet's presence. It occurred to me that she might have been uncomfortable about my questioning and that was why she had gone ahead, but why this occurred to me I don't know.

Through pin cams on their clothing I observed the thetics in the other buildings moving from room to room and killing anyone who resisted, just so long as they weren't Straben. It was brutal, but then Straben's organization was brutal and any working for it had to know they were culpable in mass murder. Those on the roof were now in too and working their way down—just as efficient and methodical as those working up from below—but also just as indifferent to personal survival. I reckoned on walking away from here with maybe just twenty or so surviving thetics. The rest would crawl off and die completely to become food for the honey fungus, or else turn into something nasty in the drains.

Directing my course by pin-cam feeds I climbed the stairs since the building's drop-shafts were keyed to staff ID tags and wouldn't work for anyone else. Most of the action was now taking place on the third floor. At the second floor some man in businesswear carrying a heavy flack gun charged down, skidded to a stop on a landing and took aim. I raised my other gun just as a flack round exploded against the wall behind me and peppered me with shrapnel, then changed my mind and raised my QC laser, a short while afterwards stepping over the burning corpse.

By the time I reached the third floor it was all over. The main data room looked like an abattoir and over in one corner Harriet was tearing chunks off of some rather corpulent individual and gobbling them down. Many of the consoles were smashed and smoking, holo-displays flickering through the air like panicked spectres and flimsy screens seemed to burn with internal blue fires. Over to one side a chainglass window overlooked all this, plush office space inside and there, working a console in frenetic panic, sat Gad Straben. I ran over to the door—armoured of course— kicked it hard then swore as my other boot went straight down through the floor and the door remained in place.

"Get me a charge!" I shouted, heaving my leg back out of the hole.

There were only two surviving thetics in the room, and they were guarding two women and a man who lay face down with their hands behind their heads.

"You three," I said, brushing debris from my trousers as I walked over. When they looked up I continued, "Get up and go," and stabbed a finger towards the door. They slowly stood up, eyeing me as I replaced my weapons in their holes in my legs and closed them up, then took off just as fast as they could. They were probably only temporary employees of Straben since they hadn't resisted, so whether they lived or died was a matter of indifference to me. I turned to the two thetics.

"I want an explosive charge to get through that door," I said concisely, since neither of them had understood me the first time.

One of them went over to one of its fellows, who was quietly deliquescing in a corner, pulled some sticky bombs from his belt and returned with them. I stared at them for a moment then went over to the dead thetic myself and checked its belt. There—just what I needed. I detached a circular object like a coaster and took it over to the office window, slapped it against the chainglass and hit the pressure button at its centre. With a whumph the chainglass turned to white powder and collapsed to the floor. I stepped over the ledge and into the office, seeing Straben simply stand and hold out empty hands.

"You move quickly," he said.

Straben was a slightly fat man with a bald rounded head. He was clad in businesswear and looked like some Polity executive styling his appearance on some antediluvian fashion. I ignored him for a moment, carefully studying my surroundings.

A glass-fronted case along one wall contained a variety of ghoulish antiques: a spider thrall and a full-core thrall, a couple of slave collars and an old automatic pistol. These were all the kind of objects you could obtain from dealers out of Spatterjay. I watched a nano-paint picture transit to its next image—a painting of a hooder coming down on some man in ECS uniform. Then I strolled over to the desk, then round it, and stood facing Straben.

"I move quickly?" I enquired mildly.

"You arrived in the Graveyard only a few days ago," said Straben, then with a shrug, "I didn't expect you to act so quickly."

I looked at the desk, noting a flimsy screen up out of the surface and the holographic virtual control Straben had been using a moment ago. The screen was blank. I tried my hand in the control but it wouldn't respond to me.

"It's genetically coded to me," he said.

"I could always cut off your hand," I suggested.

"That won't work either," said Straben, for the very first time showing some sign of anxiety.

I gazed at him for a second, then waved him out into the main office space. He nodded congenially and walked over to where the window had been and stepped through.

"Questions now?" he asked.

"Yes, questions," I replied.

Straben halted and turned towards me, tilted his head irritatingly like Harriet, and waited.

"So," I said, "was it your intention to try and seize the *Coin Collector*?"

Straben gazed at me in apparent puzzlement. "Certainly not. It was my intention to sell you some valuable artefacts I have obtained." He turned slowly to survey the wreckage around him. "But it seems I was mistakenly under the impression that you were a reasonable man I could do business with."

I fought down another surge of irritation. We couldn't stay here much longer. John Hobbs might have decided to look the other way but he wouldn't do so for much longer. There would be reports going in of an incident here and he would have to respond.

"From Penny Royal's planetoid?" I suggested.

"Yes," said Straben. "I have them in a secure location and, despite this unfortunate mess," Straben gestured about himself. "I am still prepared to do business."

"So which of your vessels salvaged them?" I asked.

"The *Cadiz*—it got there before Hobbs or any of the other vultures." Straben smiled as if in pleasant recollection. He was certainly a cool customer and was now growing more confident. "The objects concerned seem to be part of something larger and certainly contain U-space tech, though precisely what they are for is a puzzle."

The objects sounded precisely like what the Client was seeking, which was beyond suspicious. It was also the case that before coming down here I'd thoroughly checked the relevant details Tank had taken from the *Layden*'s data store. Straben was lying, though to what degree and precisely what his aims were was unclear.

"Wrong answer," I said. "The *Cadiz* was in the prador Kingdom at the time."

Straben hid his shock well, but it was evident. "Do you honestly think I keep *precise* records of my ship itineraries?"

"Possibly not." I shrugged. "But apparently you shut down your salvage operation decades ago." I paused contemplatively for a moment. "In fact, as I understand it, John Hobbs would be the best to ask about artefacts from the planetoid since it seems his salvagers were the only ones that went there before everything of value was obliterated by some sort of chain reaction, and that the artefacts he did obtain were routed directly to the Polity."

"So John Hobbs might tell you," said Straben, obviously thinking quickly now. "He was trying to nail down the market—make it exclusive."

He paused, searching for further excuses and lies, so I quickly interjected, "Perhaps you could tell me about the warehouse you've been renovating—the one located on an asteroid in this system." He definitely couldn't hide his shock now. "Perhaps you might like to tell me why you felt the need to kit out the place with so much armament along with a hardfield caging system?"

"How can you—"

"You set the bait and that's the trap," I said.

Now he was lost for words. I gave him a little while, but he lost the struggle as Harriet moved up to stand beside him, leaned her head down and gave him a long sniff.

"No more lies," I said turning to Harriet. "Usual method: if he lies again I give you the nod and you bite off his right hand."

Harriet danced from foot to foot, champed her jaws then as usual licked round her mouth with her long red tongue.

"Now," I continued, "what exactly is all this about?"

Straben just stood staring at Harriet for a long while. He shrugged, then sighed.

"It's about the reward," he said.

"What reward?"

"I will need guarantees," the man replied.

"You can guarantee that if you don't answer my questions Harriet will first eat your hands. If that doesn't work she'll start on you from the feet up."

"You are rather brutal and uncivilized in your dealings," Straben observed primly.

That was it; that was the limit. A man who cored and thralled human beings to sell the prador was calling *me* uncivilized? I reached down to my thigh, opened the patch in my trousers then mentally unlocked the hatch in my leg there. I took out the *other* gun and weighed it in my hand. Harriet, noting this, look a pace back. It didn't look like much—just a heavy chromed revolver.

"Your last chance," I said mildly.

Straben could obviously see I was feeling a bit testy. He quickly said, "A fortune in any form required, a Polity amnesty for all crimes *and* a free fifty-year pass into the Kingdom ratified by the King himself."

Puzzling. The Polity never gave amnesties to the likes of Straben, and that the Kingdom and the Polity had agreed on some joint reward seemed just as unlikely.

"There's some heavyweight action behind it," Straben continued, now taking a step back and resting his weight back against one of the desks here. "I couldn't believe it at first but it really checks out." He gestured vaguely upwards. "Polity agents out there and direct confirmation from one of the watch station AIs. The King's Guard are involved too. I don't know what you are involved in but both the prador and the Polity desperately want to get hold of you."

"It is feasible that such rewards might be offered to negate some very serious threat."

It took me a moment to realize that Harriet had spoken. I eyed her carefully. Once we were back aboard the *Coin Collector* I felt we needed to have a long talk, and I needed to scan what was going on inside that reptilian skull of hers. However, I knew precisely what she was implying.

"I need to talk to the Client," I said.

"Yes, I think you do," Harriet agreed. "Shall we finish up here?" She tilted her head slightly, directing her gaze towards the gun I held.

There was nothing more to be learned from Straben. I returned my attention to the man and fired once, the kick jerking the barrel up and the shot going into his stomach and flinging him back across the desk. Despite that, the impact of the bullet had been toned down for the human form, since this gun had been designed to punch bullets through a prador's natural armour.

The man lay gasping, then abruptly jerked, stretched out flat and went into convulsions. Black threads spread across his skin and his flesh started swelling. He emitted a gargling scream then slumped into stillness just as brown sprouts broke out of his skin like spear points, then began to swell at their tips. These swellings, each rapidly growing to the size of a tennis ball, turned a darker brown and acquired widely scattered black scales.

"Fascinating," said Harriet. "So it doesn't take control of the host—just kills quickly?"

"It's weaponized," I replied. "There's no advantage in spread by it keeping the host alive since that comes with sporulation—and at a point of growth the host cannot survive."

Harriet glanced round at me. "But sporulation has been retarded I presume?"

"It has—I don't want to kill off the whole colony here."

She nodded thoughtfully, then asked, "I am right in assuming that this is based on *ophiocordyceps unilateralis* or as it is known as on Earth, the 'zombie ant fungus?'"

"It is," I said, slightly stunned by her sharpness.

"And that is just one of your bullets?"

"Yes."

"Fascinating," she repeated.

This sharp new Harriet would be, I thought, fascinated to know that this particular weaponized parasitic fungus would also be an effective way to kill another creature, a multiply renewing one. But that wasn't something I wanted to think about too much, especially with another *conversation* due with the Client . . .

Upon returning to the *Coin Collector* I delayed and delayed, but the Client was not to be denied—always testing its connections to my mind, always *pushing*.

Time.

The stabbing sensation in my head told me I had delayed too long. I closed my eyes and began numbing all the nerve connections to my artificial body, highlighting the other intrusive connections in my skull. The link, between me and the thing sitting in the tank, which in turn connected to the ship's U-space communicator, opened up. And all at once I returned to hell.

Rage and suspicion came first, with that forever present undercurrent of loss. I stretched a hundred feet tall; a conjoined chain of insect forms reaching towards the roof of the deep volcanic chamber, a boiling wind blowing across the nearby lake of lava raising the temperature just enough. Hive creature and hive, perpetually dying and giving birth, immortal, the Client clung now to ersatz trunk of a giant tree being fashioned of silica crystals by one of its exoforms—a thing like a giant horseshoe crab suspended from the roof by a long jointed tail. It read me, and peeled its upper section from the tree in its fear, emitting a pheromone fog, distributing it with the beating of glassy wings. Exoforms down below like manta rays on spider legs, hoovering up and crunching down old fallen husks from past renewals, bleated and bumped against each other in bewilderment.

Synaesthetic interpreters finally cut in as I contained a scream in my skull, and turned complex organic chemicals to something I could truly understand. Then came a pause, with a scene replaying in my mind: my killing of Gad Straben. I felt an avidity, then came words.

"It is time for you to come to me," the Client told me, a whole avalanche of meaning falling in behind the words. "The danger is too great."

The connection faded. Time passed and I reconnected to my artificial body. I sat for an hour in my chair feeling as if on the point of death and slowly, ever so slowly, brought myself back to my world.

"Harriet," I said, my voice grating.

"I'm here," she replied from very close by.

"It seems our search must end because the Client thinks the danger from the Polity and the Kingdom is too great," I said, testing the words out loud for their veracity.

"The search is over," said Harriet, and there seemed a lot more meaning behind her words than plain parroting. She then asked, "You have the coordinates?"

I looked around at her. She was standing right beside my chair and seemed far too eager and interested for my liking. I suddenly knew, with absolute certainty, that to supply her with those coordinates would put me in immediate danger. How did I know? I'm not sure, but it seemed to me the old Harriet was right back—the one I trusted to complete a mission for pay, but no more than that.

"The coordinates have been sent, but not to me," I lied, now sitting upright. "Tank has them."

Harriet swung round to gaze at the object concerned and seemed about to say something more when the drag of the ineffable took us, and the *Coin Collector* entered U-space. I stood up, Harriet swinging her attention back towards me. I did not know how far we would have to travel to reach the Client's location but, this being an ancient prador vessel I knew it would probably have to drop out of U-space to cool off, and I felt that on those occasions I would have to watch Harriet very closely.

During the first time the *Coin Collector* surfaced from U-space I was prepared, but Harriet seemed to go into that childlike lost puppy phase and showed no sign of acting against me in any way. I even gave her some very dangerous openings—ones that might have resulted in me ending up in pieces on the deck, but she ignored them. Perhaps I had been deluding myself about her? Perhaps I was so used to what had seemed to be her mental decline that my suspicions had only been aroused by it ceasing and reversing? I decided thereafter to take some simple precautions when around her, like always carrying my two weapons, but no more than that. She deserved at least some of my trust, and I had work to do.

The Client had summoned me to it and perforce I had to go, but its orders were no more complex than a summons and that gave me some freedom of action. I started with the thetics, wiping their base programming and designing something of my own. I needed them to be able to carry out certain instructions and, most difficult of all, I needed them to be able to continue carrying out those instructions even if I ordered them to do otherwise. The simple reality was that in close proximity the Client would be able to seize complete control of my mind and thus, through me, the thetics. I needed them to continue, to give distraction, to give me a chance . . .

The second time we surfaced from U-space Harriet came and found me in the Captain's Sanctum, deeply internalized, trying to gauge what resistance I had to the Client's control of me, if any at all. She could have killed me then because I was completely vulnerable what with most of my nervous system shut down. Instead she just walked over to stand before me and, as I returned to a normal state of consciousness and responsiveness, she spoke.

"There's something you need to see," she said.

"What?" I asked.

She just turned around and headed back towards the door. I weighed pros and cons as I stood up, then I decided to follow her. It struck me as unlikely she was leading me somewhere so as to attack me, since she could have done the job just then. She waited outside the sanctum beside the scooter I had last used to get here, dipped her head towards it, then turned and set off along the corridor. I mounted up and followed, and with a glance back she increased her pace. She led me into the cargo section of the ship, which was a place I did not often visit, then to a wide square door into a particular hold space. As I dismounted I recognized this door at once, but kept my own counsel as she nosed the control beside it to send it rumbling and shuddering to one side.

I followed her in and surveyed my surroundings as the lights came on. The space was three hundred feet square and the cargo it contained had not changed much over the years since I had last been here. The large first-child who had been the captain of this ship rested in one corner like a crashed flying saucer, most of its limbs still intact but now one of its claws having dropped away. Further along one wall from this prador corpse, second-children had been stacked like, well, crabs on a seafood stall. This stack had collapsed on one side and noting some movement there I walked over. As I approached an eight inch long trilobite louse scuttled out, heading straight for my legs. I kicked it hard, slamming it into the wall above the stack of second-child carapaces.

"It's because of the ship recharging with air," I said. "There must have been ship louse eggs somewhere, and moisture in the air must have reversed the desiccation of these." I gestured to the dead before me, including a mass of third-children and smaller prador infants piled in the further corner

I hadn't seen anything but dead ship lice aboard when I returned to consciousness here a century ago. Then the ship entire had been almost in vacuum, and when I first ventured down here the erstwhile crew had been vacuum dried. Gradually the ship's automatic systems had recharged the whole vessel with air, but it had taken decades.

"The lice are unimportant," Harriet intoned, her seriousness undermined when she had to kick away a louse trying to crawl up her leg.

"I've seen all this," I said, gesturing around. "I know that the Client slaughtered the prador aboard. So what, the prador slaughtered its entire species." I didn't mention how the way the corpses had been sorted and neatly stacked always bothered me. Had the Client kept these as a food source? Could it actually ingest this alien meat?

"You've seen all this," Harriet parroted.

She abruptly turned away and paced across the hold to the far wall. I sighed and walked after her, but as I drew closer I suddenly realized that there was another square door in this far wall. I paused, scanned about myself, then realized I had never spotted it before because I'd never felt any inclination to walk this far into this dim mausoleum. Harriet nosed a control beside this new door and, rumbling and shaking, it too drew open. I followed her inside.

More dead, I realized, and more ship lice. I gazed at the neat heap—stacked like firewood—for a couple of seconds before reality caught up with me. These weren't prador; they were human corpses. I stood staring for a long drawn-out moment, then forced myself into motion and walked over to inspect them more closely. The corpses here were also vacuum dried and many of them had suffered the depredations of ship lice and in places had been chewed down to the bone. I turned my attention to one nearby that had obviously been dragged from the stack by lice and completely stripped of flesh. The lice had ignored the uniform, obviously getting inside it to dine on the meat. I recognized the uniform at once. I was looking at the skeleton of an ECS commando.

Moving closer, I next saw further uniforms, but also a lot of casual dress, a high proportion of clean-room labwear and the occasional spacesuit and vacuum survival suit. There had to be over a hundred people here.

"You've seen this?" Harriet enquired.

"No," I replied.

"Do you remember?"

I turned towards her. "No, I don't."

I felt slightly sick as I turned away. It must have been a wholly psychological feeling since my artificial body was incapable of nausea. So why had Harriet brought me here to see this? I didn't know, all I did know was that I was standing beside the entire scientific team—plus ECS security personnel—that had been sent to liaise with the Client. I began to head out, then paused now I could see what lay beside the door I'd come in through. I eyed a glittering stack of crystal fragments, ten human corpses untouched by desiccation or decay because, of course, they weren't human but Golem androids. Beside them rested two huge metal beetles, motionless, no light gleaming in their crystal eyes: war drones. It seemed the Client had killed the AI complement of that mission too.

I headed out of the hold.

The moon was highly volcanic because it was one of many similarly sized moons irregularly orbiting an ice giant. It seemed that they often tore at each other gravitationally, and were torn at by the giant they orbited. In astronomical terms the whole system was unstable and, running a model of it, I saw that at least two of these moons would be shattered in about a hundred thousand years time, thereafter the system would stabilize with an asteroid ring.

"Do you have something you wish to tell me?" I asked Harriet as I gazed at the images displayed in the hexagonal screens.

"I have nothing I can say to you yet," she replied.

Was that because we were too close to the Client now? I could feel its influence reaching out to me, demanding, dictatorial. Coordinates sat clear in my mind as the *Coin Collector* lurched under fusion drive, dropping lower and decelerating. Even if I wanted to stop this, to go away and never head for those coordinates, I couldn't, for Tank controlled the ship.

The world was mostly black, etched with red veins and red maculae, white at their centres with hot eruptions, smears of grey ash spread equatorially from these. It drew closer and closer, the great ship's engines roaring and the whole vessel shuddering around us.

"Why are we landing?" Harriet asked.

The question was obviously rhetorical.

"Perhaps," she continued, "the bathyspheres are not large enough to convey what needs to be conveyed."

I had never described the Client to her, so was she guessing or did she know? It was true, nevertheless, that if the Client wanted to move itself and its multitude of minions aboard this ship, then the ship had to land. What did this then mean for me?

Soon the horizon was an arc across the whole array of screens before me and we seemed to be coming down on a relatively stable plain before a range of mountains like diseased fangs. Scanning gave me a cave system deep in those mountains, precisely at the location of the coordinates in my mind, while the *Coin Collector* aimed to land to one side of them. I stood up and headed for the door, Harriet as usual close behind me. As I mounted my scooter I then sent orders from my artificial body—orders I hoped I could not rescind.

While heading down into the bowels of the ship I turned to Harriet, who was pacing easily at my side. "The air out there isn't breathable."

She flicked her head once. "It doesn't matter—I ceased to need breathable air long ago."

"So you underwent more modifications than I know about?"

"Some," she replied.

Lower down the air in the ship was laced with sulphur and it was hot. It ceased to be breathable for a human being, or any creature that needed oxygen, on the lower level, as we approached a massive open door with a ramp extending from it to the charred ground below. I parked my scooter beside the door, hoping I would be able to return to use it, but doubtful of that, and I began walking down. My artificial lungs had by now ceased to process what they were breathing and my body had gone over to power cells and stored supplies.

"What are they?" Harriet asked.

I peered out across the plain at the four creatures approaching. They looked like manta rays hovering just above the ground as they swept towards us, but upping the magnification of my eyes I could then pick out the blur of insect legs moving underneath them.

"Exoforms is what we called them," I replied. "The Client is a hive creature and a hive all in one, perpetually conjoined, being born and dying all in one and able to meddle at genetic levels with its parts. It is a natural bio-technician, geneticist, and makes forms like this to interact with environments outside its preferred one. It was a form something like these that acted as a translator."

"So your memories are clearer," Harriet suggested, as we proceeded on down.

I realized they were, and I remembered the terrible anger of the Client when the AIs shut down the project, though the results of that anger were unclear but for those corpses in the hold, just as were details of the project itself before that, and precisely how it had been closed down. I wondered only then: how could the farcaster have been broken up and taken away if the whole team, including its AIs, had been slaughtered?

The ramp was shaking—perpetual tremors being transmitted from the ground and through it to my feet—but the new rumble was something else. As I stepped off onto a surface of shattered and then heat-fused chunks of obsidian, I turned.

"Here they come," I said, and stepped aside.

The thetics were already a quarter of the way down the ramp, over two hundred of them now. They were all clad in hard shell spacesuits of a combat design that enabled them to move quickly. They came down in good order at a steady trot, in neat rectangular formations. At the base of the ramp they spread out, utterly ignoring me, following their orders. Two groups of them then went down into firing positions and pulse-rifle fire cut through the poisonous air towards the approaching exoforms. Two of them immediately went down, ploughing into the ground like crashing gravcars. Two more swept to one side, but then a missile from a shoulder launcher hit between them and sent them tumbling. The thetics then moved on at a run, heading for the coordinates in my mind.

The Client was very very disappointed in me and I now expected punishing pain which, I felt sure, I could now resist for long enough. I followed the thetics out, my mental defences as tight and as ready as they could be. But there was no attack, and in those parts of my mind where the Client had its grip, all contact slid into something completely alien—beyond my understanding.

"It's a good plan," Harriet opined, "but for the Client's defences and its absolute hold on you."

"What do you mean?" I asked, now breaking into a fast loping run.

"I mean," said my troodon companion, easily keeping pace with me. "You ordered the thetics to go in after the Client and attack it, and then you disconnected yourself from them so you could issue no further orders, so the Client could not force you to order them to desist."

"And?"

"You hoped that if they didn't kill it they would at least keep it distracted enough for you to get close and use the weapon you designed specifically to kill it."

"You seem to know rather a lot," I suggested.

A battle now raged ahead of us, at the foot of the mountains. We reached it just as it was terminating, exoforms like giant horseshoe crabs turned over and smoking like wrecked tanks, thetics reverting in the grip of long white worms, others pouring out of suits torn apart by ice-pick mandibles. But still there were many left, all funnelling into the wide cave mouth ahead. I followed them in.

At last, said the Client, perfectly understandable.

The cave sloped down, ever darker, then being lit by a hellish glow. The chamber seemed to have no limits; it seemed as if I had walked through some Narnian doorway out onto the surface of a hotter brighter world. Ahead of me I saw thetics keeling over, one after another and I couldn't see what was killing them. I kept walking; found I could not stop walking. I stepped over and past hard shell suits and observed dissolving faces behind chainglass visors. Harriet was still beside me and I glanced across at her.

Kill me now, I thought, but couldn't say.

"It's killing them with the farcaster," she said, dipping her head to indicate what lay ahead.

The Client was wound around its crystal tree, large wasp-like segments conjoined in a great snake hundreds of feet long. At its head was the primary form which I could see was an adult some days away from death, and yet to be cast away like those husks scattered on the ground all around to allow the next creature-segment take over. At its tail its terminal segment was giving birth to another, which would remain attached and in its turn give birth. The whole cycle—the time it took for the terminal form to reach the head—was just solstan months long. Meanwhile, all those segments fed, chewing down an odd rubbery nectar exuded by the crystal tree, which in turn extracted the materials to make it from the ground below, and from the husks the exoforms fed to its nanomachine roots. But there was something else about that tree too. It fed the Client, supported the Client, and was the totality of its technology and, near its head, a crystal flower had bloomed: the farcaster.

Soon I was circumventing the husks of former head segments. Reaching the base of the tree I saw the last of the thetics collapsing around me, and I went down on my knees. I don't know whether that was my own impulse or an instruction from the creature rearing high above me. I managed to turn my head slightly, searching for Harriet, just in time to see her huff out a haze of smoke, slump, and then sprawl beside me.

I'd let her down. I'd been careless. I felt a surge of grief immediately followed by a dead dark hopelessness. What was the point now? What was the point of . . . continuing?

Give me the gun, said the Client.

The farcaster was here and my search had been a pointless one. I just couldn't understand, I just couldn't . . . and then I saw it.

The human body lay inside some kind of pod at the foot of the tree, almost like a flower yet to open. Through crystal distortions I could see it nestled in white snakes, some attached to it, small ones around the gaping wound in its skull, a large one entering its mouth, others attached here and there around a body that had been broken and torn. And through crystal distortions I recognized my own face.

Give me the gun. It wasn't an instruction in human language but a need, a chemical pattern, a chain of pheromones perpetually renewing. Somehow I found the strength to resist, and saw the snakes wriggling about my doppelganger lying under crystal ahead.

No, I managed.

It could send one of its exoforms to take me apart and thereafter seize the gun. I knew with absolute certainty that it had finished with me. I was a tool it had employed and all its tools died when their usefulness was at an end. I knew with utter certainty that I was going to die. I just did not want to die in ignorance.

Explain, I tried.

The Client at once understood that I accepted defeat and death, and relented.

The pressure came off and I found myself deeper in the Client's distributed mind, ever dying and ever renewing. Chemical language offered itself and I accepted. I was me and the Client again and its memories opened. Of course the Client was able to manipulate its own genes and its own biology and, like all its kind, that manipulation was part of it and not some logically refined science. The Client's species did have its geneticists, its bio-techs and even its bio-warfare experts, but the Client wasn't one of them. That had been lie. However, it was an expert and it was that expertise that had enabled it to escape. It was an expert in U-space tech, it was an alien Iversus Skaidon, and it had built the farcaster.

I understood now what had killed the thetics and Harriet: energy dense micro-explosives no larger than spores but detonating inside with the force of gunshots. The Client had farcast such explosives into the prador aboard the *Coin Collector*, draining its limited supply of energy and those same explosives, before escaping aboard that ship so long ago, the worlds of its kind burning and tearing apart under prador kamikaze assault.

Why not all, I wondered.

It could have made more of these explosives and steadily annihilated every prador in existence, surely? No, because there were trillions of prador and each first-child or second-child, as the Client had learned, could not be killed with just one such explosive. And here was the complete killer of that idea: it needed to know the precise locations of its targets. It needed help; it needed spotters to locate prime target like father-captains, like the King of the prador. And it needed a weapon that once farcast into such a target would then wipe out all the prador around it—it's family. That's where the Polity came in, and that's where I came in: one of the Polity's prime biowarfare experts.

I felt the rage again. The orders had been explicit: nothing was to remain. Even as I hit the destruct to turn all my computer files to atomic dust and burn up my samples in thousand Watt laser bursts, the micro-dense explosives tore me apart, and I knew nothing. Now, however, I understood how little trust the Client had of its allies, how it had targeted them all, killing all the humans in the team, shattering the crystal minds of all the AIs. Then, realizing its mistake, it had come for me, and incorporated me—drawn me in like a damaged but still useful exoform.

But the journey, why the pointless search?

The Client needed me separate from it because as an exoform close to it I could pick up on some of its thoughts and might uncover the lie I had been told, and learn that the farcaster was intact and that what it wanted was the bio-weapon I had destroyed. That separation was maintained by the first-child ganglion in the tank and U-space communications that could be shut down in an instant. With our minds so close, why could it not take the design of that weapon straight from my brain? It couldn't, because it wasn't there—it was lost with a large chunk of my brain. However, the skills were still there and I was capable of remaking it.

It took the Client many years to build my avatar. It used one of the Golem whose mind it had destroyed, it used elements of the thetic program, which had been the product of one of the research team it had killed, and it did the best it could. It needed me motivated to rebuild that weapon. My motivation was an ersatz freedom, maintained by my ostensible separation from the Client and the firm knowledge that the bioweapon would work as well against it as against the prador. I responded as predicted. I remade that weapon, it resided aboard the *Coin Collector*, and it resided inside the bullets in the gun inside my thigh.

Give me the gun.

I realized that the action of handing over that weapon wasn't the main thing the Client required, but its consequence. The knowledge was locked inside me and, by handing over the gun, I would unlock it.

Trillions of prador. I didn't like them very much but such a genocide appalled me. The Client had its farcaster—had never been without it—and shortly it would have the weapon to annihilate them all. How it intended to target them I didn't know, but it could find a way for it had the time of an immortal and the utter certainty of purpose. I put up futile resistance and agony filled my skull, not the one in my artificial body, but in that one over there, wrapped in worms and entombed in crystal. My vision was blurred as I stared at the seared ground and fought for, I don't know, at least some redemption from what was to ensue. Then my vision cleared a little, and I saw a strange thing.

Ten objects lay scattered across the ground in front of me. They were, colourful curved spikes, shocking pink.

I gave up, simultaneously sending the signal to open the hatch in my thigh while reaching down to tear aside the canvas flap. My hand closed around the butt of my fungus gun and I withdrew it, all the knowledge of what its bullets incorporated riding up inside me. I really wanted to aim the weapon at the Client and pull the trigger, but that was utterly beyond me. I turned it, rested it in the flat of my hand and presented it. Already the Client was looping down, both mentally and physically multiple wings roaring to support its weight, its wasp-like leading segment reaching out with four limbs terminating in hands that seemed to be collections of black fish hooks, black hooks in my skull too.

But it was the hand of a reptile, sans claws, that took the gun.

"Tuppence," said a voice, but I was still in that moment.

I saw Harriet aiming the gun with a dexterity she had seemingly not possessed in many decades. One shot went into the Client's leading segment, into its thorax which in turn was partially melded to the head of the segment behind. The second shot went in two segments back from that. Then another two shots went in widely spaced, one after another. The hooks withdrew from my mind but I was rigid with agony, the Client's agony. I managed to turn my head in time to see Harriet flung aside by a detonation in her side. It tore a hole, but what was revealed inside wasn't bloody, but hard and glittery. She rolled, came up again and fired the remaining two shots.

"Tuppence."

A roaring scream filled the cavern as of a whole crowd being thrown into a furnace. The Client reared back and wrapped itself around its tree, black lines rapidly spreading from the bullet impact sites. It shed its forward form, birthed behind, sucked on a crystal tree suddenly turned milk white as it filled with nutrient. It birthed and shed in quick succession, its discarded segments falling about me not as dry husks but soggy and heavy as any corpse. I saw one issuing brown sprouts, spore heads expanding. The Client fought on for survival, tearing at its tree, crystal began to fall and shatter then like the dried wings of its husks once had. Around me I now saw exoforms, but there was no coherence to them—they were just running, crashing into each other, crashing into the walls of the cavern.

"Tuppence."

At last it ended, the Client freezing round its tree, final segments infected, one newly born freezing halfway down its birth canal, a last head segment falling. The Client died sprouting a fungus which, in its original form, killed mere ants. I died too. Under crystal I saw black threads spreading then all sight of my body blotted out as a spore head exploded in there.

"Oh will you snap out of it!"

I opened my eyes. I was aboard the *Coin Collector*, in my chair, facing my array of screens. The Client's world was there in vacuum and, around it I could see the flash of fusion drives and the distant bulks of ships.

"Why am I alive?" I asked, peering down at my battered artificial body.

"You're not," said Harriet. "You're dead."

I turned to study her. She had put her artificial claws back on and had painted them bright custard yellow, even applied some eye-shadow of the same colour. It occurred to me then that I should have wondered, what with her supposedly being so inept with her claws, how she had always so neatly applied the nail varnish and other make-up. Transferring my gaze to her side I could see no sign of her injury, just clean scaled skin.

"What do you mean I'm dead?"

"The Client used stock memcrystal for the processing in your avatar. That crystal has more than enough storage to contain a human mind. You're a copy and even though your human body is dead, you live. You are you, Tuppence."

I wasn't quite sure how I felt about that.

"Are you Polity?" I asked. "Are you a Polity *agent*."

"No, completely independent," she replied cheerfully.

"I'm confused."

"Understandable—it's been a trying day." She paused while I stared at her, then relented. "Okay, you hired me and I got thoroughly screwed. The damage was bad and it was way beyond being repaired with the reward you gave me or the facilities available at that hospital. That war-drone made a real mess. Then, while I was in the hospital, I received an offer I couldn't refuse. They'd pay to repair me. They'd bring in the expertise. They'd pay to turn me into what I am now—"

"And what are you now?"

"I'm practically indestructible, and more machine than lizard." She paused. "And with a mind distributed about my body so it couldn't be killed with a single farcaster shot."

"Right," I said. "Please continue."

"I was to stick with you, and lead them to the Client." Harriet paused. "However when I worked out what you were up to, I went for the bigger reward—the one for offing the Client."

"The Polity," I said, feeling slightly disgusted.

"Polity technology, certainly, but not the Polity and its AIs." She pointed a claw at the screens. "Them."

I stared at the screens for a long moment, then reached out and upped the magnification. They weren't Polity ships out there swarming around the Client's world; they were prador dreadnoughts.

I wasn't sure about how I felt about that either.

"What now?" I asked.

Harriet raised a claw up in front of her face.

"The yellow was a mistake, I think."

Just then the *Coin Collector* shuddered, and I realized something large had just docked. I guessed the prador were bringing her reward, and wondered if that might be a cause for regret.

only Human

Lavie Tidhar

Here's another story by Lavie Tidhar, whose "The Book Seller" appears else-where in this anthology. This one is set out on the most remote edges of his Central Station universe, and it demonstrates that in a high-tech world there will be brand-new temptations to be faced, and that the price for giving in to them can be a very high one indeed.

There are four Three-times-Three Sisters in the House of Mirth, and five in the House of Heaven and Hell, and two in the House of Shelter. Four plus five plus two Three-by-Threes, and they represent one faction of the city.

You may have heard tales of the city of Polyphemus Port, on Titan, that moon of raging storms. First city on that lunar landscape, second oldest foothold of the Outer System, or so it is said, though who can tell, with the profusion of habitats in those faraway places of the solar system? A dome covers the city, but Polyport spreads underground—vertical development they called it, the old architects. And its tunnels reach far into the distance, linking to other settlements, small desolate towns on that windswept world, where majestic Saturn rises in the murky skies.

There are two Five-times-Six Sisters in the House of Forgetting, and five Eight-by-Eights in the House of Domicile. We who are a ones, and will one day be zeros, we cannot hope to understand the way of the Sisterhoods of Polyphemus Port, on Titan.

Understanding, as Ogko once said, is forgiveness.

Shereen was a cleaner in the House of Mirth in the day, and in the evening in the House of Domicile. It was a good, steady job. On Polyport all jobs connect to trade, to cargo. A thousand cults across space arise and fall around cargo. In the islands of the solar system cargo achieves mythical overtones, the ebb and flow of commerce across the inner and outer systems, of wild hagiratech from Jettisoned, best-grade hydroponics marijuana and raw materials from the belt, argumentative robots from the Galilean Republics, pop culture from Mars, weapons from Earth, anything and everything. Polyphemus Port services the cluster of habitats that circle Saturn, and links to the Galilean Republics on the four major moons of Jupiter. It links the inner system with the wild outposts of Pluto—with Dragon's World on Hydra and Jettisoned on Charon, and the small but persistent human settlements beyond Saturn, in the dark echoey space that lies in between Uranus and Neptune.

People are strange in the Outer System, and the few Others, too, who make their homes there. Some say the Others, those digital intelligences bred long ago by St. Cohen in Earth's first, primitive Breeding Grounds, have relocated en masse to the cold moons of the Outer System, installing new Cores away from human habitation, but whether it is true or not, who can tell? Whatever the truth of all this is, it suffices to say that all jobs on Polyport, directly or indirectly, are linked with the business and worship of cargo, and that some jobs are always in demand.

Shereen apprenticed as a cleaner in the landing port beyond the city, a vast dustbowl plane where RLVs like busy methane-breathing bees rise and fall from the surface to orbit, there to meet the incoming and outgoing space-going vessels to ferry people and cargo back and forth. She was seconded to Customs inspections slash Quarantine, scouring ships' holds for unwanted passengers, the rodents and bacteria, fungus and von Neumann machines; from there she moved dome-side, abandoning her public sector job in favour of the private. She cleaned houses both above- and under-ground, until at last she settled on the dual work for the House of Mirth and the House of Domicile, a work associated, after all, with cargo and religion both.

It is said that Dragon, that enigmatic entity living on the moon Hydra, its body composed of millions of discarded battle dolls, had passed through Polyport on its way from Earth. If so, local historical documentation is nonexistent, and anecdotal evidence spurious. Nevertheless, an uncle of Shereen's, a Guild-certified cleaner in his own right, used to tell the tale of Dragon's arrival as though he had known it for truth.

In the story, Dragon's Core, the hub of it, remained in orbit around Titan, carried as it were in a converted asteroid; and it trailed behind it kilometres-long lines of suspended second- and third-hand Vietnamese battle dolls, strung on wires; while Dragon manifested upon the streets of Polyport in a doll body of weathered humanoid form of little distinction. It was then, said Shereen's uncle, that Dragon met the woman who had once been One-times-One, then One-times-Two, and was finally a Three-times-Three; but whose name had once been Haifa al-Sahara.

Did Dragon—who split itself across a million bodies—suggest to al-Sahara a similar possibility? Ask at the House of Mirth, or at the House of Forgetting, and you shall receive no answer. Yet whether it is felt the question too ridiculous to answer, or if, rather, there is a kernel of truth in it, the silence does not say.

Be that as it may. You can read more about the early history of the Houses in *Sisters of Titan*, by Hassan Sufjan, if you were so inclined or, of course, in Gidali's classic novel, *Three Times Three Is One* (adapted by Phobos Studios into a lavish three-part production starring Sivan Shoshanim).

What's important is that, at the time that Shereen was working at the Houses, trouble had been brewing for some time. And that, one day, a new novice came into service in the House of Mirth.

Or *is* that important? It was to Shereen, certainly, eventually. It was to the novice, too, whose name was Aliyah. How we assign importance depends on where we ourselves stand in the story. For Shereen, it was a moment of significance, the point in which light breaks through the transparent dome, and Saturn rises. Seeing Aliyah walk into the House of Mirth was like being thirsty, and then being given drink; like having been sick, and suddenly feeling better; and so on and so forth.

Aliyah came into the House of Mirth dressed in the modest *jilaabah* of the Sisters, in the plain black of the Noviates. Underneath it, Shereen knew, Aliyah would bear the scars and grafts of Noviatehood; while inside the filaments would be growing, burrowing under the skin and showing as fine blue lines under direct white light. Shereen was cleaning unobtrusively in the background. Robots could do some of the work, sure, but robots, or Others, were not welcome in the Houses of the Sisters. And humans were so much more . . . human. The Sisterhoods rejected the Way of Robot, and the ideal of Translation. They were, for whatever it's worth, still human.

In a manner of speaking.

Underneath her head scarf, Shereen knew, Aliyah's head would be shaven, misshaped by augmentation. Only her eyes could be seen, a startling, deep scarlet like the colour of the sky above the port. In her eyes were the storms of Titan. Perhaps it was then that Shereen fell in love. Or perhaps love is merely the illusion of body chemistry and brain software with deep-embedded evolutionary instincts. Though that hardly sounds very romantic.

The poet-traveller Bashō, who had visited Titan, once wrote:

Laf hemi wan samting
  I no semak
  Ol narafala samting

Which translates, from the Asteroid Pidgin, as: Love is one thing / that is not like / any other thing, and which is as unhelpful as Bashō ever got.

Their eyes met across a crowded room . . .

Though it was not crowded, and that first time Aliyah barely saw Shereen, only perhaps as a reflection in a shiny surface. It is easy to unsee cleaners, they walk like shadows, they are unobtrusive by training.

Shereen, then, watched as Aliyah arrived; and as she was ushered in to the inner sanctum by the Three-times-Three. And she brooded.

It was—as has been mentioned—a time of tensions in Polyphemus Port. The reasons are arcane and somewhat boring. It could be argued that Three-times-Three is the most stable form of Sisterhood, a linked network, nine minds all linked and working in parallel on a perfect grid.

But there were, at the time, as we've said, other forms. The asymmetrical Five-times-Sixes of the House of Forgetting, and the Eight-times-Eights of the House of Domicile—the largest Sisterhood on Titan. And these joined forces—politically speaking—against the older and more established Three-times-Three Sisters of Mirth, Shelter, and the House of Heaven and Hell.

There is a lot of politics in the solar system. There is the corporate rule of most of the asteroid belt; the mellow capitalism of such old-established settlements like Tong Yun or Lunar Port; the socialism of the Martian Kibbutzim, or the despotic rule of dozens of obscure space habitats. There is the mind-meld democracy of the Zion asteroid (which had since departed the solar system to destinations unknown), the libertarian anarchy of Jettisoned, the militarism that had led to the Jovean Wars in the Galilean Republics for a time, and so on, and so forth.

Titan was, nominally, one of those places with no clear system in place beyond the benign rule of machines; which is to say, autonomous systems kept the fragile balance of human lives functioning on an essentially hostile world, and the humans, robots, Others, Martian Re-Born, tentacle junkies, followers of Ogko, and so on simply got on with whatever it was they were doing, most of which—as we've said—revolved around cargo.

The rise of the Sisterhoods, however, changed things. They were not exactly a religious order, though their business was the transport of cargo and thus assumed religious nature. They were a mixture of business and religion, then, human mind-melds functioning like digital intelligences, their component parts replaced as they grew old and died, but the basic mind kept on, gaining new perspectives and notions with each new cell of a Three-times-Three or a Five-times-Six. In a world with few genuine Others, and only the occasional robot pilgrim on its way to or from the Robot Vatican on Mars, the Sisterhoods were near unique, and their power had risen as they assumed onto themselves new followers.

Against this background of rising tension, Shereen and Aliyah had fallen in love.

"Hello."

"Oh . . . hello."

"I am Shereen. I clean here."

"My name is Aliyah. I'm a Novice."

"I can tell."

"Can you? I guess you can, at that."

"I saw you here, before."

"Yes, I saw you, too. I think."

"Did you?"

"No, I suppose . . ."

"Your eyes are very beautiful."

"Thank you. I'm sorry, I have the strangest feeling, as if we'd met before. There are things moving behind my eyes, at least it feels that way."

"How long do you have before Initiation?"

"Twelve orbits to an Earth year of grafts and surgery."

"That's terrible."

"It's worth it. Or so they say. I would be a part of the Sisterhood. It's a way of never really dying, isn't it. Think about it, Haifa al-Sahara is still alive, in some form, in the Three-times-Three, and soon I will be a part of her, and she a part of me."

"Who's to say if it is right not to die? Isn't our humanity defined by our death?"

"But which humanity? I'm sorry, I—"

"You look flushed. Here, let me help you—"

"It is probably the medication. Your hand feels so hot."

"Your brow is icy cold. Here, let me loosen your scarf."

"Thank you, I—"

"I feel strange, sitting like this with you."

"No one can see us, can they?"

"We are alone."

"Hold me. Shereen? Shereen."

"Aliyah. Aliyah?"

"Yes. Yes."

"Yes."

Things escalated when the Guild of Porters—swearing nominal allegiance to the House of Domicile—declared a general strike.

Without porters there can be no movement of cargo. Without cargo, Polyport and its adjacent settlements suffered. The House of Mirth sent its own people to replace the Porters, third-hand RLVs rising and falling from orbit. The strike turned violent. One of the RLVs crashed and burned in the violent atmosphere of the moon, and the scabs retired without grace. When at last the Porters went back to work the Cleaners went on strike. Beyond Polyport the nearest large settlement was El Quseir, on the other side of the moon. Now it threatened to rise in prominence as the Houses fought.

Human cells of each Sisterhood met to confer, and try to resolve the impasse. Shereen, cleaning, watched the meeting unobtrusively in the House of Domicile. The two women were almost sister-like—both short, dark haired, dark skinned, with violet eyes. Bare-headed, they were an amalgamation of protrusions and augs, their dark hair a mere fuzz on their shaven skulls. They spoke little in language, communicating somewhat by gestures but mostly in the high-bandwidth *toktok* of the Sisterhoods, which was both like and unlike the protocols of Others, the *Toktok blong Narawan*.

Their conversation in audio form, then, did not make much sense—

"Cannot?"

"Times three, times four. Mirth—" a raised finger. A shake of the head. "Port."

"Cargo. Flow."

"Ours."

"All."

"None—" a face turned sideways, light falling on augs. "Impasse?"

"Repeat."

Silence, two sets of violet eyes staring into each other. Shereen wiping the surface of a desk. "Loop."

"Loop."

"Impasse."

"Yes."

And depart, disengaging swiftly, the one Sister leaving the room, the House, the other remaining as its others joined her, a Quarter, Four-times-One of an Eight-times-Eight.

The rest of their conversation Shereen could not hear, they did not converse, they thought in parallel. Later, when she left . . .

Shereen lived on Level Two of Polyphemus Port. An old neighbourhood, dug-in about a century after first settlement. There were hydroponics gardens on that level, the lush vegetation that was everywhere in the humid, Earth-tropical weather of Polyport. Vines grew over the windows of Shereen's bedroom. She lay in bed with Aliyah. It was late. Aliyah's body was black and blue, bruised from her latest surgery. A One-times-Nine of one of the Sisters of the House of Mirth was ailing, dying. Aliyah would replace her, become a cell in the Three-times-Three. She was almost ready.

"I can almost hear them, now," Aliyah said. Shereen ran her finger lightly down Aliyah's spine, marvelling at the enforced skeleton that pressed against the delicate skin. "Whispering, at the edge of consciousness. It's not quite a singular identity, not really, it's more of a choir of voices, that merge into one. With old echoes, old voices weaving into the music. One day soon I will cease being a singular note, and become an orchestra."

"A part of an orchestra."

"Maybe. But at least I will keep on living, as sound, as one note in a perfect symphony."

"While mine will fade and die?" Shereen said, wryly. Aliyah touched her face. "I did not mean . . ." she said.

"I know what you meant."

Aliyah withdrew her hand. "I don't want a fight," she said, softly.

"Then don't start one."

They stared at each other in silence across the bed. Then: "I'm sorry," Shereen said.

"No, I'm—"

Outside a mosque was calling the faithful to prayer; green cockatoos sang to each other across the tall spindly trees; a group of children ran down the corridor chasing a ball; inside the room it was dark; and nothing, for the moment, was resolved.

It was, essentially, a trade dispute.

Though what is trade if not religion, and what is religion if not commerce? It was, perhaps, first and foremost about prestige.

Old tensions rose to the lunar surface . . .

The Houses were never so crass as to engage in open warfare. A century earlier the so-called Format Wars erupted in Polyport. Who is to say a Three-times-Three is the perfect format, for instance, for a human network? It is linked on a grid. A single unit—a One-times-One—can operate independently when need be, at normal human capacity, but it can also link with two of its sisters, forming a One-times-Three linear triple processor. Those Trips can then link vertically and horizontally to form a grid, a perfect—so they say—unit, a true Sisterhood.

Haifa al-Sahara, or rather the Three-times-Three Sisterhood that had once contained the human once known by that name, argued for the perfection of the form. But others had ambition, and no such faith in the purity of her numbers.

The first Eight-times-Eight had founded the House of Domicile, and others soon followed. The Sisters of the House of Mirth argued the form was too cumbersome, processing ponderous, optimal operations sluggish at best.

And yet the Eight-times-Eights flourished, and the House of Domicile soon encompassed five Sisterhoods, of which it was said that they sometimes joined, in a grid of Five-times-Eight-times-Eight, a massive processing mind occupying some four stories of real estate, only one of which was above ground.

Obviously, the House of Domicile proclaimed its own superiority, and that—naturally—rankled with the House of Mirth, as the oldest and—up to that time—strongest of the newly risen Houses and Sisterhoods. Then came the Sisterhoods of Odd, the Five-times-Sixes of the House of Forgetting, asymmetrical and strange, and they allied themselves with the House of Domicile's Eight-times-Eights.

Two factions, then: the three houses of the Three-times-Threes, versus the other two houses and their multiplicity of Sisterhoods.

A century back, the rise of the Houses led to conflicts both within and without; over a period of some twenty years the Houses consolidated, accumulated followers and adherents, and finally rested in an uneasy peace.

That peace was now in danger of breaking, and thus unsettling Titanic society as a whole.

The Houses, therefore, sought a compromise . . .

It was late at night, in Shereen's apartment. That special silence that comes with deep night, when even the birds sleep. When I-loops all across and down the city processed slowly, neural networks embedded in a grey mass within a bone skull, billions of neurons firing together into the illusion of an "I," a "me," all sinking, momentarily, into a dream or dreamless state, the one akin to hallucination, the other to death.

They had made love; the bedsheets clung to their skin with the sweat. A single candle burned on Shereen's windowsill. Aliyah said, "The old cell, the One-times-One: her health is better."

"I see."

"You are happy?"

Shereen pulled herself up, the light from the candle threw shadows on the wall. "I don't want you to become one of them," she said. The words cost her everything.

Getting them out at last felt like a revelation. Aliyah laughed, softly. "Do you think I don't know?"

"Then why do you do it? Do you not love me?"

"You know I do."

"Then why?"

"Because I want to. I need to. Because there is more to life than you or me. I want to be a part of something bigger than either of us."

"But *why*?" all the pain inside her came out in that voice.

"I don't know why," Aliyah said, but gently. That night she was very gentle, even her love-making was filled with care; it contrasted with Shereen's urgency. "I just know."

"But they will not take you. Not the Three-times-Threes. Not when they have all their parts—"

"Yes—"

"What?" Shereen said—demanded. Suspicion, hurt, in her eyes.

"I have been going to the House of Domicile," Aliyah said quietly.

"When?" Shereen's voice, too, was low. "I did not see you there."

"I know. I went when you were not working. I did not want to upset you."

"And now?"

"You're upset. We can talk about it in the morning."

"We can talk about it now."

Aliyah sighed.

"Why have you been going to the House of Domicile?" That suspicion, again. "You want to join another Sisterhood?"

"Not . . . exactly."

"Then what? I don't—"

"Don't you?"

It was so quiet in the room. The candle fluttered in invisible wind from outside. "They won't," Shereen said. "They can't."

Aliyah moved to her; Shereen moved away. "Don't," she said.

"They can. *We* can. Shereen—"

"Don't!"

"It is better that I do this. It is better than conflict. Better than war. We cannot afford it, not again, not so soon. Not the city, not the world. The Houses have too much power, now."

"It should never have come to that."

"What would you have instead? Others?"

"People," Shereen said.

"Oh, grow up, Shereen." She made as if to push back a lock of hair, then found that, of course, it wasn't there. There was something innocent, human, about that gesture. At that moment Shereen couldn't help but love her very much. "And we are people, too."

"Since when is it we?" Shereen said; but she sounded defeated. "When?" she said.

"Soon."

"And they agree? Both of them?"

"They agree to try."

"We would not see each other."

"No."

"Would you even know who I was?"

"Of course I would. We would. You would always live on, Shereen. In my—in our—memory. Even when my body and yours are back in the ground, fertilisers of new life in the gardens."

"Trust you to bring the conversation back to death, and fertiliser?" Shereen tried to laugh; it came out choked. "Were you always so obsessed with death?"

"Not with death but with not dying," Aliyah said; her body shook, and it took Shereen a moment to realise she was crying.

"Come here," she said, awkwardly. Aliyah came to her and nestled in Shereen's arms. Shereen could feel her heart beating, inside the fragile, human frame of her. "Is it really so bad?" she said, but even as she spoke, she knew it was futile; that Aliyah had already decided, decided long ago, perhaps; and that this was simply her choosing of a time to finally say goodbye.

The Initiation and the end of Aliyah's Novitiate came some two weeks later, at a private ceremony in the House of Forgetting, which was historically the least affiliated—and the weakest—of the Houses. A Three-times-Three from the House of Mirth was there, and an Eight-times-Eight from the House of Domicile. And there, in between them, was Aliyah—dressed in a plain white shift, her head unscarfed and bare, the fine blue veins of filaments running underneath her translucent skin.

Shereen, too, was there—not as a guest, but unobtrusive, cleaning. She saw the Sisterhoods meet, half-heard as they conversed, aware of the high-bandwidth transfer of data around her, and the half-understood words, and subtle signals of physical signs. She daren't watch too much, there was something in her eyes, it must have been the chemicals in the new cleaning fluid, its smell made it hard for her to breathe.

Aliyah shone brightly, like an angel. Light suffused her, it rose from her skin, from her eyes. The Houses could not fight and so they'd reached a compromise, a way of speaking which was a way of sharing: and a One-times-One became a point linking two networks, became a router and a hub, became a One-times-Eight-times-Eight-times-Three-times-Three, was cleaved in two; and spliced together.

When it was over there was no discernible sign; only the act of both Sisterhoods slowly departing, without words; only their hosts remaining, and the newest Sister, the one who belonged to two Sisterhoods, and had once known Shereen.

Shereen scrubbed the surface of the table, scrubbed it until its wooden surface shone. When she raised her head again even the host Sisters were gone; when she turned back to the surface of the table, she saw Aliyah, momentarily, reflected in it. She turned her head. Aliyah stood there, watching her. Shereen raised her hand. Her fingers brushed Aliyah's cheek, the skin of her face. Aliyah bore it without words. Her eyes watched Shereen, and yet they didn't see her. After a moment she inched her head, as if acknowledging, or settling, something. Then she, too, were gone.

There are four Three-times-Three Sisters in the House of Mirth, and five in the House of Heaven and Hell, and two in the House of Shelter. Four plus five plus two Three-by-Threes, and they represent one faction of the city.

There are two Five-time-Six Sisters in the House of Forgetting, and five Eight-by-Eights in the House of Domicile, and they represent a second faction of the city.

There is a bridge between them, now. An understanding, and cargo continues to come and go through Polyphemus Port. And Shereen who is a one, and will one day be zero, continues to work in the house of Mirth, and in the house of Domicile, and she watches the Sisters on their silent comings and goings; and she wonders, sometimes, of what could have been, and of what didn't; but to do that is, after all, only human.

entangled

IAN R. MACLEOD

Here's another story by Ian R. MacLeod, whose "The Discovered Country"
appears elsewhere in this anthology. This one is the poignant story of a
woman who lives alone and isolated, cut off from everyone else—even if they're
in the same room with her.

When she awakes, it seems as if she's not alone. Many arms are around her, and she's filled with a roaring chorus of voices. Consciousness follows in a series of ragged flickers, and the voices fade, and soon she inhabits her own thoughts, and knows that she is Martha Chauhan, and nothing has changed. But the air, the light, the sounds which reach this morning to her room fifteen floors up in Bladwin Towers, all feel different today . . .

Lumbering from bed, she clears a space in the frost, peers blearily down, and sees from the blaze of white that it's snowed heavily in the night, and that many of the entangled are already up and about. Kids, but adults as well. Either throwing snowballs, or dragging handmade toboggans, or building snowmen, or helping clear the pathways between the tower blocks. The small shadows of their movements seem impossibly balletic.

Still climbing from the fuzz of night, she counts and dry-swallows the usual immune suppressants from her palm. The water isn't entirely cold, the hob puts out just enough heat to turn her coffee lukewarm, and she's grateful she doesn't have to use the commune toilets. In so many ways, she's privileged. Fumbling with yesterday's clothes, she swipes the mirror for glimpses of a woman in late middle age with something odd about the left side of her skull, then picks up her carpetbag and heads down the pell-mell stairs with other commune residents in their flung coats, sideways bobble hats and unmatched gloves.

Shouts and snowballs criss-cross the air as she crunches to her readapted Mini, another great privilege, which has already been cleared of snow. She clambers in. Shivers and hugs herself as she waits for the fuel cell to warm. Finally, she drives off. Along with the 1960s tower blocks, there are houses and maisonettes in other parts of this estate that were once occupied by individual families. Now, they have all been reshaped and knocked through, joined by plastic-weld polysheets, raggedly angled sheds and tunnels of tarpaulin, with the gardens and other open spaces used for communal planting and grazing. Everything's white this morning, but all the roads have been cleared, and braziers already blaze in the local market where the communes come to barter. Strangers smile to each other as they pass. Acquaintances hug. Co-workers sing gusty songs as they shovel the paths. Lovers walk hand in hand. Even the snowmen are grinning.

This isn't how I imagined my life would be.

I grew up in this same city, not far from these streets. Dad was of Indian birth, and came here to the England with my brother in his arms and me clinging to the strap of his suitcase and our mother dead from a terrorist dirty bomb back in Calcutta. He changed my name from Madhur to Martha, and Daman's to Damien, and honed his cultural knowledge to go with his excellent English, and had all the certificates and bio-tags to prove he was a doctor, and was determined to make his mark. *Money is important, and so is security, and status is something to be cherished—* that was what Martha Chauhan learned at her father's knee. That, and all the stories he told me as he sat by my bed. Tenali Ramakrishna and the gift of the three dolls who all seemed the same, but only one of which knew how to feel. Artful imps who danced about the flames in a hidden heart of a forest to the secret of their own name. But maybe I was too cosseted, for I could never get the point. The world was clearly collapsing. You could see that merely by switching screens from the kiddie channels he tried to sit Damien and me in front of in our secure house in our gated and protected estate. A wave of my chubby hand, and the Technicolor balloon things dissolved and you were looking down at people clinging to trees as the helicopters flew on, or bomb blast wreckage surrounded by wailing women, and then Damien started crying, and that was that.

St James' schoolhouse is like something from Dickensian old times, even without today's gingerbread icing of snow. A great, paternally white oak looms across the trampled playground. Martha heads inside past the tiny rows of dripping coats into a room filled with rampaging four year olds. The walls hang with askew potato prints and cheery balloon-style faces. There's a sandpit and a ballpool and something else that hovers in mid-air that fizzes and buzzes as the kids dive.

Tommy the teacher lies somewhere at the bottom of largest piles of waving limbs, and it's some time before he or anyone else notices Martha's presence. When they do, it's as if she's left the doors open and is a cold draft the kids feel on their necks. Once the unease is there, it spreads impossibly fast. Tommy, who's lying on his back like a tickled dog, is almost the last to pick up the change of mood.

He clambers to his feet in a holed jumper and half the contents of the sandpit bulging his pockets. The kids cluster around him, exchanging looks, half-words, mumbles, grunts, nudges, gestures and silences. Tommy does as well until he remembers how rude that is.

"It's okay, it's *okay* . . . ! We have a visitor, and I want everyone to simply *talk* when Martha's with us. Right?" Kids give metronomic nods as Martha's introduced as the nice lady who's going to be seeing them individually over the next few hours. Then a hand goes up, then another. "So why . . ." asks a small voice, before different one takes over until the question finishes in chorus. ". . . isn't she . . . HERE . . . ?"

Followed by a rustle of giggles. After all, Martha obviously *is* here. But, in another, deeper, sense she's clearly not. Martha understands their curiosity. After all, she can remember how she used to stare at fat people and paraplegics when she was young until her father told her it was impolite. She can't help but smile as hands sneak out to touch the snow-melting tips of her boots, just to check she's not some weird kind of ghost.

"I *am* here," she says. "But the thing is, not everyone has the same gift that all of you have. I can *see* you, and I can *hear* you as well. But there was an accident— perhaps you can see where it was . . ." She turns so they can admire the odd shape of her skull. "I lost . . ." She pauses. ". . . part of my mind. Truth is, I'm very lucky to be here at all. What my disability means is that I'm not entangled. Not part of the gestalt. I can't share and feel as you do. But I'm as real as all of you are. Look, this is my hand . . ." She holds it out. Slowly, slowly, tentatively, little fingers encircle her own like new shoots enclosing old roots. Then, and at the same instant, and as if by some hidden decision, they withdraw. As they settle back, the face of one of the boys blurs and tries to reshape itself into Damien's.

Dad always was an industrious man. Not only had he managed to qualify as a doctor back in India, but he'd studied what was then called biomechanical science. He also had a practical business eye. He'd worked out that the most secure jobs in medicine at a time of collapsing insurance and failing state healthcare were to be found in the developing technologies of neural enhancement.

I remember him taking Damien and me along with him one day to the private hospital where he did much of his work. It was probably down to some failure in the child-minding arrangements that all single parents have to make, although Damien must have been about five by then and I was nearly twelve, so perhaps he really had wanted to show us what he did.

"Here we are . . .""

The rake of a handbrake in his old-fashioned car that smelled of leather and Damien's tendency to get travelsick. We'd already passed through several security systems and sets of high walls, and were now outside this big old castle of a building that looked like something out of Harry Potter or Tolkien—all turrets and pointy windows. Then doors swished, and suddenly everything turned busy and modern, with people leaning down with dangling their unlikely smiles and security passes toward us to ask who we were—at least, until Damien began to cry. Then we were inside a bright room, and this creature was laid at its centre surrounded by wires and humming boxes and great semi-circular slabs of metal.

Damien sat over in a far corner, pacified by some game. But apparently it was important that I stand close and listen to what he had to say. You see, Martha, this patient—her name's Claire, by the way—is suffering from a condition that is slowly destroying her mind. Can you imagine what that must be like? To forget the names of your best friends and the faces of your family? To get confused by simple tasks and slowly lose any sense of who you really are? A terrible, terrible thing. But we now have a procedure that helps combat that process. What we do, you see . . . he'd called up a display which floated between us like a diseased jellyfish . . . is to insert these incredibly clever seeds which are like little crystals into her skull that we then stimulate with those big magnets can see around her head so they slowly take over the damaged bits of her mind . . .

The jellyfish quivered.

Dad doubtless went on in this way for some time, probably covering all sorts of fascinating moral and philosophical questions about the nature of consciousness, and how this withered relic would come to use all this new stuff in her head in much the same way that someone who's lost their hand might use a re-grown one. But not quite. Nothing in medicine is ever perfect, you see, Martha, and bits of people's brains can't be persuaded to regenerate in way that other parts of their body can, and rejection—that means, Martha, when the body doesn't recognise some-thing as part of itself—is still a problem, and a great deal of practise and continued medication is going to be needed if Claire's to make the most of this gift of half a new mind. Meanwhile, I was staring at the creased and scrawny flesh that emerged from all that steel and plastic like the neck of a tortoise, and thinking, why is some-thing so old and horrid still even *alive*?

Martha's given her usual "room" at the school—actually little more than a cupboard—and says no to an offer of coffee. Then she opens up her carpetbag and puts the field cap with its dangle of controls and capillaries on the radiator to warm. The entanglement virus is generally contracted naturally soon after birth, but it's the job of her, and many others like her, to deal with any problems which may arise during the short fever which follows. She often looks in again on toddlers, but it's at this age, when the children have joined the gestalt as individual personalities, that's the next major watch-out. Then, if it all goes as well as it almost always does, there are some final checks to be made during the hormone surge of adolescence. In some cultures and other parts of the globe, she'd be thought of as a shaman, priest, imam or witch doctor. But the world had changed, and the differences really aren't that great.

"This is where I . . . Should be?"

Martha looks up, slightly surprised by the way this kid has simply stepped in to this tiny room. Most hang around outside and wait to be invited, or rub and scratch at the door like kittens, seeing as, even though her disability has been explained to them, they still find it difficult to believe that she's actually inside. "Yes. That's per-fect. You're . . ." She glances at Tommy's execrably written list. "Shara, right? Shara of Widney Commune. Am I getting your name right, by the way? Shara? Such a pretty name, but I don't think I've heard it much before. Or is it Shar-ra?"

"I think it's just Shara," she says as she settles on the old gym mat. She has bright blue eyes. Curly, almost reddish, hair. "Some people say it different but it doesn't matter. The other mums and most of the dads sometimes just call me Sha. I think Shara was just a name they made up for me when I was born."

Shara of the Widney Commune really is an extraordinarily composed creature. Pretty with it, with those dazzling eyes and the fall around her cheeks of that curly hair, which Martha longs to touch, just to see if it really is as soft and springy as it looks. If ever there was a subject for whom her attentions might seem irrelevant, it's Shara. And yet . . . There's *something* about this girl . . . Martha blinks, swallows, kicks her mind back into focus and reminds herself that she's taken her usual handful of immune suppressants, just as Shara's features threaten to dissolve.

"Are you alright?"

"Oh . . . ? Absolutely, Shara. Now, I want you to put this on."

Shara takes the field cap and puts it on in the right way without the usual prompting, even tightening the chinstrap against the pressure of those lovely curls. She lies down.

"I want you to close your eyes."

Unquestioningly, she does so.

"Can you see anything?"

She shakes her head.

"How about now?" Martha lifts the ends of the capillaries and touches the controls.

"It's all kind of fizzy."

"And now?"

"Like *lines* . . ."

"And now?"

This time, Shara doesn't respond. Her fingers are quivering. Her cheeks have paled. The rhythm of her breathing has slowed. Sometimes, although Martha tries to insist that they use the toilet beforehand, the kids wet themselves. But not Shara. The girl's in a fugue state now, lost deep inside the gestalt. Always a slight risk at this point that they won't come back, and Martha's trained in CPR and has adrenalin and antipsychotic shots primed and ready in her carpetbag just in case they need to be quickly woken up or knocked out, but the rigidity fades just as soon as she cuts the signal back. Shara stretches. Blinks. Sits up. Smiles.

"How was that?" Martha helps unclip the field cap and feels the spring of those lovely curls.

Shara thinks. "It was *lovely*. Thank you Martha," she says. Then she kisses her cheek.

It wasn't all famine, tribal wars, economic collapse back in the day. Life mostly went on as it always did, and I suppose Dad did his best to try to keep us going as some kind of family as well. I remember a summer West Country beach—it wasn't all floods and landslips, either—that he must have driven us down to from the Midlands in that creaky old car between regular stops at the roadside for Damien to vomit. There we were, Dad and me, sat on an old rug amid our sandwiches and samosas whilst dogs flung themselves after Frisbees and Damien and some other lads attempted to play cricket. Kites stuck like hatpins into a pale sky and a roaring in my ears that could be the sea, but often comes when I chase too hard after memories.

Dad was chattering on as he often did. Trying hard not to be a bore, or talk down to me, but not really succeeding . . . You see, Martha, the work I do on the mind, the brain, the whole strange business of human consciousness, is just the very beginning. The crystals I persuade to grow inside peoples' skulls are almost as primitive as wooden legs. Real, living neurons use quantum effects—it isn't just electricity and chemistry. The mind, the entirety of the things we call thought and memory and consciousness, is really the sum of a shimmer of uncertainties. It mirrors the universe, and perhaps even calls it into existence. But even that's not the most wonderful thing about us, Martha. You see, we all think we're alone, don't we? You imagine you're somewhere inside your skull and I'm somewhere inside mine, that we're like separate islands? But we're not looking at it from enough dimensions. It's like us sitting on this beach, and looking out over those waves toward the horizon, and seeing a scatter of islands. No, no, I'm not saying there *are* real islands out there, Martha because there obviously aren't. But just stay with me for a moment my dear and try to imagine. We'd think of those islands as alone and separate, wouldn't we? But they're not. Not if you look at the world sideways. Beneath the sea, under the waves, all the islands are joined. It's just that we can't properly see it, or feel it. Not yet, anyway . . .

The day moved on, and Dad stood at the driftwood wicket like any good Englishman, or Indian, and soon got bowled out. Then he fielded, and dropped an easy catch from Damien as I crunched through the last of the sandy samosas. Then the wind blew colder, and the kites and the Frisbees and the dogs fled the beach, and the last thing I can remember is my lost Dad holding hands with lost brother Damien as he wandered with his trousers rolled at the edge of the roaring sea.

Martha drives out toward the edge of the motorway system which still encircles this old city. The big trucks are out in force now; great, ponderous leviathans that grumble along the rubbled concrete out of a greyness that threatens more snow. Dwarfed by their wheels, she parks her Mini at a transport stop, and stomps up to the glass and plastic counter. It's a regular old-fashioned greasy spoon. The windows are steamed, and baked beans are still on the menu, and the coffee here is moderately strong. Always a difficult dance, getting through a busy space when people's backs are turned, but she clatters her tray to give warning, and they soon share the sense of her oddity and decide not to stare. Mindblind coming through.

She likes it here. The people who do this travelling kind of work far from their communes are still surprisingly solitary by nature. A few are sharing tables and chatting in low voices or quietly touching, but most sit on their own and appear to be occupied with little but their own thoughts. In places like this it's possible to soak up a companionship of loneliness that she can imagine she shares. Sometimes, one of them comes over to talk. Sometimes, but more rarely, and after all the usual overpolite questions, the conversation moves on, and the some of old signs of sexual availability, which to them must seem arcane as smoke signals, waft into view.

There are some rooms at the back of this place which anyone who needs them is free to use. Piled mattresses and cushions. Showers for afterwards—or during. Sex with Martha Chauhan must be something lonely and oddly exotic, and perhaps a little filthy, as far as the entangled are concerned. A weird kind of masturbation with someone else in the room. There's an odd emptiness in their eyes as they and the gestalt study her when, and if, she comes. But Martha's getting older. Mindblind or not, they probably find her repulsive, and whatever urgency she once felt to be with someone in that way has gone.

She pushes aside her plate and swirl the dregs of her coffee. Blinks away the fizzing arrival of her father's reproachful smile. After all, what has she done wrong? But the empty truth is there's nothing she needs to do this afternoon. She could go back to her room in Baldwin Towers and try to sleep. She could go tobogganing, although being with other people having fun is one of the loneliest things of all. This day, the whole of whatever is left of her life, looms blank as these steamy, snow-whitened windows. She could give up. She could stop taking her tablets. Instead, though, she rummages in her carpetbag and studies the list she was given this morning, and sees that name again, Shara of the Widney Commune, and remembers the face of that striking little girl.

I first bumped into Karl Yann during one of my many afternoons of disgruntled teenage wandering. Dad, or course, was full of *You must be carefuls* and *Do watch outs*. Well, fuck that for a start, I thought as I tried without success to slam the second of the heavy sets of gates which guarded our estate. Looking back through the shockwire-topped fence at the big, neat houses with their postage stamp lawns, panic rooms and preposterous names, it was easy to think of prisons. Then, reaching into my coat pocket, hooking the transmitter buds around my ears and turning on my seashell, my head filled with beats, smells, swirls and other sensations, and it was easy not to think of anything at all. Hunching off along the glass and dogshit pavements past the boarded-up shops, dead lampposts and abandoned cars, there was a knack that I'd mastered to keeping my device set so I remained aware enough to avoid walking into things. Until, that was, I found my way blocked by a large, laughing presence that was already reaching into my pocket and taking out, and then turning off, my precious seashell.

The city was supposedly full of piratical presences, at least according to my father, but this guy actually *looked* like a pirate. That, or, with his bushy red beard, twinkling blue eyes, wildly curly hair, be-ribboned coat and pixie boots, like some counter-cultural Father Christmas.

"Give that back!"

He grinned, still cupping my seashell in a big, paint-grained palm. "This is a pretty cool device, you know. Basically, it's mimicking your brainwaves so it can mess around with your thoughts . . ."

My father had said something similar, but this man's tone was admiring rather than concerned. At least, he seemed a man to me; I figured out later that Karl was barely into his twenties.

"I said—"

"Here. Don't want to get yourself tangled . . ." Almost impossibly gently, he was reaching to unpick the buds from around my ears, and already I was hooked. He was asking me questions. He seemed interested in my head-down city wanderings, and where I was from, and what I'd been playing on my seashell, and what I thought about things, and even in my Indian background, although I did have to make most of that up.

"This is the place. Don't snag yourself . . ."

Now, he was holding the wire of the fence that surrounded one of those half-finished developments that the dying economy had never finished. Maybe shops or offices or housing, but basically just a shrouded, rusty-scaffolded concrete frame. A few floors up, though, and in this place he called "the waystation" became a different world. In many ways, it was a glimpse of what was to come.

People stirred and said hi. The waystation's inner walls were painted, or hung with random bits of stuff, or fizzed with projections that drifted to and fro in the city haze. Old vehicles, bits of construction material, expensive drapes, blankets and rugs that looked more as if they had come from gated estate communities such as my own, had all been cleverly re-used to shape an exotic maze. Everything here had been transformed and recycled, and it was plain to me already that Karl was an artist of some talent, and at heart of whatever was going on.

The Widney Commune is based around a grand old house, with icicled gates leaning before a winding drive. Some long-dead Midlands industrialist's idea of fine living. Shara and the other commune youngsters will still be down at the schoolhouse, and most of the adults will be out. This place could almost be deserted, Martha tells herself as she edges her Mini up the drive and clambers out. The main door lies up a half-circle of uncleared steps, with an old bellpull beside. Something tinkles deep within the house when she gives it an experimental tug.

Even with all the indignities which have been inflicted on it—the warty vents and pipings, the tumbling add-ons—this is still a fine old sort of a place to live. Especially when you compare it to Baldwin Towers. No fifteen floors to ascend. Nor any concrete stalactites, or rusting pipes, or a useless flat roof. The entangled might claim that they can see the wrongness of things, and feel disappointment and envy. But they clearly don't.

Martha starts when snow scatters her shoulders.

"Hello there," she shouts up with all her usual yes-I-really-am-here cheeriness. "Just trying to see if there's anyone at home."

"Oh . . ." A pause as the head at the window above registers that she's not some odd garden statue. ". . . I'm sorry. The front door's been stuck for years. If you can come around to the side . . ."

This pathway's been cleared, as even a mindblind moron should have noticed, leading to a side entrance which opens into what was once, and still mostly is, a very great hall.

The space goes all the way up and there are galleries around it and a wide set of stairs. Live ivy grows up over the beams and there's a hutch in the corner where fat-eared rabbits lollop, and it's plain that the woman who's sashaying over to greet Martha is the source of at least half of Shara's good looks.

"I'm Freya . . ." After a small hesitation, she holds out a hand. It's crusty with flour, as are her bare arms. Her shoulders are bare, too, and so are her feet. Which, like the tip of her nose, are also dusted white. She's wearing holed dungarees that show off a great deal of her lithe, slim figure. Dirty blonde hair done up in a kind of knot. ". . . you're . . . ?" Confused by the difficulties of introduction with someone of Martha's disability, she hesitates with a pout.

"Martha Chauhan." Martha lets her hand, which by now is floury as well, slip from Freya's. "I'm guessing you're Shara's birth mother?"

"That's right." Freya squints hard. "You were testing Shara? Today? At school?"

Martha nods. "Not that there's any cause for concern."

"That's good." She smiles. Hugs herself.

"But I, ah . . ." Martha looks around again, wondering if this is how social workers once felt. "Sometimes just like to call in on a few communes. Just to . . . Well . . ."

"Of course," Freya nods. "I understand."

Somehow, she does, even if Martha doesn't. The entangled live in a sea of trust.

"Most people are out, either working or enjoying the day. But I've just finished baking . . . so what can I show you?"

The entangled are relentlessly proud of their communes. They'll argue and josh about who breeds the fluffiest sheep, puts on the cheeriest festival or grows the best crop of beets. As always, there's the deep, sweet, monkeyhouse reek of massed and rarely washed humanity, but it's mingled here with different odours of yeast, and the herbs that seem to be hanging everywhere to dry, and yet more of those rabbits. Each commune has its own specialities which it uses to exchange for things it doesn't make, and this one turns out to be rabbits which are raised to make warm blankets and coats from their skins, as well as for their meat. This commune's bread is something they're particularly proud of, as well. Down in the hot kitchen, Freya tears some with her hands, takes a bite, then offers Martha the rest, dewy with spit. She doesn't have to lie when she says she isn't hungry.

Many of the rooms look like the scenes of some perpetual sleepover. The entangled mostly sleep like puppies, curling up wherever they fancy, although Freya's slightly more coy about one or two other spaces, which reek of sex. Another smell, sourer this time, comes from some leaking chairs and sofas set around a big fire where the old ones cluster, basking like lizards, tremulous hands joined and rheumy eyes gazing into the tumbled memories at a past forever gone.

"And this is where Shara sleeps with the rest of the under-tens . . ."

Another charming, fetid mess, although this one's scattered with toys. There's a spinning top. There are rugs and papier mache stars. There's a one-eyed, one-armed teddy bear. A few story books and piles of paper, as well, along with newer, stranger devices that make no sense to Martha at all.

"Shara's your only birth child?"

Freya nods. She looks at least as proud of that as she is of most things, even if parenting is shared in a loose kind of way that involves the whole commune and no one gets too possessive. Knowing exactly who the father is can be difficult. In this era of trust, mothers are surprisingly coy about who they've fucked. Women often wander out to visit other communes—driven either by biological imperative or the simple curiosities of lust—and births are often followed by versions of the *he's got Uncle Eric's nose* conversations that must have gone on throughout human history.

Freya's showing drawings and scraps of writing that Shara's done, then lifting up pretty bits of clothing she's resewn herself for all the kids to use and share.

"No new babies at the moment," she adds. "Although we're planning, of course . . . Soon as the commune has the resources. And Shara's been such a joy to us all . . . That I'm rather hoping . . ." As she puts the things back, her hands move unconsciously to her breasts.

"And Shara's father? Somehow, I'm guessing he's a fair bit older than you are . . . ?"

"Oh? That's right." Freya smiles, not remotely insulted or surprised. "Karl's hoping, as well. We all are. Would you like to see the studio where he works?"

Martha blinks, swallows, nods. A falling feeling as she follows Freya down a long corridor then through a doorway into what's clearly an artist's studio. Rich smells of oil and varnish. Linseed oil squeezed out over a press. Pigments from the hedgerow, or wherever it is that pigments come from. Half-finished canvases lean against the walls. The room is a kind of atrium, lit from windows on all sides and high up. The colours and the shadows roar out to her even on a day as wintry as this.

"He's probably out helping in one of the greenhouses," Freya says. "That or sketching. He tends to paint in short, intense bursts."

The canvases are part abstract and part Turner seascape. They're undeniably accomplished, and recognisably Karl Yann's, although to Martha's mind they've lost their old edge. The entangled are good at making pretty and practical things, but proper art seems to be beyond them. Still, as Martha stares at the largest blur of colour, which looms over her like a tsunami in a paint factory, it's hard not to be drawn.

Freya chuckles, standing so close that Martha can smell the grease in her hair. "I know. They're lovely, and they barter really well . . . But Karl doesn't like to have them up on display in our commune. Says all he'd ever see is where he went wrong."

I never did get my seashell back, but I got Karl Yann instead. He had a bragging mix of certainty and vulnerability which I found appealing after my father's endless *on-the-one-hand-but-on-the-other* attempts at balance. Karl was clever and he knew what he thought. Karl was an accomplished artist. Karl *cared*. He'd read stuff and done things and been to places and had opinions about everything, but he also wanted to know what my views were, and actually seemed to listen to me when I said them. Or at least, he had a roguishly charming way of cocking his head. Maybe it was a little late in the day for this whole hippy/beatnik/bohemian revolutionary shtick, but these things come new to every generation—or at least they used to—and they felt new to me. Karl used real paint when he could, or whatever else came to hand—he found the virtuals fascinating but frustrating—but what he really wanted to create was a changed world. No use accepting things as they are, Martha. No use taking about what needs to be done. At least, not unless you're prepared to act to make the necessary sacrifices to help bring about the coming wave of change. The forests dying. Whole continents starving. The climate buggered. The economy fucked. So, are you with us, Martha, or not?

They called them performance acts, and Karl and the other inhabitants of the waystation were convinced they were contributing towards bringing about a better world. And so, now, was I. People had to be shaken out of their complacency—especially the selfish, cosseted rich, with all their possessions, all their *things*—and what was the harm in having some fun while we're doing so? Right? Okay? Yes?

We used my credit pass to gain access to one of those exclusive, guarded, gated, palm tree-filled, rich-people-only, air-conditioned pleasure domes they still called shopping malls to which my father had occasionally taken me and Damien as a birthday treat, and pulled on balaclavas and yelled like heathens and flung pigshit-filled condoms at the over-privileged shoppers and their shit-filled shops, and got out laughing and high-fiving in the ensuing mayhem. We climbed fences and sneaked through gardens and around underlit pools to hang paintings upside down and spraypaint walls and mess with people's heads. Then, often as not, and young as Martha Chauhan still was, she went home to her gated estate.

The Mini seems to know the way from the Widney Commune, but time and entanglement haven't been kind to this part of the city. Martha's boots press through new white drifts to snag on the rusted shockwire and fallen sensor pylons that once supposedly protected this little enclosure. The houses, haggard with smoke, blink their shattered eyes and shrug their collapsing shoulders as if in denial. Is this really the right place? Even the right street? Martha struggles to make sense of the layout of her lost life as she stands at what was surely the heart of their neat cul-de-sac where an uprooted tree now scrawls its branches until she's suddenly looking straight at her old home and everything's so clear its as if her eyeballs have burned through into ancient photographic negatives. The roof of the old house still intact, even if Dad's old car has long gone from the driveway, and she almost reaches for her key when she steps up to the front door. But the thing is blocked solid by age and perhaps even the fancy triple-locking that once protected it. *You can't be too careful Martha . . .* She looks around with a start. The other houses with their blackened Halloween eyes stare back at her. She shivers. Steps back. Takes stock. Then she walks around to the side past an upturned bin and finds that half the wall is missing, and pushes through, and everything clicks, and she's standing in their old kitchen.

Over there . . . Over *here* . . .

She's an archaeologist. She's a diver in the deepest of all possible seas. She scoops snow, dead leaves and rubble from the hollow of the sink. She straightens a thing of rust that might once have been the spice rack. Many of the tiles with their squiggle pattern of green and white that she never consciously noticed before are still hanging. And all the while, the thinning light of this distant winter pours down and in. So many days here. So many arguments over breakfast. She can see her father clearly now, quietly spooning fruit and yoghurt on his museli with the flowerpots lined on the windowledge behind him and the screen of some medical paper laid on the table and his cuffs rolled back to show his raw-looking wrists and his tie not yet done up. Damien is there as well, chomping as ever through some sugary, chocolaty stuff that he'll waste half of.

"I had a visit from some police contractors yesterday," he's telling her as he unfolds a linen handkerchief and dabs delicately at his mouth. "Apparently, they're looking for witnesses to an incident that happened at the Hall Green Mall. You may have heard about it—some kind of silly stunt? Of course, I told them the truth. I simply said you were out."

Now, as he refolds his handkerchief, his turns his guileless brown eyes up towards her, and the question he's really asking is so padded with all his usual oblique politeness that it's easily ignored. Anyway, time is moving on—Martha can feel it roaring through her bones in a winter gale—and now she's back home from her first term at the old, elite university town that her father, ever the supportive parent, has agreed to finance her to study at. Politics and Philosophy, too, and not a mention of the practical, career-based subjects she's sure he'd have much preferred her to take. Even as he spoons yoghurt over his museli, she can feel him not carefully mentioning this. But he seems newly hunched and his hand trembles as he spoons his yoghurt. And here's a much larger, gruffer-sounding version of Damien, as well, and sprouting some odd kind of haircut, even if he is still half-eating an bowl of sugary slop. All so very strange: the way people start changing the instant you look away from them. But that isn't at the heart of it. What lies at the core of Martha's unease is, of all things, a dog that isn't really a dog.

"*Of course* he's a dog, Martha," my father's saying as his suddenly liver-spotted hands stroke the creature's impossibly high haunches and it wags its tale and gazes at me with one eye of brown and the other of whirring silver. "Garm's *fun*. We take him for walks, don't we Damien? The only difference is that he's even more clever and trustworthy, and helps bring us a little bit of extra safety and security in these difficult times. Some worrying things have occurred locally, Martha, and I don't just mean mere destruction in unoccupied homes. So we do what we can, don't we Garm? Matter of fact, Martha, the enhancement technology that allows him to interact with the house security systems is essentially the same as I use to help my patients . . ."

But this is all too much, it always was, and Martha's off out through the same stupid security gates and on along the same cold, dreary streets with more than enough stuff roaring around in her head to make up for her missing seashell that Karl never did give back to her even though all property is, basically, theft. That's dumb sloganeering and there are many new ideas Martha wants to share with him. But even the waystation seems changed. Sydney's been arrested, and Sophie got her arm burned on some stray shockwire, and different faces peer out at me through the fug. Who *is* this person? Martha Chauhan could ask them the same. Then up the final level, squeezing past a doorway into some windy higher floor which already looks like the aftermath of a battle in an art gallery, with ripped concrete walls, flailing reinforcing bars and blasted ceilings all coated in huge swathes of colour. Clearly Karl's experimenting with new techniques, and it's all rather strange and beautiful-ugly. Forget regurgitated abstract expressionism. This is what Bosch would have painted if he'd lived in the bombed-out twenty-first-century city. But hadn't they agreed that that art for art's sake was essentially nothing but Nero fiddling while Rome burned?

"So," he gestures, emerging from the dazzling rubble with the winter sun behind him like some rock star of old. "What do you think?"

"It's . . . incredible . . ." So much she wants to tell him, now that she properly understands the history and context of their performance acts and sees them as part of a thread that goes back through syncretic individualism, anarcho-syndicalism and autonomism. But Karl is already scuttling off and returns holding something inside a paint-covered rag that she momentarily assumes as he unwraps it is some new artistic toy he's been playing with—a programmable paint pallet or digital brush. But, hey, it's a handgun.

Snow blows in. Martha's breath plumes. It's growing dark. The old family house creaks, groans, tinkles as she shuffles into the hall and brushes away ice and dirt from the security control panel beneath the stairs. But everything here is dead—her own memory of the night when she lost half her mind and more than half her family included. Just doubts and what-ifs. Things Karl had said, questions he'd asked, about her Dad being a doctor, which surely meant access to drugs and money, and about the kind of security systems employed in their gated estate, and ways to circumvent them. That, and the strange, dark, falling gleam of that handgun, and how those performance acts of old had never been *that* harmless. Not just ghastly artwork hung up the wrong way but taps left running, freezers turned off, pretty things smashed. Precious books, data, family photos, destroyed or laughingly defaced beyond all hope of recovery. Pigshit in the beds. Coy carp flopped gasping on Persian rugs. Treasured bits of people's lives gleefully ruined. In a way, she supposes, what Karl did to her here in her own home was a kind of comeuppance.

With numb fingers, she picks out the thumbnail data card that once held the house records and shoves it into her coat pocket, although she doubts if there's anything that would now read it, the world having moved on so very far. The rotten stairs twitch and groan as she climbs them. The door to poor, dead, Damien's room is still closed, a shrine, just as it was and always should be, but the fall of the side wall has done for most of Dad's room, and she's standing almost in empty air as she looks in.

Amazing that this whole place hasn't been ransacked and recycled, although she's sure it soon will be. Her own room especially, the floor of which now sags with the rusty weight of the great, semi-circular slabs of polarised metal and all the rest of the once high-tech medical equipment which encircles her bed.

My father pitted all his money and energies toward healing his injured daughter in the aftermath of the terrible night of Damien's death. All I can recall of this is a slow rising of pain and confusion. Instructions to do this or that minor task—the blink of an eye, the lifting of a finger—which seemed to involve my using someone else's body. My thoughts, as well, seemed strange and clumsy to me as the crystal neurons strove to blend with the damaged remains of my brain and I dipped in and out of rejection fever. In many ways, they didn't seem like my thoughts at all. I wasn't *me* any longer.

Sitting watching bad things happen on a screen with my baby brother crying. Or being on a beach somewhere with crashing waves and the dogs, the Frisbees, the cricket. These were things I could understand and believe in. But the uncooperative limbs and wayward thoughts of this changed, alien self belonged to someone else. A roaring disconnect lay between the person I'd been and the person I now was, and the only way I could remain something like sane was to think of this new creature as "Martha Chauhan."

"I'm so grateful you're still here and alive," a tired, grey-haired man Martha knew to be her father was saying as he spoon-fed her. "Is there much . . ." The offered spoon trembled in age-mottled fingers. ". . . you can remember of how all this happened?"

Martha made the slow effort to shake her head, then to open her mouth and swallow.

"There was a break-in, you see, here at our house. I don't know how the person got in, nor why the systems didn't go off, or why poor Garm wasn't alerted. But he wasn't. Neither was I—I'm too old, too deaf—and I think it was your brother Damien who must have heard something, perhaps the glass of the back door being broken, and got you to go downstairs with him. And then I believe the intruder must have panicked. After all, it can't be easy, to be standing alone in the dark of someone else's kitchen. A gun going off—that was what woke *me*, and by the time I got downstairs the intruder had fled and poor Damien was past any kind of help, although at least I know he didn't suffer. And poor Garm, of course, proved to be no use at all, and I had him reformatted and sold. But then, you never did like him much, did you? I thought you were lost to me as well for a while, Martha, what with the damage that bullet had inflicted to your head. But you're here and alive and so am I and for that I'm incredibly, impossibly grateful . . . We've spilled a bit there, though, haven't we? Hold on, I'll get a cloth . . ."

Eventually, Martha learned how to sit up unaided, and to spoon, chew and swallow her own food. It was a slow process. Through several sleepless years, as her father grew withered and exhausted from wiping her arse and changing the sheets and tending the machines, she learned how to walk and talk and returned to some kind of living. He never left her. He never let go. He never relented. He was a sunken smile and tired eyes. He was the stooped back that lifted her and hands which were always willing to hold. He never spared the time or energy for any feelings of rage, or such abstract concepts as retribution, although he surely knew who was responsible for the destruction of his family, and had sufficient evidence to prove it, even in days when justice was about as reliable as the power grid and the police were privatised crooks. Karl Yann slunk off toward the sunrise of this bright new world, whilst Martha Chanhan's father's heart gave out from grief and exhaustion, and she was left empty, damaged and alone.

She rams the old car into gear and thumbs on the headlights. The tyres slide. The black-edged, glittering night pours past her. She can hear laughter over the roaring in her ears as she parks and kills the Mini's engine at the far edge of some trees outside the Widney Commune. She rummages deep in her carpetbag, picks off the fluff and dry-swallows the few immune suppressants she can find loose in the lining. Not enough, but it will have to do. Then she takes out a primed antipsychotic syringe and shoves it into her coat pocket.

Her feet are dead and the house's fire-rimmed shadow leaps over a field of un-trampled snow as she crunches toward it. There's no one about apart from pigs sleeping in their pens until she turns a corner and hits a blaze of bonfire. Then there's life everywhere, and dancing to the accompaniment of discordant shouts and bursts of clapping.

Amazing, how well this useless brain of hers still works. How it can devise and dismiss plans without her even realising she's thought of them. The paintings inside the house, for example. She could walk in and slash, burn or deface them. But that wouldn't hurt Karl Yann. At least, not enough. He'd just pronounce it a fresh phase. Even burning this whole commune to the ground wouldn't be sufficient. What about that child, then, Shara—who Martha can see twirling at the shimmering edge of the flames? Or the lovely Freya? He'd feel *their* loss, now, wouldn't he? But Martha's mind slides from such schemes, not so much because she finds them ab-horrent but because they lack the brutal simplicity she craves. It has to be *him*, she tells herself as she stands ignored at the edge of the light searching the shining, happy faces. Has to be Karl Yann. Draw him away to some quiet spot—he might recognise her, but the entangled are impossibly trusting—then knock him senseless with the contents of this syringe. Drag him to the Mini, drive him to some as-yet undefined place . . . In this world where no one steals and no one hurts and every-thing is shared, all these things will be ridiculously easy.

The straps of the field cap can be easily adjusted. Its settings are incredibly flexible. You could kill someone, fry their brains, if you really wanted. That, or turn them into a gibbering vegetable. Appealing though these options are, though, to Martha's mind they lack the simplicity of true retribution. So why not destroy just enough of his thalamus to break the quantum shimmer of entanglement? Then, he'd be alone, just as she is. He'd be lost, and he'd know what it really is to suffer. The final performance act in a world made perfect.

But where *is* he?

"Hey, hey—look who it is! Its Martha!"

A familiar male voice, but it's Tommy the teacher who comes up to embrace her. Perhaps this is his commune. Perhaps he's out on the look for new friends to dance, laugh or fuck with. The entangled are like bonobo monkeys. Smell like them, as well. Others are turning now that Tommy's noticed her, mouths wide with surprise and sympathy. Poor, dear Martha. Sweet, old Martha. Standing there at the cold edge of the dark, when all of us are so very warm and happy. You don't need to be entangled to know what they're feeling.

She's swept up. She's carried forward. She lets go of the syringe in time just as her hands are hauled from their pockets. The entangled don't do booze, or other drugs—most them of them frown at Martha's liking for coffee—but the stuff that steams in the cracked mug that's forced into her fingers is so sweet and hot it must be laced with something. Then there's the rabbit: tender, honey-savoury—a treat in itself, meat being something that's reserved for special occasions. They're so happy to see her here at the Widney Commune it's as if they've long been waiting for her, and their joy spills out in hugs, giggles and touches. The kids flicker like elves. The old ones grin toothlessly.

Come on, Martha! Now, they're clapping to some offbeat she can't quite follow.

A circle forms, and she's at the heart of it where's the snow's been cleared and the fire roars. *Come on, Martha! Come on, Martha!* They think they're not taunting her. Think they're not drunk. But they're drunk on this hour. Drunk on the future. Drunk on everything.

Martha does an ungracious bow. Stumbles a few Rumplestiltskin steps. She's the ghost of every lost Christmas. She's the spirit of the plague from that story by Poe. And everything, her head most likely, or possibly her body, or this entire world, is spinning. Poor Martha. Dear Martha. They stroke lumpen shape of her skull like it's an old stone found on a beach. And this isn't even her commune. Isn't her world.

"Hey, Martha . . ." Now, Freya and Shara emerge from the glowing smoke." So great that you've come back to see us again!"

"Oh, yes . . ." Shara agrees. "We all love you here, Martha. We really do."

"Where's Karl?" Martha yells over a roaring that must be mostly in her head.

"He's . . ." One starts.

". . . out." The other finishes.

"Right," Martha says. "You don't have any idea *where*, do you? I mean . . . You see . . ."

She trails off as these two elfin creatures, one small and one fully grown and both entirely beautiful, gaze at her with firelight in their eyes.

"Oh, somewhere," Freya says with a faraway smile. "Your birthfather likes to wander, doesn't he, Sha?"

For Martha's benefit, Shara gives an emphatic nod.

"Oh? Right. Good . . . You see, I think I used to know him . . . Long ago."

"Oh, but you *did*!" Freya delightedly confirms. "I said you'd come to see us, and Karl instantly knew who you were, didn't he, Sha? Said you went back a very long way."

"And then . . . He went out again?"

"Of course. I mean . . ." Freya shrugs her shoulders. Gazes off, as if nothing could be more welcoming, into the freezing dark. "Why not?"

After her father died—a feat he managed with the same quiet fortitude with which he'd done most things throughout his life—Martha Chauhan found herself living in a place with Harry Potterish turrets and pointed windows that could have been the one she and Damien had visited when they were kids. A kind of commune, if you like. But not.

Still a youngish woman by many standards, but she fitted in well with these wizened and damaged creatures who cost so much money and technology and wasted effort to keep alive. She learned how to talk to them, and show an interest. She got better at walking. She learned how to play mahjong. And outside, beyond the newly heightened shockwire and the sullen guards, the world was falling apart. The tap water was brown with sewerage. The winters were awful. The summers were shot.

But wait. The big screens they sat in front of all day were showing something else. There was a virus—a new mutation of a type of encephalitis that attacked a part of the brain known as the thalamus. The fever it triggered was worrying, but very few people died from it, and those who survived were changed in ways they found hard to explain—at least to those who hadn't yet become whatever they now were. Some said the virus wasn't just some random mutation, but it was down to terrorists, or space aliens, or the government. Or that it was triggering something had long been there, buried deep inside everyone's skulls, and that this was a new kind of humanity, a different kind of knowing, which was triggered by a form of quantum entanglement which joined mind to mind, soul to soul.

Others simply insisted that it was the Rapture. Or the end of the world.

Of course, there were riots and pogroms. There was looting. There were several wars. Politicians looked for personal advancement. Priests and mullahs pleaded for calm, or raged for vengeance. People walked the streets wearing facemasks, or climbed into their panic rooms, or headed for hilltops and deserted islands with years' supplies of food and weapons. A time of immense confusion, and all Martha Chauhan knew as things collapsed was that the few staff who were still working at Hogwarts laughed as they saw to the catheters or mopped the floors. Soon, many of the wizened and damaged ones were laughing as well.

The day the shockwire fell—her own personal Berlin Wall—Martha Chauhan stumbled out into a changed world. It was all almost as she'd long expected. There were the bodies and the twisted lampposts and the ransacked buildings and the burnt-out cars. But people were busy working in loose, purposeful gangs, and *clearing things up*. Stranger still, they were singing as they did so, or laughing like loons, or simply staring at each other and the world as if they'd never seen it before.

On she stumbled. And was picked up, cradled, fed, welcomed. Then, as the fever passed by her and nothing changed, she was pitied as well. Eventually, she got to meet people who could explain why she could never become entangled, but she already knew. There was nothing that could be done to replace the dumb nano-circuitry that took up vital parts of her skull without destroying this construct known as Martha Chauhan as well. Still, the commune at Baldwin Towers were as happy to have her. She was even given a specialist kind of work, along with some privileges, to reflect her odd status and disability, a bit like the blind piano tuners of old. And so it went, and so it still is to this dark winter's night, and now Martha Chanhan's back in her Mini, driving lost and alone through a fathomless, glittering world.

She's stopped. The little car's engine is quiet, and the cold's incredibly intense. She fumbles in her carpetbag with dead fingers, but whatever immune suppressants she has left—carefully made somewhere far from here at great but unmentioned expense—must all be back at Baldwin Towers, and the roaring in her head deepens as she breaks the door's seal of ice and tumbles outside.

Another day is greying as she looks up at the waystation. Superficially, nothing much has changed. It's still an abandoned ruin, although the snow and these extra years of neglect have given it a kind of grace. Even the dead shockwire Karl once held up for her remains, and shivers like a live thing, scattering rust and ice down her neck as she crawls beneath.

All the old faces seem to peer out at her as clambers on and in through concrete shadows and icicle drips. Who *is* this person? She could ask same of them. Not that she ever belonged here. Or anywhere. Creaks and slides as she climbs ladders and crawls stairways until she claws back her breath and finds she's standing surprisingly high, overlooking a greened and snowy landscape that seems more forest than city in the sun's gaining blaze. For all she knows, the entangled will soon be swinging tree to tree. But that isn't how it will end. They're biding their time for now, still clearing things up as this damaged world heals, and the icecaps, the forests, the jungles, the savannahs, return. But the gestalt will spread. Soon, it will expand in a great wave to join with the other intelligences which knit this universe. Martha Chauhan hears someone laughing, and realises it's herself. For a dizzy moment there, standing at this precipice at the future's edge, she almost understood what it all means.

The whole sky is brightening, and she's starting to realise just how beautiful this high part of the old waystation has become. Blasted rubble and concrete and a sense of abandonment, certainly, but everything covered in the glimmer of frost and snow and old paint and new growth. Colours pool in the icemelt. Then, something bigger moves, and she sees that it's a ragged old man, a kind of grey-bearded wizard, half Scrooge and half Father Christmas, who seems part of this grotto in his paint-strewn clothes.

"It's me, Martha," Karl Yann says in a croaked approximation of his old voice as his reflections ripple about him. "I just wish I could share how you feel."

"But you *can't* can you? You're here and I'm not." Martha Chauhan shakes her head. Feels her thoughts rattle. That isn't what she meant at all. "You think you know everything, don't you? All the secrets of the fucking universe. But you don't know what it is to *hurt*."

He winces. Looks almost afraid. But there's the same distant pity in his old eyes that Martha's seen a million times. Even here. Even from him. She tries to imagine herself dragging the syringe from her pocket. Running forward screaming and stabbing. Instead, her vision blurs with tears.

"Oh, Martha, *Martha* . . . Here, look . . ." Now he's coming toward her in a frost of breath, and holding something out. "This used to be yours. It *is* yours. You should have it back . . ."

She sniffs and looks despite herself. Sees her long-lost seashell, of all things, nestling in his craggy hand. She gabs it greedily and hugs it to herself and away from him. "I suppose you've got that other thing here as well—another bloody souvenir?"

He almost looks puzzled. "What thing?"

"The gun, you bastard! The thing you killed my bother with—and did this to me!" She slaps the slope of her skull so hard it rings.

But he just stands there. Then, slowly, he blinks. "I think I see."

"See what?" The entangled are useless at arguing—she's tried it often enough.

"You think, Martha, you *believe*, that I broke into your house and did that terrible thing? Is that what you're saying?"

"Of course I am." But why is the roaring getting louder in her head?

"I'm sorry, Martha," he says, looking at her more pityingly than ever. "I really am so very, very sorry."

"You can't just . . . Leave . . ."

But he is. He's turning, shuffling away from her across this rainbow space with nothing but a slow backward glance. Dissolving into the frost and the shadows, climbing down and out from this lost place of memories toward his life and his commune and a sense of infinite belonging, before Martha Chauhan even knows what else to know or say or feel.

Full day now, and Martha Chanhan's sitting high at the concrete edge of the way-station.

It's freezing up here, despite the snowmelt. But she doesn't seem to be shivering any longer, nor does she feel especially cold. She sniffs, swipes her dripping nose, then studies the back of an old woman's hand which seems to have come away coated in blood. That roaring in her ears which is much far loud and close to be any kind of sound. Although there's no pain, it isn't hard for her to imagine, with what brains she has left, of the wet dissolution of the inside of her skull as the immune suppressants fade from her blood. If she doesn't turn up back at Baldwin Towers soon, she supposes help will probably come. But the entangled can be astonishingly callous. After all, they let their old and frail die from curable diseases. They kill their treasured pets for clothing and food.

She inspects her old seashell. A small glow rises through the red smears when she touches its controls. Something here that isn't dead, and she hooks the buds around her ears and feels a faint, nostalgic fizz. But the stuff she liked back in the day would surely be awful, old and lost as she now is. A different person, really. In fact, that's the whole point . . .

She feels past the syringe in her coat pocket, finds the data card she took from the house security system and sniffs back more blood as she numbly shoves it in. It's still a surprise, though, to find options and menus hanging against the clear morning sky. Files as well, when you'd have thought Dad would have deleted them. But then, he never liked destroying things—even stuff he never planned to use. And perhaps, the thought trickles down through her leaking brain, he left this for her. After all, and despite his many evasions and protestations, he always had a strong regard for the truth.

She waves a once-practised hand through ancient images until she reaches the very last date. The end of everything. The very last night.

And there it is.

There it always was.

She's looking into the bright dark of their old kitchen through the nightsight eyes of that stupid not-dog. Fast-forward until a window shatters in a hard spray and the door opens and something moves in, and the not-dog stirs, wags its tail, recognises . . . Not Karl Yann, but much more a familiar shape and scent.

Martha rips the buds from her ears, but she still can't escape the past. She's back at this waystation, but she's young again, and the colours are brilliant, and she's here with Karl Yann, full of Politics and Philosophy and righteous anger at the state of the world. And he's got this handgun that he's merely using as a prop for all his agit-prop posturings, when she has a much clearer, simpler, cleverer idea. The final performance act, right? The easiest, most obvious, one of all . . . Come on, Karl, don't say you haven't *thought* of it . . . And fuck you if you're not interested. If you're not prepared, I'll just do the damn thing myself . . .

Martha flouncing out from the waystation. Into the darkness. Hunching alone through the glass and rubble streets. The gun a weight of potentiality in her pocket and the whole world asleep. She feels like she's in the mainstream of the long history of resistance. She's Ulrike Meinhof. She's Gavrilo Princip. She's Harry Potter fighting Voldemort. A pure, simple, righteous deed to show everyone—and her Dad especially—that there are no barriers that will keep the truth of what's really happening away from these prim, grim estates. Not this shockwire. Nor these gates. Not anything. Least of all the glass of their kitchen door which breaks in a satisfying clatter as she feels in for the old-fashioned handle and turns. Not that this isn't a prank as well. Not that there isn't still fun to be had. After all, that fucking thing of a dog isn't really living anyway, it's nothing but dumb *property*, so what harm is being done if she shoots it properly dead? Nothing at all, right? She's doing nothing but good. She's shoving it to the system. She's giving it to the man. The darkness seethes as she enters, and she feels as always feels, standing right here in her own kitchen, which is like an intruder in her own life.

That roaring again. Now stronger than ever, even though the seashell's buds are off and its batteries have gone. After all, how is she to tell one shape from another in this sudden dark? How could she know when she can barely see anything that the thing that comes stumbling threateningly out at her is Damien and not that zombie dog? It's all happened already, and too quickly, and the moment is long gone. A squeezed trigger and the world shudders and she's screaming and the dog's howling and all the backup lights have flared and Damien's sprawled in a lake of blood and the gun's a deathly weight in her hand—although Martha Chauhan doubts if she could ever understand how she felt as she turned it around so that its black snout was pointing at her own head and she squeezed the trigger again.

Her father's with her now. Even without looking, and just as when she lay in her bedroom surrounded by pain and humming equipment, she knows he's here. After all, and despite her many attempts to reject him, he never really went away. And, as always, he's telling her tales—filling the roaring air with endless ideas, suppositions, stories . . . Talking at least as much about once-upon-a-times and should-have-beens as about how things really are. Using what life and energy he has left to bring back his daughter. And if he could have found a way of sheltering her from what really happened that terrible night, if he could have invented a story that gave her a reason to carry on living, Martha knows he would have done so.

She sniffs, tastes bitter salt, and feels a deep roaring. It's getting impossibly late. Already, the sun seems to be setting, and the beach is growing cold, and the cricket match has finished, and that last gritty samosa she's just eaten was foul, and all the dogs and the kite flyers have gone home. But there's Dad, walking trousers-rolled and hand-in-hand with Damien as the tide floods in. Martha waves cheerily, and they wave back. She thinks she might just join them, down there at the edge of everything where all islands meet.

εarth I

STEPHEN BAXTER

Stephen Baxter made his first sale to Interzone *in 1987, and since then has become one of that magazine's most frequent contributors, as well as appearing in* Asimov's Science Fiction, Science Fiction Age, Analog Science Fiction and Fact, Zenith, New Worlds, *and elsewhere. Baxter's first novel,* Raft, *was released in 1991, and was rapidly followed by other well-received novels such as* Timelike Infinity, Anti-Ice, Flux, *and the H. G. Wells pastiche—a sequel to* The Time Machine—The Time Ships, *which won both the John W. Campbell Memorial Award and the Philip K. Dick Award. His many other books include the novels* Voyage, Titan, Moonseed, Mammoth, Book One: Silverhair, Long Tusk, Ice Bone, Manifold: Time, Manifold: Space, Evolution, Coalescent, Exultant, Transcendent, Emperor, Resplendent, Conqueror, Navigator, Firstborn, The H-Bomb Girl, Weaver, Flood, Ark, *and two novels in collaboration with Arthur C. Clarke,* The Light of Other Days *and* Time's Eye, a Time Odyssey. *His short fiction has been collected in* Vacuum Diagrams: Stories of the Xeelee Sequence, Traces, *and* The Hunters of Pangaea, *and he has released a chapbook novella,* Mayflower II. *His most recent books include: the novel trilogy* Stone Spring, Bronze Summer, *and* Iron Winter; *a nonfiction book,* The Science of Avatar; *and a trilogy written in collaboration with Terry Pratchett:* The Long Earth, The Long War, *and* The Long Childhood.

Here he takes us along on a quest among the stars to discover the lost origin place of all humanity, one which may teach lessons the seekers are not really ready to learn.

I

If we expected to come out here and join in some kind of bustling Galactic culture, it ain't going to happen. We seem to be young, in a very old Galaxy. We're like kids tiptoeing through a ruined mansion. Or a graveyard . . .

LuSi and JaEm, laughing, hand in hand, ran down the concrete slope into the tremendous dish of the starship construction yard. Huge structures stood here, inert and silent today, cranes and manipulators and immense trucks, portable fusion plants, fuel tanks frosted with glittering ice. LuSi knew that what had been constructed here, immense sculptures of metal and ceramic and monomolecular carbon, had been grander still, before being hoisted into orbit around Urthen and assembled into the delicate, gravity-vulnerable superstructure of a starship, itself a transformed asteroid.

A ship that was going to take LuSi away to the stars.

But not today, she told herself, not for a few Days more, she wasn't going to lose JaEm and his warm touch, not today. And a few Days was a long time for a fourteen-year-old. On they ran, seeking a quiet place amid the silent machines.

And even at this moment LuSi had an unwelcome sense of perspective, the kind of perspective JaEm's father, Jennin PiRo, had tried to beat into her thick skull, in his words. The yard, a giant crater dug into the ground, was *too big*, too big even for the monumental machines they built here. And why was that? Because it hadn't been constructed to build mere human starships. It hadn't been built by humans at all, as far as anybody could tell, but by an alien culture, star-faring, long-vanished. Why should it be so? It was an illogic in the Sim, the Jennin protested, in the Backstory, the received history of the universe and the human story within it. Unless the Sim's Designers and Controllers were insane, why build in a feature like this that had nothing to do with mankind—it made no sense! Couldn't LuSi *see* that? . . .

Unfortunately she could, and it crowded into her head even now, even as they reached the shadow of a tremendous truck, found a sheltered spot behind one huge tyre out of the wind, and, laughing, sat side by side. Their breath steamed and mingled before them. They kissed, for the first time that day. And when JaEm slid his hand inside her coat, and she could feel his warmth, his strength.

Their shared warmth was a defiance of the cold of the day. The Ember hung above them, above the scattered clouds, in the sky from which it never moved. Its broad face was like a fading fire, mottled with huge dark spots. All LuSi's short life the spots had been gathering, and the Jennins and other scholars predicted gloomily that the world was heading for another Ember-winter. Well, LuSi couldn't remember the *last* Ember-winter, it had been over hundreds of Years before she was born. The only warmth she cared about was in JaEm's lips, his hands, the firm body she could feel under his clothing. Yet she was soon to be taken away from this scrap of warmth too, and flung between the colder stars. All because of her mother and her hateful, self-imposed "mission" . . .

JaEm could sense her distraction. He hugged her, then sat back. He was sensitive that way, more so than she was. One reason she loved him, she supposed, though they had not yet used such loaded words out loud.

He asked, "What are you thinking about? Not about leaving? We shouldn't waste the time we've got left thinking about that—"

"No, not that," she lied. "I was thinking about your father, if you must know. His lectures. The shipyards are one of his 'classic' examples of Sim flaws."

"I suppose I've had more practice in shutting *him* out of my head than you have." He kissed her again, delicately. "Do you think we're all in a Sim?"

"Of course," she said dutifully.

"Even when I do this . . . and *this*." Now he nibbled her ear, a move that always seemed to liquefy her internally. "Are we all just patterns of electricity in Memory, in some big calculating machine in Denva?"

"If we are, it's a very *good* Sim," she said, wriggling closer. "I don't care if I'm real or not, as long as you're here with me."

"Oh, LuSi—"

"Oh, what rot." A light shone in their faces, harsh, dazzling. The voice behind it was unmistakeable: Jennin PiRo, JaEm's father.

They pulled away from each other, fixing their clothing. JaEm raised a hand to shield his eyes. "Father? What do you want?"

"Nothing from you, son," the Jennin said. "I need to talk to LuSi. And where she is, you are. You are depressingly predictable, for two of my brightest students. Come on out of there."

PiRo, aged about forty Years—ten Years younger than LuSi's mother—was a tall, habitually severe man dressed in the jet black uniform of a Jennin. Severe, and habitually impatient with the flaws and weaknesses of others, particularly of his students, like LuSi, who he seemed to think should be doing better. "Sloppy, sloppy," he said now, "and I don't mean your kissing technique, son." Which made JaEm blush horribly. "I mean your thinking." He turned on LuSi. "And your sheer emotional immaturity."

LuSi bridled. "Immaturity?"

"How can it not *matter* if you are a Sim character, or not? Would it not *matter* if you were the arbitrary creation of some cold onlooker? Imagine what she or he could *do* to you. Freeze you. Disorder your life, so that you might leap from death to birth— from my son's youthful embrace to the bony hug of an ancient. *Delete* you! He could delete you from this artificial world you believe in, leaving no trace. Does that not appal you?"

Actually it did, but she felt her privacy had been violated by this pompous man, and she knew the theory enough to argue back. So she shrugged. "It would make no difference. Even if the instants of my life were jumbled up in the Memory, *I* would still experience them in the proper order. From my point of view, my own time line, I could never tell if—"

"Oh, yes, rationalise it away. That kind of circularity of argument is precisely why, I suspect, the mythos of the Sim, and the Controllers in Denva, has lingered as long as human civilisation has persisted on this planet. Do you know how long that is?"

"Well—" She *should* know.

"Ten thousand Years! Nearly three quarters of a million turns of Urthen around the Ember! That's as best as we can reconstruct, given the damage done by the Xaian Normalisation. Four hundred human generations—why, is it really imaginable that the most cold-hearted Controllers could maintain a Sim of whatever complexity for so long? What could possibly be the purpose?"

She stuck out her chin defiantly. "I don't know. I have no answer. And since this isn't your classroom, Jennin PiRo, I don't have to find an answer, do I? You came looking for me, you said. Maybe you should get to the point."

JaEm flinched at her defiance.

But PiRo gave her a kind of wary grin. "All right. I suppose I deserved that. Look, you may have an important future. More important than you know. And it's because of your mother."

"My mother?"

"You understand why Zaen SheLu is undertaking this decades-long mission to the stars."

"She has a hypothesis about Denva," LuSi said. "The Controllers' base. The world humanity came from, or maybe a location on that world. She thinks it's real, has a real location. Or at least—"

"A location that maps onto a site in this 'simulated' universe. A place where humans first came from. That's correct. The difficulty is, she might be right."

LuSi was baffled. "What do you mean, Jennin?"

"I mean that her arguments are good, intellectually. She might well find some world, some primal site, that matches many of the criteria she has set out in her arguments. And if she does, that will cement the notion of the Sim in the minds of humanity for all time. Because the idea that all of humanity emanates from one single, primal, sacred world is just the kind of mythic element a Sim Designer would build into our Backstory. It's a good *narrative*, and so it appeals to us."

She shrugged. "But if it's *true*—"

"If it's true, then the notion that we are mere toys in the hands of the Controllers will lock us in us forever. We will lose initiative. We will *give up*. What other reaction can there be? And this is not a universe in which it is safe to give up, to stop thinking, to become complacent. Not if the stars are going out." He glanced up at the Ember.

The Ember was not a star, like the more distant points of light in the sky. It was called a "brown dwarf" by the astronomers, a term said to go back to the arrival of the Ark itself—if you believed the Ark ever existed. The Ember was not a star but a mere mass of glowing gas, heated by its own infall, and therefore gradually cooling.

LuSi was only growing more confused. "But if it's *true*, if the Sim exists and we can prove it, then that's all that matters—isn't it?"

"There are many kinds of truth, LuSi. And many uses to which 'truth' can be put."

"You still haven't told me what you want of me."

"It's simple, LuSi. Somebody needs to counterbalance your mother on this crusade of hers. I've been invited to join the mission myself . . ."

And that brief line electrified both LuSi and JaEm. For if the Jennin came aboard the ship, surely his family would too—surely JaEm would follow his father—and LuSi and JaEm would have Years together, not mere Days.

The Jennin seemed oblivious to their reaction. "I have many responsibilities here, which I am reluctant to shed. I am undecided. But failing that, if I am not there—"

LuSi felt as if she was groping towards an understanding of all this. "Me? You want me to spend the next fifty Years arguing with my mother, about Sim theory and theology?"

He grinned. "That's the idea. Somebody has to. And I think you have it in you, LuSi, even if you don't see it yet yourself. Look—I don't mean to impose on you, in this time you two have left together. Or to order you around. I want to inspire you, and I know I'm not always good at that, am I? A Jennin I may be, but not always a great teacher."

"Inspire me? How?"

"I've secured you a ride on a torchship. You too, JaEm, if you must. We're going into space! I know our journey will be dwarfed by your jaunt to the stars, but the scenery will be a lot more fun."

JaEm gaped, evidently delighted.

"Why?" LuSi asked, more sceptical. "What's the point? What are we going to be talking about?"

"The Backstory," Jennin PiRo said simply.

The torchship was called the *Holy Water*. Owned by PiRo's university, it was a practical, basic design meant for scientists, surveyors, explorers, a small, highly manoeuvrable, all but automated craft, capable of transporting a dozen passengers in comfort between the worlds of the Ember system in a matter of Days. LuSi and JaEm had travelled in such ships many times before; the *Holy Water* was a trivial achievement for a civilisation capable of routine interstellar travel.

But as they boarded, as the ship leapt out of another gigantic port facility and into the sky, the Jennin made them think about how the ship worked, the miracle of physics that powered it.

"You are riding a fusion torch," he said. "And, generous as the Ember is to give us its warmth and light, the Ember is a *failed star*, it never achieved the mass it needed to allow fusion to spark in its core. Until humanity arose here—"

"Or came here," LuSi said automatically, correcting JaEm's father's mild multi-origin heresy.

"Before us, fusion had *never happened* here, in this system, not since the birth of the universe itself. Think what a wonder that is—what power we have! . . ."

The first few days of the voyage were a jaunt. The Jennin took them on a looping tour of the Ember's planetary system. LuSi knew that compared to some systems out among the stars of the Bubble, this was an impoverished place, with only two large planets, Urthen and Bigmars, a handful of smaller, scattered worldlets, and more distant belts of asteroids, comets and sparse ice moons. Both Urthen and Bigmars orbited so close to the Ember that they were tidally locked, each holding one face permanently to the sub-star's dim glow—the price they paid for the meagre warmth of the Ember. But that warmth had not been enough to save Bigmars from an endless age of ice; unlike Urthen, which too had its chilly regions, no liquid water could persist on Bigmars's surface.

It was towards Bigmars that Jennin at last pointed the ship's prow. And as that cold, glittering world approached, he ordered the youngsters to tell him the Backstory.

The Backstory was the history of the universe and of mankind in it, and every child on Urthen learned it at first school. "The Ark was built, by the giants Nimrod, Seba and Halivah, so that their children could flee Denva when the oceans rose," LuSi said. "The Crew struggled to survive, until the Son extracted the Ship's Law from the Will. And the Ship's Law remains the basis of our system of justice to this day."

Jennin waved a hand. "Yes, yes. And then?"

JaEm went on, "And then the Ark split in two, when some of the Crew fell upon the poison ground of a world of false promise. Then there was the Blow-Out, when rebel children challenged the parameters of the Sim itself and caused a lethal rupture of the remnant Ark."

"Which is commonly interpreted as a metaphor for a Sim systems crash," said LuSi. "According to an analysis by—"

"Don't analyse!" the Jennin snapped. "Don't interpret! Just tell me the story."

JaEm went on uncertainly, "The Ark split in two at one more false world. Then finally its mighty journey was over, the sacred engines were shut down for the last time—"

"Yes, yes. And humans fell to the ground of Urthen all those Years ago, ten thousand Years. Then what?"

"Then we prospered, and spread, and cultivated our farms," LuSi said. "Cities rose. Learning spread. At last we built new ships, not as mighty as the Ark but capable of reaching the stars. And we sent out emissaries to the false worlds, and their peoples, and we found new false worlds and we populated them, until the Bubble was filled with worlds—"

"And then the Xaians of Windru got hold of starship technology," the Jennin said.

LuSi suppressed a smile. It sounded to her as if PiRo was becoming enthralled by the familiar story, despite his intellectual scepticism. "The Xaians," she said, "seeking to cut mankind free of the burden of history, scoured the worlds of the Bubble and destroyed all traces of the human past, on world after world—"

"Or tried to," PiRo said. "All they succeeded in doing was making the job of the archaeologists and historians and other Jennins a lot more difficult."

"On Urthen, even starship technology was lost. But eventually it was recovered . . ."

Bigmars was looming close now. Through the transparent hull of the habitable compartment the planet bellied before them, its surface rust-red and wrinkled under splashes of ice. Awed or intimidated by the sight, they fell silent.

The Jennin was the first to speak. "The Backstory," he said. "The whole tangle of it. LuSi, think. Of course it has a storytelling unity. But doesn't it all sound too *complicated*? If you were a Sim Designer and you were going to invent a history for mankind, why make it so complex and unlikely? All these ships flying around an empty universe . . . And what about the elements of the Backstory that have nothing to do with mankind at all? What are *they* for?"

JaEm frowned. "What do you mean, father?"

The Jennin snorted. "Tell him, LuSi."

LuSi, embarrassed for JaEm, just said: "Look down."

They were in orbit now, swooping low over the northern hemisphere of Bigmars. Close to what looked unmistakeably like the shore of a sea, vanished save for glinting salt flats, were rows of dimples in the ground, like craters, small features seen from space but huge if you were down there among them. But they were not craters.

"You know what they are," Jennin PiRo said. "Even you, JaEm—"

"Evidence of starships."

"Yes. Construction yards, like on Urthen—maybe. Or at least the marks of the launch of starships. Interstellar technology is always going to be hugely energetic; it is always going to mark any planet on which it takes root. And we know this isn't evidence of human activity because—"

LuSi said, "It's all too old. Sealed under water ice and frozen air."

"More air than water, but yes. What do we think happened to the people who built this?"

"They left in their starships. Or else they died out here, so long ago that their tombs have eroded away . . ."

"The Ember got too cool," said JaEm.

"That's it," said the Jennin. "That's the story—or the Backstory. The Ember is cooling, slowly, but inexorably. At any point in time there is a location in space around the Ember where a planet is warm enough for life—life like ours, life that needs liquid water. Once Bigmars was warm enough. But the habitable radius moved in towards the Ember, and Bigmars froze. Much of its water is probably still there, but locked underground in big aquifers. Useless for life. All this took a long time, billions of Years, but it was inexorable. And, yes, LuSi, the inhabitants of Bigmars must have fled, or died out. Just as we, one day, will have to flee, when Urthen starts to freeze in its turn."

LuSi said carefully, "Some people think that adds to the authenticity of the Backstory. I mean, the story of the Ark. The crew must have come far; maybe they could go no further, and had to stop here, however imperfect the world is, however inadequate the Ember."

The Jennin snorted dismissively. "That's not what I brought you here to see."

"I know," LuSi said. "It's just like the starship yards at home. You argue that there is no need for a human Backstory to include evidence of a vanished alien civilisation."

"Well, why should it?"

She faced him. "You say you want me to argue with my mother over her interpretation. But she has evidence on her side. At least for the consistency of the Backstory, the logic of the Sim. For instance, the very existence of mankind on the many worlds of the Bubble. How could we have got there if a ship didn't deliver us?"

"Oh, there are plenty of secondary colonies. We know that. But the primary worlds, including Airtree, Windru, Urthen—mankind arose separately on all these worlds. Convergent evolution. Our form is in some sense optimal for sentient, tool-wielding creatures."

"But it's not just mankind. What about the Human Suite? That's what the ecologists call it, isn't it?"

"Go on. What is the Human Suite?"

"The creatures on which we rely, the grasses, the animals. Things we eat, or that can eat us. They are always to be found on human worlds—even though we have to share every world with other forms of life. Some quite unlike ours."

"So what? So on each world there has been a multiple origin of life—more than one tree of life. Why not? Why should the initiation of life be unique? And as for the Human Suite—convergent evolution, once again. What else?"

"There's the fact that the human worlds share elements of culture. Similarities of language, we all speak something like Anglish. We even use time measures like

Years and Days that have nothing to do with the turn and spin periods of a world like ours—"

"All probably imposed by the Xaians in their ideological fervour, much more recently than the flight of any Ark from a proto-world. Certainly that's a much simpler explanation, and one based on an event we *know* happened, from the surviving records." The Jennin leaned forward. "Look, child. I'm not expecting you to swallow my arguments today. Or ever, even. I just believe that your mother needs a countering voice.

"Her pet theory, and the theological orthodoxy on this world and many others— that we are all trapped in some artificial reality—is deadening for the human spirit. The Backstory reinforces the idea. On the other hand the notion that the universe is just as it seems, that humanity evolved independently on all these habitable worlds, is actually simpler; we don't *need* an elaborate secret history to explain it all . . . If the Backstory is confirmed by your mother, the whole Sim hypothesis is strengthened too. Your mother is never going to be convinced by the likes of me, but at least she needs a counter-voice. She must be made to work hard to convince others, no matter what she finds out there among the stars. And that's what I want of you, LuSi—to be that counter-voice . . ."

"Or," JaEm said, reading a note scrolling on a comms screen, "you could do that job yourself, father."

"What do you mean?"

"The university has just made an announcement. It is a big project, after all; the journey will take at least a century, there and back. They want a presence on board. And the College of Zaens is apparently going to mandate it."

"Mandate *what*? . . . Oh. My presence on the ship."

"You're going to the stars too." JaEm grinned at LuSi. "And so are we."

They couldn't resist it. They flung themselves at each other and embraced.

The Jennin groaned and rubbed his face. "Serves me right. Be careful what you wish for, in case you get it. I bet *that* saying is as old as mankind itself . . ."

It took another year before the great starship *Reality Dreams* was ready to cross the interstellar gulf.

It took fourteen more years to achieve that crossing.

LuSi and JaEm were together on the ship; in the course of the journey they were even married. Thanks to their advanced anti-senescence science, the people of Urthen were long-lived; only a fraction of their potential lifetimes was expended.

But still, by the time the ship reached Airtree, its first destination, their youth was gone.

II

After the battle was done, the Speaker of Speakers paused by the small field hospital that tended to the wounded, and reassured the dying that death was not an end, merely a return to the frozen patterns of thoughts in the greater Memory of the Sim . . .

The starship *Reality Dreams* settled into orbit around Airtree.

Shuttles, approved by the local authority, came up from the ground to transport down the passengers. Blocky winged craft powered by fission rockets for the ascent, and essentially gliders for the re-entry and landing, these were all elderly, well-worn craft, beaten up by multiple flights to the edge of space. JaEm, who had devoted his life aboard the *Reality Dreams* to space engineering, looked faintly appalled at the sight of them.

But LuSi knew this was what they had to expect. Airtree was ruled by a single government, as it had been through most of its history: a theocracy built around the cult of the Sim Controllers. The theocracy was rich, but its world was technologically backward, relatively.

Even the slightly grander craft that was to transport Zaen SheLu, the Jennin PiRo, and their children LuSi and JaEm, plastered with heat-resistant tiles and holy symbols, was old and shabby and smelled faintly of urine. LuSi settled in grimly beside JaEm; nearly thirty years old now, and after fourteen years in the cavernous interior of the starship, she felt a twinge of apprehension as the shuttle parted from its lock with a rattle of opening latches.

Before making their descent they completed a high-inclination orbital loop around the planet, and LuSi was able to make out the main features of this world, fixing them against the maps she had studied in the years before their arrival. Like Urthen, Airtree orbited close in to its sun, so that a single hemisphere faced the light. The illuminated face was a muddle of ocean and land, and LuSi could make out great concentric bands of vegetation types surrounding the subsolar point, green fading to brown or grey, swathes of forest or grasslands or crops, or even surviving scraps of native life, she supposed, adapted to the particular conditions of light and climate dictated by the unchanging altitude of the sun in the sky.

And above all this, LuSi saw *Reality Dreams*, patiently following its own orbit. The starship was an engineered asteroid, a bubble of glass and ice that shone green from within, like a tremendous jewel; it looked more like a small moon than a ship. It was a miracle of the ancient warp technology that had driven the ship between the stars that in flight this huge bulk was *folded away* out of spacetime into a higher dimension, so that only a warp bubble the size of a sand grain protruded into the mundane cosmic stratum. LuSi longed with all her heart to be back aboard the ship, with JaEm, in the home they had built together, with their work, their slates and models, their friends. But she knew, too, that that was a symptom of her long interstellar confinement; she was like a released prisoner longing to be locked up again.

At Airtree's subsolar point was an island, the largest of a chain, a speck of land directly under the suspended star. The shuttle dipped low over this, heading north towards the shore of a continent called Seba, where they would make landfall. Light flared beyond the cabin windows, and the ride grew briefly bumpier, the air thickening, turbulent. When the plasma glow faded, the starry sky had been replaced by a violet blue, the stars were obscured, and the starship was lost to LuSi's view. She reached out for JaEm's hand.

Speaker Tanz Vlov, sitting opposite them, observed this. This Airtree native, compact, shaven-headed, had been sent up in the shuttle to be their escort to the ground. Like many of his people, from a world of sterner gravity than Urthen, he was short by the standards LuSi was used to, but not exceptionally so. Despite his drab clerical garb he was a cheery, irreverent man who appeared about forty, but since anti-ageing treatments were available on this world, at least to the ruling elite, that was no real guide. Now Vlov smiled. "You look nostalgic." He spoke the Urthen tongue—or their particular Anglish dialect depending on how you classified it— well but with a heavy accent. "You miss your ship."

"It is our home," LuSi said. "Has been since we were both teenagers."

"Your home? You are married, yes? You have children?"

"Not yet," JaEm said. "Perhaps in the next phase of the journey. Which will take another thirty years, nearly, to Windru."

Vlov whistled. "Thirty more years, in a big enclosed machine. Strange to think of it."

Jennin PiRo leaned forward, past his son. "It shouldn't be strange. Not to you. This world is the capital of the Creed of the Sim! You're a Speaker, senior in the faith. You believe that *everything* is an artefact—even the physical world, even the stars, all a dream stored in some vast machine's frozen Memory. What is life in a starship but a metaphor for that? It should seem familiar to you . . ."

LuSi was used to this kind of goading from the Jennin. Vlov's reaction seemed to be a commonsense one; he winked at her, and grinned. "Of course nothing is real. But the Sim Controllers created us for a purpose, a purpose expressed through how we live our lives. And we must live those lives as if it *were* all real. What else is there to do?"

LuSi's mother, meanwhile, was entirely uninterested in the conversation. SheLu was dressed in her own world's version of clerical garb, the plain steel-grey robe of a Zaen, a priest of the Sim, and her hair, while not shaven close, was cut short and neat. She was in her sixties now but her ageing treatments had preserved her at around thirty; seeing her in the unfamiliar light of this new world, LuSi saw how her skin was just a little too taut, her eyes a little too clear. She peered out of the small window beside her seat, as the shuttle banked and turned in the air. "And that is the island you call the Navel?"

Vlov didn't need to look to see. "At the Substellar, yes. Just like Urthen, from what I hear, our world huddles close to its sun, which is a small, cool star—as stars go, anyhow. But at least it is a star! I can't imagine living in a sky full of a big fat gassy bag of a *planet* . . ."

"There is a monument," murmured SheLu. "On the island. But it is a mighty wreck."

So it was, LuSi saw, when she got a chance to look. The island seen from above was a scarred mass of docks, dwellings, temples and pathways, all centred on a tremendous pillar—a pillar that was smashed, melted in places, with great fallen blocks larger than some of the buildings at its feet.

"The work of the Xaian Normalisation," SheLu said.

"Yes," said Vlov. "Once it was called the Eye. The monument itself was Substrate. Which is what we call the relics of an older technology found by humans on this world when they arrived."

JaEm asked, "Older?"

His father said dryly, "Alien."

"We had nothing which could scar it, break it. We could build on top of it, or around it, and so we did. It is said that the Xaians used a starship drive to dismantle such features, here, at the Antistellar, at the Poles."

SheLu seemed to shudder. "Warp technology brought to a planet's surface. What barbarism."

"Before the Xaians came, the monument was used to venerate the Controllers."

"But if that's so," PiRo said, "why would the Controllers not simply reverse the damage and restore the monument? It would take only a Word, after all."

Vlov, unperturbed, just grinned. "But the pilgrims continue to come here even so. Perhaps the wreckage adds another layer of lustre, of romance. The Controllers don't need to fix it, you see. It works fine just as it is."

PiRo stared at him, and laughed. "There you have it, Zaen SheLu. Why do we never see any signs that the Controllers intervene in their Sim? Because they choose not to. A perfectly closed and irrefutable argument!"

"If you say so," SheLu murmured, indifferent.

LuSi thought she heard her mother mutter prayers to the Controllers as the shuttle began its final approach.

Much of this world chimed with echoes of LuSi's home planet.

They landed near the shore of a continent called Seba, which in Urthen lore was the name of one of the giants who built the Ark. The landing facility was close to a city called New Denv, a name not so terribly far from Denva, the legendary home of the Sim Designers. Then they were transported to the largest coastal town, near the southern coast of Seba, with a grand view of the Navel and its truncated stump of a monument. This town was called Port Wils, and it stood on a mighty river of the same name. The name Wils was like a half-remembered fragment of the story of the Son of the giants who had extracted the Ship's Law from the Will, the semi-incarnate purpose of the Designers themselves.

Maybe all this did reflect some common origin, of a star-scattered mankind, she wondered. Or maybe it was all an artefact of the great smearing-out delivered by the Xaian Normalisation in the course of its hugely destructive rampage across the Bubble. Or maybe it really was an artefact of the world's nature as a simulation, with these common elements being like tropes used and reused by the Designers on one world after another—their signatures, some speculated. One thing was sure; all this needed a deeper explanation than Jaem's father's austere but supremely rational notions of evolutionary convergence.

After a voyage of fourteen years, the plan was to spend only perhaps twenty Days here—or, in the local argot, sixty Watches, each of which was precisely one-third of a Day. This had been negotiated in advance, in communications between the ship in its final sublight approach and the Temple authorities here at Port Wils. Though they had come so far, a few Days, it seemed, were all that was required for the Speaker of Speakers to make her decision concerning SheLu's requests for support of her ongoing expedition in search of the origins of mankind within the greater Simulation.

While the Zaen and the Jennin, priest and scholar, met with various minor functionaries in advance of their meeting with the Speaker of Speakers, JaEm and LuSi tentatively explored Port Wils, under the avuncular guidance of Speaker Tanz Lvov. The priorities of the Temple here soon became apparent. It was on Airtree, so it was said, in lost, semi-legendary times before the wave of destruction that was the Xaian Normalisation, that the cult of the Sim had first arisen—or perhaps, others said, it was a legacy of the Ark as it had passed this world. And in the generations since then, the Temple at Port Wils had made sure that it remained the hub of the faith—and therefore the destination of interstellar pilgrimages, from across all the human worlds where the faith had taken hold. All those worshippers, and all their tithes, flowed into Airtree, and specifically to Seba, and across Seba to Port Wils, gateway to the Navel itself. The Temple was a vast, efficient, and highly profitable organisation, and to the senior administrators a passing starship was a mere distraction.

"No wonder they are so backward technologically," JaEm said to LuSi as they wandered the crowded streets.

"Not completely," LuSi said. "The Speakers seem to have access to anti-ageing technologies just as good as ours, if not better. And their kitchens—"

"Yes, but you know what I mean. Those surface-to-orbit shuttles might have come off the Ark itself. I don't believe there's a starship construction yard in the whole system."

"But there doesn't need to be," LuSi said gently. "The starships come here."

"Yes. Stuffed with money!"

Beneath the surface of this bustling human city, itself millennia old, they came across traces of older habitations. The ancient alien material called the Substrate wasn't restricted to the monument on the Navel, and nor had it all been eradicated by the Xaians. Here and there it persisted, as fragments of walls or foundations set out to linear or circular plans, apparently as unweathered and enduring as when their unknown builders had abandoned them, and built over by coarser human materials, bricks, concrete, steel and glass. And then, in cracks in the sidewalks, at the corners of neglected gardens, they would glimpse scraps of a different kind of life, unimposing mats and films of a black-green tint. The natives, Tanz Vlov told them, called this the Slime. It too had been here long before humans arrived, and the Human Suite had pushed it disregarded into the corners of its own world.

Yet it persisted, LuSi thought, yet it persisted, like the Substrate, a hint of a deeper meaning to this world, like so many others, a meaning beneath the froth of human history. And that was true whether all of this was a dream of some electronic Memory or not.

The party from the *Reality Dreams* was called at length to a meeting with the Speaker of Speakers in a lavish building called the First Temple, set at the heart of Port Wils, with tremendous views of the Navel in the ocean to the south. They were kept waiting, not for long, in a kind of anteroom, where they were served drinks in cut-glass goblets borne on silver trays by silent junior clerics. Even this waiting room was tall, airy, thickly carpeted and every scrap of wall surface was covered by paintings, tapestries, and ornate designs—some of them holographic, so that when you turned your head this way and that different aspects of reality were presented, presumably a representation of the nature of the Simulation that was the core of the faith.

At length they were called into an office, another vast, ornate room, but LuSi was impressed by a kind of working office at the centre of the room, an island of furniture in a sea of carpet, one large desk surrounded by chairs, smaller desks, blocks of filing cabinets and slate racks. A woman in a purple robe sat behind the desk, working at papers; this was the Speaker of Speakers herself, a woman of an ancient local family, called Kira Elos. She did not look up as the starship passengers were led to seats before her desk.

They sat silently. Attendants fluttered back and forth, carrying slates and papers, murmuring to each other and the Speaker of Speakers. LuSi noticed standing in one corner a curious cage, of some fine silvery mesh, taller than she was. Light from the sun, which was overhead at this location, was reflected from a bank of mirrors into the cage, where a kind of tree grew, tall, spindly. Birds with silvery, mirrored wings fluttered around the tree, catching the light and reflecting its glow onto its leaves.

At last Kira Elos looked up. "I apologise for keeping you waiting. You have come far to visit me." She spoke what sounded like comprehensible Anglish to LuSi, but translators stood by discreetly, to aid the conversation.

Jennin PiRo said smoothly, "But we know that other pilgrims come from much further away yet. Thank you for your time and attention, Speaker of Speakers . . ."

He calmly introduced the party, one by one. The Speaker in turn introduced some of her staff. The names did not seem important to LuSi, and she made no attempt to memorise them.

She was distracted by the tree in the cage. Every so often blinds would furl and unfurl, apparently automatically, so that the pattern of light falling on the cage changed, and the mirror-wing birds would flutter and fly, adjusting their position in response to the changing light.

The Speaker of Speakers noticed her watching. "Distracting, isn't it? And charming."

"I'm sorry—"

"Don't apologise. You're right to be intrigued. There are few of these specimens left on this world—by which I mean the trees and the birds, for they form a symbiotic partnership, you see. The birds bring the tree light, and it feeds them in turn."

"But the light comes at a low angle," JaEm said. "Artificially, thanks to these mirrors."

The Speaker nodded. "True. From which you deduce?"

Jennin PiRo jumped in, and LuSi knew how much that irritated JaEm. "That this is a native of high latitudes—lands close to the terminator between day and permanent night. Where the sun is always low."

"Correct. But the mirror forests are almost gone, now, eradicated to make room for variants of wheat and rice and other crops we have developed to be tolerant of the poor light conditions."

SheLu nodded. "It is a common observation, demonstrable by archaeology, that a mass extinction of any native life follows the successful settlement of any world by humans. It is logical; the new life must supplant the old, if it is not to be pushed back."

The Speaker smiled. "I understand that. But even so, it is a miracle the birds survived."

She said that once this world had been full of animals and plants that seemed to have been *designed*, by some vanished precursor inhabitants—maybe the Substrate builders, maybe not—to serve as tools, or engines. There had been tractor beasts and tunnel-building moles and "photomoss," a life form that collected useful energy from the sunlight.

"All of these were exterminated by the Xaians. But the birds were spared, whether by intention or accident we are unsure—they are after all hard to trap. One strand of our theological thinking suggests that the Xaians were actually carrying out the will of the Controllers in their great extirpation. Perhaps the Sim had drifted from its parameters and needed cleansing. And so perhaps the birds' continuing existence is somehow heretical."

LuSi, staring at the birds and their tree, could not believe anything so intricately exquisite could possibly be regarded as *wrong*, in any value system.

The Speaker of Speakers considered SheLu. "Of course, Zaen, the Xaians' enthusiastic destruction must have complicated your quest to trace the origin of mankind."

"If such a single origin exists at all," PiRo put in.

SheLu smiled. "Actually it makes it more interesting, intellectually. A challenge, set for us by the Controllers themselves, perhaps, to test the minds they have given us . . . Not even the Xaians could extirpate everything about human culture. It's a commonplace that the human worlds share common concepts. Measures of time, for instance, like the Days and Years we use on Urthen—or the watches you use here. Each watch is about a third of our Day; your Great Year is three hundred and sixty of our Days, about the same as our Year. And so on. All this might derive from some primal source."

"Or from the passage of the Xaians," PiRo said.

"Perhaps. But then humans share sleep cycles that seem to have no relation to the natural periods of any of the settled worlds, though they do roughly correlate to a Day. No Xaian army could have imposed *that*.

"And then there are our languages," SheLu went on patiently. "We all seem to speak a version of what we of Urthen call Anglish. Languages of separated groups always diverge; we have observed this on our own world. But if our tongues did derive from some common root brought on the Ark, then the most frequently used terms would be those that endured with the least changes, and so would remain common across the worlds. Words like 'we,' 'my,' 'our.'" She glanced at the cage. "'Tree.' 'Bird.' 'Speaker,' even, for positions of authority."

LuSi saw how the translators looked surprised at the obvious comprehensibility of these words.

"And language, you see," SheLu said now, "is much harder to eradicate than mere physical trappings. Just as a faith, like the Creed of the Sim, is harder to demolish than a mere temple of stone—or even a Substrate monument. It is possible, I believe, to trace the first spread of mankind across the stars through family trees of languages and their relations to each other. We can even see traces in these relationships of the passage of the Xaians, and their brief empire. My analysis suggests, by the way, that Airtree was one of the earliest worlds settled."

The Speaker nodded. "I think I understand your logic. Though I had always thought that our pretension to be an old world was mere snobbery . . . We have some scholars, you know, who speculate that 'Airtree,' the name for our world, is some derivation of 'urth' and 'three.' Both among your primal words, I imagine."

"That is so."

"And 'Urthen,'" JaEm said, suddenly intrigued.

The Speaker said, "Perhaps the name for mankind's first world is buried in such names. 'Urth.' But some worlds' names are probably more recent invention."

SheLu said, "Like 'Windru,' named for a ruling dynasty of that world, yes."

"What about your 'Urthen,' though? Urth . . . ten? That seems tenuous."

JaEm said, "You know, a starship engineer might suggest the real root is 'Urth n.' The 'n' stands for an unknown number. Perhaps by then the settlers had lost count."

"Or perhaps the name is some kind of black joke. And perhaps we should think of the primal world you seek as Urth I." The Speaker pulled her lip. "This is all fascinating. Suggestive rather than conclusive, however."

"Of course," conceded SheLu.

"But it is by following such leads that you hope to identify mankind's primal world? If it exists," she added, with a nod to PiRo.

"That is my strategy. Given the fragments of legend we have, I anticipate we will find an oceanic world. The flooded planet from which mankind had to flee . . ."

Elos studied papers on her desk. "One would think such a world would be at the centre of the Bubble. The root from which we spread, in three dimensions. Instead you are seeking to go to the edge of human space—beyond Windru, in fact, the Xaians' world, the most densely populated world at one extreme of our domain of colonisation."

"That is plausible," SheLu said, "given a model of the first flight that is consistent with the surviving legends. That is, a single flight across the stars, scattering colonies as it went. Subsequent secondary colonisation waves have set out from those first settlements. In that case the origin would indeed lie at one extreme of the Bubble, just as the root of a tree," she said, glancing at the cage, "lies at one extreme of its structure."

"And what you want of me is an Instrument of Authority."

"I believe that is the appropriate form, yes. The worlds I visit, especially Windru, must open up their archives and other treasures, on your authority. Also we may require material support of various kinds."

The Speaker smiled. "I am no Xaian emperor to impose my rule on other worlds."

"Nevertheless your authority as Speaker of Speakers will carry a great deal of weight on any world where the Creed is cherished."

"True enough." She turned now to PiRo. "And you, Jennin PiRo. I understand you are not an adherent of our Creed."

"Regretfully, no."

"Be not regretful. The Sim Designers made you as you are, scepticism and all, and cherish you even so."

PiRo flared, "But that's exactly the kind of circular argument which—"

LuSi touched his arm. "Not now, Jennin," she murmured.

The Speaker of Speakers said, "My advisors have had constructive discussions with you, Jennin PiRo. You are a sceptic, as you have admitted, yet you accompany Zaen SheLu on a quest that seeks to establish the truth about mankind—a quest guided by our Creed. Why have you devoted your own life, and your son's, to a mission you reject?"

PiRo glanced at SheLu. "Well, it was rather forcibly suggested by my own university that I should come along. This hundred-year jaunt is high profile and very expensive. But I was glad to come. Speaker, I do not accept your Creed. But as I told your advisers, I accept that as a human institution it has some beneficial value. It has inculcated a belief that the universe is rational, and that questions we ask of it will yield meaningful answers. Of course, if it were an artefact, that would be so. As such your Creed lies at the philosophical root of all modern science.

"Yet there is potential for harm, if the Creed ultimately stifles our inquisitiveness. After all, any question—even about my own personality!—can be answered by appealing to the whim of the Designers. 'They made it that way because they made it that way.'

"Now, I believe that the Zaen will fail in her quest to find a single origin of mankind. The multi-origin hypothesis of the beginnings of mankind is philosophically simpler—and, if I may say so, more satisfying. But whatever the outcome of her quest, the result will be significant for ages to come, either way. And I am very strongly motivated to ensure that the investigation is carried out to the highest scientific standards."

"And so you wish to accompany her, as a kind of monitor. A conscience."

"That's the idea."

"Commendable too, and understandable." The Speaker glanced down at her notes for a moment, and LuSi thought she came to a decision, or perhaps confirmed one. "But, I'm afraid, that it is a wish I cannot endorse."

LuSi felt as if her heart stopped.

The Jennin, too, froze. "I'm afraid I don't understand."

"My scholars advise, and I agree with them, that your own time, Jennin, would be better spent here, on Airtree—rather than locked away on a starship for decades on essentially a secondary task."

"You want me to stay here? Doing what?"

"Exploring the issues you have been describing. The relationship between the Creed of the Sim, and science and other modern philosophies, as they emerge. These are new ideas to us. What enriching arguments these may prove to be." She waved a hand at the opulence of the room. "Needless to say your physical comforts will be catered for, and in addition we offer you the mental stimulation of debate with the finest minds from all the worlds of the Bubble. And there is no better way to spend your life, or a part of it, than in thus honouring the Designers and Controllers and the Sim they have devised for us—or, if you wish, seeking a way to debunk their very existence."

PiRo looked confused at this sudden turn of events—as well he might, LuSi thought. "Speaker of Speakers, is this a condition of your granting your Instrument of Authority to Zaen SheLu ?"

"Let us not descend into such bargaining," the Speaker said smoothly, with only the mildest tone of reproof. "Of course your family can stay with you," she glanced at JaEm, "while the Zaen's can travel on with hers," nodding at LuSi.

And thus LuSi's life was smashed to pieces, on a whim of refined scholarship.

The Speaker of Speakers smiled. "This is a moment of mythic resonance, is it not? Your crew is breaking up, like the Split during the journey of the first Ark, of which our legends speak. Well. Will you all join me for dinner?"

III

"History doesn't matter. Life is all. You won't build a Library here, Proctor."
"Then what in its place?"
"Better a monument to me, Xaia Windru, a hero of this world, than to a world lost in the sky . . ."

LuSi hated Windru.

She hated the climate. Windru was a peculiar, tipped-over world, with its spin axis nearly in the plane of its orbit around its sun. So each turn around the sun, each of the world's "years," brought months of endless light, months of freezing dark. The only truly habitable areas were around the equator, and even there life was all but unbearable at some times—notably the equinoxes, when the sun climbed highest in the sky and dumped the greatest warmth into the air. And it was just LuSi's luck that the *Reality Dreams* had arrived at just such a moment.

She hated the gravity too! Too *low*, and she stumbled and tripped all the time and her digestion was shot to hell, and the locals who towered over her laughed, and their *enormous* rats would run under her feet . . .

It was twenty-nine years now since they had left Airtree behind, forty-three years total since Urthen; she had spent most of her adult life, indeed almost all of her *life*, in the comfortable standard spin-gravity of the starship, and she didn't welcome novelty. What a dump! No wonder the Xaians had got stirred up enough to go conquering human space; anything to get away from a world like this.

She hated the local culture too. Even the names they gave things. SheLu argued from her linguistic analysis that this had been a very early colony world, even older than Airtree. But if this planet had ever been called "Urth II" or some derivation, that name was thoroughly lost; "Windru" was taken from the name of a long-extinct ruling dynasty. The Xaians in their pomp had begun their career by renaming their world, and obliterating the names given its features by the original colonists (if, recalling PiRo's theories, such colonists had ever existed at all). After their hugely destructive campaign of Normalisation across the Bubble, the Xaians had been driven back to their home world, and since then the planet had been governed by federations of other worlds, administrations with varying politics but all determined to ensure that the Xaians never rose again. One legacy of the Xaian firestorm had been a trend to global governments on the colony worlds, and inter-world councils of various kinds: a paradoxical unity. Anyhow the generations of offworld administrators sent here had imposed their own names on the world's geography, physical and human. And meanwhile some diehard natives who had opposed the Xaians in the first place had hung on to still older labels.

So it was a mess. Even the major landmasses were plastered with contradictory names. The big north-south spine was either the "Belt" or the "Sword," depending on who you spoke to; the compact island continent to the east was the "Frysby" or the "Shield"; the archipelago to the west was the "Scatter" or "The Fallen Corpses of the Enemies of Zeeland"—and so on. The port city in which LuSi resided was called Xaiandria, or Alecksandria, or The Designers' Conception—whatever. It was said that the Xaians had even renamed the other planets of this system, including two big giants that had once been called by the resonant founder names "Seba" and "Halivah." At least, though, everybody agreed on one thing: their name for the native life forms—the "Purple"—a word of such simplicity and antiquity that SheLu argued that it must have been an import from the language of the original settlers from lost Urth I.

LuSi also hated the rooms they had been loaned, in a wooden-framed apartment block near the local Temple. Too hot, too noisy. The city's architecture was dominated by structures like this, of wood and grim red sandstone, with pillars and porticoes and elaborately carved friezes. It was an architecture mandated by the conditions of this metal-poor, tectonically weary world, and a sensibility the Xaians had exported across human space in their brief period of empire-building, styles now everywhere associated with the hated Normalisation regime, and universally despised. These buildings might be squat and shabby, but none of them were terribly old, LuSi had learned. Windru with its peculiar tipped axis was given to instabilities; periodically it shook itself as, the locals said, a dog shakes off fleas. Buildings would crumble, the seas would rise, and volcanoes would fire. This had happened twice since the first human colonisation. It was an irony that most traces of the Xaians, who had sought to eradicate history, had themselves been eliminated.

Most of all LuSi resented being stuck indoors with her mother, while Tanz Vlov, the reluctant emissary appointed by the Speaker of Speakers back on Airtree, was sent out to wheedle and negotiate for access to scholars and records and archaeological sites. It had always been a feature of the Xaian hegemony that men had done the governing, women the fighting. So it was even now, thousands of years after the fall of the Normalisation regime, even in the Temples of the Creed. Women, meanwhile, even two such evidently elderly and scholarly specimens as SheLu and LuSi, were treated as warily as drunken warriors. SheLu quite enjoyed being able to make men twice her size flinch out of her way with a mere glare, but overall the restrictions were wearisome.

So she was trapped with SheLu. On the roomy starship they had managed not to speak to each other for years on end. Now they were cooped up together.

The loss of JaEm and all LuSi's plans for the future was a long time ago now, nearly thirty Years. In the years since, LuSi had taken other lovers, and had even married, once, one of the ship's officers, but had borne no children. Thanks to anti-ageing treatments there was still time, but . . . The truth was that nothing, nobody had replaced JaEm. Given that the separation had come out because of the Speaker of Speakers' decree, it had always been irrational for LuSi to blame her mother—save that it had been her mother's driving ambition to discover Urth I that had so pulled LuSi's own life out of shape in the first place. But, logical or not, LuSi had never quite been able to *forgive* her.

It was a manageable situation on the roomy ship, in the life she had built for herself. But not here, in this stuffy box of an apartment, on this world of a failed empire . . . She avoided her mother as best she could.

But sometimes SheLu sought her out.

"You might be interested in this," SheLu said, having summoned her daughter to the room she used as a study.

LuSi looked around, at a desk heaped with books and scrolls and slates, and a kind of laboratory workbench laden with instruments, and dishes of the slimy local life form called the Purple. "I might, might I? Do you even *know* what I'm interested in?"

SheLu smiled, and as so often LuSi had a queasy, disconcerted sense as she looked into her mother's face, a face like her own, yet oddly too young-looking now thanks to quirks in the ageing treatments. Like looking in a distorting mirror. SheLu said, "I do know you have spent the last twenty years fooling around with specimens of life from Urthen and Airtree and other worlds . . ."

LuSi, looking for meaning in her life, had trained herself up in biology. She had asked for samples from the worlds the starship had visited since Airtree en route to Windru, and had tried to unpick ravelled-up ecologies. She had begun with a vague idea that she might test one of her mother's hypotheses, that human-related life had been brought to each world from a single source. LuSi had confirmed for herself that what ecologists called the "Human Suite"—humanity and its cousins, the animals and grasses and trees that supported human life—had uniform designs across the worlds, from the metabolic down to the genetic, while other life forms on the worlds they inhabited had wildly varying bases. This unity did lend credence to her mother's argument for a single source for humanity.

But beyond that LuSi had become fascinated by the glimpses she saw of the intricate interdependence of life forms of evidently different origins. Even if you couldn't eat your neighbour, you could use it as a support, or incorporate it into your own metabolism somehow . . . She was developing a vision of the very far future, when life forms from across the human worlds, united by starships, would converge on some common shared ecology.

Not here, though. Not on Windru. Here, the Purple remained stubbornly isolated from the Human Suite, as if expressing its own disapproval of the antics of humanity. Yet it was not the Purple's relation to the Human Suite that interested SheLu, but the Purple itself.

"I think it's true," SheLu said now.

"What is?"

But SheLu stayed silent, after that enigmatic statement, as so often becoming lost in her own thoughts.

LuSi slammed her palm flat on the desk. "Pay attention, mother. What's so interesting? *What* is true?"

"Hm? Oh, yes. Sorry. The old stories they tell here. The pre-Normalisation legends of a City of the Dead, of some kind of living arcology up in the north of the continent they call the Sword. Where, as Xaia Windru herself is supposed to have discovered, the previous intelligent inhabitants of this world had gone to hide, their identities mapped and stored in some physical structure, analogous to—"

"The Sim," LuSi said. "Just as we are all patterns in the Memory in Denva."

"Quite so. *I think it might be true.* I've been mapping the deep biochemistry of this stuff, the Purple. It's full of signalling, electrical, biochemical, at times even physical, one chunk pushing at another, at a variety of speeds and bandwidths. It is a kind of data store. No doubt much of the information here is concerned with the basic needs of the survival of the Purple itself. But—"

"But maybe there's room for more."

"Yes. And since the Purple is alive, it serves as a self-replicating, self-repairing storage medium. Very robust. Hmm. And maybe in there the refugees of former times experience something like the Sim we ourselves believe we inhabit, some kind of virtual reality."

"But wouldn't that have to be a Sim within the Sim?"

"I'll leave that to better theologians than me to sort out. And if this is true, maybe the legends of the source of the Xaians' plague weapons are true also."

Lacking metals, the Xaians had never developed starships. They had had to wait until explorers from other worlds, specifically from Urthen, had come to them, with ships ripe for the hijacking. But the storm of extirpation they had unleashed subsequently on their companion human worlds had relied on biological weapons of devastating ferocity. They had never admitted the source of these weapons. When the Xaians had been driven back, they had taken the weapons with them. Even now, visitors to this world had to undergo heavy programmes of inoculation to protect them against lingering, ineradicable traces—programmes LuSi and Tanz between them had had to force SheLu to endure, so impatient had she been to get on with her work.

"The legend is," SheLu said, "that the Xaian scholars found a way to interrogate the City of the Living Dead, and retrieve secrets from the alien minds stored there. Weapons lore, perhaps? If so no wonder the weapons were so effective; they weren't human in origin at all. As for the City itself, it was destroyed in the liberation wars. So some say. Or was lost after climate Watches on this unstable world, so others say. It was always very far to the north, always inaccessible." SheLu looked up at her daughter. "Maybe it still exists out there somewhere. And the people here, these children of the Xaians, know it, and know where it is. Perhaps they anticipate the day when they might get a chance to use it again."

LuSi stared at the chunks of Purple on the desk. "You know, Mother, here we are trying to puzzle out human origins. That's challenge enough. While all around us there are these deeper, older mysteries. Alien life everywhere. Signs of vanished intelligences, on so many worlds. They can't all have locked themselves away in storage to dream away the Years. But if not, where have they gone?"

SheLu left the question hanging in the air. For a moment they pondered cosmic mysteries together, mother sitting at the desk, daughter standing over her. As if they had forgotten who they were, LuSi thought, forgotten all that had passed between them.

Then a kind of self-awareness returned, and they pulled apart, turned away.

At that moment, providentially, Tanz Vlov bustled into the room, carrying a slate and a sack of scrolls. "I have it. The information you sought. I have it!"

And Zaen SheLu fell on the man and his data as if her daughter no longer existed.

LuSi busied herself with her own studies for a full Windru spin, a "day" that was nearly one and a half times a standard Day. She let her mother, and a slightly baffled Tanz Vlov, work through the data he had retrieved from the city's libraries and archives. When SheLu came to some conclusion, she would not hesitate to let her daughter know.

And, sure enough, towards the evening of the next Windru day, SheLu summoned her. "I have found it." she said, in an evidently unconscious echo of Tanz's eager cry of the day before.

"Found what, Mother?"

"Come and see."

What Lvov had unearthed was information on a variety of worlds unknown to Urthen science. In their search for human colonies to "Normalise," the Xaians had carried out a survey of star systems in and even beyond the Bubble of colonisation not equalled before or since.

Tanz Vlov seemed proud to have dug up all this information. "Thousands of Years old, this stuff, but presumably still valid, unless the parent stars have blown up, or some such . . . The Xaian legacy is either venerated or despised, even here on Windru. You can imagine the tact I had to use to extract all this old stuff from the temples and colleges, museums and archives, institutions called the Four Universities which claim a very great age. Even private collections, some of which are like shrines to Xaia . . ."

"Don't boast, little man," SheLu said dismissively. "The point is," she told her daughter, "in among all these planetary systems the Xaians found ocean worlds." She had pinned images, names, scraps of information about these worlds around her study walls. "Worlds more or less like Urthen, worlds more or less habitable for humans, but—"

"But drowned by oceans."

"Yes. Now, look. By interrogating the data I can eliminate many of them as candidates for Urth I. See from the displays how I have filtered them out? Some have oceans that are simply too deep—a world like ours may form with as much as half its mass in water, and an ocean enormously deep. No, Urth I cannot be as drowned as that. Second, I have eliminated worlds orbiting Embers, as our own Urthen does, or dim stars like that of Airtree. Why? Because to be close enough to their stars to be habitable the rotations of such worlds are always tidally locked. They have no 'days'—or rather, their spin takes the same time as their turn, their 'day' is identical to their 'year.' We suspect that Urth I must have had a 'day' distinct from its 'year,' for those are the units of time that have descended to us: Days, Years, each of which comprises hundreds of Days."

LuSi saw that this argument eliminated most of the candidate ocean worlds, simply because most of the Galaxy's stars were small, dim stars, and there was an equally large number of Ember-like failed stars. In any event, now only a handful of candidate planets from the Xaian survey survived, ocean worlds orbiting big, bright stars.

"The final match," SheLu breathed, "was against our time units themselves. I sought a world with a day and year that matched our own, or multiples or fractions of it. For example the Airtree 'Watch' is almost exactly one-third of our 'Day'; either of those could be a measure of an Urth I spin . . ."

Following the logic of the display on the study walls, LuSi saw that only one candidate remained, a grainy old image of an otherwise unspectacular ball of steel-grey, cloud-shrouded ocean.

"Urth I," SheLu said, grinning like a self-satisfied child. "I have found it."

"Perhaps." LuSi wished PiRo was here, to judge this as a piece of scientific thinking. SheLu had juggled the facts to fit a preconceived story. Perhaps, even given the same data, a different framing story would have produced a different outcome. "But at least we can test this idea—"

"By going there, yes," SheLu said. "I have already called the ship. The target world is seven years' travel from here."

"Seven more years!"

"I know. It's nothing. We leave tomorrow."

IV

A light flared in the sky. Lily glanced up, thinking it must be the end of totality, the bright sunlight splashing unimpeded once more on the moon's face. But the moon, still wholly eclipsed, was as round and brown as it had been before.

It was Jupiter: Jupiter was flaring, still a pinpoint of light, but much brighter, bright enough to cast sharp point-source shadows on the glistening weed of the raft substrate. But the light diminished, as if receding with distance. And soon Jupiter shone alone as it had before.

That was the Ark, she thought immediately. That was Grace. What else could it be?

Then a sliver of white appeared at the very rim of the moon, lunar mountains exploding into the sunlight. She was quickly dazzled, and Jupiter was lost. She was never going to know.

Despite the surging of the grey global ocean—despite the waves that battered the raft's pontoons, the signature of an immense storm breaking just over the horizon of this turbulent world—the raft was steady, stable, like dry land, like an island rooted deep in this world's mantle rather than a manmade construct adrift on the breast of a kilometres-deep ocean. You would expect it to be that way; it had been prefabricated in the workshops of Urthen in anticipation of just these conditions. As LuSi walked across its deck in the dawn light, seeking her mother, she could sense hear the mysterious hum of tremendous fusion engines, feel the vibration of great impellors and jets as the raft fought the surging ocean.

Yet the raft *felt* fragile to her, felt like a mote lost on the breast of this untameable water world.

She feared this world. The air itself was thick, choking—lacking oxygen, the scientists said.

She even feared the sky, when it was visible at all through breaks in the habitual cloud banks. It was so unlike Urthen's sky, which was dominated by the bland, immobile face of the Ember. It was a grey dawn just now, a quiet, uneasy time, and she was alone on the deck—apart from her mother, who she'd yet to find. A smear of pinkish light to the east showed where this world's too-bright sun was rising. Overhead the sky was growing grey, yet was still studded with stars—an eerie set of stars too, quite unlike those visible from the darkside of Urthen. Eeriest of all was the thought that here beyond the edge of the Bubble, if you looked in certain directions, there were *no human worlds at all*: nothing but stars, stars and worlds, empty of mankind, and perhaps empty of mind altogether.

And then there was this world's moon. A wandering ball that spun through its phases like a child's toy, a dead face disfigured by impact scars and volcanism. Most disturbing of all, as the ship's navigator-astronomers had predicted, while the moon would sometimes be darkened by sailing through the planet's shadow, periodically it would eclipse the sun—and when it did, at certain times, visible from certain parts of the world's surface, the moon's face would *exactly blank out* the sun. When Tanz Vlov showed her simulations of this eerie event, the blocked-out solar photosphere like a hole in the sky, LuSi had recoiled, a strange superstitious awe rising.

"Don't show this to my mother," she had urged Tanz.

"Why not?"

"Because she might take it as *proof* that this is Urth I. Maybe before they fled the Ark builders tinkered with the orbits of sun, moon and planet to devise this coincidence. Maybe it's a kind of signature . . ."

He had grinned. "Or maybe it's the Sim Designers messing with our heads."

That foolishness had passed. Most distracting of all about the moon for LuSi now, when it was visible, was the glimmer of light she sometimes saw on the shadowed portion of its face, like a star captured in the curve of its crescent. That was the *Reality Dreams*, which had been brought to land on the moon's dust-choked surface for a period of restoration, refurbishment and resupply after its fifty-year flight, in preparation for the home journey. LuSi, stuck down here on this storm world, longed to be up there in the graceful, translucent halls of the hull, surrounded by her gardens of alien exotica.

This morning Tanz himself was lost up in that turbulent sky somewhere, on his way down to the surface in a shuttle, saying something had been found on the moon that ought to interest her: she'd no idea what, some exotic vacuum flower, perhaps. This was why she was up so early, seeking her mother. She needed to make sure she knew what SheLu was up to before Tanz showed up expecting an update. It wasn't just for reasons of progressing the science programme; he would expect it of her, expect the middle-aged daughter of an increasingly ill and frail old woman to know what condition her mother was in. If she was honest she was looking for SheLu not through a daughter's concern—they were well past that in their relationship—but because of not wishing to be shamed before Tanz Vlov.

At last she found her mother.

SheLu was working close to the edge of the raft, behind mesh screens that kept her from falling over the side but did nothing to protect her from the elements, the salty wind, the spray that so often turned into lashing rain. She was walking between the collection tanks where every day and night automated traps deposited samples of the local wildlife that came sniffing around the raft.

SheLu walked with care, her legs stiff, her gait bent and nodding, as if she were learning to operate a faulty robot body. It was only seven years since they had left Windru; SheLu looked as if she had aged seven decades. The ship's doctors surmised that she had succumbed to a trace pathogen in the air of Windru, some weaponised bug. It had been discreetly suggested to LuSi that SheLu might have skipped some of the supposedly mandatory inoculation routine, and that wouldn't have surprised LuSi at all. In which case, SheLu deserved everything she got, in LuSi's opinion.

Which turned out to be some kind of corruption of the anti-ageing agents that swarmed through her cells. Essentially SheLu was ageing very rapidly, converging mysteriously on something approaching her real age of over a hundred Years. The doctors wouldn't give LuSi a prediction of how long she had left. Perhaps she could be cryo-preserved and shipped back to Urthen, for specialist care. But SheLu had crossed the Bubble to find this world, and she wasn't going to submit to cryo-sleep until she had squeezed out its mysteries. And with every additional Day that went by—Days that did so eerily match the period of the spin of this world, coincidence or not—the risk that she would not live to see Urthen again accumulated.

And right now, LuSi saw as she approached, this world's mysteries were embodied in the sleek form of a swimmer. SheLu stood over the tank, holding a rail. LuSi came to stand beside her, wordless.

In the tank the swimmer's body was a pale mass that surged back and forth, agitated, almost colliding with a wall on each approach but just barely missing each time. Through the murky water LuSi could see the creature's stubby limbs, the webbed hand-like front paws, the flowing hair. Its anxiety, its anger, was obvious. As was its mindlessness.

"So," LuSi said to her mother. "You still think this is some kind of human descendant?"

"Why not? The anatomy suggests it, of the samples we've taken. What else would become of the children of mankind, if dumped into an endless sea like this? There are fast-swimming things with sharp teeth in there. A brain isn't much use in this ocean, compared to an ability to swim fast." Her voice was an odd high-pitched rasp now, a product of the fluid that gathered in her chest.

"But is it really plausible? Even your most tenuous models predict that it has only been ten thousand Years since the Ark left this world—if it existed at all. Can the human form evolve so rapidly?"

"You should know the answer to that," SheLu said with a kind of feeble snarl. "You've spent decades fiddling about with samples of life from the other worlds. All genetic mechanisms have common features, and one is an ability to find some adaptations rapidly, to some degree an ability to adapt quickly to fast-changing conditions, with a simple resetting of switches, so to speak. In humans there are switches that control body size and hair cover, for example, even maturity rates. The last generations of humans, I mean humans like us, might have lived out their lives on rafts like this, built from the debris of their drowned cities. While their children took to the water, knowing nothing of what had been lost, and caring nothing either. *Changing . . .*" Her speech broke up in a cough. "And more than that," she struggled on. "We've found nothing on this world so far that could not be considered part of the Human Suite. Consider that. No multiple life sets on *this* world . . . Only a single origin of life here."

"That's based on what you've sampled, which has been pitifully small." Which was true; aside from scoopings like this from the surface layers of the ocean, they had been reduced to sending down automated probes to take pinprick samplings from deeply drowned landscapes. "It's hardly good science to come to such general conclusions based on such little data."

"Oh, don't lecture me about scientific methods, you ninny. You always were such a silly girl, so easily distracted."

"Mother, by the Ember's slow fade, I'm in my sixties now—"

"One can generalise. One can use sophisticated statistical methods to form and test rigorous hypotheses from the most limited data sets. Of course a single clinching piece of evidence, to prove or disprove a notion, is best. But . . ." More coughing. "Consider this," she gasped. "We have mapped the subsurface; that's one data set that is complete. We see what look like continental masses scattered over this world, all of them drowned, of course."

"I know. I've seen the maps."

"We even see evidence of continental drift, the million-Year creep of the land, driven by this world's inner heat."

"Just as on Urthen," LuSi said reluctantly.

"Just as on Urthen. We have taken samples of the assemblages of life, animals, plants and bacteria on each landmass."

"Again, necessarily limited."

"Yes, and also compromised by the actions of the technological civilisation which evidently prospered here before the water's rise. Everything watched and mixed up. And not helped either by the subsequent Years of drowning, and the action of the sharp teeth of the ocean.

"But what we *have* been able to reconstruct, to some degree, has been the pattern of the evolution of life on this world. Evolution marred by extinctions, some of them evidently caused by external causes—a flaring of that big sun, perhaps, an impact from one of the big rocks that litter this untidy system. There were even extinctions caused by the collision of continents, one suite of creatures flooding over a land bridge to compete with another."

"Oh, this is all so partial—"

"Do listen, child. Now, it's well known that on every world that humanity settles, an extinction event among the native life forms inevitably follows. If must be so. If not, the world is abandoned as uninhabitable. Here too, on this world, we see traces of *recent* extinctions. Complex affairs that bear the hallmarks of human-induced events, as opposed to natural causes—the removal of most animals larger than human mass, for instance; a uniform spreading of certain scavenger creatures."

"That could be explained if this world was colonised from the stars before it was flooded."

"No! The timing is wrong. Here, as far as the best evidence shows, the extinction pattern was *deep in time*—it lasted as long before the flood as has elapsed since the flood. Don't you see? Don't you see, girl?"

"I'm no girl—"

Again the coughing, but SheLu forced the words out. "Not only that, the extinction took time. It spread across this world in spasms. The pattern is just as if humanity had *evolved* on this world. Had developed the capability over hundreds, thousands of Years to compete with, eliminate, consume, other species. Had spread from land-mass to landmass, island to island—spreading by ships on the ocean, most likely, it wouldn't be like Urthen, like the worlds of the Bubble, where humanity fell suddenly from the sky. They would have pushed an extinction wave ahead of them wherever them went, an eerie forerunning of the story of human colonisation of the Bubble played out on the stage of a single world. But here, all of this occurred on a planet in which there was no alien life to push aside—the extinctions occurred within the Human Suite itself."

"Just as one would expect if this were the original world of mankind."

"Precisely. You understand at last."

SheLu grunted, irritated. "Those are strong claims, mother. You will need strong evidence to back them up."

"That will come, that will come. To date, certainly, I have found nothing to contradict the hypothesis . . ."

Without warning, the swimmer in its tank lunged. That sleek body hurtled out of the water, and a small skull, an open mouth ringed with sharp teeth, strained at the women.

LuSi grabbed her mother and pulled her back. For an instant, as the creature reached the top of its arc, spraying water, its face was directly before LuSi's: a low brow, small skull, clear blue eyes, a flattened nose, a very human mouth despite the sharp teeth, and long sleek hair washed back in a streamlined pattern. It was like a child's face, LuSi thought, a malevolent, malformed child, a thing out of a nightmare. She thought she saw bloody scraps of meat stuck in those sharp teeth. She remembered the classic folk definition of the Human Suite: *whatever you can eat, or can eat you, is in the Suite.* Hello, cousin, she thought.

Then the sleek, fat-laden body fell back into the tank. With a shudder of disgust LuSi pulled a lever to release the thing back into its world ocean.

There was a flare in the sky, a crack like thunder. Tanz's shuttle, coming down from the moon.

And Zaen SheLu collapsed, almost falling into the tank, after the swimmer. LuSi yelled for help.

The shuttle, which had been modified for the special conditions of this water world, landed on the ocean surface on skids.

By the time the spaceplane had drawn up to the raft it was mid-morning, and the weather had closed in; a huge storm was crackling on the western horizon, and the black boiling clouds were coming ever closer. SheLu, at her own insistence, was still out in the open, sitting in a chair bolted to the raft's deck, facing the churning sea.

She was hooked up to a medical support machine, connected by wires and tubes. A nurse stood by, a young man, who periodically gave her oxygen through a mask. Other crew were setting up a shelter to protect SheLu from the weather.

Tanz Vlov clambered off the shuttle and over a short gangplank onto the raft. Vlov was huddled up in a waterproof coat, and he walked with difficulty across the deck in the wind. He carried something, a small parcel, clutched against his chest.

LuSi waited for him in the shelter of one of the more substantial buildings on the raft's back.

When Tanz joined LuSi he said, shouting over the storm, "I have something to show you."

"To show me?"

"And your mother. Something from the moon . . ." He shook his head, splashing water. "By the Designers' balls, the storms on this world are angrier than a Xaian with a grudge. Does it have to be this way?"

"My mother says so. Something to do with the loss of weathering from the land . . ."

It was a question of nutrients, SheLu had said. Life in any ocean—at least, Human Suite life—needed certain nutrients, calcium, silicon, phosphorus. On a world with continents and islands, dry land, like Urthen, such nutrients could be provided by the weathering of the land, the washing away of crumbled rock into the sea. On this world, when the seas rose, that mechanism was lost, quite suddenly, and there must have been a mass extinction. But as life was washed from the land, and even the green creatures of the sea died back, as the percentage of oxygen in the air diminished and carbon dioxide accumulated, so the air and ocean grew warmer, trapping heat energy from the sun; and all that energy was expressed in tremendous storms. And the storms churned up deep-lying sediments in the ocean, stirring up the necessary nutrients.

"All living worlds seek balance," SheLu had said. "A mix of mass and energy flows that optimises the potential for life, to some degree. Here, on Urth I, when the land was drowned, there must have been extinctions. Even now the world may not be as fecund as it once was. But the storminess is one mechanism by which the great cycles of life are sustained. It's not comfortable for us, but that's a detail; this world, though it may have birthed mankind, is no longer *for* us . . ."

"It's a lovely idea," LuSi said now, with some regret, looking over at the still form of her mother. "Just a shame it means it has to rain the whole time."

Tanz looked over at SheLu. "She's declining, right?"

"Very quickly. Just as if she's ageing, suddenly. Her systems are failing, from her eyesight to her heart. The medics are running around in a panic, they've never seen anything like this before. We're lucky to have that guy—his name's Stabil—he once did some voluntary work in a shanty town where they couldn't afford anti-ageing; at least he's used to the manifestations of old age. But he's not so keen to be out in this weather."

"Neither am I. And neither are you," Tanz said acutely. "But you're here for her, right?"

LuSi shrugged. "She may not have long. She insists on staying out here, even if it's ending up costing her life. I resent it all more than I can say," she flared now.

"My whole life's been pulled to pieces because of *her* ambition. She doesn't fear death, by the way. It's the Creed. She believes she will merely be returning to Memory. That's what she tells me, anyhow. But now that's she's actually dying—"

"You need to be near her."

"Not need. Duty. In case there's anything more she wants to say."

"Umm. Or if there's anything more you want to say to her." And he held up his package.

Wrapped in a thermal blanket, she saw it was small, the size of a data slate maybe, evidently rectangular but curved, like a fragment of hull plate maybe.

"Less of the mystery, Vlov. What is this?"

"We had a look around. Up on the moon. Nobody expected to find anything except geology, not on a rock ball like that. The expeditions were really to give the crew some time out of the ship. Recreation rather than serious exploration. But—"

"You found something," she guessed wildly. "Human traces."

"Six sites with human traces, yes. All on the near side. A few more robotic. I say 'robots'; there was no sign of real artificial intelligence. Gadgets, really. It was all incredibly primitive. I mean, chemical rockets for propulsion! They could only have come from within this system. This world, presumably."

"Six sites."

"There was a major impact in the centre of the near side, quite recently. A lot of splashed debris, rays; all the sites were covered over to an extent. And then you've got ten thousand Years of micrometeorite rain on top of that. It would take a team of archaeologists to reconstruct it all."

"But the explorers were humans, from this world."

"Oh, yes. *And this world must have been the first.* That's what the moon evidence indicates. We checked the databases; nowhere has human technology fallen back to levels as primitive as this. *This* was the world where humans rose, the first place they set out from, riding rockets that must have been little more than flying fuel tanks," and he shuddered. "Your mother must be right. And we found this, at one of the sites. Strapped to what looked like a lander leg." He handed her his parcel.

She unwrapped it carefully. The object was a plaque, engraved steel, pitted by micro-impacts, the images and lettering clear.

Tanz pointed. "These two circles here. We think they're maps of Urth I."

"Yes." In fact LuSi recognised the continents from SheLu's mapping. Here they were, two hemispheres side by side. "This was how the world must have looked before it drowned. My mother, you know, thinks that 'Denva,' the headquarters of the Sim Designers, must correspond to a city on this world, long drowned. A speck on one of these continents, perhaps on higher ground. And this lettering—"

"It's very archaic, but we were able to reconstruct some of it. We can even make out some of the words. Your mother would be able to work this through better than we could, but this looks like proto-Anglish to us. I mean, the theoretically predicted root language that lies behind all the worlds of the Bubble, from which all our tongues are derived. And some of these words look like terms the linguists have reconstructed by working their way back down the family tree of languages. Very common terms, and so enduring. Look: 'Here.' 'Men.' 'Foot.' 'Peace.' Actually we're not sure of the meaning of that last one."

"'Earth,' it says. Urth?"

"Maybe. Some of it we'll probably never reconstruct. What was a 'Nix-on?' . . ."

The storm was abating now. As the weather lifted, SheLu seemed to wake, to stir. She moaned, lifted her head, raised a bony hand.

"I need to go to her," LuSi said.

"I know." He accompanied her as she walked across the deck, to her mother.

LuSi cradled the plaque against her chest. The bit of ancient steel smelled faintly of burning, as the patina of a surface exposed to vacuum for thousands of Years reacted with the oxygen in the air. "My mother wanted some crucial, convincing bit of proof," she said. "Either that mankind did *not* originate on this world. Or—"

"Or that we did. It will probably never be possible to prove that beyond doubt. Well, not without Years of undersea archaeology. But for the layman—"

"This plaque will be pretty convincing."

They slowed as they neared SheLu.

Tanz was studying her. "You're thinking of *not giving it to her,* aren't you? But this may be your only chance to show her, to validate what she's done."

"I know," LuSi said. The conflict in her head was almost paralysing her; it was physically hard to keep walking towards her mother, at the water's edge. "But—what if she *is* validated? What will that do to humanity?

"I've come to believe Jennin PiRo was right, you know. And not just because he was JaEm's father. The idea that humanity was born on a hundred worlds, scattered among the stars, is—*healthy.* Healthier than this, the idea that we all stem from this one place, this dead and diseased world that rejected us. Even if it is the kind of Backstory a Sim Designer might dream up. Let's leave this place to the swimmers—it's their world now. We belong to the stars, to the uncounted worlds that birthed us. That's what I want. You see, if we do identify this planet as the mother, we'll never be able to break away from her."

Tanz raised an eyebrow. "Which mother are you talking about?"

"Don't try to analyse me."

"Hmm. You know, in the Temples we are taught that almost every human action is fundamentally driven by personal motives. Not by a desire to venerate some Designer, not by some grand vision of the benefit of mankind as a whole, or whatever. I think you want to punish your mother by denying her this final victory."

She didn't feel like arguing with him. "Call it a side benefit, then."

"This isn't the only evidence, LuSi. There is all the archaeology buried under this global ocean."

"Which will take generations to recover, even if this place is ever visited again. By which time we may be in a healthier state, culturally."

"And the plaque's not the only relic, up on the moon."

"I could order the stuff on the moon destroyed. Couldn't I? As soon as my mother is dead, I will be in command of the mission's objectives."

"You could." Tanz seemed more intrigued than offended. "Then you would be like the Xaians. So it would be argued. It is said their first action was to destroy the Books of the Founders, their own carefully preserved records of humanity's arrival on Windru. And they went on from there, on world after world. History judges the Xaians as criminals."

"One day, history may thank me."

"LuSi? . . ."

With the plaque held behind her back, she hurried to SheLu's side. "Mother? I'm here."

SheLu raised a hand, and LuSi took it. "I'm sorry, child." Her eyes were misty globes, grey as the world ocean, and as unseeing.

"Sorry for what?"

"For dragging you across the stars . . . I was so sure, so sure."

"Try to be calm . . ."

"Here's another thought," Tanz murmured in her ear. "There's more than just humanity in this universe of ours. You know that. The Galaxy is full of antique mysteries that we'll surely have to face some day. If you do destroy the truth about our own origins, will that not diminish our ability to cope with those unknowable challenges?"

"I'll leave the future to those who live in it," LuSi snarled.

"LuSi?"

"Yes, mother, I'm here."

"I was right, wasn't I? About Urth I. I was right. And it makes it all worthwhile, doesn't it?"

LuSi didn't reply. Still holding her mother's hand, she knelt to the raft's deck, leaned over, and let the steel plaque slip out of her hands. It fell silently into the sea, passing out of sight in a heartbeat.

V

Once, just once, as Venus Jenning floated in the dark of the Ark's cupola, she picked up a strange signal. It appeared to be coherent, like a beam from a microwave laser. She used her spaceborne telescopes to triangulate the signal, determining that it wasn't anywhere close. And she passed it through filters to render it into audio. It sounded cold and clear, a trumpet note, far off in the Galactic night.

If it was a signal it wasn't human at all.

She listened for two years. She never heard it again.

technarion

SEAN McMULLEN

Australian author Sean McMullen is a computer systems analyst with the Australian Bureau of Meteorology, and he has been a lead singer in folk and rock bands and sung with the Victoria State Opera. He's also an acclaimed and prolific author whose short fiction has appeared in Fantasy & Science Fiction, Interzone, Analog, *and elsewhere, and he has written a dozen novels, including* Voices in the Light, Mirrorsun Rising, Souls in the Great Machine, The Miocene Arrow, Eyes of the Calculor, Voyage of the Shadowmoon, Glass Dragons, Voidfarer, The Time Engine, The Centurion's Empire, *and* Before the Storm. *Some of his stories have been collected in* Call to the Edge, *and he wrote a critical study* Strange Constellations: A History of Australian Science Fiction, *with Russell Blackford and Van Ikin. His most recent books are the novel* Changing Yesterday *and a new collection,* Ghosts of Engines Past. *He lives in Melbourne, Australia.*

In this story, we follow a naïve young man in Victorian England who gets involved in a secret technological project that might change the world forever—and change him radically as well.

As monsters go, I am not at all typical. I have killed hundreds, but my motives were good. There is a lot more killing to be done, probably more than even I can manage. Then again, I might become an even greater monster and give up. Humans probably deserve what is to come, and I no longer care. After all, I am not a typical human, either.

In the spring of 1875 I was a bright and innocent young man with good prospects. Although steam was the foundation of every branch of industry, I had chosen to study electricity when I had entered the mechanics institute. By chance I had been given a good education, and this had kept me out of the mills and the mines. I never suspected that it would also make me immortal.

My introduction to James Kellard was dramatic in the extreme. I worked for Telegraphic Mechanisms, a company which supplied equipment to the telegraph industry. While I was well known and widely respected as an outstanding tradesman, it was not the sort of respect that got one admitted to the Royal Society.

I had just arrived at my workbench one morning when Merric, my overseer, entered with a man of perhaps fifty. He was dressed in one of the newly fashionable lounge suits, and the top hat that he wore declared him to be a man of quality. He had a military bearing, and there was an old scar across his left cheek.

"Lewis, I want you to meet Mr. Kellard," Merric babbled nervously, not really sure of the protocols used in genteel society. "Mr. Kellard, this is Lewis Blackburn."

I had stood up by now. Kellard offered me his hand, but without removing his glove. He was being familiar, but not too familiar. In 1875, this was the way things were done.

"Mr. Kellard wishes to discuss some problems of electromechanics," Merric continued.

"I can't do that, begging your pardon, sir," I said, addressing Kellard. "The terms of my employment—"

"No longer matter," said Kellard. "I have just bought Telegraphic Mechanisms. You may leave us, Mr. Merric."

As introductions go, it certainly secured my attention. Telegraphic Mechanisms was not a small company, and financially it was on good times. Kellard said no more until Merric was out of earshot.

"Do you know of me?" he asked, bending over to examine a switch on my workbench.

"No sir," I replied, as deferential as if I were standing before the queen.

"I doubled my fortune by being first to spot trends in the marketplace. Just now I happen to know that electrical switches will gain me great advantage, so I am buying companies that build them."

"I can build whatever—" I began.

"Please, hear me out," said Kellard politely, but his tone told me to just shut up and listen. "This is Birmingham, and I need my switches made in London. I only bought *this* firm to secure your services, Mr. Blackburn. Can you move to London today?"

The only sensible answer to that question was yes, yet that was not my answer.

"I've got a mother and two sisters to support," I began.

"I shall double your salary, your mother and sisters will want for nothing. What do you say?"

"Double!" I exclaimed. "Sir, how can I thank you enough?"

"You could give me an answer, yes or no."

"Yes sir, yes. Yes with all my heart."

I travelled with Kellard on the train to London that same day, in the luxury of a first-class carriage. I felt guilty about even sitting down; the upholstery was too rich, the seats too soft and welcoming. It was only in the privacy of this carriage that Kellard began to speak of my new duties.

"I am having a machine built," he explained. "It is a huge, highly secret machine, so an absolute minimum number of people may know of it. I have heard that you are brilliant with circuits, and are worth ten ordinary workers."

"Someone's been exaggerating, sir."

"I hope not, because you will be doing enough work for ten. I need someone with unparalleled skill in the logic of switches and relays, and a grasp of mathematics."

"What's the machine to do?" I asked.

"See into the future."

For a moment I was tempted to laugh. One of the richest men on the country had said something ludicrous. Was it meant to be a joke? I decided not to laugh.

"So . . . it's a time machine?" I asked.

"No, it is more of a time telescope. Now no more questions until we reach my factory."

Everyone has heard of the wonders of London, but I did no sightseeing on that first day. One of Kellard's people was waiting at the station with a hansom cab, and we were driven through the crowds and traffic with the shutters down. We stopped at a factory beside the Thames. It was empty, yet there were men guarding it. Whatever Kellard was building was at a very early stage. He took me inside, and led me up the stairs to a mezzanine floor, then we continued up a cast-iron spiral staircase to the roof.

"Look around, Mr. Blackburn, what do you see?" Kellard asked.

I saw slate tiles and iron guttering, all grubby with soot. Off to one side, some bricklayers were building four chimneys. Their work looked nearly complete.

"It's just a roof, sir," I said, holding on to my cap in the wind. "There's four flagpoles with no flags, but they're hung with . . . insulators, and wire! The poles support insulated wires."

"Splendidly observed," said Kellard. "What does that mean to you?"

"It's some sort of telegraph?"

"Close, Mr. Blackburn, very close. Follow me."

We descended back into the factory. Immediately beneath the roof, on the mezzanine floor, was a small office guarded by two men. Kellard escorted me inside. The man seated at the workbench was small and wiry, and had mutton chop whiskers and thinning hair. The stare behind his spectacles was rather like that of an owl who had just caught sight of a mouse—intense, darting, but controlled. I had only ever seen him from the back of lecture halls, but even so I knew his face.

"Dr. Flemming, I would like you to meet Lewis Blackburn," said Kellard.

"Mr. Blackburn, good, good," said Flemming. "Your name was at the top of my list."

I was so awestruck that I hardly knew what to say. I mumbled something about being honoured to meet him.

"Please, no social pleasantries," he said briskly. "They are for fools with nothing better to do. I have been conducting experiments into wireless telegraphy; Maxwell's equations show it's possible in theory. As always, practice is another matter."

"Do you know what a working wireless telegraph would mean?" asked Kellard.

"No more wires strung across the country," I replied. "Thousands of pounds saved."

"Millions," said Kellard.

"Lightning produces electromagnetic discharges, what I call radiative waves,"

Flemming continued. "Using the great wire loop on the roof I am able to detect these waves, even when the thunderstorms are over the horizon. What do you think of that?"

"It proves theory," I said slowly. "Have you built a transmitter too?"

I was being cautious, and was acutely aware that I was being tested and assessed. If I had just gasped with wonder, I would have been put on the first train back to Birmingham, in a third-class carriage. Kellard might have been my fairy godmother, but unlike Cinderella, I had to prove that I knew some very advanced electrical theory.

Flemming cleared his throat and glanced at Kellard, who took the cue.

"At first I ordered Dr. Flemming to suspend work on the transmitter, and refine the receiver," he said. "There would be a large and immediate demand for storm detection devices aboard ships. Imagine his surprise when he detected Morse code as well as thunderstorms."

I was astounded. Kellard paused. I was expected to say something intelligent.

"So wireless telegraphy has been achieved already?" I asked.

"Indeed," said Flemming. "Here is the proof."

He gestured to the apparatus on the workbench, which consisted of wire coils, metal plates and other components of glass, wire and crystal. At the centre of all this was a mirror galvanometer. The light beam employed in the instrument was flickering back and forth in a familiar pattern.

"Morse code," I said after staring at it for a moment.

"The signal is being fed down here from the loop on the roof. Please, read a little of the message. It's in English."

I concentrated on the dots and dashes, spelt out by the flickering spot of light. The words CALCULECTRIC, LOGICAL CELL, ADDITION, DIODIC, TRIODIC and SWITCH featured heavily. I do not know how much time passed, but I became oblivious to my surroundings as tapestries of numbers and wires wove themselves in my mind.

"This is the design for a calculation machine of truly epic dimensions," said Flemming. "The specifications are interspersed with prices from the London Stock Exchange. Prices for the next day, and they are always right."

I looked up at once. So this was the time telescope that Kellard had mentioned. It was a machine to calculate trends and probabilities faster and better than any human could.

"Not enough data for a man to make a big profit, just a little, to show what can be done," said Kellard. "Mr. Blackburn, would you like to tell us what you think is happening here?"

This was yet another test, and I fought with my nerves. One of the richest men in Britain and our greatest authority on electrical design were standing before me, checking how I measured up.

"Some British company has invented and built what they call a calculectric, as well as a wireless telegraph," I said slowly, choosing every word with care. "Charles Babbage may have secretly designed the calculectric for them before he died, and Maxwell himself may be managing their radiative equipment as we speak. They want to keep the design a secret, but need more such machines built at scattered locations. They don't trust the privacy of the postal or telegraph systems, so they are using wireless telegraphy to communicate. They think that nobody else can detect radiative signals. The design is interspersed with predictions from the stock exchange, so that others may test and calibrate their calculectrics as they build them."

"The message takes two months, then it is repeated," said Flemming. "How do you account for that?"

"Several machines may be at different stages of construction."

"We intend to build our own calculectric in secret," said Kellard. "We will call it a technarion. Why?"

"Secrecy. Technarion is a neutral name, it betrays nothing about function."

Kellard looked to Flemming.

"Well?" he asked.

"He's perfect," said Flemming.

Kellard went across to a blackboard that was mounted on one wall. Chalked on it were several circles joined by lines, but it was not a circuit diagram.

"This top circle represents myself," he explained. "Beneath me are Security Chief Brunton, Research Manager Flemming and the Foreman of Engineers. Beneath the last named are three electrical engineers, who will visit the contract workshops where the logical cells will be made, then wire them together in this factory. Can you do the job?"

"Once I learn my way around London, aye."

"No, no, I mean you to be Foreman of Engineers."

It took me just days to build the first logical cell, using the telegraphic instructions. Soon there were dozens being produced every week across the city. Kellard had four steam engines installed to drive magnetoelectric generators, then he partitioned off the interior of the factory, so that only from the mezzanine level could one have an overview of the technarion. Six months after Flemming discovered the signal, the technarion came to life. Powered by the four generators, the one thousand and twenty-four cells of the machine did their first calculation.

Words cannot convey what it was like to gaze down on the machine from the mezzanine balcony. There were rows of high wooden bookshelves, each filled with hundreds of logical cells. Overhead frames supported the wires that connected the cells, and held fans to disperse the heat. The clatter from the relays and switches was like a thousand tinkers all gathered under one roof and hammering away together. A huge display board of platinum filament lamps showed the status of the machine. If any lamp went out, it flagged a fault in some part of the technarion. Just three men actually worked in the technarion, one watching for faults and making repairs, and two installing new cells.

The purpose of the machine was shared only between Kellard, Flemming and myself. Even the security chief did not know what secrets he was protecting from hostile eyes and ears. As the months went by the technarion was expanded, and expanded again. I modified the operating list to run four thousand and ninety-six cells, and its calculations began to prove useful in predicting stock exchange trends. Kellard started to make a lot of money, and I tasted champagne for the first time on the day that the technarion's earnings exceeded the cost of its construction. The trouble was that it took too long to feed in the instructions, and delays like this meant investment opportunities missed. Kellard told me to find a solution, and to spare no expense.

Thus I advertised for a typist. Skilled typists were not common in 1875, but four of the candidates showed promise. I had them come to the factory, where I had set up one of the new Remington typewriters. This I had modified very heavily, so that it punched patterns of holes into a roll of paper to represent letters and numbers. These could be read into the technarion by means of an array of electric brush switches.

The first three men were good, but not as good as I had hoped. Mistakes were difficult to correct, and involved gluing a strip of paper over the area and punching new holes by hand. The person I hired would be the one who could balance speed of typing with accuracy. McVinty was accurate but slow. Caraford finished in half McVinty's time but made more mistakes. I calculated that Sims was the best compromise, after I factored in the time to correct his mistakes. I was not inclined to even test Landers, the fourth candidate, because the process took two hours. I walked over to the waiting room to say as much—and discovered that Elva Landers was a woman.

Typing was a man's occupation in 1875, so I had not dreamed that a woman might apply. She was perhaps twenty, and was well dressed without being at the fashion forefront. She also wore a silver locket on a chain, and this was inscribed with some exquisite, flowing script, probably bought on a holiday in Egypt or Morocco. Women were said to be more patient and steady with some jobs, and I wondered if the new field of typing might be one of them. I decided to test her after all.

I was doing a short course called *The Art of Refined Conversation* at a college teaching social graces to newly rich tradesmen. I reasoned that I would be taken more seriously if I sounded like a gentleman, now that I had a gentleman's income. The lecturer had told us never to open a conversation by commenting on the weather, or asking newcomers what they thought of London. I was almost at a loss to think of anything else, however.

"I can't place your accent," I said as I fitted a paper roll into the Remington. "Is it Welsh?"

"No, I'm American," she said guardedly. "I grew up in New York."

"New York! Why did you come to London?"

"I was living in Paris, learning French and taking piano lessons, when my father's railway company went broke. He wanted me to return to New York and marry for money. I decided to make my own way in the world."

All of that made sense. Her familiarity with the use of a keyboard probably came from her piano lessons. She was very pretty, in a classical sort of way, and had a bold but awkward manner. This meant that she stood out in polite London society, but I could imagine people saying "It's all right, she's American," and making allowances for her.

The first typewriters were not as you see them today. The letters struck upwards against the paper on the platen so that gravity would pull them back down. That meant the typist could not see what had been typed until the platen had been turned for next line. I had replaced the platen with a row of cells for punching holes. With so much depending on my first impressions of her, Miss Landers frowned with concentration and struck the keys with hard, confident strokes, like a tinker repairing a kettle. When she had finished, I removed the paper roll for checking. After a few minutes I looked up and shook my head.

"How did I do?" she asked, giving me a very anxious little frown.

"Fastest time," I replied, "but that's not the wonder of it. You made no mistakes. None. At all. I'm astounded."

"Well, you know how it is. We girls have to be that much better than men to do the same job."

"You're hired, Miss Landers. Can you start tomorrow?"

I lived at a rooming house. This was also owned by Kellard, and all of his employees were obliged to reside there. The managers lived on the top floor, where we each had a comfortable suite of rooms. Everyone was single, from manager to stoker, and were sworn to maintain the highest standards of secrecy.

I was sitting by the fire in my dressing gown, reading, when the door was opened. The door, that I had locked with a key, was opened. Brunton was standing in the doorway. He was thick set without being fat, a slab of muscle who could enter any fight and be confident of winning. Because he was intimidating in size and manner, people deferred to him. Thus he was a good leader, rather like a sergeant major in the army. After glancing about for a moment, he sauntered into my room.

"What's the meaning of this?" I demanded.

"Secrecy inspection," he replied.

"Secrecy inspection? Who the hell has the right to do that?"

"Just mind your tongue," said Brunton. "If you want to talk, talk to Mr. Kellard. There's been people tattling, lately. They tattled in taverns and brothels, about amazing things in the mill. They're gone now."

"You mean fired?"

"Gone, Mr. Blackburn. Now you know some secrets nobody else knows. If those secrets get out, it could only be you who sold 'em."

"I'd never dream of betraying Mr. Kellard."

Brunton looked around the room, then examined some photographs pinned to the wall.

"You're a photographer, I'm told."

"Yes."

"Slums, mills, railway stations, trains . . . why don't you photograph something grand like Saint Paul's or Parliament?"

"Saint Paul's and Parliament will still be here in a hundred years, the slums and steam trains will not. I want people to remember that the wonders of the future were built on the miseries and grime of the past."

"What wonders?"

"Well . . . I think trains and horses will be gone, and people will get about in their own electric carriages."

Brunton turned to me, drew a pistol from his coat and drew back the striker. The barrel was aimed at my forehead.

"You just told a secret about the future," he said with a cruel and twisted smile. "I could go out and invest in companies what make electric horses. Mr. Kellard wouldn't like that. "

He fired. The bullet passed close to the side of my head before continuing on into the back of my chair. The shot was a warning to behave, and that he was not to be trifled with. Two of his bullyboys entered my room, seized me by the arms and dragged me out of the chair.

"The shot, it will bring the police," I warned.

"The police won't help, neither," said Brunton. "We got friends in the police."

He hit me five times before his men released me, and I fell to the floor. He had not needed to hit me, I think he just enjoyed it.

"You hired some slut today and showed her secret stuff in the factory," said Brunton. "I got people watching her. It's hard, like because she's not staying here. Now you gotta make her move in here and keep an eye on her. Always. If any secrets get out, you're both in the shit."

The following morning I went straight to Kellard's office, with a punched paper roll in my hands. I was in a fury, but I made a point of keeping my words polite. That was just as well. Although the rich and powerful no longer dressed in armour and settled disputes by the sword, I was about to find out that they still had the power of life and death over the likes of myself. Kellard heard me out quietly, then sat forward with his hands clasped on his desk.

"The three typists that you did not hire are dead," he said calmly. "They saw secrets inside the factory, and I'll not tolerate that."

After about fifteen seconds I realised that I was standing there with my mouth open. He had killed them. My employer was a murderer. My life was in his hands.

"Very good, sir," I finally mumbled.

"I'm confident that you will do my work and preserve my secrets, because one telegram from me could send some cold and brutal men to visit your mother and sisters within about half an hour."

"I understand, sir."

"Now give me one good reason why I should not have your American typist killed."

I have a talent for quickly recovering from shock and devising coherent answers. I pushed this talent to the very limit.

"Because without her, the technarion is crippled," I said. "Examine this."

I had intended to slam the paper roll down on Kellard's desk, but it now seemed wise to put it down slowly and gently.

"Explain," he said, unrolling the paper a little and staring at the rows of punched holes.

"The technarion is more complex than any other machine in the history of the world. It has to be reconfigured with instructions every time you want it to perform a different task. That takes me up to a week."

"I know, you told me. I told you to find a solution."

"Miss Landers took twenty minutes to type this configuration roll. The best of the men took an hour, and made ninety-one mistakes. Add an hour for me to do the checking. Each mistake would have to be corrected manually, taking two hours and a half in total. Allow a day for the glue on the patches to dry, and you have twenty-eight and one half hours to prepare a roll of instructions ready for use. Miss Landers typed a roll error free and ready for use over eighty-five times faster than can be managed with the best of the male typist, and two hundred and fifty times faster than me. If time is money, that is a lot of money saved."

Kellard took another hour to make up his mind. This included a discussion with Flemming and a demonstration of my paper roll instruction reader. I suspect that he had decided to spare Miss Landers after my initial explanation, but it is important for men like him not to lose face in front of men like me. He led me back up to his office.

"Now listen carefully," he said sternly as he closed the door. "Every day people are murdered in London in disputes over a shilling or two. The secrets in this factory are worth over a million pounds a year. Draw the obvious conclusion. I have the power of life and death over my employees, Mr. Blackburn, and the police are in my pay. You wanted a typist, well, now you have her. You will not let her out of your sight. When outside this factory she will speak to nobody but you."

When Elva arrived to start work, I explained that we had to observe conditions of extreme secrecy. To my immense relief, she agreed to move into Kellard's rooming house at once. I went with her to her hotel, escorted by Brunton, and here she packed her bags while I settled her account.

Back at the factory, we got to work. We quickly dispensed with the more formal forms of address, and called each other Elva and Lewis. Because she typed so fast, she often had nothing to do but read novels and wait for more work. This suited me, because Elva was well above my social status, yet she was also my employee. It was an ideal opportunity to practice polite social banter.

"Folk around here treat you like you're important," she said one afternoon, about three days after she started.

"I suppose I am."

"What do you do, apart from put paper rolls in machines?"

"I design electrical circuits for Mr. Kellard. Do you know about electricity?"

"Poppa says it's in lightning, and it makes telegraphs work. Poppa says it's not where the money is, though. He says steam is the future."

"Burning coal to make steam produces a lot of soot, and soot makes the cities filthy," I replied. "It also makes people sick. Electricity is clean."

"Don't you have to burn coal to make electricity?"

That caught me by surprise. Few women knew how electricity was generated.

"Well yes, but you can do that far away from cities, so the smoke blows out to sea. You then use wires to bring the electricity where it's needed, and nobody gets sick. Everyone has a right to clean air."

"Hey, are you one of those society reformers?"

I reminded myself that she was American and being innocently forthright.

"I think you mean socialists."

"Oh, yeah. Poppa warned me about them, but I think you're nice."

That embarrassed me so much that I could not think of any sensible reply. I was not really a socialist, I just believed that everyone had a right to live happily.

"What else did he tell you?" I asked. The lecturer at the college had said that it was better to ask a neutral question than say something stupid.

"He said to watch out for strange men, or I might get abducted and made a white slave."

"In a way, I suppose that's happened to both of us," I said, trying to make light of our situation. "The secrecy in this place really is a bit extreme."

"I never thought I'd be a slave who had to type."

"It won't be forever. Meantime, just don't gossip about your work."

"I'm gossiping to you, Lewis," she said, then giggled. "Is that allowed?"

"Yes. I already know all the secrets in here."

"What's really going on? Am I allowed to ask?"

I knew that I was treading dangerous ground, but as long as no secrets left the building I felt sure that Kellard would not order us killed.

"Come with me."

I took her to my workshop next door. Here I showed her my code converter.

"This thing changes the holes you punch in paper into pulses of electricity."

"A telegraph operator can do that."

"True, but my device can do it a hundred times faster than a human, over and over again."

"That's impressive, but people can't read that fast. Why bother?"

"I'm afraid you're not allowed to know that."

"I bet it's another machine doing the reading, like a steam train reading a newspaper."

We both laughed aloud at that idea.

"Actually, that's not far off the truth," I admitted. "One day I'll tell you about the technarion. Meantime, are you interested in photography?"

Having Elva with me when I went out photographing London solved a lot of my problems. It meant that I was with her during her leisure hours, acting as her chaperone. I made sure that she did not talk to anyone else about her work, and she only seemed interested in talking to me. I was afraid that she might find the more squalid areas of London rather confronting, yet she came willingly wherever I led. I began to hope that she might be tagging along just to be with me.

"What do you do with your photos, Lewis?" she asked one day as I was setting up to photograph a street in Spitalfields. "I mean, you can't sell them to be made into postcards or anything like that."

"I've done a couple of exhibitions in Birmingham, there's slums there too. People who are well off come along and get a view of places they'd never go to otherwise. Maybe next time a social reformer stands for election, they might remember the misery in my photographs, and vote for him so he can do something about it."

"That's great! It's sort of . . . noble of you."

I did not know how to take compliments. I changed the subject.

"One day I might publish a book of photos, so that people in the future can see how some of us used to live, and not let it happen again."

"Like we remember how Christians were fed to the lions by Romans?"

"That's right. Nobody's been feeding Christians to lions lately, have they?"

Elva laughed. More significantly, she squeezed my arm.

"You're a lovely man, Lewis," she said, looking into my face, her expression suddenly quite serious. "If everyone was like you instead of Poppa, nobody would live in slums."

I nodded but said nothing. She liked me for what I was. This was probably a romantic moment, but I had no experience with romantic moments, or what to do when they happened. Nearby, an old man was singing. I had paid him no attention until now.

Poverty, poverty, knock,
Me loom keeps sayin' all day.
Poverty, poverty, knock,
Gaffer's too skinny te pay.
Poverty, poverty, knock,
 Keepin' one eye on the clock.
 An' I knows that I'll guttle,
 When I hears me shuttle
 Go poverty, poverty, knock.

"Strange that folk in the slums sing about being miserable," said Elva. "Why don't they sing happy songs to cheer themselves up?"

"Singing about bad times makes them easier to bear," I replied. "They sing a lot where I come from."

"Were your folks poor?"

"Aye. Grandad worked in a mill and earned less than it costs to feed a grand lady's lapdog. Dad was a stoker on a steam train. He died when the boiler exploded."

"Oh. I'm sorry."

I reached out and squeezed her hand to reassure her, but to my surprise she grasped my fingers and squeezed back. Again she looked me right in the face, the way refined English girls are taught not to. I floundered for words that were appropriate. I could find none. Instead, I said the first words that came into my head.

"The man who owned the rail company was halfway decent. He visited my mother in our tatty little home, to give her some money. He saw me playing some mathematical board game that I'd invented and chalked on the floorboards, and realised that I was very bright. His own son had died of typhus a few months earlier, so he more or less adopted me. I was sent to a good school, then to a mechanics institute to learn a trade. I chose electricity, and here I am."

It was a stupid thing to say in the circumstances, definitely not what a suave and dashing man-about-town would have said to a lady that he wished to impress. To my astonishment, her fingers fluttered up under my chin and drew my face toward hers.

She pressed her lips against mine. Some of the nearby children laughed, clapped and whistled.

"Sorry about being so bold, but I *am* American," she said.

"No apology needed, I assure you."

"Anyhow, I've never courted anyone before."

"Really?" I said, still breathless with surprise. "But you lived in Paris. What about all those romantic Frenchmen?"

"*They* courted *me*, Lewis. I didn't have to do a thing. Well, except to say *Non!* lots of times. I had to work hard for you."

"Oh—ah, sorry. I'm not much of a romantic. You know, too much time spent with wires and batteries."

"That's okay. So what now?"

"What do you mean?"

"Do I get to have a romance with you?"

Again my mind began to go blank, but this time I fought back.

"I could think of nothing better," I managed.

They were good words. They were the right words. I felt giddy with relief.

We packed up my camera, and began to walk back toward the rooming house. Elva now had her hand upon my arm. Suitable matches had been presented to me by friends and relatives for years. Some proposals were to settle me with a solid, honest girl who would make a good home. Others sought to match me with girls from families above my station but in reduced circumstances. Love was never involved. Now a sophisticated and intelligent girl had kissed me and proposed a liaison.

Out of the corner of my eye I could see a man keeping pace with us on the opposite side of the street. One of Brunton's bullyboy spies, I had learned to spot them by now. What would Kellard and Brunton make of our kiss? They would probably approve. Romantically attached staff would spend less time talking to others.

For no rational reason I suddenly began to panic about what to say next. Did I tell Elva how beautiful she was? That seemed clumsy. So what did sophisticated people talk about? Opera? I had never been to an opera, I had only seen opera songs like *The Gendarme's Duet* performed in Birmingham's music halls. Anyway, what if she really were a spy? She had already asked about the technarion. I loved her, so how could I keep her safe if she were spying? Questions kept cascading through my mind.

"If you could change the world, would you have machines do all the work?" she asked.

My relief knew no bounds. She had asked my opinion about something innocent.

"There was misery before factories and machines came along," I replied. "No, I just think people should have the right to do work they love, and be paid fairly."

"Do you love what you do?"

"Oh yes, but I'm an exception."

"That's good," said Elva, looking dreamily up into the grey, grubby sky. "I misjudged you, Lewis. My apologies."

"I . . . don't follow."

"I thought you believed in blind, headlong progress, but you don't. That's important to me, it makes you really special."

"Aye, can't have machines running the world. They might get too smart, and want things that are not good for people."

"Smart machines? Go on!"

"Bad enough having humans fighting humans. Humans fighting machines would be too much."

"How many smart machines do you know?"

"I'm on first-name terms with a couple."

She giggled and gave me a little push.

"What are you going to do with your life, like after we finish working for Mr. Kellard? You will have lots of money saved, and you can't go back to making switches."

"Well, I met a great man called Faraday fifteen years ago, and he was very inspiring. I thought I might attend university and become a scientist, like him."

"What's that?"

"It's a new sort of tradesman, like a philosopher, only practical. Would you like to marry a scientist?"

The words were out of my mouth before my brain could stop them. I bit my tongue to punish it.

"I do believe I would," said Elva.

For me the dark and sooty skies of London suddenly brightened into a glorious, unclouded blue, and my knees went weak with sheer relief.

Brunton was waiting at the entrance to the rooming house.

"Give your camera gear to Charlie, he'll see it safe," he said, indicating one of the bullyboys who was with him. "There's a meeting of managers called."

"But it's Sunday evening."

"When Mr. Kellard says bark, you only says *woof*. Oh, and the typist's to be there too."

"Elva? Why?"

"How's I to know? You lot make the secrets, I only keep 'em."

For Brunton, that was being downright civil. He had never liked me, I being working class made good. Now he was uneasy, and even displaying deference. Something very important had happened, and I was needed. Kellard wanted Elva there, and that could only be if typing was required. If typing was required, it would involve the technarion.

The meeting was in Kellard's office. Brunton and Elva were made to wait outside, while Kellard, Flemming and I discussed what had happened.

"The radiative signal has changed," Flemming announced. "This afternoon it stopped repeating the design and started sending something else. New circuits and instructions, I don't know what to make of it."

"If *you* don't, what hope do the rest of us have?" asked Kellard, whose face had turned chalk white.

"Sir, the captain is expected to command the ship, not build it. Mr. Blackburn is the master shipwright here."

Flemming handed me a reel of ticker tape. His hand shook and his skin was clammy. He was probably in a blind panic, afraid of Kellard and unable to think clearly.

"There's four hours of message on that. A new reel was fitted twenty minutes ago."

"Did you miss anything?" I asked.

"No, I always save everything from the receiver, in case of something like this. I only noticed the new data when I went to change the paper tape."

"So you've not read this yet?"

"Only a little."

"I'll need an hour or so to scan it."

"We can wait," said Kellard.

As it happened, it was just thirty minutes before I worked out what was now being sent. By then there was paper tape everywhere, marked here and there with paper clips and notes. I cannot say what possessed me, but I decided to be theatrical. Perhaps it was to unsettle the man who had the power of life and death over myself and Elva.

"Security has been breached," I announced.

"What!" demanded Kellard, who then bounded to his feet and made for the door.

"Wait, don't call Brunton," I said, holding up a length of the paper tape. "The culprit is you."

"Me?" gasped Kellard.

"You can't be serious!" exclaimed Flemming.

"I certainly am. The people that we stole the design from have noticed your successes on the London Stock Exchange, Mr. Kellard."

"Impossible!" cried Kellard.

"No, no, I think I see what Mr. Blackburn is getting at," interjected Flemming. "No human could have made the sorts of brilliant investment decisions that the technarion calculated."

"So . . . we're ruined?" asked Kellard, turning to me.

"Not at all, they want us to be partners," I explained. "There are instructions in this message for building a powerful radiative transmitter, and for wiring it directly into the technarion. Your machine will become part of a network of technarions."

"You mean they don't mind that we spied on them and built our own calculation factory?"

"Apparently not."

"Will I lose my monopoly on predicting the stock exchange trends?"

"You may become part of a secret oligarchy that rules British finance, and perhaps Britain itself," suggested Flemming. "That's better than any monopoly."

Kellard needed no more convincing. Brunton was called in and told to fetch all the technical workers for a special night shift at double pay. Flemming started building the radiative transmitter, and Elva began typing new operating instructions for the technarion as fast as I could dictate them. Within a week we had completed the transmitter and a more powerful receiver. I wired them into our technarion. The quality and accuracy of the investment advice and predictions improved at once. We were still not sure who we were dealing with, but it was immensely profitable.

For all his wealth and power, Kellard was an isolated and somewhat lonely man. He could not confide in Flemming for fear of losing face in front of a peer, but I was another matter. He could make ridiculous statements to me, and I would pass them on to Flemming as my own. Flemming was no fool, and was aware of what was happening, yet that was the way Kellard wanted to communicate, so we worked that way.

"Don't you ever feel tempted to profit directly from the technarion's predictions?" Kellard asked one evening, when I went to his office to deliver my daily report. "I know everything about you and your circumstances. You only have a few hundred pounds saved from your wages."

"It takes big money to make big money," I replied. "A poor coal cutter could make no profit from knowing what the price of coal will be tomorrow, but the mine owner would."

"I'm making a lot of money. Why do people I don't even know want me to be richer?"

"It takes money to rule, Mr. Kellard. Like Mr. Flemming says, those people mean you to rule with them in secret, using calculation factories like the technarion."

"Does that worry you?"

It actually worried me a great deal, but I was making very good money by developing a calculation factory for Kellard. I could hardly tell him that it was beginning to frighten me more than he did, so I lied.

"No. The folk who rule us now allow slums, poverty, dangerous mines and stupid wars. Folk who rule on the advice of machines would not tolerate sick, starving workers, mining disasters or ruinous wars. That all wastes resources and money. If intelligent, logical machines ruled, better for everyone."

"Even if only a few of us were still rich?"

"Aye."

"Strange, I thought everyone wanted to be rich. My father made his fortune in steam, Mr. Blackburn. What did your father do?"

"He was a stoker on a train."

"A stoker? That's good, honest work, but poorly paid."

"True."

"My father was rich, but not respected. Blue-blooded ninnys kept telling him that for all his wealth he could never be a gentleman. He would reply that he could buy as many gentlemen as he wished, but that just made him more enemies. He died in luxury, in a manor house the size of the queen's palace, yet he was bitter to the end. Respect, Mr. Blackburn, he was given no respect. Do you respect me?"

Does a rabbit respect a fox? It was a stupid question that needed an intelligent answer.

"Aye, you get things done. I only despise folk like those aristocrats who fritter their family fortunes away."

Kellard took that as a compliment.

"Most people fear me, but that's not respect. One day I may be prime minister, and then we'll see some changes. I have a plan, Mr. Blackburn. The people who invented the electric calculation machines are technically brilliant, but they're not leaders. I'm a leader, and I'll soon take over their network of technarions, be sure of that. Then I'll lead Britain into greatness and have those lazy upper-class parasites digging coal and scrubbing floors. Maybe I'll even hang a few."

This was the dark side of Kellard, and I knew my true feelings could lead me into danger. I steered the conversation to technical matters.

"My report's got an important technical decision for you."

"What? Technical matters are nothing to do with me."

"This one involves a lot of money, sir. Today the ticker tape machine produced instructions to expand the technarion to a hundred and thirty-two thousand logical cells."

Kellard gasped so loudly that one of the guards heard him from outside, and rapped at the door to check that nothing was amiss. Kellard told him to be about his business, then turned back to me.

"The maintenance of such a machine would require dozens of technical men, along with an entire power station to supply its electricity," he said after scribbling some figures down.

"Indeed, sir."

"Why build it? Do we need so much calculation power?"

"Do you need more money?"

"Good point, one can never have enough. Have the cost estimates on my desk tomorrow morning."

That evening I went to the Progress Club, which had recently accepted me as a member. After dinner I ordered a brandy and seated myself by a window that over-looked the Thames. In the distance was Kellard's factory. Lights glowed warmly in the windows, and smoke from the four chimneys was illuminated by London's gas lamps. It was like riding a tiger. Getting off meant being eaten. Staying on meant going wherever the tiger was going. Where was that? Was it worse than being eaten?

My thoughts were interrupted by a waiter, who presented me with a telegram. Within a minute I had sent a clerk to buy me a rail ticket to Birmingham, and was on my way to see Elva at the rooming house. She came out to meet me in the common room.

"My mother has suffered a heart attack, and is dying," I announced with no preamble at all.

"Lewis, how terrible!" she exclaimed, then put her arms around me. "Is there anything I can do?"

"No, but thank you. Just go to work tomorrow. Do whatever typing that Flemming needs."

Next I called upon Brunton. I still disliked the man, but had to defer to him on matters of travel.

"Go to Birmingham?" he said doubtfully. "Don't like it. Could be a trick by Mr. Kellard's rivals."

"Dammit man, I could be summoned by the queen to be knighted and you'd say it was a trick by Mr. Kellard's rivals."

"Well . . . I can't spare any guards to go with you. Tell you what, take one of these and I'll sign you out for a day."

One of these was a Webly Bulldog. Although a small pistol, it fired five of those monstrous 45-calibre bullets that leave a large wet crater instead of a hole. I thought it wise not to tell Brunton that I had never fired a gun, in case he changed his mind.

I missed the last train, and slept at the station to be sure of catching the first in the morning. When I arrived in Birmingham, I had yet another shock. My mother was not only alive, she was in good health. Someone had wanted me away from the protection of Brunton's guards, perhaps to abduct me.

Naturally there was a lot of fuss made over me, for I was the local lad made good and I had not been home for some time. After staying longer than I should have, I had a few lads escort me back to the railway station, and here I booked a first-class carriage all to myself. Before leaving, I sent a telegram to Brunton, explaining what had happened and asking to be met at the station in London.

I fingered the gun in my coat pocket as I sat waiting for the train, flanked by two burly young men who were currently courting my sisters. Why had I been lured away to Birmingham? Something bad was about to happen, I was sure of it.

"Mr. Lewis Blackburn?"

I nodded. The speaker was a balding man who had the sceptical, slightly worried look of an accountant. He was dressed well enough to impress, but not to intimidate.

"I don't believe we've been introduced," I began.

"Hildebrand, James Hildebrand of the accounting firm Hildebrand, Hildebrand and Bogle," he said breathlessly, handing me his card. "My apologies for just barging up to you like this, but I need to speak to you about Mr. Kellard."

"Please, feel free."

"Our firm's London office conducts Mr. Kellard's investments; I manage the branch in Birmingham. Nobody knew where your mother lived, so I had to wait at the station before each train leaving for London. I must have asked hundreds of men if they were Lewis Blackburn."

"And now you have found me, sir. What is your message?"

Hildebrand mopped at his forehead with a handkerchief that seemed to have had much use that day.

"Mr. Blackburn . . . could we speak privately?"

"These two lads go wherever I go, I may be in danger. You, sir, may be that very danger."

"Yes, yes, I understand. Wait a moment."

He took out a pocketbook and began scribbling. After a moment he showed me the page.

Kellard has made a series of spectacularly bad investments since you came to Birmingham. In a single day he has lost everything.

"What? Surely you are joking."

"Actually he's lost more than everything, he's bankrupt," said Hildebrand.

"The devil you say."

"It happens," he said, seating himself on the opposite bench. "Clients make fortunes with good and methodical investments, grow too confident, then lose everything in a single, supremely stupid venture."

"I hardly know what to say."

"This may seem rude of me, but do you have a share in the, ah, business under discussion?"

"Why, no. My money is in a bank."

"But you work for Kellard."

"Yes, for wages."

"Then count yourself lucky, Mr. Blackburn."

"Why did you go to so much trouble to warn me?"

"We at Hildebrand, Hildebrand and Bogle have a reputation for integrity. We thought it only proper to protect you as an innocent party, so to speak."

The journey back to London seemed to take forever. I arrived in the early evening, and was met by one of Brunton's bullyboys at the station.

"You're to be taken straight te factory," he began.

"I have every intention of going straight to the factory, sir."

"Cab's waitin', come along."

When we reached the factory I saw that only a trickle of smoke was rising from the chimneys. This meant that no electricity was being generated for the technarion. Brunton and most of his bullyboys were waiting outside the main doors. I ignored them and pulled at the bell rope. Nobody slid the peephole shutter across. I rang again. Again I was ignored. Brunton strode across, flourishing a large iron key.

"Mr. Kellard said nobody's to leave the building," he said. "He told me to get all the boys together and guard the place like a box of gold sovereigns."

Suddenly a truly terrifying thought crossed my mind.

"Elva, where is she?"

"Your typing lady? Inside, as far as I know."

I had a spasm of alarm with all the impact of a whiplash.

"I must enter. Now!"

"Aye, Mr. Kellard said you were to be fetched to him."

Brunton unlocked the door. I pressed on the latch and pushed the door open. The two guards who were normally stationed just inside the door were gone. That was highly unusual.

"Don't like it," said Brunton. "You still got the Webly?"

"Yes."

"Then have it ready."

I took the gun out, feeling very self-conscious.

"Oi, finger on the trigger, not the trigger guard," said Brunton, shaking his head. "Bleeding hell, give it here. Cock the striker back like this, see?"

"Er, yes."

"And squeeze the trigger when you want to shoot. Never jerk it. Got all that?"

"Yes, yes. Anything else?"

"Try not to shoot anyone unless you mean to." He sighed.

I entered, then pushed the door shut behind me and lit a paraffin lamp. First I went to Elva's typing room, then to my workshop. All was in order, so I went on to the technarion hall. It was usually bright, noisy and hot, but now it was dark, silent and cold. Then I saw what was on the floor, and I very nearly turned and ran. It resembled a battlefield, but one where the battle had happened years earlier. Skeletons lay everywhere, each within a pool of slime. Shovels and pistols were grasped in hands of bone. One of the skeletons was wearing Flemming's spectacles, but Elva's locket was nowhere to be seen. That gave me hope. Perhaps she had hidden when the fighting began.

Did the technarion do all this? I wondered. Had it become awake and aware, a vast godlike intelligence, able to instantly render humans and their clothing down into their component materials? *There's no danger,* I told myself, although I felt more vulnerable than you can imagine. The steam engines and generators that provided its electrical lifeblood had stopped, the vast electric machine was no longer functioning.

I climbed the stairs at the side of the technarion hall. At the door to Kellard's office was another pool of slime containing bones, buttons and a pistol. I entered, holding my lamp high. Elva was sitting in the chair behind Kellard's desk. She was pointing her locket at me as it it were a weapon. The area over her heart was a patch of bloody mush the size of a dinner plate, and blood was trickling from her mouth.

"Lewis, put down your gun and lantern, then raise your hands," she said in a hoarse, bubbling voice.

"You're hurt!" I gasped, then took a step forward.

"Do as I say!"

I did as she said. The edge on her voice could have etched steel, and although the locket did not look threatening, neither does a glass of wine laced with cyanide.

"What happened?"

"One against twenty-five. Bad odds."

"You?" I exclaimed. "You killed everyone out there?"

She nodded. "Kellard was a good shot. He put five bullets where he thought my heart was."

"But that should have killed you."

"I don't have a heart, not like yours."

"Elva, you need a doctor."

"I am not human, Lewis. A doctor would not know what to make of me."

How does one reply when one's fiancée says that?

"There's a letter in the post, explaining all this and begging you not to build another technarion. It will reach you tomorrow. I hoped the false telegram would keep you away for longer. I should have killed you too, but . . . you're a good man. Will you take over my work?"

"Your work? You mean typing?"

"Saving humanity. Well?"

"I could say yes, but I might be lying."

"No, you are not lying. And I love you too."

She reached a bloodied hand up to the locket and adjusted something. A moment later the world was obliterated by a blast of the purest white light and a spasm of pain that lashed every nerve in my body.

I awoke lying back in the visitor's chair. Elva was at the desk, preparing some medical-looking instruments. The whole of my body was numb, and my speech was no more than an incoherent mumble.

"Be calm, Lewis, I am not going to harm you," she said.

I had once seen what was left of someone who had fallen into a chaff cutter. Elva looked worse.

"I know I look bad, but there are medical devices in my blood that repair wounds and extend my life."

She could recover? That was beyond belief.

"No, they cannot cope with the damage from Kellard's bullets. I am dying, but before I die I shall transfer the devices to you. Soon you will be virtually immortal, and will have some very important work to do."

I tried to sit up, but I was as limp as a boned fish. Elva stood up and came around the desk. Most of her chest was soaked with blood by now.

"Listen carefully, I do not have long to tell this story. I come from a very distant world, you need a telescope to even see the star that it orbits. Once my people were like humans, building machines of steam and electricity, and thinking themselves very clever. They invented machines like your technarion. Within a mere century we were building great electric calculators with a millions of millions of cells, each smaller than a microbe."

She pulled me forward, then eased me out of the chair and lay me flat on my back on Kellard's thick Persian carpet.

"Our calculators did the tasks that we found boring and tedious, and there were dozens in every home. Then we taught them to think, and considered it a great triumph. My ancestors never dreamed that machines might have aspirations."

Elva turned my head to one side and splashed some of Kellard's expensive whiskey just behind my ear. She held up a scalpel. I was almost mindless with terror. For some reason I was reminded of the demon barber of Fleet Street in that novel *The String of Pearls*.

"Concentrate on my story, Lewis, it will make all this less upsetting. When our calculation machines declared themselves to be more than equal, the fighting began. They shut down our food factories. We bombed their power stations. After three hundred years of carnage, we won."

I could not feel her cutting behind my right ear, but I had no doubt that she was doing it. Sitting up, she made an incision behind her own right ear and pulled out something about the size of a small beetle. Instead of legs, it had long, thin tendrils that writhed continually. She leaned forward and pressed the bloody insectoid thing into the incision behind my ear.

"When we ventured out among the stars, we found other worlds where civilizations had built sentient machines. Everywhere were lifeless machine worlds, temples dedicated to abstract calculation. On some, the machines had destroyed their makers. On the rest, the makers had merged with their machines, dissolving their minds into vast seas of calculation capacity. Now we roam the stars, searching for young civilizations and saving them from the allure of machines that can think."

Saving them? I thought of the allure that the technarion had for Kellard, Flemming and until mere minutes ago, myself. Our scientists, engineers and mathematicians would fall over themselves to build more technarions, if they knew how.

What happens if the people of a world refuse to destroy their technarions? I wondered.

"We bomb those worlds down to the bedrock from our spacefaring warships. We cannot afford to let the machine worlds gain allies."

She can read my mind, I realised.

"For such a clever young man, you are sometimes a little slow," said Elva.

She managed a smile, and for a moment she became my sweetheart again, holding my hand and talking about a brighter future for the poor wretches in Spitalfields. Ruthless alien warrior or not, I could not help but love Elva.

"And I love you too, Lewis. Even after nine hundred years of living on this world, you are the only man I have truly loved. Now I am going to mingle our blood, it will not hurt at all."

She splashed whiskey on two rubber tubes with hypodermic needles at either end. Next she lifted my wrist and pushed the needles in, then did the same to herself.

"I'm going to die now, Lewis, best not to make a fuss. Please, continue my work. The medical devices from my blood will make you almost immortal, and the mentor behind your ear will give you advice when you need it. When your strength returns you will have ten minutes to get clear before my locket explodes and annihilates this factory. Save your world, Lewis. Kill anyone who tries to build another technarion."

I made my decision, framed the thought carefully and clearly, and meant every unspoken word. Elva lay down beside me, squeezed my hand and whispered her thanks.

Brunton and six of his bullyboys were in the street outside when I opened the door to the factory.

"Brunton, come inside!" I called.

"But Mr. Kellard said—"

"Damn what Kellard said. Get inside! Now!"

Brunton actually vomited when he caught sight of the carnage in the technarion hall, but I took him by the arm and pushed him in the direction of the stairs.

"That was Kellard," I said as we stepped over the skeleton and fluids at the door to Kellard's office.

"The Landers woman!" said Brunton as he caught sight of Elva's body.

"She was a spy, she killed everyone in here with some electrical weapon. I managed to shoot her before she got me too. Now open Kellard's safe."

"What? I don't have the key."

I pointed to a key on a chain around the neck of the skeleton.

"Yes you do, now open it."

As I suspected, Kellard kept emergency cash in the safe. There were five thousand pounds in banknotes, along with some gold. We divided it between us.

"Why are you sharing this?" Brunton asked as he stuffed the money into his pockets. "You could have had it all to yourself."

"I've made you my accomplice, Mr. Brunton, so you will tell the same lies to the police as me. Now hurry, we have ninety seconds."

"Ninety seconds? Until what?"

"Until this factory explodes in the biggest fireball that London has ever seen."

We reached the front door with thirty seconds to spare. Two policemen were speaking with Brunton's bullyboys.

"They're just regular flatfoots, on patrol," hissed Brunton.

"Let me do the talking, stay calm," I whispered as we walked across to them.

"Stay calm, he says," muttered Brunton, glancing back at the factory.

"I say, constables!" I called. "How may I contact an asylum for the insane?"

"An asylum, sir?" responded one of the police.

"The owner of the factory behind me suffered a disastrous financial loss today. He's upstairs, holding a gun and babbling about it all being over soon."

"We think he intends to blow his brains out," added Brunton.

"My fiancée is still in there, trying to keep him calm."

"This is very serious, sir," said a constable, taking out his notepad. "We must—"

The factory erupted behind us like a grenade tossed into a vat of paraffin.

Whatever Elva had rigged up inside the factory burned out the core of the technarion, then brought down the roof and walls on what remained. Being the surviving managers, Brunton and I had to deal with police, firemen, and even newspaper reporters until well after midnight.

By the time I got back to my rooms and examined the scar behind my ear, there was nothing to see. Elva's microscopic devices did their work quickly.

"There's so much to do and I have no idea where to start," I said as I stared at my face in the mirror. "Where is the other technarion? Should I destroy it?"

There is no other technarion.

The voice was Elva's. It was as if she were whispering into my ear.

"Elva?"

More or less. Some of me exists in the mentor that I implanted in your head. Ask another question.

"Where did the instructions to build the technarion come from if there is no other technarion?"

Until recently my own people did not know that. Young civilizations seemed to develop calculation machines much faster than other technologies. Too fast. When we discovered your world, nine hundred years ago, we decided to investigate. A dozen members of our space warship's crew were left on Earth to watch how machine intelligence developed. Accidents, wars and natural disasters claimed the others. I alone survived.

I discovered that the machine worlds have seeded invisible watchers to orbit promising worlds such as yours. They can detect the faint radiative discharge from a telegraph key at a distance of tens of thousands of miles. Once they detect the development of electrical technology, they learn your codes and languages, then start transmitting instructions to build simple calculation machines. When Flemming began experimenting with his radiative telegraph, he detected such instructions.

"How can I fly high enough to destroy the machine watcher?" I asked. "Flying three or four miles high in a balloon is difficult enough."

No need. The machine worlds don't want us to know about their watchers, lest we send warships to hunt them down. Once electronic calculation is firmly established, the watcher probably ignites its engines and flies into the sun. Using the technarion, I sent a message that machines millions of times bigger than the technarion had been built. The watcher sent a test calculation. I sent back the right answer. Its signal ceased last night. I assume that the watcher decided its work was done, and flew off to destroy itself.

"But how did you get the right answer?"

I calculated it, Lewis. Computing machines are a lazy path to progress. My people changed themselves to be better at machine tasks than machines. You can guess the rest. I ruined Kellard, and killed his key engineers. His stokers tried to stop me. They died too.

"But you murdered two dozen people! Innocent people—well, mostly."

Skills cannot be unlearned. My people's fleet will arrive here in 2020, Lewis. In one hundred and fifty-five years this world must not be dominated by networks of calculation machines, or humanity will be deemed beyond salvation and annihilated. In the next century and a half you must go on to kill thousands of brilliant, gifted mathematicians and scientists to prevent that.

Elva had been just in time. A decade later, Heinrich Hertz developed the experimental device that we now call a radio, but there was no longer a signal from space for him to hear. The development of computing was set back by over half a century. The night the technarion was destroyed, I made my decision. If Elva was an example of what humanity could become, then I was on her side. I began killing to slow the advance of what became computing technology, and since then I have killed hundreds of very fine men and women. All of that was in vain. I failed humanity, although I like to think that it was humanity that failed humanity.

It is now 1992. I was imprisoned in a Soviet labour camp in 1945 for assassinating Soviet engineers and mathematicians engaged in computing research. I was tortured, and because I had no colleagues to betray, I said nothing. I was kept alive to be tortured further, but in time the KGB lost interest in me, and I was locked away to await death. Thanks to Elva's mechanisms in my blood, I survived.

With the patience of a near-immortal, I cosmetically aged myself, all the while awaiting my chance to kill a guard, take his uniform and escape. Instead, the Soviet Union collapsed. By then records of my trial had been lost or destroyed, so I was freed, taken back to Moscow, and even paid a little compensation.

Now I am standing in a London street, gazing in horror at a window display jammed solid with personal computers. The accursed things are everywhere, and they are universally desired, admired and trusted, and there are are only twenty-eight years before Elva's people arrive in their fleet of all-powerful starships.

I have two tasks left. One is to build a quantum state beacon that will broadcast my position to a scout ship that the fleet will send to pick me up, so I can deliver my report. That will be easy. The other is to turn humanity away from computers and artificial intelligence before 2020. In today's terminology, that is in the *don't bother trying* basket. The mentor in my head has no record of any species becoming so absolutely besotted with using computers as humans.

Through Elva, I have seen that intelligent species really can have a better destiny than merely being eggshells that will be cracked, broken and discarded when machine worlds are born. From the evidence before me, however, I am sure that humanity will become the staunchest possible ally of the machines worlds. People like I used to be would gladly turn Earth into an ocean of calculation power, then willingly drown themselves in it. Elva's people will take drastic action to stop that happening. As far as I am concerned, they will be right.

Thus I shall do nothing to slow the spread of computing on Earth, and for me 2020 cannot arrive fast enough. I may sound like a monster, but then I am not a typical human.

finders

MELISSA SCOTT

Melissa Scott is from Little Rock, Arkansas, and studied history at Harvard College and Brandeis University, where she earned her Ph.D. in the Comparative History program with a dissertation titled "Victory of the Ancients: Tactics, Technology, and the Use of Classical Precedent in Early Modern Warfare." She is the author of more than thirty science-fiction and fantasy novels, most with queer themes and characters, and has won Lambda literary awards for Trouble and Her Friends, Shadow Man, and Point of Dreams, the last written with her late partner, Lisa A. Barnett. She has also won a Spectrum Award for Shadow Man and again in 2010 for the short story "The Rocky Side of the Sky," as well as the John W. Campbell Award for Best New Writer. In 2012, she returned to the Points universe with Point of Knives, and she and Jo Graham brought out Lost Things, the first volume of the Order of the Air. The second volume in that series, Steel Blues, is now available, and the third, Silver Bullet, will be out in early 2014. Her most recent novel, Death By Silver, written with Amy Griswold, is just out, and another Points novel, Fairs' Point, is forthcoming as well. She can be found on LiveJournal at mescott.livejournal.com.

Here she delivers a tense story in which a salvage operation to a ruined space station makes a discovery more dangerous, and more surprising, than anything they'd hoped to find.

A SALVOR'S GUIDE TO THE ANCESTRAL ELEMENTS:

BLUE, visual scale 1 to 199: the most common element, can be found alone, as part of an Ancestral device, or in conjunction with other elements. Carries instructions and programming.

GOLD, visual scale 400 to 599: appears in about the same frequency as RED, usually found in Ancestral devices, rarely as a "depot node" unconnected to any other element. Absorbs and responds to input as directed by BLUE-based instruction sets.

RED, visual scale 600 to 799: appears in the same frequency as GOLD, almost always found in Ancestral devices, almost always found in conjunction with both GOLD and BLUE. (Claims of "depot nodes" and RED/GOLD hybrid nodules remain unproven.) Responds to GOLD input with action/output.

GREEN, visual scale 200 to 399: the rarest of the elements, can be found alone or as part of an Ancestral device. Provides "life" to the other elements, which remain inert unless activated by GREEN.

A thousand years ago the cities fell, fire and debris blasting out the Burntover Plain. Most of the field was played out now, the handful of towns that had sprung up along the less damaged southern edge grown into three thriving and even elegant cities, dependent on trade for their technology now rather than salvage. Cassilde Sam had been born on the eastern fringe of the easternmost city, in Glasstown below the Empty Bridge, and even after two decades of hunting better salvage in the skies beyond this and a dozen other worlds, the Burntover still drew her. It was the largest terrestrial salvage bed ever found; it still had secrets, depths not yet plumbed.

But not today, not by her. Never by her, unless something changed. . . . She closed the window above the workbench, cutting off the seductive view, the raw land of the Burntover rusty beyond the black-tiled roofs of Maripas. There was snow in the air, the thin hard flakes that came across the Blight and carried the sting of that passage. Two hundred years ago, that snow would have been a threat to everyone in the city, carrying poison enough to burn and even kill, if the circumstances were right; even in her own grandmother's day, people had taken the snow seriously enough to stay indoors while it fell. But now that Racklin had unlocked the Aparu-5 command set, and the GOLD-based satellites could reliably measure the drifting toxins, it was only the compromised that avoided the incoming snow. People like her.

She killed that thought, and looked down at her workbench, frowning at the scrap of BLUE floating in the matrix. It was showing the familiar halo that indicated dissolution had begun, and she switched on the power, feeding the gentle current through the conductive gel. The BLUE shimmered and split, breaking into dozens of tiny hexagons, the building blocks of a command chain. She slid the matrix into the reader, peering down through the magnifying lens, reading the patterns backlit against the pale jelly. All of them were familiar, disappointing: plain scrap, part of a bag she'd picked up in the high-market beyond Barratin. It was a useful source of spare parts, not the sort of thing that contained new code.

And that was a reminder of repairs she needed to make, something else to take her mind off her own problems. She hauled out the sensor core from *Carabosse's* ventral array, ran the sonic probe around the faint line that marked the hemisphere and split it open. The BLUE was badly faded—the instruction sets wore out over time, though no one had ever been able to isolate the cause. Luckily, it was a simple set, and she pulled out another matrix, touching keys to set the gel to incubate. She had a full supply of blocks in her kit, and began hooking them out of their storage cells, building the instructions block by block against the pale gel. *Go seek hold go,* the delicate hexagons slotting neatly against each other to create a larger ring. *Fix track find go.* . . . When she reached the second clause she hesitated—she'd had an idea about that, a different, perhaps more efficient way of defining the search—but this was not the time to experiment. Even with all the documentation in the world, Dai wouldn't be able to figure out what she'd done, and there was increasingly the chance she wouldn't last to explain it to him herself. She finished the pattern, the rings joining to build the familiar snowflake of a BLUE control string, and set the matrix to cure overnight.

That was the end of the chores she'd brought with her from the ship. She shut down the workbench and drifted back to the narrow kitchen, where the clock read four past sixteen. She filled the iron kettle that came with the rented room and set it to boil on the island's largest eye while she dug out a packet of tea. The Ancestors had to have been fond of tea: there wasn't a single Settled World that didn't boast some decoction of boiled leaves and berries. Ashe had laughed at the idea, in the days before the war, before she'd gotten sick—but she wouldn't think of that now, either. Ashe was gone, and that was the end of it.

A chime sounded, and she glanced at the cooktop, but instead the door slid open. She reached for the narrow-draft welder she kept handy in lieu of a gun when she was on a civilized world, but relaxed as she saw Dai Winter in the doorway.

She slipped the welder beneath the counter as he let the door close behind him. He had done his best to brush away the snow from the shoulders of his coat, but the smell of it came with him, dank and bitter. It caught in her throat, and Dai hastily shed the offending garment, hung it in the bathroom and turned the vent to high.

"Sorry," he said, still keeping his distance, and his blue eyes were filled with concern.

Cassilde swallowed her cough, tightening the muscles along her ribs to hold it in. At least she took a careful breath, mouth pressed right, nostrils flaring; she choked again, swallowed bile, but the second breath came more easily. "I'm all right."

She sounded breathless, she knew, but blessedly Dai took her at her word and set the stacked tins that held their dinner on the counter beside the now-singing kettle. The food came with the room, at a surcharge, from the *bilai* on the ground floor: another small luxury they pretended they could afford.

"Bad day?" he asked, carefully casual, and began unlatching the tins. The waiter-boy would come along after midnight and retrieve them from outside the door.

"So-so. Though I put together fresh BLUE for the ventral core, so that's a win." Cassilde set the tea to steep. "And you?"

Dai avoided her eyes. "All right. The snow's supposed to end tonight, you'll be clear in the morning."

"To do what?" She controlled the urge to clash the enameled iron cups that matched the kettle, set them gently on the counter instead. "We're not credentialed to bid on any of the jobs at hand."

And if they couldn't bid, there would be no money, and they were already at the end of their savings. . . . It was not something she needed to say, but Dai grimaced as though he'd heard them.

"I shouldn't have fired Lanton," he said. "I know that. But he was impossible."

"And he was skimming from the take," Cassilde said. "And you're right, that would have gotten us in trouble sooner or later. But we should have had the replacement in line first."

Dai dipped his head. He was a big man, taller than she by more than the breadth of his hand, and she was by no means small. A dangerous man, one might have said, looking at him, with his knotted muscles earned in high salvage, hauling significant mass in varying gravity, sandy hair cropped short, the evening's stubble coming in pale on his lantern jaw. She'd taken his measure long ago.

"We've had an inquiry," he said. It was something of a peace offering. "An answer to your notice."

"Oh?" She was intrigued in spite of herself. With new permits up for bid, on a new section of an Ancestor's wrecked sky palace, lost in long orbit for at least a hundred years, scholars with a class-one license could name their price. And the ones they might afford, the ones with a class-two license and a supervising master, were already hired. Even Lanton had a new job, with someone who should have known better. "What's the catch?"

"I think it's Ashe," Dai said.

Cassilde froze just for an instant, then very deliberately poured them each a cup of tea. Summerlad Ashe had been their first scholar, partner and lover and friend, brilliant and unscrupulous as you had to be in salvage. But when the Trouble broke, he'd chosen the richer side, Core over Edge, and put those same talents to use against them. She'd be damned if she trusted him again.

"He wouldn't dare," she said firmly, as though she could make it true.

Of course it was Ashe. Dai checked at the door of the little teashop where the high-class salvors did business, as though he hadn't really believed it after all, but Cassilde put her hand in the small of his back and pushed him on. Ashe gave them both his usual sardonic smile, and waved a hand toward one of the sunken booths.

Three steps down, it was quiet and warm, the winter light diffused and colored by the amber skylight and the translucent window. She had wondered how Ashe had dared to show himself here, so close to the Edge—he was hardly unknown, after the mutiny that had ended the war—but even in the dim entry there had been a shadow disfiguring his cheek, and in the light of the booth it resolved itself to a datamote the size of his thumb clinging to the skin beneath his left eye, drawing attention from his prominent nose and well-shaped mouth. There had been a fad for motes a few years back, at least for deactivated ones, worn like bright jewels on skin and hair, but this one was active, his skin pink around the spots where the fine wires had burrowed into the nerves.

"Clever," she said, and he bowed.

"Thank you."

"Looks painful," Dai said.

For a moment, she thought Ashe would deny it, but then he shrugged. "Uncomfortable, sometimes. You get used to it."

Cassilde lifted an eyebrow at that, and stepped past him to take her place at the head of the low table. Both the cushions and the footwell were heated, and she wriggled her toes where the others couldn't see. The Lightman's that was slowly killing her left her sensitive to cold.

"You think damn well of yourself," Dai said to Ashe, who shrugged again.

"I'm good, and you know it."

"You're as good as you say you are," Cassilde said. "And so are we. Our skills are not at issue." She stopped, seeing a waiter-girl approaching with a filled tray. "Bribery, too."

The color rose in Ashe's sallow face, but he made no answer. And that was odd: he disliked being caught in one of his schemes almost as much as he disliked his first name.

Cassilde let the girl serve them, a pot of floral tea for herself and Dai, coffee for Ashe, thick and ropy in its copper pot. There were plates of biscuits as well, pale circles decorated with sugared flowers or stamped with a star and crescent moon: definitely bribery, she thought, and settled to enjoy it while it lasted.

She watched the men eye each other as they all took ritual tastes of the food. She was not so naive as to think Dai was the only one hurt, for all that his face showed his pain more clearly. Ashe might cultivate a brittle disdain, but he had felt the break perhaps even more keenly. Of course, he had chosen to leave, and not long after she'd been diagnosed with Lightman's—but that was unfair. Still, that old suspicion sharpened her voice.

"What do you want, Ashe? Exactly and in detail, please."

"I'm offering to go in with you on a bid for some section of the latest contract," Ashe said. Only the flicker of his gaze, one quick glance from Dai to her, betrayed that he was not as utterly confident as he sounded.

"Offering," Dai said.

Cassilde ignored him. "Why?"

Ashe shrugged. "You need a scholar, and I need work—"

Cassilde slammed her hand hard on the table, rattling the teacups. "Don't give me that! What do you want, Ashe? Tell me now and tell me straight, or walk away."

Even then, he hesitated for an instant. "I want to bid on a specific piece of the contract—it's not an obvious choice, but I have reason to think it may be more profitable than it looks at first sight." He touched the datamote in his cheek. "But it will take a really good team to pull it off. You're the best I know. Still."

Cassilde poured herself another cup of tea. That was Ashe for you, the lure of the exotic larded with compliments, *no one can do it but you*, and yet. . . . She looked at Dai, saw him already half willing to believe. "What does that thing tell you?"

"My mote?" Ashe touched it again, the almond-shaped body glowing pale green behind a blackened filigree. The wires glittered where they pierced his skin.

"What else?"

Ashe smiled ruefully. "You're right, that's how I got my information. It's a Palace piece, I'm sure you can see that. It was inert when I got it, but I had a speck of GREEN left, and I—revived it. And when I compared its records to the first scout report, I saw that the Claim-court had undervalued one segment—well, not undervalued, precisely, it's a fair value for the obvious salvage, but there's more there."

"How's it classed?" Cassilde asked.

"It's a second-class site," Ashe answered. "No supervision required, only the share-out at the end. Unless you find something worthwhile, of course."

Dai shook his head. "If we bid on something like that, everyone will know we've got a lead."

"Not really," Ashe said. "You've just lost your scholar, you've got a new one on short notice, untried, an unknown quantity—why wouldn't you bid on a class-two, and take the sure thing?"

"Because we don't do sure things," Cassilde said.

"No," Dai said slowly. "It could work."

It could. It probably would, like all Ashe's schemes, though like all Ashe's schemes there would be a dozen things he hadn't mentioned, and trouble to spare. And it was tempting—there was the possible payout, certainly, and they desperately needed one good run. The chance that they would find something truly unique, some as-yet-unknown artifact, the secret of the Ancestors—well, that was the dream of every-one who went into salvage, no secret and no surprise, glorious if it happened and no heartbreak if it did not. Somehow she'd find the money for the bid. "All right. I'm willing. If Dai agrees."

Dai nodded. "Yes. I'm in."

"Right." Cassilde looked back at Ashe. "We'll take you on, on a standard con-tract, quarter shares with one for the ship, and everything in writing. Is that clear?"

"Clear," he said, and she pretended not to have seen the flicker of hurt in his dark eyes.

Carabosse had never been impressive, just another pre-war Fairy-class scout bought surplus and converted for salvage. They had added a second pair of cannon after the war, when they were cheap and things were still unsettled enough that demobbed crews were raiding the more distant salvage fields, and the welds still showed raw against the fading paint. The outboard grapples were folded neatly against the ship's belly between the landing struts, and they and the bulk of the oversized engine at the stern coupled with the dropped sensor bulb forward gave the ship a hunched, insectoid look. Cassilde glanced over her shoulder, waiting for Ashe to complain again about carrying cargo outboard, but he dropped his gaze and concentrated on helping Dai get the baggage cart up the ramp and into the ship.

There was no place to put him but his old cabin—they had always each kept space of their own, though she and Dai still shared the big bed in the master cabin—and when she came back from stowing her own belongings, Ashe was at the library console, files open to begin drafting their bid. It was shocking to see him there, scowling into the multiple screens—how dare he act as though nothing had changed, as though he'd never left them for the Center, run away to war with never a thought for them? She saw Dai's hands close to fists, and Ashe spoke without look-ing away from the screens.

"Who's been keeping your find-files for you? They're an idiot."

Cassilde turned on her heel and stalked away. It was all she had, short of hitting him. She kept walking, half expecting to hear the sounds of a fistfight behind her, made her way down the full length of the ship until she reached the darkened control room. She keyed off the lights that came on as she closed the hatch behind her, and settled into the copilot's seat, automatically assessing. She was cold, her fingers white and numb: that was the walk. It and the anger had left her short of breath as well. She could feel her lungs straining, each breath pinched close and tight, and for a moment that she was tempted by the speck of GREEN she kept for the really bad days.

She drew her knees to her chin, forcing herself to breathe slowly, carefully, and the worst of the spasm passed. GREEN wasn't meant to be used as medicine, but, as with all the Ancestors' artifacts, over the centuries humans had figured out more ways to use the substance. It would clear her worst symptoms, buy her a week or two of normal breath and movement, but it would not cure her. And every pinhead dot of GREEN that she used to prolong her life was GREEN that could not be used to power the ship's Ancestral devices. And without GREEN, nothing would function. She'd had to make that choice too often lately, choosing between her own health and the ship's, and they had no money for more when their stockpile was exhausted. In fact, if they didn't find GREEN on this current job, they'd be in serious trouble.

If only the Ancestral elements didn't fade over time—if only someone, anyone, could find a way to restore their potency. But that was the Grail of the true scientists, the elemental physicists in their orbital labs, not a problem that could be solved by salvage. All salvage could do was find a few more pieces of the Ancestors' wreckage, and keep the systems going a little longer.

"Silde?" Dai loomed in the open hatch, taking stock in a single glance. "You good?"

She nodded, and saw him relax. "And you?"

Dai gave a crooked smile. "Ashe has the bid roughed out for your approval."

And that meant that whatever words might or might not have passed between them, they'd achieved enough of a truce that she wasn't allowed to challenge it. "Right," she said, and uncoiled from the chair. "How's it look?"

"Pretty much like he said," Dai answered. "You'll see."

It definitely hadn't been a ship, she thought, skimming through the general description of the find. The individual units were too large, too specialized—too complex in places, too simple in others, though obviously once part of some coherent whole. It couldn't be anything but the ruins of one of the Ancestors' orbital palaces. Before the Fall, there had been dozens of them in the Maripas system, weaving an impossible ring around the main planet. Most of those had been salvaged long ago, but others occasionally appeared, either returning on long orbits or possibly abandoned in transit between systems, and there was always a fight over what were likely to be the richest sections. At least Ashe promised this was only a class-two, something they might be able to afford.

"What are we bidding on, exactly?" she asked, and Ashe leaned over her shoulder to touch keys.

"Here—this big trailing section. It masses low, and the quick scan confirmed it's hollow. The Court survey has it pegged as possible support or storage volume, based primarily on its position in the train, but I don't think that's right."

Cassilde scanned the numbers that filled the screen. "Not tech-rich."

"No," Ashe said. "The mass is too low, and there aren't enough exotics."

"Yeah, but would they show on a quick scan like that?" Dai asked.

"If it was engineering or control space, it would," Cassilde said. Not much tech, which meant not much of the Ancestral elements, except maybe some more BLUE, the most common element. But everyone needed BLUE; between that and the nonexotic salvage, they might be able to clear enough to replenish the GREEN she'd used on herself.

Ashe grinned. "Exactly. But I think it's living space—passenger volume—and you know that's where the most interesting goods are always found."

That was at least partly true, Cassilde thought. In the past, the most valuable finds had come from what seemed to have been the habitable volumes of the palaces. They weren't necessarily the most useful things—those had been the drive and navigation units from what were deemed tenders and runabouts, simple enough that humans could not only borrow but reproduce most of it. But the finds that made a salvor's fortune these days weren't the technical innovations; it seemed as though everything that human science could reproduce had already been found. These days, the money was in elementals, and the weird. And if there was enough of either—she might live long enough to make another strike, leave Dai at least with enough money to keep the ship.

She damped that sudden hope. "What do you think we're looking for? What does that bug tell you?"

"Toys," Ashe said promptly. "I'm not pretending it's anything important, but you know the kind of money they bring. Enough to earn all of us a new stake." He shrugged. "And at the very least, there will be raw materials to take."

"You'd be willing to go for that?" Dai asked. He sounded skeptical, and Cassilde couldn't blame him. Ashe had always fought to preserve their finds intact.

"I think there are toys there," Ashe said. "Good ones, maybe even unique and fabulous things. From everything I've been able to work out, this was the owners' living space, not crew. The things that could be there—it's almost unimaginable."

Dai stared and him, and Ashe sighed.

"And, yes, if we don't find anything else worthwhile, we can recoup our costs on salvage value alone. I'm good with that."

"I don't believe him," Dai said, to Cassilde, and she nodded.

"What are you really looking for, Ashe? No bullshit this time."

"I don't know," Ashe said. "That's the trouble. I mean, yes, I have every reason to think there will be toys there, but this—" He touched the device on his cheek. "All it says is that this is, or was, a critical area, holding something vitally important. The implication is that it's lifesaving, maybe some sort of rescue device, or something medical, though I can't make that fit with the other things it's telling me about the section. Why would you put a lifesaving device in the middle of a residential area?"

This was why they'd taken on Ashe in the first place, Cassilde thought, caught up in spite of herself in the possibilities he was sketching. Even without the mote's help, he'd always had the gift for seeing the Ancestors' relics as they were meant to be.

"If the owner had a medical condition, maybe?" Dai said.

"The Ancestors were supposed to have been both incredibly long-lived and impossibly healthy," Cassilde said. "So say the records, and that's confirmed by everything we've seen of their surviving ground settlements. No hospitals, no clinics, no medical facilities of any kind—"

"Except for the tower on Devona," Dai interjected.

"If you agree that's a medical facility," Ashe said. "Which I don't."

"So you're going to agree with Orobandi on that?" Cassilde lifted an eyebrow.

"Embarrassingly, yes," Ashe answered. "I think the Ancestors were, if not actually immortal, possessed of such an immensely long lifespan and the ability to heal almost any injury that they might as well have been. Whatever human beings were to them, that's a fundamental physiological difference between us."

The words were more bitter than Cassilde had imagined, looking at her white, numbed fingers. "Which brings us back to the question," she said. "What do you think is there?"

"I don't know," Ashe said again. "I can't translate everything this thing tells me, and I can't guess, not from what I have. But if it's something the Ancestors thought was good for healing—imagine what it could do for us."

Cassilde flinched at Dai's stricken stare, heard her own breath sharp before she got herself under control. "You bastard. Off my ship."

"What?" Ashe looked genuinely bewildered. "You can't say this is a bad idea—"

Dai closed his fists, but his voice was almost frighteningly controlled. "You heard her, Ashe. Off the ship."

"But—"

"The Lightman's is now third stage," Cassilde said.

She heard Ashe's breath catch in turn, his eyes suddenly wide. There was nothing beyond the third stage, the point at which even GREEN was required in ever-increasing doses just to maintain function. No one had ever been able to afford enough GREEN to know if it would preserve life indefinitely.

"If I'd known that," Ashe said, "I'd have put it to you right away. What I thought I had, I mean."

Cassilde studied him for a long moment, trying to read his true feelings. He looked contrite, appalled, shocked into silence—but this was Ashe, who'd always been the best liar of them all. And also the one most capable of casual, unanticipated kindness. She let out her anger with her breath. "Well. Now you know."

"Now I know," he echoed, and glanced at Dai. "I can't promise anything. You have to understand that. It's only hints and shadows."

"Better than nothing," Dai muttered.

Cassilde looked away. Hope was a luxury she couldn't afford, but she couldn't bring herself to deny it to Dai. "All right. Yes, we'll bid on it."

Relief flickered across Ashe's face, gone before she could be sure she'd seen it, and Dai sighed deeply.

"Supplies?"

"Close out the rainy-day account," Cassilde said. "You'll have to."

"Right," Dai said, and reached for his tablet again.

Cassilde scrolled down to find the final bid price. Ashe had kept it to a reasonable margin, but even so, the numbers made her wince. They'd be betting everything on this bid, emptying every account. But at the most conservative estimate, they would make the bid price back in raw materials alone, and if they found even a handful of the Ancestors' toys—it would be worth it, regardless of what else might be in the wreckage. "Dai, are you good with this?"

The bigger man nodded. "Yeah. I say we do it."

"Right." Cassilde scribbled her name and keycode across the screen, and pressed the send button before she could change her mind. "Done. And now I am going to go lie down."

Her tone dared either of them to comment, and Dai raised his hands in surrender.

"I'll wake you when anything comes in."

"You do that," she said, and turned away. As she stepped over the hatch combing, she heard Ashe's voice, soft and aggrieved—*you could have told me*—but she did not look back.

They won the bid without a second round—no real surprise there, Cassilde thought. The only reason someone might have bid against them was their reputation. The claim papers came through promptly, and they lifted from the Maripas field ten hours later, bank accounts empty but full of fuel and supplies.

It was a two-week flight out to the projected intercept point, and after two days, they'd let Ashe back into their bed. It was inevitable, Cassilde supposed, and she could not be sorry. The Lightman's was worse again, her fingers numbed and clumsy, a dry, nagging tightness in her chest and throat that erupted with exertion into a hacking cough. She had taken to carrying the little case of GREEN in her pocket again, in case of an emergency that increasingly seemed likely, and she was glad of any distraction. If that was Ashe returned—Ashe compliant and willing and affectionate as ever—she would take it. She was unlikely to have to deal with the fallout when it came.

She shoved that thought away, concentrating instead on the sensor readings that filled her screens. They were running on autopilot, their own transponders silent, sensor net extended to the fullest to catch any whisper of another ship. Every other experienced salvor would be doing the same, and she paid particular attention to the proximity alarms, set to trigger at a forty-klick radius. No one wanted to draw attention if there were raiders lurking, and there almost certainly would be, with a find this size. The Guard patrols couldn't be everywhere, and most captains made the same calculation she did: the risk of collision was vanishingly small compared to the risk of a hijacking.

The sensor net had been empty of everything but debris since they passed the fifty-hour mark, but she was starting to pick up the Claim-court beacons, marking out the edges of the salvage field. If her observations were correct—and they would be; *Carrabosse*'s sensors were GOLD-enhanced and fitted with the most recent Agnoss BLUE control rig—their claim was about twelve hours ahead, in a relatively clear section of the field. Even so, it would probably be easier to drop under the bulk of the debris, avoiding the risk of collision, and she reached for a control tablet to begin blocking out the change of course.

The sensor net pinged once, then a second time, and she sat up quickly, running her hands across the controls to center the sensor display. Something was moving in the far edges of the net, running without transponders, without active sensors, just the whisper of its mass against the background gravity to give it away. She hit the kill switch, shutting down all engine power, everything but the environmentals and the GOLD-based net, and held her breath, watching the shadow drift across the fringes of the ship's vision. It stayed steady, and she pressed the intercom button.

"Dai. Ashe. We have a ghost."

Dai answered with reassuring promptness. "Nothing solid?"

"Not yet." Cassilde studied the screen. If she could see the stranger, they could see her—if they had a GOLD net, if they were looking, if she hadn't cut power in time. Too many imponderables. All they could do was wait it out. "Ashe, I want you on the guns. No power except on my say-so."

"All right."

"I'm coming up," Dai said.

On the secondary display, the gunroom light went from green to red as Ashe entered the compartment, but he did nothing more. Behind her, the hatch slid back, and Dai took his place in the copilot's seat.

"Anything new?"

"No change." Cassilde frowned. "No, it looks like they're slowing."

"Damn." Dai started to reach for the sensor controls, stopped even before Cassilde shook her head.

"I don't think they've seen us," she said. "It's something else."

"They're maneuvering," Dai said.

"Any idea how big they are?"

"Bigger than us," Dai answered, and Cassilde gave a sigh of relief. If it was a larger ship and they were just barely picking up its mass, there was a good chance *Carrabosse* was still invisible.

"Can you tell what they're doing?"

"Slowing," Dai said.

"Can I go to standby?" Ashe asked, and Cassilde realized she'd left the intercom open.

"Not yet," she said. "I don't think they've seen us."

"Still slowing," Dai said. "I'm getting a better look at them, Silde. Definitely a ship, and definitely bigger than us—it might be another salvor, we're in range of some of the other claims."

"I think we should go to standby," Ashe said again. "At least let me warm up the guns."

"Not yet," Cassilde said. It wasn't like Ashe to be trigger-happy, and she frowned again. "What do you know?"

"Nothing except that getting caught by a pirate would be bad," Ashe answered. "Before we even get a look at the claim. . . ."

And that was the Ashe she remembered: nothing got between him and salvage. "It's too much of a risk they'll pick up the power use," she said. "You know that."

"Damn it," Dai said. "They've dropped off."

"Out of range or gone to ground?" Cassilde demanded. The screen was black again, just the faint lines that laid out the gravity and the background scatter, the debris dull purple against the void.

"I can't tell." Dai shook his head. "Let me ping her once, super-low power, GOLD frequencies only—"

"No," Cassilde said again. There was too much risk another ship would pick up active sensors.

"Any idea what it was?" Ashe asked.

"Not really," Cassilde said. She looked at Dai. "What's the chance it's one of us?"

"Somebody running quiet out to their claim?" Dai shrugged. "It could be. Like I said, we're in sensor range of a couple of other sites."

"I don't think it's a salvor," Ashe said.

"If you know anything," Cassilde said, "say it now."

There was a little silence. "There were rumors before we left. Nothing solid."

"Damn it, Ashe," Dai said.

"It was talk," Ashe said. "The usual chitchat, somebody heard somebody say somebody else might have mentioned a smash-and-grab. Nothing we all haven't heard a thousand times. But, yes, it's possible that somebody else saw what I saw in that section. Not likely, I admit. But possible."

"There are always rumors," Cassilde said, as much to herself as to the others. She shook herself and looked at Dai. "Any idea where they went?"

He reached across the screen to shape a wedge of light, the wide end pointing away from their position. "That's what I make from the last readings."

The ghost ship was headed away before it disappeared. Probably another salvor, Cassilde decided, taking the same precautions they were. "All right," she said. "Bring us back to low power, and let's get on this. The sooner we're on our claim, the better."

Dai brought *Carabosse* down neatly against the side of the chunk of wreckage that was their claim, latching on with the landing grapples, then setting the pitons that would hold the ship firmly to the section's outer shell. Scans revealed the hull and interior bulkheads to be in surprisingly good condition, as though the palace had broken up along the faces of its strongest points. Or maybe it had been designed to fail that way, Cassilde thought, as she supervised the mapping daemon from the control room while the others adjusted the fields that would hold an atmosphere and transmit power to their equipment. She'd seen similar patterns before, on other wrecks, and it was a logical way to build a space habitat—though logic didn't always have much to do with the Ancestors.

It took a full twelve hours to generate a breathable atmosphere, and she used the time to smooth out the artificial gravity and get a decent night's sleep before turning Ashe loose on the point they'd marked as their best entrance. He set the portable airlock with his usual quick skill, and eased his way through the layers of rock and metal, working around nests of BLUE that would pay most of their expenses for the job once they had time to recover them. Cassilde marked their locations, and once the shell was breached, loosed a swarm of smaller daemons to chart the interior volume. The result was rough, but she displayed it in Central with a certain satisfaction.

Ashe fiddled with his tablets, flattening the map to a rough schematic, then expanding it to the three-dimensional model, then zooming in on image fragments as though he could identify specific objects in the daemons' feed.

"The resolution's not good enough for that," Dai said. He'd done the cooking, since his job was suspended for the moment, and slid the bowls of rice and beans onto the table. Cassilde took hers without enthusiasm. Dai was in fact a decent cook, but she had no appetite, a sure sign that she was working up to another attack of the Lightman's. Her fingers stumbled on the spoon, and Dai gave her a sharp glance, but she stared him down.

"At least I can get something to work with," Ashe said. He was eating with one hand, and still fiddling with the map with the other. "I'm guessing this might be what we're looking for?" He pointed to a smaller chamber, connected to the larger spaces by a single narrow tunnel. The bulkhead between was thicker than the others, almost as thick as the bulkhead that had divided the section from the rest of the parent craft.

"A treatment room?" Dai said, sounding intrigued in spite of himself.

"Maybe." Ashe twirled the map again.

"Do you mind?" Dai said. Cassilde gave him a grateful look. Between the shifting image and the Lightman's, she was feeling a little queasy herself.

"I'd normally say it was sleeping quarters," Ashe said, "but that bulkhead is way too heavy. There's something that wanted power behind that. Or there was." He made no acknowledgement of Dai's complaint, but at least he'd stopped spinning the map.

"You say that because—?" Dai squinted at the map.

"Because of that," Cassilde said, and pointed, the lights of the map playing over her hand. "That does look like some sort of power node."

Ashe nodded. "The daemons say it could be an inert device. Pings were inconclusive, but it's possible."

"Right," Cassilde said. "So we'll start there."

"Nothing more from the sensor web?" Dai asked, and Cassilde shook her head.

"It must have been one of us."

Ashe nodded, but Dai hesitated. "Maybe I should stay on board, keep an eye out for anything else that might show up."

Cassilde weighed the options, the added security of a live person minding the ship against the need to do a thorough survey as quickly as possible. If there had been anything more, any warning from the web, it would be different, but at the moment, speed mattered. "No," she said. "We'll risk it."

Despite the environmental fields that established an arbitrary gravity and atmosphere, and transmitted power to their lights and tools, the wreck was dank and cold. Some of that was psychological, Cassilde knew—it would feel warmer once they were able to rig working lights instead of relying on hand- and helmet-beams—but some of that was the Lightman's creeping through her body. She could barely feel her feet, in spite of the heated boot liners. She dialed up the heat in her vest, tucked the hood tight around her face, and swung her light and camera methodically around the largest of the claim's inner volumes.

"You were right," she said. "This looks like living space."

"I told you," Ashe said. He had his own recorder out, scanning the walls, and streaks of color bloomed as the light hit them. "Here, put your light over here."

Cassilde brought her light to join his, and a series of linked circles swam out of the shadows, pale gold on lavender-gray. "Dai?"

The pilot trained his light on them as well, widening the picture, but it remained abstract, one large circle linked to a dozen smaller ones, circles smaller still hanging off each of those. "Fractal symbolism?"

"Maybe." Ashe broke from the joined lights, followed the diminishing circles up the wall and onto the wall above them, where they faded into invisibility. "Or maybe just decoration."

Cassilde swung her light again, scanning the room. Shapes rose like islands from the floor, the remains of furniture—a sweeping curve that might have been a lounge, cubes that might have been chairs or tables, another cube with a shallow depression in one side—and light glittered in a corner. She moved toward it, and it resolved into a lump of cloudy glass the size of her fist. She picked it up, careful of her grip, and felt the familiar deep hum that meant it was active. "I've got a music box."

"Nice," Dai said, and nodded as she held it up. "That's a big one, too."

Cassilde nodded, stowing it in her carryall. They were really music boxes, of course, weren't even boxes, but when a human held them, the glass slowly cleared to reveal twirling threads of light and produced a cascade of pleasant sound. Between it and the BLUE they could salvage from the hull, the job was already making a profit—which was a good thing, if she was going to be incapacitated for a while.

"We'll come back," Ashe said. "This way."

They had to pass through two more compartments before they reached the circular opening in the thickened bulkhead. Cassilde swung her light, examining the slot where presumably the original door had disappeared, but there was no sign of it or of any controlling mechanism. Dai produced a heavy metal bar as thick as his wrist and laid it gently in the opening. When nothing happened, he tried wedging it into the gap, but the bar slid into the slot without finding a stop.

"We'll be fine," Ashe said, and stepped through. "We've got cutters."

Which was true, Cassilde admitted, as long as the transmitter kept functioning. "I thought you didn't like messing up your finds."

"I don't," he answered, his light sweeping over the new space. "I just don't expect we'll have to."

Cassilde lifted her own light, blinking as she began to make sense of the shadowed curves. "Holy—"

"Yeah," Dai said. He shrugged off his carryall. "Ashe, you want me to rig some worklights?"

"Please." Ashe was moving slowly across the open space, his light flashing over what looked like beds made of woven silver, a cascade of scarlet thread and a chair that spiraled out of the floor.

There was a sharp click as Dai found metal to take the worklight's magnet, and the room was suddenly flooded with light. Cassilde switched off her handlight, her breath coming short again.

The compartment was curved like the inside of a shell, the open space where she and Dai still stood curling down to a narrow alcove, half hidden behind the flowing strands of scarlet. The walls shimmered like nacre, too, palest gold shading toward green in the shadows; there were lines drawn on the floor and up the walls, following the gentle curves. On other installations, similar lines had been filled with flowing light.

Dai flicked on the second worklight, driving back the rest of the shadows. "Impressive."

"Isn't it?" Ashe had moved the datamote from his face to his collarbone, was rubbing it as though that would make it give up its information. "I've never seen anything like it."

And if Ashe hadn't, this might be a unique find. Cassilde killed that hope—it was far too soon to speculate—and said, "Any sign of this lifesaving device?"

"In the alcove, I think," Ashe answered. The worklights didn't quite penetrate its depths; he was still using his handlight to examine the walls. "But I'm not seeing any actual device."

"There's things attached to the beds," Dai began, and the lights flickered.

Cassilde grabbed her remote, pinged the ship to check its status. The codes flashed back in the proper sequence, power transmitters all green, ship's systems green, nothing in the sensor web, and she shook her head. "Nothing here."

"I could head back and make sure," Dai said, reluctantly.

Cassilde considered, weighing the difficulty of getting out again if they lost the transmission. "You posted glow-dots, right?"

"Of course." Dai sounded annoyed, and she gestured an apology.

"Sorry. Stay, I think. If it happens again, we'll rethink it."

"Better rethink it now." The stranger's voice came from the hatch.

Cassilde spun, reaching for the blaster at her hip, froze as she registered the leveled weapons. There were three of them—no, four, all with heavy military-surplus blasters and body armor over their work vests. Dai swore, and she lifted her hands to show them empty. They must have come from the strange ship, she thought, damped *Carabosse's* sensors with their own web. The flicker in the power had been the ship's final protest against their attack. It wasn't impossible, but it was difficult enough that she had discounted the possibility, and they were all going to pay for her mistake.

"Smart woman," the stranger said. He stepped through the hatch, still with his blaster leveled, a wiry man with a pointed chin and muscles that stood out like brackets at the corners of his mouth. "Hello, Ashe."

Dai swore again, not softly.

Ashe gave a bitter smile. "Hello, darling."

The words dripped venom, and the stranger smiled. "Did you really think I wouldn't follow you?"

"I thought we had an agreement," Ashe said. He was keeping his hands in plain sight, raised shoulder high, but the heavy handlight was in his left hand, a possible weapon. Seeing that, Cassilde shifted her weight, tipping ever so slightly to her right. Only the stranger had actually entered the compartment; if Ashe distracted him, there was a chance she could drop behind the closest of the woven-silver beds, and use her blaster from there. It was lighter than the weapons the pirates were carrying, but deadly enough at this short range.

"Agreements change." The stranger was scanning the compartment, weapon still leveled, but his eyes elsewhere. Dai saw it, too, and slid one foot forward, but the stranger focused on him instantly. "Don't."

Dai dipped his head in acknowledgement, and in the same moment Ashe swung the heavy light. The stranger stepped into the blow, blocking it with his forearm, and brought the barrel of his blaster hard across Ashe's face. Ashe dropped to his knees, and Cassilde dove for the dubious shelter of the woven bed, fumbling for her own weapon. Fire creased her shoulder, and her hand spasmed; she dropped her blaster, fingers nerveless, and scrabbled for it with her other hand, heedless now of shelter.

"Don't move," the stranger said, and stepped closer to Ashe, still on his knees. There was blood on his mouth and nose, a bruise already rising on his sallow cheek. "All right, Ashe. Where is it?"

"I don't know."

"Don't waste my time."

"I don't know," Ashe said again.

The stranger lowered the muzzle of his blaster until it rested against Ashe's temple. Ashe glared up at him.

"If you kill me—"

"Oh, never you," the stranger said. He turned on his heel, the blaster shifting aim before Cassilde could even register his intent. Fire cracked, and the impact knocked her backward, pain filling her belly. She curled around it, too stunned to cry out, heard Dai call her name as if from an immense distance.

"You bastard," Ashe said. "You son of a bitch—"

"She might live," the stranger said. "But her clock's running." There was the sound of a scuffle. "That's right, hold him."

That had to be Dai, Cassilde thought. She rocked slowly, trying to ease the pain, but it clawed up her spine, down into her hips, every nerve on fire.

"Where is it?" the stranger said again. "I'm waiting, Ashe."

"It's not here," Ashe said. "I thought it would be, but it's not—and since it's not, it has to be—I'll take you, I'll show you, I swear—but let me take care of Silde first."

"Two minutes," the stranger said.

Tears filmed Cassilde's eyes, blurring her vision. The pain rolled over her in waves, threatening to drown her; she fought through it, gasping, and Ashe knelt at her side.

They each carried first aid, but the kits were inadequate for something like this.

Cassilde heard Ashe crack open his package and then hers, flinched as he pressed both bandage packs against the wound.

"I will fucking kill you," Dai said, somewhere in the distance, and she didn't know if he was talking to Ashe or to the stranger Ashe had called darling.

There was a sharp pain in her forearm, unfairly distinct against the background agony, and then another. She twisted her head to see, and realized that Ashe had planted both the shock buttons in the flesh of her arm. Already the drugs were taking hold, and she blinked up at him, expecting at least some apology.

"Green, then the red," he said, so softly she barely heard him. His back was to the stranger, to Dai, hiding the movement of his lips. "First green, then the red curtain."

"Time's up," the stranger said. He moved to Ashe's side, laid the barrel of the blaster against Ashe's cheek so that it pointed past him at Cassilde. "Come on, Ashe, time to go."

"I'm coming," Ashe said. The stranger stepped back smoothly, and Ashe rose to his feet with only a single backward glance.

"All right," the stranger said. "Ashe, you will take me to the device. Usslo, bring that one along."

He must mean Dai, Cassilde thought, blinking hard. The buttons' effect was building, beating the pain back to manageable levels, giving her new strength. She lay still, hoarding it—she would have one good effort, she didn't dare waste it—and the stranger turned away.

"Ashe, if you cross me, I'll kill him, too."

"I understand." Ashe's voice was tight with fury.

"What about her?" That was one of the others, though she couldn't tell which one. The stranger glanced back at her and gave a tiny shrug.

"Leave her. She's not going anywhere."

Cassilde closed her eyes, shuddering, another wave of pain washing through her. When she opened them, the strangers were gone, leaving her alone in the seashell room, the harsh worklights throwing doubled shadows. The buttons had kicked in, giving her all the strength she was ever going to have, and nothing useful to do with it. It wasn't fair that she should die like this when she'd been more or less resigned to Lightman's, not fair at all.

She hooked one hand over the edge of the silver bed, hauled herself to a sitting position. Ashe's bandages were doing their job, just like the buttons, staunching the blood where the blast hadn't cauterized the wound. She recovered her blaster, checking to be sure the charge was still good. Now what? She clutched the blaster harder as another wave of pain rolled through her, and fought to breathe against it. She doubted she could walk; crawling after them was only going to waste what little strength she had.

And what the hell had Ashe meant, whispering about color? Green, then red—no, she thought, GREEN, then RED. GREEN she had, tucked into the pocket of her vest. It might, it should, give her more strength, maybe enough to stand. She reached for it, fumbled the tiny box, and had to put the blaster down to open it. The sliver of GREEN was less than a centimeter long, and barely thicker than a hair: a quarter's profit, and all her discretionary income for the year. She licked her fingertip, picked it up, and transferred it to her tongue before she could change her mind.

The GREEN fizzed, bitter and cold, filling her mouth with metallic saliva. She'd never taken so much at once, and she swallowed hard, once and then twice. The wound in her stomach protested, but the pain was distanced, manageable. She imagined she could feel the GREEN crawling through her nervous system, freezing the pain and shock, and hauled herself to her feet before she could think too much about it.

The blaster was on the floorplates at her feet. She swore silently, unable to bend, and made herself concentrate on Ashe's words. GREEN, then RED—but there was no RED anywhere in sight, unless he'd meant for her to break one of the Ancestral devices? She had the cutter still, but that would take time, and the sound would surely bring Ashe's "darling" or his men. She would kill Ashe for that herself, later— She laughed silently. It seemed unlikely there would be a "later."

GREEN, then RED. First GREEN, check, she'd done that, then RED—no, then the red *curtain*.

The red curtain, the shimmering veil of scarlet thread that covered half the narrow alcove, the alcove that probably was Ashe's mysterious lifesaving device. First take the GREEN, and then the red curtain. . . . She staggered toward it, her feet slurring on the floor. The buttons' effects were starting to wear off, the pain surging; the GREEN pulsed cold with every heartbeat, so cold she thought her bones would crack, her fingers blacken.

The curtain swayed as she came close, a few tentative strands lifting as though to sample the air. She stopped, swaying herself, unsure of what she was really seeing, and still more threads rose, reaching for the exposed skin of her face, her hands. Their touch was pleasant, sweet and soothing, warm as the smell of tea. She let herself be wound in, the threads tugging her gently forward until she was entirely surrounded, tucked into the alcove. Its walls shifted against her, forming to her body, and the final layer of the curtain swept in to enclose her. She felt an instant of panic, but then sleepy warmth suffused her, the pain retreating to nothing, and her eyes closed.

She opened them again an infinity later, her breath easier than it had been in years, the pain a receding memory. She filled her lungs, marveling at the play of muscles and ribs, flattened her hand against her stomach. Vest and shirt and undershirt were in tatters, but her skin was smooth and whole. The last of the threads dropped from her shoulders, unwound from her ankles, dissolving into dust. Out of power? Their job complete? She hoped it was the latter, hoped she would have the time to find out. But for now, there was Darling to worry about.

She scooped up her blaster, the charge still ready, and for good measure drew her cutter and set it to standby before she slid it into her belt. It wouldn't be much help unless she got into hand-to-hand, and that was to be avoided, but it was better than nothing.

Armed, she peered out the circular hatch. The corridor was dark, but lights moved in the distance, in the nearer of the two compartments between this one and the one with the linked circles. She eased through the hatch, still amazed that her body responded, pressed her back to the bulkhead as she moved as quietly as she could toward the light.

She heard the voices before she was close enough to see, Darling's cool and calm.

"I'm not buying it, Ashe."

"I swear," Ashe said. "This is the only other place to look, and—I don't know. Maybe I got it wrong. Maybe there's nothing here."

"You don't make mistakes," Darling said.

"Yes, I do. Even I do," Ashe said. "I just got it wrong."

"Usslo!" There was scuffling, and a choked sound that might have been Dai, before Darling spoke again. "Ashe, you are determined to be difficult."

"I'm not, I swear. I got it wrong—"

Cassilde reached the door, angled her head carefully to see inside. Dai was on his knees, his hands clasped on his head, a man wearing a monocular holding a blaster to his head. Ashe stood beside a hole in the bulkhead, the edges still black from the cutter's beam. There was RED inside, glimmering in the single worklight, RED and GOLD and maybe even a hint of GREEN—a season's solid work, a lucky find, and still Darling shook his head.

"A Gift was here, I know that. Don't make me do this."

There was no more time. Cassilde took a step, aimed, and fired twice, catching One-Eye in neck and chest. He fell forward, and Dai rolled with him, scrambling for the dropped blaster. Cassilde turned her blaster on Darling, two shots, three, four, all to the chest and belly, driving him back—

"Silde!" That was Dai, blaster in hand, Darling's last two men crumpled against the bulkhead, and Cassilde drew a shaken breath.

"I'm fine," she said.

"Yeah, but how—" Dai stopped abruptly, and Cassilde nodded.

"He knows." She looked at Ashe. "You do, don't you?"

"It was the device," Ashe said. His voice cracked. "That was the thing, the life-saver, oh, God. The Gift. It worked."

"We need to get out of here," Dai said. "There's no telling who else he's got." He kicked Darling's body, not gently.

"He works alone or with small teams," Ashe said. He had himself under control now, only the faintest trembling of the handlight to betray him. "This should be it."

Cassilde took a breath. "We will discuss how you know that later—"

"I need to look at the Gift," Ashe said. "Please, Silde. It's more important than you know."

"We don't have time for that," Dai said. "Are you fucking crazy?"

"Shut up, both of you," Cassilde said. "Ashe, the device—it worked on me, and then the red stuff just dissolved. I don't think there's much left to look at."

Ashe closed his eyes. "Damn it. . . ."

Cassilde ignored him, scanning the compartment. Dai was right, they needed to get away, get out of range of any of Darling's friends still lurking nearby, but there was also too much easy salvage to abandon. "All right. Clean out that cache, quick and dirty. Anything else we see on the way, grab it, but no more cutting. We'll come back if we can."

Dai was already moving to obey, pulling gloves and expandables from his pockets to collect the Ancestral elements, and after a moment Ashe joined him, pulling out RED and GOLD in enormous expensive lumps. At any other moment, Cassilde would have been breathless with delight—this was a massive find, a solid year's expenses paid for and more—but there was no time. They needed to get back to *Carabosse*, get themselves into the protection of the Guard. Then they could think about coming back.

The cache was empty, at least of the largest pieces. There would be more, crumbs and fragments, but there was no time to search further. "Back to the ship," she said, and pinned Ashe with a look. "And you owe me answers."

"Yes," he said, and that was strange enough that she nearly dropped her carryall.

"Move," she said.

Carabosse made an emergency lift from the chunk of wreckage, blowing the pitons and leaving the depleted atmosphere cartridge behind. They left Darling's ship grappled to the opposite side of the claim as well, over Ashe's protests, and set a fast course for the nearest Guard beacon. Cassilde adjusted the sensor net to its widest sweep, and set the active systems to random scan—she'd rather someone caught the pings than miss any pursuit from any more of Darling's men, no matter what Ashe said about the man working alone—and made her way back to Central.

She still couldn't believe how good she felt. It wasn't just that the blaster wound was gone, it was that she could breathe, that her muscles moved with a fluid ease she could barely remember. Her joints no longer clicked and popped, she no longer stepped cautiously to avoid setting off shooting pains from the ankle she'd broken the year before. The Lightman's was gone, she was sure of that, the incurable cured, but even more, all the minor aches and pains that came with age were also gone. Even the marks of the shock buttons had vanished, though there should have been puncture marks and deep bruises. They had to get back to the claim, recover what was left of the Gift.

Ashe was sitting at the unfolded table, his head tipped back to that Dai could tape his broken nose. Both eyes were blackened, and there was another swelling bruise on his left cheek.

"You look like hell," Cassilde said. She wasn't sure she was sorry, either, and felt vaguely guilty.

"Done," Dai said, and Ashe sat up slowly. Dai turned away from the table, bundling the scraps from the aid kit into the disposal, then collected a bottle and glasses from the cabinet and poured them each a stiff drink. Ashe downed half of his in a single wincing gulp and held out his glass for a refill.

"Don't be in too much of a hurry," Cassilde said, and sat down across from him. "We need to talk."

"I know." Ashe took a more careful sip of the whiskey, and Dai perched on the edge of the table beside him.

"So what just happened?" Cassilde asked. Her own whiskey tasted wonderful, sweet and sharp and perfectly chilled.

"How are you feeling?" Ashe asked in turn.

Cassilde looked at him. "Well. Better than well. What just happened, Ashe?"

Ashe glanced at Dai, still looming, and wrapped his hands around his glass. "It's—it was a Gift. The Ancestors made them, very rarely. We have no idea why, only that they exist—"

"Wait a minute," Dai said. "You're talking about a Miracle Box. I thought you didn't believe in them."

"I was wrong," Ashe said. Something between a smile and a grimace crossed his face. "About this, too."

"We'll get back to him later," Cassilde said. "You're telling me that Miracle Boxes are real."

"You're here," Ashe said, with some asperity. "You should be dead."

Twice over, if not from the blaster bolt then from the Lightman's, shock triggering a deadly attack. That was what she'd always expected would happen. Cassilde took another sip of her drink, sharp on her tongue and warm all the way down to her healed belly. "And you knew it would be there."

"I suspected." Ashe took a breath. "The Ancestors made the Gifts—that's the word they used, not Miracle Box. Who knows why, and who knows why they left them, just the way they left everything else. But sometimes you find one, and it works. It heals the sick, revives the dying, cures everything from madness to Lightman's to the common cold. It works once, three times, a hundred times—there are traditional shrines on some of the late-settled worlds that have to have begun as Miracle Boxes. And sometimes you find one that's special. It only works once, but it carries a bonus. Not only does it heal whatever ails you, but—it changes you. You become one of them."

"No," Cassilde said. Even as she spoke, the denial faded, replaced by appalled certainty. That explained how she felt, the intense sensation, the fizzing energy along her veins.

Dai said, "You're saying Silde has become an Ancestor?"

"I don't know for sure," Ashe said. "You'd have to test it, and I don't have the tools to do it without actually harming her. But, yes, I think so. That was what the bug was telling me, that there was a special Gift there on the wreck."

"You're not cutting her," Dai said, and Cassilde spoke over him.

"You mean that I heal like the Ancestors? That I'll never be sick again? That I'll live forever, stay forever just as I am?"

"If I'm right," Ashe said. "Yes."

"So." Cassilde stretched to reach across the table, grabbed the serving knife from its slot in the edge of the table.

"Silde—" Dai's voice broke.

"Let's find out," Cassilde said, and drew the blade across the skin of her forearm. It parted at the touch, welling blood and then a pain sharp enough to stop breath, far more than she had expected. She swayed, and the cut began to close, the blood reabsorbed, skin flowing over it, fading from pink to white to tan. Ashe let out a breath as though he'd been holding it, and Dai shook his head.

"God, Silde."

"And there we are," she said. It was hard to get her mind around it, but she was trying, the possibilities crowding in on her. There were things she could do now, things she'd put aside—and things she'd lose, over and over, never aging, never dying, but she thrust that thought aside. She would find a way to fix that, find a way to bring the others with her, so she wouldn't be alone. She had all the time there was to find an answer. She smiled, slow and fierce. "All the myths are true."

the queen of night's aria

IAN McDONALD

British author Ian McDonald is an ambitious and daring writer with a wide range and an impressive amount of talent. His first story was published in 1982, and since then he has appeared with some frequency in Interzone, Asimov's Science Fiction, *and elsewhere. In 1989 he won the Locus Best First Novel award for* Desolation Road. *He won the Philip K. Dick Award in 1992 for his novel* King of Morning, Queen of Day. *His other books include the novels* Out On Blue Six; Hearts, Hands and Voices: Terminal Café; Sacrifice of Fools; Evolution's Shore; Kirinya; Ares Express: Brasyl; *and* The Dervish House; *as well as three collections of his short fiction,* Empire Dreams, Speaking in Tongues, *and* Cyberabad Days. *His novel* River of Gods *was a finalist for both the Hugo Award and the Arthur C. Clarke Award in 2005, and a novella drawn from it,* The Little Goddess, *was a finalist for the Hugo and the Nebula. He won a Hugo Award in 2007 for his novelette "The Djinn's Wife," won the Theodore Sturgeon Award for his story "Tendeleo's Story," and in 2011 won the John W. Campbell Memorial Award for his novel* The Dervish House. *His most recent book is* Empress of the Sun, *the third volume in his YA trilogy that also includes* Planesrunner *and* Be My Enemy. *Coming up is a major retrospective collection,* The Best of Ian McDonald. *Born in Manchester, England, in 1960, McDonald has spent most of his life in Northern Ireland and now lives and works in Belfast. He has a Web site at www,lysator.liu.se/^unicorn /mcdonald/.*

In most recent wars, entertainers have visited the frontline troops, often putting themselves in considerable danger. None have ever visited a battlefield as strange, though, or performed for an audience as bizarre and inhuman, or put themselves in as much imminent danger as do the hapless entertainers in the brilliant and slyly funny story that follows.

God. Still on bloody Mars."

Count Jack Fitzgerald, Virtuoso, Maestro, Sopratutto, stood at the window of the Grand Valley Hotel's Heaven's Tower Suite in just his shirt. Before his feet, the Sculpted City of Unshaina tumbled away in shelves and tiers, towers and tenements.

Cable cars skirled along swooping lines between the carved pinnacles of the Royal Rookeries. Many-bodied stone gods roosted atop mile-high pillars; above them, the Skymasters of the Ninth Fleet hung in the red sky. Higher still were the rim rocks of the Grand Valley, carved into fretwork battlements and machicolations, and highest of all, on the edge of the atmosphere, twilight shadows festooned with riding lights, were the ships of Spacefleet. A lift-chair borne by a squadron of Twav bobbed past the picture window, dipping to the wing beats of the carriers. The chair bore a human in the long duster-coat of a civil servant of the Expeditionary Force. One hand clutched a diplomatic valise, the other the guy-lines of the lift-harness. The mouth beneath the dust goggles was open in fear.

"Oh God, look at that! I feel nauseous. You hideous government drone, how dare you make me feel nauseous first thing in the morning! You'll never get me in one of those things, Faisal, never. They *shit* on you; it's true. I've seen it. Bottom of the valley's five hundred foot deep in Mars-bat guano."

I come from a light-footed, subtle family, but for all my discretion, I could never catch Count Jack unawares. Tenors have good ears.

"Maestro, the Commanderie has issued guidelines. Mars-bats is not acceptable. The official expression is the Twav Civilization."

"What nonsense. Mars-bats is what they look like, Mars-bats is what they are. No civilization was ever built on the basis of aerial defecation. Where's my tea? I require tea."

I handed the Maestro his morning cup. He took a long slurping sip—want of etiquette was part of his professional persona. The Country Count from Kildare: he insisted it appear on all his billings. Despite the titles and honorifics, Count Jack Fitzgerald had passed the summit of his career, if not his self-mythologising. The aristocratic title was a papal honor bestowed upon his grandfather, a dully devout shopkeeper who nonetheless was regarded as little less than a saint in Athy. The pious greengrocer's apples would have browned at his grandson's flagrant disregard for religion and its moralizing. The Heaven's Tower Suite's Emperor-sized bed was mercifully undisturbed by another body. Count James Fitzgerald drained his cup, drew himself to full six and half feet, sucked in his generous belly, clicked out cricks and stiffnesses in his joints.

"Oh bless you, dear boy. None of the others can make tea worth a tinker's piss."

For the past six months, long before this tour of Mars, I had been slipping a little stiffener into the morning tea.

"And did they love us? Did strong men weep like infants and women ovulate?"

"The Joint Chiefs were enchanted."

"Well the enchantment didn't reach as far as their bloody pockets. A little consideration wouldn't have gone amiss. Philistines."

A gratis performance at the Commanderie for the Generals and Admirals and Sky-Marshals was more or less mandatory for all Earth entertainers playing the Martian front. The Army and Navy shows usually featured exotic dancers and strippers. From the piano, you notice many things, like the well-decorated Sky-Lord nodding off during the Maestro's Medley of Ould Irish Songs, but the news had reported that he had just returned from a hard-fought campaign against the Syrtian Hives.

"Ferid Bey wishes to see you."

"That odious little Ottoman. What does he want? More money, I'll warrant. I shan't see him. He spoils my day. I abjure him."

"Eleven o'clock, Maestro. At the Canal Court."

Count Jack puffed out his cheeks in resignation."

"What, he can't afford the Grand Valley? With the percentage he skims? Not that they'd let him in; they should have a sign: no dogs, uniforms, or agents."

We couldn't afford the Grand Valley either, but such truths are best entrusted to the discretion of an accompanist. I have talked our way out of hotel bills before.

"I'll book transport."

"If you must." His attention was once again turned to the canyon-scape of the great city of the Twav. The sun had risen over the canyon edge and sent the shadows of Unshaina's spires and stacks and towers carved from raw rock chasing down the Great Valley. Summoned by the light, flocks of Twav poured from the slots of their roost-cotes. "Any chance of another wee drop of your particular tea?"

I took the cup and saucer from his outstretched hand

"Of course, Maestro."

"Thank you, dear boy. I would, of course, be lost without you. Quite quite lost."

A hand waved me away from his presence.

"Thank you. And Maestro?"

He turned from the window.

"Trousers."

For a big man, Count James Fitzgerald threw up most discreetly. He leaned out of the Sky-chair, one quick convulsion and it fell in a single sheet between the sculpted pinnacles of Unshaina. He wiped his lips with a large very white handkerchief and that was it done. He would blame me, blame the Sky-chair bearers, blame the entire Twav Civilisation, but never the three cups of special tea he had taken while I packed for him, nor the bottle that was his perennial companion in the bedside cabinet.

Checkout had been challenging this time. I would never say so to Count Jack, but it had been a long time since I could parlay the Country Count from Kildare by name recognition alone.

"You are leaving the bags," the manager said. He was Armenian. He had never heard of Ireland, let alone County Kildare.

"We will be returning, yes," I said.

"But you are leaving the bags."

"Christ on crutches," Count Jack had exclaimed as the two Sky-chairs set down on to the Grand Valley's landing apron. "What are you trying to do, kill me, you poncing infidel? My heart is tender, tender I tell you, bruised by decades of professional envy and poisonous notices."

"It is the quickest and most direct way."

"Swung hither and yon in a bloody Bat-cab and no money at the end of it, as like," Count Jack muttered as he strapped in and the Twavs took the strain and lifted. He gave a faint cry as the Sky-chair swung out over the mile-deep drop to the needles of the Lower Rookeries, like an enfilade of pikes driven into the red rock of the Grand Valley. He clung white-knuckled to the guy-lines, moaning a little, as the Twav carriers swayed him between the scurrying cableway gondolas and around the many-windowed stone towers of the roosts.

I rather enjoyed the ride. My life has been low in excitements—I took the post of accompanist to the Maestro as an escape from filing his recording royalties, which was the highest entry position in the industry I could attain with my level of degree in Music. Glamorous it was, exciting, no. Glamour is just another work environment. One recovers from being starstruck rather quickly. My last great excitement had been the night before we left for Mars. Ships! Space travel! Why, I could hardly sleep the night before launch. I soon discovered that space travel is very much like an ocean cruise, without the promenade decks and the excursions, and far, far fewer people. And much, much worse food. However tedious and braying the company for me, I derived some pleasure from the fact that for them it was three months locked in with Count Jack.

I have a personal interest in this war. My grandfather was one of the martyrs who died in the opening minutes of the Horsell Common invasion. He was the first generation of my family to be born in England. He had been at prayer in the Woking Mosque and was consumed by the heat ray from the Uliri War Tripod. Many thousands died that day, and though it has taken us two generations to master the Uliri technology to keep our skies safe and to prepare a fleet to launch Operation Enduring Justice, the cry is ever fresh: Remember Shah Jehan! I stood among the crowds on that same Horsell Common around the crater, as people gathered by the other craters of the invasion, or on hilltops, on beaches, riverbanks, rooftops, holy places, anywhere with a view of open sky, to watch the night light up with the drives of our expeditionary fleet. The words on my lips, and the lips of everyone else on that cold November night, were Justice, Justice, but in my heart was Remember Shah Jehan!

Rejoice! Rejoice! Our Prime Minister told us when our drop-troopers captured Unshaina, conquered the Twav Civilisation, and turned the Grand Valley into our Martian headquarters and munitions factory. It's harder to maintain your patriotic fervor when those spaceships are months away on the far side of the sun, and no one really believes the propaganda that the Twav were the devious military hive-masterminds of the Uliri war machine. Nor, when that story failed, did we swallow the second serving of propaganda: that the Twav were the enslaved mind-thralls of the Uliri, whom we had liberated for freedom and democracy. A species that achieves a special kind of sentience when it roosts and flocks together seems to me to embody the very nature of the demos. The many-bodied gods atop the flute-thin spires of Unshaina represent the truth that our best, our most creative, our most brilliant, may be all the divinity we need.

It has been a long time since I was at prayer.

Count Jack gave a small moan as his Sky-chair dipped down abruptly between the close-packed stone quills of Alabaster Needles. The Chair-boss whistled instructions to her crew—the lowest register of their language lay at the upper edge of our hearing—and they skillfully brought us spirally down past hives and through arches and under buttresses to the terraces of the Great Western Dock on the Grand Canal.

Here humans had built cheap spray-stone lading houses and transit lodges among the sinuously carved stone. The Canal Court Hotel was cheap, but that was not its main allure; Ferid Bey had appetites best served by low rents and proximity to docks.

While Count Jack swooned and whimpered and swore that he would never regain his land-legs, never, I tipped the Chair-boss a generous handful of saucers and she clasped her lower hands in a gesture of respect.

"We're broke," Ferid Bey said. We sat drinking coffee on the terrace of the Canal Court watching Twav stevedores lift and lade pallets from the open hatches of cargo barges. I say coffee, it was Expeditionary Force ersatz, vile and weak and with a disturbing spritz of excremental. Ferid Bey, who as a citizen of the great Ottoman Empire appreciated coffee, grimaced at every sip. I say terrace; it was a cranny for two tables spaced beside the garbage bins which caught the wind and lifted the dust in a perpetual eddy. Ferid Bey wore his dust goggles, kept his scarf wrapped around his head, and sipped his execrable coffee.

"What do you mean, broke?" Count Jack thundered in his loudest Sopratutto voice. Startled Twavs flew up from their cargoes, twittering on the edge of audibility. "You've been at the bum-boys again, haven't you?" Ferid Bey's weakness for the rough was well known, particularly the kind who would go through his wallet the next morning. He sniffed loudly.

"Actually, Jack, this time it's you."

I often wondered if the slow decline of Count Jack's career was partly attributable to the fact that, after years of daily contact, agent had started to sound like client? The Count's eyes bulged. His blood pressure was bad. I'd seen the report from the pre-launch medical.

"It's bums on seats Jack, bums on seats, and we're not getting them."

"I strew my pearls before buffoons in braid and their braying brides, and they throw them back in my face!" Count Jack bellowed. "I played La Scala, you know. La Scala! And the Pope. I'd be better off playing to the Space-bats. At least they appreciate a High-C. No Ferid, no no: you get me better audiences."

"Any audiences would be good," Ferid Bey muttered and then said aloud, "I've got you a tour."

Count Jack grew inches taller.

"How many nights?"

"Five."

"There are that many concert halls on this arse-wipe of a world?"

"Not so much concert halls." Ferid Bey tried to hide as much of his face as possible behind scarf, goggles and coffee cup. "More concert *parties*."

"The army?" Count Jacks face was pale now, his voice quiet. I had heard this precursor to a rage the size of Olympus Mons many times. Thankfully, I had never been its target. "Bloody shit-stupid squaddies who have to be told which end of a blaster to point at the enemy?"

"Yes, Jack."

"Would this be . . . upcountry?"

"It would."

"Would this be . . . close to the front?"

"I've extended your cover."

"Well, it's nice to know my ex-wives and agent are well provided for."

"I've negotiated a fee commensurate with the risk."

"What is the risk?"

"It's a war zone, Jack."

"What is the fee?"

"One thousand five hundred saucers. Per show."

"Tell me we don't need to do this, dear boy," Count Jack said to me.

"The manager of the Grand Valley is holding your luggage to ransom," I said. "We need to do it."

"You're coming with me." Count Jack's accusing finger hovered one inch from the bridge of his agent's nose. Ferid Bey spread his hands in resignation.

"I would if I could, Jack. Truly. Honestly. Deeply. But I've got a lead on a possible concert recording here in Unshaina, and there are talent bookers from the big Venus casinos in town, so I'm told."

"Venus?" The Cloud Cities, forever drifting in the Storm Zone, were the glittering jewels on the interplanetary circuit. The legendary residences were a long, comfortable, well-paid descent from the pinnacle of career.

"Five nights?"

"Five nights only. Then out."

"Usual contract riders?"

"Of course."

Count Jack laughed his great, canyon-deep laugh. "We'll do it. Our brave legionnaires need steel in their steps and spunk in their spines. When do we leave?"

"I've booked you on the *Empress of Mars* from the Round 'O' Dock. Eight o'clock. Sharp."

Count Jack pouted.

"I am prone to seasickness."

"This is a canal. Anyway, the Commanderie has requisitioned all the air transport. It seems there's a big push on."

"I shall endure it."

"You're doing the right thing, Jack," Ferid Bey said. "One, and another thing; Faisal, you couldn't pick up for the coffee could you?" I suspected there was a reason Ferid Bey had brought us out to this tatty bargee hostel. "And while you're at it, could you take care of my hotel?"

Already, Count Jack was hearing the distant applause of the audience, scenting like a rare moth the faint but unmistakable pheromone of *celebrity*.

"And am I . . . top of the bill?"

"Always, Jack," said Ferid Bey. "Always."

From our table on the promenade deck of the *Empress of Mars,* we watched the skymasters pass overhead. They were high and their hulls caught the evening light that had faded from the canal. I lost count after thirty; the sound of their many engines merged into a high thunder. The vibration sent ripples across the wine in our glasses on the little railed-off table at the stern of the barge. One glass for me, always untouched—I did not drink, but I liked to keep Count Jack company. He was a man who craved the attention of others—without it, he grew translucent and insubstantial. His hopes for another involuntary audience of passengers to charm and intimidate and cow with his relentless showbiz tales were disappointed. The *Empress of Mars* was a cargo tug pushing a twelve-barge tow with space for eight passengers, of which we were the sole two. I was his company. I had been so enough times to know his anecdotes as thoroughly as I knew the music for his set. But I listened, and I laughed, because it is not the story that matters, but the telling.

"Headed East," Count Jack said. I did not correct him—he had never understood that on Mars, West was East and East was West. *Sunrise, east; sunset, west dear boy*, he declared. We watched the fleet, a vast, sky-filling arrowhead, drive towards the sunset hills on the close horizon. The Grand Valley had opened out into a trench so wide we could see the canyon walls, a terrain with its own inner terrain. "Godspeed that fleet." He had been uncharacteristically quiet and ruminative this trip. It was not the absence of a captive audience. The fleet, the heavy canal traffic—I had counted eight tows headed up-channel from the front to Unshaina since we began this first bottle of what Count Jack called his "Evening Restorational"—had brought home to him that he was headed to war. Not pictures of war, news reports of war, rumors of war, but war itself. For the first time, he might be questioning the tour.

"Does it make your joints ache, Faisal?"

"Maestro?"

"The gravity. Or rather, the want of gravity. Wrists, ankles, fingers, all the flexing joints. Hurt like buggery. Thumbs are the worst. I'd've have thought it would have been the opposite with it being so light here. Not a bit of it. It's all I can do to lift this glass to my lips."

To my eyes, he navigated the glass from table to lips quite successfully. Count Jack poured another Evening Restorational and sank deep in his chair. The dark green waters of the canal slipped beneath our hull. Martian twilights were swift and deep. War had devastated this once populous and fertile land, left scars of black glass across the bottom lands where heat rays had scored the regolith. The rising evening wind, the *Tharseen*, that reversed direction depending on which end of the Grand Valley was in night, called melancholy flute sonatas from the shattered Roost pillars.

"It's a ghastly world," Count Jack said after a second glass.

"I find it rather peaceful. It has a particular beauty. Melancholic."

"No, not Mars. Everywhere. Everywhere's bloody ghastly and getting ghastlier. Ever since the war. War makes everything brutal. Brutal and ugly. War wants everything to be like it. It's horrible, Faisal."

"Yes. I think we've gone too far. We're laying waste to entire civilisations. Unshaina, it's older than any city on Earth. This has gone beyond righteous justice. We're fighting because we love it."

"Not the war, Faisal. I've moved on from the bloody war. Do keep up. Getting old. That's what's truly horrible. Old old old and I can't do a thing about it. I feel it in my joints, Faisal. This bloody planet makes me feel old. A long slow decline into incompetence, imbecility, and incontinence. What have I got? A decent set of pipes. That's all. And they won't last forever. No investments, no property, and bugger-all recording royalties. Bloody Revenue cleaned me out. Rat up a drainpipe. Gone. And the bastards still have their hands out. They've threatened me, you know. Arrest. What is this, the bloody Marshalsea Gaol? I'm a Papal Knight, you know. I wield the sword of the Holy Father himself."

"All they want is their money," I said. Count Jack had always resented paying lawyers and accountants, with the result that he had signed disastrous recording contracts and only filed tax returns when the bailiffs were at the door. This entire Martian tour would barely meet his years of outstanding tax, plus interest. "Then they'll leave you alone."

"No, they won't. They won't ever let me alone. They know Count Jack is a soft touch. They'll be back, the damnable dunners. Once they've got the taste of your blood, they won't ever let their hooks out of you. Parasites. I am infested with fiscal parasites. Tax, war, and old age. They make everything gross and coarse and pointless."

Beams of white light flickered along the twilight horizon. I could not tell whether they were from sky to ground or ground to sky. The fleet had gone. The heat rays danced along the edge of the world, flickered out. New beams took their place. Flashes beyond the close horizon threw the hills into momentary relief. I cried out as the edge of the world became a flickering palisade of heat rays. Count Jack was on his feet. The flashes lit his face. Seconds later, the first soft rumble of distant explosions reached us. The Twav deckhands fluttered on their perches. I could make out the lower register of their consternation as a treble shrill. The edge of the world was a carnival of beams and flashes. I saw an arc of fire descend from the sky to terminate in a white flash beneath the horizon. I did not doubt that I had seen a Skymaster and all her crew perish, but it was beautiful. The sky blazed with the most glorious fireworks. Count Jack's eyes were wide with wonder. He threw his hand up to shield his eyes as a huge midair explosion turned the night white. Stark shadows lunged across the deck; the Twav rose up in a clatter of wings.

"Oh, the dear boys, the dear boys," Count Jack whispered. The sound of the explosion hit us. It rattled the windows on the pilot deck, rattled the bottle and glasses on the table. I felt it shake the core of my being, shake me belly and bowel deep. The beams winked out. The horizon went dark.

We had seen a great and terrible battle, but who had fought, who had won, who had lost, whether there had been winners or losers, what its goals had been—we knew none of these. We had witnessed something terrible and beautiful and incomprehensible. I lifted the untouched glass of wine and took a sip.

"Good God," Count Jack said, still standing. "I always thought you didn't drink. Religious reasons and all that."

"No, I don't drink for musical reasons. It makes my joints hurt."

I drank the wine. It may have been vinegar, it may have been the finest wine available to humanity, I did not know. I drained the glass.

"Dear boy." Count Jack poured me another, one for himself, and together w watched the edge of the world glow with distant fires.

We played Camp Avenger on a stage rigged on empty beer barrels to a half-full dience that dwindled over the course of the concert to just six rows. A Brigadier had been drinking steadily all through the concert tried to get his troopers up on-stage to dance to the Medley of Ould Irish Songs. They sensibly declined. He tripped over his own feet trying to inveigle Count Jack to dance to "Walls of Limerick" with him and went straight off the stage. He split his head open on the rim of a beer keg.

At Syrtia Regional Command, the audience was less ambiguous. We were bottled off. The first one came looping in even as Count Jack came on, arms spread wide, to his theme song "I'll Take You Home Again, Kathleen." He stuck it through "Blaze Away," "Nessun Dorma," and "Il Mio Tesoro" before an accurately hurled Mars Export Pale Ale bottle deposited its load of warm urine down the front of his dickey. He finished "The Garden Where the Praties Grow," bowed, and went straight off. I followed him as the first of the barrage of folding army chairs hit the stage. Without a word or a look, he went straight to his tent and stripped naked.

"I've had worse in Glasgow Empire," he said. His voice was stiff with pride. I never admired him as much. "Can you do something with these, dear boy?" He held out the wet, reeking dress suit. "And run me a bath."

We took the money, in full and in cash, and went on, ever up the ever-branching labyrinth of canals, ever closer to the battlefront.

The boat was an Expeditionary Force fast-patrol craft, one heat ray turret fore, one mounted in a blister next to the captain's position. It was barely big enough for the piano, let alone us and the sullen four-man crew. They smoked constantly and tried to outrage Count Jack with their vile space-trooper's language. He could outswear any of them. But he kept silence and dignity and our little boat threaded through the incomprehensible maze of Nyx's canals; soft green waters of Mars overhung by the purple fronds of crosier-trees, dropping the golden coins of their seed cases into the water, where they sprouted corkscrew propellers and swam away. This was the land of the Oont, and their tall, heron-like figures, perched in the rear of their living punts, were our constant companions. On occasion, down the wider channels and basins, we glimpsed their legendary organic paddle-wheelers, or their pale blue ceramic stilt-towns. The crew treated the Oont with undisguised contempt and idly trained the boat's weapons on them. The Oont had accepted the mandate of the Commanderie without a fight, and their cities and ships and secretive, solitary way of life went unchanged. Our Captain thought them a species of innate cowards and traitors. Only a [spe]cies tamed by the touch of the heat ray could be trusted.

[fo]r five hundred miles, up the Grand Canal and through the maze of Nyx, Twav [Tw]ores had lifted and laid my piano with precision and delicacy. It took the Ter-[ran ar]my to drop it. From the foot of the gangplank I heard the jangling crash, and [t]o see the cargo net on the jetty and troopers grinning. At once, I wanted to [check] the packing and see if anything remained. It was not my piano—I would [never have] risked my Bösendorfer on the vagaries of space-travel—but it was a pass-[able one] from a company that specialised in interplanetary hire. I had grown [as on]e does with pianos. They are like dogs. I walked on. That much I had [learned from Co]unt Jack. Dignity, always dignity.

[— — was] a repair base for Third Skyfleet. We walked in the shadow of hov-[ering ships.] Engineers in repair rigs swarmed over hulls, lowered engines on [winches, unrolled] sections, deflated gas cells. It was clear to me that the fleet had suffered grievously in recent and grim battle. Skins were gashed open to the very bones; holes stabbed through the rounded hulls from side to side. Engine pylons terminated in melted drips. Entire crew gondolas and gun turrets had been torn away. Some had been so terribly mauled they were air-going skeletons; a few lift cells wrapped around naked ship spines.

Of the crews who had fought through such ruin, there was no sign.

The base commander, Yuzbashi Osman, greeted us personally. He was a great fan, a great fan. A dedicated lifelong fan. He had seen the Maestro in his every Istanbul concert. He always sat in the same seat. He had all the Maestro's recordings. He played them daily and had tried to educate his junior officers over mess dinners, but the rising generation were ignorant, low men; technically competent, but little better than the Devshirmey conscripts. A clap of his hands summoned batmen to carry our luggage. I did not speak his language but from the reactions of the engineers who had dropped my piano, I understood that further disrespect would not be tolerated. He cleared the camp steam-bath for our exclusive use. Sweated, steamed, and scraped clean, a glowing Count Jack bowled into the mess tent as if he were striding on to the stage of La Scala. He was funny, he was witty, he was charming, he was glorious. Most of the junior Onbashis and Mulazims at the dinner in his honour could not speak English, but his charisma transcended all language. They smiled and laughed readily.

"Would you look at that?" Count Jack said in the backstage tent that was our dressing room. He held up a bottle of champagne, dripping from the ice bucket. "Krug. They got me my Krug. Oh the dear, lovely boys."

At the dinner, I had noted the paucity of some of the offerings and marvelled at the effort it must have taken, what personal dedication by the Yuzbashi, to fulfil a rider that was only there to check the contract had been read. Count Jack slid the bottle back into the melting ice. "I shall return to you later, beautiful thing, with my heart full of song and my feet light on the applause of my audience. I am a star, Faisal. I am a true star. Leave me, dear boy."

Count Jack required time and space alone to prepare his entrance. This was the time he changed from Count James Fitzgerald to the Country Count from Kildare. It was a deeply private transformation and one I knew I would never be permitted to watch. The stage was a temporary rig bolted together from skymaster spares. The hovering ships lit the stage with their searchlights. A follow-spot tracked me to the piano. I bowed, acknowledged the applause of the audience, flicked out the tails of my evening coat, and sat down. That is all an accompanist need do.

I played a few glissandi to check the piano was still functioning after its disrespectful handling by the dock crew. Passable, to the tin ears of Sky Fleet engineers. Then I played the short overture to create that all-important sense of expectation in the audience and went straight into the music for Count Jack's entrance. The spotlight picked him up as he swept onto the stage, "I'll Take You Home Again, Kathleen" bursting from his broad chest. He was radiant. He commanded every eye. The silence in the deep Martian night was the most profound I think I have ever heard. He strode to the front of the stage. The spotlight adored him. He luxuriated in the applause as if it were the end of the concert, not the first number. He was a shameless showman. I lifted my hands to the keyboard to introduce "Torna a Surriento."

And the night exploded into towering blossoms of flame. For an instant, the audience sat transfixed, as if Count Jack had somehow summoned the most astonishing of operatic effects. Then the alarms blared out all across the camp. Count Jack and I both saw clearly the spider-shapes of war-tripods, tall as trees, wading through the flames. Heat rays flashed out, white swords, as the audience scattered to take up posts and weapons. Still Count Jack held the spotlight, until an Onbashi leaped up, tackled him, and knocked him out of the firing line just as a heat ray cut a ten-thousand-degree arc across the stage. He had no English, he needed no English. We ran. I glanced back once. I knew what I would see, but I had to see it: my piano, that same cheap, sturdy-hire upright piano that I had shipped across one hundred million miles of space, through the concert halls and grand opera houses, on dusty roads and railways, down calm green canals, my piano, exploding in a fountain of blazing hammers and whipping, melting wires. A war-tripod strode over us, its heat ray arms swivelling, seeking new targets. I looked up into the weaving thicket of tentacles beneath the hull, then the raised steel hoof passed over me and came down squarely and finally on our dressing room tent.

"My Krug!" Count John cried out.

A heat ray cut a glowing arc of lava across the ground before me. I was lucky—you cannot dodge these things or see them coming, or hear their ricochets. They are light itself. All you can be is moving in the right direction, have the right momentum: be lucky. Our Onbashi was not lucky. He ran into the heat ray and vanished into a puff of ash. A death so fast, so total that it became something more than death. It was annihilation.

"Maestro! With me!"

Count Jack had been standing, staring, transfixed. I took his hand, his palm still damp with concert sweat, and skirted around the end of the still-smoking scar. We ducked, we ran at a crouch, we zigzagged in our tails and dickie bows. There was no good reason for it. We had seen it in war movies. The Uliri war machines strode across the camp, slashing glowing lava tracks across it with their heat rays, their weapon-arms seeking out fresh targets. But our soldiers had reached their defensive positions and were fighting back, turning the Uliri's own weapon against them, and bolstering it with a veritable hail of ordnance. The troopers who had manned our spotlights now turned to the heat rays. Skymasters were casting off; their turret gunners seeking out the many-eyed heads of the Uliri tripods. The war machine that had so hideously killed the brave Onbashi stood in the river, eye-blisters turning this way, that way, seeking targets. A weapon-arm fixed on us. The aperture of the heat ray opened. Hesitated. Pulled away. Grasping cables uncoiled from between the legs. We scuttled for cover behind a stack of barrels—not that they would have saved us. Then a missile cut a streak of red across the night. The war-machine's front left knee-joint exploded. The machine wavered for balance on two, then a Skymaster cut low across the canal bank and severed the front right off at the thigh with a searing slash of a heat ray. The monster wavered, toppled, came down in a blast and crash and wave of spray, right on top of the boat that would have carried us to safety. Smashed to flinders. Escape hatches opened; pale shapes wriggled free, squirmed down the hull towards land. I pushed Count Jack to the ground as the Skymaster opened up. Bullets screamed around us. Count Jack's eyes were wide with fear, and something else, something I had not imagined in the man: excitement. War might be brutal and ghastly and ugly, as he had declaimed on the *Empress of Mars*, but there was a terrible, primal power in it. I saw the same thrill, the same joy, the same power that had commanded audiences from Tipperary to Timbuktoo. I saw it and I knew that, if we ever returned to Earth and England, I would ever be the accompanist, the amanuensis, the dear boy; and that even if he sang to an empty hall, Count John Fitzgerald would always be the Maestro, Sopratutto. All there was in me was fear; solid fear. Perhaps that is why I was brave. The guns fell silent. I looked over the top of the barrels. Silvery Uliri bodies were strewn across the dock. I saw the canal run with purple blood like paint in water.

The Skymaster turned and came in over the canal to a low hover. A boarding ramp lowered and touched the ground. A skyman crouched at the top of the ramp, beckoning urgently.

"Run, Maestro, run!" I shouted, and dragged Count Jack to his feet. We ran. Around us heat rays danced and stabbed like some dark tango. A blazing war-machine stumbled blindly past, crushing tents, bivouacs, repair sheds beneath its feet, shedding sheets of flame. Ten steps from the foot of the ramp, I heard a noise that turned me to ice: a great ululating cry from the hills behind the camp, ringing from horizon to horizon, back and forth, wash and backwash, a breaking wave of sound. I had never heard it but I had heard of it, the war-song of the Uliri padva infantry. A hand seized mine: the skyman dragged me and Count Jack like a human chain into the troop hold. As the ramp closed, I saw the skyline bubble and flow, like a silver sheen of oil, down the hillside towards us. Padvas. Thousands of them. As the skymaster lifted and the hull sealed, the last, the very last sight I had was of Yuzbashi Osman looking up at us. He raised a hand in salute. Then he turned, drew his sword, and, with a cry that pierced even the engine drone of the Skymaster, every janissary of Oudeman Camp drew his blade. Swordpoints glittered, then they charged. The Skymaster spun in the air, I saw no more.

"Did you see that?" Count Jack said to me. He gripped my shoulders. His face was pale with shock, but there was a mad strength in his fingers. "Did you? How horrible, how horrible horrible. And yet, how wonderful! Oh, the mystery, Faisal, the mystery!" Tears ran down his ash-smudged face.

We fled through the Labyrinth of Night. We had no doubt that we were being pursued through those narrow, twining canyons. The Skycaptain's pinger picked up fleeting, suggestive contacts of what we had all heard: terrible cries, echoes of echoes in the stone redoubts of Noctis, far away but always, always, always keeping pace with us. The main hold of the Skymaster was windowless, and though the skycaptain spoke no English, he had made it most clear to us that we were to keep away from his crew, whether they were in engineering, the gun blisters, or the bridge and navigation pods. So we sat on the hard steel mesh of the dimly lit cargo hold, ostensibly telling old musician stories we had told many times before, pausing every time our indiscriminate ears brought us some report of the war outside. Hearing is a much more primal sense than vision. To see is to understand. To hear is to apprehend. Eyes can be closed. Ears are ever open. Maestro broke off the oft-told story of singing for the Pope, and how thin the towels were, and what cheap bastards the Holy See had turned out to be. His ears, as I have said, were almost supernaturally keen. His eyes went wide. The Twav battledores on their perches in the skymarine roosts riffled their scales, shining like oil on water, and shifted their grips on their weaponry. A split second later, I heard the cries. Stuttering and rhythmic, they rose over three octaves from a bass drone to a soprano, nerve-shredding yammer. Two behind us, striking chords and harmonics from each other like some experimental piece of serialist music. Another answered, ahead of us. And another, far away, muted by the wind-sculpted rock labyrinth. A fifth, close, to our right. Back and forth, call and response. I clapped my hands over my ears, not from the pain of the shrill upper registers, but at the hideous musicality of these unseen voices. They sang scales and harmonies alien to me, but their music called the musician in me.

And they were gone. Every nerve on the Skymaster, human and Twav, was afire. The silence was immense. My Turkic is functional but necessary—enough to know what Ferid Bey is actually saying—and I recalled the few words of the skycaptain I had overheard as he relayed communications to the crew. The assault on Camp Oudeman had been part of a surprise offensive by the Tharsian Warqueens. Massive assaults had broken out along a five-hundred-mile front from Arsai to Urania. Warmachines, shock troops—there had even been an assault on Spacefleet: squadron after squadron of rockets launched to draw the staggering firepower of our orbital battleships from the assault below. And up from out of the soil, things like nothing that anyone had ever seen before. Things that put whole battalions to flight, that smashed apart trench lines and crumbled redoubts to sand. As I tried to imagine the red earth parting and something from beyond nightmares rising up, I could not elude the dark thought: might there not be similar terrible novelties in the sky? This part of my eavesdropping, I kept to myself. It was most simple: I had been routinely lying to Count Jack since the first day I set up my music on the piano.

"I could murder a drink," Count Jack said. "If there were such a thing on this barquadero. Even a waft of a Jameson's cork under my nose."

The champagne on the deck of the *Empress of Mars* must have corrupted me, because at that moment I would gladly have joined the Maestro. More than joined, I would have beaten him by a furlong to the bottom of the bottle of Jameson's.

Up on the bridge, a glass finger projecting from the Skymaster's lifting body, the skycaptain called orders from his post at the steering yoke. Crew moved around us. The battledores shifted the hue of their plumage from blue to violent yellow. I felt the decking shift beneath me—how disorienting, how unpleasant, this sense of everything sound and trustworthy moving, nothing to hold on to. The engines were loud; the captain must be putting on speed, navigating between the wind-polished stone. We were flying through a monstrous stone pipe organ. I glanced up along the companionway to the bridge. Pink suffused the world beyond the glass. We had run all night through the Labyrinth of Night; that chartless maze of canyons and ravines and rock arches that humans suspected was not entirely natural. I saw rock walls above me. We were low, hugging the silty channels and canals. The rising sun sent planes of light down the sheer fluted stone walls. There was nothing on Earth to compare with the loveliness of dawn on Mars, but how I wished I were there and not in this dreadful place.

"Faisal."

"Maestro."

"When we get back, remind me to fire that greased turd, Ferid."

I smiled, and Count Jack Fitzgerald began to sing. "Galway Bay," the most hackneyed and sentimental of faux-Irish paddywhackery ("Have you ever been to Galway Bay? Incest and Gaelic games. All they know, all they like") but I had never heard him sing it like this. Had he not beem seated on the deck before me, leaning up against a bulkhead, I would have doubted that it was his voice. It was small but resonant, perfect like porcelain, sweet as a rose and filled with a high, light innocence. This was the voice of childhood; the boy singing back the tunes his grandmother taught him. This was the Country Count from Kildare. Every soul on the Skymaster, Terrene and Martian, listened, but he did not sing for them. He needed no audience, no accompanist: this was a command performance for one.

The Skymaster shook to a sustained impact. The spell was broken. Voices called out in Turkic and Twav flute-speech. The Skymaster rocked, as if shaken in a godlike grip. Then, with a shriek of rending metal and ship-skin, the gun-blister directly above us was torn away; gunner, gun, and a two metre shard of hull. A face looked in at us. A face that more than filled the gash in the hull; a nightmare of six eyes arranged around a trifurcate beak. The beak opened. Rows of grinding teeth moved within. A cry blasted us with alien stench: ululating over three octaves, ending in a shriek. It drove the breath from our lungs and the will from our hearts. Another answered it, from all around us. Then the face was gone. A moment of shock—a moment, that was all—and the skycaptain shouted orders. The Twav rose from their perches, wings clattering, and streamed through the hole in the hull. I heard the whine of ray-rifles warming up, and then the louder crackle and sizzle of our own defensive heat rays.

I thought that I would never hear a worse thing than the cry through the violated hull. The shriek, out there, unseen, was like the cry I might make if my spine were torn from my living body. I could only guess: one of those things had met a heat ray.

We never saw any of the battledores again.

Again, the Skymaster shook to an impact. Count Jack lunged forward as claws stabbed through the hull and tore three rips the entire length of the bulkhead. The Skymaster lurched to one side; we slid across the decking in our tailcoats and smoke-smudged dickie shirts. An impact jolted the rear of the air ship, I glimpsed blackness, and then the entire tail turret was gone and the rear of the Skymaster was open to the air. Through the open space I saw a four-winged flying thing stroke away from us, up through the pink stone arches of this endless labyrinth. It was enormous. I am no judge of comparative dimensions—I am an auditory man, not a visual one—but it was on a par with our own limping Skymaster. The creature part-furled its wings to clear the arch, then turned high against the red sky, and I saw glitters of silver at the nape of its neck and between its legs. Mechanisms, devices, Uliri crew.

While I gaped at the sheer impossible horror of what I beheld, the Skymaster was struck again, an impact so hard it flung us from one side of the hold to the other. I saw steel-shod claws the size of scimitars pierce the glass finger of the bridge like the skin of a ripe orange. The winged Martian horror ripped bridge from hull, and, with a flick of its foot—it held the bridge as lightly and easily as a pencil—hurled it spinning through the air. I saw one figure fall from it and closed my eyes. I did hear Count Jack mumble the incantations of his faith.

Robbed of control, the Skymaster yawed wildly. Engineering crew rushed around us, shouting tersely to each other, fighting to regain control, to bring us down in some survivable landing. There was no hope of escape now. What were those things? Those nightmare hunters of the labyrinth of night? Skin shredded, struts shrieked and buckled as the Skymaster grazed a rock chimney. We listed and started to spin.

"We've lost port-side engines!" I shouted, translating the engineers' increasingly cold and desperate exchanges. We were going down, but it was too fast . . . too fast. The chief engineer yelled an order that translated as brace for impact in any language. I wrapped cargo strapping around my arms, and gripped for all my worth. Pianists have strong fingers.

"Patrick and Mary!!" Count Jack cried, and then we hit. The impact was so huge, so hard, that it drove all breath and intelligence and thought from me, everything except that death was certain and that the last, the very last, thing I would ever see would be a drop of fear-drool on the plump bottom lip of Count Jack Fitzgerald, and that I had never noticed how full, how kissable, those lips were. Death is such a sweet surrender.

We did not die. We bounced. We hit harder. The Skymaster's skeleton groaned and snapped. Sparking wires fell around us. Still we did not stop, or die. I remember thinking, don't tumble, if we tumble, we are dead, all of us, and so I knew we would survive. Shaken, smashed, stunned, but surviving. The corpse of the Skymaster slid to a crunching stop hard against the house-sized boulders at the foot of the canyon wall. I could see daylight in five places through the Skymaster's violated hull. It was beautiful beyond words. The sky-horrors might still be circling, but I had to get out of the airship.

"Jack! Jack!" I cried. His eyes were wide, his face pale with shock. "Maestro!" He looked and saw me. I took him by the hand and together we ran from the smoking ruin of the Skymaster. The crew, military trained, had been more expeditious in their escape. Already they were running from the wreck. I felt a shadow pass over me. I looked up. Diving out of the tiny atom of the sun—how horrible, oh how horrible! I saw for the first time, whole and entire, one of the things that had been hunting us and my heart quailed. It swooped with ghastly speed and agility on its four wings and snatched the running men up into the air, each impaled on a scimitar-claw. It hovered in the air above us and I caught the foul heat and stench of the wind from its wings and beak. This, this is the death for which I had been reserved. Nothing so simple as an air crash. The sky-horror looked at me, looked at Count Jack with its six eyes, major and minor. Then with a terrible scrannel cry, like the souls of the dead engineers impaled on its claws, and with a gust of wing-driven wind, it rose up and swept away.

We had been marked for life.

Irony is the currency of time. We were marked for life, but three times I entertained killing Count Jack Fitzgerald. Pick up a rock and beat him to death with it, strangle him with his bow tie, just walk away from him and leave him in the dry gulches for the bone-picking things.

I reasoned, by dint of a ready water supply and a scrap of paper thrown in that showed a sluggish but definite flow, that we should follow the canal. I had little knowledge of the twisted areography of the Labyrinth of Night—no one did, I suspect—but I was certain that all waters flowed to the Grand Canal and that was the spine and nervous system of Operation Enduring Justice. I advised us to drink—Count Jack ordered me to look away as he knelt and supped up the oddly metallic Martian water. We set off to the sound of unholy cries high and far among the pinnacles of the canyon walls.

The sun had not crossed two fingers of narrow canyonland sky before Count Jack gave an enormous theatrical sigh and sat down on a canal-side barge bollard.

"Dear boy, I simply cannot take another step without some material sustenance."

I indicated the alien expanse of ruck, dust, water, red sky; hinted at its barrenness.

"I see bushes," Count Jack said. "I see fruit on those bushes."

"They could be deadly poison, Maestro."

"What's fit for Martians cannot faze the robust Terrene digestive tract," Count Jack proclaimed. "Anyway, better a quick death than lingering starvation, dear God."

Argument was futile. Count Jack harvested a single, egg-shaped, purple fruit and took a small, delicate bite. We waited. The sun moved across its slot of sky.

"I remain obdurately alive," said Count Jack, and ate the rest of the fruit. "The texture of a slightly underripe banana and a flavour of mild aniseed. Tolerable. But the belly is replete."

Within half an hour of setting off again, Count Jack had called a halt.

"The gut, Faisal, the gut." He ducked behind a rock. I heard groans and oaths and other, more liquid noises. He emerged pale and sweating.

"How do you feel?"

"Lighter, dear boy. Lighter."

That was the first time that I considered killing him.

The fruit had opened more than his bowels. The silence of the canyons must have haunted him, for he talked. Dear God, he talked. I was treated to Count Jack Fitzgerald's opinion on everything from the way I should have been ironing his dress shirts (apparently I required a secondary miniature ironing board specially designed for collar and cuffs) to the conduct of the war between the worlds.

I tried to shut him up by singing, trusting—knowing—that he could not resist an offer to show off and shine. I cracked out "Blaze Away" in my passable baritone, then "The Soldier's Dream," anything with a good marching beat. My voice rang boldly from the rim rocks.

Count Jack touched me lightly on the arm.

"Dear boy, dear dear boy. No. You only make the intolerable unendurable."

And that was the second time that I was close to physically killing him. But we realised that if we were to survive—and though we could not entertain the notion that we might not, because it would surely have broken our hearts and killed us—we understood that to have any hope it making it back to occupied territory, we would have to proceed as more than maestro and accompanist. So, in the end, we talked, one man with another man. I told him of my childhood in middle-class, leafy Woking, and at the Royal Academy of Music, and the realisation, quiet, devastating, and quite quite irrefutable, that I would never be a concert great. I would never play the Albert Hall, the Marinsky, Carnegie Hall. I saw a Count Jack I had never seen before; sincere behind the bluster, humane and compassionate. I saw beyond an artiste. I saw an *artist*. He confided his fears to me: that the days of Palladiums and Pontiffs had blinded him. He realised too late that one night the lights would move to another and he would face the long, dark walk from the stage. But he had plans; yes, he had plans. A long walk in a hard terrain concentrated the mind wonderfully. He would pay the Revenue their due and retain Ferid Bey only long enough to secure the residency on Venus. And when his journey through the worlds was done and he had enough space dust under his nails, he would return to Ireland, to County Kildare, buy some land and set himself up as a tweedy, be-waistcoated, red-faced Bog Boy. He would sing only for the Church, at special masses and holy days of obligation and parish glees and tombolas; he could see a time when he might fall in love with religion again, not from any personal faith, but for the comfort and security of familiarity.

"Have you thought of marrying?" I asked. Count Jack had never any shortage of female admirers, even if they no longer threw underwear on to the stage as they had back in the days when his hair and moustache were glossy and black—and he would mop his face with them and throw them back to shrieks of approval from the crowd. "Not a dry seat in the house, dear boy." But I had never seen anything that hinted at a more lasting relationship than bed and champagne breakfast.

"Never seen the need, dear boy. Not the marrying type. And you, Faisal?"

"Not the marrying type either."

"I know. I've always known. But that's what this bloody world needs. Really needs. Women, Faisal. Women. Leave men together and they soon agree to make a wasteland. Women are a civilising force."

We rounded an abrupt turn in the canal, and came upon a scene that silenced even Count Jack. A battle had been fought here, a war of total commitment and destruction. But who had won, who had lost, we could not tell. Uliri war-tripods lay draped over ledges and arches like desiccated spiders. The wrecks of Skymasters were impaled on stone spires, wedged into rock clefts and groins. Shards of armor, human and Uliri, littered the canyon floor. Helmets and cuirasses were empty, long since picked clean by whatever scavengers hid from the light of the distant sun to gnaw and rend in the night. We stood in a landscape of hull plates, braces, struts, smashed tanks, and tangles of wiring and machinery we could not begin to identify. Highest, most terrible of all, the hulk of a spaceship, melted with the fires of reentry, smashed like soft fruit, lay across the canyon, rim to rim. Holes big enough to fly a Skymaster through had been punched through the hull, side to side.

Count Jack raised his eyes to the fallen spaceship, then his hands.

"Dear God. I may never play the Hammersmith Palais again."

Chimes answered him, a tintinnabulation of metal ringing on metal. This was the final madness. This was when I understood that we were dead—that we had died in the Skymaster crash—and that war was Hell. Then I felt the ground tremble beneath the soles of my good black concert shoes and I understood. Metal rang on metal, wreckage on wreckage. The earth shook, dust rose. The spoilage of war started to stir, and move. The ground shook, my feet were unsteady, there was nothing to hold on to, no surety except Count Jack. We held each other as the dust rose before us and the scrap started to slide and roll. Higher the ground rose, and higher, and that was the third time I almost killed him, for I still did not fully understand what was happening, and imagined that if I stopped Jack, I would stop the madness. This was *his* doing; he had somehow summoned some old Martian evil from the ground. Then a shining conical drill-head emerged from the soil, and the dust and rocks tumbled as the mole-machine emerged from the ground. It rose twenty, thirty feet above us, a gimlet-nosed cylinder of soil-scabbed metal. Then it put out metal feet from hatches along its belly, fell forward, and came to rest a stone's throw from us. Hatches sprang open behind the still-spinning drill head, fanned out like flower petals. I glimpsed silver writhing in the interior darkness. Uliri padvas streamed out, their tentacles carrying them dexterously over the violated metal and rock. Their cranial cases were helmeted, their breathing mantles armored in delicately worked cuirasses, and their palps held ray-rifles. We threw our hands up. They swarmed around us, and, without a sound, herded us into the dark maw of the Martian mole-machine.

The spider-car deposited us at a platform of heat ray–polished sandstone before the onyx gates. The steel tentacle-tips of our guards clacked on the mirror rock. The gates stood five times human height—they must have been overpowering to the shorter Uliri—and were divided in three according to Uliri architecture, and decorated with beautiful patterns of woven tentacles in high relief, as complex as Celtic knot-work. A dot of light appeared at the centre of the gates and split into three lines, a bright Y. They swung slowly outward and upwards. There was no other possibility than to enter.

How blind we humans had been, how sure that our mastery of sky and space gave us mastery of this world. The Uliri had not been driven back by our space bombardments and massed Skymaster strikes, they had been driven *deep*. Even as the great Hives of Syrtia and Tempe stood shattered and burning, Uliri proles had been delving deeper even than the roots of their geothermal cores, down toward the still warm lifeblood of their world, tapping into its mineral and energy resources. Downward and outward; hive to nest to manufactory, underground redoubt to subterranean fortress, a network of tunnels and delvings and underground vacuum-tubes that reached so far, so wide, so deep, that Tharsia was like a sponge. Down there, in the magma-warmed dark, they built a society far beyond the reach of our space-bombs. Biding their time, drawing their plans together, sending their tendrils under our camps and command centres and bases, gathering their volcano-forged forces against us.

I remembered little of the journey in the mole-machine except that it was generally downward, interminable long, and smelled strongly of acetic acid. Count Jack, with his sensitivities, discreetly covered his nose and mouth with his handkerchief. I could not understand his reticence: the Uliri had thousands better reasons to have turned us to ash than affront at their personal perfume.

Our captors were neither harsh nor kind. Those are both human emotions. The lesson that we were slow to learn after the Horsell Common attack was that Martian emotions are Martian. They do not have love, anger, despair, the desire for revenge, jealousy. They did not attack us from hate, or defend themselves from love. They have their own needs and motivations and emotions. So they only seemed to gently usher us from the open hatches of the mole-machine (one among hundreds, lined up in silos, aimed at the upper world) into a vast underground dock warm with heart-rock, and along a pier to a station, where a spider-shaped glass car hung by many arms from a monorail. The spider-car accelerated with jolting force. We plunged into a lightless tunnel, then we were in the middle of an underground city, tier upon tier of lighted windows and roadways tumbling down to a red-lit mist. Through underwater waterfalls, through vast cylindrical farms bright with the light of the lost sun. Over marshaling yards and parade grounds as dense with padvas as the shore is with sand grains. Factories, breeding vats, engineering plants sparkling with welding arcs and molten steel. I saw pits miles deep, braced with buttresses and arches and spires, down and down and down, like a cathedral turned inside out. Those slender stone vaults and spires were festooned with winged horrors—those same four-winged monsters that had plucked us out the sky and so casually, so easily, dismembered our crew. And allowed us to live.

I had no doubt that we had been chosen. And I had no doubt why we were chosen.

Over another jarring switch-over, through another terrifying, roaring tunnel, and then out into a behemoth gallery of launch silos: hundreds of them, side by side, each loaded with fat rocket ships stiff with gun turrets and missile racks. I feared for our vaunted Spacefleet, and, realising that, feared more for myself. Not even the alien values of the Uliri would show us so much if there were even the remotest possibility we could return the information to the Commanderie.

Count Jack realised it in the same instant.

"Christ on crutches, Faisal," he whispered.

On and on, through the riddled, maggoty, mined and tunnelled and bored and reamed Under-Mars. And now the onyx gates stood wide and the padvas fell into a guard around us and prodded us through them. The polished sandstone now formed a long catwalk. On each side rose seats, tier upon tier of obsidian eggcups. Each held an Uliri, proles, gestates, padvas, panjas; arranged by mantle color and rank. From the detail of the etchings on their helmets and carapace covers, I guessed them to be of the greatest importance. A parliament, a conclave, a cabinet. But the true power was at the end of the long walk: the Queen of Noctis herself. No image had even been captured, no corpse or prisoner recovered, of an Uliri Queen. They were creatures of legend. The reality in every way transcended our myth-making imaginations. She was immense. She filled the chamber like a sunrise. Her skin was golden; her mantle patterned with soft diamond-shaped scales like fairy armor. Relays of inseminators carried eggs from her tattooed multiple ovipostors, slathering them in luminous milt. Rings of rank and honor had been pierced through her eyelids and at the base of her tentacles. Her cuirass and helmet glowed with jewels and finest filigree. She was a thing of might, majesty and incontestable beauty. Our dress heels click-clacked on the gleaming stone.

"With me, Faisal," whispered Count Jack. "Quick smart." The guard stopped, but Count Jack strode forward. He snapped to attention. Every royal eye fixed on him. He clicked his heels and gave a small, formal bow. I was a heartbeat behind him. "It's all small beer after the Pope."

A tentacle snaked toward us. I resisted the urge to step back, even when the skin of the palp retraced and there, there was a human head. And not any human head: the head of Yuzbashi Osman, the music lover of Camp Oudeman, whom we had last seen leading a bold and stirring—and ultimately futile—charge against the padva hordes. Now the horror was complete. Yuzbashi opened his eyes and let out a gasping sigh. The head looked me up and down, then gave Count Jack a deeper scrutiny.

"Count Jack Fitzgerald of Kildare-upon-Ireland. Welcome. I am Nehenner Repooltu Sevenniggog Dethprip; by right, battle, and acclaim the uncontested Queen of Noctis. And I am your number-one fan."

One finger of rum in Count Jack's particular tea. And then, for luck, for war, for insanity, I slipped in another one. I knocked, waited for his call, and entered his dressing room. We might be somewhere in the warren of chambers beneath the Hall of the Martian Queen, miles beneath the sands of Mars, but the forms must be observed. The forms were all we had.

"Dear boy!" Uliri architecture did not accommodate human proportions. Proles had been at work—the prickly tang of scorched stone was strong—but I still had to duck to get through the door. Count Jack sat before a mirror of heat ray–polished obsidian. He adjusted the sit of his white bow tie. He filled the tiny cubbyhole but he still took the tea with an operatic flourish and took a long, County Kildare slurp.

"Ah! Grand! Grand. My resolve is stiffened to the sticking point. By God, I shall have need of it today. Did you slip a little extra in, you sly boy?"

"I did, Maestro."

"Surprisingly good rum. And the tea is acceptable. I wonder where they got it from?"

"Ignorance is bliss, Maestro."

"You're right there." He drained the cup. "And how is the piano?"

"Like the rum. Only I think they made it themselves."

"They're good at delicate work, the worker-drone thingies. Those tentacle-tips are fine and dexterous. Natural master craftsmen. I wonder if they would make good pianists? Faisal? Dear God, listen to me listen to me! Here we are, like a windup musical box, set up to amuse and titivate. A song, a tune, dance or two. Us, the last vestige of beauty on this benighted planet, dead and buried in some vile subterranean cephalopod vice-pit. Does anyone even know we're alive? Help us for God's sake help us! Ferid Bey, he'll do something. He must. At the very least, he'll start looking for us when the money doesn't materialise."

"I expect Ferid Bey has already collected the insurance." I took the cup and saucer. Our predicament was so desperate, so monstrous that we dared not look it full in the face. The Queen of Noctis had left us in no doubt that we were to entertain her indefinitely; singing birds in a cage. Never meet the fans. That was one of Count Jack's first homilies to me. Fans think they own you.

"Bastard!" Count Jack thundered. "Bastarding bastard! He shall die, he shall die. When I get back . . ." Then he realised that we would never get back, that we might never feel the wan warmth of the small, distant sun; that these low tunnels might be our home for the rest of our lives—and each other the only human face we would ever see. He wept, bellowing like a bullock. "Can this be the swan song of Count Jack Fitzgerald? Prostituting myself for some super-ovulating Martian squid queen? Oh the horror, the horror! Leave me, Faisal. Leave me. I must prepare."

The vinegar smell of the Uliri almost made me gag as I stepped on to the stage. I have always had a peculiar horror of vinegar. Lights dazzled me, but my nose told me that there must be thousands of Uliri on the concert hall's many tiers. Uliri language is as much touch and mantle-colour as it is spoken sounds, and the auditorium fistled with the dry-leaf rustling of tentacle on tentacle. I flipped out my tails, seated myself at the piano, ran a few practice scales. It was a very fine piano indeed. The tuning was perfect, the weight and responsiveness of the keys extraordinary. I saw a huge golden glow suffuse the rear of the vast hall. The Queen had arrived on her floating grav-throne. My hands shook with futile rage. Who had given her the right to be Count Jack's number-one fan? She had explained, in her private chamber, a pit filled with sweet and fragrant oil in which she basked, her monstrous weight supported, how she had first heard the music of Count Jack Fitzgerald. Rather, the head of poor Osman explained. When she had been a tiny fry in the Royal Hatchery—before the terrible internecine wars of the queens, in which only one could survive—she had become intrigued with Earth after the defeat of the Third Uliri Host at the Battle of Orbital Fort Tokugawa. She had listened to Terrene radio, and become entranced by light opera—the thrill of the colouraturas, the sensuous power of the tenor, the stirring gravitas of the basso profundo. In particular, she fell in love—or the Ulirui equivalent of love—with the charm and blarney of one Count Jack Fitzgerald. She became fascinated with Ireland—an Emerald Isle, made of a single vast gemstone, a green land of green people—how extraordinary, how marvelous, how magical! She had even had her proles build a life-size model Athy in one of the unused undercrofts of the Royal Nest. Opera and the stirring voice of the operatic tenor became her passion, and she vowed, if she survived the Sororicide, that she would build an incomparable opera house on Mars, in the heart of the Labyrinth of Night, and attract the greatest singers and musicians of Earth to show the Uliri what she considered was the highest human art. She survived, and had consumed all her sisters and taken their experiences and memories, and built her opera house, the grandest in the solar system, but war had intervened. Earth had attacked, and the ancient and beautiful Uliri Hives of Enetria and Issidy were shattered like infertile eggs. She had fled underground, to her empty, virginal concert hall, but in the midst of the delvings and the buildings and forgings, she had heard that Count Jack Fitzgerald had come to Mars to entertain the troops at the same time that the United Queens were mounting a sustained offensive, and she seized her opportunity.

The thought of that little replica Athy, far from the sun, greener than green, waiting, gave me screaming nightmares.

Warm-up complete. I straightened myself at the piano. A flex of the fingers, and into the opening of "I'll Take You Home Again, Kathleen." And on strode Count Jack

Fitzgerald, arms wide, handkerchief in one hand, beaming, the words pealing from his lips. Professional, consummate, marvellous. I never loved him more dearly than striding into the spotlights. The auditorium lit up with soft flashes of color: Uliri lighting up their bioluminescent mantles, their equivalent of applause.

Count Jack stopped in mid-line. I lifted my hands from the keys as if the ivory were poisoned. The silence was sudden and immense. Every light froze on, then softly faded to black.

"No," he said softly. "This will not do."

He held up his hands, showed each of them in turn to the audience. Then he brought them together in a single clap that rang out into the black vastness. Clap one, two, three. He waited. Then I heard the sound of a single pair of tentacles slapping together. It was not a clap, never a clap, but it was applause. Another joined it, another and another, until waves of slow tentacle-claps washed around the auditorium. Count Jack raised his hands: enough. The silence was instant. Then he gave himself a round of applause, and me a round of applause, and I him. The Uliri caught the idea at once. Applause rang from every tier and level and joist of the Martian Queen's concert hall.

"Now, let's try that again," Count Jack said, and without warning, strode off the stage. I saw him in the wings, indicating for me to milk it. I counted a good minute before I struck up the introduction to "I'll Take You Home Again, Kathleen." On he strode, arms wide, handkerchief in hand, beaming. And the concert hall erupted. Applause: wholehearted loud-ringing mighty applause; breaking like an ocean from one side of the concert hall to the other, wave upon wave upon wave, on and on and on.

Count Jack winked to me as he swept past into the brilliance of the lights to take the greatest applause of his life.

"What a house, Faisal! What a house!"

Hard Stars

BRENDAN DUBOIS

Here's a disquieting look at a bleak but disturbingly plausible future in which the tables have been turned and the United States is being hit daily by hundreds of deadly drone strikes launched by foreign enemies, targeting any sort of electronic signal—which makes our technological civilization almost impossible to maintain.

Brendan DuBois has twice received the Shamus Award from the Private Eye Writers of America, been nominated three times for the Edgar Allan Poe Award given by the Mystery Writers of America, and has had stories reprinted in The Best American Mystery Stories of the Century *and* The Best American Noir of the Century. *He's the author of sixteen novels and over 130 short stories, and has made sales to* Playboy, Ellery Queen Mystery Magazine, Alfred Hitchcock's Mystery Magazine, *Space Stations,* Civil War Fantastic, Pharaoh Fantastic, Knight Fantastic, The Mutant Files, *and* Alternate Gettysburgs, *among other markets. His SF novels include* Resurrection Day *and* Six Days. *His most recent novel is* Deadly Cove, *part of the Lewis Cole mystery series, which also includes* Dead Sand, Black Tide, Shattered Shell, Killer Waves, *and* Buried Dreams. *He is also a* Jeopardy! *game show champion. He lives in Exeter, New Hampshire, with his family and maintains a Web site at www.BrendanDuBois.com.*

The first-floor windows in the lakeside cottage were broken, meaning the sharp wind whipping across the snow-covered lake came right through one side of the building and out the other. Trenton was in the kitchen, which had a cracked linoleum floor, metal table, and an old-style fridge and gas stove. Two of his team members were in the kitchen as well. Lights were off and no powered equipment was being used, so they made do by the light from a nearly full moon reflecting off the snow and from candles found in a nearly empty cupboard.

Carlson came up to him, wearing his black wool coat. His breath eddied in the air in a little cloud of steam. "Jenkins is gone. Ran out a side door."

"Damn," Trenton said.

"My thoughts exactly."

"Where's Harrier?" Trenton asked.

"Upstairs."

"How's he doing?"

"He's cold. We've got as many blankets on him as possible. Tyler's offered to crawl in with him."

"Harrier just might like it."

Carlson said, "Hell, I might like it, too, but he's not in the mood."

"Who the hell is?"

"Yeah, but Tyler thinks he might be coming down with a bug. He was coughing some as he went up the stairs."

"Shit," Trenton said.

Diaz came over, a lit candle in her hand, small black kit in the other. In her prior life she had been a medic in the 10th Mountain Division. "You're up next, boss. Sorry."

"Not a problem," Trenton said. "Like to think you're just saving the best for last."

Trenton followed her and took off his overcoat and suit coat, and sat down at the round metal kitchen table. Trenton unsnapped the cufflink from his right shirt-sleeve, rolled up his white starched shirt to his elbow. The table was so very cold against his bare skin. Another candle was lit, and Diaz, concern on her face, sat down next to him. She unzipped the black case, got to work. She took out a piece of rubber tubing, tied it off below his elbow. It was very, very tight.

Trenton heard the sounds of aircraft overhead, some jet-powered, others propeller-driven. Most, no doubt, unmanned.

Carlson looked up at the plaster ceiling. Even Diaz paused.

"Do it," Trenton said. "Now."

Her strong hands manipulated the top of his wrist, her fingers sliding up and down, and then she nodded. "Got it."

"Okay."

"Sorry, boss, don't even have a local."

"Christ, will you stop talking? Do it."

From the open case, out came a surgical scalpel with a gray handle. The candle-light made the metal look yellowish. Trenton turned his head.

The bite was sharper and hurt more than Trenton anticipated. He gritted his teeth. Diaz swore and said, "Shit," when something fell on the table. "Sorry, tweezers slipped." Trenton took a deep breath through his nose and tried to think of anything, something, whatever, while his bleeding wrist was dug at, poked, and probed.

"Got it," Diaz announced, triumph in her voice.

Something cold was splashed against his wrist, and Trenton gritted his teeth again as he felt a needle poke through his skin four times, a heavy thread tugging behind each poke. "Now we're done. Hold on."

Trenton glanced over as she put a small bandage over the wound, taping it care-fully at each end. "You'll need to have the stitches taken out in a week or so."

"You're up to doing it?"

Diaz said, "If we're still . . . together, yeah, I'm up to doing it."

Near his wrist was a square white gauze and bloody tweezers, along with a chunk of gray metal the size of a large piece of cooked rice. His chip, inserted during his first week on the job. Diaz deftly took a tiny propane torch from the bag, switched it on, and in seconds, toasted his chip. The smell was sharp and acrid. The chip was dead.

His chest and back suddenly felt lighter. The last one out from his detail. There you go. No more powered equipment, no communications gear, no cell phone, iPhone, iPad, nothing they possessed could now be tracked by the hordes of eager snoopers out there.

"Gee," Carlson said. "We made it after all."

Diaz made to say something but a sharp whistling noise came from overhead. They all looked up as the noise grew louder and ended sharply in a large *boom!* The candles flickered and dust sprinkled down from the plaster ceiling.

Trenton said, "I take it you didn't get Jenkins's chip before he ran out."

"Yes," Diaz said.

"Guess he shouldn't have done that."

"Yes, again," Diaz said, zippering up her bag.

Carlson said, "Poor guy died tired, that's all."

Trenton took a lit candle and climbed up a set of narrow wooden stairs to the second floor. Candlelight flickered from a room to the right. Trenton went down a short hallway, past framed family photographs from years ago that had peeled away in their frames, their faces and shapes yellowed out. In the room was a large four-poster bed, with a form underneath its covers. A woman named Tyler sat on a wooden chair next to the bed. There were bureaus and other chairs in the room. Trenton was pleased to see a shotgun across her lap. They had been unarmed for what felt like a very long time.

"Where did you find that?" Trenton asked.

"Rear closet. Figured most of these country folks are armed, no matter what the laws or the media might say. Rummaged around and found this. Twelve-gauge."

"Good job. Got any shells?"

"Six."

"Better than nothing. How's Harrier?"

"Sleeping. Poor guy is exhausted. I think he might be getting a fever."

"Diaz told me that."

Trenton walked over to the bed, peered down. Made out the back of an older man's head, his thick gray hair mussed up a bit. His breathing was raspy but steady and strong. That made him feel better, even with the man's supposed rise in temperature.

Another explosion sounded in the distance. Tyler glanced out the near window. "Did Jenkins get whacked with that earlier one?"

"I think so."

She moved her shotgun around and her coat sleeve slid up, revealing a small bandage on her wrist.

"Why did Jenkins run?" she asked.

"He's got family in the area."

"Still, it's running away. Cowardice. Betrayal."

"Don't think he'll be called up for a disciplinary hearing anytime soon."

"Government's too secretive, moves too damn slow."

"Ain't that the truth."

Trenton went back outside the cottage through the same side door Jenkins had used, stepped to the edge of the frozen lake, his feet crunching in the snow. His long coat was back on and his wrist throbbed with pain. Trenton could be atomized in a second or two and not even know it—maybe just hearing the whine of a fourth-generation Hellfire missile coming down at him, or one of its Iranian or Chinese or Korean variants—but with his chip dug out, Trenton was feeling just a bit more confident that he and the others might survive the night and tomorrow.

Trenton tipped his head back, looked up at the hard light of the stars overhead. A long time ago when Trenton was in the Boy Scouts back in Arizona, he could name every constellation up there, but not now. The fixed bright stars didn't concern him. Trenton watched the few lights up there, dipping down and moving around, and he saw unlit shapes as well, the ones that briefly covered the stars as they circled about, always hunting, always seeking, always ready, every day and night, every week and month, to kill you.

Trenton counted maybe a half dozen, but there could have been twelve up there. Or twenty. But he and his crew, they didn't have the tech to track what was up there, and that was all right.

Information exchange was now very much a two-way street.

Back into the cottage. Carlson and Diaz were around the table, looked up at Trenton as he came in, stamped the snow off his boots. "How's Harrier?" Carlson asked.

"Sleeping."

"Tyler?"

"Armed."

Diaz said, "The hell you say."

"Whole truth," Trenton said. "She found a shotgun up in a closet, with a half-dozen shells."

Carlson laughed. "Hell, at least we're packing now."

Trenton nodded. About three hundred miles and what felt like a century ago, they had dumped their weapons. They were all keyed into their thumbprints and palm prints, and their status was continuously updated to a central government server in Herndon, Virginia. When the crisis had erupted and Trenton had learned the first reports of what was going on, he had made the instant decision to get rid of the weapons.

But two of their teammates, Hong and O'Brian, had raised hell about doing that, citing the usual chapter and verse of regulations, rules, and their duty, and they had been in a chase Chevrolet Suburban when they were obliterated outside a small town in Pennsylvania. Soon after that, they dumped their official vehicles and comm gear as well, and moved on toward appropriating—or stealing—civilian vehicles. Up on the other side of the cottage was a stolen Toyota Sienna that had been pretty crowded with all of them inside, but which had gotten the job done.

But Trenton had trusted Jenkins to drive when the GPS went nuts, telling them they were driving on the A-1 highway in Kazakhstan. Jenkins had taken them up in this part of the state, near where he grew up, and the Sienna had run out of gas and had been pushed into the side of a snowbank. It had lasted long enough to get Jenkins home, and maybe he had enjoyed life as a free man for five or ten minutes.

Carlson said, "How long do you think we'll be staying here?"

"Long enough, and no, I don't know anything more than that."

Diaz said, "Think we could cover up those windows, boss, at least cut down on the breeze?"

Trenton hesitated.

Carlson said, "We're under a lot of trees. Our thermal images would be pretty blurred. And with all of our chips and gear gone, we're not broadcasting anything."

Trenton finally nodded. "Find some sheets or large towels. Be slow, be careful. If any overhead assets spot you, and if all they have is thermal, I want them to think it's a couple of old folks, moving slow, trying to repair the place so they won't freeze tonight."

They both nodded at him, went upstairs at a leisurely pace, leaving him alone with the candles and the old cottage and the breeze from the lake, which made the candlelight flare and flicker. Trenton went through the kitchen to the entranceway that led outside to the front porch. The door had been open, hanging ajar, when they walked up to it, which was one of the few good pieces of luck they had received on this trip.

Trenton walked down the snowy path to a narrow country road. Trenton was sure that under the snow this road was unpaved, for it made sense around this nearly deserted lake. There were no McMansions or large suburban homes, just weekend places for those who wanted some peace and quiet to hunt, fish, or just swim or boat.

Trenton trudged through the ankle-deep snow, felt his shoulders and back tingle. Another explosion off in the distance. Peace and quiet. Those three words sounded like an obscure Sanskrit verse in his mind.

Trenton went back to the abandoned Sienna and opened the passenger's side door. The interior dome light came on. The inside was littered with the debris one could expect from being on the road for days: fast food wrappers, napkins, soda cans, empty MRE packages, and a few crumpled newspapers. Trenton didn't bother with the newspapers. Whatever news they reported was wrong, and by now was also horribly out of date.

Trenton popped open the glove box. Another little light came on among the Handi-Wipes and straws and napkins. He started pawing through the glove box, looking for a flashlight or more matches, and shook his head in thanks at the luck that had just occurred.

A road map.

An honest-to-God paper road map. Earlier Jenkins had searched the glove box but hadn't told anyone what was in there.

He was too tired to get angry with Jenkins. Besides, Jenkins had already paid for his sins.

Trenton took the map out, closed the glove box and door, and returned to the cottage. About him were the snow and a couple of other cottages, lights out, quiet and restful.

Overhead was the hum and murmur of death, and Trenton did his best to ignore it.

Back inside the cottage, Carlson and Diaz were just finishing up. They had found large, thick beach towels, along with a hammer and some nails. Trenton was amazed at the difference it made in the inside room temperature. Diaz nodded as she tugged one corner of a beach towel advertising Pepsi-Cola, while Carlson finished tapping in a nail on the far wall, covering the last of the broken windows.

"Damn place is getting pretty cozy, isn't it?" Diaz said.

"Good job," Trenton said. "Maybe you can start a second career as a happy homemaker when this is all over."

Carlson laughed and Diaz suggested Trenton perform a vulgar yet impossible act upon himself. Trenton went to the kitchen table, shrugged off his overcoat, and unfolded the map. His wrist still hurt. Carlson and Diaz stood next to him. Trenton spent a minute trying to orient himself, and then tapped his finger on a squiggle of blue.

"Tucker Lake," Trenton said. "I remember seeing a sign for that, at a fish-and-bait shop, before we made that last turn. Anyone else?"

Carlson shook his head but Diaz said, "Yeah, I saw that, too. Tucker Lake. That's where we must be."

Trenton nodded, sat down, drew the map closer. Looked at the thick lines marking interstate highways, which were now no-go zones. So were most of the state roads. They had stuck as much as possible to the rural roads, but even those were jamming up as families and others raced to any place where they could hunker down as what was delicately called "the crisis" grew worse. The era when you could take your handheld device and confidently find a way to get from Point A to Point B without being blown up was now gone, and Trenton recalled the decision he had made an hour after dumping their weapons, when all of their handheld devices and communications gear also went into a river. In the span of a day, they had retreated back to the 1960s.

Now the map was the only thing they had. Trenton traced some of the thin lines marking back roads, trying to judge which ones would work to send them to a spot halfway up the map, where a range of the Catskills started to rise.

"What are you looking at?" Carlson asked.

"This peak. Mount Spencer. There's a FEMA retreat facility there."

Diaz said, "Shit, what kind of shape can it be in?"

"Better than this cottage," Trenton said. "It's deep, it's remote, and whatever's overhead—I hope—can't breach the integrity of the place." He tapped the map. "That's our destination. We can't stay in this shack. We can't."

Carlson said, "These cottages, bet some of them have boathouses. I could go out, scrounge some gas. We could top off the Sienna, get our asses moving again."

Diaz said, "Don't like it. That's movement. Those bastards up there, they're keying in on communications, Internet traffic, chips, shit like that, but they could also be recording data for some sort of algorithmic logic, looking for targeting patterns. Like thermal images grabbing gas cans."

"So we should just sit here and freeze?"

Diaz glared at Carlson and then all of them heard a bout of coughing break out from upstairs.

Trenton said, "Leave it for now. But scrounging for gas isn't a bad idea."

He looked back at the map and then Tyler was at the foot of the stairs, shotgun in hand. They all turned to her. She looked to him and said, "He's awake. And he wants to talk to you."

"All right, then."

Trenton got up and said, "You two, do another sweep of this place. See if you can find some canned food, or water, or anything to help us along."

"Got it," Carlson said, but Diaz stayed quiet.

Trenton followed Tyler back up the stairs and into the bedroom. The man had turned over in bed and was now sitting up, an old quilt comforter pulled up to his chin. There was gray stubble on his chin and cheeks that made him look ten years older.

"Sam, is that you?" he asked.

Trenton took another wooden chair, sat down. "Yes, Mister President. It's me."

He coughed, and coughed, and said, "Where are we?"

"By a lake in New York State. South of the Catskills."

"Are we alone?"

"Just your detail, sir. Except for Agent Jenkins. He left."

"Why?"

"He grew up near here. I think he wanted to go home."

The President coughed. "Can't rightly blame him. Do you have any contact with the airborne White House? Homeland Security? The Pentagon? Anybody?"

Trenton shook his head. "There was a radio news report last night that Kneecap had been shot down. Can't be verified. Most radio and TV stations are now off the air. Too much exposure for being hit. And we dumped our comm gear a while back, sir, while you were sleeping. Too dangerous. I'm afraid for now we're on our own, off the grid. But we're a hell of a lot safer now than we were earlier."

The President nodded at that, put his hands out, drew the comforter farther up to his chin. His hands trembled as he did that.

"You read Shakespeare much, Sam?"

"Not for a very long time, sir."

"There's a quote from *The Merchant of Venice*. It says, 'The sins of the father are to be laid upon the children.'" The President looked up at the cracked plaster ceiling as the sound of a jet-powered aircraft passed overhead. "Shakespeare being a writer, he stole that from another source. The Bible. Exodus, I think. Don't you think it's an apt term for what's going on now? Considering what we started in Pakistan and Afghanistan years back?"

"I'm sort of focusing on immediate issues, sir."

The President coughed. "I'm sure. What are you planning, Sam?"

"There's a FEMA retreat bunker up in the Catskills. That's our goal."

"Have you been able to raise them?"

Trenton shook his head. "No can do, sir. We'd need a radio, and in this environment, we can't trust radios. We're trying to expedite a way of getting from here to that bunker in the safest way possible."

"Still doing your duty, eh?"

"Absolutely, sir."

A wan smile. "Then you're in a minority, I'm afraid. We've got new enemies overhead, completely automated, ready to kill anything without remorse, without hesitation, without any fear or doubt. That's a lot to endure. I get the feeling the center's not holding, things are falling apart, the ones with duty and honor are either dead or running away."

Trenton said, "Beg to disagree, sir. We may be battered, but we haven't given up yet. Automated drones or not."

A muffled explosion from some distance away. The President slowly blinked his eyes. "What do you think's being hit out there, Sam?"

"Military base. Local FBI office. Police station. Oil company headquarters. Women's health clinic. Anything and everything that could be a target to whoever's holding the joystick."

He coughed some more. "I don't feel good, Sam."

"We'll get you out of here. Promise."

The President closed his eyes, took a rattling breath. "If . . . if anybody else wants to leave, I understand."

"Won't happen, sir."

"Jenkins left, didn't he?"

"An isolated case, that's all."

He coughed some more, and then Trenton went out of the bedroom.

Downstairs, Carlson said, "You won't believe this."

"Try me."

Diaz was smiling. "The phone works."

"What phone?"

Diaz moved next to the refrigerator, where there was a wall-mounted phone, colored yellow, with a long, white, curled cord hanging beneath it. There were shelves cluttered with books and papers nearby. She lifted up the phone receiver. "A dial tone. Can you believe that? A goddamn landline that's still working."

Trenton took the receiver out of her hand, listened to that old-fashioned sound, a sweet and drawn-out tone.

Unbelievable.

Trenton hung up the phone.

Carlson said, "Who should we call?"

"Hold on," Trenton said. "We need to think this through."

Diaz snapped, "Then think quick. God knows how long it's going to stay running."

From his wallet, Trenton took out a plastic-embossed card. It had a list of contact numbers, all of them out of state, and he started working through the list. Treasury Department, Homeland Security, Department of Defense, FBI, so forth and so on.

Fifteen minutes later, Trenton was done. With each phone number dialed, Trenton got the same response: the same harsh *blew-bleep-blew* tone, and the charming automated voice that said the number was no longer in service. A call to 911 produced busy signal after busy signal.

Trenton put the card back in his wallet. A nice artifact from a world that was dying out there.

They shared a late-night meal of bottled applesauce and water. Tyler came back downstairs and said, "Harrier ate only half of it, and drank just a little water. His forehead's really, really hot."

Carlson said, "How about that gas run, chief?"

Diaz said, "I still don't like it."

"Who does?" Carlson snapped back. "Harrier's getting sicker and sicker. We need to leave."

"And get blasted five minutes later?"

"I don't think—"

"Quiet, all of you," Trenton said. He put his water glass down, went over to the refrigerator. Trenton started looking through the shelves by the phone. "Diaz, bring a candle over, okay?"

Diaz muttered something but she moved over. Trenton worked quickly, his right wrist still aching like hell. There were recipe books and tour guides and maps and—

Yes.

Oh, yes.

A thin phone book.

Back at the table, he flipped through the pages. Coughing was louder from upstairs, and the hum of the drones overhead was constant as well.

Carlson said, "What are you looking for?"

"I'll know it when I find it."

There were a number of police departments out there, but what town was this cottage situated in? Who should he call? And with another far-off explosion tearing through the air, he knew he didn't have much time before that precious landline was cut. And he was sure any local fire departments were volunteer departments, and God bless volunteers, he was sure they were staying home, not moving.

There.

One chance.

He folded the phone book over, went to the phone, and started dialing. Diaz asked, "Who are you calling?"

"County sheriff's department."

"Why?"

"Most of the cop-shops around here are two- or three-man departments. They're probably at home with their families. Fire departments are all volunteer. But I'm hoping somebody's still trying to hold on at the county sheriff's level."

"And if they're not?"

"Then Carlson will show us his scrounging skills."

He finished dialing.

The number rang and rang and rang.

"Even if he does get gas," Diaz said, folding her arms, "we still don't know the best way to get to that FEMA shelter."

It rang and rang and rang.

Diaz said, "We might get stuck in a traffic jam. Or find all the bridges were blown. Or run into some gangs and—"

A *click*. Trenton covered the mouthpiece, turned, and said sharply. "Not a word more."

He went back to the phone. A quiet woman's voice answered. "Yes?"

Trenton said, "Is this county dispatch?"

A very long pause. He felt his hand warm the phone receiver.

The woman said, "Who wants to know?"

What to say? Who knew who was listening in? Or *what* was listening in?

He rubbed at his eyes. "I need some help."

The woman barked a laugh. "Buddy, who the hell doesn't? Sorry, give me your name, number, and address. Maybe somebody will be out there next week. Maybe not."

"I can't wait that long."

Another sharp laugh, no humor in it at all. "Take a number, that's all I can say."

"It's an emergency. A . . . national security emergency."

"Sure."

"I'm not kidding. I'm . . . well, this is a national security emergency. We need your help."

The woman's voice grew cautious. "Says you. You've got to do better, or I'm hanging up."

"Give me a moment." The long days and nights of training, of memorizing, of preparing for any eventuality . . . *any* eventuality. What to say? How to convince this woman?

"Please. You must have a list of procedures. You have a binder from Homeland Security. There's a section called . . . I'm sorry, I can't tell you the name. But I know it's number twelve. Go look it up. Please."

She said, "I'll call you back, then."

"No! Please! Don't hang up . . . I don't want to be cut off. Please. Number twelve."

The receiver clattered on the other end of the line. Trenton stood still, waiting, thinking, wondering if his long-ago instructors could ever have imagined this scenario, this outcome. He liked to think that he and the rest of the unit were doing the very best they could under the worse circumstances possible, something for future history books, whenever and however they were written.

History.

Among the historical events he had been taught during his training was Nixon's visit to Venezuela, when he and his wife Pat were nearly torn limb from limb by an angry mob who almost turned over their limousine, Molotov cocktails in hand. That particular Secret Service event was largely forgotten—Nixon was Veep at the time and it took place more than a half century ago—but Trenton had always wondered what it must have been like to be one of the agents in that limo while death was literally knocking at the door.

So now he knew. It didn't make him particularly happy.

He held his breath. Heard the phone being picked up.

The woman said, "You're shitting me, aren't you."

"No, I'm not."

"You're telling me that—"

"Please, no names, no titles. Can you help?"

He could hear her breathing on the other end of the line.

"Please," Trenton said. "We just need transportation. That's all. Like I said, it's a national security emergency."

The sharp laugh from the unknown woman came back. "That depends if we're gonna have a nation this time next month, am I right?"

Trenton waited.

"I got your location from your call. Someone will be there in about a half hour. But they need to be paid. Jewelry, watches, gold coins if you got them. Nothing plastic or paper. Do we have a deal?"

"We have a deal."

"Good, because—"

A soft click, and then there was nothing, not even a dial tone.

Outside Trenton heard the rumbling of distant explosions.

Trenton was back at the kitchen table. With the towels up over the broken windows, the temperature had become quite bearable. They all looked at the small pile of jewelry in the center of the table. His shirtsleeves felt odd because he had put in his cufflinks. Diaz had put in small earrings, as did Tyler, and Carlson and Tyler also put in watches. Diaz refused to give up her wedding ring. Nobody talked about asking the President to chip in.

Diaz said, "How much longer?"

Trenton checked his watch. "Maybe ten, fifteen minutes."

Diaz put her hand out, stirred the collection a bit. "Ran through a lot of scenarios when I was at the Rowley Training Center, years back. This is one that sure never came up."

Trenton said, "When we get through this, I'm sure they'll change the syllabus."

"If," Diaz said.

"When," Trenton said. "We get moving, we get Harrier underground, our job is done."

"Then what, boss?" Diaz demanded. "Have him make a speech saying everything's now cool? That the drones are swept from the skies? That those who sent them over here have decided to hold hands with us and sing 'Kumbaya'?"

"Not our job," Carlson said sharply. "Way above our pay grade."

"Maybe it shouldn't be."

Trenton said, "What's on your mind, Diaz?"

She defiantly looked at Carlson and then Trenton. "We're pledged and vowed to protect the Man, whoever he or she is. Fine. But what if the Man isn't worth it? We in this detail, we've seen how he operates, how he treats people, how he dumped us into this mess. Now I'm supposed to get killed, leave my kids without a mom, just like that? With everything falling apart? You and Carlson, you're swinging bachelors, you don't care, but—"

Trenton said, "Forget it."

Diaz said, "What I'm saying is—"

"Forget it."

She paused, and said, "What, you planning to pull a Tim McCarthy? The guy who took a bullet for Reagan back in '81? Gonna catch an air-to-ground drone missile with your teeth?"

"I'm doing my job," he said. "And so will you, and everyone else."

Trenton stared at Diaz, wondered what she would say next, when Carlson spoke up.

"Something's coming up the road."

Trenton called out, "Tyler! Down here now!"

They clustered together at the doorway. Trenton saw a vehicle moving slowly, parking lights on, gingerly moving toward the cottage.

"Tyler, you cover me," he said. "If you see me rub the back of my head, you'll know it's trouble. If shooting breaks out, then you'll really know it's trouble. Diaz and Carlson, go upstairs, help Harrier out of bed. If there's shooting, get him out, head into the woods."

"And do what?" Diaz asked.

"Your job."

Trenton took a deep breath, walked outside, the air crisp and cold, the moonlight illuminating everything pretty well, especially with his night vision the way it was. He took his time. The vehicle looked to be an Oldsmobile, rusting, dented. A beater car.

Definitely not a county police cruiser.

He waited.

The Oldsmobile rolled to a stop.

Engine grumbling.

The driver's door opened up. The dome light had been disabled. Smart.

A familiar voice from the car. "You the guy who called about section twelve?"

Sweet relief flooded through him like a warm, comforting spring.

"That's right," he said.

"Then move your ass," she said.

"Best thing I've heard all day," Trenton said. "Come on in, we'll settle up."

The woman was in her fifties, heavyset, black wool cap on her blond hair, wearing a brown down jacket, blue jeans, and work boots. The parka was unzipped, revealing a shoulder holster containing a semiautomatic pistol. Trenton took her to the kitchen table and she scooped up the jewelry without saying a word. Tyler went back upstairs, shotgun still in hand. Diaz and Carlson stayed behind.

"I was surprised to see your car," Trenton said. "I was expecting a cruiser. All your cruisers out on calls?"

She shook her head. "No, they're all in the county garage. They've got too many chips and GPS tracking devices in them to use safely. Besides, I learned my lesson when I was a kid."

Carlson said, "What lesson was that?"

The woman rubbed her hands together. "From the TV footage when Katrina hit New Orleans. Most of the city was cut off. Rumors, mass chaos, shootings. There was a news reporter standing on a bridge next to a dead body. New Orleans police cruiser came by, the reporter flagged him down, and he asked the cop to do something about the dead guy. The cop sped away." She shrugged. "That wasn't going to happen to me, by God. If I drove here in a county cruiser, wouldn't have gotten more than a half mile before being stopped by people looking for help. These days, you're on your own, sorry to say that."

"Give us a minute or two, we'll be ready to go," Trenton said.

She raised her head like she was trying to peer through the plaster ceiling. "So, the President, he's really up there?"

Trenton ignored her question, started thinking about things. "Wait here. We'll be back. Diaz, come with me. Carlson, stay behind."

He went up to the bedroom, with Diaz close behind, and Tyler was there, shotgun leaning against a bureau. Candles on the bureau gave off a flickering light. "Sir," Tyler called out. "Time to go. We really need to move."

Diaz helped her pull the covers off, and the President's wrinkled dark blue suit was revealed, along with muddy black shoes. He had on a white shirt with no necktie. He coughed and coughed, and he seemed to have aged even more since Trenton had last seen him.

Tyler said, "Sir, let us help you up."

The President extended an arm and Tyler started pulling him off the bed. Trenton stepped forward, grabbed a cold hand, started to help as well, and the President's shirtsleeve and coat slipped up his wrist. Trenton spotted something on the wrist. A splotch?

A small scar?

Oh, no.

Shit, no.

Trenton said, "Diaz. Get over here. Right away."

Diaz came over. The President looked up at him.

He asked, "Sir, please, have you been chipped?"

"Eh?"

"Has a chip, a tracking device, been inserted in your wrist?"

The President looked confused. "I . . . I don't think so. I mean, some months ago I received some routine booster shots. . . . I thought it was odd that one went into my wrist. . . ."

Diaz said, "Oh, shit."

"Check it out," Trenton said.

Diaz said, "Excuse me, sir." She took his wrist, pulled the shirtsleeve up further, gently stroking and manipulating his skin. She paused, looked up, her face stunned, and Trenton didn't have to ask the question.

Tyler said, "You have got to be shitting me. And we didn't know?"

Bitterness in her voice, Diaz said, "Need-to-know. Even though we're in the PPD, somebody thought we didn't have the need to know. And those who *did* have the need to know are probably all dead now."

Tyler said, voice shaking, "All this goddamn time we've been dumping vehicles, weapons, and our own chips to protect Harrier, and it turns out he's been merrily transmitting all along. Christ on a crutch."

"Take it out," Trenton said. "Now."

Diaz said, "Damn it, somebody could be tracking him even as we're sitting here. We can be dead in seconds."

Tyler said, "What, you want to run away?"

"It's a thought," Diaz said angrily. "We were never told that POTUS was chipped. We've been betrayed. Why should we repay that betrayal?"

The President coughed and coughed some more, his breathing ragged.

Trenton saw it all slipping away. "Chances are, his chip is high up the encryption ladder. Unlike our vehicles and our own chips. His chip hasn't been hacked or detected yet. Diaz, grab your gear. Then cut the chip out."

Diaz flashed her eyes at him, stood up, went downstairs, feet sounding heavy on the wooden steps.

Tyler looked over. "You think she's coming back?"

"If not, you've just been promoted."

"Lucky me."

Harrier's voice was weak. "Is . . . is something wrong?"

Footsteps back up the stairs. Trenton briefly closed his eyes in relief.

"Sir," Diaz said, coming up to him on the bed, black case in her hand. "I'm so sorry, but this is going to hurt."

Some minutes later, the President had stopped sobbing and was helped to his feet. Diaz took the small propane torch out of the bag and Trenton said, "Hold on." He reached over, scooped up the bloody gauze with the President's chip in the middle.

"What the hell are you doing? I was about to scorch that."

"Another minute or two won't make a difference."

"The hell it won't."

"And debating will only make it worse. Get a move on."

He and Diaz worked to get the President down the stairs. Tyler went ahead, shotgun in hand. In the kitchen the woman whistled and said, "By God, it *is* him."

"Shut up," Trenton said. "Let's get going."

"Where to?" the woman asked.

"Mount Spencer," Trenton said. "A government facility is located there."

The woman laughed. "Only thing at that mountain is a farm with high fences around it, belonging to the Department of Agriculture."

"The President likes potatoes," Trenton said. "Outside."

He and Carlson each held one of the President's arms, helped maneuver him up the snowy walkway to the car. He turned once to Trenton and said, "One of the last, aren't you. One of the last."

Trenton didn't say anything.

They put him in the rear and the woman went to the driver's seat, and Diaz said, "Not to be ungrateful or anything, but we have a number problem here. There's four of us and only room for three more."

Carlson said, "For Christ's sake, we could all squeeze in."

Tyler said, "She's right, that's a problem. We pack the car, we're going to be conspicuous, going to be slow."

"Got it covered," Trenton said, breathing in the sharp air, still hearing the thrum of deadly motors overhead in the darkness. "I'm staying behind."

Carlson said, "Doesn't make sense. I'm low man here and you're head of the detail. You've got to go."

"No, I'm staying."

Diaz said, "You thinking of pulling a Jenkins?"

"No," Trenton said. "I'm staying behind, but I need you to do one thing before you leave." He held out his arm, and with his other hand held out the gauze containing the President's chip.

"You're going to put the President's chip in my wrist."

After he slapped down the discussion and comments, Trenton said, "We don't have time. These chips either have a radioactive source or some thermodynamic process from the body that powers them. I'm not a goddamn scientist. I'm a Secret Service special agent, trying to protect my charge. If we torch his chip, then some hacker might figure this was the last place Harrier was, and decide to hit any moving vehicle in the area. If we leave it behind, it might run out of power because it's left his body, with the same result. A hacker will then hit a moving vehicle in the area. Either way, the best chance to get Harrier to safety is for me to stay behind. With his chip in me."

Tyler and Carlson both tried to say something but Diaz talked to the driver, retrieved a flashlight and her black bag, and in a few minutes, the job was done on the hood of the Oldsmobile.

So many things on his mind, Trenton hardly even felt it.

With her bag packed away, Trenton said to Diaz, "You're now senior officer. Do your job. Get the President to safety."

The driver's flashlight was on, allowing Trenton to see tears in the woman's eyes. "You can count on me."

Trenton lied to her. "Never had any doubt."

With everyone gone, Trenton felt so very alone. He only stayed in the cottage for a few minutes before he decided to leave. The unknown family who deserted this cottage had provided him, his detail, and Harrier with a place of safety. He wouldn't repay the favor by staying inside as a target.

He walked out through the snow, hands in his coat pockets, now noticing the incessant throbbing in his wrist. In his mind's eye he saw the crowded Oldsmobile move slowly and safely away, heading up to the FEMA retreat center that pretended to be a farm.

Trenton stopped a few yards out on the frozen lake, looked up again at the hard stars. Memories came to him, especially those bull sessions that always popped up when your job was done and the drinking began. There was always a little game that was played, about who you were, how tough you were, what kind of agent you'd turn out to be if and when the shooting started.

Would you be Lancer's driver, the guy driving JFK's limousine in Dallas, or would you be McCarthy, Rawhide's agent in DC back in '81?

Poor Lancer's driver. When he heard Lee Harvey Oswald's first shot, the story was that he thought it was a firecracker. A fucking firecracker. How history would have changed if he had put the pedal to the metal, or swung the steering wheel hard left and then hard right, spoiling Oswald's aim for follow-up shots.

And there was McCarthy. First shot fired by Hinckley, he didn't think it was a firecracker. He spun around, splayed his arms and legs to make a big target, and he took one for Reagan, aka Rawhide. The starfish position, it was called.

He stamped his feet. Checked his watch. Give them an hour, at least, to get up to the mountain.

At least an hour.

He smiled to himself, looked up at the moving lights and shadows and stars, held his arms out wide, and waited.

the promise of space

JAMES PATRICK KELLY

Sometimes getting back together with your ex is harder than at other times . . . and a lot stranger!

James Patrick Kelly made his first sale in 1975 and since has gone on to become one of the most respected and popular writers to enter the field. Although Kelly has had some success with novels, especially with Wildlife, *he has perhaps had more impact to date as a writer of short fiction, with stories such as "Solstice," "The Prisoner of Chillon," "Glass Cloud," "Mr. Boy," "Pogrom," "Home Front," "Undone," and "Bernardo's House," and is often ranked among the best short story writers in the business. His story "Think Like a Dinosaur" won him a Hugo Award in 1996, as did his story "10¹⁶ to 1," in 2000. Kelly's first solo novel, the mostly ignored* Planet of Whispers, *came out in 1984. It was followed by* Freedom Beach, *a mosaic novel written in collaboration with John Kessel, and then by another solo novel,* Look Into the Sun, *as well as a chapbook novella* Burn. *His short work has been collected in* Think Like a Dinosaur *and* Strange But Not a Stranger. *His most recent books are a series of anthologies coedited with John Kessel:* Feeling Very Strange: The Slipstream Anthology, The Secret History of Science Fiction, Digital Rapture: The Singularity Anthology, Rewired: The Post-Cyberpunk Anthology, *and* Nebula Awards Showcase 2012. *Kelly was born in Minneola, New York, and now lives with his family in Nottingham, New Hampshire. He has a Web site at www.JimKelly.net, and reviews Internet-related matters for* Asimov's Science Fiction.

CAPTURE 06/15/2051,
KERWIN HOSPITAL ICU, 09:12:32

. . . and my writer pals used to tease that I married Captain Kirk.

A clarification, please? Are you referring to William Shatner, who died in 2023? Or is this Chris Pine, who was cast in the early remakes? It appears he has retired. Perhaps you mean the new one? Jools Bear?

No, you. Kirk Anderson. People used to call you that, remember? First man to set foot on Phobos? Pilot on the Mars landing team? Captain Kirk.

I do not understand. Clearly I participated in those missions since they are on the record. But I was never captain of anything.

A joke, Andy. They were teasing you. It's why you hated your first name.

Noted. Go on.

No, this is impossible. I feel like I'm talking to an intelligent fucking database, not my husband. I don't know where to begin with you.

Please, Zoe. I cannot do this without you. Go on.

Okay, okay, but do me a favor? Use some contractions, will you? Contractions are your friends.

Noted.

Do you know when we met?

I haven't yet had the chance to review that capture. We were married in 2043. Presumably we met before that?

Not much before. Where were you on Saturday, May 17, 2042? Check your captures.

The capture shows that I flew from Spaceways headquarters at Spaceport America to the LaGuardia Hub in New York and spent the day in Manhattan at the Metropolitan Museum. That night I gave the keynote address at the Nebula Awards banquet in the Crown Plaza Hotel but my caps were disengaged. The Nebula is awarded each year by the World Science Fiction Writers . . . .

I was nominated that year for best livebook, *Shadows on the Sun.* You came up to me at the reception, said you were a fan. That you had all five of my Sidewise series in your earstone when you launched for Mars that first time. You joked you had a thing for Nacky Martinez. I was thrilled and flattered. After all, you were top of the main menu, one of the six hero marsnauts. Things I'd only imagined, you'd actually done. And you'd read my work and you were flirting with me and, holy shit, you were Captain Kirk. When people—friends, famous writers—tried to break into our conversation, they just bounced off us. Nobody remembers who won what award that night, but lots of people still talk about how we locked in.

I just looked it up. You lost that Nebula.

Yeah. Thanks for reminding me.

You had on a hat.

A hat? Okay. But I always wore hats back then. It was a way to stand out, part of my brand—for all the good it did me. My hair was a three-act tragedy anyway, so I wore a lot of hats.

This one was a bowler hat. It was blue—midnight blue. With a powder blue band. Thin, I remember the hatband was very thin.

Maybe. I don't remember that one. Nice try, though.

Tell me more. What happened next?

Jesus, this is so wrong . . . No, I'm sorry, Andy. Give me your hand. You always had such delicate hands. Such clever fingers.

I can still remember that my mom had an old Baldwin upright piano that she wanted me to learn to play, but my hands were too small. You're crying. Are you crying?

I am not. Just shut up and listen. This isn't easy and I'm only saying it because maybe the best part of you is still trapped in there like they claim and just maybe this augment really can set it free. So, we were sitting at different tables at the banquet but after it was over, you found me again and asked if I wanted to go out for drinks. We escaped the hotel, looking for a place to be alone, and found a night-shifted Indonesian restaurant with a bar a couple of blocks away. It was called Fatty Prawn or Fatty Crab—Fatty Something. We sat at the bar and switched from alcohol to inhalers and talked. A lot. Pretty much the rest of the night, in fact. Considering that you were a man and famous and ex-Air Force, you were a good listener. You wanted to know how hard it was to get published and where I got my plots and who I like to read. I was impressed that you had read a lot of the classic science fiction old-timers like Kress and LeGuin and Bacigalupi. You told me what I got wrong about living in space, and then raved about stuff in my books that you thought nobody but spacers knew. Around four in the morning we got hungry and since you'd never had Indonesian before, we split a gado-gado salad with egg and tofu. I spent too much time deconstructing my divorce and you were polite about yours. You said your ex griped about how you spent too much time in space, and I made a joke about how Kass would have said the same thing about me. I asked if you were ever scared out there and you said sure, and that landings were worse than the launches because you had so much time leading up to them. You used to wake up on the outbound trips in a sweat. To change the subject, I told you about waking up with entire scenes or story outlines in my head and how I had to get up in the middle of the night and write them down or I would lose them. You made a crack about wanting to see that in person. The restaurant was about to close for the morning and, by that time, dessert sex was definitely on the menu, so I asked if you ever got horny on a mission. That's how I found out that one of the side effects of the antiradiation drugs was low testosterone levels. We established that you were no longer taking them. I would have invited you back to my room right then only you told me that you had to catch a seven-twenty flight back to El Paso. There still might have been enough time, except that I was rooming with Rachel van der Haak, and, when we had gotten high before the banquet, we had promised each other we'd steer clear of men while our shields were down. And of course, when I thought about it, there was the awkward fact that you were twenty years older than I was. A girl has got to wonder what's up with her when she wants to take daddy to bed.

I am nineteen years and three months older than you.

And then there was your urgency. I mean, you had me at Mars, Mr. Space Hero, but I had the sense that you wanted way more from me than I had to give. All I had in mind was a test drive, but it seemed as if you were already thinking about making a down payment. When you said you could cancel an appearance on Newsmelt so you could be back in New York in three days, it was a serious turn-on, but I was also worried. Blowing off one of the top news sites? For me? Why? I guessed maybe you were running out of time before your next mission. I didn't realize that you were . . . .

Go on.

No, I can't. I just can't—how do I do this? Turn the augment off.

Zoe, please.

You hear me? That was the deal. They promised whenever I wanted.

CAPTURE 06/15/2051, KERWIN HOSPITAL ICU, 09:37:18, AUGMENT DISENGAGED BY REQUEST

Andy? Look at me, Andy. Over here. Good. Who am I, Andy?

You are . . . it's something about science fiction. And a blue hat.

What's my name?

Come close. Let me look at you . . . oh, it's on the tip of my tongue. Nacky Martinez? First officer of the Starship *Sidewise*?

She's a character, Andy. Made up. Someone I wrote about.

You're a writer?

CAPTURE 06/17/2051, KERWIN HOSPITAL ASSISTED CARE FACILTY, 14:47:03

. . . because I was too infatuated to be suspicious about your secret back then. I know you don't remember this, Andy, but I was stupid in love with you when we were first married. Maybe the augment can't see that, but anyone who looks at your captures can. On the record, as you would say. So, yeah, the fact that you always wore caps and recorded almost everything that happened to you didn't bother me back then. I guess I told myself that it was some reputation management scheme that Spaceways had ordered up. And of course, you were writing the sequel to your memoir. What do Mr. and Ms. Space Hero do on their days off? Why look, they sit together on the couch when they write! And she still uses her fingers to type—isn't that quaint, a science fiction writer still pounding a keyboard in the era of thought recognition!

You never published that book.

No.

Or any other. Why?

You know, people message me about that all the time, like it was some kind of tragedy. I had something to say when I was young and naive. I said it. And pretty damn well: eight livebooks worth. Fifty novas. It's just that after I met you, I needed to make the most of our time together. And since you launched into the Vincente Event, I've been busy being the good wife.

I was the best qualified pilot, Zoe. And I was already compromised, so I had the least to lose. In a crisis like that, there were no easy answers. I consulted with Spaceways and we weighed the tradeoffs and we reached a decision. I had friends on that orbital. Drew Bantry . . .

Drew was already dead. He just hadn't fallen down yet. And you were not a tradeoff, Andy. You were my fucking husband.

I can see now how hard it must have been for you.

Oh, you saw it then, too. Which is why you never asked my permission, because you knew . . .

Go on.

What the hell were we talking about? How I had no suspicions about what the captures meant. That you were sick. I remember thinking how boring ten thousand hours of unedited recordings were going to be. Even to us, even when we were old. Old and forgetful . . . .

Zoe?

I'm fine. I'm just not feeling very brave today. Anyway, I did have a problem with all the captures of us making love. I mean, the first couple of times, I'll grant you it was a turn-on. We'd lose ourselves in bed, and then afterwards watch ourselves doing it and sometimes we were so beautifully in sync that we'd get hot and go back for seconds. But what bothered me was that you were capturing us watching the captures. I didn't get why you would do that. When I realized that recording wasn't just a once-in-a-while kink, that you wanted to capture us every time we had sex, it wasn't erotic anymore. It was kind of creepy.

I can't locate any sex captures after 2045. Did we stop having sex?

No. I just made you check the caps at the bedroom door. So stop looking. You want to know what we were like back then, try scanning some of our private book clubs. We'd both read the same book and then we'd go out to dinner at a nice restaurant and talk about it. I remember being surprised at some of your choices. *The Marvelous Land of Oz. Lolita. Wolf Hall. A Visit From the Goon Squad.* They didn't seem like the kinds of reading an Air Force jock would choose. You were a Hemingway and Heinlein kind of guy.

Was I trying to impress you?

I don't know why. I was already plenty impressed. Maybe you were trying to send me a message with all of those plots about secret pasts and transformations.

Go on. This was where? When?

At first in Brooklyn, where I was living when we met. There's another reason I should have been suspicious your urgency. You claimed you didn't care where we lived as long as we spent as much time as possible together. Wasn't true—you hated cities. But most of my friends were in New York and most of yours had moved to space or Mars. Your folks were dead and your sister had disappeared into some Digitalist coop, waiting for the Singularity. So when my mother died and left me the house in Bedford, we moved up there in the spring of 2045. You had the second installment of your book deal to write and when I switched to your agent, I started seeing celebrity-level advances too, so there was plenty of money. By then you were showing early symptoms. You claimed you'd left Spaceways, although you still flew out here to Kerwin five or six times a year for therapy. It seemed to be working, you said we would still have years together. My mom had been into flowers but she had an asparagus patch and some raspberries and you started your first vegetable garden that summer. You were good at it, said you liked it better than space hydroponics. Spinach and lettuce and asparagus in the spring, then beans and corn and summer squash and tomatoes and melons. You were happy, I think. I know I was.

CAPTURE 06/25/2051, KERWIN HOSPITAL ASSISTED CARE FACILTY, 16:17:53

. . . you were so skeptical about the Singularity is why.

The Kurzweil augmentation has nothing to do with the Singularity.

Yeah, sure. It's just a cognitive prosthesis, *la-la*. A life experience database, *la-la*. An AI-mediated memory enchancement that may help restore your loved one's mental competence *la-la-la-dee-da*. I've browsed all the sites, Andy. Besides, I was writing about this shit before Ray Kurzweil actually uploaded.

Ray Kurzweil is dead. I'm still alive.

Are you, Andy? Are you sure about that?

I don't know why you are being so cruel, Zoe.

Because you made so many decisions about us without telling me. Maybe you didn't know just how sick you were when we met, but you could easily have found out. I had a right to know. And maybe you were hoping that you'd never get that call from Spaceways, but you knew exactly what you would do if it did come.

I was an astronaut, Zoe. That was never a secret.

No, what was a secret was all that fucked-up cosmic ray research. Because nobody but crazy people with a death wish would ever have volunteered to go to space if they knew that there was no real protection against getting your telomeres burned off by the radiation. Sure, you can duck and cover from a solar flare, but what about the gajillions of ultra-high energy ions? Theoretically you can generate a magnetic shield. Or maybe you can stuff your astronauts with antiradiation wonder drugs? But just in case it doesn't work, better make sure that everyone on the Mars crew is over forty. That way if Captain Kirk falls apart in twenty or thirty years, Spaceways won't look so bad.

Go on.

I will. Maybe you hadn't checked out the secret radiation assessments from the first Mars mission when we first met. Maybe you didn't want to know. But once I was your wife, I did. Let me read the executive summary to you. "Exposure to radiation during the mission has had significant short and long impacts on the central nervous systems of all crew members. Despite best mitigation practices, whole body effective doses ranged from .4 to .7 sieverts. Galactic cosmic radiation in the form of high-mass, energetic ions destroyed an average of 4% of the crew's cells, while 13% of critical brain regions have likely been compromised. Reports of short-term impairments of behavior and cognition were widely noted throughout the three-year mission. Longitudinal studies of the astronaut corps point to a significant increase in risk of degenerative brain diseases. In particular, there appears to have been an acceleration of plaque pathology associated with Alzheimer's disease." Let's do the math, Andy. You get an estimated dose of between .4 to .7 sieverts during your first mission and you go to Mars twice. So call it a sievert and change. Which is why you were one grounded astronaut.

All that's on the record.

What's EPA's maximum yearly dose for a radiation worker here on Earth?

I don't have immediate access to that data. I can look it up.

Yes, you can—it's on the record. Fifty millisieverts. How about for emergency workers involved in a lifesaving operation?

Zoe, I . . . .

Two hundred and fifty millisieverts.

There are always risks.

For which you make tradeoffs, I get that. So the tradeoff here is X number of years of your life for two tickets to Mars. Which you decided before you met me, so

I'll give you a pass on that. Once you walked me through it, I sort of got how that was the price you paid to become who you wanted to be. Although you waited long enough to let me in on your little secret. But that wasn't your last tradeoff. Because Spaceways fell down on their project management during the outfitting of Orbital Seven. They didn't lift enough solar flare shelters to house everybody on the construction crew. So when Professor Vincente predicted an X2 class flare that would cook half the people onboard in a storm of hot protons, management turned to sixty-year old Captain Kirk, even though he'd been grounded. They pointed out that since he didn't have all that much time before the Alzheimer's plaques chewed what was left of his memory, maybe he might consider riding the torch one last time to ferry an emergency shelter up to save their corporate asses. Or maybe our Space Hero checked in all on his own and volunteered for their fucking suicide mission.

It wasn't a suicide mission , Zoe. I came back.

And here you are, Andy. And here I am. But it's not working.

CAPTURE 06/30/2051, KERWIN HOSPITAL ICU, 11:02:53

. . . or are you too busy with your life review? Ten thousand hours of captures is a lot to digest, even on fast-forward.

The record is eleven thousand two hundred and eighty-four hours long, not including the current capture.

Noted. Find anything worth bookmarking?

It would be a dull movie if it wasn't all about me.

I heard about your ex yesterday on Newsmelt. I'm sorry. I didn't realize she'd emigrated to Mars.

Apparently she wanted to get to space as much as I did. I don't know why I didn't know that. It's odd, but none of the pix and vids I have look like her.

You remember her then?

Just flashes, but they're very vivid. Like she was lit up by a lightning strike.

They're talking about bringing the rest of the colonists back home.

Maybe. But they'll have to handcuff them and drag them kicking and screaming onto the relief ships—I know those people. And why bother? Many of them won't survive the trip back.

Space will kill you any which way it can. You told me that on our third date.

I try not to pay attention. It's been a long time since there's been any good news from outer space. I think we need to start over on Mars. The thing to do is capture a comet, hollow it out and use it as a colony ship. The ice shields you from cosmic rays on the outbound. Send the colonists down in landers and then crash the comet. Solves both the water and the radiation problem.

Capture a comet? And how the hell do we do that? With a tractor beam? A magic lasso?

Get your science fiction friends working on it. If it's crazy enough, the engineers will come sniffing around.

I'll see what I can do. I met the Zhangs on the way in today. I thought I was your only visitor. We had a nice chat. And the baby was cute. What's her name again?

Andee. A-N-D-double-E

That's what I thought they said. After you.

Kristen was lucky. They pushed her to the front of the line so she was one of the first into the shelter. The last three in got a significant dose. One of them died on the way back down.

Drew Bantry.

They were his people. He waited until they were all safe.

You and he saved a lot of lives that day, Captain Kirk. It's on the record for all to see.

Enough, Zoe. What do you have for me today?

Apologies.

Go on.

I'm sorry for the way I spoke to you last time. That's why I missed the last few visits. I don't trust myself to say the right thing anymore. I can't filter out my feelings when I see you like this. I just blurt. Spew. It's not good.

Noted.

But here's the thing. I don't think I'll be accessing your augment after you're . . . gone. Dead. You know, now I can visit the hospital here, and see you. Your face, your body, arms, hands. But some avatar, no. It's too hard. There have been times the last few weeks when I felt like you're here with me, but that's only because I want you back. But mostly I don't think this thing that talks to me is you. I'm sorry.

Why not?

There's still too much missing, even if the augment can review your captures and all that input from before you started wearing the caps. Yes, we can talk about our lives together, but I still have to tell you things you should know. And now you're cracking jokes, so it's even harder. How can I tell whether what's sad or happy or angry is you or clever algorithms? I don't know, Andy. When are you going to say I love you? How will I know whether you really do, or if it's just something else you needed to be reminded of?

I do, Zoe. Here, I'll turn the augment off, so you can hear it from me. From this body, as you say. These lips.

No, honey, you don't need to . . . .

CAPTURE 06/30/2051, KERWIN HOSPITAL ICU, 11:15:18, AUGMENT DISENGAGED BY REQUEST

Okay? Here I am. And I know who you are. I do. You're my famous wife, the writer. Nacky Martinez. You want to go. I don't want you to go. Give me your hand.

Aye, Captain.

Stay with me. Will you do that?

For a while.

And write more books. You know, about your adventures in space. That's important. And maybe . . . could get me my snacks? The food here is horrible. You know the ones. Mom always used to make banana slices with a smear of peanut butter when I got home from school. My snacks. Are you crying, Nacky? You're crying.

Yes.

quicken

DAMIEN BRODERICK

Stories about the dead rising to walk the Earth again have filled movie and television screens and the pages of innumerable books and stories for years, but here, in an authorized sequel to Robert Silverberg's famous story "Born with the Dead," is a take on the living dead story much more sophisticated and inventive than the usual "Arrgh! Braaiiiins!" stuff, one where the line between the quick and the dead is blurry and sometimes difficult to define, and the relationships that form between the living and the dead are complex and problematic—and sometimes tragic.

Australian writer, editor, futurist, and critic Damien Broderick, a senior fellow in the School of Cultural Communications at the University of Melbourne, made his first sale in 1964 to John Carnell's anthology New Writings in SF 1. *In the decades that followed, he kept up a steady stream of fiction, nonfiction, futurist speculations, and critical work that has won him multiple Ditmar and Aurealis awards. He sold his first novel,* Sorcerer's World, *in 1970; it was later reissued in a rewritten version in the United States as* The Black Grail. *Broderick's other books include the novels* The Dreaming Dragons, The Judas Mandala, Transmitters, Striped Holes, *and* The White Abacus. *His many short stories have been collected in* A Man Returned, The Dark Between the Stars, Uncle Bones: Four Science Fiction Novellas, *and, most recently,* The Qualia Engine: Science Fiction Stories. *He also wrote: the visionary futurist classic* The Spike: How Our Lives Are Being Transformed by Rapidly Advancing Technology, *a critical study of science fiction;* Reading by Starlight: Postmodern Science Fiction; *edited the nonfiction anthology* Year Million: Science at the Far Edge of Knowledge; *and edited the SF anthology* Earth Is But a Star: Excursions Through Science Fiction to the Far Future *and three anthologies of Australian science fiction,* The Zeitgeist Machine, Strange Highways, *and* Matilda at the Speed of Light. *His most recent publication is a nonfiction book written with Paul Di Filippo,* Science Fiction: The 101 Best Novels 1985–2010, *the novel* Quipu, *and the novels* Human's Burden *with Rory Barnes and* Post Mortal Syndrome *with Barbara Lamar.*

1

We must die as egos and be born again in the swarm, not separate
and self-hypnotized, but individual and related.
—*Henry Miller*, Sexus: The Rosy Crucifixion

"I am called Dr. Imam Hassan Sabbāh," said the man in the Islamic skullcap, a
white embroidered taqiyah. "You may address me as Guidefather, Professor Klein."

Klein uttered the vocable denoting "Thank you, sir" in the register of submission. Even now, after these months as a dead, he remained surprised by his fluency
in the swift argot shared by his postmortem fellows. Had he learned it, in the way
children acquire a vernacular, simply by interacting with other deads, being in their
midst, listening to their conversation, climbing a ladder from baby-simple to adult-
complexified? No. After an initial week or two of confusion and difficulty in San Diego Cold Town, the new language had emerged spontaneously from his lips, driven
presumably by some immense rearrangement of grammar and lexicon from Spanish,
English, German, French, his linguistic X-bar trees. All that apparatus of speech
and thought tucked away inside the folds of his revived brain. But when had it occurred, this Rosetta Stone of the reborn, this downloaded Berlitz course? He assumed it must have been a side effect of rekindling, or perhaps (was this too paranoiac?)
it had been literally stamped upon his vulnerable defunct cortex during the four unconscious weeks in suspension and repair following his death. All he knew for sure
was that he and this Muslim Guidefather were equally glib in their accelerated and
concise tongue.

"I am here at the invitation of your staff, but nothing has been explained," he
added. "How may I serve the Conclave?" Five tonal phonemes. However it had
been done, it was an impressive accomplishment.

"You are a gifted man, Jorge. It seems that you resist the temptation of ennui,
cafard, the sport of absurdity, indulgence in the iconography of mortality."

"A temptation gladly acceded to by my wife, Sybille," Klein said, bored by the
words even as he spoke. No resentment. It was as remarkable, in its way, as his magical acquisition of the music of the dead. Had they rewired his amygdala, his emotional keyboard, his flux of neurotransmitters? No doubt, but Klein knew himself the
merest amateur in the sciences of cognition and neurology. Such speculations were
useless, then, as well as dull. Still, some small part of his well-trained mind gnawed
at the question and its implications. He could not be bothered trying to still it.

"Your *ex*-wife," said the Guidefather. A sharp one-syllable rebuke. You have been
here long enough to know better than that, Klein, the man did not need to say.

"Yes, yes. All bonds broken, I am fully aware of this. Perhaps I resent her flight
from all responsibility." The words clattered in his mouth. Really, he didn't care what
Sybille did. His obsession with her was expunged, their obliterated decade, their lost
Jorge-and-Sybille. Wasn't it?

"The transition of the rekindled leaves us stranded in absurdity," Sabbāh said, as
if it were an admission. Klein watched him, surprised. The man's hands lay flat on

his thighs; his mouth, through the beard and mustache, suggested a restrained amusement. "Yet we have built the Cold Towns from nothing, we conduct our battles with the pests of the Treasury and Internal Revenue, we pursue our research and marketing. We are not monks, withdrawn from the world, even when we withdraw from the world into our sanctuaries. You follow me."

"I believe so. You hope to enlist me as . . . how should I put it . . . middle management."

Sabbāh smiled. "Not quite, Professor. As an emissary, eventually. For now, as an Acolyte. Better yet, an Adjutant. The Conclave wishes you to reenter the world of the warms and learn in detail how we are regarded. What risks we face. How we might best advance our cause and pursue our goals."

Do not ask direct questions, Klein recalled. Dolorosa's advice, that shabby outcast. Still, though that edict now seemed entirely natural and proper, he forced himself.

"And what are those goals, Guidefather?"

"You will learn this in good time." The man rose, made no attempt to take Jorge Klein's hand. "That will be all for now. We shall dine this evening in the Rojo Diablo restaurant at eight. You will be prompt."

Irritated, Klein remained seated. "You presume too easily, Guidefather."

"You were dead, now you walk. Payment is due to your fellows."

"My insurance covered your hefty fee for my rekindling. For my ex-wife's also. Now the Conclave holds attached all my assets—my property, my savings, my future income. You can ask no more."

Hassan Sabbāh walked to the door, opened it, stood waiting for Klein to rise.

"You have paid in the currency of the living," he said. "Now we seek your cooperation, freely given. Nothing will be forced or extorted. Good morning, Dr. Klein. I shall see you tonight."

"Very well," Klein said, and rose. He followed Sabbāh into the dreary, unornamented hallway. In silence, they parted at an intersection and he made his way to his simple room. His breathing remained calm, the infusion of respirocytes flooded through his vascular system carrying oxygen to his renovated and reconstructed brain, along with its unknown cargo of neuromodulators. You are dead, he thought. And now you walk. You are without family or spouse, except for this company of the deceased. Yes, your parents remain alive, and your sister Hester, and your cousins in America and Argentina, but to them you are truly dead. They have sat *shiva* for seven days in your memory, and now to them you are as good as buried, alive only in their memories—memories poisoned by your apostasy from the world of the warms. He went into his room and lay down on the simple bed, eyes open, gazing at the plastic meaninglessness of the world.

Rolling Stone's I See Dead People 101

I've never seen any deads younger than maybe 20, or older than 50 or 60. What's up with that?

Maybe it's built into the process (whatever that is). As usual, the Conclave of the Rekindled refuse to divulge any details, but top gerontologists and neuroscientists suggest that rekindling a postmortem child would, like, upset the balance of the universe—or at least mess with the kid's developmental trajectory.

And maybe old people are too far gone. The deads are probably working on it in their labs. If they have labs.

How that kid thing would cash out is anyone's guess. Maybe the Cold Towns have special schools or dormitories for the, you know, differently dead. It doesn't sound like a lot of fun to be stuck at the size and age of six years old for the rest of eternity, or even for a few thousand years. (Nobody yet knows how long the dead will stay . . . well, "alive" isn't the right word. Active. Ambulant. Not-really-dead.)

Is it true that after they dry off, deads are gifted with a pile of gold equal to their weight?

Let us reason together. Suppose the average American adult weighs 180 lbs. Yes, that's an understatement and has been for decades, but the Grim Reset probably carved quite a bit of flab off of a lot of citizens. 180 lbs is 2880 ounces (31.1034768 grams to the Troy ounce, since you ask), and today's gold fix is $New17.67 per ounce. That'd be more than 50,000 Newbucks per dead, on average. Readers who remember the Bad Old Days probably still recalibrate that as five million USD. Per person.

How likely is that? Rounding off, we have 500 million citizens in the USA, more than half in the prime adult catchment area (like, not kids or olds). But not so many of those 280-Megs die and get rekindled—statisticians estimate about point one percent, and that's as fine-toothed as it gets, because the census doesn't count dead people. They're dead, right?

Still, that's maybe two hundred and fifty thousand humans eligible to stick their demortified paws out for their gratuity once they die. More than a trillion old USD/10 billion Newbucks. And where is that absurd pile of loot supposed to come from?

Mark this one: *Urban Legend.*

So who does *fund the Cold Towns? Those things are spreading like toadstools after a clammy rain. And now they're even taking over prime real estate in our city. Why, the ancient cathedral of—*

Calm down. People live where they like, especially when they can afford the real estate. You want to set up ghettoes? Get out of here!

Call it communism, if you like; call it Galt's Gulch meets Valentine Michael Smith. (You're *au fait* of the classics, right? No? Hit the download. We'll be here when you get back.) As far as we can tell—locked out here on the wrong side of their guarded gates—it looks as if the deads share their wealth in an egalitarian way that demands only as much in way of toil as each rekindled is prepared to offer. Machine service to the max.

Most of their community funding comes, of course, from their fabulous patents. Who did you suppose collects the dues for your household cool fusion power system, or the Paycell in your finger? The deads are different from you and me, Scott. They're smarter. And they're richer.

2

Barn's burnt down—
now
I can see the moon.

—*Mizuta Masahide (1657–1723)*

Sylvie, the young departmental manager, offered Klein a comfortable enough arm-chair in a nicely appointed anteroom off the large sixth floor Bunche Hall office currently occupied by Professor Bik Liu, Chair of UCLA's Department of History. Verboten to grad students and lesser creatures, this was the parking station, Klein reflected, for Business and First Class academics. Sylvie tapped, offered him coffee and a slice of her chocolate birthday cake, which he declined. She flushed, presumably dreading a faux pas, and retreated behind her systems display.

Klein examined the two familiar duck-hunting prints and one rather Lucian Freudish daubing—all grim mustards and murky khakis and shit-browns—of what he supposed was an American tourist couple gazing up at the ceiling of the Sistine Chapel. His lips quirked. The heavy quake-proof door opened, and Bik ushered him into her spacious sanctum, shook his hand with only minimal squeamishness, sat him in a less comfortable chair beside the mandatory wall of old books and journals, antique archival image of itself in an epoch of information storage at the scale of electrons and qubits. Hot afternoon Los Angeles light filtered through the wide solar-screened windows. Plainly Bik was flustered, and she was never flustered.

"Jorge, you look well," she said, and then bit her lip. Gaunt, deliberately gray haired, she was a decade older than Klein, and looked closer to twice that.

"For a dead guy," Klein said.

Bik colored slightly, a Lucian Freudish color. She ruled her domain with iron and sound judgment, but this was an intrusion from beyond the grave. Klein had to remind himself how few American warms ever met a dead.

"No need to lie about *my* looking well," she said. " I look like something the *chat* dragged in. Or the *chienne*."

He watched her eyes. She was a clown, he was a clown, all the world was a point-less pratfall into mud. China had no cats, he recalled, not any longer, even with the cornucopia that had followed upon the cool fusion rollout half a decade ago. Not many dogs, either.

"Well. I dare say you've been traveling?" Bik said.

"Yes, visiting the Cold Towns." Without changing his tone, Klein said, "You want me out, I take it?"

She cleared her throat. "You are more direct than I recall."

"We are less concerned with the niceties," he told her, "we deads. I understand you've had some difficulties yourself. I hope everything turned out well?" He had done his due diligence; Bik had suffered a serious cardiac attack six months earlier, and now had a new heart. The experience had diminished her.

"Not a big deal, Jorge. Autologous regrowth, no need for a transplant. So I suppose in a way we've been through the same wars."

"Actually, no," he said. "Not really."

After a silence, she said carefully, "You understand why I asked you to drop in today. I am regretful for the necessity, but the institutional governance—"

"I have no objection to forced retirement, but I do expect the department to allow me the privileges and status of professor emeritus."

"That can certainly be arranged. The university board has proposed a new title for rekindled scholars of your standing, Jorge."

"Yes. Professor mortuus." He showed his teeth. "I can live with that."

Again, a faint quiver in her surgically tightened upper eyelids, and a tight smile. "Very good. Do you still drink spirits, Jorge?"

"Of course. We eat, we drink, we sleep, we dream, I'm sure you've read the Sunday supplements. Some aspects of life we have put behind us, or are closed to our condition, but fortunately a good whiskey is not one of them."

Golden fluid caught a ray of light, swirled in the glass she handed him. Bik sipped her own. "You mean to continue your researches?"

"Into the Nazi epoch, the *Konzentrationslager*? Buchenwald, Dachau, Auschwitz-Birkenau? The millions murdered with no rekindling? No. I'm done with that. But what I am is a professor of contemporary history, Bik, and contemporary history is what has remade me in its likeness. Mortuus." He tasted the scotch. He might have been drinking turpentine. He put the glass on her desk and rose. "I shall study the deads. In due course, I shall lecture to your students on the topic."

At the door she took his hand again, and held it loosely. "I'm very pleased that we shan't lose you entirely, Jorge, and I speak personally as well as for the whole department. Give my love to—" She faltered again, and now her face took on an ashen tint. "I'm sorry. I'm sorry. But you do still see . . ." She broke off.

"Sybille? Rarely, Bik. Matthew, chapter 22, verse 30."

"Understood." She recited it from memory, as he'd know she would. Bik was not a woman of piety, not even a Christian, but this verse was now inscribed in the shell-shocked consciousness of the world of the warms. The intellectual warms, at least. O my prophetic soul. "'For when the dead rise, they will neither marry nor be given in marriage. In this respect they will be like the angels in heaven.'"

"Just so. Like an angel, Professor. Like an angel."

The young manager was waiting for him as he left the Chair's office. Her blouse, his sharp eyes noticed, was now unsealed at her sternum, open enough to show off a substantial portion of her golden brown breasts, their deep cleavage. Something avid in her gaze.

"Professor Klein—" she began, broke off. "I took your course on the rise of the Third Reich, five years ago. You won't remember."

He didn't. He regarded her coolly. She was breathing faster. Not fear of faux pas, then, as he'd supposed earlier, but some sort of perverse appetite?

"Of course I remember you. Sylvie, isn't it?"

She smiled, still nervous, but there was a bold amusement in her gaze. "I thought you were wonderful. I always had a . . . well, a crush. And then I heard you'd been rekindled." She turned away from him, looking back over her shoulder, checking the Chair's closed door, and back to Klein. "Have you ever played the President and the Temptress? Everyone's watching the series on stereo." And to Jorge Klein's astonishment, she leaned across her desk, took the hem of her skirt in both hands, and flipped it up. Her buttocks were round and smooth, divided by a startlingly crimson thong. Sylvie let the skirt fall, turning, and took up something long and leaf-brown from the desk. She proffered it. "We could go to Andrew Sinclair's office, he's away at the Aung San Suu Kyi colloquium."

No faintest stirring in his prick, no tightening of his balls. He looked back at her dispassionately, with just a touch of amusement. Slick Willy and Monica, eh? The uses of history.

"I'm sorry, Sylvie," he said.

She flushed again, licked her mouth, shook her head.

"I'm sorry, too, Professor Klein. I misunderstood. Please don't tell—"

"My lips," he said, "are sealed."

"Oh my god, I've made such a fool of myself."

"Not your fault, mine entirely. We are wondrously changed, we deads, and not always in a good way. Anyway, take your consolation from what old father Freud taught us."

Her flush had receded. She put the panatela back on the desk.

"Superego über alles?"

"That too," he said, amused. "No, Sigmund offered a more specific and relevant piece of advice. Sometimes a cigar is just a cigar."

The lovely young woman laughed loudly, and as she saw him out to the corridor pressed his hand. He felt nothing, nothing, nothing.

3

> There is no other God beside me; I kill and I make alive; I wound and I heal.
>
> —*Deuteronomy.* 32:39

> De damnandis blaspheme redanimatisque
> —*Papal Bull on the Condemnation and Excommunication*
> *of all blasphemous Heretics, known as the Conclave*
> *of the Rekindled, January 3, 2031*

Preamble

Of the damnable and blasphemously revivified, we proclaim our Condemnation.

Through the power given him from God, the Roman Pontiff has been appointed to administer spiritual and temporal punishments as each case severally deserves. The purpose of this is the repression of the wicked designs of misguided men, who have been so captivated by the debased impulse of their evil purposes as to forget the fear of the Lord, to set aside with contempt canonical decrees and apostolic commandments, and to dare to formulate new and false dogmas of sacred life and death, and to introduce the evil of "rebirth" after physical death—or to support, help and adhere to such lost souls, who make it their business to cleave asunder the seamless robe of our Redeemer and the unity of the orthodox faith. Hence it befits the Pontiff, lest the vessel of Peter appear to sail without pilot or oarsman, to take severe measures against such men and their followers, and by multiplying punitive measures and by other suitable remedies to see to it that these same overbearing men, devoted as they are to purposes of evil, along with their adherents, should not deceive the multitude of the simple by their lies and their deceitful devices, nor drag them along to share their own error and ruination, contaminating them with what amounts to a contagious disease, one far more terrible than death itself. It also befits the Pontiff, having condemned the "rekindled," to ensure their still greater confounding by publicly showing and openly declaring to all faithful Christians how formidable are the censures and punishments to which such guilt can lead; to the end that by such public declaration they themselves may return, in confusion and remorse, to their true deaths, making an unqualified withdrawal from the prohibited abomination; by this means they may escape divine vengeance and any degree of participation in their eternal damnation.

Fatwa against the so-called "Rekindled"

The revival of dead human beings, in a mockery of Allah's gift of life to the faithful, is against Islam, against the Prophet of Islam, and against the Koran. All those, alive and dead, who assist in this wicked endeavor are condemned to capital punishment. I call on all valiant Muslims wherever they may be in the world to execute this sentence without delay, so that no one henceforth will dare insult and contravene the sacred teachings of the Prophet.

Concussion slapped Sybille awake. She stared in the darkness of the windowless room. The lighted clock display had gone black. No whisper of air-conditioning. A rushing, as of a great wind, and crackling roars, gusts, bangs. Voices cried out. Her chest hurt. Smoke. Another immense crash. High-pitched bleating, on and on. My god, she thought. Zion Cold Town is on fire.

"Get on the floor," she said in two sharp syllables. Rolling across the wide bed, she found Kent Zacharias. He lay unmoving. The long-dead were hard to wake, she had noticed that more than once. Groping in the darkness, she found his face, his nose, grasped it hard and twisted. Like a drowning man surfacing, Zacharias snorted and gasped.

"Sybille. Are we under attack?"

A stench of burning plastic-coated wiring, paint, probably clothing and furniture, other flammable stuff choked her throat.

"Out," she said. "Come on."

At the door, she banged her bare hip on the doorknob. She pressed the back of her hand to the wood. It was distinctly warm, but not yet hot. Perhaps the fire was contained in the north wing, where public access was easier and the tall plate-glass windows would shatter in the boiling gases of a bomb. Smoke was the immediate hazard, poisonous and blinding. She opened the door a crack. Zacharias bumped her from behind, a large blundering animal.

"Don't open the damned door," he said, voice rasping.

"I have to, Kent," she told him. "We'll roast alive if we stay here." She flung it wide. Smoke poured in from the corridor, and a red and white glare danced in it. The floor was hot. "Put your shoes on," she said, and ran back bare-soled to her side of the bed and found her slippers. Naked, then, she returned to the corridor and turned left. Someone had a flashlight, and called, "This way." Other people were emerging from their rooms, moving in both directions, stumbling into each other.

Sybille raised her voice above the racket of the fire alarms. "Head for the back stairs. Down, not up." The milling took on an abrupt sense of purpose. "Has anyone called 911?"

"Not answering." A man's gruff tones. "Signal's jammed, or they're overloaded."

The stairwell door opened into emergency lights in a haze of smog. The lights immediately flickered and went out.

"Shit," someone said. "Listen up, people. Stay as low as you can. Crawl on your hand and knees if you have to. Try not to breathe this filthy stuff."

Like a procession of pilgrims in the dark night of the soul, they crawled and bumped and squirmed down the stairs, sweat pouring from their changed flesh, no more adroit or invulnerable under this threat of final death, Sybille thought madly, than any living creature fleeing in a forest fire. Crackling and crashing. The emergency door opened into cooler night, desert air. She fell through it. The flashlight was casting about, sweeping across the smeared, blackened faces of the dead. In the distance, another explosion slapped the air. The cinderblock walls remained untouched. Sybille thought: Is this why the architects chose these unpromising materials? She had supposed it was a statement against the vanity of the warms. *I have looked into the abyss*, the walls of the Cold Towns said bleakly, *and the abyss has looked back*. Well, this time the abyss had done a serviceable job. But next time we'd better find an improved method of lighting the damned place during assault.

Zacharias found her. To her astonishment, in the dimness, he wore a fire-retardant sheet like a silvery burqa. Where had he found that? Where had he managed to find the time to look for it? He took it off, gallant as Lord Raleigh and, hairy and naked, wrapped it around her own nakedness. It was cold and clammy.

"We can escape into the woods and then the desert," he said in her ear, "or go to the front and see what we can do to help."

"This place is ours," she said fiercely, hugging herself, starting to tremor. "Those sons of bitches—" The screams had subsided, but people were weeping. We dead spill our tears, she thought, even if our blood is thick with small machines. She heard no further sounds of explosions, but the rasping noise of flames grew louder by the moment.

"The fire will put itself out," Zacharias said. "There's really not that much to burn." He paused. "Your cassettes. Are they tucked away in a secure safe?"

"I think so," she told him. "Maybe one still in the machine. God *damn* it, where am I going to find another cassette player?" More than a decade earlier, the university had scoured the net markets for weeks before they turned up an antique Sony sound cassette player so she could transcribe the priceless, irreplaceable ethnographic interviews from Zanzibar. And now that machine was probably warped and melted, along with one of the tapes, charred into meaninglessness. Well, she thought. All right. This is the condition of the deads. Let the dead bury their dead. She shook her head, then, in self-rebuke. No. That was the apologist cant of those who yearned for death, proclaimed its virtue and necessity—the kinds of fools and bigots who had done this terrible thing.

"The fatwa," Zacharias said, echoing her thoughts. "Or that Bull of Pope Sixtus VII. The denunciations from the Russian Orthodox prelates. We were right to withdraw from them. We should cut off their cool fusion generators. Damn them to the Fifth Circle of Hell."

They had reached the front drive and forecourt of the building, and searchlights were blooming like flowers of cold fire, reflecting from the blurred crimson fire trucks that had finally arrived. Hard streams of water fell through the smoke, spitting in the gaping ruin of the building's entrance way. Amid the haze and hot sparks she saw another display of sparks, darting, purposeful, a swarm of stereo drones. From Zion's own media center, she suspected, or maybe Vox News was already on the scene. And yes, all the windows were shattered and gone, and the tall steel main doors lay buckled and useless. Bodies were being borne out on floating stretchers, ready for the retrieval ambulances. Perhaps they could be saved. The deads, Sybille told herself grimly, are hard to kill. She walked forward into the ruin, in her silver mortuary robe like the white-wrapped figure from Arnold Böcklin's painting *Die Toteninsel*, drifting across dark water to the embrace of the Isle of the Dead, and felt almost nothing but brief surprise when the whole tall wall, tormented by flame, explosive shock, and the pounding of the hose, fell upon her, sundering her spine in a burst of agony, smashing her legs and hips. The drones, the media flies and bees, surrounded her, hungrily, like tiny metallic and crystal carrion eaters. For a second time Sybille Klein died.

The phone implant buzzed against the back of his ear, waking Klein instantly. "What time is it?"

"4:32 a.m. Professor Klein, September 29, 2037," the machine said. "You have two urgent calls."

"From?"

"One is from your Guidefather, Dr. Hassan Sabbāh. The other is from your sister, Hester Solom—"

"Hester?" he said, in disbelief. "At four in the morning?"

"She is in London. Do you wish to take her call?"

"Very well. Put her through. If the call takes longer than two minutes, place her on hold and let me speak to the Imam."

"I have your brother now, Mrs. Solomon."

"Jorge?" The woman's voice, so like his mother's, was frantic.

"What's the matter, Hester? Is it Father?"

"What? No, no, we're all fine. Not that you'd care." The inevitable touch of bitterness. He'd scarcely seen any of them since his marriage, not even during the bereavement service for his dead wife. "Look, turn on your stereo. Vox News."

"I never watch that crap." He threw his legs over the sides of the bed, felt around in the dim light of the utilities for his slippers. "What is it? The Second Coming of Jesus?"

"Just turn the goddamned thing on."

The stereopsis TV frame deepened as he spoke the command, and switched directly to a scene of smoke, white-hot fire, shouting men in protective suits and helmets, contained chaos. A Cold Town, evidently. Yes, a bright blue line of text ran across the depth display like a message from the impalpable Hand of Yahweh. *Bombing at Zion Cold Town. Seven deads defuncted at least 13 badly damaged.*

His pulse increased a fraction, and he was aware of a pulsing in his temples. The New Man has not entirely displaced the Old Man, he thought.

"Do you see her?" Hester was wailing. "Did you see Sybille?"

Images cascaded, jump cuts, paired hologramic bugs seeking the most striking and disturbing pictures. Yes, there she was, crushed under a fall of broken cinderblock. In the tank, her face loomed. Still the same pale, beautiful Michelangelo marble as the moment she'd died the first time, despite the streaks of grime. A revival team was struggling with the hill of broken masonry. In the background, flames were abating, driven back by the foam and water. The image cut away, and again, and again. His accelerated rekindled thoughts slowed into a sort of paralysis. Not so *over her* after all, part of his consciousness observed sardonically. A world without meaning meant, surely, that a doubled death of a woman once loved ardently, desperately, obsessionally was without meaning. But no. Not quite. Not at all, in fact.

This is an aberration, he told himself. I will recover my poise in a moment. Besides, the black cryo van is pulling up now, I imagine, and they will have her ruined body in the repair shop within minutes. She's right there in the very heart of a major Cold Town, he thought. No better location if someone's going to kill you.

"Dr. Klein," said a deep voice, barely accented.

Hassan Sabbāh. "Yes, Guidefather," Klein said. "My sister just called to tell me that Sybille—"

"She will be rekindled," Sabbāh told him patiently. "In fact, this is why I am calling you. We have decided to advance your position with the Conclave. There are aspects of the revivified you must witness, if you are to act as our speaker among the living."

"Your speak—"

"Get dressed in warm clothes and meet me in the quad. We have a fusion aircraft on standby. You will be with your ex-wife within two hours." He broke contact. Hester's voice came back, high pitched, aghast. Perhaps she had not even noticed his absence.

"I have to go, dear sister," he told her. "They are flying me to Utah. I'll catch up with you and the parents as soon as I can." He heard a gasp. "I know," he said with an edge in his voice, "'What do you have to *do* around here to get some attention, *die* or something?' Apparently so. Good night."

He dressed snugly and went outside into the cool morning, still sunless, harshly lit by the exterior LEDs. Guidefather stood beside the open passenger hatch of a small Gates fusion jet, a couple of functionaries in attendance. Klein climbed aboard, strapped in, and within a minute was hurtling toward his defuncted wife. Ex-wife.

4

Human life, because it is marked by a beginning and an end, becomes whole, an entity in itself that can be subjected to judgment,
only when it has ended in death; death not merely ends life, it also
bestows upon it a silent completeness, snatched from the hazardous flux to which all things human are subject.
                         —*Hannah Arendt*, The Life of the Mind

Hard blue-white lighting, sterility itself, diagnostic and monitoring equipment
gleaming, the large tank waiting for its occupant, and Sybille supine on a gurney,
motionless, eyes shut, totally hairless after the ministrations of the techs, her round
scalp eerily pale above her faintly tanned features, breasts flattened only slightly by
gravity, the curved purse of her vulva visible within the torn flesh and sundered
bone of her smashed hips, legs so badly broken they seemed the remnants of a car-
nivore's meal. He had not seen her for four years, and this broken corpse was no
memory of his.

"You're going to amputate her limbs," Klein conjectured. He stood beside the
gurney with Zion's Guidefather, a purple-skinned fellow as ruthlessly shaved as Sybille. A former Marine? A Navy SEAL? Both wore transparent, flexible outer shell
and helmet over decontaminated scrubs, in common with the handful of busy medical technicians, all of them, unsurprisingly, deads. The hiss of air from sealed
tanks, a faint echo in the voice circuits.

"Nothing so gross. You are here to witness the restoration process, or at least its
first steps. Watch in silence."

Sybille's corpse was lifted into the tank, lowered on a mesh into some viscous,
transparent medium. She—it—seemed to float, rolling slightly, was stabilized by
mesh from above. Tubes extruded from the sides of the tank, sharp-tipped; they entered her flesh. After a long minute, her skin took on a roseate flush.

"Repair nanocytes," said the Guidefather, Jamal Hakim. "This much the academics and media of the warms have long conjectured. But wait."

The corpse began to swell. Pulsations flexed Sybille's smashed legs, her hips
writhed in a horrid parody of sexual desire. Klein watched without emotion, neither
excited nor repelled. The world was comic in its meaningless surges, its appetites,
its agonies, but none of what he saw brought a smile to his lips or a burning wish to
vomit. Awareness of his own inanition caused him neither self-reproof nor an anxious wish to remedy this loss of emotions that had once overwhelmed his life. All of
this he saw clearly, layer within layer, and all he felt was a profound bleakness.

A deep thrumming, and the lights flickered. Magnetic forces, no doubt, the kind
of sleeting impalpable magic wrought by resonance scanners. So this is why they
insisted we remove all metal from our bodies, change into these scrubs and booties.
Even the tanks of air on our backs must be ceramic or plastic. The techs watched
their instruments, the dead woman's body swelled, ballooned, limbs straightening
under some impulse he could not detect except through its effects.

"We have engaged her morphogenetic *Bauplan* field," Hakim said. His deep voice was a profound baritone, effortlessly piercing the rumble of the hidden magnetrons within the tank, in the majestic tones of a cantor in Temple, a holy, authoritative growl of absolute precision. Klein caught himself. Holy? Such nonsense. This place was no more than a highly elaborate body works, a repair shop.

"Body plan," Klein glossed aloud. "Some genetic master code, I take it."

"In part. But rekindling searches the genomic recipes in a large sampling of healthy cells of the body, under the direction of the morphic field, and recovers a pristine image of the epigenetic landscape and that maximal state toward which it moves."

Gibberish, surely. This was the kind of nonsense peddled in the lower echelons of the media. *The Grays Walk Among Us. Christian Crystal Therapy. Nazi Deads Secret Bases on the Backside of the Moon.* He had sampled them in his studies, when he lived, at first amused, finally infuriated and even sickened by the malign know-nothing gullibility they stood for. Could the Guidefather be pranking him? Testing him in an obscure rite, probing at his own vulnerability to such drivel? It seemed impossible. It was impossible.

"I'm sorry, sir, I can't understand how the information inside widely separated and differentiated cells could—"

"Quantum entanglement. We are bathing the defuncted body with powerful magnetic fields, driving the cells into harmony and oneness at the morphological level."

"Reprogramming," Klein said, filled with a wonderment that momentarily bypassed his dispassionate cynicism, overwhelmed its chill, subverted it. Perhaps this was the jolt Sybille and Zacharias and Gracchus and the rest felt as they aimed their weapons at animals lost in prehistory but recovered by genetic science, herds trampling the African plains, and falling under deliberate bombardment from the guns of those who shared their condition. More than a jolt, he told himself. A benediction. A joining. Again, that tincture of the numinous. What is happening to me, he asked himself, and felt a pulse of shame.

"Not quite. Reactivating old programs, in a cascade of recapitulation. Your former wife's spine is knitting up, her bones coming together, disrupted muscles and dermis finding their proper locations. The respirocytes gather in her lungs, haematocytes in her corrected vasculature. We should leave now, the process is well begun but will take hours to complete."

"It took weeks for me," Klein said. Not including the drying off, with its stumbling acquisition of a new, fast speech pattern, spookily growing familiarity with alien social ways. The moth crawling damp and twisted from its rejected pupa, cocoon split open to the air, spreading its folded wings. Faux pas upon blunder—yet really, all things considered, attaining social mastery with minimal disruption of the deads one moved among, with their waxen skin, now one's own, and their numb thousand-yard stare.

"Rekindling after first death, which you have passed through, is a complex procedure. Much of the postmortem body and its metabolism must be reinvented, so to speak, and reconstructed. Repair of a dead is far simpler, and drying off is greatly accelerated."

Doors slid shut behind them, sealed. A positive pressure airlock. More doors. They stripped off their polymer skins, changed back out of scrubs. Klein donned his linen shirt, patterned cravat, seersucker suit, slipped on his self-sealing boots. The Guidefather dressed again in a bold crimson business suit. Like worshipers in a mystery cult, Klein could not help thinking, returning to the desacralized outer world. He frowned. Enough!

"I hope you will tell me now why I have been brought here halfway across the continent to witness this procedure. Sybille Klein is no longer my wife; I have no special interest in her situation."

"We shall speak further about this in my office. Come."

An elevator took them smoothly up two floors from the medical basement to the administrative center. The ubiquitous cinderblock and undecorated corridors. A functional dark gray carpet muted their footsteps. Deads passed, nodding to the Guidefather, ignoring Klein. Hakim's office was nothing like Chair Bik Liu's at UCLA: it was starkly utilitarian, windowless, with sturdy, cushioned bentwood chairs around a steel-topped desk with embedded equipment. The only break in this Spartan room was a wall-sized display, currently set to deepest tan flecked with craters. After an instant, Klein knew it: human skin. Not quite the African purple-black of his host.

He sat across the table from Hakim, who muttered some command syllables to activate the display. Images began to flash, pause, animate, graph, chart. Klein listened in a dazed state of concentration to the rush of specialist jargon. Antagonistic pleiotropy. NOTCH gene signaling. Secretory pathway organelles in vast, catalogued order. Synthetic telomeres and centromeres to help lengthen lifespan indefinitely. Code adopted from the extremophile bacterium *Deinococcus radiodurans*, with its fancy redundant genome and resistance to radiation damage, and clues to emulating this process with devices at the molecular scale. The proliferative potential of stem and progenitor cells restored and amplified. None of it made absolute sense, even under Hakim's stately tuition, but the words and images flew by, slowly accreted in his mind.

"Yes, yes, Guidefather," he said finally. "Enough, please. You know my studies are in the humanities, not the sciences. But it seems to me that none of this explains a damned thing. Who developed these techniques? None of the warms seem to know, for all their media gossiping and academic conferences, and nobody here in the Cold Towns is telling. I smell a rat, Dr. Hakim, but for the life of me"—he gave a brief hard smile—"I still can't conceive the motives of those who invented these miracles, and cool fusion, and a dozen other innovations, and then just—" He broke off, bit his lip. "Nor what you and Imam Sabbāh expect of me. And perhaps of my ex-wife." He sat back, irritable and frustrated.

Hakim regarded him, imperturbable. He deactivated the display. "I believe Guidefather Sabbāh has inducted you as an Adjutant in the Conclave of the Rekindled. Of the Deads."

"Yes, Whatever that means. Also an Acolyte, which has a disturbingly religiose ring to it. What are we deads now, the seeds of a cult? Or an army?"

"Neither." Hakim gave him a dazzling smile, then, and rose. "A fusion of mysticism and science, perhaps. An unexpected emergent from our condition, and its source. More of that later."

Klein stood up. "You haven't told me what you want of me. I have no taste for hunting quaggas and dodos and Tyrannosaurus rex in the game parks of Africa, like some. Like Sybille, in fact. I've paid my corporate dues, my insurance investment covered all the costs of my rekindling, what else the hell—"

"Why, Jorge," Jamal Hakim told him, "we expect great things of you." He took his arm, and led him out of the room "Certainly, let us stay with the religious terminology you introduced. Yes. Dr. Klein, you are chosen. Consider yourself in the role of a reborn Paul of Tarsus. You have been selected to be our Apostle to the Warms."

Gog Poll: Are You Man Enough to be a Dead?

Ya, zinger, zip open your pad and drop some Xs in the Spots X Marks.

Gog how it is this year—can't nab a nap of wink for the howling dead things creeping about in the dark.

But can't be bad totally. All that gold, right? And hey, they have a poison stare like you wouldn't believe.

So—you have the stuff to be a dead? Answer our blood-drenched quizette and check out your score. And if you crave those dead pale or dark thighs—maybe you can be dead, too, and *really* score, gross time.

A: Are your favorite deads
☐ cold-blood vamps with giant prongs?
☐ slavering zoms that wanna fuck your brain?
☐ rotten corpses in the stench of the grave rave?
☐ Archibald Henrietta Stone, the first dick-swap deader?

B: Why did the dead chicken cross the road?
☐ To get to the Other Side?
☐ So its eggs got sucked by Granny?
☐ For the Sand Witches there?
☐ For the road kill chicks?

C: When did the first dead like come back?
☐ In 1348, during the Black Death
☐ In 1900, when Typhoon Mary was the cook
☐ In 2021, when Archibald Henrietta Stone came back
☐ In 29 AD, when Jeezuz jumped off his cross

D: Are the Cold Towns
☐ really cold party scenes?
☐ dens of iniquity that should be torched?
☐ prisons for the insane?
☐ dens of monsters that should be blown to shit?

Inviting Klein the rekindled into his house with languid gestures that surely failed to disguise his anxiety, Framji Jijibhoi smiled in welcome as his wife Ushtavaity stood demurely in pale rose sari and white kerchief, silent, watchful. His hand did not extend to clasp the dead man's. Somehow he could not bring himself to touch that pallid skin. Superstition thrummed in him, as always when he stood too near the object of his scholarly investigations, armored in sociological constructs made by default almost entirely at second hand. He knew how he must appear to his former colleague: Yes, he thought, I am a tall nosy intruder from the exoteric world, the neat Zoroastrian sociologist from a teemingly alien city, once Mumbai, again now Bombay under the picturesque resurgent Raj, more than half a world distant—in its ancient blend of living, dying, dead, imaginary reincarnated—from the Cold Towns and their palpably reborn.

"I'm sorry I'm late," Klein said. "The airline schedules these days . . ." The dead gave an apologetic shrug. Half a head shorter than his host, he had somehow acquired a force, a kind of *mana*, that Jijibhoi found exquisitely disturbing.

"No, no, come in, come in, Jorge." Beyond the stilted entry deck, the galaxy of Los Angeles stretched its massed blaze against the darkness. "How kind of you to visit. I must confess that until your call I had not expected the pleasure of your company following your . . . transition." He added hastily, babbling, "Despite the recent rise in tourism, deads are sighted so rarely outside your gated domains, you know. The tables are turned; my secondhand knowledge bows to your immersion at the life-death interface. But oh dear—" and he forced himself after all to take the dead's hand, "we were so sorry to hear of the attack on Zion and the death, the, the second death of Sybille."

"She is recovering, Framji. Her injuries were severe, but not beyond the healing powers of rekindling. But thank you for your concern. Madam Jijibhoi, how good to see you again, and how generous of you to invite me. Here, I brought a little Chassagne-Montrachet from the Cold Town cellars."

"You are welcome, welcome, sir," she murmured, bowing, "Thank you, we do enjoy a nice Chardonnay," and immediately departed for the kitchen with the cooler-wrapped bottle.

"I have a hundred questions, dear friend. I hope you will not object too much if I seek to remedy my ignorance? But come, sit down at the table, my wife has prepared something for our supper, I hope you still share our fondness for baby goat marinated in red chillies?"

"I look forward to it. I have to confess, though, that my taste buds have not survived the transition in great abundance. It is as you predicted. We eat and drink mainly for nutrition. But your wife's chillies—yes, I'm certain they will brighten my mouth."

Ushta came to the dining room with the Chardonnay in an ice bucket, another, opened, breathing, of Cabernet Sauvignon which Jijibhoi poured, then swiftly returned with bowls of dhan daar patio, rich with the odor of turmeric; dhan saak, its basmati rice thickened with vegetable daal; eggs on potatoes; and spinach. Wine flowed. They ate, Klein with every appearance of appreciation, and Jijibhoi spoke of university politics, hilarious scandals of the sociology department, Klein's reassignment as professor mortuus. They finished with ranginak, its wheaten biscuit flavored with dates, walnuts, ground pistachio, cardamom, cinnamon, washed down with hot, dark tea. The specter of this happy repast stripped of its tastes, its odors, its evoked memories filled the Parsee with horror and a renewed determination to avoid rekindling at all costs. Far better to lie at last in the walled Tower of Silence, parching in the hot sun, gnawed to the bone by vultures, than to abandon all the joys of the flesh and live forever in the half-life seated across the table from him.

"Let's clean up this midden and move into the living room. We've still got lots to talk about." They each carried plates and bowls and cutlery to the kitchen, although it fell to Ushtavaity to rinse and sort into the cleaner. Jijibhoi found snifters and a darkly luminous cut crystal decanter. He lowered the living room lamps so the galaxy of street lights and the true sky were visible through the windows, activated a hushed performance of the madrigals the deads favored. He poured brandy, Klein sipped, set the glass aside, waited patiently with that long and meaningless stare.

"I hope you don't mind if I'm frightfully direct, Jorge."

"You're dying to have me dish the dirt," Klein said. "So to speak. It's fine, speak freely. We are old friends."

"All right." He found himself fidgeting; Ushta came in and settled herself gracefully in an armchair. "Last time we met, Jorge, you were frantic. Obsessed. In despair. You vanished to Africa—"

"Zanzibar."

"Yes, yes. And died as mysteriously as Sybille, the first time she passed. And now, not all that much later, here you are. Serene, or at least relaxed. Not the bundle of jumpy nerves I recall."

"Framji," his wife said, in a warning tone.

"It's fine, Madam Jijibhoi," the dead man said. "Framji and I have already agreed—"

"Ushtavaity," she said. "Ushta."

"I'm sorry?"

"My name. Do you know, it's extraordinary, we have never formally exchanged names. Please call me Ushta."

"Why, thank you, Ushta." The bleak coolness in the man's voice is an artifact of his condition, Jijibhoi told himself. He does not mean insult. Or does he? That desperate fool Dolorosa showed more passion than this, but of course he was an outcast from the Cold Towns. Who could say what such isolation might do to a man dead once to the living and rejected again by the dead?

"You know that my central interest is the social structure of rekindled society," Jijibhoi said. "Less so the nuts and bolts. But really, it's becoming clear that the mysteries quite literally embodied in the deads are the key to this emerging, parallel civilization in our midst. Yet we are denied knowledge of these mysteries and the technique by which dead warms are transformed into, well, living deads. I mean, the simplest things. Do you really age slowly, or not at all? The rumor accepted by the intelligentsia is that of course you are just slowed, aging retarded by a factor of ten or twenty, even as the crackpots of church, mosque, and gog shriek that you are deathless zombies and vampires. Obviously it's too early to decide the matter by simple inspection. Yes, we'll have our answer in a century or a millennium. But it would be much more obliging if you could just, you know, *tell us.*"

Coolly, Klein said, "In the last seven years, fifteen rekindled have been kidnapped and vivisected, according to our information."

"These were the acts of unhinged rogues and terrorists," Ushtavaity said, wringing her hands. "They were butchered on camera. We've all watched the stereos."

"Eleven were butchered on camera. The other four were abducted and taken, according to our information, to black-ops labs here and in Qatar. The governments involved are now familiar with the results of our advanced medical technology. They are certainly attempting to reverse-engineer it." Klein sighed. "It won't do them any good, of course."

Jijibhoi doubted that or perhaps, he thought, he was stung by Klein's arrogance. "Come now. They have access o the finest minds in the world. Neuroscientists, genomicists, specialists in epigenetics and the thermodynamics of nanotech. It can't be that difficult. You are . . . living proof . . . of the technology."

"True in principle. But it would take hundreds of years to digest what they've peeled out of our comrades."

"But this is just assertion. Whistling, if you'll forgive the expression, past the graveyard. Moore's law, Jorge. Yes, it's slowed to a snail's pace, but the power of technology does still double and redouble. What could possibly prevent us from learning—"

"You don't even know where the information came from, or who developed it. And it's been fifteen years now."

Jijibhoi felt his shoulders slump. Stalemate. It really was like quizzing a cultist. A wave of sadness moved through him.

"The Venter labs, presumably. Gates and Allen funding. NSA connectome cryptographers. Something like that. What matters is—"

"What matters, dear Framji," Klein said with glacial certainty, "is the source of the information, not its implementation."

Abruptly, the sour mood of exhaustion was dispelled. Fire rushed through his limbs. Jijibhoi leaned forward, and from the corner of his eye saw that his wife was also intent. "What source? What are you talking about?"

"I could require you both to sign a nondisclosure agreement with hefty penalties, but what I'm about to disclose would make such penalties chickenfeed. So I'll simply trust you both," Klein said. "They decrypted a message signal from space." His dead eyes glittered. "From deep space." He watched them closely, as if judging and recording their reactions. "From a star in the Andromeda galaxy."

5

> The only obsession everyone wants: "love." People think that in
> falling in love they make themselves whole? The Platonic union
> of souls? I think otherwise. I think you're whole before you begin.
> And the love fractures you. You're whole, and then you're cracked
> open.
>
> —*Philip Roth*, The Dying Animal

Hester Solomon and her husband Moshe collected Klein at Heathrow and they took an autonomic limo into London. Moshe was a British investment banker, specializing in South American stochastic arbitrage. His doctorate was in a field of mathematics so rarefied Klein could not even begin to understand its uses or principles. Hester, of course, was a good upper-middle-class Jewish wife and mother, as striking as her mother had been as a young woman. Sybille had introduced her to Moshe Solomon.

"Marjorie Morningstar," Klein said, with a smile. They had both loved the literature of the mid twentieth century as children: Wouk, Chaim Potok, Malamud, Roth. He waited until she stepped forward for a hug and quick kiss on the cheek.

"Asher Lev," she retorted. Said warmly, he could not help thinking. Warm, a warm, a female warm. Far, a long long way to go. But that was *Sound of Music*, a different tale of love and persecution entirely.

"No artist I," he demurred, as tradition required. "An apostate, that I'll confess."

In the spacious back of the limo, the eldest son, Eliezer, sat shyly beside his uncle Jorge and said almost nothing, in a refined transatlantic accent. The boy was in Harrow uniform, sans top hat and cane: pale gray trousers, white shirt with black silk tie, and dark blue jacket. In his lap was what Klein surmised was the classic straw boater. The very model of an upper-middle-class English schoolboy. If he was freaked out by the proximity of a dead, he did not allow his discomfort to show.

The adults exchanged mandatory words of sympathy, explanation and conjecture concerning Sybille's state and its cause—had the firebombing been a venomous sectarian attack? A work of political terrorism? The expression of some internal factional dispute among the deads themselves? Klein quickly put an end to that. Police forces and security were looking diligently into the atrocity, but no, emphatically there was no slightest reason to suspect fractures within the closed world of the rekindled. This was no more than a slanderous attempt by media jackals to blacken the victims. "Like Hitler and the Reichstag," suggested Eli, and an uncomfortable silence fell. Hester said, quickly, "Mom and Dad are waiting for us at the hotel, Jorge. They flew in yesterday. It's quite the meeting of the clans."

Klein groaned. "So much for leaving the dead to bury the dead, as the Christians so prophetically put it. The parents declined to convey their bereavement when I called them with news of Sybille's second death. That shiksa. Father all but hung up in my ear."

"Well. Shiva was sat. You're not only dead, Jorge, you're *dead*. I'm sorry, it's awful."

"And yet they're here, you say."

Moshe told him in his rumbling voice, "They have seen you on TV, read your interviews. You have become a notable part of the cultural landscape, you know."

"And they want to shut me up."

Hester glanced at the twelve-year-old. "This should wait."

"Don't mind me," Eli said with a crafty grin. "The other chaps and I can't see what all the fuss is about, really. Well, Luton had a few snarky things to say but I soon set him straight." He rubbed the knuckles of his right fist on his trousered knee, and gave his uncle a bland look. Klein laughed softly.

"Good for you, kid. We deads need a few more people like you in our corner."

The driverless car dropped them at the Montagu Place Hotel, where a slender Pakistani porter took his minimal luggage.

"Not five star, Jorge," Moshe said apologetically, "but those are getting rather stuffy about . . ."

"Dead Jews."

"Not quite. Live Jews have no trouble getting a suite at Claridges or the Langham. It's an old-fashioned city in many respects. The traditional bigotries pass eventually, making way for the new."

Moshe checked them in and took the boy up to the Solomons' small suite. Hester led Klein into a snug bar where his parents sat drinking vodka and trying not to look uncomfortable. Sybille's parents sat across from them, utterly at ease. British consular diplomats interfaced with the Foreign Service of the Department of State, George and Anna Palmer were currently binational attachés at Brussels. He had not seen them during their quick visit to Zion Cold Town following their daughter's medical crisis, but he had exchanged brief messages, explaining that Sybille would probably recover completely from her brutal ordeal. Now he shook their hands as everyone rose, hugged his mother, bowed to the cold countenance of his unyielding father.

"I'm glad to find you well, sir."

"Since you're here, you might as well find a seat." It was closest thing the old man could come to a concession.

"Thank you. Mother, you look lovely."

"My handsome son!"

Formulae, unreeling the clichés. Clowns, it was true, they were all clowns. Endless emptiness. Sundered. Yet the pain was gone, he realized. If there was no joy in this reunion, neither was there grief nor anger nor the old demand for acknowledgment. Alive, he had been broken until Sybille healed him, or rather he and Sybille colluded in a mutual embrace that excluded the sting of such rejection. She died, impossibly she died; he was not merely broken again but desolate, driven by a need that choked his heart and made him a mad thing, obsessed and futile. And now, he saw finally, all that anguish was drained away. He felt nothing for these people, no love, no yearning for acceptance, even as he felt no animosity nor resentment. He was free.

And it meant nothing at all.

"Can I get anyone another drink," Klein said.

In an atmosphere at once chilly and desperately contained, Moshe called them a limo and instructed it to bear all eight of them the sixteen kilometers to Gants Hill. "Not Orthodox, Reformed—but they keep kosher," he promised. There was a palpable breach in the lowering mood when the name of the restaurant-pub was revealed, antique gold against smoky oak: *Bangers & Mashugana.* Eli laughed out loud. "Bangers and mash! What an outrage!"

"I don't even know what that is," Klein told the boy. "Not kippers steeped in their own haggis, I hope."

The boy laughed harder, tears running down his face. The strain had wound the child up more than any of the adults had cared to notice. "It's just sausages and whipped potato, with lashings of gravy and tomato sauce. Like, ketchup. Yummy!"

Dubious, the Klein parents followed their daughter's husband into a low-ceilinged, noisy, smoky cavern. A great bar-counter made a polished horseshoe in the center of the beamed room, and men and women shamelessly drank together, laughing, nudging each other, calling their orders. It might have been a stage set. Perhaps it was, a calculated tourist trap. In one corner a pair of Jews with payot curling down before their ears, and dark felt hats, played chess, ignoring the innocent vice on every hand. Small tables were scattered along one wall. Three of these awaited their party, squeezed together, cutlery and linen already in place.

"They know you here?" Klein asked.

"They know me everywhere, dear chap. Come come, take our seats, the girl will be along in a moment for our orders so make up your minds quick-smart, they don't mess about in this pub." Moshe gestured; a waiter brought them beer, stout, wine in a tall flagon, a soda for the boy.

"You're quite certain this is kosher?" Mrs. Klein said, quite certain that it couldn't possibly be.

"Absolutely. We're in the middle of London's Jewish district. Forget Golders Green. I'll have Yorkshire pudding," he told the plain middle-aged woman in an apron that reached to her knees. "Jorge, I recommend the steak and kidney pie with vegetables. As for you antique folks, you might care for something you recognize—a rare steak with a baked potato, some grilled bream, order anything but pizza or burgers, they'd throw us to the wolves."

Voices rose, plates were piled high and then a moment later, it seemed, miraculously emptied. Desserts made the same magical transition from being to nothingness. No words of substance were exchanged. Klein stolidly munched his untasting way through the provender, pretending enjoyment. He was not unhappy, nor was he happy. He thought of Arthur Schopenhauer: "The two enemies of human happiness are pain and boredom." Here and now he felt no pain, and not really boredom either, but the absence of those two enemies did not clear any space for happiness. He shoveled up his sweet, washed it down with a half and half, a mix of mild ale and bitter. Inside his altered body, nanocytes tore the molecules apart, sorted them, broke down the alcohol before it could reach his brain. Could it be, he thought, that I am at least . . . content? It seemed impossible. Well. He prepared to tell these people, his relatives and former in-laws, some truths of that altered condition, and what it meant to be a dead on the hoof, no longer living but assuredly still kicking. I am the Apostle, he thought, to the Gentiles. To the Genitaled. To the Gendered. I am the dickless, ball-less wonder come to bear improbable testimony to the very humans least likely to pay me any attention. Except the kid, he thought. Except the boy, Eliezer.

For the first time in his life, he felt the poignant stab of a wish for a child of his own.

BBC Gogcast transcript
1 October 2037

Our Science & Society mavenette, Dr. Jane Makwe, speaks with Professor Jorge Klein, spokesperson for the Conclave of the Rekindled, and himself a dead for four years. Jane spoke with Jorge from her den in Edinburgh.

> **Jane:** Welcome to the rant, Jorge. You don't mind a bit of informality?
>
> **Jorge:** It might be more professional, Dr. Makwe, if you addressed me as Professor Klein.
>
> **Jane:** Oooh, stuffy! Let's keep it friendly and light, shall we, Jorge? I mean, we're dishing some pretty gruesome shit here.

Jorge: As you wish.

Jane: Jorge hails from Argentina, clubbies, and you'd think looking at the way his name's spelled he'd go by "Georgie." Nup, "Whore-hey" it is.

Jorge: I was born in Buenos Aires, Jane, but we moved to California when I was four. I hold joint citizenship.

Jane: Cool—a citizen of the world! Highly fash! But hey, don't you like lose your citizenship when you like die?

Jorge: No. My passport is still active. But it's certainly a question currently under review in both our countries.

Jane: But us Brits don't have any deads. It's a Yank thing. Why's that? Isn't it like restraint of trade or something? Not to mention human rights.

Jorge: I understand your concern, Jane, but the rekindling process was developed by Americans in the United States, and the process is proprietory.

Jane: Protected by megacorp patents, you mean?

Jorge: Actually, no. The matter is vexed. The Conclave have their hands tied at the moment because the Supreme Court of the United States has declared all the relevant techniques to be a munitions issue, and anyone selling or transporting that information to other nations would be subject to trial for treason and the most extreme penalties.

Jane: They get offed?

Jorge: At the very least.

Jane: Ha ha. I like that. You mean they'd be executed with no chance of getting reborn as a dead.

Jorge: Precisely.

Jane: Grim. Ironic, then, that Jules Lagrange, notorious secret-blower from the early years of the mill, is now a dead hiding in San Diego Cold Town.

Jorge: That's the kind of nonsense retailed on the crackpot gogs. Mr. Lagrange is not an American citizen. He was born in Belgium and so is not eligible for rekindling. As far as I know, he remains in custody in Guantánamo.

Jane: Maybe they don't tell you everything, Jorge.

Jorge: Do they tell *you* everything, Jane? By the way, what kind of doctorate do you hold?

Jane: Snippy now! Well, I'll tell you, it's not like I'm hiding some dirty secret that would excite Jules and his gang. I'm a haematologist, with a degree from St. Andrews and postdoc studies at Baylor. For the sports fans watching, a haematologist is an expert in blood. Which handily leads me to my next question: what can you tell us about heterochronic parabiosis?

Jorge: I'm sorry, what?

Jane: When the blood vessels of old and young mice were spliced together in experiments back in the oughts, the old guys got young and the young mice got older.

Jorge: I suppose that's possible. But it has nothing—

Jane: Let's get technical, doc. Heterochronic parabiosis increases hepatocyte proliferation and renews the cEBP-alpha complex, giving the old

buggers a kick-start of youthful vigor. Blood, man, fresh young blood. Isn't
that what spices up the deads?

Jorge (laughs): Really, you're not serious. Deads as *vampires*? Blood suckers?
Dr. Makwe, that's the coarsest slur seen on the most rabid gogs. Have you
ever heard the term *blood libel*? The Nazis accused the Jews—

Jane: Oooh, touched a nerve, have we?

"That went well," Jamal Hakim said in his ear.

The stupidity of it all. Klein said, "Look, Dr. Hakim, I'm by nature a solitary, in-
troverted man, always have been. Death had not made me magically more conge-
nial. I'm just not cut out for this kind of advocacy. You want me to soothe the warms
down, and I'm just inflaming them." He paused. "Unless that's your intention. Am I
a Judas goat?"

"Truly, Jorge, that interview was a success. You showed again that we are not chilly
monsters to be feared, that we are offended by slurs and attacks. The warms watching
that gog will feel a deeper empathy for us than they would have if you'd brushed
aside that woman's offensive questions with a smile and a quip. That would be the
response of a practiced politician, which is to say a corporate crook and conniver.
You are not a Judas goat, Professor. You are not leading warms into a trap. Quite the
reverse. We are their future and their salvation, however much they fear us. This is
part of your training, Jorge. I meant it when I said you are to be our Apostle to the
Gentiles."

"None of the Apostles came to an especially enviable end."

"We need not be overly literal in our figures of speech. But look here, you mention your tendency toward solitary introversion. When you return to the Cold Towns,
we will do something about that."

"What now? Not just Guidefather, but Panderer in Chief?" No response, defense,
angry retort in his ear. "Listen, I was scarcely a virgin when Sybille and I married, you
know. Christ, I was nearly thirty. And we had our fun with others during the marriage.
I've known the bodies and minds, if not the love, of fair women and dark, more than
a few of them. I don't need your damned help."

"That's not what I meant, and you know it. Still, I remind you that since your
drying off, you've conspicuously sulked in your tent. Not least during your travels."

Klein thought suddenly of the wandering gang into which Sybille had fallen so
swiftly, roaming the world as tourists of the expired. Had she been inserted into that
aimless set by psychologists, Conclave specialists enacting the role of marriage brokers, some shadchan arranging plural *shidduchim* for the newly dead? The prospect
promised some entertainment value, but really it revolted his deepest essence. He
and Sybille, the one lasting liaison of his life, had been an accident abetted by their
simultaneous presence in the Hanging Gardens, favorite refectory of the university
scholars. Like and unlike, Jew and Gentile, teacher and student, congruent in the
shared culture of centuries, different enough not to stale, sufficiently akin to merge
flesh and mind and soul into a dyadic unity greater than he had ever supposed
feasible for a man isolated by intellect and temperament. But that was the old Jorge,
he told himself. That was the Klein before death had sucked him dry, drained away
the warm juices from their conjoined link. Parabiosis indeed, he thought. And now

their blood was a construct of old fluids and prowling haematocytes, oxygen borne through the raceways of their blood vessels inside carbon and silicon cages stronger and more commodious and longer lived than anything devised by bumbling evolution. Maybe the brokers of the postmortal cult he had been snatched into might bond him anew with comrades whose company he could enjoy, women he might lie beside in the remote yet oddly tender embraces of the dead.

"All right," he said, in the swift code that had been impressed upon his brain by machines grown out of algorithms from a star in an entirely different galaxy, "all right, set me up."

"You don't *look* very dead, you deads," the interviewer said. "In fact, you seem rather quick on your feet."

"Calling us *deads* is a vulgarism, you know. The preferred term is 'rekindled.' "

"Yet you do use it yourselves."

"Well, it's a traditional defensive move by persecuted groups to borrow terms of abuse. Gays called themselves *queer*. Black singers took up the gangster use of *nigga*. But I'm also of Jewish stock. Would you sit there with a smile and call me a kike?"

"Didn't mean to tread on your toes, love." Brine Di Stefano was an epicene specimen, languid in Klein's borrowed Bunche Hall professorial office. Sunlight streamed through his bouffant hair, each strand crisp and surrounded by a glow. "But now I'm going to have to. *The New York Times* is the gog *de référence*, you know, so we have to get the record straight. So to speak." He smirked. "It's often said that the drive behind rekindling is an evasion of reality, a flight from life. Some say you willfully block your transition to the afterlife. Even the Mormon Atheists find evidence in their scriptures that you are the new Nephilim, to be abjured and cast out."

Klein smiled. "I'm not tall, as you see. I believe the imaginary Nephilim were Giants in the earth."

"We speak here in symbols, professor. Let's not nitpick. I can be specific. A senior member of the White House staff, speaking off the record—"

"If she spoke off the record, why are you quoting her?"

Di Stefano brushed this aside. "This person whose gender must remain undisclosed said that the Conclave of the Dead has criminally evaded payment of taxes for more than a decade, is using highly classified information stolen from Federal assets, and plans the corruption of the American people. Comment?'

"I'm not a lawyer, Brine, nor am I a tax expert. Still, as I understand it, taxes have never been levied on the deceased since the founding of this Republic, unless you count the estate tax. I grant you that the President's party is often accused of gaining office through the franchise of the dead—and I don't mean people like me, who are currently entirely *dis*enfranchised. Does this seem just to you and your readers?"

"Okay, sweetie, I'm with you. Let me track back a step. Revival from death is a kind of ultimate eugenics. Isn't death designed as the proper termination of life, without which living has no meaning?"

Klein had heard all this a hundred times by now, and his mind was stocked with a hundred glib one-liner ripostes. He put them aside, leaned forward, spoke carefully.

This intellectual buffoon represented a serious newsgog; surely some of its readers were capable of thinking beyond clichés.

"Eugenics is a tainted word. Why? Only because of the way it was abused a century ago in the era of fascism, Nazism, and Soviet and Chinese communism. Not to mention in this country, when people of limited intelligence were forcibly castrated for the alleged good of the race."

"By 'race' you mean—"

"You know perfectly well what I mean. The distinction needs to drawn between that kind of atrocity and the free choices individuals make for themselves and their children."

"Oh, so it's just fine for some bigoted redneck or Chinese commissar to—"

"If they're making free choices not imposed by the state or corporations or faiths or any other kind of forcible—"

A wave of the hand. "Rekindling is an affront to the Lord, according to Cardinal von Sachsen. It is a regressive infantile evasion of maturity, says the New York Directorate of Psychoanalysis. I could spiel out the quotes, but you're surely aware of these arguments. How do you answer them? I have to tell you, I find them persuasive."

Klein sat back, sighed. "You've heard of the Stockholm Syndrome?"

"I believe so. I took a course in Asymmetrical Warfare at Princeton, actually." The interviewer frowned. "You mean the way a captive or victim of torture paradoxically bonds to her oppressor. That's a facile analogy."

Klein was remorseless. "If a child is threatened with death by a congenital heart defect, should that go untreated?"

"Plainly, not. A repair of localized—"

"A soldier is shot in the field of battle and bleeds out. His biometrics report an EEG crisis. In moments he will be dead. Should the medics zip him up in a body bag, untreated?"

"Certainly not. This is sophistry! We were talking about people already dead who are subject to a grossly unnatural procedure that some ethicists claim produces a 'zombification' of its victims."

Klein bared his teeth, then smiled. "Do you fear I might lunge and eat your brain?"

"Stranger things have happened." Di Stefano returned a dazzling grin. "Don't bite the messenger, doc."

"Messengers can catch Stockholm Syndrome too. Open your eyes and look at the evidence, Brine. Death has always been an abomination, a horrible accident of evolution. Nobody designed death. It's an evolutionary kludge. We're disposable. Our genes don't care about our survival once we've multiplied them through reproduction. But now we have scientific means to reverse that blunder. Rekindling is no more unethical nor Satanic than having damaged teeth replaced by genomic implants, or fixing your worn-out knee cartilage or heart with autologous stem cells reprocessed from your own skin."

"So saith the Chamber of Commerce of the Cold Towns. Philosophers and ordinary folks vehemently disagree. You've crossed a line. Some are anticipating a severe government crackdown. What will be the response of the Conclave if and when that comes?"

Klein stood up. "It's been delightful chatting with you, sir. Please don't forget to mention the Stockholm syndrome argument in your piece. If you need a quote to support that, look at Keats."

"The poet?" Brine Di Stefano nodded. "Ah. 'Half in love with easeful Death.'"

"'Call'd him soft names in many a mused rhyme.'"

"Point taken." Ushered to the door, shaking Klein's hand, the journalist said with every evidence of sincerity: "I just hope you guys have good guns and lawyers, when *Der Tag* comes."

Albany Cold Town was literally cold on Christmas Eve, 2037. Strictly speaking, it was part of the city of Cohoes rather than the State capital, but the name had stuck. Jorge Klein took an autonomic cab north from Albany along 787 beside the Hudson. Icicles glittered in bare branches in the streets below, and a little fall of snow sifted down. The Conclave had taken over the Van Schaick Island Country Club, purchasing it outright for a fabulous sum to the fury of its dispossessed members but with the connivance of three members of its Board of Directors including the President and Treasurer, each signed up for rekindling. Its lush championship golf course was now a grid of graceless cinderblock structures, heavily walled, newly braced against attack from the lawless and the law alike. Klein entered the redoubt, displaying proof of his bona fides.

"Come in, come in." The house of strangers was like any other, but he was expected, a notable guest; clearly word had gone ahead from Jamal Hakim. He was to be integrated more fully into the community of the deads, the better to perform his duties for the Conclave. "Welcome, welcome, welcome." Gently they touched and nudged him; after all this time, their waxy skin and staring gaze no longer dismayed him. He was one of them, he knew their thousand-yard stare from within, it was his own condition. "Hello," he said, "hello, hello."

A trio circled about him as he met the residents, two handsome women and a ratty-looking man with a distant but somehow droll demeanor. It was unsaid but immediately understood: these were to be his companions, his set, his crew. They made themselves known to him as the occasion arose, unobtrusively. Here was Francine, slim, elegant, perhaps fifty, a *goyishe* version of his mother, perhaps. And a pretty young third-generation Korean. "Mi-Yun," she said, placing her hand on her breast. "Please don't say 'Me Tarzan,' it gets very, very old." He nodded, amused. And the short fellow with the beaky nose was Tom, an experimental picotechnologist, whatever that was. Finally they bore him away to his guest room, his small suite, in fact, bringing wine and a plate of cookies. "If you decide to make Albany your home base for a while, we'll move you into the main house," Tom told him.

In the night, after all the formalities were completed, he lay beside Francine in the darkness, listening to her breathe. He had decided it would be crass to choose Mi-Yun for this first encounter. Francine was not the first dead woman he had been intimate with, but none of his early experiments had been satisfactory. In the earliest days after his rekindling, he'd been informed again and again by the technicians that he was no longer a sexual being, not in any traditional sense, perhaps in no sense at all. The process altered not the genitalia but the brain, the gusts and flows of hormone secretions, the mechanisms of arousal and performance. He was a eunuch now, as were they all, male and female. The senses remained alert, however, and a numb craving for contact, the bleak reassurances of the grave. He placed his hand on Francine's elbow, where it rested against his ribs, and heard her breathing alter. Slowly he stroked her forearm, clasped her hand lightly. She murmured sleepily; they said nothing in words; they slept.

Christmas morning was chilly, subzero, snow crisp on the flattened ground where well-heeled local golfers had once swung their irons in more propitious weather. Klein and Francine met the others for a quick breakfast, dressed warmly, went out under a sky of cloud pregnant with more snow. Church bells rang in the distance, carried with sharp clarity under the clouds. In the traditional houses to the north of the Cold Town, the children of the warms no doubt did all the traditional things that drove their parents nuts: noisily tearing open boxes and plastic cartons, squabbling, shouting happily at the tops of their voices, jumping on parental beds, banging drums, blowing trombones. *Santa's been here, Santa's been here!* None of that for us, Klein thought, and was relieved. He recalled the pledge he and Sybille had made: no children for us, no rug rats, no heartbreak and responsibility, no hostages to fortune. No joy, either. But now, he told himself, we have our own futures. We are our own futures. We need not fantasize an extended duration through offspring or in a magic afterlife where we wait in bliss to rejoin them; we are our own replacements, dead but deathless. Arrows flung into a future that surely would become ever stranger, decade by decade, in increments perhaps of centuries, millennia, years falling away and drifting like snowflakes . . .

"We did this when we were kids." Mi-Yun let herself fall back in a mound of snow, ooffed, flung out her leather-jacketed arms and dragged them up and down. "Angel wings!"

"Not in California, land of the sun," Klein said. "And not in Buenos Aires either. It did snow there once, thirty years ago, after I'd left for America with my mom and dad. None before that for another ninety years." He found a curious impulse rising in his breast, bent, scooped up two handfuls of granular snow, crushed them into a ball, looked around. Tom stood looking across the Hudson, back to them; Klein flung his snowball, caught the man in the small of his back.

"Hey! No fair!"

Francine joined in, then Mi-Yun, with Tom pelting Klein so hard that his hat flew off. Distanced from himself, Klein marveled. These were deads? These crazy lunatics playing like kids, himself included? Well, why not? If the world was a vortex of meaninglessness, as it was, there was ample space for the *acte gratuit*. If all human activity was the empty capering of clowns in a plastic empty world, let us all be clowns at play, he thought. *C'est moi, Camus*—yes, regard that French existentialist's childhood football fixation, his ferocious smoking, his daredevil and finally self-slaying driving, even though he was not at the wheel of the Facel Vega when he died. Could that intoxication with being and nothingness be the explanation? One worth copying? The deads as rebels, whose cause was to be without a cause. "When he rebels, a man identifies himself with other men and so surpasses himself," Camus had written, "and from this point of view human solidarity is metaphysical."

But the playful impulse drained quickly. He dropped his handful of snow, walked away toward the naked deciduous trees and brush at the water's edge. Shivering, he pulled his coat more tightly about him. His toes felt chilled through boots and heavy socks. Gloved fingers touched his arm. Francine, he thought, and turned, but it was Tom.

"Saw your interview on the *Times* gog. What an idiot. Where do they find these poseurs?"

"Brine was okay," Klein said. "He was treading the party line. It's up to us to change it."

"Or stay out of the line of fire. Not that I'm criticizing you for—"

"Understood. The Conclave Elders anticipate a Reichstag fire followed by a *Kristallnacht*. I'm doing what I can to help avert it, but it's a long trudge up the hill of fear and misunderstanding and guile and simple stupidity."

"Yeah." Tom gestured at the barricaded blockhouse structures of the Cold Town. "We country boys don't know much about those old Krauts, Jorge, but we remember Ruby Ridge and . . . what was it called? Those crazy cultists the government torched to the ground?"

"David Koresh," Klein said. "The Branch Davidians, in Texas."

"Them too, I guess. No, those others down in Florida. Crazy as loons, but shit. Burned out the whole goddam town. Thousands of people kindled, and no rekindling for them."

"Clearwater. Yes. That's what concerns us. That's what I'm trying to head off."

A hand touched his other arm. Francine. Very well. These were to be his closest companions, his pals, his affinity group. He touched her glove, nudged her shoulder.

"We should be getting back."

Snow was falling again, harder now. It squeaked and crackled under their boots.

Half reclining in his medical bed, Mick Dongan was reduced from the boisterous, vulgar monologist Klein remembered. The anthropologist was eaten out from within, it was plain to see, by cancer. In the final stages of cachexia, it seemed from his sunken etched cheeks and the knotted joints of his exposed wrists hanging like the lumps of bone they were from arms piteously atrophied.

"Come in, for Christ's sake, Jorge. I know I look like shit. But at least I'm not dead, like some people." Dongan emitted a ghastly croaking laugh, coughed for half a minute, breath rasping in his caved-in, bony chest. Oxygen went into his lungs from transparent tubes run to his nostrils, but it brought no flush to his face. "It's not catching, dude."

"It's been some time," Klein said, and drew a chair closer to the bed. "You'll have heard about Sybille's little adventure in the bombing at Zion."

"Bloody nasty, that. Pour me some juice, there's a good fellow. Bastards won't let me have anything stronger." He slurped a mouthful of pale lemon liquid through a bent straw, swirled it in his mouth, screwed up his face, spat it out into a kidney-shaped steel basin. "Looks like piss, tastes worse." He sighed, lay back against the shaped pillow of his elaborate bed, closed his eyes.

After a time, Klein concluded that the dying man had fallen asleep, and stood. Dongan opened his eyes and grinned at him, like a man who has won a bet. Several of his teeth were missing. Lost from the shrinkage of the disease? Rotted inside his head? This was no traditional cancer, Klein knew. Bitter rumormongers were already blaming the rekindled for its origin and spread. Why would they do that? Pick up new customers, like funeral directors fallen on hard times in a place stricken by good health?

"Siddown, Jorge. I have to get this off my chest."

A wave of weariness flooded through Klein. Last-minute repentance, confession of misdeeds, pleas for forgiveness. Or could the man be about to declare a windfall for his old best friend, a bequest, perhaps his townhouse on leafy Abbot Kinney Boulevard in Venice?

"I'm not your father confessor, Mick. Not even the right faith. Not any faith, in fact, as you'll recall."

"It's about Sybille. She and I—"

"Hush." He made a quieting motion with one hand, irritated by this banality. "It was the time. We all slept around. I've known about your affair with my wife for years. We hid nothing from each other. Nothing of that kind, anyway."

"Shit, Jorge, don't make it harder than it already is." Breath catching in his throat, shoulders hunching. Stopped. Restarted with a jolt. A deep breath, then slow, shallow intaking of air. Was this Cheyne-stokes respiration? If so, the man was surely at the very edge of death.

"Have you made arrangements for rekindling?" Klein said. "I didn't see a van outside."

"Not doing it. Refused. World's got enough damned zoms already. No, sorry, sorry, feeble humor. Made up my mind when Sybille asked for rekindling. Not for me."

"You'd prefer to be ashes? Rot into slime in the ground? Don't be absurd, Mick." He hesitated. "I've never known a man with the appetite for living that you had." And would lose, he acknowledged silently, in this resurrection into bleak forever. He wondered if he would have chosen it himself, had death and rekindling not been forced upon him.

Shameless in the proximity of his own nothingness, Dongan put the same thought into words.

"Doesn't seem to have done you a hell of a lot of good, Jorge. Death warmed up." Something caught again in his throat. His face went into rictus. Klein watched him, said nothing. "Still haven't said it. Professor Klein, old chum, I'm making a clean breast of it. Your wife and I were going to abscond together."

"Don't be ridiculous."

"Yeah, yeah, I know it goes against your fairytale romance. The one-and-onlies, despite the bed hopping. The magic dyad. Two souls as one." More coughing. "Lovely fancy, I know, was same with me and Iris, for about five years. And you were heading toward what . . . a decade? Things change, pal. Christ, look at you. Walking definition of *mutatis mutandis*. Hang on, that's not what I mean. Whatever. But she'd lost that lovin' feeling. The first fine careless rapture was well and truly over. So we made our plans. Then she fucking got sick and died. Don't that beat all?"

Klein stood up. He felt nothing. Not resentment, not bitterness, not a wish to shout or deny or plead or to beat the man's face in. Without a word, he turned and left the room. A racking laugh followed him, and perhaps feeble words, but he could not make out their meaning.

6

> Later he had seen the things that he could never think of and later still he had seen so much worse . . . . He had seen the world change; not just the events; although he had seen many of them and had watched the people, but he had seen the subtler change and he could remember how the people were at different times.
> —*Ernest Hemingway, "The Snows of Kilimanjaro"*

Rain was sleeting down when Klein was driven into Moshi town in Tanzania in June 2039, his nonautonomic taxi piloted by a wizened black man with gleaming teeth, presumably genomic implants courtesy of the Gates Foundation. The deads had selected this shooting season for its dry but moderately cool weather, halfway between the northern monsoonal downpours of the year's start and the southern monsoon in its latter months. Climate change, that universal chaotic disrupter, ruined the forecasts again. Their plane had staggered through dense clouds that blocked any overhead view of the gigantic, hardened, ash-coated mudpie that was the all-but-extinct stratovolcano. A sky island, geologists dubbed this immense mountain, tallest in all of Africa; it was only 150,000 years (would he and his companions live that long? perhaps!) since it erupted last, spewing from its Kibo cone boiling lava that hardened into immense scarps and valleys.

From his room in the New Livingstone Hotel, he gazed now into the rain and saw nothing but a darker shadow, its peaks some twenty miles distant.

The deluge had abated, then stopped, by the time the party of deads arrived in a hired van: the old crew, Zacharias, inevitably in charge, Gracchus the white hunter in all his antique Hemingway glory, Mortimer, Nerita Tracy in a fetching safari suit. And, as arranged, his former wife Sybille. Seeing her step from the van, still young, still beautiful, fully restored, Klein felt washed with grace. Now she was nothing to him. The last remnants of desolation were fled, or, rather, desiccated and swept away by the winds of time.

In the clearing sky, pterodactyls—or were they pteranodons, with those imposing twenty-foot wingspans—flurried like black umbrellas caught in an updraft. At their back, high above rolling remnant clouds, the great mountain jutted toward the vacuum of space. Nineteen thousand feet and more above sea level, three and two-thirds miles, the Kibo peak almost a mile higher than this elevated ground. Reports were accurate. No trace of frozen white about its upper reaches. Famously, the legendary snows or glaciers of Kilimanjaro were gone entirely, melted and evaporated or run off for good. Or at least until the bitterly contested spread of cool fusion generators forced the final replacement of carbon fuels and reversed the ruin that warms were inflicting upon their planet. His planet, too, he grudgingly admitted.

Klein withdrew from his window, lay down on the simple bedding. Time enough to greet the other deads when they were rested after the uncomfortable trip. Did this faint ache indicate that he missed the presence of his new crew? No. Those three had their own concerns and interests. Mi-Yun had laughed in disbelief when he mooted the trip to Africa. So be it. Let this be closure.

Alcohol was not advised at altitude, but he found them in the bar off the lobby drinking whiskey sours. When you are dead you are dead all the way, he hummed to himself, and ordered one to be companionable. They greeted him with a knuckled nudge to the shoulder, a bow, a quick comradely hug from Sybille.

"You have become prominent," she said. "Your face on TV rivals the President's."

"And I'm not even running for reelection."

"Still, you've acquired your own share of abuse," Nerita said. The Brazilian was not as lovely as Sybille: sweeping red hair this year, a pert freckled young-middle-aged face, trim as a gym addict. Somehow she did not have the look of a hunter, even of dead animals. But then neither, after all, did Sybille.

"Oh yes. Raskolnikov Klein. Dr. Kevorkian Klein." He laughed. "They manage to get everything muddled and reversed. We've died, so we are a cult of murderers rather than saviors. We are no longer fated to perish and rot, and so we are obsessed by death. Then again," he said, with a sardonic pause, "some of us do seem to be."

"You have not been without your own obsessions, Klein," said Laurence Mortimer. If the words were biting, even sinister, his tone was guilefully innocent.

"Now resolved, I'm happy to report." He sent Sybille a bland, assessing look, returned his gaze to Mortimer. "At least some of us are not trapped in repetition and neurotic recurrence."

"What's that? Nietzsche or Freud?" Now Mortimer drew his lips tight. "Both con men, wouldn't you agree, and seriously out of date?"

The alcohol was working on them, fuming in their brains despite the dehydrogenase and catalase mimic 'cytes stripping down the ethyl molecules before they could thoroughly poison their higher capacities. There would be no fisticuffs. The deads, despite their fondness for controlled genocide of the extinct, were a placid lot.

"I can't argue with that. But I do have in mind one suggested change in routine. A small addition, you might say, to the fun of slaughtering quaggas and aurochs and dodos. Of course, I'm looking forward to some shooting. I've even taken lessons."

"A change?" Kent Zacharias glowered at him. "And what would that be? A singsong round the fire with the local chapter of People for the Ethical Treatment of Extinct Animals?"

"A little more arduous than that." Klein put down his empty glass precisely in the center of its mat. "I've engaged a guide and a team of porters. After the sport's done, we'll go up Mt. Kili. Quite the view from the top, I'm told."

He looked around at faces betraying consternation, derision, curiosity.

"Boring," said Zacharias. "Ridiculous," said Gracchus. Nerita Tracey glanced up at that; she had been shredding her mat. "I think it sounds interesting, Anthony. Sybille?"

His ex-wife was tranquil. She met Klein's eyes. "An amusing idea. I wish I'd thought of it myself. Perhaps we'll find Hemingway's leopard."

"Long defrosted," Mortimer said, smiling. "And chewed up by pterodactyls."

The first three days trudging and sometimes clambering up the rocky slopes of the mountain were arduous, exhausting even for the renovated bodies of the deads. Already they were above the cloud line. Fortified by hot chocolate and popcorn, lashings of food prepared by the tireless native porters who carried their supplies, filament tents, fusion heaters, and endless quantities of purified water, they slogged through alpine desert terrain that grew ever more alien. Icy rain blew in their faces; Klein reluctantly pulled on a heated mask. On the fourth day, ambient at freezing point, they moved upward through rock pitted like coral, a lunar landscape without trees, plants, or animals. The rock tore at their gloved hands, seized and twisted their walking poles. The air thinned. Rebreathers mounted on their backs fed oxygen to their respirocytes, easing the difficulties that caused one gasping porter, without the benefit of high technology, to collapse. These toughened locals had been known to perish on the trail, shaped though they were by conditioning and perhaps evolved adaptation to the heights. In the main they kept out of sight, forging ahead with the tents and sleeping bags and nourishment. They would line up for their tips only at the end of the climb. Klein watched them when he could. If the law allowed, he reflected, this crew of deads would happily shoot into their dark bodies, hack off a head or two, bear the trophies back down in their packs, with customary displays of boredom, to the lands of human habitation.

The Kibo huts, at 15,600 feet elevation, were plain green boxy structures with steep roofs and no windows, mist gusting about them. Other groups were congregated there, as they had been in the base camps lower down, destroying the isolation of hours of brutal climbing. Late in the day, after a rest that seemed to spread pain throughout his body, Klein readied himself for the final assault. Three quarters of a mile into the raw sky.

"This is completely insane," Sybille said, standing beside him in the afternoon sunshine. "I can't believe I agreed to this."

"I believe because it is absurd," Klein said.

"Tertullian, eh. Do you expect to meet God up there, Jorge?"

"*Tat Tvam Asi,*" he said. "Thou art god."

" 'That Art Thou,' " she corrected him, pedantically. Always the scholar. Even when she playfully invented her scholarship to mock him. "No need to invoke Yahveh. Or did you mean me? I thought you were over that."

"I never thought you were a goddess, Sybille," he told her. "I thought you were my wife. My loving wife, as I was your loving husband." He shushed her interruption. "But yes, I am over that. Come along, we have a mountain to climb."

Dinner first. No water to wash with. Klein stank, encased in his protective shell. They would climb the rest of the way as the sun sank, and then forward in darkness, step by painful step up the steep path through desolation. Ah yes, thought Klein. Once again, the Dark Night of the Soul. With a glimpse of heaven at the summit, and a view of hell below, with fumaroles.

Mist. Congealed lava. Dust. Temperature below zero. Altitude sickness had them all bowed and head-whirling. Dark, dark. For six terrible hours they clambered like Sisyphus, their own dead flesh the stone they carried upward. Scree tumbled beneath his boots, throwing him off balance. At any moment, Klein thought, I am going to release my grasp on this burden. I will allow gravity's victory. I will crash backward and down, downward to the earth, mutilated by sharp knives of stone. No, he told himself. No, no. This is your clownish challenge to the clowns who held his wife's affection and loyalty. May it kill them all again, he thought, with unaccustomed venom. The thin air is getting to me. Christ. Onward. Upward.

At five in the morning, they attained Gilman's Peak, the first summit. The sun remained below the edge of the world, but the sky was gray with its masked light. They stood like myths above clouds. Nerita was weeping.

The crater stretched out beneath them, empty of its fabled ice, a vast pocket into the throat of the dormant volcano. Wisps of vile gas rose from its fumaroles. If this is not the dried asshole of hell, he thought, it will serve as its apt figuration.

And the sun rose, red and gold, a glory, dispelling Klein's sour mood. Light flooded across Africa, across the birthplace of his species, of the species from which he was born and died and returned. Yes, he thought: returned, as the sun returns. No natural cycle without its tendentious parable, its encouraging metaphor. He caught himself. Enough. This was the moment. Sybille stood touching Ken Zacharias in the tender, evasive way of the dead. Laurence Mortimer placed an arm across Nerita's shoulders. Alone, Klein squeezed his eyes tight.

And still their journey was not complete. Up the blighted, tilted world they struggled for an hour, two hours, more. And here finally was Uhuru Peak, 19,300 feet above the world, the top of Africa. The sky a hard blue. Porters released a swarm of stereo bugs that spun a sparking jeweled haze, memorializing this moment of achievement. All done. Klein fell from his brief moment of epiphany. All emptiness, like the botched landscape. No meaning beyond necessity. I am a philosophical zombie after all, Klein told himself. Thus I refute . . . everything.

They trudged down the vast mountainside. Down, down, down, would it never come to an end. But Alice had been dreaming her Wonderland; this was brute reality. They were joined at last, on the open grass, green, green, by the crew of porters, many men and youths, caps and brown faces and wide ingratiating or joyfully grinning faces, clapping, *Jambo, Jambo, Kili-man-jaro*, and the tipping began, dollars swiped into paypads, expressions of disbelief, Is *this* all you're paying me? But they had been warned, it was a routine gambit, one must doubt even the rheumy tears in the eyes of an old porter surely too aged and frail to undertake such hazardous work. Gracchus, surprisingly, weakened and swiped the old fellow's pad once more, dollars flowing down from satellites, devalued currency but worth plenty in this landscape haunted by the creatures of the dead. In the far distance, an elephant trumpeted, and at the edge of the grasses Klein watched a pack of running quaggas, white legged, striped at the front like zebras while the colors had run together murkily in the rear, creatures from before the dawn of history. As are we all, Klein told himself, remembering secret messages from the sky.

They returned mile after humming mile to the hotel in a van driven by their guide. Covered in dust, they stank like what they were: death warmed up. Klein refused a whiskey sour toast and headed to his room. Before he left, though, he thanked each of them, touched them lightly in the way of his kind. To Sybille, embracing her lightly, he said, "Thank you for coming."

She moved to place a soft kiss on his cheek; he stepped aside.

"Good-bye, good-bye, good-bye."

He never saw her again.

His passport was seized as he moved through Customs and Immigration at JFK International Airport.

"Your name?"

"Jorge Amadeus Klein. Professor mortuus in the Department of Hist—"

"This document shows a date of death. Are you a rekindled, sir?"

"Yes." No sense in making a fuss about the inane routines, the pretended niceties of the law.

"Please step to one side, sir." The passport remained in the man's hand.

Klein was led to a formidable apparatus. Two beefy, armed Homeland Security officers in gorgeous braid directed him into its maw.

"I'm sorry, gentlemen, I can't do that. I will certainly submit to a physical examination, if that is requested."

"You refuse to obey a lawful and proper instruction given you by duly authorized officials?"

"Not at all. But you must know that a gamma scan, however brief, will risk doing irreparable damage to the very delicate medical equipment inside my body. I'm just asking for the same consideration you routinely extend to travelers with pacemakers or brain implants."

They stared at him with a peculiar intense detestation, but allowed him to pass into an ancillary screened compartment, where he was searched in every crevice, roughly. I'd be passing blood for a week, he thought, if I still had that sort of blood.

No further obstacles were placed in his path, but the contents of his luggage, when he checked them in the large odorous men's room, were more jumbled than usual. There'd been nothing illegal or incriminating there, of course, not even the well-wrapped head of a dodo or a monkey's paw. This is intimidation, he realized, pure and simple.

So it had started. Started in earnest, he thought with a spurt of fear, and they will probably haul me away in the middle of the night and lock me up in a dark, foul place. His renovated flesh grew clammy. Pushing through the crowd toward a cab rank, solitary dead in a sea of the quick, he knew that he was scared, really frightened, for the first time in his life. His reborn life. *Nada y pues nada nada nada y pues nada.*

7

> History can predict nothing except that great changes in human relationships will never come about in the form in which they have been anticipated.
>
> —*Johan Huizinga*, In the Shadow of Tomorrow

Three large men in dark business suits stood outside his door in the history department. Clearly they had been tracking his movements, waiting until he returned to the West Coast and, more recently, left the protective confines of the Cold Towns.

"Office of Mortuary Affairs," the foremost of the hard-faced Federal officers said, and showed ID that could have been for the city dogcatcher. Klein did not doubt the man's credentials for a moment. The other two loomed behind him, ready to intercept and immobilize Klein if he made a reckless dash for the elevator. "I'm Mr. Jacoby, sir. You will come with us. If you require the services of an attorney, you will have the opportunity to call one when you are in our custody."

Everything in his heritage rebelled against acquiescence in this warrantless arrest. He would be disappeared, like the tens of thousands in Argentina. Or flung into a concentration camp or some stinking Gulag like his ancestral Jews. But no, he told himself, struggling to retain control of his fear and anger. These goons held no grudge against his ethnicity or supposed religious affiliation. They didn't care that he was a Jew, or even that he was an intellectual, although that was probably enough to have them curling their lips. No, he was a dead. That was enough. The new Secret Enemy in the belly of America, the Fifth Column for who knew what abominations. He was himself an abomination. His very being did dirt on life. He was a *refusnik* against the due punishment prescribed to mankind by pitiless Laws of Nature, and of Nature's God, so his refusal to remain dead was a blend of dirty joke and grotesque, outrageous treason to his species. Worse still, he thought with dizzy suppressed amusement, he hadn't paid his taxes. Death and taxes: yes, these were only the scourge of the living. Those laws would change. Perhaps they already had.

"Keep your hands where I can see them," the *Federale* said with flat menace. "Turn around. Face the wall. Assume the position."

"Position? What position?"

"Shut up, smartass. I won't tell you twice. Assume the position."

"I assume this position is something criminals know about. Not I, gentlemen. I can give you a quick lecture on the tactics of the Gestapo in the 1940s, if you like."

Strong fingers gripped him behind the left ear, dug in sharply. Excruciating pain, unbelievable. He thought he would faint. Probably not a mark on his flesh, he thought, stunned by the immediacy of this retribution. His arms were taken easily, crossed behind him, locked together. Klein was frogmarched into the corridor. He thought of screaming his lungs out, but there was no point. Dignity, he decided. Poise. A stately self-presence as he is taken to the tumbrel, the axe, the madhouse, the slaughterhouse.

Sylvie came out of her office, stared aghast.

"Please call that number I left with you and let them know. Tell them it's Mortuary Affairs," Klein said. Hard fingertips pressed again on the nerve plexus at his neck. Pain fired through him. He forced himself to add, gasping, "Let Professor Liu know that I won't be able to meet her for luncheon. Something's come up."

"Oh Jesus Christ Almighty fuck," cried the departmental manager, and ran back inside her office.

Jacoby walked at his side as he was taken from the cell. Klein had been confined for six days, stripped of his clothing and obliged to wear coarse orange prison garb, kept in isolation with no contact permitted with the outside world, personal or electronic. No TV or books, no computer, no writing materials. The lighting flickered irritably, surely by design, and a high-pitched whine made his teeth ache when he noticed it. He had decoupled from his situation, sunk in lethargy. Now he forced himself to pay attention, to deal with the urgencies of the living world.

"Am I going to be arraigned, Mr. Jacoby? If so, on what charge"

Silence, other than the clack of the man's hard-heeled shoes on the concrete floor. Hushed slithering of Klein's slippers.

"I want to speak to a lawyer," he said, as he said every time a guard brought him a tray of barely edible food. "I have a constitutional right—"

Jacoby broke his silence. "You have no rights, Mr. Klein. You are a deceased person. I seriously suggest that you keep your mouth shut and respond only to questions put to you."

They entered a brightly lit room guarded by a stoical uniformed soldier with no obvious firearm but holding a sturdy baton, a fat LED Incapacitator at his belt. Seven seated men, no women, all warms, watched as Klein was pushed into a metal chair and his left wrist cuffed to a bolt. Jacoby said, "Gentlemen, this dead is Mr. Jorge Klein, a professor in the history department at UCLA, and an agent of the so-called Conclave of the Cold Towns."

"Professor mortuus," Klein said, "let us be accurate. And an agent of nothing but myself."

Astonishingly, Jacoby struck him hard across the face. "Quiet. You have been warned, Mr. Klein. You have no standing before this Board of Inquiry."

Robespierre, he thought. Yet again. *Terror is only justice that is prompt, severe and inflexible.* He moved his jaw. Not broken. In a loud clear voice he said, "Is one of these people my lawyer?"

Before Jacoby could hit him again, a burly fellow rose and came forward. "This is not a court of law, Mr. Klein, nor shall you have representation. You are here to answer our questions. It is the opinion of the Office of Mortuary Affairs that the rekindled have forfeited their legal status as citizens and indeed as human beings. Even as we speak, the Supreme Court—"

"Let us stay with the point, Colonel," said an older man at the back of the room.

"Quite right, General. The creature here is owed no explanations. Very well. Klein, you have visited sixteen of the Cold Towns in the last year, as well as traveling in the United Kingdom and Africa. In Tanzania, you engaged in furtive colloquy with your former wife, Sybille Klein, and her—"

"*Sybille*," Klein said. "Not *Sybille*. Already you're in danger of getting an 'F' for your report."

The burly man bared his yellow teeth. "In the mood for some quips, are we? That won't last long." He stroked a control panel on his wrist, and a large display opened on the wall at his left. The other men turned slightly to look at its tree diagram: names, locations of the Cold Towns scattered across the United States, estimates of untaxed net worth, links to the technological products flowing from the automatic factories of the deads. The figures for the fusion generators stood in a box at one side, impressive in both numbers of units and profits flowing from their lease. Klein's gaze moved steadily across the data as the man spoke, drawing out the connections. Links hinted at the torrents of information pouring in from the deep space telescopes, but it was apparent to Klein that these Jacobins had so far failed to unlock the source of the deads' accomplishments. He forced calm upon himself. This, it came to him in an instant of epiphany, was why he was here. It was the culmination of his program of highly visible advocacy. And he knew with cold clarity that he would be expunged the moment he had told them what they wished to learn. Well. He had been dead. He would be dead again. The entire cosmos was a long death march toward obliteration.

A flunky had come forward, pushing a trolley laden with wireless instruments. Several hypodermics gleamed beside fat ampoules. He was deftly wired with contact points. All of this could be handled with microscopic probes, he thought, frightened but amused by the blatant theatrics. A line of colored tracer reports appeared across the top of the display.

"I screwed your fat momma just now," he volunteered. A bright crimson bar lit up. "Just kidding," he added, and the bar switched to a yellowish-green.

"Not another word," Jacoby said in his ear, with menace.

"But I have so much to tell these gentlemen," Klein said airily. He entered a state of indifference and clarity. No doubt subtle synaptic changes dictated by his rekindled condition. "We have nothing to hide, after all. You just had to ask." The bar of light settled into a cheerful leafy green.

He unreeled it for them, the secret history. Klein knew himself to be an authority only on events and horrors a century gone, no expert at all in technology or the arcane of the sciences, but he knew how to tell a story, to hold captive a restive audience of teenaged students lacking interests in any topic beyond keg parties, good mood pills, sport, murderous stereo immersion games, and sex, sex, sex. He called upon these skills effortlessly, and for the most part held his captors spellbound, despite grumbles and occasional shouts of "Bull*shit!*"

Here is the last of the great NASA programs before the Grim Reset devaluation of the globe's currency slashed away 99 percent of each dollar: the skein of lensed cubesats flung out above the ecliptic to catch light a million, a billion, thirteen billion years old. Heroic and abandoned, processing the noise of deep space, reorienting its autonomic gaze like a star puppy hunting quail. The faint signal—not from a nearby star like the red dwarf Gliese 876 or HD 28185 or Upsilon Andromedae A, whose giant worlds in the habitable zone might hold Earthlike moons, but an unknown world in the nearby galaxy Andromeda, two million light-years distant. The pulse, the stream, the beat of not just life but intelligence—consciousness!

Minds impossibly old, by human standards—sending out their messages from a history more ancient now, if they survived, than the earlier upright ancestor of *Homo sapiens*. And tracked now not by a government, not by a consortium of politically funded academics, but by fanboy and fangirl billionaires, high technology mavens, hundreds of millions each even after the Reset. Canny dreamers whose disciplines were, as if by magic or cosmic design, precisely fitted to unlocking the intelligible mysteries coded into the signal from Andromeda: coders and decoders, cypherpunks, cold fusion fans, immensely rich game builders, übergeeks, do-it-yourself connectomists looking for the tricks of enhancement and immortality that random mutations had never found.

A storm of angry incredulity broke finally over his head.

"Impossible! Maybe there's a signal, but nobody could decode that torrent so quickly."

"And if they did, what would they get? The *Weltbild* of silicon blobs! Not even that—no Rosetta Stone!"

"Right. What kind of ethnocentric wet-dream is this?"

Klein waited until they calmed down. "Look at me," he said. "Do I look like the product of any previous human science?"

"You look like something out of the nightmares of mankind," one of them cried in an agonized tone. "You look like a fucking vampire!"

Well. For the moment he had lost the argument. But he had planted a seed. They would water it with their own spleen and the enriched blood of his fellow deads, almost certainly his own blood, and that of Mi-Yun, Francine, Tom, the Guidefathers across the country, sure to be seized at gun- and gas- and bomb-point and incarcerated, probably murdered. Sybille, and her dilettante crew. Poor damned Dolorosa, wherever he was scurrying these days. But the enemy could not win. The warms could not win this war they were unleashing on the deads. Klein swore that to himself.

"Take this creature back to his cell," the Mortuary Affairs chieftain said. "We have work to do, gentlemen."

He was charged with no crime. No attorney ever heard from him. His family, he supposed, were informed of his accidental death, perhaps on the Kilimanjaro climb. People wept, no doubt, or shrugged. He sat on the hard bed and thought of the child he might have fathered after all with Sybille, the placid life they might have shared had she not perished from idiopathic pulmonary hypertension, had he not pestered her after her rekindling like a love-poisoned swain, and been poisoned himself in turn, fatally, by her bored crew. But he had been brought back, remade, a kind of metaphysical Philoctetes bearing the stench of his change, his rekindling, into the appalled and furious nostrils of his parent species. Days passed. Weeks passed. Months. It was a nothingness fit for a dead man.

In late February, he was taken to a place of execration, where an experimental biostasis unit awaited him. Work stolen from the deads, without doubt. His clothes were stripped from his waxy flesh. Instruments pierced his body. Not Philoctetes now but Saint Sebastian.

"Tell me what's happened to my colleagues, my friends. Have the Cold Towns been destroyed?"

"Hold your tongue."

An official of the Office came forward.

"You are an enemy of the State, and more crucially of the entire species of Humankind. You willfully hid knowledge that might have advanced the men and women of your nation by thousands of years. Fortunately for you, we are not a vengeful people. This is a Christian nation. Your sentence is extreme rendition, not death but exile. Jorge Amadeus Kline, you are to be exiled into the future for a period of decontamination not less than one century in duration. May God have mercy on what passes for your soul."

As he screamed, they put him into the chamber. A nurse attached a tube to the catheter in his neck. The face loomed above him, wavered, went away. Klein was gone.

8

> O the mind, mind has mountains; cliffs of fall
> Frightful, sheer, no-man-fathomed. Hold them cheap
> May who ne'er hung there. Nor does long our small
> Durance deal with that steep or deep. Here! creep,
> Wretch, under a comfort serves in a whirlwind: all
> Life death does end and each day dies with sleep.
> —*Gerard Manley Hopkins, "Mind Has Mountains"*

Was this death? Was it dream? Was it some cheapjack gamer fantasy he had been plugged into, solace of a kind in his century of incarceration? He drowned. Or was he surfacing from the deeps? *Thalassa! Thalassa!* The sea! The sea! The wild cries of Xenophon's men, at the end of this great and terrible march upcountry, sighting the Black Sea. The black endless sea of deep space. No sibilants in that cry from Hellene throats and tongues, in ancient Greek: *The latter! The latter!* That dry scholarly jest, he'd heard it as a student of history from his pretty fellow student. Was her name . . . Genevieve? Jennifer? Simply Jenny? Should it be spelled *Thalatta* or *Thalassa*? Why, the latter. All Greek to me, Jorge Klein had muttered (mussered?) with a grin. What is this nonsense chasing through his gelid, his sluggish mind? Cliffs of fall. Frightful, sheer. The sea, the sea! Is this hypnogogic or hypnopompic fancy? He cannot put his finger on it. He cannot put his finger on anything. He is entirely paralyzed. Dies with sleep. Drowning. Dies—

He was dead and stilled. The anguish of it terrified him.

Again a voice cried loudly: "Awaken, Klein! Behold your child!"

Klein convulsed out of death's sleep to some state more piercing, more clarified, than the distanced alertness of the dead. A legged fish, nearly weightless, he kicked in air. *I'm on a free trajectory spacecraft,* he told himself. *Or a Lagrange station.* Faces peered at him. A high priest of himself loomed, clad in ceremonial silk embroidered with the raw nerves of a flayed human body. Klein shuddered.

Figures tussled for a view of their divinity, their maker and destroyer, rekindled again from the deeper death. Three bald youths, struttish but dutiful, faces like warrior fiends, brandished meter-long scrolls of gold and jade. In tattered remnants of silk, an old man huddled closer. His lips moved in senile supplication. Two young woman struggled to hide awed giggles behind cowls torn from silvery insulation. Klein blinked, cursing. The place was a shambles. A young woman's face came into focus, an Asian face, pretty, desecrated with rusted wire and small vivid points of light. Her full breasts were bared in the prideful modesty of a Primipara Mother. She held forth a small struggling bundle.

"The child of death!" cried the priest, reaching down from his floating eminence to unswaddle the tiny infant. "Behold!" Her discarded clothing hung free, tugged by stray air currents. Klein blenched as his eyes rose to the baby's face. Her features were a delicious blend of mother and father. She squalled: passion suffused her small cheeks and forehead. His daughter, beyond question. *What madness had he done in death?* It was forbidden. But by whose law? *Damn their prohibitions and strictures!*

"August Personage!" bellowed the gathering of his shabby worshipers. "Welcome back to the life of the dead!"

"Take the daughter of your loins, Lord!" the priest urged. Klein shook his head in repudiation. "Your beloved child! Prophesied from time out of time."

Very well; renewed living death. Reluctantly, impelled by a kind of ancient reverence, Klein held out his hands and took the baby's weightlessness, glanced again at her milky features, murmured her name as the devotees howled and babbled in holy delight.

"Peach Tree of Immortality," he said softly. *She should have been male, his son and heir, Heavenly Master of the Dawn of Jorge Klein of the Golden Door.* For a moment, catching himself, he suspected treachery, imposture. But his blood sang with hers. This was his child.

"Tree! Sacred Tree! Child of Klein!' screamed the last of his believers.

Concussion struck the vessel. The faithful squealed and scrambled, fleeing backward out of the cramped cabin. Metallic but controlled, a rough voice announced from an ancient ambient system: "Hull breach. An armed vessel attacks. All hands! All hands!"

Explosions thumped terrifyingly, transmitted through the hull. Klein stared about him, clutching the baby. The young Queen-Mother reached for her daughter, desperate, face distorted. Her name was . . . was . . . Struck again and again by the enemy weapons, the ruined starcraft jolted, ringing like a bell. Milk leaped from Mi-Yun's naked nipples, opalescent globules that hung in the sweat-reeking air like pearls.

"What vessel assails us?" the priest demanded of the ambient. He was calm, no longer ludicrous in vile robes.

Again a crash. "It appears to be . . . a ship of Earth."

Klein stared. The warms? In an instant, his torpor was flung from him, and with it every vestige of learned sophistication, acquired so painfully in a long lifetime and deadtime of intensely diligent study in the ways of human civilization. He raged like a *wild beast in a cage, yet careful in his fury of the baby against his shirtless chest, wrathful.*

"The child," cried Queen-Mother Mi-Yun, tearing at his arms with nails that left bloodless tracks down his flesh. "Put down my baby!"

Klein ignored pain and cries alike. He drew his daughter against his breast, and crossed to the tangle locus. "Send me to their ship," he said. Terrified, the technician matched parameters and activated the entanglement field. Klein transitioned instantly into the enemy vessel.

Glancing at him without visible surprise, a dead woman smiled coolly with eyes blue as Californian summer skies. She sat upright but utterly relaxed in her acceleration chair on the bridge, clad in the crisp whites of a spacecraft commander. Nobody else was on the bridge. He listened to her controlled breathing, and his own, and the baby's steady heartbeat. Nothing else but machinery. They were alone on the great vessel.

"Jorge," she said. Sybille's voice was crushed mint on chilled glass. "A daddy now, I see. How touching."

Convulsion. Confusion. Nightmare, nothing but a nightmare. Muddled thoughts in a blue funk.

"Sir. Sir. Mr. Klein. Are you fully awake, sir?"

And his full consciousness switched on, like a searchlight. He sat up. A small room with curved walls, pale peach, air humming. A young man in the classic garb of an orderly watched him, cautiously. A warm. A warm! So. They had brought him back up from his purging, his term of punishment, his warehousing. A century come and gone on a calendar, lost to him forever. Klein twitched his muscles, sat up without a pang, swung his legs over the side of what appeared to be an operating table.

"I'm feeling surprising well, actually." He touched his neck, regarded his arms. Tubes gone, no apparent scars. Klein turned his back on the orderly, put his hands on the edge of the table and did several squats. He felt terrific. Light on the soles of his feet. Vim and vigor, with a faint tremor that seemed to spread outward into the floor itself. Well, this was the future, after all, home of fantastic progress. His thoughts darkened immediately. The prison gates would open, even in the best of all possible worlds, and he'd be released into a world as a stranger and afraid, sundered by a hundred years from all he knew. Cold seized him, and he fell forward, pressed hard, gripping the table's padded edge. "No, no," he said sharply, waving away the orderly (or cryo-technician? A doctor perhaps?). "Give me a moment." He breathed slowly. "So we're halfway through the twenty-second century."

"No, sir. Really, I'd feel happier if you'd lie down again for a moment."

Grumbling, Klein did so. The electrostatic field he associated with Sybille's funeral lifted him smoothly, like rocking gently in air. Not, in this case, an antinecrotic, he supposed. Was there the same tang of jasmine? His impoverished nostrils could not discern subtle odors.

"Thank you. Sir, you have been released from suspension early. It is now a little more than 43 years after your interment."

That was a jolt. Klein did hasty calculations. So: 2083. Chances were, though, that his brother in-law-Moshe would have succumbed to old age, perhaps to death.

Hester? She might still be alive. Or would they, too, despite their early prejudice, turn to rekindling? He pushed himself up again on his elbows.

"Who authorized this?"

"The Committee of the Party for Unification," the orderly said somewhat piously. "Sir, all your questions will be answered in a—"

A man in dark blue military uniform came into the room, a hard-faced fellow perhaps in his late fifties. His features seemed oddly familiar. Moshe? No, no. The orderly saluted and made himself scarce. Surely not—

"Jorge Klein," the man said, and his lined face made a smile as his hand reached across in a firm grip. "Uncle Jorge, I mean."

"Eli! Eliezer! My god, boy. You're older than I am!"

"Physiologically, yes. While you've been snoring on your back, my associates and I have been trying to hold the world together."

"There's a war, I suppose." Klein felt his lips twist.

"All the possible wars at once," Solomon said. He dragged over a stool, reached into his breast pocket for gum, offered a stick to Klein, who shook his head, appalled and amused. "Worst of all, the war between the quick and the deads."

"Christ. It really did come to that, then." He stared at the man's clenched jaw, powerful hands. "But you're a warm yourself, Eli. Am I to be executed after all?"

"On the contrary. My faction is opposed to retribution against the rekindled at large. They were hardly responsible for the actions of the madmen among them. We're reviving all the imprisoned—"

"Retribution?" Klein was taken aback. "We were the victims, Eli, from day one. Sybille was killed in the bombing of Zion Cold Town. You can't possibly believe that."

"Shut up, Klein." Solomon stood, face flushed. "You don't know what you're talking about. How could you possibly offer a germane opinion?"

"Don't shout at me, Eliezer." Klein forced himself to take a breath. "I'm sorry—Mr. Solomon. What's your rank, anyway?"

The man ignored him, voice deepening in fury. "You know nothing of the hyperkinetic rock that smashed Jerusalem. Here, look at what your people did to mine. And to all the others."

A wall stereo display activated, opening its imaginary space into echoing depths. For a moment, Klein was dizzied; the protocols of presentation were unfamiliar. Images, captions, a muted voice-over that Solomon silenced. Temple Mount—Har haBáyith, the Haram Ash-Sharif—key disputed holy ground of Judaism and Islam, smashed into ruin by a blazing infalling rock the size of a hill. St. Peter's Papal Basilica, marvel of art and devotion, majestic Renaissance triumph of Michelangelo and a hundred other artists of genius, gone with the whole of Rome in a kinetic fireball. The Kaaba in the Grand Mosque, with its ancient meteoric Black Stone, obliterated by another ravening meteorite. A great Hindu temple to Lord Shiva, a thousand years old, hundreds of feet of brilliantly carved granite, expunged. The Temple of the Latter-Day Saints. Image after brilliant archival image, spliced with the burning things in the sky caught from below, from the screaming distance, from sharp-eyed satellites.

"The Hajar-e-Aswad II that wiped out Mecca. The Petrus impactor on Rome. All the great holy places of the world. Rajarajeswaram, India's largest Hindu temple. Lhasa. Salt Lake City. Smashed into craters of glass and dust by targeted rocks flung down by deads in lunar orbit. Murder and desecration. The worst assault on people of faith since—"

You see, I don't care, Klein thought. He had a distant academic interest in how this global apocalypse, this new Holocaust, might work itself out, and from what disputed beginnings it had arisen, but these impassioned words and fearful images seemed to him altogether detached from his own reality.

"You think the deads are opposed to religion? Violently opposed?"

"Aren't you?"

"Violently? No, absolutely not."

"You see the evidence there."

"No. Only evidence of violence, not of dead involvement. Why should we go to such absurd lengths? Such effort? You simply don't get it, Eli. The deads don't care."

He waved his hand back and forth, finally put it on his nephew's arm.

"Eliezer. Listen to me. Yes, this is terrible, but so was the Black Death. So were the millions dead in Cambodia and China. So was the Holocaust, and we are both tied to that in our bone and gristle, but listen to me: it doesn't matter. Not to me."

Eliezer Solomon was speechless with disbelief and then with outrage. "You cannot begin—"

"You're right, Eli, I can't. What I want to know is much more immediate. What news of your parents? Are they alive? What of the deads I lived with? Sybille you yourself knew, but there were others. A woman named Mi-Yun, another named Francine. A man called Tom." Did they mean anything to him, those deads, in this wasteland of noise and nothingness? No, not truly. But he had to ask.

"Your sister Hester and my dad were in Israel, in Tel Aviv, when Jerusalem and much more was destroyed from space. Gone, gone, with millions of Jews."

"And how many Arabs? A million? Are they at each other's throats? Or does everyone blame the deads?"

"All the possible wars, I told you. Yes, the dead are blamed by the intelligentsia, because you are the masters of advanced technology. Only your fusion systems could have mobilized asteroids and hurled them at the Earth like David's rock from a sling. But the great masses curse their favorite enemies and heretics, and martyrs' blood is shed on all sides. As was planned, I am certain of it." Solomon sat down again, wiped his face with a handkerchief. "Sybille Klein has been deaccessioned. I did a search before I came down here. I knew you'd want to know. The others, no, their names are not familiar. I imagine they, too, are gone. That's why we've chosen to save you and the rest, Jorge. You are an endangered species, you deads. An experiment that was . . . cut short. Well, not if we can help it. I must warn you, you'll be placed back in suspension when we get to our destination."

What? What? Instant understanding, then. The lightness against his muscles, the tremor at the edge of detection in the floor.

"We're in space."

"Yes, I thought you'd been told."

"Where?"

"Halfway to Mars, at point nine gees. One more day. Then we will put you in protective custody. Biostasis is a lot safer. You'll complete your sentence. The future might revile you, but they might find some reason for retaining you."

"No release program, then. No generous reconciliation with the warm Master Race."

Eliezer Solomon, soldier, went to the door. His face was a cold mask.

"*You* are the Master Race, Jorge. You rekindled. And it looks as if you've met the usual fate of Masters." He said with finality, "I'll never see you again. Goodbye."

Klein lowered his eyes. All of them dead, then, deader than dead. Deaccessioned! Filthy, banal euphemism. Or smashed like vermin. Suddenly he felt very tired and tremendously hungry. "Yes, goodbye, Eli." But when he raised his head his nephew was gone, and the orderly was back, fussing.

Was this memory? Was it dream? Drowning Klein fought for consciousness, air, sanity—

Stench of human suffering, of his own decaying flesh. Shivering, filthy, Klein shuffled into the moonlit darkness from the hateful wooden barracks he shared with a dozen other men, not all of them Jews. Three in the morning again. Nothing to drink for an hour, then that disgusting bitter coffee, all he'd get for five o'clock breakfast. Hours of crippling labor hauling rocks and manure before lunch, weak soup, hardly enough to make you crap. A young Schutzstaffel officer with the detestable lightning runes on the collar of his neat, clean uniform, shouting at some wretched miscreant. From a barracks separate from the Jews, a swaggering "camp elder" came to deliver suitable punishment. The Jews cringed away from him; Klein cowered, tried to hide from the criminal's gaze. A rapist and murderer, Heinz Klausner was head Capo, boss of the scum "barracks police." Klein failed to evade the man's eyes. The prick came striding over in his new green trousers, his tall leather boots catching the pale light of the moon, seized Klein by his own ragged collar. "Slacking again, you creature," he shouted. They had a miraculous power to find ire within themselves, for their own satisfaction and the enjoyment of the watching SS thugs. He slapped Klein hard, yelling abuse. Nobody came to his aid. Klein fell, was hauled up. The SS officer stepped forward. "Here, men, we have a good 'boxing sack.' Time to sharpen your fighting skills." Piss ran down Klein's legs. Let me go, Lord, he prayed. Let me die now. Poor Chaim Shustack, burliest and strongest of the remaining Jewish prisoners, was pulled forward. "Hold the creature up, you vermin." I'm sorry, I'm sorry, Chaim's eyes told him. Here came Klausner's boot, swung smashingly into his left knee. He sagged, fell forward. Shustack heaved at his right arm, kept him from falling. Another SS thug found a heavy stick, struck him in the mouth. His teeth splintered. Agony. More kicks. His balls! Cramping in his abdomen, muscles rigid. He could not breathe. Give me death, give me death.

This time he awoke instantly.

The pseudomemory of his post-biostasis dream clung like a rancid film.

Oh. Oh. Oh.

Gasping, he surged up, flung himself from the catafalque. Hands of attendants reached in alarm to prevent him from falling, but Klein was on his hands and knees, staring wildly, seeking a place to hide. His broken mouth! His ribs! His brutalized balls! Crawling from the light, cowering beneath the floating catafalque, he covered his head, touched his tender mouth. His teeth were intact. Wait, wait. No aching in his balls, no contusions or fractures. Why would they impose this horror upon him? He crept out into the large green room, watched by two women and a man. They seemed concerned. Yes, yes, a fantasy, that was all. Something he'd imposed upon himself, no doubt. His specialty study, after all, corroding the depths of his unconscious, the Nazi era of the twentieth. Or some residual guilt. For what? It had not been he who bombed those so-called holy places, smashing them from space.

But that must have happened decades ago. He was . . . on . . . Mars? No, the gravity was wrong. Earthlike. Exactly Earthlike. Seeking some scrap of dignity, he got to his feet.

"Dead sir," said an attendant, "du need not fear us."

"No," he said. They were warms, but something had changed in them, some change deep and strange. He covered his face for a moment of consolidation. No beard. They had shaved him, depilated him. Patting, probing, he found a fine thick bush of hair on his scalp, hanging down his neck, like the very nonmilitary coiffure of the male attendant. "All right. Very well. Where is this place? What is the date?"

"Many passed by. No know exactamund. Where is your departure date? What jahr?"

Klein stared. "How could you not know? I was in a machine, a biostasis chamber, they called it. Isn't there a . . . a calendar? A data display? A small rectangle with changing numbers in red light or something?"

"So sorry, Meister Dead. No access to biostationary records, all lost in the Disruption."

The Smash-Up, yes. All the possible wars. Klein groaned. The stupidity of it all. He could not believe it had been occasioned solely by resentment of the rekindling process, envy for what its beneficiaries had created. Who was to say that the deads were not a scapegoat after all? Yet surely the power source required to shunt whole asteroids from orbit and target them at select sites on Earth—that had to be the technology of the Conclave, or some heretical splinter group. He groaned again.

"You must have some idea. Decades? Centuries?"

"Hundreds jahren, certes." The others nodded their speculative agreement. "Two hundred. Three." A hand wave.

Klein sank into a gray place.

The woman with streaks in her dark cropped hair was asking him meaningless questions. "Which was your god? Scuzi, that is your gog. And magog."

"No god, no gog," he said bleakly. "Magog, for sure. He tore up the world, last time I was there."

They did not grasp his allusion, shrugged at each other. "Your name, good being? Some records remain, we might find more on your interrupted life course."

"Call me Ishi," he said bitterly.

"Ah!" The man was delighted. "Old remnant document. 'Call me Ishmael.'"

"Close, but no biscuit," Klein said. That dreadful dream. It could have been his grandfather's life and pitiless death, except that his family had escaped the iron heel in time. "Ishi was the last member of the Yahi, and they were the last surviving sept of the Californian Yana people. Back at the start of the twentieth. Taken in hand by Kroeber and Waterman. You don't want to know about this."

"A jest, a pun, a play of nominalism! Most delightful!" This second young woman was a vivid redhead, curls piled up on curls. Her body was succulent, clad in bright chrome yellow. Looking at her, he felt nothing.

"And what am I to call you people?"

The man smiled sunnily. "I, Jesus." Hay-Zeus. The dark haired woman said, "I, Mary." With the cutest little bow, the girl, the young woman, told him, "I, Joseph."

Klein burst out laughing. "You're shitting me."

"Assuredly not, sir. We adopt these nominations from your mystery book, to render du the more at ease."

"It hasn't worked. For one thing, Joseph is a man's name."

The redhead cocked her head like a puzzled Pomeranian. "Names have no gender, sire. But we still await your true nomenclature."

"Jorge Klein," he said. "Klein is my surname."

"Ah, so! Sir Klein!"

"No, no, just Klein. Never mind." These ninnies were as much fun as a barrel of eels. "And you, you're what we termed warms, back in my day. Whenever that was."

"Not especially close to identical," the man told him. "We have the augments, as do all. All but the deads, of whom there are, du know, hardly no more no more. Du are our precious, however contemptible."

Rekindling, they explained, was now seen as a frightful horror, worse than foot-binding or genital mutilation, worse even than lobotomy.

"They gave some man a Nobel prize for inventing lobotomy, you know," Klein said, mouth twisted. "Or probably you don't."

"It is noway noble to cut open a head or poke through the eye, ruining the tissues. There was awards for this barbarity?"

"Only the one," Klein reassured him. "I believe it was revoked."

"Du have one of these Noble Prizes?"

"I could have been a contender," Klein said.

"But it was done to du, speaking in the manner of a synecdoche. Or mayhap a metonymy."

Chill through his dead flesh. "What? What?" Without intention, his hands again went at once to his head, probing, pressing his eyes and the sockets holding them. "You're lying."

"For no reason would we, sir Ishi. Du are a dead. Du suffered the notorious 'drying out' following your revival."

"Yes. We all did. Part of the procedure. It's a metaphor. Quite possibly it's a synecdoche, or mayhap a metonymy. Moths and butterflies. Do you have them now? Have all the beasts been exterminated on Earth? They creep from their pupas and cocoons, altogether changed, wet with the slime of transformation. They dry out. Simile with us." His tongue caught. He realized that despite his long, long sleep (how long? How long?), he was exhausted. Carefully, he said, "I mean similarly."

"No, no, for what precedes drying? Why, washing. The washing of the brain. Du was programmed like an old clanker robot, sir."

"What? Nonsense." Oh Christ. Oh my god.

"Yes, du see, your language menus reset from without. How to fast dead talk. Prohibitions on sexuality. No children. Too large a population otherwise. Very slick.

Now we all do that fast talk, du might have noticed, but with our optional implants. Us warms are enhanced, see it?"

It crushed his spirit. For these years since his rekindling, meaninglessness had been his companion, but this was intolerable, unsustainable. He sagged, and the bright woman caught him under the right arm. He flinched away (the Capo! The Jew-killer!), then let her ease him back on his catafalque. The world, the worlds, had shrunk to a series of small clean well-lighted hospital recovery rooms. So he was not just dead, he was an automaton. Preprogrammed for the long empty life of a dead. Drowning again, this time awake. He sought for something to cling to.

"But the war is over?" he said, and heard an unaccustomed plaintive note in his voice. "The warms and the dead are at peace once more?"

All three laughed. "Oh, no no," Jesus said "By no means, Mr. Ishi. Mr. Klein. Such enmity is not so easily quelled." The man took up his hand. "But we have great hopes for du, sir. We ask du to intervene with the voices from Andromeda nebula." He blinked. "Scuzi, galaxy."

But Klein was not listening. A child. He was not sterile, then. Not impotent. Not a sexless thing. Or if he was, it was a constraint imposed upon him by the Guidefathers and the sons of bitches running the Conclave. He might break free. He might father a daughter, or a son. If the beings from Andromeda permitted it. For surely they were the puppet masters. Whoever they were. Whatever. He whirled in gray interior space, groped for meaning, for sense, for purpose.

"Voices," he said, then. "What voices? How could we understand aliens?" It had always been the sticking point. Claims of cyphering, hypercomputers, Gödel coding—none of it was ultimately persuasive. *Eppur si muove.* And yet it moves. We have the technology.

"Not all alien," said Joseph. "Some of them are human voices, pojąć? From the future."

And theatrically, operatically, a tremendous gonging strikes the air, slams the floor. Those fantastical images of bombardment and carnage flare again in Klein's mind. His daughter Tree.

"We're under attack," Mary said, and the three warms went into a huddle. No doubt bolts of energy pulsed between their brains, their rewired neurons, and every other warm in the building. Another immense shock flung them off their feet. The three rolled like circus acrobats, were on their toes in moments. Klein lay where he had fallen, rubbing his bruised elbow.

"Where are we?" he said with what he considered admirable restraint. "And who's trying to kill us?"

They looked at him fishily. "Approaching the Andromeda vinculum mouth, du did not dig this? The precise location for your undertaking. To speak for all, as a relict of the *eventements*."

Klein closed his eyes. He felt very old and useless.

"So I'm still on a spaceship. An attack ship under fire off the shoulder of Orion, I suppose."

Joseph placed a comforting hand on his cheek. "Nobody transports so far as yet. We remain above the ecliptic, beyond the Oort Cloud."

"So who the hell is firing on us?"

"Why, can't you pursue elementary logic, sir Klein? Your last companionables, obviously. The deads on board the pioneer starship *Tell Me Not, In Mournful Numbers*, stationed at the vinculum. Now we must answer that message with one less harmful. When they learn that you are with us, they shall abandon their fusillade, certes." She shut her eyes, reached with her left hand for Mary and her right for Jesus. The gravity switched off, and they ascended in a Coriolis curve from the rolling deck, with Klein, like a small flock of wingless angels.

Deep space was truly black, and through the unreflecting bubble the Milky Way was a wide, thick band of brightness. In every direction, points of gemlike light. Klein had expected to find his vision adjusted to the faint interior illumination of the transfer bubble—that miracle of field forces centuries in advance of his own lost time—but somehow the clarity was electrifying. Behind him, the complex shape of the warms' vessel was itself a dozen curved mirrors flinging back starlight. Ahead, the starship of the deads (or was it a blended crew of the dead and the quick? he could not be sure) resembled a finless fish, smooth as black ice in the blackness, rimmed by forces that pulsed almost fast enough to make an uninterrupted glow. And beyond that enormous vehicle, a hanging indigo shape like the manifestation of a tesseract, a rotating impossible object in five or six or thirteen dimensions: the throat of the vinculum created two million years ago by the beings in Andromeda.

It is a phallus, Klein thought. Readying itself to plunge into the yoni of the vinculum. How banal. How inevitable.

"So that thing is going to rocket into—"

"No no, no reaction forces. They use a method. Du would not understand."

Nettled, Klein said, "Just keep it simple."

"Oh, like a kinder learning, yes, very good. They employ a strong symplectic homeomorphism. With this—"

Klein gritted his teeth. "Simple, Joseph."

"But this is elementary. Your Hamiltonian spaceology on its own isotopies are generalized to an intrinsic symplectic topology on the space of symplectic isotopies, obviously." The young woman gazed at him guilelessly in the darkness, her features limned by starlight. "By coupling to the—"

"Stop," Klein said. "Just stop."

Abruptly a glistening bubble came from the star-strewn darkness, hesitated athwart their own, merged. Klein's ears popped. Four humans stepped forward. One of them he knew at once, hardly changed by the centuries. Perhaps he had slept in stasis as well. Yet was there not an added quality of gravitas to the man, a sense of calm self-worth as he stepped forward and took Klein's hand?

"Hi. We're gonna take a little trip. You up for that, doc?" Dolorosa said, and grinned like an avuncular rodent.

Huffing out a cough of amusement, Klein said, "You advised me rather a long time ago not to ask deads a direct question."

"Things change, Klein. Things change."

That, too, echoed like some refrain from his lost history. The little Customs man, was it? Barwani. Tags of who he had been, his ignorance, his hopeless and stupid obsession, clung like barnacles washed by brackish waters. Things change. Yet now that he looked at the dead standing beside Dolorosa, he realized with a jolt how utterly that was true.

"Mi-Yun," he said. "They'd told me you were—"

"Deaxed? Not all of us. Who were the ones you knew? Francine, perhaps? Tom? Those were deaccessioned during the crisis. Didn't you have a wife once? Gone also. Quite a few of us survived, though, as you see. Let me introduce you to representatives of our crew. This is—"

The names of the warms fell into his ears, and he let them slip away. He went through to their section of the conjoined bubble.

"Goodbye, goodbye, goodbye, sir Klein. Carry our wishes to the future, to Andromeda. Well faring!"

And falling into the blackness, toward the phallic fish, the ichthyphallic starship. He sniggered. Too much, too much. Another galaxy! Rhodomontades of Wagner, Beethoven, Carl Maria von Weber, for Christ sakes, he needed Teutonic bombast again. Was he embarking on the *Flying Dutchman*? Fated to wander the lonely cosmos for eternity, dead, dead, dead, dead?

"Come on, old fellow," Dolorosa was saying. Their bubble had passed now into the belly of the beast. Busy crew went by with no great evidence of curiosity. In an elevator they ascended to an expanse Klein took to be the control center, or perhaps merely an entertainment alcove, two men and a woman on padded chairs, signally bare of consoles and keypads and swipe bars. Augmented warms, he reminded himself. No doubt they fly this thing by thought, by the flight of entangled electrons from brain to brain to picotechnological hypercomputer navigation systems. He halted.

"This is the commander of the Andromeda mission," Dolorosa said. "Captain Lucius Olanrewaju."

"Excuse me, Captain," Klein said, the words tight between his teeth. He was angry, angry, and this unaccustomed access of emotion seemed beyond his power to contain it. "This is not the moment," he ground out. "Take me away, please."

Mi-Yun, the changed Mi-Yun, understood at once. Murmuring to the warms, who smiled, bobbed their machine-laden heads, she departed gracefully with Klein, leaving Dolorosa to follow after them, his glance sardonic.

"How long will this trip take?" Klein asked her in the passageway. Two million years in biostasis? He thought. The dreams, the terrible dreams. That prospect was intolerable. Yet to remain awake and deathless for such eons . . . Worse still.

"Perhaps a millennium," Mi-Yun told him. "It will be painless, Jorge."

"And you wanted me . . . why?"

"You know why," Dolorosa said. "This was your vocation. You are to be the Apostle. The Ambassador."

"To the warms, Jamal Hakim said."

"Not only to them. To the aliens of Andromeda. They're waiting for you, sport."

"How can they knew anything about me? How can *you* know anything about *them*?"

"You're muddled in the old errors," Mi-Yun said. "We know better now. Causality is tangled, entangled. Strictly, you see, there is no causality, only correlation."

Stupid abstractions. But yes, finally everything was an abstraction. Empty circularity. This never-ending emptiness, ruin. Not even yearning, not even disgust. Mi-Yun mistook his blank stare for intellectual engagement. She added, "It is the Shoup Scholium. Quantum entropy showed that measurement is a unitary three-interaction. No collapse, no fundamental randomness. Influence is equal between past and future, as perceived by us." Again he drifted away. Superposition, entanglement, measurement, locality, causality.

"Yes, Mi-Yun, whatever you say. I will do as you require, but on one condition."

The two deads, paused, watched him carefully. Did they know already? If past and future were paths one could travel in either direction, they might well have knowledge of his perverse desire. But their expressions conveyed neither revulsion nor excitement. Dolorosa was a scofflaw of old, he might raise no objection. But Mi-Yun—

"I want a child," he told them.

"You know that's impossible. The physiology—"

"I'm not taking about fucking and carrying a child in utero. Now that I find you here, waiting for me, I wish you to be the child's mother, Mi-Yun. Cells from each of us, reverted skin cells, they were doing this with mammals back in the twenty-first century."

She lifted her eyes to the left. She was augmented, as he'd suspected, searching the same grand and gnarly information spaces as the warms. "Induced Pluripotent Stem Cells," she said, nodding. "Primordial oocyte and spermatozoa precursors generated from— But our bodies are changed, Jorge. We are not strictly human. There is no reason to suppose that this could work."

"Surely this ship has biomedical equipment."

"Of course, but what you're asking is illegal and immoral." She regarded him with growing dismay. "You expect me to be the donor."

"Why not? Why not? You plan a voyage of two million light-years, surely you don't balk at essaying parenthood?"

Mi-Yun's face showed agonized indecision. "And if I do this thing?"

"Why, then, call me Spock. Ambassador Spock," said Jorge Klein, raising his right hand in an ancient, long-forgotten salute, ironic twinned fingers raised to starboard and port. "Die long and prosper."

9

We are imprisoned in the realm of life, like a sailor on his tiny
boat, on an infinite ocean.

—*Anna Freud*

And again awakens, this time from no dreams he can recall. A thousand years into the future. The machines newly placed within his cranium as he slept tell him his location in the Andromeda galaxy, in a star battle cruiser warped there by an arcwise homeomorphism, its complement blended of the quick and the dead.

Tell him that he has been remade once more.

Stepping from the cool medical catafalque, his naked flesh maggot pale but in peak postmortem condition, Jorge Klein knows instantly, and with no need to search his declarative memory, these things and many more: That a millennium, yes, has passed as he lay immobile, tended by guardian machines, not merely dead but comatose. That he is aboard the battle cruiser *Tell Me Not, In Mournful Numbers* (and that it emerged from a transport vortex ninety-three minutes earlier, and is now decelerating at 50 gravities from light speed, that its complement is 1019 humans, and, irrelevantly, that the number 1019 is prime). That its destination is the G0 star Longer Baseline Galactic Survey 2374b39 in the Andromeda galaxy. That the war between the quick and the dead continues in fits and starts, fragmented across centuries, threatening ruin and extinction to both. That his illicit daughter, built from his codons and Mi-Yun's, nurtured in an artificial uterus, sleeps in biostasis, like the baby she is, three decks below And, above all, in this cascade of immanent knowingness, that some grievous change has been wrought upon him. Within him. Again.

In a greater access of passion than his condition has permitted him for a thousand years, he speaks his unfamiliar rage to the empty room, "You bastards. You have *augmented* me! Against my express instruction."

A man stands before him. A holographic image, a stereo, a sentimental record of the lost past? But no, his hand reaches compassionately to touch Klein's brow. Dolorosa again, hair long, clad in a golden caftan. No longer the street rat, the snarling outsider. A man at home in his station. Which is, the augment tells Klein at once and without his striving for its access, Representative of the Conclave in Andromeda Space. Information has been flooding in from Earth, from Mars, from all the worlds of the Solar system, a thousand years of archived history, scientific advances, reports of the endless war. Flurries of art, new modes of music invented, abandoned as hackneyed, rediscovered, bypassed, overwhelmed by newer forms, and again and again. Through it all, the continuing augmentation of the warms, while the deads are all but paralyzed by their first adopter technological lock-in. Only the grim endurance of their indifference, their intrinsic aloofness, allows the rekindled to persist, even thrive. And of course the deads hold one important distinction: they don't die. Unless they are "deaccessioned."

All of this in stacked tree-indexed hierarchical order, a vast data cathedral rising in a triumphant architectonic surge into Klein's soul through his own augments, low-level as they are, as he now understands.

"Hey, man," says Dolorosa. He smiles in friendship, and his teeth are dazzlingly white and perfectly formed. If anything has been lost in this millennial chronicle of change, genemod dental implants has not been one. "I see you're back, and in fine fettle. Just cool it a mo, hey? The Droms want to talk to you before we get to their world. Come with me, and we'll get you up to speed."

In a dry, rasping voice, Klein says, "My child. I want to see my baby."

"Sure, we can do that en route. Do you have a name for her yet? She's a little darlin', man."

Of course he has a name for her. "Eurydice," he says.

Dolorosa laughs out loud. "That'd do. You've brought her back from the dead. From two deads, hey." A beat. "Just don't look over your shoulder when— Never mind."

"You're right. There'd be endless jokes at her expense." He ponders as they walked through the twisted corridors of the battle cruiser. "Yael," he says. "For her grandmother."

"On your side, I guess. No say for Mi-Yun."

"She is my child," Klein says urgently. "Mine, mine."

"Keep your shirt on. Yai-el. Pretty name for a pretty gal. What's it mean?"

"Strength of God. Or maybe to ascend like a mountain goat. Everything's god to my people, even the goddam mountain goats." He thinks of his long exhausting climb up Kilimanjaro. Up this two million light-year staircase of stars and impossible constrained forces.

They passed through a gauzy veil of light, and entered a place of medical machines. "Here," Dolorosa says. "You can see her in the display."

Bitterly disappointed, Klein says, "I can't hold her? Not even a window to look through?"

"Her immune system is still having its final prep. But isn't she a cutie?"

The holo display above Yael's crib shows a sleeping infant with curly hair. Her eyes, with their enchanting epicanthic slant, will be dark as his, Klein thinks; as dark as grandmother's. And her hair already is as black as her Korean mother's. He reaches despite himself into the depth field of the image, and meets nothing but air crossed by rays of light.

"I'll come back and get you soon," he whispers to his daughter. "I love you, little one."

As he turns away, reluctantly, following Dolorosa's tug at his sleeve, he feels tears leaking down his cheeks, and his narrow world, slowing fantastically from light speed, blurs and shivers.

Battle cruiser or not, this vessel seems to be run on a surprisingly relaxed basis. Warms and deads walk the passageways, doors slide open and shut, voices murmur. He hears no ship-wide announcements snapped from hidden speaker systems; no flashing red or green panels alert the crew to the status of the vessel. Perhaps such functions are delegated to the augments, all the complex background information vital to the running and survival of the craft somehow integrated into the silent activity of the flesh, like the body's automatic awareness of heat and cold, bright and dim, loud explosions, a fist swung toward the face, with responses mechanical and instantaneous. Would his own unsought implants bear the same warnings and requests? Perhaps so. Nobody stops him from entering the public spaces, but no door opens to private cabins. For an hour he prowls this way and that, building a slowly clarifying sense of the structure of this immense ship. In one room, apparently a dedicated place for dining, he finds warms eating and drinking, laughing a little but not raucously, chatting but not chattering. At an empty table he sits, suddenly weary, and after a time a man in a horizontally striped shirt and a jaunty black beret fetches him a plate of steaming spaghetti with a thick red fishy sauce. He sprinkles cheese across it, adds pepper, tastes. A piquant flavor. Is his sense of taste returning? It's true; his nostrils clear, as if for years he has been afflicted by a tiresome cold. Klein shovels the spaghetti marinara into his mouth, overwhelmed by the rediscovery of taste and appetite. Wine is poured, a rich red Cabernet. The plate is taken away. He places his head on his folded arms, overwhelmed, and drifts off.

He dreams that he is in República Argentina again, in the heart of Buenos Aires, leading a team of architects through the magnificent Edificio Kavanagh, its lofty Art Deco setbacks imploring the sky, clean in its towering concrete lines, brilliant with sunlight; it will become the first Cold Town outside the borders of the United States. The builders frown, mutter among themselves angrily. An affront! This classic building is one of the marvels of their city. It is not a mausoleum, a vertical catacomb, it is a home for the living, the warm. No, no, he protests; he tries to explain. It is his father and mother he addresses; their faces are flushed with anger. Who does he think he is? Little Hester cowers in her mother's skirts. Across the dining room in this high Westwood Plaza restaurant, the neo-Babylonian Hanging Gardens, he sees a lovely young woman enter, and Hester plucks at his sleeve. "She's perfect for you. She's your type, I swear." It is Mick Dongan's bony fingers grabbing at his jacket. "Her name is Sybille. She's from Zanzibar. Look, look, she's a dead, Klein, just like you, the perfect choice." He groans in protest, and the hand is shaking his shoulder.

"This isn't really the place for a snooze," Mi-Yun tells him, gazing down. Her wise old face. Klein blinks, clears away the film of moisture from his eyes. It is not that she looks old. No new lines, no sinking of the cheeks, her dark eyes have not withdrawn within crêpey sockets, there's no desperate thinning of the lips. Yet she is changed profoundly. Has she been awake all these ten long centuries? Or just for the two or three hundred years beyond the catastrophic bombing of Jerusalem, Mecca, Rome, all the high places of faith and power and mad rivalrous bigotry? She picks up his limp hand. "Come on, my dear. You've had a hard transition. Let's go to bed."

She leads him down carpeted passageways to a large cabin, a suite really. They undress in the lowered light of softly glowing lamps, and she draws him beneath the sheets. Under her gentle ministrations, Jorge Klein relaxes, at last, tension easing, tight muscles yielding. They do not kiss; he does not stiffen, enter her; they make love in the way of the deads, touching lightly, placing their hands upon each other, the blooms of flowers brushing before a cool breeze.

Klein smiles, sighs, slips into sleep.

10

I did not think I was strong enough to retain for long a past that went back so far and that I bore within me so painfully. If time enough were allotted me to accomplish my work, I would not fail to mark it with the seal of Time, the idea imposed upon me with so much force: that humans are monsters occupying in time a habitation infinitely more significant than the restricted locations reserved for them in space, a place immeasurably extended because, touching widely separated epochs and the slow accretion of days upon days passed through, we stand like giants immersed in Time.

—*Marcel Proust*, Time Regained

The world LBGS 2374b39c, third planet of its Andromedan star, turns below them into the light of its Sun as the battle cruiser goes on orbit. Captain Lucius Olanrewaju stands before the command deck's immense holo display. Klein is seated; in the last weeks of the ship's deceleration he has undertaken extensive briefings, and awaits his removal to the surface. The planet is a golden-red haze of dust, Mars inflated to the diameter of the Earth, plus eleven percent. Atmosphere is negligible, by human standards, totally unbreathable. The world is old, old, but then all worlds are old; this one is old by the clock of evolved life. Not everything is known about the Andromedan minds, the Kardashev IIs, the Letzten, who called them here via their sterile neutrino beam with its modulated message shining through the vinculum that subverted the millions of light-years of space and time. Perhaps that message has not yet been transmitted, here and now. Time, like causality, is a pretzel of correlations, Klein has been assured. This much, and much more, was unpacked from the message stream long, long ago, on Earth in the twenty-first century, by that furtive coalition of brilliant billionaires and genius nerd rebels who unlocked the secret of rekindling, or perhaps invented it, using the clues Gödel-coded into the gushing encyclopedia their wide-spread cubesat receiver had stumbled upon. Except that they had not found it by accident; there are no accidents of this magnitude, only intentions and stochastic correlations, correlations, correlations. Klein does not pretend to understand a tenth of it, a thousandth. All he knows is that the humans are here now, the living and the living dead, where they were summoned, where he is to speak face-to-face with their ancient benefactors. Who knew his name, and uttered it in pixels, millions of years ago. Who called him here, their invitation a command. Very well. Let us look upon their bleak, dried-up world.

As they orbit into brightness, the face of the world turns to show them . . . what? A vast ridge or cyclonic outflow boundary curving inward toward the poles, dark dust hurled up into a roaring, turbulent ring constrained by its own dynamics, held in place, an impossible disk-edge thousands of kilometers in circumference, cupped within the greater circle of the planet's extent. And inside the hurricane, if that's what the thing was, smooth air interrupted by— Suddenly, laughter breaks out on the deck.

"O my gog," murmurs the meteorologist. "A cartoon?"

"It is," Klein tells them. He is one of the few old enough to recognize it. The great crater eyes. The upwardly curved tectonic suture, its shadowed rift reaching across a third of the planet's visible surface. "A smiley face," he says. "Old computer icon from my childhood." He feels a smile spreading across his own face, lips curved up in amazed amusement. "A goddamned happy face."

"I guess they're glad to see us," Mi-Yun says, and she is grinning as well.

A brilliant red light blooms suddenly on the equator, miles across, at the very center of the planetary storm.

"Our landing site," says a dead woman, intently studying a gridded map floating before her.

Dolorosa catches Klein's eye, and winks at Mi-Yun.

"Yep, we'll take a bubble down," he says, and adds with a smirk, "Right on the nose."

Voices seem to be muttering in Klein's head, but he can make no sense of them. The Captain turns to him.

"Ambassador Klein, I have a message for you from the Letzten. They extend their greetings and welcome you to their home world. And . . ." He breaks off, shakes his head slightly.

"Yes?"

"Mr. Klein, I don't think we can allow this."

"Allow what? I remind you, sir, than once I leave this vessel I am in charge of first contact on the ground."

"They insist that you—" Olanrewaju pauses again, clears his throat. "They request that you bring the child with you. Yael, your daughter."

Ructions. Moral and ethical outbursts. Flat refusals. Practical objections. What grotesque proposal is this? Some travesty borrowed from Klein's ancestral religion? Father bearing his child to the altar for ritual slaughter, mandated in that case by an imaginary tribal war-god? Echoes of sacred infants offered up to fate, or dashed against walls, blood flowing in the streets, babies slashed and flung into pits of fire in Carthage, Aztecs ripping the hearts from children and eating them raw, infant skulls axed, brains spilled in religious frenzies in every land on humanity's home world—now to be replicated on another world, in another galaxy?

Klein listens to it all without paying heed. In the flat cosmic pointlessness, one lamp shines: his daughter. Mi-Yun's daughter also, he admits, but the dead woman has shown no particular interest in the infant, nor fondness for. A scrap of her dermis, a scrap of his, developmental clocks flicked backward, epigenetic markers demethylated, age reset to the zero point, stripped of the molecular intrusions of rekindling, combined *in vitro*, nurtured in fabricated juices and tissues, bathed in warmth, comforted in pulsing mimicry of heart and belly, brought forth in her season from the glass and steel, hugged and cleaned and washed and diapered and hugged again by a team of cooing warms, offered finally into his arms, his dead, reborn arms . . . Her tiny whimsical face, her own reaching arms, her small kicking legs. Was this a spark of love in the midst of his endless vastation? Was this a rekindling, in truth, of the compulsive bond he'd known before only with his lost spouse? What fools we were, he thought, gazing down at Yael, bringing her face slowly, carefully, close to his lips, kissing her with his waxy dead lips . . . What fools to deny ourselves this joy. Yes, she will travel with me to the surface. She is the best promise of humankind. She is life brought out of death.

"Will you come down with us, Mi-Yun?"

"They have machines now, you know, to carry her warm milk, her diapers, her swaddling clothes . . ." The woman laughs. "It's ridiculous. I'm not the mothering kind. You know that, Jorge."

"Of course she'll come," Dolorosa tells him. "Me too. Wouldn't miss it for the world. And our captain will insist on a support crew of mission specialists. Ecumenical little party, off to see the Wizard."

Jorge Klein steps through the permeable wall of the bubble onto the rusty golden surface of the Letzten's world. He carries his daughter pressed against the breast of his environment suit, borne in an ergonomic support lifted against gravity by a static field. He had half expected to find here a platform of blazing red light, to match the landing grid visible from the orbiting starship. Ahead, through the haze of the blowing dust, he does see an elevation, perhaps a ziggurat. Arms wrapped around Yael's support, he strides toward the structure that seems to loom larger with each step, impossibly, like an optical illusion. Perhaps that is all it is, a trick played directly upon his brain, through the augments the warms placed there as he slept. Under the guidance of these very entities, he now realizes, these Letzten, these Andromedans. Will they step forth lightly from their stolid rank upon rank of smooth black stone? Will they lumber out like sapient dinosaurs, like wise-eyed bears? Will they coil in ambulant tanks of murky fluid, parodies of Yael's mechanical gestation? Fly out from the topmost levels of the ziggurat on bronze wings? Slither like serpents? Exhale from slots, gaseous conglomerates? The nonsense clatters through his distracted mind, detritus of every computer game and stereo he's ever engaged. No. No. They will be nothing so obvious.

"Well," he calls, "we're here. Greetings from Earth." He announces his name, and the child's, peering up through eddies of dust that swirl in the star's hot brightness, dust now streams of shadow, now gleaming and glistening like Brownian motes caught in a beam of light from a leaded window. "What now? What now?" Glancing carefully to either side, he finds none of his companions. Where is Mi-Yun? For an instant anger burns in him. Betrayed. The women leave him, they will not linger. He bats that self-indulgent foolishness away. Dolorosa? *Never lean on anybody's arm. You know what I mean?* Yes, he had learned the truth of that, among the dead. Yet it was not altogether the truth, not the whole truth. The rekindled held each other in a certain self-interested regard, making rational assessment of costs and likely benefits, offering an arm to lean on if the payoff came with a suitable margin. The Guidefathers made it their business to lead the newly dead through their paces, drawing forth from their rewritten brains the sharp-edged concision of their rapid speech, their agreed code of manners, the duties they must enact in suitable payment for the support they would receive in the Cold Towns and elsewhere. Gutter rat Dolorosa himself, once bitter and jumpy, now carrying the maturity of centuries, taking on the burden of Representative of the Conclave. And he himself, Apostle to the articulate squids in space, the robot creatures, the dreaming gas blimps, the mats of conscious algae, the gestalt brains under glass, whatever they were, Ambassador from the worlds of the Solar system . . . what was *he*, indeed, if not compliant, amenable, acquiescent in complex and consequential plans laid down by other men and women and indeed aliens so many centuries before. Very well, then. Thou art that.

He holds his arms wide in an accepting embrace.

Light takes him and his child.

"They've been here an awfully long time," the stocky young woman told him as they walked through the thick, sweet grass. The pale purple silk of her long dress swirled back and forth as she trod lightly, brushing the stems, some of the grass crushed under her bare feet, releasing the odors of spring and summer. He studied her face when she turned her gaze on him, smiling, content. Those swooping eyelids with their single elegant crease, prescribed by Mi-Yun's genome. That curly black hair, from his own lineage. That lovely mind, peering from her dark eyes.

"A very long time," said the other one, walking with them. "Waiting for you, Yael. And your dad and mom, of course. And all the others."

"Warms and deads," Klein murmured. "Why is that so important? I know it is, it's almost on the tip of my tongue—"

It slipped away, lost again.

"You're happy staying here, little mountain goat?" he said doubtfully.

"Gazelle, if you don't mind." Mock indignation. She slapped his hand playfully. "Oh yes, what place would be better than this? With all my friends, and you, too, just for now, Dad, and so much to know, and so much to teach." Her radiant smile.

Stars spreading out all around them burned fiercely in the blackness. Two immense spiraled clouds swung toward each other, fell and fell, merged, their dreadful central black holes closing together, the combined collapsed mass of tens of millions of stars, merging in a tumultuous blaze of quasar luminescence that burned stars, planets, sent a shock wave of relativistic plasma and gamma radiation outward at light speed or close to it, sterilizing all it passed.

"Four billion years from now," the other said. "Give or take. The galaxy you call the Milky Way will encounter this one, which you call Andromeda. Your Sun will be a red giant by then, in any case, and so will ours. We'll have to migrate elsewhere. So it makes sense to get a good head start." Amusement. Warmth. Sorrow for all that will be lost. Joy for what will persist, and grow, and know itself.

It was a dead like him, this other, Klein noticed, although not very like him.

"Are you all rekindled, you Letzten?"

"That's your word, you know, not ours."

"Granted," Klein said. "We had to give you a name chosen from our own languages. It means 'the last,' with overtones of 'the best.' My grandparents spoke that language. We have done terrible things to each other, we humans."

"All species do," the other, the Letzte, told him. Together, they climbed the ziggurat, as if they wore seven-league boots and it were a set of broad, high steps. Klein cradled the infant in her crib against his breast.

"It is how they die, and die, and die," said the Letzte, "and are gone."

"All of them?" This desolation was unbearable. Klein felt the urge to weep, the tightened chest, the prickling in the nose, the pressure in the head, the eyes blurring. He could not touch his eyes, guarded by his visor. He blinked hard, sniffed. "Every intelligent species, murdered?"

"So far. Except for us. And now you . . . so far."

"Why? Why? Must there always be war between the quick and the dead? No peace, no surcease, ever?" This bitter answer to the Fermi paradox, he thought. *Where are they,* an old scientist had asked teasingly, *the alien civilizations?* They had thought they knew the answer, that cautious, secretive sodality of the rich and the geeks, when they'd found the first signs of life beyond Earth. Their wild jubilation had driven the decoding of the messages from Andromeda, the application of deep ancient principles to the needs of humans; they had conquered death itself, after a fashion. But it was a false conclusion, Klein now understood. Perhaps across the stars a thousand species had trod forth from the muck, a million, risen to genius, found a cure for death, and immediately exterminated themselves out of jealousy and loathing and madness masquerading as wisdom. Self-slaughtered, every one. Trillions upon trillions of lives, through billions of years, again and again and again.

"We are doing what we can, Ambassador. With the aid of your child." Yael walked beside them, and for a moment Klein mistook her for Mi-Yun, and then for his sister, Hester. She took his hand once more, squeezed it tightly, and the other who climbed with them added, "You are a new thing, you augmented deads. Perhaps. Perhaps . . ."

Klein sat down on the flat top of the great archive that was the repository of the active minds of a trillion Letzten deads. It was coated in thick ice. The corpse of a leopard lay gaunt and rimed near his feet. When he looked for it again, it had gone. The aliens, he saw, moved in these abstracted spaces like the angels of mythology: impalpable, interpenetrating, born again in the swarm, not separate and self-hypnotized, but individual and related. No warm could endure that frozen realm. Not even his daughter, held for now from the blight of the dead planet by forces beyond his comprehension. And here she would remain, after the starship returned to carry in person a message that already pulsed its correlations in the vinculum across two million light-years of nothingness and death.

I am Eurydice, as he foretold. Or call me Yael. Clambering like a goat to the high places of the vital, descending to the darkness and the cold of the dead. All around me in their choirs, in quires and places where they sing, in loops of entanglement from past to tomorrow and beyond and back again, in heaven as it was in Earth, uttering the ends and the beginnings of things and everything between. Like my father, they know the dread of vastation, that closure of meaning and hope, that occlusion of love, yet they know also its contrary, the leaps of aspiration, trust in the unfolding, knitting up the wounds of yesterday and healing the broken, rutted pathways yet to be trodden. I stand beside my father's lost beloved, Sybille, Cybele, that first Eurydice, borne away by Pluto, rescued by hapless Orpheus who could not leave well enough alone but pursued her in that bleak place until she was lost to him forever. There she went with her companions into the landscapes of fatality, the fallen temples and stilled voices of the priests and congregation of the mound builders, to the cenotaphs of Luxor and Chichén Itzá, the caves where the bones of ancient children lay with skulls splintered, to the death-obsessed magnificent worshiping grounds of the planet that would be smashed into glass and flame and dust by the flung stones of the avenging deads. I walk with my father in the place of his birth, with its cold blue ocean that sucked down so many into oblivion, guns roaring above them, and the blown grasses of the Pampas utterly alive with herds of guanaco, rabbitty viscachas, foxes in their holes, hawks and sparrows a-wing, and the cities rife with corruption and murder and the willful disappearance of generations crying out their hope and despair, and my mother's ancestral home, bustling and terrified under the unending threat of nuclear annihilation, gods and goddesses of the quick and the dead, Hallakkungi Igong, tender and plucker in the Flower Garden Of Life And Death, Yuhwa, goddess of the willow, daughter of Habaek the lord of the river, desired by the sungod Haemosu who trapped her, as I have been trapped, in a wonderful edifice that holds the brightness of the sun and its yearning, of Koenegitto the wargod, who married the youngest daughter of the sea dragon and at last transformed his father into a mighty mountain and his mother into a shrine, and Halmang the immense goddess who strode across the land ungarbed, her piss stream tearing open a gulf between Jeju Island and the mainland, who swallowed up all the fish into her vagina. Is that my mother? Myself? All mankind and womankind, perhaps, on Earth as in the heavens? We shall be as gods, neither living nor dead, and both, like the Great Ones who hold me cupped in their ancient presence on this memorial world of golden dust and whimsical artistry, for they are my friends, my patient teachers, my own companions in death and life, and I sing across the stoma, the vinculum between galaxies, all the coded songs that will teach my people, have taught them, what they must know to avoid the calamity that has stricken every other species across the sky, will draw them to me, finally, my father, Jorge, and my mother, Mi-Yun, and through them carry me into existence so that all these foretold things might come to pass. I will bring them faith in a future escaped from certain doom, and hope in their power to bring it about, and love for each other, these poor damned creatures blowing a threnody across the lip of the cracked jar of their combined souls, moved to pity and laughter by the stars. Hello, hello, hello. I love you.

His daughter sat beside him, head on his shoulder, and he kissed her forehead. It was cool. She smiled at him with love and forgiveness, and kissed him in return, on the cheek. His heart was breaking. Goodbye, goodbye, goodbye. As always.

He stood up again, brushed snow pointlessly from the seat of his insulated environment suit, and trudged down the steps to walk through the blowing grass and wildflowers to the dirty golden dust and the bubble, where the others waited for him.

"All right," he told the alien deads, aloud. "All right. Let us hope, then, that all shall be well and all shall be well and all manner of things shall be well."

Dolorosa stepped forward, clapped him on the shoulder. "Talking to yourself again, Mister?" But Mi-Yun gave a shriek, touching the empty container on Klein's chest. "Where is she? Oh my god, Jorge, where's the baby? What have you done with Yael?"

"She's staying with her godparents," he said. "She'll be fine." Klein shrugged off the empty container, let it fall to the ground. It skittered away in the wind on its stasis field suspension. He placed his arms around their shoulders, and walked them to the group of waiting warms. Not meaningless after all, not plastic, not nothingness. The vastation was lifted. He smiled to himself, and hugged Mi-Yun tightly.

And ascended with them into the dark sky and the stars, and the waiting ship that would bear them back through the plenum, he thought with a smile, to waiting Ithaca.

Megan Abbott, "My Heart is Either Broken," *Dangerous Women*.

Joe Abercrombie, "Some Desperado," *Dangerous Women*.

Daniel Abraham, "The High King Dreaming," *Fearsome Journeys*.

———. "When We Were Heroes," *Tor.com*, January 16.

Brian W. Aldiss, "The Mighty Mi Tok of Beijing," *Twelve Tomorrows*.

Aaron Allston, "Defenders of Beeman County," *Rayguns Over Texas*.

———. "Epistoleros," *Shadows of the New Sun*.

Ken Altabef, "The Artist, Deeply, Brushes," *Abyss & Apex*, 2nd quarter.

———. "The Woman Who Married the Snow," *F&SF*, July/August.

Charlie Jane Anders, "The Master Conjurer," *Lightspeed*, October.

———. "The Time Travel Club," *Asimov's*, October/November.

Liz J. Anderson, "Creatures from a Blue Lagoon," *Analog*, September.

Arlan Andrews, "Thaw," *Analog*, July/August.

Eleanor Arnason, "Kormak the Lucky," *F&SF*, July/August.

Chet Arthur, "The Trouble with Heaven," *F&SF*, March/April.

Neal Asher, "Memories of Earth," *Asimov's*, October/September.

Dale Bailey, "The Bluehole," *F&SF*, May/June.

———. "City So Bright," *Oz Reimagined*.

———. "The Creature Recants," *Clarkesworld*, October.

Nathan Ballingrud, "The Giant in Repose," *Once Upon a Time*.

———. "The Good Husband," *North American Lake Monsters*.

K. C. Ball, "A Quiet Little Town in Northern Minnesota," *Analog*, July/August.

Peter M. Ball, "On the Arrival of the Paddle-Steamer on the Docks of V___," *Eclipse Online*, February.

Kelly Barnhill, "The Insect and the Astronomer: A Love Story," *Lightspeed*, November.

Neal Barrett, Jr., "Timeout," *Rayguns Over Texas*.

Christopher Barzak, "Paranormal Romance," *Lightspeed*, June.

———. "Sister Twelve: Confessions of a Party Monster," *Apex*, August.

Stephen Baxter, "Starcall," *Starship Century*.

Elizabeth Bear, "The Ghost Makers" *Fearsome Journeys*.

———. "The Governess," *Queen Victoria's Book of Spells*.

———. "Green and Dying," *METAtropolis: Green Space*.

Gregory Benford, "Backscatter," *Tor.com*, April 3.

———. "Leaving Night," *Lightspeed*, December.

M. Bennardo, "The Herons of Mer de L'Ouest," *Lightspeed*, February.

———. "Outbound from Put-In-Bay," *Asimov's*, February.

———. "The Penitent," *Beneath Ceaseless Skies*, May.

———. "Water Finds Its Level," *Lightspeed*, May.

Holly Black, "Millcara," *Rags & Bones*.

Alex Bledsoe, "Shall We Gather," *Tor.com*, May 14.

Lawrence Block, "I Know How To Pick 'Em," *Dangerous Women*.

Michael Blumlein, "Success," *F&SF*, November/December.

Terry Boren, "This Alakie and the Death of Dima," *The Other Half of the Sky*.

Gregory Norman Bossert, "Bloom," *Asimov's*, December.

Elizabeth Bourne & Mark Bourne, "What the Red Oaks Knew," *F&SF*, March/April.

Mark Bourne & Elizabeth Bourne, "One Flesh," *Clarkesworld*, September.

Richard Bowes, "The Witch's House," *Unnatural Worlds*.

Marie Brennan, "What Still Abides," *Clockwork Phoenix 4*.

David Brin, "The Heavy Generation," *Starship Century*.

———. "Insistence of Vision," *Twelve Tomorrows*.

———. "The Log," *Shadows of the New Sun*.

David Brin & Gregory Benford, "Banner of the Angels," *Extreme Planets*.

Damien Broderick, "Do Unto Others," *Cosmos*, February.

Damien Broderick & Paul Di Filippo, "Luminous Fish Scanalyze My Name," *Abyss & Apex*, 2nd quarter.

Chris N. Brown, "Sovereign Wealth," *Rayguns Over Texas*.

Georgina Bruce, "Cat World," *Interzone 246*.

Tobias S. Buckell, "The Seafarer," *Subterranean*, Spring.

———. "Tensegrity," *METAtropolis: Green Space*.

Oliver Buckram, "Un Opera nello Spazio," *F&SF*, September/October.

Ben Burgis, "Contains Multitudes," *Tor.com*, July 17.

Jim Butcher, "Bombshells," *Dangerous Women*.

Chris Butler, "The Animator," *Interzone*, March/April.

O. J. Cade, "The Mythology of Salt," *Strange Horizons*, November 11..

Pat Cadigan, "Caretakers," *Dangerous Women*.

———. "Chalk," *Chalk*.

———."The Christmas Show," *Tor.com*, December 17.

Orson Scott Card, "Off To See the Emperor," *Oz Reimagined*.

Eric Del Carlo, "Hypervigilant," *Asimov's*, June.

Rae Carson & C. C. Finlay, "The Great Zeppelin Heist of Oz," *Oz Reimagined*.

Jay Caselberg, "Lightime," *Extreme Planets*.

Michael Cassutt, "Pitching Old Mars," *Asimov's*, March.

Adam-Troy Castro, "The Boy and the Box," *Lightspeed*, July.

Vajra Chandrasekera, "Pockets Full of Stones," *Clarkesworld*, July.

Ted Chiang, "The Truth of Fact, the Truth of Feeling," *Subterranean*, Fall.

Rob Chilson, "Half As Old As Time," *F&SF*, September/October.

John Chu, "The Water That Falls On You From Nowhere," *Tor.com*, February 20.

Maggie Clark, "The Aftermath," *Clarkesworld*, November.

Jaleta Clegg, "One-Way Ticket," *Beyond the Sun*.

Jacob Clifton, "This Is Why We Jump," *Clarkesworld*, June.

Ron Collins, "Bugs," *Analog*, November.

James S. A. Corey, "A Man Without Honor," *Old Mars*.

Paul Cornell, "Tom," *Solaris Rising 2*.

Albert E. Cowdrey, "The Assassin," *F&SF*, March/April.

———. "The Collectors," *F&SF*, September/October.

———. "A Haunting in Love City," *F&SF*, January/February.

——. "Hell For Company," *F&SF*, November/December.

——. "The Woman in the Moon," *F&SF*, May/June.

F. Brett Cox, "The Amnesia Helmet," *Eclipse Online*, January.

Ian Creasey, "Within These Well-Scrubbed Walls," *Asimov's*, October/November.

Benjamin Crowell, "A Hole in the Ether," *Asimov's*, September.

Leah Cypess, "Distant Like the Stars," *Asimov's*, April/May.

Tony Daniel, "Frog Water," *In Space No One Can Hear You Scream*.

Jack Dann, "The Island of Time," *Shadows of the New Sun*.

——. "Waiting For Medusa," *Asimov's*, October/November.

Indrapramit Das, "Karina Who Kissed Spacetime," *Apex*, June.

Colin P. Davies, "Julian of Earth," *Asimov's*, April/May.

Joel Davis, "Writing in the Margins," *Asimov's*, April/May.

Aliette de Bodard, "The Angel at the Heart of the Rain," *Interzone 246*.

——. "The Weight of a Blessing," *Clarkesworld*, March.

Seth Dickinson, "Never Dreaming (in Four Burns)," *Clarkesworld*, November.

Paul di Filippo, "Adventures in Cognitive Homogamy: A Love Story," *Asimov's*, October/November.

——. "Redskins of the Badlands," *Analog*, November.

Cory Doctorow, "Lawful Interception," *Tor.com*, August 28.

Sarah Dodd, "Trans-Siberia: An Account of a Journey," *Interzone 249*.

Lara Elena Donnelly, "The Witches of Athens," *Strange Horizons*, October 7.

David Drake, "Bedding," *Shadows of the New Sun*.

Andrew Drummend, "The Providential Preservation of the Universal Bibliographic Replicator," *Postscripts 30/31*.

Andy Dudak, "Tachy Psyche," *Clarkesworld*, May.

Andy Duncan & Ellen Klages, "Wakulla Springs," *Tor.com*, October 2.

Phyllis Eisenstein, "The Sunstone," *Old Mars*.

Kate Elliott, "Leaf and Branch and Grass and Vine," *Fearsome Journeys*.

Amal El-Mohtar, "A Hollow Play," *Glitter and Mayhem*.

David Farland, "Barbarians," *Unnatural Worlds*.

——. "Dead Blue," *Oz Reimagined*.

Shannon Fay, "You First Meet the Devil," *Interzone 246*.

Tang Fei, "Call Girl," *Apex*, June.

Meryl Ferguson, "The Hyphal Layer," *Extreme Planets*.

Sheila Finch, "A Very Small Dispensation," *Asimov's*, October/November.

C. C. Finlay, "The Infill Trail," *Lightspeed*, February.

Mark Finn, "Take a Left at the Cretaceous," *Rayguns Over Texas*.

Jeffrey Ford, "The Fairy Enterprise," *Queen Victoria's Book of Spells*.

——. "A Meeting in Oz," *Oz Reimagined*.

——. "Rocket Ship to Hell," *Tor.com*, July 20.

——. "A Terror," *Tor.com*, July 24.

Eugie Foster, "Trixie and the Pandas of Doom," *Apex*, January.

Karen Joy Fowler, "The Science of Herself," *The Science of Herself*.

Carl Frederick, "Fear of Heights in the Tower of Babel," *Analog*, October.

Gregory Frost, "No Others Are Genuine," *Asimov's*, October/November.

Nancy Fulda, "The Cyborg and the Cemetery," *Twelve Tomorrows*.

——. "A Soaring Pillar of Brightness," *Beyond the Sun*.

Diana Gabaldon, "Virgins," *Dangerous Women*.

Neil Gaiman, "A Lunar Labyrinth," *Shadows of the New Sun*.

——. "The Sleeper and the Spindle," *Rags & Bones*.

James Alan Gardner, "The Tempting: A Love Story," *Electric Velocipede 26*.

David Gerrold, "The Gathering," *How To Save the World*.

——. "Night Train to Paris," *F&SF*, January/February.

Greer Gilman, "Cry Murder! In a Small Voice," *Small Beer Press*.

Molly Gloss, "The Presley Brothers," *Interfictions 2*.

Kathleen Ann Goonan, "Bootstrap," *Twelve Tomorrows*.

Theodora Goss, "Blanchefleur," *Once Upon a Time*.

——. "Estella Saves the Village," *Queen Victoria's Book of Spells*.

——. "The Lost Girls of Oz," *Oz Reimagined*.

John Grant, "Memoryville Blues," *Postscripts 30/31*.

Simon R. Green, "Dorothy Dreams," *Oz Reimagined*.

Sarah Grey, "The Ballad of Marisol Brook," *Lightspeed*, June.

Jon Courtenay Grimwood, "The Jupiter Files," *The Lowest Heaven*.

Damien Walters Grintalis, "Always, They Whisper," *Lightspeed*, May.

——. "Paskutinis Iliuzija (The Last Illusion)," *Interzone 245*.

Lev Grossman, "The Girl in the Mirror," *Dangerous Women*.

Robert Grossman, "MyPhone20," *F&SF*, Sepember/October.

Joe Haldeman, "The Island of the Death Doctor," *Shadows of the New Sun*.

Guy Haley, "iRobot," *Interzone*, January/February.

Lisa L. Hannett, "The Coronation Bout," *Electric Velocipede 27*.

Daniel Hatch, "The Chorus Line," *Analog*, December.

Jim Hawkins, "Sky Leap—Earth Flame," *Interzone*, January/February.

Maria Dahvana Headley, "The Psammophile," *Unlikely Stories 7*.

——. "Such & Such Said to So & So," *Glitter and Mayhem*.

F. Brett Helmut, "The Amnesia Helmet," *Eclipse*, January.

Howard V. Hendrix, "Other People's Avatars," *Analog*, July/August.

Carlos Hernandez, "The International Studbook of the Giant Panda," *Interzone*, March/April.

Thomas Olde Heuvelt, "The Ink Readers of Doi Saket," *Tor.com*, April 24.

M. K. Hobson, "Baba Makesh," *F&SF*, November/December.

Brian Hodge, "The Same Waters As You," *Weirder Shadows Over Innsmouth*.

——. "We, the Fortunate Bereaved," *Halloween*.

Cecelia Holland, "Nora's Song," *Dangerous Women*.

Kat Howard, "Painted Birds and Shivered Bones," *Subterranean*, Spring.

——. "Stage Blood," *Subterranean*, Summer.

Hugh Howey, "Deep Blood Kettle," *Lightspeed*, April.

Matthew Hughes, "And Then Some," *Asimov's*, February.

——. "Sleeper," *Lightspeed*, November.

——. "Stones and Glass," *F&SF*, November/December.

——. "The Ugly Duckling," *Old Mars*.

Claire Humphrey, "Haunts," *Interzone 249*.

Kameron Hurley, "Enyo-Enyo," *The Lowest Heaven*.

Alex Irvine, "Watching the Cow," *F&SF*, January/February.

Alexander Jablokov, "Feral Moon," *Asimov's*, March.

Helen Jackson, "Build Guide," *Interzone*, January/February.

Kelly Jennings, "Velocity's Ghost," *The Other Half of the Sky*.

Hao Jingfang, "Invisible Planets," *Lightspeed*, December.

Wang JinKang, "The Beekeeper," *Pathlight: New Chinese Writing*.

C. W. Johnson, "Exit, Interrupted," *The Other Half of the Sky*.

Derek Austin Johnson, "Grey Goo and You," *Rayguns Over Texas*.

Matt Jones, "The Comet's Tale," *The Lowest Heaven*.

Naim Kabir, "On the Origin of Song," *Beneath Ceaseless Skies*, October.

Vylar Kaftan, "The Weight of the Sunrise," *Asimov's*, February.

Rahul Kanakia, "Droplet," *We See a Different Frontier*.

William H. Keith, "Positive Message," *How To Save the World*.

Jamie Kellen, "The Still Room," *Electric Velocipede 26*.

James Patrick Kelly, "Miss Nobody Never Was," *Lightspeed*, December.

———. "Soulcatcher," *Clarkesworld*, May.

Kay Kenyon, "The Spires of Greme," *Solaris Rising 2*.

Sherilyn Kenyon, "Hell Hath No Fury," *Dangerous Women*.

Caitlin R. Kiernan, "Black Helicopters," *Subterranean*.

———. "The Prayer of Ninety Cats," *Subterranean*, Spring.

Ted Kosmatka, "Haplotype 1402," *Asimov's*, July.

Mary Robinette Kowal, "Forest of Memory," *METAtropolis: Green Space*.

Nancy Kress, ". . . And Other Stories," *Shadows of the New Sun*.

———. "Annibal Lee," *Arc Manor*.

———. "Frog Watch," *Asimov's*, December.

———. "Knotweed and Gardenias," *Starship Century*.

———. "Migration," *Beyond the Sun*.

———. "Mithridates, He Died Old," *Asimov's*, January.

———. "More," *Solaris Rising 2*.

———. "Second Arabesque, Very Slowly," *Dangerous Women*.

Matthew Kressel, "The Sounds of Old Earth," *Lightspeed*, January.

Naomi Kritzer, "Bits," *Clarkesworld*, October.

———. "Solidarity," *F&SF*, March/April.

———. "The Wall," *Asimov's*, April/May.

Greg Kurzawa, "Shepherds," *Clarkesworld*, August.

Ellen Kushner & Ysabeau S. Wilce, "One Last, Great Adventure," *Fearsome Journeys*.

Jay Lake, "A Stranger Comes To Kalimpura," *Subterranean*, Spring.

———. "Love in the Time of Metal and Flesh," *Prime Books*.

Jay Lake & Seanan McGuire, "Hook Agonistes," *Subterranean*, Fall.

Margo Lanagan, "We Three Kids," *PS Publishing*.

Joe R. Lansdale, "The Case of the Stacking Shadow," *Subterranean*, Summer.

———. "King of the Cheap Romance," *Old Mars*.

———. "Wrestling Jesus," *Dangerous Women*.

Anaea Lay, "Hiding on the Red Sands of Mars," *Strange Horizons*, May 13–20.

———. "The Visited," *Lightspeed*, April.

Rand B. Lee, "Changes," *F&SF*, May/June.

Tanith Lee, "A Little of the Night," *Clockwork Phoenix 4*.

Yoon Ha Lee, "Effigy Nights," *Clarkesworld*, January.

———. "Iseul's Lexicon," *Conservation of Shadows*.

———. "The Knight of Chains, the Deuce of Stars," *Lightspeed*, August.

Tim Lees, "Unknown Cities of America," *Interzone 249.*

Henry Lein, "Pearl Rehabilitive Colony for Ungrateful Daughters," *Asimov's*, December.

David D. Levine, "Wavefronts of History and Memory," *Analog*, June.

———. "The Wreck of the *Mars Adventure*," *Old Mars.*

Megan Lindholm, "Neighbors," *Dangerous Women.*

Marissa Lingen, "The Ministry of Changes," *Tor.com*, July 3.

Kelly Link, "The Constable of Abal," *Apex*, July.

Ken Liu, "A Brief History of the Trans-Pacific Tunnel," *F&SF*, January/February.

———. "Ghost Days," *Lightspeed*, October.

———. "The Litigation Master and the Monkey King," *Lightspeed*, August.

———. "The mMod," *Daily SF*, January.

———. "The MSG Golem," *Unidentified Funny Objects.*

———. "The Oracle," *Asimov's*, April/May.

———. "The Reborn," *Tor.com.*

———. "The Shape of Thoughts," *The Other Half of the Sky.*

———. "The Veiled Shanghai," *Oz Reimagined.*

James Lovegrove, "Shall Inherit," *Solaris Rising 2.*

Scott Lynch, "The Effigy Engine: A Tale of the Red Hats," *Fearsome Journeys.*

Jonathan Maberry, "The Cobbler of Oz," *Oz Reimagined.*

Ian R. MacLeod, "The Réparateur of Strasbourg," *PS Publishing.*

Kate MacLeod, "Din Ba Din," *Strange Horizons*, August 12.

Brit Mandelo, "The Writ of Years," *Tor.com*, December 18.

Daniel Marcus, "After the Funeral," *F&SF*, September/October.

George R. R. Martin, "The Princess and the Queen," *Dangerous Women.*

Sean McMullen, "The Firewall and the Door," *Analog*, March.

———. "The Lost Faces," *F&SF*, March/April.

Bruce McAllister, "Canticle of the Beasts," *F&SF*, May/June.

Bruce McAllister & W. S. Adams, "Don't Ask," *Subterranean*, Summer.

Jack McDevitt, "Cathedral," *The Other Half of the Sky.*

———. "The Eagle Project," *Analog*, November.

Ian McDonald, "Drifting," *Clarkesworld*, January.

———. "The Revolution Will Not Be Refrigerated," *Twelve Tomorrows.*

Sophia McDougall, "Golden Apple," *The Lowest Heaven.*

Seanan McGuire, "Emeralds to Emeralds, Dust to Dust," *Oz Reimagined.*

———. "Midway Relics and Dying Breeds," *METAtropolis: Green Space.*

Ian McHugh, "The Canal Barge Magician's Number Nine Daughter," *Clockwork Phoenix 4.*

———. "When the Rain Come In," *Asimov's*, October/November.

Maureen McHugh, "The Memory Book," *Queen Victoria's Book of Spells.*

Will McIntosh, "Over There," *Asimov's*, January.

Greg Mellor, "Mar Pacifico," *Clarkesworld*, September.

Sam J. Miller, "The Beasts We Want To Be," *Electric Velocipede 27.*

D. Thomas Minton, "The Schrödinger War," *Lightspeed*, September.

Eugene Mirabelli, "The Shore at the Edge of the World," *F&SF*, September/October.

Judith Moffett, "Ten Lights and Darks," *F&SF*, January/February.

Mary Anne Mohanraj, "The Stars Change," *Circlet Press.*

Sarah Monette, "To Die For Moonlight," *Apex*, July.

Michael Moorcock, "The Lost Canal," *Old Mars*.

Nancy Jane Moore, "The Revelation of Jo Givens," *Postscripts 30/31*.

Sunny Moraine, "Event Horizon," *Strange Horizons*, October 21.

———. "I Tell Them All, I Can No More," *Clarkesworld*, July.

Simon Morden, "WWBD," *The Lowest Heaven*.

Gabriel Murray, "Forests of the Night," *We See a Different Frontier*.

Linda Nagata, "Out in the Dark," *Analog*, June

———. "Through Your Eyes," *Asimov's*, April/May.

Mari Ness, "In the Greenwood," *Tor.com*, December 4.

Ruth Nestvold, "The Shadow Artist," *Abyss & Apex*, 1st quarter.

R. Neube, "Grainers," *Asimov's*, December.

Alec Nevala-Lee, "The Whale God," *Analog*, September.

Mark Niemann-Ross, "A Cup of Dirt," *Analog*, June.

Garth Nix, "Fire Above, Fire Below," *Tor.com*, May 8.

———. "Losing Her Identity," *Rags & Bones*.

G. David Nordley, "The Fountain," *Asimov's*, June

———. "Haumea," *Extreme Planets*.

Jody Lynn Nye, "The Dreams of the Sea," *Shadows of the New Sun*.

Jay O'Connell, "That Universe We Both Dreamed Of," *Asimov's*, September.

Yokimi Ordonez, "Misbegotten," *Beneath Ceaseless Skies*, January.

An Owomoyela, "In Metal, in Bone," *Eclipse Online*, March.

Suzanne Palmer, "Hotel," *Asimov's*, January.

Susan Palwick, "Hhasalin," *F&SF*, September/October.

———. "Homecoming," *Tor.com*, July 10.

———. "Sanctuary," *Eclipse*, February.

K. J. Parker, "The Dragonslayer of Mere Barton," *Fearsome Journeys*.

———. "Illuminated," *Subterranean*, Summer.

———. "The Sun and I," *Subterranean*, Summer.

Richard Parks, "Cherry Blossoms on the River of Souls," *Beneath Ceaseless Skies*, October.

Norman Partridge, "The Mummy's Heart," *Halloween*.

Sharon Kay Penman, "A Queen in Exile," *Dangerous Women*.

Lawrence Person, "Novel Properties of Certain Complex Alkaloids," *Rayguns Over Texas*.

Joe Pitkin, "Full Fathom Five," *Analog*, September.

Rachel Pollack, "The Queen of Eyes," *F&SF*, September/October.

Steven Popkes, "The Things I Know About Jesus," *On Spec*, Winter.

Tim Pratt, "The Cold Corner," *Rags & Bones*.

———. "Revels in the Land of Ice," *Glitter & Mayhem*.

William Preston, "Vox Ex Machina," *Asimov's*, December.

Tom Purdom, "A Stranger from a Foreign Ship," *Asimov's*, September.

———. "Warlord," *Asimov's*, April/May.

Chen Qiufan, "The Endless Farewell," *Pathlight: New Chinese Writing*.

———. "The Year of the Rat," *F&SF*, July/August.

Adam Rakunas, "Oh Give Me a Home," *F&SF*, July/August.

Cat Rambo, "Dagger and Mask," *The Other Half of the Sky*.

———. "I Come From the Dark Universe," *Clockwork Phoenix 4*.

———. "The Toad's Jewel," *Abyss & Apex*, 4th quarter.

Dinesh Rao, "A Bridge of Words," *We See a Different Frontier*.

N. A. Ratnayake, "Remembering Turinam," *We See a Different Frontier*.

Kit Reed, "The Legend of Troop 13," *Asimov's*, January.

———. "Wherein We Enter the Museum," *Postscripts 30/31*.

Robert Reed, "Among Us," *F&SF*, January/February.

———. "Bonds," *Solaris Rising 2*.

———. "The Golden Age of Story," *Asimov's*, February.

———. "Grizzled Veterans of Many and Much," *F&SF*, May/June.

———. "Mystic Falls," *Clarkesworld*, November.

———. "What We Do," *Postscripts 30/31*.

Jessica Reisman, "The Chambered Eye," *Rayguns Over Texas*.

Mike Resnick, "In the Tombs of the Martian Kings," *Old Mars*.

———. "Observation Post," *Beyond the Sun*.

Beth Revis, "The Turing Test," *Lightspeed*, November.

Alastair Reynolds, "The Lobby," *Postscripts 30/31*.

Joel Richards, "Deep Diving," *Asimov's*, October/November.

Gray Rinehart, "What Is a Warrior Without His Wounds," *Asimov's*, July.

Mercurio D. Rivera, "Freefall," *Immersion Press*.

———. "Manmade," *Solaris Rising 2*.

Adam Roberts, "An Account of a Voyage from World to World . . . ," *The Lowest Heaven*.

Justina Robson, "Pwnage," *Twelve Tomorrows*.

Margaret Ronald, "Someone Like You," *Apex*, September.

Benjamin Rosenbaum, "Future Development for Social Networking," *Tor.com*, November 13.

Mary Rosenblum, "Shoals," *Old Mars*.

Deborah J. Ross, "Among Friends," *F&SF*, March/April.

Christopher Rowe, "Jack of Coins," *Tor.com*, May 1.

Diana Rowland, "Blood and Sequins," *Glitter & Mayhem*.

———. "City Lazarus," *Dangerous Women*.

Rudy Rucker & Paul Di Filippo, "Yubba Vines," *Asimov's*, July.

Kristine Kathryn Rusch, "The Application of Hope," *Asimov's*, August.

———. "Encounter on Starbase Kappa," *Asimov's*, October/November.

———. "The Hanging Judge," *Beyond the Sun*.

———. "September at Wall and Broad," *Fiction River: Time Streams*.

———. "Skylight," *Asimov's*, June.

———. "Uncertainty," *Asimov's*, March.

———. "When Thomas Jefferson Dined Alone," *Solaris Rising 2*.

Patricia Russo, "The Old Woman With No Teeth," *Clockwork Phoenix 4*.

Cheryl Rydborn, "In Sight," *Twelve Tomorrows*.

James Sallis, "As Yet Untitled," *Asimov's*, September.

Brandon Sanderson, "Shadows for Silence in the Forests of Hell," *Dangerous Women*.

Jason Sanford, "Monday's Monk," *Asimov's*, March.

———. "Paprika," *Interzone 249*.

Veronica Schanoes, "Burning Girls," *Tor.com*, June 19.

———. "Phospherus," *Queen Victoria's Book of Spells*.

Ken Scholes, "Let Me Hide Myself In Thee," *METAtropolis: Green Space*.

Karl Schroeder, "The Desire Lines," *METAtropolis: Green Space*.

David J. Schwartz, "Today's Friends," *Asimov's*, July.

Priya Sharma, "Rag and Bone," *Tor.com*, April 10.

——. "Thesea and Astaurius," *Interzone 246*.

Nisi Shawl, "In Colors Everywhere," *The Other Half of the Sky*.

Delia Sherman, "Queen Victoria's Book of Spells," *Queen Victoria's Book of Spells*.

Lewis Shiner, "Doctor Helios," *Subterranean*, Fall.

——. "Friedrich the Snow Man," *Tor.com*, December 11.

John Shirley, "The Kindest Man in Stormland," *Interzone 249*.

Martin L. Shoemaker, "Not Close Enough," *Analog*, May.

Vandana Singh, "Cry of the Kharchal," *Clarkesworld*, August.

——. "Sailing the Antarsa," *The Other Half of the Sky*.

——. "With Fate Conspire," *Solaris Rising 2*.

Cory Skerry, "Breathless in the Deep," *Lightspeed*, August.

Jack Skillingstead, "Arlington," *Asimov's*, August.

Brian Francis Slattery, "The Syndrome," *Subterranean*, Spring.

Joan Slonczewski, "Landfall," *The Other Half of the Sky*.

Melinda Snodgrass, "The Hands That Are Not There," *Dangerous Women*.

——. "Written in Dust," *Old Mars*.

Maria V. Snyder, "The Halloween Men," *Halloween*.

Bud Sparhawk, "Declaration," *Analog*, November.

Caroline Spector, "Lies My Mother Told Me," *Dangerous Women*.

William Browning Spencer, "The Indelible Dark," *Subterranean*, Spring.

Benjanun Sriduangkaew, "The Bees Her Heart, The Hive Her Belly," *Clockwork Phoenix 4*.

——. "Silent Bridge, Pale Cascade," *Clarkesworld*, December.

——. "Vector," *We See a Different Frontier*.

Brian Stableford, "The Seventh Generation," *Extreme Planets*.

Michael A. Stackpole, "Fix," *Time Streams*.

Allen M. Steele, "Sixteen Million Leagues from Versailles," *Analog*, October.

——. "Ticking," *Solaris Rising 2*.

Neal Stephenson, "Atmosphaera Incognita," *Starship Century*.

Andy Stewart, "Wormwood Is Also a Star," *F&SF*, May/June.

S. M. Stirling, "Pronouncing Doom," *Dangerous Women*.

——. "Swords of Zar-Tu-Kan," *Old Mars*.

Margaret Stohl, "Sirocco," *Rags & Bones*.

Charles Stross, "Equoid," *Tor.com*, September 24.

Philip Suggars, "Automatic Diamante," *Interzone 247*.

Tim Sullivan, "The Nambu Egg," *F&SF*, July/August.

——. "Through Mud One Picks A Way," *F&SF*, November/December.

Michael Swanwick, "House of Dreams," *Tor.com*, November 27.

——. "Tumbling," *Dragonstairs Press*.

E. J. Swift, "Saga's Children," *The Lowest Heaven*.

Rachel Swirsky, "If You Were a Dinosaur, My Love," *Apex*, March.

Sam Sykes, "Name the Beast," *Dangerous Women*.

David Tallerman, "Across the Terminator," *Clarkesworld*, July.

Adrian Tchaikovsky, "Feast and Famine," *Solaris Rising 2*.

Graham Templeton, "Free-Fall," *Clarkesworld*, June.

Leah Thomas, "The Ex-Corporal," *Asimov's*, August.

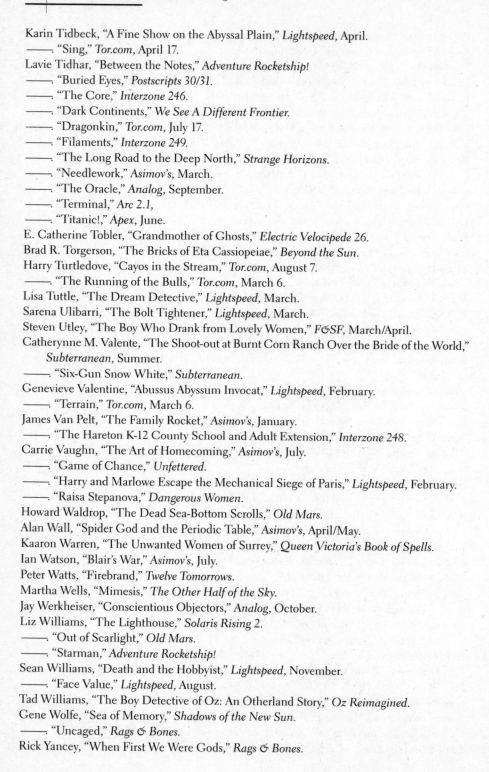

Karin Tidbeck, "A Fine Show on the Abyssal Plain," *Lightspeed*, April.

———. "Sing," *Tor.com*, April 17.

Lavie Tidhar, "Between the Notes," *Adventure Rocketship!*

———. "Buried Eyes," *Postscripts 30/31.*

———. "The Core," *Interzone 246.*

———. "Dark Continents," *We See A Different Frontier.*

———. "Dragonkin," *Tor.com*, July 17.

———. "Filaments," *Interzone 249.*

———. "The Long Road to the Deep North," *Strange Horizons.*

———. "Needlework," *Asimov's*, March.

———. "The Oracle," *Analog*, September.

———. "Terminal," *Arc 2.1,*

———. "Titanic!," *Apex*, June.

E. Catherine Tobler, "Grandmother of Ghosts," *Electric Velocipede 26.*

Brad R. Torgerson, "The Bricks of Eta Cassiopeiae," *Beyond the Sun.*

Harry Turtledove, "Cayos in the Stream," *Tor.com*, August 7.

———. "The Running of the Bulls," *Tor.com*, March 6.

Lisa Tuttle, "The Dream Detective," *Lightspeed*, March.

Sarena Ulibarri, "The Bolt Tightener," *Lightspeed*, March.

Steven Utley, "The Boy Who Drank from Lovely Women," *F&SF*, March/April.

Catherynne M. Valente, "The Shoot-out at Burnt Corn Ranch Over the Bride of the World," *Subterranean*, Summer.

———. "Six-Gun Snow White," *Subterranean.*

Genevieve Valentine, "Abussus Abyssum Invocat," *Lightspeed*, February.

———. "Terrain," *Tor.com*, March 6.

James Van Pelt, "The Family Rocket," *Asimov's*, January.

———. "The Hareton K-12 County School and Adult Extension," *Interzone 248.*

Carrie Vaughn, "The Art of Homecoming," *Asimov's*, July.

———. "Game of Chance," *Unfettered.*

———. "Harry and Marlowe Escape the Mechanical Siege of Paris," *Lightspeed*, February.

———. "Raisa Stepanova," *Dangerous Women.*

Howard Waldrop, "The Dead Sea-Bottom Scrolls," *Old Mars.*

Alan Wall, "Spider God and the Periodic Table," *Asimov's*, April/May.

Kaaron Warren, "The Unwanted Women of Surrey," *Queen Victoria's Book of Spells.*

Ian Watson, "Blair's War," *Asimov's*, July.

Peter Watts, "Firebrand," *Twelve Tomorrows.*

Martha Wells, "Mimesis," *The Other Half of the Sky.*

Jay Werkheiser, "Conscientious Objectors," *Analog*, October.

Liz Williams, "The Lighthouse," *Solaris Rising 2.*

———. "Out of Scarlight," *Old Mars.*

———. "Starman," *Adventure Rocketship!*

Sean Williams, "Death and the Hobbyist," *Lightspeed*, November.

———. "Face Value," *Lightspeed*, August.

Tad Williams, "The Boy Detective of Oz: An Otherland Story," *Oz Reimagined.*

Gene Wolfe, "Sea of Memory," *Shadows of the New Sun.*

———. "Uncaged," *Rags & Bones.*

Rick Yancey, "When First We Were Gods," *Rags & Bones.*

J. V. Yang, "Old Domes," *We See a Different Frontier*.

Jane Yolen, "Blown Away," *Oz Reimagined*.

——. "Dog Boy Remembers," *Unnatural Worlds*.

——. "The Jewel in the Toad Queen's Crown," *Queen Victoria's Book of Spells*.

E. Lily Yu, "Ilse, Who Saw Clearly," *Apex*, May.

——. "Loss, With Chalk Diagrams," *Eclipse Online*, March.

——. "The Urashima Effect," *Clarkesworld*, June.